100p

1750

WILKIE COLLINS

The Complete Shorter Fiction

WILKIE COLLINS

The Complete Shorter Fiction

Edited by

Julian Thompson

Carroll & Graf Publishers, Inc.
NEW YORK

Carroll & Graf Publishers, Inc.
260 Fifth Avenue
New York
NY 10001

This collection published in the UK by Robinson Publishing
Ltd 1995

First Carroll & Graf edition 1995

ISBN 0-7867-0134-X

Typeset in the UK

Printed and bound in the USA

10 9 8 7 6 5 4 3 2 1

Contents

Introduction

Collins is surely the most readable of all major English writers. As T.S. Eliot pointed out he has the 'immense merit . . . of being never dull.'[1] Whether he is offering up a slight jest, a glorified potboiler, or a striking tour-de-force, there is always a confidence that the eye will be propelled profitably from page to page (Collins after all believed that 'the primary object of a work of fiction should be to tell a story'), and that the plants Collins puts down will all be taken up. His rich gifts for characterisation and the sustenance of narrative constitute a major part of his appeal.

Not the whole of it, however. As a sensational writer Collins delights in extraordinary events and peculiar states of mind. Life in the small hours, hereditary madness, violent abductions, the sufferings of women: Collins permits us to glimpse areas of Victorian society usually hidden from fictional consideration, as befits a man with two mistresses, two households and a lifelong disinclination for marriage. He knows his nether world well – Collins's healthy rakishness was a major part of his appeal for the more conventional Dickens – and insinuates something of its arduousness and strangeness into our memory of his most bustling stories.

Collins is probably best known for his tales of the occult. His ghosts are extraordinarily convincing. As G.K. Chesterton points out,[2] they sidle softly and solidly as Count Fosco, and disturb and satisfy the reader in the same weightily insouciant way. Collins's repeated use of the double is striking, too – but it is grounded much more firmly in the actual, and is much less theoretic than the conventional Gothic *doppelganger*, which stiffly allegorises the human soul. In Godwin's *Caleb Williams* (1794), Falkland's guilt and Caleb's fear are recto and verso of the same emotion. Similarly, Poe's William Wilson must acknowledge his shadowy persecutor, Frankenstein struggle to regain his lost monster-self, Jekyll take responsibility for Hyde. The effect may be complex, but the intention is clear: 'This thing of darkness I acknowledge mine.'[3] By contrast the moral fable in Collins's stories such as 'The Dead Hand' or the original version of 'The Dream Woman' seems much less articulate. This is partly because Collins is not as serious as his rivals: his motive is more openly to entertain. But it is also because Collins refuses the portentousness that can so easily overtake Romantic-Gothic gestures: he is in some ways closer than his masters to that canny accommodation of mystery and uncertainty that Keats called negative capability. None of Collins's stories seems to work better in this way than the very early *Mad Monkton* (1852), where the ghost of a dead profligate uncle is superimposed on the living figure of the hero's fiancée:

'Think of the calm angel-face and the tortured spectre-face being always together, whenever my eyes meet hers!' The contortion of sexuality and personal obsession in Monkton's imagination is appalling and naked; the uncle's festering sensuality, drifting for ever about the hero's consciousness as his unburied corpse drifts along the ocean tides, is a fearful reality for Monkton, and becomes one both for the story's sceptical narrator and eventually for the reader. It is quite unnecessary to raise the whole thing to an abstract plane, and mutter about ineluctable dualism. Collins was capable at his best of 'a sort of involuntary mysticism which dealt wholly with the darker side of the human soul' (Chesterton again).[4] Robert Aickman suggests that the story seems to be written 'by the light of gas-flares.'[5]

Throughout his career Collins continues to brush the nerves with a thrill of the *unheimlich*. As the clergyman discovers when the spectre of Miss Jéromette hardens like guilt out of his past, 'the chill of the mist was in the wine'. The effect often seems to hinge on the audacity with which Collins juxtaposes the mysterious and the everyday. Catherine Peters has brilliantly pointed out a moment of compelling subtlety in the undervalued story 'Nine o'Clock!': 'A young man, standing beside his brother, sees the brother's projection or shadow-self simultaneously walking in the garden with their father. The father, though sympathetically presented, cannot tell the shadow from the real son: a fleeting but effective image of parental obtuseness.'[6] Even where the component parts seem to vibrate uncomfortably, the stories have a still centre where powerful effects are achieved. In 'Gabriel's Marriage' the white spectre women riding the waves seem to create the taste by which the story's vision of atonement is relished. The grisly glamour of Notman's Arctic experience emphasises rather than overpowers the moralistic fable in 'The Devil's Spectacles'. The sensation of the young man's panic in 'A Terribly Strange Bed' is wonderfully involved with the description of the apparently dissolving picture on the wall. Most striking of all is the effect in 'The Black Cottage'. This is Collins's most brutal story: the persecution of the lonely wife in her isolated homestead is carried on so luridly as to resemble melodrama or even pantomime. And yet even here Collins achieves a fabular grandeur – despite the coarseness of the treatment, the story becomes an embodied nightmare, and recognisably a mythic presentation of a woman's worst fears.

But Collins did not only confine his attentions to ghost stories and psychological fables. His best-known novels, *The Woman in White* (1860) and *The Moonstone* (1868), eschew supernatural machinery, and Collins's 'daylight work' retains its power to shock and energise, or at the very least to keep us turning the pages. As an untried author he felt the need to display a range of wares. His first surviving fiction, 'The Last Stage Coachman' (1843), is a piece of magic realism; his second published story, 'The Twin Sisters' (1851), is a study in the incorrigibility of sexual choice; his third, 'A Passage in the Life of Perugino Potts' (1852), is a skit on artistic egotism; his fourth is the brazenly sensational 'A Terribly Strange Bed' (1852). The variety is impressive but some of Collins's early stories are (by the standards of the time) also formidably inventive: almost singlehanded he effected the importation into England of the detective story on Poe's model, but with an unassuming control of humour (for instance, in 'The Biter Bit') and character (the private investigator in 'A Plot in Private Life') that seems quite beyond the range of Poe. By the mid 1850s Collins had accumulated sufficient short stories to want to preserve some of them in book form, and his ability to produce page-turning copy (especially early in his career) is wonderfully illustrated by the framing-narratives he concocted to support this republication. It is beyond the scope of the present volume to reproduce these, but the reader is urged to seek out both *After Dark* (1856) and *The Queen of Hearts* (1859) to see how neatly Collins wove very disparate stories into sustained omnibus entertainment. In *After Dark* the device is that a portrait painter has suffered an eye infection and cannot paint. At his wife's instigation he turns instead to telling stories – and the stories he tells are those told to him in the course of the protracted sittings that make up his working life. In *The Queen of Hearts* the framing-narrative is if anything even more colourful. Three crusty old bachelors, living in a Peacock-like hermitage on the Welsh borders, have to keep a spry young girl from quitting them for the delights of the town – the arrival of the eligible son of one of them is imminent. Like Scheherazade they hit on the idea of telling her stories, and the stories they tell are those Collins had been purveying in *Household Words* and elsewhere in the previous three or four years. Both *After Dark* and *The Queen of Hearts* are highly readable collections: the plays-without-the-play being quite as good as the main entertainment.

Part of the secret of Collins's charm lies in his skill in creating and sustaining serviceable characters. In the great novels, Frederick Fairlie's hypochondria and the imperturbability of Sergeant Cuff take plenty of time to assert themselves. In the short story Collins must work faster, and he does. The old Capuchin in 'Mad Monkton' is as vivid a time-waster as the vestry clerk at Welmingham in *The Woman in White*. The bitter baroness in 'Mr Medhurst and the Princess' deprecates English modesty with Fosco-like brio. In 'Mr Percy and the Prophet' the egoistic Mr Bowmore fusses that his speeches must be delivered correctly in his absence (an objective correlative for the one right of man this radical reserves above all others, 'the right of using his tongue'). Equally well done (among many other examples) are the Galt-like prissiness of the Minister of Cauldkirk in 'Mr Marmaduke and the Minister', and the brittle feistiness of the young governess in 'Miss Morris and the Stranger'.

Collins's stories show other aspects of his command of characterisation. What Miss Mina in 'Miss Mina and the Groom' calls 'the influence that men have on women *because* they are men' was no mystery to Collins. As J.I.M. Stewart has pointed out, Collins is 'able to portray women with a fidelity much in advance of some more famous Victorian novelists. Perhaps because he himself lived . . . outside the ring-fence of Victorian convention, he was more willing to endow women with intellect, passion and strength-of-will than were many of his more famous contemporaries.'[7] Not only does he deal sympathetically and fully with disadvantaged women – governesses ('Miss Morris and the Stranger'), work-girls ('Anne Rodway'), serving-girls ('Mr Policeman and the Cook'), the daughters of stone-cutters ('The Black Cottage') and lodge-keepers ('Mr Lepel and the Housekeeper').[8] He is also never slow to signal female sexuality (much quicker than Dickens), though strictly within the bounds of magazine propriety. Miss Mina's glands have not yet been activated, as her rather striking confession illustrates: 'When a man pressed my hand, I felt it in my rings, instead of my heart.' The South-Sea island girl in 'Mr Captain and the Nymph', on the other hand, has the 'fearless candour of a child. "Squeeze me again. I like it!"' Nancy Morris, in 'Miss Morris and the Stranger' has the temerity to cut through her suitor's plot-bound scruples, and demand to be taken with her money; whereas Salome Skirton, in 'Fie! Fie! or, The Fair Physician' has all the Byronic languor of a sofa-bound Dudu. But despite the confidence with which Collins portrays women as sexual beings, it would be unreasonable to claim him as an unqualified champion of women's rights. The medical examinations of 'Fie! Fie! or, the Fair Physician' are full of male chauvinist double entendre: '[The female doctor's] pretty hand grasped his shoulder, and her little rosy ear pressed (medically pressed) Sir John's broad back.' The story seems brusquely unaware that if female doctors are subject to universal flirtatiousness, the problem lies not in feminism, but in unreconstructed male sexuality. But then, as 'Miss Dulane and My Lord' makes clear, Collins believed that 'very few women . . . mean No when they say No.'

It is often pointed out that Collins's later stories are thinner in texture than his early ones, and show the scars of having been wrung from an ailing mind and body. Certainly some of them leave possibilities unfulfilled. Hardy, for instance, would have made so much of the quasi-mythic ironies and ambiguities that mark the situation in 'Mr Lismore and the Widow', where the sexually eligible young woman impersonates an aged woman to secure her marriage contract, and then seduces her husband in the persona of her younger self. The denouement of Collins's story is striking, certainly, but the interest springs (in a manner familiar with Collins when his imagination is not wholly engaged) more from the extraordinary situation than its psychological convolution and suggestiveness. Similarly 'Mr Captain and the Nymph', a tale of the South Seas, despite purple sub-Coleridgean visions of volcanic fires, burning skies and 'empty and endless seas', never aspires to the tragic resonance which Stevenson or Conrad might tease out of similar material, nor to the racial allegories of Melville's *Typee* or *Omoo*.

Some of the late stories also show evidence of reworking of old themes in a lower key, or with a more perfunctory treatment. 'Miss Jéromette and the Clergyman', in bringing the false lover and the timid clergyman together (both have led lives of sexual irregularity), recalls Collins's favourite 'double' motif – and also reworks in somewhat jaded fashion the 'pursuer as nemesis' theme that had done such sterling service in his early novel *Basil*. The ghostly duellist in 'Miss Bertha and the Yankee' brings us back to familiar territory from 'Mad Monkton', but this time Collins injures the effect (as in 'Miss Dulane and My Lord') with a somewhat stretched rational explanation. Although individual stories (and parts of stories) from the last decade or so of Collins's career have a kind of desperate flair and power – as of a candle guttering in the socket – reading them collectively one does get the impression of narrative weariness, and of involuntary repetition. By the mid 1880s the short story was moving on, and leaving Collins behind. Kipling had published his collection of life-histories in three pages, *Plain Tales From the Hills* (1886). In comparison Collins looks leisurely and old-fashioned: a writer of the mid-century increasingly out of the swing of the literary world. But the best of his short stories withstand the test of time. In conclusion I shall quote (as many have quoted) the literary creed of the hard-to-please young lady who listens to the yarns of the old men in *The Queen of Hearts*. In many ways it precisely expresses Collins's own:

'I'm sick to death of novels with an earnest purpose. I'm sick to death of outbursts of eloquence, and large-minded philanthropy, and graphic descriptions, and unsparing anatomy of the human heart, and all that sort of thing. Good gracious me! isn't it the original intention or purpose, or whatever you call it, of a work of fiction to set out distinctly by telling a story? . . . Oh, dear me! what I want is something that seizes hold of my interest, and makes me forget when it is time to dress for dinner; something that keeps me reading, reading, reading, in a breathless state to find out the end.'[9]

JULIAN THOMPSON
Brackley 1994

NOTES

1 T.S. Eliot, *Selected Essays* (1932; Faber, 1951), p. 468.
2 G.K. Chesterton, *The Victorian Age in Literature* (London: Williams and Norgate, 1913), p. 132.
3 *The Tempest*, V. i. 275–6.
4 *The Victorian Age in Literature*, p. 130.
5 Introduction to Robert Aickman, ed. *The Fourth Fontana Book of Great Ghost Stories* (1967), p. 10.
6 Catherine Peters, *The King of Inventors* (London: Secker and Warburg, 1991), p. 112.
7 J.I.M. Stewart, Introduction to *The Moonstone* (Harmondsworth: Penguin, 1966), pp. 9–10.
8 Collins's championship of marginal women has led to feminist studies of his work in recent years. See Tamar Heller's *Dead Secrets: Wilkie Collins and the Female Gothic* (1992).
9 Wilkie Collins, *The Queen of Hearts* (London: Hurst and Blackett, 1859), Vol. I, pp. 94–5.

A Note on the Texts

There is no full scholarly edition of Collins's writings, and no one has yet compiled an authoritative bibliography. The present collection is based on R.V. Andrew's 'A Wilkie Collins Check List' (*English Studies in Africa* 3, 1960), with Andrew's known errors and mis-attributions filtered out. I have tried to include all the fiction under novella length published by Collins in his lifetime. For this purpose a novella has been deemed to contain 30,000 words.

In this collection the stories are arranged, as far as can be established, in order of composition; failing that, in order of first publication. The texts are reproduced from the first edition in book form, except in the case of the uncollected stories, where the original magazine text has been used.

The titling of Collins's short stories is a confused business. Collins often made use of the same story (occasionally slightly dishonestly) several times, and a regular device for squeezing maximum profits seems to have been re-jigging of titles. I have generally preferred to use the revised titles of the stories, as these are the best-known; I have, however, abbreviated the titles used in the volumes *After Dark* and *The Queen of Hearts* which draw too much attention to the framing narratives (here omitted). The revised titles of the stories included in *Little Novels* have, after much heart-searching, been retained, although they often seem to reflect undue pressure on Collins's part to bring the contents page into uniform format.

Several of Collins's fictional contributions to the Christmas numbers of *Household Words* and *All The Year Round* do not seem to me to be sufficiently self-contained to merit reprinting here. I have therefore omitted 'John Steadiman's Account' in *The Wreck of the Golden Mary* (1856), 'Over the Way' and 'Trottle's Report', two sections of *A House to Let* (1858), and 'The Seafaring Man', Chapter 4 of *A Message From the Sea* (1860).

Most of the stories made their first appearance in periodical form, Collins later gathering them into one or other of five omnibus collections (an account of the publishing history of each story is given in its headnote). Stories which remained uncollected are as follows:

'The Last Stage Coachman'
'The Twin Sisters'
'A Passage in the Life of Mr Perugino Potts'
'Nine o'Clock!'
'A Fair Penitent'
'The Devil's Spectacles'

'Fie! Fie! or, the Fair Physician'
'Love's Random Shot'
'The Poetry Did It: An Incident in the Life of Major Evergreen'
'The First Officer's Confession'

'The Yellow Tiger' (*Household Words*, 8 August 1857), often described as Collins's, is in fact by Percy Fitzgerald.

Acknowledgement

I should like to thank my wife Catherine for help given throughout the preparation of this edition. I also wish to express my warmest gratitude to the Secretary of the Wilkie Collins Society, Andrew Gasson, who supplied the texts of some of the stories; and to Ms Catherine Peters who answered several queries, and to whose biography of Collins, *The King of Inventors* (1991), I am much indebted.

The Last Stage Coachman

Originally appeared in Douglas Jerrold's *The Illuminated Magazine*, August 1843. Never reprinted. This is the first signed work by 'W. Wilkie Collins' traced, and appeared when he was nineteen and a half years old. On its original appearance the story was garnished with four superbly lugubrious illustrations: the broken skeleton of a coach-horse and a shattered wheel-rim lying amid tangled undergrowth; a coachman's coat, cape and hat doing duty as a scarecrow; top-boots and other coaching impedimenta hung up among cobwebs; and the epitaph of 'The Last Stage Coach Man' engraved on what appears to be a tombstone. Written at the height of Railway Mania (which it roundly stigmatises), Collins's meditation is topical if far from original: Collins's cockney stage coachman sounds like Tony Weller, and his phantom stage coach in the clouds may have been suggested by the ghostly mail coaches in Dickens's story of the Bagman's uncle (*Pickwick Papers*, ch. 49). Of the 'chance outside passengers' at the end of Collins's 'Vision', the only common factor seems to be that all died before the railway-age. Julius Caesar (d. 44 BC), Mrs Hannah More (d. 1833, proponent of Sunday schools and author of evangelical literature) and Sir Joseph Banks (d. 1820, a somewhat Draconian President of the Royal Society) might all be viewed as apostles of progress, and therefore sympathetic to the introduction of railways, but it is hard to see Mrs Elizabeth Brownrigg in that light. She was a London midwife executed in 1767 for torturing her apprentices.

T HE LAST STAGE Coachman! It falls upon the ear of every one but a
        shareholder in railways, with a boding, melancholy sound. In spite of
our natural reverence for the wonders of science, our hearts grow heavy
at the thought of never again beholding the sweet-smelling nosegay, the
unimpeachable top boots, and fair white breeches; once so prominent as the
uniform of the fraternity. With all our respect for expeditious and business-like
travelling, we experience a feeling nearly akin to disgust, at being marshalled to
our places by a bell and a fellow with a badge on his shoulder; instead of hearing
the cheery summons 'Now then, gentlemen,' and being regaled by a short and
instructive conversation with a ruddy-faced personage in a dustless olive green
coat and prismatic belcher handkerchief. What did we want with smoke? Had
we not the coachman's cigar, if we were desirous of observing its shapes and
appearances? Who would be so unreasonable as to languish for steam, when
he could inhale it on a cool, autumnal morning, naturally concocted from the
backs of four blood horses? Who! – Alas! we may propose questions and find
out answers to the end of the chapter, and yet fail in reforming the perverted
taste of the present generation; we know that the attempt is useless, and we
give up in sorrowful and philosophic resignation, and proceed undaunted by
the probable sneers of railway directors, to the recital of—

A VISION

Methought I walked forth one autumn evening to observe the arrival of a stage
coach. I wandered on, yet nothing of the kind met my eye. I tried many an
old public road – they were now grass-grown and miry, or desecrated by
the abominable presence of a 'station.' I wended my way towards a famous
road-side inn: it was desolate and silent, or in other words, 'To Let.' I looked
for 'the commercial room:' not a pot of beer adorned the mouldering tables,
and not a pipe lay scattered over the wild and beautiful seclusions of its once
numerous 'boxes.' It was deserted and useless; the voice of the traveller rung
no longer round its walls, and the merry horn of the guard startled no more the
sleepy few, who once congregated round its hospitable door. The chill fire-place
and broad, antiquated mantel-piece presented but one bill – the starting time
of an adjacent railroad; surmounted by a representation of those engines of
destruction, in dull, frowsy lithograph.

I turned to the yard. Where was the oastler with his unbraced breeches and
his upturned shirt sleeves? Where was the stable boy with his wisp of straw and
his sieve of oats? Where were the coquettish mares and the tall blood horses?
Where was the manger and the stable door? – All gone – all disappeared: the
buildings dilapidated and tottering – of what use is a stable to a stoker? The
oastler and stable boy had passed away – what fellowship have either with a
boiler? *The inn yard was no more!* The very dunghill in its farthest corner was
choked by dust and old bricks, and the cock, the pride of the country round,
clamoured no longer on the ruined and unsightly wall. I thought it was possible
that he had satisfied long since the cravings of a railway committee; and I sat
down on a ruined water-tub to give way to the melancholy reflections called
up by the sight before me.

I know not how long I meditated. There was no officious waiter to ask me,
'What I would please to order?' No chambermaid to simper out 'This way,

Sir,' – not even a stray cat to claim acquaintance with the calves of my legs, or a horse's hoof to tread upon my toe. There was nothing to disturb my miserable reverie, and I anathematised railways without distinction or exception.

The distant sound of slow and stealthy footsteps at last attracted my attention. I looked to the far end of the yard. Heavens above! a stage coachman was pacing its worn and weedy pavement.

There was no mistaking him – he wore the low-crowned, broad-brimmed, whitey-brown, well-brushed hat; the voluminous checked neckcloth; the ample-skirted coat; the striped waistcoat; the white cords; and last, not least, the immortal boots. But alas! the calf that had once filled them out, had disappeared; they clanked heavily on the pavement, instead of creaking tightly and noisily wherever he went. His waistcoat, evidently once filled almost to bursting, hung in loose, uncomfortable folds about his emaciated waist: large wrinkles marred the former beauty of the fit of his coat: and his face was all lines and furrows, instead of smiles and jollity. The spirit of the fraternity had passed away from him – he was the stage coachman only in dress.

He walked backwards and forwards for some time without turning his head one way or the other, except now and then to peer into the deserted stable, or to glance mournfully at the whip he held in his hand: at last the sound of the arrival of a train struck upon his ear!

He drew himself up to his full height, slowly and solemnly shook his clenched fist in the direction of the sound, and looked – Oh that look! it spoke annihilation to the mightiest engine upon the rail, it scoffed at steam, and flashed furious derision at the largest terminus that ever was erected; it was an awfully comprehensive look – the concentrated essence of the fierce and deadly enmity of all the stage coachmen in England to steam conveyance.

To my utter astonishment, not, it must be owned, unmixed with fear, he suddenly turned his eyes towards my place of shelter, and walked up to me.

'That's the rail,' said he, between his set teeth.

'It is,' said I, considerably embarrassed.

'Damn it!' returned the excited Stage Coachman.

There was something inexpressibly awful about this execration; and I confess I felt a strong internal conviction that the next day's paper would teem with horrible railway accidents in every column.

'I did my utmost to hoppose 'em,' said the Stage Coachman, in softened accents. 'I wos the *last* that guv' in, I kep' a losing day after day, and yet I worked on; I wos determined to do my dooty, and I drove a coach the last day with an old hooman and a carpet bag inside, and three little boys and seven whopping empty portmanteaus outside. I wos determined my last kick to have *some* passengers to show to the rail, so I took my wife and children 'cos nobody else wouldn't go, and then we guv' in. Hows'ever, the last time as *I* wos on the road I did'nt go and show 'em an empty coach – we wasn't full, but we wasn't empty; we wos game to the last!'

A grim smile of triumph lit up the features of the deposed Coachman as he gave vent to this assertion. He took hold of me by the button-hole, and led the way into the house.

'This landlord wos an austerious sort of a man,' said he; 'he used to hobserve, that he only wished a Railway Committee would dine at his house, he'd pison 'em all, and emigrate; and he'd ha' done it, too!'

I did not venture to doubt this, so the stage coachman continued.

'I've smoked my pipe by the hour together in that fire-place; I've read 'The Times' adwertisements and Perlice Reports in that box till I fell asleep; I've walked up and down this here room a saying all sorts of things about the rail, and a busting for happiness. Outside this wery door I've bin a drownded in thankys from ladies for never lettin' nobody step through their band-boxes. The chambermaids used to smile, and the dogs used to bark, wherever I came. – But it's all hover now – the poor feller as kep' this place takes tickets at a Station, and the chambermaids makes scalding hot tea behind a mahuggany counter for people as has no time to drink it in!'

As the Stage Coachman uttered these words, a contemptuous sneer puckered his sallow cheek. He led me back into the yard; the ruined appearance of which, looked doubly mournful, under the faint rays of moonlight that every here and there stole through the dilapidated walls of the stable. An owl had taken up his abode, where the chief oastler's bedroom had once rejoiced in the grotesque majesty of huge portraits of every winner of every 'Derby,' since the first days of Epsom. The bird of night flew heavily off at our approach, and my companion pointed gloomily up to the fragments of mouldy, worm-eaten wood, the last relics of the stable loft.

'He wos a great friend of mine, was that h'ostler,' said the Coachman, 'but he's left this railway-bothered world – he was finished by the train.'

At my earnest entreaty to hear further, he continued,

'When this h'old place, wos guv'up and ruinated; the h'oastler as 'ud never look at the rail before, went down to have a sight of it, and as he wos a leaning his elbows on the wall, and a wishing as how he had the stabling of all the steam h'ingines (he'd ha' done 'em justice!) wot should he see, but one of his osses as wos thrown out of employ by the rail, a walking along jist where the train was coming. Bill jumped down, and as he wos a leading of him h'off, up comes the train, and went over his leg and cut the'os in two – "Tom," says he to me when we picked him up; 'I'm a going eleven mile an hour, to the last stage as is left for me to do. I've always done my dooty with the osses; I've bin and done it now – bury that ere poor os and me out of the noise of the rail.' We got the surgeons to him, but he never spoke no more, Poor Bill! Poor Bill!'

This last recollection seemed too much for the Stage Coachman, he wrung my hand, and walked abruptly to the furthest corner of the yard.

I took care not to interrupt him, and watched him carefully from a distance.

At first, the one expression of his countenance was melancholy; but by degrees, other thoughts came crowding from his mind, and mantled on his woe-be-gone visage. Poor fellow, I could see that he was again in imagination the beloved of the ladies and the adored of the chambermaids: a faint reflection of the affable, yet majestic demeanour, required by his calling, flitted occasionally over his pinched, attenuated features: and brightened the cold, melancholy expression of his countenance.

As I still looked, it grew darker and darker, yet the face of the Stage Coachman was never for an instant hidden from me. The same artificial expression of pleasure characterized its lineaments as before. Suddenly I heard a strange, unnatural noise in the air – now it seemed like the distant trampling of horses; and now again, like the rumbling of a heavily laden coach along a public road. A faint, sickly light, spread itself over that part of the Heavens whence the sounds proceeded; and after an interval, a fully equipped Stage

Coach appeared in the clouds, with a railway director strapped fast to each wheel, and a stoker between the teeth of each of the four horses.

In place of luggage, fragments of broken steam carriages, and red carpet bags filled with other mementos of railway accidents, occupied the roof. Chance passengers appeared to be the only tenants of the outside places. In front sat Julius Caesar and Mrs Hannah Moore; and behind, Sir Joseph Banks and Mrs Brownrigge. Of all the 'insides,' I could, I grieve to say, see nothing.

On the box was a little man with fuzzy hair and large iron grey whiskers; clothed in a coat of engineers' skin, with gloves of the hide of railway police. He pulled up opposite my friend, and bowing profoundly motioned him to the box seat.

A gleam of unutterable joy irradiated the Stage Coachman's countenance, as he stepped lightly into his place, seized the reins, and with one hearty 'good night,' addressed to an imaginary inn-full of people, started the horses.

Off they drove! my friend in the plenitude of his satisfaction cracking the whip every instant as he drove the phantom coach into the air. And amidst the shrieks of the railway directors at the wheel, the groans of *James Watt*, the bugle of the guard, and the tremendous cursing of the invisible 'insides,' fast and furiously disappeared from my eyes.

The Twin Sisters

Originally appeared in *Bentley's Miscellany*, March 1851. Signed 'W. Wilkie Collins, Author of *Antonina*.' Never reprinted. Though Collins assures us in his subtitle that this is 'A True Story', it is not clear what episode lies behind it. Collins had twin cousins, William and Percy Carpenter, and later in the 1850s (after the story was published) got to know Eliza and Janet Chambers who, according to Catherine Peters, 'played the usual substitution tricks that identical twins delight in' (*The King of Inventors*, p. 92). But in 'The Twin Sisters' the twins are not precisely identical – the hero, at least, finds plenty to choose between them. Nor are they deliberately hoodwinking him. It is plain bad luck that he ends up engaged to the one he doesn't fancy. It is most likely Collins is experimenting with the theme of the 'Double': a theme that will crop up again and again in his fiction, most memorably in the highly suggestive story 'The Dead Hand' (see below) and in the coupling of Anne Catherick and Laura Fairlie in *The Woman in White* (1860). 'The Twin Sisters', like *Basil*, the novel Collins was to write the next year, is a story of love at first sight, where the hero is later desperately disappointed in the choice he has made. Collins attempted to revive the story in 1859 as the basis of a one-act farce 'to keep the audience roaring with laughter all through'. He offered it to the management of the Olympic Theatre, but it was never produced (see *The King of Inventors*, pp. 183–4).

A MONG THOSE WHO attended the first of the King's *levées*, during the London season of 18—, was an unmarried gentleman of large fortune, named Streatfield. While his carriage was proceeding slowly down St James's Street, he naturally sought such amusement and occupation as he could find in looking on the brilliant scene around him. The day was unusually fine; crowds of spectators thronged the street and the balconies of the houses on either side of it, all gazing at the different equipages with as eager a curiosity and interest, as if fine vehicles and fine people inside them were the rarest objects of contemplation in the whole metropolis. Proceeding at a slower and slower pace, Mr Streatfield's carriage had just arrived at the middle of the street, when a longer stoppage than usual occurred. He looked carelessly up at the nearest balcony; and there, among some eight or ten ladies, all strangers to him, he saw one face that riveted his attention immediately.

He had never beheld anything so beautiful, anything which struck him with such strange, mingled, and sudden sensations, as this face. He gazed and gazed on it, hardly knowing where he was, or what he was doing, until the line of vehicles began again to move on. Then – after first ascertaining the number of the house – he flung himself back in the carriage, and tried to examine his own feelings, to reason himself into self-possession; but it was all in vain. He was seized with that amiable form of social monomania, called 'love at first sight.'

He entered the palace, greeted his friends, and performed all the necessary Court ceremonies, feeling the whole time like a man in a trance. He spoke mechanically, and moved mechanically – the lovely face in the balcony occupied his thoughts, to the exclusion of everything else. On his return home, he had engagements for the afternoon and the evening – he forgot and broke them all; and walked back to St James's Street as soon as he had changed his dress.

The balcony was empty; the sight-seers, who had filled it but a few hours before, had departed – but obstacles of all sorts now tended only to stimulate Mr Streatfield; he was determined to ascertain the parentage of the young lady, determined to look on the lovely face again – the thermometer of his heart had risen already to Fever Heat! Without loss of time, the shopkeeper to whom the house belonged was bribed to loquacity by a purchase. All that he could tell, in answer to inquiries, was that he had let his lodgings to an elderly gentleman and his wife, from the country, who had asked some friends into their balcony to see the carriages go to the *levée*. Nothing daunted, Mr Streatfield questioned and questioned again. What was the old gentleman's name? – Dimsdale. – Could he see Mr Dimsdale's servant? – The obsequious shopkeeper had no doubt that he could: Mr Dimsdale's servant should be sent for immediately.

In a few minutes the servant, the all-important link in the chain of Love's evidence, made his appearance. He was a pompous, portly man, who listened with solemn attention, with a stern judicial calmness, to Mr Streatfield's rapid and somewhat confused inquiries, which were accompanied by a minute description of the young lady, and by several explanatory statements, all very fictitious, and all very plausible. Stupid as the servant was, and suspicious as all stupid people are, he had nevertheless sense enough to perceive that he was addressed by a gentleman, and gratitude enough to feel considerably mollified by the handsome *douceur* which was quietly slipped into his hand. After much pondering and doubting, he at last arrived at the conclusion that the fair object of Mr Streatfield's inquiries was a Miss Langley, who had joined the party in the balcony that morning, with her sister; and who was the daughter of Mr Langley, of Langley Hall, in — shire. The family were now staying in London, at — Street. More information than this, the servant stated that he could not afford – he was certain that he had made no mistake, for the Miss Langleys were the only very young ladies in the house that morning – however, if Mr Streatfield wished to speak to his master, he was ready to carry any message with which he might be charged.

But Mr Streatfield had already heard enough for his purpose, and departed at once for his club, determined to discover some means of being introduced in due form to Miss Langley, before he slept that night – though he should travel round the whole circle of his acquaintance – high and low, rich and poor – in making the attempt. Arrived at the club, he began to inquire resolutely, in all directions, for a friend who knew Mr Langley, of Langley Hall. He disturbed gastronomic gentlemen at their dinner; he interrupted agricultural gentlemen who were moaning over the prospects of the harvest; he startled literary gentlemen who were deep in the critical mysteries of the last Review; he invaded billiard-room, dressing-room, smoking-room; he was more like a frantic ministerial whipper-in, hunting up stray members for a division, than an ordinary man; and the oftener he was defeated in his object, the more determined he was to succeed. At last, just as he had vainly inquired of everybody that he knew, just as he was standing in the hall of the club-house thinking where he should go next, a friend entered, who at once relieved him of all his difficulties – a precious, an inestimable man, who was on intimate terms with Mr Langley, and had been lately staying at Langley Hall. To this friend all the lover's cares and anxieties were at once confided; and a fitter depositary for such secrets of the heart could hardly have been found. He made no jokes – for he was not a bachelor; he abstained from shaking his head and recommending prudence – for he was not a seasoned husband, or an experienced widower; what he really did, was to enter heart and soul into his friend's projects – for he was precisely in that position, the only position, in which the male sex generally take a proper interest in match-making: he was a newly married man.

Two days after, Mr Streatfield was the happiest of mortals – he was introduced to the lady of his love, to Miss Jane Langley. He really enjoyed the priceless privilege of looking once more on the face in the balcony, and looking on it almost as often as he wished. It was perfect Elysium. Mr and Mrs Langley saw little, or no company – Miss Jane was always accessible, never monopolised – the light of her beauty shone, day after day, for her adorer alone; and his love blossomed in it, fast as flowers in a hot-house. Passing quickly by all the minor details of the wooing to arrive the sooner at the grand fact of the winning, let us simply relate that Mr Streatfield's object in seeking an introduction to Mr Langley was soon explained, and was indeed visible enough long before the explanation. He was a handsome man, an accomplished man, and a rich man. His two first qualifications conquered the daughter, and his third the father. In six weeks Mr Streatfield was the accepted suitor of Miss Jane Langley.

The wedding-day was fixed – it was arranged that the marriage should take place at Langley Hall, whither the family proceeded, leaving the unwilling lover in London, a prey to all the inexorable business formalities of the occasion. For ten days did the ruthless lawyers – those dead weights that burden the back of Hymen – keep their victim imprisoned in the metropolis, occupied over settlements that never seemed likely to be settled. But even the long march of the Law has its end like other mortal things: at the expiration of the ten days all was completed, and Mr Streatfield found himself at liberty to start for Langley Hall.

A large party was assembled at the house to grace the approaching nuptials. There were to be *tableaux*, charades, boating-trips, riding-excursions, amusements of all sorts – the whole to conclude (in the play-bill phrase) with the grand climax of the wedding. Mr Streatfield arrived late; dinner was ready; he had barely time to dress, and then bustle into the drawing-room, just as the guests were leaving it, to offer his arm to Miss Jane – all greetings with friends and introductions to strangers being postponed till the party met round the dining-table.

Grace had been said; the covers were taken off; the loud, cheerful hum of conversation was just beginning, when Mr Streatfield's eyes met the eyes of a young lady who was seated opposite, at the table. The guests near him, observing at the same moment, that he continued standing after every one else had been placed, glanced at him inquiringly. To their astonishment and alarm, they observed that his face had suddenly become deadly pale – his rigid features looked struck by paralysis. Several of his friends spoke to him; but for the first few moments he returned no answer. Then, still fixing his eyes upon the young lady opposite, he abruptly exclaimed in a voice, the altered tones of which startled every one who heard him: '*That* is the face I saw in the balcony! – *that* woman is the only woman I can ever marry!' The next instant, without a word more either of explanation or apology, he hurried from the room.

One or two of the guests mechanically started up, as if to follow him; the rest remained at the table, looking on each other in speechless surprise. But, before any one could either act or speak, almost at the moment when the door closed on Mr Streatfield, the attention of all was painfully directed to Jane Langley. She had fainted. Her mother and sisters removed her from the room immediately, aided by the servants. As they disappeared, a dead silence again sank down over the company – they all looked round with one accord to the master of the house.

Mr Langley's face and manner sufficiently revealed the suffering and suspense that he was secretly enduring. But he was a man of the world – neither by word nor action did he betray what was passing within him. He resumed his place at the table, and begged his guests to do the same. He affected to make light of what had happened; entreated every one to forget it, or, if they remembered it at all, to remember it only as a mere accident which would no doubt be satisfactorily explained. Perhaps it was only a jest on Mr Streatfield's part – rather too serious a one, he must own. At any rate, whatever was the cause of the interruption to the dinner which had just happened, it was not important enough to require everybody to fast around the table of the feast. He asked it as a favour to himself, that no further notice might be taken of what had occurred. While Mr Langley was speaking thus, he hastily wrote a few lines on a piece of paper, and gave it to one of the servants. The note was directed to Mr Streatfield; the lines contained only these words: 'Two hours hence, I shall expect to see you alone in the library.'

The dinner proceeded; the places occupied by the female members of the Langley family, and by the young lady who had attracted Mr Streatfield's notice in so extraordinary a manner, being left vacant. Every one present endeavoured to follow Mr Langley's advice, and go through the business of the dinner, as if nothing had occurred; but the attempt failed miserably. Long, blank pauses occurred in the conversation; general topics were started, but never pursued; it was more like an assembly of strangers, than a meeting of friends; people neither eat nor drank, as they were accustomed to eat and drink; they talked in altered voices, and sat with unusual stillness, even in the same positions. Relatives, friends, and acquaintances, all alike perceived that some great domestic catastrophe had happened; all foreboded that some serious, if not fatal, explanation of Mr Streatfield's conduct would ensue: and it was vain and hopeless – a very mockery of self-possession – to attempt to shake off the sinister and chilling influences that recent events had left behind them, and resume at will the thoughtlessness and hilarity of ordinary life.

Still, however, Mr Langley persisted in doing the honours of his table, in proceeding doggedly through all the festive ceremonies of the hour, until the ladies rose and retired. Then, after looking at his watch, he beckoned to one of his sons to take his place; and quietly left the room. He only stopped once, as he crossed the hall, to ask news of his daughter from one of the servants. The reply was, that she had had a hysterical fit; that the medical attendant of the family had been sent for; and that since his arrival she had become more composed. When the man had spoken, Mr Langley made no remark, but proceeded at once to the library. He locked the door behind him, as soon as he entered the room.

Mr Streatfield was already waiting there – he was seated at the table, endeavouring to maintain an appearance of composure, by mechanically turning over the leaves of the books before him. Mr Langley drew a chair near him; and in low, but very firm tones, began the conversation thus:

'I have given you two hours, Sir, to collect yourself, to consider your position fully – I presume, therefore, that you are now prepared to favour me with an explanation of your conduct at my table, to-day.'

'What explanation can I make? – what can I say, or think of this most terrible of fatalities?' exclaimed Mr Streatfield, speaking faintly and confusedly; and still not looking up – 'There has been an unexampled error committed! – a fatal mistake, which I could never have anticipated, and over which I had no control!'

'Enough, sir, of the language of romance,' interrupted Mr Langley, coldly; 'I am neither of an age nor a disposition to appreciate it. I come here to ask plain questions honestly, and I insist, as my right, on receiving answers in the same spirit. *You*, Mr Streatfield, sought an introduction to *me* – you professed yourself attached to my daughter Jane – your proposals were (I fear unhappily for *us*) accepted – your wedding-day was fixed – and now, after all this, when you happen to observe my daughter's twin-sister sitting opposite to you—'

'Her twin-sister!' exclaimed Mr Streatfield; and his trembling hand crumpled the leaves of the book, which he still held while he spoke. 'Why is it, intimate as I have been with your family, that I now know for the first time that Miss Jane Langley has a twin-sister?'

'Do you descend, sir, to a subterfuge, when I ask you for an explanation?'

returned Mr Langley, angrily. 'You must have heard, over and over again, that my children, Jane and Clara, were twins.'

'On my word and honour, I declare that—'

'Spare me all appeals to your word or your honour, sir; I am beginning to doubt both.'

'I will not make the unhappy situation in which we are all placed, still worse, by answering your last words, as I might, at other times, feel inclined to answer them,' said Mr Streatfield, assuming a calmer demeanour than he had hitherto displayed. 'I tell you the truth, when I tell you that, before to-day, I never knew that any of your children were twins. Your daughter, Jane, has frequently spoken to me of her absent sister, Clara, but never spoke of her as her twin-sister. Until to-day, I have had no opportunity of discovering the truth; for until to-day, I have never met Miss Clara Langley since I saw her in the balcony of the house in St James's Street. The only one of your children who was never present during my intercourse with your family, in London, was your daughter Clara – the daughter whom I now know, for the first time, as the young lady who really arrested my attention on my way to the levée – whose affections it was really my object to win in seeking an introduction to you. To *me*, the resemblance between the twin-sisters has been a fatal resemblance; the long absence of one, a fatal absence.'

There was a momentary pause, as Mr Streatfield sadly and calmly pronounced the last words. Mr Langley appeared to be absorbed in thought. At length he proceeded, speaking to himself:

'It *is* strange! I remember that Clara left London on the day of the *levée*, to set out on a visit to her aunt; and only returned here two days since, to be present at her sister's marriage. Well, sir,' he continued, addressing Mr Streatfield, 'granting what you say, granting that we all mentioned my absent daughter to you, as we are accustomed to mention her among ourselves, simply as "Clara," you have still not excused your conduct in my eyes. Remarkable as the resemblance is between the sisters, more remarkable even, I am willing to admit, than the resemblance usually is between twins, there is yet a difference, which, slight, indescribable though it may be, is nevertheless discernible to all their relations and to all their friends. How is it that you, who represent yourself as so vividly impressed by your first sight of my daughter Clara, did not discover the error when you were introduced to her sister Jane, as the lady who had so much attracted you?'

'You forget, sir,' rejoined Mr Streatfield, 'that I have never beheld the sisters together until to-day. Though both were in the balcony when I first looked up at it, it was Miss Clara Langley alone who attracted my attention. Had I only received the smallest hint that the absent sister of Miss Jane Langley was her *twin-sister*, I would have seen her, at any sacrifice, before making my proposals. For it is my duty to confess to you, Mr Langley (with the candour which is your undoubted due), that when I was first introduced to your daughter Jane, I felt an unaccountable impression that she was the same as, and yet different from, the lady whom I had seen in the balcony. Soon, however, this impression wore off. Under the circumstances, could I regard it as anything but a mere caprice, a lover's wayward fancy? I dismissed it from my mind; it ceased to affect me, until to-day, when I first discovered that it was a warning which I had most unhappily disregarded; that a terrible error had been committed, for which no one of us was to blame, but which was fraught with misery, undeserved misery, to us all!'

'These, Mr Streatfield, are explanations which may satisfy *you*,' said Mr Langley, in a milder tone, 'but they cannot satisfy *me*; they will not satisfy the world. You have repudiated, in the most public and most abrupt manner, an engagement, in the fulfilment of which the honour and the happiness of my family are concerned. You have given me reasons for your conduct, it is true; but will those reasons restore to my daughter the tranquillity which she has lost, perhaps for ever? Will they stop the whisperings of calumny? Will they carry conviction to those strangers to me, or enemies of mine, whose pleasure it may be to disbelieve them? You have placed both yourself and me, sir, in a position of embarrassment – nay, a position of danger and disgrace, from which the strongest reasons and the best excuses cannot extricate us.'

'I entreat you to believe,' replied Mr Streatfield, 'that I deplore from my heart the error – the fault, if you will – of which I have been unconsciously guilty. I implore your pardon, both for what I said and did at your table to-day; but I cannot do more. I cannot and I dare not pronounce the marriage vows to your daughter, with my lips, when I know that neither my conscience nor my heart can ratify them. The commonest justice, and the commonest respect towards a young lady who deserves both, and more than both, from every one who approaches her, strengthen me to persevere in the only course which it is consistent with honour and integrity for me to take.'

'You appear to forget,' said Mr Langley, 'that it is not merely your own honour, but the honour of others, that is to be considered in the course of conduct which you are now to pursue.'

'I have by no means forgotten what is due to *you*,' continued Mr Streatfield, 'or what responsibilities I have incurred from the nature of my intercourse with your family. Do I put too much trust in your forbearance, if I now assure you, candidly and unreservedly, that I still place all my hopes of happiness in the prospect of becoming connected by marriage with a daughter of yours? Miss Clara Langley—'

Here the speaker paused. His position was becoming a delicate and a dangerous one; but he made no effort to withdraw from it. Almost bewildered by the pressing and perilous emergency of the moment, harassed by such a tumult of conflicting emotions within him as he had never known before, he risked the worst, with all the blind-fold desperation of love. The angry flush was rising on Mr Langley's cheek; it was evidently costing him a severe struggle to retain his assumed self-possession; but he did not speak. After an interval, Mr Streatfield proceeded thus:

'However unfortunately I may express myself, I am sure you will do me the justice to believe that I am now speaking from my heart on a subject (to *me*) of the most vital importance. Place yourself in my situation, consider all that has happened, consider that this may be, for aught I know to the contrary, the last opportunity I may have of pleading my cause; and then say whether it is possible for me to conceal from you that I can only look to your forbearance and sympathy for permission to retrieve my error, to – to – Mr Langley! I cannot choose expressions at such a moment as this. I can only tell you that the feeling with which I regarded your daughter Clara, when I first saw her, still remains what it was. I cannot analyse it; I cannot reconcile its apparent inconsistencies and contradictions; I cannot explain how, while I may seem to you and to every one to have varied and vacillated with insolent caprice, I have really remained, in my own heart and to my own conscience, true to my first sensations and my first convictions. I can only implore you not to condemn me to a life of disappointment and misery, by judging me with hasty irritation. Favour me, so far at least, as to relate the conversation which has passed between us to your two daughters. Let me hear how it affects each of them towards me. Let me know what they are willing to think and ready to do under such unparalleled circumstances as have now occurred. I will wait *your* time, and *their* time; I will abide by *your* decision and *their* decision, pronounced after the first poignant distress and irritation of this day's events have passed over.'

Still Mr Langley remained silent; the angry word was on his tongue; the contemptuous rejection of what he regarded for the moment as a proposition equally ill-timed and insolent, seemed bursting to his lips; but once more he restrained himself. He rose from his seat, and walked slowly backwards and forwards, deep in thought. Mr Streatfield was too much overcome by his own agitation to plead his cause further by another word. There was a silence in the room now, which lasted for some time.

We have said that Mr Langley was a man of the world. He was strongly attached to his children; but he had a little of the selfishness and much of the reverence for wealth of a man of the world. As he now endeavoured to determine mentally on his proper course of action – to disentangle the whole case from all its mysterious intricacies – to view it, extraordinary as it was, in its proper bearings, his thoughts began gradually to assume what is called, 'a practical turn.' He reflected that he had another daughter, besides the twin-sisters, to provide for; and that he had two sons to settle in life. He was not rich enough to portion three daughters; and he had not interest enough to start his sons favourably in a career of eminence. Mr Streatfield, on the contrary, was a man of great wealth, and of great 'connections' among people in power. Was such a son-in-law to be rejected, even after all that had happened, without at least consulting his wife and daughters first? He thought not. Had not Mr Streatfield, in truth, been the victim of a remarkable fatality, of an incredible accident, and were no allowances, under such circumstances, to be made for him? He began to think there were. Reflecting thus, he determined at length to proceed with moderation and caution at all hazards; and regained composure enough to continue the conversation in a cold, but still in a polite tone.

'I will commit myself, sir, to no agreement or promise whatever,' he began, 'nor will I consider this interview in any respect as a conclusive one, either on your side or mine; but if I think, on consideration, that it is desirable that our conversation should be repeated to my wife and daughters, I will make them acquainted with it, and will let you know the result. In the meantime, I think you will agree with me, that it is most fit that the next communications between us should take place by letter alone.'

Mr Streatfield was not slow in taking the hint conveyed by Mr Langley's last words. After what had occurred, and until something was definitely settled, he felt that the suffering and suspense which he was already enduring would be increased tenfold if he remained longer in the same house with the twin-sisters – the betrothed of one, the lover of the other! Murmuring a few inaudible words of acquiescence in the arrangement which had just been proposed to him, he left the room. The same evening he quitted Langley Hall.

The next morning the remainder of the guests departed, their curiosity to know all the particulars of what had happened remaining ungratified. They were simply informed that an extraordinary and unexpected obstacle had arisen to delay the wedding; that no blame attached to any one in the matter; and that as soon as everything had been finally determined, everything would be explained. Until then, it was not considered necessary to enter in any way into particulars. By the middle of the day every visitor had left the house; and a strange and melancholy spectacle it presented when they were all gone. Rooms were now empty and silent, which the day before had been filled with animated groups, and had echoed with merry laughter. In one apartment, the fittings for the series of 'Tableaux' which had been proposed, remained half completed: the dresses that were to have been worn, lay scattered on the floor; the carpenter who had come to proceed with his work, gathered up his tools in ominous silence, and departed as quickly as he could. Here lay books still open at the last page read; there was an album, with the drawing of the day before unfinished, and the colour-box unclosed by its side. On the deserted billiard-table, the positions of the 'cues' and balls showed traces of an interrupted game. Flowers were scattered on the rustic tables in the garden, half-made into nosegays, and beginning to wither already. The very dogs wandered in a moody, unsettled way about the house, missing the friendly hands that had fondled and fed them for so many days past, and whining impatiently in the deserted drawing-rooms. The social desolation of the scene was miserably complete in all its aspects.

Immediately after the departure of his guests, Mr Langley had a long interview with his wife. He repeated to her the conversation which had taken place between Mr Streatfield and himself, and received from her in return such an account of the conduct of his daughter, under the trial that had befallen her, as filled him with equal astonishment and admiration. It was a new revelation to him of the character of his own child.

'As soon as the violent symptoms had subsided,' said Mrs Langley, in answer to her husband's first inquiries, 'as soon as the hysterical fit was subdued, Jane seemed suddenly to assume a new character, to become another person. She begged that the doctor might be released from his attendance, and that she might be left alone with me and with her sister Clara. When every one else had quitted the room, she continued to sit in the easy chair where we had at first placed her, covering her face with her hands. She entreated us not to speak to her for a short time, and, except that she shuddered occasionally, sat quite still and silent. When she at last looked up, we were shocked to see the deadly paleness of her face, and the strange alteration that had come over her expression; but she spoke to us so coherently, so solemnly even, that we were amazed; we knew not what to think or what to do; it hardly seemed to be *our* Jane who was now speaking to us.'

'What did she say?' asked Mr Langley, eagerly.

'She said that the first feeling of her heart, at that moment, was gratitude on her own account. She thanked God that the terrible discovery had not been made too late, when her married life might have been a life of estrangement and misery. Up to the moment when Mr Streatfield had uttered that one fatal exclamation, she had loved him, she told us, fondly and fervently; *now*, no explanation, no repentance (if either were tendered), no earthly persuasion or command (in case Mr Streatfield should think himself bound, as a matter of atonement, to hold to his rash engagement), could ever induce her to become his wife.'

'Mr Streatfield will not test her resolution,' said Mr Langley, bitterly; 'he deliberately repeated his repudiation of his engagement in this room; nay, more, he—'

'I have something important to say to you from Jane on this point,' interrupted Mrs Langley. 'After she had spoken the first few words which I have already repeated to you, she told us that she had been thinking – thinking more calmly perhaps than we could imagine – on all that had happened; on what Mr Streatfield had said at the dinner-table; on the momentary glance of recognition which she had seen pass between him and her sister Clara, whose accidental absence, during the whole period of Mr Streatfield's intercourse with us in London, she now remembered and reminded me of. The cause of the fatal error, and the manner in which it had occurred, seemed to be already known to her, as if by intuition. We entreated her to refrain from speaking on the subject for the present; but she answered that it was her duty to speak on it – her duty to propose something which should alleviate the suspense and distress we were all enduring on her account. No words can describe to you her fortitude, her noble endurance –' Mrs Langley's voice faltered as she pronounced the last words. It was some minutes ere she became sufficiently composed to proceed thus:

'I am charged with a message to you from Jane – I should say, charged with her entreaties, that you will not suspend our intercourse with Mr Streatfield, or view his conduct in any other than a merciful light – as conduct for which accident and circumstances are alone to blame. After she had given me this message to you, she turned to Clara, who sat weeping by her side, completely overcome; and kissing her, said that *they* were to blame, if any one was to be blamed in the matter, for being so much alike as to make all who saw them apart doubt which was Clara and which was Jane. She said this with a faint smile, and an effort to speak playfully, which touched us to the heart. Then, in a tone and manner which I can never forget, she asked her sister – charging her, on their mutual affection and mutual confidence, to answer sincerely – if *she* had noticed Mr Streatfield on the day of the levée, and had afterwards remembered him at the dinner-table, as *he* had noticed and remembered *her*? It was only after Jane had repeated this appeal, still more earnestly and affectionately, that Clara summoned courage and composure enough to confess that she *had* noticed Mr Streatfield on the day of the levée, had thought of him afterwards during her absence from London, and had recognised him at our table, as he had recognised her.'

'Is it possible! I own I had not anticipated – not thought for one moment of that,' said Mr Langley.

'Perhaps,' continued his wife, 'it is best that you should see Jane now, and judge for yourself. For *my* part, her noble resignation under this great trial, has so astonished and impressed me, that I only feel competent to advise as she advises, to act as she thinks fit. I begin to think that it is not *we* who are to guide *her*, but *she* who is to guide *us*.'

Mr Langley lingered irresolute for a few minutes; then quitted the room, and proceeded alone to Jane Langley's apartment.

When he knocked at the door, it was opened by Clara. There was an expression partly of confusion, partly of sorrow on her face; and when her father stopped as if to speak to her, she merely pointed into the room, and hurried away without uttering a word.

Mr Langley had been prepared by his wife for the change that had taken place in his daughter since the day before; but he felt startled, almost overwhelmed, as he now looked on her. One of the poor girl's most prominent personal attractions, from her earliest years, had been the beauty of her complexion; and now, the freshness and the bloom had entirely departed from her face; it seemed absolutely colourless. Her expression, too, appeared to Mr Langley's eyes, to have undergone a melancholy alteration; to have lost its youthfulness suddenly; to have assumed a strange character of firmness and thoughtfulness, which he had never observed in it before. She was sitting by an open window, commanding a lovely view of wide, sunny landscape; a Bible which her mother had given her, lay open on her knees; she was reading in it as her father entered. For the first time in his life, he paused, speechless, as he approached to speak to one of his own children.

'I am afraid I look very ill,' she said, holding out her hand to him; 'but I am better than I look; I shall be quite well in a day or two. Have you heard my message, father? have you been told?'

'My love, we will not speak of it yet; we will wait a few days,' said Mr Langley.

'You have always been so kind to me,' she continued, in less steady tones, 'that I am sure you will let me go on. I have very little to say, but that little must be said now, and then we need never recur to it again. Will you consider all that has happened, as something forgotten? You have heard already what it is that I entreat you to do; will you let *him* – Mr Streatfield –' (She stopped, her voice failed for a moment, but she recovered herself again almost immediately.) 'Will you let Mr Streatfield remain here, or recall him if he is gone, and give him an opportunity of explaining himself to my sister? If poor Clara should refuse to see him for my sake, pray do not listen to her. I am sure this is what ought to be done; I have been thinking of it very calmly, and I feel that it is right. And there is something more I have to beg of you, father; it is, that, while Mr Streatfield is here, you will allow me to go and stay with my aunt. You know how fond she is of me. Her house is not a day's journey from home. It is best for everybody (much the best for *me*) that I should not remain here at present; and – and – dear father! I have always been your spoiled child; and I know you will indulge me still. If you will do what I ask you, I shall soon get over this heavy trial. I shall be well again if I am away at my aunt's – if—'

She paused; and putting one trembling arm round her father's neck, hid her face on his breast. For some minutes, Mr Langley could not trust himself to answer her. There was something, not deeply touching only, but impressive and sublime, about the moral heroism of this young girl, whose heart and mind – hitherto wholly inexperienced in the harder and darker emergencies of life – now rose in the strength of their native purity superior to the bitterest, cruellest trial that either could undergo; whose patience and resignation, called forth for the first time by a calamity which suddenly thwarted the purposes and paralysed the affections that had been destined to endure for a life, could thus appear at once in the fullest maturity of virtue and beauty. As the father thought on these things; as he vaguely and imperfectly estimated the extent of the daughter's sacrifice; as he reflected on the nature of the affliction that had befallen her – which combined in itself a fatality that none could have foreseen, a fault that could neither be repaired nor resented, a judgment against which there was no appeal – and then remembered how this affliction had been borne, with what words and what actions it had been met, he felt that it would be almost a profanation to judge the touching petition just addressed to him, by the criterion of *his* worldly doubts and *his* worldly wisdom. His eye fell on the Bible, still open beneath it; he remembered the little child who was set in the midst of the disciples, as teacher and example to all; and when at length he spoke in answer to his daughter, it was not to direct or to advise, but to comfort and comply.

They delayed her removal for a few days, to see if she faltered in her resolution, if her bodily weakness increased; but she never wavered; nothing in her appearance changed, either for better or for worse. A week after the startling scene at the dinner-table, she was living in the strictest retirement in the house of her aunt.

About the period of her departure, a letter was received from Mr Streatfield. It was little more than a recapitulation of what he had already said to Mr Langley – expressed, however, on this occasion, in stronger and, at the same time, in more respectful terms. The letter was answered briefly: he was informed that nothing had, as yet, been determined on, but that the next communication would bring him a final reply.

Two months passed. During that time, Jane Langley was frequently visited at her aunt's house, by her father and mother. She still remained calm and resolved; still looked pale and thoughtful, as at first. Doctors were consulted: they talked of a shock to the nervous system; of great hope from time, and their patient's strength of mind; and of the necessity of acceding to her wishes in all things. Then, the advice of the aunt was sought. She was a woman of an eccentric, masculine character, who had herself experienced a love-disappointment in early life, and had never married. She gave her opinion unreservedly and abruptly, as she always gave it. 'Do as Jane tells you!' said the old lady, severely; 'that poor child has more moral courage and determination than all the rest of you put together! I know better than anybody what a sacrifice she has had to make; but she has made it, and made it nobly – like a heroine, as some people would say; like a good, high-minded, courageous girl, as *I* say! Do as she tells you! Let that poor, selfish fool of a man have his way, and marry her sister – he has made one mistake already about a face – see if he doesn't find out, some day, that he has made another, about a wife! Let him! – Jane is too good for *him*, or for any man! Leave her to me; let her stop here; she shan't lose by what has happened! You know this place is mine – I mean it to be hers, when I'm dead. You know I've got some money – I shall leave it to her. I've made my will: it's all done and settled! Go back home; send for the man, and tell Clara to marry him without any more fuss! You wanted my opinion – there it is for you!'

At last, Mr Langley decided. The important letter was written, which recalled Mr Streatfield to Langley Hall. As Jane had foreseen, Clara at first refused to hold any communication with him; but a letter from her sister, and the remonstrances of her father, soon changed her resolution. There was nothing in common between the twin-sisters but their personal resemblance. Clara had been guided all her life by the opinions of others, and she was guided by them now.

Once permitted the opportunity of pleading his cause, Mr Streatfield did not neglect his own interests. It would be little to our purpose to describe the doubts and difficulties which delayed at first the progress of his second courtship – pursued as it was under circumstances, not only extraordinary, but unprecedented. It is no longer, with him, or with Clara Langley, that the interest of our story is connected. Suffice it to say, that he ultimately overcame all the young lady's scruples; and that, a few months afterwards, some of Mr Langley's intimate friends found themselves again assembled round his table as wedding-guests, and congratulating Mr Streatfield on his approaching union with Clara, as they had already congratulated him, scarcely a year back, on his approaching union with Jane!

The social ceremonies of the wedding-day were performed soberly – almost sadly. Some of the guests (especially the unmarried ladies) thought that Miss Clara had allowed herself to be won too easily – others were picturing to themselves the situation of the poor girl who was absent; and contributed little towards the gaiety of the party. On this occasion, however, nothing occurred to interrupt the proceedings; the marriage took place; and, immediately after it, Mr Streatfield and his bride started for a tour on the Continent.

On their departure, Jane Langley returned home. She made no reference whatever to her sister's marriage; and no one mentioned it in her presence. Still the colour did not return to her cheek, or the old gaiety to her manner. The shock that she had suffered had left its traces on her for life. But there was no evidence that she was sinking under the remembrances which neither time nor resolution could banish. The strong, pure heart had undergone a change, but not a deterioration. All that had been brilliant in her character was gone; but all that was noble in it remained. Never had her intercourse with her family and her friends been so affectionate and so kindly as it was now.

When, after a long absence, Mr Streatfield and his wife returned to England, it was observed, at her first meeting with them, that the momentary confusion and embarrassment were on *their* side, not on *hers*. During their stay at Langley Hall, she showed not the slightest disposition to avoid them. No member of the family welcomed them more cordially; entered into all their plans and projects more readily; or bade them farewell with a kinder or better grace, when they departed for their own home.

Our tale is nearly ended: what remains of it, must comprise the history of many years in the compass of a few words.

Time passed on; and Death and Change told of its lapse among the family at Langley Hall. Five years after the events above related, Mr Langley died; and was followed to the grave, shortly afterwards, by his wife. Of their two sons, the eldest was rising into good practice at the bar; the youngest had become *attaché* to a foreign embassy. Their third daughter was married, and living at the family seat of her husband, in Scotland. Mr and Mrs Streatfield had children of their own, now, to occupy their time and absorb their care. The career of life was over for some – the purposes of life had altered for others – Jane Langley alone, still remained unchanged.

She now lived entirely with her aunt. At intervals – as their worldly duties and worldly avocations permitted them – the other members of her family, or one or two intimate friends, came to the house. Offers of marriage were made to her, but were all declined. The first, last love of her girlish days – abandoned as a hope, and crushed as a passion; living only as a quiet grief, as a pure remembrance – still kept its watch, as guardian and defender, over her heart. Years passed on and worked no change in the sad uniformity of her life, until the death of her aunt left her mistress of the house in which she had hitherto been a guest. Then it was observed that she made fewer and fewer efforts to vary the tenor of her existence, to forget her old remembrances for awhile in the society of others. Such invitations as reached her from relations and friends were more frequently declined than accepted. She was growing old herself now; and, with each advancing year, the busy pageant of the outer world presented less and less that could attract her eye.

So she began to surround herself, in her solitude, with the favourite books that she had studied, with the favourite music that she had played, in the days of her hopes and her happiness. Everything that was associated, however slightly, with that past period, now acquired a character of inestimable value in her eyes, as aiding her mind to seclude itself more and more strictly in the sanctuary of its early recollections. Was it weakness in her to live thus; to abandon the world and the world's interests, as one who had no hope, or part in either? Had she earned the right, by the magnitude and resolution of her sacrifice, thus to indulge in the sad luxury of fruitless remembrance? Who shall say! – who shall presume to decide that cannot think with *her* thoughts, and look back with *her* recollections!

Thus she lived – alone, and yet not lonely; without hope, but with no despair; separate and apart from the world around her, except when she approached it by her charities to the poor, and her succour to the afflicted; by her occasional interviews with the surviving members of her family and a few old friends, when they sought her in her calm retreat; and by the little presents which she constantly sent to brothers' and sisters' children, who worshipped, as their invisible good genius, 'the kind lady' whom most of them had never seen. Such was her existence throughout the closing years of her life: such did it continue – calm and blameless – to the last.

Reader, when you are told, that what is impressive and pathetic in the Drama of Human Life has passed with a past age of Chivalry and Romance, remember Jane Langley, and quote in contradiction the story of the Twin Sisters!

A Passage in the Life of Perugino Potts

Originally appeared in *Bentley's Miscellany*, February 1852. Never reprinted. This inventive comic sketch features an arch narrator typical of Collins's early non-fiction and travel books. The painting background derives partly from Collins's own early experiments as a visual artist, but mainly from observation of his father and brother. Collins broke off the composition of his first novel *Antonina* to write the biography of his recently dead father (see *Memoirs of the Life of William Collins, Esq., R.A.* (1848)). His brother was Charles Allston Collins, most famous as the painter of 'Convent Thoughts', now in the Ashmolean Museum, Oxford. 'A Passage in the Life of Mr Perugino Potts' mirrors Charles Collins's Bohemian agonies about establishing his true 'vocation'. It also features parodies of most of the contemporary genres of painting, including a swipe or two at Pre-Raphaelitism, then at its height. Catherine Peters points out that the opening of the story is a pastiche of William Collins's gently self-regarding journal entry for 1844 (*The King of Inventors*, p. 105). Wilkie Collins's first collection of short stories, *After Dark* (1856), features a painter as its framing device, and his novel *Hide and Seek* (1854) includes yet more 'glimpses at that artist-life which circumstances have afforded me peculiar opportunities of studying' (Preface to *After Dark*).

December 7th, 18— I have just been one week in Rome, and have determined to keep a journal. Most men in my situation would proceed to execute such a resolution as this, by writing about the antiquities of the 'Eternal City': I shall do nothing of the sort; I shall write about a much more interesting subject – myself.

I may be wrong, but my impression is that, as an Historical Painter, my biography will be written some of these days: personal particulars of me will then be wanted. I have great faith in the affectionate remembrance of any surviving friends I may leave behind me; but, upon the whole, I would rather provide these particulars myself. My future biographer shall have P.P. sketched by P.P. I paint my own pictures; why should I not paint my own character? The commencement of a new journal offers the opportunity of doing this – let me take it!

I was destined to be an artist from my cradle; my father was a great connoisseur, and a great collector of pictures; he christened me 'Perugino,' after the name of his favourite master, left me five hundred a-year, and told me with his last breath to be Potts, R.A., or perish in the attempt. I determined to obey him; but, though I have hitherto signally failed in becoming an R.A., I have not the slightest intention even of so much as *beginning* to perish, in compliance with the alternative suggested to me by my late lamented parent. Let the Royal Academy perish first! I mean to exist for the express purpose of testifying against that miserably managed institution as long as I possibly can.

This may be thought strong language: I will justify it by facts. For seven years I have vainly sought a place at the annual exhibition – for seven years has modest genius knocked for admission at the door of the Royal Academy, and invariably the answer of the Royal Academicians has been, 'not at home!' The first year I painted, 'the Smothering of the Princes in the Tower,' muscular murderers, flabby children, florid colouring; quite in the Rubens' style – turned out! The second year I tried the devotional and severe, 'the Wise and Foolish Virgins'; ten angular women, in impossible attitudes, with a landscape background, painted from the anti-perspective point of view – turned out! The third year I changed to the sentimental and pathetic; it was Sterne's 'Maria,' this time, with her goat; Maria was crying, the goat was crying, Sterne himself (in the background) was crying, with his face buried in a white cambric pocket-handkerchief, wet through with tears – turned out! The fourth year I fell back on the domestic and familiar: a young Housemaid in the kitchen, plighting her troth, at midnight, to a private in the Grenadier Guards, while the policeman of the neighbourhood, a prey to jealousy and despair, flashed his 'bull's-eye' on them through the window, from the area railings above, – turned out! The fifth year I gave up figures, and threw my whole soul into landscape, – classical landscape. I sent in a picture of three ruined columns, five pine-trees, a lake, a temple, distant mountains, and a gorgeous sun-set, the whole enlivened by a dance of nymphs in Roman togas, in front of the ruined columns to be sold for the ludicrously small price of fifty guineas – turned out! The sixth year, I resolved to turn mercenary in self-defence; and, abandoning high art, to take to portraiture. I produced a 'portrait of a lady' (she was a professional model, who sat at a shilling an hour – but no matter); I depicted her captivatingly clothed in white satin, and grinning serenely; in the background appeared a red curtain, gorgeously bound books on a round table, and thunder-storm clouds – turned out! The seventh year I humbly resigned myself to circumstances, and sank at once to 'still life,' represented on the smallest possible scale. A modest canvas, six inches long by four inches broad, containing striking likenesses of a pot of porter, a pipe, and a plate of bread and cheese, and touchingly entitled, 'the Labourer's best Friends,' was my last modest offering; and this – even this! the poor artist's one little ewe-lamb of a picture, was – turned out! The eighth year was the year when I started in disgust to seek nobler fields for pictorial ambition in the regions of Italian Art! The eighth year has brought me to Rome – here I am! – I, Perugino Potts! vowed to grapple with Raphael and Michael Angelo on their own ground! Grand idea!

Personally (when I have my high-heeled boots on) I stand five feet, three inches high. Let me at once acknowledge – for I have no concealments. from posterity – that I am, outwardly, what is termed a little man. I have nothing great about me but my mustachios and my intellect; I am of the light-complexioned order of handsome fellows, and have hitherto discovered nothing that I can conscientiously blame in my temper and general disposition. The fire of artistic ambition that burns within me, shoots upward with a lambent glow – in a word, I am a good-humoured man of genius. This is much to say, but I could add yet more; were I not unhappily writing with an Italian pen on Italian paper: the pen splutters inveterately; the paper absorbs my watery ink like a blotting-book – human patience can stand it no longer: I give up for the day, in despair!

8th – Intended to proceed with my interesting autobiographical particulars, but was suddenly stopped at the very outset by an idea for a new picture. Subject: The primitive Father Polycarp, writing his Epistles; to be treated in the sublime style of Michael Angelo's Prophets, on the ceiling of the Sistine Chapel. Polycarp to be several sizes larger than life, and well developed about the beard and muscles.

9th – Made inquiries for a good model, and found the very man I wanted. When I entered his humble abode, he was preparing his breakfast; the meal was characterised by a primitive simplicity and a strong smell. He first pulled out his stiletto knife, and cut off a large crust of bread: the outside of this crust he rubbed with garlic till it shone like a walnut-wood table in an English farm-house; the inside he saturated with oil and vinegar. By the time he had done that, the whole crust looked like a cold poultice in a polished calf-leather saucer. He ate this remarkable compound with voracious enjoyment, while I looked at him. I found him rather a difficult man to estimate in a physiognomical point of view; nothing was to be seen of his face but two goggle eyes and a hook nose, peering out of a forest of hair – such hair! just the iron-grey sort of thing I wanted. Such a beard! the most devotional I ever saw. I engaged him on the spot, and jocosely christened him Polycarp the Second, in allusion to the character he was to represent on my canvas.

10th – Polycarp the Second came to sit; he was polite, talkative, and apparently somewhat infested by fleas. I had an explanation with him on the last-mentioned of his personal characteristics. He asserted consolingly, that the fleas were not likely to leave *him* to go to *me* – they patriotically preferred Italian to English pasturage. Trusting he was right, I changed the subject and asked about his history. His answer tended to show that he had been ill-used and misunderstood by everybody from his very cradle.

His father, his mother, his relations, the priests, the police, the high populace and the low populace, throughout every degree – they had all maltreated, persecuted, falsely accused, and unrelentingly pursued Polycarp the Second. He attributed this miserable state of things partly to the invincible piety and honesty of his character, which, of course, exposed him to the malice of the world; and partly to his strong and disinterested attachment to the English nation, which lowered him in the eyes of his prejudiced countrymen. He wept as he said this – his beard became a disconsolate beard with the tears that trickled down it. Excellent-hearted Polycarp! I sympathise with him already in spite of the fleas.

11th – Another sitting from my worthy model. The colossal figure is, by this time (so rapid a workman am I) entirely sketched in. My physical exertions are tremendous. My canvas is fourteen feet high; and Polycarp reaches from top to bottom. I can only pursue my labour by incessantly getting up and down a pair of steps; by condemning myself heroically to a sort of pictorial treadmill. Already, however, I have tasted the compensating sweets of triumph. My model is in raptures with my design – he was so profoundly affected that he cried over it, just as he cried over his own history. What taste these Italians naturally possess! What impressibility! What untaught sympathies with genius! How delightfully different their disposition from the matter-of-fact English character! How stolid is a British Royal Academician, compared to Polycarp the Second!

12th – Model again. Crying again. Previous history again. Raptures again. I wish he would not smell quite so strong of garlic. At present he repels my nose as powerfully as he attracts my heart. Sent him on an errand, to buy me lamp-black and flake-white: I mean to lay it on rather thick when I come to Polycarp's beard. Gave him the money to pay for the paint – about fourpence English. The honest creature showed himself worthy of my confidence, by bringing me back one halfpenny of change with the colours. Poor Polycarp! Poor persecuted, lost sheep! the malicious world has singed the wool off your innocent back: be it mine to see it grow again under the British artist's fostering care!

13th, 14th, 15th, 16th – Too much occupied to make regular entries in my journal. I must have been up and down several miles of steps, during my four days' labour on my fourteen feet of canvas. The quantity of paint I am obliged to use is so enormous that it quite overpowers all Polycarp's garlic, and will, I imagine, in process of time poison all Polycarp's fleas. I feel fatigued, especially in the calves of my legs; but with such a design as I am producing, to cheer me on; and with such a model as I have got, to appreciate my genius and run my errands, fatigue itself becomes an enjoyment. Physically as well as intellectually, I feel the Samson of High Art!

17th – Horror! humiliation! disenchantment! despair! – Polycarp the Second is off with my watch, chain, and purse containing Roman money to the amount of five pounds English. I feel the most forlorn, deluded, miserable ass under the canopy of Heaven! I have been the dupe of a hypocritical, whimpering scoundrel! The scent of his garlic still floats aggravatingly on the atmosphere of my studio, outraging my nose and my feelings both together. But I can write no more on this disastrous day: I must either go mad, or go to dinner immediately. Let me embrace the latter alternative, while it is still within my power. Away! away to forget myself in the national Roman dish of kid's flesh and pistachio nuts!

18th – The national Roman dish has disagreed with me: I sit bilious before my fourteen canvas feet of thickly-painted but still unfinished Polycarp. This is an opportunity for relating in a proper spirit of lamentation the history of my discomfiture. It happened thus: Powerfully as my legs are made, they gave way under me on the morning of the 17th, after I had been three hours engaged in incessantly getting up the steps to put hairs on Polycarp's beard, and incessantly getting down again to go to the other end of the room and look at the effect of them. I told my perfidious model that he might take a rest, and set him the example by taking a rest myself. Overpowered by weariness, and the pressure of ideas, I fell asleep – unaccountably and barbarously fell asleep in my chair – before my own picture. The toil-worn British artist innocently reposed; and the whimpering Italian scoundrel took advantage of his slumbers! The bearded villain must have coolly taken my chain off my neck, my watch out of my waistcoat, my purse out of my pocket, while I was asleep. When I awoke it was dusk: I yawned loudly – no notice taken of it: I called out more loudly – no answer: I struck a light – no chain, no watch, no purse, no Polycarp. After a moment of bewilderment and horror, I rushed to the traitor's dwelling. The people of the house knew nothing about him, except that he was not at home. I proclaimed my wrongs furiously to the rest of the lodgers. Another bearded man among them threatened me with assassination if I did not immediately hold my tongue: I held it. The bearded man's mother recommended me to go home (ominously swinging a saucepan full of dirty water towards me, while she spoke): I took her advice. When I am in a den of thieves I do not find the courageous part of my character quite so fully developed as I could wish.

19th – Sought redress and restitution from the Police. They appeared to consider my application first as a joke, and then as an insult. Could they not catch Polycarp the Second? (I asked.) – Yes; they might possibly catch him in process of time. Then, why not set about his capture at once? – in the sacred name of Justice, why not? Because it was of no use: he must have sold the watch and chain, and spent the money by this time. Besides, suppose him caught, it would be inconvenient to punish him, for the prisons were all full – there was no room for him anywhere. I was an Englishman, therefore rich, and therefore able to put up with my loss. Surely I had better go away, and not make a fuss about the business in bad Italian. Shade of Brutus! can this be Roman justice?

20th – A visit from a brother artist – a German who chirps his national songs all day; paints in the severe style; and lives on an income of forty pounds a year. This esteemed fellow-labourer gave me some advice, on hearing of my disaster. He assured me that I should get no assistance from the police without bribing them handsomely to do their work. Supposing they really took decisive steps, after that; it was more than probable that Polycarp, or some of his friends, would put me out of their way in the night, by sticking an inch or two of stiletto into my ribs. I had better not move in the matter, if I valued either my pocket or my life. 'This,' said the German student, lighting his pipe, 'this, O Anglo-Saxon brother, is not thy fatherland. At Rome, the mind-and-body-comforting virtues they practise not – they grant no justice, and they quaff no beer.'

21st – After mature consideration, arrived at the conclusion that I had better leave Rome. To go on with my picture, after what has happened, is impossible.

The train of thought in which it originated, is broken up for ever. Moreover, envious fellow-students are already beginning to make a joke of my disaster; and, for aught I know to the contrary, Polycarp the Second may be lying in wait for my life, every night, at the corner of the street. Pursued by ridicule, and threatened by assassination, no course is left me but dignified retreat. Rome, farewell! Romans! one more master spirit that dwelt among ye has now been outraged and proscribed! CORIOLANUS – POTTS.

22nd – Early in the morning, took my canvas off the stretcher; rolled it up, and deposited it in the studio of my friend, the German artist. He promises to complete my design, as soon as he can afford paint enough to cover so colossal a canvas. I wrung his hand in silence, and left him my lamp-black, as a stock-in-trade of colours to begin with. Half an hour afterwards I was on the road to Florence, hastening to seek intellectual consolation at the feet of the Venus de Medici.

24th – Arrived at the Tuscan capital late in the evening. Rain, hail, snow, wind rising to a hurricane. People who praise the climate of Italy must be the paid agents of Italian innkeepers. I have never suffered such cold as this in England in my life.

25th – Called on an Italian gentleman, to whom I had a letter of introduction, for the purpose of inquiring about lodgings. Told him I only wanted a bedroom and a studio. He informed me that I could get both (the studio fifty feet long, if I liked it), at the palace of the Marchesa —. 'Lodgings at a palace!' cried I. 'Yes, and very cheap, too,' answered my new friend. Cheap! Can a Marchioness drive bargains? Readily. The Marchioness has not fifty pounds of your money for her whole yearly income. 'Has she any children?' 'One unmarried daughter, the Marchesina.' 'What's that?' 'A diminutive term of endearment; it means, the little Marchioness, my dear sir, in your language.' This last reply decided me. Serene visions of a future Marchesina Potts swam benignant before my eyes. In an evil hour, and little thinking into what fatal embarrassments I was plunging myself, I asked for the address of the palace, and determined to lodge with the Marchioness. (Christmas-day; and no roast-beef or plum-pudding. I wish I was back in England, in spite of my brilliant prospects with the Italian aristocracy.)

26th – Went to my noble landlady's, having dreamt all night of Polycarp the Second. (Is this a warning that I am to see that miscreant again?) Found the palace situated in a back street; an enormous building in a very deficient state of repair. The flag-stones of the courtyard grass-grown; the fountain in the middle throwing up no water, and entirely surrounded by weeds and puddles; the staircase rugged with hard dirt – but for thinking of the Marchesina, I should have run away at my first external view of my future lodgings. Saw the Marchesa. Where does all the flesh of all the old women in Italy go to? What substance absorbs, what grave receives it? Why is there no such thing as a fat lady of sixty in the whole Peninsula? Oh, what a thoroughly Italian old woman was this Marchesa! She was little, crooked, fleshless; her yellow skin had shrivelled up tight over her bones; her nose looked preternaturally aquiline, without an atom of cheek to relieve it; her hair was white; her eyes were blazing black; and to crown all, she was as stealthily civil as any watering-place landlady in England that I ever met with. She must have exercised some hideous fascination over me, for I fell into her toils, and chartered a bedroom and studio before I had been in her presence ten minutes. The bedroom was comparatively small for a palace, only about thirty feet long by twenty broad. The studio was a vasty mausoleum of a drawing-room: sixty feet by forty of marble floor, without a fire-place or a single article of furniture on any part of it, do not look comfortable in the month of February, when the snow is falling out of doors. I shall have to sit and paint in a sentry-box!

27th – Removed to my dungeon – I can call it nothing else. . . . I have just seen the Marchesina, and feel faint and giddy after the sight. 'The little Marchioness' – to use my friend's translation of her name – stands five feet eleven in her slippers; her hair and eyes are as black as ink; her arm is as thick as my leg; her complexion is sallow. She is as fleshy a subject as I ever remember to have met with. I know where all the old woman's fat has gone now; it has gone to the Marchesina. My first intuitive resolve, on being introduced to this magnificent aristocrat, was as follows: 'I must make friends with you, madam, for I see that you can thrash me!'

28th – The domestic life of the two noble ladies exhibits some peculiarities. I have observed that neither of them appears to possess such a thing as a gown; they are both swaddled in quantities of shapeless, dark-coloured robes, wrapped about them in a very mysterious manner. They appear to live exclusively on salad. They make salads not only of every kind of vegetable, but of bread, nuts and sponge-cakes. If the Marchesina by any accident ever set herself on fire, I feel assured that she would blaze like a beacon, from the quantity of oil she imbibes. Both the ladies keep me company in my studio, because I have got a chafing-dish of charcoal in it to preserve me from freezing, and they like to be economical in point of fire. But, besides *my* fire, they have their own, which they carry in their laps. An earthenware pipkin a-piece, with an arched handle, and with a small provision of burning charcoal in it, is the extraordinary portable fire that they hold on their knees all day long. I suspect the Marchesina of having a second pipkin full of live charcoal, under her robes, for the purpose of warming her feet and so forth. But of this I am not yet certain.

29th – The mighty Marchesina has proposed a subject to me to paint – a life-size portrait of herself in the character of a Sibyl. Ah, merciful Heaven! I must have another huge canvas for this! It will be another 'Polycarp,' in female form! More getting up and down steps! More gallons of black paint! But I must submit. The Marchesina has been hitherto very kind, sometimes even alarmingly affectionate. Nevertheless, if I oppose, or neglect her, I feel perfectly certain that she is capable of knocking me down! – Why! why did I ever come to Italy?

January 1st – I mark this day's entry with red ink. The new year has begun for me with one of the most astounding adventures that ever happened to anybody – Baron Munchausen included. Let me note it down in these pages.

I had just begun this morning to make a sketch for the future Sibyl picture, when the Sibyl herself burst into my studio in a great hurry. She had her bonnet on; and was dressed for the first time, since I had seen her, in something which really looked like a petticoat.

'Industrious little man,' said the Marchesina, with an air of jocular authority, 'put on your hat, and come out with me.'

Of course I obeyed directly. We were going to the nunnery church of Santa So-and-so (I am afraid of being prosecuted for libel if I write the real name), to see the live object of the last new miracle, which had set all Florence in an uproar of astonishment and admiration. This object was a poor man who had been miraculously restored from blindness, by praying to a certain statue of the Madonna. He had only pursued his devotions for two days, when he was 'cured in an instant,' like the man with the toothache, on the outside cover of a certain quack medicine bottle, that I remember in England. Besides gaining his sight, he gained a great deal of money, subscribed for him by the devout rich. He was exhibited every day in the church; and it was the great sight of Florence to go and see him.

Well! we got to the church. Such a scene inside! Crowds of people; soldiers in full uniform to keep order; the organ thundering sublimely; the choir singing hosannas; clouds of incense floating through the church; devotees, some kneeling, some prostrate on their faces, wherever they could find room, – all the magnificence of the magnificent Roman Catholic worship, was displayed before us in its grandest festival garb. My companion was right, this was a sight worth seeing indeed.

The Marchesina being a person of some weight, both in respect of physical formation and social standing, made her way victoriously through the crowd, dragging me after her in triumph. At the inner extremity of the church we saw the wonder-working statue of the Madonna, raised on high, and profusely decorated with the jewels presented to it by the faithful. To get a view of the man on whom the miracle had been wrought was, however, by no means easy. He was closely surrounded by a circle of gazers five deep. Ere long, however, the indomitable Marchesina contrived to force her way and mine through every obstacle. We reached the front row, I looked eagerly under a tall man's elbow; and saw—

Portentous powers of scoundrelism and hypocrisy! It was – yes! there was no mistaking him – it was POLYCARP THE SECOND!!!

I never really knew what it was to doubt my own eyes before; and yet there was no doubt here. There, kneeling beneath the statue of the Madonna, in an elegant pose of adoration, was my wide-awake miscreant of a model, changed to the hero of the most fashionable miracle of the day. The tears were trickling over his villainous beard, exactly as they trickled in my studio; I just detected the smell of garlic faintly predominant over the smell of incense, as I used to detect it at Rome. My sham model had turned sham blind man to all Florence, sham miracle-subject to a convent of illustrious nuns. The fellow had reached the sublime *acme* of rascality at a single stride.

The shock of my first recognition of him deprived me of my presence of mind. I forgot where I was, forgot all the people present, and unconsciously uttered aloud our national English ejaculation of astonishment, 'Hullo!' The spectators in my neighbourhood all turned round upon me immediately. A priest among the number beckoned to a soldier standing near, and said, 'Remove the British heretic.' This was rather too violent a proceeding to be patiently borne. I was determined to serve the cause of truth, and avenge myself on Polycarp the Second at the same time.

'Sir,' said I to the priest, 'before I am taken away, I should like to speak in private to the lady abbess of this convent.'

'Remove the heretic!' reiterated the furious bigot.

'Remove the heretic!' echoed the indignant congregation.

'If you *do* remove me,' I continued resolutely, 'without first granting what

I ask, I will publicly proclaim, before you can get me out at the door of the church, a certain fact which you would give the best jewel on that statue up there to keep concealed. Will you let me see the abbess, or will you not?'

My naturally limpid and benevolent eye must have flashed lightnings of wrath as I spoke, my usually calm and mellow voice must have sounded like a clarion of defiance; for the priest suddenly changed his tactics. He signed to the soldier to let me go.

'The Englishman is mad; and must be managed by persuasion, not force,' said the wily churchman to the congregation.

'He is not mad, – he is only a genius,' exclaimed my gigantic and generous Marchesina, taking my part.

'Leave him to me, and hold your peace, all of you,' said the priest, taking my arm, and leading me quickly out of the crowd.

He showed me into a little room behind the body of the church: shut the door carefully, and turning quickly and fiercely on me, said:

'Now, you fanatic of an Englishman, what do you want?'

'Bigot of an Italian!' I answered, in a rage, 'I want to prove your miracle man there, to be a thief and impostor. I know him. He was no more blind, when he came to Florence, than I am.'

The priest turned ghastly with rage, and opened his mouth to speak again, when, by a second door at the other end of the room, in came the abbess herself.

She tried at first the same plan as the priest. I never saw a fiercer, leaner, sharper old woman in my life. But bullying me would not do. I knew I was right: and stuck manfully to my point. After stating the whole of the great Polycarp robbery case, I wound up brilliantly by announcing my intention of sending to Rome for witnesses who could prove the identity of *my* thief of a model, and *their* sham of a miracle man, beyond the possibility of refutation. This threat conquered; the abbess got frightened in real earnest, and came to terms; or, in other words, began to humbug me on the spot.

In the course of my life I have known a great many wily old women. The tart-seller at school was a wily old woman; a maternal aunt of mine, who wheedled my father out of a special legacy, was a wily old woman; the laundress I employed in London was a wily old woman; the Marchioness I now lodge with is a wily old woman; but the abbess was wilier than all four put together. She flattered and cringed, lamented and shed tears, prayed *for* me and *to* me, all in a breath. Even the magnificent depths of humbug displayed by Polycarp the Second, looked shallow and transparent by contrast with the unfathomable profundities of artifice exhibited by the lady abbess!

Of course, the petitions that the abbess now poured on me in torrents were all directed towards the one object of getting me to hold my tongue for ever on the subject of Signor Polycarp's assumed blindness. Of course, her defence of the miracle-exhibition going on in her church was, that she and the whole nunnery (officiating priests included) had been imposed on by the vagabond stranger who had come to them from Rome. Whether this was true or not I really cannot say. I had a faint consciousness all the time the abbess was speaking that she was making a fool of me; and yet, for the life of me, I could not help believing some of the things she said; I could not refrain from helplessly granting her all that she asked. In return for this docility on my part, she gratefully promised that Polycarp should be ignominiously turned out of the church, without receiving a single farthing of the sums collected for him; which happened to be still remaining in the convent cash-box. Thus avenged on my pickpocket model, I felt perfectly satisfied, and politely assured the abbess (who undertook to account satisfactorily to the public for the disappearance of the miracle-man) that whatever her story was, I would not contradict it. This done, the pious old lady gave me her blessing; the priest 'followed on the same side;' and I left them writing down my name, to be prayed for among the convent list of personages of high rank, who were all to be benefited by the abbess's interest with Heaven! Rather different this from being removed as a heretic in the custody of a soldier!

2nd – A quiet day at home, after yesterday's excitement. The behaviour of the Marchesina begins to give me serious uneasiness. Gracious powers! – does she mean to fall in love with me? It seems awfully like it. On returning to the palace yesterday she actually embraced me! I was half suffocated by her congratulatory hug. The hug over, she playfully pinned me into a corner, till she made me tell her the whole of my adventure in the church. And, worse than all! not half an hour since, she coolly desired me to pull the foot-warming pipkin from under her robes – (I was right about her having one there), to poke the embers, and then to put it back again; speaking just as composedly as if she were only asking me to help her on with her shawl! This looks very bad. What had I better do? – run away?

3rd – Another adventure! A fearful, life-and-death adventure this time. This evening somebody gave the Marchesina a box at the opera. She took me with her. Confound the woman, she *will* take me with her everywhere! Being a beautiful moonlight night, we walked home. As we were crossing the 'Piazza' I became aware that a man was following us, and proposed to the Marchesina that we should mend our pace. 'Never!' exclaimed that redoubtable woman. 'None of my family have ever known what fear was. I am a worthy daughter of the house, and *I* don't know! Courage, Signor Potts, and keep step with me!'

This was all very well, but *my* house was the house of Potts, and every member of it had, at one time or other, known fear quite intimately. My position was dreadful. The resolute Marchesina kept tight hold of my arm, and positively slackened her pace rather than otherwise! The man still followed us, always at the same distance, evidently bent on robbery or assassination, or perhaps both. I would gladly have given the Marchesina five pounds to forget her family dignity and run.

On looking over my shoulder for about the five hundredth time, just as we entered the back street where the palace stood, I missed the mysterious stranger, to my infinite relief. The next moment, to my unutterable horror, I beheld him before us, evidently waiting to intercept our progress. We came up with him in the moonshine. Death and destruction! Polycarp the Second again!

'I know you!' growled the ruffian, grinding his teeth at me. 'You got me turned out of the church! Body of Bacchus! I'll be revenged on you for that!'

He thrust his hand into his waistcoat. Before I could utter even the faintest cry for help, the heroic Marchesina had caught him fast by the beard and wrist, and had pinned him helpless against the wall. 'Pass on, Signor Potts!' said this lioness of a woman, quite complacently. 'Pass on; there's plenty of room now.' Just as I passed on I heard the sound of a kick behind me, and, turning round, saw Polycarp the Second prostrate in the kennel. 'La, la, la-la-la-la-la – la!'

sang the Marchesina from 'Suoni la Tromba' (which we had just heard at the Opera), as she took my arm once more, and led me safely up the palace stairs – 'La, la, la-la – la! We'll have a salad for supper to-night, Signor Potts!' Majestic, Roman matron-minded woman! She could kick an assassin and talk of a salad both at the same moment!

4th – A very bad night's rest: dreams of gleaming stilettos and midnight assassination. The fact is, my life is no longer safe in Florence. I can't take the Marchesina about with me everywhere as a body-guard (she is a great deal too affectionate already); and yet, without my Amazonian protectress what potent interposition is to preserve my life from the blood-thirsty Polycarp, when he next attempts it? I begin to be afraid that I am not quite so brave a man as I have been accustomed to think myself. Why have I not the courage to give the Marchesina and her mother warning, and so leave Florence? Oh, Lord! here comes the tall woman to sit for the Sibyl picture! She will embrace me again, I know she will! She's got into a habit of doing it; she takes an unfair advantage of her size and strength. Why can't she practise fair play, and embrace a man of her own weight and inches?

5th – Another mess! I shall be dead soon; killed by getting into perpetual scrapes, if I am not killed by a stiletto! I've been stabbing an innocent man now; and have had to pay something like three pounds of compensation-money. This was how the thing happened: Yesterday I got away from the Marchesina (she hugged me, just as I foretold she would) about dusk, and immediately went and bought a sword-stick, as a defence against Polycarp. I don't mind confessing that I was afraid to return to the palace at night without a weapon of some sort. They never shut the court-yard door till everybody is ready to go to bed; the great staircase is perfectly dark all the way up, and affords some capital positions for assassination on every landing-place. Knowing this, I drew my new sword (a murderous-looking steel skewer, about three feet long) out of the stick, as I advanced towards home, and began to poke for Polycarp in the darkness, the moment I mounted the first stair. Up I went, stabbing every inch of my way before me, in the most scientific and complete manner; spitting invisible assassins like larks for supper. I was just exploring the corners of the second landing-place on this peculiar defensive system of my own, when my sword-point encountered a soft substance, and my ears were instantly greeted by a yell of human agony. In the fright of the moment, I echoed the yell, and fell down flat on my back. The Marchesina rushed out on the stairs at the noise, with a lamp in her hand. I sat up and looked round in desperation. There was the miserable old porter of the palace, bleeding and blubbering in a corner, and there was my deadly skewer of a sword stuck in a piece of tough Italian beef by his side! The meat must have attracted the skewer, like a magnet; and it saved the porter's life. He was not much hurt; the beef (stolen property with which he was escaping to his lodge, when my avenging sword-point met him) acted like a shield, and was much the worse wounded of the two. The Marchesina found this out directly; and began to upbraid the porter for thieving. The porter upbraided me for stabbing, and I, having nobody else to upbraid, upbraided Destiny for leading me into a fresh scrape. The uproar we made was something quite indescribable; we three outscreamed all Billingsgate-market in the olden time. At last I calmed the storm by giving the porter every farthing I had about me, and asking the Marchesina to accept the sword part of my sword stick as a new spit to adorn the kitchen department of the palace. She called me 'an angel;' and hugged me furiously on the spot. If this hugging is not stopped by to-morrow I shall put myself under the protection of the British ambassador – I will, or my name isn't Potts!

6th – No protection is henceforth available! No British ambassador can now defend my rights! No threats of assassination from Polycarp the Second can terrify me more! – All my other calamities are now merged in one enormous misfortune that will last for the rest of my life: the Marchesina has declared her intention of marrying me!

It was done at supper last night, after I had pinked the porter. We sat round the inevitable, invariable salad, on which we are condemned to graze – the Nebuchadnezzars of modern life – in this accursed gazebo of a palace. My stomach began to ache beforehand as I saw the Marchesina pouring in the vinegar, and heard her, at the same time, dropping certain hints in my direction – frightfully broad hints, with which she has terrified and bewildered me for the last three or four days. I sat silent. In England I should have rushed to the window and screamed for the police; but I was in Florence, defenceless and a stranger, before an Amazon who was fast ogling me into terrified submission to my fate. She soon got beyond even the ogling. When we were all three helped to salad, just at the pause before eating, the Marchesina looked round at her fleshless, yellow old parent.

'Mother,' says she, 'shall I have him?'

'Beloved angel,' was the answer, 'you are of age, I leave your choice to yourself; pick where you like?'

'Very well then,' pursued the Amazonian daughter, 'very well! Potts! here is my hand.' She held out her mighty fist towards me, with a diabolical grin. I felt I must either take it or have my head broken. I now sincerely wish I had preferred the latter alternative; but an unlucky emotion of terror misled me into accepting the former. I received an amorous squeeze that made the bones of my fingers crack again.

'You are a little man, and not noble,' observed the Marchesina, critically looking me over, as if I had been a piece of meat that she was purchasing in the market, 'but you get both size and rank in getting *me*. Let us therefore be perfectly happy, and proceed with our salad.'

'I beg your pardon,' said I, faintly shivering all over in a sort of cold horror, 'I beg your pardon; but really—'

'Come, come!' interrupted the Marchesina, crushing my hand with another squeeze; 'too much diffidence is a fault; you have genius and wealth to offer in exchange for all I confer on you, you have, you modest little cherub of a man! As for the day, my venerated mother!' she continued, turning towards the old woman; 'shall we say this day week?'

'Certainly, this day week,' said mamma, looking yellower than ever, as she mopped up all the oil and vinegar in her plate with a large spoon. The next minute I received the old woman's blessing; I was ordered to kiss the Marchesina's hand; I was wished good night, – and then found myself alone with three empty salad plates; 'left for execution' that very day week; left without the slightest chance of a reprieve!

I write these lines at the dead of night, – myself, more dead than alive. I am in my bed-room; the door is locked and barricaded against the possible entrance of the Marchesina and her mamma. I am covered from head to foot with a cold perspiration, but am nevertheless firm in my resolution to run away to-morrow. I must leave all my luggage behind me, and resort to stratagem or I shall not get off. Tomorrow, the moment the palace gate is opened, I shall take to my heels, carrying with me nothing but my purse, my passport, and my nightcap. Hush! a stealthy breathing sounds outside the door – an eye is at the key-hole – it is the old woman watching me! Hark! a footstep in the street outside – Polycarp the Second, with his stiletto lying in wait before the house! I shall be followed, I know I shall, however cunningly and secretly I get away to-morrow! Marriage and murder – murder and marriage, will alternately threaten me for the remainder of my life! Art, farewell! henceforth the rest of my existence is dedicated to perpetual flight!

[NOTE BY THE EDITOR OF THE FOREGOING FRAGMENTS]

With the ominous word 'flight,' the journal of Mr Potts abruptly ends. I became possessed of the manuscript in this manner: The other day, while I was quietly sitting in my study in London, the door of the room was flung violently open, and the ill-fated Potts himself rushed in, his eyes glaring, his hair dishevelled.

'Print that!' cried my gifted, but unhappy friend; 'enlist for me the sympathies, procure for me the protection, of the British public! The Marchesina is after me – she has followed me to England – she is at the bottom of the street! Farewell, farewell, for ever!'

'Who is the Marchesina? Where are you going to?' I exclaimed, aghast.

'To Scotland! To hide myself in the inaccessible caverns of the most desolate island I can find among the Hebrides!' cried Potts, dashing out of the room like a madman. I ran to my window, which opens on the street, just in time to see my friend fly past, at the top of his speed. The next passenger proceeding in the same direction was a woman of gigantic stature, striding over the pavement in a manner awful to behold. Could that be the Marchesina? For my friend's sake I devoutly hope not.

Mad Monkton

Written in February 1852 as a prospective contribution for *Household Words*, but rejected by Dickens on the grounds that its presentation of the 'horrible affliction of hereditary insanity' might prove distressing to his 'family' readership. Originally appeared in *Fraser's Magazine*, November-December 1855, under the title 'The Monktons of Wincot Abbey', and described as 'edited by Wilkie Collins'. Reprinted in *The Queen of Hearts* (1859) under the title 'Brother Griffith's Story of Mad Monkton'. In *Basil* (1852) Collins defines 'monomania' (Monkton's complaint) as 'some fixed idea that never leaves him day or night.' According to Dorothy Goldman the term was of fairly recent date in 1852. The French critic Emile Forgues's influential discussion of Collins's early work in the *Revue des Deux Mondes* (October-December 1855) included significant comment on 'Mad Monkton'. A. Gasson (in *Wilkie Collins: A Collector's Challenge*) has suggested that the narrator's discovery of Stephen Monkton's corpse represents the first case solved by an amateur detective in fiction.

I

The Monktons of Wincot Abbey bore a sad character for want of sociability in our county. They never went to other people's houses, and excepting my father, and a lady and her daughter living near them, never received anybody under their own roof.

Proud as they all certainly were, it was not pride but dread which kept them thus apart from their neighbours. The family had suffered for generations past from the horrible affliction of hereditary insanity, and the members of it shrank from exposing their calamity to others, as they must have exposed it if they had mingled with the busy little world around them. There is a frightful story of a crime committed in past times by two of the Monktons, near relatives, from which the first appearance of the insanity was always supposed to date, but it is needless for me to shock anyone by repeating it. It is enough to say that at intervals almost every form of madness appeared in the family; monomania being the most frequent manifestation of the affliction among them. I have these particulars, and one or two yet to be related, from my father.

At the period of my youth but three of the Monktons were left at the Abbey: Mr and Mrs Monkton, and their only child, Alfred, heir to the property. The one other member of this, the elder, branch of the family who was then alive, was Mr Monkton's younger brother, Stephen. He was an unmarried man, possessing a fine estate in Scotland; but he lived almost entirely on the Continent, and bore the reputation of being a shameless profligate. The family at Wincot held almost as little communication with him as with their neighbours.

I have already mentioned my father, and a lady and her daughter, as the only privileged people who were admitted into Wincot Abbey.

My father had been an old school and college friend of Mr Monkton, and accident had brought them so much together in later life, that their continued intimacy at Wincot was quite intelligible. I am not so well able to account for the friendly terms on which Mrs Elmslie (the lady to whom I have alluded) lived with the Monktons. Her late husband had been distantly related to Mrs Monkton, and my father was her daughter's guardian. But even these claims to friendship and regard never seemed to me strong enough to explain the intimacy between Mrs Elmslie and the inhabitants of the Abbey. Intimate however they certainly were, and one result of the constant interchange of visits between the two families in due time declared itself: Mr Monkton's son and Mrs Elmslie's daughter became attached to each other.

I had no opportunities of seeing much of the young lady; I only remember her at that time as a delicate, gentle, lovable girl, the very opposite in appearance, and apparently in character also, to Alfred Monkton. But perhaps that was one reason why they fell in love with each other. The attachment was soon discovered, and was far from being disapproved by the parents on either side. In all essential points, except that of wealth, the Elmslies were nearly the equals of the Monktons, and want of money in a bride was of no consequence to the heir of Wincot. Alfred, it was well known, would succeed to thirty thousand a year on his father's death.

Thus, though the parents on both sides thought the young people not old enough to be married at once, they saw no reason why Ada and Alfred should not be engaged to each other, with the understanding that they should be united when young Monkton came of age, in two years' time. The person to be consulted in the matter, after the parents, was my father in his capacity of Ada's guardian. He knew that the family misery had shown itself many years ago in Mrs Monkton, who was her husband's cousin. The *illness*, as it was significantly called, had been palliated by careful treatment, and was reported to have passed away. But my father was not to be deceived. He knew where the hereditary taint still lurked; he viewed with horror the bare possibility of its reappearing one day in the children of his friend's only daughter; and he positively refused his consent to the marriage engagement.

The result was that the doors of the Abbey and the doors of Mrs Elmslie's house were closed to him. This suspension of friendly intercourse had lasted but a very short time, when Mrs Monkton died. Her husband, who was fondly attached to her, caught a violent cold while attending her funeral. The cold was neglected, and settled on his lungs. In a few months' time, he followed his wife to the grave, and Alfred was left master of the grand old Abbey, and the fair lands that spread all around it.

At this period Mrs Elmslie had the indelicacy to endeavour a second time to procure my father's consent to the marriage engagement. He refused it again more positively than before. More than a year passed away. The time was approaching fast when Alfred would be of age. I returned from college to spend the long vacation at home, and made some advances towards bettering my acquaintance with young Monkton. They were evaded – certainly with perfect politeness, but still in such a way as to prevent me from offering my friendship to him again. Any mortification I might have felt at this petty repulse, under ordinary circumstances, was dismissed from my mind by the occurrence of a real misfortune in our household. For some months past my father's health had been failing, and, just at the time of which I am now writing, his sons had to mourn the irreparable calamity of his death.

This event, through some informality or error in the late Mr Elmslie's will, left the future of Ada's life entirely at her mother's disposal. The consequence was the immediate ratification of the marriage engagement to which my father had so steadily refused his consent. As soon as the fact was publicly announced, some of Mrs Elmslie's more intimate friends, who were acquainted with the reports affecting the Monkton family, ventured to mingle with their formal congratulations one or two significant references to the late Mrs Monkton, and some searching inquiries as to the disposition of her son.

Mrs Elmslie always met these polite hints with one bold form of answer. She first admitted the existence of those reports about the Monktons which her friends were unwilling to specify distinctly; and then declared that they were infamous calumnies. The hereditary taint had died out of the family generations back. Alfred was the best, the kindest, the sanest of human beings. He loved study and retirement; Ada sympathised with his tastes, and had made her choice unbiased; if any more hints were dropped about sacrificing her by her marriage, those hints would be viewed as so many insults to her mother, whose affection for her it was monstrous to call in question. This way of talking silenced people, but did not convince them. They began to suspect, what was indeed the actual truth, that Mrs Elmslie was a selfish, worldly, grasping woman, who wanted to get her daughter well married, and cared nothing for consequences as long as she saw Ada mistress of the greatest establishment in the whole county.

It seemed, however, as if there was some fatality at work to prevent the attainment of Mrs Elmslie's great object in life. Hardly was one obstacle to the ill-omened marriage removed by my father's death, before another succeeded it, in the shape of anxieties and difficulties caused by the delicate state of Ada's health. Doctors were consulted in all directions, and the result of their advice was that the marriage must be deferred, and that Miss Elmslie must leave England for a certain time, to reside in a warmer climate; the south of France, if I remember rightly. Thus it happened that just before Alfred came of age, Ada and her mother departed for the Continent, and the union of the two young people was understood to be indefinitely postponed.

Some curiosity was felt in the neighbourhood as to what Alfred Monkton would do under these circumstances. Would he follow his lady-love? Would he go yachting? Would he throw open the doors of the old Abbey at last, and endeavour to forget the absence of Ada and the postponement of his marriage in a round of gaieties? He did none of these things. He simply remained at Wincot, living as suspiciously strange and solitary a life as his father had lived before him. Literally, there was now no companion for him at the Abbey but the old priest – the Monktons, I should have mentioned before, were Roman Catholics – who had held the office of tutor to Alfred from his earliest years. He came of age, and there was not even so much as a private dinner-party at Wincot to celebrate the event. Families in the neighbourhood determined to forget the offence which his father's reserve had given them, and invited him to their houses. The invitations were politely declined. Civil visitors called resolutely at the Abbey, and were as resolutely bowed away from the doors as soon as they had left their cards. Under this combination of sinister and aggravating circumstances, people in all directions took to shaking their heads mysteriously when the name of Mr Alfred Monkton was mentioned, hinting at the family calamity, and wondering peevishly or sadly, as their tempers inclined them, what he could possibly do to occupy himself month after month in the lonely old house.

The right answer to this question was not easy to find. It was quite useless, for example, to apply to the priest for it. He was a very quiet, polite old gentleman; his replies were always excessively ready and civil, and appeared at the time to convey an immense quantity of information, but when they came to be reflected on, it was universally observed that nothing tangible could ever be got out of them. The housekeeper, a weird old woman, with a very abrupt and repelling manner, was too fierce and taciturn to be safely approached. The few indoor servants had all been long enough in the family to have learnt to hold their tongues in public as a regular habit. It was only from the farm-servants who supplied the table at the Abbey, that any information could be obtained; and vague enough it was when they came to communicate it.

Some of them had observed the 'young master' walking about the library with heaps of dusty papers in his hands. Others had heard odd noises in the uninhabited parts of the Abbey, had looked up, and had seen him forcing open the old windows, as if to let light and air into rooms supposed to have been shut close for years and years; or had discovered him standing on the perilous summit of one of the crumbling turrets, never ascended before within their memories, and popularly considered to be inhabited by the ghosts of the monks who had once possessed the building. The result of these observations and discoveries, when they were communicated to others, was of course to impress every one with a firm belief that 'poor young Monkton was going the way that the rest of the family had gone before him:' which opinion always appeared to be immensely strengthened in the popular mind by a conviction – founded on no particle of evidence – that the priest was at the bottom of all the mischief.

Thus far I have spoken from hearsay evidence mostly. What I have next to tell will be the result of my own personal experience.

II

About five months after Alfred Monkton came of age I left college, and resolved to amuse and instruct myself a little by travelling abroad.

At the time when I quitted England, young Monkton was still leading his secluded life at the Abbey, and was, in the opinion of everybody, sinking rapidly, if he had not already succumbed, under the hereditary curse of his family. As to the Elmslies, report said that Ada had benefited by her sojourn abroad, and that mother and daughter were on their way back to England to resume their old relations with the heir of Wincot. Before they returned, I was away on my travels, and wandered half over Europe, hardly ever planning whither I should shape my course beforehand. Chance, which thus led me everywhere, led me at last to Naples. There I met with an old school-friend, who was one of the *attachés* at the English embassy; and there began the extraordinary events in connexion with Alfred Monkton which form the main interest of the story I am now relating.

I was idling away the time one morning with my friend the *attaché*, in the garden of the Villa Reale, when we were passed by a young man, walking alone, who exchanged bows with my friend.

I thought I recognised the dark eager eyes, the colourless cheeks, the strangely-vigilant, anxious expression which I remembered in past times as characteristic of Alfred Monkton's face, and was about to question my friend on the subject, when he gave me unasked the information of which I was in search.

'That is Alfred Monkton,' said he; 'he comes from your part of England. You ought to know him.'

'I do know a little of him,' I answered; 'he was engaged to Miss Elmslie when I was last in the neighbourhood of Wincot. Is he married to her yet?'

'No; and he never ought to be. He has gone the way of the rest of the family; or, in plainer words, he has gone mad.'

'Mad! But I ought not to be surprised at hearing that, after the reports about him in England.'

'I speak from no reports; I speak from what he has said and done here before me, and before hundreds of other people. Surely you must have heard of it?'

'Never. I have been out of the way of news from Naples or England for months past.'

'Then I have a very extraordinary story to tell you. You know, of course, that Alfred had an uncle, Stephen Monkton. Well, some time ago, this uncle fought a duel in the Roman states, with a Frenchman, who shot him dead. The seconds and the Frenchman (who was unhurt) took to flight in different directions, as it is supposed. We heard nothing here of the details of the duel till a month after it happened, when one of the French journals published an account of it, taken from papers left by Monkton's second, who died at Paris of consumption. These papers stated the manner in which the duel was fought, and how it terminated, but nothing more. The surviving second and the Frenchman have never been traced from that time to this. All that anybody knows, therefore, of the duel is that Stephen Monkton was shot; an event which nobody can regret, for a greater scoundrel never existed. The exact place where he died, and what was done with his body, are still mysteries not to be penetrated.'

'But what has all this to do with Alfred?'

'Wait a moment, and you will hear. Soon after the news of his uncle's death reached England, what do you think Alfred did? He actually put off his marriage with Miss Elmslie, which was then about to be celebrated, to come out here in search of the burial-place of his wretched scamp of an uncle. And no power on earth will now induce him to return to England and to Miss Elmslie, until he has found the body, and can take it back with him to be buried with all the other dead Monktons, in the vault under Wincot Abbey Chapel. He has squandered his money, pestered the police, exposed himself to the ridicule of the men and the indignation of the women for the last three months, in trying to achieve his insane purpose, and is now as far from it as ever. He will not assign to anybody the smallest motive for his conduct. You can't laugh him out of it, or reason him out of it. When we met him just now, I happen to know that he was on his way to the office of the police minister, to send out fresh agents to search and inquire through the Roman states for the place where his uncle was shot. And mind, all this time, he professes to be passionately in love with Miss Elmslie, and to be miserable at his separation from her. Just think of that! And then think of his self-imposed absence from her here, to hunt after the remains of a wretch who was a disgrace to the family, and whom he never saw but once or twice in his life. Of all the 'Mad Monktons,' as they used to call them in England, Alfred is the maddest. He is actually our principal excitement in this dull opera season; though, for my own part, when I think of the poor girl in England, I am a great deal more ready to despise him than to laugh at him.'

'You know the Elmslies, then?'

'Intimately. The other day my mother wrote to me from England, after having seen Ada. This escapade of Monkton's has outraged all her friends. They have been entreating her to break off the match, which it seems she could do if she liked. Even her mother, sordid and selfish as she is, has been obliged at last, in common decency, to side with the rest of the family; but the good faithful girl won't give Monkton up. She humours his insanity, declares he gave her a good reason, in secret, for going away; says she could always make him happy when they were together in the old Abbey, and can make him still happier when they are married; in short, she loves him dearly, and will therefore believe in him to the last. Nothing shakes her; she has made up her mind to throw away her life on him, and she will do it.'

'I hope not. Mad as his conduct looks to us, he may have some sensible reason for it that we cannot imagine. Does his mind seem at all disordered when he talks on ordinary topics?'

'Not in the least. When you can get him to say anything, which is not often, he talks like a sensible, well-educated man. Keep silence about his precious errand here, and you would fancy him the gentlest and most temperate of human beings. But touch the subject of his vagabond of an uncle, and the Monkton madness comes out directly. The other night a lady asked him, jestingly of course, whether he had ever seen his uncle's ghost. He scowled at her like a perfect fiend, and said that he and his uncle would answer her question together some day, if they came from hell to do it. We laughed at his words, but the lady fainted at his looks, and we had a scene of hysterics and hartshorn in consequence. Any other man would have been kicked out of the room for nearly frightening a pretty woman to death in that way; but "Mad Monkton," as we have christened him, is a privileged lunatic in Neapolitan society, because he is English, good-looking, and worth thirty thousand a year. He goes out everywhere, under the impression that he may meet with somebody who has been let into the secret of the place where the mysterious duel was fought. If you are introduced to him, he is sure to ask you whether you know anything about it; but beware of following up the subject after you have answered him, unless you want to make sure that he is out of his senses. In that case, only talk of his uncle, and the result will rather more than satisfy you.'

A day or two after this conversation with my friend the *attaché*, I met Monkton at an evening party.

The moment he heard my name mentioned, his face flushed up; he drew me away into a corner, and referring to his cool reception of my advance, years ago, towards making his acquaintance, asked my pardon for what he termed his inexcusable ingratitude with an earnestness and an agitation which utterly astonished me. His next proceeding was to question me, as my friend had said he would, about the place of the mysterious duel.

An extraordinary change came over him while he interrogated me on this point. Instead of looking into my face as they had looked hitherto, his eyes wandered away, and fixed themselves intensely, almost fiercely, either on the perfectly empty wall at our side, or on the vacant space between the wall and ourselves – it was impossible to say which. I had come to Naples from Spain by sea, and briefly told him so, as the best way of satisfying him that I could not assist his inquiries. He pursued them no further; and mindful of my friend's warning, I took care to lead the conversation to general topics. He looked back at me directly, and as long as we stood in our corner, his eyes never wandered away again to the empty wall or the vacant space at our side.

Though more ready to listen than to speak, his conversation, when he did talk, had no trace of anything the least like insanity about it. He had evidently read, not generally only, but deeply as well, and could apply his reading with singular felicity to the illustration of almost any subject under discussion, neither obtruding his knowledge absurdly, nor concealing it affectedly. His manner was in itself a standing protest against such a nickname as 'Mad Monkton.' He was so shy, so quiet, so composed and gentle in all his actions, that at times I should have been almost inclined to call him effeminate. We had a long talk together on the first evening of our meeting; we often saw each other afterwards, and never lost a single opportunity of bettering our acquaintance. I felt that he had taken a liking to me, and in spite of what I had heard about his behaviour to Miss Elmslie, in spite of the suspicions which the history of his family and his own conduct had arrayed against him,

I began to like 'Mad Monkton' as much as he liked me. We took many a quiet ride together in the country, and sailed often along the shores of the Bay on either side. But for two eccentricities in his conduct which I could not at all understand, I should soon have felt as much at my ease in his society as if he had been my own brother.

The first of these eccentricities consisted in the reappearance on several occasions of the odd expression in his eyes, which I had first seen when he asked me whether I knew anything about the duel. No matter what we were talking about, or where we happened to be, there were times when he would suddenly look away from my face, now on one side of me, now on the other, but always where there was nothing to see, and always with the same intensity and fierceness in his eyes. This looked so like madness – or hypochondria, at the least – that I felt afraid to ask him about it, and always pretended not to observe him.

The second peculiarity in his conduct was that he never referred, while in my company, to the reports about his errand at Naples, and never once spoke of Miss Elmslie, or of his life at Wincot Abbey. This not only astonished me, but amazed those who had noticed our intimacy, and who had made sure that I must be the depositary of all his secrets. But the time was near at hand when this mystery, and some other mysteries of which I had no suspicion at that period, were all to be revealed.

I met him one night at a large ball, given by a Russian nobleman, whose name I could not pronounce then, and cannot remember now. I had wandered away from reception-room, ball-room, and card-room, to a small apartment at one extremity of the palace, which was half conservatory, half boudoir, and which had been prettily illuminated for the occasion, with Chinese lanthorns. Nobody was in the room when I got there. The view over the Mediterranean, bathed in the bright softness of Italian moon-light, was so lovely, that I remained for a long time at the window, looking out, and listening to the dance music which faintly reached me from the ball-room. My thoughts were far away with the relations I had left in England, when I was startled out of them by hearing my name softly pronounced.

I looked round directly, and saw Monkton standing in the room. A livid paleness overspread his face, and his eyes were turned away from me with the same extraordinary expression in them to which I have already alluded.

'Do you mind leaving the ball early to-night?' he asked, still not looking at me.

'Not at all,' said I. 'Can I do anything for you? Are you ill?'

'No, at least nothing to speak of. Will you come to my rooms?'

'At once, if you like.'

'No, not at once. *I* must go home directly; but don't you come to me for half an hour yet. You have not been at my rooms before, I know; but you will easily find them out, they are close by. There is a card with my address. I *must* speak to you to-night; my life depends on it. Pray come! for God's sake come when the half hour is up!'

I promised to be punctual, and he left me directly.

Most people will be easily able to imagine the state of nervous impatience and vague expectation in which I passed the allotted period of delay, after hearing such words as those Monkton had spoken to me. Before the half hour had quite expired, I began to make my way out through the ballroom.

At the head of the staircase, my friend the *attaché* met me.

'What! going away already?' said he.

'Yes; and on a very curious expedition. I am going to Monkton's rooms, by his own invitation.'

'You don't mean it! Upon my honour, you're a bold fellow to trust yourself alone with "Mad Monkton" when the moon is at the full.'

'He is ill, poor fellow. Besides, I don't think him half as mad as you do.'

'We won't dispute about that; but mark my words, he has not asked you to go where no visitor has ever been admitted before, without a special purpose. I predict that you will see or hear something to-night which you will remember for the rest of your life.'

We parted. When I knocked at the courtyard gate of the house where Monkton lived, my friend's last words on the palace staircase recurred to me; and though I had laughed at him when he spoke them, I began to suspect even then that his prediction would be fulfilled.

III

The porter who let me into the house where Monkton lived, directed me to the floor on which his rooms were situated. On getting up stairs, I found his door on the landing ajar. He heard my footsteps, I suppose, for he called to me to come in before I could knock.

I entered, and found him sitting by the table, with some loose letters in his hand, which he was just tying together into a packet. I noticed, as he asked me to sit down, that his expression looked more composed, though the paleness had not yet left his face. He thanked me for coming; repeated that he had something very important to say to me; and then stopped short, apparently too much embarrassed to proceed. I tried to set him at his ease by assuring him that if my assistance or advice could be of any use, I was ready to place myself and my time heartily and unreservedly at his service.

As I said this, I saw his eyes beginning to wander away from my face – to wander slowly, inch by inch as it were, until they stopped at a certain point, with the same fixed stare into vacancy which had so often startled me on former occasions. The whole expression of his face altered as I had never yet seen it alter; he sat before me, looking like a man in a death-trance.

'You are very kind,' he said, slowly and faintly, speaking, not to me, but in the direction in which his eyes were still fixed. 'I know you can help me; but—'

He stopped; his face whitened horribly, and the perspiration broke out all over it. He tried to continue; said a word or two; then stopped again. Seriously alarmed about him, I rose from my chair, with the intention of getting him some water from a jug which I saw standing on a side table.

He sprang up at the same moment. All the suspicions I had ever heard whispered against his sanity flashed over my mind in an instant; and I involuntarily stepped back a pace or two.

'Stop,' he said, seating himself again; 'don't mind me; and don't leave your chair. I want – I wish, if you please, to make a little alteration, before we say anything more. Do you mind sitting in a strong light?'

'Not in the least.'

I had hitherto been seated in the shade of his reading-lamp, the only light in the room.

As I answered him, he rose again; and going into another apartment, returned with a large lamp in his hand; then took two candles from the side table, and two others from the chimney-piece; placed them all, to my amazement, together, so as to stand exactly between us; and then tried to light them. His hand trembled so, that he was obliged to give up the attempt, and allow me to come to his assistance. By his direction I took the shade off the reading-lamp, after I had lit the other lamp and the four candles. When we sat down again, with this concentration of light between us, his better and gentler manner began to return; and while he now addressed me, he spoke without the slightest hesitation.

'It is useless to ask whether you have heard the reports about me,' he said; 'I know that you have. My purpose to-night is to give you some reasonable explanation of the conduct which has produced those reports. My secret has been hitherto confided to one person only; I am now about to trust it to your keeping, with a special object which will appear as I go on. First, however, I must begin by telling you exactly what the great difficulty is which obliges me to be still absent from England. I want your advice and your help; and, to conceal nothing from you, I want also to test your forbearance and your friendly sympathy, before I can venture on thrusting my miserable secret into your keeping. Will you pardon this apparent distrust of your frank and open character – this apparent ingratitude for your kindness towards me ever since we first met?'

I begged him not to speak of these things, but to go on.

'You know,' he proceeded, 'that I am here to recover the body of my Uncle Stephen, and to carry it back with me to our family-burial place in England; and you must also be aware that I have not yet succeeded in discovering his remains. Try to pass over for the present whatever may seem extraordinary and incomprehensible in such a purpose as mine is; and read this newspaper article, where the ink-line is traced. It is the only evidence hitherto obtained on the subject of the fatal duel in which my uncle fell; and I want to hear what course of proceeding the persual of it may suggest to you as likely to be best on my part.'

He handed me an old French newspaper. The substance of what I read there is still so firmly impressed on my memory, that I am certain of being able to repeat correctly, at this distance of time, all the facts which it is necessary for me to communicate to the reader.

The article began, I remember, with editorial remarks on the great curiosity then felt in regard to the fatal duel between the Count St Lo and Mr Stephen Monkton, an English gentleman. The writer proceeded to dwell at great length on the extraordinary secrecy in which the whole affair had been involved from first to last; and to express a hope that the publication of a certain manuscript, to which his introductory observations referred, might lead to the production of fresh evidence from other and better informed quarters. The manuscript had been found among the papers of Monsieur Foulon, Mr Monkton's second, who had died at Paris of a rapid decline, shortly after returning to his home in that city from the scene of the duel. The document was unfinished, having been left incomplete at the very place where the reader would most wish to find it continued. No reason could be discovered for this, and no second manuscript bearing on the all-important subject had been found, after the strictest search among the papers left by the deceased.

The document itself then followed.

It purported to be an agreement privately drawn up between Mr Monkton's second, Monsieur Foulon, and the Count St Lo's second, Monsieur Dalville; and contained a statement of all the arrangements for conducting the duel. The paper was dated 'Naples, February 22nd' and was divided into some seven or eight clauses.

The first clause described the origin and nature of the quarrel – a very disgraceful affair on both sides, worth neither remembering nor repeating. The second clause stated that the challenged man having chosen the pistol as his weapon, and the challenger (an excellent swordsman) having, on his side, thereupon insisted that the duel should be fought in such a manner as to make the first fire decisive in its results, the seconds, seeing that fatal consequences must inevitably follow the hostile meeting, determined, first of all, that the duel should be kept a profound secret from everybody, and that the place where it was to be fought should not be made known beforehand, even to the principals themselves. It was added that this excess of precaution had been rendered absolutely necessary, in consequence of a recent address from the Pope to the ruling powers in Italy, commenting on the scandalous frequency of the practice of duelling, and urgently desiring that the laws against duellists should be enforced for the future with the utmost rigour.

The third clause detailed the manner in which it had been arranged that the duel should be fought.

The pistols having been loaded by the seconds on the ground, the combatants were to be placed thirty paces apart, and were to toss up for the first fire. The man who won was to advance ten paces – marked out for him beforehand – and was then to discharge his pistol. If he missed, or failed to disable his opponent, the latter was free to advance, if he chose, the whole remaining twenty paces before he fired in his turn. This arrangement ensured the decisive termination of the duel at the first discharge of the pistols, and both principals and seconds pledged themselves on either side to abide by it.

The fourth clause stated that the seconds had agreed that the duel should be fought *out* of the Neapolitan states, but left themselves to be guided by circumstances as to the exact locality in which it should take place. The remaining clauses, so far as I remember them, were devoted to detailing the different precautions to be adopted for avoiding discovery. The duellists and their seconds were to leave Naples in separate parties; were to change carriages several times; were to meet at a certain town, or, failing that, at a certain post-house on the high road from Naples to Rome; were to carry drawing-books, colour-boxes, and camp-stools, as if they had been artists out on a sketching tour; and were to proceed to the place of the duel on foot, employing no guides, for fear of treachery. Such general arrangements as these, and others for facilitating the flight of the survivors after the affair was over, formed the conclusion of this extraordinary document, which was signed, in initials only, by both the seconds.

Just below the initials, appeared the beginning of a narrative, dated 'Paris,' and evidently intended to describe the duel itself with extreme minuteness. The hand-writing was that of the deceased second.

Monsieur Foulon, the gentleman in question, stated his belief that circumstances might transpire which would render an account by an eye-witness of the hostile meeting between St Lo and Mr Monkton an important document. He proposed, therefore, as one of the seconds, to testify that the duel had been fought in exact accordance with the terms of the agreement, both the principals conducting themselves like men of gallantry and honour (!). And he further announced that, in order not to compromise any one, he should place the paper containing his testimony in safe hands, with strict directions that it was on no account to be opened, except in a case of the last emergency.

After this preamble, Monsieur Foulon related that the duel had been fought two days after the drawing up of the agreement, in a locality to which accident had conducted the duelling party. (The name of the place was not mentioned, nor even the neighbourhood in which it was situated.) The men having been placed according to previous arrangement, the Count St Lo had won the toss for the first fire, had advanced his ten paces, and had shot his opponent in the body. Mr Monkton did not immediately fall, but staggered forward some six or seven paces, discharged his pistol ineffectually at the count, and dropped to the ground a dead man. Monsieur Foulon then stated that he tore a leaf from his pocket-book, wrote on it a brief description of the manner in which Mr Monkton had died, and pinned the paper to his clothes; this proceeding having been rendered necessary by the peculiar nature of the plan organized on the spot for safely disposing of the dead body. What this plan was, or what was done with the corpse, did not appear, for at this important point the narrative abruptly broke off.

A foot-note in the newspaper merely stated the manner in which the document had been obtained for publication, and repeated the announcement contained in the editor's introductory remarks, that no continuation had been found by the persons entrusted with the care of Monsieur Foulon's papers. I have now given the whole substance of what I read, and have mentioned all that was then known of Mr Stephen Monkton's death.

When I gave the newspaper back to Alfred, he was too much agitated to speak; but he reminded me by a sign that he was anxiously waiting to hear what I had to say. My position was a very trying and a very painful one. I could hardly tell what consequences might not follow any want of caution on my part, and could think at first of no safer plan that questioning him carefully before I committed myself either one way or the other.

'Will you excuse me if I ask you a question or two before I give you my advice?' said I.

He nodded impatiently.

'Yes, yes; any questions you like.'

'Were you at any time in the habit of seeing your uncle frequently?'

'I never saw him more than twice in my life: on each occasion, when I was a mere child.'

'Then you could have had no very strong personal regard for him?'

'Regard for him! I should have been ashamed to feel any regard for him. He disgraced us wherever he went.'

'May I ask if any family motive is involved in your anxiety to recover his remains?'

'Family motives may enter into it among others – but why do you ask?'

'Because, having heard that you employ the police to assist your search,

I was anxious to know whether you had stimulated their superiors to make them do their best in your service, by giving some strong personal reasons at head-quarters for the very unusual project which has brought you here.'

'I give no reasons. I pay for the work I want done, and in return for my liberality I am treated with the most infamous indifference on all sides. A stranger in the country, and badly acquainted with the language, I can do nothing to help myself. The authorities, both at Rome and in this place, pretend to assist me, pretend to search and inquire as I would have them search and inquire, and do nothing more. I am insulted, laughed at, almost to my face.'

'Do you not think it possible – mind, I have no wish to excuse the misconduct of the authorities, and do not share in any such opinion myself – but, do you not think it likely that the police may doubt whether you are in earnest?'

'Not in earnest!' he cried, starting up and confronting me fiercely, with wild eyes and quickened breath. 'Not in earnest! *You* think I'm not in earnest, too. I know you think it, though you tell me you don't. Stop! before we say another word, your own eyes shall convince you. Come here – only for a minute – only for one minute!'

I followed him into his bed-room, which opened out of the sitting-room. At one side of his bed stood a large packing-case of plain wood, upwards of seven feet in length.

'Open the lid, and look in,' he said, 'while I hold the candle so that you can see.'

I obeyed his directions, and discovered, to my astonishment, that the packing-case contained a leaden coffin, magnificently emblazoned with the arms of the Monkton family, and inscribed in old-fashioned letters with the name of 'Stephen Monkton,' his age and the manner of his death being added underneath.

'I keep his coffin ready for him,' whispered Alfred, close at my ear. 'Does that look like earnest?'

It looked more like insanity – so like that I shrank from answering him.

'Yes! yes! I see you are convinced,' he continued, quickly; 'we may go back into the next room, and may talk without restraint on either side now.'

On returning to our places, I mechanically moved my chair away from the table. My mind was by this time in such a state of confusion and uncertainty about what it would be best for me to say or do next, that I forgot for the moment the position he had assigned to me when we lit the candles. He reminded me of this directly.

'Don't move away,' he said, very earnestly; 'keep on sitting in the light; pray do! I'll soon tell you why I am so particular about that. But first give me your advice; help me in my great distress and suspense. Remember, you promised me you would.'

I made an effort to collect my thoughts, and succeeded. It was useless to treat the affair otherwise than seriously in his presence; it would have been cruel not to have advised him as I best could.

'You know,' I said, 'that two days after the drawing up of the agreement at Naples, the duel was fought out of the Neapolitan states. This fact has of course led you to the conclusion that all inquiries about localities had better be confined to the Roman territory?'

'Certainly: the search, such as it is, has been made there, and there only.

If I can believe the police, they and their agents have inquired for the place where the duel was fought (offering a large reward in my name to the person who can discover it), all along the high-road from Naples to Rome. They have also circulated – at least, so they tell me – descriptions of the duellists and their seconds; have left an agent to superintend investigations at the post-house, and another at the town mentioned as meeting-points in the agreement; and have endeavoured by correspondence with foreign authorities to trace the Count St Lo and Monsieur Dalville to their place or places of refuge. All these efforts, supposing them to have been really made, have hitherto proved utterly fruitless.'

'My impression is,' said I, after a moment's consideration, 'that all inquiries made along the high-road, or anywhere near Rome, are likely to be made in vain. As to the discovery of your uncle's remains, that is, I think, identical with the discovery of the place where he was shot; for those engaged in the duel would certainly not risk detection by carrying a corpse any distance with them in their flight. The place, then, is all that we want to find out. Now, let us consider for a moment. The duelling-party changed carriages; travelled separately, two and two; doubtless took roundabout roads; stopped at the post-house and the town as a blind; walked, perhaps, a considerable distance unguided. Depend upon it, such precautions as these (which we know they must have employed) left them very little time out of the two days – though they might start at sunrise, and not stop at nightfall – for straightforward travelling. My belief therefore is, that the duel was fought somewhere near the Neapolitan frontier; and if I had been the police agent who conducted the search, I should only have pursued it parallel with the frontier, starting from west to east till I got up among the lonely places in the mountains. That is my idea: do you think it worth anything?'

His face flushed all over in an instant. 'I think it an inspiration!' he cried. 'Not a day is to be lost in carrying out our plan. The police are not to be trusted with it. I must start myself, tomorrow morning; and you—'

He stopped; his face grew suddenly pale; he sighed heavily; his eyes wandered once more into the fixed look at vacancy; and the rigid, deathly expression fastened again upon all his features.

'I must tell you my secret before I talk of to-morrow,' he proceeded, faintly. 'If I hesitated any longer at confessing everything, I should be unworthy of your past kindness, unworthy of the help which it is my last hope that you will gladly give me when you have heard all.'

I begged him to wait until he was more composed, until he was better able to speak; but he did not appear to notice what I said. Slowly, and struggling as it seemed against himself, he turned a little away from me; and, bending his head over the table, supported it on his hand. The packet of letters with which I had seen him occupied when I came in, lay just beneath his eyes. He looked down on it steadfastly when he next spoke to me.

IV

'You were born, I believe, in our county,' he said; perhaps therefore you may. have heard at some time of a curious old prophecy about our family, which is still preserved among the traditions of Wincot Abbey?'

'I have heard of such a prophecy,' I answered; 'but I never knew in what terms it was expressed. It professed to predict the extinction of your family, or something of that sort, did it not?'

'No inquiries,' he went on, 'have traced back that prophecy to the time when it was first made; none of our family records tell us anything of its origin. Old servants and old tenants of ours remember to have heard it from their fathers and grandfathers. The monks, whom we succeeded in the Abbey in Henry the Eighth's time, got knowledge of it in some way; for I myself discovered the rhymes in which we know the prophecy to have been preserved from a very remote period, written on a blank leaf of one of the Abbey manuscripts. These are the verses, if verses they deserve to be called:

> When in Wincot vault a place
> Waits for one of Monkton's race;
> When that one forlorn shall lie
> Graveless under open sky,
> Beggared of six feet of earth,
> Though lord of acres from his birth—
> That shall be a certain sign
> Of the end of Monkton's line.
> Dwindling ever faster, faster,
> Dwindling to the last-left master;
> From mortal ken, from light of day,
> Monkton's race shall pass away.

'The prediction seems almost vague enough to have been uttered by an ancient oracle,' said I, observing that he waited, after repeating the verses, as if expecting me to say something.

'Vague or not, it is being accomplished,' he returned. 'I am now the "Last-left Master" – the last of that elder line of our family at which the prediction points; and the corpse of Stephen Monkton is not in the vaults of Wincot Abbey. Wait, before you exclaim against me! I have more to say about this. Long before the Abbey was ours, when we lived in the ancient manor-house near it (the very ruins of which have long since disappeared), the family-burying place was in the vault under the Abbey chapel. Whether in those remote times the prediction against us was known and dreaded, or not, this much is certain: everyone of the Monktons (whether living at the Abbey or on the smaller estate in Scotland) was buried in Wincot vault, no matter at what risk or what sacrifice. In the fierce fighting days of the olden time, the bodies of my ancestors who fell in foreign places were recovered and brought back to Wincot, though it often cost, not heavy ransom only, but desperate bloodshed as well, to obtain them. This superstition, if you please to call it so, has never died out of the family from that time to the present day; for centuries the succession of the dead in the vault at the Abbey has been unbroken – absolutely unbroken – until now. The place mentioned in the prediction as waiting to be filled is Stephen Monkton's place; the voice that cries vainly to the earth for shelter is the spirit-voice of the dead. As surely as if I saw it, I know that they have left him unburied on the ground where he fell!'

He stopped me before I could utter a word in remonstrance, by slowly rising to his feet, and pointing in the same direction towards which his eyes had wandered a short time since.

'I can guess what you want to ask me,' he exclaimed, sternly and loudly; 'you want to ask me how I can be mad enough to believe in a doggerel prophecy, uttered in an age of superstition to awe the most ignorant hearers. I answer' (at those words his voice sank suddenly to a whisper), 'I answer, because *Stephen Monkton himself stands there at this moment, confirming me in my belief.*'

Whether it was the awe and horror that looked out ghastly from his face as he confronted me, whether it was that I had never hitherto fairly believed in the reports about his madness, and that the conviction of their truth now forced itself upon me on a sudden, I know not; but I felt my blood curdling as he spoke, and I knew in my own heart, as I sat there speechless, that I dare not turn round and look where he was still pointing close at my side.

'I see there,' he went on in the same whispering voice, 'the figure of a dark-complexioned man, standing up with his head uncovered. One of his hands, still clutching a pistol, has fallen to his side; the other presses a bloody handkerchief over his mouth. The spasm of mortal agony convulses his features; but I know them for the features of a swarthy man, who twice frightened me by taking me up in his arms when I was a child, at Wincot Abbey. I asked the nurses at the time who that man was, and they told me it was my uncle, Stephen Monkton. Plainly, as if he stood there living, I see him now at your side, with the death-glare in his great black eyes; and so have I ever seen him since the moment when he was shot; at home and abroad, waking or sleeping, day and night, we are always together wherever I go!'

His whispering tones sank into almost inaudible murmuring as he pronounced these last words. From the direction and expression of his eyes, I suspected that he was speaking to the apparition. If I had beheld it myself at that moment, it would have been, I think, a less horrible sight to witness than to see him, as I saw him now, muttering inarticulately at vacancy. My own nerves were more shaken than I could have thought possible by what had passed. A vague dread of being near him in his present mood came over me, and I moved back a step or two.

He noticed the action instantly.

'Don't go! – pray, pray don't go! Have I alarmed you? Don't you believe me? Do the lights make your eyes ache? I only asked you to sit in the glare of the candles, because I could not bear to see the light that always shines from the phantom there at dusk, shining over you as you sat in the shadow. Don't go – don't leave me yet!'

There was an utter forlornness, an unspeakable misery in his face as he spoke these words, which gave me back my self-possession by the simple process of first moving me to pity. I resumed my chair, and said that I would stay with him as long as he wished.

'Thank you a thousand times! You are patience and kindness itself,' he said, going back to his former place, and resuming his former gentleness of manner. 'Now that I have got over my first confession of the misery that follows me in secret wherever I go, I think I can tell you calmly all that remains to be told. You see, as I said, my uncle Stephen,' – he turned away his head quickly, and looked down at the table as the name passed his lips – 'my uncle Stephen came twice to Wincot while I was a child, and on both occasions frightened me dreadfully. He only took me up in his arms, and spoke to me – very kindly, as I afterwards heard, for *him* – but he terrified me, nevertheless. Perhaps I was frightened at his great stature, his swarthy complexion, and his thick black hair and moustache, as other children might have been; perhaps the mere sight of him had some strange influence on me which I could not then understand, and cannot now explain. However it was, I used to dream of him long after he had gone away; and to fancy that he was stealing on me to catch me up in his arms, whenever I was left in the dark. The servants who took care of me found this out, and used to threaten me with my uncle Stephen whenever I was perverse and difficult to manage. As I grew up, I still retained my vague dread and abhorrence of our absent relative. I always listened intently, yet without knowing why, whenever his name was mentioned by my father or my mother – listened with an unaccountable presentiment that something terrible had happened to him, or was about to happen to me. This feeling only changed when I was left alone in the Abbey; and then it seemed to merge into the eager curiosity which had begun to grow on me, rather before that time, about the origin of the ancient prophecy predicting the extinction of our race. Are you following me?'

'I follow every word with the closest attention.'

'You must know, then, that I had first found out some fragments of the old rhyme, in which the prophecy occurs, quoted as a curiosity in an antiquarian book in the library. On the page opposite this quotation, had been pasted a rude old woodcut, representing a dark-haired man, whose face was so strangely like what I remembered of my uncle Stephen, that the portrait absolutely startled me. When I asked my father about this – it was then just before his death – he either knew, or pretended to know, nothing of it; and when I afterwards mentioned the prediction he fretfully changed the subject. It was just the same with our chaplain when I spoke to him. He said the portrait had been done centuries before my uncle was born; and called the prophecy doggerel and nonsense. I used to argue with him on the latter point, asking why we Catholics, who believed that the gift of working miracles had never departed from certain favoured persons, might not just as well believe that the gift of prophecy had never departed either? He would not dispute with me; he would only say that I must not waste time in thinking of such trifles, that I had more imagination than was good for me, and must suppress instead of exciting it. Such advice as this only irritated my curiosity. I determined secretly to search throughout the oldest uninhabited part of the Abbey, and to try if I could not find out from forgotten family records what the portrait was, and when the prophecy had been first written or uttered. Did you ever pass a day alone in the long-deserted chambers of an ancient house?'

'Never; such solitude as that is not at all to my taste.'

'Ah! what a life it was when I began my search. I should like to live it over again! Such tempting suspense, such strange discoveries, such wild fancies, such enthralling terrors, all belonged to that life! Only think of breaking open the door of a room which no living soul had entered before you for nearly a hundred years; think of the first step forward into a region of airless, awful stillness, where the light falls faint and sickly through closed windows and rotting curtains; think of the ghostly creaking of the old floor that cries out on you for treading on it, step as softly as you will; think of arms, helmets, weird tapestries of bygone days, that seem to be moving out on you from the walls as you first walk up to them in the dim light; think of prying into great cabinets and iron-clasped chests, not knowing what horrors may appear when you tear them open; of poring over their contents till twilight stole on you, and darkness grew terrible in the lonely place; of trying to leave it, and not being able to go, as if something held you; of wind wailing at you outside; of shadows darkening round you, and closing you up in obscurity within – only think of these things, and you may imagine the fascination of suspense and terror in such a life as mine was in those past days!'

(I shrunk from imagining that life: it was bad enough to see its results, as I saw them before me now.)

'Well, my search lasted months and months; then it was suspended a little, then resumed. In whatever direction I pursued it, I always found something to lure me on. Terrible confessions of past crimes, shocking proofs of secret wickedness that had been hidden securely from all eyes but mine, came to light. Sometimes these discoveries were associated with particular parts of the Abbey, which have had a horrible interest of their own for me ever since. Sometimes with certain old portraits in the picture gallery, which I actually dreaded to look at, after what I had found out. There were periods when the results of this search of mine so horrified me, that I determined to give it up entirely; but I never could persevere in my resolution, the temptation to go on seemed at certain intervals to get too strong for me, and then I yielded to it again and again. At last I found the book that had belonged to the monks, with the whole of the prophecy written in the blank leaf. This first success encouraged me to get back further yet in the family records. I had discovered nothing hitherto of the identity of the mysterious portrait, but the same intuitive conviction which had assured me of its extraordinary resemblance to my uncle Stephen, seemed also to assure me that he must be more closely connected with the prophecy, and must know more of it than anyone else. I had no means of holding any communication with him, no means of satisfying myself whether this strange idea of mine were right or wrong, until the day when my doubts were settled for ever by the same terrible proof which is now present to me in this very room.'

He paused for a moment, and looked at me intently and suspiciously. Then asked if I believed all he had said to me so far. My instant reply in the affirmative seemed to satisfy his doubts, and he went on.

'On a fine evening in February, I was standing alone in one of the deserted rooms of the western turret at the Abbey, looking at the sunset. Just before the sun went down, I felt a sensation stealing over me which it is impossible to explain. I saw nothing, heard nothing, knew nothing. This utter self-oblivion came suddenly; it was not fainting, for I did not fall to the ground, did not move an inch from my place. If such a thing could be, I should say it was the temporary separation of soul and body, without death; but all description of my situation at that time is impossible. Call my state what you will, trance or catalepsy, I know that I remained standing by the window utterly unconscious – dead, mind and body – until the sun had set. Then I came to my senses again; and then, when I opened my eyes, there was the apparition of Stephen Monkton standing opposite to me, faintly luminous, just as it stands opposite me at this very moment by your side.'

'Was this before the news of the duel reached England?' I asked.

'*Two weeks before* the news of it reached us at Wincot. And even when we heard of the duel, we did not hear of the day on which it was fought. I only found that out when the document which you have read was published in the French newspaper. The date of that document, you will remember, is February 22nd, and it is stated that the duel was fought two days afterwards. I wrote down in my pocket-book, on the evening when I saw the phantom, the day of the month on which it first appeared to me. That day was the 24th of February.'

He paused again as if expecting me to say something. After the words he had just spoken, what could I say? what could I think?

'Even in the first horror of first seeing the apparition,' he went on, 'the prophecy against our house came to my mind, and with it the conviction that I beheld before me, in that spectral presence, the warning of my own doom. As soon as I recovered a little, I determined, nevertheless, to test the reality of what I saw; to find out whether I was the dupe of my own diseased fancy or not. I left the turret; the phantom left it with me. I made an excuse to have the drawing-room at the Abbey brilliantly lighted up; the figure was still opposite me. I walked out into the park; it was there in the clear starlight. I went away from home, and travelled many miles to the seaside; still the tall dark man in his death-agony was with me. After this, I strove against the fatality no more. I returned to the Abbey, and tried to resign myself to my misery. But this was not to be. I had a hope that was dearer to me than my own life; I had one treasure belonging to me that I shuddered at the prospect of losing; and when the phantom presence stood a warning obstacle between me and this one treasure, this dearest hope, then my misery grew heavier than I could bear. You must know what I am alluding to; you must have heard often that I was engaged to be married?'

'Yes, often. I have some acquaintance myself with Miss Elmslie.'

'You never can know all that she has sacrificed for me – never can imagine what I have felt for years and years past' – his voice trembled, and the tears came into his eyes – 'but I dare not trust myself to speak of that; the thought of the old happy days in the Abbey almost breaks my heart now. Let me get back to the other subject. I must tell you that I kept the frightful vision which pursued me, at all times and in all places, a secret from everybody knowing the vile reports about my having inherited madness from my family, and fearing that an unfair advantage would be taken of any confession that I might make. Though the phantom always stood opposite to me, and therefore always appeared either before or by the side of any person to whom I spoke, I soon schooled myself to hide from others that I was looking at it, except on rare occasions – when I have perhaps betrayed myself to you. But my self-possession availed me nothing with Ada. The day of our marriage was approaching.'

He stopped and shuddered. I waited in silence till he had controlled himself.

'Think,' he went on, 'think of what I must have suffered at looking always on that hideous vision, whenever I looked on my betrothed wife! Think of my taking her hand, and seeming to take it through the figure of the apparition! Think of the calm angel-face and the tortured spectre-face being always together, whenever my eyes met hers! Think of this, and you will not wonder that I betrayed my secret to her. She eagerly entreated to know the worst – nay more, she insisted on knowing it. At her bidding I told all; and then left her free to break our engagement. The thought of death was in my heart as I spoke the parting words – death by my own act, if life still held out after our separation. She suspected that thought; she knew it, and never left me till her good influence had destroyed it for ever. But for her, I should not have been alive now – but for her, I should never have attempted the project which has brought me here.'

'Do you mean that it was at Miss Elmslie's suggestion that you came to Naples?' I asked in amazement.

'I mean that what she said, suggested the design which has brought me to Naples,' he answered. 'While I believed that the phantom had appeared to me as the fatal messenger of death, there was no comfort, there was misery rather in hearing her say that no power on earth should make her desert me, and that she would live for me, and for me only, through every trial. But it was far different when we afterwards reasoned together about the purpose which the apparition had come to fulfil – far different when she showed me that its mission might be for good, instead of for evil; and that the warning it was sent to give, might be to my profit instead of to my loss. At those words, the new idea which gave the new hope of life came to me in an instant. I believed then, what I believe now, that I have a supernatural warrant for my errand here. In that faith I live; without it I should die. *She* never ridiculed it, never scorned it as insanity. Mark what I say! The spirit that appeared to me in the Abbey, that has never left me since, that stands there now by your side, warns me to escape from the fatality which hangs over our race, and commands me, if I would avoid it, to bury the unburied dead. Mortal loves and mortal interests must bow to that awful bidding. The spectre-presence will never leave me till I have sheltered the corpse that cries to the earth to cover it! I dare not return – I dare not marry till I have filled the place that is empty in Wincot vault.'

His eyes flashed and dilated; his voice deepened; a fanatic ecstasy shone in his expression as he uttered these words. Shocked and grieved as I was, I made no attempt to remonstrate or to reason with him. It would have been useless to have referred to any of the usual common-places about optical delusions, or diseased imaginations – worse than useless to have attempted to account by natural causes for any of the extraordinary coincidences and events of which he had spoken. Briefly as he had referred to Miss Elmslie, he had said enough to show me that the only hope of the poor girl who loved him best and had known him longest of any one, was in humouring his delusions to the last. How faithfully she still clung to the belief that she could restore him! How resolutely was she sacrificing herself to his morbid fancies, in the hope of a happy future that might never come! Little as I knew of Miss Elmslie, the mere thought of her situation, as I now reflected on it, made me feel sick at heart.

'They call me "Mad Monkton!"' he exclaimed, suddenly breaking the silence between us during the last few minutes. 'Here and in England everybody believes I am out of my senses, except Ada and you. She has been my salvation; and you will be my salvation too. Something told me that, when I first met you walking in the Villa Reale. I struggled against the strong desire that was in me to trust my secret to you; but I could resist it no longer when I saw you to-night at the ball – the phantom seemed to draw me on to you, as you stood alone in the quiet room. Tell me more of that idea of yours about finding the place where the duel was fought. If I set out to-morrow to seek for it myself, where must I go to first? – where?' He stopped; his strength was evidently becoming exhausted, and his mind was growing confused. 'What am I to do? I can't remember. You know everything – will you not help me? My misery has made me unable to help myself!'

He stopped, murmured something about failing if he went to the frontier alone, and spoke confusedly of delays that might be fatal; then tried to utter the name of 'Ada;' but in pronouncing the first letter his voice faltered, and turning abruptly from me he burst into tears.

My pity for him got the better of my prudence at that moment, and without thinking of responsibilities, I promised at once to do for him whatever he asked. The wild triumph in his expression, as he started up and seized my hand, showed me that I had better have been more cautious; but it was too late now to retract what I had said. The next best thing to do was to try if I could not induce him to compose himself a little, and then to go away and think coolly over the whole affair by myself.

'Yes, yes,' he rejoined, in answer to the few words I now spoke to try and calm him, 'don't be afraid about me. After what you have said, I'll answer for my own coolness and composure under all emergencies. I have been so long used to the apparition that I hardly feel its presence at all except on rare occasions. Besides, I have here, in this little packet of letters, the medicine for every malady of the sick heart. They are Ada's letters; I read them to calm me whenever my misfortune seems to get the better of my endurance. I wanted that half hour to read them in tonight, before you came, to make myself fit to see you; and I shall go through them again after you are gone. So, once more don't be afraid about me. I know I shall succeed with your help; and Ada shall thank you as you deserve to be thanked when we get back to England. If you hear the fools at Naples talk about my being mad, don't trouble yourself to contradict them: the scandal is so contemptible that it must end by contradicting itself.'

I left him, promising to return early the next day.

When I got back to my hotel, I felt that any idea of sleeping, after all that I had seen and heard, was out of the question. So I lit my pipe, and sitting by the window – how it refreshed my mind just then to look at the calm moonlight! – tried to think what it would be best to do. In the first place, any appeal to doctors or to Alfred's friends in England was out of the question. I could not persuade myself that his intellect was sufficiently disordered to justify me, under existing circumstances, in disclosing the secret which he had entrusted to my keeping. In the second place, all attempts on my part to induce him to abandon the idea of searching out his uncle's remains would be utterly useless after what I had incautiously said to him. Having settled these two conclusions, the only really great difficulty which remained to perplex me was whether I was justified in aiding him to execute his extraordinary purpose.

Supposing that with my help he found Mr Monkton's body, and took it back with him to England, was it right in me thus to lend myself to promoting the marriage which would most likely follow these events – a marriage which it might be the duty of everyone to prevent at all hazards? This set me thinking about the extent of his madness, or to speak more mildly and more correctly, of his delusion. Sane he certainly was on all ordinary subjects; nay, in all the narrative parts of what he had said to me on this very evening he had spoken clearly and connectedly. As for the story of the apparition, other men, with intellects as clear as the intellects of their neighbours, had fancied themselves pursued by a phantom, and had even written about it in a high strain of philosophical speculation. It was plain that the real hallucination in the case now before me lay in Monkton's conviction of the truth of the old prophecy, and in his idea that the fancied apparition was a supernatural warning to him to evade its denunciations. And it was equally clear that both delusions had been produced, in the first instance, by the lonely life he had led, acting on a naturally excitable temperament, which was rendered further liable to moral disease by an hereditary taint of insanity.

Was this curable? Miss Elmslie, who knew him far better than I did, seemed by her conduct to think so. Had I any reason or right to determine off-hand that she was mistaken? Supposing I refused to go to the frontier with him, he would then most certainly depart by himself, to commit all sorts of errors, and perhaps to meet with all sorts of accidents; while I, an idle man, with my time entirely at my own disposal, was stopping at Naples, and leaving him to his fate after I had suggested the plan of his expedition, and had encouraged him to confide in me. In this way I kept turning the subject over and over again in my mind – being quite free, let me add, from looking at it in any other than a practical point of view. I firmly believed, as a derider of all ghost stories, that Alfred was deceiving himself in fancying that he had seen the apparition of his uncle before the news of Mr Monkton's death reached England; and I was on this account therefore uninfluenced by the slightest infection of my unhappy friend's delusions, when I at last fairly decided to accompany him in his extraordinary search. Possibly my harum-scarum fondness for excitement at that time, biassed me a little in forming my resolution; but I must add, in common justice to myself, that I also acted from motives of real sympathy for Monkton, and from a sincere wish to allay, if I could, the anxiety of the poor girl who was still so faithfully waiting and hoping for him far away in England.

Certain arrangements preliminary to our departure, which I found myself obliged to make after a second interview with Alfred, betrayed the object of our journey to most of our Neapolitan friends. The astonishment of everybody was of course unbounded, and the nearly universal suspicion that I must be as mad in my way as Monkton himself, showed itself pretty plainly in my presence. Some people actually tried to combat my resolution by telling me what a shameless profligate Stephen Monkton had been – as if I had a strong personal interest in hunting out his remains! Ridicule moved me as little as any arguments of this sort; my mind was made up, and I was as obstinate then as I am now.

In two days' time I had got everything ready, and had ordered the travelling carriage to the door some hours earlier than we had originally settled. We were jovially threatened with 'a parting cheer' by all our English acquaintances, and I thought it desirable to avoid this on my friend's account; for he had been more excited, as it was, by the preparations for the journey than I at all liked. Accordingly, soon after sunrise, without a soul in the street to stare at us, we privately left Naples.

Nobody will wonder, I think, that I experienced some difficulty in realising my own position, and shrank instinctively from looking forward a single day into the future, when I now found myself starting, in company with 'Mad Monkton,' to hunt for the body of a dead duellist all along the frontier line of the Roman states!

V

I had settled it in my own mind that we had better make the town of Fondi, close on the frontier, our head-quarters, to begin with; and I had arranged, with the assistance of the Embassy, that the leaden coffin should follow us so far, securely nailed up in its packing case. Besides our passports, we were well furnished with letters of introduction to the local authorities at most of the important frontier towns, and to crown all, we had money enough at our command (thanks to Monkton's vast fortune) to make sure of the services of anyone whom we wanted to assist us, all along our line of search. These various resources ensured us every facility for action – provided always that we succeeded in discovering the body of the dead duellist. But, in the very probable event of our failing to do this, our future prospects – more especially after the responsibility I had undertaken – were of anything but an agreeable nature to contemplate. I confess I felt uneasy, almost hopeless, as we posted, in the dazzling Italian sunshine, along the road to Fondi.

We made an easy two days' journey of it; for I had insisted, on Monkton's account, that we should travel slowly.

On the first day the excessive agitation of my companion a little alarmed me; he showed, in many ways, more symptoms of a disordered mind than I had yet observed in him. On the second day, however, he seemed to get accustomed to contemplate calmly the new idea of the search on which we were bent, and, except on one point, he was cheerful and composed enough. Whenever his dead uncle formed the subject of conversation, he still persisted – on the strength of the old prophecy, and under the influence of the apparition which he saw, or thought he saw, always – in asserting that the corpse of Stephen Monkton, wherever it was, lay yet unburied. On every other topic he deferred to me with the utmost readiness and docility; on this he maintained his strange opinion with an obstinacy which set reason and persuasion alike at defiance.

On the third day we rested at Fondi. The packing case, with the coffin in it, reached us, and was deposited in a safe place under lock and key. We engaged some mules, and found a man to act as guide who knew the country thoroughly. It occurred to me that we had better begin by confiding the real object of our journey only to the most trustworthy people we could find among the better educated classes. For this reason we followed, in one respect, the example of the fatal duelling-party, by starting, early on the morning of the fourth day, with sketch-books and colour-boxes, as if we were only artists in search of the picturesque.

After travelling some hours in a northerly direction within the Roman frontier, we halted to rest ourselves and our mules at a wild little village, far out of the track of tourists in general.

The only person of the smallest importance in the place was the priest, and to him I addressed my first inquiries, leaving Monkton to await my return with the guide. I spoke Italian quite fluently and correctly enough for my purpose, and was extremely polite and cautious in introducing my business, but, in spite of all the pains I took, I only succeeded in frightening and bewildering the poor priest more and more with every fresh word I said to him. The idea of a duelling-party and a dead man seemed to scare him out of his senses. He bowed, fidgeted, cast his eyes up to heaven, and piteously shrugging his shoulders, told me, with rapid Italian circumlocution, that he had not the faintest idea of what I was talking about. This was my first failure. I confess I was weak enough to feel a little dispirited when I rejoined Monkton and the guide.

After the heat of the day was over, we resumed our journey.

About three miles from the village, the road, or rather cart-track, branched off in two directions. The path to the right, our guide informed us, led up among the mountains to a convent about six miles off. If we penetrated beyond the convent, we should soon reach the Neapolitan frontier. The path to the left led far inwards on the Roman territory, and would conduct us to a small town where we could sleep for the night. Now, the Roman territory presented the first and fittest field for our search, and the convent was always within reach, supposing we returned to Fondi unsuccessful. Besides, the path to the left led over the widest part of the country we were starting to explore; and I was always for vanquishing the greatest difficulty first – so we decided manfully on turning to the left. The expedition in which this resolution involved us lasted a whole week, and produced no results. We discovered absolutely nothing, and returned to our head-quarters at Fondi, so completely baffled that we did not know whither to turn our steps next.

I was made much more uneasy by the effect of our failure on Monkton than by the failure itself. His resolution appeared to break down altogether as soon as we began to retrace our steps. He became first fretful and capricious, then silent and desponding. Finally, he sank into a lethargy of body and mind that seriously alarmed me. On the morning after our return to Fondi, he showed a strange tendency to sleep incessantly, which made me suspect the existence of some physical malady in his brain. The whole day he hardly exchanged a word with me, and seemed to be never fairly awake. Early the next morning I went into his room, and found him as silent and lethargic as ever. His servant, who was with us, informed me that Alfred had once or twice before exhibited such physical symptoms of mental exhaustion as we were now observing, during his father's lifetime at Wincot Abbey. This piece of information made me feel easier, and left my mind free to return to the consideration of the errand which had brought us to Fondi.

I resolved to occupy the time until my companion got better, in prosecuting our search by myself. That path to the right hand which led to the convent had not yet been explored; if I set off to trace it, I need not be away from Monkton more than one night, and I should at least be able on my return to give him the satisfaction of knowing that one more uncertainty regarding the place of the duel had been cleared up. These considerations decided me. I left a message for my friend, in case he asked where I had gone, and set out once more for the village at which we had halted when starting on our first expedition.

Intending to walk to the convent, I parted company with the guide and the mules where the track branched off, leaving them to go back to the village and await my return.

For the first four miles the path gently ascended through an open country, then became abruptly much steeper, and led me deeper and deeper among thickets and endless woods. By the time my watch informed me that I must have nearly walked my appointed distance, the view was bounded on all sides, and the sky was shut out overhead, by an impervious screen of leaves and branches. I still followed my only guide, the steep path; and in ten minutes, emerging suddenly on a plot of tolerably clear and level ground, I saw the convent before me.

It was a dark, low, sinister-looking place. Not a sign of life or movement was visible anywhere about it. Green stains streaked the once white façade of the chapel in all directions. Moss clustered thick in every crevice of the heavy scowling wall that surrounded the convent. Long lank weeds grew out of the fissures of roof and parapet, and drooping far downward, waved wearily in and out of the barred dormitory windows. The very cross opposite the entrance-gate, with a shocking life-sized figure in wood nailed to it, was so beset at the base with crawling creatures, and looked so slimy, green and rotten all the way up, that I absolutely shrank from it.

A bell-rope with a broken handle hung by the gate. I approached it – hesitated, I hardly knew why – looked up at the convent again, and then walked round to the back of the building, partly to gain time to consider what I had better do next; partly from an unaccountable curiosity that urged me, strangely to myself, to see all I could of the outside of the place before I attempted to gain admission at the gate.

At the back of the convent I found an outhouse, built on to the wall – a clumsy, decayed building, with the greater part of the roof fallen in, and with a jagged hole in one of its sides, where in all probability a window had once been. Behind the outhouse the trees grew thicker than ever. As I looked towards them, I could not determine whether the ground beyond me rose or fell – whether it was grassy, or earthy, or rocky. I could see nothing but the all-pervading leaves, brambles, ferns, and long grass.

Not a sound broke the oppressive stillness. No bird's note rose from the leafy wilderness around me; no voices spoke in the convent garden behind the scowling wall; no clock struck in the chapel-tower; no dog barked in the ruined outhouse. The dead silence deepened the solitude of the place inexpressibly. I began to feel it weighing on my spirits – the more because woods were never favourite places with me to walk in. The sort of pastoral happiness which poets often represent when they sing of life in the woods, never, to my mind, has half the charm of life on the mountain or in the plain. When I am in a wood, I miss the boundless loveliness of the sky, and the delicious softness that distance gives to the earthly view beneath. I feel oppressively the change which the free air suffers when it gets imprisoned among leaves, and I am always awed, rather than pleased, by that mysterious still light which shines with such a strange dim lustre in deep places among trees. It may convict me of want of taste and absence of due feeling for the marvellous beauties of vegetation, but I must frankly own that I never penetrate far into a wood without finding that the getting out of it again is the pleasantest part of my walk – the getting out on to the barest down, the wildest hill-side, the bleakest mountain-top – the getting out anywhere so that I can see the sky over me and the view before me as far as my eye can reach.

After such a confession as I have now made, it will appear surprising to no one that I should have felt the strongest possible inclination, while I stood by the ruined outhouse, to retrace my steps at once, and make the best of my way out of the wood. I had indeed actually turned to depart, when the remembrance of the errand which had brought me to the convent suddenly stayed my feet. It seemed doubtful whether I should be admitted into the building if I rang the bell; and more than doubtful, if I were let in, whether the inhabitants would be able to afford me any clue to the information of which I was in search. However, it was my duty to Monkton to leave no means of helping him in his desperate object untried; so I resolved to go round to the front of the convent again, and ring the gate-bell at all hazards.

By the merest chance I looked up as I passed the side of the outhouse where the jagged hole was, and noticed that it was pierced rather high in the wall.

As I stopped to observe this, the closeness of the atmosphere in the wood seemed to be affecting me more unpleasantly than ever.

I waited a minute and untied my cravat.

Closeness? – surely it was something more than that. The air was even more distasteful to my nostrils than to my lungs. There was some faint, indescribable smell loading it – some smell of which I had never had any previous experience – some smell which I thought (now that my attention was directed to it) grew more and more certainly traceable to its source the nearer I advanced to the outhouse.

By the time I had tried the experiment two or three times, and had made myself sure of this fact, my curiosity became excited. There were plenty of fragments of stone and brick lying about me. I gathered some of them together, and piled them up below the hole, then mounted to the top, and, feeling rather ashamed of what I was doing, peeped into the outhouse.

The sight of horror that met my eyes the instant I looked through the hole, is as present to my memory now as if I had beheld it yesterday. I can hardly write of it at this distance of time without a thrill of the old terror running through me again to the heart.

The first impression conveyed to me, as I looked in, was of a long recumbent object, tinged with a lightish blue colour all over, extended on trestles, and bearing a certain hideous half-formed resemblance to the human face and figure. I looked again, and felt certain of it. There were the prominences of the forehead, nose, and chin, dimly shown as under a veil – there, the round outline of the chest, and the hollow below it – there, the points of the knees, and the stiff, ghastly, upturned feet. I looked again, yet more attentively. My eyes got accustomed to the dim light streaming in through the broken roof; and I satisfied myself, judging by the great length of the body from head to foot, that I was looking at the corpse of a man – a corpse that had apparently once had a sheet spread over it – and that had lain rotting on the trestles under the open sky long enough for the linen to take the livid, light-blue tinge of mildew and decay which now covered it.

How long I remained with my eyes fixed on that dread sight of death, on that tombless, terrible wreck of humanity, poisoning the still air, and seeming even to stain the faint descending light that disclosed it, I know not. I remember a dull, distant sound among the trees, as if the breeze were rising – the slow, creeping on of the sound to near the place where I stood – the noiseless whirling fall of a dead leaf on the corpse below me, through the gap in the outhouse roof – and the effect of awakening my energies, of relaxing the heavy strain on my mind, which even the slight change wrought in the scene I beheld by the falling leaf, produced in me immediately. I descended to the ground, and, sitting down on the heap of stones, wiped away the thick perspiration which covered my face, and which I now became aware of for the first time. It was something more than the hideous spectacle unexpectedly offered to my eyes, which had shaken my nerves, as I felt that they were shaken now.

Monkton's prediction that, if we succeeded in discovering his uncle's body, we should find it unburied, recurred to me the instant I saw the trestles and their ghastly burden. I felt assured on the instant that I had found the dead man – the old prophecy recurred to my memory – a strange yearning sorrow, a vague foreboding of ill, an inexplicable terror, as I thought of the poor lad who was awaiting my return in the distant town, struck through me with a chill of superstitious dread, robbed me of my judgment and resolution, and left me, when I had at last recovered myself, weak and dizzy, as if I had just suffered under some pang of overpowering physical pain.

I hastened round to the convent gate, and rang impatiently at the bell – waited a little while, and rang again – then heard footsteps.

In the middle of the gate, just opposite my face, there was a small sliding panel, not more than a few inches long; this was presently pushed aside from within. I saw, through a bit of iron grating, two dull, light grey eyes staring vacantly at me, and heard a feeble husky voice saying:

'What may you please to want?'

'I am a traveller –' I began.

'We live in a miserable place. We have nothing to show travellers here.'

'I don't come to see anything. I have an important question to ask, which I believe some one in this convent will be able to answer. If you are not willing to let me in, at least come out and speak to me here.'

'Are you alone?'

'Quite alone.'

'Are there no women with you?'

'None.'

The gate was slowly unbarred; and an old Capuchin, very infirm, very suspicious, and very dirty, stood before me. I was far too excited and impatient to waste any time in prefatory phrases; so telling the monk at once how I had looked through the hole in the outhouse, and what I had seen inside, I asked him in plain terms who the man had been whose corpse I had beheld, and why the body was left unburied?

The old Capuchin listened to me with watery eyes that twinkled suspiciously. He had a battered tin snuff-box in his hand; and his finger and thumb slowly chased a few scattered grains of snuff round and round the inside of the box all the time I was speaking. When I had done, he shook his head, and said 'that was certainly an ugly sight in their outhouse; one of the ugliest sights, he felt sure, that ever I had seen in all my life!'

'I don't want to talk of the sight,' I rejoined, impatiently; 'I want to know who the man was, how he died, and why he is not decently buried. Can you tell me?'

The monk's finger and thumb having captured three or four grains of snuff at last, he slowly drew them into his nostrils, holding the box open under his nose the while, to prevent the possibility of wasting even one grain, sniffed once or twice, luxuriously – closed the box – then looked at me again, with his eyes watering and twinkling more suspiciously than before.

'Yes,' said the monk, 'that's an ugly sight in our outhouse – a very ugly sight, certainly!'

I never had more difficulty in keeping my temper in my life, than at that moment. I succeeded, however, in repressing a very disrespectful expression on the subject of monks in general, which was on the tip of my tongue, and made another attempt to conquer the old man's exasperating reserve. Fortunately for my chances of succeeding with him, I was a snuff-taker myself; and I had a box full of excellent English snuff in my pocket, which I now produced as a bribe. It was my last resource.

'I thought your box seemed empty just now,' said I, 'will you try a pinch out of mine?'

The offer was accepted with an almost youthful alacrity of gesture. The Capuchin took the largest pinch I ever saw held between any man's finger and thumb, inhaled it slowly, without spilling a single grain – half closed his eyes – and, wagging his head gently, patted me paternally on the back.

'Oh, my son!' said the monk, 'what delectable snuff! Oh, my son and amiable traveller, give the spiritual father who loves you, yet another tiny, tiny pinch!'

'Let me fill your box for you. I shall have plenty left for myself.'

The battered tin snuff-box was given to me before I had done speaking – the paternal hand patted my back more approvingly than ever – the feeble, husky voice grew glib and eloquent in my praise. I had evidently found out the weak side of the old Capuchin; and, on returning him his box, I took instant advantage of the discovery.

'Excuse my troubling you on the subject again,' I said, 'but I have particular reasons for wanting to hear all that you can tell me in explanation of that horrible sight in the outhouse.'

'Come in,' answered the monk.

He drew me inside the gate, closed it, and then leading the way across a grass grown courtyard, looking out on a weedy kitchen garden, showed me into a long room with a low ceiling, a dirty dresser, a few rudely-carved stall seats, and one or two grim mildewed pictures for ornaments. This was the refectory.

'There's nobody here, and it's nice and cool,' said the old Capuchin. It was so damp that I actually shivered. 'Would you like to see the church?' said the monk; 'a jewel of a church, if we could only keep it in repair; but we can't. Ah! malediction and misery, we are too poor to keep our church in repair!'

Here he shook his head, and began fumbling with a large bunch of keys.

'Never mind the church now!' said I. 'Can you, or can you not, tell me what I want to know.'

'Everything, from beginning to end – absolutely everything! Why, I answered the gate bell – I always answer the gate bell here,' said the Capuchin.

'What, in heaven's name, has the gate bell to do with the unburied corpse in your outhouse?'

'Listen, son of mine, and you shall know. Some time ago – some months – ah, me, I'm old; I've lost my memory; I don't know how many months – ah! miserable me, what a very old, old monk I am!' Here he comforted himself with another pinch of my snuff.

'Never mind the exact time,' said I. 'I don't care about that.'

'Good,' said the Capuchin. 'Now I can go on. Well, let us say, it is some months ago – we in this convent are all at breakfast – wretched, wretched breakfasts, son of mine, in this convent! – we are at breakfast, and we hear *bang! bang!* twice over. "Guns," says I. "What are they shooting for?" says brother Jeremy. "Game," says brother Vincent. "Aha! game," says brother Jeremy.

"If I hear more, I shall send out and discover what it means," says the father superior. We hear no more, and we go on with our wretched breakfasts.'

'Where did the report of fire-arms come from?' I inquired.

'From down below, beyond the big trees at the back of the convent, where there's some clear ground – nice ground, if it wasn't for the pools and puddles. But, ah misery! how damp we are in these parts! how very, very damp!'

'Well, what happened after the report of fire-arms?'

'You shall hear. We are still at breakfast, all silent – for what have we to talk about here? What have we but our devotions, our kitchen garden, and our wretched, wretched bits of breakfasts and dinners? I say we are all silent, when there comes suddenly such a ring at the bell as never was heard before – a very devil of a ring – a ring that caught us all with our bits – our wretched, wretched bits! – in our mouths, and stopped us before we could swallow them. "Go, brother of mine!" says the father superior to me – "go, it is your duty – go to the gate." I am brave – a very lion of a Capuchin. I slip out on tip-toe – I wait – I listen – I pull back our little shutter in the gate – I wait, I listen again – I peep through the hole – nothing, absolutely nothing, that I can see. I am brave – I am not to be daunted. What do I do next? I open the gate. Ah! Sacred Mother of Heaven, what do I behold lying all along our threshold? A man – dead! – a big man; bigger than you, bigger than me, bigger than anybody in this convent – buttoned up tight in a fine coat, with black eyes, staring, staring up at the sky; and blood soaking through and through the front of his shirt. What do I do? I scream once – I scream twice – and run back to the father superior!'

All the particulars of the fatal duel which I had gleaned from the French newspaper in Monkton's room at Naples, recurred vividly to my memory. The suspicion that I had felt when I looked into the outhouse, became a certainty as I listened to the old monk's last words.

'So far I understand,' said I. 'The corpse I have just seen in the outhouse, is the corpse of the man whom you found dead outside your gate. Now tell me why you have not given the remains decent burial?'

'Wait – wait – wait,' answered the Capuchin. 'The father superior hears me scream, and comes out; we all run together to the gate; we lift up the big man, and look at him close. Dead! dead as this' (smacking the dresser with his hand). 'We look again, and see a bit of paper pinned to the collar of his coat. Aha! son of mine, you start at that. I thought I should make you start at last.'

I had started indeed. That paper was doubtless the leaf mentioned in the second's unfinished narrative as having been torn out of his pocket-book, and inscribed with the statement of how the dead man had lost his life. If proof positive were wanted to identify the dead body, here was such proof found.

'What do you think was written on the bit of paper?' continued the Capuchin. 'We read, and shudder. This dead man has been killed in a duel – he, the desperate, the miserable, has died in the commission of mortal sin; and the men who saw the killing of him, ask us Capuchins, holy men, servants of Heaven, children of our lord the pope – they ask *us* to give him burial! Oh! but we are outraged when we read that; we groan, we wring our hands, we turn away, we tear our beards, we—'

'Wait one moment,' said I, seeing that the old man was heating himself with his narrative, and was likely, unless I stopped him, to talk more and more fluently to less and less purpose – 'wait a moment. Have you preserved the paper that was pinned to the dead man's coat; and can I look at it?'

The Capuchin seemed on the point of giving me an answer, when he suddenly checked himself. I saw his eyes wander away from my face, and at the same moment heard a door softly opened and closed again behind me.

Looking round immediately, I observed another monk in the refectory – a tall, lean, black-bearded man, in whose presence my old friend with the snuff-box suddenly became quite decorous and devotional to look at. I suspected I was in the presence of the father superior; and I found that I was right the moment he addressed me.

'I am the father superior of this convent,' he said in quiet, clear tones, and looking me straight in the face while he spoke, with coldly attentive eyes. 'I have heard the latter part of your conversation, and I wish to know why you are so particularly anxious to see the piece of paper that was pinned to the dead man's coat?'

The coolness with which he avowed that he had been listening, and the quietly imperative manner in which he put his concluding question perplexed and startled me. I hardly knew at first what tone I ought to take in answering him. He observed my hesitation, and attributing it to the wrong cause, signed to the old Capuchin to retire. Humbly stroking his long grey beard, and furtively consoling himself with a private pinch of the 'delectable snuff,' my venerable friend shuffled out of the room, making a profound obeisance at the door, just before he disappeared.

'Now,' said the father superior, as coldly as ever; 'I am waiting, sir, for your reply.'

'You shall have it in the fewest possible words,' said I, answering him in his own tone. 'I find to my disgust and horror that there is an unburied corpse in an outhouse attached to your convent. I believe that corpse to be the body of an English gentleman of rank and fortune, who was killed in a duel. I have come into this neighbourhood, with the nephew and only relation of the slain man, for the express purpose of recovering his remains; and I wish to see the paper found on the body, because I believe that paper will identify it to the satisfaction of the relative to whom I have referred. Do you find my reply sufficiently straightforward? And do you mean to give me permission to look at the paper?'

'I am satisfied with your reply, and see no reason for refusing you a sight of the paper,' said the father superior; 'but I have something to say first. In speaking of the impression produced on you by beholding the corpse, you used the words "disgust" and "horror." This licence of expression in relation to what you have seen in the precincts of a convent, proves to me that you are out of the pale of the Holy Catholic Church. You have no right, therefore, to expect any explanation; but I will give you one, nevertheless, as a favour. The slain man died, unabsolved, in the commission of mortal sin. We infer so much from the paper which we found on his body; and we know, by the evidence of our own eyes and ears, that he was killed on the territories of the church, and in the act of committing direct violation of those special laws against the crime of duelling, the strict enforcement of which the holy father himself has urged on the faithful throughout his dominions, by letters signed with his own hand. Inside this convent the ground is consecrated; and we Catholics are not accustomed to bury the outlaws of our religion, the enemies of our Holy Father, and the violators of our most sacred laws, in consecrated ground. Outside this convent, we have no rights and no power; and, if we had both, we should remember that we are monks, not gravediggers, and that the only burial with which *we* can have any concern, is burial with the prayers of the church. That is all the explanation I think it necessary to give. Wait for me here, and you shall see the paper.' With those words the father superior left the room as quietly as he had entered it.

I had hardly time to think over this bitter and ungracious explanation, and to feel a little piqued by the language and manner of the person who had given it to me, before the father superior returned with the paper in his hand. He placed it before me on the dresser; and I read hurriedly traced in pencil, the following lines:

This paper is attached to the body of the late Mr Stephen Monkton, an Englishman of distinction. He has been shot in a duel, conducted with perfect gallantry and honour on both sides. His body is placed at the door of this convent, to receive burial at the hands of its inmates, the survivors of the encounter being obliged to separate and secure their safety by immediate flight. I, the second of the slain man, and the writer of this explanation, certify, on my word of honour as a gentleman, that the shot which killed my principal on the instant was fired fairly, in the strictest accordance with the rules laid down beforehand for the conduct of the duel.

(Signed) F.

'F.' I recognised easily enough as the initial letter of Monsieur Foulon's name, the second of Mr Monkton, who had died of consumption at Paris.

The discovery and the identification were now complete. Nothing remained but to break the news to Alfred, and to get permission to remove the remains in the outhouse. I began almost to doubt the evidence of my own senses, when I reflected that the apparently impracticable object with which we had left Naples was already, by the merest chance, virtually accomplished.

'The evidence of the paper is decisive,' said I, handing it back. 'There can be no doubt that the remains in the outhouse are the remains of which we have been in search. May I inquire if any obstacles will be thrown in our way, should the late Mr Monkton's nephew wish to remove his uncle's body to the family burial-place in England?'

'Where is this nephew?' asked the father superior.

'He is now awaiting my return at the town of Fondi.'

'Is he in a position to prove his relationship?'

'Certainly; he has papers with him which will place it beyond a doubt.'

'Let him satisfy the civil authorities of his claim, and he need expect no obstacle to his wishes from anyone here.'

I was in no humour for talking a moment longer with my sour-tempered companion than I could help. The day was wearing on fast; and, whether night overtook me or not, I was resolved never to stop on my return till I got back to Fondi. Accordingly, after telling the father superior that he might expect to hear from me again immediately, I made my bow, and hastened out of the refectory.

At the convent gate stood my old friend with the tin snuff-box, waiting to let me out.

'Bless you, my son,' said the venerable recluse, giving me a farewell pat on the shoulder; 'come back soon to your spiritual father, who loves you; and amiably favour him with another tiny, tiny pinch of the delectable snuff.'

VI

I returned at the top of my speed to the village where I had left the mules, had the animals saddled immediately, and succeeded in getting back to Fondi a little before sunset.

While ascending the stairs of our hotel, I suffered under the most painful uncertainty as to how I should best communicate the news of my discovery to Alfred. If I could not succeed in preparing him properly for my tidings, the results – with such an organization as his – might be fatal. On opening the door of his room, I felt by no means sure of myself; and when I confronted him, his manner of receiving me took me so much by surprise that, for a moment or two, I lost my self-possession altogether.

Every trace of the lethargy in which he was sunk when I had last seen him had disappeared. His eyes were bright, his cheeks deeply flushed. As I entered, he started up, and refused my offered hand.

'You have not treated me like a friend,' he said, passionately; 'you had no right to continue the search unless I searched with you – you had no right to leave me here alone. I was wrong to trust you: you are no better than all the rest of them.'

I had by this time recovered a little from my first astonishment, and was able to reply before he could say anything more. It was quite useless, in his present state, to reason with him, or to defend myself. I determined to risk everything, and break my news to him at once.

'You will treat me more justly, Monkton, when you know that I have been doing you good service during my absence,' I said. 'Unless I am greatly mistaken, the object for which we have left Naples may be nearer attainment by both of us than—'

The flush left his cheeks almost in an instant. Some expression in my face, or some tone in my voice, of which I was not conscious, had revealed to his nervously-quickened perception more than I had intended that he should know at first. His eyes fixed themselves intently on mine; his hand grasped my arm; and he said to me in an eager whisper:

'Tell me the truth at once. Have you found him?'

It was too late to hesitate. I answered in the affirmative.

'Buried or unburied?'

His voice rose abruptly as he put the question, and his unoccupied hand fastened on my other arm.

'Unburied.'

I had hardly uttered the word before the blood flew back into his cheeks; his eyes flashed again as they looked into mine, and he burst into a fit of triumphant laughter, which shocked and startled me inexpressibly.

'What did I tell you? What do you say to the old prophecy now?' he cried, dropping his hold on my arms, and pacing backward and forwards in the room.

'Own you were wrong. Own it, as all Naples shall own it, when once I have got him safe in his coffin!'

His laughter grew more and more violent. I tried to quiet him in vain. His servant and the landlord of the inn entered the room; but they only added fuel to the fire, and I made them go out again. As I shut the door on them, I observed lying on a table near at hand the packet of letters from Miss Elmslie, which my unhappy friend preserved with such care, and read and re-read with such unfailing devotion. Looking towards me just when I passed by the table, the letters caught his eye. The new hope for the future, in connexion with the writer of them, which my news was already awakening in his heart, seemed to overwhelm him in an instant at sight of the treasured memorials that reminded him of his betrothed wife. His laughter ceased, his face changed, he ran to the table, caught the letters up in his hand, looked from them to me for one moment with an altered expression which went to my heart, then sank down on his knees at the table, laid his face on the letters, and burst into tears. I let the new emotion have its way uninterruptedly, and quitted the room without saying a word. When I returned, after a lapse of some little time, I found him sitting quietly in his chair, reading one of the letters from the packet which rested on his knee.

His look was kindness itself; his gesture almost womanly in its gentleness as he rose to meet me, and anxiously held out his hand.

He was quite calm enough now to hear in detail all that I had to tell him. I suppressed nothing but the particulars of the state in which I had found the corpse. I assumed no right of direction as to the share he was to take in our future proceedings, with the exception of insisting beforehand that he should leave the absolute superintendence of the removal of the body to me, and that he should be satisfied with a sight of M. Foulon's paper, after receiving my assurance that the remains placed in the coffin were really and truly the remains of which we had been in search.

'Your nerves are not so strong as mine,' I said, by way of apology for my apparent dictation; 'and for that reason I must beg leave to assume the leadership in all that we have now to do, until I see the leaden coffin soldered down and safe in your possession. After that, I shall resign all my functions to you.'

'I want words to thank you for your kindness,' he answered. 'No brother could have borne with me more affectionately, or helped me more patiently, than you.'

He stopped, and grew thoughtful, then occupied himself in tying up slowly and carefully the packet of Miss Elmslie's letters, and then looked suddenly towards the vacant wall behind me, with that strange expression the meaning of which I knew so well. Since we had left Naples, I had purposely avoided exciting him by talking on the useless and shocking subject of the apparition by which he believed himself to be perpetually followed. Just now, however, he seemed so calm and collected – so little likely to be violently agitated by any allusion to the dangerous topic – that I ventured to speak out boldly.

'Does the Phantom still appear to you,' I asked, 'as it appeared at Naples?'

He looked at me and smiled.

'Did I not tell you that it followed me everywhere?' His eyes wandered back again to the vacant space, and he went on speaking in that direction as if he had been continuing the conversation with some third person in the room. 'We shall part,' he said slowly and softly, 'when the empty place is filled in Wincot vault. Then I shall stand with Ada before the altar in the Abbey chapel; and when my eyes meet hers, they will see the tortured face no more.'

Saying this, he leaned his head on his hand, sighed, and began repeating softly to himself the lines of the old prophecy:

> When in Wincot vault a place
> Waits for one of Monkton's race;
> When that one forlorn shall lie
> Graveless under open sky,
> Beggared of six feet of earth,
> Though lord of acres from his birth—
> That shall be a certain sign
> Of the end of Monkton's line.
> Dwindling ever faster, faster,
> Dwindling to the last left master;
> From mortal ken, from light of day,
> Monkton's race shall pass away.

Fancying that he pronounced the last lines a little incoherently, I tried to make him change the subject. He took no notice of what I said, and went on talking to himself.

'Monkton's race shall pass away!' he repeated; 'but not with *me*. The fatality hangs over *my* head no longer. I shall bury the unburied dead; I shall fill the vacant place in Wincot vault. And then – then the new life, the life with Ada!' – That name seemed to recall him to himself. He drew his travelling desk towards him, placed the packet of letters in it, and then took out a sheet of paper. 'I am going to write to Ada,' he said, turning to me, 'and tell her the good news. Her happiness, when she knows it, will be even greater than mine.'

Worn out by the events of the day, I left him writing, and went to bed. I was, however, either too anxious or too tired to sleep. In this waking condition, my mind naturally occupied itself with the discovery at the convent, and with the events to which that discovery would in all probability lead. As I thought on the future, a depression for which I could not account weighed on my spirits. There was not the slightest reason for the vaguely melancholy forebodings that oppressed me. The remains, to the finding of which my unhappy friend attached so much importance, had been traced; they would certainly be placed at his disposal in a few days; he might take them to England by the first merchant vessel that sailed from Naples; and, the gratification of his strange caprice thus accomplished, there was at least some reason to hope that his mind might recover its tone, and that the new life he would lead at Wincot might result in making him a happy man. Such considerations as these were, in themselves, certainly not calculated to exert any melancholy influence over me; and yet, all through the night, the same inconceivable, unaccountable depression weighed heavily on my spirits – heavily through the hours of darkness – heavily, even when I walked out to breathe the first freshness of the early morning air.

With the day came the all-engrossing business of opening negotiations with the authorities.

Only those who have had to deal with Italian officials can imagine how our patience was tried by every one with whom we came in contact. We were bandied about from one authority to the other, were stared at, cross-questioned, mystified – not in the least because the case presented any special difficulties or intricacies, but because it was absolutely necessary that every civil dignitary to whom we applied should assert his own importance by leading us to our object in the most roundabout manner possible. After our first day's experience of official life in Italy, I left the absurd formalities, which we had no choice but to perform, to be accomplished by Alfred alone, and applied myself to considering the really serious question of how the remains in the convent outhouse were to be safely removed.

The best plan that suggested itself to me was to write to a friend at Rome, where I knew that it was a custom to embalm the bodies of high dignitaries of the church, and where, I consequently inferred, such chemical assistance as was needed in our emergency might be obtained. I simply stated in my letter that the removal of the body was imperative, then described the condition in which I had found it, and engaged that no expense on our part should be spared if the right person or persons could be found to help us. Here again more difficulties interposed themselves, and more useless formalities were to be gone through, but, in the end, patience, perseverance, and money triumphed, and two men came expressly from Rome to undertake the duties we required of them.

It is unnecessary that I should shock the reader by entering into any detail in this part of my narrative. When I have said that the progress of decay was so far suspended by chemical means as to allow of the remains being placed in the coffin, and to ensure their being transported to England with perfect safety and convenience, I have said enough. After ten days had been wasted in useless delays and difficulties, I had the satisfaction of seeing the convent outhouse empty at last; passed through a final ceremony of snuff-taking, or rather, of snuff-giving, with the old Capuchin, and ordered the travelling carriages to be ready at the inn door. Hardly a month had elapsed since our departure, when we entered Naples, successful in the achievement of a design which had been ridiculed as wildly impracticable by every friend of ours who had heard of it.

The first object to be accomplished on our return was to obtain the means of carrying the coffin to England – by sea, as a matter of course. All inquiries after a merchant vessel on the point of sailing for any British port led to the most unsatisfactory results. There was only one way of ensuring the immediate transportation of the remains to England, and that was to hire a vessel. Impatient to return, and resolved not to lose sight of the coffin till he had seen it placed in Wincot vault, Monkton decided immediately on hiring the first ship that could be obtained. The vessel in port, which we were informed could soonest be got ready for sea, was a Sicilian brig; and this vessel my friend accordingly engaged. The best dockyard artisans that could be got were set to work, and the smartest captain and crew to be picked up on an emergency in Naples, were chosen to navigate the brig.

Monkton, after again expressing in the warmest terms his gratitude for the services I had rendered him, disclaimed any intention of asking me to accompany him on the voyage to England. Greatly to his surprise and delight, however, I offered of my own accord to take passage in the brig. The strange coincidences I had witnessed, the extraordinary discovery I had hit on, since our first meeting in Naples, had made his one great interest in life my one great interest for the time being, as well. I shared none of his delusions, poor fellow; but it is hardly an exaggeration to say that my eagerness to follow our remarkable adventure to its end was as great as his anxiety to see the coffin laid in Wincot vault. Curiosity influenced me, I am afraid, almost as strongly as friendship, when I offered myself as the companion of his voyage home.

We set sail for England on a calm and lovely afternoon.

For the first time since I had known him, Monkton seemed to be in high spirits. He talked and jested on all sorts of subjects, and laughed at me for allowing my cheerfulness to be affected by the dread of sea-sickness. I had really no such fear; it was my excuse to my friend for a return of that unaccountable depression under which I had suffered at Fondi. Everything was in our favour; everybody on board the brig was in good spirits. The captain was delighted with the vessel; the crew, Italians and Maltese, were in high glee at the prospect of making a short voyage on high wages in a well-provisioned ship. I alone felt heavy at heart. There was no valid reason that I could assign to myself for the melancholy that oppressed me, and yet I struggled against it in vain.

Late on our first night at sea, I made a discovery which was by no means calculated to restore my spirits to their usual equilibrium. Monkton was in the cabin, on the floor of which had been placed the packing-case containing the coffin; and I was on deck. The wind had fallen almost to a calm, and I was lazily watching the sails of the brig as they flapped from time to time against the masts, when the captain approached, and, drawing me out of hearing of the man at the helm, whispered in my ear—

'There's something wrong among the men forward. Did you observe how suddenly they all became silent just before sunset?'

I had observed it, and told him so.

'There's a Maltese boy on board,' pursued the captain, 'who is a smart lad enough, but a bad one to deal with. I have found out that he has been telling the men there is a dead body inside that packing case of your friend's in the cabin.'

My heart sank as he spoke. Knowing the superstitious irrationality of sailors – of foreign sailors especially – I had taken care to spread a report on board the brig, before the coffin was shipped, that the packing-case contained a valuable marble statue which Mr Monkton prized highly, and was unwilling to trust out of his own sight. How could this Maltese boy have discovered that the pretended statue was a human corpse? As I pondered over the question, my suspicions fixed themselves on Monkton's servant, who spoke Italian fluently, and whom I knew to be an incorrigible gossip. The man denied it when I charged him with betraying us, but I have never believed his denial to this day.

'The little imp won't say where he picked up this notion of his about the dead body,' continued the captain. 'It's not my place to pry into secrets; but I advise you to call the crew aft, and contradict the boy, whether he speaks the truth or not. The men are a parcel of fools who believe in ghosts, and all the rest of it. Some of them say they would never have signed our articles if they had known they were going to sail with a dead man; others only grumble; but I'm afraid we shall have some trouble with them all, in case of rough weather, unless the boy is contradicted by you or the other gentleman. The men say that if either you or your friend tell them on your words of honour that the Maltese is a liar, they will hand him up to be rope's-ended accordingly; but that if you won't, they have made up their minds to believe the boy.'

Here the captain paused, and awaited my answer. I could give him none. I felt hopeless under our desperate emergency. To get the boy punished by giving my word of honour to support a direct falsehood, was not to be thought of even for a moment. What other means of extrication from this miserable dilemma remained? None that I could think of. I thanked the captain for his attention to our interests, told him I would take time to consider what course I should pursue, and begged that he would say nothing to my friend about the discovery he had made. He promised to be silent, sulkily enough, and walked away from me.

We had expected the breeze to spring up with the morning, but no breeze came. As it wore on towards noon, the atmosphere became insufferably sultry, and the sea looked as smooth as glass. I saw the captain's eye turn often and anxiously to windward. Far away in that direction, and alone in the blue heaven, I observed a little black cloud, and asked if it would bring us any wind.

'More than we want,' the captain replied, shortly; and then, to my astonishment, ordered the crew aloft to take in sail. The execution of this manoeuvre showed but too plainly the temper of the men; they did their work sulkily and slowly, grumbling and murmuring among themselves. The captain's manner, as he urged them on with oaths and threats, convinced me we were in danger. I looked again to windward. The one little cloud had enlarged to a great bank of murky vapour, and the sea at the horizon had changed in colour.

'The squall will be on us before we know where we are,' said the captain. 'Go below; you will be only in the way here.'

I descended to the cabin, and prepared Monkton for what was coming. He was still questioning me about what I had observed on deck, when the storm burst on us. We felt the little brig strain for an instant as if she would part in two, then she seemed to be swinging round with us, then to be quite still for a moment, trembling in every timber. Last, came a shock which hurled us from our seats, a deafening crash, and a flood of water pouring into the cabin. We clambered, half-drowned, to the deck. The brig had, in the nautical phrase, 'broached to,' and she now lay on her beam ends.

Before I could make out anything distinctly in the horrible confusion, except the one tremendous certainty that we were entirely at the mercy of the sea, I heard a voice from the fore part of the ship which stilled the clamouring and shouting of the rest of the crew in an instant. The words were in Italian, but I understood their fatal meaning only too easily. We had sprung a leak, and the sea was pouring into the ship's hold like the race of a millstream. The captain did not lose his presence of mind in this fresh emergency. He called for his axe to cut away the foremast, and ordering some of the crew to help him, directed the others to rig out the pumps.

The words had hardly passed his lips, before the men broke into open mutiny. With a savage look at me, their ringleader declared that the passengers might do as they pleased, but that he and his messmates were determined to take to the boat, and leave the accursed ship, and *the dead man in her* to go to the bottom together. As he spoke there was a shout among the sailors, and I observed some of them pointing derisively behind me. Looking round, I saw Monkton, who had hitherto kept close at my side, making his way back to the cabin. I followed him directly, but the water and confusion on deck, and the impossibility, from the position of the brig, of moving the feet without the slow assistance of the hands, so impeded my progress that it was impossible for me to overtake him. When I had got below, he was crouched upon the coffin, with the water on the cabin floor whirling and splashing about him, as the ship heaved and plunged. I saw a warning brightness in his eyes, a warning flush on his cheek, as I approached and said to him:

'There is nothing left for it, Alfred, but to bow to our misfortune, and do the best we can to save our lives.'

'Save yours,' he cried, waving his hand to me, 'for *you* have a future, before you. Mine is gone when this coffin goes to the bottom. If the ship sinks, I shall know that the fatality is accomplished, and shall sink with her.'

I saw that he was in no state to be reasoned with or persuaded, and raised myself again to the deck. The men were cutting away all obstacles, so as to launch the long boat, placed amidships, over the depressed bulwark of the brig, as she lay on her side; and the captain, after having made a last vain exertion to restore his authority, was looking on at them in silence. The violence of the squall seemed already to be spending itself, and I asked whether there was really no chance for us if we remained by the ship. The captain answered that there might have been the best chance if the men had obeyed his orders, but that now there was none. Knowing that I could place no dependence on the presence of mind of Monkton's servant, I confided to the captain, in the fewest and plainest words, the condition of my unhappy friend, and asked if I might depend on his help. He nodded his head, and we descended together to the cabin. Even at this day it costs me pain to write of the terrible necessity to which the strength and obstinacy of Monkton's delusion reduced us, in the last resort. We were compelled to secure his hands, and drag him by main force to the deck. The men were on the point of launching the boat, and refused at first to receive us into it.

'You cowards!' cried the captain, 'have we got the dead man with us this time? Isn't he going to the bottom along with the brig? Who are you afraid of when we get into the boat?'

This sort of appeal produced the desired effect; the men became ashamed of themselves, and retracted their refusal.

Just as we pushed off from the sinking ship Alfred made an effort to break from me, but I held him firm, and he never repeated the attempt. He sat by me, with drooping head, still and silent, while the sailors rowed away from the vessel: still and silent when, with one accord, they paused at a little distance off, and we all waited and watched to see the brig sink: still and silent, even when that sinking happened, when the labouring hull plunged slowly into a hollow of the sea – hesitated, as it seemed, for one moment – rose a little again – then sank to rise no more.

Sank with her dead freight: sank, and snatched for ever from our power the corpse which we had discovered almost by a miracle – those jealously-preserved remains on the safe-keeping of which rested so strangely the hopes and the love-destinies of two living beings! As the last signs of the ship disappeared in the depths of the waters, I felt Monkton trembling all over as he sat close at my side, and heard him repeating to himself, sadly, and many times over, the name of 'Ada.'

I tried to turn his thoughts to another subject, but it was useless. He pointed over the sea to where the brig had once been, and where nothing was left to look at but the rolling waves.

'The empty place will now remain empty for ever in Wincot vault.'

As he said those words, he fixed his eyes for a moment sadly and earnestly on my face, then looked away, leant his cheek upon his hand, and spoke no more.

We were sighted long before nightfall by a trading-vessel, were taken on board, and landed at Cartagena in Spain. Alfred never held up his head, and never once spoke to me of his own accord, the whole time we were at sea in the merchantman. I observed, however, with alarm, that he talked often and incoherently to himself – constantly muttering the lines of the old prophecy – constantly referring to the fatal place that was empty in Wincot vault – constantly repeating in broken accents, which it affected me inexpressibly to hear, the name of the poor girl who was awaiting his return to England. Nor were these the only causes for the apprehension that I now felt on his account. Towards the end of our voyage he began to suffer from alternations of fever fits and shivering fits, which I ignorantly imagined to be attacks of ague. I was soon undeceived. We had hardly been a day on shore before he became so much worse that I secured the best medical assistance Cartagena could afford. For a day or two the doctors differed, as usual, about the nature of his complaint, but ere long alarming symptoms displayed themselves. The medical men declared that his life was in danger, and told me that his disease was brain fever.

Shocked and grieved as I was, I hardly knew how to act at first under the fresh responsibility now laid upon me. Ultimately I decided on writing to the old priest who had been Alfred's tutor, and who, as I knew, still resided at Wincot Abbey. I told this gentleman all that had happened, begged him to break my melancholy news as gently as possible to Miss Elmslie, and assured him of my resolution to remain with Monkton to the last.

After I had despatched my letter, and had sent to Gibraltar to secure the best English medical advice that could be obtained, I felt that I had done my best, and that nothing remained but to wait and hope.

Many a sad and anxious hour did I pass by my poor friend's bedside. Many a time did I doubt whether I had done right in giving any encouragement to his delusion. The reasons for doing so which had suggested themselves to me, after my first interview with him, seemed, however, on reflection, to be valid reasons still. The only way of hastening his return to England and to Miss Elmslie, who was pining for that return, was the way I had taken. It was not my fault that a disaster which no man could foresee had overthrown all his projects and all mine. But now that the calamity had happened and was irretrievable, how, in the event of his physical recovery, was his moral malady to be combated?

When I reflected on the hereditary taint in his mental organisation, on that first childish fright of Stephen Monkton from which he had never recovered, on the perilously secluded life that he had led at the Abbey, and on his firm persuasion of the reality of the apparition by which he believed himself to be constantly followed, I confess I despaired of shaking his superstitious faith in every word and line of the old family prophecy. If the series of striking coincidences which appeared to attest its truth had made a strong and lasting impression on *me* (and this was assuredly the case), how could I wonder that they had produced the effect of absolute conviction on *his* mind, constituted as it was? If I argued with him, and he answered me, how could I rejoin? If he said, 'The prophecy points at the last of the family: *I* am the last of the family. The prophecy mentions an empty place in Wincot vault: there is such an empty place there at this moment. On the faith of the prophecy I told you that Stephen Monkton's body was unburied, and you found that it was unburied,' – if he said this, what use would it be for me to reply, 'These are only strange coincidences, after all?'

The more I thought of the task that lay before me, if he recovered, the more I felt inclined to despond. The oftener the English physician who attended on him said to me, 'He may get the better of the fever, but he has a fixed idea, which never leaves him night or day, which has unsettled his reason, and which will end in killing him, unless you or some of his friends can remove it,' – the oftener I heard this, the more acutely I felt my own powerlessness, the more I shrank from every idea that was connected with the hopeless future.

I had only expected to receive my answer from Wincot in the shape of a letter. It was consequently a great surprise, as well as a great relief, to be informed one day that two gentlemen wished to speak with me, and to find that of these two gentlemen the first was the old priest, and the second a male relative of Mrs Elmslie.

Just before their arrival the fever-symptoms had disappeared, and Alfred had been pronounced out of danger. Both the priest and his companion were eager to know when the sufferer would be strong enough to travel. They had come to Cartagena expressly to take him home with them, and felt far more hopeful than I did of the restorative effects of his native air. After all the questions connected with the first important point of the journey to England had been asked and answered, I ventured to make some inquiries after Miss Elmslie. Her relative informed me that she was suffering both in body and in mind from excess of anxiety on Alfred's account. They had been obliged to deceive her as to the dangerous nature of his illness, in order to deter her from accompanying the priest and her relation on their mission to Spain.

Slowly and imperfectly as the weeks wore on, Alfred regained something of his former physical strength, but no alteration appeared in his illness as it affected his mind.

From the very first day of his advance towards recovery, it had been discovered that the brain fever had exercised the strangest influence over his faculties of memory. All recollection of recent events was gone from him. Everything connected with Naples, with me, with his journey to Italy, had dropped in some mysterious manner entirely out of his remembrance. So completely had all late circumstances passed from his memory that, though he recognised the old priest and his own servant easily on the first days of his convalescence, he never recognised me, but regarded me with such a wistful, doubting expression, that I felt inexpressibly pained when I approached his bedside. All his questions were about Miss Elmslie and Wincot Abbey; and all his talk referred to the period when his father was yet alive.

The doctors augured good rather than ill from this loss of memory of recent incidents, saying that it would turn out to be temporary, and that it answered the first great healing purpose of keeping his mind at ease. I tried to believe them – tried to feel as sanguine, when the day came for his departure, as the old friends felt who were taking him home. But the effort was too much for me. A foreboding that I should never see him again oppressed my heart, and the tears came into my eyes as I saw the worn figure of my poor friend half helped, half lifted into the travelling carriage, and borne away gently on the road towards home.

He had never recognised me, and the doctors had begged that I would give him, for some time to come, as few opportunities as possible of doing so. But for this request I should have accompanied him to England. As it was, nothing better remained for me to do than to change the scene, and recruit as I best could my energies of body and mind, depressed of late by much watching and anxiety. The famous cities of Spain were not new to me, but I visited them again, and revived old impressions of the Alhambra and Madrid. Once or twice I thought of making a pilgrimage to the East, but late events had sobered and altered me. That yearning, unsatisfied feeling which we call 'home-sickness,' began to prey upon my heart, and I resolved to return to England.

I went back by way of Paris, having settled with the priest that he should write to me at my banker's there, as soon as he could after Alfred had returned to Wincot. If I had gone to the East, the letter would have been forwarded to me. I wrote to prevent this; and, on my arrival at Paris, stopped at the banker's before I went to my hotel.

The moment the letter was put into my hands, the black border on the envelope told me the worst. He was dead.

There was but one consolation – he had died calmly, almost happily, without once referring to those fatal chances which had wrought the fulfilment of the ancient prophecy. 'My beloved pupil,' the old priest wrote, 'seemed to rally a little the first few days after his return, but he gained no real strength, and soon suffered a slight relapse of fever. After this he sank gradually and gently day by day, and so departed from us on the last dread journey. Miss Elmslie (who knows that I am writing this) desires me to express her deep and lasting gratitude for all your kindness to Alfred. She told me when we brought him back, that she had waited for him as his promised wife, and that she would nurse him now as a wife should; and she never left him. His face was turned towards her, his hand was clasped in hers when he died. It will console you to know that he never mentioned events at Naples, or the shipwreck that followed them, from the day of his return to the day of his death.'

Three days after reading the letter I was at Wincot, and heard all the details of Alfred's last moments from the priest. I felt a shock which it would not be very easy for me to analyse or explain, when I heard that he had been buried, at his own desire, in the fatal Abbey vault.

The priest took me down to see the place – a grim, cold subterranean building, with a low roof, supported on heavy Saxon arches. Narrow niches, with the ends only of coffins visible within them, ran down each side of the vault. The nails and silver ornaments flashed here and there as my companion moved past them with a lamp in his hand. At the lower end of the place he stopped, pointed to a niche, and said: 'He lies there, between his father and mother.' I looked a little further on, and saw what appeared at first like a long dark tunnel. 'That is only an empty niche,' said the priest, following me. 'If the body of Mr Stephen Monkton had been brought to Wincot, his coffin would have been placed there.'

A chill came over me, and a sense of dread which I am ashamed of having felt now, but which I could not combat then. The blessed light of day was pouring down gaily at the other end of the vault through the open door. I turned my back on the empty niche, and hurried into the sunlight and the fresh air.

As I walked across the grass glade leading down to the vault, I heard the rustle of a woman's dress behind me, and, turning round, saw a young lady advancing, clad in deep mourning. Her sweet sad face, her manner as she held out her hand, told me who it was in an instant.

'I heard that you were here,' she said, 'and I wished' – her voice faltered a little. My heart ached as I saw how her lip trembled, but before I could say anything, she recovered herself, and went on – 'I wished to take your hand, and thank you for your brotherly kindness to Alfred; and I wanted to tell you that I am sure, in all you did, you acted tenderly and considerately for the best. Perhaps you may be soon going away from home again, and we may not meet any more. I shall never, never forget that you were kind to him when he wanted a friend, and that you have the greatest claim of any one on earth to be gratefully remembered in my thoughts as long as I live.'

The inexpressible tenderness of her voice, trembling a little all the while she spoke, the pale beauty of her face, the artless candour in her sad, quiet eyes, so affected me that I could not trust myself to answer her at first, except by gesture. Before I recovered my voice, she had given me her hand once more and had left me.

I never saw her again. The chances and changes of life kept us apart. When I last heard of her, years and years ago, she was faithful to the memory of the dead, and was Ada Elmslie still for Alfred Monkton's sake.

A Terribly Strange Bed

Originally appeared in *Household Words*, 24 April 1852. Included in
After Dark (1852) as 'The Traveller's Story of a Terribly Strange
Bed.' This is still the best-known story Collins wrote, and used
to be reckoned his finest work after *The Woman in White* and *The
Moonstone* (surely an unreasonable judgement). In the Preface to
After Dark, Collins acknowledged indebtedness to the artist W.S.
Herrick, who furnished 'the curious and interesting facts on which
the tales of "The Terribly Strange Bed" and "The Yellow Mask"
are founded.' Though the situation and events are quite different,
most readers note a general indebtedness to Edgar Allan Poe's
'The Pit and the Pendulum' (1842), especially in the handling of
the victim's psychological responses. In turn Collins's story seems
to have influenced Joseph Conrad's 'The Inn of the Two Witches:
A Find' (*Pall Mall Gazette*, March 1913). When Conrad reprinted
the story in his collection *Within the Tides* he denied knowledge of 'A
Terribly Strange Bed'. 'A bed of the sort was discovered in an Inn
on the road between Rome and Naples at the end of the eighteenth
century,' he wrote. 'Where I picked up the information I cannot say
now but I am certain it was not in a tale.' 'A Terribly Strange Bed'
was the first of many Collins contributions to *Household Words* over
the next few years. Dickens valued Collins's inventiveness, reliability
and capacity for hard work, and after four years invited him to join
the editorial staff of the magazine. The *Household Words* version of 'A
Terribly Strange Bed' introduces the framing-device of the painter
Kerby (hence the references to sketches on p. 85ff), which Collins
later expanded to key the narratives of his collection *After Dark*. A.
Gasson suggests that this story represents the first appearance of a
police officer in British short fiction.

S HORTLY AFTER MY education at college was finished, I happened to be staying at Paris with an English friend. We were both young men then, and lived, I am afraid, rather a wild life, in the delightful city of our sojourn. One night we were idling about the neighbourhood of the Palais Royal, doubtful to what amusement we should next betake ourselves. My friend proposed a visit to Frascati's; but his suggestion was not to my taste. I knew Frascati's, as the French saying is, by heart; had lost and won plenty of five-franc pieces there, merely for amusement's sake, until it was amusement no longer, and was thoroughly tired, in fact, of all the ghastly respectabilities of such a social anomaly as a respectable gambling-house. 'For Heaven's sake,' said I to my friend, 'let us go somewhere where we can see a little genuine, blackguard, poverty-stricken gaming, with no false gingerbread glitter thrown over it at all. Let us get away from fashionable Frascati's, to a house where they don't mind letting in a man with a ragged coat, or a man with no coat, ragged or otherwise.' – 'Very well,' said my friend, 'we needn't go out of the Palais Royal to find the sort of company you want. Here's the place just before us; as blackguard a place, by all report, as you could possibly wish to see.' In another minute we arrived at the door, and entered the house, the back of which you have drawn in your sketch.

When we got up stairs, and had left our hats and sticks with the doorkeeper, we were admitted into the chief gambling-room. We did not find many people assembled there. But, few as the men were who looked up at us on our entrance, they were all types – lamentably true types – of their respective classes.

We had come to see blackguards; but these men were something worse. There is a comic side, more or less appreciable, in all blackguardism – here there was nothing but tragedy – mute, weird tragedy. The quiet in the room was horrible. The thin, haggard, long-haired young man, whose sunken eyes fiercely watched the turning up of the cards, never spoke; the flabby, fat-faced, pimply player, who pricked his piece of pasteboard perseveringly, to register how often black won, and how often red – never spoke; the dirty, wrinkled old man, with the vulture eyes and the darned greatcoat, who had lost his last *sou*, and still looked on desperately, after he could play no longer – never spoke. Even the voice of the croupier sounded as if it were strangely dulled and thickened in the atmosphere of the room. I had entered the place to laugh; but the spectacle before me was something to weep over. I soon found it necessary to take refuge in excitement from the depression of spirits which was fast stealing on me. Unfortunately I sought the nearest excitement, by going to the table, and beginning to play. Still more unfortunately, as the event will show, I won – won prodigiously; won incredibly; won at such a rate, that the regular players at the table crowded round me; and staring at my stakes with hungry, superstitious eyes, whispered to one another, that the English stranger was going to break the bank.

The game was *Rouge et Noir*. I had played at it in every city in Europe, without, however, the care or the wish to study the Theory of Chances – that philosopher's stone of all gamblers! And a gambler, in the strict sense of the word, I had never been. I was heart-whole from the corroding passion for play. My gaming was a mere idle amusement. I never resorted to it by necessity, because I never knew what it was to want money. I never practised it so incessantly as to lose more than I could afford, or to gain more than I could coolly pocket without being thrown off my balance by my good luck. In short, I had hitherto frequented gambling-tables – just as I frequented ball-rooms and opera-houses – because they amused me, and because I had nothing better to do with my leisure hours.

But on this occasion it was very different – now, for the first time in my life, I felt what the passion for play really was. My success first bewildered, and then, in the most literal meaning of the word, intoxicated me. Incredible as it may appear, it is nevertheless true, that I only lost when I attempted to estimate chances, and played according to previous calculation. If I left everything to luck, and staked without any care or consideration, I was sure to win – to win in the face of every recognised probability in favour of the bank. At first, some of the men present ventured their money safely enough on my colour; but I speedily increased my stakes to sums which they dared not risk. One after another they left off playing, and breathlessly looked on at my game.

Still, time after time, I staked higher and higher, and still won. The excitement in the room rose to fever pitch. The silence was interrupted by a deep, muttered chorus of oaths and exclamations in different languages, every time the gold was shovelled across to my side of the table – even the imperturbable croupier dashed his rake on the floor in a (French) fury of astonishment at my success. But one man present preserved his self-possession; and that man was my friend. He came to my side, and whispering in English, begged me to leave the place satisfied with what I had already gained. I must do him the justice to say, that he repeated his warnings and entreaties several times; and only left me and went away, after I had rejected his advice (I was to all intents and purposes gambling-drunk) in terms which rendered it impossible for him to address me again that night.

Shortly after he had gone, a hoarse voice behind me cried: 'Permit me, my dear sir! – permit me to restore to their proper place two Napoleons which you have dropped. Wonderful luck, sir! I pledge you my word of honour as an old soldier, in the course of my long experience in this sort of thing, I never saw such luck as yours! – never! Go on, sir – *Sacré mille bombes!* Go on boldly, and break the bank!'

I turned round and saw, nodding and smiling at me with inveterate civility, a tall man, dressed in a frogged and braided surtout.

If I had been in my senses, I should have considered him, personally, as being rather a suspicious specimen of an old soldier. He had goggling blood-shot eyes, mangy mustachios, and a broken nose. His voice betrayed a barrack-room intonation of the worst order, and he had the dirtiest pair of hands I ever saw – even in France. These little personal peculiarities exercised, however, no repelling influence on me. In the mad excitement, the reckless triumph of that moment, I was ready to 'fraternize' with anybody who encouraged me in my game. I accepted the old soldier's offered pinch of snuff; clapped him on the back, and swore he was the honestest fellow in the world – the most glorious relic of the Grand Army that I had ever met with. 'Go on!' cried my military friend, snapping his fingers in ecstasy – 'Go on, and win! Break the bank – *Mille tonnerres!* my gallant English comrade, break the bank!'

And I *did* go on – went on at such a rate, that in another quarter of an hour the croupier called out: 'Gentlemen! the bank has discontinued for tonight.' All the notes, and all the gold in that 'bank,' now lay in a heap under my hands; the whole floating capital of the gambling-house was waiting to pour into my pockets!

'Tie up the money in your pocket-handkerchief, my worthy sir,' said the old soldier, as I wildly plunged my hands into my heap of gold. 'Tie it up, as we used to tie up a bit of dinner in the Grand Army; your winnings are too heavy for any breeches pockets that ever were sewed. There! that's it! – shovel them in, notes and all! *Credié!* what luck! – Stop! another Napoleon on the floor! *Ah! sacré petit polisson de Napoleon!* have I found thee at last? Now then, sir – two tight double knots each way with your honourable permission, and the money's safe. Feel it! feel it, fortunate sir! hard and round as a cannon ball – *Ah, bah!* if they had only fired such cannon balls at us at Austerlitz – *nom d'une pipe!* if they only had! And now, as an ancient grenadier, as an ex-brave of the French army, what remains for me to do? I ask what? Simply this: to entreat my valued English friend to drink a bottle of champagne with me, and toast the goddess Fortune in foaming goblets before we part!'

"Excellent ex-brave! Convivial ancient grenadier! Champagne by all means! An English cheer for an old soldier! Hurrah! hurrah! Another English cheer for the goddess Fortune! Hurrah! hurrah! hurrah!"

'Bravo! the Englishman; the amiable, gracious Englishman, in whose veins circulates the vivacious blood of France! Another glass? *Ah, bah!* – the bottle is empty! Never mind! *Vive le vin!* I, the old soldier, order another bottle, and half-a-pound of *bon-bons* with it!'

'No, no, ex-brave; never – ancient grenadier! *Your* bottle last time; *my* bottle this. Behold it! Toast away! The French Army! – the great Napoleon! – the present company! the croupier! the honest croupier's wife and daughters – if he has any! the Ladies generally! Everybody in the world!'

By the time the second bottle of champagne was emptied, I felt as if I had been drinking liquid fire – my brain seemed all a-flame. No excess in wine had ever had this effect on me before in my life. Was it the result of a stimulant acting upon my system when I was in a highly excited state? Was my stomach in a particularly disordered condition? Or was the champagne amazingly strong?

'Ex-brave of the French Army!' cried I, in a mad state of exhilaration, '*I* am on fire! how are *you?* You have set me on fire! Do you hear; my hero of Austerlitz? Let us have a third bottle of champagne to put the flame out!'

The old soldier wagged his head, rolled his goggle eyes, until I expected to see them slip out of their sockets; placed his dirty forefinger by the side of his broken nose; solemnly ejaculated 'Coffee!' and immediately ran off into an inner room.

The word pronounced by the eccentric veteran seemed to have a magical effect on the rest of the company present. With one accord they all rose to depart. Probably they had expected to profit by my intoxication; but finding that my new friend was benevolently bent on preventing me from getting dead drunk, had now abandoned all hope of thriving pleasantly on my winnings. Whatever their motive might be, at any rate they went away in a body. When the old soldier returned, and sat down again opposite to me at the table, we had the room to ourselves. I could see the croupier, in a sort of vestibule which opened out of it, eating his supper in solitude. The silence was now deeper than ever.

A sudden change, too, had come over the 'ex-brave.' He assumed a portentously solemn look; and when he spoke to me again, his speech was ornamented by no oaths, enforced by no finger-snapping, enlivened by no apostrophes or exclamations.

'Listen, my dear sir,' said he, in mysteriously confidential tones – 'listen to an old soldier's advice. I have been to the mistress of the house (a very charming woman, with a genius for cookery!) to impress on her the necessity of making us some particularly strong and good coffee. You must drink this coffee in order to get rid of your little amiable exaltation of spirits before you think of going home – you *must*, my good and gracious friend! With all that money to take home to-night, it is a sacred duty to yourself to have your wits about you. You are known to be a winner to an enormous extent by several gentlemen present to-night, who, in a certain point of view, are very worthy and excellent fellows; but they are mortal men, my dear sir, and they have their amiable weaknesses! Need I say more? Ah, no, no! you understand me! Now, this is what you must do – send for a cabriolet when you feel quite well again – draw up all the windows when you get into it – and tell the driver to take you home only through the large and well-lighted thoroughfares. Do this; and you and your money will be safe. Do this; and to-morrow you will thank an old soldier for giving you a word of honest advice.'

Just as the ex-brave ended his oration in very lachrymose tones, the coffee came in, ready poured out in two cups. My attentive friend handed me one of the cups with a bow. I was parched with thirst, and drank it off at a draught. Almost instantly afterwards, I was seized with a fit of giddiness, and felt more completely intoxicated than ever. The room whirled round and round furiously; the old soldier seemed to be regularly bobbing up and down before me like the piston of a steam-engine. I was half deafened by a violent singing in my ears; a feeling of utter bewilderment, helplessness, idiocy, overcame me, I rose from my chair, holding on by the table to keep my balance; and stammered out, that I felt dreadfully unwell – so unwell that I did not know how I was to get home.

'My dear friend,' answered the old soldier, and even his voice seemed to be bobbing up and down as he spoke – 'my dear friend, it would be madness to go home in *your* state; you would be sure to lose your money; you might be robbed and murdered with the greatest ease. *I* am going to sleep here: do *you* sleep here, too – they make up capital beds in this house – take one; sleep off the effects of the wine, and go home safely with your winnings to-morrow – to-morrow, in broad daylight.'

I had but two ideas left: one, that I must never let go hold of my handkerchief full of money; the other, that I must lie down somewhere immediately, and fall off into a comfortable sleep. So I agreed to the proposal about the bed, and took the offered arm of the old soldier, carrying my money with my disengaged hand. Preceded by the croupier, we passed along some passages and up a flight of stairs into the bed-room which I was to occupy. The ex-brave shook me warmly by the hand; proposed that we should breakfast together, and then, followed by the croupier, left me for the night.

I ran to the wash-hand stand; drank some of the water in my jug; poured the rest out, and plunged my face into it – then sat down in a chair and tried to compose myself. I soon felt better. The change for my lungs, from the fetid atmosphere of the gambling-room to the cool air of the apartment I now occupied; the almost equally refreshing change for my eyes, from the glaring gas-lights of the 'Salon' to the dim, quiet flicker of one bedroom candle; aided wonderfully the restorative effects of cold water. The giddiness left me, and I began to feel a little like a reasonable being again. My first thought was of the risk of sleeping all night in a gambling-house; my second, of the still greater risk of trying to get out after the house was closed, and of going home alone at night, through the streets of Paris with a large sum of money about me. I had slept in worse places than this on my travels, so I determined to lock, bolt, and barricade my door, and take my chance till the next morning.

Accordingly, I secured myself against all intrusion; looked under the bed, and into the cupboard; tried the fastening of the window; and then, satisfied that I had taken every proper precaution, pulled off my upper clothing, put my light, which was a dim one, on the hearth among a feathery litter of wood ashes, and got into bed, with the handkerchief full of money under my pillow.

I soon felt not only that I could not go to sleep, but that I could not even close my eyes. I was wide awake, and in a high fever. Every nerve in my body trembled – every one of my senses seemed to be preternaturally sharpened. I tossed and rolled, and tried every kind of position, and perseveringly sought out the cold corners of the bed, and all to no purpose. Now, I thrust my arms over the clothes; now, I poked them under the clothes; now, I violently shot my legs straight out down to the bottom of the bed; now, I convulsively coiled them up as near my chin as they would go; now, I shook out my crumpled pillow, changed it to the cool side, patted it flat, and lay down quietly on my back; now, I fiercely doubled it in two, set it up on end, thrust it against the board of the bed, and tried a sitting-posture. Every effort was in vain; I groaned with vexation, as I felt that I was in for a sleepless night.

What could I do? I had no book to read. And yet, unless I found out some method of diverting my mind, I felt certain that I was in the condition to imagine all sorts of horrors; to rack my brain with forebodings of every possible and impossible danger; in short, to pass the night in suffering all conceivable varieties of nervous terror.

I raised myself on my elbow, and looked about the room – which was brightened by a lovely moonlight pouring straight through the window – to see if it contained any pictures or ornaments that I could at all clearly distinguish. While my eyes wandered from wall to wall, a remembrance of Le Maistre's delightful little book, 'Voyage autour de ma Chambre,' occurred to me. I resolved to imitate the French author, and find occupation and amusement enough to relieve the tedium of my wakefulness, by making a mental inventory of every article of furniture I could see, and by following up to their sources the multitude of associations which even a chair, a table, or a wash-hand stand may be made to call forth.

In the nervous unsettled state of my mind at that moment, I found it much easier to make my inventory than to make my reflections, and thereupon soon gave up all hope of thinking in Le Maistre's fanciful track – or, indeed, of thinking at all. I looked about the room at the different articles of furniture, and did nothing more.

There was, first, the bed I was lying in; a four-post bed, of all things in the world to meet with in Paris! – yes, a thorough clumsy British four-poster, with the regular top lined with chintz – the regular fringed valance all round – the regular stifling unwholesome curtains, which I remembered having mechanically drawn back against the posts without particularly noticing the bed when I first got into the room. Then there was the marble-topped wash-hand stand, from which the water I had spilt, in my hurry to pour it out, was still dripping, slowly and more slowly, on to the brick-floor. Then two small chairs, with my coat, waistcoat, and trousers flung on them. Then a large elbow-chair covered with dirty-white dimity, with my cravat and shirt-collar thrown over the back. Then a chest of drawers with two of the brass handles off, and a tawdry, broken china inkstand placed on it by way of ornament for the top. Then the dressing-table, adorned by a very small looking-glass, and a very large pin-cushion. Then the window – an unusually large window. Then a dark old picture, which the feeble candle dimly showed me. It was the picture of a fellow in a high Spanish hat, crowned with a plume of towering feathers. A swarthy sinister ruffian, looking upward, shading his eyes with his hand, and looking intently upward – it might be at some tall gallows at which he was going to be hanged. At any rate, he had the appearance of thoroughly deserving it.

This picture put a kind of constraint upon me to look upward too – at the top of the bed. It was a gloomy and not an interesting object, and I looked back at the picture. I counted the feathers in the man's hat – they stood out in relief – three white, two green. I observed the crown of his hat, which was of a conical shape, according to the fashion supposed to have been favoured by Guido Fawkes. I wondered what he was looking up at. It couldn't be at the stars; such a desperado was neither astrologer nor astronomer. It must be at the high gallows, and he was going to be hanged presently. Would the executioner come into possession of his conical crowned hat and plume of feathers? I counted the feathers again – three white, two green.

While I still lingered over this very improving and intellectual employment, my thoughts insensibly began to wander. The moonlight shining into the room reminded me of a certain moonlight night in England – the night after a picnic party in a Welsh valley. Every incident of the drive homeward, through lovely scenery, which the moonlight made lovelier than ever, came back to my remembrance, though I had never given the picnic a thought for years; though, if I had *tried* to recollect it, I could certainly have recalled little or nothing of that scene long past. Of all the wonderful faculties that help to tell us we are immortal, which speaks the sublime truth more eloquently than memory? Here was I, in a strange house of the most suspicious character, in a situation of uncertainty, and even of peril, which might seem to make the cool exercise of my recollection almost out of the question; nevertheless, remembering, quite involuntarily, places, people, conversations, minute circumstances of every kind, which I had thought forgotten for ever, which I could not possibly have recalled at will even under the most favourable auspices. And what cause had produced in a moment the whole of this strange, complicated, mysterious effect? Nothing but some rays of moonlight shining in at my bedroom window.

I was still thinking of the picnic – of our merriment on the drive home – of the sentimental young lady who *would* quote Childe Harold because it was moonlight. I was absorbed by these past scenes and past amusements, when, in an instant, the thread on which my memories hung snapped asunder: my attention immediately came back to present things more vividly than ever, and I found myself, I neither knew why nor wherefore, looking hard at the picture again.

Looking for what?

Good God, the man had pulled his hat down on his brows! – No! the hat itself was gone! Where was the conical crown? Where the feathers – three white, two green? Not there! In place of the hat and feathers, what dusky object was it that now hid his forehead, his eyes, his shading hand?

Was the bed moving?

I turned on my back and looked up. Was I mad? drunk? dreaming? giddy again? or was the top of the bed really moving down – sinking slowly, regularly, silently, horribly, right down throughout the whole of its length and breadth – right down upon Me, as I lay underneath?

My blood seemed to stand still. A deadly paralyzing coldness stole all over me, as I turned my head round on the pillow, and determined to test whether the bed-top was really moving or not, by keeping my eye on the man in the picture.

The next look in that direction was enough. The dull, black, frowsy outline of the valance above me was within an inch of being parallel with his waist. I still looked breathlessly. And steadily, and slowly – very slowly – I saw the figure, and the line of frame below the figure, vanish, as the valance moved down before it.

I am, constitutionally, anything but timid. I have been on more than one occasion in peril of my life, and have not lost my self-possession for an instant; but when the conviction first settled on my mind that the bed-top was really moving, was steadily and continuously sinking down upon me, I looked up shuddering, helpless, panic-stricken, beneath the hideous machinery for murder, which was advancing closer and closer to suffocate me where I lay.

I looked up, motionless, speechless, breathless. The candle, fully spent, went out; but the moonlight still brightened the room. Down and down, without pausing and without sounding, came the bed-top, and still my panic-terror seemed to bind me faster and faster to the mattress on which I lay – down and down it sank, till the dusty odour from the lining of the canopy came stealing into my nostrils.

At that final moment the instinct of self-preservation startled me out of my trance, and I moved at last. There was just room for me to roll myself sideways off the bed. As I dropped noiselessly to the floor, the edge of the murderous canopy touched me on the shoulder.

Without stopping to draw my breath, without wiping the cold sweat from my face, I rose instantly on my knees to watch the bed-top. I was literally spell-bound by it. If I had heard footsteps behind me, I could not have turned round; if a means of escape had been miraculously provided for me, I could not have moved to take advantage of it. The whole life in me was, at that moment, concentrated in my eyes.

It descended – the whole canopy, with the fringe round it, came down – down – close down; so close that there was not room now to squeeze my finger between the bed-top and the bed. I felt at the sides, and discovered that what had appeared to me from beneath to be the ordinary light canopy of a four-post bed, was in reality a thick, broad mattress, the substance of which was concealed by the valance and its fringe. I looked up and saw the four posts rising hideously bare. In the middle of the bed-top was a huge wooden screw that had evidently worked it down through a hole in the ceiling, just as ordinary presses are worked down on the substance selected for compression. The frightful apparatus moved without making the faintest noise. There had been no creaking as it came down; there was now not the faintest sound from the room above. Amid a dead and awful silence I beheld before me – in the nineteenth century, and in the civilized capital of France – such a machine for secret murder by suffocation as might have existed in the worst days of the Inquisition, in the lonely inns among the Hartz Mountains, in the mysterious tribunals of Westphalia! Still, as I looked on it, I could not move, I could hardly breathe, but I began to recover the power of thinking, and in a moment I discovered the murderous conspiracy framed against me in all its horror.

My cup of coffee had been drugged, and drugged too strongly. I had been saved from being smothered by having taken an overdose of some narcotic. How I had chafed and fretted at the fever-fit which had preserved my life by keeping me awake! How recklessly I had confided myself to the two wretches who had led me into this room, determined, for the sake of my winnings, to kill me in my sleep by the surest and most horrible contrivance for secretly accomplishing my destruction! How many men, winners like me, had slept, as I had proposed to sleep, in that bed, and had never been seen or heard of more! I shuddered at the bare idea of it.

But, erelong, all thought was again suspended by the sight of the murderous canopy moving once more. After it had remained on the bed – as nearly as I could guess – about ten minutes, it began to move up again. The villains who worked it from above evidently believed that their purpose was now accomplished. Slowly and silently, as it had descended, that horrible bed-top rose towards its former place. When it reached the upper extremities of the four posts, it reached the ceiling too. Neither hole nor screw could be seen; the bed became in appearance an ordinary bed again – the canopy an ordinary canopy, even to the most suspicious eyes.

Now, for the first time, I was able to move – to rise from my knees – to dress myself in my upper clothing – and to consider of how I should escape. If I betrayed, by the smallest noise, that the attempt to suffocate me had failed, I was certain to be murdered. Had I made any noise already? I listened intently, looking towards the door.

No! no footsteps in the passage outside – no sound of a tread, light or heavy, in the room above – absolute silence everywhere. Besides locking and bolting my door, I had moved an old wooden chest against it, which I had found under the bed. To remove this chest (my blood ran cold as I thought what its contents *might* be!) without making some disturbance was impossible; and, moreover, to think of escaping through the house, now barred up for the night, was sheer insanity. Only one chance was left me – the window. I stole to it on tiptoe.

My bedroom was on the first floor, above an *entresol*, and looked into the back street, which you have sketched in your view. I raised my hand to open the window, knowing that on that action hung, by the merest hair's-breadth, my chance of safety. They keep vigilant watch in a House of Murder. If any part of the frame cracked, if the hinge creaked, I was a lost man! It must have occupied me at least five minutes, reckoning by time – five *hours*, reckoning by suspense – to open that window. I succeeded in doing it silently – in doing it with all the dexterity of a housebreaker – and then looked down into the street. To leap the distance beneath me would be almost certain destruction! Next, I looked round at the sides of the house. Down the left side ran the thick water-pipe which you have drawn – it passed close by the outer edge of the window. The moment I saw the pipe, I knew I was saved. My breath came and went freely for the first time since I had seen the canopy of the bed moving down upon me!

To some men the means of escape which I had discovered might have seemed difficult and dangerous enough – to *me* the prospect of slipping down the pipe into the street did not suggest even a thought of peril. I had always been accustomed, by the practice of gymnastics, to keep up my schoolboy powers as a daring and expert climber; and knew that my head, hands, and feet would serve me faithfully in any hazards of ascent or descent. I had already got one leg over the window-sill, when I remembered the handkerchief filled with money under my pillow. I could well have afforded to leave it behind me, but I was revengefully determined that the miscreants of the gambling-house should miss their plunder as well as their victim. So I went back to the bed and tied the heavy handkerchief at my back by my cravat.

Just as I had made it tight and fixed it in a comfortable place, I thought I heard a sound of breathing outside the door. The chill feeling of horror ran through me again as I listened. No! dead silence still in the passage – I had only heard the night-air blowing softly into the room. The next moment I was on the window-sill – and the next I had a firm grip on the water-pipe with my hands and knees.

I slid down into the street easily and quietly, as I thought I should, and immediately set off at the top of my speed to a branch 'Prefecture' of Police, which I knew was situated in the immediate neighbourhood. A 'Sub-prefect,' and several picked men among his subordinates, happened to be up, maturing, I believe, some scheme for discovering the perpetrator of a mysterious murder which all Paris was talking of just then. When I began my story, in a breathless hurry and in very bad French, I could see that the Sub-prefect suspected me of being a drunken Englishman who had robbed somebody; but he soon altered his opinion as I went on, and before I had anything like concluded, he shoved all the papers before him into a drawer, put on his hat, supplied me with another (for I was bare-headed), ordered a file of soldiers, desired his expert followers to get ready all sorts of tools for breaking open doors and ripping up brick-flooring, and took my arm, in the most friendly and familiar manner possible, to lead me with him out of the house. I will venture to say, that when the Sub-prefect was a little boy, and was taken for the first time to the Play, he was not half as much pleased as he was now at the job in prospect for him at the gambling-house!

Away we went through the streets, the Sub-prefect cross-examining and congratulating me in the same breath as we marched at the head of our formidable *posse comitatus*. Sentinels were placed at the back and front of the house the moment we got to it; a tremendous battery of knocks was directed against the door; a light appeared at a window; I was told to conceal myself behind the police – then came more knocks, and a cry of 'Open in the name of the law!' At that terrible summons bolts and locks gave way before an invisible hand, and the moment after the Sub-prefect was in the passage, confronting a waiter half-dressed and ghastly pale. This was the short dialogue which immediately took place:

'We want to see the Englishman who is sleeping in this house?'

'He went away hours ago.'

'He did no such thing. His friend went away; *he* remained. Show us to his bedroom!'

'I swear to you, Monsieur le Sous-prefet, he is not here! he—'

'I swear to you, Monsieur le Garçon, he is. He slept here – he didn't find your bed comfortable – he came to us to complain of it – here he is among my men – and here am I ready to look for a flea or two in his bedstead. Renaudin! (calling to one of the subordinates, and pointing to the waiter) collar that man, and tie his hands behind him. Now, then, gentlemen, let us walk up stairs!'

Every man and woman in the house was secured – the 'Old Soldier' the first. Then I identified the bed in which I had slept, and then we went into the room above.

No object that was at all extraordinary appeared in any part of it. The Sub-prefect looked round the place, commanded everybody to be silent, stamped twice on the floor, called for a candle, looked attentively at the spot he had stamped on, and ordered the flooring there to be carefully taken up. This was done in no time. Lights were produced, and we saw a deep raftered cavity between the floor of this room and the ceiling of the room beneath. Through this cavity there ran perpendicularly a sort of case of iron thickly greased; and inside the case appeared the screw, which communicated with the bed-top below. Extra lengths of screw, freshly oiled; levers covered with felt; all the complete upper works of a heavy press – constructed with infernal ingenuity so as to join the fixtures below, and when taken to pieces again to go into the smallest possible compass – were next discovered and pulled out on the floor. After some little difficulty the Sub-prefect succeeded in putting the machinery together, and, leaving his men to work it, descended with me to the bedroom. The smothering canopy was then lowered, but not so noiselessly as I had seen it lowered. When I mentioned this to the Sub-prefect, his answer, simple as it was, had a terrible significance. 'My men,' said he, 'are working down the bed-top for the first time – the men whose money you won were in better practice.'

We left the house in the sole possession of two police agents – every one of the inmates being removed to prison on the spot. The Sub-prefect, after taking down my '*procès-verbal*' in his office, returned with me to my hotel to get my passport. 'Do you think,' I asked, as I gave it to him, 'that any men have really been smothered in that bed, as they tried to smother *me?*'

'I have seen dozens of drowned men laid out at the Morgue,' answered the Sub-prefect, 'in whose pocket-books were found letters, stating that they had committed suicide in the Seine, because they had lost everything at the gaming-table. Do I know how many of those men entered the same gambling-house that *you* entered? won as *you* won? took that bed as *you* took it? slept in it? were smothered in it? and were privately thrown into the river, with a letter of explanation written by the murderers and placed in their pocket-books? No man can say how many or how few have suffered the fate from which you have escaped. The people of the gambling-house kept their bedstead machinery a secret from *us* – even from the police! The dead kept the rest of the secret for them. Good night, or rather good morning, Monsieur Faulkner! Be at my office again at nine o'clock – in the meantime, *au revoir!*'

The rest of my story is soon told. I was examined and re-examined; the gambling-house was strictly searched all through from top to bottom; the prisoners were separately interrogated; and two of the less guilty among them made a confession. *I* discovered that the Old Soldier was the master of the gambling-house – *justice* discovered that he had been drummed out of the army as a vagabond years ago; that he had been guilty of all sorts of villanies since; that he was in possession of stolen property, which the owners identified; and that he, the croupier, another accomplice, and the woman who had made my cup of coffee, were all in the secret of the bedstead. There appeared some reason to doubt whether the inferior persons attached to the house knew anything of the suffocating machinery; and they received the benefit of that doubt, by being treated simply as thieves and vagabonds. As for the Old Soldier and his two head-myrmidons, they went to the galleys; the woman who had drugged my coffee was imprisoned for I forget how many years; the regular attendants at the gambling-house were considered 'suspicious,' and placed under 'surveillance;' and I became, for one whole week (which is a long time), the head 'lion' in Parisian society. My adventure was dramatised by three illustrious playmakers, but never saw theatrical daylight; for the censorship forbade the introduction on the stage of a correct copy of the gambling-house bedstead.

One good result was produced by my adventure which any censorship must have approved: it cured me of ever again trying *Rouge et Noir* as an amusement. The sight of a green cloth, with packs of cards and heaps of money on it, will henceforth be for ever associated in my mind with the sight of a bed-canopy descending to suffocate me in the silence and darkness of the night.

Nine o'Clock!

Originally appeared in *Bentley's Miscellany*, Vol. 32, 1852. Never reprinted. Catherine Peters suggests that the occult element in this story may have derived from experiments that Collins made in the fashionable pseudo-sciences of hypnotism and clairvoyance, which he wrote up in a series of articles on 'Magnetic Evenings at Home', which appeared in *The Leader* in 1852 (*The King of Inventors*, p. 109). One of Collins's late novels, *The Two Destinies* (1876), involves telepathic communication. The Girondin deputy who memorably condemned the 'creatures of Robespierre' was Lasource. The dark mirror within the wardrobe recalls the prophetic mirror of polished coal in Collins's nonfictional sketch 'My Black Mirror' (*Household Words*, 1856). For another more famous treatment of the French Revolution by Collins, see the novella 'Sister Rose', included in *After Dark* (1856).

T HE NIGHT OF the 30th of June, 1793, is memorable in the prison annals of Paris, as the last night in confinement of the leaders of the famous Girondin party in the first French Revolution. On the morning of the 31st, the twenty-one deputies who represented the department of the Gironde, were guillotined to make way for Robespierre and the Reign of Terror.

With these men fell the last revolutionists of that period who shrank from founding a republic on massacre; who recoiled from substituting for a monarchy of corruption, a monarchy of bloodshed. The elements of their defeat lay as much in themselves, as in the events of their time. They were not, as a party, true to their own convictions; they temporized; they fatally attempted to take a middle course amid the terrible emergencies of a terrible epoch, and they fell – fell before worse men, because those men were in earnest.

Condemned to die, the Girondins submitted nobly to their fate; their great glory was the glory of their deaths. The speech of one of them on hearing his sentence pronounced, was a prophecy of the future, fulfilled to the letter.

'*I* die,' he said to the Jacobin judges, the creatures of Robespierre, who tried him. '*I* die at a time when the people have lost their reason; *you* will die on the day when they recover it.' Valazé was the only member of the condemned party who displayed a momentary weakness; he stabbed himself on hearing his sentence pronounced. But the blow was not mortal – he died on the scaffold, and died bravely with the rest.

On the night of the 30th the Girondins held their famous banquet in the prison; celebrated, with the ferocious stoicism of the time, their last social meeting before the morning on which they were to die. Other men, besides the twenty-one, were present at this supper of the condemned. They were prisoners who held Girondin opinions, but whose names were not illustrious enough for history to preserve. Though sentenced to confinement they were not sentenced to death. Some of their number, who had protested most boldly against the condemnation of the deputies, were ordered to witness the execution on the morrow, as a timely example to terrify them into submission. More than this, Robespierre and his colleagues did not, as yet, venture to attempt: the Reign of Terror was a cautious reign at starting.

The supper-table of the prison was spread; the guests, twenty-one of their number stamped already with the seal of death, were congregated at the last Girondin banquet; toast followed toast; the *Marseillaise* was sung; the desperate triumph of the feast was rising fast to its climax, when a new and ominous subject of conversation was started at the lower end of the table, and spread electrically, almost in a moment, to the top.

This subject (by whom originated no one knew) was simply a question as to the hour in the morning at which the execution was to take place. Every one of the prisoners appeared to be in ignorance on this point; and the gaolers either could not, or would not, enlighten them. Until the cart for the condemned rolled into the prison-yard, not one of the Girondins could tell whether he was to be called out to the guillotine soon after sunrise, or not till near noon.

This uncertainty was made a topic for discussion, or for jesting on all sides. It was eagerly seized on as a pretext for raising to the highest pitch the ghastly animation and hilarity of the evening. In some quarters, the recognised hour of former executions was quoted as a precedent sure to be followed by the executioners of the morrow; in others, it was asserted that Robespierre and his party would purposely depart from established customs in this, as in previous instances. Dozens of wild schemes were suggested for guessing the hour by fortune-telling rules on the cards; bets were offered and accepted among the prisoners who were not condemned to death, and witnessed in stoical mockery by the prisoners who were. Jests were exchanged about early rising and hurried toilets; in short, every man contributed an assertion, a contradiction, or a witticism to keep up the new topic of conversation, with one solitary exception. That exception was the Girondin, Duprat, one of the deputies who was sentenced to die by the guillotine.

He was a younger man than the majority of his brethren, and was personally remarkable by his pale, handsome, melancholy face, and his reserved yet gentle manners. Throughout the evening, he had spoken but rarely; there was something of the silence and serenity of a martyr in his demeanour. That he feared death as little as any of his companions was plainly visible in his bright, steady eye; in his unchanging complexion; in his firm, calm voice, when he occasionally addressed those who happened to be near him. But he was evidently out of place at the banquet; his temperament was reflective, his disposition serious; feasts were at no time a sphere in which he was calculated to shine.

His taciturnity, while the hour of the execution was under discussion, had separated him from most of those with whom he sat, at the lower end of the table. They edged up towards the top, where the conversation was most general and most animated. One of his friends, however, still kept his place by Duprat's side, and thus questioned him anxiously, but in low tones, on the cause of his immovable silence:

'Are you the only man of the company, Duprat, who has neither a guess nor a joke to make about the time of the execution?'

'I never joke, Marigny,' was the answer, given with a slight smile which had something of the sarcastic in it; 'and as for guessing at the time of the execution, I never guess at things which I *know*.'

'Know! You know the hour of the execution! Then why not communicate your knowledge to your friends around you?'

'Because not one of them would believe what I said.'

'But, surely, you could prove it. Somebody must have told you.'

'Nobody has told me.'

'You have seen some private letter, then; or you have managed to get sight of the execution-order; or—'

'Spare your conjectures, Marigny. I have not read, as I have not been told, what is the hour at which we are to die to-morrow.'

'Then how on earth can you possibly know it?'

'I do *not* know when the execution will begin, or when it will end. I only know that it will be *going on* at nine o'clock to-morrow morning. Out of the twenty-one who are to suffer death, one will be guillotined exactly at that hour. Whether he will be the first whose head falls, or the last, I cannot tell.'

'And pray who may this man be, who is to die exactly at nine o'clock? Of course, prophetically knowing so much, you know that!'

'I *do* know it. I am the man whose death by the guillotine will take place exactly at the hour I have mentioned.'

'You said just now, Duprat, that you never joked. Do you expect me to believe that what you have just spoken is spoken in earnest?'

'I repeat that I never joke; and I answer that I expect you to believe me. I know the hour at which my death will take place tomorrow, just as certainly as I know the fact of my own existence tonight.'

'But how? My dear friend, can you really lay claim to supernatural intuition, in this eighteenth century of the world, in this renowned Age of Reason?'

'No two men, Marigny, understand that word, supernatural, exactly in the same sense; you and I differ about its meaning, or, in other words, differ about the real distinction between the doubtful and the true. We will not discuss the subject: I wish to be understood, at the outset, as laying claim to no superior intuitions whatever; but I tell you, at the same time, that even in this Age of Reason, I have reason for what I have said. My father and my brother both died at nine o'clock in the morning, and were both warned very strangely of their deaths. I am the last of my family; I was warned last night, as they were warned; and I shall die by the guillotine, as they died in their beds, at the fatal hour of nine.'

'But, Duprat, why have I never heard of this before? As your oldest and, I am sure, your dearest friend, I thought you had long since trusted me with all your secrets.'

'And you shall know this secret; I only kept it from you till the time when I could be certain that my death would substantiate my words, to the very letter. Come! you are as bad supper-company as I am; let us slip away from the table unperceived, while our friends are all engaged in conversation. Yonder end of the hall is dark and quiet – we can speak there uninterruptedly, for some hours to come.'

He led the way from the supper-table, followed by Marigny. Arrived at one of the darkest and most retired corners of the great hall of the prison, Duprat spoke again:

'I believe, Marigny,' he said, 'that you are one of those who have been ordered by our tyrants to witness my execution, and the execution of my brethren, as a warning spectacle for an enemy to the Jacobin cause?'

'My dear, dear friend! it is too true; I am ordered to witness the butchery which I cannot prevent – our last awful parting will be at the foot of the scaffold. I am among the victims who are spared – mercilessly spared – for a little while yet.'

'Say the martyrs! We die as martyrs, calmly, hopefully, innocently. When I am placed under the guillotine to-morrow morning, listen, my friend, for the striking of the church clocks; listen for the hour while you look your last on me. Until that time, suspend your judgment on the strange chapter of family history which I am now about to relate.'

Marigny took his friend's hand, and promised compliance with the request. Duprat then began as follows:

'You knew my brother Alfred, when he was quite a youth, and you knew something of what people flippantly termed, the eccentricities of his character. He was three years my junior; but, from childhood, he showed far less of a child's innate levity and happiness than his elder brother. He was noted for his seriousness and thoughtfulness as a boy; showed little inclination for a boy's usual lessons, and less still for a boy's usual recreations, – in short, he was considered by everybody (my father included) as deficient in intellect; as a vacant dreamer, and an inveterate idler, whom it was hopeless to improve. Our tutor tried to lead him to various studies, and tried in vain. It was the same when the cultivation of his mind was given up, and the cultivation of his body was next attempted. The fencing-master could make nothing of him; and the dancing-master, after the first three lessons, resigned in despair. Seeing that it was useless to set others to teach him, my father made a virtue of necessity, and left him, if he chose, to teach himself.

'To the astonishment of every one, he had not been long consigned to his own guidance, when he was discovered in the library, reading every old treatise on astrology which he could lay his hands on. He had rejected all useful knowledge for the most obsolete of obsolete sciences – the old, abandoned delusion of divination by the stars! My father laughed heartily over the strange study to which his idle son had at last applied himself, but made no attempt to oppose his new caprice, and sarcastically presented him with a telescope on his next birthday. I should remind you here, of what you may perhaps have forgotten, that my father was a philosopher of the Voltaire school, who believed that the summit of human wisdom was to arrive at the power of sneering at all enthusiasms, and doubting of all truths. Apart from his philosophy, he was a kind-hearted, easy man, of quick, rather than of profound intelligence. He could see nothing in my brother's new occupation, but the evidence of a new idleness, a fresh caprice which would be abandoned in a few months. My father was not the man to appreciate those yearnings towards the poetical and the spiritual, which were part of Alfred's temperament, and which gave to his peculiar studies of the stars and their influences, a certain charm altogether unconnected with the more practical attractions of scientific investigation.

'This idle caprice of my brother's, as my father insisted on terming it, had lasted more than a twelvemonth, when there occurred the first of a series of mysterious and – as I consider them – supernatural events, with all of which Alfred was very remarkably connected. I was myself a witness of the strange circumstance, which I am now about to relate to you.

'One day – my brother being then sixteen years of age – I happened to go into my father's study, during his absence, and found Alfred there, standing close to a window, which looked into the garden. I walked up to him, and observed a curious expression of vacancy and rigidity in his face, especially in his eyes. Although I knew him to be subject to what are called fits of absence, I still thought it rather extraordinary that he never moved, and never noticed me when I was close to him. I took his hand, and asked if he was unwell. His flesh felt quite cold; neither my touch nor my voice produced the smallest sensation in him. Almost at the same moment when I noticed this, I happened to be looking accidentally towards the garden. There was my father walking along one of the paths, and there, by his side, walking with him, was *another Alfred!* – Another, yet exactly the same as the Alfred by whose side I was standing, whose hand I still held in mine!

'Thoroughly panic-stricken, I dropped his hand, and uttered a cry of terror. At the loud sound of my voice, the statue-like presence before me immediately began to show signs of animation. I looked round again at the garden. The figure of my brother, which I had beheld there, was gone, and I saw to my horror, that my father was looking for it – looking in all directions for the companion (spectre, or human being?) of his walk!

'When I turned towards Alfred once more, he had (if I may so express it) come to life again, and was asking, with his usual gentleness of manner and kindness of voice, why I was looking so pale? I evaded the question by making some excuse, and in my turn inquired of him, how long he had been in my father's study.

"'Surely you ought to know best," he answered with a laugh, "for you must have been here before me. It is not many minutes ago since I was walking in the garden with—'"

'Before he could complete the sentence my father entered the room.

"'Oh! here you are, Master Alfred," said he. "May I ask for what purpose you took it into your wise head to vanish in that extraordinary manner? Why you slipped away from me in an instant, while I was picking a flower! On my word, sir, you're a better player at hide-and-seek than your brother, – *he* would only have run into the shrubbery, *you* have managed to run in here, though how you did it in the time passes my poor comprehension. I was not a moment picking the flower, yet in that moment you were gone!'"

'Alfred glanced suddenly and searchingly at me; his face became deadly pale, and, without speaking a word, he hurried from the room.

"'Can *you* explain this?" said my father, looking very much astonished.

'I hesitated a moment, and then told him what I had seen. He took a pinch of snuff – a favourite habit with him when he was going to be sarcastic, in imitation of Voltaire.

"'One visionary in a family is enough," said he; "I recommend you not to turn yourself into a bad imitation of your brother Alfred! Send your ghost after me, my good boy! I am going back into the garden, and should like to see him again!'"

'Ridicule, even much sharper than this, would have had little effect on me. If I was certain of anything in the world, I was certain that I had seen my brother in the study – nay, more, had touched him, – and equally certain that I had seen his double – his exact similitude, in the garden. As far as any man could know that he was in possession of his own senses, I knew myself to be in possession of mine. Left alone to think over what I had beheld, I felt a supernatural terror creeping through me – a terror which increased, when I recollected that, on one or two occasions friends had said they had seen Alfred out of doors, when we all knew him to be at home. These statements, which my father had laughed at, and had taught me to laugh at, either as a trick, or a delusion on the part of others, now recurred to my memory as startling corroborations of what I had just seen myself. The solitude of the study oppressed me in a manner which I cannot describe. I left the apartment to seek Alfred, determined to question him, with all possible caution, on the subject of his strange trance, and his sensations at the moment when I had awakened him from it.

'I found him in his bed-room, still pale, and now very thoughtful. As the first words in reference to the scene in the study passed my lips, he started violently, and entreated me, with very unusual warmth of speech and manner, never to speak to him on that subject again, – never, if I had any love or regard for him! Of course, I complied with his request. The mystery, however, was not destined to end here.

'About two months after the event which I have just related, we had arranged, one evening, to go to the theatre. My father had insisted that Alfred should be of the party, otherwise he would certainly have declined accompanying us; for he had no inclination whatever for public amusements of any kind. However, with his usual docility, he prepared to obey my father's desire, by going up-stairs to put on his evening dress. It was winter-time, so he was obliged to take a candle with him.

'We waited in the drawing-room for his return a very long time, so long, that my father was on the point of sending up-stairs to remind him of the lateness of the hour, when Alfred reappeared without the candle which he had taken with him from the room. The ghastly alteration that had passed over his face – the hideous, death-look that distorted his features I shall never forget, – I shall see it to-morrow on the scaffold!

'Before either my father or I could utter a word, my brother said: 'I have been taken suddenly ill; but I am better now. Do you still wish me to go to the theatre?'

'"Certainly not, my dear Alfred," answered my father; "we must send for the doctor immediately."

'"Pray do not call in the doctor, sir; he would be of no use. I will tell you why, if you will let me speak to you alone."

'My father, looking seriously alarmed, signed to me to leave the room. For more than half an hour I remained absent, suffering almost unendurable suspense and anxiety on my brother's account. When I was recalled, I observed that Alfred was quite calm, though still deadly pale. My father's manner displayed an agitation which I had never observed in it before. He rose from his chair when I re-entered the room, and left me alone with my brother.

'"Promise me," said Alfred, in answer to my entreaties to know what had happened, "promise that you will not ask me to tell you more than my father has permitted me to tell. It is his desire that I should keep certain things a secret from you.'

'I gave the required promise, but gave it most unwillingly. Alfred then proceeded.

'"When I left you to go and dress for the theatre, I felt a sense of oppression all over me, which I cannot describe. As soon as I was alone, it seemed as if some part of the life within me was slowly wasting away. I could hardly breathe the air around me, big drops of perspiration burst out on my forehead, and then a feeling of terror seized me which I was utterly unable to control. Some of those strange fancies of seeing my mother's spirit, which used to influence me at the time of her death, came back again to my mind. I ascended the stairs slowly and painfully, not daring to look behind me, for I heard – yes, heard! – something following me. When I had got into my room, and had shut the door, I began to recover my self-possession a little. But the sense of oppression was still as heavy on me as ever, when I approached the wardrobe to get out my clothes. Just as I stretched forth my hand to turn the key, I saw, to my horror, the two doors of the wardrobe opening of themselves, opening slowly and silently. The candle went out at the same moment, and the whole inside of the wardrobe became to me like a great mirror, with a bright light shining in the middle of it. Out of that light there came a figure, the exact counterpart of myself. Over its breast hung an open scroll, and on that I read the warning of my own death, and a revelation of the destinies of my father and his race. Do not ask me what were the words on the scroll, I have given my promise not to tell you. I may only say that, as soon as I had read all, the room grew dark, and the vision disappeared."

'Forgetful of my promise, I entreated Alfred to repeat to me the words on the scroll. He smiled sadly, and refused to speak on the subject any more. I next sought out my father, and begged him to divulge the secret. Still sceptical to the last, he answered that one diseased imagination in the family was enough, and that he would not permit me to run the risk of being infected by Alfred's mental malady. I passed the whole of that day and the next in a state of agitation and alarm which nothing could tranquillize. The sight I had seen in the study gave a terrible significance to the little that my brother had told me. I was uneasy if he was a moment out of my sight. There was something in his expression, – calm and even cheerful as it was, – which made me dread the worst.

'On the morning of the third day after the occurrence I have just related, I rose very early, after a sleepless night, and went into Alfred's bedroom. He was awake, and welcomed me with more than usual affection and kindness. As I drew a chair to his bedside, he asked me to get pen, ink, and paper, and write down something from his dictation. I obeyed, and found to my terror and distress, that the idea of death was more present to his imagination than ever. He employed me in writing a statement of his wishes in regard to the disposal of all his own little possessions, as keepsakes to be given, after he was no more, to my father, myself, the house-servants, and one or two of his own most intimate friends. Over and over again I entreated him to tell me whether he really believed that his death was near. He invariably replied that I should soon know, and then led the conversation to indifferent topics. As the morning advanced, he asked to see my father, who came, accompanied by the doctor, the latter having been in attendance for the last two days.

'Alfred took my father's hand, and begged his forgiveness of any offence, any disobedience of which he had ever been guilty. Then, reaching out his other hand, and taking mine, as I stood on the opposite side of the bed, he asked what the time was. A clock was placed on the mantel-piece of the room, but not in a position in which he could see it, as he now lay. I turned round to look at the dial, and answered that, it was just on the stroke of nine.

'"Farewell!" said Alfred, calmly; "in this world, farewell for ever!"

'The next instant the clock struck. I felt his fingers tremble in mine, then grow quite still. The doctor seized a hand-mirror that lay on the table, and held it over his lips. He was dead – dead, as the last chime of the hour echoed through the awful silence of the room!

'I pass over the first days of our affliction. You, who have suffered the loss of a beloved sister, can well imagine their misery. I pass over these days, and pause for a moment at the time when we could speak with some calmness and resignation on the subject of our bereavement. On the arrival of that period, I ventured, in conversation with my father, to refer to the vision which had been seen by our dear Alfred in his bedroom, and to the prophecy which he described himself as having read upon the supernatural scroll.

'Even yet my father persisted in his scepticism; but now, as it seemed to me, more because he was afraid, than because he was unwilling, to believe. I again recalled to his memory what I myself had seen in the study. I asked him to recollect how certain Alfred had been beforehand, and how fatally right, about the day and hour of his death. Still I could get but one answer; my brother had died of a nervous disorder (the doctor said so); his imagination had been diseased from his childhood; there was only one way of treating the vision which he described himself as having seen, and that was, not to speak of it again between ourselves; never to speak of it at all to our friends.

'We were sitting in the study during this conversation. It was evening. As my father uttered the last words of his reply to me, I saw his eye turn suddenly and uneasily towards the further end of the room. In dead silence, I looked in the same direction, and saw the door opening slowly of itself. The vacant space beyond was filled with a bright, steady glow, which hid all outer objects in the hall, and which I cannot describe to you by likening it to any light that we are accustomed to behold either by day or night. In my terror, I caught my father by the arm, and asked him, in a whisper, whether he did not see something extraordinary in the direction of the doorway?

'"Yes," he answered, in tones as low as mine, "I see, or fancy I see, a strange light. The subject on which we have been speaking has impressed our feelings as it should not. Our nerves are still unstrung by the shock of the bereavement we have suffered: our senses are deluding us. Let us look away towards the garden."

'"But the opening of the door, father; remember the opening of the door!"

'"Ours is not the first door which has accidentally flown open of itself."

'"Then why not shut it again?"

'"Why not, indeed. I will close it at once." He rose, advanced a few paces, then stopped, and came back to his place. "It is a warm evening," he said, avoiding my eyes, which were eagerly fixed on him, "the room will be all the cooler, if the door is suffered to remain open."

'His face grew quite pale as he spoke. The light lasted for a few minutes longer, then suddenly disappeared. For the rest of the evening my father's manner was very much altered. He was silent and thoughtful, and complained of a feeling of oppression and languor, which he tried to persuade himself was produced by the heat of the weather. At an unusually early hour he retired to his room.

'The next morning, when I got down stairs, I found, to my astonishment, that the servants were engaged in preparations for the departure of somebody from the house. I made inquiries of one of them who was hurriedly packing a trunk. "My master, sir, starts for Lyons the first thing this morning," was the reply. I immediately repaired to my father's room, and found him there with an open letter in his hand, which he was reading. His face, as he looked up at me on my entrance, expressed the most violent emotions of apprehension and despair.

'"I hardly know whether I am awake or dreaming; whether I am the dupe of a terrible delusion, or the victim of a supernatural reality more terrible still," he said in low awe-struck tones as I approached him. "One of the prophecies which Alfred told me in private that he had read upon the scroll, has come true! He predicted the loss of the bulk of my fortune – here is the letter, which informs me that the merchant at Lyons in whose hands my money was placed, has become a bankrupt. Can the occurrence of this ruinous calamity be the chance fulfilment of a mere guess? Or was the doom of my family really revealed to my dead son? I go to Lyons immediately to know the truth: this letter may have been written under false information; it may be the work of an impostor. And yet, Alfred's prediction – I shudder to think of it!"'

'"The light, father!" I exclaimed, "the light we saw last night in the study!"

'"Hush! don't speak of it! Alfred said that I should be warned of the truth of the prophecy, and of its immediate fulfilment, by the shining of the same supernatural light that he had seen – I tried to disbelieve what I beheld last night – I hardly know whether I dare believe it even now! This prophecy is not the last: there are others yet to be fulfilled – but let us not speak, let us not think of them! I must start at once for Lyons; I must be on the spot, if this horrible news is true, to save what I can from the wreck. The letter – give me back the letter! – I must go directly!"

'He hurried from the room. I followed him; and, with some difficulty, obtained permission to be the companion of his momentous journey. When we arrived at Lyons, we found that the statement in the letter was true. My father's fortune was gone: a mere pittance, derived from a small estate that had belonged to my mother, was all that was left to us.

'My father's health gave way under this misfortune. He never referred again to Alfred's prediction, and I was afraid to mention the subject; but I saw that it was affecting his mind quite as painfully as the loss of his property. Over, and over again, he checked himself very strangely when he was on the point of speaking to me about my brother. I saw that there was some secret pressing heavily on his mind, which he was afraid to disclose to me. It was useless to ask for his confidence. His temper had become irritable under disaster; perhaps, also, under the dread uncertainties which were now evidently tormenting him in secret. My situation was a very sad, and a very dreary one, at that time: I had no remembrances of the past that were not mournful and affrighting remembrances; I had no hopes for the future that were not darkened by a vague presentiment of troubles and perils to come; and I was expressly forbidden by my father to say a word about the terrible events which had cast an unnatural gloom over my youthful career, to any of the friends (yourself included) whose counsel and whose sympathy might have guided and sustained me in the day of trial.

'We returned to Paris; sold our house there; and retired to live on the small estate, to which I have referred, as the last possession left us. We had not been many days in our new abode, when my father imprudently exposed himself to a heavy shower of rain, and suffered, in consequence from a violent attack of cold. This temporary malady was not dreaded by the medical attendant; but it was soon aggravated by a fever, produced as much by the anxiety and distress of mind from which he continued to suffer, as by any other cause. Still the doctor gave hope; but still he grew daily worse – so much worse, that I removed my bed into his room, and never quitted him night or day.

'One night I had fallen asleep, overpowered by fatigue and anxiety, when I was awakened by a cry from my father. I instantly trimmed the light, and ran to his side. He was sitting up in bed, with his eyes fixed on the door, which had been left ajar to ventilate the room. I saw nothing in that direction, and asked what was the matter. He murmured some expressions of affection towards me, and begged me to sit by his bedside till the morning; but gave no definite answer to my question. Once or twice, I thought he wandered a little; and I observed that he occasionally moved his hand under the pillow, as if searching for something there. However, when the morning came, he appeared to be quite calm and self-possessed. The doctor arrived; and pronouncing him to be better, retired to the dressing-room to write a prescription. The moment his back was turned, my father laid his weak hand on my arm, and whispered faintly: "Last night I saw the supernatural light again – the second prediction – true, true – my death this time – the same hour as Alfred's – nine – nine o'clock, this morning." He paused a moment through weakness; then added: "Take that sealed paper – under the pillow – when I am dead, read it – now go into the dressing-room – my watch is there – I have heard the church clock strike eight; let me see how long it is now till nine – go – go quickly!"

'Horror-stricken, moving and acting like a man in a trance, I silently obeyed him. The doctor was still in the dressing-room: despair made me catch eagerly at any chance of saving my father; I told his medical attendant what I had just heard, and entreated advice and assistance without delay.

'"He is a little delirious," said the doctor – "don't be alarmed: we can cheat him out of his dangerous idea, and so perhaps save his life. Where is the watch?" (I produced it) – "See: it is ten minutes to nine. I will put back the hands one hour; that will give good time for a composing draught to operate. There! take him the watch, and let him see the false time with his own eyes. He will be comfortably asleep before the hour hand gets round again to nine."

'I went back with the watch to my father's bed-side. "Too slow," he murmured, as he looked at the dial – "too slow by an hour – the church clock – I counted eight."

'"Father! dear father! you are mistaken," I cried, "*I* counted also: it was only seven."

'"Only seven!" he echoed faintly, "another hour then – another hour to live!" He evidently believed what I had said to him. In spite of the fatal experiences of the past, I now ventured to hope the best from our stratagem, as I resumed my place by his side.

'The doctor came in; but my father never noticed him. He kept his eyes fixed on the watch, which lay between us, on the coverlid. When the minute hand was within a few seconds of indicating the false hour of eight, he looked round at me, murmured very feebly and doubtingly, "another hour to live!" and then gently closed his eyes. I looked at the watch, and saw that it was just eight o'clock, according to our alteration of the right time. At the same moment, I heard the doctor, whose hand had been on my father's pulse, exclaim, "My God! it's stopped! He *has* died at nine o'clock!"

'The fatality, which no human stratagem or human science could turn aside, was accomplished! I was alone in the world!

'In the solitude of our little cottage, on the day of my father's burial, I opened the sealed letter, which he had told me to take from the pillow of his death-bed. In preparing to read it, I knew that I was preparing for the knowledge of my own doom; but I neither trembled nor wept. I was beyond all grief: despair such as mine was then, is calm and self-possessed to the last.

'The letter ran thus: "After your father and your brother have fallen under the fatality that pursues our house, it is right, my dear son, that you should be warned how *you* are included in the last of the predictions which still remains unaccomplished. Know then, that the final lines read by our dear Alfred on the scroll, prophesied that *you* should die, as *we* have died, at the fatal hour of nine; but by a bloody and violent death, the day of which was not foretold. My beloved boy! you know not, you never will know, what I suffered in the possession of this terrible secret, as the truth of the former prophecies forced itself more and more plainly on my mind! Even now, as I write, I hope against all hope; believe vainly and desperately against all experience, that this last, worst doom may be avoided. Be cautious; be patient; look well before you at each step of your career. The fatality by which you are threatened is terrible; but there is a Power above fatality; and before that Power my spirit and my child's spirit now pray for you. Remember this when your heart is heavy, and your path through life grows dark. Remember that the better world is still before you, the world where we shall all meet! Farewell!''

'When I first read those lines, I read them with the gloomy, immovable resignation of the Eastern fatalists; and that resignation never left me afterwards. Here, in this prison, I feel it, calm as ever. I bowed patiently to my doom, when it was only predicted: I bow to it as patiently now, when it is on the eve of accomplishment. You have often wondered, my friend, at the tranquil, equable sadness of my manner: after what I have just told you, can you wonder any longer?

'But let me return for a moment to the past. Though I had no hope of escaping the fatality which had overtaken my father and my brother, my life, after my double bereavement, was the existence of all others which might seem most likely to evade the accomplishment of my predicted doom. Yourself and one other friend excepted, I saw no society; my walks were limited to the cottage garden and the neighbouring fields, and my every-day, unvarying occupation was confined to that hard and resolute course of study, by which alone I could hope to prevent my mind from dwelling on what I had suffered in the past, or on what I might still be condemned to suffer in the future. Never was there a life more quiet and more uneventful than mine!

'You know how I awoke to an ambition, which irresistibly impelled me to change this mode of existence. News from Paris penetrated even to my obscure retreat, and disturbed my self-imposed tranquillity. I heard of the last errors and weaknesses of Louis the Sixteenth; I heard of the assembling of the States-General; and I knew that the French Revolution had begun. The tremendous emergencies of that epoch drew men of all characters from private to public pursuits, and made politics the necessity rather than the choice of every Frenchman's life. The great change preparing for the country acted universally on individuals, even to the humblest, and it acted on *me*.

'I was elected a deputy, more for the sake of the name I bore, than on account of any little influence which my acquirements and my character might have exercised in the neighbourhood of my country abode. I removed to Paris, and took my seat in the Chamber, little thinking at that time, of the crime and the bloodshed to which our revolution, so moderate in its beginning, would lead; little thinking that I had taken the first, irretrievable step towards the bloody and the violent death which was lying in store for me.

'Need I go on? You know how warmly I joined the Girondin party; you know how we have been sacrificed; you know what the death is which I and my brethren are to suffer to-morrow. On now ending, I repeat what I said at the beginning: Judge not of my narrative till you have seen with your own eyes what really takes place in the morning. I have carefully abstained from all comment, I have simply related events as they happened, forbearing to add my own views of their significance, my own ideas on the explanation of which they admit. You may believe us to have been a family of nervous visionaries, witnesses of certain remarkable contingencies; victims of curious, but not impossible chances, which we have fancifully and falsely interpreted into supernatural events. I leave you undisturbed in this conviction (if you really feel it); to-morrow you will think differently; to-morrow you will be an altered man. In the mean time, remember what I now say, as you would remember my dying words: Last night I saw the supernatural radiance which warned my father and my brother; and which warns *me*, that, whatever the time when the execution begins, whatever the order in which the twenty-one Girondins are chosen for death, I shall be the man who kneels under the guillotine, as the clock strikes nine!'

It was morning. Of the ghastly festivities of the night no sign remained. The prison-hall wore an altered look, as the twenty-one condemned men (followed by those who were ordered to witness their execution) were marched out to the carts appointed to take them from the dungeon to the scaffold.

The sky was cloudless, the sun warm and brilliant, as the Girondin leaders and their companions were drawn slowly through the streets to the place of execution. Duprat and Marigny were placed in separate vehicles: the contrast in their demeanour at that awful moment was strongly marked. The features of the doomed man still preserved their noble and melancholy repose; his glance was steady; his colour never changed. The face of Marigny, on the contrary, displayed the strongest agitation; he was pale even to his lips. The terrible narrative he had heard, the anticipation of the final and appalling proof by which its truth was now to be tested, had robbed him, for the first time in his life, of all his self-possession. Duprat had predicted truly; the morrow had come, and he was an altered man already.

The carts drew up at the foot of the scaffold which was soon to be stained with the blood of twenty-one human beings. The condemned deputies mounted it; and ranged themselves at the end opposite the guillotine. The prisoners who were to behold the execution remained in their cart. Before Duprat ascended the steps, he took his friend's hand for the last time: 'Farewell!' he said, calmly. 'Farewell! I go to my father, and my brother! Remember my words of last night.'

With straining eyes, and bloodless cheeks, Marigny saw Duprat take his position in the middle row of his companions, who stood in three ranks of seven each. Then the awful spectacle of the execution began. After the first seven deputies had suffered there was a pause; the horrible traces of the judicial massacre were being removed. When the execution proceeded, Duprat was the third taken from the middle rank of the condemned. As he came forward, and stood for an instant erect under the guillotine, he looked with a smile on his friend, and repeated in a clear voice the word, '*Remember!*' – then bowed himself on the block. The blood stood still at Marigny's heart, as he looked and listened, during the moment of silence that followed. That moment past, the church clocks of Paris struck. He dropped down in the cart, and covered his face with his hands; for through the heavy beat of the hour he heard the fall of the fatal steel.

'Pray, sir, was it nine or ten that struck just now?' said one of Marigny's fellow-prisoners to an officer of the guard who stood near the cart.

The person addressed referred to his watch, and answered—

'Nine o'clock!'

Gabriel's Marriage

Originally appeared in *Household Words*, 16–23 April 1853. Reprinted in *After Dark* (1856), as 'The Nun's Story of Gabriel's Marriage'. In the framing narrative the Painter visits a nunnery in a 'quiet little valley in the West of England' to make a copy of a Correggio that hangs over the altar there. In the convent parlour he is surprised to see 'an old worm-eaten wooden cross, made in the rudest manner, hanging by itself on a slip of wall between two windows.' He asks how it comes to be there and, in answer, the simple and gentle Mother Martha tells him the story of 'Gabriel's Marriage'. The convent is based on Collins's visit to the House of Lanhearne in the Vale of Mawgan, Cornwall, on his walking-tour in the summer of 1850. See 'The Nuns of Mawgan', *Rambles Beyond Railways*, ch. 12. (In order to bring out the moral it has been necessary to retain Mother Martha's brief appearance at the close of the tale.) Both the travel-book and 'Gabriel's Marriage', like the earlier 'Mad Monkton', show Collins to be well-disposed to 'that vigilant and indestructible Papal religion, which defies alike hidden conspiracy and open persecution', though late in his career he was to write a sensational anti-Jesuit novel, 'The Black Robe' (1881). In 1855 Collins adapted 'Gabriel's Marriage' to form the two-act play, 'The Lighthouse', which was successfully staged at the Olympic Theatre, London in 1857.

I

One night, during the period of the first French Revolution, the family of François Sarzeau, a fisherman of Brittany, were all waking and watching at a late hour in their cottage on the peninsula of Quiberon. François had gone out in his boat that evening, as usual, to fish. Shortly after his departure, the wind had risen, the clouds had gathered; and the storm, which had been threatening at intervals throughout the whole day, burst forth furiously about nine o'clock. It was now eleven; and the raging of the wind over the barren, heathy peninsula still seemed to increase with each fresh blast that tore its way out upon the open sea; the crashing of the waves on the beach was awful to hear; the dreary blackness of the sky terrible to behold. The longer they listened to the storm, the oftener they looked out at it, the fainter grew the hopes which the fisherman's family still strove to cherish for the safety of François Sarzeau and of his younger son who had gone with him in the boat.

There was something impressive in the simplicity of the scene that was now passing within the cottage.

On one side of the great rugged black fireplace crouched two little girls; the younger half asleep, with her head in her sister's lap. These were the daughters of the fisherman; and opposite to them sat their eldest brother Gabriel. His right arm had been badly wounded in a recent encounter at the national game of the *Soule*, a sport resembling our English football; but played on both sides in such savage earnest by the people of Brittany as to end always in bloodshed, often in mutilation, sometimes even in loss of life. On the same bench with Gabriel sat his betrothed wife – a girl of eighteen – clothed in the plain, almost monastic black and white costume of her native district. She was the daughter of a small farmer living at some little distance from the coast. Between the groups formed on either side of the fireplace, the vacant space was occupied by the foot of a truckle bed. In this bed lay a very old man, the father of François Sarzeau. His haggard face was covered with deep wrinkles; his long white hair flowed over the coarse lump of sacking which served him for a pillow, and his light grey eyes wandered incessantly, with a strange expression of terror and suspicion, from person to person, and from object to object, in all parts of the room. Whenever the wind and sea whistled and roared at their loudest, he muttered to himself and tossed his hands fretfully on his wretched coverlid. On these occasions his eyes always fixed themselves intently on a little delft image of the Virgin placed in a niche over the fireplace. Every time they saw him look in this direction Gabriel and the young girls shuddered and crossed themselves; and even the child, who still kept awake, imitated their example. There was one bond of feeling at least between the old man and his grandchildren, which connected his age and their youth unnaturally and closely together. This feeling was reverence for the superstitions which had been handed down to them by their ancestors from centuries and centuries back, as far even as the age of the Druids. The spirit-warnings of disaster and death which the old man heard in the wailing of the wind, in the crashing of the waves, in the dreary monotonous rattling of the casement, the young man and his affianced wife and the little child who cowered by the fireside, heard too. All differences in sex, in temperament, in years, Superstition was strong enough to strike down to its own dread level, in the fisherman's cottage, on that stormy night.

Besides the benches by the fireside and the bed, the only piece of furniture in the room was a coarse wooden table, with a loaf of black bread, a knife, and a pitcher of cider placed on it. Old nets, coils of rope, tattered sails, hung about the walls and over the wooden partition which separated the room into two compartments. Wisps of straw and ears of barley drooped down through the rotten rafters and gaping boards that made the floor of the granary above.

These different objects, and the persons in the cottage, who composed the only surviving members of the fisherman's family, were strangely and wildly lit up by the blaze of the fire and by the still brighter glare of a resin torch stuck into a block of wood in the chimney-corner. The red and yellow light played full on the weird face of the old man as he lay opposite to it, and glanced fitfully on the figures of the young girl, Gabriel, and the two children; the great gloomy shadows rose and fell, and grew and lessened in bulk about the walls like visions of darkness, animated by a supernatural spectre-life, while the dense obscurity outside spreading before the curtainless window seemed as a wall of solid darkness that had closed in for ever around the fisherman's house. The night-scene within the cottage was almost as wild and as dreary to look upon as the night-scene without.

For a long time the different persons in the room sat together without speaking, even without looking at each other. At last, the girl turned and whispered something into Gabriel's ear.

'Perrine, what were you saying to Gabriel?' asked the child opposite, seizing the first opportunity of breaking the desolate silence – doubly desolate at her age – which was preserved by all around her.

'I was telling him,' answered Perrine simply, 'that it was time to change the bandages on his arm; and I also said to him, what I have often said before, that he must never play at that terrible game of the *Soule* again.'

The old man had been looking intently at Perrine and his grandchild as they spoke. His harsh, hollow voice mingled with the last soft tones of the young girl, repeating over and over again the same terrible words: 'Drowned! drowned! Son and grandson, both drowned! both drowned!'

'Hush! grandfather,' said Gabriel, 'we must not lose all hope for them yet. God and the Blessed Virgin protect them!' He looked at the little delft image, and crossed himself; the others imitated him, except the old man. He still tossed his hands over the coverlid, and still repeated 'Drowned! drowned!'

'Oh that accursed *Soule!*' groaned the young man. 'But for this wound I should have been with my father. The poor boy's life might at least have been saved; for we should then have left him here.'

'Silence!' exclaimed the harsh voice from the bed. 'The wail of dying men rises louder than the loud sea; the devil's psalm-singing roars higher than the roaring wind! Be silent, and listen! François drowned! Pierre drowned! Hark! Hark!'

A terrific blast of wind burst over the house as he spoke, shaking it to its centre, overpowering all other sounds, even to the deafening crash of the waves. The slumbering child awoke, and uttered a scream of fear. Perrine, who had been kneeling before her lover binding the fresh bandages on his wounded arm, paused in her occupation, trembling from head to foot. Gabriel looked towards the window: his experience told him what must be the hurricane fury of that blast of wind out at sea, and he sighed bitterly as he murmured to himself, 'God help them both – man's help will be as nothing to them now!'

'Gabriel!' cried the voice from the bed in altered tones – very faint and trembling.

He did not hear, or did not attend to the old man. He was trying to soothe and encourage the young girl at his feet.

'Don't be frightened, love,' he said, kissing her very gently and tenderly on the forehead. 'You are as safe here as anywhere. Was I not right in saying that it would be madness to attempt taking you back to the farm-house this evening? You can sleep in that room, Perrine, when you are tired – you can sleep with the two girls.'

'Gabriel! brother Gabriel!' cried one of the children. 'O! look at grand-father!'

Gabriel ran to the bedside. The old man had raised himself into a sitting position; his eyes were dilated, his whole face was rigid with terror, his hands were stretched out convulsively towards his grandson. 'The White Women!' he screamed. 'The White Women! the grave-diggers of the drowned are out on the sea!'

The children, with cries of terror, flung themselves into Perrine's arms; even Gabriel uttered an exclamation of horror, and started back from the bedside.

Still the old man reiterated, 'The White Women! The White Women! Open the door, Gabriel! look out westward, where the ebb-tide has left the sand dry. You'll see them bright as lightning in the darkness, mighty as the angels in stature, sweeping like the wind over the sea, in their long white garments, with their white hair trailing far behind them! Open the door, Gabriel! You'll see them stop and hover over the place where your father and your brother have been drowned; you'll see them come on till they reach the sand; you'll see them dig in it with their naked feet, and beckon awfully to the raging sea to give up its dead. Open the door, Gabriel – or, though it should be the death of me, I will get up and open it myself!'

Gabriel's face whitened even to his lips, but he made a sign that he would obey. It required the exertion of his whole strength to keep the door open against the wind while he looked out.

'Do you see them, grandson Gabriel? Speak the truth, and tell me if you see them,' cried the old man.

'I see nothing but darkness – pitch darkness,' answered Gabriel, letting the door close again.

'Ah! Woe! Woe!' groaned his grandfather, sinking back exhausted on the pillow. 'Darkness to *you*; but bright as lightning to the eyes that are allowed to see them. Drowned! drowned! Pray for their souls, Gabriel – *I* see the White Women even where I lie, and dare not pray for them. Son and grandson drowned! both drowned!'

The young man went back to Perrine and the children.

'Grandfather is very ill to-night,' he whispered.

'You had better all go into the bedroom, and leave me alone to watch by him.'

They rose as he spoke, crossed themselves before the image of the Virgin, kissed him one by one, and, without uttering a word, softly entered the little room on the other side of the partition. Gabriel looked at his grandfather, and saw that he lay quiet now, with his eyes closed as if he were already dropping asleep. The young man then heaped some fresh logs on the fire, and sat down by it to watch till morning.

Very dreary was the moaning of the night-storm; but it was not more dreary than the thoughts which now occupied him in his solitude – thoughts darkened and distorted by the terrible superstitions of his country and his race. Ever since the period of his mother's death he had been oppressed by the conviction that some curse hung over the family. At first they had been prosperous, they had got money, a little legacy had been left them. But this good fortune had availed only for a time; disaster on disaster strangely and suddenly succeeded. Losses, misfortunes, poverty, want itself had overwhelmed them; his father's temper had become so soured, that the oldest friends of François Sarzeau declared he was changed beyond recognition. And now, all this past misfortune – the steady, withering, household blight of many years – had ended in the last worst misery of all – in death. The fate of his father and his brother admitted no longer of a doubt – he knew it, as he listened to the storm, as he reflected on his grandfather's words, as he called to mind his own experience of the perils of the sea. And this double bereavement had fallen on him just as the time was approaching for his marriage with Perrine; just when misfortune was most ominous of evil, just when it was hardest to bear! Forebodings which he dared not realize began now to mingle with the bitterness of his grief, whenever his thoughts wandered from the present to the future; and as he sat by the lonely fireside, murmuring from time to time the Church prayer for the repose of the dead, he almost involuntarily mingled with it another prayer, expressed only in his own simple words, for the safety of the living – for the young girl whose love was his sole earthly treasure; for the motherless children who must now look for protection to him alone.

He had sat by the hearth a long, long time, absorbed in his thoughts, not once looking round towards the bed, when he was startled by hearing the sound of his grandfather's voice once more.

'Gabriel,' whispered the old man, trembling and shrinking as he spoke, 'Gabriel, do you hear a dripping of water – now slow, now quick again – on the floor at the foot of my bed?'

'I hear nothing, grandfather, but the crackling of the fire, and the roaring of the storm outside.'

'Drip, drip, drip! Faster and faster; plainer and plainer. Take the torch, Gabriel; look down on the floor – look with all your eyes. Is the place wet there? Is it the rain from heaven that is dropping through the roof?'

Gabriel took the torch with trembling fingers, and knelt down on the floor to examine it closely. He started back from the place, as he saw that it was quite dry – the torch dropped upon the hearth – he fell on his knees before the statue of the Virgin and hid his face.

'Is the floor wet? Answer me, I command you – Is the floor wet?' – asked the old man quickly and breathlessly.

Gabriel rose, went back to the bedside, and whispered to him that no drop of rain had fallen inside the cottage. As he spoke the words, he saw a change pass over his grandfather's face – the sharp features seemed to wither up on a sudden; the eager expression to grow vacant and death-like in an instant. The voice too altered; it was harsh and querulous no more; its tones became strangely soft, slow, and solemn, when the old man spoke again.

'I hear it still,' he said, 'drip! drip! faster and plainer than ever. That ghostly dropping of water is the last and the surest of the fatal signs which have told of your father's and your brother's deaths to-night, and I know from the place where I hear it – the foot of the bed I lie on – that it is a warning to me of my own approaching end. I am called where my son and my grandson have gone before me: my weary time in this world is over at last. Don't let Perrine and the children come in here, if they should awake – they are too young to look at death.'

Gabriel's blood curdled, when he heard these words – when he touched his grandfather's hand, and felt the chill that it struck to his own – when he listened to the raging wind, and knew that all help was miles and miles away from the cottage. Still, in spite of the storm, the darkness, and the distance, he thought not for a moment of neglecting the duty that had been taught him from his childhood – the duty of summoning the priest to the bedside of the dying. 'I must call Perrine,' he said, 'to watch by you while I am away.'

'Stop!' cried the old man, 'Stop, Gabriel; I implore, I command you not to leave me!'

'The priest, grandfather – your confession—'

'It must be made to you. In this darkness and this hurricane no man can keep the path across the heath. Gabriel! I am dying – I should be dead before you got back, Gabriel! For the love of the Blessed Virgin, stop here with me till I die – my time is short – I have a terrible secret that I must tell to somebody before I draw my last breath! Your ear to my mouth – quick! quick!'

As he spoke the last words, a slight noise was audible on the other side of the partition, the door half opened, and Perrine appeared at it, looking affrightedly into the room. The vigilant eyes of the old man – suspicious even in death – caught sight of her directly.

'Go back!' he exclaimed faintly, before she could utter a word, 'go back – push her back, Gabriel, and nail down the latch in the door, if she won't shut it of herself!'

'Dear Perrine! go in again,' implored Gabriel. 'Go in and keep the children from disturbing us. You will only make him worse – you can be of no use here!'

She obeyed without speaking, and shut the door again.

While the old man clutched him by the arm, and repeated, 'Quick! quick! – your ear close to my mouth,' Gabriel heard her say to the children (who were both awake), 'Let us pray for grandfather.' And as he knelt down by the bedside, there stole on his ear the sweet, childish tones of his little sisters, and the soft, subdued voice of the young girl who was teaching them the prayer, mingling divinely with the solemn wailing of wind and sea, rising in a still and awful purity over the hoarse, gasping whispers of the dying man.

'I took an oath not to tell it, Gabriel – lean down closer! I'm weak, and they mustn't hear a word in that room – I took an oath not to tell it; but death is a warrant to all men for breaking such an oath as that. Listen; don't lose a word I'm saying! Don't look away into the room: the stain of blood-guilt has defiled it for ever! – Hush! Hush! Hush! Let me speak. Now your father's dead, I can't carry the horrid secret with me into the grave. Just remember, Gabriel – try if you can't remember the time before I was bedridden – ten years ago and more – it was about six weeks, you know, before your mother's death; you can remember it by that. You and all the children were in that room with your mother; you were all asleep, I think; it was night, not very late – only nine o'clock. Your father and I were standing at the door, looking out at the heath in the moonlight. He was so poor at that time, he had been obliged to sell his own boat, and none of the neighbours would take him out fishing with them – your father wasn't liked by any of the neighbours. Well; we saw a stranger coming towards us; a very young man, with a knapsack on his back. He looked like a gentleman, though he was but poorly dressed. He came up, and told us he was dead tired, and didn't think he could reach the town that night, and asked if we would give him shelter till morning. And your father said yes, if he would make no noise, because the wife was ill, and the children were asleep. So he said all he wanted was to go to sleep himself before the fire. We had nothing to give him but black bread. He had better food with him than that, and undid his knapsack to get at it – and – and Gabriel! I'm sinking – drink! something to drink – I'm parched with thirst.'

Silent and deadly pale, Gabriel poured some of the cider from the pitcher on the table into a drinking-cup, and gave it to the old man. Slight as the stimulant was, its effect on him was almost instantaneous. His dull eyes brightened a little, and he went on in the same whispering tones as before.

'He pulled the food out of his knapsack rather in a hurry, so that some of the other small things in it fell on the floor. Among these was a pocket-book, which your father picked up and gave him back; and he put it in his coat-pocket – there was a tear in one of the sides of the book, and through the hole some bank-notes bulged out. I saw them, and so did your father (don't move away, Gabriel; keep close, there's nothing in me to shrink from). Well, he shared his food, like an honest fellow, with us; and then put his hand in his pocket, and gave me four or five livres, and then lay down before the fire to go to sleep. As he shut his eyes, your father looked at me in a way I didn't like. He'd been behaving very bitterly and desperately towards us for some time past; being soured about poverty, and your mother's illness, and the constant crying out of you children for more to eat. So when he told me to go and buy some wood, some bread, and some wine with the money I had got, I didn't like, somehow, to leave him alone with the stranger; and so made excuses, saying (which was true) that it was too late to buy things in the village that night. But he told me in a rage to go and do as he bid me, and knock the people up if the shop was shut. So I went out, being dreadfully afraid of your father – as indeed we all were at that time – but I couldn't make up my mind to go far from the house: I was afraid of something happening, though I didn't dare to think what. I don't know how it was; but I stole back in about ten minutes on tip-toe to the cottage; and looked in at the window; and saw – O! God forgive him! O, God forgive me! – I saw – I – more to drink, Gabriel! I can't speak again – more to drink!'

The voices in the next room had ceased; but in the minute of silence which now ensued, Gabriel heard his sisters kissing Perrine, and wishing her good night. They were all three trying to go to sleep again.

'Gabriel, pray yourself, and teach your children after you to pray, that your father may find forgiveness where he is now gone. I saw him as plainly as I now see you, kneeling with his knife in one hand over the sleeping man. He was taking the little book with the notes in it out of the stranger's pocket. He got the book into his possession, and held it quite still in his hand for an instant, thinking. I believe – oh, no! no! – I'm sure he was repenting; I'm sure he was going to put the book back; but just at that moment the stranger moved, and raised one of his arms, as if he was waking up. Then, the temptation of the devil grew too strong for your father – I saw him lift the hand with the knife in it – but saw nothing more. I couldn't look in at the window – I couldn't move away – I couldn't cry out; I stood with my back turned towards the house, shivering all over, though it was a warm summer-time, and hearing no cries, no noises at all, from the room behind me. I was too frightened to know how long it was before the opening of the cottage-door made me turn round; but when I did, I saw your father standing before me in the yellow moonlight, carrying in his arms the bleeding body of the poor lad who had shared his food with us and slept on our hearth. Hush! hush! Don't groan and sob in that way! Stifle it with the bed-clothes. Hush! you'll wake them in the next room!'

'Gabriel – Gabriel!' exclaimed a voice from behind the partition. 'What has happened? Gabriel! let me come out and be with you?'

'No! no!' cried the old man, collecting the last remains of his strength in the attempt to speak above the wind, which was just then howling at the loudest; 'stay where you are – don't speak – don't come out, I command you! – Gabriel' (his voice dropped to a faint whisper), 'raise me up in bed – you must hear the whole of it, now – raise me; I'm choking so that I can hardly speak. Keep close and listen – I can't say much more. Where was I? – Ah, your father! He threatened to kill me if I didn't swear to keep it secret; and in terror of my life I swore. He made me help him to carry the body – we took it all across the heath – oh! horrible, horrible, under the bright moon – (lift me higher, Gabriel). You know the great stones yonder, set up by the heathens; you know the hollow place under the stones they call "The Merchant's Table" – we had plenty of room to lay him in that, and hide him so; and then we ran back to the cottage. I never dared go near the place afterwards; no, nor your father either! (Higher, Gabriel! I'm choking again.) We burnt the pocket-book and the knapsack – never knew his name – we kept the money to spend. (You're not lifting me! you're not listening close enough!) Your father said it was a legacy, when you and your mother asked about the money. (You hurt me, you shake me to pieces, Gabriel, when you sob like that.) It brought a curse on us, the money; the curse has drowned your father and your brother; the curse is killing me; but I've confessed – tell the priest I confessed before I died. Stop her; stop Perrine! I hear her getting up. Take his bones away from The Merchant's Table, and bury them for the love of God! – and tell the priest – (lift me higher: lift me till I'm on my knees) – if your father was alive, he'd murder me – but tell the priest – because of my guilty soul – to pray – and – remember The Merchant's Table – to bury, and to pray – to pray always for—'

As long as Perrine heard faintly the whispering of the old man – though no word that he said reached her ear – she shrank from opening the door in the partition. But, when the whispering sounds – which terrified her she knew not how or why – first faltered, then ceased altogether; when she heard the sobs that followed them; and when her heart told her who was weeping in the next room – then, she began to be influenced by a new feeling which was stronger than the strongest fear, and she opened the door without hesitating – almost without trembling.

The coverlid was drawn up over the old man; Gabriel was kneeling by the bedside, with his face hidden. When she spoke to him, he neither answered nor looked at her. After a while, the sobs that shook him ceased; but still he never moved – except once when she touched him, and then he shuddered – shuddered under *her* hand! She called in his little sisters, and they spoke to him, and still he uttered no word in reply. They wept. One by one, often and often, they entreated him with loving words; but the stupor of grief which held him speechless and motionless was beyond the power of human tears, stronger even then the strength of human love.

It was near daybreak, and the storm was lulling – but still no change occurred at the bedside. Once or twice, as Perrine knelt near Gabriel, still vainly endeavouring to arouse him to a sense of her presence, she thought she heard the old man breathing feebly, and stretched out her hand towards the coverlid; but she could not summon courage to touch him or to look at him. This was the first time she had ever been present at a deathbed; the stillness in the room, the stupor of despair that had seized on Gabriel, so horrified her, that she was almost as helpless as the two children by her side. It was not till the dawn looked in at the cottage-window – so coldly, so drearily, and yet so reassuringly – that she began to recover her self-possession at all. Then she knew that her best resource would be to summon assistance immediately from the nearest house. While she was trying to persuade the two children to remain alone in the cottage with Gabriel during her temporary absence, she was startled by the sound of footsteps outside the door. It opened; and a man appeared on the threshold, standing still there for a moment in the dim uncertain light.

She looked closer – looked intently at him. It was François Sarzeau himself!

II

The fisherman was dripping with wet; but his face – always pale and inflexible – seemed to be but little altered in expression by the perils through which he must have passed during the night. Young Pierre lay almost insensible in his arms. In the astonishment and fright of the first moment, Perrine screamed as she recognised him.

'There! there! there!' he said, peevishly, advancing straight to the hearth with his burden; 'don't make a noise. You never expected to see us alive again, I dare say. We gave ourselves up as lost, and only escaped after all by a miracle.'

He laid the boy down where he could get the full warmth of the fire; and then, turning round, took a wicker-covered bottle from his pocket, and said, 'If it hadn't been for the brandy! –' He stopped suddenly – started – put down the bottle on the bench near him – and advanced quickly to the bedside.

Perrine looked after him as he went; and saw Gabriel, who had risen when the door was opened, moving back from the bed as François approached. The young man's face seemed to have been suddenly struck to stone – its blank ghastly whiteness was awful to look at. He moved slowly backward and backward till he came to the cottage-wall – then stood quite still, staring on his father with wild vacant eyes, moving his hands to and fro before him, muttering, but never pronouncing one audible word.

François did not appear to notice his son; he had the coverlid of the bed in his hand.

'Anything the matter here?' he asked, as he drew it down.

Still Gabriel could not speak. Perrine saw it, and answered for him.

'Gabriel is afraid that his poor grandfather is dead,' she whispered nervously.

'Dead!' There was no sorrow in the tone as he echoed the word. 'Was he very bad in the night before his death happened? Did he wander in his mind? He has been rather light-headed lately.'

'He was very restless, and spoke of the ghostly warnings that we all know of: he said he saw and heard many things which told him from the other world that you and Pierre – Gabriel!' she screamed, suddenly interrupting herself. 'Look at him! Look at his face! Your grandfather is not dead!'

At that moment, François was raising his father's head to look closely at him. A faint spasm had indeed passed over the deathly face; the lips quivered, the jaw dropped. François shuddered as he looked, and moved away hastily from the bed. At the same instant Gabriel started from the wall: his expression altered, his pale cheeks flushed suddenly, as he snatched up the wicker-cased bottle, and poured all the little brandy that was left in it down his grandfather's throat.

The effect was nearly instantaneous; the sinking vital forces rallied desperately. The old man's eyes opened again, wandered round the room, then fixed themselves intently on François, as he stood near the fire. Trying and terrible as his position was at that moment, Gabriel still retained self-possession enough to whisper a few words in Perrine's ear. 'Go back again into the bedroom, and take the children with you,' he said. 'We may have something to speak about which you had better not hear.'

'Son Gabriel, your grandfather is trembling all over,' said François. 'If he is dying at all, he is dying of cold: help me to lift him, bed and all, to the hearth.'

'No, no! don't let him touch me!' gasped the old man. 'Don't let him look at me in that way! Don't let him come near me, Gabriel! Is it his ghost? or is it himself?'

As Gabriel answered, he heard a knocking at the door. His father opened it; and disclosed to view some people from the neighbouring fishing-village, who had come – more out of curiosity than sympathy – to inquire whether François and the boy Pierre had survived the night. Without asking any one to enter, the fisherman surlily and shortly answered the various questions addressed to him, standing in his own doorway. While he was thus engaged, Gabriel heard his grandfather muttering vacantly to himself – 'Last night – how about last night, grandson? What was I talking about last night? Did I say your father was drowned? Very foolish to say he was drowned, and then see him come back alive again! But it wasn't that – I'm so weak in my head, I can't remember! What was it, Gabriel? Something too horrible to speak of? Is that what you're whispering and trembling about? I said nothing horrible. A crime? Bloodshed? I know nothing of any crime or bloodshed here – I must have been frightened out of my wits to talk in that way! The Merchant's Table? Only a big heap of old stones! What with the storm, and thinking I was going to die, and being afraid about your father, I must have been light-headed. Don't give another thought to that nonsense, Gabriel! I'm better now. We shall all live to laugh at poor grandfather for talking nonsense about crime and bloodshed in his sleep. Ah! poor old man – last night – light-headed – fancies and nonsense of an old man – why don't you laugh at it? I'm laughing – so light-headed – so light— !'

He stopped suddenly. A low cry, partly of terror and partly of pain, escaped him; the look of pining anxiety and imbecile cunning which had distorted his face while he had been speaking, faded from it for ever. He shivered a little – breathed heavily once or twice – then became quite still.

Had he died with a falsehood on his lips?

Gabriel looked round and saw that the cottage-door was closed, and that his father was standing against it. How long he had occupied that position, how many of the old man's last words he had heard, it was impossible to conjecture, but there was a lowering suspicion in his harsh face as he now looked away from the corpse to his son, which made Gabriel shudder; and the first question that he asked, on once more approaching the bedside, was expressed in tones which, quiet as they were, had a fearful meaning in them.

'What did your grandfather talk about last night?' he asked.

Gabriel did not answer. All that he had heard, all that he had seen, all the misery and horror that might yet be to come, had stunned his mind. The unspeakable dangers of his present position were too tremendous to be realized. He could only feel them vaguely in the weary torpor that oppressed his heart: while in every other direction the use of his faculties, physical and mental, seemed to have suddenly and totally abandoned him.

'Is your tongue wounded, son Gabriel, as well as your arm?' his father went on with a bitter laugh. 'I come back to you, saved by a miracle; and you never speak to me. Would you rather I had died than the old man there? He can't hear you now – why shouldn't you tell me what nonsense he was talking last night? – You won't? I say you shall!' (He crossed the room and put his back to the door.) 'Before either of us leave this place, you shall confess it! You know that my duty to the Church bids me to go at once and tell the priest of your grandfather's death. If I leave that duty unfulfilled, remember it is through your fault! *You* keep me here – for here I stop till I am obeyed. Do you hear that, idiot? Speak! Speak instantly, or you shall repent it to the day of your death! I ask again – what did your grandfather say to you when he was wandering in his mind, last night?'

'He spoke of a crime, committed by another, and guiltily kept secret by him,' answered Gabriel slowly and sternly. 'And this morning he denied his own words with his last living breath. But last night, if he spoke the truth—'

'The truth!' echoed François. 'What truth?'

He stopped, his eyes fell, then turned towards the corpse. For a few minutes he stood steadily contemplating it; breathing quickly, and drawing his hand several times across his forehead. Then he faced his son once more. In that short interval he had become in outward appearance a changed man: expression, voice, and manner, all were altered.

'Heaven forgive me!' he went on, 'but I could almost laugh at myself, at this solemn moment, for having spoken and acted just now so much like a fool! Denied his words, did he? Poor old man! they say sense often comes back to light-headed people just before death; and he is a proof of it. The fact is, Gabriel, my own wits must have been a little shaken – and no wonder – by what I went through last night and what I have come home to this morning.

As if you, or anybody, could ever really give serious credit to the wandering speeches of a dying old man! (Where is Perrine? Why did you send her away?) I don't wonder at your still looking a little startled, and feeling low in your mind, and all that – for you've had a trying night of it; trying in every way. He must have been a good deal shaken in his wits last night, between fears about himself and fears about me. (To think of my being angry with you, Gabriel, for being a little alarmed – very naturally – by an old man's queer fancies!) Come out, Perrine – come out of the bedroom whenever you are tired of it: you must learn sooner or later to look at death calmly. Shake hands, Gabriel; and let us make it up, and say no more about what has passed. You won't? Still angry with me for what I said to you just now? – Ah! you'll think better about it by the time I return. Come out, Perrine, we've no secrets here.'

'Where are you going to?' asked Gabriel, as he saw his father hastily open the door.

'To tell the priest that one of his congregation is dead, and to have the death registered,' answered François. 'These are *my* duties, and must be performed before I take any rest.'

He went out hurriedly as he said these words. Gabriel almost trembled at himself, when he found that he breathed more freely, that he felt less horribly oppressed both in mind and body, the moment his father's back was turned. Fearful as thought was now, it was still a change for the better to be capable of thinking at all. Was the behaviour of his father compatible with innocence? Could the old man's confused denial of his own words in the morning and in the presence of his son, be set for one instant against the circumstantial confession that he had made during the night alone with his grandson? These were the terrible questions which Gabriel now asked himself; and which he shrank involuntarily from answering. And yet that doubt, the solution of which would one way or the other irrevocably affect the whole future of his life, must sooner or later be solved at any hazard!

Was there any way of setting it at rest? Yes, one way: to go instantly while his father was absent, and examine the hollow place under the Merchant's Table. If his grandfather's confession had really been made while he was in possession of his senses, this place (which Gabriel knew to be covered in from wind and weather) had never been visited since the commission of the crime by the perpetrator, or by his unwilling accomplice: though time had destroyed all besides, the hair and the bones of the victim would still be left to bear witness to the truth – if truth had indeed been spoken. As this conviction grew on him, the young man's cheek paled; and he stopped irresolute half-way between the hearth and the door. Then he looked down doubtfully at the corpse on the bed; and then there came upon him suddenly a revulsion of feeling. A wild feverish impatience to know the worst without another instant of delay possessed him. Only telling Perrine that he should be back soon, and that she must watch by the dead in his absence, he left the cottage at once, without waiting to hear her reply, even without looking back as he closed the door behind him.

There were two tracks to the Merchant's Table. One, the longer of the two, by the coast cliffs; the other across the heath. But this latter path was also, for some little distance, the path which led to the village and the church. He was afraid of attracting his father's attention here, so he took the direction of the coast. At one spot the track trended inland, winding round some of the many Druid monuments scattered over the country. This place was on high ground, and commanded a view, at no great distance, of the path leading to the village, just where it branched off from the heathy ridge which ran in the direction of the Merchant's Table. Here Gabriel descried the figure of a man standing with his back towards the coast.

This figure was too far off to be identified with absolute certainty, but it looked like, and might well be, François Sarzeau. Whoever he was, the man was evidently uncertain which way he should proceed. When he moved forward, it was first to advance several paces towards the Merchant's Table – then he went back again towards the distant cottages and the church. Twice he hesitated thus: the second time pausing long before he appeared finally to take the way that led to the village.

Leaving the post of observation among the stones, at which he had instinctively halted for some minutes past, Gabriel now proceeded on his own path. Could this man really be his father? And if it were so, why did François Sarzeau only determine to go to the village where his business lay, after having twice vainly attempted to persevere in taking the exactly opposite direction of the Merchant's Table? Did he really desire to go there? Had he heard the name mentioned, when the old man referred to it in his dying words? And had he failed to summon courage enough to make all safe by removing – ? This last question was too horrible to be pursued: Gabriel stifled it affrightedly in his own heart as he went on.

He reached the great Druid monument without meeting a living soul on his way. The sun was rising, and the mighty storm-clouds of the night were parting asunder wildly over the whole eastward horizon. The waves still leapt and foamed gloriously: but the gale had sunk to a keen fresh breeze. As Gabriel looked up, and saw how brightly the promise of a lovely day was written in the heavens, he trembled as he thought of the search which he was now about to make. The sight of the fair fresh sunrise jarred horribly with the suspicions of committed murder that were rankling foully in his heart. But he knew that his errand must be performed, and he nerved himself to go through with it; for he dared not return to the cottage until the mystery had been cleared up at once and for ever.

The Merchant's Table was formed by two huge stones resting horizontally on three others. In the troubled times of more than half a century ago, regular tourists were unknown among the Druid monuments of Brittany; and the entrance to the hollow place under the stones – since often visited by strangers – was at this time nearly choked up by brambles and weeds. Gabriel's first look at this tangled nook of briars convinced him that the place had not been entered – perhaps for years – by any living being. Without allowing himself to hesitate (for he felt that the slightest delay might be fatal to his resolution), he passed as gently as possible through the brambles, and knelt down at the low, dusky, irregular entrance of the hollow place under the stones.

His heart throbbed violently, his breath almost failed him; but he forced himself to crawl a few feet into the cavity, and then groped with his hand on the ground about him.

He touched something! Something which it made his flesh creep to handle; something which he would fain have dropped, but which he grasped tight in spite of himself. He drew back into the outer air and sunshine. Was it a human bone? No! he had been the dupe of his own morbid terror – he had only taken up a fragment of dried wood!

Feeling shame at such self-deception as this, he was about to throw the wood from him before he re-entered the place, when another idea occurred to him.

Though it was dimly lighted through one or two chinks in the stones, the far part of the interior of the cavity was still too dusky to admit of perfect examination by the eye, even on a bright sunshiny morning. Observing this, he took out the tinderbox and matches, which – like the other inhabitants of the district – he always carried about with him for the purpose of lighting his pipe, determining to use the piece of wood as a torch which might illuminate the darkest corner of the place when he next entered it. Fortunately the wood had remained so long and had been preserved so dry in its sheltered position, that it caught fire almost as easily as a piece of paper. The moment it was fairly aflame Gabriel went into the cavity – penetrating at once – this time – to its farthest extremity.

He remained among the stones long enough for the wood to burn down nearly to his hand. When he came out, and flung the burning fragment from him, his face was flushed deeply, his eyes sparkled. He leaped carelessly on to the heath, over the bushes through which he had threaded his way so warily but a few minutes before, exclaiming, 'I may marry Perrine with a clear conscience now – I am the son of as honest a man as there is in Brittany!'

He had closely examined the cavity in every corner, and not the slightest sign that any dead body had ever been laid there was visible in the hollow place under the Merchant's Table.

III

'I may marry Perrine with a clear conscience now!'

There are some parts of the world where it would be drawing no natural picture of human nature to represent a son as believing conscientiously that an offence against life and the laws of hospitality, secretly committed by his father, rendered him, though innocent of all participation in it, unworthy to fulfil his engagement with his affianced wife. Among the simple inhabitants of Gabriel's province, however, such acuteness of conscientious sensibility as this was no extraordinary exception to all general rules. Ignorant and superstitious as they might be, the people of Brittany practised the duties of hospitality as devoutly as they practised the duties of the national religion. The presence of the stranger-guest, rich or poor, was a sacred presence at their hearths. His safety was their especial charge – his property their especial responsibility. They might be half-starved, but they were ready to share the last crust with him nevertheless, as they would share it with their own children.

Any outrage on the virtue of hospitality, thus born and bred in the people, was viewed by them with universal disgust, and punished with universal execration. This ignominy was uppermost in Gabriel's thoughts by the side of his grandfather's bed; the dread of this worst dishonour, which there was no wiping out, held him speechless before Perrine, shamed and horrified him so that he felt unworthy to look her in the face; and when the result of his search at the Merchant's Table proved the absence there of all evidence of the crime spoken of by the old man, the blessed relief, the absorbing triumph of that discovery, was expressed entirely in the one thought which had prompted his first joyful words: He could marry Perrine with a clear conscience, for he was the son of an honest man!

When he returned to the cottage, François had not come back. Perrine was astonished at the change in Gabriel's manner; even Pierre and the children remarked it. Rest and warmth had by this time so far recovered the younger brother, that he was able to give some account of the perilous adventures of the night at sea. They were still listening to the boy's narrative when François at last returned. It was now Gabriel who held out his hand, and made the first advances towards reconciliation.

To his utter amazement, his father recoiled from him. The variable temper of François had evidently changed completely during his absence at the village. A settled scowl of distrust darkened his face as he looked at his son.

'I never shake hands with people who have once doubted me,' he exclaimed loudly and irritably; 'for I always doubt them for ever after. You are a bad son! You have suspected your father of some infamy that you dare not openly charge him with, on no other testimony than the rambling nonsense of a half-witted, dying old man. Don't speak to me! I won't hear you! An innocent man and a spy are bad company. Go and denounce me, you Judas in disguise! I don't care for your secret or for you. What's that girl Perrine doing here still? Why hasn't she gone home long ago? The priest's coming; we don't want strangers in the house of death. Take her back to the farm-house, and stop there with her, if you like: nobody wants you here!'

There was something in the manner and look of the speaker as he uttered these words, so strange, so sinister, so indescribably suggestive of his meaning much more than he said, that Gabriel felt his heart sink within him instantly; and almost at the same moment this fearful question forced itself irresistibly on his mind – might not his father have followed him to the Merchant's Table?

Even if he had been desired to speak, he could not have spoken now, while that question and the suspicion that it brought with it were utterly destroying all the reassuring hopes and convictions of the morning. The mental suffering produced by the sudden change from pleasure to pain in all his thoughts, reacted on him physically. He felt as if he were stifling in the air of the cottage, in the presence of his father; and when Perrine hurried on her walking attire, and with a face which alternately flushed and turned pale with every moment, approached the door, he went out with her as hastily as if he had been flying from his home. Never had the fresh air and the free daylight felt like heavenly and guardian influences to him until now!

He could comfort Perrine under his father's harshness, he could assure her of his own affection which no earthly influence could change, while they walked together towards the farm-house; but he could do no more. He durst not confide to her the subject that was uppermost in his mind: of all human beings she was the last to whom he could reveal the terrible secret that was festering at his heart. As soon as they got within sight of the farm-house, Gabriel stopped; and, promising to see her again soon, took leave of Perrine with assumed ease in his manner and with real despair in his heart. Whatever the poor girl might think of it, he felt, at that moment, that he had not courage to face her father, and hear him talk happily and pleasantly, as his custom was, of Perrine's approaching marriage.

Left to himself, Gabriel wandered hither and thither over the open heath, neither knowing nor caring in what direction he turned his steps. The doubts about his father's innocence which had been dissipated by his visit to the Merchant's Table, that father's own language and manner had now revived – had even confirmed, though he dared not yet acknowledge so much to himself. It was terrible enough to be obliged to admit that the result of his morning's search was, after all, not conclusive – that the mystery was in very truth not yet cleared up. The violence of his father's last words of distrust; the extraordinary and indescribable changes in his father's manner while uttering them – what did these things mean? Guilt or innocence? Again, was it any longer reasonable to doubt the deathbed confession made by his grandfather? Was it not, on the contrary, far more probable that the old man's denial in the morning of his own words at night had been made under the influence of a panic terror, when his moral consciousness was bewildered, and his intellectual faculties were sinking? – The longer Gabriel thought of these questions, the less competent – possibly also the less willing – he felt to answer them. Should he seek advice from others wiser than he? No: not while the thousandth part of a chance remained that his father was innocent.

This thought was still in his mind, when he found himself once more in sight of his home. He was still hesitating near the door, when he saw it opened cautiously. His brother Pierre looked out, and then came running towards him. 'Come in, Gabriel; oh, do come in!' said the boy earnestly. 'We are afraid to be alone with father. He's been beating us for talking of you.'

Gabriel went in. His father looked up from the hearth where he was sitting, muttered the word 'Spy!' and made a gesture of contempt – but did not address a word directly to his son. The hours passed on in silence; afternoon waned into evening, and evening into night; and still he never spoke to any of his children. Soon after it was dark, he went out, and took his net with him – saying that it was better to be alone on the sea than in the house with a spy.

When he returned the next morning, there was no change in him. Days passed – weeks, months even elapsed, and still, though his manner insensibly became what it used to be towards his other children, it never altered towards his eldest son. At the rare periods when they now met, except when absolutely obliged to speak, he preserved total silence in his intercourse with Gabriel. He would never take Gabriel out with him in the boat; he would never sit alone with Gabriel in the house; he would never eat a meal with Gabriel; he would never let the other children talk to him about Gabriel; and he would never hear a word in expostulation, a word in reference to anything his dead father had said or done on the night of the storm, from Gabriel himself.

The young man pined and changed so that even Perrine hardly knew him again, under this cruel system of domestic excommunication; under the wearing influence of the one unchanging doubt which never left him; and, more than all, under the incessant reproaches of his own conscience, aroused by the sense that he was evading a responsibility which it was his solemn, his immediate duty to undertake. But no sting of conscience, no ill-treatment at home, and no self-reproaches for failing in his duty of confession as a good Catholic, were powerful enough in their influence over Gabriel to make him disclose the secret, under the oppression of which his very life was wasting away. He knew that if he once revealed it, whether his father was ultimately proved to be guilty or innocent, there would remain a slur and a suspicion on the family, and on Perrine besides, from her approaching connexion with it, which in their time and in their generation could never be removed. The reproach of the world is terrible even in the crowded city, where many of the dwellers in our abiding-place are strangers to us – but it is far more terrible in the country, where none near us are strangers, where all talk of us and know of us, where nothing intervenes between us and the tyranny of the evil tongue. Gabriel had not courage to face this, and dare the fearful chance of lifelong ignominy – no, not even to serve the sacred interests of justice, of atonement, and of truth.

IV

While Gabriel still remained prostrated under the affliction that was wasting his energies of body and mind, Brittany was visited by a great public calamity, in which all private misfortunes were overwhelmed for a while.

It was now the time when the ever-gathering storm of the French Revolution had risen to its hurricane climax. Those chiefs of the new republic were in power, whose last, worst madness it was to decree the extinction of religion and the overthrow of everything that outwardly symbolized it throughout the whole of the country that they governed. Already this decree had been executed to the letter in and around Paris; and now the soldiers of the republic were on their way to Brittany, headed by commanders whose commission was to root out the Christian religion in the last and the surest of the strongholds still left to it in France.

These men began their work in a spirit worthy of the worst of their superiors who had sent them to do it. They gutted churches, they demolished chapels, they overthrew roadside crosses wherever they found them. The terrible guillotine devoured human lives in the villages of Brittany, as it had devoured them in the streets of Paris; the musket and the sword, in highway and byway, wreaked havoc on the people – even on women and children kneeling in the act of prayer; the priests were tracked night and day from one hiding-place where they still offered up worship to another, and were killed as soon as overtaken – every atrocity was committed in every district; but the Christian religion still spread wider than the widest bloodshed; still sprang up with ever-renewed vitality from under the very feet of the men whose vain fury was powerless to trample it down. Everywhere the people remained true to their Faith; everywhere the priests stood firm by them in their sorest need. The executioners of the republic had been sent to make Brittany a country of apostates: they did their worst, and left it a country of martyrs.

One evening while this frightful persecution was still raging, Gabriel happened to be detained unusually late at the cottage of Perrine's father. He had lately spent much of his time at the farm-house: it was his only refuge now from that place of suffering, of silence, and of secret shame, which he had once called home! Just as he had taken leave of Perrine for the night, and was about to open the farm-house door, her father stopped him, and pointed to a chair in the chimney-corner. 'Leave us alone, my dear,' said the old man to his daughter; 'I want to speak to Gabriel. You can go to your mother in the next room.'

The words which Père Bonan – as he was called by the neighbours – had now to say in private, were destined to lead to very unexpected events. After referring to the alteration which had appeared of late in Gabriel's manner, the old man began by asking him, sorrowfully but not suspiciously, whether he still preserved his old affection for Perrine. On receiving an eager answer in the affirmative, Père Bonan then referred to the persecution still raging through the country, and to the consequent possibility that he, like others of his countrymen, might yet be called to suffer and perhaps to die for the cause of his religion. If this last act of self-sacrifice were required of him, Perrine would be left unprotected, unless her affianced husband performed his promise to her, and assumed, without delay, the position of her lawful guardian. 'Let me know that you will do this,' concluded the old man. 'I shall be resigned to all that may be required of me, if I can only know that I shall not die leaving Perrine unprotected.' Gabriel gave the promise – gave it with his whole heart. As he took leave of Père Bonan, the old man said to him:

'Come here to-morrow; I shall know more then than I know now – I shall be able to fix with certainty the day for the fulfilment of your engagement with Perrine.'

Why did Gabriel hesitate at the farm-house door, looking back on Père Bonan as though he would fain say something, and yet not speaking a word? Why, after he had gone out and had walked onward several paces, did he suddenly stop, return quickly to the farm-house, stand irresolute before the gate, and then retrace his steps sighing heavily as he went, but never pausing again on his homeward way? Because the torment of his horrible secret had grown harder to bear than ever, since he had given the promise that had been required of him. Because, while a strong impulse moved him frankly to lay bare his hidden dread and doubt to the father whose beloved daughter was soon to be his wife, there was a yet stronger passive influence which paralyzed on his lips the terrible confession that he knew not whether he was the son of an honest man, or the son of an assassin and a robber. Made desperate by his situation, he determined, while he hastened homeward, to risk the worst and ask that fatal question of his father in plain words. But this supreme trial for parent and child was not to be. When he entered the cottage, François was absent. He had told the younger children that he should not be home again before noon on the next day.

Early in the morning Gabriel repaired to the farm-house, as he had been bidden. Influenced by his love for Perrine, blindly confiding in the faint hope (which in despite of heart and conscience he still forced himself to cherish) that his father might be innocent, he now preserved the appearance at least of perfect calmness. 'If I tell my secret to Perrine's father, I risk disturbing in him that confidence in the future safety of his child, for which I am his present and only warrant' – Something like this thought was in Gabriel's mind, as he took the hand of Père Bonan, and waited anxiously to hear what was required of him on that day.

'We have a short respite from danger, Gabriel,' said the old man. 'News has come to me that the spoilers of our churches and the murderers of our congregations, have been stopped on their way hitherward by tidings which have reached them from another district. This interval of peace and safety will be a short one – we must take advantage of it while it is yet ours. My name is among the names on the list of the denounced. If the soldiers of the Republic find me here! – but we will say nothing more of this: it is of Perrine and of you that I must now speak. On this very evening, your marriage may be solemnized with all the wonted rites of our holy religion, and the blessing may be pronounced over you by the lips of a priest. This evening, therefore, Gabriel, you must become the husband and the protector of Perrine. Listen to me attentively, and I will tell you how.'

This was the substance of what Gabriel now heard from Père Bonan:

Not very long before the persecutions broke out in Brittany, a priest, known generally by the name of Father Paul, was appointed to a curacy in one of the northern districts of the province. He fulfilled all the duties of his station in such a manner as to win the confidence and affection of every member of his congregation, and was often spoken of with respect, even in parts of the country distant from the scene of his labours. It was not, however, until the troubles broke out, and the destruction and bloodshed began, that he became renowned far and wide, from one end of Brittany to another. From the date of the very first persecutions the name of Father Paul was a rallying cry of the hunted peasantry; he was their great encouragement under oppression, their example in danger, their last and only consoler in the hour of death. Wherever havoc and ruin raged most fiercely, wherever the pursuit was hottest and the slaughter most cruel, there the intrepid priest was sure to be seen pursuing his sacred duties in defiance of every peril. His hairbreadth escapes from death; his extraordinary re-appearances in parts of the country where no one ever expected to see him again, were regarded by the poorer classes with superstitious awe. Wherever Father Paul appeared, with his black dress, his calm face, and the ivory crucifix which he always carried in his hand, the people reverenced him as more than mortal; and grew at last to believe that, single-handed, he would successfully defend his religion against the armies of the republic. But their simple confidence in his powers of resistance was soon destined to be shaken. Fresh reinforcements arrived in Brittany, and overran the whole province from one end to the other. One morning, after celebrating service in a dismantled church, and after narrowly escaping with his life from those who pursued him, the priest disappeared. Secret inquiries were made after him in all directions; but he was heard of no more.

Many weary days had passed, and the dispirited peasantry had already mourned him as dead, when some fishermen on the northern coast observed a ship of light burden in the offing, making signals to the shore. They put off to her in their boats; and on reaching the deck saw standing before them the well-remembered figure of Father Paul.

The priest had returned to his congregations; and had founded the new altar that they were to worship at on the deck of a ship! Razed from the face of the earth, their church had not been destroyed – for Father Paul and the priests who acted with him had given that church a refuge on the sea. Henceforth, their children could still be baptized, their sons and daughters could still be married, the burial of their dead could still be solemnized, under the sanction of the old religion for which, not vainly, they had suffered so patiently and so long.

Throughout the remaining time of trouble, the services were uninterrupted on board the ship. A code of signals was established by which those on shore were always enabled to direct their brethren

at sea towards such parts of the coast as happened to be uninfested
by the enemies of their worship. On the morning of Gabriel's visit to
the farmhouse, these signals had shaped the course of the ship towards
the extremity of the peninsula of Quiberon. The people of the district
were all prepared to expect the appearance of the vessel some time in
the evening, and had their boats ready at a moment's notice to put off
and attend the service. At the conclusion of this service Père Bonan
had arranged that the marriage of his daughter and Gabriel was to
take place.

They waited for evening at the farm-house. A little before sunset the ship was
signalled as in sight; and then Père Bonan and his wife, followed by Gabriel
and Perrine, set forth over the heath to the beach. With the solitary exception
of François Sarzeau, the whole population of the neighbourhood was already
assembled there; Gabriel's brother and sisters being among the number.

It was the calmest evening that had been known for months. There was not
a cloud in the lustrous sky – not a ripple on the still surface of the sea. The
smallest children were suffered by their mothers to stray down on the beach as
they pleased; for the waves of the great ocean slept as tenderly and noiselessly
on their sandy bed, as if they had been changed into the waters of an inland
lake. Slow, almost imperceptible, was the approach of the ship – there was
hardly a breath of wind to carry her on – she was just drifting gently with
the landward set of the tide at that hour, while her sails hung idly against
the masts. Long after the sun had gone down, the congregation still waited
and watched on the beach. The moon and stars were arrayed in their glory
of the night, before the ship dropped anchor. Then the muffled tolling of a bell
came solemnly across the quiet waters; and then, from every creek along the
shore, as far as the eye could reach, the black forms of the fishermen's boats
shot out swift and stealthy into the shining sea.

By the time the boats had arrived alongside of the ship, the lamp had been
kindled before the altar, and its flame was gleaming red and dull in the radiant
moonlight. Two of the priests on board were clothed in their robes of office,
and were waiting in their appointed places to begin the service. But there was
a third, dressed only in the ordinary attire of his calling, who mingled with the
congregation, and spoke a few words to each of the persons composing it, as,
one by one, they mounted the sides of the ship. Those who had never seen
him before knew by the famous ivory crucifix in his hand that the priest who
received them was Father Paul. Gabriel looked at this man, whom he now
beheld for the first time, with a mixture of astonishment and awe; for he saw
that the renowned chief of the Christians of Brittany was, to all appearance,
but little older than himself.

The expression on the pale calm face of the priest was so gentle and kind,
that children just able to walk tottered up to him, and held familiarly by
the skirts of his black gown, whenever his clear blue eyes rested on theirs,
while he beckoned them to his side. No one would ever have guessed from
the countenance of Father Paul what deadly perils he had confronted, but for
the scar of a sabre-wound, as yet hardly healed, which ran across his forehead.
That wound had been dealt while he was kneeling before the altar, in the last
church in Brittany which had escaped spoliation. He would have died where
he knelt, but for the peasants who were praying with him, and who, unarmed

as they were, threw themselves like tigers on the soldiery, and at awful sacrifice of their own lives saved the life of their priest. There was not a man now on board the ship who would have hesitated, had the occasion called for it again, to have rescued him in the same way.

The service began. Since the days when the primitive Christians worshipped amid the caverns of the earth, can any service be imagined nobler in itself, or sublimer in the circumstances surrounding it, than that which was now offered up? Here was no artificial pomp, no gaudy profusion of ornament, no attendant grandeur of man's creation. All around this church spread the hushed and awful majesty of the tranquil sea. The roof of this cathedral was the immeasurable heaven, the pure moon its one great light, the countless glories of the stars its only adornment. Here were no hired singers or rich priest-princes; no curious sight-seers, or careless lovers of sweet sounds. This congregation and they who had gathered it together, were all poor alike, all persecuted alike, all worshipping alike, to the overthrow of their worldly interests, and at the imminent peril of their lives. How brightly and tenderly the moonlight shone upon the altar and the people before it! – how solemnly and divinely the deep harmonies, as they chanted the penitential Psalms, mingled with the hoarse singing of the freshening night-breeze in the rigging of the ship! – how sweetly the still rushing murmur of many voices, as they uttered the responses together, now died away and now rose again softly into the mysterious night!

Of all the members of the congregation – young or old – there was but one over whom that impressive service exercised no influence of consolation or of peace: that one was Gabriel. Often, throughout the day, his reproaching conscience had spoken within him again and again. Often, when he joined the little assembly on the beach, he turned away his face in secret shame and apprehension from Perrine and her father. Vainly, after gaining the deck of the ship, did he try to meet the eye of Father Paul as frankly, as readily, and as affectionately as others met it. The burden of concealment seemed too heavy to be borne in the presence of the priest – and yet, torment as it was, he still bore it! But when he knelt with the rest of the congregation and saw Perrine kneeling by his side – when he felt the calmness of the solemn night and the still sea filling his heart – when the sounds of the first prayers spoke with a dread spiritual language of their own to his soul – then, the remembrance of the confession which he had neglected, and the terror of receiving unprepared the sacrament which he knew would be offered to him – grew too vivid to be endured: the sense that he merited no longer, though once worthy of it, the confidence in his perfect truth and candour placed in him by the woman with whom he was soon to stand before the altar, overwhelmed him with shame: the mere act of kneeling among that congregation, the passive accomplice by his silence and secrecy, for aught he knew to the contrary, of a crime which it was his bounden duty to denounce, appalled him as if he had already committed sacrilege that could never be forgiven. Tears flowed down his cheeks, though he strove to repress them: sobs burst from him, though he tried to stifle them. He knew that others besides Perrine were looking at him in astonishment and alarm; but he could neither control himself, nor move to leave his place, nor raise his eyes even – until suddenly he felt a hand laid on his shoulder. That touch, slight as it was, ran through him instantly. He looked up, and saw Father Paul standing by his side.

Beckoning him to follow, and signing to the congregation not to suspend their devotions, he led Gabriel out of the assembly – then paused for a moment, reflecting – then beckoning again, took him into the cabin of the ship, and closed the door carefully.

'You have something on your mind,' he said, simply and quietly, taking the young man by the hand. 'I may be able to relieve you, if you tell me what it is.'

As Gabriel heard these gentle words, and saw, by the light of a lamp which burned before a cross fixed against the wall, the sad kindness of expression with which the priest was regarding him, the oppression that had lain so long on his heart seemed to leave it in an instant. The haunting fear of ever divulging his fatal suspicions and his fatal secret had vanished, as it were, at the touch of Father Paul's hand. For the first time, he now repeated to another ear – the sounds of prayer and praise rising grandly the while from the congregation above – his grandfather's death-bed confession, word for word almost, as he had heard it in the cottage on the night of the storm.

Once, and once only, did Father Paul interrupt the narrative, which in whispers was addressed to him. Gabriel had hardly repeated the first two or three sentences of his grandfather's confession, when the priest, in quick altered tones, abruptly asked him his name and place of abode.

As the question was answered, Father Paul's calm face became suddenly agitated; but the next moment, resolutely resuming his self-possession, he bowed his head, as a sign that Gabriel was to continue; clasped his trembling hands, and raising them as if in silent prayer, fixed his eyes intently on the cross. He never looked away from it while the terrible narrative proceeded. But when Gabriel described his search at the Merchant's Table; and, referring to his father's behaviour since that time, appealed to the priest to know whether he might, even yet, in defiance of appearances, be still filially justified in doubting whether the crime had been really perpetrated – then Father Paul moved near to him once more, and spoke again.

'Compose yourself, and look at me,' he said with his former sad kindness of voice and manner. 'I can end your doubts for ever. Gabriel, your father was guilty in intention and in act; but the victim of his crime still lives. I can prove it.'

Gabriel's heart beat wildly; a deadly coldness crept over him, as he saw Father Paul loosen the fastening of his cassock round the throat.

At that instant the chanting of the congregation above ceased; and then, the sudden and awful stillness was deepened rather than interrupted by the faint sound of one voice praying. Slowly and with trembling fingers the priest removed the band round his neck – paused a little – sighed heavily – and pointed to a scar which was now plainly visible on one side of his throat. He said something at the same time; but the bell above tolled while he spoke. It was the signal of the elevation of the Host. Gabriel felt an arm passed round him, guiding him to his knees, and sustaining him from sinking to the floor. For one moment longer he was conscious that the bell had stopped, that there was dead silence, that Father Paul was kneeling by him beneath the cross, with bowed head – then all objects around vanished; and he saw and knew nothing more.

When he recovered his senses, he was still in the cabin – the man whose life his father had attempted was bending over him, and sprinkling water on his face – and the clear voices of the women and children of the congregation were joining the voices of the men in singing the *Agnus Dei*.

'Look up at me without fear, Gabriel,' said the priest. 'I desire not to avenge injuries: I visit not the sins of the father on the child. Look up, and listen! I have strange things to speak of; and I have a sacred mission to fulfil before the morning, in which you must be my guide.'

Gabriel attempted to kneel and kiss his hand, but Father Paul stopped him, and said, pointing to the cross: 'Kneel to that – not to me: not to your fellow-mortal, and your friend – for I will be your friend, Gabriel; believing that God's mercy has ordered it so. And now listen to me,' he proceeded, with a brotherly tenderness in his manner which went to Gabriel's heart. 'The service is nearly ended. What I have to tell you must be told at once; the errand on which you will guide me must be performed before to-morrow dawns. Sit here near me; and attend to what I now say!'

Gabriel obeyed: Father Paul then proceeded thus:

'I believe the confession made to you by your grandfather to have been true in every particular. On the evening to which he referred you, I approached your cottage, as he said, for the purpose of asking shelter for the night. At that period I had been studying hard to qualify myself for the holy calling which I now pursue; and, on the completion of my studies, had indulged in the recreation of a tour on foot through Brittany, by way of innocently and agreeably occupying the leisure time then at my disposal, before I entered the priesthood. When I accosted your father I had lost my way, had been walking for many hours, and was glad of any rest that I could get for the night. It is unnecessary to pain you now, by reference to the events which followed my entrance under your father's roof. I remember nothing that happened from the time when I lay down to sleep before the fire, until the time when I recovered my senses at the place which you call the Merchant's Table. My first sensation was that of being moved into the cold air: when I opened my eyes I saw the great Druid stones rising close above me, and two men on either side of me rifling my pockets. They found nothing valuable there, and were about to leave me where I lay, when I gathered strength enough to appeal to their mercy through their cupidity. Money was not scarce with me then, and I was able to offer them a rich reward (which they ultimately received as I had promised) if they would take me to any place where I could get shelter and medical help. I suppose they inferred by my language and accent – perhaps also by the linen I wore, which they examined closely – that I belonged to the higher ranks of the community, in spite of the plainness of my outer garments; and might therefore be in a position to make good my promise to them. I heard one say to the other, "Let us risk it;" and then they took me in their arms, carried me down to a boat on the beach, and rowed to a vessel in the offing. The next day they disembarked me at Paimboeuf, where I got the assistance which I so much needed. I learnt through the confidence they were obliged to place in me, in order to give me the means of sending them their promised reward, that these men were smugglers, and that they were in the habit of using the cavity in which I had been laid, as a place of concealment for goods, and for letters of advice to their accomplices. This accounted for their finding me. As to my wound, I was informed by the surgeon who attended me, that it had missed being inflicted in a mortal part by less than a quarter of an inch, and that, as it was, nothing but the action of the night air in coagulating the blood over the place had, in the first instance, saved my life. To be brief, I recovered after a long illness, returned to Paris, and was called to the priesthood. The will of my superiors obliged me to perform the first duties of my vocation in the great city; but my own wish was to be appointed to a cure of souls in your province, Gabriel. Can you imagine why?'

The answer to this question was in Gabriel's heart; but he was still too deeply awed and affected by what he had heard to give it utterance.

'I must tell you then what my motive was,' said Father Paul. 'You must know first that I uniformly abstained from disclosing to any one where and by whom my life had been attempted. I kept this a secret from the men who rescued me – from the surgeon – from my own friends even. My reason for such a proceeding was, I would fain believe, a Christian reason. I hope I had always felt a sincere and humble desire to prove myself, by the help of God, worthy of the sacred vocation to which I was destined. But my miraculous escape from death made an impression on my mind, which gave me another and an infinitely higher view of this vocation – the view which I have since striven, and shall always strive for the future, to maintain. As I lay, during the first days of my recovery, examining my own heart, and considering in what manner it would be my duty to act towards your father when I was restored to health, a thought came into my mind which calmed, comforted, and resolved all my doubts. I said within myself – "In a few months more I shall be called to be one of the chosen ministers of God. If I am worthy of my vocation, my first desire towards this man who has attempted to take my life, should be, not to know that human justice has overtaken him, but to know that he has truly and religiously repented and made atonement for his guilt. To such repentance and atonement let it be my duty to call him; if he reject that appeal, and be hardened only the more against me because I have forgiven him my injuries, then it will be time enough to denounce him for his crimes to his fellow-men. Surely it must be well for me here and hereafter, if I begin my career in the holy priesthood by helping to save from hell the soul of the man who, of all others, has most cruelly wronged me." It was for this reason, Gabriel – it was because I desired to go straightway to your father's cottage, and reclaim him after he had believed me to be dead – that I kept the secret and entreated of my superiors that I might be sent to Brittany. But this, as I have said, was not to be at first, and when my desire was granted, my place was assigned me in a far district. The persecution under which we still suffer broke out; the designs of my life were changed; my own will became no longer mine to guide me. But, through sorrow and suffering, and danger and bloodshed, I am now led after many days to the execution of that first purpose which I formed on entering the priesthood. Gabriel! when the service is over, and the congregation are dispersed, you must guide me to the door of your father's cottage.'

He held up his hand, in sign of silence, as Gabriel was about to answer. Just then, the officiating priests above were pronouncing the final benediction. When it was over, Father Paul opened the cabin-door. As he ascended the steps, followed by Gabriel, Père Bonan met them. The old man looked doubtfully and searchingly on his future son-in-law, as he respectfully whispered a few words in the ear of the priest. Father Paul listened attentively, answered in a whisper, and then turned to Gabriel, first begging the few people near them to withdraw a little.

'I have been asked whether there is any impediment to your marriage,' he said, 'and have answered that there is none. What you have said to me has been said in confession, and is a secret between us two. Remember that; and forget not, at the same time, the service which I shall require of you to-night, after the marriage ceremony is over. Where is Perrine Bonan?' he added aloud, looking round him. Perrine came forward. Father Paul took her hand, and placed it in Gabriel's. 'Lead her to the altar steps,' he said, 'and wait there for me.'

It was more than an hour later; the boats had left the ship's side; the congregation had dispersed over the face of the country – but still the vessel remained at anchor. Those who were left in her watched the land more anxiously than usual; for they knew that Father Paul had risked meeting the soldiers of the republic by trusting himself on shore. A boat was awaiting his return on the beach; half of the crew, armed, being posted as scouts in various directions on the high land of the heath. They would have followed and guarded the priest to the place of his destination; but he forbade it; and, leaving them abruptly, walked swiftly onward with one young man only for his companion.

Gabriel had committed his brother and his sisters to the charge of Perrine. They were to go to the farm-house that night with his newly married wife and her father and mother. Father Paul had desired that this might be done. When Gabriel and he were left alone to follow the path which led to the fisherman's cottage, the priest never spoke while they walked on – never looked aside either to the right or the left – always held his ivory crucifix clasped to his breast. They arrived at the door.

'Knock,' whispered Father Paul to Gabriel, 'and then wait here with me.'

The door was opened. On a lovely moonlight night François Sarzeau had stood on that threshold, years since, with a bleeding body in his arms. On a lovely moonlight night, he now stood there again, confronting the very man whose life he had attempted, and knowing him not.

Father Paul advanced a few paces, so that the moonlight fell fuller on his features, and removed his hat.

François Sarzeau looked, started, moved one step back, then stood motionless and perfectly silent, while all traces of expression of any kind suddenly vanished from his face. Then the calm, clear tones of the priest stole gently on the dead silence. 'I bring a message of peace and forgiveness from a guest of former years,' he said; and pointed, as he spoke, to the place where he had been wounded in the neck.

For one moment, Gabriel saw his father trembling violently from head to foot – then his limbs steadied again – stiffened suddenly, as if struck by catalepsy. His lips parted, but without quivering; his eyes glared, but without moving in their orbits. The lovely moonlight itself looked ghastly and horrible, shining on the supernatural panic-deformity of that face! Gabriel turned away his head in terror. He heard the voice of Father Paul saying to him: 'Wait here till I come back,' – then, there was an instant of silence again – then a low groaning sound, that seemed to articulate the name of God; a sound unlike his father's voice, unlike any human voice he had ever heard – and then the noise of a closing door. He looked up, and saw that he was standing alone before the cottage.

Once, after an interval, he approached the window.

He just saw through it the hand of the priest holding on high the ivory crucifix; but stopped not to see more, for he heard such words, such sounds, as drove him back to his former place. There he stayed, until the noise of something falling heavily within the cottage, struck on his ear. Again he advanced towards the door; heard Father Paul praying; listened for several minutes; then heard a moaning voice, now joining itself to the voice of the priest, now choked in sobs and bitter wailing. Once more he went back out of hearing, and stirred not again from his place. He waited a long and a weary time there – so long that one of the scouts on the look-out came towards him, evidently suspicious of the delay in the priest's return. He waved the man back, and then looked again towards the door. At last, he saw it open – saw Father Paul approach him, leading François Sarzeau by the hand.

The fisherman never raised his downcast eyes to his son's face; tears trickled silently over his cheeks; he followed the hand that led him, as a little child might have followed it, listening anxiously and humbly at the priest's side to every word that he spoke.

'Gabriel,' said Father Paul, in a voice which trembled a little for the first time that night – 'Gabriel, it has pleased God to grant the perfect fulfilment of the purpose which brought me to this place; I tell you this, as all that you need – as all, I believe, that you would wish – to know of what has passed while you have been left waiting for me here. Such words as I have now to speak to you, are spoken by your father's earnest desire. It is his own wish that I should communicate to you his confession of having secretly followed you to the Merchant's Table, and of having discovered (as you discovered) that no evidence of his guilt remained there. This admission he thinks will be enough to account for his conduct towards yourself from that time to this. I have next to tell you (also at your father's desire) that he has promised in my presence, and now promises again in yours, sincerity of repentance in this manner: When the persecution of our religion has ceased – as cease it will, and that speedily, be assured of it! – he solemnly pledges himself henceforth to devote his life, his strength, and what worldly possessions he may have, or may acquire, to the task of re-erecting and restoring the roadside crosses which have been sacrilegiously overthrown and destroyed in his native province, and to doing good, good where he may. I have now said all that is required of me, and may bid you farewell – bearing with me the happy remembrance that I have left a father and son reconciled and restored to each other. May God bless and prosper you, and those dear to you, Gabriel! May God accept your father's repentance, and bless him also throughout his future life!'

He took their hands, pressed them long and warmly, then turned and walked quickly down the path which led to the beach. Gabriel dared not trust himself yet to speak; but he raised his arm, and put it gently round his father's neck. The two stood together so, looking out dimly through the tears that filled their eyes, to the sea. They saw the boat put off in the bright track of the moonlight, and reach the vessel's side; they watched the spreading of the sails, and followed the slow course of the ship till she disappeared past a distant headland from sight.

After that, they went into the cottage together. They knew it not then, but they had seen the last, in this world, of Father Paul.

V

The events foretold by the good priest happened sooner even than he had anticipated. A new government ruled the destinies of France, and the persecution ceased in Brittany.

Among other propositions which were then submitted to the parliament, was one advocating the restoration of the roadside crosses throughout the province. It was found, however, on inquiry, that these crosses were to be counted by thousands, and that the mere cost of the wood required to re-erect them necessitated an expenditure of money which the bankrupt nation could ill afford to spare. While this project was under discussion, and before it was finally rejected, one man had undertaken the task which the government shrank from attempting. When Gabriel left the cottage, taking his brother and sisters to live with his wife and himself at the farm-house, François Sarzeau left it also, to perform in highway and byway his promise to Father Paul. For months and months he laboured without intermission at his task; still, always doing good, and rendering help and kindness and true charity to all whom he could serve. He walked many a weary mile, toiled through many a hard day's work, humbled himself even to beg of others, to get wood enough to restore a single cross. No one ever heard him complain, ever saw him impatient, ever detected him in faltering at his task. The shelter in an outhouse, the crust of bread and drink of water, which he could always get from the peasantry, seemed to suffice him. Among the people who watched his perseverance, a belief began to gain ground that his life would be miraculously prolonged until he had completed his undertaking from one end of Brittany to the other. But this was not to be.

He was seen one cold autumn evening, silently and steadily at work as usual, setting up a new cross on the site of one which had been shattered to splinters in the troubled times. In the morning he was found lying dead beneath the sacred symbol which his own hands had completed and erected in its place during the night. They buried him where he lay; and the priest who consecrated the ground allowed Gabriel to engrave his father's epitaph in the wood of the cross. It was simply the initial letters of the dead man's name, followed by this inscription: '*Pray for the repose of his soul: he died penitent, and the doer of good works.*'

Once, and once only, did Gabriel hear anything of Father Paul. The good priest showed, by writing to the farm-house, that he had not forgotten the family so largely indebted to him for their happiness. The letter was dated 'Rome.' Father Paul said, that such services as he had been permitted to render to the Church in Brittany, had obtained for him a new and a far more glorious trust than any he had yet held. He had been recalled from his curacy, and appointed to be at the head of a mission which was shortly to be despatched to convert the inhabitants of a savage and a far distant land to the Christian faith. He now wrote, as his brethren with him were writing, to take leave of all friends for ever in this world, before setting out – for it was well known to the chosen persons intrusted with the new mission, that they could only hope to advance its object by cheerfully risking their own lives for the sake of their religion. He gave his blessing to François Sarzeau, to Gabriel, and to his family; and bade them affectionately farewell for the last time.

There was a postscript to the letter, which was addressed to Perrine, and which she often read afterwards with tearful eyes. The writer begged that, if she should have any children, she would show her friendly and Christian remembrance of him by teaching them to pray (as he hoped she herself would pray) that a blessing might attend Father Paul's labours in the distant land.

The priest's loving petition was never forgotten. When Perrine taught its first prayer to her first child, the little creature was instructed to end the few simple words pronounced at its mother's knees, with: 'God bless Father Paul.'

In those words the nun concluded her narrative. After it was ended, she pointed to the old wooden cross, and said to me:

'That was one of the many that he made. It was found, a few years since, to have suffered so much from exposure to the weather, that it was unfit to remain any longer in its old place. A priest in Brittany gave it to one of the nuns in this convent. Do you wonder now that the Mother-Superior always calls it a Relic?'

'No,' I answered. 'And I should have small respect indeed for the religious convictions of any one who could hear the story of that wooden cross, and not feel that the Mother-Superior's name for it is the very best that could have been chosen.'

A Stolen Letter

Originally appeared as 'The Fourth Poor Traveller' in *The Seven Poor Travellers*, the Extra Christmas Number of *Household Words* for 1854. This was a collection of short stories with framing-narrative to which Dickens, G.A. Sala, Adelaide Anne Procter and Eliza Lynn also contributed. Reprinted in *After Dark* (1856) as 'The Lawyer's Story of a Stolen Letter.' In *The Seven Poor Travellers* the narrator is an out-of-work and down-at-heel lawyer who had once been 'an attorney in a large practice in a bursting big country town'; in *After Dark*, which supplies the present text, he is replaced by the superbly prosperous and combative Mr Boxsious, who tells the story while sitting for his portrait. It is often pointed out that many features of the story parallel those in Poe's 'The Purloined Letter' (Julian Symons has called it 'almost a crib'). It is often claimed to be the first English detective story; certainly, in V.S. Pritchett's phrase, it is the first 'properly uniformed and impressive' one. Catherine Peters points out that the story refers in passing to the early experiences of Wilkie Collins's mother. 'The young man in the story, whose father objects to his marrying a governess, must retrieve a letter which implicates her father in a forgery.' Like Wilkie's grandfather, the governess's father in the story lost all his money after selling out of the army. See *The King of Inventors*, p. 145. In America, *Harper's Magazine* pirated the story and tried to pass it off as the work of Dickens.

I SERVED MY time – never mind in whose office – and I started in business for myself in one of our English country towns – I decline stating which. I hadn't a farthing of capital, and my friends in the neighbourhood were poor and useless enough, with one exception. That exception was Mr Frank Gatliffe, son of Mr Gatliffe, member for the county, the richest man and the proudest for many a mile round about our parts. – Stop a bit, Mr Artist! you needn't perk up and look knowing. You won't trace any particulars by the name of Gatliffe. I'm not bound to commit myself or anybody else by mentioning names. I have given you the first that came into my head.

Well, Mr Frank was a stanch friend of mine, and ready to recommend me whenever he got the chance. I had contrived to get him a little timely help – for a consideration, of course – in borrowing money at a fair rate of interest: in fact, I had saved him from the Jews. The money was borrowed while Mr Frank was at college. He came back from college, and stopped at home a little while, and then there got spread about all our neighbourhood a report that he had fallen in love, as the saying is, with his young sister's governess, and that his mind was made up to marry her. – What! you're at it again, Mr Artist! You want to know her name, don't you? What do you think of Smith?

Speaking as a lawyer, I consider Report, in a general way, to be a fool and a liar. But in this case report turned out to be something very different. Mr Frank told me he was really in love, and said upon his honour (an absurd expression which young chaps of his age are always using) he was determined to marry Smith the governess – the sweet darling girl, as *he* called her; but I'm not sentimental, and *I* call her Smith the governess. Well, Mr Frank's father, being as proud as Lucifer, said 'No' as to marrying the governess, when Mr Frank wanted him to say 'Yes.' He was a man of business, was old Gatliffe, and he took the proper business course. He sent the governess away with a first-rate character and a spanking present, and then he looked about him to get something for Mr Frank to do. While he was looking about, Mr Frank bolted to London after the governess, who had nobody alive belonging to her to go to but an aunt – her father's sister. The aunt refuses to let Mr Frank in without the squire's permission. Mr Frank writes to his father, and says he will marry the girl as soon as he is of age, or shoot himself. Up to town comes the squire and his wife and his daughter, and a lot of sentimentality, not in the slightest degree material to the present statement, takes place among them; and the upshot of it is that old Gatliffe is forced into withdrawing the word No, and substituting the word Yes.

I don't believe he would ever have done it, though, but for one lucky peculiarity in the case. The governess's father was a man of good family – pretty nigh as good as Gatliffe's own. He had been in the army: had sold out: set up as a wine-merchant – failed – died: ditto his wife, as to the dying part of it. No relation, in fact, left for the squire to make inquiries about but the father's sister – who had behaved, as old Gatliffe said, like a thorough-bred gentlewoman in shutting the door against Mr Frank in the first instance. So, to cut the matter short, things were at last made up pleasant enough. The time was fixed for the wedding, and an announcement about it – Marriage in High Life and all that – put into the county paper. There was a regular biography, besides, of the governess's father, so as to stop people from talking – a great flourish about his pedigree, and a long account of his services in the army; but not a word, mind ye, of his having turned wine-merchant afterwards. Oh, no – not a word about that!

I knew it, though, for Mr Frank told me. He hadn't a bit of pride about him. He introduced me to his future wife one day when I met them out walking, and asked me if I did not think he was a lucky fellow. I don't mind admitting that I did, and that I told him so. Ah! but she was one of my sort, was that governess. Stood, to the best of my recollection, five foot four. Good lissome figure, that looked as if it had never been boxed up in a pair of stays. Eyes that made me feel as if I was under a pretty stiff cross-examination the moment she looked at me. Fine red, fresh, kiss-and-come-again sort of lips. Cheeks and complexion – No, Mr Artist, you would'nt identify her by her cheeks and complexion, if I drew you a picture of them this very moment. She has had a family of children since the time I'm talking of; and her cheeks are a trifle fatter and her complexion is a shade or two redder now than when I first met her out walking with Mr Frank.

The marriage was to take place on a Wednesday. I decline mentioning the year or the month. I had started as an attorney on my own account – say six weeks, more or less, and was sitting alone in my office on the Monday morning before the wedding-day, trying to see my way clear before me and not succeeding particularly well, when Mr Frank suddenly bursts in, as white as any ghost that ever was painted, and says he's got the most dreadful case for me to advise on, and not an hour to lose in acting on my advice.

'Is this in the way of business, Mr Frank?' says I, stopping him just as he was beginning to get sentimental. 'Yes or no, Mr Frank?' rapping my new office paper-knife on the table to pull him up short all the sooner.

'My dear fellow' – he was always familiar with me – 'it's in the way of business, certainly; but friendship'—

I was obliged to pull him up short again and regularly examine him as if he had been in the witness-box, or he would have kept me talking to no purpose half the day.

'Now, Mr Frank,' says I, 'I can't have any sentimentality mixed up with business matters. You please to stop talking, and let me ask questions. Answer in the fewest words you can use. Nod when nodding will do instead of words.'

I fixed him with my eye for about three seconds, as he sat groaning and wriggling in his chair. When I'd done fixing him, I gave another rap with my paper-knife on the table to startle him up a bit. Then I went on.

'From what you have been stating up to the present time,' says I, 'I gather that you are in a scrape which is likely to interfere seriously with your marriage on Wednesday?'

(He nodded, and I cut in again before he could say a word): –

'The scrape affects your young lady, and goes back to the period of a transaction in which her late father was engaged, don't it?'

(He nods, and I cut in once more): –

'There is a party who turned up after seeing the announcement of your marriage in the paper, who is cognizant of what he oughtn't to know, and who is prepared to use his knowledge of the same to the prejudice of the young lady and of your marriage, unless he receives a sum of money to quiet him? Very well. Now, first of all, Mr Frank, state what you have been told by the young lady herself about the transaction of her late father. How did you first come to have any knowledge of it?'

'She was talking to me about her father one day so tenderly and prettily, that she quite excited my interest about him,' begins Mr Frank; 'and I asked her, among other things, what had occasioned his death. She said she believed it was distress of mind in the first instance; and added that this distress was connected with a shocking secret, which she and her mother had kept from everybody, but which she could not keep from me, because she was determined to begin her married life by having no secrets from her husband.' Here Mr Frank began to get sentimental again, and I pulled him up short once more with the paper-knife.

'She told me,' Mr Frank went on, 'that the great mistake of her father's life was his selling out of the army and taking to the wine trade. He had no talent for business; things went wrong with him from the first. His clerk, it was strongly suspected, cheated him'—

'Stop a bit,' says I. 'What was that suspected clerk's name?'

'Davager,' says he.

'Davager,' says I, making a note of it. 'Go on, Mr Frank.'

'His affairs got more and more entangled,' says Mr Frank; 'he was pressed for money in all directions; bankruptcy, and consequent dishonour (as he considered it), stared him in the face. His mind was so affected by his troubles that both his wife and daughter, towards the last, considered him to be hardly responsible for his own acts. In this state of desperation and misery, he' – Here Mr Frank began to hesitate.

We have two ways in the law of drawing evidence off nice and clear from an unwilling client or witness. We give him a fright or we treat him to a joke. I treated Mr Frank to a joke.

'Ah!' says I, 'I know what he did. He had a signature to write; and, by the most natural mistake in the world, he wrote another gentleman's name instead of his own – eh?'

'It was to a bill,' says Mr Frank, looking very crest-fallen, instead of taking the joke. 'His principal creditor wouldn't wait till he could raise the money, or the greater part of it. But he was resolved, if he sold off everything, to get the amount and repay'—

'Of course!' says I, 'drop that. The forgery was discovered. When?'

'Before even the first attempt was made to negotiate the bill. He had done the whole thing in the most absurdly and innocently wrong way. The person whose name he had used was a stanch friend of his, and a relation of his wife's: a good man as well as a rich one. He had influence with the chief creditor, and he used it nobly. He had a real affection for the unfortunate man's wife, and he proved it generously.'

'Come to the point,' says I. 'What did he do? In a business way what did he do?'

'He put the false bill into the fire, drew a bill of his own to replace it, and then – only then – told my dear girl and her mother all that had happened. Can you imagine anything nobler?' asks Mr Frank.

'Speaking in my professional capacity, I can't imagine anything greener,' says I. 'Where was the father? Off, I suppose?'

'Ill in bed,' says Mr Frank, colouring. 'But, he mustered strength enough to write a contrite and grateful letter the same day, promising to prove himself worthy of the noble moderation and forgiveness extended to him, by selling off everything he possessed to repay his money-debt. He did sell off everything, down to some old family pictures that were heirlooms; down to the little plate he had; down to the very tables and chairs that furnished his drawing-room. Every farthing of the debt was paid; and he was left to begin the world again, with the kindest promises of help from the generous man who had forgiven him. It was too late. His crime of one rash moment – atoned for though it had been – preyed upon his mind. He became possessed with the idea that he had lowered himself for ever in the estimation of his wife and daughter, and'—

'He died,' I cut in. 'Yes, yes, we know that. Let's go back for a minute to the contrite and grateful letter that he wrote. My experience in the law, Mr Frank, has convinced me that if everybody burnt everybody else's letters, half the Courts of Justice in this country might shut up shop. Do you happen to know whether the letter we are now speaking of contained anything like an avowal or confession of the forgery?'

'Of course it did,' says he. 'Could the writer express his contrition properly without making some such confession?'

'Quite easy, if he had been a lawyer,' says I. 'But never mind that; I'm going to make a guess, – a desperate guess, mind. Should I be altogether in error, if I thought that this letter had been stolen; and that the fingers of Mr Davager, of suspicious commercial celebrity, might possibly be the fingers which took it?'

'That is exactly what I wanted to make you understand,' cries Mr Frank.

'How did he communicate the interesting fact of the theft to you?'

'He has not ventured into my presence. The scoundrel actually had the audacity'—

'Aha!' says I. 'The young lady herself! Sharp practitioner, Mr Davager.'

'Early this morning when she was walking alone in the shrubbery,' Mr Frank goes on, 'he had the assurance to approach her, and to say that he had been watching his opportunity of getting a private interview for days past. He then showed her – actually showed her – her unfortunate father's letter; put into her hands another letter directed to me; bowed, and walked off; leaving her half-dead with astonishment and terror. If I had only happened to be there at the time – !' says Mr Frank, shaking his fist murderously in the air by way of a finish.

'It's the greatest luck in the world that you were not,' says I. 'Have you got that other letter?'

He handed it to me. It was so remarkably humorous and short, that I remember every word of it at this distance of time. It began in this way:

To Francis Gatliffe, Esq., jun.

Sir, I have an extremely curious autograph letter to sell. The price is a Five hundred pound note. The young lady to whom you are to be married on Wednesday will inform you of the nature of the letter, and the genuineness of the autograph. If you refuse to deal, I shall send a copy to the local paper, and shall wait on your highly respected father with the original curiosity, on the afternoon of Tuesday next. Having come down here on family business, I have put up at the family hotel – being to be heard of at the Gatliffe Arms. Your very obedient servant,

ALFRED DAVAGER

'A clever fellow that,' says I, putting the letter into my private drawer.

'Clever!' cries Mr Frank, 'he ought to be horsewhipped within an inch of his life. I would have done it myself; but she made me promise, before she told me a word of the matter, to come straight to you.'

'That was one of the wisest promises you ever made,' says I. 'We can't afford to bully this fellow, whatever else we may do with him. Do you think I am saying anything libellous against your excellent father's character when I assert that if he saw the letter he would certainly insist on your marriage being put off, at the very least?'

'Feeling as my father does about my marriage, he would insist on its being dropped altogether, if he saw this letter,' says Mr Frank, with a groan. 'But even that is not the worst of it. The generous, noble girl herself says, that if the letter appears in the paper, with all the unanswerable comments this scoundrel would be sure to add to it, she would rather die than hold me to my engagement – even if my father would let me keep it.'

As he said this his eyes began to water. He was a weak young fellow, and ridiculously fond of her. I brought him back to business with another rap of the paper-knife.

'Hold up, Mr Frank,' says I. 'I have a question or two more. Did you think of asking the young lady, whether, to the best of her knowledge, this infernal letter was the only written evidence of the forgery now in existence?'

'Yes, I did think directly of asking her that,' says he; 'and she told me she was quite certain that there was no written evidence of the forgery except that one letter.'

'Will you give Mr Davager his price for it?' says I.

'Yes,' says Mr Frank, quite peevish with me for asking him such a question. He was an easy young chap in money-matters, and talked of hundreds as most men talk of sixpences.

'Mr Frank,' says I, 'you came here to get my help and advice in this extremely ticklish business, and you are ready, as I know without asking, to remunerate me for all and any of my services at the usual professional rate. Now, I've made up my mind to act boldly – desperately if you like – on the hit or miss – win-all-or-lose-all principle – in dealing with this matter. Here is my proposal. I'm going to try if I can't do Mr Davager out of his letter. If I don't succeed before to-morrow afternoon, you hand him the money, and I charge you nothing for professional services. If I do succeed, I hand you the letter instead of Mr Davager; and you give me the money instead of giving it to him. It's a precious risk for me, but I'm ready to run it. You must pay your five hundred any way. What do you say to my plan? Is it Yes, Mr Frank – or No?'

'Hang your questions!' cries Mr Frank, jumping up; 'you know it's Yes ten thousand times over. Only you earn the money and'—

'And you will be too glad to give it to me. Very good. Now go home. Comfort the young lady – don't let Mr Davager so much as set eyes on you – keep quiet – leave everything to me – and feel as certain as you please that all the letters in the world can't stop your being married on Wednesday.' With these words I hustled him off out of the office; for I wanted to be left alone to make my mind up about what I should do.

The first thing, of course, was to have a look at the enemy. I wrote to Mr Davager, telling him that I was privately appointed to arrange the little business-matter between himself and 'another party' (no names!) on friendly terms; and begging him to call on me at his earliest convenience. At the very beginning of the case, Mr Davager bothered me. His answer was, that it would not be convenient to him to call till between six and seven in the evening. In this way, you see, he contrived to make me lose several precious hours, at a time when minutes almost were of importance. I had nothing for it but to be patient, and to give certain instructions, before Mr Davager came, to my boy Tom.

There never was such a sharp boy of fourteen before, and there never will be again, as my boy Tom. A spy to look after Mr Davager was, of course, the first requisite in a case of this kind; and Tom was the smallest, quickest, quietest, sharpest, stealthiest little snake of a chap that ever dogged a gentleman's steps and kept cleverly out of range of a gentleman's eyes. I settled it with the boy that he was not to show at all, when Mr Davager came; and that he was to wait to hear me ring the bell when Mr Davager left. If I rang twice he was to show the gentleman out. If I rang once, he was to keep out of the way and follow the gentleman wherever he went till he got back to the inn. Those were the only preparations I could make to begin with; being obliged to wait, and let myself be guided by what turned up.

About a quarter to seven my gentleman came.

In the profession of the law we get somehow quite remarkably mixed up with ugly people, blackguard people, and dirty people. But far away the ugliest and dirtiest blackguard I ever saw in my life was Mr Alfred Davager. He had greasy white hair and a mottled face. He was low in the forehead, fat in the stomach, hoarse in the voice, and weak in the legs. Both his eyes were bloodshot, and one was fixed in his head. He smelt of spirits, and carried a toothpick in his mouth. 'How are you? I've just done dinner,' says he – and he lights a cigar, sits down with his legs crossed, and winks at me.

I tried at first to take the measure of him in a wheedling confidential way; but it was no good. I asked him in a facetious smiling manner, how he had got hold of the letter. He only told me in answer that he had been in the confidential employment of the writer of it, and that he had always been famous since infancy for a sharp eye to his own interests. I paid him some compliments; but he was not to be flattered. I tried to make him lose his temper; but he kept it in spite of me. It ended in his driving me to my last resource – I made an attempt to frighten him.

'Before we say a word about the money,' I began, 'let me put a case, Mr Davager. The pull you have on Mr Francis Gatliffe is, that you can hinder his marriage on Wednesday. Now, suppose I have got a magistrate's warrant to apprehend you in my pocket? Suppose I have a constable to execute it in the next room? Suppose I bring you up to-morrow – the day before the marriage – charge you only generally with an attempt to extort money, and apply for a day's remand to complete the case? Suppose, as a suspicious stranger, you can't get bail in this town? Suppose'—

'Stop a bit,' says Mr Davager: 'Suppose I should not be the greenest fool that ever stood in shoes? Suppose I should not carry the letter about me? Suppose I should have given a certain envelope to a certain friend of mine in a certain place in this town? Suppose the letter should be inside that envelope, directed to old Gatliffe, side by side with a copy of the letter directed to the editor of the local paper? Suppose my friend should be instructed to open the envelope, and take the letters to their right address, if I don't appear to claim them from him this evening? In short, my dear sir, suppose you were born yesterday, and suppose I wasn't?' says Mr Davager, and winks at me again.

He didn't take me by surprise, for I never expected that he had the letter about him. I made a pretence of being very much taken aback, and of being quite ready to give in. We settled our business about delivering the letter and handing over the money in no time. I was to draw out a document which he was to sign. He knew the document was stuff and nonsense just as well as I did, and told me I was only proposing it to swell my client's bill. Sharp as he was, he was wrong there. The document was not to be drawn out to gain money from Mr Frank, but to gain time from Mr Davager. It served me as an excuse to put off the payment of the five hundred pounds till three o'clock on the Tuesday afternoon. The Tuesday morning Mr Davager said he should devote to his amusement, and asked me what sights were to be seen in the neighbourhood of the town. When I had told him, he pitched his toothpick into my grate, yawned, and went out.

I rang the bell once – waited till he had passed the window – and then looked after Tom. There was my jewel of a boy on the opposite side of the street, just setting his top going in the most playful manner possible! Mr Davager walked away up the street, towards the market-place. Tom whipped his top up the street towards the market-place too.

In a quarter-of-an-hour he came back, with all his evidence collected in a beautifully clear and compact state. Mr Davager had walked to a public-house just outside the town, in a lane leading to the high road. On a bench outside the public-house there sat a man smoking. He said 'All right?' and gave a letter to Mr Davager, who answered 'All right,' and walked back to the inn. In the hall he ordered hot rum and water, cigars, slippers, and a fire to be lit in his room. After that he went up stairs, and Tom came away.

I now saw my road clear before me – not very far on, but still clear. I had housed the letter, in all probability for that night, at the Gatliffe Arms. After tipping Tom, I gave him directions to play about the door of the inn, and refresh himself when he was tired at the tart-shop opposite, eating as much as he pleased, on the understanding that he crammed all the time with his eye on the window. If Mr Davager went out, or Mr Davager's friend called on him, Tom was to let me know. He was also to take a little note from me to the head chambermaid – an old friend of mine – asking her to step over to my office, on a private matter of business, as soon as her work was done for that night. After settling these little matters, having half-an-hour to spare, I turned to and did myself a bloater at the office-fire, and had a drop of gin and water hot, and felt comparatively happy.

When the head chambermaid came, it turned out, as good luck would have it, that Mr Davager had drawn her attention rather too closely to his ugliness, by offering her a testimony of his regard in the shape of a kiss. I no sooner mentioned him than she flew into a passion; and when I added, by way of clinching the matter, that I was retained to defend the interests of a very beautiful and deserving young lady (name not referred to, of course) against the most cruel underhand treachery on the part of Mr Davager, the head chambermaid was ready to go any lengths that she could safely to serve my cause. In few words I discovered that Boots was to call Mr Davager at eight the next morning, and was to take his clothes down stairs to brush as usual.

If Mr D. had not emptied his own pockets overnight, we arranged that Boots was to forget to empty them for him, and was to bring the clothes down stairs just as he found them. If Mr D.'s pockets were emptied, then, of course, it would be necessary to transfer the searching process to Mr D.'s room. Under any circumstances, I was certain of the head chambermaid; and under any circumstances also, the head chambermaid was certain of Boots.

I waited till Tom came home, looking very puffy and bilious about the face; but as to his intellects, if anything rather sharper than ever. His report was uncommonly short and pleasant. The inn was shutting up; Mr Davager was going to bed in rather a drunken condition; Mr Davager's friend had never appeared. I sent Tom (properly instructed about keeping our man in view all the next morning) to his shake-down behind the office-desk, where I heard him hicupping half the night, as even the best boys will, when over-excited and too full of tarts.

At half-past seven next morning, I slipped quietly into Boots's pantry.

Down came the clothes. No pockets in trousers. Waistcoat pockets empty. Coat pockets with something in them. First, handkerchief; secondly, bunch of keys; thirdly, cigar-case; fourthly, pocket-book. Of course I wasn't such a fool as to expect to find the letter there, but I opened the pocket-book with a certain curiosity, notwithstanding.

Nothing in the two pockets of the book but some old advertisements cut out of newspapers, a lock of hair tied round with a dirty bit of ribbon, a circular letter about a loan society, and some copies of verses not likely to suit any company that was not of an extremely free-and-easy description. On the leaves of the pocket-book, people's addresses scrawled in pencil, and bets jotted down in red ink. On one leaf, by itself, this queer inscription:

Mem. 5 Along. 4 Across.

I understood everything but those words and figures, so of course I copied them out into my own book. Then I waited in the pantry till Boots had brushed the clothes and had taken them up stairs. His report when he came down was, that Mr D. had asked if it was a fine morning. Being told that it was, he had ordered breakfast at nine, and a saddle-horse to be at the door at ten, to take him to Grimwith Abbey – one of the sights in our neighbourhood which I had told him of the evening before.

'I'll be here, coming in by the back way, at half-past ten,' says I to the head chambermaid.

'What for?' says she.

'To take the responsibility of making Mr Davager's bed off your hands for this morning only,' says I.

'Any more orders?' says she.

'One more,' says I. 'I want to hire Sam for the morning. Put it down in the order-book that he's to be brought round to my office at ten.'

In case you should think Sam was a man, I'd better perhaps tell you he was a pony. I'd made up my mind that it would be beneficial to Tom's health, after the tarts, if he took a constitutional airing on a nice hard saddle in the direction of Grimwith Abbey.

'Anything else?' says the head chambermaid.

'Only one more favour,' says I. 'Would my boy Tom be very much in the way if he came, from now till ten, to help with the boots and shoes, and stood at his work close by this window which looks out on the staircase?'

'Not a bit,' says the head chambermaid.

'Thank you,' says I; and stepped back to my office directly.

When I had sent Tom off to help with the boots and shoes, I reviewed the whole case exactly as it stood at that time.

There were three things Mr Davager might do with the letter. He might give it to his friend again before ten – in which case, Tom would most likely see the said friend on the stairs. He might take it to his friend, or to some other friend, after ten – in which case Tom was ready to follow him on Sam the pony. And, lastly, he might leave it hidden somewhere in his room at the inn – in which case, I was all ready for him with a search-warrant of my own granting, under favour always of my friend the head chambermaid. So far I had my business arrangements all gathered up nice and compact in my own hands. Only two things bothered me; the terrible shortness of the time at my disposal, in case I failed in my first experiments for getting hold of the letter, and that queer inscription which I had copied out of the pocket-book.

MEM. 5 ALONG. 4 ACROSS.

It was the measurement most likely of something, and he was afraid of forgetting it; therefore, it was something important. Query – something about himself? Say '5' (inches) 'along' – he does'nt wear a wig. Say '5' (feet) 'along' – it can't be coat, waistcoat, trousers, or underclothing. Say '5' (yards) 'along' – it can't be anything about himself, unless he wears round his body the rope that he's sure to be hanged with one of these days. Then it is *not* something about himself. What do I know of that is important to him besides? I know of nothing but the Letter. Can the memorandum be connected with that? Say, yes. What do '5 along' and '4 across' mean then? The measurement of something he carries about with him? – or the measurement of something in his room? I could get pretty satisfactorily to myself as far as that; but I could get no further.

Tom came back to the office, and reported him mounted for his ride. His friend had never appeared. I sent the boy off, with his proper instructions, on Sam's back – wrote an encouraging letter to Mr Frank to keep him quiet – then slipped into the inn by the back way a little before half-past ten. The head chambermaid gave me a signal when the landing was clear. I got into his room without a soul but her seeing me, and locked the door immediately.

The case was, to a certain extent, simplified now. Either Mr Davager had ridden out with the letter about him, or he had left it in some safe hiding-place in his room. I suspected it to be in his room, for a reason that will a little astonish you – his trunk, his dressing-case, and all the drawers and cupboards were left open. I knew my customer, and I thought this extraordinary carelessness on his part rather suspicious.

Mr Davager had taken one of the best bedrooms at the Gatliffe Arms. Floor carpeted all over, walls beautifully papered, four-poster, and general furniture first-rate. I searched, to begin with, on the usual plan, examining everything in every possible way, and taking more than an hour about it. No discovery. Then I pulled out a carpenter's rule which I had brought with me. Was there anything in the room which – either in inches, feet, or yards – answered to '5 along' and '4 across'? Nothing. I put the rule back in my pocket – measurement was no good, evidently. Was there anything in the room that would count up to 5 one way and 4 another, seeing that nothing would measure up to it? I had got obstinately persuaded by this time that the letter must be in the room –

principally because of the trouble I had had in looking after it. And persuading myself of that, I took it into my head next, just as obstinately, that '5 along' and '4 across' must be the right clue to find the letter by – principally because I had'nt left myself, after all my searching and thinking, even so much as the ghost of another guide to go by. '5 along' – where could I count five along the room, in any part of it?

Not on the paper. The pattern there was pillars of trellis-work and flowers, enclosing a plain green ground – only four pillars along the wall and only two across. The furniture? There were not five chairs or five separate pieces of any furniture in the room altogether. The fringes that hung from the cornice of the bed? Plenty of them, at any rate! Up I jumped on the counterpane, with my penknife in my hand. Every way that '5 along' and '4 across' could be reckoned on those unlucky fringes I reckoned on them – probed with my penknife – scratched with my nails – crunched with my fingers. No use; not a sign of a letter; and the time was getting on – oh, Lord! how the time did get on in Mr Davager's room that morning.

I jumped down from the bed, so desperate at my ill-luck that I hardly cared whether anybody heard me or not. Quite a little cloud of dust rose at my feet as they thumped on the carpet.

'Hullo!' thought I, 'my friend the head chambermaid takes it easy here. Nice state for a carpet to be in, in one of the best bedrooms at the Gatliffe Arms.' Carpet! I had been jumping up on the bed, and staring up at the walls, but I had never so much as given a glance down at the carpet. Think of me pretending to be a lawyer, and not knowing how to look low enough!

The carpet! It had been a stout article in its time; had evidently begun in a drawing-room; then descended to a coffee-room; then gone upstairs altogether to a bedroom. The ground was brown, and the pattern was bunches of leaves and roses speckled over the ground at regular distances. I reckoned up the bunches. Ten along the room – eight across it. When I had stepped out five one way and four the other, and was down on my knees on the centre bunch, as true as I sit on this chair I could hear my own heart beating so loud that it quite frightened me.

I looked narrowly all over the bunch, and I felt all over it with the ends of my fingers, and nothing came of that. Then I scraped it over slowly and gently with my nails. My second finger-nail stuck a little at one place. I parted the pile of the carpet over that place, and saw a thin slit which had been hidden by the pile being smoothed over it – a slit about half an inch long, with a little end of brown thread, exactly the colour of the carpet-ground, sticking out about a quarter of an inch from the middle of it. Just as I laid hold of the thread gently, I heard a footstep outside the door.

It was only the head chambermaid. 'Haven't you done yet?' she whispers.

'Give me two minutes,' says I, 'and don't let anybody come near the door – whatever you do, don't let anybody startle me again by coming near the door.'

I took a little pull at the thread, and heard something rustle. I took a longer pull, and out came a piece of paper, rolled up tight like those candle-lighters that the ladies make. I unrolled it – and, by George! there was the letter!

The original letter! – I knew it by the colour of the ink. The letter that was worth five hundred pound to me! It was all I could do to keep myself at first from throwing my hat into the air, and hooraying like mad. I had to take a chair and sit quiet in it for a minute or two, before I could cool myself down to my proper business level. I knew that I was safely down again when I found myself pondering how to let Mr Davager know that he had been done by the innocent country attorney after all.

It was not long before a nice little irritating plan occurred to me. I tore a blank leaf out of my pocket-book, wrote on it with my pencil 'Change for a five hundred pound note,' folded up the paper, tied the thread to it, poked it back into the hiding-place, smoothed over the pile of the carpet, and then bolted off to Mr Frank. He in his turn bolted off to show the letter to the young lady, who first certified to its genuineness, then dropped it into the fire, and then took the initiative for the first time since her marriage engagement, by flinging her arms round his neck, kissing him with all her might, and going into hysterics in his arms. So at least Mr Frank told me, but that's not evidence. It is evidence, however, that I saw them married with my own eyes on the Wednesday; and that while they went off in a carriage and four to spend the honeymoon, I went off on my own legs to open a credit at the Town and County Bank with a five hundred pound note in my pocket.

As to Mr Davager, I can tell you nothing more about him, except what is derived from hearsay evidence, which is always unsatisfactory evidence, even in a lawyer's mouth.

My inestimable boy, Tom, although twice kicked off by Sam the pony, never lost hold of the bridle, and kept his man in sight from first to last. He had nothing particular to report, except that on the way out to the Abbey Mr Davager had stopped at the public-house, had spoken a word or two to his friend of the night before, and had handed him what looked like a bit of paper. This was no doubt a clue to the thread that held the letter, to be used in case of accidents. In every other respect Mr D. had ridden out and ridden in like an ordinary sightseer. Tom reported him to me as having dismounted at the hotel about two. At half-past, I locked my office door, nailed a card under the knocker with 'not at home till to-morrow' written on it, and retired to a friend's house a mile or so out of the town for the rest of the day.

Mr Davager, I have been since given to understand, left the Gatliffe Arms that same night with his best clothes on his back, and with all the valuable contents of his dressing-case in his pockets. I am not in a condition to state whether he ever went through the form of asking for his bill or not; but I can positively testify that he never paid it, and that the effects left in his bedroom did not pay it either. When I add to these fragments of evidence that he and I have never met (luckily for me, you will say) since I jockeyed him out of his bank-note, I have about fulfilled my implied contract as maker of a statement with you, sir, as hearer of a statement. Observe the expression, will you? I said it was a Statement before I began; and I say it's a Statement now I've done. I defy you to prove it's a Story! – How are you getting on with my portrait? I like you very well, Mr Artist; but if you have been taking advantage of my talking to shirk your work, as sure as you're alive I'll split upon you to the Town Council!'

The Dream Woman

Originally appeared as 'The Ostler', the second story in *The Holly Tree Inn*, the Christmas Number of *Household Words* for 1855. The other contributors were Dickens, William Howitt, Adelaide Anne Procter, and Harriet Parr. In 1859 the story was lengthened, and included in *The Queen of Hearts* as 'Brother Morgan's Story of the Dream Woman.' Collins later expanded the story to form a two-hour public-reading text, which he used several times on his American Lecture Tour in 1873–4. When he returned home he expanded the story yet again, and reprinted it in *The Frozen Deep and Other Stories* (1874), explaining in his 'Introductory Lines' that 'the limits of time in the case of a public reading [rendered] it imperatively necessary to abridge without mercy developments of character and incident which are essential to the due presentation of a work in its literary form.' Critics are unanimous in pointing out that the redundant contextual detail introduced in 1874 deforms the outline of the story; by adding a sequel in which the woman does murder her husband Collins also destroys the eerie open-endedness of his original version. For the sake of completeness I print the story in its most extensive form – but urge the reader to seek out its earlier texts for purposes of comparison. These have been widely anthologised, most recently in *Mad Monkton and Other Stories*, ed. Norman Page (World's Classics, 1994). Catherine Peters wonders if the prophetic dream of the fatal woman embodies some of Collins's deepest fears about the nature of marriage (*The King of Inventors*, p. 155). Robert Ashley suggests that 'the story anticipates the more famous and more complex dream technique of *Armadale*' (*Wilkie Collins*, p. 54).

PERSONS OF THE MYSTERY.

FRANCIS RAVEN	(*Ostler*).
MRS RAVEN	(*His mother*).
MRS CHANCE	(*His aunt*).
PERCY FAIRBANK } MRS FAIRBANK }	(*His master and mistress*).
JOSEPH RIGOBERT	(*His fellow-servant*).
ALICIA WARLOCK	(*His wife*).

PERIOD – THE PRESENT TIME.

SCENE – PARTLY IN ENGLAND, PARTLY IN FRANCE.

THE FIRST NARRATIVE

INTRODUCTORY STATEMENT OF THE FACTS
BY PERCY FAIRBANK

'Hullo, there! Ostler! Hullo-o-o!'

'My dear! why don't you look for the bell?'

'I *have* looked – there is no bell.'

'And nobody in the yard. How very extraordinary! Call again, dear.'

'Ostler! Hullo, there! Ostler-r-r!'

My second call echoes through empty space, and rouses nobody – produces, in short, no visible result. I am at the end of my resources – I don't know what to say or what to do next. Here I stand in the solitary inn yard of a strange town, with two horses to hold, and a lady to take care of. By way of adding to my responsibilities, it so happens that one of the horses is dead lame, and that the lady is my wife.

Who am I? – you will ask.

There is plenty of time to answer the question. Nothing happens; and nobody appears to receive us. Let me introduce myself and my wife.

I am Percy Fairbank – English gentleman – age (let us say) forty – no profession – moderate politics – middle height – fair complexion – easy character – plenty of money.

My wife is a French lady. She was Mademoiselle Clotilde Delorge – when I was first presented to her at her father's house in France. I fell in love with her – I really don't know why. It might have been because I was perfectly idle, and had nothing else to do at the time. Or it might have been because all my friends said she was the very last woman whom I ought to think of marrying. On the surface, I must own, there is nothing in common between Mrs Fairbank and me. She is tall; she is dark; she is nervous, excitable, romantic; in all her opinions she proceeds to extremes. What could such a woman see in me? what could I see in her? I know no more than you do. In some mysterious manner we exactly suit each other. We have been man and wife for ten years, and our only regret is, that we have no children. I don't know what *you* may think; *I* call that – upon the whole – a happy marriage.

So much for ourselves. The next question is – what has brought us into the inn yard? and why am I obliged to turn groom, and hold the horses?

We live for the most part in France – at the country house in which my wife and I first met. Occasionally, by way of variety, we pay visits to my friends in England. We are paying one of those visits now. Our host is an old college friend of mine, possessed of a fine estate in Somersetshire; and we have arrived at his house – called Farleigh Hall – towards the close of the hunting-season.

On the day of which I am now writing – destined to be a memorable day in our calendar – the hounds meet at Farleigh Hall. Mrs Fairbank and I are mounted on two of the best horses in my friend's stables. We are quite unworthy of that distinction; for we know nothing, and care nothing, about hunting. On the other hand, we delight in riding, and we enjoy the breezy spring morning and the fair and fertile English landscape surrounding us on every side. While the hunt prospers, we follow the hunt. But when a check occurs – when time passes and patience is sorely tried; when the bewildered dogs run hither and thither, and strong language falls from the lips of exasperated sportsmen – we fail to take any further interest in the proceedings. We turn our horses' heads in the direction of a grassy lane, delightfully shaded by trees. We trot merrily along the lane, and find ourselves on an open common. We gallop across the common, and follow the windings of a second lane. We cross a brook, we pass through a village, we emerge into pastoral solitude among the hills. The horses toss their heads, and neigh to each other, and enjoy it as much as we do. The hunt is forgotten. We are as happy as a couple of children; we are actually singing a French song – when in one moment our merriment comes to an end. My wife's horse sets one of his fore-feet on a loose stone, and stumbles. His rider's ready hand saves him from falling. But, at the first attempt he makes to go on, the sad truth shows itself – a tendon is strained; the horse is lame.

What is to be done? We are strangers in a lonely part of the country. Look where we may, we see no signs of a human habitation. There is nothing for it but to take the bridle-road up the hill, and try what we can discover on the other side. I transfer the saddles, and mount my wife on my own horse. He is not used to carry a lady; he misses the familiar pressure of a man's legs on either side of him; he fidgets, and starts, and kicks up the dust. I follow on foot, at a respectful distance from his heels, leading the lame horse. Is there a more miserable object on the face of creation than a lame horse? I have seen lame men and lame dogs who were cheerful creatures; but I never yet saw a lame horse who didn't look heartbroken over his own misfortune.

For half-an-hour my wife capers and curvets sideways along the bridle-road. I trudge on behind her; and the heartbroken horse halts behind *me*. Hard by the top of the hill, our melancholy procession passes a Somersetshire peasant at work in a field. I summon the man to approach us; and the man looks at me stolidly, from the middle of the field, without stirring a step. I ask at the top of my voice how far it is to Farleigh Hall. The Somersetshire peasant answers at the top of *his* voice,

'Vourteen mile. Gi' oi a drap o' zyder.'

I translate (for my wife's benefit) from the Somersetshire language into the English language. We are fourteen miles from Farleigh Hall; and our friend in the field desires to be rewarded for giving us that information, with a drop of cider. There is the peasant, painted by himself! Quite a bit of character, my dear! Quite a bit of character!

Mrs Fairbank doesn't view the study of agricultural human nature with my relish. Her fidgety horse will not allow her a moment's repose; she is beginning to lose her temper.

'We can't go fourteen miles in this way,' she says. 'Where is the nearest inn? Ask that brute in the field!'

I take a shilling from my pocket and hold it up in the sun. The shilling exercises magnetic virtues. The shilling draws the peasant slowly towards me from the middle of the field. I inform him that we want to put up the horses, and to hire a carriage to take us back to Farleigh Hall. Where can we do that? The peasant answers (with his eye on the shilling):

'At Oonderbridge, to be zure.' (At Underbridge, to be sure.)

'Is it far to Underbridge?'

The peasant repeats, 'Var to Oonderbridge?' – and laughs at the question. 'Hoo-hoo-hoo!' (Underbridge is evidently close by – if we could only find it.) 'Will you show us the way, my man?' 'Will you gi' oi a drap o' zyder?' I courteously bend my head, and point to the shilling. The agricultural intelligence exerts itself. The peasant joins our melancholy procession. My wife is a fine woman, but he never once looks at my wife – and, more extraordinary still, he never even looks at the horses. His eyes are with his mind – and his mind is on the shilling.

We reach the top of the hill – and, behold on the other side, nestling in a valley, the shrine of our pilgrimage, the town of Underbridge! Here our guide claims his shilling, and leaves us to find out the inn for ourselves. I am constitutionally a polite man. I say 'Good morning' at parting. The guide looks at me with the shilling between his teeth to make sure that it is a good one. 'Marnin!' he says savagely – and turns his back on us, as if we had offended him. A curious product, this, of the growth of civilisation. If I didn't see a church spire at Underbridge, I might suppose that we had lost ourselves on a savage island.

Arriving at the town, we have no difficulty in finding the inn. The town is composed of one desolate street; and midway in that street stands the inn – an ancient stone building sadly out of repair. The painting on the signboard is obliterated. The shutters over the long range of front windows are all closed. A cock and his hens are the only living creatures at the door. Plainly, this is one of the old inns of the stage-coach period, ruined by the railway. We pass through the open arched doorway, and find no one to welcome us. We advance into the stable yard behind; I assist my wife to dismount – and there we are in the position already disclosed to view at the opening of this narrative. No bell to ring. No human creature to answer when I call. I stand helpless, with the bridles of the horses in my hand. Mrs Fairbank saunters gracefully down the length of the yard, and, does – what all women do, when they find themselves in a strange place. She opens every door as she passes it, and peeps in. On my side, I have just recovered my breath, I am on the point of shouting for the ostler for the third and last time, when I hear Mrs Fairbank suddenly call to me.

'Percy! come here!'

Her voice is eager and agitated. She has opened a last door at the end of the yard, and has started back from some sight which has suddenly met her view. I hitch the horses' bridles on a rusty nail in the wall near me, and join my wife. She has turned pale, and catches me nervously by the arm.

'Good Heavens!' she cries; 'look at that!'

I look – and what do I see?

I see a dingy little stable, containing two stalls. In one stall a horse is munching his corn. In the other a man is lying asleep on the litter.

A worn, withered, woe-begone man in an ostler's dress. His hollow wrinkled cheeks, his scanty grizzled hair, his dry yellow skin, tell their own tale of past sorrow or suffering. There is an ominous frown on his eyebrows – there is a painful nervous contraction on one side of his mouth. I hear him breathing convulsively when I first look in; he shudders and sighs in his sleep. It is not a pleasant sight to see, and I turn round instinctively to the bright sunlight in the yard. My wife turns me back again in the direction of the stable door.

'Wait!' she says. 'Wait! he may do it again.'

'Do what again?'

'He was talking in his sleep, Percy, when I first looked in. He was dreaming some dreadful dream. Hush! he's beginning again.'

I look and listen. The man stirs on his miserable bed. The man speaks, in a quick fierce whisper, through his clenched teeth. 'Wake up! Wake up, there! Murder!'

There is an interval of silence. He moves one lean arm slowly until it rests over his throat; he shudders, and turns on his straw; he raises his arm from his throat, and feebly stretches it out; his hand clutches at the straw on the side towards which he has turned; he seems to fancy that he is grasping at the edge of something; I see his lips begin to move again; I step softly into the stable; my wife follows me, with her hand fast clasped in mine. We both bend over him. He is talking once more in his sleep – strange talk, mad talk, this time.

'Light grey eyes' (we hear him say), 'and a droop in the left eyelid – flaxen hair, with a gold-yellow streak in it – all right, mother! fair, white arms with a down on them – little, lady's hand, with a reddish look round the finger-nails – the knife – the cursed knife – first on one side, then on the other – aha, you she-devil! where is the knife?'

He stops and grows restless on a sudden. We see him writhing on the straw. He throws up both his hands and gasps hysterically for breath. His eyes open suddenly. For a moment they look at nothing, with a vacant glitter in them – then they close again in deeper sleep. Is he dreaming still? Yes; but the dream seems to have taken a new course. When he speaks next, the tone is altered; the words are few – sadly and imploringly repeated over and over again. 'Say you love me! I am so fond of *you*. Say you love me! say you love me!' He sinks into deeper and deeper sleep, faintly repeating those words. They die away on his lips. He speaks no more.

By this time, Mrs Fairbank has got over her terror. She is devoured by curiosity now. The miserable creature on the straw has appealed to the imaginative side of her character. Her illimitable appetite for romance hungers and thirsts for more. She shakes me impatiently by the arm. 'Do you hear? There is a woman at the bottom of it, Percy! There is love and murder in it, Percy! Where are the people of the inn? Go into the yard, and call to them again.'

My wife belongs, on her mother's side, to the South of France. The South of France breeds fine women with hot tempers. I say no more. Married men will understand my position. Single men may need to be told that there are occasions when we must not only love and honour – we must also obey – our wives.

I turn to the door to obey *my* wife, and find myself confronting a stranger who has stolen on us unawares. The stranger is a tiny, sleepy, rosy old man, with a vacant pudding-face, and a shining bald head. He wears drab breeches and gaiters, and a respectable square-tailed ancient black coat. I feel instinctively that here is the landlord of the inn.

'Good morning, sir,' says the rosy old man. 'I'm a little hard of hearing. Was it you that was a-calling just now in the yard?'

Before I can answer, my wife interposes. She insists (in a shrill voice, adapted to our host's hardness of hearing) on knowing who that unfortunate person is sleeping on the straw? 'Where does he come from? Why does he say such dreadful things in his sleep? Is he married or single? Did he ever fall in love with a murderess? What sort of a looking woman was she? Did she really stab him or not? In short, dear Mr Landlord, tell us the whole story!'

Dear Mr Landlord waits drowsily until Mrs Fairbank has quite done – then delivers himself of his reply as follows:

'His name's Francis Raven. He's an Independent Methodist. He was forty-five year old last birthday. And he's my ostler. That's his story.'

My wife's hot Southern temper finds its way to her foot, and expresses itself by a stamp on the stable yard.

The landlord turns himself sleepily round, and looks at the horses. 'A fine pair of horses, them two in the yard. Do you want to put 'em up in my stables?' I reply in the affirmative by a nod. The landlord, bent on making himself agreeable to my wife, addresses her once more. 'I'm a-going to wake Francis Raven. He's an Independent Methodist. He was forty-five year old last birthday. And he's my ostler. That's his story.'

Having issued this second edition of his interesting narrative, the landlord enters the stable. We follow him, to see how he will wake Francis Raven, and what will happen upon that. The stable broom stands in a corner; the landlord takes it – advances towards the sleeping ostler – and coolly stirs the man up with the broom as if he was a wild beast in a cage. Francis Raven starts to his feet with a cry of terror – looks at us wildly, with a horrid glare of suspicion in his eyes – recovers himself the next moment – and suddenly changes into a decent, quiet, respectable serving-man.

'I beg your pardon, ma'am. I beg your pardon, sir.'

The tone and manner in which he makes his apologies are both above his apparent station in life. I begin to catch the infection of Mrs Fairbank's interest in this man. We both follow him out into the yard, to see what he will do with the horses. The manner in which he lifts the injured leg of the lame horse tells me at once that he understands his business. Quickly and quietly, he leads the animals into an empty stable; quickly and quietly, he gets a bucket of hot water, and puts the lame horse's leg into it. 'The warm water will reduce the swelling, sir. I will bandage the leg afterwards.' All that he does, is done intelligently; all that he says, he says to the purpose. Nothing wild, nothing strange about him, now. Is this the same man whom we heard talking in his sleep? the same man who woke with that cry of terror and that horrid suspicion in his eyes? I determine to try him with one or two questions.

'Not much to do here,' I say to the ostler.

'Very little to do sir,' the ostler replies.

'Anybody staying in the house?'

'The house is quite empty, sir.'

'I thought you were all dead. I could make nobody hear me.'

'The landlord is very deaf, sir, and the waiter is out on an errand.'

'Yes; and *you* were fast asleep in the stable. Do you often take a nap in the daytime?'

The worn face of the ostler faintly flushes. His eyes look away from my eyes for the first time. Mrs Fairbank furtively pinches my arm. Are we on the eve of a discovery at last? I repeat my question. The man has no civil alternative but to give me an answer. The answer is given in these words:

'I was tired out, sir. You wouldn't have found me asleep in the daytime but for that.'

'Tired out, eh? You had been hard at work, I suppose?'

'No, sir.'

'What was it, then?'

'He hesitates again, and answers unwillingly, 'I was up all night.'

'Up all night? Anything going on in the town?'

'Nothing going on, sir.'

'Anybody ill?'

'Nobody ill, sir.'

That reply is the last. Try as I may, I can extract nothing more from him. He turns away and busies himself in attending to the horse's leg. I leave the stable, to speak to the landlord about the carriage which is to take us back to Farleigh Hall. Mrs Fairbank remains with the ostler, and favours me with a look at parting. The look says plainly, '*I* mean to find out why he was up all night. Leave him to Me.'

The ordering of the carriage is easily accomplished. The inn possesses one horse and one chaise. The landlord has a story to tell of the horse, and a story to tell of the chaise. They resemble the story of Francis Raven – with this exception, that the horse and chaise belong to no religious persuasion. 'The horse will be nine year old next birthday. I've had the shay for four and twenty year. Mr Max of Underbridge, he bred the horse; and Mr Pooley of Yeovil, he built the shay. It's my horse and my shay. And that's *their* story!' Having relieved his mind of these details, the landlord proceeds to put the harness on the horse. By way of assisting him, I drag the chaise into the yard. Just as our preparations are completed, Mrs Fairbank appears. A moment or two later the ostler follows her out. He has bandaged the horse's leg, and is now ready to drive us to Farleigh Hall. I observe signs of agitation in his face and manner, which suggest that my wife has found her way into his confidence. I put the question to her privately in a corner of the yard. 'Well? Have you found out why Francis Raven was up all night?'

Mrs Fairbank has an eye to dramatic effect. Instead of answering plainly, Yes or No, she suspends the interest and excites the audience by putting a question on her side.

'What is the day of the month, dear?'

'The day of the month is the first of March.'

'The first of March, Percy, is Francis Raven's birthday.'

I try to look as if I was interested – and don't succeed.

'Francis was born,' Mrs Fairbank proceeds gravely, 'at two o'clock in the morning.'

I begin to wonder whether my wife's intellect is going the way of the landlord's intellect. 'Is that all?' I ask.

'It is *not* all,' Mrs Fairbank answers. 'Francis Raven sits up on the morning of his birthday, because he is afraid to go to bed.'

'And why is he afraid to go to bed?'

'Because he is in peril of his life.'

'On his birthday?'

'On his birthday. At two o'clock in the morning. As regularly as the birthday comes round.'

There she stops. Has she discovered no more than that? No more thus far. I begin to feel really interested by this time. I ask eagerly what it means? Mrs Fairbank points mysteriously to the chaise – with Francis Raven (hitherto our ostler, now our coachman) waiting for us to get in. The chaise has a seat for two in front, and a seat for one behind. My wife casts a warning look at me, and places herself on the seat in front.

The necessary consequence of this arrangement is, that Mrs Fairbank sits by the side of the driver, during a journey of two hours and more. Need I state the result? It would be an insult to your intelligence to state the result. Let me offer you my place in the chaise. And let Francis Raven tell his terrible story in his own words.

THE SECOND NARRATIVE

The Ostler's Story. Told By Himself

It is now ten years ago, since I got my first warning of the great trouble of my life, in the Vision of a Dream.

I shall be better able to tell you about it, if you will please suppose yourselves to be drinking tea along with us in our little cottage in Cambridgeshire, ten years since.

The time was the close of day, and there were three of us at the table, namely, my mother, myself, and my mother's sister, Mrs Chance. These two were Scotch-women by birth, and both were widows. There was no other resemblance between them that I can call to mind. My mother had lived all her life in England, and had no more of the Scotch brogue on her tongue than I have. My aunt Chance had never been out of Scotland until she came to keep house with my mother after her husband's death. And when *she* opened her lips you heard broad Scotch, I can tell you, if ever you heard it yet!

As it fell out, there was a matter of some consequence in debate among us that evening. It was this: whether I should do well or not to take a long journey on foot the next morning.

Now the next morning happened to be the day before my birthday; and the purpose of the journey was to offer myself for a situation as groom at a great house in the neighbouring county to ours. The place was reported as likely to fall vacant in about three weeks' time. I was as well fitted to fill it as any other man. In the prosperous days of our family, my father had been manager of a training-stable, and he had kept me employed among the horses from my boyhood upward. Please to excuse my troubling you with these small matters. They all fit into my story further on, as you will soon find out.

My poor mother was dead against my leaving home on the morrow.

'You can never walk all the way there and all the way back again by to-morrow night,' she says. 'The end of it will be that you will sleep away from home on your birthday. You have never done that yet, Francis, since your father's death. I don't like your doing it now. Wait a day longer, my son – only one day.'

For my own part, I was weary of being idle, and I couldn't abide the notion of delay. Even one day might make all the difference. Some other man might take time by the forelock, and get the place.

'Consider how long I have been out of work,' I says, 'and don't ask me to put off the journey. I won't fail you, mother. I'll get back by to-morrow night, if I have to pay my last sixpence for a lift in a cart.'

My mother shook her head. 'I don't like it, Francis – I don't like it!' There was no moving her from that view. We argued and argued, until we were both at a dead lock. It ended in our agreeing to refer the difference between us to my mother's sister, Mrs Chance.

While we were trying hard to convince each other, my aunt Chance sat as dumb as a fish, stirring her tea and thinking her own thoughts. When we made our appeal to her, she seemed, as it were, to wake up. 'Ye baith refer it to my puir judgment?' she says, in her broad Scotch. We both answered Yes. Upon that my aunt Chance first cleared the tea-table, and then pulled out from the pocket of her gown a pack of cards.

Don't run away, if you please, with the notion that this was done lightly, with a view to amuse my mother and me. My aunt Chance seriously believed that she could look into the future by telling fortunes on the cards. She did nothing herself without first consulting the cards. She could give no more serious proof of her interest in my welfare than the proof which she was offering now. I don't say it profanely; I only mention the fact – the cards had, in some incomprehensible way, got themselves jumbled up together with her religious convictions. You meet with people nowadays who believe in spirits working by way of tables and chairs. On the same principle (if there *is* any principle in it) my aunt Chance believed in Providence working by way of the cards.

'Whether *you* are right, Francie, or your mither – whether ye will do weel or ill, the morrow, to go or stay – the cairds will tell it. We are a' in the hands of Proavidence. The cairds will tell it.'

Hearing this, my mother turned her head aside, with something of a sour look in her face. Her sister's notions about the cards were little better than flat blasphemy to her mind. But she kept her opinion to herself. My aunt Chance, to own the truth, had inherited, through her late husband, a pension of thirty pounds a year. This was an important contribution to our house-keeping, and we poor relations were bound to treat her with a certain respect. As for myself, if my poor father never did anything else for me before he fell into difficulties, he gave me a good education, and raised me (thank God) above superstitions of all sorts. However, a very little amused me in those days; and I waited to have my fortune told, as patiently as if I believed in it too!

My aunt began her hocus-pocus by throwing out all the cards in the pack under seven. She shuffled the rest, with her left hand, for luck; and then she gave them to me to cut. 'Wi' yer left hand, Francie. Mind that! Pet yer trust in Proavidence – but dinna forget that yer luck's in yer left hand!' A long and roundabout shifting of the cards followed, reducing them in number, until there were just fifteen of them left, laid out neatly before my aunt in a half circle. The card which happened to lay outermost, at the right-hand end of the circle, was, according to rule in such cases, the card chosen to represent Me. By way of being appropriate to my situation as a poor groom out of work, the card was – the King of Diamonds.

'I tak' up the King o' Diamants,' says my aunt. 'I count seven cairds fra' richt to left; and I humbly ask a blessing on what follows.' My aunt shut her eyes as if she was saying grace before meat, and held up to me the seventh card. I called the seventh card – the Queen of Spades. My aunt opened her eyes again in a hurry, and cast a sly look my way. 'The Queen o' Spades means a dairk woman. Ye'll be thinking in secret, Francie, of a dairk woman?'

When a man has been out of place for more than three months, his mind isn't troubled much with thinking of women – light or dark. I was thinking of the groom's place at the great house, and I tried to say so. My aunt Chance wouldn't listen. She treated my interruption with contempt. 'Hoot-toot! there's the caird in your hand! If ye're no thinking of her the day, ye'll be thinking of her the morrow. Where's the harm of thinking of a dairk woman! I was aince a dairk woman myself, before my hair was grey. Haud yer peace, Francie, and watch the cairds.'

I watched the cards as I was told. There were seven left on the table. My aunt removed two from one end of the row and two from the other, and desired me to call the two outermost of the three cards now left on the table. I called the Ace of Clubs and the Ten of Diamonds. My aunt Chance lifted her eyes to the ceiling with a look of devout gratitude which sorely tried my mother's patience. The Ace of Clubs and the Ten of Diamonds, taken together, signified – first, good news (evidently the news of the groom's place!); secondly, a journey that lay before me (pointing plainly to my journey to-morrow!); thirdly and lastly, a sum of money (probably the groom's wages!) waiting to find its way into my pockets. Having told my fortune in these encouraging terms, my aunt declined to carry the experiment any further. 'Eh, lad! it's a clean tempting of Proavidence to ask mair o' the cairds than the cairds have tauld us noo. Gae yer ways to-morrow to the great hoose. A dairk woman will meet ye at the gate; and she'll have a hand in getting ye the groom's place, wi' a' the graitifications and pairquisites appertaining to the same. And, mebbe, when yer poaket's full o' mony, ye'll no' be forgetting yer aunt Chance, maintaining her ain unbleemished widowhood – wi' Proavidence assisting – on thratty punds a year!'

I promised to remember my aunt Chance (who had the defect, by the way, of being a terribly greedy person after money) on the next happy occasion when my poor empty pockets were to be filled at last. This done, I looked at my mother. She had agreed to take her sister for umpire between us, and her sister had given it in my favour. She raised no more objections. Silently, she got on her feet, and kissed me, and sighed bitterly – and so left the room.

My aunt Chance shook her head. 'I doubt, Francie, yer puir mither has but a heathen notion of the vairtue of the cairds!'

By daylight the next morning I set forth on my journey. I looked back at the cottage as I opened the garden gate. At one window was my mother, with her handkerchief to her eyes. At the other stood my aunt Chance, holding up the Queen of Spades by way of encouraging me at starting. I waved my hand to both of them in token of farewell, and stepped out briskly into the road. It was then the last day of February. Be pleased to remember, in connection with this, that the first of March was the day, and two o'clock in the morning the hour, of my birth.

Now you know how I came to leave home. The next thing to tell is, what happened on the journey.

I reached the great house in reasonably good time considering the distance. At the very first trial of it, the prophecy of the cards turned out to be wrong. The person who met me at the lodge gate was not a dark woman – in fact, not a woman at all – but a boy. He directed me on the way to the servants' offices; and there again the cards were all wrong. I encountered, not one woman, but three – and not one of the three was dark. I have stated that I am not superstitious, and I have told the truth. But I must own that I did feel a certain fluttering at the heart when I made my bow to the steward, and told him what business had brought me to the house. His answer completed the discomfiture of aunt Chance's fortune-telling. My ill-luck still pursued me. That very morning another man had applied for the groom's place, and had got it.

I swallowed my disappointment as well as I could, and thanked the steward, and went to the inn in the village to get the rest and food which I sorely needed by this time.

Before starting on my homeward walk I made some enquiries at the inn, and ascertained that I might save a few miles, on my return, by following a new road. Furnished with full instructions, several times repeated, as to the various turnings I was to take, I set forth, and walked on till the evening with only one stoppage for bread and cheese. Just as it was getting towards dark, the rain came on and the wind began to rise; and I found myself, to make matters worse, in a part of the country with which I was entirely unacquainted, though I guessed myself to be some fifteen miles from home. The first house I found to enquire at, was a lonely roadside inn, standing on the outskirts of a thick wood. Solitary as the place looked, it was welcome to a lost man who was also hungry, thirsty, footsore, and wet. The landlord was civil and respectable-looking; and the price he asked for a bed was reasonable enough. I was grieved to disappoint my mother. But there was no conveyance to be had, and I could go no further afoot that night. My weariness fairly forced me to stop at the inn.

I may say for myself that I am a temperate man. My supper simply consisted of some rashers of bacon, a slice of home-made bread, and a pint of ale. I did not go to bed immediately after this moderate meal, but sat up with the landlord, talking about my bad prospects and my long run of ill-luck, and diverging from these topics to the subjects of horse-flesh and racing. Nothing was said either by myself, my host, or the few labourers who strayed into the tap-room, which could, in the slightest degree, excite my mind, or set my fancy – which is only a small fancy at the best of times – playing tricks with my common sense.

At a little after eleven the house was closed. I went round with the landlord, and held the candle while the doors and lower windows were being secured. I noticed with surprise the strength of the bolts, bars, and iron-sheathed shutters.

'You see, we are rather lonely here,' says the landlord. 'We never have had any attempts to break in yet, but it's always as well to be on the safe side. When nobody is sleeping here, I am the only man in the house. My wife and daughter are timid, and the servant-girl takes after her missuses. Another glass of ale, before you turn in? – No! – Well, how such a sober man as you comes to be out of place is more than I can understand for one. – Here's where you're to sleep. You're the only lodger to-night, and I think you'll say my missus has done her best to make you comfortable. You're quite sure you won't have another glass of ale? – Very well. Good night.'

It was half-past eleven by the clock in the passage as we went upstairs to the bedroom. The window looked out on the wood at the back of the house.

I locked my door, set my candle on the chest of drawers, and wearily got me ready for bed. The bleak wind was still blowing, and the solemn, surging moan of it in the wood was very dreary to hear through the night silence. Feeling strangely wakeful, I resolved to keep the candle alight until I began to grow sleepy. The truth is, I was not quite myself. I was depressed in mind by my disappointment of the morning; and I was worn out in body by my long walk. Between the two, I own I couldn't face the prospect of lying awake in the darkness, listening to the dismal moan of the wind in the wood.

Sleep stole on me before I was aware of it; my eyes closed, and I fell off to rest, without having so much as thought of extinguishing the candle.

The next thing that I remember was a faint shivering that ran through me from head to foot, and a dreadful sinking pain at my heart, such as I had never felt before. The shivering only disturbed my slumbers – the pain woke me instantly. In one moment I passed from a state of sleep to a state of wakefulness – my eyes wide open – my mind clear on a sudden as if by a miracle.

The candle had burnt down nearly to the last morsel of tallow, but the unsnuffed wick had just fallen off, and the light was, for the moment, fair and full.

Between the foot of the bed and the closed door, I saw a person in my room. The person was a woman, standing looking at me, with a knife in her hand.

It does no credit to my courage to confess it – but the truth *is* the truth. I was struck speechless with terror. There I lay with my eyes on the woman; there the woman stood (with the knife in her hand) with *her* eyes on *me*.

She said not a word as we stared each other in the face; but she moved after a little – moved slowly towards the left-hand side of the bed.

The light fell full on her face. A fair, fine woman, with yellowish flaxen hair, and light grey eyes, with a droop in the left eyelid. I noticed these things and fixed them in my mind, before she was quite round at the side of the bed. Without saying a word; without any change in the stony stillness of her face; without any noise following her footfall, she came closer and closer; stopped at the bed-head, and lifted the knife to stab me. I laid my arm over my throat to save it; but, as I saw the blow coming, I threw my hand across the bed to the right side, and jerked my body over that way, just as the knife came down within a hair's-breadth of my shoulder.

My eyes fixed on her arm and her hand – she gave me time to look at them as she slowly drew the knife out of the bed. A white, well-shaped arm, with a pretty down lying lightly over the fair skin. A delicate lady's hand, with a pink flush round the finger-nails.

She drew the knife out, and passed back again slowly to the foot of the bed; she stopped there for a moment looking at me; then she came on without saying a word; without any change in the stony stillness of her face; without any noise following her footfall – came on to the side of the bed where I now lay.

Getting near me, she lifted the knife again, and I drew myself away to the left side. She struck, as before, right into the mattress, with a swift downward action of her arm; and she missed me, as before, by a hair's-breadth. This time my eyes wandered from *her* to the knife. It was like the large clasp-knives which labouring men use to cut their bread and bacon with. Her delicate little fingers did not hide more than two-thirds of the handle; I noticed that it was made of buck-horn, clean and shining as the blade was, and looking like new.

For the second time she drew the knife out of the bed, and suddenly hid it away in the wide sleeve of her gown. That done, she stopped by the bedside, watching me. For an instant I saw her standing in that position – then the wick of the spent candle fell over into the socket. The flame dwindled to a little blue point, and the room grew dark.

A moment, or less if possible, passed so – and then the wick flamed up, smokily, for the last time. My eyes were still looking for her over the right-hand side of the bed when that last flash of light came. Look as I might, I could see nothing. The woman with the knife was gone.

I began to get back to myself again. I could feel my heart beating; I could hear the woeful moaning of the wind in the wood; I could leap up in bed, and give the alarm before she escaped from the house. 'Murder! Wake up there! Murder!'

Nobody answered to the alarm. I rose and groped my way through the darkness to the door of the room. By that way she must have got in. By that way she must have gone out.

The door of the room was fast locked, exactly as I had left it on going to bed!

I looked at the window. Fast locked too!

Hearing a voice outside, I opened the door. There was the landlord, coming towards me along the passage, with his burning candle in one hand, and his gun in the other.

'What is it?' he says, looking at me in no very friendly way.

I could only answer him in a whisper. 'A woman, with a knife in her hand. In my room. A fair, yellow-haired woman. She jabbed at me with the knife, twice over.'

He lifted his candle, and looked at me steadily from head to foot.

'She seems to have missed you twice over.'

'I dodged the knife as it came down. It struck the bed each time. Go in, and see.'

The landlord took his candle into the bedroom immediately. In less than a minute he came out again into the passage in a violent passion.

'The devil fly away with you and your woman with the knife! There isn't a mark in the bedclothes anywhere. What do you mean by coming into a man's place and frightening his family out of their wits by a dream?'

A dream? The woman who had tried to stab me, not a living human being like myself? I began to shake and shiver. The horrors got hold of me at the bare thought of it.

'I'll leave the house,' I said. 'Better out on the road in the rain and dark, than back again in that room, after what I've seen in it. Lend me the light to get my clothes by, and tell me what I'm to pay.'

The landlord led the way back with his light into the bedroom. 'Pay?' says he. 'You'll find your score on the slate when you go downstairs. I wouldn't have taken you in for all the money you've got about you, if I had known your dreaming, screeching ways beforehand. Look at the bed – where's the cut of a knife in it? Look at the window – is the lock bursted? Look at the door (which I heard you fasten yourself) – is it broke in? A murdering woman with a knife in my house! You ought to be ashamed of yourself!'

My eyes followed his hand as it pointed first to the bed – then to the window – then to the door. There was no gainsaying it. The bed sheet was as sound as on the day it was made. The window was fast. The door hung on its hinges as steady as ever. I huddled my clothes on without speaking. We went downstairs together. I looked at the clock in the bar room. The time was twenty minutes past two in the morning. I paid my bill; and the landlord let me out. The rain had ceased; but the night was dark, and the wind was bleaker than ever. Little did the darkness, or the cold, or the doubt about the way home matter to *me*. My mind was away from all these things. My mind was fixed on the vision in the bedroom. What had I seen trying to murder me? The creature of a dream? Or that other creature from the world beyond the grave, whom men call ghost? I could make nothing of it as I walked along in the night; I had made nothing of it by midday – when I stood at last, after many times missing my road, on the doorstep of home.

My mother came out alone to welcome me back. There were no secrets between us two. I told her all that had happened, just as I have told it to you.

She kept silence till I had done. And then she put a question to me.

'What time was it, Francis, when you saw the Woman in your Dream?'

I had looked at the clock when I left the inn, and had noticed that the hands pointed to twenty minutes past two. Allowing for the time consumed in speaking to the landlord, and in getting on my clothes, I answered that I must have first seen the Woman at two o'clock in the morning. In other words, I had not only seen her on my birthday, but at the hour of my birth.

My mother still kept silence. Lost in her own thoughts, she took me by the hand, and led me into the parlour. Her writing-desk was on the table by the fire-place. She opened it, and signed to me to take a chair by her side.

'My son! your memory is a bad one, and mine is fast failing me. Tell me again what the woman looked like. I want her to be as well known to both of us, years hence, as she is now.'

I obeyed; wondering what strange fancy might be working in her mind. I spoke; and she wrote the words as they fell from my lips:

'Light grey eyes, with a droop in the left eyelid. Flaxen hair, with a gold-yellow streak in it. White arms, with a down upon them. Little, lady's hands, with a rosy-red look about the finger-nails.'

'Did you notice how she was dressed, Francis?'

'No, mother.'

'Did you notice the knife?'

Yes. A large clasp-knife, with a buck-horn handle as good as new.'

My mother added the description of the knife. Also the year, month, day of the week, and hour of the day when the Dream Woman appeared to me at the inn. That done, she locked up the paper in her desk.

'Not a word, Francis, to your aunt. Not a word to any living soul. Keep your Dream a secret between you and me.'

The weeks passed, and the months passed. My mother never returned to the subject again. As for me, time, which wears out all things, wore out my remembrance of the Dream. Little by little, the image of the Woman grew dimmer and dimmer. Little by little, she faded out of my mind.

The story of the warning is now told. Judge for yourself if it was a true warning or a false, when you hear what happened to me on my next birthday.

In the summer time of the year, the Wheel of Fortune turned the right way for me at last. I was smoking my pipe one day, near an old stone-quarry at the entrance to our village, when a carriage accident happened, which gave a new turn, as it were, to my lot in life. It was an accident of the commonest kind – not worth mentioning at any length. A lady driving herself; a runaway horse; a cowardly man-servant in attendance, frightened out of his wits; and the stone-quarry too near to be agreeable – that is what I saw, all in a few moments, between two whiffs of my pipe. I stopped the horse at the edge of the quarry, and got myself a little hurt by the shaft of the chaise. But that didn't matter. The lady declared I had saved her life; and her husband, coming with her to our cottage the next day, took me into his service then and there. The lady happened to be of a dark complexion; and it may amuse you to hear that my aunt Chance instantly pitched on that circumstance as a means of saving the credit of the cards. Here was the promise of the Queen of Spades performed to the very letter, by means of 'a dark woman,' just as my aunt had told me! 'In the time to come, Francie, beware o' pettin' yer ain blinded intairpretation on the cairds. Ye're ower ready, I trow, to murmur under dispensations of Proavidence that ye canna fathom – like the Eesraelites of auld. I'll say nae mair to ye. Mebbe when the mony's powering into yer poakets, ye'll no forget yer aunt Chance, left like a sparrow on the housetop, wi' a sma' annuitee o' thratty punds a year.'

I remained in my situation (at the West-end of London) until the spring of the New Year.

About that time, my master's health failed. The doctors ordered him away to foreign parts, and the establishment was broken up. But the turn in my luck still held good. When I left my place, I left it – thanks to the generosity of my kind master – with a yearly allowance granted to me, in remembrance of the day when I had saved my mistress's life. For the future, I could go back to service or not, as I pleased; my little income was enough to support my mother and myself.

My master and mistress left England towards the end of February. Certain matters of business to do for them detained me in London until the last day of the month. I was only able to leave for our village by the evening train, to keep my birthday with my mother as usual. It was bedtime when I got to the cottage; and I was sorry to find that she was far from well. To make matters worse, she had finished her bottle of medicine on the previous day, and had omitted to get it replenished, as the doctor had strictly directed. He dispensed his own medicines, and I offered to go and knock him up. She refused to let me do this; and, after giving me my supper, sent me away to my bed.

I fell asleep for a little, and woke again. My mother's bedchamber was next to mine. I heard my aunt Chance's heavy footsteps going to and fro in the room, and, suspecting something wrong, knocked at the door. My mother's pains had returned upon her; there was a serious necessity for relieving her sufferings as speedily as possible. I put on my clothes, and ran off, with the medicine-bottle in my hand, to the other end of the village, where the doctor lived. The church clock chimed the quarter to two on my birthday just as I reached his house. One ring at the night-bell brought him to his bedroom window to speak to me. He told me to wait, and he would let me in at the surgery door. I noticed, while I was waiting, that the night was wonderfully fair and warm for the time of year. The old stone-quarry where the carriage accident had happened was within view. The moon in the clear heavens lit it up almost as bright as day.

In a minute or two, the doctor let me into the surgery. I closed the door, noticing that he had left his room very lightly clad. He kindly pardoned my mother's neglect of his directions, and set to work at once at compounding the medicine. We were both intent on the bottle; he filling it, and I holding the light – when we heard the surgery door suddenly opened from the street.

Who could possibly be up and about in our quiet village at the second hour of the morning?

The person who had opened the door appeared within range of the light of the candle. To complete our amazement, the person proved to be a woman!

She walked up to the counter, and standing side-by-side with me, lifted her veil. At the moment when she showed her face, I heard the church clock strike two. She was a stranger to me, and a stranger to the doctor. She was also, beyond all comparison, the most beautiful woman I have ever seen in my life.

'I saw the light under the door,' she said. 'I want some medicine.'

She spoke quite composedly, as if there was nothing at all extraordinary in her being out in the village at two in the morning, and following me into the surgery to ask for medicine! The doctor stared at her as if he suspected his own eyes of deceiving him. 'Who are you?' he asked. 'How do you come to be wandering about at this time in the morning?'

She paid no heed to his questions. She only told him coolly what she wanted.

'I have got a bad toothache. I want a bottle of laudanum.'

The doctor recovered himself when she asked for the laudanum. He was on his own ground, you know, when it came to a matter of laudanum; and he spoke to her smartly enough this time.

'Oh, you have got the toothache, have you? Let me look at the tooth.'

She shook her head, and laid a two-shilling piece on the counter.

'I won't trouble you to look at the tooth,' she said. 'There is the money. Let me have the laudanum, if you please.'

The doctor put the two-shilling piece back again in her hand.

'I don't sell laudanum to strangers,' he answered. 'If you are in any distress of body or mind, that is another matter. I shall be glad to help you.'

She put the money back in her pocket. '*You* can't help me,' she said, as quietly as ever. 'Good morning.'

With that, she opened the surgery door to go out again into the street.

So far, I had not spoken a word on my side. I had stood with the candle in my hand (not knowing I was holding it) – with my eyes fixed on her, with my mind fixed on her – like a man bewitched. Her looks betrayed, even more plainly than her words, her resolution, in one way or another, to destroy herself. When she opened the door, in my alarm at what might happen I found the use of my tongue.

'Stop!' I cried out. 'Wait for me. I want to speak to you before you go away.'

She lifted her eyebrows with a look of careless surprise, and a mocking smile on her lips.

'What can *you* have to say to me?' She stopped, and laughed to herself. 'Why not?' she says. 'I have got nothing to do, and nowhere to go.' She turned back a step, and nodded to me. 'You're a strange man – I think I'll humour you – I'll wait outside.' The door of the surgery closed on her. She was gone.

I am ashamed to own what happened next. The only excuse for me is that I was really and truly a man bewitched. I turned me round to follow her out, without once thinking of my mother. The doctor stopped me.

'Don't forget the medicine,' he said. 'And, if you will take my advice, don't trouble yourself about that woman. Rouse up the constable. It's his business to look after her – not yours.'

I held out my hand for the medicine in silence: I was afraid I should fail in respect if I trusted myself to answer him. He must have seen, as I saw, that she wanted the laudanum to poison herself. He had, to my mind, taken a very heartless view of the matter. I just thanked him when he gave me the medicine – and went out.

She was waiting for me as she had promised; walking slowly to and fro – a tall, graceful, solitary figure in the bright moonbeams. They shed over her fair complexion, her bright golden hair, her large grey eyes, just the light that suited them best. She looked hardly mortal when she first turned to speak to me.

'Well?' she said. 'And what do you want?'

In spite of my pride, or my shyness, or my better sense – whichever it might be – all my heart went out to her in a moment. I caught hold of her by the hands, and owned what was in my thoughts, as freely as if I had known her for half a lifetime.

'You mean to destroy yourself,' I said. 'And I mean to prevent you from doing it. If I follow you about all night, I'll prevent you from doing it.'

She laughed. 'You saw yourself that he wouldn't sell me the laudanum. Do you really care whether I live or die?' She squeezed my hands gently as she put the question: her eyes searched mine with a languid, lingering look in them that ran through me like fire. My voice died away on my lips; I couldn't answer her.

She understood, without my answering. 'You have given me a fancy for living, by speaking kindly to me,' she said. 'Kindness has a wonderful effect on women and dogs, and other domestic animals. It is only men who are superior to kindness. Make your mind easy – I promise to take as much care of myself as if I was the happiest woman living! Don't let me keep you here, out of your bed. Which way are you going?'

Miserable wretch that I was, I had forgotten my mother – with the medicine in my hand!

'I am going home,' I said. 'Where are you staying? At the inn?'

She laughed her bitter laugh, and pointed to the stone-quarry. 'There is *my* inn for to-night,' she said. 'When I got tired of walking about, I rested there.'

We walked on together, on my way home. I took the liberty of asking her if she had any friends.

'I thought I had one friend left,' she said, 'or you would never have met me in this place. It turns out I was wrong. My friend's door was closed in my face some hours since: my friend's servants threatened me with the police. I had nowhere else to go, after trying my luck in your neighbourhood; and nothing left but my two-shilling piece and these rags on my back. What respectable innkeeper would take *me* into his house? I walked about, wondering how I could find my way out of the world without disfiguring myself, and without suffering much pain. You have no river in these parts. I didn't see my way out of the world, till I heard you ringing at the doctor's house. I got a glimpse at the bottles in the surgery, when he let you in, and I thought of the laudanum directly. What were you doing there? Who is that medicine for? Your wife?'

'I am not married.'

She laughed again. 'Not married! If I was a little better dressed there might be a chance for ME. Where do you live? Here?'

We had arrived, by this time, at my mother's door. She held out her hand to say good-bye. Houseless and homeless as she was, she never asked me to give her a shelter for the night. It was *my* proposal that she should rest under my roof, unknown to my mother and my aunt. Our kitchen was built out at the back of the cottage: she might remain there unseen and unheard until the household was astir in the morning. I led her into the kitchen, and set a chair for her by the dying embers of the fire. I dare say I was to blame – shamefully to blame, if you like. I only wonder what *you* would have done in my place. On your word of honour as a man, would *you* have let that beautiful creature wander back to the shelter of the stone-quarry like a stray dog? God help the woman who is foolish enough to trust and love you, if you would have done that!

I left her by the fire, and went to my mother's room.

If you have ever felt the heart-ache, you will know what I suffered in secret when my mother took my hand, and said, 'I am sorry, Francis, that your night's rest has been disturbed through *me*.' I gave her the medicine; and I waited by her till the pains abated. My aunt Chance went back to her bed; and my mother and I were left alone. I noticed that her writing-desk, moved from its customary place, was on the bed by her side. She saw me looking at it. 'This is your birthday, Francis,' she said. 'Have you anything to tell me?' I had so completely forgotten my Dream, that I had no notion of what was passing in her mind when she said those words. For a moment there was a guilty fear in me that she suspected something. I turned away my face, and said, 'No, mother; I have nothing to tell.' She signed to me to stoop down over the pillow and kiss her. 'God bless you, my love!' she said; 'and many happy returns of the day.' She patted my hand, and closed her weary eyes, and, little by little, fell off peaceably into sleep.

I stole downstairs again. I think the good influence of my mother must have followed me down. At any rate, this is true: I stopped with my hand on the closed kitchen door, and said to myself, 'Suppose I leave the house, and leave the village, without seeing her or speaking to her more?'

Should I really have fled from temptation in this way, if I had been left to myself to decide? Who can tell? As things were, I was not left to decide. While my doubt was in my mind, she heard me, and opened the kitchen door. My eyes and her eyes met. That ended it.

We were together, unsuspected and undisturbed, for the next two hours. Time enough for her to reveal the secret of her wasted life. Time enough for her to take possession of me as her own, to do with me as she liked. It is needless to dwell here on the misfortunes which had brought her low: they are misfortunes too common to interest anybody.

Her name was Alicia Warlock. She had been born and bred a lady. She had lost her station, her character, and her friends. Virtue shuddered at the sight of her; and Vice had got her for the rest of her days. Shocking, and common, as I told you. It made no difference to *me*. I have said it already – I say it again – I was a man bewitched. Is there anything so very wonderful in that? Just remember who I was. Among the honest women in my own station in life, where could I have found the like of *her*? Could *they* walk as she walked? and look as she looked? When *they* gave me a kiss, did their lips linger over it as hers did? Had *they* her skin, her laugh, her foot, her hand, her touch? *She* never had a speck of dirt on her: I tell you her flesh was a perfume. When she embraced me, her arms folded round me like the wings of angels; and her smile covered me softly with its light like the sun in heaven. I leave you to laugh at me, or to cry over me, just as your temper may incline. I am not trying to excuse myself – I am trying to explain. You are gentlefolks; what dazzled and maddened *me*, is everyday experience to *you*. Fallen or not, angel or devil, it came to this – she was a lady; and I was a groom.

Before the house was astir, I got her away (by the workmen's train) to a large manufacturing town in our parts.

Here – with my savings in money to help her – she could get her outfit of decent clothes, and her lodging among strangers who asked no questions so long as they were paid. Here – now on one pretence and now on another – I could visit her, and we could both plan together what our future lives were to be. I need not tell you that I stood pledged to make her my wife. A man in my station always marries a woman of her sort.

Do you wonder if I was happy at this time? I should have been perfectly happy, but for one little drawback. It was this: I was never quite at my ease in the presence of my promised wife.

I don't mean that I was shy with her, or suspicious of her, or ashamed of her. The uneasiness I am speaking of was caused by a faint doubt in my mind, whether I had not seen her somewhere, before the morning when we met at the doctor's house. Over and over again, I found myself wondering whether her face did not remind me of some other face – *what* other I never could tell. This strange feeling, this one question that could never be answered, vexed me to a degree that you would hardly credit. It came between us at the strangest times – oftenest, however, at night, when the candles were lit. You have known what it is to try and remember a forgotten name – and to fail, search as you may, to find it in your mind.

That was my case. I failed to find my lost face, just as you failed to find your lost name.

In three weeks, we had talked matters over, and had arranged how I was to make a clean breast of it at home. By Alicia's advice, I was to describe her as having been one of my fellow-servants, during the time when I was employed under my kind master and mistress in London. There was no fear now of my mother taking any harm from the shock of a great surprise. Her health had improved during the three weeks' interval. On the first evening when she was able to take her old place at tea-time, I summoned my courage, and told her I was going to be married. The poor soul flung her arms round my neck, and burst out crying for joy. 'Oh, Francis!' she says, 'I am so glad you will have somebody to comfort you and care for you when I am gone!' As for my aunt Chance, you can anticipate what *she* did, without being told. Ah, me! If there had really been any prophetic virtue in the cards, what a terrible warning they might have given us that night!

It was arranged that I was to bring my promised wife to dinner at the cottage on the next day.

I own I was proud of Alicia when I led her into our little parlour at the appointed time. She had never, to my mind, looked so beautiful as she looked that day. I never noticed any other woman's dress: I noticed hers as carefully as if I had been a woman myself! She wore a black silk gown, with plain collar and cuffs, and a modest lavender-coloured bonnet, with one white rose in it placed at the side. My mother, dressed in her Sunday best, rose up, all in a flutter, to welcome her daughter-in-law that was to be. She walked forward a few steps, half smiling, half in tears – she looked Alicia full in the face – and suddenly stood still. Her cheeks turned white in an instant; her eyes stared in horror; her hands dropped helplessly at her sides. She staggered back, and fell into the arms of my aunt, standing behind her. It was no swoon: she kept her senses. Her eyes turned slowly from Alicia to me. 'Francis,' she said, 'does that woman's face remind you of nothing?'

Before I could answer, she pointed to her writing-desk on the table at the fireside. 'Bring it!' she cried, 'bring it!'

At the same moment, I felt Alicia's hand laid on my shoulder, and saw Alicia's face red with anger – and no wonder!

'What does this mean?' she asked. 'Does your mother want to insult me?'

I said a few words to quiet her, what they were I don't remember – I was so confused and astonished at the time. Before I had done, I heard my mother behind me.

My aunt had fetched her desk. She had opened it; she had taken a paper from it. Step by step, helping herself along by the wall, she came nearer and nearer, with the paper in her hand. She looked at the paper – she looked in Alicia's face – she lifted the long, loose sleeve of her gown, and examined her hand and arm. I saw fear suddenly take the place of anger in Alicia's eyes. She shook herself free of my mother's grasp. 'Mad!' she said to herself, 'and Francis never told me!' With those words she ran out of the room.

I was hastening out after her, when my mother signed me to stop. She read the words written on the paper. While they fell slowly, one by one, from her lips, she pointed towards the open door.

'Light grey eyes, with a droop in the left eyelid. Flaxen hair, with a gold-yellow streak in it. White arms, with a down upon them. Little, lady's hand, with a rosy-red look about the finger nails. The Dream-Woman, Francis! The Dream-Woman!'

Something darkened the parlour window as those words were spoken. I looked sidelong at the shadow. Alicia Warlock had come back! She was peering in at us over the low window-blind. There was the fatal face which had first looked at me in the bedroom of the lonely inn! There, resting on the window-blind, was the lovely little hand which had held the murderous knife. I *had* seen her before we met in the village. The Dream-Woman! The Dream-Woman!

I expect nobody to approve of what I have next to tell of myself.

In three weeks from the day when my mother had identified her with the Woman of the Dream, I took Alicia Warlock to church, and made her my wife. I was a man bewitched. Again and again I say it, I was a man bewitched!

During the interval before my marriage, our little household at the cottage was broken up. My mother and my aunt quarrelled. My mother, believing in the Dream, entreated me to break off my engagement. My aunt, believing in the cards, urged me to marry.

This difference of opinion produced a dispute between them, in the course of which my aunt Chance – quite unconscious of having any superstitious feelings of her own – actually set out the cards which prophesied happiness to me in my married life, and asked my mother whether anybody but 'a blinded heathen could be fule enough, after seeing those cairds, to believe in a dream!' This was, naturally, too much for my mother's patience; hard words followed on either side; Mrs Chance returned in dudgeon to her friends in Scotland. She left me a written statement of my future prospects, as revealed by the cards, and with it an address at which a Post-office order would reach her. 'The day was no that far off,' she remarked, 'when Francie might remember what he owed to his aunt Chance, maintaining her ain unbleemished widowhood on thratty punds a year.'

Having refused to give her sanction to my marriage, my mother also refused to be present at the wedding, or to visit Alicia afterwards. There was no anger at the bottom of this conduct on her part. Believing as she did in the Dream, she was simply in mortal fear of my wife. I understood this, and I made allowances for her. Not a cross word passed between us. My one happy remembrance now – though I did disobey her in the matter of my marriage – is this: I loved and respected my good mother to the last.

As for my wife, she expressed no regret at the estrangement between her mother-in-law and herself. By common consent, we never spoke on that subject. We settled in the manufacturing town which I have already mentioned; and we kept a lodging-house. My kind master, at my request, granted me a lump sum in place of my annuity. This put us into a good house, decently furnished. For a while, things went well enough. I may describe myself at this time of my life as a happy man.

My misfortunes began with a return of the complaint from which my mother had already suffered. The doctor confessed, when I asked him the question, that there was danger to be dreaded this time. Naturally, after hearing this, I was a good deal away at the cottage. Naturally, also, I left the business of looking after our house, in my absence, to my wife. Little by little, I found her beginning to alter towards me. While my back was turned, she formed acquaintances with people of the doubtful and dissipated sort. One day, I observed something in her manner which forced the suspicion on me that she had been drinking. Before the week was out, my suspicion was a certainty. From keeping company with drunkards, she had grown to be a drunkard herself.

I did all a man could do to reclaim her. Quite useless! She had never really returned the love I felt for her: I had no influence; I could do nothing. My mother, hearing of this last worst trouble, resolved to try what her influence could do. Ill as she was, I found her one day dressed to go out.

'I am not long for this world, Francis,' she said. 'I shall not feel easy on my death-bed, unless I have done my best to the last to make you happy. I mean to put my own fears and my own feelings out of the question, and to go with you to your wife, and try what I can do to reclaim her. Take me home with you, Francis. Let me do all I can to help my son, before it's too late.'

How could I disobey her? We took the railway to the town: it was only half an hour's ride. By one o'clock in the afternoon we reached my house. It was our dinner hour, and Alicia was in the kitchen. I was able to take my mother quietly into the parlour, and then prepare my wife for the visit. She had drunk but little at that early hour, and, luckily, the devil in her was tamed for the time.

She followed me into the parlour, and the meeting passed off better than I had ventured to forecast; with this one drawback, that my mother – though she tried hard to control herself – shrank from looking my wife in the face when she spoke to her. It was a relief to me when Alicia began to prepare the table for dinner.

She laid the cloth, brought in the bread-tray, and cut some slices for us from the loaf. Then she returned to the kitchen. At that moment, while I was still anxiously watching my mother, I was startled by seeing the same ghastly change pass over her face which had altered it on the morning when Alicia and she first met. Before I could say a word, she started up with a look of horror.

'Take me back! – home, home again, Francis! Come with me, and never go back more!'

I was afraid to ask for an explanation; I could only sign to her to be silent, and help her quickly to the door. As we passed the bread-tray on the table, she stopped and pointed to it.

'Did you see what your wife cut your bread with?' she asked.

'No, mother; I was not noticing. What was it?'

'Look!'

I did look. A new clasp-knife, with a buck-horn handle, lay with the loaf in the bread-tray. I stretched out my hand to possess myself of it. At the same moment, there was a noise in the kitchen, and my mother caught me by the arm.

'The knife of the Dream! Francis, I'm faint with fear – take me away before she comes back!'

I couldn't speak, to comfort or even to answer her. Superior as I was to superstition, the discovery of the knife staggered me. In silence, I helped my mother out of the house, and took her home.

I held out my hand to say good-bye. She tried to stop me.

'Don't go back, Francis! don't go back!'

'I must get the knife, mother. I must go back by the next train.'

I held to that resolution. By the next train I went back.

My wife had, of course, discovered our secret departure from the house. She had been drinking. She was in a fury of passion. The dinner in the kitchen was flung under the grate; the cloth was off the parlour table. Where was the knife?

I was foolish enough to ask for it. She refused to give it to me. In the course of the dispute between us which followed, I discovered that there was a horrible story attached to the knife. It had been used in a murder – years since – and had been so skilfully hidden that the authorities had been unable to produce it at the trial. By help of some of her disreputable friends, my wife had been able to purchase this relic of a bygone crime. Her perverted nature set some horrid unacknowledged value on the knife. Seeing there was no hope of getting it by fair means, I determined to search for it, later in the day, in secret. The search was unsuccessful. Night came on, and I left the house to walk about the streets. You will understand what a broken man I was by this time, when I tell you I was afraid to sleep in the same room with her!

Three weeks passed. Still she refused to give up the knife; and still that fear of sleeping in the same room with her possessed me. I walked about at night, or dozed in the parlour, or sat watching by my mother's bedside. Before the end of the first week in the new month, the worst misfortune of all befell me – my mother died. It wanted then but a short time to my birthday. She had longed to live till that day. I was present at her death. Her last words in this world were addressed to me.

'Don't go back, my son – don't go back!'

I was obliged to go back, if it was only to watch my wife. In the last days of my mother's illness she had spitefully added a sting to my grief by declaring that she would assert her right to attend the funeral. In spite of all that I could do or say, she held to her word. On the day appointed for the burial she forced herself – inflamed and shameless with drink – into my presence, and swore she would walk in the funeral procession to my mother's grave.

This last insult – after all I had gone through already – was more than I could endure. It maddened me. Try to make allowances for a man beside himself. I struck her.

The instant the blow was dealt, I repented it. She crouched down, silent, in a corner of the room, and eyed me steadily. It was a look that cooled my hot blood in an instant. There was no time now to think of making atonement. I could only risk the worst, and make sure of her till the funeral was over. I locked her into her bedroom.

When I came back, after laying my mother in the grave, I found her sitting by the bedside, very much altered in look and bearing, with a bundle on her lap. She faced me quietly; she spoke with a curious stillness in her voice – strangely and unnaturally composed in look and manner.

'No man has ever struck me yet,' she said. 'My husband shall have no second opportunity. Set the door open, and let me go.'

She passed me, and left the room. I saw her walk away up the street.

Was she gone for good?

All that night I watched and waited. No footstep came near the house.

The next night, overcome by fatigue, I lay down in bed in my clothes, with the door locked, the key on the table, and the candle burning. My slumber was not disturbed. The third night, the fourth, the fifth, the sixth, passed, and nothing happened. I lay down on the seventh night, still suspicious of something happening; still in my clothes; still with the door locked, the key on the table, and the candle burning.

My rest was disturbed. I woke twice, without any sensation of uneasiness. The third time, that horrid shivering of the night at the lonely inn, that awful sinking pain at the heart, came back again, and roused me in an instant.

My eyes turned towards the left-hand side of the bed. And there stood, looking at me—

The Dream-Woman again? No! My wife. The living woman, with the face of the Dream – in the attitude of the Dream – the fair arm up; the knife clasped in the delicate white hand.

I sprang upon her on the instant; but not quickly enough to stop her from hiding the knife. Without a word from me, without a cry from her, I pinioned her in a chair. With one hand I felt up her sleeve; and there, where the Dream-Woman had hidden the knife, my wife had hidden it – the knife with the buck-horn handle, that looked like new.

What I felt when I made that discovery I could not realise at the time, and I can't describe now. I took one steady look at her with the knife in my hand.

'You meant to kill me?' I said.

'Yes,' she answered; 'I meant to kill you.' She crossed her arms over her bosom, and stared me coolly in the face. 'I shall do it yet,' she said. 'With that knife.'

I don't know what possessed me – I swear to you I am no coward; and yet I acted like a coward. The horrors got hold of me. I couldn't look at her – I couldn't speak to her. I left her (with the knife in my hand), and went out into the night.

There was a bleak wind abroad, and the smell of rain was in the air. The church clocks chimed the quarter as I walked beyond the last houses in the town. I asked the first policeman I met what hour that was, of which the quarter past had just struck.

The man looked at his watch, and answered, 'Two o'clock.' Two in the morning. What day of the month was this day that had just begun? I reckoned it up from the date of my mother's funeral. The horrid parallel between the dream and the reality was complete – it was my birthday!

Had I escaped the mortal peril which the dream foretold? or had I only received a second warning?

As that doubt crossed my mind I stopped on my way out of the town. The air had revived me – I felt in some degree like my own self again. After a little thinking, I began to see plainly the mistake I had made in leaving my wife free to go where she liked and to do as she pleased.

I turned instantly, and made my way back to the house.

It was still dark. I had left the candle burning in the bedchamber. When I looked up to the window of the room now, there was no light in it. I advanced to the house door. On going away I remembered to have closed it; on trying it now, I found it open.

I waited outside, never losing sight of the house till daylight. Then I ventured in-doors – listened, and heard nothing – looked into the kitchen, scullery, parlour, and found nothing – went up at last into the bedroom. It was empty.

A pick-lock lay on the floor, which told me how she had gained entrance in the night. And that was the one trace I could find of the Dream-Woman.

I waited in the house till the town was astir for the day, and then I went to consult a lawyer. In the confused state of my mind at the time, I had one clear notion of what I meant to do: I was determined to sell my house and leave the neighbourhood. There were obstacles in the way which I had not counted on. I was told I had creditors to satisfy before I could leave – I, who had given my wife the money to pay my bills regularly every week! Enquiry showed that she had embezzled every farthing of the money that I had entrusted to her. I had no choice but to pay over again.

Placed in this awkward position, my first duty was to set things right, with the help of my lawyer. During my forced sojourn in the town I did two foolish things. And, as a consequence that followed, I heard once more, and heard for the last time, of my wife.

In the first place, having got possession of the knife, I was rash enough to keep it in my pocket. In the second place, having something of importance to say to the lawyer, at a late hour of the evening, I went to his house after dark – alone and on foot. I got there safely enough. Returning, I was seized on from behind by two men; dragged down a dark passage, and robbed – not only of the little money I had about me, but also of the knife. It was the lawyer's opinion (as it was mine) that the thieves were among the disreputable acquaintances formed by my wife, and that they had attacked me at her instigation. To confirm this view I received a letter the next day, without date or address, written in Alicia's hand. The first line informed me that the knife was back again in her possession. The second line reminded me of the day when I had struck her. The third line warned me that she would wash out the stain of that blow in my blood, and repeated the words, 'I shall do it with the knife!'

These things happened a year ago. The law laid hands on the men who had robbed me; but from that time to this the law has failed completely to find a trace of my wife.

My story is told. When I had paid the creditors and paid the legal expenses, I had barely five pounds left out of the sale of my house; and I had the world to begin over again. Some months since – drifting here and there – I found my way to Underbridge. The landlord at the inn had known something of my father's family in times past. He gave me (all he had to give) my food, and shelter in the yard. Except on market-days, there is nothing to do. In the coming winter the inn is to be shut up, and I shall have to shift for myself. My old master would help me if I applied to him – but I don't like to apply: he has done more for me already than I deserve. Besides, in another year who knows but my troubles may all be at an end? Next winter will bring me nigh to my next birthday, and my next birthday may be the day of my death. Yes! it's true I sat up all last night; and I heard two in the morning strike: and nothing happened. Still, allowing for that, the time to come is a time I don't trust. My wife has got the knife – my wife is looking for me. I am above superstition, mind! I don't say I believe in dreams; I only say, Alicia Warlock is looking for me. It is possible I may be wrong. It is possible I may be right. Who can tell?

THE THIRD NARRATIVE

THE STORY CONTINUED BY PERCY FAIRBANK

We took leave of Francis Raven at the door of Farleigh Hall, with the understanding that he might expect to hear from us again.

The same night Mrs Fairbank and I had a discussion in the sanctuary of our own room. The topic was 'The Ostler's Story'; and the question in dispute between us turned on the measure of charitable duty that we owed to the ostler himself.

The view I took of the man's narrative was of the purely matter-of-fact kind. Francis Raven had, in my opinion, brooded over the misty connection between his strange dream and his vile wife, until his mind was in a state of partial delusion on that subject. I was quite willing to help him with a trifle of money, and to recommend him to the kindness of my lawyer, if he was really in any danger and wanted advice. There my idea of my duty towards this afflicted person began and ended.

Confronted with this sensible view of the matter, Mrs Fairbank's romantic temperament rushed, as usual, into extremes. 'I should no more think of losing sight of Francis Raven when his next birthday comes round,' says my wife, 'than I should think of laying down a good story with the last chapters unread. I am positively determined, Percy, to take him back with us, when we return to France, in the capacity of groom. What does one man more or less among the horses matter to people as rich as we are?' In this strain the partner of my joys and sorrows ran on, perfectly impenetrable to everything that I could say on the side of common sense. Need I tell my married brethren how it ended? Of course I allowed my wife to irritate me, and spoke to her sharply. Of course my wife turned her face away indignantly on the conjugal pillow, and burst into tears. Of course, upon that, 'Mr' made his excuses, and 'Mrs' had her own way.

Before the week was out we rode over to Underbridge, and duly offered to Francis Raven a place in our service as supernumerary groom.

At first the poor fellow seemed hardly able to realise his own extraordinary good fortune. Recovering himself, he expressed his gratitude modestly and becomingly. Mrs Fairbank's ready sympathies overflowed, as usual, at her lips. She talked to him about our home in France, as if the worn, grey-headed ostler had been a child. 'Such a dear old house, Francis; and such pretty gardens! Stables ten times as big as your stables here: quite a choice of rooms for you. You must learn the name of our house – it is called Maison Rouge. Our nearest town is Metz. We are within a walk of the beautiful river Moselle. And when we want a change we have only to take the railway to the frontier, and find ourselves in Germany.'

Listening, so far, with a very bewildered face, Francis started and changed colour when my wife reached the end of her last sentence.

'Germany?' he repeated.

'Yes. Does Germany remind you of anything?'

The ostler's eyes looked down sadly on the ground. 'Germany reminds me of my wife,' he replied.

'Indeed? How?'

'She once told me she had lived in Germany – long before I knew her – in the time when she was a young girl.'

'Was she living with relations or friends?'

'She was living as governess in a foreign family.'

'In what part of Germany?'

'I don't remember, ma'am. I doubt if she told me.'

'Did she tell you the name of the family?'

'Yes, ma'am. It was a foreign name, and it has slipped my memory long since. The head of the family was a wine-grower in a large way of business – I remember that.'

'Did you hear what sort of wine he grew? There are wine-growers in our neighbourhood. Was it Moselle wine?'

'I couldn't say, ma'am. I doubt if I ever heard.'

There the conversation dropped. We engaged to communicate with Francis Raven before we left England, and took our leave.

I had made my arrangements to pay our round of visits to English friends, and to return to Maison Rouge in the summer. On the eve of departure, certain difficulties in connection with the management of some landed property of mine in Ireland, obliged us to alter our plans. Instead of getting back to our house in France in the summer, we only returned a week or two before Christmas. Francis Raven accompanied us, and was duly established, in the nominal capacity of stable-helper, among the servants at Maison Rouge.

Before long, some of the objections to taking him into our employment, which I had foreseen and had vainly mentioned to my wife, forced themselves on our attention in no very agreeable form.

Francis Raven failed (as I had feared he would) to get on smoothly with his fellow-servants. They were all French; and not one of them understood English. Francis, on his side, was equally ignorant of French. His reserved manners, his melancholy temperament, his solitary ways – all told against him. Our servants called him 'the English Bear.' He grew widely known in the neighbourhood under his nick-name. Quarrels took place, ending once or twice in blows. It became plain, even to Mrs Fairbank herself, that some wise change must be made. While we were still considering what the change was to be, the unfortunate ostler was thrown on our hands for some time to come by an accident in the stables. Still pursued by his proverbial ill-luck, the poor wretch's leg was broken by a kick from a horse.

He was attended to by our own surgeon, in his comfortable bedroom at the stables. As the date of his birthday drew near he was still confined to his bed.

Physically speaking, he was doing very well. Morally speaking, the surgeon was not satisfied. Francis Raven was suffering under some unacknowledged mental disturbance, which interfered seriously with his rest at night. Hearing this, I thought it my duty to tell the medical attendant what was preying on the patient's mind. As a practical man, he shared my opinion that the ostler was in a state of delusion on the subject of his Wife and his Dream. 'Curable delusion, in my opinion,' the surgeon added, 'if the experiment could be fairly tried.'

'How can it be tried?' I asked.

Instead of replying, the surgeon put a question to me, on his side.

'Do you happen to know,' he said, 'that this year is Leap Year?'

'Mrs Fairbank reminded me of it yesterday,' I answered. 'Otherwise I might *not* have known it.'

'Do you think Francis Raven knows that this year is Leap Year?'

(I began to see dimly what my friend was driving at.)

'It depends,' I answered, 'on whether he has got an English almanack. Suppose he has *not* got the almanack – what then?'

'In that case,' pursued the surgeon, 'Francis Raven is innocent of all suspicion that there is a twenty-ninth day in February this year. As a necessary consequence – what will he do? He will anticipate the appearance of the Woman with the Knife at two in the morning on the twenty-ninth of February, instead of the first of March. Let him suffer all his superstitious terrors on the wrong day. Leave him, on the day that is really his birthday, to pass a perfectly quiet night, and to be as sound asleep as other people at two in the morning. And then, when he wakes comfortably in time for his breakfast, shame him out of his delusion by telling him the truth.'

I agreed to try the experiment. Leaving the surgeon to caution Mrs Fairbank on the subject of Leap Year, I went to the stables to see Francis Raven.

The poor fellow was full of forebodings of the fate in store for him on the ominous first of March. He eagerly entreated me to order one of the men-servants to sit up with him on the birthday morning. In granting his request, I asked him to tell me on which day of the week his birthday fell. He reckoned the days on his fingers; and proved his innocence of all suspicion that it was Leap Year by fixing on the twenty-ninth of February, in the full persuasion that it was the first of March. Pledged to try the surgeon's experiment, I left his error uncorrected, of course. In so doing, I took my first step blindfold towards the last act in the drama of the Ostler's Dream.

The next day brought with it a little domestic difficulty, which indirectly and strangely associated itself with the coming end.

My wife received a letter, inviting us to assist in celebrating the 'Silver Wedding' of two worthy German neighbours of ours – Mr and Mrs Beldheimer. Mr Beldheimer was a large wine-grower on the banks of the Moselle. His house was situated on the frontier line of France and Germany; and the distance from our house was sufficiently considerable to make it necessary for us to sleep under our host's roof. Under these circumstances, if we accepted the invitation, a comparison of dates showed that we should be away from home on the morning of the first of March. Mrs Fairbank – holding to her absurd resolution to see with her own eyes what might, or might not, happen to Francis Raven on his birthday – flatly declined to leave Maison Rouge. 'It's easy to send an excuse,' she said, in her off-hand manner.

I failed, for my part, to see any easy way out of the difficulty. The celebration of a 'Silver Wedding' in Germany is the celebration of twenty-five years of happy married life; and the host's claim upon the consideration of his friends on such an occasion is something in the nature of a Royal 'command.' After considerable discussion, finding my wife's obstinacy invincible, and feeling that the absence of both of us from the festival would certainly offend our friends, I left Mrs Fairbank to make her excuses for herself, and directed her to accept the invitation so far as I was concerned. In so doing, I took my second step, blindfold, towards the last act in the drama of the Ostler's Dream.

A week elapsed; the last days of February were at hand. Another domestic difficulty happened; and, again, this event also proved to be strangely associated with the coming end.

My head groom at the stables was one Joseph Rigobert. He was an ill-conditioned fellow, inordinately vain of his personal appearance, and by no means scrupulous in his conduct with women. His one virtue consisted in his fondness for horses, and in the care he took of the animals under his charge. In a word, he was too good a groom to be easily replaced, or he would have quitted my service long since. On the occasion of which I am now writing, he was reported to me by my steward as growing idle and disorderly in his habits. The principal offence alleged against him was, that he had been seen that day in the city of Metz, in the company of a woman (supposed to be an Englishwoman), whom he was entertaining at a tavern, when he ought to have been on his way back to Maison Rouge. The man's defence was that 'the lady' (as he called her) was an English stranger, unacquainted with the ways of the place, and that he had only shown her where she could obtain some refreshment, at her own request. I administered the necessary reprimand, without troubling myself to enquire further into the matter. In failing to do this, I took my third step, blindfold, towards the last act in the drama of the Ostler's Dream.

On the evening of the twenty-eighth, I informed the servants at the stables that one of them must watch through the night by the Englishman's bedside. Joseph Rigobert immediately volunteered for the duty – as a means, no doubt, of winning his way back to my favour. I accepted his proposal.

That day, the surgeon dined with us. Towards midnight he and I left the smoking-room, and repaired to Francis Raven's bed-side. Rigobert was at his post, with no very agreeable expression on his face. The Frenchman and the Englishman had evidently not got on well together, so far. Francis Raven lay helpless on his bed, waiting silently for two in the morning, and the Dream-Woman.

'I have come, Francis, to bid you goodnight,' I said, cheerfully. 'To-morrow morning I shall look in at breakfast time, before I leave home on a journey.'

'Thank you for all your kindness, sir. You will not see me alive to-morrow morning. She will find me this time. Mark my words – she will find me this time.'

'My good fellow! she couldn't find you in England. How in the world is she to find you in France?'

'It's borne in on my mind, sir, that she will find me here. At two in the morning on my birthday I shall see her again, and see her for the last time.'

'Do you mean that she will kill you?'

'I mean that, sir. She will kill me – with the knife.'

'And with Rigobert in the room to protect you?'

'I am a doomed man. Fifty Rigoberts couldn't protect me.'

'And yet you wanted somebody to sit up with you?'

'Mere weakness, sir. I don't like to be left alone on my death-bed.'

I looked at the surgeon. If he had encouraged me, I should certainly, out of sheer compassion, have confessed to Francis Raven the trick that we were playing him. The surgeon held to his experiment; the surgeon's face plainly said – 'No.'

The next day (the twenty-ninth of February) was the day of the 'Silver Wedding.' The first thing in the morning, I went to Francis Raven's room. Rigobert met me at the door.

'How has he passed the night?' I asked.

'Saying his prayers, and looking for ghosts,' Rigobert answered. 'A lunatic asylum is the only proper place for him.'

I approached the bedside. 'Well, Francis, here you are, safe and sound, in spite of what you said to me last night.'

His eyes rested on mine with a vacant, wondering look.

'I don't understand it,' he said.

'Did you see anything of your wife when the clock struck two?'

'No, sir.'

'Did anything happen?'

'Nothing happened, sir.'

'Doesn't *this* satisfy you that you were wrong?'

His eyes still kept their vacant, wondering look. He only repeated the words he had spoken already:

'I don't understand it.'

I made a last attempt to cheer him. 'Come, come, Francis! keep a good heart. You will be out of bed in a fortnight.'

He shook his head on the pillow. 'There's something wrong,' he said. 'I don't expect you to believe me, sir. I only say, there's something wrong – and time will show it.'

I left the room. Half an hour later I started for Mr Beldheimer's house; leaving the arrangements for the morning of the first of March in the hands of the doctor and my wife.

The one thing which principally struck me when I joined the guests at the 'Silver Wedding,' is also the one thing which it is necessary to mention here. On this joyful occasion a noticeable lady present was out of spirits. That lady was no other than the heroine of the festival, the mistress of the house!

In the course of the evening I spoke to Mr Beldheimer's eldest son on the subject of his mother. As an old friend of the family, I had a claim on his confidence which the young man willingly recognised.

'We have had a very disagreeable matter to deal with,' he said; 'and my mother has not recovered the painful impression left on her mind. Many years since, when my sisters were children, we had an English governess in the house. She left us, as we then understood, to be married. We heard no more of her until a week or ten days since, when my mother received a letter, in which our ex-governess described herself as being in a condition of great poverty and distress. After much hesitation she had ventured – at the suggestion of a lady who had been kind to her – to write to her former employers, and to appeal to their remembrance of old times. You know my mother: she is not only the most kind-hearted, but the most innocent of women – it is impossible to persuade her of the wickedness that there is in the world. She replied by return of post, inviting the governess to come here and see her, and enclosing the money for her travelling expenses. When my father came home, and heard what had been done, he wrote at once to his agent in London to make enquiries, enclosing the address on the governess's letter. Before he could receive the agent's reply the governess arrived. She produced the worst possible impression on his mind. The agent's letter, arriving a few days later, confirmed his suspicions. Since we had lost sight of her, the woman had led a most disreputable life. My father spoke to her privately: he offered – on condition of her leaving the house – a sum of money to take her back to England. If she refused, the alternative would be an appeal to the authorities and a public scandal. She accepted the money, and left the house. On her way back to England she appears to have stopped at Metz. You will understand what sort of woman she is, when I tell you that she was seen the other day in a tavern with your handsome groom, Joseph Rigobert.'

While my informant was relating these circumstances, my memory was at work. I recalled what Francis Raven had vaguely told us of his wife's experience in former days, as governess in a German family. A suspicion of the truth suddenly flashed across my mind.

'What was the woman's name?' I asked.

Mr Beldheimer's son answered:

'Alicia Warlock.'

I had but one idea when I heard that reply – to get back to my house without a moment's needless delay. It was then ten o'clock at night – the last train to Metz had left long since. I arranged with my young friend – after duly informing him of the circumstances – that I should go by the first train in the morning, instead of staying to breakfast with the other guests who slept in the house.

At intervals during the night I wondered uneasily how things were going on at Maison Rouge. Again and again, the same question occurred to me, on my journey home in the early morning – the morning of the first of March. As the event proved, but one person in my house knew what really happened at the stables on Francis Raven's birthday. Let Joseph Rigobert take my place as narrator, and tell the story of the end to You – as he told it, in times past, to his lawyer and to Me.

FOURTH (AND LAST) NARRATIVE.

THE STATEMENT OF JOSEPH RIGOBERT: ADDRESSED TO THE BARRISTER WHO DEFENDED HIM AT HIS TRIAL

Respected Sir, – On the twenty-seventh of February I was sent, on business connected with the stables at Maison Rouge, to the city of Metz. On the public promenade I met a magnificent woman. Complexion blonde. Nationality, English. We mutually admired each other; we fell into conversation. (She spoke French perfectly – with the English accent.) I offered refreshment; my proposal was accepted. We had a long and interesting interview – we discovered that we were made for each other. So far, Who is to blame?

Is it my fault that I am a handsome man – universally agreeable, as such, to the fair sex? Is it a criminal offence to be accessible to the amiable weakness of love? I ask again, Who is to blame? Clearly, Nature. Not the beautiful lady – not my humble self.

To resume. The most hard-hearted person living will understand that two beings made for each other could not possibly part without an appointment to meet again.

I made arrangements for the accommodation of the lady in the village near Maison Rouge. She consented to honour me with her company at supper, in my apartment at the stables, on the night of the twenty-ninth. The time fixed on was the time when the other servants were accustomed to retire – eleven o'clock.

Among the grooms attached to the stables was an Englishman, laid up with a broken leg. His name was Francis. His manners were repulsive; he was ignorant of the French language. In the kitchen he went by the nick-name of 'the English Bear.' Strange to say, he was a great favourite with my master and my mistress. They even humoured certain superstitious terrors to which this repulsive person was subject – terrors into the nature of which I, as an advanced freethinker, never thought it worth my while to enquire.

On the evening of the twenty-eighth, the Englishman, being a prey to the terrors which I have mentioned, requested that one of his fellow-servants might sit up with him for that night only. The wish that he expressed was backed by Mr Fairbank's authority. Having already incurred my master's displeasure – in what way, a proper sense of my own dignity forbids me to relate – I volunteered to watch by the bedside of the English Bear. My object was to satisfy Mr Fairbank that I bore no malice, on my side, after what had occurred between us. The wretched Englishman passed a night of delirium. Not understanding his barbarous language, I could only gather from his gestures that he was in deadly fear of some fancied apparition at his bedside. From time to time, when this madman disturbed my slumbers, I quieted him by swearing at him. This is the shortest and best way of dealing with persons in his condition.

On the morning of the twenty-ninth, Mr Fairbank left us on a journey.

Later in the day, to my unspeakable disgust, I found that I had not done with the Englishman yet. In Mr Fairbank's absence, Mrs Fairbank took an incomprehensible interest in the question of my delirious fellow-servant's repose at night. Again, one or other of us was to watch by his bedside, and to report it, if anything happened. Expecting my fair friend to supper, it was necessary to make sure that the other servants at the stables would be safe in their beds that night. Accordingly, I volunteered once more to be the man who kept watch. Mrs Fairbank complimented me on my humanity. I possess great command over my feelings. I accepted the compliment without a blush.

Twice, after nightfall, my mistress and the doctor (this last staying in the house, in Mr Fairbank's absence) came to make enquiries. Once, *before* the arrival of my fair friend – and once *after*. On the second occasion (my apartment being next door to the Englishman's) I was obliged to hide my charming guest in the harness room. She consented, with angelic resignation, to immolate her dignity to the servile necessities of my position. A more amiable woman (so far) I never met with!

After the second visit I was left free. It was then close on midnight. Up to that time, there was nothing in the behaviour of the mad Englishman to reward Mrs Fairbank and the doctor for presenting themselves at his bedside. He lay half awake, half asleep, with an odd, wondering kind of look in his face. My mistress at parting warned me to be particularly watchful of him towards two in the morning. The doctor (in case anything happened) left me a large hand-bell to ring, which could easily be heard at the house.

Restored to the society of my fair friend, I spread the supper-table. A pâté, a sausage, and a few bottles of generous Moselle wine, composed our simple meal. When persons adore each other, the intoxicating illusion of Love transforms the simplest meal into a banquet. With immeasurable capacities for enjoyment, we sat down to table. At the very moment when I placed my fascinating companion in a chair, the infamous Englishman in the next room took that occasion, of all others, to become restless and noisy once more. He struck with his stick on the floor; he cried out, in a delirious access of terror, 'Rigobert! Rigobert!'

The sound of that lamentable voice, suddenly assailing our ears, terrified my fair friend. She lost all her charming colour in an instant. 'Good heavens!' she exclaimed. 'Who is that in the next room?'

'A mad Englishman.'

'An Englishman?'

'Compose yourself, my angel. I will quiet him.'

The lamentable voice called out on me again. 'Rigobert! Rigobert!'

My fair friend caught me by the arm. 'Who is he? What is his name?'

Something in her face struck me as she put that question. A spasm of jealousy shook me to the soul. 'You know him?' I said.

'His name!' she vehemently repeated; 'his name!'

'Francis,' I answered.

'Francis – *what?*'

I shrugged my shoulders. I could neither remember nor pronounce the barbarous English surname. I could only tell her it began with an 'R.'

She dropped back into the chair. Was she going to faint? No; she recovered, and more than recovered, her lost colour. Her eyes flashed superbly. What did it mean? Profoundly as I understand women in general, I was puzzled by *this* woman!

'You know him?' I repeated.

She laughed at me. 'What nonsense! How should I know him? Go and quiet the wretch.'

My looking-glass was near. One glance at it satisfied me that no woman in her senses could prefer the Englishman to Me. I recovered my self-respect. I hastened to the Englishman's bedside.

The moment I appeared he pointed eagerly towards my room. He overwhelmed me with a torrent of words in his own language. I made out, from his gestures and his looks, that he had, in some incomprehensible manner, discovered the presence of my guest; and, stranger still, that he was scared by the idea of a person in my room. I endeavoured to compose him on the system which I have already mentioned – that is to say, I swore at him in *my* language. The result not proving satisfactory, I own I shook my fist in his face, and left the bedchamber.

Returning to my fair friend, I found her walking backwards and forwards in a state of excitement wonderful to behold. She had not waited for me to fill her glass – she had begun the generous Moselle in my absence. I prevailed on her with difficulty to place herself at the table. Nothing would induce her to eat. 'My appetite is gone,' she said. 'Give me wine.'

The generous Moselle deserves its name – delicate on the palate, with prodigious 'body.' The strength of this fine wine produced no stupefying effect on my remarkable guest. It appeared to strengthen and exhilarate her – nothing more. She always spoke in the same low tone, and always, turn the conversation as I might, brought it back with the same dexterity to the subject of the Englishman in the next room. In any other woman this persistency would have offended me. My lovely guest was irresistible; I answered her questions with the docility of a child. She possessed all the amusing eccentricity of her nation. When I told her of the accident which confined the Englishman to his bed, she sprang to her feet. An extraordinary smile irradiated her countenance.

She said, 'Show me the horse who broke his leg! I must, and will, see that horse!' I took her down to the stables. She kissed the horse – on my word of honour, she kissed the horse! That struck me. I said, 'You *do* know the man; and he has wronged you in some way.' No! she would not admit it, even then. 'I kiss all beautiful animals,' she said. 'Haven't I kissed *you*?' With that charming explanation of her conduct, she ran back up the stairs. I only remained behind to lock the stable door again. When I rejoined her, I made a startling discovery. I caught her coming out of the Englishman's room.

'I was just going downstairs again to call you,' she said. 'The man in there is getting noisy once more.'

The mad Englishman's voice assailed our ears again.

'Rigobert! Rigobert!'

He was a frightful object to look at when I saw him this time. His eyes were staring wildly; the perspiration was pouring over his face. In a panic of terror he clasped his hands; he pointed up to heaven. By every sign and gesture that a man can make, he entreated me not to leave him again. I really could not help smiling. The idea of my staying with *him*, and leaving my fair friend by herself in the next room!

I turned to the door. When the mad wretch saw me leaving him he burst out into a screech of despair – so shrill that I feared it might awaken the sleeping servants.

My presence of mind in emergencies is proverbial among those who know me. I tore open the cupboard in which he kept his linen – seized a handful of his handkerchiefs – gagged him with one of them, and secured his hands with the others. There was now no danger of his alarming the servants. After tying the last knot, I looked up.

The door between the Englishman's room and mine was open. My fair friend was standing on the threshold – watching *him* as he lay helpless on the bed; watching *me* as I tied the last knot.

'What are you doing there?' I asked. 'Why did you open the door?'

She stepped up to me, and whispered her answer in my ear, with her eyes all the time upon the man on the bed.

'I heard him scream.'

'Well?'

'I thought you had killed him.'

I drew back from her in horror. The suspicion of me which her words implied, was sufficiently detestable in itself. But her manner when she uttered the words was more revolting still. It so powerfully affected me that I started back from that beautiful creature, as I might have recoiled from a reptile crawling over my flesh.

Before I had recovered myself sufficiently to reply, my nerves were assailed by another shock. I suddenly heard my mistress's voice, calling to me from the stable yard.

There was no time to think – there was only time to act. The one thing needed was to keep Mrs Fairbank from ascending the stairs, and discovering – not my lady-guest only – but the Englishman also, gagged and bound on his bed. I instantly hurried to the yard. As I ran down the stairs I heard the stable clock strike the quarter to two in the morning.

My mistress was eager and agitated. The doctor (in attendance on her) was smiling to himself, like a man amused at his own thoughts.

'Is Francis awake or asleep?' Mrs Fairbank enquired.

'He has been a little restless, madam. But he is now quiet again. If he is not disturbed' (I added those words to prevent her from ascending the stairs), 'he will soon fall off into a quiet sleep.'

'Has nothing happened since I was here last?'

'Nothing, madam.'

The doctor lifted his eyebrows with a comical look of distress.

'Alas, alas, Mrs Fairbank!' he said. 'Nothing has happened! The days of romance are over!'

'It is not two o'clock yet,' my mistress answered, a little irritably.

The smell of the stables was strong on the morning air. She put her handkerchief to her nose and led the way out of the yard, by the north entrance – the entrance communicating with the gardens and the house. I was ordered to follow her, along with the doctor. Once out of the smell of the stables, she began to question me again. She was unwilling to believe that nothing had occurred in her absence. I invented the best answers I could think of on the spur of the moment; and the doctor stood by, laughing. So the minutes passed, till the clock struck two. Upon that, Mrs Fairbank announced her intention of personally visiting the Englishman in his room. To my great relief, the doctor interfered to stop her from doing this.

'You have heard that Francis is just falling asleep,' he said. 'If you enter his room you may disturb him. It is essential to the success of my experiment that he should have a good night's rest, and that he should own it himself, before I tell him the truth. I must request, madam, that you will not disturb the man. Rigobert will ring if anything happens.'

My mistress was unwilling to yield. For the next five minutes at least, there was a warm discussion between the two. In the end, Mrs Fairbank was obliged to give way – for the time. 'In half an hour,' she said, 'Francis will either be sound asleep, or awake again. In half an hour I shall come back.' She took the doctor's arm. They returned together to the house.

Left by myself, with half an hour before me, I resolved to take the English-woman back to the village – then, returning to the stables, to remove the gag and the bindings from Francis, and to let him screech to his heart's content. What would his alarming the whole establishment matter to *me*, after I had got rid of the compromising presence of my guest?

Returning to the yard I heard a sound like the creaking of an open door on its hinges. The gate of the north entrance I had just closed with my own hand. I went round to the west entrance at the back of the stables. It opened on a field crossed by two footpaths, in Mr Fairbank's grounds. The nearest footpath led to the village. The other led to the high road and the river.

Arriving at the west entrance I found the door open – swinging to and fro slowly in the fresh morning breeze. I had myself locked and bolted that door after admitting my fair friend at eleven o'clock. A vague dread of something wrong stole its way into my mind. I hurried back to the stables.

I looked into my own room. It was empty. I went to the harness room. Not a sign of the woman was there. I returned to my room, and approached the door of the Englishman's bedchamber. Was it possible that she had remained there during my absence? An unaccountable reluctance to open the door made me hesitate, with my hand on the lock. I listened. There was not a sound inside. I called softly. There was no answer. I drew back a step, still hesitating. I noticed something dark, moving slowly in the crevice between the bottom of the door and the boarded floor. Snatching up the candle from the table, I held it low, and looked. The dark, slowly-moving object was a stream of blood!

That horrid sight roused me. I opened the door.

The Englishman lay on his bed – alone in the room. He was stabbed in two places – in the throat and in the heart. The weapon was left in the second wound. It was a knife of English manufacture, with a handle of buck-horn as good as new.

I instantly gave the alarm. Witnesses can speak to what followed. It is monstrous to suppose that I am guilty of the murder. I admit that I am capable of committing follies; but I shrink from the bare idea of a crime. Besides, I had no motive for killing the man. The woman murdered him in my absence. The woman escaped by the west entrance while I was talking to my mistress. I have no more to say. I swear to you what I have here written is a true statement of all that happened on the morning of the first of March.

Accept, sir, the assurance of my sentiments of profound gratitude and respect.

JOSEPH RIGOBERT

LAST LINES

ADDED BY PERCY FAIRBANK

Tried for the murder of Francis Raven, Joseph Rigobert was found Not Guilty; the papers of the assassinated man presenting ample evidence of the deadly animosity felt towards him by his wife.

The investigations pursued on the morning when the crime was committed showed that the murderess, after leaving the stable, had taken the footpath which led to the river. The river was dragged – without result. It remains doubtful to this day whether she died by drowning or not. The one thing certain is – that Alicia Warlock was never seen again.

So – beginning in mystery, ending in mystery – the Dream-Woman passes from your view. Ghost; demon; or living human creature – say for yourselves which she is. Or, knowing what unfathomed wonders are around you, what unfathomed wonders are *in* you, let the wise words of the greatest of all poets be explanation enough:

> We are such stuff
> As dreams are made of, and our little life
> Is rounded with a sleep.

The Lady of Glenwith Grange

Unusually this story had no magazine publication, and was first published in *After Dark* (1856). The framing-narrative is an integral part of the story, and has been reproduced as its 'Prologue'. Robert Ashley points out that the story's sinister house anticipates Satis House in *Great Expectations* (1860), while its 'double identity plot . . . antedates the double identity plots of both *A Tale of Two Cities* (1859) and *The Woman in White* (1860)' (*Wilkie Collins*, p. 49). Norman Page has recently argued that 'the relationship between Ida and her sister Rosamond . . . surely represents a first sketch for that between Marion Halcombe and her half-sister Laura Fairlie in *The Woman in White*: a relationship part sisterly, part maternal' (Introduction to *Mad Monkton and Other Stories*, p. xix).

PROLOGUE

My practice in the art of portrait-painting, if it has done nothing else, has at least fitted me to turn my talents (such as they are) to a great variety of uses. I have not only taken the likenesses of men, women, and children, but have also extended the range of my brush, under stress of circumstances, to horses, dogs, houses, and in one case even to a bull – the terror and glory of his parish, and the most truculent sitter I ever had. The beast was appropriately named 'Thunder and Lightning,' and was the property of a gentleman-farmer named Garthwaite, a distant connexion of my wife's family.

How it was that I escaped being gored to death before I had finished my picture, is more than I can explain to this day. 'Thunder and Lightning' resented the very sight of me and my colour-box, as if he viewed the taking of his likeness in the light of a personal insult. It required two men to coax him, while a third held him by a ring in his nostrils, before I could venture on beginning to work. Even then he always lashed his tail, and jerked his huge head, and rolled his fiery eyes with a devouring anxiety to have me on his horns for daring to sit down quietly and look at him. Never, I can honestly say, did I feel more heartily grateful for the blessings of soundness of limb and wholeness of skin, than when I had completed the picture of the bull!

One morning, when I had but little more than half done my unwelcome task, my friend and I were met on our way to the bull's stable by the farm-bailiff, who informed us gravely that 'Thunder and Lightning' was just then in such an especially surly state of temper as to render it quite unsafe for me to think of painting him. I looked inquiringly at Mr Garthwaite, who smiled with an air of comic resignation, and said: 'Very well, then, we have nothing for it but to wait till to-morrow. What do you say to a morning's fishing, Mr Kerby, now that my bull's bad temper has given us a holiday?'

I replied, with perfect truth, that I knew nothing about fishing. But Mr Garthwaite, who was as ardent an angler in his way as Izaak Walton himself, was not to be appeased even by the best of excuses. 'It is never too late to learn,' cried he. 'I will make a fisherman of you in no time, if you will only attend to my directions.' It was impossible for me to make any more apologies, without the risk of appearing discourteous. So I thanked my host for his friendly intentions, and with some secret misgivings, accepted the first fishing-rod that he put into my hands.

'We shall soon get there,' said Mr Garthwaite. 'I am taking you to the best mill-stream in the neighbourhood.' It was all one to me whether we got there soon or late, and whether the stream was good or bad. However, I did my best to conceal my unsportsmanlike apathy; and tried to look quite happy and very impatient to begin, as we drew near to the mill, and heard louder and louder the gushing of many waters all around it.

Leading the way immediately to a place beneath the falling stream, where there was a deep, eddying pool, Mr Garthwaite baited and threw in his line before I had fixed the joints of my fishing-rod. This first difficulty overcome, I involuntarily plunged into some excellent, but rather embarrassing, sport with my line and hook. I caught every one of my garments, from head to foot; I angled for my own clothes with the dexterity and success of Izaak Walton himself. I caught my hat, my jacket, my waistcoat, my trousers, my fingers, and my thumbs – some devil possessed my hook; some more than eel-like vitality twirled and twisted in every inch of my line. By the time my host arrived to assist me, I had attached myself to my fishing-rod, apparently for life. All difficulties yielded, however, to his patience and skill; my hook was baited for me, and thrown in; my rod was put into my hand; my friend went back to his place; and we began at last to angle in earnest.

We certainly caught a few fish (in *my* case, I mean, of course, that the fish caught themselves); but they were scanty in number and light in weight. Whether it was the presence of the miller's foreman – a gloomy personage, who stood staring disastrously upon us from a little flower-garden on the opposite bank – that cast an adverse influence over our sport; or whether my want of faith and earnestness as an angler acted retributively on my companion as well as myself, I know not; but it is certain that he got almost as little reward for his skill as I got for my patience. After nearly two hours of intense expectation on my part, and intense angling on his, Mr Garthwaite jerked his line out of the water in a rage, and bade me follow him to another place, declaring that the stream must have been netted by poachers in the night, who had taken all the large fish away with them, and had thrown in the small ones to grow until their next visit. We moved away, further down the bank, leaving the imperturbable foreman still in the flower-garden, staring at us speechlessly on our departure, exactly as he had already stared at us on our approach.

'Stop a minute,' said Mr Garthwaite suddenly, after we had walked some distance in silence by the side of the stream, 'I have an idea. Now we *are* out for a day's angling, we won't be baulked. Instead of trying the water here again, we will go where I know, by experience, that the fishing is excellent. And, what is more, you shall be introduced to a lady whose appearance is sure to interest you, and whose history, I can tell you beforehand, is a very remarkable one.'

'Indeed,' I said. 'May I ask in what way.'

'She is connected,' answered Mr Garthwaite, 'with an extraordinary story, which relates to a family once settled in an old house in this neighbourhood. Her name is Miss Welwyn; but she is less formally known among the poor people about here, who love her dearly, and honour her almost superstitiously, as The Lady of Glenwith Grange. Wait till you have seen her before you ask me to say anything more. She lives in the strictest retirement: I am almost the only visitor who is admitted. Don't say you had rather not go in. Any friend of mine will be welcome at the Grange (the scene of the story, remember), for my sake – the more especially because I have never abused my privilege of introduction. The place is not above two miles from here, and the stream (which we call in our county dialect, Glenwith Beck), runs through the grounds.'

As we walked on, Mr Garthwaite's manner altered. He became unusually silent and thoughtful. The mention of Miss Welwyn's name had evidently called up some recollections which were not in harmony with his every-day mood. Feeling that to talk to him on any indifferent subject would be only to interrupt his thoughts to no purpose, I walked by his side in perfect silence, looking out already with some curiosity and impatience for a first view of Glenwith Grange. We stopped, at last, close by an old church, standing on the outskirts of a pretty village. The low wall of the churchyard was bounded on one side by a plantation, and was joined by a park paling, in which I noticed a small wicket-gate. Mr Garthwaite opened it, and led me along a shrubbery-path, which conducted us circuitously to the dwelling-house.

We had evidently entered by a private way, for we approached the building by the back. I looked up at it curiously, and saw standing at one of the windows on the lower floor a little girl watching us as we advanced. She seemed to be about nine or ten years old. I could not help stopping a moment to look up at her, her clear complexion, and her long dark hair, were so beautiful. And yet there was something in her expression – a dimness and vacancy in her large eyes, a changeless unmeaning smile on her parted lips – which seemed to jar with all that was naturally attractive in her face; which perplexed, disappointed, and even shocked me, though I hardly knew why. Mr Garthwaite, who had been walking along thoughtfully, with his eyes on the ground, turned back when he found me lingering behind him; looked up where I was looking; started a little, I thought; then took my arm, whispered rather impatiently, 'Don't say anything about having seen that poor child when you are introduced to Miss Welwyn; I'll tell you why afterwards,' and led me round hastily to the front of the building.

It was a very dreary old house, with a lawn in front thickly sprinkled with flower-beds, and creepers of all sorts climbing in profusion about the heavy stone porch and the mullions of the lower windows. In spite of these prettiest of all ornaments clustering brightly round the building – in spite of the perfect repair in which it was kept from top to bottom – there was something repellent to me in the aspect of the whole place: a deathly stillness hung over it, which fell oppressively on my spirits. When my companion rang the loud, deep-toned bell, the sound startled me as if we had been committing a crime in disturbing the silence. And when the door was opened by an old female servant (while the hollow echo of the bell was still vibrating in the air), I could hardly imagine it possible that we should be let in. We were admitted, however, without the slightest demur. I remarked that there was the same atmosphere of dreary repose inside the house which I had already observed, or rather felt, outside it. No dogs barked at our approach – no doors banged in the servants' offices – no heads peeped over the banisters – not one of the ordinary domestic consequences of an unexpected visit in the country met either eye or ear. The large shadowy apartment, half library, half breakfast-room, into which we were ushered, was as solitary as the hall of entrance; unless I except such drowsy evidences of life as were here presented to us, in the shape of an Angola cat and a gray parrot – the first lying asleep in a chair, the second sitting ancient, solemn, and voiceless in a large cage. Mr Garthwaite walked to the window when we entered, without saying a word. Determining to let his taciturn humour have its way, I asked him no questions, but looked around the room to see what information it would give me (and rooms often do give such information) about the character and habits of the owner of the house.

Two tables covered with books were the first objects that attracted me. On approaching them, I was surprised to find that the all-influencing periodical literature of the present day – whose sphere is already almost without limit; whose readers, even in our time, may be numbered by millions – was entirely unrepresented on Miss Welwyn's table. Nothing modern, nothing contemporary in the world of books, presented itself. Of all the volumes beneath my hand, not one bore the badge of the circulating library, or wore the flaring modern livery of gilt cloth. Every work that I took up had been written at least fifteen or twenty years since. The prints hanging round the walls (towards which I next looked) were all engraved from devotional subjects by the old masters: the music-stand contained no music of later date than the compositions of Haydn and Mozart. Whatever I examined besides, told me, with the same consistency, the same strange tale. The owner of these possessions lived in the bygone time; lived among old recollections and old associations – a voluntary recluse from all that was connected with the passing day. In Miss Welwyn's house, the stir, the tumult, the 'idle business' of the world, evidently appealed in vain to sympathies which grew no longer with the growing hour.

As these thoughts were passing through my mind, the door opened, and the lady herself appeared.

She looked certainly past the prime of life; longer past it, as I afterwards discovered, than she really was. But I never remember, in any other face, to have seen so much of the better part of the beauty of early womanhood still remaining, as I saw in hers. Sorrow had evidently passed over the fair calm countenance before me, but had left resignation there as its only trace. Her expression was still youthful – youthful in its kindness and its candour especially. It was only when I looked at her hair, that was now growing gray – at her wan thin hands – at the faint lines marked round her mouth – at the sad serenity of her eyes, that I fairly detected the mark of age; and, more than that, the token of some great grief, which had been conquered, but not banished. Even from her voice alone – from the peculiar uncertainty of its low calm tones when she spoke – it was easy to conjecture that she must have passed through sufferings, at some time of her life, which had tried to the quick the noble nature that they could not subdue.

Mr Garthwaite and she met each other almost like brother and sister: it was plain that the friendly intimacy between them had been of very long duration. Our visit was a short one. The conversation never advanced beyond the commonplace topics suited to the occasion: it was, therefore, from what I saw, and not from what I heard, that I was enabled to form my judgment of Miss Welwyn. Deeply as she had interested me – far more deeply than I at all know how to explain in fitting words – I cannot say that I was unwilling to depart when we rose to take leave. Though nothing could be more courteous and more kind than her manner towards me during the whole interview, I could still perceive that it cost her some effort to repress in my presence the shades of sadness and reserve which seemed often ready to steal over her. And I must confess that when I once or twice heard the half-sigh stifled, and saw the momentary relapse into thoughtfulness suddenly restrained, I felt an indefinable awkwardness in my position which made me ill at ease; which set me doubting whether, as a perfect stranger, I had done right in suffering myself to be introduced where no new faces could awaken either interest or curiosity; where no new sympathies could ever be felt, no new friendships ever be formed.

As soon as we had taken leave of Miss Welwyn, and were on our way to the stream in her grounds, I more than satisfied Mr Garthwaite that the impression the lady had produced on me was of no transitory kind, by overwhelming him with questions about her – not omitting one or two incidental inquiries on the subject of the little girl whom I had seen at the back window. He only rejoined that his story would answer all my questions; and that he would begin to tell it as soon as we had arrived at Glenwith Beck, and were comfortably settled to fishing.

Five minutes more of walking brought us to the bank of the stream, and showed us the water running smoothly and slowly, tinged with the softest green lustre from the reflections of trees which almost entirely arched it over. Leaving me to admire the view at my ease, Mr Garthwaite occupied himself with the necessary preparations for angling, baiting my hook as well as his own. Then, desiring me to sit near him on the bank, he at last satisfied my curiosity by beginning his story. I shall relate it in his own manner, and, as nearly as possible, in his own words.

THE ANGLER'S STORY OF THE LADY OF GLENWITH GRANGE

I have known Miss Welwyn long enough to be able to bear personal testimony to the truth of many of the particulars which I am now about to relate. I knew her father, and her younger sister Rosamond; and I was acquainted with the Frenchman who became Rosamond's husband. These are the persons of whom it will be principally necessary for me to speak; they are the only prominent characters in my story.

Miss Welwyn's father died some years since. I remember him very well – though he never excited in me, or in any one else that I ever heard of, the slightest feeling of interest. When I have said that he inherited a very large fortune, amassed during his father's time, by speculations of a very daring, very fortunate, but not always very honourable kind, and that he bought this old house with the notion of raising his social position, by making himself a member of our landed aristocracy in these parts, I have told you as much about him, I suspect, as you would care to hear. He was a thoroughly commonplace man, with no great virtues and no great vices in him. He had a little heart, a feeble mind, an amiable temper, a tall figure, and a handsome face. More than this need not, and cannot, be said on the subject of Mr Welwyn's character.

I must have seen the late Mrs Welwyn very often as a child; but I cannot say that I remember anything more of her than that she was tall and handsome, and very generous and sweet-tempered towards me when I was in her company. She was her husband's superior in birth, as in everything else; was a great reader of books in all languages; and possessed such admirable talents as a musician, that her wonderful playing on the organ is remembered and talked of to this day among the old people in our country houses about here. All her friends, as I have heard, were disappointed when she married Mr Welwyn, rich as he was; and were afterwards astonished to find her preserving the appearance, at least, of being perfectly happy with a husband who, neither in mind nor heart, was worthy of her.

It was generally supposed (and I have no doubt correctly), that she found her great happiness and her great consolation in her little girl Ida – now the lady from whom we have just parted. The child took after her mother from the first – inheriting her mother's fondness for books, her mother's love of music, her mother's quick sensibilities, and, more than all, her mother's quiet firmness, patience, and loving-kindness of disposition. From Ida's earliest years, Mrs Welwyn undertook the whole superintendence of her education. The two were hardly ever apart, within doors or without. Neighbours and friends said that the little girl was being brought up too fancifully, was not enough among other children, was sadly neglected as to all reasonable and practical teaching, and was perilously encouraged in those dreamy and imaginative tendencies of which she had naturally more than her due share. There was, perhaps, some truth in this; and there might have been still more, if Ida had possessed an ordinary character, or had been reserved for an ordinary destiny. But she was a strange child from the first, and a strange future was in store for her.

Little Ida reached her eleventh year without either brother or sister to be her playfellow and companion at home. Immediately after that period, however, her sister Rosamond was born. Though Mr Welwyn's own desire was to have had a son, there were, nevertheless, great rejoicings yonder in the old house on the birth of this second daughter. But they were all turned, only a few months afterwards, to the bitterest grief and despair: the Grange lost its mistress. While Rosamond was still an infant in arms, her mother died.

Mrs Welwyn had been afflicted with some disorder after the birth of her second child, the name of which I am not learned enough in medical science to be able to remember. I only know that she recovered from it, to all appearance, in an unexpectedly short time; that she suffered a fatal relapse, and that she died a lingering and a painful death. Mr Welwyn (who, in after-years, had a habit of vaingloriously describing his marriage as 'a love-match on both sides') was really fond of his wife in his own frivolous feeble way, and suffered as acutely as such a man could suffer, during the latter days of her illness, and at the terrible time when the doctors, one and all, confessed that her life was a thing to be despaired of. He burst into irrepressible passions of tears, and was always obliged to leave the sick-room whenever Mrs Welwyn spoke of her approaching end. The last solemn words of the dying woman, the tenderest messages that she could give, the dearest parting wishes that she could express, the most earnest commands that she could leave behind her, the gentlest reasons for consolation that she could suggest to the survivors among those who loved her, were not poured into her husband's ear, but into her child's. From the first period of her illness, Ida had persisted in remaining in the sick-room, rarely speaking, never showing outwardly any signs of terror or grief, except when she was removed from it; and then bursting into hysterical passions of weeping, which no expostulations, no arguments, no commands – nothing, in short, but bringing her back to the bedside – ever availed to calm. Her mother had been her playfellow, her companion, her dearest and most familiar friend; and there seemed something in the remembrance of this which, instead of overwhelming the child with despair, strengthened her to watch faithfully and bravely by her dying parent to the very last.

When the parting moment was over, and when Mr Welwyn, unable to bear the shock of being present in the house of death at the time of his wife's funeral, left home and went to stay with one of his relations in a distant part of England, Ida, whom it had been his wish to take away with him, petitioned earnestly to be left behind. 'I promised mamma before she died that I would be as good to my little sister Rosamond as she had been to me,' said the child simply; 'and she told me in return that I might wait here and see her laid in her grave.' There happened to be an aunt of Mrs Welwyn, and an old servant of the family, in the house at this time, who understood Ida much better than her father did, and they persuaded him not to take her away. I have heard my mother say that the effect of the child's appearance at the funeral on her, and on all who went to see it, was something that she could never think of without the tears coming into her eyes, and could never forget to the last day of her life.

It must have been very shortly after this period that I saw Ida for the first time.

I remember accompanying my mother on a visit to the old house we have just left, in the summer, when I was at home for the holidays. It was a lovely, sunshiny morning; there was nobody in-doors, and we walked out into the garden. As we approached that lawn yonder, on the other side of the shrubbery, I saw, first, a young woman in mourning (apparently a servant) sitting reading; then a little girl, dressed all in black, moving towards us slowly over the bright turf, and holding up before her a baby whom she was trying to teach to walk. She looked, to my ideas, so very young to be engaged in such an occupation as this, and her gloomy black frock appeared to be such an unnaturally grave garment for a mere child of her age, and looked so doubly dismal by contrast with the brilliant sunny lawn on which she stood, that I quite started when I first saw her, and eagerly asked my mother who she was. The answer informed me of the sad family story, which I have just been relating to you. Mrs Welwyn had then been buried about three months; and Ida, in her childish way, was trying, as she had promised, to supply her mother's place to her infant sister Rosamond.

I only mention this simple incident, because it is necessary, before I proceed to the eventful part of my narrative, that you should know exactly in what relation the sisters stood towards one another from the first. Of all the last parting words that Mrs Welwyn had spoken to her child, none had been oftener repeated, none more solemnly urged, than those which had commended the little Rosamond to Ida's love and care. To other persons, the full, the all-trusting dependence which the dying mother was known to have placed in a child hardly eleven years old, seemed merely a proof of that helpless desire to cling even to the feeblest consolations which the approach of death so often brings with it. But the event showed that the trust so strangely placed had not been ventured vainly when it was committed to young and tender hands. The whole future existence of the child was one noble proof that she had been worthy of her mother's dying confidence when it was first reposed in her. In that simple incident which I have just mentioned, the new life of the two motherless sisters was all foreshadowed.

Time passed. I left school – went to college – travelled in Germany, and stayed there some time to learn the language. At every interval when I came home, and asked about the Welwyns, the answer was, in substance, almost always the same. Mr Welwyn was giving his regular dinners, performing his regular duties as a county magistrate, enjoying his regular recreations as an amateur farmer and an eager sportsman. His two daughters were never separate. Ida was the same strange, quiet, retiring girl, that she had always been; and was still (as the phrase went) 'spoiling' Rosamond in every way in which it was possible for an elder sister to spoil a younger by too much kindness.

I myself went to the Grange occasionally, when I was in this neighbourhood, in holiday and vacation time; and was able to test the correctness of the picture of life there which had been drawn for me. I remember the two sisters, when

Rosamond was four or five years old; and when Ida seemed to me, even then, to be more like the child's mother than her sister. She bore with her little caprices as sisters do not bear with one another. She was so patient at lesson-time, so anxious to conceal any weariness that might overcome her in play-hours, so proud when Rosamond's beauty was noticed, so grateful for Rosamond's kisses when the child thought of bestowing them, so quick to notice all that Rosamond did, and to attend to all that Rosamond said, even when visitors were in the room; that she seemed, to my boyish observation, altogether different from other elder sisters, in other family circles into which I was then received.

I remember them, again, when Rosamond was just growing to womanhood, and was in high spirits at the prospect of spending a season in London, and being presented at Court. She was very beautiful at that time – much handsomer than Ida. Her 'accomplishments' were talked of far and near in our country circles. Few, if any, of the people, however, who applauded her playing and singing, who admired her water-colour drawings, who were delighted at her fluency when she spoke French, and amazed at her ready comprehension when she read German, knew how little of all this elegant mental cultivation and nimble manual dexterity she owed to her governesses and masters, and how much to her elder sister. It was Ida who really found out the means of stimulating her when she was idle; Ida who helped her through all her worst difficulties; Ida who gently conquered her defects of memory over her books, her inaccuracies of ear at the piano, her errors of taste when she took the brush or pencil in hand. It was Ida alone who worked these marvels, and whose all-sufficient reward for her hardest exertions was a chance word of kindness from her sister's lips. Rosamond was not unaffectionate, and not ungrateful; but she inherited much of her father's commonness and frivolity of character. She became so accustomed to owe everything to her sister – to resign all her most trifling difficulties to Ida's ever-ready care – to have all her tastes consulted by Ida's ever watchful kindness – that she never appreciated, as it deserved, the deep devoted love of which she was the object. When Ida refused two good offers of marriage, Rosamond was as much astonished as the veriest strangers, who wondered why the elder Miss Welwyn seemed bent on remaining single all her life.

When the journey to London, to which I have already alluded, took place, Ida accompanied her father and sister. If she had consulted her own tastes, she would have remained in the country; but Rosamond declared that she should feel quite lost and helpless twenty times a-day, in town, without her sister. It was in the nature of Ida to sacrifice herself to any one whom she loved, on the smallest occasions as well as the greatest. Her affection was as intuitively ready to sanctify Rosamond's slightest caprices as to excuse Rosamond's most thoughtless faults. So she went to London cheerfully, to witness with pride all the little triumphs won by her sister's beauty; to hear, and never tire of hearing, all that admiring friends could say in her sister's praise.

At the end of the season, Mr Welwyn and his daughters returned for a short time to the country; then left home again to spend the latter part of the autumn and the beginning of the winter in Paris.

They took with them excellent letters of introduction, and saw a great deal of the best society in Paris, foreign as well as English. At one of the first of the evening parties which they attended, the general topic of conversation was the conduct of a certain French nobleman, the Baron Franval, who had returned to his native country after a long absence, and who was spoken of in terms of high eulogy by the majority of the guests present. The history of who Franval was, and of what he had done, was readily communicated to Mr Welwyn and his daughters, and was briefly this:

The Baron inherited little from his ancestors besides his high rank and his ancient pedigree. On the death of his parents, he and his two unmarried sisters (their only surviving children) found the small territorial property of the Franvals, in Normandy, barely productive enough to afford a comfortable subsistence for the three. The Baron, then a young man of three-and-twenty, endeavoured to obtain such military or civil employment as might become his rank; but, although the Bourbons were at that time restored to the throne of France, his efforts were ineffectual. Either his interest at Court was bad, or secret enemies were at work to oppose his advancement. He failed to obtain even the slightest favour; and, irritated by undeserved neglect, resolved to leave France, and seek occupation for his energies in foreign countries, where his rank would be no bar to his bettering his fortunes, if he pleased, by engaging in commercial pursuits.

An opportunity of the kind that he wanted unexpectedly offered itself. He left his sisters in care of an old male relative of the family at the château in Normandy, and sailed, in the first instance, to the West Indies; afterwards extending his wanderings to the continent of South America, and there engaging in mining transactions on a very large scale. After fifteen years of absence (during the latter part of which time false reports of his death had reached Normandy), he had just returned to France; having realized a handsome independence, with which he proposed to widen the limits of his ancestral property, and to give his sisters (who were still, like himself, unmarried) all the luxuries and advantages that affluence could bestow. The Baron's independent spirit, and generous devotion to the honour of his family and the happiness of his surviving relatives, were themes of general admiration in most of the social circles of Paris. He was expected to arrive in the capital every day; and it was naturally enough predicted that his reception in society there could not fail to be of the most flattering and most brilliant kind.

The Welwyns listened to this story with some little interest; Rosamond, who was very romantic, being especially attracted by it, and openly avowing to her father and sister, when they got back to their hotel, that she felt as ardent a curiosity as anybody to see the adventurous and generous Baron. The desire was soon gratified. Franval came to Paris, as had been anticipated – was introduced to the Welwyns – met them constantly in society – made no favourable impression on Ida, but won the good opinion of Rosamond from the first; and was regarded with such high approval by their father, that when he mentioned his intention of visiting England in the spring of the new year, he was cordially invited to spend the hunting season at Glenwith Grange.

I came back from Germany about the same time that the Welwyns returned from Paris: and at once set myself to improve my neighbourly intimacy with the family. I was very fond of Ida; more fond, perhaps, than my vanity will now allow me to – but that is of no consequence. It is much more to the purpose to tell you, that I heard the whole of the Baron's story enthusiastically related by Mr Welwyn and Rosamond; that he came to the Grange at the appointed time; that I was introduced to him; and that he produced as unfavourable an impression upon me as he had already produced upon Ida.

It was whimsical enough, but I really could not tell why I disliked him, though I could account very easily, according to my own notions, for his winning the favour and approval of Rosamond and her father. He was certainly a handsome man, as far as features went; he had a winning gentleness and graceful respect in his manner when he spoke to women; and he sang remarkably well, with one of the sweetest tenor voices I ever heard. These qualities alone were quite sufficient to attract any girl of Rosamond's disposition: and I certainly never wondered why he was a favourite of hers.

Then, as to her father, the Baron was not only fitted to win his sympathy and regard in the field, by proving himself an ardent sportsman and an excellent rider, but was also, in virtue of some of his minor personal peculiarities, just the man to gain the friendship of his host. Mr Welwyn was as ridiculously prejudiced, as most weak-headed Englishmen are, on the subject of foreigners in general. In spite of his visit to Paris, the vulgar notion of a Frenchman continued to be *his* notion, both while he was in France and when he returned from it. Now, the Baron was as unlike the traditional 'Mounseer' of English songs, plays, and satires, as a man could well be; and it was on account of this very dissimilarity that Mr Welwyn first took a violent fancy to him, and then invited him to his house. Franval spoke English remarkably well; wore neither beard, moustachios, nor whiskers; kept his hair cut almost unbecomingly short; dressed in the extreme of plainness and modest good taste; talked little in general society; uttered his words, when he did speak, with singular calmness and deliberation; and, to crown all, had the greater part of his acquired property invested in English securities. In Mr Welwyn's estimation, such a man as this was a perfect miracle of a Frenchman, and he admired and encouraged him accordingly.

I have said that I disliked him, yet could not assign a reason for my dislike; and I can only repeat it now. He was remarkably polite to me; we often rode together in hunting, and sat near each other at the Grange table; but I could never become familiar with him. He always gave me the idea of a man who had some mental reservation in saying the most trifling thing. There was a constant restraint, hardly perceptible to most people, but plainly visible, nevertheless, to me, which seemed to accompany his lightest words, and to hang about his most familiar manner. This, however, was no just reason for my secretly disliking and distrusting him as I did. Ida said as much to me, I remember, when I confessed to her what my feelings towards him were, and tried (but vainly) to induce her to be equally candid with me in return. She seemed to shrink from the tacit condemnation of Rosamond's opinion which such a confidence on her part would have implied. And yet she watched the growth of that opinion, or, in other words, the growth of her sister's liking for the Baron, with an apprehension and sorrow which she tried fruitlessly to conceal. Even her father began to notice that her spirits were not so good as usual, and to suspect the cause of her melancholy. I remember he jested, with all the dense insensibility of a stupid man, about Ida having invariably been jealous, from a child, if Rosamond looked kindly upon anybody except her elder sister.

The spring began to get far advanced towards summer. Franval paid a visit to London; came back in the middle of the season to Glenwith Grange; wrote to put off his departure for France; and, at last (not at all to the surprise of anybody who was intimate with the Welwyns) proposed to Rosamond, and was accepted. He was candour and generosity itself when the preliminaries of the marriage settlement were under discussion. He quite overpowered Mr Welwyn and the lawyers with references, papers, and statements of the distribution and extent of his property, which were found to be perfectly correct. His sisters were written to, and returned the most cordial answers: saying that the state of their health would not allow them to come to England for the marriage; but adding a warm invitation to Normandy for the bride and her family. Nothing, in short, could be more straightforward and satisfactory than the Baron's behaviour, and the testimonies to his worth and integrity which the news of the approaching marriage produced from his relatives and his friends.

The only joyless face at the Grange now was Ida's. At any time it would have been a hard trial to her to resign that first and foremost place, which she had held since childhood in her sister's heart, as she knew she must resign it when Rosamond married. But, secretly disliking and distrusting Franval as she did, the thought that he was soon to become the husband of her beloved sister filled her with a vague sense of terror which she could not explain to herself, which it was imperatively necessary that she should conceal, and which, on those very accounts, became a daily and hourly torment to her that was almost more than she could bear.

One consolation alone supported her: Rosamond and she were not to be separated. She knew that the Baron secretly disliked her as much as she disliked him; she knew that she must bid farewell to the brighter and happier part of her life on the day when she went to live under the same roof with her sister's husband; but, true to the promise made, years and years ago, by her dying mother's bed, true to the affection which was the ruling and beautiful feeling of her whole existence, she never hesitated about indulging Rosamond's wish, when the girl, in her bright light-hearted way, said that she could never get on comfortably in the marriage state unless she had Ida to live with her and help her just the same as ever. The Baron was too polite a man even to *look* dissatisfied when he heard of the proposed arrangement; and it was therefore settled from the beginning that Ida was always to live with her sister.

The marriage took place in the summer, and the bride and bridegroom went to spend their honeymoon in Cumberland. On their return to Glenwith Grange, a visit to the Baron's sisters, in Normandy, was talked of; but the execution of this project was suddenly and disastrously suspended by the death of Mr Welwyn from an attack of pleurisy.

In consequence of this calamity, the projected journey was of course deferred; and when autumn and the shooting season came, the Baron was unwilling to leave the well-stocked preserves of the Grange. He seemed, indeed, to grow less and less inclined, as time advanced, for the trip to Normandy; and wrote excuse after excuse to his sisters, when letters arrived from them urging him to pay the promised visit. In the winter-time, he said he would not allow his wife to risk a long journey. In the spring, his health was pronounced to be delicate. In the genial summertime, the accomplishment of the proposed visit would be impossible; for at that period the Baroness expected to become a mother. Such were the apologies which Franval seemed almost glad to be able to send to his sisters in France.

The marriage was, in the strictest sense of the term, a happy one. The Baron, though he never altogether lost the strange restraint and reserve of his manner, was, in his quiet, peculiar way, the fondest and kindest of husbands.

He went to town occasionally on business, but always seemed glad to return to the Baroness; he never varied in the politeness of his bearing towards his wife's sister; he behaved with the most courteous hospitality towards all the friends of the Welwyns: in short, he thoroughly justified the good opinion which Rosamond and her father had formed of him when they first met at Paris. And yet no experience of his character thoroughly reassured Ida. Months passed on quietly and pleasantly; and still that secret sadness, that indefinable, unreasonable apprehension on Rosamond's account, hung heavily on her sister's heart.

At the beginning of the first summer months, a little domestic inconvenience happened, which showed the Baroness, for the first time, that her husband's temper could be seriously ruffled – and that by the veriest trifle. He was in the habit of taking in two French provincial newspapers – one published at Bordeaux, and the other at Havre. He always opened these journals the moment they came, looked at one particular column of each with the deepest attention for a few minutes, then carelessly threw them aside into his waste-paper basket. His wife and her sister were at first rather surprised at the manner in which he read his two papers; but they thought no more of it when he explained that he only took them in to consult them about French commercial intelligence, which might be, occasionally, of importance to him.

These papers were published weekly. On the occasion to which I have just referred, the Bordeaux paper came on the proper day, as usual; but the Havre paper never made its appearance. This trifling circumstance seemed to make the Baron seriously uneasy. He wrote off directly to the country post-office, and to the newspaper agent in London. His wife, astonished to see his tranquillity so completely overthrown by so slight a cause, tried to restore his good-humour by jesting with him about the missing newspaper. He replied by the first angry and unfeeling words that she had heard issue from his lips. She was then within about six weeks of her confinement, and very unfit to bear harsh answers from anybody – least of all from her husband.

On the second day no answer came. On the afternoon of the third, the Baron rode off to the post-town to make inquiries. About an hour after he had gone, a strange gentleman came to the Grange, and asked to see the Baroness. On being informed that she was not well enough to receive visitors, he sent up a message that his business was of great importance, and that he would wait down stairs for a second answer.

On receiving this message, Rosamond turned, as usual, to her elder sister for advice. Ida went down stairs immediately to see the stranger. What I am now about to tell you of the extraordinary interview which took place between them, and of the shocking events that followed it, I have heard from Miss Welwyn's own lips.

She felt unaccountably nervous when she entered the room. The stranger bowed very politely, and asked, in a foreign accent, if she were the Baroness Franval. She set him right on this point, and told him she attended to all matters of business for the Baroness; adding, that, if his errand at all concerned her sister's husband, the Baron was not then at home.

The stranger answered that he was aware of it when he called, and that the unpleasant business on which he came could not be confided to the Baron – at least in the first instance.

She asked why. He said he was there to explain; and expressed himself as feeling greatly relieved at having to open his business to her, because she would, doubtless, be best able to prepare her sister for the bad news that he was, unfortunately, obliged to bring. The sudden faintness which overcame her, as he spoke those words, prevented her from addressing him in return. He poured out some water for her from a bottle which happened to be standing on the table, and asked if he might depend on her fortitude. She tried to say 'Yes;' but the violent throbbing of her heart seemed to choke her. He took a foreign newspaper from his pocket, saying that he was a secret agent of the French police – that the paper was the *Havre Journal* for the past week, and that it had been expressly kept from reaching the Baron, as usual, through his (the agent's) interference. He then opened the newspaper, and begged that she would nerve herself sufficiently (for her sister's sake) to read certain lines, which would give her some hint of the business that brought him there. He pointed to the passage as he spoke. It was among the 'Shipping Entries,' and was thus expressed:

> Arrived, the *Berenice*, from San Francisco, with a valuable cargo of hides. She brings one passenger, the Baron Franval, of Château Franval, in Normandy.

As Miss Welwyn read the entry, her heart, which had been throbbing violently but the moment before, seemed suddenly to cease from all action, and she began to shiver, though it was a warm June evening. The agent held the tumbler to her lips, and made her drink a little of the water, entreating her very earnestly to take courage and listen to him. He then sat down, and referred again to the entry; every word he uttered seeming to burn itself in for ever (as she expressed it) on her memory and her heart.

He said: 'It has been ascertained beyond the possibility of doubt that there is no mistake about the name in the lines you have just read. And it is as certain as that we are here, that there is only *one* Baron Franval now alive. The question, therefore, is, whether the passenger by the *Berenice* is the true Baron, or – I beg you most earnestly to bear with me and to compose yourself – or the husband of your sister. The person who arrived last week at Havre was scouted as an impostor by the ladies at the château, the moment he presented himself there as their brother, returning to them after sixteen years of absence. The authorities were communicated with, and I and my assistants were instantly sent for from Paris.

'We wasted no time in questioning the supposed impostor. He either was, or affected to be, in a perfect frenzy of grief and indignation. We just ascertained, from competent witnesses, that he bore an extraordinary resemblance to the real Baron, and that he was perfectly familiar with places and persons in and about the château: we just ascertained that, and then proceeded to confer with the local authorities, and to examine their private entries of suspected persons in their jurisdiction, ranging back over a past period of twenty years or more. One of the entries thus consulted contained these particulars: "Hector Auguste Monbrun, son of a respectable proprietor in Normandy. Well educated; gentlemanlike manners. On bad terms with his family. Character: bold, cunning, unscrupulous, self-possessed. Is a clever mimic. May be easily recognised by his striking likeness to the Baron Franval. Imprisoned at twenty for theft and assault."'

Miss Welwyn saw the agent look up at her after he had read this extract from the police-book, to ascertain if she was still able to listen to him. He asked, with some appearance of alarm, as their eyes met, if she would like some more water. She was just able to make a sign in the negative. He took a second extract from his pocket-book, and went on.

He said: 'The next entry under the same name was dated four years later, and ran thus: "H. A. Monbrun, condemned to the galleys for life, for assassination, and other crimes not officially necessary to be here specified. Escaped from custody at Toulon. Is known, since the expiration of his first term of imprisonment, to have allowed his beard to grow, and to have worn his hair long, with the intention of rendering it impossible for those acquainted with him in his native province to recognise him, as heretofore, by his likeness to the Baron Franval." There were more particulars added, not important enough for extract. We immediately examined the supposed impostor: for, if he was Monbrun, we knew that we should find on his shoulder the two letters of the convict brand, "T.F." (standing for *Travaux Forcés*). After the minutest examination with the mechanical and chemical tests used on such occasions, not the slightest trace of the brand was to be found. The moment this astounding discovery was made, I started to lay an embargo on the forthcoming numbers of the *Havre Journal* for that week, which were about to be sent to the English agent in London. I arrived at Havre on Saturday (the morning of publication), in time to execute my design. I waited there long enough to communicate by telegraph with my superiors in Paris, then hastened to this place. What my errand here is, you may—'

He might have gone on speaking for some moments longer; but Miss Welwyn heard no more.

Her first sensation of returning consciousness was the feeling that water was being sprinkled on her face. Then she saw that all the windows in the room had been set wide open, to give her air; and that she and the agent were still alone. At first, she felt bewildered, and hardly knew who he was; but he soon recalled to her mind the horrible realities that had brought him there, by apologizing for not having summoned assistance when she fainted. He said it was of the last importance, in Franval's absence, that no one in the house should imagine that anything unusual was taking place in it. Then, after giving her an interval of a minute or two to collect what little strength she had left, he added that he would not increase her sufferings by saying anything more, just then, on the shocking subject of the investigation which it was his duty to make – that he would leave her to recover herself, and to consider what was the best course to be taken with the Baroness in the present terrible emergency – and that he would privately return to the house between eight and nine o'clock that evening, ready to act as Miss Welwyn wished, and to afford her and her sister any aid and protection of which they might stand in need. With these words he bowed, and noiselessly quitted the room.

For the first few awful minutes after she was left alone, Miss Welwyn sat helpless and speechless; utterly numbed in heart, and mind, and body – then a sort of instinct (she was incapable of thinking) seemed to urge her to conceal the fearful news from her sister as long as possible. She ran up stairs to Rosamond's sitting-room, and called through the door (for she dared not trust herself in her sister's presence) that the visitor had come on some troublesome business from their late father's lawyers, and that she was going to shut herself up, and write some long letters in connexion with that business. After she had got into her own room, she was never sensible of how time was passing – never conscious of any feeling within her, except a baseless, helpless hope that the French police might yet be proved to have made some terrible mistake – until she heard a violent shower of rain come on a little after sunset. The noise of the rain, and the freshness it brought with it in the air, seemed to awaken her as if from a painful and a fearful sleep. The power of reflection returned to her; her heart heaved and bounded with an overwhelming terror, as the thought of Rosamond came back vividly to it; her memory recurred despairingly to the long past day of her mother's death, and to the farewell promise she had made by her mother's bedside. She burst into an hysterical passion of weeping that seemed to be tearing her to pieces. In the midst of it she heard the clatter of a horse's hoofs in the court-yard, and knew that Rosamond's husband had come back.

Dipping her handkerchief in cold water, and passing it over her eyes as she left the room, she instantly hastened to her sister.

Fortunately, the daylight was fading in the old-fashioned chamber that Rosamond occupied. Before they could say two words to each other, Franval was in the room. He seemed violently irritated; said that he had waited for the arrival of the mail – that the missing newspaper had not come by it – that he had got wet through – that he felt a shivering fit coming on – and that he believed he had caught a violent cold. His wife anxiously suggested some simple remedies. He roughly interrupted her, saying there was but one remedy, the remedy of going to bed; and so left them without another word. She just put her handkerchief to her eyes, and said softly to her sister, 'How he is changed!' – then spoke no more. They sat silent for half an hour or longer. After that, Rosamond went affectionately and forgivingly to see how her husband was. She returned, saying that he was in bed, and in a deep, heavy sleep; and predicting hopefully that he would wake up quite well the next morning. In a few minutes more the clock struck nine; and Ida heard the servant's step ascending the stairs. She suspected what his errand was, and went out to meet him. Her presentiment had not deceived her; the police agent had arrived, and was waiting for her down stairs.

He asked her if she had said anything to her sister, or had thought of any plan of action, the moment she entered the room; and, on receiving a reply in the negative, inquired further if 'the Baron' had come home yet. She answered that he had; that he was ill and tired, and vexed, and that he had gone to bed. The agent asked in an eager whisper if she knew that he was asleep, and alone in bed? and, when he received her reply, said that he must go up into the bed-room directly.

She began to feel the faintness coming over her again, and with it sensations of loathing and terror that she could neither express to others nor define to herself. He said that if she hesitated to let him avail himself of this unexpected opportunity, her scruples might lead to fatal results. He reminded her that if 'the Baron' were really the convict Monbrun, the claims of society and of justice demanded that he should be discovered by the first available means; and that if he were not – if some inconceivable mistake had really been committed – then, such a plan for getting immediately at the truth as was now proposed, would ensure the delivery of an innocent man from suspicion, and at the same time spare him the knowledge that he had ever been suspected. This last argument had its effect on Miss Welwyn. The baseless, helpless hope that the French authorities might yet be proved to be in error, which she had already felt in her own room, returned to her now. She suffered the agent to lead her up stairs.

He took the candle from her hand when she pointed to the door; opened it softly; and, leaving it ajar, went into the room.

She looked through the gap, with a feverish, horror-struck curiosity. Franval was lying on his side in a profound sleep, with his back turned towards the door. The agent softly placed the candle upon a small reading-table between the door and the bed-side, softly drew down the bed-clothes a little way from the sleeper's back, then took a pair of scissors from the toilette table, and very gently and slowly began to cut away, first the loose folds, then the intervening strips of linen from the part of Franval's night-gown, that was over his shoulders. When the upper part of his back had been bared in this way, the agent took the candle and held it near the flesh. Miss Welwyn heard him ejaculate some word under his breath, then saw him looking round to where she was standing, and beckoning to her to come in.

Mechanically she obeyed; mechanically she looked down where his finger was pointing. It was the convict Monbrun – there, just visible under the bright light of the candle, were the fatal letters 'T. F.' branded on the villain's shoulder!

Though she could neither move nor speak, the horror of this discovery did not deprive her of her consciousness. She saw the agent softly draw up the bed-clothes again into their proper position, replace the scissors on the toilet-table, and take from it a bottle of smelling-salts. She felt him removing her from the bed-room, and helping her quickly down stairs, giving her the salts to smell by the way. When they were alone again, he said, with the first appearance of agitation that he had yet exhibited, 'Now, madam, for God's sake, collect all your courage, and be guided by me. You and your sister had better leave the house immediately. Have you any relatives in the neighbourhood, with whom you could take refuge?' They had none. 'What is the name of the nearest town where you could get good accommodation for the night?' Harleybrook (he wrote the name down on his tablets). 'How far off is it?' Twelve miles. 'You had better have the carriage out at once, to go there with as little delay as possible: leaving me to pass the night here. I will communicate with you to-morrow at the principal hotel. Can you compose yourself sufficiently to be able to tell the head-servant, if I ring for him, that he is to obey my orders till further notice?'

The servant was summoned, and received his instructions, the agent going out with him to see that the carriage was got ready quietly and quickly. Miss Welwyn went up stairs to her sister.

How the fearful news was first broken to Rosamond, I cannot relate to you. Miss Welwyn has never confided to me, has never confided to anybody, what happened at the interview between her sister and herself that night. I can tell you nothing of the shock they both suffered, except that the younger and the weaker died under it; that the elder and the stronger has never recovered from it, and never will.

They went away the same night, with one attendant, to Harleybrook, as the agent had advised. Before daybreak Rosamond was seized with the pains of premature labour. She died three days after, unconscious of the horror of her situation; wandering in her mind about past times, and singing old tunes that Ida had taught her, as she lay in her sister's arms.

The child was born alive, and lives still. You saw her at the window as we came in at the back way to the Grange. I surprised you, I dare say, by asking you not to speak of her to Miss Welwyn. Perhaps you noticed something vacant in the little girl's expression. I am sorry to say that her mind is more vacant still. If 'idiot' did not sound like a mocking word, however tenderly and pityingly one may wish to utter it, I should tell you that the poor thing had been an idiot from her birth.

You will, doubtless, want to hear now what happened at Glenwith Grange, after Miss Welwyn and her sister had left it. I have seen the letter which the police agent sent the next morning to Harleybrook; and, speaking from my recollection of that, I shall be able to relate all you can desire to know.

First, as to the past history of the scoundrel Monbrun, I need only tell you that he was identical with an escaped convict, who, for a long term of years, had successfully eluded the vigilance of the authorities all over Europe, and in America as well. In conjunction with two accomplices, he had succeeded in possessing himself of large sums of money by the most criminal means. He also acted secretly as the 'banker' of his convict brethren, whose dishonest gains were all confided to his hands for safe keeping. He would have been certainly captured, on venturing back to France, along with his two associates, but for the daring imposture in which he took refuge; and which, if the true Baron Franval had really died abroad, as was reported, would, in all probability, never have been found out.

Besides his extraordinary likeness to the Baron, he had every other requisite for carrying on his deception successfully. Though his parents were not wealthy, he had received a good education. He was so notorious for his gentlemanlike manners among the villainous associates of his crimes and excesses, that they nicknamed him 'the Prince.' All his early life had been passed in the neighbourhood of the Château Franval. He knew what were the circumstances which had induced the Baron to leave it. He had been in the country to which the Baron had emigrated. He was able to refer familiarly to persons and localities, at home and abroad, with which the Baron was sure to be acquainted. And, lastly, he had an expatriation of fifteen years to plead for him as his all-sufficient excuse, if he made any slight mistakes before the Baron's sisters, in his assumed character of their long-absent brother. It will be, of course, hardly necessary for me to tell you, in relation to this part of the subject, that the true Franval was immediately and honourably reinstated in the family rights of which the impostor had succeeded for a time in depriving him.

According to Monbrun's own account, he had married poor Rosamond purely for love; and the probabilities certainly are, that the pretty innocent English girl had really struck the villain's fancy for the time; and that the easy, quiet life he was leading at the Grange pleased him, by contrast with his perilous and vagabond existence of former days. What might have happened if he had had time enough to grow wearied of his ill-fated wife and his English home, it is now useless to inquire. What really did happen on the morning when he awoke after the flight of Ida and her sister can be briefly told.

As soon as his eyes opened they rested on the police-agent, sitting quietly by the bedside, with a loaded pistol in his hand. Monbrun knew immediately that he was discovered; but he never for an instant lost the self-possession for which he was famous. He said he wished to have five minutes allowed him to deliberate quietly in bed, whether he should resist the French authorities on English ground, and so gain time by obliging the one government to apply specially to have him delivered up by the other – or whether he should accept the terms officially offered to him by the agent, if he quietly allowed himself to be captured. He chose the latter course – it was suspected, because he wished to communicate personally with some of his convict associates in France, whose fraudulent gains were in his keeping, and because he felt boastfully confident of being able to escape again, whenever he pleased. Be his secret motives, however, what they might, he allowed the agent to conduct him peaceably from the Grange; first writing a farewell letter to poor Rosamond, full of heartless French sentiment, and glib sophistries about Fate and Society. His own fate was not long in overtaking him. He attempted to escape again, as it had been expected he would, and was shot by the sentinel on duty at the time. I remember hearing that the bullet entered his head and killed him on the spot.

My story is done. It is ten years now since Rosamond was buried in the churchyard yonder; and it is ten years also since Miss Welwyn returned to be the lonely inhabitant of Glenwith Grange. She now lives but in the remembrances that it calls up before her of her happier existence of former days. There is hardly an object in the old house which does not tenderly and solemnly remind her of the mother, whose last wishes she lived to obey; of the sister, whose happiness was once her dearest earthly care. Those prints that you noticed on the library walls, Rosamond used to copy in the past time, when her pencil was often guided by Ida's hand. Those music-books that you were looking over, she and her mother have played from together, through many a long and quiet summer's evening. She has no ties now to bind her to the present but the poor child whose affliction it is her constant effort to lighten, and the little peasant population around her, whose humble cares and wants and sorrows she is always ready to relieve. Far and near her modest charities have penetrated among us; and far and near she is heartily beloved and blessed in many a labourer's household. There is no poor man's hearth, not in this village only, but for miles away from it as well, at which you would not be received with the welcome given to an old friend, if you only told the cottagers that you knew the Lady of Glenwith Grange!

Anne Rodway

[taken from her diary]

Originally appeared in *Household Words* on 19 and 26 July 1856 as
'The Diary of Anne Rodway'. The story was included in *The Queen of
Hearts* as 'Brother Owen's Story of Anne Rodway'. It is often argued
that Anne is the first female detective in shorter fiction. Collins also
supplies the first female detective in a full-length novel in *The Law
and the Lady* (1874). Dickens was fulsome in his praise of the story. 'I
cannot tell you what a high opinion I have of "Anne Rodway"', he
wrote, 'I read the first part at the office with strong admiration, and
read the second on the railway coming back here . . . My behaviour
before my fellow passengers was weak in the extreme, for I cried as
much as you could possibly desire. Apart from the genuine force
and beauty of the little narrative, and the admirable presentation
of the girl's identity and point of view, it is done with an amount
of honest pains and devotion to the work which few men can have
better reason to appreciate than I, and which no man can have a
more profound respect for. I think it excellent, feel a personal pride
and pleasure in it which is a delightful sensation, and know no-one
else who could have done it' (*The Letters of Charles Dickens*, ed. Walter
Dexter, Vol. II, p. 792).

MARCH 3RD, 1840. A long letter to-day from Robert, which surprised and vexed me so, that I have been sadly behind-hand with my work ever since. He writes in worse spirits than last time, and absolutely declares that he is poorer even than when he went to America, and that he has made up his mind to come home to London.

How happy I should be at this news, if he only returned to me a prosperous man! As it is, though I love him dearly, I cannot look forward to the meeting him again, disappointed and broken down and poorer than ever, without a feeling almost of dread for both of us. I was twenty-six last birthday, and he was thirty-three; and there seems less chance now than ever of our being married. It is all I can do to keep myself by my needle; and his prospects, since he failed in the small stationery business three years ago, are worse, if possible, than mine.

Not that I mind so much for myself; women, in all ways of life, and especially in my dressmaking way, learn, I think, to be more patient than men. What I dread is Robert's despondency, and the hard struggle he will have in this cruel city to get his bread – let alone making money enough to marry me. So little as poor people want to set up in house-keeping and be happy together, it seems hard that they can't get it when they are honest and hearty, and willing to work. The clergyman said in his sermon, last Sunday evening, that all things were ordered for the best, and we are all put into the stations in life that are properest for us. I suppose he was right, being a very clever gentleman, who fills the church to crowding; but I think I should have understood him better if I had not been very hungry at the time, in consequence of my own station in life being nothing but Plain Needlewoman.

March 4th. Mary Mallinson came down to my room to take a cup of tea with me. I read her bits of Robert's letter, to show her that if she has her troubles, I have mine too; but I could not succeed in cheering her. She says she is born to misfortune, and that, as long back as she can remember, she has never had the least morsel of luck to be thankful for. I told her to go and look in my glass, and to say if she had nothing to be thankful for then; for Mary is a very pretty girl, and would look still prettier if she could be more cheerful and dress neater. However, my compliment did no good. She rattled her spoon impatiently in her tea-cup, and said, 'If I was only as good a hand at needlework as you are, Anne, I would change faces with the ugliest girl in London.' 'Not you!' says I, laughing. She looked at me for a moment, and shook her head, and was out of the room before I could get up and stop her. She always runs off in that way when she is going to cry, having a kind of pride about letting other people see her in tears.

March 5th. A fright about Mary. I had not seen her all day, as she does not work at the same place where I do; and in the evening she never came down to have tea with me, or sent me word to go to her. So just before I went to bed, I ran up-stairs to say good-night.

She did not answer when I knocked; and when I stepped softly into the room, I saw her in bed, asleep, with her work, not half done, lying about the room in the untidiest way. There was nothing remarkable in that, and I was just going away on tip-toe, when a tiny bottle and wine-glass on the chair by her bedside caught my eye. I thought she was ill and had been taking

physic, and looked at the bottle. It was marked in large letters, 'Laudanum –
Poison.'

My heart gave a jump as if it was going to fly out of me. I laid hold of her
with both hands, and shook her with all my might. She was sleeping heavily,
and woke slowly, as it seemed to me – but still she did wake. I tried to pull
her out of bed, having heard that people ought to be always walked up and
down when they have taken laudanum; but she resisted, and pushed me away
violently.

'Anne!' says she, in a fright. 'For gracious sake, what's come to you? Are
you out of your senses?'

'Oh, Mary! Mary!' says I, holding up the bottle before her, 'If I hadn't
come in when I did –' And I laid hold of her to shake her again.

She looked puzzled at me for a moment – then smiled (the first time I had
seen her do so for many a long day) – then put her arms round my neck.

'Don't be frightened about me, Anne,' she says, 'I am not worth it, and
there is no need.'

'No need!' says I, out of breath. 'No need, when the bottle has got Poison
marked on it!'

'Poison, dear, if you take it all,' says Mary, looking at me very tenderly;
'and a night's rest if you only take a little.'

I watched her for a moment, doubtful whether I ought to believe what she
said, or to alarm the house. But there was no sleepiness now in her eyes,
and nothing drowsy in her voice; and she sat up in bed quite easily without
anything to support her.

'You have given me a dreadful fright, Mary,' says I, sitting down by her
in the chair, and beginning, by this time, to feel rather faint after being
startled so.

She jumped out of bed to get me a drop of water, and kissed me, and said
how sorry she was, and how undeserving of so much interest being taken in
her. At the same time, she tried to possess herself of the laudanum-bottle,
which I still kept cuddled up tight in my own hands.

'No,' says I. 'You have got into a low-spirited despairing way. I won't trust
you with it.'

'I am afraid I can't do without it,' says Mary, in her usual quiet, hopeless
voice. 'What with work that I can't get through as I ought, and troubles that
I can't help thinking of, sleep won't come to me unless I take a few drops out
of that bottle. Don't keep it away from me, Anne; it's the only thing in the
world that makes me forget myself.'

'Forget yourself!' says I. 'You have no right to talk in that way, at your age.
There's something horrible in the notion of a girl of eighteen sleeping with a
bottle of laudanum by her bedside every night. We all of us have our troubles.
Haven't I got mine?'

'You can do twice the work I can, twice as well as me,' says Mary. 'You are
never scolded and rated at for awkwardness with your needle; and I always
am. You can pay for your room every week; and I am three weeks in debt
for mine.'

'A little more practice,' says I, 'and a little more courage, and you will soon
do better. You have got all your life before you—'

'I wish I was at the end of it,' says she, breaking in. 'I'm alone in the world,
and my life's no good to me.'

'You ought to be ashamed of yourself for saying so,' says I. 'Haven't you got me for a friend? Didn't I take a fancy to you when first you left your stepmother, and came to lodge in this house? And haven't I been sisters with you ever since? Suppose you are alone in the world, am I much better off? I'm an orphan, like you. I've almost as many things in pawn as you; and, if your pockets are empty, mine have only got nine-pence in them, to last me for all the rest of the week.'

'Your father and mother were honest people,' says Mary, obstinately. 'My mother ran away from home, and died in a hospital. My father was always drunk, and always beating me. My stepmother is as good as dead, for all she cares about me. My only brother is thousands of miles away in foreign parts, and never writes to me, and never helps me with a farthing. My sweetheart—'

She stopped, and the red flew into her face. I knew, if she went on that way, she would only get to the saddest part of her sad story, and give both herself and me unnecessary pain.

'*My* sweetheart is too poor to marry me, Mary,' I said. 'So I'm not so much to be envied, even there. But let's give over disputing which is worst off. Lie down in bed, and let me tuck you up. I'll put a stitch or two into that work of yours while you go to sleep.'

Instead of doing what I told her, she burst out crying (being very like a child in some of her ways), and hugged me so tight round the neck, that she quite hurt me. I let her go on, till she had worn herself out, and was obliged to lie down. Even then, her last few words, before she dropped off to sleep, were such as I was half sorry, half frightened, to hear.

'I won't plague you long, Anne,' she said. 'I haven't courage to go out of the world as you seem to fear I shall. But I began my life wretchedly, and wretchedly I am sentenced to end it.'

It was of no use lecturing her again, for she closed her eyes.

I tucked her up as neatly as I could, and put her petticoat over her; for the bed-clothes were scanty, and her hands felt cold. She looked so pretty and delicate as she fell asleep, that it quite made my heart ache to see her, after such talk as we had held together. I just waited long enough to be quite sure that she was in the land of dreams; then emptied the horrible laudanum-bottle into the grate, took up her half-done work, and, going out softly, left her for that night.

March 6th. Sent off a long letter to Robert, begging and entreating him not to be so down-hearted, and not to leave America without making another effort. I told him I could bear any trial except the wretchedness of seeing him come back a helpless, broken-down man, trying uselessly to begin life again, when too old for a change.

It was not till after I had posted my own letter, and read over parts of Robert's again, that the suspicion suddenly floated across me, for the first time, that he might have sailed for England immediately after writing to me. There were expressions in the letter which seemed to indicate that he had some such headlong project in his mind. And yet, surely, if it were so, I ought to have noticed them at the first reading. I can only hope I am wrong in my present interpretation of much of what he has written to me – hope it earnestly for both our sakes.

This has been a doleful day for me. I have been uneasy about Robert and uneasy about Mary. My mind is haunted by those last words of hers: 'I began my life wretchedly, and wretchedly I am sentenced to end it.' Her usual melancholy way of talking never produced the same impression on me that I feel now. Perhaps the discovery of the laudanum-bottle is the cause of this. I would give many a hard day's work to know what to do for Mary's good. My heart warmed to her when we first met in the same lodging-house, two years ago; and, although I am not one of the over-affectionate sort myself, I feel as if I could go to the world's end to serve that girl. Yet, strange to say, if I was asked why I was so fond of her, I don't think I should know how to answer the question.

March 7th. I am almost ashamed to write it down, even in this journal, which no eyes but mine ever look on; yet I must honestly confess to myself, that here I am, at nearly one in the morning, sitting up in a state of serious uneasiness, because Mary has not yet come home.

I walked with her, this morning, to the place where she works, and tried to lead her into talking of the relations she has got who are still alive. My motive in doing this was to see if she dropped anything in the course of conversation which might suggest a way of helping her interests with those who are bound to give her all reasonable assistance. But the little I could get her to say to me led to nothing. Instead of answering my questions about her stepmother and her brother, she persisted at first, in the strangest way, in talking of her father, who was dead and gone, and of one Noah Truscott, who had been the worst of all the bad friends he had, and had taught him to drink and game. When I did get her to speak of her brother, she only knew that he had gone out to a place called Assam, where they grew tea. How he was doing, or whether he was there still, she did not seem to know, never having heard a word from him for years and years past.

As for her stepmother, Mary, not unnaturally, flew into a passion the moment I spoke of her. She keeps an eating-house at Hammersmith, and could have given Mary good employment in it; but she seems always to have hated her, and to have made her life so wretched with abuse and ill-usage, that she had no refuge left but to go away from home, and do her best to make a living for herself. Her husband (Mary's father) appears to have behaved badly to her; and, after his death, she took the wicked course of revenging herself on her step-daughter. I felt, after this, that it was impossible Mary could go back, and that it was the hard necessity of her position, as it is of mine, that she should struggle on to make a decent livelihood without assistance from any of her relations. I confessed as much as this to her; but I added that I would try to get her employment with the persons for whom I work, who pay higher wages, and show a little more indulgence to those under them, than the people to whom she is now obliged to look for support.

I spoke much more confidently than I felt, about being able to do this; and left her, as I thought, in better spirits than usual. She promised to be back to-night to tea, at nine o'clock, and now it is nearly one in the morning, and she is not home yet. If it was any other girl, I should not feel uneasy, for I should make up my mind that there was extra work to be done in a hurry, and that they were keeping her late, and I should go to bed. But Mary is so unfortunate in everything that happens to her, and her own melancholy talk about herself keeps hanging on my mind so, that I have fears on her account which would not distress me about any one else. It seems inexcusably silly to think such a thing, much more to write it down; but I have a kind of nervous dread upon me that some accident—

What does that loud knocking at the street door mean? And those voices and heavy footsteps outside? Some lodger who has lost his key, I suppose. And yet, my heart – What a coward I have become all of a sudden!

More knocking and louder voices. I must run to the door and see what it is. O Mary! Mary! I hope I am not going to have another fright about you; but I feel sadly like it.

March 8th.
March 9th.
March 10th.

March 11th. O me! all the troubles I have ever had in my life are as nothing to the trouble I am in now. For three days I have not been able to write a single line in this journal, which I have kept so regularly ever since I was a girl. For three days I have not once thought of Robert – I, who am always thinking of him at other times.

My poor, dear, unhappy Mary! the worst I feared for you on that night when I sat up alone was far below the dreadful calamity that has really happened. How can I write about it, with my eyes full of tears and my hand all of a tremble? I don't even know why I am sitting down at my desk now, unless it is habit that keeps me to my old everyday task, in spite of all the grief and fear which seem to unfit me entirely for performing it.

The people of the house were asleep and lazy on that dreadful night, and I was the first to open the door. Never, never could I describe in writing, or even say in plain talk, though it is so much easier, what I felt when I saw two policemen come in, carrying between them what seemed to me to be a dead girl, and that girl Mary! I caught hold of her, and gave a scream that must have alarmed the whole house; for frightened people came crowding downstairs in their night-dresses. There was a dreadful confusion and noise of loud talking, but I heard nothing, and saw nothing, till I had got her into my room, and laid on my bed. I stooped down, frantic-like, to kiss her, and saw an awful mark of a blow on the left temple, and felt, at the same time, a feeble flutter of her breath on my cheek. The discovery that she was not dead seemed to give me back my senses again. I told one of the policemen where the nearest doctor was to be found, and sat down by the bedside, while he was gone, and bathed her poor head with cold water. She never opened her eyes, or moved, or spoke; but she breathed, and that was enough for me, because it was enough for life.

The policeman left in the room was a big, thick-voiced, pompous man, with a horrible unfeeling pleasure in hearing himself talk before an assembly of frightened, silent people. He told us how he had found her, as if he had been telling a story in a tap-room, and began with saying, 'I don't think the young woman was drunk.'

Drunk! My Mary, who might have been a born lady for all the spirits she ever touched – drunk! I could have struck the man for uttering the word, with her lying, poor suffering angel, so white and still and helpless before him. As it was, I gave him a look; but he was too stupid to understand it, and went droning on, saying the same thing over and over again in the same words. And yet the story of how they found her was, like all the sad stories I have ever heard told in real life, so very, very short. They had just seen her lying along on the kerb-stone, a few streets off, and had taken her to the station-house. There she had been searched, and one of my cards, that I give to ladies who promise me employment, had been found in her pocket, and so they had brought her to our house. This was all the man really had to tell. There was nobody near her when she was found, and no evidence to show how the blow on her temple had been inflicted.

What a time it was before the doctor came, and how dreadful to hear him say, after he had looked at her, that he was afraid all the medical men in the world could be of no use here! He could not get her to swallow anything, and the more he tried to bring her back to her senses, the less chance there seemed of his succeeding. He examined the blow on her temple, and said he thought she must have fallen down in a fit of some sort, and struck her head against the pavement, and so have given her brain what he was afraid was a fatal shake. I asked what was to be done if she showed any return to sense in the night. He said, 'Send for me directly;' and stopped for a little while afterwards, stroking her head gently with his hand, and whispering to himself, 'Poor girl, so young and so pretty!' I had felt, some minutes before, as if I could have struck the policeman; and I felt now as if I could have thrown my arms round the doctor's neck and kissed him. I did put out my hand, when he took up his hat, and he shook it in the friendliest way. 'Don't hope, my dear,' he said, and went out.

The rest of the lodgers followed him, all silent and shocked, except the inhuman wretch who owns the house, and lives in idleness on the high rents he wrings from poor people like us.

'She's three weeks in my debt,' says he, with a frown and an oath. 'Where the devil is my money to come from now?' – Brute! brute!

I had a long cry alone with her that seemed to ease my heart a little. She was not the least changed for the better when I had wiped away the tears, and could see her clearly again. I took up her right hand, which lay nearest to me. It was tight clenched. I tried to unclasp the fingers, and succeeded after a little time. Something dark fell out of the palm of her hand as I straightened it.

I picked the thing up, and smoothed it out, and saw that it was an end of a man's cravat.

A very old, rotten, dingy strip of black silk, with thin lilac lines, all blurred and deadened with dirt, running across and across the stuff in a sort of trellis-work pattern. The small end of the cravat was hemmed in the usual way, but the other end was all jagged, as if the morsel then in my hands had been torn off violently from the rest of the stuff. A chill ran all over me as I looked at it; for that poor, stained, crumpled end of a cravat seemed to be saying to me, as though it had been in plain words – 'If she dies, she has come to her death by foul means, and I am the witness of it.'

I had been frightened enough before, lest she should die suddenly and quietly without my knowing it, while we were alone together; but I got into a perfect agony now, for fear this last worst affliction should take me by surprise. I don't suppose five minutes passed all that woeful night through, without my getting up and putting my cheek close to her mouth, to feel if the faint breaths still fluttered out of it. They came and went just the same as at first, though the fright I was in often made me fancy they were stilled for ever.

Just as the church clocks were striking four, I was startled by seeing the room door open. It was only Dusty Sal (as they call her in the house), the maid-of-all-work. She was wrapped up in the blanket off her bed; her hair was all tumbled over her face; and her eyes were heavy with sleep, as she came up to the bedside where I was sitting.

'I've two hours good before I begin to work,' says she, in her hoarse, drowsy voice, 'and I've come to sit up and take my turn at watching her. You lay down and get some sleep on the rug. Here's my blanket for you – I don't mind the cold – it will keep me awake.'

'You are very kind – very, very kind and thoughtful, Sally,' says I, 'but I am too wretched in my mind to want sleep, or rest, or to do anything but wait where I am, and try and hope for the best.'

'Then I'll wait too,' says Sally. 'I must do something; if there's nothing to do but waiting, I'll wait.'

And she sat down opposite me at the foot of the bed, and drew the blanket close round her with a shiver.

'After working so hard as you do, I'm sure you must want all the little rest you can get,' says I.

'Excepting only you,' says Sally, putting her heavy arm very clumsily, but very gently at the same time, round Mary's feet, and looking hard at the pale, still face on the pillow. 'Excepting you, she's the only soul in this house as never swore at me, or give me a hard word, that I can remember. When you made puddings on Sundays, and give her half, she always give me a bit. The rest of 'em calls me Dusty Sal. Excepting only you, again, she always called me Sally, as if she knowed me in a friendly way. I ain't no good here, but I ain't no harm neither; and I shall take my turn at the sitting up – that's what I shall do!'

She nestled her head down close at Mary's feet as she spoke those words, and said no more. I once or twice thought she had fallen asleep, but whenever I looked at her, her heavy eyes were always wide open. She never changed her position an inch till the church clocks struck six; then she gave one little squeeze to Mary's feet with her arm, and shuffled out of the room without a word. A minute or two after, I heard her down below, lighting the kitchen fire just as usual.

A little later, the doctor stepped over before his breakfast-time, to see if there had been any change in the night. He only shook his head when he looked at her, as if there was no hope. Having nobody else to consult that I could put trust in, I showed him the end of the cravat, and told him of the dreadful suspicion that had arisen in my mind when I found it in her hand.

'You must keep it carefully, and produce it at the inquest,' he said. 'I don't know, though, that it is likely to lead to anything. The bit of stuff may have been lying on the pavement near her, and her hand may have unconsciously clutched it when she fell. Was she subject to fainting fits?'

'Not more so, sir, than other young girls who are hard-worked and anxious, and weakly from poor living,' I answered.

'I can't say that she may not have got that blow from a fall,' the doctor went on, looking at her temple again. 'I can't say that it presents any positive appearance of having been inflicted by another person. It will be important, however, to ascertain what state of health she was in last night. Have you any idea where she was yesterday evening?'

I told him where she was employed at work, and said I imagined she must have been kept there later than usual.

'I shall pass the place this morning,' said the doctor, 'in going my rounds among my patients, and I'll just step in and make some inquiries.'

I thanked him, and we parted. Just as he was closing the door, he looked in again.

'Was she your sister?' he asked.

'No, sir, only my dear friend.'

He said nothing more; but I heard him sigh, as he shut the door softly. Perhaps he once had a sister of his own, and lost her. Perhaps she was like Mary in the face.

The doctor was hours gone away. I began to feel unspeakably forlorn and helpless. So much so, as even to wish selfishly that Robert might really have sailed from America, and might get to London in time to assist and console me.

No living creature came into the room but Sally. The first time she brought me some tea; the second and third times she only looked in to see if there was any change, and glanced her eye towards the bed. I had never known her so silent before; it seemed almost as if this dreadful accident had struck her dumb. I ought to have spoken to her, perhaps, but there was something in her face that daunted me; and, besides, the fever of anxiety I was in began to dry up my lips, as if they would never be able to shape any words again. I was still tormented by that frightful apprehension of the past night, that she would die without my knowing it – die without saying one word to clear up the awful mystery of this blow, and set the suspicions at rest for ever which I still felt whenever my eyes fell on the end of the old cravat.

At last the doctor came back.

'I think you may safely clear your mind of any doubts to which that bit of stuff may have given rise,' he said. 'She was, as you supposed, detained late by her employers, and she fainted in the work-room. They most unwisely and unkindly let her go home alone, without giving her any stimulant, as soon as she came to her senses again. Nothing is more probable, under these circumstances, than that she should faint a second time on her way here. A fall on the pavement, without any friendly arm to break it, might have produced even a worse injury than the injury we see. I believe that the only ill-usage to which the poor girl was exposed was the neglect she met with in the work-room.'

'You speak very reasonably, I own, sir,' said I, not yet quite convinced. 'Still, perhaps she may—'

'My poor girl, I told you not to hope,' said the doctor, interrupting me. He went to Mary, and lifted up her eyelids, and looked at her eyes while he spoke, then added: 'If you still doubt how she came by that blow, do not encourage the idea that any words of hers will ever enlighten you. She will never speak again.'

'Not dead! Oh, sir, don't say she's dead!'

'She is dead to pain and sorrow – dead to speech and recognition. There is more animation in the life of the feeblest insect that flies, than in the life that is left in her. When you look at her now, try to think that she is in heaven. That is the best comfort I can give you, after telling the hard truth.'

I did not believe him. I could not believe him. So long as she breathed at all, so long I was resolved to hope. Soon after the doctor was gone, Sally came in again, and found me listening (if I may call it so) at Mary's lips. She went to where my little hand-glass hangs against the wall, took it down, and gave it to me.

'See if the breath marks it,' she said.

Yes; her breath did mark it, but very faintly. Sally cleaned the glass with her apron, and gave it back to me. As she did so, she half stretched out her hand to Mary's face, but drew it in again suddenly, as if she was afraid of soiling Mary's delicate skin with her hard, horny fingers. Going out, she stopped at the foot of the bed, and scraped away a little patch of mud that was on one of Mary's shoes.

'I always used to clean 'em for her,' said Sally, 'to save her hands from getting blacked. May I take 'em off now, and clean 'em again?'

I nodded my head, for my heart was too heavy to speak. Sally took the shoes off with a slow, awkward tenderness, and went out.

An hour or more must have passed, when, putting the glass over her lips again, I saw no mark on it. I held it closer and closer. I dulled it accidentally with my own breath, and cleaned it. I held it over her again. Oh, Mary, Mary, the doctor was right! I ought to have only thought of you in heaven!

Dead, without a word, without a sign – without even a look to tell the true story of the blow that killed her! I could not call to anybody, I could not cry, I could not so much as put the glass down and give her a kiss for the last time. I don't know how long I had sat there with my eyes burning, and my hands deadly cold, when Sally came in with the shoes cleaned, and carried carefully in her apron for fear of a soil touching them. At the sight of that—

I can write no more. My tears drop so fast on the paper that I can see nothing.

March 12th. She died on the afternoon of the eighth. On the morning of the ninth, I wrote, as in duty bound, to her stepmother, at Hammersmith. There was no answer. I wrote again; my letter was returned to me this morning, unopened. For all that woman cares, Mary might be buried with a pauper's funeral. But this shall never be, if I pawn everything about me, down to the very gown that is on my back.

The bare thought of Mary being buried by the workhouse gave me the spirit to dry my eyes, and go to the undertaker's, and tell him how I was placed. I said, if he would get me an estimate of all that would have to be paid, from first to last, for the cheapest decent funeral that could be had, I would undertake to raise the money. He gave me the estimate, written in this way, like a common bill:

A walking funeral complete	£1	13	8
Vestry	0	4	4
Rector	0	4	4
Clerk	0	1	0
Sexton	0	1	0
Beadle	0	1	0
Bell	0	1	0
Six feet of ground	0	2	0
Total	£2	8	4

If I had the heart to give any thought to it, I should be inclined to wish that the Church could afford to do without so many small charges for burying poor people, to whose friends even shillings are of consequence. But it is useless to complain; the money must be raised at once. The charitable doctor – a poor man himself, or he would not be living in our neighbourhood – has subscribed ten shillings towards the expenses; and the coroner, when the inquest was over, added five more. Perhaps others may assist me. If not, I have fortunately clothes and furniture of my own to pawn. And I must set about parting with them without delay; for the funeral is to be to-morrow, the thirteenth.

The funeral – Mary's funeral! It is well that the straits and difficulties I am in, keep my mind on the stretch. If I had leisure to grieve, where should I find the courage to face to-morrow?

Thank God, they did not want me at the inquest. The verdict given – with the doctor, the policeman, and two persons from the place where she worked, for witnesses – was Accidental Death. The end of the cravat was produced, and the coroner said that it was certainly enough to suggest suspicion; but the jury, in the absence of any positive evidence, held to the doctor's notion that she had fainted and fallen down, and so got the blow on her temple. They reproved the people where Mary worked for letting her go home alone, without so much as a drop of brandy to support her, after she had fallen into a swoon from exhaustion before their eyes. The coroner added, on his own account, that he thought the reproof was thoroughly deserved. After that, the cravat-end was given back to me, by my own desire, the police saying that they could make no investigations with such a slight clue to guide them. They may think so, and the coroner, and doctor, and jury may think so; but, in spite of all that has passed, I am now more firmly persuaded than ever that there is some dreadful mystery in connection with that blow on my poor lost Mary's temple which has yet to be revealed, and which may come to be discovered through this very fragment of a cravat that I found in her hand. I cannot give any good reason why I think so, but I know that if I had been one of the jury at the inquest, nothing should have induced me to consent to such a verdict as Accidental Death.

After I had pawned my things, and had begged a small advance of wages at the place where I work, to make up what was still wanting to pay for Mary's funeral, I thought I might have had a little quiet time to prepare myself as I best could for to-morrow. But this was not to be. When I got home, the landlord met me in the passage. He was in liquor, and more brutal and pitiless in his way of looking and speaking than ever I saw him before.

'So you're going to be fool enough to pay for her funeral, are you?' were his first words to me.

I was too weary and heart-sick to answer – I only tried to get by him to my own door.

'If you can pay for burying her,' he went on, putting himself in front of me, 'you can pay her lawful debts. She owes me three weeks' rent. Suppose you raise the money for that next, and hand it over to me? I'm not joking, I can promise you. I mean to have my rent; and if somebody don't pay it, I'll have her body seized and sent to the workhouse!'

Between terror and disgust, I thought I should have dropped to the floor at his feet. But I determined not to let him see how he had horrified me, if I could possibly control myself. So I mustered resolution enough to answer that I did not believe the law gave him any such wicked power over the dead.

'I'll teach you what the law is!' he broke in; 'you'll raise money to bury her like a born lady, when she's died in my debt, will you? And you think I'll let my rights be trampled upon like that, do you? See if I do! I'll give you till to-night to think about it. If I don't have the three weeks she owes before to-morrow, dead or alive, she shall go to the workhouse!'

This time I managed to push by him, and get to my own room, and lock the door in his face. As soon as I was alone, I fell into a breathless, suffocating fit of crying that seemed to be shaking me to pieces. But there was no good and no help in tears; I did my best to calm myself after a little while, and tried to think whom I should run to for help and protection.

The doctor was the first friend I thought of; but I knew he was always out seeing his patients of an afternoon. The beadle was the next person who came into my head. He had the look of being a very dignified, unapproachable kind of man when he came about the inquest; but he talked to me a little then, and said I was a good girl, and seemed, I really thought, to pity me. So to him I determined to apply in my great danger and distress.

Most fortunately, I found him at home. When I told him of the landlord's infamous threats, and of the misery I was suffering in consequence of them, he rose up with a stamp of his foot, and sent for his gold-laced cocked hat that he wears on Sundays, and his long cane with the ivory top to it.

'I'll give it to him,' said the beadle. 'Come along with me, my dear. I think I told you you were a good girl at the inquest – if I didn't, I tell you so now. I'll give it to him! Come along with me.'

And he went out, striding on with his cocked-hat and his great cane, and I followed him.

'Landlord!' he cries, the moment he gets into the passage, with a thump of his cane on the floor. 'Landlord!' with a look all round him as if he was king of England calling to a beast, 'come out!'

The moment the landlord came out and saw who it was, his eye fixed on the cocked-hat, and he turned as pale as ashes.

'How dare you frighten this poor girl?' says the beadle. 'How dare you bully her at this sorrowful time with threatening to do what you know you can't do? How dare you be a cowardly, bullying braggadocio of an unmanly landlord? Don't talk to me – I won't hear you! I'll pull you up, sir! If you say another word to the young woman, I'll pull you up before the authorities of this metropolitan parish! I've had my eye on you, and the authorities have had their eye on you, and the rector has had his eye on you. We don't like the look of your small shop round the corner; we don't like the look of some of the customers who deal at it; we don't like disorderly characters; and we don't, by any manner of means, like *you*. Go away! Leave the young woman alone! Hold your tongue, or I'll pull you up! If he says another word, or interferes with you again, my dear, come and tell me; and, as sure as he's a bullying, unmanly braggadocio of a landlord, I'll pull him up!'

With those words, the beadle gave a loud cough to clear his throat, and another thump of his cane on the floor – and so went striding out again, before I could open my lips to thank him. The landlord slunk back into his room without a word. I was left alone and unmolested at last, to strengthen myself for the hard trial of my poor love's funeral to-morrow.

March 13th. It is all over. A week ago, her head rested on my bosom. It is laid in the churchyard now – the fresh earth lies heavy over her grave. I and my dearest friend, the sister of my love, are parted in this world for ever.

I followed her funeral alone through the cruel, bustling streets. Sally, I thought, might have offered to go with me; but she never so much as came into my room. I did not like to think badly of her for this, and I am glad I restrained myself – for, when we got into the churchyard, among the two or three people who were standing by the open grave, I saw Sally, in her ragged gray shawl and her patched black bonnet. She did not seem to notice me till the last words of the service had been read, and the clergyman had gone away. Then she came up and spoke to me.

'I couldn't follow along with you,' she said, looking at her ragged shawl; 'for I havn't a decent suit of clothes to walk in. I wish I could get vent in crying for her, like you; but I can't; all the crying's been drudged and starved out of me, long ago. Don't you think about lighting your fire when you get home. I'll do that, and get you a drop of tea to comfort you.'

She seemed on the point of saying a kind word or two more, when, seeing the Beadle coming towards me, she drew back, as if she was afraid of him, and left the churchyard.

'Here's my subscription towards the funeral,' said the Beadle, giving me back his shilling fee. 'Don't say anything about it, for it mightn't be approved of in a business point of view, if it came to some people's ears. Has the landlord said anything more to you? – no, I thought not. He's too polite a man to give me the trouble of pulling him up. Don't stop crying here, my dear. Take the advice of a man familiar with funerals, and go home.'

I tried to take his advice; but it seemed like deserting Mary to go away when all the rest forsook her.

I waited about till the earth was thrown in, and the man had left the place – then I returned to the grave. Oh, how bare and cruel it was, without so much as a bit of green turf to soften it! Oh, how much harder it seemed to live than to die, when I stood alone looking at the heavy piled-up lumps of clay, and thinking of what was hidden beneath them!

I was driven home by my own despairing thoughts. The sight of Sally lighting the fire in my room eased my heart a little. When she was gone, I took up Robert's letter again, to keep my mind employed on the only subject in the world that has any interest for it now.

This fresh reading increased the doubts I had already felt relative to his having remained in America after writing to me. My grief and forlornness have made a strange alteration in my former feelings about his coming back. I seem to have lost all my prudence and self-denial, and to care so little about his poverty, and so much about himself, that the prospect of his return is really the only comforting thought I have now to support me. I know this is weak in me, and that his coming back poor can lead to no good result for either of us. But he is the only living being left me to love; and – I can't explain it – but I want to put my arms round his neck and tell him about Mary.

March 14th. I locked up the end of the cravat in my writing-desk. No change in the dreadful suspicions that the bare sight of it rouses in me. I tremble if I so much as touch it.

March 15th, 16th, 17th. Work, work, work. If I don't knock up, I shall be able to pay back the advance in another week; and then, with a little more pinching in my daily expenses, I may succeed in saving a shilling or two to get some turf to put over Mary's grave – and perhaps even a few flowers besides to grow round it.

March 18th. Thinking of Robert all day long. Does this mean that he is really coming back? If it does, reckoning the distance he is at from New York, and the time ships take to get to England, I might see him by the end of April or the beginning of May.

March 19th. I don't remember my mind running once on the end of the cravat yesterday, and I am certain I never looked at it. Yet I had the strangest dream concerning it at night. I thought it was lengthened into a long clue, like the silken thread that led to Rosamond's Bower. I thought I took hold of it, and followed it a little way, and then got frightened and tried to go back, but found that I was obliged, in spite of myself, to go on. It led me through a place like the Valley of the Shadow of Death, in an old print I remember in my mother's copy of the Pilgrim's Progress. I seemed to be months and months following it without any respite, till at last it brought me, on a sudden, face to face with an angel whose eyes were like Mary's. He said to me, 'Go on, still; the truth is at the end, waiting for you to find it.' I burst out crying, for the angel had Mary's voice as well as Mary's eyes, and woke with my heart throbbing and my cheeks all wet. What is the meaning of this? Is it always superstitious, I wonder, to believe that dreams may come true?

*   *   *

April 30th. I have found it! God knows to what results it may lead; but it is as certain as that I am sitting here before my journal, that I have found the cravat from which the end in Mary's hand was torn! I discovered it last night; but the flutter I was in, and the nervousness and uncertainty I felt, prevented me from noting down this most extraordinary and unexpected event at the time when it happened. Let me try if I can preserve the memory of it in writing now.

I was going home rather late from where I work, when I suddenly remembered that I had forgotten to buy myself any candles the evening before, and that I should be left in the dark if I did not manage to rectify this mistake in some way. The shop close to me, at which I usually deal, would be shut up, I knew, before I could get to it; so I determined to go into the first place I passed where candles were sold. This turned out to be a small shop with two counters, which did business on one side in the general grocery way, and on the other in the rag and bottle and old iron line.

There were several customers on the grocery side when I went in, so I waited on the empty rag side till I could be served. Glancing about me here at the worthless-looking things by which I was surrounded, my eye was caught by a bundle of rags lying on the counter, as if they had just been brought in and left there. From mere idle curiosity, I looked close at the rags, and saw among them something like an old cravat. I took it up directly, and held it under a gas-light. The pattern was blurred lilac lines, running across and across the dingy black ground in a trellis-work form. I looked at the ends: one of them was torn off.

How I managed to hide the breathless surprise into which this discovery threw me, I cannot say; but I certainly contrived to steady my voice somehow, and to ask for my candles calmly, when the man and woman serving in the shop, having disposed of their other customers, inquired of me what I wanted.

As the man took down the candles, my brain was all in a whirl with trying to think how I could get possession of the old cravat without exciting any suspicion. Chance, and a little quickness on my part in taking advantage of it, put the object within my reach in a moment. The man, having counted out the candles, asked the woman for some paper to wrap them in. She produced a piece much too small and flimsy for the purpose, and declared, when he called for something better, that the day's supply of stout paper was all exhausted. He flew into a rage with her for managing so badly. Just as they were beginning to quarrel violently, I stepped back to the rag-counter, took the old cravat carelessly out of the bundle, and said, in as light a tone as I could possibly assume:

'Come, come! don't let my candles be the cause of hard words between you. Tie this ragged old thing round them with a bit of string, and I shall carry them home quite comfortably.'

The man seemed disposed to insist on the stout paper being produced; but the woman, as if she was glad of an opportunity of spiting him, snatched the candles away, and tied them up in a moment in the torn old cravat. I was afraid he would have struck her before my face, he seemed in such a fury; but, fortunately, another customer came in, and obliged him to put his hands to peaceable and proper uses.

'Quite a bundle of all-sorts on the opposite counter there,' I said to the woman, as I paid her for the candles.

'Yes, and all hoarded up for sale by a poor creature with a lazy brute of a husband, who lets his wife do all the work, while he spends all the money,' answered the woman, with a malicious look at the man by her side.

'He can't surely have much money to spend, if his wife has no better work to do than picking up rags,' said I.

'It isn't her fault if she hasn't got no better,' says the woman, rather angrily. 'She's ready to turn her hand to anything. Charing, washing, laying-out, keeping empty houses – nothing comes amiss to her. She's my half-sister, and I think I ought to know.'

'Did you say she went out charing?' I asked, making believe as if I knew of somebody who might employ her.

'Yes, of course I did,' answered the woman; 'and if you can put a job into her hands, you'll be doing a good turn to a poor hard-working creature as wants it. She lives down the Mews here to the right – name of Horlick, and as honest a woman as ever stood in shoe-leather. Now then, ma'am, what for you?'

Another customer came in just then, and occupied her attention. I left the shop, passed the turning that led down to the Mews, looked up at the name of the street, so as to know how to find it again, and then ran home as fast as I could. Perhaps it was the remembrance of my strange dream striking me on a sudden, or perhaps it was the shock of the discovery I had just made, but I began to feel frightened, without knowing why, and anxious to be under shelter in my own room.

If Robert should come back! Oh, what a relief and help it would be now if Robert should come back!

May 1st. On getting in-doors last night, the first thing I did, after striking a light, was to take the ragged cravat off the candles, and smooth it out on the table. I then took the end that had been in poor Mary's hand out of my writing-desk, and smoothed that out too. It matched the torn side of the cravat exactly. I put them together, and satisfied myself that there was not a doubt of it.

Not once did I close my eyes that night. A kind of fever got possession of me – a vehement yearning to go on from this first discovery and find out more, no matter what the risk might be. The cravat now really became, to my mind, the clue that I thought I saw in my dream – the clue that I was resolved to follow. I determined to go to Mrs Horlick this evening, on my return from work.

I found the Mews easily. A crook-backed dwarf of a man was lounging at the corner of it, smoking his pipe. Not liking his looks, I did not inquire of him where Mrs Horlick lived, but went down the Mews till I met with a woman, and asked her. She directed me to the right number. I knocked at the door, and Mrs Horlick herself – a lean, ill-tempered, miserable-looking woman – answered it. I told her at once that I had come to ask what her terms were for charing. She stared at me for a moment, then answered my question civilly enough.

'You look surprised at a stranger like me finding you out,' I said. 'I first came to hear of you last night, from a relation of yours, in rather an odd way.'

And I told her all that had happened in the chandler's shop, bringing in the bundle of rags, and the circumstance of my carrying home the candles in the old torn cravat, as often as possible.

'It's the first time I've heard of anything belonging to him turning out any use,' said Mrs Horlick, bitterly.

'What, the spoilt old neck-handkerchief belonged to your husband, did it?' said I at a venture.

'Yes; I pitched his rotten rag of a neck-'andkercher into the bundle along with the rest; and I wish I could have pitched him in after it,' said Mrs Horlick. 'I'd sell him cheap at any rag-shop. There he stands, smoking his pipe at the end of the Mews, out of work for weeks past, the idlest humpbacked pig in all London!'

She pointed to the man whom I had passed on entering the Mews. My cheeks began to burn and my knees to tremble; for I knew that in tracing the cravat to its owner I was advancing a step towards a fresh discovery. I wished Mrs Horlick good evening, and said I would write and mention the day on which I wanted her.

What I had just been told put a thought into my mind that I was afraid to follow out. I have heard people talk of being light-headed, and I felt as I have heard them say they felt, when I retraced my steps up the Mews. My head got giddy, and my eyes seemed able to see nothing but the figure of the little crook-backed man, still smoking his pipe in his former place, I could see nothing but that; I could think of nothing but the mark of the blow on my poor lost Mary's temple. I know that I must have been light-headed, for as I came close to the crook-backed man, I stopped without meaning it. The minute before, there had been no idea in me of speaking to him. I did not know how to speak, or in what way it would be safest to begin. And yet, the moment I came face to face with him, something out of myself seemed to stop me, and to make me speak without considering beforehand, without thinking of consequences, without knowing, I may almost say, what words I was uttering till the instant when they rose to my lips.

'When your old neck-tie was torn, did you know that one end of it went to the rag-shop, and the other fell into my hands?'

I said these bold words to him suddenly, and, as it seemed, without my own will taking any part in them.

He started, stared, changed colour. He was too much amazed by my sudden speaking to find an answer for me. When he did open his lips, it was to say, rather to himself than me:

'You're not the girl.'

'No,' I said, with a strange choking at my heart. 'I'm her friend.'

By this time he had recovered his surprise, and he seemed to be aware that he had let out more than he ought.

'You may be anybody's friend you like,' he said brutally, 'so long as you don't come jabbering nonsense here. I don't know you, and I don't understand your jokes.'

He turned quickly away from me when he had said the last words. He had never once looked fairly at me since I first spoke to him.

Was it his hand that had struck the blow?

I had only sixpence in my pocket, but I took it out and followed him. If it had been a five-pound note, I should have done the same in the state I was in then.

'Would a pot of beer help you to understand me?' I said, and offered him the sixpence.

'A pot ain't no great things,' he answered, taking the sixpence doubtfully.

'It may lead to something better,' I said.

His eyes began to twinkle, and he came close to me. Oh, how my legs trembled! – How my head swam!

'This is all in a friendly way, is it?' he asked in a whisper.

I nodded my head. At that moment, I could not have spoken for worlds.

'Friendly, of course,' he went on to himself, 'or there would have been a policeman in it. She told you, I suppose, that I wasn't the man?'

I nodded my head again. It was all I could do to keep myself standing upright.

'I suppose it's a case of threatening to have him up, and make him settle it quietly for a pound or two? How much for me if you lay hold of him?'

'Half.'

I began to be afraid that he would suspect something if I was still silent. The wretch's eyes twinkled again, and he came yet closer.

'I drove him to the Red Lion, corner of Dodd Street and Rudgely Street. The house was shut up, but he was let in at the jug and bottle-door, like a man who was known to the landlord. That's as much as I can tell you, and I'm certain I'm right. He was the last fare I took up at night. The next morning master give me the sack. Said I cribbed his corn and his fares. I wish I had!'

I gathered from this that the crook-backed man had been a cab-driver.

'Why don't you speak?' he asked suspiciously. 'Has she been telling you a pack of lies about me? What did she say when she came home?'

'What ought she to have said?'

'She ought to have said my fare was drunk, and she came in the way as he was going to get into the cab. That's what she ought to have said, to begin with.'

'But after.'

'Well, after, my fare, by way of larking with her, puts out his leg for to trip her up, and she stumbles and catches at me for to save herself, and tears off one of the limp ends of my rotten old tie. "What do you mean by that, you brute?" says she, turning round, as soon as she was steady on her legs, to my fare. Says my fare to her, "I means to teach you to keep a civil tongue in your head." And he ups with his fist, and – what's come to you, now? What are you looking at me like that for? How do you think a man of my size was to take her part, against a man big enough to have eaten me up? Look as much as you like, in my place you would have done what I done – drew off when he shook his fist at you, and swore he'd be the death of you if you didn't start your horse in no time.'

I saw he was working himself up into a rage; but I could not, if my life had depended on it, have stood near him, or looked at him, any longer. I just managed to stammer out that I had been walking a long way, and that, not being used to much exercise, I felt faint and giddy with fatigue. He only changed from angry to sulky, when I made that excuse. I got a little further away from him, and then added, that if he would be at the Mews entrance the next evening, I should have something more to say, and something more to give him. He grumbled a few suspicious words in answer, about doubting whether he should trust me to come back. Fortunately, at that moment, a policeman passed on the opposite side of the way. He slunk down the Mews immediately, and I was free to make my escape.

How I got home, I can't say, except that I think I ran the greater part of the way. Sally opened the door, and asked if anything was the matter the moment she saw my face. I answered, 'Nothing! nothing!' She stopped me as I was going into my room, and said:

'Smooth your hair a bit, and put your collar straight. There's a gentleman in there waiting for you.'

My heart gave one great bound – I knew who it was in an instant, and rushed into the room like a mad woman.

'Oh, Robert! Robert!'

All my heart went out to him in those two little words.

'Good God, Anne! has anything happened? Are you ill?'

'Mary! my poor, lost, murdered, dear, dear Mary!'

That was all I could say before I fell on his breast.

May 2nd. Misfortunes and disappointments have saddened him a little; but towards me he is unaltered. He is as good, as kind, as gently and truly affectionate as ever. I believe no other man in the world could have listened to the story of Mary's death with such tenderness and pity as he. Instead of cutting me short anywhere, he drew me on to tell more than I had intended; and his first generous words, when I had done, were to assure me that he would see himself to the grass being laid and the flowers planted on Mary's grave. I could almost have gone on my knees and worshipped him when he made me that promise.

Surely, this best, and kindest, and noblest of men cannot always be unfortunate! My cheeks burn when I think that he has come back with only a few pounds in his pocket, after all his hard and honest struggles to do well in America. They must be bad people there, when such a man as Robert cannot get on among them. He now talks calmly and resignedly of trying for any one of the lowest employments by which a man can earn his bread honestly in this great city – he who knows French, who can write so beautifully! Oh, if the people who have places to give away only knew Robert as well as I do, what a salary he would have, what a post he would be chosen to occupy!

I am writing these lines alone, while he has gone to the Mews to treat with the dastardly, heartless wretch with whom I spoke yesterday.

Robert says the creature – I won't call him a man – must be humoured and kept deceived about poor Mary's end, in order that we may discover and bring to justice the monster whose drunken blow was the death of her. I shall know no ease of mind till her murderer is secured, and till I am certain that he will be made to suffer for his crimes. I wanted to go with Robert to the Mews; but he said it was best that he should carry out the rest of the investigation alone; for my strength and resolution had been too hardly taxed already. He said more words in praise of me for what I have been able to do up to this time, which I am almost ashamed to write down with my own pen. Besides, there is no need – praise from his lips is one of the things that I can trust my memory to preserve to the latest day of my life.

May 3rd. Robert was very long last night before he came back to tell me what he had done. He easily recognised the hunchback at the corner of the Mews, by my description of him; but he found it a hard matter, even with the help of money, to overcome the cowardly wretch's distrust of him as a stranger and a man. However, when this had been accomplished, the main difficulty was conquered. The hunchback, excited by the promise of more money, went at once to the Red Lion to inquire about the person whom he had driven there in his cab. Robert followed him, and waited at the corner of the street. The tidings brought by the cabman were of the most unexpected kind. The murderer – I can write of him by no other name – had fallen ill on the very night when he was driven to the Red Lion, had taken to his bed there and then, and was still confined to it at that very moment. His disease was of a kind that is brought on by excessive drinking, and that affects the mind as well as the body. The people at the public-house called it the Horrors.

Hearing these things, Robert determined to see if he could not find out something more for himself, by going and inquiring at the public-house, in the character of one of the friends of the sick man in bed upstairs. He made two important discoveries. First, he found out the name and address of the doctor in attendance. Secondly, he entrapped the barman into mentioning the murderous wretch by his name. This last discovery adds an unspeakably fearful interest to the dreadful misfortune of Mary's death. Noah Truscott, as she told me herself in the last conversation I ever had with her, was the name of the man whose drunken example ruined her father; and Noah Truscott is also the name of the man whose drunken fury killed her. There is something that makes one shudder, something supernatural in this awful fact. Robert agrees with me that the hand of Providence must have guided my steps to that shop from which all the discoveries since made took their rise. He says he believes we are the instruments of effecting a righteous retribution; and, if he spends his last farthing, he will have the investigation brought to its full end in a court of justice.

May 4th. Robert went to-day to consult a lawyer whom he knew in former times. The lawyer was much interested, though not so seriously impressed as he ought to have been, by the story of Mary's death and of the events that have followed it. He gave Robert a confidential letter to take to the doctor in attendance on the double-dyed villain at the Red Lion. Robert left the letter, and called again and saw the doctor, who said his patient was getting better, and would most likely be up again in ten days or a fortnight. This statement Robert communicated to the lawyer, and the lawyer has undertaken to have the public-house properly watched, and the hunchback (who is the most important witness) sharply looked after for the next fortnight, or longer if necessary. Here, then, the progress of this dreadful business stops for awhile.

May 5th. Robert has got a little temporary employment in copying for his friend the lawyer. I am working harder than ever at my needle, to make up for the time that has been lost lately.

May 6th. To-day was Sunday, and Robert proposed that we should go and look at Mary's grave. He, who forgets nothing where a kindness is to be done, has found time to perform the promise he made to me on the night when we first met. The grave is already, by his orders, covered with turf, and planted round with shrubs. Some flowers, and a low head-stone, are to be added to make the place look worthier of my poor lost darling who is beneath it. Oh, I hope I shall live long after I am married to Robert! I want so much time to show him all my gratitude!

May 20th. A hard trial to my courage today. I have given evidence at the police-office, and have seen the monster who murdered her.

I could only look at him once. I could just see that he was a giant in size, and that he kept his dull, lowering, bestial face turned towards the witness box, and his bloodshot, vacant eyes staring on me. For an instant I tried to confront that look; for an instant I kept my attention fixed on him – on his blotched face, on the short grizzled hair above it – on his knotty, murderous right hand, hanging loose over the bar in front of him, like the paw of a wild beast over the edge of its den. Then the horror of him – the double horror of confronting him, in the first place, and afterwards of seeing that he was an old man – overcame me; and I turned away, faint, sick, and shuddering. I never faced him again; and at the end of my evidence, Robert considerately took me out.

When we met once more at the end of the examination, Robert told me that the prisoner never spoke, and never changed his position. He was either fortified by the cruel composure of a savage, or his faculties had not yet thoroughly recovered from the disease that had so lately shaken them. The magistrate seemed to doubt if he was in his right mind; but the evidence of the medical man relieved him from this uncertainty, and the prisoner was committed for trial on a charge of manslaughter.

Why not on a charge of murder? Robert explained the law to me when I asked that question. I accepted the explanation, but it did not satisfy me. Mary Mallinson was killed by a blow from the hand of Noah Truscott. That is murder in the sight of God. Why not murder in the sight of the law also?

* * *

June 18th. To-morrow is the day appointed for the trial at the Old Bailey.

Before sunset this evening, I went to look at Mary's grave. The turf has grown so green since I saw it last; and the flowers are springing up so prettily. A bird was perched, dressing his feathers, on the low white headstone that bears the inscription of her name and age. I did not go near enough to disturb the little creature. He looked innocent and pretty on the grave, as Mary herself was in her life time. When he flew away, I went and sat for a little by the headstone, and read the mournful lines on it. Oh, my love, my love! what harm or wrong had you ever done in this world, that you should die at eighteen by a blow from a drunkard's hand?

June 19th. The trial. My experience of what happened at it is limited, like my experience of the examination at the police-office, to the time occupied in giving my own evidence. They made me say much more than I said before the magistrate. Between examination and cross-examination, I had to go into almost all the particulars about poor Mary and her funeral that I have written in this journal; the jury listening to every word I spoke with the most anxious attention. At the end, the judge said a few words to me approving of my conduct, and then there was a clapping of hands among the people in court. I was so agitated and excited that I trembled all over when they let me go out into the air again.

I looked at the prisoner both when I entered the witness-box and when I left it. The lowering brutality of his face was unchanged, but his faculties seemed to be more alive and observant than they were at the police-office. A frightful blue change passed over his face, and he drew his breath so heavily that the gasps were distinctly audible, while I mentioned Mary by name, and described the mark of the blow on her temple. When they asked me if I knew anything of the prisoner, and I answered that I only knew what Mary herself had told me about his having been her father's ruin, he gave a kind of groan, and struck both his hands heavily on the dock. And when I passed beneath him on my way out of court, he leaned over suddenly, whether to speak to me or to strike me I can't say, for he was immediately made to stand upright again by the turnkeys on either side of him. While the evidence proceeded (as Robert described it to me), the signs that he was suffering under superstitious terror became more and more apparent; until, at last, just as the lawyer appointed to defend him was rising to speak, he suddenly cried out, in a voice that startled everyone, up to the very judge on the bench, 'Stop!'

There was a pause, and all eyes looked at him. The perspiration was pouring over his face like water, and he made strange, uncouth signs with his hands to the judge opposite. 'Stop all this!' he cried again; 'I've been the ruin of the father and the death of the child. Hang me before I do more harm! Hang me for God's sake, out of the way!' As soon as the shock produced by this extraordinary interruption had subsided, he was removed, and there followed a long discussion about whether he was of sound mind or not. The matter was left to the jury to decide by their verdict. They found him guilty of the charge of manslaughter, without the excuse of insanity. He was brought up again, and condemned to transportation for life. All he did, on hearing the dreadful sentence, was to reiterate his desperate words, 'Hang me before I do more harm! Hang me, for God's sake, out of the way!'

June 20th. I made yesterday's entry in sadness of heart, and I have not been better in my spirits to-day. It is something to have brought the murderer to the punishment that he deserves. But the knowledge that this most righteous act of retribution is accomplished, brings no consolation with it. The law does indeed punish Noah Truscott for his crime; but can it raise up Mary Mallinson from her last resting-place in the churchyard?

While writing of the law, I ought to record that the heartless wretch who allowed Mary to be struck down in his presence without making an attempt to defend her, is not likely to escape with perfect impunity. The policeman who looked after him, to insure his attendance at the trial, discovered that he had committed past offences, for which the law can make him answer. A summons was executed upon him, and he was taken before the magistrate the moment he left the court after giving his evidence.

I had just written these few lines, and was closing my journal, when there came a knock at the door. I answered it, thinking Robert had called on his way home to say good-night, and found myself face to face with a strange gentleman, who immediately asked for Anne Rodway. On hearing that I was the person inquired for, he requested five minutes conversation with me. I showed him into the little empty room at the back of the house, and waited, rather surprised and fluttered, to hear what he had to say.

He was a dark man, with a serious manner and a short, stern way of speaking. I was certain that he was a stranger, and yet there seemed something in his face not unfamiliar to me. He began by taking a newspaper from his pocket, and asking me if I was the person who had given evidence at the trial of Noah Truscott on a charge of manslaughter. I answered immediately that I was.

'I have been for nearly two years in London seeking Mary Mallinson, and always seeking her in vain,' he said. 'The first and only news I have had of her I found in the newspaper report of the trial yesterday.'

He still spoke calmly, but there was something in the look of his eyes which showed me that he was suffering in spirit. A sudden nervousness overcame me, and I was obliged to sit down.

'You knew Mary Mallinson, sir?' I asked, as quietly as I could.

'I am her brother.'

I clasped my hands and hid my face in despair. Oh! the bitterness of heart with which I heard him say those simple words.

'You were very kind to her,' said the calm, tearless man. 'In her name, and for her sake, I thank you.'

'Oh, sir,' I said, 'why did you never write to her when you were in foreign parts?'

'I wrote often,' he answered; 'but each of my letters contained a remittance of money. Did Mary tell you she had a stepmother? If she did, you may guess why none of my letters were allowed to reach her. I now know that this woman robbed my sister. Has she lied in telling me that she was never informed of Mary's place of abode?'

I remembered that Mary had never communicated with her stepmother after the separation, and could therefore assure him that the woman had spoken the truth.

He paused for a moment after that, and sighed. Then he took out a pocket-book, and said:

'I have already arranged for the payment of any legal expenses that may have been incurred by the trial; but I have still to reimburse you for the funeral charges which you so generously defrayed. Excuse my speaking bluntly on this subject; I am accustomed to look on all matters where money is concerned purely as matters of business.'

I saw that he was taking several bank-notes out of the pocket-book, and stopped him.

'I will gratefully receive back the little money I actually paid, sir, because I am not well off, and it would be an ungracious act of pride in me to refuse it from you,' I said. 'But I see you handling bank-notes, any one of which is far beyond the amount you have to repay me. Pray put them back, sir. What I did for your poor lost sister, I did from my love and fondness for her. You have thanked me for that; and your thanks are all I can receive.'

He had hitherto concealed his feelings, but I saw them now begin to get the better of him. His eyes softened, and he took my hand and squeezed it hard.

'I beg your pardon,' he said. 'I beg your pardon, with all my heart.'

There was silence between us, for I was crying; and I believe, at heart, he was crying too. At last, he dropped my hand, and seemed to change back, by an effort, to his former calmness.

'Is there no one belonging to you to whom I can be of service?' he asked. 'I see among the witnesses on the trial the name of a young man who appears to have assisted you in the inquiries which led to the prisoner's conviction. Is he a relation?'

'No, sir; at least, not now – but I hope—'

'What?'

'I hope that he may, one day, be the nearest and dearest relation to me that a woman can have.' I said those words boldly, because I was afraid of his otherwise taking some wrong view of the connection between Robert and me.

'One day?' he repeated. 'One day may be a long time hence.'

'We are neither of us well off, sir,' I said. 'One day means the day when we are a little richer than we are now.'

'Is the young man educated? Can he produce testimonials to his character? Oblige me by writing his name and address down on the back of that card.'

When I had obeyed, in a handwriting which I am afraid did me no credit, he took out another card, and gave it to me.

'I shall leave England to-morrow,' he said. 'There is nothing now to keep me in my own country. If you are ever in any difficulty or distress (which, I pray God, you may never be), apply to my London agent, whose address you have there.'

He stopped, and looked at me attentively – then took my hand again.

'Where is she buried?' he said suddenly, in a quick whisper, turning his head away.

I told him, and added that we had made the grave as beautiful as we could with grass and flowers.

I saw his lips whiten and tremble.

'God bless and reward you!' he said, and drew me towards him quickly and kissed my forehead. I was quite overcome, and sank down and hid my face on the table. When I looked up again, he was gone.

*   *   *

June 25th, 1841. I write these lines on my wedding morning, when little more than a year has passed since Robert returned to England.

His salary was increased yesterday to one hundred and fifty pounds a year. If I only knew where Mr Mallinson was, I would write and tell him of our present happiness. But for the situation which his kindness procured for Robert, we might still have been waiting vainly for the day that has now come.

I am to work at home for the future, and Sally is to help us in our new abode. If Mary could have lived to see this day! I am not ungrateful for my blessings; but, oh, how I miss that sweet face, on this morning of all others!

I got up to-day early enough to go alone to the grave, and to gather the nosegay that now lies before me from the flowers that grow round it. I shall put it in my bosom when Robert comes to fetch me to the church. Mary would have been my bridesmaid if she had lived; and I can't forget Mary, even on my wedding-day.

The Black Cottage

Originally appeared in *Harper's Monthly Magazine*, February 1857, as 'The Siege of the Black Cottage'. The story was included in *The Queen of Hearts* as 'Brother Owen's Story of the Black Cottage'. Catherine Peters points out that the narrator of the story is the daughter of a stonemason, which was the occupation of the father-in-law of Collins's mistress, Caroline Graves (*The King of Inventors*, p. 210).

To BEGIN AT the beginning, I must take you back to the time after my mother's death, when my only brother had gone to sea, when my sister was out at service, and when I lived alone with my father, in the midst of a moor in the West of England.

The moor was covered with great limestone rocks, and intersected here and there by streamlets. The nearest habitation to ours was situated about a mile and a half off, where a strip of the fertile land stretched out into the waste, like a tongue. Here the out-buildings of the great Moor Farm, then in the possession of my husband's father, began. The Farm-lands stretched down gently into a beautiful rich valley, lying nicely sheltered by the high platform of the moor. When the ground began to rise again, miles and miles away, it led up to a country-house, called Holme Manor, belonging to a gentleman named Knifton. Mr Knifton had lately married a young lady whom my mother had nursed, and whose kindness and friendship for me, her foster-sister, I shall remember gratefully to the last day of my life. These, and other slight particulars, it is necessary to my story that I should tell you; and it is also necessary that you should be especially careful to bear them well in mind.

My father was by trade a stone-mason. His cottage stood a mile and a half from the nearest habitation. In all other directions we were four or five times that distance from neighbours. Being very poor people, this lonely situation had one great attraction for us – we lived rent free on it. In addition to that advantage, the stones, by shaping which my father gained his livelihood, lay all about him at his very door; so that he thought his position, solitary as it was, quite an enviable one. I can hardly say that I agreed with him, though I never complained. I was very fond of my father, and managed to make the best of my loneliness with the thought of being useful to him. Mrs Knifton wished to take me into her service when she married, but I declined, unwillingly enough, for my father's sake. If I had gone away, he would have had nobody to live with him; and my mother made me promise on her death-bed, that he should never be left to pine away alone in the midst of the bleak moor. Our cottage, small as it was, was stoutly and snugly built, with stone from the moor as a matter of course. The walls were lined inside and fenced outside with wood, the gift of Mr Knifton's father to my father. This double covering of cracks and crevices, which would have been superfluous in a sheltered position, was absolutely necessary, in our exposed situation, to keep out the cold winds which, excepting just the summer months, swept over us continually, all the year round. The outside boards, covering our roughly-built stone walls, my father protected against the wet with pitch and tar. This gave to our little abode a curiously dark, dingy look, especially when it was seen from a distance; and so it had come to be called in the neighbourhood, even before I was born, the Black Cottage.

I have now related the preliminary particulars which it is desirable that you should know, and may proceed at once to the pleasanter task of telling you my story.

One cloudy autumn day, when I was rather more than eighteen years old, a herdsman walked over from Moor Farm with a letter which had been left there for my father. It came from a builder, living at our county town, half a day's journey off, and it invited my father to come to him and give his judgment about an estimate for some stone-work on a very large scale. My father's expenses for loss of time were to be paid, and he was to have his share of employment afterward, in preparing the stone. He was only too glad, therefore, to obey the directions which the letter contained, and to prepare at once for his long walk to the county town.

Considering the time at which he received the letter, and the necessity of resting before he attempted to return, it was impossible for him to avoid being away from home for one night at least. He proposed to me, in case I disliked being left alone in the Black Cottage, to lock the door and to take me to Moor Farm to sleep with any one of the milkmaids who would give me a share of her bed. I by no means liked the notion of sleeping with a girl whom I did not know, and I saw no reason to feel afraid of being left alone for only one night; so I declined. No thieves had ever come near us; our poverty was sufficient protection against them; and of other dangers there were none that even the most timid person could apprehend. Accordingly, I got my father's dinner, laughing at the notion of my taking refuge under the protection of a milkmaid at Moor Farm. He started for his walk as soon as he had done, saying he should try and be back by dinner-time the next day, and leaving me and my cat Polly to take care of the house.

I had cleared the table and brightened up the fire, and had sat down to my work, with the cat dozing at my feet, when I heard the trampling of horses; and, running to the door, saw Mr and Mrs Knifton, with their groom behind them, riding up to the Black Cottage. It was part of the young lady's kindness never to neglect an opportunity of coming to pay me a friendly visit; and her husband was generally willing to accompany her for his wife's sake. I made my best curtsey, therefore, with a great deal of pleasure, but with no particular surprise at seeing them. They dismounted and entered the cottage, laughing and talking in great spirits. I soon heard that they were riding to the same county town for which my father was bound; and that they intended to stay with some friends there for a few days, and to return home on horseback, as they went out.

I heard this, and I also discovered that they had been having an argument, in jest, about money matters, as they rode along to our cottage. Mrs Knifton had accused her husband of inveterate extravagance, and of never being able to go out with money in his pocket without spending it all, if he possibly could, before he got home again. Mr Knifton had laughingly defended himself by declaring that all his pocket-money went in presents for his wife, and that, if he spent it lavishly, it was under her sole influence and superintendence.

'We are going to Cliverton now,' he said to Mrs Knifton, naming the county town, and warming himself at our poor fire just as pleasantly as if he had been standing on his own grand hearth. 'You will stop to admire every pretty thing in every one of the Cliverton shop-windows; I shall hand you the purse, and you will go in and buy. When we have reached home again, and you have had time to get tired of your purchases, you will clasp your hands in amazement and declare that you are quite shocked at my habits of inveterate extravagance. I am only the banker who keeps the money – you, my love, are the spendthrift who throws it all away!'

'Am I, sir?' said Mrs Knifton, with a look of mock indignation. 'We will see if I am to be misrepresented in this way with impunity. Bessie, my dear,' (turning to me), 'you shall judge how far I deserve the character which that unscrupulous man has just given to me. *I* am the spendthrift, am I? And you are only the banker? Very well. Banker! give me my money at once, if you please.'

Mr Knifton laughed, and took some gold and silver from his waistcoat pocket.

'No, no,' said Mrs Knifton. 'You may want what you have got there for necessary expenses. Is that all the money you have about you? What do I feel here?' and she tapped her husband on the chest, just over the breast-pocket of his coat.

Mr Knifton laughed again, and produced his pocket-book. His wife snatched it out of his hand, opened it, and drew out some bank-notes, put them back again immediately, and closing the pocket-book, stepped across the room to my poor mother's little walnut-wood book-case – the only bit of valuable furniture we had in the house.

'What are you going to do there?' asked Mr Knifton, following his wife.

Mrs Knifton opened the glass door of the book-case, put the pocket-book in a vacant place on one of the lower shelves, closed and locked the door again, and gave me the key.

'You called me a spendthrift just now,' she said. 'There is my answer. Not one farthing of that money shall you spend at Cliverton on *me*. Keep the key in your pocket, Bessie, and, whatever Mr Knifton may say, on no account let him have it until we call again on our way back. No, Sir, I won't trust you with that money in your pocket in the town of Cliverton. I will make sure of your taking it all home again, by leaving it here in more trustworthy hands than yours, until we ride back. Bessie, my dear, what do you say to that, as a lesson in economy inflicted on a prudent husband by a spendthrift wife?'

She took Mr Knifton's arm while she spoke, and drew him away to the door. He protested, and made some resistance, but she easily carried her point, for he was far too fond of her to have a will of his own in any trifling matter between them. Whatever the men might say, Mr Knifton was a model husband in the estimation of all the women who knew him.

'You will see us as we come back, Bessie. Till then, you are our banker, and the pocket-book is yours,' cried Mrs Knifton, gaily, at the door. Her husband lifted her into the saddle, mounted himself, and away they both galloped over the moor, as wild and happy as a couple of children.

Although my being trusted with money by Mrs Knifton was no novelty (in her maiden days she always employed me to pay her dress-maker's bills), I did not feel quite easy at having a pocket-book full of bank notes left by her in my charge. I had no positive apprehensions about the safety of the deposit placed in my hands; but it was one of the odd points in my character then (and I think it is still), to feel an unreasonably strong objection to charging myself with money responsibilities of any kind, even to suit the convenience of my dearest friends. As soon as I was left alone, the very sight of the pocket-book behind the glass-door of the book-case began to worry me; and instead of returning to my work, I puzzled my brains about finding a place to lock it up in, where it would not be exposed to the view of any chance passers-by, who might stray into the Black Cottage.

This was not an easy matter to compass in a poor house like ours, where we had nothing valuable to put under lock and key. After running over various hiding-places in my mind, I thought of my teacaddy, a present from Mrs Knifton, which I always kept out of harm's way in my own bedroom. Most unluckily – as it afterwards turned out – instead of taking the pocket-book to the tea-caddy, I went into my room first to take the tea-caddy to the pocket-book. I only acted in this roundabout way from sheer thoughtlessness, and severely enough I was punished for it, as you will acknowledge yourself when you have read a page or two more of my story.

I was just getting the unlucky tea-caddy out of my cupboard, when I heard footsteps in the passage, and running out immediately, saw two men walk into the kitchen – the room in which I had received Mr and Mrs Knifton. I inquired what they wanted, sharply enough, and one of them answered immediately that they wanted my father. He turned towards me, of course, as he spoke, and I recognised him as a stonemason, going among his comrades by the name of Shifty Dick. He bore a very bad character for everything but wrestling – a sport for which the working men of our parts were famous all through the county. Shifty Dick was champion, and he had got his name from some tricks in wrestling, for which he was celebrated. He was a tall, heavy man, with a lowering, scarred face, and huge hairy hands – the last visitor in the whole world that I should have been glad to see under any circumstances. His companion was a stranger, whom he addressed by the name of Jerry – a quick, dapper, wicked-looking man, who took off his cap to me with mock politeness, and showed, in so doing, a very bald head with some very ugly-looking knobs on it. I distrusted him worse than I did Shifty Dick, and managed to get between his leering eyes and the bookcase, as I told the two that my father was gone out, and that I did not expect him back till the next day.

The words were hardly out of my mouth before I repented that my anxiety to get rid of my unwelcome visitors had made me incautious enough to acknowledge that my father would be away from home for the whole night.

Shifty Dick and his companion looked at each other when I unwisely let out the truth, but made no remark, except to ask me if I would give them a drop of cider. I answered, sharply, that I had no cider in the house – having no fear of the consequences of refusing them drink, because I knew that plenty of men were at work within hail, in a neighbouring quarry. The two looked at each other again, when I denied having any cider to give them; and Jerry (as I am obliged to call him, knowing no other name by which to distinguish the fellow) took off his cap to me once more, and, with a kind of blackguard gentility upon him, said they would have the pleasure of calling the next day, when my father was at home. I said good afternoon as ungraciously as possible; and, to my great relief, they both left the cottage immediately afterwards.

As soon as they were well away, I watched them from the door. They trudged off in the direction of Moor Farm; and, as it was beginning to get dusk, I soon lost sight of them.

Half an hour afterwards I looked out again.

The wind had lulled with the sunset, but the mist was rising, and a heavy rain was beginning to fall. Never did the lonely prospect of the moor look so dreary as it looked to my eyes that evening. Never did I regret any slight thing more sincerely than I then regretted the leaving of Mr Knifton's pocket-book in my charge. I cannot say that I suffered under any actual alarm, for I felt next to certain that neither Shifty Dick nor Jerry had got a chance of setting eyes on so small a thing as the pocket-book, while they were in the kitchen; but there was a kind of vague distrust troubling me – a suspicion of the night – a dislike at being left by myself, which I never remember having experienced before. This feeling so increased, after I had closed the door and gone back to the kitchen, that, when I heard the voices of the quarrymen, as they passed our cottage on their way home to the village in the valley below Moor Farm, I stepped out into the passage with a momentary notion of telling them how I was situated, and asking them for advice and protection.

I had hardly formed this idea, however, before I dismissed it. None of the quarrymen were intimate friends of mine. I had a nodding acquaintance with them, and believed them to be honest men, as times went. But my own common sense told me that what little knowledge of their characters I had, was by no means sufficient to warrant me in admitting them into my confidence in the matter of the pocket-book. I had seen enough of poverty and poor men to know what a terrible temptation a large sum of money is to those whose whole lives are passed in scraping up sixpences by weary hard work. It is one thing to write fine sentiments in books about incorruptible honesty, and another thing to put those sentiments in practice, when one day's work is all that a man has to set up in the way of an obstacle between starvation and his own fireside.

The only resource that remained was to carry the pocket-book with me to Moor Farm, and ask permission to pass the night there. But I could not persuade myself that there was any real necessity for taking such a course as this; and, if the truth must be told, my pride revolted at the idea of presenting myself in the character of a coward before the people at the farm. Timidity is thought rather a graceful attraction among ladies, but among poor women it is something to be laughed at. A woman with less spirit of her own than I had, and always shall have, would have considered twice in my situation before she made up her mind to encounter the jokes of ploughmen and the jeers of milkmaids. As for me, I had hardly considered about going to the farm before I despised myself for entertaining any such notion. 'No, no,' thought I, 'I am not the woman to walk a mile and a half through rain, and mist, and darkness, to tell a whole kitchenful of people that I am afraid. Come what may, here I stop till father gets back.'

Having arrived at that valiant resolution, the first thing I did was to lock and bolt the back and front doors, and see to the security of every shutter in the house.

That duty performed, I made a blazing fire, lighted my candle, and sat down to tea, as snug and comfortable as possible. I could hardly believe now, with the light in the room, and the sense of security inspired by the closed doors and shutters, that I had ever felt even the slightest apprehension earlier in the day. I sang as I washed up the tea-things; and even the cat seemed to catch the infection of my good spirits. I never knew the pretty creature so playful as she was that evening.

The tea-things put by, I took up my knitting, and worked away at it so long that I began at last to get drowsy. The fire was so bright and comforting that I could not muster resolution enough to leave it and go to bed. I sat staring lazily into the blaze, with my knitting on my lap – sat till the splashing of the rain outside, and the fitful, sullen sobbing of the wind, grew fainter and fainter on my ear. The last sounds I heard before I fairly dozed off to sleep were the cheerful crackling of the fire and the steady purring of the cat, as she basked luxuriously in the warm light on the hearth. Those were the last sounds before I fell asleep. The sound that woke me was one loud bang at the front door.

I started up, with my heart (as the saying is) in my mouth, with a frightful momentary shuddering at the roots of my hair – I started up breathless, cold, and motionless; waiting in the silence, I hardly knew for what; doubtful, at first, whether I had dreamed about the bang at the door, or whether the blow had really been struck on it.

In a minute, or less, there came a second bang, louder than the first. I ran out into the passage.

'Who's there?'

'Let us in,' answered a voice, which I recognized immediately as the voice of Shifty Dick.

'Wait a bit, my dear, and let me explain,' said a second voice, in the low, oily, jeering tones of Dick's companion – the wickedly clever little man whom he called Jerry. 'You are alone in the house, my pretty little dear. You may crack your sweet voice with screeching, and there's nobody near to hear you. Listen to reason, my love, and let us in. We dont want cider this time – we only want a very neat-looking pocket-book which you happen to have, and your late excellent mother's four silver tea spoons, which you keep so nice and clean on the chimney-piece. If you let us in, we won't hurt a hair of your head, my cherub, and we promise to go away the moment we have got what we want, unless you particularly wish us to stop to tea. If you keep us out, we shall be obliged to break into the house, and then—'

'And then,' burst in Shifty Dick, 'we'll *mash* you!'

'Yes,' said Jerry, 'we'll mash you, my beauty. But you won't drive us to doing that, will you? You will let us in?'

This long parley gave me time to recover from the effect which the first bang at the door had produced on my nerves. The threats of the two villains would have terrified some women out of their senses; but the only result they produced on *me* was violent indignation. I had, thank God, a strong spirit of my own; and the cool, contemptuous insolence of the man Jerry effectually roused it.

'You cowardly villains!' I screamed at them through the door. 'You think you can frighten me because I am only a poor girl left alone in the house. You ragamuffin thieves, I defy you both! Our bolts are strong, our shutters are thick. I am here to keep my father's house safe; and keep it I will against an army of you!'

You may imagine what a passion I was in when I vapoured and blustered in that way. I heard Jerry laugh, and Shifty Dick swear a whole mouthful of oaths. Then there was a dead silence for a minute or two; and then the two ruffians attacked the door.

I rushed into the kitchen and seized the poker, and then heaped wood on the fire, and lighted all the candles I could find; for I felt as though I could keep up my courage better if I had plenty of light. Strange and improbable as it may appear, the next thing that attracted my attention was my poor pussy, crouched up, panic-stricken, in a corner. I was so fond of the little creature that I took her up in my arms and carried her into my bedroom, and put her inside my bed. A comical thing to do in a situation of deadly peril, was it not? But it seemed quite natural and proper at the time.

All this while the blows were falling faster and faster on the door. They were dealt, as I conjectured, with heavy stones picked up from the ground outside. Jerry sang at his wicked work, and Shifty Dick swore. As I left the bedroom, after putting the cat under cover, I heard the lower panel of the door begin to crack.

I ran into the kitchen and huddled our four silver spoons into my pocket; then took the unlucky book with the bank-notes and put it in the bosom of my dress. I was determined to defend the property confided to my care with my life. Just as I had secured the pocket-book I heard the door splintering, and rushed into the passage again with my heavy kitchen poker lifted in both hands.

I was in time to see the bald head of Jerry, with the ugly-looking knobs on it, pushed into the passage through a great rent in one of the lower panels of the door.

'Get out, you villain, or I'll brain you on the spot!' I screeched, threatening him with the poker.

Mr Jerry took his head out again much faster than he put it in.

The next thing that came through the rent was a long pitchfork, which they darted at me from the outside, to move me from the door. I struck at it with all my might, and the blow must have jarred the hand of Shifty Dick up to his very shoulder, for I heard him give a roar of rage and pain. Before he could catch at the fork with his other hand, I had drawn it inside. By this time, even Jerry lost his temper, and swore more awfully than Dick himself.

Then there came another minute of respite. I suspected they had gone to get bigger stones, and I dreaded the giving way of the whole door.

Running into the bedroom as this fear beset me, I laid hold of my chest of drawers, dragged it into the passage, and threw it down against the door. On the top of that I heaped my father's big tool chest, three chairs, and a scuttleful of coals – and last, I dragged out the kitchen-table and rammed it as hard as I could against the whole barricade. They heard me as they were coming up to the door with fresh stones. Jerry said, 'Stop a bit,' and then the two consulted together in whispers. I listened eagerly, and just caught these words:

'Let's try it the other way.'

Nothing more was said, but I heard their footsteps retreating from the door.

Were they going to besiege the backdoor now?

I had hardly asked myself that question when I heard their voices at the other side of the house. The back-door was smaller than the front; but it had this advantage in the way of strength – it was made of two solid oak boards, joined longwise, and strengthened inside by heavy cross pieces. It had no bolts like the front door, but was fastened by a bar of iron, running across it in a slanting direction, and fitting at either end into the wall.

'They must have the whole cottage down before they can break in at that door,' I thought to myself. And they soon found out as much for themselves. After five minutes of banging at the back door, they gave up any farther attack in that direction, and cast their heavy stones down with curses of fury awful to hear.

I went into the kitchen and dropped on the window-seat to rest for a moment. Suspense and excitement together were beginning to tell upon me. The perspiration broke out thick on my forehead, and I began to feel the bruises I had inflicted on my hands in making the barricade against the front door. I had not lost a particle of my resolution, but I was beginning to lose strength. There was a bottle of rum in the cupboard, which my brother the sailor had left with us the last time he was ashore. I drank a drop of it. Never before or since have I put anything down my throat that did me half so much good as that precious mouthful of rum.

I was still sitting in the window seat drying my face, when I suddenly heard their voices close behind me.

They were feeling the outside of the window against which I was sitting. It was protected, like all the other windows in the cottage, by iron bars. I listened in dreadful suspense for the sound of filing, but nothing of the sort was audible. They had evidently reckoned on frightening me easily into letting them in, and had come unprovided with house-breaking tools of any kind. A fresh burst of oaths informed me that they had recognized the obstacle of the iron bars. I listened breathlessly for some warning of what they were going to do next, but their voices seemed to die away in the distance. They were retreating from the window. Were they also retreating from the house altogether? Had they given up the idea of effecting an entrance in despair?

A long silence followed – a silence which tried my courage even more severely than the tumult of their first attack on the cottage.

Dreadful suspicions now beset me of their being able to accomplish by treachery what they had failed to effect by force. Well as I knew the cottage, I began to doubt whether there might not be ways of cunningly and silently entering it against which I was not provided. The ticking of the clock annoyed me; the crackling of the fire startled me. I looked out twenty times in a minute into the dark corners of the passage, straining my eyes, holding my breath, anticipating the most unlikely events, the most impossible dangers. Had they really gone? or were they still prowling about the house? Oh, what a sum of money I would have given, only to have known what they were about in that interval of silence!

I was startled at last out of my suspense in the most awful manner. A shout from one of them reached my ears on a sudden down the kitchen chimney. It was so unexpected and so horrible in the stillness, that I screamed for the first time since the attack on the house. My worst forebodings had never suggested to me that the two villains might mount upon the roof.

'Let us in, you she devil!' roared a voice down the chimney.

There was another pause. The smoke from the wood fire, thin and light as it was in the red state of the embers at that moment, had evidently obliged the man to take his face from the mouth of the chimney. I counted the seconds while he was, as I conjectured, getting his breath again. In less than half a minute there came another shout:

'Let us in, or we'll burn the place down over your head.'

Burn it? Burn what? There was nothing easily combustible but the thatch on the roof; and that had been well soaked by the heavy rain which had now fallen incessantly for more than six hours. Burn the place over my head? How?

While I was still casting about wildly in my mind to discover what possible danger there could be of fire, one of the heavy stones placed on the thatch to keep it from being torn up by high winds, came thundering down the chimney. It scattered the live embers on the hearth all over the room. A richly furnished place, with knickknacks and fine muslin about it, would have been set on fire immediately. Even our bare floor and rough furniture gave out a smell of burning at the first shower of embers which the first stone scattered.

For an instant I stood quite horror-struck before this new proof of the devilish ingenuity of the villains outside. But the dreadful danger I was now in recalled me to my senses immediately. There was a large canful of water in my bedroom, and I ran in at once to fetch it. Before I could get back to the kitchen, a second stone had been thrown down the chimney, and the floor was smouldering in several places.

I had wit enough to let the smouldering go on for a moment or two more, and to pour the whole of my canful of water over the fire before the third stone came down the chimney. The live embers on the floor I easily disposed of after that. The man on the roof must have heard the hissing of the fire as I put it out, and have felt the change produced in the air at the mouth of the chimney; for after the third stone had descended, no more followed it. As for either of the ruffians themselves dropping down by the same road along which the stones had come, that was not to be dreaded. The chimney, as I well knew by our experience in cleaning it, was too narrow to give passage to anyone above the size of a small boy.

I looked upwards as that comforting reflection crossed my mind – I looked up, and saw, as plainly as I see the paper I am now writing on, the point of a knife coming through the inside of the roof just over my head. Our cottage had no upper storey, and our rooms had no ceilings. Slowly and wickedly the knife wriggled its way through the dry inside thatch between the rafters. It stopped for a while, and there came a sound of tearing. That, in its turn, stopped too; there was a great fall of dry thatch on the floor; and I saw the heavy, hairy hand of Shifty Dick, armed with the knife, come through after the fallen fragments. He tapped at the rafters with the back of the knife, as if to test their strength. Thank God, they were substantial and close together! Nothing lighter than a hatchet would have sufficed to remove any part of them.

The murderous hand was still tapping with the knife, when I heard a shout from the man Jerry, coming from the neighbourhood of my father's stone-shed in the back yard. The hand and knife disappeared instantly. I went to the back door and put my ear to it, and listened.

Both men were now in the shed. I made the most desperate efforts to call to mind what tools and other things were left in it, which might be used against me. But my agitation confused me. I could remember nothing except my father's big stone saw, which was far too heavy and unwieldy to be used on the roof of the cottage. I was still puzzling my brains and making my head swim to no purpose, when I heard the men dragging something out of the shed. At the same instant when the noise caught my ear, the remembrance flashed across me like lightning of some beams of wood which had lain in the shed for years past. I had hardly time to feel certain that they were removing one of these beams, before I heard Shifty Dick say to Jerry:

'Which door?'

'The front,' was the answer. 'We've cracked it already; we'll have it down now in no time.'

Senses less sharpened by danger than mine would have understood but too easily, from these words, that they were about to use the beam as a battering-ram against the door. When that conviction overcame me, I lost courage at last. I felt that the door must come down. No such barricade as I had constructed could support it, for more than a few minutes, against such shocks as it was now to receive.

'I can do no more to keep the house against them,' I said to myself, with my knees knocking together, and the tears at last beginning to wet my cheeks. 'I must trust to the night and the thick darkness, and save my life by running for it while there is yet time.'

I huddled on my cloak and hood, and had my hand on the bar of the back-door, when a piteous mew from the bed-room reminded me of the existence of poor Pussy. I ran in, and huddled the creature up in my apron. Before I was out in the passage again, the first shock from the beam fell on the door.

The upper hinge gave way. The chairs and the coal-scuttle forming the top of my barricade were hurled, rattling, on to the floor; but the lower hinge of the door, and the chest of drawers and tool-chest, still kept their places.

'One more,' I heard the villains cry – 'one more run with the beam, and down it comes!'

Just as they must have been starting for that 'one more run,' I opened the back door and fled out into the night, with the book full of bank-notes in my bosom, the silver spoons in my pocket, and the cat in my arms. I threaded my way easily enough through the familiar obstacles in the back-yard, and was out in the pitch darkness of the moor, before I heard the second shock, and the crash which told me that the whole door had given way.

In a few minutes they must have discovered the fact of my flight with the pocket-book, for I heard shouts in the distance as if they were running out to pursue me. I kept on at the top of my speed, and the noise soon died away. It was so dark that twenty thieves, instead of two, would have found it useless to follow me.

How long it was before I reached the farm-house – the nearest place to which I could fly for refuge – I cannot tell you. I remember that I had just sense enough to keep the wind at my back (having observed in the beginning of the evening that it blew toward Moor Farm), and to go on resolutely through the darkness. In all other respects, I was by this time half-crazed by what I had gone through. If it had so happened that the wind had changed after I had observed its direction early in the evening, I should have gone astray, and have probably perished of fatigue and exposure on the moor. Providentially, it still blew steadily as it had blown for hours past, and I reached the farm-house with my clothes wet through, and my brain in a high fever. When I made my alarm at the door, they had all gone to bed but the farmer's eldest son, who was sitting up late over his pipe and newspaper. I just mustered strength enough to gasp out a few words, telling him what was the matter, and then fell down at his feet, for the first time in my life, in a dead swoon.

That swoon was followed by a severe illness. When I got strong enough to look about me again, I found myself in one of the farm-house beds – my father, Mrs Knifton, and the doctor, were all in the room – my cat was asleep at my feet, and the pocket-book that I had saved lay on the table by my side.

There was plenty of news for me to hear, as soon as I was fit to listen to it. Shifty Dick and the other rascal had been caught, and were in prison, waiting their trial at the next assizes. Mr and Mrs Knifton had been so shocked at the danger I had run – for which they blamed their own want of thoughtfulness in leaving the pocket-book in my care – that they had insisted on my father's removing from our lonely home to a cottage on their land, which we were to inhabit rent free. The bank-notes that I had saved were given to me to buy furniture with, in place of the things that the thieves had broken. These pleasant tidings assisted so greatly in promoting my recovery, that I was soon able to relate to my friends at the farm house the particulars that I have written here. They were all surprised and interested; but no one, as I thought, listened to me with such breathless attention as the farmer's eldest son. Mrs Knifton noticed this, too, and began to make jokes about it, in her light-hearted way, as soon as we were alone. I thought little of her jesting at the time; but when I got well, and we went to live at our new home, 'the young farmer,' as he was called in our parts, constantly came to see us, and constantly managed to meet me out of doors. I had my share of vanity, like other young women, and I began to think of Mrs Knifton's jokes with some attention. To be brief, the young farmer managed one Sunday – I never could tell how – to lose his way with me in returning from Church, and before we found out the right road home again, he had asked me to be his wife.

His relations did all they could to keep us asunder and break off the match, thinking a poor stonemason's daughter no fit wife for a prosperous yeoman. But the farmer was too obstinate for them. He had one form of answer to all their objections. 'A man, if he is worth the name, marries according to his own notions, and to please himself,' he used to say. 'My notion is, that when I take a wife I am placing my character and my happiness – the most precious things I have to trust – in one woman's care. The woman I mean to marry had a small charge confided to her care, and showed herself worthy of it at the risk of her life. That is proof enough for me that she is worthy of the greatest charge I can put into her hands. Rank and riches are fine things, but the certainty of getting a good wife is something better still. I'm of age, I know my own mind, and I mean to marry the stonemason's daughter.'

And he did marry me. Whether I proved myself worthy or not of his good opinion is a question which I must leave you to ask my husband. All that I had to relate about myself and my doings is now told. Whatever interest my perilous adventure may excite, ends, I am well aware, with my escape to the farmhouse. I have only ventured on writing these few additional sentences, because my marriage is the moral of my story. It has brought me the choicest blessings of happiness and prosperity; and I owe them all to my night-adventure in *The Black Cottage*.

The Family Secret

Originally appeared in *The National Magazine*, May 1857, as 'Uncle George or the Family Mystery'. The story was included in *The Queen of Hearts* as 'Brother Griffith's Story of the Family Secret'.

I

Was it an Englishman or a Frenchman who first remarked that every family had a skeleton in its cupboard? I am not learned enough to know; but I reverence the observation, whoever made it. It speaks a startling truth through an appropriately grim metaphor – a truth which I have discovered by practical experience. Our family had a skeleton in the cupboard; and the name of it was Uncle George.

I arrived at the knowledge that this skeleton existed, and I traced it to the particular cupboard in which it was hidden, by slow degrees. I was a child when I first began to suspect that there was such a thing, and a grown man when I at last discovered that my suspicions were true.

My father was a doctor, having an excellent practice in a large country-town. I have heard that he married against the wishes of his family. They could not object to my mother on the score of birth, breeding, or character – they only disliked her heartily. My grandfather, grandmother, uncles, and aunts, all declared that she was a heartless, deceitful woman; all disliked her manners, her opinions, and even the expression of her face – all, with the one exception of my father's youngest brother, George.

George was the unlucky member of our family. The rest were all clever; he was slow in capacity. The rest were all remarkably handsome; he was the sort of man that no woman ever looks at twice. The rest succeeded in life; he failed. His profession was the same as my father's; but he never got on when he started in practice for himself. The sick poor, who could not choose, employed him, and liked him. The sick rich, who could – especially the ladies – declined to call him in when they could get anybody else. In experience he gained greatly by his profession; in money and reputation he gained nothing.

There are very few of us, however dull and unattractive we may be to outward appearance, who have not some strong passion, some germ of what is called romance, hidden more or less deeply in our natures. All the passion and romance in the nature of my Uncle George lay in his love and admiration for my father.

He sincerely worshipped his eldest brother, as one of the noblest of human beings. When my father was engaged to be married, and when the rest of the family, as I have already mentioned, did not hesitate to express their unfavourable opinion of the disposition of his chosen wife, Uncle George, who had never ventured on differing with any one before, to the amazement of every body undertook the defence of his future sister-in-law in the most vehement and positive manner. In his estimation, his brother's choice was something sacred and indisputable. The lady might, and did, treat him with unconcealed contempt, laugh at his awkwardness, grow impatient at his stammering – it made no difference to Uncle George. She was to be his brother's wife; and, in virtue of that one great fact, she became, in the estimation of the poor surgeon, a very queen, who, by the laws of the domestic constitution, could do no wrong.

When my father had been married a little while, he took his youngest brother to live with him as his assistant.

If Uncle George had been made President of the College of Surgeons, he could not have been prouder and happier than he was in his new position. I am afraid my father never understood the depth of his brother's affection for him. All the hard work fell to George's share: the long journeys at night, the physicking of wearisome poor people, the drunken cases, the revolting cases – all the drudging, dirty business of the surgery, in short, was turned over to him; and day after day, month after month, he struggled through it without a murmur. When his brother and his sister-in-law went out to dine with the county gentry, it never entered his head to feel disappointed at being left unnoticed at home. When the return dinners were given, and he was asked to come in at tea-time, and left to sit unregarded in a corner, it never occurred to him to imagine that he was treated with any want of consideration or respect. He was part of the furniture of the house, and it was the business as well as the pleasure of his life, to turn himself to any use to which his brother might please to put him.

So much for what I have heard from others on the subject of my Uncle George. My own personal experience of him is limited to what I remember as a mere child. Let me say something, however, first about my parents, my sister, and myself.

My sister was the eldest born and the best loved. I did not come into the world till four years after her birth; and no other child followed me. Caroline, from her earliest days, was the perfection of beauty and health. I was small, weakly, and, if the truth must be told, almost as plain-featured as Uncle George himself. It would be ungracious and undutiful in me to presume to decide whether there was any foundation or not for the dislike that my father's family always felt for my mother. All I can venture to say is, that her children never had any cause to complain of her.

Her passionate affection for my sister, her pride in the child's beauty, I remember well; as also her uniform kindness and indulgence towards me. My personal defects must have been a sore trial to her in secret, but neither she nor my father ever showed me that they perceived any difference between Caroline and myself. When presents were made to my sister, presents were made to me. When my father and mother caught my sister up in their arms and kissed her, they scrupulously gave me my turn afterwards. My childish instinct told me that there was a difference in their smiles when they looked at me and looked at her; that the kisses given to Caroline were warmer than the kisses given to me; that the hands which dried her tears, in our childish griefs, touched her more gently than the hands which dried mine. But these, and other small signs of preference like them, were such as no parents could be expected to control. I noticed them at the time rather with wonder than with repining. I recall them now without a harsh thought either towards my father or my mother. Both loved me, and both did their duty by me. If I seem to speak constrainedly of them here, it is not on my own account. I can honestly say that with all my heart and soul.

Even Uncle George, fond as he was of me, was fonder of my beautiful child-sister.

When I used mischievously to pull at his lank scanty hair, he would gently and laughingly take it out of my hands; but he would let Caroline tug at it till his dim, wandering, grey eyes winked and watered again with pain. He used to plunge perilously about the garden, in awkward imitation of the cantering of a horse, while I sat on his shoulders; but he would never proceed at any pace beyond a slow and safe walk when Caroline had a ride in her turn. When he took us out walking, Caroline was always on the side next the wall. When we interrupted him over his dirty work in the surgery, he used to tell me to go and play until he was ready for me; but he would put down his bottles, and clean his clumsy fingers on his coarse apron, and lead Caroline out again, as if she had been the greatest lady in the land. Ah, how he loved her! – and, let me be honest and grateful, and add, how he loved me too!

When I was eight years old and Caroline was twelve, I was separated from home for some time. I had been ailing for many months previously; had got benefit from being taken to the seaside; and had shown symptoms of relapsing on being brought home again to the midland county in which we resided. After much consultation it was at last resolved that I should be sent to live, until my constitution got stronger, with a maiden-sister of my mother's, who had a house at a watering-place on the south coast.

I left home, I remember, loaded with presents, rejoicing over the prospect of looking at the sea again, as careless of the future and as happy in the present as any boy could be. Uncle George petitioned for a holiday to take me to the seaside, but he could not be spared from the surgery. He consoled himself and me by promising to make me a magnificent model of a ship.

I have that model before my eyes now while I write. It is dusty with age; the paint on it is cracked, the ropes are tangled, the sails are moth-eaten and yellow. The hull is all out of proportion, and the rig has been smiled at by every nautical friend of mine who has ever looked at it. Yet, worn out and faulty as it is – inferior to the cheapest miniature vessel now-a-days in any toy-shop window – I hardly know a possession of mine in this world, that I would not sooner part with than Uncle George's ship.

My life at the seaside was a very happy one. I remained with my aunt more than a year. My mother often came to see how I was going on, and, at first, always brought my sister with her. But, during the last eight months of my stay, Caroline never once appeared. I noticed also at the same period a change in my mother's manner. She looked paler and more anxious at each succeeding visit, and always had long conferences in private with my aunt. At last she ceased to come and see us altogether, and only wrote to know how my health was getting on. My father, too, who had at the earlier periods of my absence from home, travelled to the seaside to watch the progress of my recovery as often as his professional engagements would permit, now kept away like my mother. Even Uncle George, who had never been allowed a holiday to come and see me, but who had hitherto often written and begged me to write to him, broke off our correspondence.

I was naturally perplexed and amazed by these changes, and persecuted my aunt to tell me the reason of them. At first she tried to put me off with excuses; then she admitted that there was trouble in our house; and finally she confessed that the trouble was caused by the illness of my sister. When I inquired what that illness was, my aunt said it was useless to attempt to explain it to me. I next applied to the servants. One of them was less cautious than my aunt, and answered my question, but in terms that I could not comprehend. After much explanation, I was made to understand that 'something was growing on my sister's neck that would spoil her beauty for ever, and perhaps kill her, if it could not be got rid of.' How well I remember the shudder of horror that ran through me at the vague idea of this deadly 'something!' A fearful, awe-struck curiosity to see what Caroline's illness was with my own eyes, troubled my inmost heart; and I begged to be allowed to go home and help to nurse her. The request was, it is almost needless to say, refused.

Weeks passed away, and still I heard nothing, except that my sister continued to be ill.

One day I privately wrote a letter to Uncle George, asking him in my childish way to come and tell me about Caroline's illness.

I knew where the post-office was, and slipped out in the morning unobserved and dropped my letter in the box. I stole home again by the garden, and climbed in at the window of a back parlour on the ground floor. The room above was my aunt's bed-chamber, and the moment I was inside the house, I heard moans and loud convulsive sobs proceeding from it. My aunt was a singularly quiet composed woman. I could not imagine that the loud sobbing and moaning came from her; and I ran down terrified into the kitchen to ask the servants who was crying so violently in my aunt's room.

I found the housemaid and the cook talking together in whispers, with serious faces. They started when they saw me, as if I had been a grown-up master who had caught them neglecting their work.

'He's too young to feel it much,' I heard one say to the other. 'So far as he is concerned, it seems like a mercy that it happened no later.'

In a few minutes they had told me the worst. It was my aunt who had been crying in the bed-room. Caroline was dead.

I felt the blow more severely than the servants or anyone else about me supposed. Still I was a child in years, and I had the blessed elasticity of a child's nature. If I had been older, I might have been too much absorbed in grief to observe my aunt so closely as I did, when she was composed enough to see me, later in the day.

I was not surprised by the swollen state of her eyes, the paleness of her cheeks, or the fresh burst of tears that came from her when she took me in her arms at meeting. But I was both amazed and perplexed by the look of terror that I detected in her face. It was natural enough that she should grieve and weep over my sister's death; but why should she have that frightened look, as if some other catastrophe had happened?

I asked if there was any more dreadful news from home besides the news of Caroline's death. My aunt said, No, in a strange stifled voice, and suddenly turned her face from me. Was my father dead? No. My mother? No. Uncle George? My aunt trembled all over as she said No, to that also, and bade me cease asking any more questions. She was not fit to bear them yet, she said; and signed to the servant to lead me out of the room.

The next day I was told that I was to go home after the funeral, and was taken out towards evening by the housemaid, partly for a walk, partly to be measured for my mourning clothes. After we had left the tailor's, I persuaded the girl to extend our walk for some distance along the sea-beach, telling her, as we went, every little anecdote connected with my lost sister that came tenderly back to my memory in those first days of sorrow. She was so interested in hearing, and I in speaking, that we let the sun go down before we thought of turning back.

The evening was cloudy, and it got on from dusk to dark by the time we approached the town again. The housemaid was rather nervous at finding herself alone with me on the beach, and once or twice looked behind her distrustfully as we went on. Suddenly she squeezed my hand hard, and said—

'Let's get up on the cliff as fast as we can.'

The words were hardly out of her mouth before I heard footsteps behind me – a man came round quickly to my side, snatched me away from the girl, and catching me up in his arms, without a word, covered my face with kisses. I knew he was crying, because my cheeks were instantly wet with his tears; but it was too dark for me to see who he was, or even how he was dressed. He did not, I should think, hold me half a minute in his arms. The housemaid screamed for help, I was put down gently on the sand, and the strange man instantly disappeared in the darkness.

When this extraordinary adventure was related to my aunt, she seemed at first merely bewildered at hearing of it; but in a moment more there came a change over her face, as if she had suddenly recollected or thought of something. She turned deadly pale, and said in a hurried way, very unusual with her—

'Never mind; don't talk about it any more. It was only a mischievous trick to frighten you, I dare say. Forget all about it, my dear – forget all about it.'

It was easier to give this advice than to make me follow it. For many nights after, I thought of nothing but the strange man who had kissed me and cried over me.

Who could he be? Somebody who loved me very much, and who was very sorry. My childish logic carried me to that length. But when I tried to think over all the grown-up gentlemen who loved me very much, I could never get on, to my own satisfaction, beyond my father and my Uncle George.

II

I was taken home on the appointed day to suffer the trial – a hard one even at my tender years – of witnessing my mother's passionate grief and my father's mute despair. I remember that the scene of our first meeting after Caroline's death was wisely and considerately shortened by my aunt, who took me out of the room. She seemed to have a confused desire to keep me from leaving her after the door had closed behind us; but I broke away and ran downstairs to the surgery, to go and cry for my lost playmate with the sharer of all our games, Uncle George.

I opened the surgery-door, and could see nobody. I dried my tears, and looked all round the room: it was empty. I ran upstairs again to Uncle George's garret-bedroom – he was not there; his cheap hair-brush and old cast-off razor-case, that had belonged to my grand-father, were not on the dressing-table. Had he got some other bedroom? I went out on the landing, and called softly, with an unaccountable terror and sinking at my heart:

'Uncle George!'

Nobody answered; but my aunt came hastily up the garret-stairs.

'Hush!' she said. 'You must never call that name out here again!'

She stopped suddenly, and looked as if her own words had frightened her.

'Is Uncle George dead?' I asked.

My aunt turned red and pale, and stammered.

I did not wait to hear what she said – I brushed past her, down the stairs – my heart was bursting – my flesh felt cold. I ran breathlessly and recklessly into the room where my father and mother had received me. They were both sitting there still. I ran up to them, wringing my hands, and crying out in a passion of tears—

'Is Uncle George dead?'

My mother gave a scream that terrified me into instant silence and stillness. My father looked at her for a moment, rang the bell that summoned the maid, then seized me roughly by the arm, and dragged me out of the room.

He took me down into the study, seated himself in his accustomed chair, and put me before him between his knees. His lips were awfully white, and I felt his two hands, as they grasped my shoulders, shaking violently.

'You are never to mention the name of Uncle George again,' he said in a quick, angry, trembling whisper. 'Never to me, never to your mother, never to your aunt, never to anybody in this world! Never, never, never!'

The repetition of the word terrified me even more than the suppressed vehemence with which he spoke. He saw that I was frightened, and softened his manner a little before he went on.

'You will never see Uncle George again,' he said. 'Your mother and I love you dearly; but if you forget what I have told you, you will be sent away from home. Never speak that name again – mind, never! Now kiss me, and go away.'

How his lips trembled – and, oh, how cold they felt on mine!

I shrunk out of the room the moment he had kissed me, and went and hid myself in the garden.

'Uncle George is gone; I am never to see him any more; I am never to speak of him again' – those were the words I repeated to myself, with indescribable terror and confusion, the moment I was alone. There was something unspeakably horrible to my young mind in this mystery which I was commanded always to respect, and which, so far as I then knew, I could never hope to see revealed. My father, my mother, my aunt – all appeared to be separated from me now by some impassable barrier. Home seemed home no longer with Caroline dead, Uncle George gone, and a forbidden subject of talk perpetually and mysteriously interposing between my parents and me.

Though I never infringed the command my father had given me in his study (his words and looks, and that dreadful scream of my mother's, which seemed to be still ringing in my ears, were more than enough to ensure my obedience), I also never lost the secret desire to penetrate the darkness which clouded over the fate of Uncle George.

For two years I remained at home and discovered nothing. If I asked the servants about my uncle, they could only tell me that one morning he disappeared from the house. Of the members of my father's family, I could make no inquiries. They lived far away, and never came to see us – and the idea of writing to them, at my age and in my position, was out of the question. My aunt was as unapproachably silent as my father and mother; but I never forgot how her face had altered, when she reflected for a moment, after hearing of my extraordinary adventure while going home with the servant over the sands at night. The more I thought of that change of countenance, in connection with what had occurred on my return to my father's house, the more certain I felt that the stranger who had kissed me and wept over me must have been no other than Uncle George.

At the end of my two years at home, I was sent to sea in the merchant navy by my own earnest desire. I had always determined to be a sailor from the time when I first went to stay with my aunt at the seaside – and I persisted long enough in my resolution to make my parents recognise the necessity of acceding to my wishes.

My new life delighted me; and I remained away on foreign stations more than four years. When I at length returned home, it was to find a new affliction darkening our fireside. My father had died on the very day when I sailed for my return voyage to England.

Absence and change of scene had in no respect weakened my desire to penetrate the mystery of Uncle George's disappearance. My mother's health was so delicate, that I hesitated for some time to approach the forbidden subject in her presence. When I at last ventured to refer to it, suggesting to her that any prudent reserve, which might have been necessary while I was a child, need no longer be persisted in, now that I was growing to be a young man, she fell into a violent fit of trembling, and commanded me to say no more. It had been my father's will, she said, that the reserve to which I referred should be always adopted towards me; he had not authorised her, before he died, to speak more openly; and, now that he was gone, she would not so much as think of acting on her own unaided judgment. My aunt said the same thing in effect when I appealed to her. Determined not to be discouraged even yet, I undertook a journey, ostensibly to pay my respects to my father's family, but with the secret intention of trying what I could learn in that quarter on the subject of Uncle George.

My investigations led to some results, though they were by no means satisfactory. George had always been looked upon with something like contempt by his handsome sisters and his prosperous brothers; and he had not improved his position in the family by his warm advocacy of his brother's cause at the time of my father's marriage. I found that my uncle's surviving relatives now spoke of him slightingly and carelessly. They assured me that they had never heard from him, and that they knew nothing about him, except that he had gone away to settle, as they supposed, in some foreign place, after having behaved very basely and badly to my father. He had been traced to London, where he had sold out of the funds the small share of money which he had inherited after his father's death, and he had been seen on the deck of a packet bound for France, later on the same day. Beyond this, nothing was known about him. In what the alleged baseness of his behaviour had consisted, none of his brothers and sisters could tell me. My father had refused to pain them by going into particulars, not only at the time of his brother's disappearance, but afterwards whenever the subject was mentioned. George had always been the black sheep of the flock, and he must have been conscious of his own baseness, or he would certainly have written to explain and to justify himself.

Such were the particulars which I gleaned during my visit to my father's family. To my mind, they tended rather to deepen than to reveal the mystery. That such a gentle, docile, affectionate creature as Uncle George should have injured the brother he loved, by word or deed, at any period of their intercourse, seemed incredible; but that he should have been guilty of an act of baseness at the very time when my sister was dying, was simply and plainly impossible. And yet, there was the incomprehensible fact staring me in the face, that the death of Caroline and the disappearance of Uncle George had taken place in the same week! Never did I feel more daunted and bewildered by the family secret, than after I had heard all the particulars in connection with it that my father's relatives had to tell me.

I may pass over the events of the next few years of my life briefly enough.

My nautical pursuits filled up all my time, and took me far away from my country and my friends. But, whatever I did, and wherever I went, the memory of Uncle George, and the desire to penetrate the mystery of his disappearance, haunted me like familiar spirits. Often, in the lonely watches of the night at sea, did I recall the dark evening on the beach, the strange man's hurried embrace, the startling sensation of feeling his tears on my cheeks, the disappearance of him before I had breath or self-possession enough to say a word. Often did I think over the inexplicable events that followed, when I had returned, after my sister's funeral, to my father's house; and oftener still did I puzzle my brains vainly, in the attempt to form some plan for inducing my mother or my aunt to disclose the secret which they had hitherto kept from me so perseveringly. My only chance of knowing what had really happened to Uncle George, my only hope of seeing him again, rested with those two near and dear relatives. I despaired of ever getting my mother to speak on the forbidden subject after what had passed between us; but I felt more sanguine about my prospects of ultimately inducing my aunt to relax in her discretion. My anticipations, however, in this direction were not destined to be fulfilled. On my next visit to England I found my aunt prostrated by a paralytic attack, which deprived her of the power of speech. She died soon afterwards in my arms, leaving me her sole heir. I searched anxiously among her papers for some reference to the family mystery, but found no clue to guide me. All my mother's letters to her sister at the time of Caroline's illness and death had been destroyed.

III

More years passed; my mother followed my aunt to the grave; and still I was as far as ever from making any discoveries in relation to Uncle George. Shortly after the period of this last affliction, my health gave way, and I departed, by my doctor's advice, to try some baths in the south of France.

I travelled slowly to my destination, turning aside from the direct road, and stopping wherever I pleased. One evening, when I was not more than two or three days' journey from the baths to which I was bound, I was struck by the picturesque situation of a little town placed on the brow of a hill at some distance from the main road, and resolved to have a nearer look at the place, with a view to stopping there for the night, if it pleased me. I found the principal inn clean and quiet – ordered my bed there – and after dinner strolled out to look at the church. No thought of Uncle George was in my mind when I entered the building; and yet, at that very moment, chance was leading me to the discovery which, for so many years past, I had vainly endeavoured to make – the discovery which I had given up as hopeless since the day of my mother's death.

I found nothing worth notice in the church, and was about to leave it again, when I caught a glimpse of a pretty view through a side door, and stopped to admire it.

The churchyard formed the foreground, and below it the hill-side sloped away gently into the plain, over which the sun was setting in full glory. The *curé* of the church was reading his breviary, walking up and down a gravel-path that parted the rows of graves. In the course of my wanderings I had learnt to speak French as fluently as most Englishmen; and when the priest came near me I said a few words in praise of the view, and complimented him on the neatness and prettiness of the churchyard. He answered with great politeness, and we got into conversation together immediately.

As we strolled along the gravel-walk, my attention was attracted by one of the graves standing apart from the rest. The cross at the head of it differed remarkably, in some points of appearance, from the crosses on the other graves. While all the rest had garlands hung on them, this one cross was quite bare; and, more extraordinary still, no name was inscribed on it.

The priest, observing that I stopped to look at the grave, shook his head and sighed.

'A countryman of yours is buried there,' he said. 'I was present at his death. He had borne the burden of a great sorrow among us, in this town, for many weary years, and his conduct had taught us to respect and pity him with all our hearts.'

'How is it that his name is not inscribed over his grave?' I inquired.

'It was suppressed by his own desire,' answered the priest, with some little hesitation. 'He confessed to me in his last moments that he had lived here under an assumed name. I asked his real name, and he told it to me, with the particulars of his sad story. He had reasons for desiring to be forgotten after his death. Almost the last words he spoke were, 'Let my name die with me.' Almost the last request he made was, that I would keep that name a secret from all the world excepting only one person.'

'Some relative, I suppose?' said I.

'Yes – a nephew,' said the priest.

The moment the last word was out of his mouth, my heart gave a strange answering bound. I suppose I must have changed colour also, for the *curé* looked at me with sudden attention and interest.

'A nephew,' the priest went on, 'whom he had loved like his own child. He told me that if this nephew ever traced him to his burial-place, and asked about him, I was free in that case to disclose all I knew. "I should like my little Charley to know the truth," he said. "In spite of the difference in our ages, Charley and I were playmates years ago."'

My heart beat faster, and I felt a choking sensation at the throat, the moment I heard the priest unconsciously mention my Christian name in reporting the dying man's last words.

As soon as I could steady my voice and feel certain of my self-possession, I communicated my family name to the *curé*, and asked him if that was not part of the secret that he had been requested to preserve.

He started back several steps, and clasped his hands amazedly.

'Can it be?' he said in low tones, gazing at me earnestly, with something like dread in his face.

I gave him my passport, and looked away towards the grave. The tears came into my eyes as the recollections of past days crowded back on me. Hardly knowing what I did, I knelt down by the grave, and smoothed the grass over it with my hand. O Uncle George, why not have told your secret to your old playmate? Why leave him to find you *here?*

The priest raised me gently, and begged me to go with him into his own house. On our way there, I mentioned persons and places that I thought my uncle might have spoken of, in order to satisfy my companion that I was really the person I represented myself to be. By the time we had entered his little parlour, and had sat down alone in it, we were almost like old friends together.

I thought it best that I should begin by telling all that I have related here on the subject of Uncle George, and his disappearance from home. My host listened with a very sad face, and said, when I had done:

'I can understand your anxiety to know what I am authorised to tell you – but pardon me if I say first that there are circumstances in your uncle's story which it may pain you to hear –' he stopped suddenly.

'Which it may pain me to hear, as a nephew?' I asked.

'No,' said the priest, looking away from me, – 'as a son.'

I gratefully expressed my sense of the delicacy and kindness which had prompted my companion's warning, but I begged him at the same time to keep me no longer in suspense, and to tell me the stern truth, no matter how painfully it might affect me as a listener.

'In telling me all you knew about what you term the Family Secret,' said the priest, 'you have mentioned as a strange coincidence that your sister's death and your uncle's disappearance took place at the same time. Did you ever suspect what cause it was that occasioned your sister's death?'

'I only knew what my father told me, and what all our friends believed – that she died of a tumour in the neck, or, as I sometimes heard it stated, from the effect on her constitution of a tumour in the neck.'

'She died under an operation for the removal of that tumour,' said the priest, in low tones. 'And the operator was your Uncle George.'

In those few words all the truth burst upon me.

'Console yourself with the thought that the long martyrdom of his life is over,' the priest went on. 'He rests: he is at peace. He and his little darling understand each other, and are happy now. That thought bore him up to the last, on his death-bed. He always spoke of your sister as his "little darling." He firmly believed that she was waiting to forgive and console him in the other world – and who shall say he was deceived in that belief?'

Not I! Not anyone who has ever loved and suffered, surely!

'It was out of the depths of his self-sacrificing love for the child that he drew the fatal courage to undertake the operation,' continued the priest. 'Your father naturally shrank from attempting it. His medical brethren, whom he consulted, all doubted the propriety of taking any measures for the removal of the tumour, in the particular condition and situation of it when they were called in. Your uncle alone differed with them. He was too modest a man to say so, but your mother found it out. The deformity of her beautiful child horrified her; she was desperate enough to catch at the faintest hope of remedying it that anyone might hold out to her; and she persuaded your uncle to put his opinion to the proof. Her horror at the deformity of the child, and her despair at the prospect of its lasting for life, seem to have utterly blinded her to all natural sense of the danger of the operation. It is hard to know how to say it to you, her son, but it must be told, nevertheless, that, one day, when your father was out, she untruly informed your uncle that his brother had consented to the performance of the operation, and that he had gone purposely out of the house because he had not nerve enough to stay and witness it. After that, your uncle no longer hesitated. He had no fear of results, provided he could be certain of his own courage. All he dreaded was the effect on him of his love for the child, when he first found himself face to face with the dreadful necessity of touching her skin with the knife.'

I tried hard to control myself; but I could not repress a shudder at those words.

'It is useless to shock you by going into particulars,' said the priest, considerately. 'Let it be enough if I say that your uncle's fortitude failed to support him when he wanted it most. His love for the child shook the firm hand which had never trembled before. In a word, the operation failed. Your father returned, and found his child dying. The frenzy of his despair, when the truth was told him, carried him to excesses which it shocks me to mention – excesses which began in his degrading his brother by a blow, which ended in his binding himself by an oath to make that brother suffer public punishment, for his fatal rashness, in a court of law. Your uncle was too heart-broken by what had happened to feel those outrages as some men might have felt them. He looked for one moment at his sister-in-law (I do not like to say your mother, considering what I have now to tell you), to see if she would acknowledge that she had encouraged him to attempt the operation, and that she had deceived him in saying that he had his brother's permission to try it. She was silent, and when she spoke, it was to join her husband in denouncing him as the murderer of their child. Whether fear of your father's anger, or revengeful indignation against your uncle most actuated her, I cannot presume to inquire in your presence. I can only state facts.'

The priest paused, and looked at me anxiously. I could not speak to him at that moment – I could only encourage him to proceed by pressing his hand.

He resumed in these terms:

'Meanwhile, your uncle turned to your father, and spoke the last words he was ever to address to his eldest brother in this world. He said: "I have deserved the worst your anger can inflict on me, but I will spare you the scandal of bringing me to justice in open court. The law, if it found me guilty, could at the worst but banish me from my country and my friends. I will go of my own accord. God is my witness that I honestly believed I could save the child from deformity and suffering. I have risked all, and lost all. My heart and spirit are broken. I am fit for nothing, but to go and hide myself and my shame and misery from all eyes that have ever looked on me. I shall never come back, never expect your pity or forgiveness. If you think less harshly of me when I am gone, keep secret what has happened; let no other lips say of me what yours and your wife's have said. I shall think that forbearance atonement enough, atonement greater than I have deserved. Forget me in this world. May we meet in another, where the secrets of all hearts are opened, and where the child who is gone before may make peace between us!" He said those words and went out. Your father never saw him or heard from him again.'

I knew the reason now why my father had never confided the truth to anyone, his own family included. My mother had evidently confessed all to her sister, under the seal of secrecy. And there the dreadful disclosure had been arrested.

'Your uncle told me,' the priest continued, 'that before he left England, he took leave of you by stealth, in a place you were staying at by the seaside. He had not the heart to quit his country and his friends for ever, without kissing you for the last time. He followed you in the dark, and caught you up in his arms, and left you again before you had a chance of discovering him. The next day he quitted England.'

'For this place?' I asked.

'Yes: he had spent a week here once with a student friend, at the time when he was a pupil in the Hôtel Dieu. And to this place he returned to hide, to suffer, and to die. We all saw that he was a man crushed and broken by some great sorrow, and we respected him and his affliction. He lived alone, and only came out of doors towards evening, when he used to sit on the brow of the hill yonder, with his head on his hand, looking towards England. That place seemed a favourite with him, and he is buried close by it. He revealed the story of his past life to no living soul here but me; and to me he only spoke when his last hour was approaching. What he had suffered during his long exile, no man can presume to say. I, who saw more of him than anyone, never heard a word of complaint fall from his lips. He had the courage of the martyrs while he lived, and the resignation of the saints when he died. Just at the last his mind wandered. He said he saw his little darling waiting by the bedside to lead him away; and he died with a smile on his face – the first I had ever seen there.'

The priest ceased, and we went out together in the mournful twilight, and stood for a little while on the brow of the hill where Uncle George used to sit, with his face turned towards England. How my heart ached for him, as I thought of what he must have suffered in the silence and solitude of his long exile! Was it well for me that I had discovered the Family Secret at last? I have sometimes thought not. I have sometimes wished that the darkness had never been cleared away which once hid from me the fate of Uncle George.

A Fair Penitent

Originally appeared in *Household Words*, 18 July 1857. Never reprinted. This rather sensational treatment of Catholic materials anticipates Collins's anti-Jesuit novel *The Black Robe* (1881).

C HARLES PINEAU DUCLOS was a French writer of biographies and novels, who lived and worked during the first half of the eighteenth century. He prospered sufficiently well, as a literary man, to be made secretary to the French Academy, and to be allowed to succeed Voltaire in the office of historiographer of France. He has left behind him, in his own country, the reputation of a lively writer of the second class, who addressed the public of his day with fair success, and who, since his death, has not troubled posterity to take any particular notice of him.

Among the papers left by Duclos, two manuscripts were found, which he probably intended to turn to some literary account. The first was a brief Memoir, written by himself, of a Frenchwoman, named Mademoiselle Gautier, who began life as an actress and who ended it as a Carmelite nun. The second manuscript was the lady's own account of the process of her conversion, and of the circumstances which attended her moral passage from the state of a sinner to the state of a saint. There are certain national peculiarities in the character of Mademoiselle Gautier and in the narrative of her conversion, which are perhaps interesting enough to be reproduced with some chance of pleasing the reader of the present day.

It appears, from the account given of her by Duclos, that Mademoiselle Gautier made her appearance on the stage of the Théâtre François in the year seventeen hundred and sixteen. She is described as a handsome woman, with a fine figure, a fresh complexion, a lively disposition, and a violent temper. Besides possessing capacity as an actress, she could write very good verses, she was clever at painting in miniature, and, most remarkable quality of all, she was possessed of prodigious muscular strength. It is recorded of Mademoiselle, that she could roll up a silver plate with her hands, and that she covered herself with distinction in a trial of strength with no less a person than the famous soldier, Marshal Saxe.

Nobody who is at all acquainted with the social history of the eighteenth century in France, need be told that Mademoiselle Gautier had a long list of lovers, – for the most part, persons of quality, marshals, counts, and so forth. The only man, however, who really attached her to him, was an actor at the Théâtre François, a famous player in his day, named Quinault Dufresne. Mademoiselle Gautier seems to have loved him with all the ardour of her naturally passionate disposition. At first, he returned her affection; but, as soon as she ventured to test the sincerity of his attachment by speaking of marriage, he cooled towards her immediately, and the connection between them was broken off. In all her former love-affairs, she had been noted for the high tone which she adopted towards her admirers, and for the despotic authority which she exercised over them even in her gayest moments. But the severance of her connection with Quinault Dufresne wounded her to her heart. She had loved the man so dearly, had made so many sacrifices for him, had counted so fondly on the devotion of her whole future life to him, that the first discovery of his coldness towards her broke her spirit at once and for ever. She fell into a condition of hopeless melancholy, looked back with remorse and horror at her past life, and abandoned the stage and the society in which she had lived, to end her days repentantly in the character of a Carmelite nun.

So far, her history is the history of hundreds of other women before her time and after it. The prominent interest of her life, for the student of human nature, lies in the story of her conversion, as told by herself. The greater part of the narrative – every page of which is more or less characteristic of the Frenchwoman of the eighteenth century – may be given, with certain suppressions and abridgments, in her own words. The reader will observe, at the outset, one curious fact. Mademoiselle Gautier does not so much as hint at the influence which the loss of her lover had in disposing her mind to reflect on serious subjects. She describes her conversion as if it had taken its rise in a sudden inspiration from Heaven. Even the name of Quinault Dufresne is not once mentioned from one end of her narrative to the other.

On the twenty-fifth of April, seventeen hundred and twenty-two (writes Mademoiselle Gautier), while I was still leading a life of pleasure – according to the pernicious ideas of pleasure which pass current in the world – I happen to awake, contrary to my usual custom, between eight and nine o'clock in the morning. I remember that it is my birthday; I ring for my people; and my maid answers the bell, alarmed by the idea that I am ill. I tell her to dress me that I may go to mass. I go to the Church of the Cordeliers, followed by my footman, and taking with me a little orphan whom I had adopted. The first part of the mass is celebrated without attracting my attention; but, at the second part the accusing voice of my conscience suddenly begins to speak. 'What brings you here?' it says. 'Do you come to reward God for making you the attractive person that you are, by mortally transgressing His laws every day of your life?' I hear that question, and I am unspeakably overwhelmed by it. I quit the chair on which I have hitherto been leaning carelessly, and I prostrate myself in an agony of remorse on the pavement of the church.

The mass over, I send home the footman and the orphan, remaining behind myself, plunged in inconceivable perplexity. At last I rouse myself on a sudden; I go to the sacristy; I demand a mass for my own proper advantage every day; I determine to attend it regularly; and, after three hours of agitation, I return home, resolved to enter on the path that leads to justification.

Six months passed. Every morning I went to my mass: every evening I spent in my customary dissipations.

Some of my friends indulged in considerable merriment at my expense when they found out my constant attendance at mass. Accordingly, I disguised myself as a boy, when I went to church, to escape observation. My disguise was found out, and the jokes against me were redoubled. Upon this, I began to think of the words of the Gospel, which declare the impossibility of serving two masters. I determined to abandon the service of Mammon.

The first vanity I gave up was the vanity of keeping a maid. By way of further accustoming myself to the retreat from the world which I now began to meditate, I declined all invitations to parties under the pretext of indisposition. But the nearer the Easter time approached at which I had settled in my own mind definitely to turn my back on worldly temptations and pleasures, the more violent became my internal struggles with myself. My health suffered under them to such an extent that I was troubled with perpetual attacks of retching and sickness, which, however, did not prevent me from writing my general confession, addressed to the vicar of Saint Sulpice, the parish in which I lived.

Just Heaven! what did I not suffer some days afterwards, when I united around me at dinner, for the last time, all the friends who had been dearest to me in the days of my worldly life! What words can describe the tumult of my heart when one of my guests said to me, 'You are giving us too good a dinner for a Wednesday in Passion Week'; and when another answered, jestingly, 'You forget that this is her farewell dinner to her friends!' I felt ready to faint while they were talking, and rose from table pretexting as an excuse, that I had a payment to make that evening, which I could not in honour defer any longer. The company rose with me, and saw me to the door. I got into my carriage, and the company returned to table. My nerves were in such a state that I shrieked at the first crack of the coachman's whip; and the company came running down again to know what was the matter. One of my servants cleverly stopped them from all hurrying out to the carriage together, by declaring that the scream proceeded from my adopted orphan. Upon this they returned quietly enough to their wine, and I drove off with my general confession to the vicar of Saint Sulpice.

My interview with the vicar lasted three hours. His joy at discovering that I was in a state of grace was extreme. My own emotions were quite indescribable. Late at night I returned to my own house, and found my guests all gone. I employed myself in writing farewell letters to the manager and company of the theatre, and in making the necessary arrangements for sending back my adopted orphan to his friends, with twenty pistoles. Finally, I directed the servants to say, if anybody enquired after me the next day, that I had gone out of town for some time; and after that, at five o'clock in the morning, I left my home in Paris never to return to it again.

By this time I had thoroughly recovered my tranquillity. I was as easy in my mind at leaving my house as I am now when I quit my cell to sing in the choir. Such already was the happy result of my perpetual masses, my general confession, and my three hours' interview with the vicar of Saint Sulpice.

Before taking leave of the world, I went to Versailles to say good-bye to my worthy patrons, Cardinal Fleury and the Duke de Gesvres. From them, I went to mass in the King's Chapel; and after that, I called on a lady of Versailles whom I had mortally offended, for the purpose of making my peace with her. She received me angrily enough. I told her I had not come to justify myself, but to ask her pardon. If she granted it, she would send me away happy. If she declined to be reconciled, Providence would probably be satisfied with my submission, but certainly not with her refusal. She felt the force of this argument; and we made it up on the spot.

I left Versailles immediately afterwards, without taking anything to eat; the act of humility which I had just performed being as good as a meal to me.

Towards evening, I entered the house of the Community of Saint Perpetua at Paris. I had ordered a little room to be furnished there for me, until the inventory of my worldly effects was completed, and until I could conclude my arrangements for entering a convent. On first installing myself, I began to feel hungry at last, and begged the Superior of the Community to give me for supper anything that remained from the dinner of the house. They had nothing but a little stewed carp, of which I eat with an excellent appetite. Marvellous to relate, although I had been able to keep nothing on my stomach for the past three months, although I had been dreadfully sick after a little rice soup on the evening before, the stewed carp of the sisterhood of Saint Perpetua, with some nuts afterwards for dessert, agreed with me charmingly, and I slept all through the night afterwards as peacefully as a child!

When the news of my retirement became public, it occasioned great talk in Paris. Various people assigned various reasons for the strange course that I had taken. Nobody, however, believed that I had quitted the world in the prime of my life (I was then thirty-one years old), never to return to it again. Meanwhile, my inventory was finished and my goods were sold. One of my friends sent a letter, entreating me to reconsider my determination. My mind was made up, and I wrote to say so. When my goods had been all sold, I left Paris to go and live incognito as a parlour-boarder in the Convent of the Ursuline nuns of Pondevaux. Here I wished to try the mode of life for a little while before I assumed the serious responsibility of taking the veil. I knew my own character – I remembered my early horror of total seclusion, and my inveterate dislike to the company of women only; and, moved by these considerations, I resolved, now that I had taken the first important step, to proceed in the future with caution.

The nuns of Pondevaux received me among them with great kindness. They gave me a large room, which I partitioned off into three small ones. I assisted at all the pious exercises of the place. Deceived by my fashionable appearance and my plump figure, the good nuns treated me as if I was a person of high distinction. This afflicted me, and I undeceived them. When they knew who I really was, they only behaved towards me with still greater kindness. I passed my time in reading and praying, and led the quietest, sweetest life it is possible to conceive.

After ten months' sojourn at Pondevaux, I went to Lyons, and entered (still as parlour-boarder only) the House of Anticaille, occupied by the nuns of the Order of Saint Mary. Here, I enjoyed the advantage of having for director of my conscience that holy man, Father Deveaux. He belonged to the Order of the Jesuits; and he was good enough, when I first asked him for advice, to suggest that I should get up at eleven o'clock at night to say my prayers, and should remain absorbed in devotion until midnight. In obedience to the directions of this saintly person, I kept myself awake as well as I could till eleven o'clock. I then got on my knees with great fervour, and I blush to confess it, immediately fell as fast asleep as a dormouse. This went on for several nights, when Father Deveaux finding that my midnight devotions were rather too much for me, was so obliging as to prescribe another species of pious exercise, in a letter which he wrote to me with his own hand. The holy father, after deeply regretting my inability to keep awake, informed me that he had a new act of penitence to suggest to me by the performance of which I might still hope to expiate my sins. He then, in the plainest terms, advised me to have recourse to the discipline of flagellation, every Friday, using the cat-o'-nine-tails on my bare shoulders for the length of time that it would take to repeat a Miserere. In conclusion, he informed me that the nuns of Anticaille would probably lend me the necessary instrument of flagellation; but, if they made any difficulty about it, he was benevolently ready to furnish me with a new and special cat-o'-nine-tails of his own making.

Never was woman more amazed or more angry than I, when I first read this letter. 'What!' cried I to myself, 'does this man seriously recommend me to lash my own shoulders? Just Heaven, what impertinence! And yet, is it not my duty to put up with it? Does not this apparent insolence proceed from the pen of a holy man? If he tells me to flog my wickedness out of me, is it not my bounden duty to lay on the scourge with all my might immediately? Sinner that I am! I am thinking remorsefully of my plump shoulders and the dimples on my back, when I ought to be thinking of nothing but, the cat-o'-nine-tails and obedience to Father Deveaux?'

These reflections soon gave me the resolution which I had wanted at first. I was ashamed to ask the nuns for an instrument of flagellation; so I made one for myself of stout cord, pitilessly knotted at very short intervals. This done, I shut myself up while the nuns were at prayer, uncovered my shoulders, and rained such a shower of lashes on them, in the first fervour of my newly-awakened zeal, that I fairly flogged myself down on the ground, flat on my nose, before I had repeated more of the Miserere than the first two or three lines.

I burst out crying, shedding tears of spite against myself when I ought to have been shedding tears of devotional gratitude for the kindness of Father Deveaux. All through the night, I never closed my eyes, and in the morning I found my poor shoulders (once so generally admired for their whiteness) striped with all the colours of the rainbow. The sight threw me into a passion, and I profanely said to myself while I was dressing, 'The next time I see Father Deveaux, I will give my tongue full swing, and make the hair of that holy man stand on end with terror!' A few hours afterwards, he came to the convent, and all my resolution melted away at the sight of him. His imposing exterior had such an effect on me that I could only humbly entreat him to excuse me from inflicting a second flagellation on myself. He smiled benignantly, and granted my request with a saintly amiability. 'Give me the cat-o'-nine-tails,' he said, in conclusion, 'and I will keep it for you till you ask me for it again. You are sure to ask for it again, dear child – to ask for it on your bended knees!'

Pious and prophetic man! Before many days had passed his words came true. If he had persisted severely in ordering me to flog myself, I might have opposed him for months together; but, as it was, who could resist the amiable indulgence he showed towards my weakness? The very next day after my interview, I began to feel ashamed of my own cowardice; and the day after that I went down on my knees, exactly as he had predicted, and said, 'Father Deveaux, give me back my cat-o'-nine-tails.' From that time I cheerfully underwent the discipline of flagellation, learning the regular method of practising it from the sisterhood, and feeling, in a spiritual point of view, immensely the better for it.

The nuns, finding that I cheerfully devoted myself to every act of self-sacrifice prescribed by the rules of their convent, wondered very much that I still hesitated about taking the veil. I begged them not to mention the subject to me till my mind was quite made up about it. They respected my wish, and said no more; but they lent me books to read which assisted in strengthening my wavering resolution. Among these books was the Life of Madame de Montmorenci, who, after the shocking death of her husband, entered the Order of St Mary. The great example of this lady made me reflect seriously, and I communicated my thoughts, as a matter of course, to Father Deveaux. He assured me that the one last greatest sacrifice which remained for me to make was the sacrifice of my liberty. I had long known that this was my duty, and I now felt, for the first time, that I had courage and resolution enough boldly to face the idea of taking the veil.

While I was in this happy frame of mind, I happened to meet with the history of the famous Rancé, founder, or rather reformer, of the Order of La Trappe. I found a strange similarity between my own worldly errors and those of this illustrious penitent. The discovery had such an effect on me, that

I spurned all idea of entering a convent where the rules were comparatively easy, as was the case at Anticaille, and determined, when I did take the veil, to enter an Order whose discipline was as severe as the discipline of La Trappe itself. Father Deveaux informed me that I should find exactly what I wanted among the Carmelite nuns; and, by his advice, I immediately put myself in communication with the Archbishop of Villeroi. I opened my heart to this worthy prelate, convinced him of my sincerity, and gained from him a promise that he would get me admitted among the Carmelite nuns of Lyons. One thing I begged of him at parting, which was, that he would tell the whole truth about my former life and about the profession that I had exercised in the world. I was resolved to deceive nobody, and to enter no convent under false pretences of any sort.

My wishes were scrupulously fulfilled; and the nuns were dreadfully frightened when they heard that I had been an actress at Paris. But the Archbishop promising to answer for me, and to take all their scruples on his own conscience, they consented to receive me. I could not trust myself to take formal leave of the nuns of Anticaille, who had been so kind to me, and towards whom I felt so gratefully. So I wrote my farewell to them after privately leaving their house, telling them frankly the motives which animated me, and asking their pardon for separating myself from them in secret.

On the fourteenth of October, seventeen hundred and twenty-four, I entered the Carmelite convent at Lyons, eighteen months after my flight from the world, and my abandonment of my profession – to adopt which, I may say, in my own defence, that I was first led through sheer poverty. At the age of seventeen years, and possessing (if I may credit report) remarkable personal charms, I was left perfectly destitute through the spendthrift habits of my father. I was easily persuaded to go on the stage, and soon tempted, with my youth and inexperience, to lead an irregular life. I do not wish to assert that dissipation necessarily follows the choice of the actress's profession, for I have known many estimable women on the stage. I, unhappily, was not one of the number. I confess it to my shame, and, as the chief of sinners, I am only the more grateful to the mercy of Heaven which accomplished my conversion.

When I entered the convent, I entreated the prioress to let me live in perfect obscurity, without corresponding with my friends, or even with my relations. She declined to grant this last request, thinking that my zeal was leading me too far. On the other hand, she complied with my wish to be employed at once, without the slightest preparatory indulgence or consideration, on any menial labour which the discipline of the convent might require from me. On the first day of my admission a broom was put into my hands. I was appointed also to wash up the dishes, to scour the saucepans, to draw water from a deep well, to carry each sister's pitcher to its proper place, and to scrub the tables in the refectory. From these occupations I got on in time to making rope shoes for the sisterhood, and to taking care of the great clock of the convent; this last employment requiring me to pull up three immensely heavy weights regularly every day. Seven years of my life passed in this hard work, and I can honestly say that I never murmured over it.

To return, however, to the period of my admission into the convent.

After three months of probation, I took the veil on the twentieth of January, seventeen hundred and twenty-five. The Archbishop did me the honour to preside at the ceremony; and, in spite of the rigour of the season, all Lyons poured into the church to see me take the vows. I was deeply affected; but I never faltered in my resolution. I pronounced the oaths with a firm voice, and with a tranquillity which astonished all the spectators, – a tranquillity which has never once failed me since that time.

Such is the story of my conversion. Providence sent me into the world with an excellent nature, with a true heart, with a remarkable susceptibility to the influence of estimable sentiments. My parents neglected my education, and left me in the world, destitute of everything but youth, beauty, and a lively temperament. I tried hard to be virtuous; I vowed, before I was out of my teens, and when I happened to be struck down by a serious illness, to leave the stage, and to keep my reputation unblemished, if anybody would only give me two hundred livres a year to live upon. Nobody came forward to help me, and I fell. Heaven pardon the rich people of Paris who might have preserved my virtue at so small a cost! Heaven grant me courage to follow the better path into which its mercy has led me, and to persevere in a life of penitence and devotion to the end of my days!

So this singular confession ends. Besides the little vanities and levities which appear here and there on its surface, there is surely a strong under-current of sincerity and frankness which fit it to appeal in some degree to the sympathy as well as the curiosity of the reader. It is impossible to read the narrative without feeling that there must have been something really genuine and hearty in Mademoiselle Gautier's nature; and it is a gratifying proof of the honest integrity of her purpose to know that she persevered to the last in the life of humility and seclusion which her conscience had convinced her was the best life that she could lead. Persons who knew her in the Carmelite convent, report that she lived and died in it, preserving to the last, all the better part of the youthful liveliness of her character. She always received visitors with pleasure, always talked to them with surprising cheerfulness, always assisted the poor, and always willingly wrote letters to her former patrons in Paris to help the interests of her needy friends. Towards the end of her life, she was afflicted with blindness; but she was a trouble to no one in consequence of this affliction, for she continued, in spite of it, to clean her own cell, to make her own bed, and to cook her own food just as usual. One little characteristic vanity – harmless enough, surely? – remained with her to the last. She never forgot her own handsome face, which all Paris had admired in the by-gone time; and she contrived to get a dispensation from the Pope which allowed her to receive visitors in the convent parlour without a veil.

The Dead Hand

Originally appeared in *Household Words*, 10 October 1857, as 'The Double-Bedded Room', where it forms part of the second chapter of *The Lazy Tour of Two Idle Apprentices*, and purports to be the product of Dickens's and Collins's meeting with an extravagantly depressed doctor's assistant in Cumberland. The story was included in *The Queen of Hearts* as 'Brother Morgan's Story of the Dead Hand.' The setting is based on Dickens's and Collins's trip to Doncaster in September 1857, ostensibly to visit the races, but really to get a sight of the Ternan girls (Ellen Ternan was soon to become Dickens's mistress) acting at the Theatre Royal. See Claire Tomalin, *The Invisible Woman: The Story of Nelly Ternan and Charles Dickens* (Viking, 1990, pp. 102–5). Dickens's account of the Doncaster races is to be found in the fifth chapter of *The Lazy Tour*. This is one of Collins's most celebrated and anthologised short stories, and one of his most effective treatments of the theme of the double, anticipating the relationship between Alan Armadale and Ozias Midwinter in *Armadale* (1866); Mr Lorn also reappears in *The Moonstone* (1868) as the shadowy doctor, Ezra Jennings. Like 'Mr Cosway and the Landlady' the story may have been suggested by an anecdote in J.G. Lockhart's *Life of Sir Walter Scott* (Robert Cadell: Edinburgh, 1837–8). 'Sir Walter mentioned having once arrived at a country inn, when he was told there was no bed for him. "No place to lie down at all?" said he. "No," said the people of the house – "None, except a room in which there is a corpse lying." "Well," said he, "did the person die of any contagious disorder?" "Oh no – not at all," said they. "Well, then," continued he, "let me have the other bed. So," said Sir Walter, "I laid me down, and have never had a better night's sleep in my life"' (Vol. 5, pp. 384–5).

W HEN THIS PRESENT nineteenth century was younger by a good many years than it is now, a certain friend of mine, named Arthur Holliday, happened to arrive in the town of Doncaster exactly in the middle of the race-week, or, in other words, in the middle of the month of September.

He was one of those reckless, rattlepated, open-hearted, and open-mouthed young gentlemen who possess the gift of familiarity in its highest perfection, and who scramble carelessly along the journey of life, making friends, as the phrase is, wherever they go. His father was a rich manufacturer, and had bought landed property enough in one of the midland counties to make all the born squires in his neighbourhood thoroughly envious of him. Arthur was his only son, possessor in prospect of the great estate and the great business after his father's death; well supplied with money, and not too rigidly looked after, during his father's lifetime. Report, or scandal, whichever you please, said that the old gentleman had been rather wild in his youthful days, and that, unlike most parents, he was not disposed to be violently indignant when he found that his son took after him. This may be true or not. I myself only knew the elder Mr Holliday when he was getting on in years; and then he was as quiet and as respectable a gentleman as ever I met with.

Well, one September, as I told you, young Arthur comes to Doncaster, having decided all of a sudden, in his hare-brained way, that he would go to the races. He did not reach the town till towards the close of evening, and he went at once to see about his dinner and bed at the principal hotel. Dinner they were ready enough to give him; but as for a bed, they laughed when he mentioned it. In the race week at Doncaster, it is no uncommon thing for visitors who have not bespoken apartments to pass the night in their carriages at the inn doors. As for the lower sort of strangers, I myself have often seen them, at that full time, sleeping out on the doorsteps for want of a covered place to creep under. Rich as he was, Arthur's chance of getting a night's lodging (seeing that he had not written beforehand to secure one) was more than doubtful. He tried the second hotel, and the third hotel, and two of the inferior inns after that; and was met everywhere with the same form of answer. No accommodation for the night of any sort was left. All the bright golden sovereigns in his pocket would not buy him a bed at Doncaster in the race-week.

To a young fellow of Arthur's temperament, the novelty of being turned away into the street like a penniless vagabond, at every house where he asked for a lodging, presented itself in the light of a new and highly amusing piece of experience. He went on with his carpet-bag in his hand, applying for a bed at every place of entertainment for travellers that he could find in Doncaster, until he wandered into the outskirts of the town.

By this time the last glimmer of twilight had faded out, the moon was rising dimly in a mist, the wind was getting cold, the clouds were gathering heavily, and there was every prospect that it was soon going to rain.

The look of the night had rather a lowering effect on young Holliday's good spirits. He began to contemplate the houseless situation in which he was placed, from the serious rather than the humorous point of view; and he looked about him for another public-house to inquire at, with something very like downright anxiety in his mind on the subject of a lodging for the night.

The suburban part of the town towards which he had now strayed was hardly lighted at all, and he could see nothing of the houses as he passed them, except that they got progressively smaller and dirtier the farther he went. Down the winding road before him shone the dull gleam of an oil lamp, the one faint lonely light that struggled ineffectually with the foggy darkness all round him. He resolved to go on as far as this lamp, and then, if it showed him nothing in the shape of an Inn, to return to the central part of the town and to try if he could not at least secure a chair to sit down on, through the night, at one of the principal hotels.

As he got near the lamp, he heard voices; and, walking close under it, found that it lighted the entrance to a narrow court, on the wall of which was painted a long hand in faded flesh colour, pointing, with a lean forefinger, to this inscription:

THE TWO ROBINS

Arthur turned into the court without hesitation, to see what The Two Robins could do for him. Four or five men were standing together round the door of the house, which was at the bottom of the court, facing the entrance from the street. The men were all listening to one other man, better dressed than the rest, who was telling his audience something, in a low voice, in which they were apparently very much interested.

On entering the passage, Arthur was passed by a stranger with a knapsack in his hand, who was evidently leaving the house.

'No,' said the traveller with the knapsack, turning round and addressing himself cheerfully to a fat, sly-looking, bald-headed man, with a dirty white apron on, who had followed him down the passage. 'No, Mr Landlord, I am not easily scared by trifles; but I don't mind confessing that I can't quite stand *that*.'

It occurred to young Holliday, the moment he heard these words, that the stranger had been asked an exorbitant price for a bed at The Two Robins; and that he was unable or unwilling to pay it. The moment his back was turned, Arthur, comfortably conscious of his own well-filled pockets, addressed himself in a great hurry, for fear any other benighted traveller should slip in and forestall him, to the sly-looking landlord with the dirty apron and the bald head.

'If you have got a bed to let,' he said, 'and if that gentleman who has just gone out won't pay your price for it, I will.'

The sly landlord looked hard at Arthur.

'Will you, sir?' he asked, in a meditative, doubtful way.

'Name your price,' said young Holliday, thinking that the landlord's hesitation sprang from some boorish distrust of him. 'Name your price, and I'll give you the money at once, if you like.'

'Are you game for five shillings?' inquired the landlord, rubbing his stubbly double chin, and looking up thoughtfully at the ceiling above him.

Arthur nearly laughed in the man's face; but thinking it prudent to control himself, offered the five shillings as seriously as he could. The sly landlord held out his hand, then suddenly drew it back again.

'You're acting all fair and above-board by me,' he said; 'and, before I take your money, I'll do the same by you. Look here, this is how it stands. You can have a bed all to yourself for five shillings; but you can't have more than a half-share of the room it stands in. Do you see what I mean, young gentleman?'

'Of course I do,' returned Arthur, a little irritably. 'You mean that it is a double-bedded room, and that one of the beds is occupied?'

The landlord nodded his head, and rubbed his double chin harder than ever. Arthur hesitated, and mechanically moved back a step or two towards the door. The idea of sleeping in the same room with a total stranger did not present an attractive prospect to him. He felt more than half inclined to drop his five shillings into his pocket, and to go out into the street once more.

'Is it yes, or no?' asked the landlord. 'Settle it as quick as you can, because there's lots of people wanting a bed at Doncaster tonight, besides you.'

Arthur looked towards the court, and heard the rain falling heavily in the street outside. He thought he would ask a question or two before he rashly decided on leaving the shelter of The Two Robins.

'What sort of man is it who has got the other bed?' he inquired. 'Is he a gentleman? I mean, is he a quiet, well-behaved person?'

'The quietest man I ever came across,' said the landlord, rubbing his fat hands stealthily one over the other. 'As sober as a judge, and as regular as clock-work in his habits. It hasn't struck nine, not ten minutes ago, and he's in his bed already. I don't know whether that comes up to your notion of a quiet man: it goes a long way a-head of mine, I can tell you.'

'Is he asleep, do you think?' asked Arthur.

'I know he's asleep,' returned the landlord. 'And, what's more, he's gone off so fast, that I'll warrant you don't wake him. This way, sir,' said the landlord, speaking over young Holliday's shoulder, as if he was addressing some new guest who was approaching the house.

'Here you are,' said Arthur, determined to be before-hand with the stranger, whoever he might be. 'I'll take the bed.' And he handed the five shillings to the landlord, who nodded, dropped the money carelessly into his waistcoat-pocket, and lighted a candle.

'Come up and see the room,' said the host of The Two Robins, leading the way to the staircase quite briskly, considering how fat he was.

They mounted to the second floor of the house. The landlord half opened a door, fronting the landing, then stopped, and turned round to Arthur.

'It's a fair bargain, mind, on my side as well as on yours,' he said. 'You give me five shillings; I give you in return a clean, comfortable bed; and I warrant, before-hand, that you won't be interfered with, or annoyed in any way, by the man who sleeps in the same room with you.' Saying those words, he looked hard, for a moment, in young Holliday's face, and then led the way into the room.

It was larger and cleaner than Arthur had expected it would be. The two beds stood parallel with each other – a space of about six feet intervening between them. They were both of the same medium size, and both had the same plain white curtains, made to draw, if necessary, all round them.

The occupied bed was the bed nearest the window. The curtains were all drawn round it, except the half curtain at the bottom, on the side of the bed farthest from the window. Arthur saw the feet of the sleeping man raising the scanty clothes into a sharp little eminence, as if he was lying flat on his back. He took the candle, and advanced softly to draw the curtain – stopped half-way, and listened for a moment – then turned to the landlord.

'He is a very quiet sleeper,' said Arthur.

'Yes,' said the landlord, 'very quiet.'

Young Holliday advanced with the candle, and looked in at the man cautiously.

'How pale he is,' said Arthur.

'Yes,' returned the landlord, 'pale enough, isn't he?'

Arthur looked closer at the man. The bedclothes were drawn up to his chin, and they lay perfectly still over the region of his chest. Surprised and vaguely startled, as he noticed this, Arthur stooped down closer over the stranger; looked at his ashy, parted lips; listened breathlessly for an instant; looked again at the strangely still face, and the motionless lips and chest; and turned round suddenly on the landlord, with his own cheeks as pale, for the moment, as the hollow cheeks of the man on the bed.

'Come here,' he whispered, under his breath. 'Come here, for God's sake! The man's not asleep – he is dead.'

'You have found that out sooner than I thought you would,' said the landlord composedly. 'Yes, he's dead, sure enough. He died at five o'clock to-day.'

'How did he die? Who is he?' asked Arthur, staggered for the moment by the audacious coolness of the answer.

'As to who is he,' rejoined the landlord, 'I know no more about him than you do. There are his books and letters and things, all sealed up in that brown paper parcel, for the Coroner's inquest to open to-morrow or next day. He's been here a week, paying his way fairly enough, and stopping in doors, for the most part, as if he was ailing. My girl brought him up his tea at five to-day, and as he was pouring of it out, he fell down in a faint, or a fit, or a compound of both, for anything I know. We couldn't bring him to – and I said he was dead. And the doctor couldn't bring him to – and the doctor said he was dead. And there he is. And the Coroner's inquest's coming as soon as it can. And that's as much as I know about it.'

Arthur held the candle close to the man's lips. The flame still burnt straight up, as steadily as ever. There was a moment of silence; and the rain pattered drearily through it against the panes of the window.

'If you haven't got nothing more to say to me,' continued the landlord, 'I suppose I may go. You don't expect your five shillings back, do you? There's the bed I promised you, clean and comfortable. There's the man I warranted not to disturb you, quiet in this world for ever. If you're frightened to stop alone with him, that's not my look out. I've kept my part of the bargain, and I mean to keep the money. I'm not Yorkshire myself, young gentleman; but I've lived long enough in these parts to have my wits sharpened; and I shouldn't wonder if you found out the way to brighten up yours, next time you come among us.'

With these words, the landlord turned towards the door, and laughed to himself softly, in high satisfaction at his own sharpness.

Startled and shocked as he was, Arthur had by this time sufficiently recovered himself to feel indignant at the trick that had been played on him, and at the insolent manner in which the landlord exulted in it.

'Don't laugh,' he said, sharply, 'till you are quite sure you have got the laugh against me. You shan't have the five shillings for nothing, my man. I'll keep the bed.'

'Will you?' said the landlord. 'Then I wish you a good night's rest.' With that brief farewell, he went out, and shut the door after him.

A good night's rest! The words had hardly been spoken, the door had hardly been closed, before Arthur half repented the hasty words that had just escaped him. Though not naturally over-sensitive, and not wanting in courage of the moral as well as the physical sort, the presence of the dead man had an instantaneously chilling effect on his mind when he found himself alone in the room – alone, and bound by his own rash words to stay there till the next morning. An older man would have thought nothing of those words, and would have acted, without reference to them, as his calmer sense suggested. But Arthur was too young to treat the ridicule, even of his inferiors, with contempt – too young not to fear the momentary humiliation of falsifying his own foolish boast, more than he feared the trial of watching out the long night in the same chamber with the dead.

'It is but a few hours,' he thought to himself, 'and I can get away the first thing in the morning.'

He was looking towards the occupied bed, as that idea passed through his mind, and the sharp angular eminence made in the clothes by the dead man's upturned feet again caught his eye. He advanced and drew the curtains, purposely abstaining, as he did so, from looking at the face of the corpse, lest he might unnerve himself at the outset by fastening some ghastly impression of it on his mind. He drew the curtain very gently, and sighed involuntarily as he closed it.

'Poor fellow,' he said, almost as sadly as if he had known the man. 'Ah, poor fellow!'

He went next to the window. The night was black, and he could see nothing from it. The rain still pattered heavily against the glass. He inferred, from hearing it, that the window was at the back of the house; remembering that the front was sheltered from the weather by the court and the buildings over it.

While he was still standing at the window – for even the dreary rain was a relief, because of the sound it made; a relief, also, because it moved, and had some faint suggestion, in consequence, of life and companionship in it – while he was standing at the window, and looking vacantly into the black darkness outside, he heard a distant church-clock strike ten. Only ten! How was he to pass the time till the house was astir the next morning?

Under any other circumstances, he would have gone down to the public-house parlour, would have called for his grog, and would have laughed and talked with the company assembled as familiarly as if he had known them all his life. But the very thought of whiling away the time in this manner was now distasteful to him. The new situation in which he was placed seemed to have altered him to himself already. Thus far, his life had been the common, trifling, prosaic, surface-life of a prosperous young man, with no troubles to conquer, and no trials to face. He had lost no relation whom he loved, no friend whom he treasured. Till this night, what share he had of the immortal inheritance that is divided amongst us all, had lain dormant within him. Till this night, Death and he had not once met, even in thought.

He took a few turns up and down the room – then stopped. The noise made by his boots on the poorly carpeted floor jarred on his ear. He hesitated a little, and ended by taking the boots off, and walking backwards and forwards noiselessly.

All desire to sleep or to rest had left him. The bare thought of lying down on the unoccupied bed instantly drew the picture on his mind of a dreadful mimicry of the position of the dead man. Who was he? What was the story of his past life? Poor he must have been, or he would not have stopped at such a place as The Two Robins Inn – and weakened, probably, by long illness, or he could hardly have died in the manner which the landlord had described. Poor, ill, lonely – dead in a strange place; dead, with nobody but a stranger to pity him. A sad story: truly, on the mere face of it, a very sad story.

While these thoughts were passing through his mind, he had stopped insensibly at the window, close to which stood the foot of the bed with the closed curtains. At first he looked at it absently; then he became conscious that his eyes were fixed on it; and then, a perverse desire took possession of him to do the very thing which he had resolved not to do, up to this time – to look at the dead man.

He stretched out his hand towards the curtains; but checked himself in the very act of undrawing them, turned his back sharply on the bed, and walked towards the chimney-piece, to see what things were placed on it, and to try if he could keep the dead man out of his mind in that way.

There was a pewter inkstand on the chimney-piece, with some mildewed remains of ink in the bottle. There were two coarse china ornaments of the commonest kind; and there was a square of embossed card, dirty and fly-blown, with a collection of wretched riddles printed on it, in all sorts of zig-zag directions, and in variously coloured inks. He took the card, and went away to read it at the table on which the candle was placed; sitting down, with his back resolutely turned to the curtained bed.

He read the first riddle, the second, the third, all in one corner of the card – then turned it round impatiently to look at another. Before he could begin reading the riddles printed here, the sound of the church-clock stopped him.

Eleven.

He had got through an hour of the time, in the room with the dead man.

Once more he looked at the card. It was not easy to make out the letters printed on it, in consequence of the dimness of the light which the landlord had left him – a common tallow candle, furnished with a pair of heavy old-fashioned steel snuffers. Up to this time, his mind had been too much occupied to think of the light. He had left the wick of the candle unsnuffed, till it had risen higher than the flame, and had burnt into an odd penthouse shape at the top, from which morsels of the charred cotton fell off, from time to time, in little flakes. He took up the snuffers now, and trimmed the wick. The light brightened directly, and the room became less dismal.

Again he turned to the riddles; reading them doggedly and resolutely, now in one corner of the card, now in another. All his efforts, however, could not fix his attention on them. He pursued his occupation mechanically, deriving no sort of impression from what he was reading. It was as if a shadow from the curtained bed had got between his mind and the gaily printed letters – a shadow that nothing could dispel. At last, he gave up the struggle, threw the card from him impatiently, and took to walking softly up and down the room again.

The dead man, the dead man, the *hidden* dead man on the bed!

There was the one persistent idea still haunting him. Hidden! Was it only the body being there – or was it the body being there, *concealed*, that was preying on his mind? He stopped at the window, with that doubt in him; once more listening to the pattering rain, once more looking out into the black darkness.

Still the dead man!

The darkness forced his mind back upon itself, and set his memory at work, reviving, with a painfully vivid distinctness the momentary impression it had received from his first sight of the corpse. Before long the face seemed to be hovering out in the middle of the darkness, confronting him through the window, with the paleness whiter, with the dreadful dull line of light between the imperfectly closed eye-lids broader than he had seen it – with the parted lips slowly dropping farther and farther away from each other – with the features growing larger and moving closer, till they seemed to fill the window and to silence the rain and to shut out the night.

The sound of a voice shouting below stairs woke him suddenly from the dream of his own distempered fancy. He recognised it as the voice of the landlord.

'Shut up at twelve, Ben,' he heard it say. 'I'm off to bed.'

He wiped away the damp that had gathered on his forehead, reasoned with himself for a little while, and resolved to shake his mind free of the ghastly counterfeit which still clung to it, by forcing himself to confront, if it was only for a moment, the solemn reality. Without allowing himself an instant to hesitate, he parted the curtains at the foot of the bed, and looked through.

There was the sad, peaceful, white face, with the awful mystery of stillness on it, laid back upon the pillow. No stir, no change there! He only looked at it for a moment before he closed the curtains again – but that moment steadied him, calmed him, restored him – mind and body – to himself.

He returned to his old occupation of walking up and down the room; persevering in it, this time, till the clock struck again.

Twelve.

As the sound of the clock-bell died away, it was succeeded by the confused noise, down stairs, of the drinkers in the tap-room leaving the house. The next sound, after an interval of silence, was caused by the barring of the door, and the closing of the shutters, at the back of the Inn. Then the silence followed again, and was disturbed no more.

He was alone now – absolutely, hopelessly alone with the dead man, till the next morning.

The wick of the candle wanted trimming again. He took up the snuffers – but paused suddenly on the very point of using them, and looked attentively at the candle – then back, over his shoulder, at the curtained bed – then again at the candle. It had been lighted, for the first time, to show him the way upstairs, and three parts of it, at least, were already consumed. It another hour it would be burnt out. In another hour – unless he called at once to the man who had shut up the Inn, for a fresh candle – he would be left in the dark.

Strongly as his mind had been affected since he had entered the room, his unreasonable dread of encountering ridicule, and of exposing his courage to suspicion, had not altogether lost its influence over him even yet.

He lingered irresolutely by the table, waiting till he could prevail on himself to open the door, and call, from the landing, to the man who had shut up the Inn. In his present hesitating frame of mind, it was a kind of relief to gain a few moments only by engaging in the trifling occupation of snuffing the candle. His hand trembled a little, and the snuffers were heavy and awkward to use. When he closed them on the wick, he closed them a hair's breadth too low. In an instant the candle was out, and the room was plunged in pitch darkness.

The one impression which the absence of light immediately produced on his mind was distrust of the curtained bed – distrust which shaped itself into no distinct idea, but which was powerful enough, in its very vagueness, to bind him down to his chair, to make his heart beat fast, and to set him listening intently. No sound stirred in the room but the familiar sound of the rain against the window, louder and sharper now than he had heard it yet.

Still the vague distrust, the inexpressible dread, possessed him, and kept him in his chair. He had put his carpet-bag on the table when he first entered the room; and he now took the key from his pocket, reached out his hand softly, opened the bag, and groped in it for his travelling writing-case, in which he knew that there was a small store of matches. When he had got one of the matches, he waited before he struck it on the coarse wooden table, and listened intently again, without knowing why. Still there was no sound in the room but the steady, ceaseless, rattling sound of the rain.

He lighted the candle again, without another moment of delay; and, on the instant of its burning up, the first object in the room that his eyes sought for was the curtained bed.

Just before the light had been put out, he had looked in that direction, and had seen no change, no disarrangement of any sort, in the folds of the closely-drawn curtains.

When he looked at the bed now, he saw, hanging over the side of it, a long white hand.

It lay perfectly motionless, midway on the side of the bed, where the curtain at the head and the curtain at the foot met. Nothing more was visible. The clinging curtains hid everything but the long white hand.

He stood looking at it, unable to stir, unable to call out; feeling nothing, knowing nothing; every faculty he possessed gathered up and lost in the one seeing faculty. How long that first panic held him, he never could tell afterwards. It might have been only for a moment; it might have been for many minutes together. How he got to the bed – whether he ran to it headlong, or whether he approached it slowly – how he wrought himself up to unclose the curtains and look in, he never has remembered, and never will remember, to his dying day. It is enough that he did go to the bed, and that he did look inside the curtains.

The man had moved. One of his arms was outside the clothes; his face was turned a little on the pillow; his eyelids were wide open. Changed as to position, and as to one of the features, the face was otherwise fearfully and wonderfully unaltered. The dead paleness and the dead quiet were on it still.

One glance showed Arthur this – one glance before he flew breathlessly to the door, and alarmed the house.

The man whom the landlord called 'Ben' was the first to appear on the stairs. In three words, Arthur told him what had happened, and sent him for the nearest doctor.

I, who tell you this story, was then staying with a medical friend of mine, in practice at Doncaster, taking care of his patients for him during his absence in London; and I, for the time being, was the nearest doctor. They had sent for me from the Inn, when the stranger was taken ill in the afternoon; but I was not at home, and medical assistance was sought for elsewhere. When the man from The Two Robins rang the night-bell, I was just thinking of going to bed. Naturally enough, I did not believe a word of his story about 'a dead man who had come to life again.' However, I put on my hat, armed myself with one or two bottles of restorative medicine, and ran to the Inn, expecting to find nothing more remarkable, when I got there, than a patient in a fit.

My surprise at finding that the man had spoken the literal truth was almost, if not quite, equalled by my astonishment at finding myself face to face with Arthur Holliday as soon as I entered the bedroom. It was no time then for giving or seeking explanations. We just shook hands amazedly; and then I ordered everybody but Arthur out of the room, and hurried to the man on the bed.

The kitchen fire had not been long out. There was plenty of hot water in the boiler, and plenty of flannel to be had. With these, with my medicines, and with such help as Arthur could render under my direction, I dragged the man, literally, out of the jaws of death. In less than an hour from the time when I had been called in, he was alive and talking in the bed on which he had been laid out to wait for the Coroner's inquest.

You will naturally ask me what had been the matter with him; and I might treat you, in reply, to a long theory, plentifully sprinkled with what the children call hard words. I prefer telling you that, in this case, cause and effect could not be satisfactorily joined together by any theory whatever. There are mysteries in life, and the conditions of it, which human science has not fathomed yet; and I candidly confess to you, that, in bringing that man back to existence, I was, morally speaking, groping hap-hazard in the dark. I know (from the testimony of the doctor who attended him in the afternoon) that the vital machinery, so far as its action is appreciable by our senses, had, in this case, unquestionably stopped; and I am equally certain (seeing that I recovered him) that the vital principle was not extinct. When I add that he had suffered from a long and complicated illness, and that his whole nervous system was utterly deranged, I have told you all I really know of the physical condition of my dead-alive patient at the Two Robins Inn.

When he 'came to,' as the phrase goes, he was a startling object to look at, with his colourless face, his sunken cheeks, his wild black eyes, and his long black hair. The first question he asked me about himself, when he could speak, made me suspect that I had been called in to a man in my own profession. I mentioned to him my surmise, and he told me that I was right.

He said he had come last from Paris, where he had been attached to a hospital. That he had lately returned to England, on his way to Edinburgh, to continue his studies; that he had been taken ill on the journey; and that he had stopped to rest and recover himself at Doncaster. He did not add a word about his name, or who he was; and of course I did not question him on the subject. All I inquired, when he ceased speaking, was what branch of the profession he intended to follow.

'Any branch,' he said, bitterly, 'which will put bread into the mouth of a poor man.'

At this, Arthur, who had been hitherto watching him in silent curiosity, burst out impetuously in his usual good-humoured way:

'My dear fellow!' (everybody was 'my dear fellow' with Arthur) 'now you have come to life again, don't begin by being down-hearted about your prospects. I'll answer for it, I can help you to some capital thing in the medical line – or, if I can't, I know my father can.'

The medical student looked at him steadily.

'Thank you,' he said coldly. Then added, 'May I ask who your father is?'

'He's well enough known all about this part of the country,' replied Arthur. 'He is a great manufacturer, and his name is Holliday.'

My hand was on the man's wrist during this brief conversation. The instant the name of Holliday was pronounced I felt the pulse under my fingers flutter, stop, go on suddenly with a bound, and beat afterwards for a minute or two at the fever rate.

'How did you come here?' asked the stranger, quickly, excitably, passionately almost.

Arthur related briefly what had happened from the time of his first taking the bed at the Inn.

'I am indebted to Mr Holliday's son then for the help that has saved my life,' said the medical student, speaking to himself, with a singular sarcasm in his voice. 'Come here!'

He held out, as he spoke, his long, white, bony right hand.

'With all my heart,' said Arthur, taking his hand cordially. 'I may confess it now,' he continued, laughing, 'upon my honour, you almost frightened me out of my wits.'

The stranger did not seem to listen. His wild black eyes were fixed with a look of eager interest on Arthur's face, and his long bony fingers kept tight hold of Arthur's hand. Young Holliday, on his side, returned the gaze, amazed and puzzled by the medical student's odd language and manners. The two faces were close together; I looked at them; and, to my amazement, I was suddenly impressed by the sense of a likeness between them – not in features or complexion, but solely in expression. It must have been a strong likeness, or I should certainly not have found it out, for I am naturally slow at detecting resemblances between faces.

'You have saved my life,' said the strange man, still looking hard in Arthur's face, still holding tightly by his hand. 'If you had been my own brother, you could not have done more for me than that.'

He laid a singularly strong emphasis on those three words 'my own brother,' and a change passed over his face as he pronounced them – a change that no language of mine is competent to describe.

'I hope I have not done being of service to you yet,' said Arthur. 'I'll speak to my father as soon as I get home.'

'You seem to be fond and proud of your father,' said the medical student. 'I suppose, in return, he is fond and proud of you?'

'Of course he is,' answered Arthur, laughing. 'Is there anything wonderful in that? Isn't *your* father fond—'

The stranger suddenly dropped young Holliday's hand, and turned his face away.

'I beg your pardon,' said Arthur. 'I hope I have not unintentionally pained you. I hope you have not lost your father?'

'I can't well lose what I have never had,' retorted the medical student, with a harsh mocking laugh.

'What you have never had!'

The strange man suddenly caught Arthur's hand again, suddenly looked once more hard in his face.

'Yes,' he said, with a repetition of the bitter laugh. 'You have brought a poor devil back into the world, who has no business there. Do I astonish you? Well!

I have a fancy of my own for telling you what men in my situation generally keep a secret. I have no name and no father. The merciful law of Society tells me I am Nobody's Son! Ask your father if he will be my father too, and help me on in life with the family name.'

Arthur looked at me more puzzled than ever.

I signed to him to say nothing, and then laid my fingers again on the man's wrist. No! In spite of the extraordinary speech that he had just made, he was not, as I had been disposed to suspect, beginning to get light-headed. His pulse, by this time, had fallen back to a quiet, slow beat, and his skin was moist and cool. Not a symptom of fever or agitation about him.

Finding that neither of us answered him, he turned to me, and began talking of the extraordinary nature of his case, and asking my advice about the future course of medical treatment to which he ought to subject himself. I said the matter required careful thinking over, and suggested that I should send him a prescription a little later. He told me to write it at once, as he would, most likely, be leaving Doncaster in the morning, before I was up. It was quite useless to represent to him the folly and danger of such a proceeding as this. He heard me politely and patiently, but held to his resolution, without offering any reasons or explanations, and repeated to me, that if I wished to give him a chance of seeing my prescription, I must write it at once.

Hearing this, Arthur volunteered the loan of a travelling writing-case, which, he said, he had with him; and, bringing it to the bed, shook the note paper out of the pocket of the case forthwith in his usual careless way. With the paper, there fell out, on the counterpane of the bed, a small packet of sticking-plaster and a little water-colour drawing of a landscape.

The medical student took up the drawing and looked at it. His eye fell on some initials, neatly written, in cipher, in one corner. He started, and trembled; his pale face grew whiter than ever; his wild black eyes turned on Arthur, and looked through and through him.

'A pretty drawing,' he said, in a remarkably quiet tone of voice.

'Ah! and done by such a pretty girl,' said Arthur. 'Oh, such a pretty girl! I wish it was not a landscape – I wish it was a portrait of her!'

'You admire her very much?'

Arthur, half in jest, half in earnest, kissed his hand for answer.

'Love at first sight,' said young Holliday, putting the drawing away again. 'But the course of it doesn't run smooth. It's the old story. She's monopolised, as usual. Trammelled by a rash engagement to some poor man who is never likely to get money enough to marry her. It was lucky I heard of it in time, or I should certainly have risked a declaration when she gave me that drawing. Here, doctor! Here is pen, ink, and paper, all ready for you.'

'When she gave you that drawing! Gave it. Gave it.'

He repeated the words slowly to himself, and suddenly closed his eyes. A momentary distortion passed across his face, and I saw one of his hands clutch up the bedclothes and squeeze them hard. I thought he was going to be ill again, and begged that there might be no more talking. He opened his eyes when I spoke, fixed them once more, searchingly, on Arthur, and said, slowly and distinctly:

'You like her, and she likes you. The poor man may die out of your way. Who can tell that she may not give you herself as well as her drawing, after all?'

Before young Holliday could answer, he turned to me, and said in a whisper,

'Now for the prescription.' From that time, though he spoke to Arthur again, he never looked at him more.

When I had written the prescription, he examined it, approved of it, and then astonished us both by abruptly wishing us good night. I offered to sit up with him, and he shook his head. Arthur offered to sit up with him, and he said, shortly, with his face turned away, 'No.' I insisted on having somebody left to watch him. He gave way when he found I was determined, and said he would accept the services of the waiter at the Inn.

'Thank you both,' he said, as we rose to go. 'I have one last favour to ask – not of you, doctor, for I leave you to exercise your professional discretion – but of Mr Holliday.' His eyes, while he spoke, still rested steadily on me, and never once turned towards Arthur. 'I beg that Mr Holliday will not mention to any one – least of all to his father – the events that have occurred, and the words that have passed, in this room. I entreat him to bury me in his memory, as, but for him, I might have been buried in my grave. I cannot give my reasons for making this strange request. I can only implore him to grant it.'

His voice faltered for the first time, and he hid his face on the pillow. Arthur, completely bewildered, gave the required pledge. I took young Holliday away with me, immediately afterwards, to the house of my friend; determining to go back to the Inn, and to see the medical student again before he had left in the morning.

I returned to the Inn at eight o'clock, purposely abstaining from waking Arthur, who was sleeping off the past night's excitement on one of my friend's sofas. A suspicion had occurred to me, as soon as I was alone in my bedroom; which made me resolve that Holliday and the stranger whose life he had saved should not meet again, if I could prevent it.

I have already alluded to certain reports, or scandals, which I knew of, relating to the early life of Arthur's father. While I was thinking, in my bed, of what had passed at the Inn – of the change in the student's pulse when he heard the name of Holliday; of the resemblance of expression that I had discovered between his face and Arthur's; of the emphasis he had laid on those three words, 'my own brother;' and of his incomprehensible acknowledgment of his own illegitimacy – while I was thinking of these things, the reports I have mentioned suddenly flew into my mind, and linked themselves fast to the chain of my previous reflections. Something within me whispered, 'It is best that those two young men should not meet again.' I felt it before I slept; I felt it when I woke; and I went, as I told you, alone to the Inn the next morning.

I had missed my only opportunity of seeing my nameless patient again. He had been gone nearly an hour when I inquired for him.

I have now told you everything that I know for certain, in relation to the man whom I brought back to life in the double-bedded room of the Inn at Doncaster. What I have next to add is matter for inference and surmise, and is not, strictly speaking, matter of fact.

I have to tell you, first, that the medical student turned out to be strangely and unaccountably right in assuming it as more than probable that Arthur Holliday would marry the young lady who had given him the water-colour drawing of the landscape. That marriage took place a little more than a year after the events occurred which I have just been relating.

The young couple came to live in the neighbourhood in which I was then established in practice. I was present at the wedding, and was rather surprised to find that Arthur was singularly reserved with me, both before and after his marriage, on the subject of the young lady's prior engagement. He only referred to it once, when we were alone, merely telling me, on that occasion, that his wife had done all that honour and duty required of her in the matter, and that the engagement had been broken off with the full approval of her parents. I never heard more from him than this. For three years he and his wife lived together happily. At the expiration of that time, the symptoms of a serious illness first declared themselves in Mrs Arthur Holliday. It turned out to be a long, lingering, hopeless malady. I attended her throughout. We had been great friends when she was well, and we became more attached to each other than ever when she was ill. I had many long and interesting conversations with her in the intervals when she suffered least. The result of one of those conversations I may briefly relate, leaving you to draw any inferences from it that you please.

The interview to which I refer occurred shortly before her death.

I called one evening, as usual, and found her alone, with a look in her eyes which told me she had been crying. She only informed me, at first, that she had been depressed in spirits; but, by little and little, she became more communicative, and confessed to me that she had been looking over some old letters, which had been addressed to her, before she had seen Arthur, by a man to whom she had been engaged to be married. I asked her how the engagement came to be broken off. She replied that it had not been broken off, but that it had died out in a very mysterious way. The person to whom she was engaged – her first love, she called him – was very poor, and there was no immediate prospect of their being married. He followed my profession, and went abroad to study. They had corresponded regularly, until the time when, as she believed, he had returned to England. From that period she heard no more of him. He was of a fretful, sensitive temperament; and she feared that she might have inadvertently done or said something to offend him. However that might be, he had never written to her again; and, after waiting a year, she had married Arthur. I asked when the first estrangement had begun, and found that the time at which she ceased to hear anything of her first lover exactly corresponded with the time at which I had been called in to my mysterious patient at The Two Robins Inn.

A fortnight after that conversation, she died. In course of time Arthur married again. Of late years, he has lived principally in London, and I have seen little or nothing of him.

I have some years to pass over before I can approach to anything like a conclusion of this fragmentary narrative. And even when that later period is reached, the little that I have to say will not occupy your attention for more than a few minutes.

One rainy autumn evening, while I was still practising as a country doctor, I was sitting alone, thinking over a case, then under my charge, which sorely perplexed me, when I heard a low knock at the door of my room.

'Come in,' I cried, looking up curiously to see who wanted me.

After a momentary delay, the lock moved, and a long, white, bony hand stole round the door as it opened, gently pushing it over a fold in the carpet which hindered it from working freely on the hinges. The hand was followed by a man whose face instantly struck me with a very strange sensation. There was something familiar to me in the look of him; and yet it was also something that suggested the idea of change.

He quietly introduced himself as 'Mr Lorn,' presented to me some excellent professional recommendations; and proposed to fill the place, then vacant, of my assistant. While he was speaking, I noticed it as singular that we did not appear to be meeting each other like strangers; and that, while I was certainly startled at seeing him, he did not appear to be at all startled at seeing me.

It was on the tip of my tongue to say that I thought I had met with him before. But there was something in his face, and something in my own recollections – I can hardly say what – which unaccountably restrained me from speaking, and which, as unaccountably, attracted me to him at once, and made me feel ready and glad to accept his proposal.

He took his assistant's place on that very day. We got on together as if we had been old friends from the first; but, throughout the whole time of his residence in my house, he never volunteered any confidences on the subject of his past life; and I never approached the forbidden topic except by hints, which he resolutely refused to understand.

I had long had a notion that my patient at the Inn might have been a natural son of the elder Mr Holliday's, and that he might also have been the man who was engaged to Arthur's first wife. And, now, another idea occurred to me, that Mr Lorn was the only person in existence who could, if he chose, enlighten me on both those doubtful points. But he never did choose – and I was never enlightened. He remained with me till I removed to London to try my fortune there, as a physician, for the second time; and then he went his way, and I went mine, and we have never seen one another since.

I can add no more. I may have been right in my suspicion, or I may have been wrong. All I know is, that, in those days of my country practice, when I came home late, and found my assistant asleep, and woke him, he used to look, in coming to, wonderfully like the stranger at Doncaster, as he raised himself in the bed on that memorable night.

A Plot in Private Life

Originally appeared in *Harper's Monthly Magazine*, February 1858, as 'A Marriage Tragedy'. The story was included in *The Queen of Hearts* as 'Brother Griffith's Story of A Plot in Private Life'. The private investigator, Mr Dark, is often held to foreshadow the portrait of Sergeant Cuff in *The Moonstone* (1868), while, as Robert Ashley points out, 'the incident of the bloodstained nightgown anticipates the paintstained gown' in the same novel (*Wilkie Collins*, p. 56).

I

The first place I got, when I began going out to service, was not a very profitable one. I certainly gained the advantage of learning my business thoroughly, but I never had my due in the matter of wages. My master was made a bankrupt, and his servants suffered with the rest of his creditors.

My second situation, however, amply compensated me for my want of luck in the first. I had the good fortune to enter the service of Mr and Mrs Norcross. My master was a very rich gentleman. He had the Darrock house and lands in Cumberland, an estate also in Yorkshire, and a very large property in Jamaica, which produced at that time, and for some years afterwards, a great income. Out in the West Indies he met with a pretty young lady, a governess in an English family, and, taking a violent fancy to her, married her, though she was a good five-and-twenty years younger than himself. After the wedding they came to England; and it was at this time that I was lucky enough to be engaged by them as a servant.

I lived with my new master and mistress three years. They had no children. At the end of that period Mr Norcross died. He was sharp enough to foresee that his young widow would marry again; and he bequeathed his property so that it all went to Mrs Norcross first, and then to any children she might have by a second marriage, and, failing that, to relations and friends of his own. I did not suffer by my master's death, for his widow kept me in her service. I had attended on Mr Norcross all through his last illness, and had made myself useful enough to win my mistress's favour and gratitude. Besides me, she also retained her maid in her service – a quadroon woman named Josephine, whom she brought with her from the West Indies. Even at that time I disliked the half-breed's wheedling manners, and her cruel, tawny face, and wondered how my mistress could be so fond of her as she was. Time showed that I was right in distrusting this woman. I shall have much more to say about her when I get further advanced with my story.

Meanwhile I have next to relate that my mistress broke up the rest of her establishment, and, taking me and the lady's maid with her, went to travel on the Continent.

Among other wonderful places, we visited Paris, Genoa, Venice, Florence, Rome, and Naples, staying in some of those cities for months together. The fame of my mistress's riches followed her wherever she went; and there were plenty of gentlemen, foreigners as well as Englishmen, who were anxious enough to get into her good graces and to prevail on her to marry them. Nobody succeeded, however, in producing any very strong or lasting impression on her; and when we came back to England, after more than two years of absence, Mrs Norcross was still a widow, and showed no signs of wanting to change her condition.

We went to the house on the Yorkshire estate first; but my mistress did not fancy some of the company round about, so we moved again to Darrock Hall, and made excursions from time to time in the lake district, some miles off. On one of these trips Mrs Norcross met with some old friends, who introduced her to a gentleman of their party bearing the very common, and very uninteresting, name of Mr James Smith.

He was a tall, fine young man enough, with black hair, which grew very long, and the biggest, bushiest pair of black whiskers I ever saw. Altogether he had a rakish, unsettled look, and a bounceable way of talking, which made him the prominent person in company. He was poor enough himself, as I heard from his servant, but well connected – a gentleman by birth and education, though his manners were so free. What my mistress saw to like in him I don't know; but when she asked her friends to stay with her at Darrock, she included Mr James Smith in the invitation. We had a fine, gay, noisy time of it at the Hall – the strange gentleman, in particular, making himself as much at home as if the place belonged to him. I was surprised at Mrs Norcross putting up with him as she did; but I was fairly thunderstruck, some months afterwards, when I heard that she and her free and easy visitor were actually going to be married! She had refused offers by dozens abroad, from higher and richer and better-behaved men. It seemed next to impossible that she could seriously think of throwing herself away upon such a hare-brained, headlong, penniless young gentleman as Mr James Smith.

Married, nevertheless, they were, in due course of time; and, after spending the honeymoon abroad, they came back to Darrock Hall.

I soon found that my new master had a very variable temper. There were some days when he was as easy and familiar and pleasant with his servants as any gentleman need be. At other times some devil within him seemed to get possession of his whole nature. He flew into violent passions, and took wrong ideas into his head, which no reasoning or remonstrance could remove. It rather amazed me, considering how gay he was in his tastes, and how restless his habits were, that he should consent to live at such a quiet, dull place as Darrock. The reason for this, however, soon came out. Mr James Smith was not much of a sportsman; he cared nothing for in-door amusements, such as reading, music, and so forth; and he had no ambition for representing the county in Parliament. The one pursuit that he was really fond of was yachting. Darrock was within sixteen miles of a seaport town, with an excellent harbour; and to this accident of position the Hall was entirely indebted for recommending itself as a place of residence to Mr James Smith.

He had such an untiring enjoyment and delight in cruising about at sea, and all his ideas of pleasure seemed to be so closely connected with his remembrance of the sailing trips he had taken on board different yachts belonging to his friends, that I verily believe his chief object in marrying my mistress was to get the command of money enough to keep a vessel for himself. Be that as it may, it is certain that he prevailed on her, some time after their marriage, to make him a present of a fine schooner yacht, which was brought round from Cowes to our coast-town, and kept always waiting ready for him in the harbour.

His wife required some little persuasion before she could make up her mind to let him have the vessel. She suffered so much from sea-sickness, that pleasure-sailing was out of the question for her; and, being very fond of her husband, she was naturally unwilling that he should engage in an amusement which took him away from her. However, Mr James Smith used his influence over her cleverly, promising that he would never go away without first asking her leave, and engaging that his terms of absence at sea should never last for more than a week or ten days at a time. Accordingly, my mistress, who was the kindest and most unselfish woman in the world, put her own feelings aside, and made her husband happy in the possession of a vessel of his own.

While my master was away cruising, my mistress had a dull time of it at the Hall. The few gentlefolks there were in our part of the county lived at a distance, and could only come to Darrock when they were asked to stay there for some days together. As for the village near us, there was but one person living in it whom my mistress could think of asking to the Hall; and that person was the clergyman who did duty at the church.

This gentleman's name was Mr Meeke. He was a single man, very young, and very lonely in his position. He had a mild, melancholy, pasty-looking face, and was as shy and soft-spoken as a little girl – altogether, what one may call, without being unjust or severe, a poor, weak creature, and, out of all sight, the very worst preacher I ever sat under in my life. The one thing he did, which, as I heard, he could really do well, was playing on the fiddle. He was uncommonly fond of music – so much so that he often took his instrument out with him when he went for a walk. This taste of his was his great recommendation to my mistress, who was a wonderfully fine player on the piano, and who was delighted to get such a performer as Mr Meeke to play duets with her. Besides liking his society for this reason, she felt for him in his lonely position; naturally enough I think, considering how often she was left in solitude herself. Mr Meeke, on his side, when he got over his first shyness, was only too glad to leave his lonesome little parsonage for the fine music room at the Hall, and for the company of a handsome, kind-hearted lady, who made much of him and admired his fiddle-playing with all her heart. Thus it happened that, whenever my master was away at sea, my mistress and Mr Meeke were always together, playing duets as if they had their living to get by it. A more harmless connection than the connection between those two never existed in this world; and yet, innocent as it was, it turned out to be the first cause of all the misfortunes that afterward happened.

My master's treatment of Mr Meeke was, from the first, the very opposite of my mistress's. The restless, rackety, bounceable Mr James Smith felt a contempt for the weak, womanish, fiddling little parson; and, what was more, did not care to conceal it. For this reason, Mr Meeke (who was dreadfully frightened by my master's violent language and rough ways) very seldom visited at the Hall, except when my mistress was alone there. Meaning no wrong, and therefore stooping to no concealment, she never thought of taking any measures to keep Mr Meeke out of the way when he happened to be with her at the time of her husband's coming home, whether it was only from a riding excursion in the neighbourhood, or from a cruise in the schooner. In this way it so turned out that whenever my master came home, after a long or short absence, in nine cases out of ten he found the parson at the Hall.

At first he used to laugh at this circumstance, and to amuse himself with some coarse jokes at the expense of his wife and her companion. But, after a while, his variable temper changed, as usual. He grew sulky, rude, angry, and, at last, downright jealous of Mr Meeke. Though too proud to confess it in so many words, he still showed the state of his mind clearly enough to my mistress to excite her indignation. She was a woman who could be led anywhere by any one for whom she had a regard; but there was a firm spirit within her that rose at the slightest show of injustice or oppression, and that resented tyrannical usage of any sort, perhaps a little too warmly. The bare suspicion that her husband could feel any distrust of her, set her all in a flame; and she took the most unfortunate, and yet, at the same time, the most natural way for a woman, of resenting it. The ruder her husband was to Mr Meeke, the more kindly she behaved to him. This led to serious disputes and dissensions, and thence, in time, to a violent quarrel. I could not avoid hearing the last part of the altercation between them, for it took place in the garden-walk, outside the dining-room window, while I was occupied in laying the table for lunch.

Without repeating their words – which I have no right to do, having heard by accident what I had no business to hear – I may say generally, to show how serious the quarrel was, that my mistress charged my master with having married from mercenary motives, with keeping out of her company as much as he could, and with insulting her by a suspicion which it would be hard ever to forgive, and impossible ever to forget. He replied by violent language directed against herself, and by commanding her never to open the doors again to Mr Meeke; she, on her side, declaring that she would never consent to insult a clergyman and a gentleman in order to satisfy the whim of a tyrannical husband. Upon that he called out, with a great oath, to have his horse saddled directly, declaring that he would not stop another instant under the same roof with a woman who had set him at defiance; and warning his wife that he would come back, if Mr Meeke entered the house again, and horsewhip him, in spite of his black coat, all through the village.

With those words he left her, and rode away to the sea-port where his yacht was lying. My mistress kept up her spirit till he was out of sight, and then burst into a dreadful screaming passion of tears, which ended by leaving her so weak that she had to be carried to her bed like a woman who was at the point of death.

The same evening my master's horse was ridden back by a messenger, who brought a scrap of note-paper with him, addressed to me. It only contained these lines: 'Pack up my clothes, and deliver them immediately to the bearer. You may tell your mistress that I sail to-night, at eleven o'clock, for a cruise to Sweden. Forward my letters to the Post-office, Stockholm.'

I obeyed the orders given to me, except that relating to my mistress. The doctor had been sent for, and was still in the house. I consulted him upon the propriety of my delivering the message. He positively forbade me to do so, that night; and told me to give him the slip of paper and leave it to his discretion to show it to her, or not, the next morning.

The messenger had hardly been gone an hour when Mr Meeke's housekeeper came to the Hall with a roll of music for my mistress. I told the woman of my master's sudden departure, and of the doctor being in the house. This news brought Mr Meeke himself to the Hall in a great flutter.

I felt so angry with him for being the cause – innocent as he might be – of the shocking scene which had taken place, that I exceeded the bounds of my duty, and told him the whole truth. The poor, weak, wavering, childish creature flushed up red in the face, then turned as pale as ashes, and dropped into one of the hall chairs, crying – literally crying fit to break his heart! 'Oh, William!' says he, wringing his little, frail, trembling, white hands, as helpless as a baby. 'Oh, William, what am I to do?'

'As you ask me that question, sir,' says I, 'you will excuse me, I hope, if, being a servant, I plainly speak my mind notwithstanding. I know my station well enough to be aware that, strictly speaking, I have done wrong, and far exceeded my duty, in telling you as much as I have told you already. But

I would go through fire and water, sir,' says I, feeling my own eyes getting moist, 'for my mistress's sake. She has no relation here who can speak to you; and it is even better that a servant like me should risk being guilty of an impertinence, than that dreadful and lasting mischief should arise from the right remedy not being applied at the right time. This is what I should do, sir, in your place. Saving your presence, I should leave off crying, and go back home and write to Mr James Smith, saying that I would not, as a clergyman, give him railing for railing, but would prove how unworthily he had suspected me, by ceasing to visit at the Hall from this time forth, rather than be a cause of dissension between man and wife. If you will put that into proper language, sir, and will have the letter ready for me in half an hour's time, I will call for it on the fastest horse in our stables, and, at my own risk, will give it to my master before he sails to-night. I have nothing more to say, sir, except to ask your pardon for forgetting my proper place, and for making bold to speak on a very serious matter as equal to equal, and as man to man.'

To do Mr Meeke justice, he had a heart, though it was a very small one. He shook hands with me, and said he accepted my advice as the advice of a friend; and so went back to his parsonage to write the letter. In half an hour I called for it on horseback, but it was not ready for me. Mr Meeke was ridiculously nice about how he should express himself when he got a pen into his hand. I found him with his desk littered with rough copies, in a perfect agony about how to turn his phrases delicately enough in referring to my mistress. Every minute being precious, I hurried him as much as I could, without standing on any ceremony. It took half an hour more, with all my efforts, before he could make up his mind that the letter would do. I started off with it at a gallop, and never drew rein till I got to the sea-port town.

The harbour-clock chimed the quarter past eleven as I rode by it, and when I got down to the jetty, there was no yacht to be seen. She had been cast off from her moorings ten minutes before eleven, and as the clock struck she had sailed out of the harbour. I would have followed in a boat, but it was a fine starlight night, with a fresh wind blowing; and the sailors on the pier laughed at me when I spoke of rowing after a schooner-yacht which had got a quarter of an hour's start of us, with the wind abeam and the tide in her favour.

I rode back with a heavy heart. All I could do now was to send the letter to the Post-office, Stockholm.

The next day the doctor showed my mistress the scrap of paper with the message on it from my master; and an hour or two after that, a letter was sent to her in Mr Meeke's handwriting, explaining the reason why she must not expect to see him at the Hall, and referring to me in terms of high praise, as a sensible and faithful man who had spoken the right word at the right time. I am able to repeat the substance of the letter, because I heard all about it from my mistress, under very unpleasant circumstances so far as I was concerned.

The news of my master's departure did not affect her as the doctor had supposed it would. Instead of distressing her, it roused her spirit and made her angry; her pride, as I imagine, being wounded by the contemptuous manner in which her husband had notified his intention of sailing to Sweden, at the end of a message to a servant about packing his clothes. Finding her in that temper of mind, the letter from Mr Meeke only irritated her the more. She insisted on getting up, and as soon as she was dressed and down stairs, she vented her violent humour on me, reproaching me for impertinent interference in the affairs of my betters, and declaring that she had almost made up her mind to turn me out of my place for it. I did not defend myself, because I respected her sorrows and the irritation that came from them; also, because I knew the natural kindness of her nature well enough to be assured that she would make amends to me for her harshness the moment her mind was composed again. The result showed that I was right. That same evening she sent for me, and begged me to forgive and forget the hasty words she had spoken in the morning, with a grace and sweetness that would have won the heart of any man who listened to her.

Weeks passed after this, till it was more than a month since the day of my master's departure, and no letter in his handwriting came to Darrock Hall.

My mistress, taking this treatment of her more angrily than sorrowfully, went to London to consult her nearest relations, who lived there. On leaving home, she stopped the carriage at the parsonage, and went in (as I thought, rather defiantly) to say good-bye to Mr Meeke. She had answered his letter, and received others from him, and had answered them likewise. She had also, of course, seen him every Sunday at church, and had always stopped to speak to him after the service. But this was the first occasion on which she had visited him at his house. As the carriage stopped, the little parson came out, in great hurry and agitation, to meet her at the garden-gate.

'Don't look alarmed, Mr Meeke,' says my mistress, getting out. 'Though you have engaged not to come near the Hall, I have made no promise to keep away from the parsonage.' With those words she went into the house.

The quadroon maid, Josephine, was sitting with me in the rumble of the carriage, and I saw a smile on her tawny face as the parson and his visitor went into the house together. Harmless as Mr Meeke was, and innocent of all wrong as I knew my mistress to be, I regretted that she should be so rash as to despise appearances, considering the situation she was placed in. She had already exposed herself to be thought of disrespectfully by her own maid; and it was hard to say what worse consequences might not happen after that.

Half an hour later, we were away on our journey. My mistress stayed in London two months. Throughout all that long time no letter from my master was forwarded to her from the country-house.

II

When the two months had passed, we returned to Darrock Hall. Nobody there had received any news in our absence of the whereabouts of my master and his yacht.

Six more weary weeks elapsed; and in that time but one event happened at the Hall to vary the dismal monotony of the lives we now led in the solitary place. One morning Josephine came down, after dressing my mistress, with her face downright livid to look at, except on one cheek, where there was a mark as red as burning fire. I was in the kitchen at the time, and I asked what was the matter.

'The matter!' says she, in her shrill voice and her half-foreign English. 'Use your own eyes, if you please, and look at this cheek of mine. What! have you lived so long a time with your mistress, and don't you know the mark of her hand yet?'

I was at a loss to understand what she meant, but she soon explained herself. My mistress, whose temper had been sadly altered for the worse by the trials and humiliations she had gone through, had got up that morning more out of humour than usual; and, in answer to her maid's inquiry as to how she had passed the night, had began talking about her weary, miserable life in an unusually fretful and desperate way. Josephine, in trying to cheer her spirits, had ventured, most improperly, on making a light, jesting reference to Mr Meeke, which had so enraged my mistress that she turned round sharp on the half-breed, and gave her – to use the common phrase – a smart box on the ear. Josephine confessed that the moment after she had done this, her better sense appeared to tell her that she had taken a most improper way of resenting undue familiarity. She had immediately expressed her regret for having forgotten herself, and had proved the sincerity of it by a gift of half a dozen cambric handkerchiefs, presented as a peace-offering on the spot. After that, I thought it impossible that Josephine could bear any malice against a mistress whom she had served ever since she had been a girl, and I said as much to her when she had done telling me what had happened upstairs.

'I! Malice!' cries Miss Josephine, in her hard, sharp, snappish way. 'And why, and wherefore, if you please? If my mistress smacks my cheek with one hand, she gives me handkerchiefs to wipe it with the other. My good mistress, my kind mistress, my pretty mistress! I, the servant, bear malice against her, the mistress! Ah, you bad man, even to think of such a thing! Ah, fie, fie! I am quite ashamed of you.'

She gave me one look – the wickedest look I ever saw; and burst out laughing – the harshest laugh I ever heard from a woman's lips. Turning away from me directly after, she said no more, and never referred to the subject again on any subsequent occasion.

From that time, however, I noticed an alteration in Miss Josephine; not in her way of doing her work, for she was just as sharp and careful about it as ever, but in her manners and habits. She grew amazingly quiet, and passed almost all her leisure time alone. I could bring no charge against her which authorised me to speak a word of warning; but, for all that, I could not help feeling that if I had been in my mistress's place, I would have followed up the present of the cambric handkerchiefs by paying her a month's wages in advance, and sending her away from the house the same evening.

With the exception of this little domestic matter, which appeared trifling enough at the time, but which led to very serious consequences afterwards, nothing happened at all out of the ordinary way during the six weary weeks to which I have referred. At the beginning of the seventh week, however, an event occurred at last.

One morning the postman brought a letter to the Hall, addressed to my mistress. I took it upstairs, and looked at the direction as I put it on the salver. The handwriting was not my master's; was not, as it appeared to me, the handwriting of any well-educated person. The outside of the letter was also very dirty; and the seal a common office-seal of the usual lattice-work pattern. 'This must be a begging-letter,' I thought to myself as I entered the breakfast-room and advanced with it to my mistress.

She held up her hand before she opened it, as a sign to me that she had some order to give, and that I was not to leave the room till I had received it. Then she broke the seal, and began to read the letter.

Her eyes had hardly been on it a moment before her face turned as pale as death, and the paper began to tremble in her fingers. She read on to the end, and suddenly turned from pale to scarlet, started out of her chair, crumpled the letter up violently in her hand, and took several turns backwards and forwards in the room, without seeming to notice me as I stood by the door. 'You villain! you villain! you villain!' I heard her whisper to herself many times over, in a quick, hissing, fierce way. Then she stopped, and said on a sudden, 'Can it be true?' Then she looked up, and seeing me standing at the door, started as if I had been a stranger, changed colour again, and told me, in a stifled voice, to leave her and come back again in half an hour. I obeyed, feeling certain that she must have received some very bad news of her husband, and wondering, anxiously enough, what it might be.

When I returned to the breakfast-room, her face was as much discomposed as ever. Without speaking a word, she handed me two sealed letters. One, a note to be left for Mr Meeke at the parsonage; the other, a letter marked 'Immediate,' and addressed to her solicitor in London, who was also, I should add, her nearest living relative.

I left one of these letters, and posted the other. When I came back, I heard that my mistress had taken to her room. She remained there for four days, keeping her new sorrow, whatever it was, strictly to herself. On the fifth day, the lawyer from London arrived at the Hall. My mistress went down to him in the library, and was shut up there with him for nearly two hours. At the end of that time the bell rang for me.

'Sit down, William,' said my mistress when I came into the room. 'I feel such entire confidence in your fidelity and attachment that I am about, with the full concurrence of this gentleman, who is my nearest relative and my legal adviser, to place a very serious secret in your keeping, and to employ your services on a matter which is as important to me as a matter of life and death.'

Her poor eyes were very red, and her lips quivered as she spoke to me. I was so startled by what she had said that I hardly knew which chair to sit in. She pointed to one placed near herself at the table, and seemed about to speak to me again, when the lawyer interfered.

'Let me entreat you,' he said, 'not to agitate yourself unnecessarily. I will put this person in possession of the facts; and if I omit anything, you shall stop me and set me right.'

My mistress leaned back in her chair, and covered her face with her handkerchief. The lawyer waited a moment, and then addressed himself to me.

'You are already aware,' he said, 'of the circumstances under which your master left this house; and you also know, I have no doubt, that no direct news of him has reached your mistress up to this time?'

I bowed to him, and said I knew of the circumstances so far.

'Do you remember,' he went on, 'taking a letter to your mistress five days ago?'

'Yes, sir,' I replied; 'a letter which seemed to distress and alarm her very seriously.'

'I will read you that letter before we say any more,' continued the lawyer. 'I warn you beforehand that it contains a terrible charge against your master, which, however, is not attested by the writer's signature. I have already told your mistress that she must not attach too much importance to an anonymous letter; and I now tell you the same thing.'

Saying that, he took up a letter from the table and read it aloud. I had a copy of it given to me afterwards, which I looked at often enough to fix the contents of the letter in my memory. I can now repeat them, I think, word for word.

> Madam,
>
> I cannot reconcile it to my conscience to leave you in total ignorance of your husband's atrocious conduct towards you. If you have ever been disposed to regret his absence, do so no longer. Hope and pray, rather, that you and he may never meet face to face again in this world. I write in great haste, and in great fear of being observed. Time fails me to prepare you as you ought to be prepared for what I have now to disclose. I must tell you plainly, with much respect for you and sorrow for your misfortune, that your husband *has married another wife*. I saw the ceremony performed, unknown to him. If I could not have spoken of this infamous act as an eye-witness, I would not have spoken of it at all.
>
> I dare not acknowledge who I am, for I believe Mr James Smith would stick at no crime to revenge himself on me if he ever came to a knowledge of the step I am now taking, and of the means by which I got my information. Neither have I time to enter into particulars. I simply warn you of what has happened, and leave you to act on that warning as you please. You may disbelieve this letter, because it is not signed by any name. In that case, if Mr James Smith should ever venture into your presence, I recommend you to ask him suddenly what he has done with his *new wife*; and to see if his countenance does not immediately testify that the truth has been spoken by
>
> Your Unknown Friend

Poor as my opinion was of my master, I had never believed him to be capable of such villainy as this, and I could not believe it, when the lawyer had done reading the letter.

'Oh, sir!' I said; 'surely that is some base imposition? Surely it cannot be true?'

'That is what I have told your mistress,' he answered. 'But she says in return—'

'That I feel it to be true,' my mistress broke in, speaking behind the handkerchief, in a faint smothered voice.

'We need not debate the question,' the lawyer went on. 'Our business now is to prove the truth or falsehood of this letter. That must be done at once. I have written to one of my clerks, who is accustomed to conducting delicate investigations, to come to this house without loss of time. He is to be trusted with anything, and he will pursue the needful inquiries immediately. It is absolutely necessary, to make sure of committing no mistakes, that he should be accompanied by some one who is well acquainted with Mr James Smith's habits and personal appearance; and your mistress has fixed upon you to be that person. However well the inquiry is managed, it may be attended by much trouble and delay, may necessitate a long journey, and may involve some personal danger. Are you,' said the lawyer, looking hard at me, 'ready to suffer any inconvenience and to run any risk for your mistress's sake?'

'There is nothing I *can* do, sir,' said I, 'that I will not do. I am afraid I am not clever enough to be of much use. But so far as troubles and risks are concerned, I am ready for anything from this moment.'

My mistress took the handkerchief from her face, looked at me with her eyes full of tears, and held out her hand. How I came to do it I don't know, but I stooped down and kissed the hand she offered me; feeling half startled, half ashamed at my own boldness the moment after.

'You will do, my man,' said the lawyer, nodding his head. 'Don't trouble yourself about the cleverness or the cunning that may be wanted. My clerk has got head enough for two. I have only one word more to say before you go down stairs again. Remember that this investigation, and the cause that leads to it, must be kept a profound secret. Except us three, and the clergyman here (to whom your mistress has written word of what has happened) nobody knows anything about it. I will let my clerk into the secret, when he joins us. As soon as you and he are away from the house, you may talk about it. Until then, you will close your lips on the subject.'

The clerk did not keep us long waiting. He came as fast as the mail from London could bring him.

I had expected, from his master's description, to see a serious, sedate man, rather sly in his looks, and rather reserved in his manner. To my amazement, this practised hand at delicate investigations was a brisk, plump, jolly little man, with a comfortable double chin, a pair of very bright black eyes, and a big bottle-nose of the true groggy red colour. He wore a suit of black, and a limp, dingy white cravat; took snuff perpetually out of a very large box; walked with his hands crossed behind his back; and looked, upon the whole, much more like a parson of free and easy habits than a lawyer's clerk.

'How d'ye do?' says he, when I opened the door to him. 'I'm the man you expect from the office in London. Just say Mr Dark, will you? I'll sit down here till you come back; and, young man, if there is such a thing as a glass of ale in the house, I don't mind committing myself so far as to say that I'll drink it.'

I got him the ale before I announced him. He winked at me as he put it to his lips.

'Your good health,' says he. 'I like you. Don't forget that the name's Dark; and just leave the jug and glass, will you, in case my master keeps me waiting.'

I announced him at once, and was told to show him into the library.

When I got back to the hall the jug was empty, and Mr Dark was comforting himself with a pinch of snuff, snorting over it like a perfect grampus. He had swallowed more than a pint of the strongest old ale in the house; and, for all the effect it seemed to have had on him, he might just as well have been drinking so much water.

As I led him along the passage to the library, Josephine passed us. Mr Dark winked at me again, and made her a low bow.

'Lady's maid,' I heard him whisper to himself. 'A fine woman to look at, but a damned bad one to deal with.' I turned round on him, rather angry at his cool ways, and looked hard at him just before I opened the library door. Mr Dark looked hard at *me*. 'All right,' says he. 'I can show myself in.' And he knocks at the door, and opens it, and goes in with another wicked wink, all in a moment.

Half an hour later, the bell rang for me. Mr Dark was sitting between my mistress (who was looking at him in amazement) and the lawyer (who was looking at him with approval). He had a map open on his knee, and a pen in his hand. Judging by his face, the communication of the secret about my master did not seem to have made the smallest impression on him.

'I've got leave to ask you a question,' says he, the moment I appeared. 'When you found your master's yacht gone, did you hear which way she had sailed? Was it northward toward Scotland? Speak up, young man, speak up!'

'Yes,' I answered. 'The boatmen told me that, when I made inquiries at the harbour.'

'Well, sir,' says Mr Dark, turning to the lawyer, 'if he said he was going to Sweden, he seems to have started on the road to it, at all events. I think I have got my instructions now?'

The lawyer nodded, and looked at my mistress, who bowed her head to him. He then said, turning to me:

'Pack up your bag for travelling at once, and have a conveyance got ready to go to the nearest post town. Look sharp, young man – look sharp!'

'And whatever happens in the future,' added my mistress, her kind voice trembling a little, 'believe, William, that I shall never forget the proof you now show of your devotion to me. It is still some comfort to know that I have your fidelity to depend on in this dreadful trial – your fidelity and the extraordinary intelligence and experience of Mr Dark.'

Mr Dark did not seem to hear the compliment. He was busy writing, with his paper upon the map on his knee.

A quarter of an hour later, when I had ordered the dog-cart, and had got down into the hall with my bag packed, I found him there waiting for me. He was sitting in the same chair which he had occupied when he first arrived, and he had another jug of the old ale on the table by his side.

'Got any fishing-rods in the house?' says he, when I put my bag down in the hall.

'Yes,' I replied, astonished at the question. 'What do you want with them?'

'Pack a couple in cases for travelling,' says Mr Dark, 'with lines and hooks and fly-books all complete. Have a drop of the ale before you go – and don't stare, William, don't stare. I'll let the light in on you as soon as we are out of the house. Off with you for the rods! I want to be on the road in five minutes.'

When I came back with the rods and tackle, I found Mr Dark in the dog-cart.

'Money, luggage, fishing-rods, papers of directions, copy of anonymous letter, guide-book, map,' says he, running over in his mind the things wanted for the journey. 'All right so far. Drive off.'

I took the reins and started the horse. As we left the house, I saw my mistress and Josephine looking after us from two of the windows on the second floor. The memory of those two attentive faces – one so fair and so good – the other so yellow and so wicked – haunted my mind perpetually for many days afterward.

'Now, William,' says Mr Dark, when we were clear of the lodge gates, 'I'm going to begin by telling you that you must step out of your own character till further notice. You are a clerk in a bank; and I'm another. We have got our regular holiday, that comes, like Christmas, once a year; and we are taking a little tour in Scotland, to see the curiosities, and to breathe the sea air, and to get some fishing whenever we can. I'm the fat cashier who digs holes in a drawerful of gold with a copper shovel. And you're the arithmetical young man who sits on a perch behind me and keeps the books. Scotland's a beautiful country, William. Can you make whisky-toddy? I can; and what's more, unlikely as the thing may seem to you, I can actually drink it into the bargain.'

'Scotland!' says I. 'What are we going to Scotland for?'

'Question for question,' says Mr Dark. 'What are we starting on a journey for?'

'To find my master,' I answered, 'and to make sure if the letter about him is true.'

'Very good,' says he. 'How would *you* set about doing that, eh?'

'I should go and ask about him at Stockholm in Sweden, where he said his letters were to be sent.'

'Should you indeed?' says Mr Dark. 'If you were a shepherd, William, and had lost a sheep in Cumberland, would you begin looking for it at the Land's End, or would you try a little nearer home?'

'You're attempting to make a fool of me now,' says I.

'No,' says Mr Dark, 'I'm only letting the light in on you, as I said I would. Now listen to reason, William, and profit by it as much as you can. Mr James Smith says he is going on a cruise to Sweden, and makes his word good, at the beginning, by starting northward toward the coast of Scotland. What does he go in? A yacht. Do yachts carry live beasts and a butcher on board? No. Will joints of meat keep fresh all the way from Cumberland to Sweden? No. Do gentlemen like living on salt provisions? No. What follows from these three Noes? That Mr James Smith must have stopped somewhere, on the way to Sweden, to supply his sea-larder with fresh provisions. Where, in that case, must he stop? Somewhere in Scotland, supposing he didn't alter his course when he was out of sight of your sea-port. Where in Scotland? Northward on the main land, or westward at one of the islands? Most likely on the main land, where the sea-side places are largest, and where he is sure of getting all the stores he wants. Next, what is our business? Not to risk losing a link in the chain of evidence by missing any place where he has put his foot on shore. Not to overshoot the mark when we want to hit it in the bull's-eye. Not to waste money and time by taking a long trip to Sweden till we know that we must absolutely go there. Where is our journey of discovery to take us to first, then? Clearly to the north of Scotland. What do you say to that, Mr William? Is my catechism all correct, or has your strong ale muddled my head?'

It was evident by this time that no ale could do that, and I told him so. He chuckled, winked at me, and taking another pinch of snuff, said he would now turn the whole case over in his mind again, and make sure that he had got all the bearings of it quite clear.

By the time we reached the post-town, he had accomplished this mental effort to his own perfect satisfaction, and was quite ready to compare the ale at the inn with the ale at Darrock Hall. The dog-cart was left to be taken back the next morning by the ostler. A post-chaise and horses were ordered out. A loaf of bread, a Bologna sausage, and two bottles of sherry were put into the pockets of the carriage; we took our seats, and started briskly on our doubtful journey.

'One word more of friendly advice,' says Mr Dark, settling himself comfortably in his corner of the carriage. 'Take your sleep, William, whenever you feel that you can get it. You won't find yourself in bed again till we get to Glasgow.'

III

Although the events that I am now relating happened many years ago, I shall still, for caution's sake, avoid mentioning by name the various places visited by Mr Dark and myself for the purpose of making inquiries. It will be enough if I describe generally what we did, and if I mention in substance only the result at which we ultimately arrived.

On reaching Glasgow, Mr Dark turned the whole case over in his mind once more. The result was that he altered his intention of going straight to the north of Scotland, considering it safer to make sure, if possible, of the course the yacht had taken in her cruise along the western coast.

The carrying out of this new resolution involved the necessity of delaying our onward journey by perpetually diverging from the direct road. Three times we were sent uselessly to wild places in the Hebrides by false reports. Twice we wandered away inland, following gentlemen who answered generally to the description of Mr James Smith, but who turned out to be the wrong men as soon as we set eyes on them. These vain excursions – especially the three to the western islands – consumed time terribly. It was more than two months from the day when we had left Darrock Hall before we found ourselves up at the very top of Scotland at last, driving into a considerable sea-side town, with a harbour attached to it. Thus far, our journey had led to no results, and I began to despair of success. As for Mr Dark, he never got to the end of his sweet temper and his wonderful patience.

'You don't know how to wait, William,' was his constant remark whenever he heard me complaining. 'I do.'

We drove into the town towards evening in a modest little gig, and put up, according to our usual custom, at one of the inferior inns.

'We must begin at the bottom,' Mr Dark used to say. 'High company in a coffee-room won't be familiar with us. Low company in a tap-room will.' And he certainly proved the truth of his own words. The like of him for making intimate friends of total strangers at the shortest notice, I have never met with before or since. Cautious as the Scotch are, Mr Dark seemed to have the knack of twisting them round his finger as he pleased. He varied his way artfully with different men; but there were three standing opinions of his which he made a point of expressing in all varieties of company while we were in Scotland. In the first place, he thought the view of Edinburgh from Arthur's Seat the finest in the world. In the second place, he considered whisky to be the most wholesome spirit in the world. In the third place, he believed his late beloved mother to be the best woman in the world. It may be worthy of note that, whenever he expressed this last opinion in Scotland, he invariably added that her maiden name was Macleod.

Well, we put up at a modest little inn near the harbour. I was dead tired with the journey, and lay down on my bed to get some rest. Mr Dark, whom nothing ever fatigued, left me to take his toddy and pipe among the company in the tap-room.

I don't know how long I had been asleep, when I was roused by a shake on my shoulder. The room was pitch dark, and I felt a hand suddenly clapped over my mouth. Then a strong smell of whisky and tobacco saluted my nostrils, and a whisper stole into my ear—

'William! we have got to the end of our journey.'

'Mr Dark,' I stammered out,' is that you? What in heaven's name do you mean?'

'The yacht put in here,' was the answer still in a whisper, 'and your blackguard of a master came ashore—'

'Oh, Mr Dark,' I broke in, 'don't tell me that the letter is true!'

'Every word of it,' says he. 'He was married here, and he was off again to the Mediterranean with Number Two a good three weeks before we left your mistress's house. Hush! don't say a word. Go to sleep again, or strike a light and read, if you like it better. Do anything but come downstairs with me. I'm going to find out all the particulars, without seeming to want to know one of them. Yours is a very good-looking face, William, but it's so infernally honest that I can't trust it in the tap-room. I'm making friends with the Scotchmen already. They know my opinion of Arthur's Seat; they *see* what I think of whisky; and I rather think it won't be long before they hear that my mother's maiden name was Macleod.'

With those words he slipped out of the room, and left me, as he had found me, in the dark.

I was far too much agitated by what I had heard to think of going to sleep again; so I struck a light, and tried to amuse myself as well as I could with an old newspaper that had been stuffed into my carpet bag. It was then nearly ten o'clock. Two hours later, when the house shut up, Mr Dark came back to me again in high spirits.

'I have got the whole case here,' says he, tapping his forehead – 'the whole case, as neat and clean as if it was drawn in a brief. That master of yours doesn't stick at a trifle, William. It's my opinion that your mistress and you have not seen the last of him yet.'

We were sleeping that night in a double-bedded room. As soon as Mr Dark had secured the door and disposed himself comfortably in his bed, he entered on a detailed narrative of the particulars communicated to him in the tap-room. The substance of what he told me may be related as follows:

The yacht had had a wonderful run all the way to Cape Wrath. On rounding that headland, she had met the wind nearly dead against her, and had beaten every inch of the way to the seaport town, where she had put in to get a supply of provisions, and to wait for a change in the wind.

Mr James Smith had gone ashore to look about him, and to see whether the principal hotel was the sort of house at which he would like to stop for a few days. In the course of his wandering about the town, his attention had been attracted to a decent house, where lodgings were to be let, by the sight of a very pretty girl sitting at work at the parlour-window. He was so struck by her face that he came back twice to look at it, determining, the second time, to try if he could not make acquaintance with her by asking to see the lodgings. He was shown the rooms by the girl's mother, a very respectable woman, whom he discovered to be the wife of the master and part owner of a small coasting vessel, then away at sea. With a little manoeuvring he managed to get into the parlour where the daughter was at work, and to exchange a few words with her. Her voice and manner completed the attraction of her face. Mr James Smith decided, in his headlong way, that he was violently in love with her; and, without hesitating another instant, he took the lodgings on the spot for a month certain.

It is unnecessary to say that his designs on the girl were of the most disgraceful kind, and that he represented himself to the mother and daughter as a single man. Helped by his advantages of money, position, and personal appearance, he had made sure that the ruin of the girl might be effected with very little difficulty; but he soon found that he had undertaken no easy conquest.

The mother's watchfulness never slept, and the daughter's presence of mind never failed her. She admired Mr James Smith's tall figure and splendid whiskers; she showed the most encouraging partiality for his society; she smiled at his compliments, and blushed whenever he looked at her; but, whether it was cunning, or whether it was innocence, she seemed incapable of understanding that his advances towards her were of any other than an honourable kind. At the slightest approach to undue familiarity, she drew back with a kind of contemptuous surprise in her face, which utterly perplexed Mr James Smith. He had not calculated on that sort of resistance, and he could not see his way to overcoming it. The weeks passed; the month for which he had taken the lodgings expired. Time had strengthened the girl's hold on him, till his admiration for her amounted to downright infatuation; and he had not advanced one step yet towards the fulfilment of the vicious purpose with which he had entered the house.

At this time he must have made some fresh attempt on the girl's virtue, which produced a coolness between them; for, instead of taking the lodgings for another term, he removed to his yacht in the harbour, and slept on board for two nights.

The wind was now fair, and the stores were on board; but he gave no orders to the sailing-master to weigh anchor. On the third day, the cause of the coolness, whatever it was, appears to have been removed, and he returned to his lodgings on shore. Some of the more inquisitive among the townspeople observed soon afterwards, when they met him in the street, that he looked rather anxious and uneasy. The conclusion had probably forced itself upon his mind, by this time, that he must decide on pursuing one of two courses. Either he must resolve to make the sacrifice of leaving the girl altogether, or he must commit the villainy of marrying her.

Scoundrel as he was, he hesitated at encountering the risk – perhaps, also, at being guilty of the crime – involved in this last alternative. While he was still in doubt, the father's coasting vessel sailed into the harbour, and the father's presence on the scene decided him at last. How this new influence acted, it was impossible to find out, from the imperfect evidence of persons who were not admitted to the family councils. The fact, however, was certain, that the date of the father's return, and the date of Mr James Smith's first wicked resolution to marry the girl, might both be fixed, as nearly as possible, at one and the same time.

Having once made up his mind to the commission of the crime, he proceeded, with all possible coolness and cunning, to provide against the chances of detection.

Returning on board his yacht, he announced that he had given up his intention of cruising to Sweden, and that he intended to amuse himself by a long fishing tour in Scotland. After this explanation, he ordered the vessel to be laid up in the harbour, gave the sailing-master leave of absence to return to his family at Cowes, and paid off the whole of the crew, from the mate to the cabin-boy. By these means he cleared the scene, at one blow, of the only people in the town who knew of the existence of his unhappy wife. After that, the news of his approaching marriage might be made public without risk of discovery; his own common name being of itself a sufficient protection, in case the event was mentioned in the Scotch newspapers. All his friends, even his wife herself, might read a report of the marriage of Mr James Smith, without having the slightest suspicion of who the bridegroom really was.

A fortnight after the paying off of the crew, he was married to the merchant-captain's daughter. The father of the girl was well known among his fellow-townsmen as a selfish, grasping man, who was too anxious to secure a rich son-in-law to object to any proposals for hastening the marriage. He and his wife, and a few intimate relations had been present at the ceremony; and, after it had been performed, the newly-married couple left the town at once for a honeymoon trip to the Highland Lakes.

Two days later, however, they unexpectedly returned, announcing a complete change in their plans. The bridegroom (thinking, probably, that he would be safer out of England than in it) had been pleasing the bride's fancy by his descriptions of the climate and the scenery of southern parts. The new Mrs James Smith was all curiosity to see Spain and Italy; and, having often proved herself an excellent sailor on board her father's vessel, was anxious to go to the Mediterranean in the easiest way by sea. Her affectionate husband, having now no other object in life than to gratify her wishes, had given up the Highland excursion, and had returned to have his yacht got ready for sea immediately. In this explanation there was nothing to awaken the suspicions of the lady's parents. The mother thought Mr James Smith a model among bridegrooms. The father lent his assistance to man the yacht at the shortest notice, with as smart a crew as could be picked up about the town. Principally through his exertions, the vessel was got ready for sea with extraordinary dispatch. The sails were bent, the provisions were put on board, and Mr James Smith sailed for the Mediterranean with the unfortunate woman who believed herself to be his wife, before Mr Dark and myself set forth to look after him from Darrock Hall.

Such was the true account of my master's infamous conduct in Scotland, as it was related to me. On concluding, Mr Dark hinted that he had something still left to tell me, but declared that he was too sleepy to talk any more that night. As soon as we were awake the next morning, he returned to the subject.

'I didn't finish all I had to say, last night, did I?' he began.

'You unfortunately told me enough, and more than enough, to prove the truth of the statement in the anonymous letter,' I answered.

'Yes,' says Mr Dark, 'but did I tell you who wrote the anonymous letter?'

'You don't mean to say that you have found that out!' says I.

'I think I have,' was the cool answer. 'When I heard about your precious master paying off the regular crew of the yacht, I put the circumstance by in my mind, to be brought out again and sifted a little as soon as the opportunity offered. It offered in about half an hour. Says I to the gauger, who was the principal talker in the room, "How about those men that Mr Smith paid off? Did they all go as soon as they got their money, or did they stop here till they had spent every farthing of it in the public-houses?' The gauger laughs. "No such luck," says he, in the broadest possible Scotch (which I'll translate into English, William, for your benefit). "No such luck; they all went south, to spend their money among finer people than us. All, that is to say, with one exception. It was thought the steward of the yacht had gone along with the rest; when, the very day Mr Smith sailed for the Mediterranean, who should turn up unexpectedly but the steward himself? Where he had been hiding, and why he had been hiding, nobody could tell." "Perhaps he had been imitating his master, and looking out for a wife," says I. "Likely enough," says the gauger; "he gave a very confused account of himself, and he cut all questions short by going away south in a violent hurry." That was enough for me: I let the subject drop. Clear as daylight, isn't it, William? The steward suspected something wrong – the steward waited and watched – the steward wrote that anonymous letter to your mistress. We can find him, if we want him, by inquiring at Cowes; and we can send to the church for legal evidence of the marriage as soon as we are instructed to do so. All that we have got to do now is to go back to your mistress, and see what course she means to take under the circumstances. It's a pretty case, William, so far – an uncommonly pretty case, as it stands at present.'

We returned to Darrock Hall as fast as coaches and post-horses could carry us.

Having from the first believed that the statement in the anonymous letter was true, my mistress received the bad news we brought, calmly and resignedly – so far, at least, as outward appearances went. She astonished and disappointed Mr Dark, by declining to act, in any way, on the information that he had collected for her, and by insisting that the whole affair should still be buried in the profoundest secrecy. For the first time since I had known my travelling companion, he became depressed in spirits on hearing that nothing more was to be done; and although he left the Hall with a handsome present, he left it discontentedly.

'Such a pretty case, William,' says he; quite sorrowfully, as we shook hands. 'Such an uncommonly pretty case! It's a thousand pities to stop it, in this way, before it's half over.'

'You don't know what a proud lady and what a delicate lady my mistress is,' I answered. 'She would die rather than expose her forlorn situation in a public court, for the sake of punishing her husband.'

'Bless your simple heart,' says Mr Dark, 'do you really think, now, that such a case as this can be hushed up?'

'Why not,' I asked, 'if we all keep the secret?'

'That for the secret!' cries Mr Dark, snapping his fingers. 'Your master will let the cat out of the bag, if nobody else does.'

'My master!' I repeated, in amazement.

'Yes, your master,' says Mr Dark. 'I have had some experience in my time, and I say you have not seen the last of him yet. Mark my words, William. Mr James Smith will come back.'

With that prophecy, Mr Dark fretfully treated himself to a last pinch of snuff, and departed in dudgeon on his journey back to his master in London. His last words hung heavily on my mind for days after he had gone. It was some weeks before I got over a habit of starting whenever the bell was rung at the front door.

IV

Our life at the Hall soon returned to its old dreary course. The lawyer in London wrote to my mistress to ask her to come and stay for a little while with his wife. But she declined the invitation, being averse to facing company after what had happened to her. Though she tried hard to keep the real state of her mind concealed from all about her, I, for one, could see plainly enough that she was pining under the bitter injury that had been inflicted on her. What effect continued solitude might have had on her spirits, I tremble to think.

Fortunately for herself, it occurred to her, before long, to send and invite Mr Meeke to resume his musical practising with her at the Hall. She told him – and, as it seemed to me, with perfect truth – that any implied engagement which he had made with Mr James Smith was now cancelled, since the person so named had morally forfeited all his claims as a husband – first, by his desertion of her; and, secondly, by his criminal marriage with another woman. After stating this view of the matter, she left it to Mr Meeke to decide whether the perfectly innocent connection between them should be resumed or not. The little parson, after hesitating and pondering, in his helpless way, ended by agreeing with my mistress, and by coming back once more to the Hall with his fiddle under his arm. This renewal of their old habits might have been imprudent enough, as tending to weaken my mistress's case in the eyes of the world; but, for all that, it was the most sensible course she could take for her own sake. The harmless company of Mr Meeke, and the relief of playing the old tunes again in the old way, saved her, I verily believe, from sinking altogether under the oppression of the shocking situation in which she was now placed.

So, with the assistance of Mr Meeke and his fiddle, my mistress got through the weary time. The winter passed; the spring came; and no fresh tidings reached us of Mr James Smith. It had been a long, hard winter that year, and the spring was backward and rainy. The first really fine day we had was the day that fell on the fourteenth of March.

I am particular in mentioning this date, merely because it is fixed for ever in my memory. As long as there is life in me, I shall remember that fourteenth of March, and the smallest circumstances connected with it.

The day began ill, with what superstitious people would think a bad omen. My mistress remained late in her room in the morning, amusing herself by looking over her clothes, and by setting to rights some drawers in her cabinet which she had not opened for some time past. Just before luncheon, we were startled by hearing the drawing-room bell rung violently. I ran up to see what was the matter, and the quadroon, Josephine, who had heard the bell in another part of the house, hastened to answer it also. She got into the drawing-room first, and I followed close on her heels. My mistress was standing alone on the hearth-rug, with an appearance of great discomposure in her face and manner.

'I have been robbed!' she said, vehemently. 'I don't know when or how. But I miss a pair of bracelets, three rings, and a quantity of old-fashioned lace pocket handkerchiefs.'

'If you have any suspicions, ma'am,' said Josephine, in a sharp, sudden way, 'say who they point at. My boxes, for one, are quite at your disposal.'

'Who asked you about your boxes?' said my mistress, angrily. 'Be a little less ready with your answer, if you please, the next time I speak.'

She then turned to me, and began explaining the circumstances under which she had discovered her loss. I suggested that the missing things should be well searched for first; and then, if nothing came of that, that I should go for the constable, and place the matter under his direction.

My mistress agreed to this plan, and the search was undertaken immediately. It lasted till dinner-time, and led to no results. I then proposed going for the constable. But my mistress said it was too late to do anything that day, and told me to wait at table as usual, and to go on my errand the first thing the next morning. Mr Meeke was coming with some new music in the evening; and I suspect she was not willing to be disturbed at her favourite occupation by the arrival of the constable.

When dinner was over, the parson came; and the concert went on as usual through the evening. At ten o'clock I took up the tray, with the wine and soda-water and biscuits. Just as I was opening one of the bottles of soda-water, there was a sound of wheels on the drive outside, and a ring at the bell.

I had unfastened the wires of the cork, and could not put the bottle down to run at once to the door. One of the female servants answered it. I heard a sort of half scream – then the sound of a footstep that was familiar to me.

My mistress turned round from the piano, and looked me hard in the face.

'William!' she said, 'do you know that step?'

Before I could answer, the door was pushed open, and Mr James Smith walked into the room.

He had his hat on. His long hair flowed down under it over the collar of his coat: his bright black eyes, after resting an instant on my mistress, turned to Mr Meeke. His heavy eyebrows met together, and one of his hands went up to one of his bushy black whiskers, and pulled at it angrily.

'You here again!' he said, advancing a few steps toward the little parson, who sat trembling all over, with his fiddle hugged up in his arms, as if it had been a child.

Seeing her villainous husband advance, my mistress moved too, so as to face him. He turned round on her at the first step she took, as quick as lightning.

'You shameless woman!' he said. 'Can you look me in the face in the presence of that man?' He pointed, as he spoke, to Mr Meeke.

My mistress never shrank when he turned upon her. Not a sign of fear was in her face when they confronted each other. Not the faintest flush of anger came into her cheeks when he spoke. The sense of the insult and injury that he had inflicted on her, and the consciousness of knowing his guilty secret, gave her all her self-possession at that trying moment.

'I ask you again,' he repeated, finding that she did not answer him. 'How dare you look me in the face in the presence of that man?'

She raised her steady eyes to his hat, which he still kept on his head.

'Who has taught you to come into a room and speak to a lady with your hat on?' she asked, in quiet, contemptuous tones. 'Is that a habit which is sanctioned by *your new wife?*'

My eyes were on him as she said those last words. His complexion, naturally dark and swarthy, changed instantly to a livid yellow white; his hand caught at the chair nearest to him; and he dropped into it heavily.

'I don't understand you,' he said, after a moment of silence, looking about the room unsteadily while he spoke.

'You do,' said my mistress. 'Your tongue lies, but your face speaks the truth.'

He called back his courage and audacity by a desperate effort, and started up from the chair again with an oath.

The instant before this happened, I thought I heard the sound of a rustling dress in the passage outside, as if one of the women servants was stealing up to listen outside the door. I should have gone at once to see whether this was the case or not, but my master stopped me just after he had risen from the chair.

'Get the bed made in the Red Room, and light a fire there directly,' he said, with his fiercest look and in his roughest tones. 'When I ring the bell, bring me a kettle of boiling water and a bottle of brandy. As for you,' he continued, turning towards Mr Meeke, who still sat pale and speechless, with his fiddle hugged up in his arms, 'leave the house, or you won't find your cloth any protection to you.'

At this insult the blood flew into my mistress's face. Before she could say anything, Mr James Smith raised his voice loud enough to drown hers.

'I won't hear another word from you,' he cried out, brutally. 'You have been talking like a mad woman, and you look like a mad woman. You are out of your senses. As sure as you live, I'll have you examined by the doctors to-morrow. Why the devil do you stand there, you scoundrel?' he roared, wheeling round on his heel to me. 'Why don't you obey my orders?'

I looked at my mistress. If she had directed me to knock Mr James Smith down, big as he was, I think at that moment I could have done it.

'Do as he tells you, William,' she said, squeezing one of her hands firmly over her bosom, as if she was trying to keep down the rising indignation in that way. 'This is the last order of his giving that I shall ask you to obey.'

'Do you threaten me, you mad— ?'

He finished the question by a word I shall not repeat.

'I tell you,' she answered, in clear, ringing, resolute tones, 'that you have outraged me past all forgiveness, and all endurance, and that you shall never insult me again as you have insulted me to-night.'

After saying those words, she fixed one steady look on him, then turned away, and walked slowly to the door.

A minute previously, Mr Meeke had summoned courage enough to get up and leave the room quietly. I noticed him walking demurely away, close to the wall, with his fiddle held under one tail of his long frock coat, as if he was afraid that the savage passions of Mr James Smith might be wreaked on that unoffending instrument. He got to the door before my mistress. As he softly pulled it open, I saw him start, and the rustling of the gown caught my ear again from outside.

My mistress followed him into the passage, turning, however, in the opposite direction to that taken by the little parson, in order to reach the staircase that led to her own room. I went out next, leaving Mr James Smith alone.

I overtook Mr Meeke in the hall, and opened the door for him.

'I beg your pardon, sir,' I said, 'but did you come upon anybody listening outside the music-room when you left it just now?'

'Yes, William,' said Mr Meeke, in a faint voice. 'I think it was Josephine. But I was so dreadfully agitated that I can't be quite certain about it.'

Had she surprised our secret? That was the question I asked myself, as I went away to light the fire in the Red Room. Calling to mind the exact time at which I had first detected the rustling outside the door, I came to the conclusion that she had only heard the last part of the quarrel between my mistress and her rascal of a husband. Those bold words about the 'new wife' had been assuredly spoken before I heard Josephine stealing up to the door.

As soon as the fire was alight and the bed made, I went back to the music-room to announce that my orders had been obeyed. Mr James Smith was walking up and down in a perturbed way, still keeping his hat on. He followed me to the Red Room without saying a word.

Ten minutes later, he rang for the kettle and the bottle of brandy. When I took them in, I found him unpacking a small carpet-bag, which was the only luggage he had brought with him. He still kept silence, and did not appear to take any notice of me. I left him immediately, without our having so much as exchanged a single word.

So far as I could tell, the night passed quietly.

The next morning I heard that my mistress was suffering so severely from a nervous attack that she was unable to rise from her bed. It was no surprise to me to be told that, knowing, as I did, what she had gone through the night before.

About nine o'clock I went with the hot water to the Red Room. After knocking twice, I tried the door, and, finding it not locked, went in with the jug in my hand.

I looked at the bed; I looked all round the room. Not a sign of Mr James Smith was to be seen anywhere.

Judging by appearances, the bed had certainly been occupied. Thrown across the counterpane lay the night-gown he had worn. I took it up, and saw some spots on it. I looked at them a little closer. They were spots of blood.

V

The first amazement and alarm produced by this discovery deprived me of my presence of mind. Without stopping to think what I ought to do first, I ran back to the servants' hall, calling out that something had happened to my master.

All the household hurried directly into the Red Room, Josephine among the rest. I was first brought to my senses, as it were, by observing the strange expression of her countenance when she saw the bed-gown and the empty room. All the other servants were bewildered and frightened. She alone, after giving a little start, recovered herself directly. A look of devilish satisfaction broke out on her face; and she left the room quickly and quietly, without exchanging a word with any of us. I saw this, and it aroused my suspicions.

There is no need to mention what they were; for, as events soon showed, they were entirely wide of the mark.

Having come to myself a little, I sent them all out of the room, except the coachman. We two then examined the place.

The Red Room was usually occupied by visitors. It was on the ground floor, and looked out into the garden. We found the window-shutters, which I had barred overnight, open, but the window itself was down. The fire had been out long enough for the grate to be quite cold. Half the bottle of brandy had been drunk. The carpet-bag was gone. There were no marks of violence or struggling anywhere about the bed or the room. We examined every corner carefully, but made no other discoveries than these.

When I returned to the servants' hall, bad news of my mistress was awaiting me there. The unusual noise and confusion in the house had reached her ears, and she had been told what had happened, without sufficient caution being exercised in preparing her to hear it. In her weak, nervous state, the shock of the intelligence had quite prostrated her. She had fallen into a swoon, and had been brought back to her senses with the greatest difficulty. As to giving me or anybody else directions what to do, under the embarrassing circumstances which had now occurred, she was totally incapable of the effort.

I waited till the middle of the day, in the hope that she might get strong enough to give her orders; but no message came from her. At last I resolved to send and ask her what she thought it best to do. Josephine was the proper person to go on this errand; but when I asked for Josephine, she was nowhere to be found. The housemaid, who had searched for her ineffectually, brought word that her bonnet and shawl were not hanging in their usual places. The parlour-maid, who had been in attendance in my mistress's room, came down while we were all aghast at this new disappearance. She could only tell us that Josephine had begged her to do lady's-maid's duty that morning, as she was not well. Not well! And the first result of her illness appeared to be that she had left the house!

I cautioned the servants on no account to mention this circumstance to my mistress, and then went upstairs myself to knock at her door. My object was to ask if I might count on her approval if I wrote in her name to the lawyer in London, and if I afterwards went and gave information of what had occurred to the nearest justice of the peace. I might have sent to make this inquiry through one of the female servants; but by this time, though not naturally suspicious, I had got to distrust everybody in the house, whether they deserved it or not.

So I asked the question myself, standing outside the door. My mistress thanked me in a faint voice, and begged me to do what I had proposed immediately.

I went into my own bedroom and wrote to the lawyer, merely telling him that Mr James Smith had appeared unexpectedly at the Hall, and that events had occurred in consequence which required his immediate presence. I made the letter up like a parcel, and sent the coachman with it to catch the mail on its way through to London.

The next thing was to go to the justice of the peace. The nearest lived about five miles off, and was well acquainted with my mistress. He was an old bachelor, and he kept house with his brother, who was a widower. The two were much respected and beloved in the county, being kind, unaffected gentlemen who did a great deal of good among the poor. The justice was Mr Robert Nicholson, and his brother, the widower, was Mr Philip.

I had got my hat on, and was asking the groom which horse I had better take, when an open carriage drove up to the house. It contained Mr Philip Nicholson and two persons in plain clothes, not exactly servants, and not exactly gentlemen, as far as I could judge. Mr Philip looked at me, when I touched my hat to him, in a very grave, downcast way, and asked for my mistress. I told him she was ill in bed. He shook his head at hearing that, and said he wished to speak to me in private. I showed him into the library. One of the men in plain clothes followed us, and sat in the hall. The other waited with the carriage.

'I was just going out, sir,' I said, as I set a chair for him, 'to speak to Mr Robert Nicholson about a very extraordinary circumstance—'

'I know what you refer to,' said Mr Philip, cutting me short rather abruptly; 'and I must beg, for reasons which will presently appear, that you will make no statement of any sort to me until you have first heard what I have to say. I am here on a very serious and a very shocking errand, which deeply concerns your mistress and you.'

His face suggested something worse than his words expressed. My heart began to beat fast, and I felt that I was turning pale.

'Your master, Mr James Smith,' he went on, 'came here unexpectedly, yesterday evening, and slept in this house last night. Before he retired to rest, he and your mistress had high words together, which ended, I am sorry to hear, in a threat of a serious nature addressed by Mrs James Smith to her husband. They slept in separate rooms. This morning you went into your master's room and saw no sign of him there. You only found his night-gown on the bed, spotted with blood.'

'Yes, sir,' I said, in as steady a voice as I could command. 'Quite true.'

'I am not examining you,' said Mr Philip. 'I am only making a certain statement, the truth of which you can admit or deny before my brother.'

'Before your brother, sir!' I repeated. 'Am I suspected of anything wrong?'

'There is a suspicion that Mr James Smith has been murdered,' was the answer I received to that question.

My flesh began to creep all over from head to foot.

'I am shocked, I am horrified to say,' Mr Philip went on, 'that the suspicion affects your mistress, in the first place, and you in the second.'

I shall not attempt to describe what I felt when he said that. No words of mine, no words of anybody's could give an idea of it. What other men would have done in my situation, I don't know. I stood before Mr Philip, staring straight at him, without speaking, without moving, almost without breathing. If he, or any other man, had struck me at that moment, I do not believe I should have felt the blow.

'Both my brother and myself,' said Mr Philip, 'have such unfeigned respect for your mistress, such sympathy for her under these frightful circumstances, and such an implicit belief in her capability of proving her innocence, that we are desirous of sparing her in this dreadful emergency as much as possible. For those reasons, I have undertaken to come here with the persons appointed to execute my brother's warrant—'

'Warrant, sir!' I said, getting command of my voice as he pronounced that word. 'A warrant against my mistress!'

'Against her and against you,' said Mr Philip. 'The suspicious circumstances have been sworn to by a competent witness, who has declared on oath that your mistress is guilty, and that you are an accomplice.'

'What witness, sir?'

'Your mistress's quadroon maid, who came to my brother this morning, and who has made her deposition in due form.'

'And who is as false as hell,' I cried out passionately, 'in every word she says against my mistress and against me.'

'I hope – no, I will go further, and say, I believe she is false,' said Mr Philip. 'But her perjury must be proved, and the necessary examination must take place. My carriage is going back to my brother's, and you will go in it, in charge of one of my men, who has the warrant to take you into custody. I shall remain here with the man who is waiting in the hall; and before any steps are taken to execute the other warrant, I shall send for the doctor to ascertain when your mistress can be removed.'

'Oh, my poor mistress!' I said, 'this will be the death of her, sir.'

'I will take care that the shock shall strike her as tenderly as possible,' said Mr Philip. 'I am here for that express purpose. She has my deepest sympathy and respect, and shall have every help and alleviation that I can afford her.'

The hearing him say that, and the seeing how sincerely he meant what he said, was the first gleam of comfort in the dreadful affliction that had befallen us. I felt this; I felt a burning anger against the wretch who had done her best to ruin my mistress's fair name and mine; but in every other respect, I was like a man who had been stunned, and whose faculties had not perfectly recovered from the shock. Mr Philip was obliged to remind me that time was of importance, and that I had better give myself up immediately, on the merciful terms which his kindness offered to me. I acknowledged that, and wished him good morning. But a mist seemed to come over my eyes as I turned round to go away; a mist that prevented me from finding my way to the door. Mr Philip opened it for me, and said a friendly word or two, which I could hardly hear. The man waiting outside took me to his companion in the carriage at the door, and I was driven away – a prisoner for the first time in my life.

On our way to the Justice's, what little thinking faculty I had left in me, was all occupied in the attempt to trace a motive for the inconceivable treachery and falsehood of which Josephine had been guilty.

Her words, her looks, and her manner, on that unfortunate day when my mistress so far forgot herself as to strike her, came back dimly to my memory, and led to the inference that part of the motive, at least, of which I was in search, might be referred to what had happened on that occasion. But was this the only reason for her devilish vengeance against my mistress? And, even if it were so, what fancied injuries had I done her? Why should I be included in the false accusation? In the dazed state of my faculties, at that time, I was quite incapable of seeking the answer to these questions. My mind was clouded all over, and I gave up the attempt to clear it in despair.

I was brought before Mr Robert Nicholson that day, and the fiend of a quadroon was examined in my presence. The first sight of her face – with its wicked self-possession, with its smooth, leering triumph – so sickened me that I turned my head away, and never looked at her a second time throughout the proceedings. The answers she gave amounted to a mere repetition of the deposition to which she had already sworn. I listened to her with the most breathless attention, and was thunder-struck at the inconceivable artfulness with which she had mixed up truth and falsehood in her charge against my mistress and me.

This was, in substance, what she now stated in my presence:

After describing the manner of Mr James Smith's arrival at the Hall, the witness, Josephine Durand, confessed that she had been led to listen at the music-room door, by hearing angry voices inside; and she then described, truly enough, the latter part of the altercation between husband and wife. Fearing, after this, that something serious might happen, she had kept watch in her room, which was on the same floor as her mistress's. She had heard her mistress's door open softly, between one and two in the morning – had followed her mistress, who carried a small lamp, along the passage and down the stairs into the hall – had hidden herself in the porter's chair – had seen her mistress take a dagger in a green sheath from a collection of Eastern curiosities kept in the hall – had followed her again, and seen her softly enter the Red Room – had heard the heavy breathing of Mr James Smith, which gave token that he was asleep – had slipped into an empty room, next door to the Red Room, and had waited there about a quarter of an hour, when her mistress came out again with the dagger in her hand – had followed her mistress again into the hall, where she had put the dagger back into its place – had seen her mistress turn into a side passage that led to my room – had heard her knock at my door, and heard me answer and open it – had hidden again in the porter's chair – had, after a while, seen me and my mistress pass together into the passage that led to the Red Room – had watched us both into the Red Room – and had then, through fear of being discovered and murdered herself, if she risked detection any longer, stolen back to her own room for the rest of the night.

After deposing, on oath, to the truth of these atrocious falsehoods, and declaring, in conclusion, that Mr James Smith had been murdered by my mistress, and that I was an accomplice, the quadroon had further asserted, in order to show a motive for the crime, that Mr Meeke was my mistress's lover, that he had been forbidden the house by her husband, and that he was found in the house, and alone with her, on the evening of Mr James Smith's return. Here again, there were some grains of truth cunningly mixed up with a revolting lie, and they had their effect in giving to the falsehood a look of probability.

I was cautioned in the usual manner, and asked if I had anything to say.

I replied that I was innocent, but that I would wait for legal assistance before I defended myself. The Justice remanded me; and the examination was over. Three days later, my unhappy mistress was subjected to the same trial. I was not allowed to communicate with her. All I knew was that the lawyer had arrived from London to help her. Towards the evening, he was admitted to see me. He shook his head sorrowfully when I asked after my mistress.

'I am afraid,' he said, 'that she has sunk under the horror of the situation in which that vile woman has placed her. Weakened by her previous agitation, she seems to have given way under this last shock, tenderly and carefully as Mr Philip Nicholson broke the bad news to her. All her feelings appeared to be strangely blunted at the examination today. She answered the questions put to her quite correctly, but, at the same time, quite mechanically, with no change in her complexion, or in her tone of voice, or in her manner from beginning to end. It is a sad thing, William, when women cannot get their natural vent of weeping, and your mistress has not shed a tear since she left Darrock Hall.'

'But surely, sir,' I said, 'if my examination has not proved Josephine's perjury, my mistress's examination must have exposed it?'

'Nothing will expose it,' answered the lawyer, 'but producing Mr James Smith, or, at least, legally proving that he is alive. Morally speaking, I have no doubt that the Justice before whom you have been examined is as firmly convinced as we can be, that the quadroon has perjured herself. Morally speaking, he believes that those threats which your mistress unfortunately used, referred (as she said they did, to-day) to her intention of leaving the Hall early in the morning, with you for her attendant, and coming to me, if she had been well enough to travel, to seek effectual legal protection from her husband for the future. Mr Nicholson believes that; and I, who know more of the circumstances than he does, believe also that Mr James Smith stole away from Darrock Hall in the night under fear of being indicted for bigamy. But if I can't find him, if I can't prove him to be alive, if I can't account for those spots of blood on the night gown, the accidental circumstances of the case remain unexplained – your mistress's rash language, the bad terms on which she has lived with her husband, and her unlucky disregard of appearances in keeping up her intercourse with Mr Meeke, all tell dead against us – and the Justice has no alternative, in a legal point of view, but to remand you both, as he has now done, for the production of further evidence.'

'But how, then, in heaven's name, is our innocence to be proved, sir?' I asked.

'In the first place,' said the lawyer, 'by finding Mr James Smith; and, in the second place, by persuading him, when he is found, to come forward and declare himself.'

'Do you really believe, sir,' said I, 'that he would hesitate to do that, when he knows the horrible charge to which his disappearance has exposed his wife? He is a heartless villain, I know; but surely—'

'I don't suppose,' said the lawyer, cutting me short, 'that he is quite scoundrel enough to decline coming forward, supposing he ran no risk by doing so. But remember that he has placed himself in a position to be tried for bigamy, and that he believes your mistress will put the law in force against him.'

I had forgotten that circumstance. My heart sank within me when it was recalled to my memory, and I could say nothing more.

'It is a very serious thing,' the lawyer went on; 'it is a downright offence against the law of the land to make any private offer of a compromise to this man. Knowing what we know, our duty as good citizens is to give such information as may bring him to trial. I tell you plainly that, if I did not stand towards your mistress in the position of a relation, as well as a legal adviser, I should think twice about running the risk – the very serious risk – on which I am now about to venture for her sake. As it is, I have taken the right measures to assure Mr James Smith that he will not be treated according to his deserts. When he knows what the circumstances are, he will trust us – supposing always that we can find him. The search about this neighbourhood has been quite useless. I have sent private instructions by today's post to Mr Dark in London, and with them a carefully-worded form of advertisement for the public newspapers. You may rest assured that every human means of tracing him will be tried forthwith. In the meantime, I have an important question to put to you about Josephine. She may know more than we think she does; she may have surprised the secret of the second marriage, and may be keeping it in reserve to use against us. If this should turn out to be the case, I shall want some other chance against her besides the chance of indicting her for perjury. As to her motive now for making this horrible accusation, what can you tell me about that, William?'

'Her motive against me, sir?'

'No, no, not against you. I can see plainly enough that she accuses you because it is necessary to do so to add to the probability of her story – which, of course, assumes that you helped your mistress to dispose of the dead body. You are coolly sacrificed to some devilish vengeance against her mistress. Let us get at that first. Has there ever been a quarrel between them?'

I told him of the quarrel, and of how Josephine had looked and talked when she showed me her cheek.

'Yes,' he said, 'that is a strong motive for revenge with a naturally pitiless, vindictive woman. But is that all? Had your mistress any hold over her? Is there any self-interest mixed up along with this motive of vengeance? Think a little, William. Has anything ever happened in the house to compromise this woman, or to make her fancy herself compromised?'

The remembrance of my mistress's lost trinkets and handkerchiefs, which later and greater troubles had put out of my mind, flashed back into my memory while he spoke. I told him immediately of the alarm in the house when the loss was discovered.

'Did your mistress suspect Josephine and question her?' he asked, eagerly.

'No, sir,' I replied. 'Before she could say a word, Josephine impudently asked who she suspected, and boldly offered her own boxes to be searched.'

The lawyer's face turned red as scarlet. He jumped out of his chair, and hit me such a smack on the shoulder, that I thought he had gone mad.

'By Jupiter!' he cried out, 'we have got the whip hand of that she-devil at last.'

I looked at him in astonishment.

'Why, man alive,' he said, 'don't you see how it is? Josephine's the thief! I am as sure of it as that you and I are talking together. This vile accusation against your mistress answers another purpose besides the vindictive one – it is the very best screen that the wretch could possibly set up to hide herself from detection. It has stopped your mistress and you from moving in the matter; it exhibits her in the false character of an honest witness against a couple of criminals; it gives her time to dispose of the goods, or to hide them, or to do anything she likes with them. Stop! let me be quite sure that I know what the lost things are. A pair of bracelets, three rings, and a lot of lace pocket-handkerchiefs – is that what you said?'

'Yes, sir.'

'Your mistress will describe them particularly, and I will take the right steps the first thing to-morrow morning. Good-evening, William, and keep up your spirits. It shan't be my fault if you don't soon see the quadroon in the right place for her – at the prisoner's bar.'

With that farewell he went out.

The days passed, and I did not see him again until the period of my remand had expired. On this occasion, when I once more appeared before the Justice, my mistress appeared with me. The first sight of her absolutely startled me – she was so sadly altered. Her face looked so pinched and thin that it was like the face of an old woman. The dull, vacant resignation of her expression was something shocking to see. It changed a little when her eyes first turned heavily towards me; and she whispered, with a faint smile, 'I am sorry for *you*, William. I am very, very sorry for *you*.' But as soon as she had said those words, the blank look returned, and she sat with her head drooping forward, quiet and inattentive and hopeless – so changed a being that her oldest friends would hardly have known her.

Our examination was a mere formality. There was no additional evidence, either for or against us, and we were remanded again for another week.

I asked the lawyer, privately, if any chance had offered itself of tracing Mr James Smith. He looked mysterious, and only said in answer, 'Hope for the best.' I inquired, next, if any progress had been made toward fixing the guilt of the robbery on Josephine.

'I never boast,' he replied. 'But, cunning as she is, I should not be surprised if Mr Dark and I, together, turned out to be more than a match for her.'

Mr Dark! There was something in the mere mention of his name that gave me confidence in the future. If I could only have got my poor mistress's sad dazed face out of my mind, I should not have had much depression of spirits to complain of during the interval of time that elapsed between the second examination and the third.

VI

On the third appearance of my mistress and myself before the Justice, I noticed some faces in the room which I had not seen there before. Greatly to my astonishment – for the previous examinations had been conducted as privately as possible – I remarked the presence of two of the servants from the Hall, and of three or four of the tenants on the Darrock estate, who lived nearest to the house. They all sat together on one side of the justice-room. Opposite to them, and close at the side of a door, stood my old acquaintance, Mr Dark, with his big snuff-box, his jolly face, and his winking eye. He nodded to me, when I looked at him, as jauntily as if we were meeting at a party of pleasure. The quadroon woman, who had been summoned to the examination, had a chair placed opposite to the witness-box, and in a line with the seat occupied by my poor mistress, whose looks, as I was grieved to see, were not altered for the better. The lawyer from London was with her, and I stood behind her chair.

We were all quietly disposed in the room in this way, when the Justice, Mr Robert Nicholson, came in with his brother. It might have been only fancy, but I thought I could see in both their faces that something remarkable had happened since we had met at the last examination.

The deposition of Josephine Durand was read over by the clerk, and she was asked if she had anything to add to it. She replied in the negative. The Justice then appealed to my mistress's relation, the lawyer, to know if he could produce any evidence relating to the charge against his clients.

'I have evidence,' answered the lawyer, getting briskly on his legs, 'which, I believe, sir, will justify me in asking for their discharge.'

'Where are your witnesses?' inquired the Justice, looking hard at Josephine while he spoke.

'One of them is in waiting, your worship,' said Mr Dark, opening the door near which he was standing.

He went out of the room, remained away about a minute, and returned with his witness at his heels.

My heart gave a bound as if it would jump out of my body. There, with his long hair cut short, and his bushy whiskers shaved off, – there, in his own proper person, safe and sound as ever, was Mr James Smith!

The quadroon's iron nature resisted the shock of his unexpected presence on the scene with a steadiness that was nothing short of marvellous. Her thin lips closed together convulsively, and there was a slight movement in the muscles of her throat. But not a word, not a sign, betrayed her. Even the yellow tinge of her complexion remained unchanged.

'It is not necessary, sir, that I should waste time and words in referring to the wicked and preposterous charge against my clients,' said the lawyer, address-ing Mr Robert Nicholson. 'The one sufficient justification for discharging them immediately is before you at this moment, in the person of that gentleman. There, sir, stands the murdered Mr James Smith, of Darrock Hall, alive and well, to answer for himself.'

'That is not the man!' cried Josephine, her shrill voice just as high, clear, and steady as ever. 'I denounce that man as an impostor! Of my own knowledge I deny that he is Mr James Smith!'

'No doubt you do,' said the lawyer; 'but we will prove his identity for all that.'

The first witness called was Mr Philip Nicholson. He could swear that he had seen Mr James Smith, and spoken to him, at least a dozen times. The person now before him was Mr James Smith, altered as to personal appearance, by having his hair cut short, and his whiskers shaved off, but still unmistakably the man he assumed to be.

'Conspiracy!' interrupted the quadroon, hissing the word out viciously between her teeth.

'If you are not silent,' said Mr Robert Nicholson, 'you will be removed from the room. It will sooner meet the ends of justice,' he went on, addressing the lawyer, 'if you prove the question of identity by witnesses who have been in habits of daily communication with Mr James Smith.'

Upon this, one of the servants from the Hall was placed in the box.

The alteration in his master's appearance evidently puzzled the man. Besides the perplexing change already adverted to, there was also a change in Mr James Smith's expression and manner. Rascal as he was, I must do him the justice to say that he looked startled and ashamed when he first caught sight of his unfortunate wife. The servant, who was used to be eyed tyrannically by him, and ordered about roughly, seeing him now for the first time abashed and silent, stammered and hesitated on being asked to swear to his identity.

'I can hardly say for certain, sir,' said the man, addressing the Justice in a bewildered manner. 'He is like my master, and yet he isn't. If he wore whiskers and had his hair long, and if he was, saving your presence, sir, a little more rough and ready in his way, I could swear to him anywhere with a safe conscience.'

Fortunately for us, at this moment Mr James Smith's feeling of uneasiness at the situation in which he was placed, changed to a feeling of irritation at being coolly surveyed and then stupidly doubted in the matter of his identity by one of his own servants.

'Can't you say in plain words, you idiot, whether you know me, or whether you don't?' he called out, angrily.

'That's his voice!' cried the servant, starting in the box. 'Whiskers or no whiskers, that's him!'

'If there is any difficulty, your worship, about the gentleman's hair,' said Mr Dark, coming forward with a grin, 'here's a small parcel which, I may make so bold as to say, will remove it.' Saying that, he opened the parcel, took some locks of hair out of it, and held them up close to Mr James Smith's head. 'A pretty good match, your worship,' continued Mr Dark. 'I have no doubt the gentleman's head feels cooler now it's off. We can't put the whiskers on, I'm afraid, but they match the hair; and there they are in the paper (if one may say such a thing of whiskers) to speak for themselves.'

'Lies! lies! lies!' screamed Josephine, losing her wicked self-control at this stage of the proceedings.

The Justice made a sign to two of the constables present, as she burst out with those exclamations, and the men removed her to an adjoining room.

The second servant from the Hall was then put in the box, and was followed by one of the tenants. After what they had heard and seen, neither of these men had any hesitation in swearing positively to their master's identity.

'It is quite unnecessary,' said the Justice, as soon as the box was empty again, 'to examine any more witnesses as to the question of identity. All the legal formalities are accomplished, and the charge against the prisoners falls to the ground. I have great pleasure in ordering the immediate discharge of both the accused persons, and in declaring from this place that they leave the court without the slightest stain on their characters.'

He bowed low to my mistress as he said that, paused a moment, and then looked inquiringly at Mr James Smith.

'I have hitherto abstained from making any remark unconnected with the immediate matter in hand,' he went on. 'But now that my duty is done, I cannot leave this chair without expressing my strong sense of disapprobation of the conduct of Mr James Smith – conduct which, whatever may be the motives that occasioned it, has given a false colour of probability to a most horrible charge against a lady of unspotted reputation, and against a person in a lower rank of life, whose good character ought not to have been imperilled, even for a moment. Mr Smith may or may not choose to explain his mysterious disappearance from Darrock Hall, and the equally unaccountable change which he has chosen to make in his personal appearance. There is no legal charge against him; but, speaking morally, I should be unworthy of the place I hold if I hesitated to declare my present conviction that his conduct has been deceitful, inconsiderate, and unfeeling, in the highest degree.'

To this sharp reprimand, Mr James Smith (evidently tutored beforehand as to what he was to say) replied that, in attending before the Justice, he wished to perform a plain duty and to keep himself strictly within the letter of the law. He apprehended that the only legal obligation laid on him was to attend in that court to declare himself, and to enable competent witnesses to prove his identity. This duty accomplished, he had merely to add that he preferred submitting to a reprimand from the Bench to entering into explanations which would involve the disclosure of domestic circumstances of a very unhappy nature. After that brief reply, he had nothing further to say; and he would respectfully request the Justice's permission to withdraw.

The permission was accorded. As he crossed the room, he stopped near his wife, and said confusedly, in a very low tone—

'I have done you many injuries, but I never intended this. I am sorry for it. Have you anything to say to me before I go?'

My mistress shuddered and hid her face. He waited a moment, and, finding that she did not answer him, bowed his head politely, and went out. I did not know it then, but I had seen him for the last time.

After he had gone, the lawyer, addressing Mr Robert Nicholson, said that he had an application to make, in reference to the woman Josephine Durand.

At the mention of that name, my mistress hurriedly whispered a few words into her relation's ear. He looked towards Mr Philip Nicholson, who immediately advanced, offered his arm to my mistress, and led her out. I was about to follow, when Mr Dark stopped me, and begged that I would wait a few minutes longer, in order to give myself the pleasure of seeing 'the end of the case.'

In the meantime, the Justice had pronounced the necessary order to have the quadroon brought back. She came in, as bold and confident as ever. Mr Robert Nicholson looked away from her in disgust, and said to the lawyer—

'Your application is to have her committed for perjury, of course?'

'For perjury?' said Josephine, with her wicked smile. 'Very good! I shall explain some little matters that I have not explained before. You think I am quite at your mercy now? Bah! I shall make myself a thorn in your sides, yet.'

'She has got scent of the second marriage,' whispered Mr Dark to me.

There could be no doubt of it. She had evidently been listening at the door, on the night when my master came back, longer than I had supposed. She must have heard those words about 'the new wife' – she might even have seen the effect of them on Mr James Smith.

'We do not, at present, propose to charge Josephine Durand with perjury,' said the lawyer, 'but with another offence, for which it is important to try her immediately, in order to effect the restoration of property that has been stolen. I charge her with stealing from her mistress, while in her service at Darrock Hall, a pair of bracelets, three rings, and a dozen and a half of lace pocket-handkerchiefs. The articles in question were taken this morning from between the mattresses of her bed; and a letter was found in the same place, which clearly proves that she had represented the property as belonging to herself, and that she had tried to dispose of it to a purchaser in London.' While he was speaking, Mr Dark produced the jewellery, the handkerchiefs, and the letter, and laid them before the Justice.

Even Josephine's extraordinary powers of self-control now gave way at last. At the first words of the unexpected charge against her, she struck her hands together violently, gnashed her sharp white teeth, and burst out with a torrent of fierce sounding words in some foreign language, the meaning of which I did not understand then, and cannot explain now.

'I think that's check-mate for Marmzelle,' whispered Mr Dark, with his invariable wink. 'Suppose you go back to the Hall, now, William, and draw a jug of that very remarkable old ale of yours? I'll be after you in five minutes, as soon as the charge is made out.'

I could hardly realise it, when I found myself walking back to Darrock a free man again.

In a quarter of an hour's time Mr Dark joined me, and drank to my health, happiness, and prosperity, in three separate tumblers. After performing this ceremony, he wagged his head and chuckled with an appearance of such excessive enjoyment that I could not avoid remarking on his high spirits.

'It's the Case, William; it's the beautiful neatness of the Case that quite intoxicates me. Oh, Lord, what a happiness it is to be concerned in such a job as this!' cries Mr Dark, slapping his stumpy hands on his fat knees in a sort of ecstasy.

I had a very different opinion of the case, for my own part, but I did not venture on expressing it. I was too anxious to know how Mr James Smith had been discovered and produced at the examination, to enter into any arguments. Mr Dark guessed what was passing in my mind, and telling me to sit down and make myself comfortable, volunteered of his own accord to inform me of all that I wanted to know.

'When I got my instructions and my statement of particulars,' he began, 'I was not at all surprised to hear that Mr James Smith had come back (I prophesied that, if you remember, William, the last time we met). But I was a good deal astonished, nevertheless, at the turn things had taken; and I can't say I felt very hopeful about finding our man. However, I followed my master's directions, and put the advertisement in the papers. It addressed Mr James Smith by name; but it was very carefully worded as to what was wanted of him. Two days after it appeared, a letter came to our office in a woman's handwriting. It was my business to open the letters, and I opened that. The writer was short and mysterious; she requested that somebody would call from our office, at a certain address, between the hours of two and four that afternoon, in reference to the advertisement which we had inserted in the newspapers. Of course I was the somebody who went. I kept myself from building up hopes by the way, knowing what a lot of Mr James Smiths there were in London. On getting to the house, I was shown into the drawing-room; and there, dressed in a wrapper and lying on a sofa, was an uncommonly pretty woman, who looked as if she was just recovering from an illness. She had a newspaper by her side, and came to the point at once: "My husband's name is James Smith," she says, "and I have my reasons for wanting to know if he is the person you are in search of." I described our man as Mr James Smith of Darrock Hall, Cumberland. "I know no such person," says she—'

'What! was it not the second wife, after all?' I broke out.

'Wait a bit,' says Mr Dark. 'I mentioned the name of the yacht next, and she started up on the sofa as if she had been shot. "I think you were married in Scotland, ma'am?" says I. She turns as pale as ashes, and drops back on the sofa, and says, faintly, "It *is* my husband. Oh, sir, what has happened? What do you want with him? Is he in debt?" I took a minute to think, and then made up my mind to tell her everything – feeling that she would keep her husband (as she called him) out of the way, if I frightened her by any mysteries. A nice job I had, William, as you may suppose, when she knew about the bigamy business. What with screaming, fainting, crying, and blowing me up (as if *I* was to blame!) she kept me by that sofa of hers the best part of an hour – kept me there, in short, till Mr James Smith himself came back. I leave you to judge if that mended matters. He found me mopping the poor woman's temples with scent and water; and he would have pitched me out of the window, as sure as I sit here, if I had not met him and staggered him at once with the charge of murder against his wife. That stopped him, when he was in full cry, I can promise you. "Go and wait in the next room," says he, "and I'll come in and speak to you directly."'

'And did you go?' I asked.

'Of course I did,' says Mr Dark. 'I knew he couldn't get out by the drawing-room windows, and I knew I could watch the door; so away I went, leaving him alone with the lady, who didn't spare him, by any manner of means, as I could easily hear in the next room. However, all rows in this world come to an end sooner or later; and a man with any brains in his head may do what he pleases with a woman who is fond of him. Before long I heard her crying and kissing him. "I can't go home," she says, after this. "You have behaved like a villain and a monster to me – but oh, Jemmy, I can't give you up to anybody. Don't go back to your wife! Oh, don't, don't go back to your wife!" "No fear of that," says he. "My wife wouldn't have me if I did go back to her." After that, I heard the door open and went out to meet him on the landing. He began swearing the moment he saw me, as if that was any good. "Business first, if you please, sir," says I, "and any pleasure you like, in the way of swearing, afterwards." With that beginning I mentioned our terms to him, and asked the pleasure of his company to Cumberland in return. He was uncommonly suspicious at first, but I promised to draw out a legal document (mere waste paper, of no earthly use except to pacify him), engaging to hold him harmless throughout the proceedings; and what with that, and telling him of the frightful danger his wife was in, I managed, at last, to carry my point.'

'But did the second wife make no objection to his going away with you?' I inquired.

'Not she,' said Mr Dark. 'I stated the case to her, just as it stood; and soon satisfied her that there was no danger of Mr James Smith's first wife laying any claim to him. After hearing that, she joined me in persuading him to do his duty, and said she pitied your mistress from the bottom of her heart. With her influence to back me, I had no great fear of our man changing his mind. I had the door watched that night, however, so as to make quite sure of him. The next morning he was ready to time when I called; and a quarter of an hour after that, we were off together for the north road. We made the journey with post-horses, being afraid of chance passengers, you know, in public conveyances. On the way down, Mr James Smith and I got on as comfortably together as if we had been a pair of old friends. I told the story of our tracing him to the north of Scotland; and he gave me the particulars, in return, of his bolting from Darrock Hall. They are rather amusing, William – would you like to hear them?'

I told Mr Dark that he had anticipated the very question I was about to ask him.

'Well,' he said, 'this is how it was: To begin at the beginning, our man really took Mrs Smith, Number Two, to the Mediterranean, as we heard.

He sailed up the Spanish coast, and, after short trips ashore, stopped at a seaside place in France, called Cannes. There he saw a house and grounds to be sold, which took his fancy as a nice retired place to keep Number Two in. Nothing particular was wanted but the money to buy it; and, not having the little amount in his own possession, Mr James Smith makes a virtue of necessity, and goes back overland to his wife, with private designs on her purse-strings. Number Two, who objects to be left behind, goes with him as far as London. There he trumps up the first story that comes into his head, about rents in the country, and a house in Lincolnshire that is too damp for her to trust herself in; and so, leaving her for a few days in London, starts boldly for Darrock Hall. His notion was to wheedle your mistress out of the money by good behaviour; but it seems he started badly by quarrelling with her about a fiddle-playing parson—'

'Yes, yes, I know all about that part of the story,' I broke in, seeing by Mr Dark's manner that he was likely to speak both ignorantly and impertinently of my mistress's unlucky friendship for Mr Meeke. 'Go on to the time when I left my master alone in the Red Room, and tell me what he did between midnight and nine the next morning.'

'Did?' said Mr Dark. 'Why, he went to bed with the unpleasant conviction on his mind that your mistress had found him out, and with no comfort to speak of, except what he could get out of the brandy bottle. He couldn't sleep; and the more he tossed and tumbled, the more certain he felt that his wife intended to have him tried for bigamy. At last, towards the gray of the morning, he could stand it no longer, and he made up his mind to give the law the slip while he had the chance. As soon as he was dressed, it struck him that there might be a reward offered for catching him, and he determined to make that slight change in his personal appearance which puzzled the witnesses so much before the magistrate to-day. So he opens his dressing-case and crops his hair in no time, and takes off his whiskers next. The fire was out, and he had to shave in cold water. What with that, and what with the flurry of his mind, naturally enough he cut himself—'

'And dried the blood with his night-gown!' says I.

'With his night-gown,' repeated Mr Dark. 'It was the first thing that lay handy, and he snatched it up. Wait a bit, though, the cream of the thing is to come. When he had done being his own barber, he couldn't for the life of him hit on a way of getting rid of the loose hair. The fire was out, and he had no matches, so he couldn't burn it. As for throwing it away, he didn't dare do that in the house, or about the house, for fear of its being found, and betraying what he had done. So he wraps it all up in paper, crams it into his pocket, to be disposed of when he is at a safe distance from the Hall, takes his bag, gets out at the window, shuts it softly after him, and makes for the road as fast as his long legs will carry him. There he walks on till a coach overtakes him, and so travels back to London, to find himself in a fresh scrape as soon as he gets there. An interesting situation, William, and hard travelling from one end of France to the other, had not agreed together in the case of Number Two. Mr James Smith found her in bed, with doctor's orders that she was not to be moved. There was nothing for it, after that, but to lie by in London till the lady got better. Luckily for us, she didn't hurry herself; so that, after all, your mistress has to thank the very woman who supplanted her, for clearing her character by helping us to find Mr James Smith!'

'And pray how did you come by that loose hair of his which you showed before the Justice to-day?' I asked.

'Thank Number Two again,' says Mr Dark. 'I was put up to asking after it by what she told me. While we were talking about the advertisement, I made so bold as to inquire what first set her thinking that her husband and the Mr James Smith whom we wanted might be one and the same man. "Nothing," says she, "but seeing him come home with his hair cut short and his whiskers shaved off, and finding that he could not give me any good reason for disfiguring himself in that way, I had my suspicions that something was wrong, and the sight of your advertisement strengthened them directly." The hearing her say that, suggested to my mind that there might be a difficulty in identifying him after the change in his looks; and I asked him what he had done with the loose hair, before we left London. It was found in the pocket of his travelling coat, just as he had huddled it up there on leaving the Hall, worry and fright and vexation having caused him to forget all about it. Of course I took charge of the parcel; and you know what good it did as well as I do. So to speak, William, it just completed this beautifully neat case. Looking at the matter in a professional point of view, I don't hesitate to say that we have managed our business with Mr James Smith to perfection. We have produced him at the right time, and we are going to get rid of him at the right time. By to-night he will be on his way to foreign parts with Number Two, and he won't show his nose in England again if he lives to the age of Methuselah.'

It was a relief to hear that; and it was almost as great a comfort to find, from what Mr Dark said next, that my mistress need fear nothing that Josephine could do for the future.

The charge of theft, on which she was about to be tried, did not afford the shadow of an excuse in law, any more than in logic, for alluding to the crime which her master had committed. If she meant to talk about it, she might do so in her place of transportation, but she would not have the slightest chance of being listened to previously in a court of law.

'In short,' said Mr Dark, rising to take his leave, 'as I have told you already, William, it's check-mate for Marmzelle. She didn't manage the business of the robbery half as sharply as I should have expected. She certainly began well enough, by staying modestly at a lodging in the village, to give her attendance at the examinations as it might be required. Nothing could look more innocent and respectable so far. But her hiding the property between the mattresses of her bed – the very first place that any experienced man would think of looking in – was such an amazingly stupid thing to do, that I really can't account for it, unless her mind had more weighing on it than it was able to bear, which, considering the heavy stakes she played for, is likely enough. Anyhow, her hands are tied now, and her tongue too, for the matter of that. Give my respects to your mistress, and tell her that her runaway husband and her lying maid will never either of them harm her again as long as they live. She has nothing to do now but to pluck up her spirits and live happy. Here's long life to her and to you, William, in the last glass of ale; and here's the same toast to myself in the bottom of the jug.'

With those words, Mr Dark pocketed his large snuff-box, gave a last wink with his bright eye, and walked away, whistling, to catch the London coach. From that time to this, he and I have never met again.

A few last words relating to my mistress, and to the other persons chiefly concerned in this narrative, will conclude all that it is now necessary for me to say.

For some months, the relatives and friends, and I myself, felt sad misgivings on my poor mistress's account. We doubted if it was possible, with such a quick sensitive nature as her's, that she could support the shock which had been inflicted on her. But our powers of endurance are, as I have learnt to believe, more often equal to the burdens laid upon us than we are apt to imagine. I have seen many surprising recoveries from illness, after all hope had been lost – and I have lived to see my mistress recover from the grief and terror which we once thought would prove fatal to her. It was long before she began to hold up her head again; but care and kindness, and time and change, wrought their effect on her at last. She is not now, and never will be again, the woman she was once: her manner is altered; and she looks older by many a year than she really is. But her health causes us no anxiety now; her spirits are calm and equal; and I have good hope that many quiet years of service in her house are left for me still. I myself have married during the long interval of time which I am now passing over in a few words. This change in my life is, perhaps, not worth mentioning – but I am reminded of my two little children, when I speak of my mistress in her present position. I really think they make the great happiness and interest and amusement of her life, and prevent her from feeling lonely and dried up at heart. It is a pleasant reflection to me to remember this; and perhaps it may be the same to you – for which reason only I speak of it.

As for the other persons connected with the troubles at Darrock Hall, I may mention the vile woman Josephine first, so as to have the sooner done with her. Mr Dark's guess, when he tried to account for her want of cunning in hiding the stolen property, by saying that her mind might have had more weighing on it than she was able to bear, turned out to be nothing less than the plain and awful truth. After she had been found guilty of the robbery, and had been condemned to seven years transportation, a worse sentence fell upon her from a higher tribunal than any in this world. While she was still in the county jail, previous to her removal, her mind gave way; the madness breaking out in an attempt to set fire to the prison. Her case was pronounced to be hopeless from the first. The lawful asylum received her, and the lawful asylum will keep her to the end of her days.

Mr James Smith, who, in my humble opinion, deserved hanging by law, or drowning by accident at least, lived quietly abroad with his Scotch wife (or no wife) for two years; and then died in the most quiet and customary manner, in his bed, after a short illness. His end was described to me as a 'highly edifying one.' But as he was also reported to have sent his forgiveness to his wife – which was as much as to say that *he* was the injured person of the two – I take leave to consider that he was the same impudent vagabond in his last moments that he had been all his life. His Scotch widow has married again, and is now settled in London. I hope her husband is all her own property this time.

Mr Meeke must not be forgotten, although he has dropped out of the latter part of my story, because he had nothing to do with the serious events which followed Josephine's perjury. In the confusion and wretchedness of that time, he was treated with very little ceremony, and was quite passed over when we left the neighbourhood. After pining and fretting for some time, as we afterwards heard, in his lonely parsonage, he resigned his living at the first chance he got, and took a sort of under-chaplain's place in an English chapel abroad. He writes to my mistress once or twice a year to ask after her health and well-being; and she writes back to him. That is all the communication they are ever likely to have with each other. The music they once played together will never sound again. Its last notes have long since faded away – and the last words of this story, trembling on the lips of the teller, may now fade with them.

The Biter Bit

[Extracted from the Correspondence of the London Police]

Originally appeared in *The Atlantic Monthly*, April 1858, as 'Who is the Thief?' The story was included in *The Queen of Hearts* as 'Brother Griffith's Story of the Biter Bit.' 'The Biter Bit' is 'widely recognised among connoisseurs as the first humorous or satirical detective-story,' and is possibly 'the first detective story written in epistolary technique' (Robert Ashley, *Wilkie Collins*, p. 55). Catherine Peters points out that the marriage in the story is almost certainly based on the quasi-illicit (the bride was under age) marriage between Edward and Henrietta Ward, which Collins had himself helped to arrange in 1848. See *The King of Inventors*, pp. 80–1. This marriage also inspired the later novella *Miss or Mrs?* (1871).

London, 4th July, 18—

Sergeant Bulmer,

This is to inform you that you are wanted to assist in looking up a case of importance, which will require all the attention of an experienced member of the force. The matter of the robbery on which you are now engaged, you will please to shift over to the young man who brings you this letter. You will tell him all the circumstances of the case, just as they stand; you will put him up to the progress you have made (if any) towards detecting the person or persons by whom the money has been stolen; and you will leave him to make the best he can of the matter now in your hands. He is to have the whole responsibility of the case, and the whole credit of his success, if he brings it to a proper issue.

So much for the orders that I am desired to communicate to you.

A word in your ear, next, about this new man who is to take your place. His name is Matthew Sharpin; and he is to have the chance given him of dashing into our office at one jump – supposing he turns out strong enough to take it. You will naturally ask me how he comes by this privilege. I can only tell you that he has some uncommonly strong interest to back him in certain high quarters, which you and I had better not mention except under our breaths. He has been a lawyer's clerk; and he is wonderfully conceited in his opinion of himself, as well as mean and underhand to look at. According to his own account, he leaves his old trade, and joins ours, of his own free will and preference. You will no more believe that than I do. My notion is, that he has managed to ferret out some private information in connection with the affairs of one of his master's clients, which makes him rather an awkward customer to keep in the office for the future, and which, at the same time, gives him hold enough over his employer to make it dangerous to drive him into a corner by turning him away. I think the giving him this unheard of chance among us, is, in plain words, pretty much like giving him hush-money to keep him quiet. However that may be, Mr Matthew Sharpin is to have the case now in your hands; and if he succeeds with it, he pokes his ugly nose into our office, as sure as fate. I put you up to this, Sergeant, so that you may not stand in your own light by giving the new man any cause to complain of you at head-quarters, and remain yours,

FRANCIS THEAKSTONE

London, 5th July, 18—

Dear Sir,

Having now been favoured with the necessary instructions from Sergeant Bulmer, I beg to remind you of certain directions which I have received, relating to the report of my future proceedings which I am to prepare for examination at head-quarters.

The object of my writing, and of your examining what I have written, before you send it in to the higher authorities, is, I am informed, to give me, as an untried hand, the benefit of your advice, in case I want it (which I venture to think I shall not) at any stage of my proceedings. As the extraordinary circumstances of the case on which I am now engaged make it impossible for me to absent myself from the place where the robbery was committed, until I have made some progress towards discovering the thief, I am necessarily precluded from consulting you personally. Hence the necessity of my writing down the various details, which might, perhaps, be better communicated by word of mouth. This, if I am not mistaken, is the position in which we are now placed. I state my own impressions on the subject, in writing, in order that we may clearly understand each other at the outset; and have the honour to remain, your obedient servant,

MATTHEW SHARPIN

FROM CHIEF INSPECTOR THEAKSTONE TO MR MATTHEW SHARPIN

London, 5th July, 18—

Sir,

You have begun by wasting time, ink, and paper. We both of us perfectly well knew the position we stood in towards each other, when I sent you with my letter to Sergeant Bulmer. There was not the least need to repeat it in writing. Be so good as to employ your pen, in future, on the business actually in hand.

You have now three separate matters on which to write me. First, You have to draw up a statement of your instructions received from Sergeant Bulmer, in order to show us that nothing has escaped your memory, and that you are thoroughly acquainted with all the circumstances of the case which has been entrusted to you. Secondly, You are to inform me what it is you propose to do. Thirdly, you are to report every inch of your progress (if you make any) from day to day, and, if need be, from hour to hour as well. This is *your* duty. As to what *my* duty may be, when I want you to remind me of it, I will write and tell you so. In the meantime, I remain, yours,

FRANCIS THEAKSTONE

FROM MR MATTHEW SHARPIN TO CHIEF INSPECTOR THEAKSTONE

London, 6th July, 18—

Sir,

You are rather an elderly person, and, as such, naturally inclined to be a little jealous of men like me, who are in the prime of their lives and their faculties. Under these circumstances, it is my duty to be considerate towards you, and not to bear too hardly on your small failings. I decline, therefore, altogether, to take offence at the tone of your letter; I give you the full benefit of the natural generosity of my nature; I sponge the very existence of your surly communication out of my memory – in short, Chief Inspector Theakstone, I forgive you, and proceed to business.

My first duty is to draw up a full statement of the instructions I have received from Sergeant Bulmer. Here they are, at your service, according to my version of them.

At number 13, Rutherford Street, Soho, there is a stationer's shop. It is kept by one Mr Yatman. He is a married man, but has no family. Besides Mr and Mrs Yatman, the other inmates in the house are a lodger, a young single man named Jay, who occupies the front room on the second floor – a shopman, who sleeps in one of the attics, – and a servant-of-all-work, whose bed is in the back-kitchen. Once a week a charwoman comes to help this servant. These are all the persons who, on ordinary occasions, have means of access to the interior of the house, placed, as a matter of course, at their disposal.

Mr Yatman has been in business for many years, carrying on his affairs prosperously enough to realize a handsome independence for a person in his position. Unfortunately for himself, he endeavoured to increase the amount of his property by speculating. He ventured boldly in his investments, luck went against him, and rather less than two years ago he found himself a poor man again. All that was saved out of the wreck of his property was the sum of two hundred pounds.

Although Mr Yatman did his best to meet his altered circumstances, by giving up many of the luxuries and comforts to which he and his wife had been accustomed, he found it impossible to retrench so far as to allow of putting by any money from the income produced by his shop. The business has been declining of late years – the cheap advertising stationers having done it injury with the public. Consequently, up to the last week, the only surplus property possessed by Mr Yatman, consisted of the two hundred pounds which had been recovered from the wreck of his fortune. This sum was placed as a deposit in a joint-stock bank of the highest possible character.

Eight days ago, Mr Yatman and his lodger, Mr Jay, held a conversation on the subject of the commercial difficulties which are hampering trade in all directions at the present time. Mr Jay (who lives by supplying the newspapers with short paragraphs relating to accidents, offences, and brief records of remarkable occurrences in general – who is, in short, what they call a penny-a-liner) told his landlord that he had been in the city that day and heard unfavourable rumours on the subject of the joint-stock banks. The rumours to which he alluded had already reached the ears of Mr Yatman from other quarters; and the confirmation of them by his lodger had such an effect on his mind – predisposed as it was to alarm by the experience of his former losses – that he resolved to go at once to the bank and withdraw his deposit. It was then getting on toward the end of the afternoon; and he arrived just in time to receive his money before the bank closed.

He received the deposit in bank notes of the following amounts: one fifty-pound note, three twenty-pound notes, six ten-pound notes, and six five-pound notes. His object in drawing the money in this form was to have it ready to lay out immediately in trifling loans, on good security, among the small tradespeople of his district, some of whom are sorely pressed for the very means of existence at the present time. Investments of this kind seemed to Mr Yatman to be the most safe and the most profitable on which he could now venture.

He brought the money back in an envelope placed in his breast-pocket; and asked his shopman, on getting home, to look for a small flat tin cash-box, which had not been used for years, and which, as Mr Yatman remembered it, was exactly of the right size to hold the bank notes. For some time the cash-box was searched for in vain. Mr Yatman called to his wife to know if she had any idea where it was. The question was overheard by the servant-of-all-work, who was taking up the tea-tray at the time, and by Mr Jay, who was coming down stairs on his way out to the theatre. Ultimately the cash-box was found by the shopman. Mr Yatman placed the banknotes in it, secured them by a padlock, and put the box in his coat-pocket. It stuck out of the coat-pocket a very little, but enough to be seen. Mr Yatman remained at home, up stairs, all that evening. No visitors called. At eleven o'clock he went to bed, and put the cash-box under his pillow.

When he and his wife woke the next morning, the box was gone. Payment of the notes was immediately stopped at the bank of England; but no news of the money has been heard of since that time.

So far, the circumstances of the case are perfectly clear. They point unmistakably to the conclusion that the robbery must have been committed by some person living in the house. Suspicion falls, therefore, upon the servant-of-all-work, upon the shopman, and upon Mr Jay. The two first knew that the cash-box was being inquired for by their master, but did not know what it was he wanted to put into it. They would assume, of course, that it was money. They both had opportunities (the servant, when she took away the tea – and the shopman, when he came, after shutting up, to give the keys of the till to his master) of seeing the cash-box in Mr Yatman's pocket, and of inferring naturally, from its position there, that he intended to take it into his bedroom with him at night.

Mr Jay, on the other hand, had been told, during the afternoon's conversation on the subject of joint-stock banks, that his landlord had a deposit of two hundred pounds in one of them. He also knew that Mr Yatman left him with the intention of drawing that money out; and he heard the inquiry for the cash-box, afterwards, when he was coming down stairs. He must, therefore, have inferred that the money was in the house, and that the cash-box was the receptacle intended to contain it. That he could have had any idea, however, of the place in which Mr Yatman intended to keep it for the night, is impossible, seeing that he went out before the box was found, and did not return till his landlord was in bed. Consequently, if he committed the robbery, he must have gone into the bedroom purely on speculation.

Speaking of the bedroom reminds me of the necessity of noticing the situation of it in the house, and the means that exist of gaining easy access to it at any hour of the night.

The room in question is the back-room on the first-floor. In consequence of Mrs Yatman's constitutional nervousness on the subject of fire, which makes her apprehend being burnt alive in her room, in case of accident, by the hampering of the lock if the key is turned in it, her husband has never been accustomed to lock the bedroom door. Both he and his wife are, by their own admission, heavy sleepers. Consequently the risk to be run by any evil-disposed persons wishing to plunder the bedroom, was of the most trifling kind. They could enter the room by merely turning the handle of the door; and if they moved with ordinary caution, there was no fear of their waking the sleepers inside. This fact is of importance. It strengthens our conviction that the money must have been taken by one of the inmates of the house, because it tends to show that the robbery, in this case, might have been committed by persons not possessed of the superior vigilance and cunning of the experienced thief.

Such are the circumstances, as they were related to Sergeant Bulmer, when he was first called in to discover the guilty parties, and, if possible, to recover the lost bank notes. The strictest inquiry which he could institute failed of producing the smallest fragment of evidence against any of the persons on whom suspicion naturally fell. Their language and behaviour, on being informed of the robbery, was perfectly consistent with the language and behaviour of innocent people. Sergeant Bulmer felt from the first that this was a case for private inquiry and secret observation. He began by recommending Mr and Mrs Yatman to affect a feeling of perfect confidence in the innocence of the persons living under their roof; and he then opened the campaign by employing himself in following the goings and comings, and in discovering the friends, the habits, and the secrets of the maid-of-all-work.

Three days and nights of exertion on his own part, and on that of others who were competent to assist his investigations, were enough to satisfy him that there was no sound cause for suspicion against the girl.

He next practised the same precaution in relation to the shopman. There was more difficulty and uncertainty in privately clearing up this person's character without his knowledge, but the obstacles were at last smoothed away with tolerable success; and though there is not the same amount of certainty, in this case, which there was in the case of the girl, there is still fair reason for supposing that the shopman has had nothing to do with the robbery of the cash-box.

As a necessary consequence of these proceedings, the range of suspicion now becomes limited to the lodger, Mr Jay.

When I presented your letter of introduction to Sergeant Bulmer, he had already made some inquiries on the subject of this young man. The result, so far, has not been at all favourable. Mr Jay's habits are irregular; he frequents public houses, and seems to be familiarly acquainted with a great many dissolute characters; he is in debt to most of the tradespeople whom he employs; he has not paid his rent to Mr Yatman for the last month; yesterday evening he came home excited by liquor, and last week he was seen talking to a prize-fighter. In short, though Mr Jay does call himself a journalist, in virtue of his penny-a-line contributions to the newspapers, he is a young man of low tastes, vulgar manners, and bad habits. Nothing has yet been discovered, in relation to him, which redounds to his credit in the smallest degree.

I have now reported, down to the very last details, all the particulars communicated to me by Sergeant Bulmer. I believe you will not find an omission anywhere; and I think you will admit, though you are prejudiced against me, that a clearer statement of facts was never laid before you than the statement I have now made. My next duty is to tell you what I propose to do, now that the case is confided to my hands.

In the first place, it is clearly my business to take up the case at the point where Sergeant Bulmer has left it. On his authority, I am justified in assuming that I have no need to trouble myself about the maid-of-all-work and the shopman. Their characters are now to be considered as cleared up. What remains to be privately investigated is the question of the guilt or innocence of Mr Jay. Before we give up the notes for lost, we must make sure, if we can, that he knows nothing about them.

This is the plan that I have adopted, with the full approval of Mr and Mrs Yatman, for discovering whether Mr Jay is or is not the person who has stolen the cash-box:

I propose, to-day, to present myself at the house in the character of a young man who is looking for lodgings. The back room on the second-floor will be shown to me as the room to let; and I shall establish myself there tonight, as a person from the country who has come to London to look for a situation in a respectable shop or office.

By this means I shall be living next to the room occupied by Mr Jay. The partition between us is mere lath and plaster. I shall make a small hole in it, near the cornice, through which I can see what Mr Jay does in his room, and hear every word that is said when any friend happens to call on him. Whenever he is at home, I shall be at my post of observation. Whenever he goes out, I shall be after him. By employing these means of watching him, I believe I may look forward to the discovery of his secret – if he knows anything about the lost bank notes – as to a dead certainty.

What you may think of my plan of observation I cannot undertake to say. It appears to me to unite the invaluable merits of boldness and simplicity. Fortified by this conviction, I close the present communication with feelings of the most sanguine description in regard to the future, and remain your obedient servant,

MATTHEW SHARPIN

FROM THE SAME TO THE SAME

7th July

Sir,

As you have not honoured me with any answer to my last communication, I assume that, in spite of your prejudices against me, it has produced the favourable impression on your mind which I ventured to anticipate. Gratified and encouraged beyond measure by the token of approval which your eloquent silence conveys to me, I proceed to report the progress that has been made in the course of the last twenty-four hours.

I am now comfortably established next door to Mr Jay; and I am delighted to say that I have two holes in the partition, instead of one. My natural sense of humour has led me into the pardonable extravagance of giving them both appropriate names. One I call my Peep-hole, and the other my Pipe-hole. The name of the first explains itself; the name of the second refers to a small tin pipe, or tube, inserted in the hole, and twisted so that the mouth of it comes close to my ear, while I am standing at my post of observation. Thus, while I am looking at Mr Jay through my Peep-hole, I can hear every word that may be spoken in his room through my Pipe-hole.

Perfect candour – a virtue which I have possessed from my childhood – compels me to acknowledge, before I go any further, that the ingenious notion of adding a Pipe-hole to my proposed Peep-hole originated with Mrs Yatman. This lady – a most intelligent and accomplished person, simple, and yet distinguished, in her manners – has entered into all my little plans with an enthusiasm and intelligence which I cannot too highly praise. Mr Yatman is so cast down by his loss, that he is quite incapable of affording me any assistance. Mrs Yatman, who is evidently most tenderly attached to him, feels her husband's sad condition of mind even more acutely than she feels the loss of the money; and is mainly stimulated to exertion by her desire to assist in raising him from the miserable state of prostration into which he has now fallen.

'The money, Mr Sharpin,' she said to me yesterday evening, with tears in her eyes, 'the money may be regained by rigid economy and strict attention to business. It is my husband's wretched state of mind that makes me so anxious for the discovery of the thief. I may be wrong, but I felt hopeful of success as soon as you entered the house; and I believe that, if the wretch who has robbed us is to be found, you are the man to discover him.' I accepted this gratifying compliment in the spirit in which it was offered – firmly believing that I shall be found, sooner or later, to have thoroughly deserved it.

Let me now return to business – that is to say, to my Peep-hole and my Pipe-hole.

I have enjoyed some hours of calm observation of Mr Jay. Though rarely at home, as I understand from Mrs Yatman, on ordinary occasions, he has been in-doors the whole of this day. That is suspicious, to begin with. I have to report, further, that he rose at a late hour this morning (always a bad sign in a young man), and that he lost a great deal of time, after he was up, in yawning and complaining to himself of headache. Like other debauched characters, he ate little or nothing for breakfast. His next proceeding was to smoke a pipe – a dirty clay pipe, which a gentleman would have been ashamed to put between his lips. When he had done smoking, he took out pen, ink, and paper, and sat down to write with a groan – whether of remorse for having taken the bank notes, or of disgust at the task before him, I am unable to say. After writing a few lines (too far away from my Peep-hole to give me a chance of reading over his shoulder), he leaned back in his chair, and amused himself by humming the tunes of popular songs. I recognised 'My Mary Anne,' 'Bobbin' around,' and 'Old Dog Tray,' among other melodies. Whether these do or do not represent secret signals by which he communicates with his accomplices remains to be seen. After he had amused himself for some time by humming, he got up and began to walk about the room, occasionally stopping to add a sentence to the paper on his desk. Before long he went to a locked cupboard and opened it.

I strained my eyes eagerly, in expectation of making a discovery. I saw him take something carefully out of the cupboard – he turned round – and it was only a pint bottle of brandy! Having drunk some of the liquor, this extremely indolent reprobate lay down on his bed again, and in five minutes was fast asleep.

After hearing him snoring for at least two hours, I was recalled to my Peep-hole by a knock at his door. He jumped up and opened it with suspicious activity.

A very small boy, with a very dirty face, walked in, said, 'Please, sir, they're waiting for you,' sat down on a chair, with his legs a long way from the ground, and instantly fell asleep! Mr Jay swore an oath, tied a wet towel round his head, and, going back to his paper, began to cover it with writing as fast as his fingers could move the pen. Occasionally getting up to dip the towel in water and tie it on again, he continued at this employment for nearly three hours; then folded up the leaves of writing, woke the boy, and gave them to him, with this remarkable expression: 'Now, then, young sleepy-head, quick march! If you see the governor, tell him to have the money ready for me when I call for it.' The boy grinned, and disappeared. I was sorely tempted to follow 'sleepy head,' but, on reflection, considered it safest still to keep my eye on the proceedings of Mr Jay.

In half an hour's time, he put on his hat and walked out. Of course, I put on my hat and walked out also. As I went down stairs, I passed Mrs Yatman going up. The lady has been kind enough to undertake, by previous arrangement between us, to search Mr Jay's room, while he is out of the way, and while I am necessarily engaged in the pleasing duty of following him wherever he goes. On the occasion to which I now refer, he walked straight to the nearest tavern, and ordered a couple of mutton chops for his dinner. I placed myself in the next box to him, and ordered a couple of mutton chops for my dinner. Before I had been in the room a minute, a young man of highly suspicious manners and appearance, sitting at a table opposite, took his glass of porter in his hand and joined Mr Jay. I pretended to be reading the newspaper, and listened, as in duty bound, with all my might.

'Jack has been here inquiring after you,' says the young man.

'Did he leave any message?' asks Mr Jay.

'Yes,' says the other. 'He told me, if I met with you, to say that he wished very particularly to see you to-night; and that he would give you a look in, at Rutherford Street, at seven o'clock.'

'All right,' says Mr Jay. 'I'll get back in time to see him.'

Upon this, the suspicious-looking young man finished his porter, and saying that he was rather in a hurry, took leave of his friend (perhaps I should not be wrong if I said his accomplice) and left the room.

At twenty-five minutes and a half past six – in these serious cases it is important to be particular about time – Mr Jay finished his chops and paid his bill. At twenty-six minutes and three-quarters, I finished my chops and paid mine. In ten minutes more I was inside the house in Rutherford Street, and was received by Mrs Yatman in the passage. That charming woman's face exhibited an expression of melancholy and disappointment which it quite grieved me to see.

'I am afraid, Ma'am,' says I, 'that you have not hit on any little criminating discovery in the lodger's room?'

She shook her head and sighed. It was a soft, languid, fluttering sigh – and, upon my life, it quite upset me. For the moment I forgot business, and burned with envy of Mr Yatman.

'Don't despair, Ma'am,' I said, with an insinuating mildness which seemed to touch her. 'I have heard a mysterious conversation – I know of a guilty appointment – and I expect great things from my Peep-hole and my Pipe-hole to-night. Pray, don't be alarmed, but I think we are on the brink of a discovery.'

Here my enthusiastic devotion to business got the better of my tender feelings. I looked – winked – nodded – left her.

When I got back to my observatory, I found Mr Jay digesting his mutton-chops in an arm-chair, with his pipe in his mouth. On his table were two tumblers, a jug of water, and the pint-bottle of brandy. It was then close upon seven o'clock. As the hour struck, the person described as 'Jack' walked in.

He looked agitated – I am happy to say he looked violently agitated. The cheerful glow of anticipated success diffused itself (to use a strong expression) all over me, from head to foot. With breathless interest I looked through my Peep-hole, and saw the visitor – the 'Jack' of this delightful case – sit down, facing me, at the opposite side of the table to Mr Jay. Making allowance for the difference in expression which their countenances just now happened to exhibit, these two abandoned villains were so much alike in other respects as to lead at once to the conclusion that they were brothers. Jack was the cleaner man and the better dressed of the two. I admit that, at the outset. It is, perhaps, one of my failings to push justice and impartiality to their utmost limits. I am no Pharisee; and where Vice has its redeeming point, I say, let Vice have its due – yes, yes, by all manner of means, let Vice have its due.

'What's the matter now, Jack?' says Mr Jay.

'Can't you see it in my face?' says Jack. 'My dear fellow, delays are dangerous. Let us have done with suspense, and risk it the day after to-morrow.'

'So soon as that?' cries Mr Jay, looking very much astonished. 'Well, I'm ready, if you are. But, I say, Jack, is Somebody Else ready, too? Are you quite sure of that?'

He smiled, as he spoke – a frightful smile – and laid a very strong emphasis on those two words, 'Somebody Else.' There is evidently a third ruffian, a nameless desperado, concerned in the business.

'Meet us to-morrow,' says Jack, 'and judge for yourself. Be in the Regent's Park at eleven in the morning, and look out for us at the turning that leads to the Avenue Road.'

'I'll be there,' says Mr Jay. 'Have a drop of brandy and water? What are you getting up for? You're not going already?'

'Yes, I am,' says Jack. 'The fact is, I'm so excited and agitated that I can't sit still anywhere for five minutes together. Ridiculous as it may appear to you, I'm in a perpetual state of nervous flutter. I can't, for the life of me, help fearing that we shall be found out. I fancy that every man who looks twice at me in the street is a spy'—

At those words, I thought my legs would have given way under me. Nothing but strength of mind kept me at my Peep-hole – nothing else, I give you my word of honour.

'Stuff and nonsense!' cries Mr Jay, with all the effrontery of a veteran in crime. 'We have kept the secret up to this time, and we will manage cleverly to the end. Have a drop of brandy and water, and you will feel as certain about it as I do.'

Jack steadily refused the brandy and water, and steadily persisted in taking his leave.

'I must try if I can't walk it off,' he said. 'Remember to-morrow morning – eleven o'clock, Avenue Road side of the Regent's Park.'

With those words he went out. His hardened relative laughed desperately, and resumed the dirty clay pipe.

I sat down on the side of my bed, actually quivering with excitement.

It is clear to me that no attempt has yet been made to change the stolen bank notes; and I may add that Sergeant Bulmer was of that opinion also, when he left the case in my hands. What is the natural conclusion to draw from the conversation which I have just set down? Evidently, that the confederates meet to-morrow to take their respective shares in the stolen money, and to decide on the safest means of getting the notes changed the day after. Mr Jay is, beyond a doubt, the leading criminal in this business, and he will probably run the chief risk – that of changing the fifty-pound note. I shall, therefore, still make it my business to follow him – attending at the Regent's Park to-morrow, and doing my best to hear what is said there. If another appointment is made for the day after, I shall, of course, go to it. In the meantime, I shall want the immediate assistance of two competent persons (supposing the rascals separate after their meeting) to follow the two minor criminals. It is only fair to add, that, if the rogues all retire together, I shall probably keep my subordinates in reserve. Being naturally ambitious, I desire, if possible, to have the whole credit of discovering this robbery to myself.

8th July

I have to acknowledge, with thanks, the speedy arrival of my two subordinates – men of very average abilities, I am afraid; but, fortunately, I shall always be on the spot to direct them.

My first business this morning was, necessarily, to prevent possible mistakes by accounting to Mr and Mrs Yatman for the presence of two strangers on the scene. Mr Yatman (between ourselves, a poor, feeble man) only shook his head and groaned. Mrs Yatman (that superior woman) favoured me with a charming look of intelligence.

'Oh, Mr Sharpin!' she said, 'I am so sorry to see those two men! Your sending for their assistance looks as if you were beginning to be doubtful of success.'

I privately winked at her (she is very good in allowing me to do so without taking offence), and told her, in my facetious way, that she laboured under a slight mistake.

'It is because I am sure of success, Ma'am, that I send for them. I am determined to recover the money, not for my own sake only, but for Mr Yatman's sake – and for yours.'

I laid a considerable amount of stress on those last three words. She said, 'Oh, Mr Sharpin!' again – and blushed of a heavenly red – and looked down at her work. I could go to the world's end with that woman, if Mr Yatman would only die.

I sent off the two subordinates to wait, until I wanted them, at the Avenue Road gate of the Regent's Park. Half an hour afterwards I was following the same direction myself, at the heels of Mr Jay.

The two confederates were punctual to the appointed time. I blush to record it, but it is nevertheless necessary to state, that the third rogue – the nameless desperado of my report, or, if you prefer it, the mysterious 'Somebody Else' of the conversation between the two brothers – is – a woman! and, what is worse, a young woman! and, what is more lamentable still, a nice-looking woman! I have long resisted a growing conviction, that, wherever there is mischief in this world, an individual of the fair sex is inevitably certain to be mixed up in it. After the experience of this morning, I can struggle against that sad conclusion no longer. I give up the sex – excepting Mrs Yatman, I give up the sex.

The man named 'Jack' offered the woman his arm. Mr Jay placed himself on the other side of her. The three then walked away slowly among the trees. I followed them at a respectful distance. My two subordinates, at a respectful distance also, followed me.

It was, I deeply regret to say, impossible to get near enough to them to overhear their conversation, without running too great a risk of being discovered. I could only infer from their gestures and actions that they were all three talking with extraordinary earnestness on some subject which deeply interested them. After having been engaged in this way a full quarter of an hour, they suddenly turned round to retrace their steps. My presence of mind did not forsake me in this emergency. I signed to the two subordinates to walk on carelessly and pass them, while I myself slipped dexterously behind a tree. As they came by me, I heard 'Jack' address these words to Mr Jay:

'Let us say half-past ten to-morrow morning. And mind you come in a cab. We had better not risk taking one in this neighbourhood.'

Mr Jay made some brief reply, which I could not overhear. They walked back to the place at which they had met, shaking hands there with an audacious cordiality which it quite sickened me to see. They then separated. I followed Mr Jay. My subordinates paid the same delicate attention to the other two.

Instead of taking me back to Rutherford Street, Mr Jay led me to the Strand. He stopped at a dingy, disreputable-looking house, which, according to the inscription over the door, was a newspaper office, but which, in my judgement, had all the external appearance of a place devoted to the reception of stolen goods.

After remaining inside for a few minutes, he came out, whistling, with his finger and thumb in his waistcoat pocket. Some men would now have arrested him on the spot. I remembered the necessity of catching the two confederates, and the importance of not interfering with the appointment that had been made for the next morning. Such coolness as this, under trying circumstances, is rarely to be found, I should imagine, in a young beginner, whose reputation as a detective policeman is still to make.

From the house of suspicious appearance, Mr Jay betook himself to a cigar-divan, and read the magazines over a cheroot. I sat at a table near him, and read the magazines likewise over a cheroot. From the divan he strolled to the tavern and had his chops. I strolled to the tavern and had my chops. When he had done, he went back to his lodging. When I had done, I went back to mine. He was overcome with drowsiness early in the evening, and went to bed. As soon as I heard him snoring, I was overcome with drowsiness, and went to bed also.

Early in the morning my two subordinates came to make their report.

They had seen the man named 'Jack' leave the woman at the gate of an apparently respectable villa-residence, not far from the Regent's Park. Left to himself, he took a turning to the right, which led to a sort of suburban street, principally inhabited by shopkeepers. He stopped at the private door of one of the houses, and let himself in with his own key – looking about him as he opened the door, and staring suspiciously at my men as they lounged along on the opposite side of the way. These were all the particulars which the subordinates had to communicate. I kept them in my room to attend on me, if needful, and mounted to my Peep-hole to have a look at Mr Jay.

He was occupied in dressing himself, and was taking extraordinary pains to destroy all traces of the natural slovenliness of his appearance. This was precisely what I expected. A vagabond like Mr Jay knows the importance of giving himself a respectable look when he is going to run the risk of changing a stolen bank note. At five minutes past ten o'clock he had given the last brush to his shabby hat and the last scouring with bread-crumb to his dirty gloves. At ten minutes past ten he was in the street, on his way to the nearest cab-stand, and I and my subordinates were close on his heels.

He took a cab, and we took a cab. I had not overheard them appoint a place of meeting, when following them in the Park on the previous day; but I soon found that we were proceeding in the old direction of the Avenue Road gate. The cab in which Mr Jay was riding turned into the Park slowly. We stopped outside, to avoid exciting suspicion. I got out to follow the cab on foot. Just as I did so, I saw it stop, and detected the two confederates approaching it from among the trees. They got in, and the cab was turned about directly. I ran back to my own cab, and told the driver to let them pass him, and then to follow as before.

The man obeyed my directions, but so clumsily as to excite their suspicions. We had been driving after them about three minutes (returning along the road by which we had advanced) when I looked out of the window to see how far they might be ahead of us. As I did this, I saw two hats popped out of the windows of their cab, and two faces looking back at me. I sank into my place in a cold sweat; the expression is coarse, but no other form of words can describe my condition at that trying moment.

'We are found out!' I said, faintly to my two subordinates. They stared at me in astonishment. My feelings changed instantly from the depth of despair to the height of indignation.

'It is the cabman's fault. Get out, one of you,' I said, with dignity – 'get out, and punch his head.'

Instead of following my directions (I should wish this act of disobedience to be reported at head-quarters) they both looked out of the window. Before I could pull them back, they both sat down again. Before I could express my just indignation, they both grinned, and said to me, 'Please to look out, sir!'

I did look out. Their cab had stopped.

Where?

At a church door!

What effect this discovery might have had upon the ordinary run of men, I don't know. Being of a strong religious turn myself, it filled me with horror. I have often read of the unprincipled cunning of criminal persons; but I never before heard of three thieves attempting to double on their pursuers by entering a church! The sacrilegious audacity of that proceeding is, I should think, unparalleled in the annals of crime.

I checked my grinning subordinates by a frown. It was easy to see what was passing in their superficial minds. If I had not been able to look below the surface, I might, on observing two nicely dressed men and one nicely dressed woman enter a church before eleven in the morning on a week day, have come to the same hasty conclusion at which my inferiors had evidently arrived. As it was, appearances had no power to impose on *me*. I got out, and, followed by one of my men, entered the church. The other man I sent round to watch the vestry door. You may catch a weasel asleep – but not your humble servant, Matthew Sharpin!

We stole up the gallery stairs, diverged to the organ loft, and peered through the curtains in front. There they were, all three, sitting in a pew below – yes, incredible as it may appear, sitting in a pew below!

Before I could determine what to do, a clergyman made his appearance in full canonicals, from the vestry door, followed by a clerk. My brain whirled, and my eyesight grew dim. Dark remembrances of robberies committed in vestries floated through my mind. I trembled for the excellent man in full canonicals – I even trembled for the clerk.

The clergyman placed himself inside the altar rails. The three desperadoes approached him. He opened his book, and began to read. What? – you will ask.

I answer, without the slightest hesitation, the first lines of the Marriage Service.

My subordinate had the audacity to look at me, and then to stuff his pocket-handkerchief into his mouth. I scorned to pay any attention to him. After I had discovered that the man 'Jack' was the bridegroom, and that the man Jay acted the part of father, and gave away the bride, I left the church, followed by my men, and joined the other subordinate outside the vestry door. Some people in my position would now have felt rather crestfallen, and would have begun to think that they had made a very foolish mistake. Not the faintest misgiving of any kind troubled me. I did not feel in the slightest degree depreciated in my own estimation. And even now, after a lapse of three hours, my mind remains, I am happy to say, in the same calm and hopeful condition.

As soon as I and my subordinates were assembled together outside the church, I intimated my intention of still following the other cab, in spite of what had occurred. My reason for deciding on this course will appear presently. The two subordinates appeared to be astonished at my resolution. One of them had the impertinence to say to me:

'If you please, sir, who is it that we are after? A man who has stolen money, or a man who has stolen a wife?'

The other low person encouraged him by laughing. Both have deserved an official reprimand; and both, I sincerely trust, will be sure to get it.

When the marriage ceremony was over, the three got into their cab; and once more our vehicle (neatly hidden round the corner of the church, so that they could not suspect it to be near them) started to follow theirs.

We traced them to the terminus of the South-Western Railway. The newly married couple took tickets for Richmond – paying their fare with a half sovereign, and so depriving me of the pleasure of arresting them, which I should certainly have done, if they had offered a bank note. They parted from Mr Jay, saying, 'Remember the address, – 14, Babylon Terrace. You dine with us to-morrow week.' Mr Jay accepted the invitation, and added, jocosely, that he was going home at once to get off his clean clothes, and to be comfortable and dirty again for the rest of the day. I have to report that I saw him home safely, and that he is comfortable and dirty again (to use his own disgraceful language) at the present moment.

Here the affair rests, having by this time reached what I may call its first stage.

I know very well what persons of hasty judgment will be inclined to say of my proceedings thus far. They will assert that I have been deceiving myself all through, in the most absurd way; they will declare that the suspicious conversations which I have reported referred solely to the difficulties and dangers of successfully carrying out a runaway match; and they will appeal to the scene in the church, as offering undeniable proof of the correctness of their assertions. So let it be. I dispute nothing up to this point. But I ask a question, out of the depths of my own sagacity as a man of the world, which the bitterest of my enemies will not, I think, find it particularly easy to answer.

Granted the fact of the marriage, what proof does it afford me of the innocence of the three persons concerned in that clandestine transaction? It gives me none. On the contrary, it strengthens my suspicions against Mr Jay and his confederates, because it suggests a distinct motive for their stealing the money. A gentleman who is going to spend his honeymoon at Richmond wants money; and a gentleman who is in debt to all his tradespeople wants money. Is this an unjustifiable imputation of bad motives? In the name of outraged Morality, I deny it. These men have combined together, and have stolen a woman. Why should they not combine together, and steal a cash-box? I take my stand on the logic of rigid Virtue; and I defy all the sophistry of Vice to move me an inch out of my position.

Speaking of virtue, I may add that I have put this view of the case to Mr and Mrs Yatman. That accomplished and charming woman found it difficult, at first, to follow the close chain of my reasoning. I am free to confess that she shook her head, and shed tears, and joined her husband in premature lamentation over the loss of the two hundred pounds. But a little careful explanation on my part, and a little attentive listening on hers, ultimately changed her opinion. She now agrees with me, that there is nothing in this unexpected circumstance of the clandestine marriage which absolutely tends to divert suspicion from Mr Jay, or Mr 'Jack,' or the runaway lady. 'Audacious hussy' was the term my fair friend used in speaking of her, but let that pass. It is more to the purpose to record that Mrs Yatman has not lost confidence in me, and that Mr Yatman promises to follow her example and do his best to look hopefully for future results.

I have now, in the new turn that circumstances have taken, to await advice from your office. I pause for fresh orders with all the composure of a man who has got two strings to his bow. When I traced the three confederates from the church door to the railway terminus, I had two motives for doing so. First, I followed them as a matter of official business, believing them still to have been guilty of the robbery. Secondly, I followed them as a matter of private speculation, with a view of discovering the place of refuge to which the runaway couple intended to retreat, and of making my information a marketable commodity to offer to the young lady's family and friends. Thus, whatever happens, I may congratulate myself beforehand on not having wasted my time. If the office approves of my conduct, I have my plan ready for further proceedings. If the office blames me, I shall take myself off, with my marketable information, to the genteel villa-residence in the neighbourhood of the Regent's Park. Any way, the affair puts money into my pocket, and does credit to my penetration as an uncommonly sharp man.

I have only one word more to add, and it is this: If any individual ventures to assert that Mr Jay and his confederates are innocent of all share in the stealing of the cash-box, I, in return, defy that individual – though he may even be Chief Inspector Theakstone himself – to tell me who has committed the robbery at Rutherford Street, Soho.

Strong in that conviction, I have the honour to be, Your very obedient servant,

MATTHEW SHARPIN

FROM CHIEF INSPECTOR THEAKSTONE TO SERGEANT BULMER.

Birmingham, July 9th

Sergeant Bulmer,

That empty-headed puppy, Mr Matthew Sharpin, has made a mess of the case at Rutherford Street, exactly as I expected he would. Business keeps me in this town; so I write to you to set the matter straight. I enclose, with this, the pages of feeble scribble-scrabble which the creature, Sharpin, calls a report. Look them over; and when you have made your way through all the gabble, I think you will agree with me that the conceited booby has looked for the thief in every direction but the right one. You can lay your hand on the guilty person in five minutes, now. Settle the case at once; forward your report to me at this place; and tell Mr Sharpin that he is suspended till further notice. Yours,

FRANCIS THEAKSTONE

FROM SERGEANT BULMER TO CHIEF INSPECTOR THEAKSTONE.

London, July 10th

Inspector Theakstone,

Your letter and enclosure came safe to hand. Wise men, they say, may always learn something, even from a fool. By the time I had got through Sharpin's maundering report of his own folly, I saw my way clear enough to the end of the Rutherford Street case, just as you thought I should. In half an hour's time I was at the house. The first person I saw there was Mr Sharpin himself.

'Have you come to help me?' says he.

'Not exactly,' says I. 'I've come to tell you that you are suspended till further notice.'

'Very good,' says he, not taken down, by so much as a single peg, in his own estimation. 'I thought you would be jealous of me. It's very natural; and I don't blame you. Walk in, pray, and make yourself at home. I'm off to do a little detective business on my own account, in the neighbourhood of the Regent's Park. Ta-ta, sergeant, ta-ta!'

With those words he took himself out of the way – which was exactly what I wanted him to do.

As soon as the maid-servant had shut the door, I told her to inform her master that I wanted to say a word to him in private. She showed me into the parlour behind the shop; and there was Mr Yatman, all alone, reading the newspaper.

'About this matter of the robbery, sir,' says I.

He cut me short, peevishly enough – being naturally a poor, weak, womanish sort of man. 'Yes, yes, I know,' says he. 'You have come to tell me that your wonderfully clever man, who has bored holes in my second-floor partition, has made a mistake, and is off the scent of the scoundrel who has stolen my money.'

'Yes, sir,' says I. 'That *is* one of the things I came to tell you. But I have got something else to say, besides that.'

'Can you tell me who the thief is?' says he, more pettish than ever.

'Yes, sir,' says I, 'I think I can.'

He put down the newspaper, and began to look rather anxious and frightened.

'Not my shopman?' says he. 'I hope, for the man's own sake, it's not my shopman.'

'Guess again, sir,' says I.

'That idle slut, the maid?' says he.

'She is idle, sir,' says I, 'and she is also a slut; my first inquiries about her proved as much as that. But she's not the thief.'

'Then, in the name of heaven, who is?' says he.

'Will you please to prepare yourself for a very disagreeable surprise, sir?' says I. 'And in case you lose your temper, will you excuse my remarking that I am the stronger man of the two, and that, if you allow yourself to lay hands on me, I may unintentionally hurt you, in pure self-defence?'

He turned as pale as ashes, and pushed his chair two or three feet away from me.

'You have asked me to tell you, sir, who has taken your money,' I went on. 'If you insist on my giving you an answer—'

'I do insist,' he said, faintly. 'Who has taken it?'

'Your wife has taken it,' I said, very quietly, and very positively at the same time.

He jumped out of the chair as if I had put a knife into him, and struck his fist on the table, so heavily that the wood cracked again.

'Steady, sir,' says I. 'Flying into a passion won't help you to the truth.'

'It's a lie!' says he, with another smack of his fist on the table – 'a base, vile, infamous lie! How dare you—'

He stopped, and fell back into the chair again, looked about him in a bewildered way, and ended by bursting out crying.

'When your better sense comes back to you, sir,' says I, 'I am sure you will be gentleman enough to make an apology for the language you have just used. In the meantime, please to listen, if you can, to a word of explanation. Mr Sharpin has sent in a report to our inspector, of the most irregular and ridiculous kind; setting down, not only all his own foolish doings and sayings, but the doings and sayings of Mrs Yatman as well. In most cases, such a document would have been fit only for the waste-paper basket; but, in this particular case, it so happens that Mr Sharpin's budget of nonsense leads to a certain conclusion which the simpleton of a writer has been quite innocent of suspecting from the beginning to the end. Of that conclusion I am so sure, that I will forfeit my place, if it does not turn out that Mrs Yatman has been practising upon the folly and conceit of this young man, and that she has tried to shield herself from discovery by purposely encouraging him to suspect the wrong persons. I tell you that confidently; and I will even go further. I will undertake to give a decided opinion as to why Mrs Yatman took the money, and what she has done with it, or with a part of it. Nobody can look at that lady, sir, without being struck by the great taste and beauty of her dress—'

As I said those last words, the poor man seemed to find his powers of speech again. He cut me short directly, as haughtily as if he had been a duke instead of a stationer.

'Try some other means of justifying your vile calumny against my wife,' says he. 'Her milliner's bill, for the past year, is on my file of receipted accounts at this moment.'

'Excuse me, sir,' says I, 'but that proves nothing. Milliners, I must tell you, have a certain rascally custom which comes within the daily experience of our office. A married lady who wishes it can keep two accounts at her dressmaker's; one is the account which her husband sees and pays; the other is the private account, which contains all the extravagant items, and which the wife pays secretly, by instalments, whenever she can. According to our usual experience, these instalments are mostly squeezed out of the housekeeping money. In your case, I suspect no instalments have been paid; proceedings have been threatened; Mrs Yatman, knowing your altered circumstances, has felt herself driven into a corner; and she has paid her private account out of your cash-box.'

'I won't believe it,' says he. 'Every word you speak is an abominable insult to me and to my wife.'

'Are you man enough, sir,' says I, taking him up short, in order to save time and words, 'to get that receipted bill you spoke of just now off the file, and come with me at once to the milliner's shop where Mrs Yatman deals?'

He turned red in the face at that, got the bill directly, and put on his hat. I took out of my pocket-book the list containing the numbers of the lost notes, and we left the house together immediately.

Arrived at the milliner's (one of the expensive West-end houses, as I expected), I asked for a private interview, on important business, with the mistress of the concern. It was not the first time that she and I had met over the same delicate investigation. The moment she set eyes on me, she sent for her husband. I mentioned who Mr Yatman was, and what we wanted.

'This is strictly private?' inquires the husband. I nodded my head.

'And confidential?' says the wife. I nodded again.

'Do you see any objection, dear, to obliging the sergeant with a sight of the books?' says the husband.

'None in the world, love, if you approve of it,' says the wife.

All this while poor Mr Yatman sat looking the picture of astonishment and distress, quite out of place at our polite conference. The books were brought – and one minute's look at the pages in which Mrs Yatman's name figured was enough, and more than enough, to prove the truth of every word that I had spoken.

There, in one book, was the husband's account, which Mr Yatman had settled. And there, in the other, was the private account, crossed off also; the date of settlement being the very day after the loss of the cash-box. This said private account amounted to the sum of a hundred and seventy-five pounds, odd shillings; and it extended over a period of three years. Not a single instalment had been paid on it. Under the last line was an entry to this effect: 'Written to for the third time, June 23rd.' I pointed to it, and asked the milliner if that meant 'last June.' Yes, it did mean last June; and she now deeply regretted to say that it had been accompanied by a threat of legal proceedings.

'I thought you gave good customers more than three years' credit?' says I.

The milliner looks at Mr Yatman, and whispers to me – 'Not when a lady's husband gets into difficulties.'

She pointed to the account as she spoke. The entries after the time when Mr Yatman's circumstances became involved were just as extravagant, for a person in his wife's situation, as the entries for the year before that period. If the lady had economized in other things, she had certainly not economized in the matter of dress.

There was nothing left now but to examine the cash-book, for form's sake. The money had been paid in notes, the amounts and numbers of which exactly tallied with the figures set down in my list.

After that, I thought it best to get Mr Yatman out of the house immediately. He was in such a pitiable condition, that I called a cab and accompanied him home in it. At first he cried and raved like a child; but I soon quieted him – and I must add, to his credit, that he made me a most handsome apology for his language, as the cab drew up at his house-door. In return, I tried to give him some advice about how to set matters right, for the future, with his wife. He paid very little attention to me, and went upstairs muttering to himself about a separation. Whether Mrs Yatman will come cleverly out of the scrape or not seems doubtful. I should say, myself, that she will go into screeching hysterics, and so frighten the poor man into forgiving her. But this is no business of ours. So far as we are concerned, the case is now at an end; and the present report may come to a conclusion along with it. I remain, accordingly, yours to command,

THOMAS BULMER

P.S. – I have to add, that, on leaving Rutherford Street, I met Mr Matthew Sharpin coming to pack up his things.

'Only think!' says he, rubbing his hands in great spirits, 'I've been to the genteel villa-residence; and the moment I mentioned my business, they kicked me out directly. There were two witnesses of the assault; and it's worth a hundred pounds to me, if it's worth a farthing.'

'I wish you joy of your luck,' says I.

'Thank you,' says he. 'When may I pay you the same compliment on finding the thief?'

'Whenever you like,' says I, 'for the thief is found.'

'Just what I expected,' says he. 'I've done all the work; and now you cut in, and claim all the credit – Mr Jay, of course?'

'No,' says I.

'Who is it then?' says he.

'Ask Mrs Yatman,' says I. 'She's waiting to tell you.'

'All right! I'd much rather hear it from that charming woman than from you,' says he, and goes into the house in a mighty hurry.

What do you think of that, Inspector Theakstone? Would you like to stand in Mr Sharpin's shoes? I shouldn't, I can promise you!

FROM CHIEF INSPECTOR THEAKSTONE TO MR MATTHEW SHARPIN

July 12th

Sir,

Sergeant Bulmer has already told you to consider yourself suspended until further notice. I have now authority to add, that your services as a member of the Detective Police are positively declined. You will please to take this letter as notifying officially your dismissal from the force.

I may inform you, privately, that your rejection is not intended to cast any reflections on your character. It merely implies that you are not quite sharp enough for our purpose. If we *are* to have a new recruit among us, we should infinitely prefer Mrs Yatman. Your obedient servant,

Francis Theakstone

NOTE ON THE PRECEDING CORRESPONDENCE, ADDED BY MR THEAKSTONE

The Inspector is not in a position to append any explanations of importance to the last of the letters. It has been discovered that Mr Matthew Sharpin left the house in Rutherford Street five minutes after his interview outside of it with Sergeant Bulmer – his manner expressing the liveliest emotions of terror and astonishment, and his left cheek displaying a bright patch of red, which looked as if it might have been the result of what is popularly termed a smart box on the ear. He was also heard, by the shopman at Rutherford Street, to use a very shocking expression in reference to Mrs Yatman; and was seen to clench his fist vindictively, as he ran round the corner of the street. Nothing more has been heard of him; and it is conjectured that he has left London with the intention of offering his valuable services to the provincial police.

On the interesting domestic subject of Mr and Mrs Yatman still less is known. It has, however, been positively ascertained that the medical attendant of the family was sent for in a great hurry on the day when Mr Yatman returned from the milliner's shop. The neighbouring chemist received, soon afterwards, a prescription of a soothing nature to make up for Mrs Yatman. The day after, Mr Yatman purchased some smelling-salts at the shop, and afterwards appeared at the circulating library to ask for a novel, descriptive of high life, that would amuse an invalid lady. It has been inferred from these circumstances that he has not thought it desirable to carry out his threat of separating himself from his wife – at least in the present (presumed) condition of that lady's sensitive nervous system.

The Poisoned Meal

[From the Records of the French Courts]

———————

Originally appeared in *Household Words*, 18 September to 2 October 1858. Reprinted in *My Miscellanies* (1863) as a 'Case Worth Looking At'. The story stands half way between fiction and reportage, the equivalent of the modern 'faction.'

I THE POCKETS

This case takes us across the Channel to Normandy; and introduces us to a young French girl, named Marie-Françoise-Victoire Salmon.

Her father was a poor Norman labourer. Her mother died while she was a child. From an early age Marie had learnt to get her own living by going out to service. Three different mistresses tried her while she was a very young girl, and found every reason to be satisfied with her conduct. She entered her fourth place, in the family of one Monsieur Dumesnil, when she was twenty years of age. This was the turning-point in her career; and here the strange story of her life properly begins.

Among the persons who often visited Monsieur Dumesnil and his wife, was a certain Monsieur Revel, a relation of Madame Dumesnil's. He was a man of some note in his part of the country, holding a responsible legal appointment at the town of Caen in Normandy; and he honoured Marie, when he first saw her at her master's house, with his special attention and approval. She had an innocent face, and a winning manner; and Monsieur Revel became almost oppressively anxious, in a strictly paternal way, that she should better her condition, by seeking service at Caen, where places were plentiful and wages higher than in the country; and where, it is also necessary to remember, Monsieur Revel himself happened to live.

Marie's own idea, however, of the best means of improving her condition was a little at variance with the idea of her disinterested adviser. Her ambition was to gain her living independently, if she could, by being a sempstress. She left the service of Monsieur Dumesnil of her own accord, without so much as the shadow of a stain on her character, and went to the old town of Bayeux to try what she could do by taking in needlework. As a means of subsistence, needlework soon proved itself to be insufficient; and she found herself thrown back again on the old resource of going out to service. Most unfortunately, as events afterwards turned out, she now called to mind Monsieur Revel's paternal advice, and resolved to seek employment as a maid-of-all-work at Caen.

She left Bayeux with the little bundle of clothes which represented all the property she had in the world, on the first of August, seventeen hundred and eighty-one. It will be well to notice this date particularly, and to remember – in case some of the events of Marie's story should seem almost incredible – that it marks the period which immediately preceded the first outbreak of the French Revolution.

Among the few articles of the maid's apparel which the bundle contained, and to which it is necessary to direct attention at the outset, were *two pairs of pockets*, one of them being still in an unfinished condition. She had a third pair which she wore on her journey. In the last century, a country girl's pockets were an important and prominent part of her costume. They hung on each side of her, ready to her hand. They were sometimes very prettily embroidered, and they were almost always large and of a bright colour.

On the first of August, seventeen hundred and eighty-one, Marie left Bayeux, and early on the same day she reached Caen. Her good manners, her excellent character, and the modesty of her demands in the matter of wages, rendered it easy for her to find a situation. On the very evening of her arrival she was suited with a place; and her first night at Caen was passed under the roof of her new employers.

The family consisted of Marie's master and mistress, Monsieur and Madame Huet Duparc (both highly respectable people); of two sons, aged respectively twenty-one and eleven years; of their sister, aged seventeen years; and of Monsieur and Madame de Beaulieu, the father and mother of Madame Duparc, one eighty-eight years old, the other eighty-six.

Madame Duparc explained to Marie the various duties which she was expected to perform, on the evening when she entered the house. She was to begin the day by fetching some milk – that being one of the ingredients used in preparing the hasty-pudding which formed the favourite morning meal of the old gentleman, Monsieur de Beaulieu. The hasty-pudding was always to be got ready by seven o'clock exactly. When this had been done, Marie was next required to take the infirm old lady, Madame de Beaulieu, every morning to mass. She was then to go to market, and get all the provisions that were wanted for the daily use of the family; and she was, finally, to look to the cooking of the food, and to make herself additionally useful (with some occasional assistance from Madame Duparc and her daughter) in every remaining branch of household work. The yearly wages she was to receive for performing all these conflicting duties, amounted to precisely two pounds sterling of English money.

She had entered her new place on a Wednesday. On Thursday she took her first lesson in preparing the old gentleman's morning meal. One point which her mistress then particularly impressed on her was, that she was *not* to put any salt in the hasty-pudding.

On the Saturday following, when she went out to buy milk, she made a little purchase on her own account. Of course the purchase was an article of dress – a piece of fine bright orange-coloured stuff, for which she paid nearly the whole price on the spot, out of her small savings. The sum of two sous six deniers (about a penny English) was all that Marie took credit for. On her return to the house she showed the piece of stuff to Madame Duparc, and asked to be advised whether she should make an apron or a jacket of it.

The next day being Sunday, Marie marked the occasion by putting on all the little finery she had. Her pair of festive pockets, striped with blue and white, came out of her bundle along with other things. When she had put them on, she hung the old work-a-day pockets which she had worn on leaving Bayeux, to the back of a chair in her bed-chamber. This was a little room on the ground-floor, situated close to the dining-room, and perfectly easy of access to every one in the house. Long afterwards, Marie remembered how pleasantly and quietly that Sunday passed. It was the last day of happiness the poor creature was to enjoy in the house of Madame Duparc.

On the Monday morning, she went to fetch the milk as usual. But the milkwoman was not in the shop to serve her. After returning to the house, she proposed making a second attempt; but her mistress stopped her, saying that the milk would doubtless be sent before long. This turned out to be the case, and Marie, having cleaned the saucepan for Monsieur de Beaulieu's hasty-pudding, received from the hands of Madame Duparc, the earthen vessel containing the meal used in the house. She mixed this flour and put it into the saucepan in the presence of Madame Duparc and her daughter.

She had just set the saucepan on the fire, when her mistress said, with a very remarkable abruptness:

'Have you put any salt in it?'

'Certainly not, ma'am,' answered Marie, amazed by the question. 'You told me yourself that I was never to put salt in it.'

Upon this, Madame Duparc snatched up the saucepan without saying another word, turned to the dresser, stretched out her hand towards one of four salt-cellars which always stood there, and sprinkled salt into the saucepan – or (to speak with extreme correctness, the matter being important), if not salt something which she took for salt.

The hasty-pudding made, Marie poured it from the saucepan into a soup-plate which her mistress held. Madame Duparc herself then took it to Monsieur de Beaulieu. She and her daughter, and one of her sons remained with the old man, while he was eating his breakfast. Marie, left in the kitchen, prepared to clean the saucepan; but, before she could do so, she was suddenly called in two different directions, by Madame de Beaulieu, and Madame Duparc. The old lady wished to be taken to mass; and her mistress wanted to send her on a number of errands. Marie did not stop even to pour some clean water, as usual, into the saucepan. She went at once to get her instructions from Madame Duparc, and to attend on Madame de Beaulieu. Taking the old lady to church, and then running on her mistress's errands, kept her so long away from the house, that it was half-past eleven in the forenoon, before she got back to the kitchen.

The first news that met her on her return was that Monsieur de Beaulieu had been suffering, ever since nine o'clock, from a violent attack of vomiting and colic. Madame Duparc ordered her to help the old man to bed immediately; and inquired, when these directions had been followed, whether Marie felt capable of looking after him herself, or whether she would prefer that a nurse should be sent for. Being a kind-hearted, willing girl, always anxious to make herself useful, Marie replied that she would gladly undertake the nursing of the old man; and, thereupon, her bed was moved at once into Monsieur de Beaulieu's room.

Meanwhile, Madame Duparc fetched from a neighbouring apothecary's, one of the apprentices of the shop, to see her father. The lad was quite unfit to meet the emergency of the case, which was certainly serious enough to require the attention of his master, if not of a regularly qualified physician. Instead of applying any internal remedies, the apprentice stupidly tried blistering. This course of treatment proved utterly useless; but no better advice was called in. After he had suffered for hours without relief, Monsieur de Beaulieu began to sink rapidly towards the afternoon. At half-past five o'clock he had ceased to exist.

This shocking catastrophe, startling and suspicious as it was, did not appear to discompose the nerves of Madame Duparc. While her eldest son immediately left the house to inform his father (who had been absent in the country all day) of what had happened, she lost no time in sending for the nearest nurse to lay out the corpse of Monsieur de Beaulieu. On entering the chamber of death, the nurse found Marie there alone, praying by the old man's bedside.

'He died suddenly, did he not?' said the nurse.

'Very suddenly,' answered Marie. 'He was walking about only yesterday, in perfect health.'

Soon afterwards the time came when it was customary to prepare supper. Marie went into the kitchen, mechanically, to get the meal ready. Madame Duparc, her daughter, and her youngest son, sat down to it as usual. Madame de Beaulieu, overwhelmed by the dreadful death of her husband, was incapable of joining them.

When supper was over, Marie assisted the old lady to bed. Then, worn out though she was with fatigue, she went back to the nurse to keep her company in watching by the dead body. Monsieur de Beaulieu had been kind to Marie, and had spoken gratefully of the little attentions she had shown him. She remembered this tenderly now that he was no more; and she could not find it in her heart to leave a hired mourner to be the only watcher by his death-bed. All that night she remained in the room, entirely ignorant of what was passing the while in every other part of the house – her own little bed-room included, as a matter of course.

About seven o'clock the next morning, after sitting up all night, she went back again wearily to the kitchen to begin her day's work. Her mistress joined her there, and saluted her instantly with a scolding.

'You are the most careless, slovenly girl I ever met with,' said Madame Duparc. 'Look at your dress; How can you expect to be decent on a Sunday, if you wear your best pair of pockets on week-days?'

Surely Madame Duparc's grief for the loss of her father must have been slight enough, if it did not prevent her from paying the strictest attention to her servant's pockets! Although Marie had only known the old man for a few days, she had been too deeply impressed by his illness and its fatal end, to be able to think of such a trifle as the condition of her dress. And now, of all the people in the world, it was Monsieur de Beaulieu's daughter who reminded her that she had never thought of changing her pockets, only the day after the old man's dreadful death.

'Put on your old pockets, directly, you untidy girl!' said Madame Duparc.

The old pockets were of course hanging where Marie had left them, at the back of the chair in her own room – the room which was open to any one who chose to go into it – the room which she herself had not entered during the past night. She left the kitchen to obey her mistress; and taking the old pair of pockets off the chair, tied them on as quickly as possible. From that fatal moment the friendless maid-of-all-work was a ruined girl.

II THE ARSENIC

On returning to the kitchen to go on with her work, the exhaustion against which Marie had hitherto fought successfully, overpowered her the moment she sat down; her heavy head drooped, her eyes closed in spite of her, and she fell into a broken, uneasy slumber. Madame Duparc and her daughter, seeing the condition she was in, undertook the preparation of the day's dinner themselves. Among the dishes which they got ready, and which they salted from the cellars on the dresser, were two different kinds of soup – one kind for themselves, made from fresh 'stock' – the other, for Marie and the nurse, made from old 'stock.' They were engaged over their cookery, when Monsieur Duparc arrived from the country; and Marie was awakened to take the horse he had ridden to the stables, to unsaddle the animal, and to give him his feed of corn.

While she was thus engaged, Madame Duparc and her daughter remained alone in the kitchen. When she left the stable it was time for her to lay the cloth. She was told to put plates for seven persons. Only six, however, sat down to dinner. Those six were, Madame de Beaulieu, Monsieur and Madame Duparc, the youngest of their two sons, Madame Beauguillot (sister of Madame Duparc), and Monsieur Beauguillot (her son). Mademoiselle Duparc remained in the kitchen to help Marie in serving up the dinner, and only took her place at table after the soup had been put on. Her elder brother, after summoning his father home, had not returned to the house.

After the soup had been taken away, and while Marie was waiting at table during the eating of the second course, young Duparc complained that he felt something gritty between his teeth. His mother made precisely the same remark. Nobody else, however, agreed with them, and the subject was allowed to drop. When the second course was done with, the dessert followed, consisting of a plate of cherries. With the dessert there arrived a visitor, Monsieur Fergant, a relation of Madame Duparc's. This gentleman placed himself at table with the rest of the company.

Meanwhile, the nurse and Marie were making their dinner in the kitchen off the soup which had been specially provided for them – Marie having previously placed the dirty plates and the empty soup-tureen from the dining-room, in the scullery, as usual, to be washed at the proper time. While she and her companion were still engaged over their soup, young Duparc and his mother suddenly burst into the kitchen, followed by the other persons who had partaken of dinner.

'We are all poisoned!' cried Madame Duparc, in the greatest terror. 'Good heavens! I smell burnt arsenic in the kitchen!'

Monsieur Fergant, the visitor, hearing these last words, politely stepped forward to echo them.

'Burnt arsenic, beyond a doubt,' said Monsieur Fergant. When this gentleman was subsequently questioned on the subject, it may not be amiss to mention, that he was quite unable to say what burnt arsenic smelt like. Neither is it altogether out of place to inquire how Madame Duparc happened to be so amazingly apt at discovering the smell of burnt arsenic? The answer to the question does not seem easy to discover.

Having settled that they were all poisoned, and having even found out (thanks to those two intelligent amateur chemists, Madame Duparc and Monsieur Fergant) the very nature of the deadly drug that had been used to destroy them, the next thing the company naturally thought of was the necessity of summoning medical help. Young Monsieur Beauguillot obligingly ran off (it was apparently a very mild case of poisoning, so far as he was concerned) to the apothecary's shop, and fetched, not the apprentice this time, but the master. The master, Monsieur Thierry, arrived in great haste, and found the dinner-eaters all complaining of nausea and pains in the stomach. He naturally asked what they had eaten. The reply was, that they had eaten nothing but soup.

This was, to say the least of it, rather an unaccountable answer. The company had had for dinner, besides soup, a second course of boiled meat and ragout of beef, and a dessert of cherries. Why was this plain fact concealed? Why was the apothecary's attention to be fixed exclusively on the soup? Was it because the tureen was empty, and because the alleged smell of burnt arsenic might be accounted for on the theory that the remains of the soup brought from the dining-room had been thrown on the kitchen fire? But no remains of soup came down – it had been all consumed by the guests. And what is still more remarkable, the only person in the kitchen (excepting Marie and the nurse) who could not discover the smell of burnt arsenic, was the person of all others who was professionally qualified to find it out first – the apothecary himself.

After examining the tureen and the plates, and stirring up the wood ashes on the fire, and making no sort of discovery, Monsieur Thierry turned to Marie, and asked if she could account for what had happened. She simply replied, that she knew nothing at all about it; and, thereupon, her mistress and the rest of the persons present all overwhelmed her together with a perfect torrent of questions. The poor girl, terrified by the hubbub, worn out by a sleepless night and by the hard work and agitation of the day preceding it, burst into an hysterical fit of tears, and was ordered out of the kitchen to lie down and recover herself. The only person who showed her the least pity and offered her the slightest attention, was a servant-girl like herself, who lived next door, and who stole up to the room in which she was weeping alone, with a cup of warm milk and water to comfort her.

Meanwhile, the report had spread in the town that the old man, Monsieur de Beaulieu, and the whole Duparc family, had been poisoned by their servant. Madame Duparc did her best to give the rumour the widest possible circulation. Entirely forgetting, as it would seem, that she was on her own showing a poisoned woman, she roamed excitably all over the house with an audience of agitated female friends at her heels; telling the burnt-arsenic story over and over again to every fresh detachment of visitors that arrived to hear it; and finally leading the whole troop of women into the room where Marie was trying to recover herself. The poor girl was surrounded in a moment; angry faces and shrill voices met her on every side; the most insolent questions, the most extravagant accusations, assailed her; and not one word that she could say in her own defence was listened to for an instant. She had sprung up in the bed, on her knees, and was frantically entreating for permission to speak in her own defence, when a new personage appeared on the scene, and stilled the clamour by his presence. This individual was a surgeon named Hébert, a friend of Madame Duparc's, who announced that he had arrived to give the family the benefit of his assistance, and who proposed to commence operations, by searching the servant's pockets without farther delay.

The instant Marie heard him make this proposal, she untied her pockets, and gave them to Surgeon Hébert with her own hands. He examined them on the spot. In one, he found some copper money and a thimble. In the other (to use his own words, given in evidence) he discovered 'various fragments of bread, sprinkled over with some minute substance which was white and shining. He kept the fragments of bread, and left the room immediately without saying a word.' By this course of proceeding, he gave Marie no chance of stating at the outset whether she knew of the fragments of bread being in her pocket, or whether she was totally ignorant how they came there. Setting aside, for the present, the question, whether there was really any arsenic on the crumbs at all, it would clearly have been showing the unfortunate maid-of-all-work no more than common justice to have allowed her the opportunity of speaking before the bread was carried away.

It was now seven o'clock in the evening. The next event was the arrival of another officious visitor. The new friend in need belonged to the legal profession – he was an advocate named Friley. Monsieur Friley's legal instincts led him straightway to a conclusion which seriously advanced the progress of events. Having heard the statement of Madame Duparc and her daughter, he decided that it was his duty to lodge an information against Marie before the Procurator of the King, at Caen.

The Procurator of the King is, by this time, no stranger to the reader. He was the same Monsieur Revel who had taken such an amazingly strong interest in Marie's fortunes, and who had strongly advised her to try her luck at Caen. Here then, surely, was a friend found at last for the forlorn maid-of-all-work. We shall see how Monsieur Revel acted, after Friley's information had been duly lodged.

The French law of the period, and, it may be added, the commonest principles of justice also, required the Procurator to perform certain plain duties as soon as the accusation against Marie had reached his ears.

He was, in the first place, bound to proceed immediately, accompanied by his official colleague, to the spot where the alleged crime of poisoning was supposed to have taken place. Arrived there, it was his business to ascertain for himself the condition of the persons attacked with illness; to hear their statements; to examine the rooms, the kitchen utensils, and the family medicine-chest, if there happened to be one in the house; to receive any statement the accused person might wish to make; to take down her answers to his questions; and, lastly, to keep anything found on the servant (the bread-crumbs, for instance, of which Surgeon Hébert had coolly taken possession), or anything found about the house which it might be necessary to produce in evidence, in a position of absolute security, under the hand and seal of justice.

These were the plain duties which Monsieur Revel, the Procurator, was officially bound to fulfil. In the case of Marie, he not only neglected to perform any one of them, but actually sanctioned a scheme for entrapping her into prison, by sending a commissary of police to the house, in plain clothes, with an order to place her in solitary confinement. To what motive could this scandalous violation of his duties and of justice be attributed? The last we saw of Monsieur Revel, he was so benevolently disposed towards Marie that he condescended to advise her about her prospects in life, and even went the length of recommending her to seek for a situation in the very town in which he lived himself. And now, we find him so suddenly and bitterly hostile towards the former object of his patronage, that he actually lends the assistance of his high official position to sanction an accusation against her, into the truth or falsehood of which he had not made a single inquiry! Can it be that Monsieur Revel's interest in Marie was, after all, not of the purest possible kind, and that the unfortunate girl proved too stubbornly virtuous to be taught what the real end was towards which the attentions of her over-benevolent adviser privately pointed? There is no evidence attaching to the case (as how should there be?) to prove this. But is there any other explanation of Monsieur Revel's conduct, which at all tends to account for the extraordinary inconsistency of it?

Having received his secret instructions, the commissary of police – a man named Bertot – proceeded to the house of Monsieur and Madame Duparc, disguised in plain clothes. His first proceeding was to order Marie to produce the various plates, dishes, and kitchen utensils which had been used at the dinner of Tuesday, the seventh of August (that being the day on which the poisoning of the company was alleged to have taken place). Marie produced a saucepan, an earthen vessel, a stewpan, and several plates piled on each other, in one of which there were the remains of some soup. These articles Bertot locked up in the kitchen cupboard, and took away the key with him. He ought to have taken the additional precaution of placing a seal on the cupboard, so as to prevent any tampering with the lock, or any treachery with a duplicate key. But this he neglected to do.

His next proceeding was to tell Marie that the Procurator Revel wished to speak to her, and to propose that she should accompany him to the presence of that gentleman forthwith. Not having the slightest suspicion of any treachery, she willingly consented, and left the house with the commissary. A friend of the Duparcs, named Vassol, accompanied them.

Once out of the house, Bertot led his unsuspecting prisoner straight to the gaol. As soon as she was inside the gates, he informed her that she was arrested, and proceeded to search her person in the presence of Vassol, of the gaoler of the prison, and of a woman named Dujardin. The first thing found on her was a little linen bag, sewn to her petticoat, and containing a species of religious charm, in the shape of a morsel of the sacramental wafer. Her pockets came next under review (the pockets which Surgeon Hébert had previously searched). A little dust was discovered at the bottom of them, which was shaken out on paper, wrapped up along with the linen bag, sealed in one packet, and taken to the Procurator's office. Finally, the woman Dujardin found in Marie's bosom a little key, which she readily admitted to be the key of her own cupboard.

The search over, one last act of cruelty and injustice was all that remained to be committed for that day. The unfortunate girl was placed at once in solitary confinement.

III THE EVIDENCE

Thus far, the case is one of suspicion only. Waiting until the end of the trial before we decide on whom that suspicion ought to rest, let us now hear the evidence by which the Duparcs and their adherents proceeded to justify their conspiracy against the liberty and the life of a friendless girl.

Having secured Marie in solitary confinement, and having thus left the house and all that it contained for a whole night at the free disposal of the Duparcs, the Procurator Revel bethought himself, the morning after the arrest of his prisoner, of the necessity of proceeding with something like official regularity. He accordingly issued his requisition to the Lieutenant-Criminel to accompany him to the house of Monsieur Duparc, attended by the medical officers and the clerk, to inquire into the circumstances under which the suspected death by poisoning of Monsieur de Beaulieu had taken place. Marie had been imprisoned on the evening of the seventh of August, and this requisition is dated on the morning of the eight. The document betrays one remarkable informality. It mentions the death of Monsieur de Beaulieu; but is absolutely silent on the subject of the alleged poisoning of seven persons at dinner the next day. And yet, it was this latter circumstance only which first directed suspicion against Marie, and which induced Friley to lodge the information against her on which the Procurator was now acting. Probably Monsieur Revel's legal acumen convinced him, at the outset, that the story of the poisoned dinner was too weak to be relied on.

The officers of the law, accompanied by the doctors, proceeded to the house of the Duparcs on the eighth of August. After viewing the body of Monsieur de Beaulieu, the medical men were directed to open and examine it. They reported the discovery in the stomach of a reddish, brick-coloured liquid, somewhat resembling the lees of wine. The mucous membrane was detached in some places, and its internal surface was corroded. On examining the reddish liquid, they found it to contain a crystallised sediment, which, on analysation, proved to be arsenic. Upon this, the doctors delivered it as their opinion that Monsieur de Beaulieu had been poisoned, and that poison had been the cause of his death.

The event having taken this serious turn, the first duty of the Lieutenant-Criminel (according to the French law) was to send for the servant on whom suspicion rested, to question her, and to confront her with the Duparcs. He did nothing of the kind; he made no inquiry after the servant (being probably unwilling to expose his colleague, the Procurator, who had illegally arrested and illegally imprisoned her); he never examined the kitchen utensils which the Commissary had locked up; he never opened the servant's cupboard with the key that had been taken from her when she was searched in prison. All he did was to reduce the report of the doctors to writing, and to return to his office with his posse-comitatus at his heels.

It was necessary to summon the witnesses and examine them. But the Procurator Revel now conveniently remembered the story of the poisoned dinner, and he sent the Lieutenant-Criminel to examine the Duparcs and their friends at the private residence of the family, in consideration of the sickly condition of the eaters of the adulterated meal. It may be as well to observe, here as elsewhere, that these highly-indulged personages had none of them been sufficiently inconvenienced even to go to bed, or in any way to alter their ordinary habits.

On the afternoon of the eighth, the Lieutenant-Criminel betook himself to the house of Monsieur Duparc, to collect evidence touching the death by poison of Monsieur de Beaulieu. The first witness called was Monsieur Duparc.

This gentleman, it will be remembered, was away from home, on Monday, the sixth, when Monsieur de Beaulieu died, and only returned, at the summons of his eldest son, at half-past eleven on the forenoon of the seventh. He had nothing to depose connected with the death of his father-in-law, or with the events which might have taken place in the house on the night of the sixth and the morning of the seventh. On the other hand, he had a great deal to say about the state of his own stomach after the dinner of the seventh – a species of information not calculated to throw much light on the subject of inquiry, which was the poisoning of Monsieur de Beaulieu.

The old lady, Madame de Beaulieu, was next examined. She could give no evidence of the slightest importance touching the matter in hand; but, like Monsieur Duparc, she had something to say on the topic of the poisoned dinner.

Madame Duparc followed on the list of witnesses. The report of her examination – so thoroughly had she recovered from the effects of the dinner of the seventh – ran to a prodigious length. Five-sixths of it related entirely to her own sensations and suspicions, and the sensations and suspicions of her relatives and friends, after they had risen from table. As to the point at issue, the point which affected the liberty, and perhaps the life, of her unfortunate servant, she had so little to say that her testimony may be repeated here in her own words:

'The witness (Madame Duparc) deposed, that after Marie had helped Monsieur de Beaulieu to get up, she (Marie) hastened out for the milk, and, on her return with it, prepared the hasty-pudding, took it herself off the fire, and herself poured it out into the plate – then left the kitchen to accompany Madame de Beaulieu to mass. Four or five minutes after Monsieur de Beaulieu had eaten the hasty-pudding, he was seized with violent illness.'

Short as it is, this statement contains several distinct suppressions of the truth.

First, Madame Duparc is wrong in stating that Marie fetched the milk, for it was the milkwoman who brought it to the house. Secondly, Madame Duparc conceals the fact that she handed the flour to the servant to make the hasty-pudding. Thirdly, Madame Duparc does not mention that she held the plate for the pudding to be poured into, and took it to her father. Fourthly, and most important of all, Madame Duparc altogether omits to state, that she sprinkled salt, with her own hands, over the hasty-pudding – although she had expressly informed her servant, a day or two before, that salt was never to be mixed with it. At a subsequent stage of the proceedings, she was charged with having salted the hasty-pudding herself, and she could not, and did not, deny it.

The examination of Madame Duparc ended the business on the day of the eighth. The next morning, the Lieutenant-Criminel, as politely attentive as before, returned to resume his inquiry at the private residence of Monsieur Duparc.

The first witness examined on the second day was Mademoiselle Duparc. She carefully followed her mother's lead – saying as little as possible about the preparation of the hasty-pudding on the morning of Monday, and as much as possible about the pain suffered by everybody after the dinner of Tuesday. Madame Beauguillot, the next witness, added her testimony, as to the state of her own digestive organs, after partaking of the same meal – speaking at such prodigious length that the poison would appear, in her case, to have produced its principal effect (and that of a stimulating kind) on her tongue. Her son, Monsieur de Beauguillot, was next examined, quite uselessly in relation to the death by poison which was the object of inquiry. The last witness was Madame Duparc's younger son – the same who had complained of feeling a gritty substance between his teeth at dinner. In one important respect, his evidence flatly contradicted his mother's. Madame Duparc had adroitly connected Monsieur de Beaulieu's illness with the hasty-pudding, by describing the old man as having been taken ill four or five minutes after eating it. Young Duparc, on the contrary, declared that his grandfather first felt ill at nine o'clock – exactly two hours after he had partaken of his morning meal.

With the evidence of this last witness, the examinations at the private residence of Monsieur Duparc ended. Thus far, out of the seven persons, all related to each other, who had been called as witnesses, three (Monsieur Duparc himself, Madame Beauguillot, and her son) had not been in the house on the day when Monsieur de Beaulieu died. Of the other four, who had been present (Madame de Beaulieu, Madame Duparc, her son and her daughter), not one deposed to a single fact tending to fix on Marie any reasonable suspicion of having administered poison to Monsieur de Beaulieu.

The remaining witnesses, called before the Lieutenant-Criminel, were twenty-nine in number. Not one of them had been in the house on the Monday which was the day of the old man's death. Twenty-six of them had nothing to offer but hearsay evidence on the subject of the events which had taken place at, and after, the dinner of Tuesday. The testimony of the remaining three, namely, of Friley, who had lodged the information against Marie; of Surgeon Hébert, who had searched her pockets in the house; and of Commissary Bertot, who had searched her for the second time, after taking her to prison, – was the testimony on which the girl's enemies mainly relied for substantiating their charges by positively associating her with the possession of arsenic.

Let us see what amount of credit can be attached to the evidence of these three witnesses.

Friley was the first to be examined. After stating what share he had taken in bringing Marie to justice (it will be remembered that he lodged his information against her at the instance of Madame Duparc, without allowing her to say a word in her own defence), he proceeded to depose that he hunted about the bed on which the girl had lain down to recover herself, and that he discovered on the mattress seven or eight scattered grains of some substance, which resembled the powder reported to have been found on the crumbs in her pockets. He added further, that on the next day, about two hours before the body of Monsieur de Beaulieu was examined, he returned to the house; searched under the bed, with Monsieur Duparc and a soldier named Cauvin; and found there four or five grains more of the same substance which he had discovered on the mattress.

Here were two separate portions of poison found, then. What did Friley do with them? Did he seal them up immediately in the presence of witnesses, and take them to the legal authorities? Nothing of the sort. On being asked what he did with the first portion, he replied that he gave it to young Monsieur Beauguillot. Beauguillot's evidence was thereupon referred to; and it was found that he had never mentioned receiving the packet of powder from Friley. He had made himself extremely officious in examining the kitchen utensils; he had been as anxious as any one to promote the discovery of arsenic; and when he had the opportunity of producing it, if Friley were to be believed, he held it back, and said not one word about the matter. So much for the first portion of the mysterious powder, and for the credibility of Friley's evidence thus far!

On being questioned as to what he had done with the second portion, alleged to have been found under the bed, Friley replied that he had handed it to the doctors who opened the body, and that they had tried to discover what it was, by burning it between two copper pieces. A witness who had been present at this proceeding declared, on being questioned, that the experiment had been made with some remains of hasty-pudding scraped out of the saucepan. Here again was a contradiction, and here, once more, Friley's evidence was, to say the least of it, not to be depended on.

Surgeon Hébert followed. What had he done with the crumbs of bread scattered over with white powder, which he had found in Marie's pocket? He had, after showing them to the company in the drawing-room, exhibited them next to the apothecary, and handed them afterwards to another medical man. Being finally assured that there was arsenic on the bread, he had sealed up the crumbs, and given the packet to the legal authorities. When had he done that? On the day of his examination as a witness – the fourteenth of August. When did he find the crumbs? On the seventh. Here was the arsenic, in this case, then, passing about from hand to hand, and not sealed up, for seven days. Had Surgeon Hébert anything more to say? Yes, he had another little lot of arsenic to hand in, which a lady-friend of his had told him she had found on Marie's bed, and which, like the first lot, had been passed about privately for seven days, from hand to hand, before it was sealed up. To us, in these later and better days, it seems hardly credible that the judge should have admitted these two packets in evidence. It is, nevertheless, the disgraceful fact that he did so receive them.

Commissary Bertot came next. He and the man named Vassol, who had helped him to entrap Marie into prison, and to search her before she was placed in solitary confinement, were examined in succession, and contradicted each other on oath, in the flattest manner.

Bertot stated that he had discovered the dust at the bottom of her pockets; had shaken it out on paper; had placed with it the little linen bag, containing a morsel of the sacramental wafer, which had been sewn to her petticoat; had sealed the two up in one packet; and had taken the packet to the proper office. Vassol, on the other hand, swore that *he* had shaken out the pockets, and had made up the packet; and that Bertot had done nothing in the matter but lend his seal. Contradicting each other in these details, both agreed that what they had found on the girl was inclosed and sealed up in *one* packet, which they had left at the office, neglecting to take such a receipt for it as might have established its identity in writing. At this stage of the proceedings the packet was sent for. Three packets appeared instead of one! Two were composed of paper, and contained dust and a little white powder. The third was the linen bag, presented without any covering at all. Vassol, bewildered by the change, declared that of these three separate objects, he could only identify one – the linen bag. In this case, it was as clear as daylight that somebody must have tampered with the single sealed packet which Bertot and Vassol swore to having left at the office. No attempt, however, was made to investigate this circumstance; and the case for the prosecution – so far as the accusation of poisoning was concerned – closed with the examination of Bertot and Vassol.

Such was the evidence produced in support of a charge which involved nothing less than the life or death of a human being.

IV THE SENTENCE

While the inquiry was in course of progress, various details connected with it found their way out of doors. The natural sense of justice among the people which had survived the corruptions of the time, was aroused to assert itself on behalf of the maid-of-all-work. The public voice spoke as loudly as it dared, in those days, in Marie's favour, and in condemnation of the conspiracy against her.

People persisted, from the first, in inquiring how it was that arsenic had got into the house of Monsieur Duparc; and rumour answered, in more than one direction, that a member of the family had purchased the poison a short time since, and that there were persons in the town who could prove it. To the astonishment of every one, no steps were taken by the legal authorities to clear up this report, and to establish the truth or the falsehood of it, before the trial. Another circumstance, of which also no explanation was attempted, filled the public mind with natural suspicion. This was the disappearance of the eldest son of Monsieur and Madame Duparc. On the day of his grandfather's sudden death, he had been sent, as may be remembered, to bring his father back from the country; and, from that time forth, he had never reappeared at the house, and nobody could say what had become of him. Was it not natural to connect together the rumours of purchased poison and the mysterious disappearance of this young man? Was it not utterly inconsistent with any proceedings conducted in the name of justice to let these suspicious circumstances exist, without making the slightest attempt to investigate and to explain them?

But, apart from all other considerations, the charge against Marie, was on the face of it preposterously incredible. A friendless young girl arrives at a strange town, possessing excellent testimonials to her character, and gets a situation in a family every member of which is utterly unknown to her until she enters the house. Established in her new place, she instantly conceives the project of poisoning the whole family, and carries it out in five days from the time when she first took her situation, by killing one member of the household, and producing suspicious symptoms of illness in the cases of all the rest. She commits this crime having nothing to gain by it; and she is so inconceivably reckless of detection that she scatters poison about the bed on which she lies down, leaves poison sticking to crumbs in her pockets, puts those pockets on when her mistress tells her to do so, and hands them over without a moment's hesitation to the first person who asks permission to search them. What mortal evidence could substantiate such a wild charge as this? How does the evidence actually presented substantiate it? No shadow of proof that she had purchased arsenic is offered, to begin with. The evidence against her is evidence which attempts to associate her with the actual possession of poison. What is it worth? In the first place, the witnesses contradict each other. In the second place, in no one case in which powdered substances were produced in evidence against her, had those powdered substances been so preserved as to prevent their being tampered with. Two packets of the powder pass about from hand to hand for seven days; two have been given to witnesses who can't produce them, or account for what has become of them; and one, which the witnesses who made it up swear to as a single packet, suddenly expands into three when it is called for in evidence!

Careless as they were of assuming even the external decencies of justice, the legal authorities, and their friends the Duparcs, felt that there would be some risk in trying their victim for her life on such evidence as this, in a large town like Caen. It was impossible to shift their ground and charge her with poisoning accidentally; for they either could not, or would not, account on ordinary grounds for the presence of arsenic in the house. And, even if this difficulty were overcome, and if it were alleged that arsenic purchased for killing vermin, had been carelessly placed in one of the salt-cellars on the dresser, Madame Duparc could not deny that her own hands had salted the hasty-pudding on the Monday, and that her servant had been too ill through exhaustion to cook the dinner on the Tuesday. Even supposing there were no serious interests of the vilest kind at stake, which made the girl's destruction a matter of necessity, it was clearly impossible to modify the charge against her. One other alternative remained – the alternative of adding a second accusation which might help to strengthen the first, and to degrade Marie in the estimation of those inhabitants of the town who were now disposed to sympathise with her.

The poor girl's character was so good, her previous country life had been so harmless, that no hint or suggestion for a second charge against her could be found in her past history. If her enemies were to succeed, it was necessary to rely on pure invention. Having hesitated before no extremes of baseness and falsehood, thus far, they were true to themselves in regard to any vile venture which remained to be tried.

A day or two after the examination of the witnesses called to prove the poisoning had been considered complete, the public of Caen were amazed to hear that certain disclosures had taken place which would render it necessary to try Marie, on a charge of theft as well as of poisoning. She was now not only accused of the murder of Monsieur de Beaulieu, but of robbing her former mistress, Madame Dumesnil (a relation, be it remembered, of Monsieur Revel's), in the situation she occupied before she came to Caen; of robbing Madame Duparc; and of robbing the shopwoman from whom she had bought the piece of orange-coloured stuff, the purchase of which is mentioned in an early part of this narrative.

There is no need to hinder the progress of the story by entering into details in relation to this second atrocious charge. When the reader is informed that the so-called evidence in support of the accusation of theft was got up by Procurator Revel, by Commissary Bertot, and by Madame Duparc, he will know beforehand what importance to attach to it, and what opinion to entertain on the question of the prisoner's innocence or guilt.

The preliminary proceedings were now considered to be complete. During their progress, Marie had been formally interrogated, in her prison, by the legal authorities. Fearful as her situation was, the poor girl seems to have maintained self-possession enough to declare her innocence of poisoning, and her innocence of theft, firmly. Her answers, it is needless to say, availed her nothing. No legal help was assigned to her; no such institution as a jury was in existence in France. Procurator Revel collected the evidence, Procurator Revel tried the case, Procurator Revel delivered the sentence. Need the reader be told that Marie's irresponsible judge and unscrupulous enemy had no difficulty whatever in finding her guilty? She had been arrested on the seventh of August, seventeen hundred and eighty-one. Her doom was pronounced on the seventeenth of April, seventeen hundred and eighty-two. Throughout the whole of that interval she remained in prison.

The sentence was delivered in the following terms. It was written, printed, and placarded in Caen; and it is here translated from the original French:

'The Procurator Royal of the Bailiwick and civil and criminal Bench and Presidency of Caen, having taken cognizance of the documents concerning the trial specially instituted against Marie-Françoise-Victoire-Salmon, accused of poisoning; the said documents consisting of an official report of the capture of the said Marie-Françoise-Victoire-Salmon on the seventh of August last, together with other official reports, &c.,

'Requires that the prisoner shall be declared duly convicted,

'I. Of having, on the Monday morning of the sixth of August last, cooked some hasty-pudding for Monsieur Paisant de Beaulieu, father-in-law of Monsieur Huet-Duparc, in whose house the prisoner had lived in the capacity of servant from the first day of the said month of August; and of having put arsenic in the said hasty-pudding while cooking it, by which arsenic the said Monsieur de Beaulieu died poisoned, about six o'clock on the same evening.

'II. Of having on the next day, Tuesday, the seventh of August last, put arsenic into the soup which was served, at noon, at the table of Monsieur and Madame Duparc, her employers, in consequence of which all those persons who sat at table and eat of the said soup were poisoned and made dangerously ill, to the number of seven.

'III. Of having been discovered with arsenic in her possession, which arsenic was found on the said Tuesday, in the afternoon, not only in the pockets of the prisoner, but upon the mattress of the bed on which she was resting; the said arsenic having been recognised as being of the same nature and precisely similar to that which the guests discovered to have been put into their soup, as also to that which was found the next day, in the body of the aforesaid Monsieur de Beaulieu, and in the saucepan in which the hasty-pudding had been cooked, of which the aforesaid Monsieur de Beaulieu had eaten.

'IV. Of being *strongly suspected* of having put some of the same arsenic into a plate of cherries which she served to Madame de Beaulieu, on the same Tuesday morning, and again on the afternoon of the same day at the table of Monsieur and Madame Duparc.

'V. Of having, at the period of Michaelmas, seventeen hundred and eighty, committed different robberies at the house of Monsieur Dumesnil, where she lived in the capacity of servant, and notably of stealing a sheet, of which she made herself a petticoat and an apron.

'VI. Of having, at the beginning of the month of August last, stolen, in the house of Monsieur Huet-Duparc, the different articles enumerated at the trial, and which were found locked up in her cupboard.

'VII. Of being *strongly suspected* of stealing, at the beginning of the said month of August, from the woman Lefévre, a piece of orange-coloured stuff.

'For punishment and reparation of which offences, she, the said Marie-Françoise-Victoire-Salmon, shall be condemned to make atonement, in her shift, with a halter round her neck, holding in her hands a burning wax candle of the weight of two pounds, before the principal gate and entrance of the church of St Peter, to which she shall be taken and led by the executioner of criminal sentences, who will tie in front of her and behind her back, a placard, on which shall be written in large characters, these words: *Poisoner and Domestic Thief*. And there, being on her knees, she shall declare that she has wickedly committed the said robberies and poisonings, for which she repents and asks pardon of God and Justice. This done, she shall be led by the said executioner to the square of the market of Saint Saviour's, to be there fastened to a stake with a chain of iron, and to be burnt alive; her body to be reduced to ashes, and the ashes to be cast to the winds; her goods to be acquired and confiscated to the king, or to whomsoever else they may belong. Said goods to be charged with a fine of ten livres to the king, in the event of the confiscation not turning to the profit of his Majesty.

'Required, additionally, that the said prisoner shall be previously submitted to the Ordinary and Extraordinary Torture, to obtain information of her accomplices, and notably of those who either sold to her or gave to her the arsenic found in her possession. Order hereby given for the printing and placarding of this sentence, in such places as shall be judged fit. Deliberated at the bar, this seventeenth April, seventeen hundred and eighty-two.

(Signed) REVEL'

On the next day, the eighteenth, this frightful sentence was formally confirmed.

The matter had now become public, and no one could prevent the unfortunate prisoner from claiming whatever rights the law still allowed her. She had the privilege of appealing against her sentence before the parliament of Rouen. And she appealed accordingly; being transferred, as directed by the law in such cases, from the prison at Caen to the prison at Rouen, to await the decision of the higher tribunal.

On the seventeenth of May the Rouen parliament delivered its judgment, and confirmed the original sentence.

There was some difficulty, at first, in making the unhappy girl understand that her last chance for life had failed her. When the fact that her sentence was ordered to be carried out was at length impressed on her mind, she sank down with her face on the prison floor – then started up on her knees, passionately shrieking to Heaven to have pity on her, and to grant her the justice and the protection which men denied. Her agitation at the frightful prospect before her was so violent, her screams of terror were so shrill and piercing, that all the persons connected with the management of the prison hurried together to her cell. Among the number were three priests, who were accustomed to visit the prisoners and to administer spiritual consolation to them. These three men mercifully set themselves to sooth the mental agony from which the poor creature was suffering. When they had partially quieted her, they soon found her willing and anxious to answer their questions. They inquired carefully into the main particulars of her sad story; and all three came to the same conclusion, that she was innocent. Seeing the impression she had produced on them, she caught, in her despair, at the idea that they might be able to preserve her life; and the dreadful duty devolved on them of depriving her of this last hope. After the confirmation of the sentence, all that they could do was to prove their compassion by preparing her for eternity.

On the 26th of May, the priests spoke their last words of comfort to her soul. She was taken back again, to await the execution of her sentence in the prison of Caen. The day was at last fixed for her death by burning, and the morning came when the Torture-Chamber was opened to receive her.

V HUSHED-UP

The saddest part of Marie's sad story now remains to be told.

One resource was left her, by employing which it was possible, at the last moment, to avert for a few months the frightful prospect of the torture and the stake. The unfortunate girl might stoop, on her side, to use the weapons of deception against her enemies, and might defame her own character by pleading pregnancy. That one miserable alternative was all that now remained; and, in the extremity of mortal terror, with the shadow of the executioner on her prison, and with the agony of approaching torment and death at her heart, the forlorn creature accepted it. If the law of strict morality must judge her in this matter without consideration, and condemn her without appeal, the spirit of Christian mercy – remembering how sorely she was tried, remembering the frailty of our common humanity, remembering the warning word which forbade us to judge one another – may open its sanctuary of tenderness to a sister in affliction, and may offer her the tribute of its pity, without limit and without blame.

The plea of pregnancy was admitted, and, at the eleventh hour, the period of the execution was deferred. On the day when her ashes were to have been cast to the winds, she was still in her prison, a living, breathing woman. Her limbs were spared from the torture, her body was released from the stake, until the twenty-ninth of July, seventeen hundred and eighty-two. On that day her reprieve was to end, and the execution of her sentence was absolutely to take place.

During the short period of grace which was now to elapse, the situation of the friendless girl, accused of such incredible crimes and condemned to so awful a doom, was discussed far and wide in French society. The case became notorious beyond the limits of Caen. The report of it spread by way of Rouen, from mouth to mouth, till it reached Paris; and from Paris it penetrated into the palace of the King at Versailles. That unhappy man, whose dreadful destiny it was to pay the penalty which the long and noble endurance of the French people had too mercifully abstained from inflicting on his guilty predecessors, had then lately mounted the fatal steps of the throne. Louis the Sixteenth was sovereign of France when the story of the poor servant-girl obtained its first court-circulation at Versailles.

The conduct of the King, when the main facts of Marie's case came to his ears, did all honour to his sense of duty and his sense of justice. He instantly despatched his Royal order to suspend the execution of the sentence. The report of Marie's fearful situation had reached him so short a time before the period appointed for her death, that the Royal mandate was only delivered to the parliament of Rouen on the twenty-sixth of July.

The girl's life now hung literally on a thread. An accident happening to the courier, any delay in fulfilling the wearisome official formalities proper to the occasion – and the execution might have taken its course. The authorities at Rouen, feeling that the King's interference implied a rebuke of their inconsiderate confirmation of the Caen sentence, did their best to set themselves right for the future by registering the Royal order on the day when they received it. The next morning, the twenty-seventh, it was sent to Caen; and it reached the authorities there on the twenty-eighth.

That twenty-eighth of July, seventeen hundred and eighty-two, fell on a Sunday. Throughout the day and night the order lay in the office unopened. Sunday was a holiday, and Procurator Revel was not disposed to occupy it by so much as five minutes' performance of week-day work.

On Monday, the twenty-ninth, the crowd assembled to see the execution. The stake was set up, the soldiers were called out, the executioner was ready. All the preliminary horror of the torturing and burning was suffered to darken round the miserable prisoner, before the wretches in authority saw fit to open the message of mercy and to deliver it at the prison-gate.

She was now saved, as if by a miracle, for the second time! But the cell-door was still closed on her. The only chance of ever opening it – the only hope of publicly asserting her innocence, lay in appealing to the King's justice by means of a written statement of her case, presenting it exactly as it stood in all its details, from the beginning at Madame Duparc's to the end in the prison of Caen. The production of such a document as this was beset with obstacles; the chief of them being the difficulty of gaining access to the voluminous reports of the evidence given at the trial, which were only accessible in those days to persons professionally connected with the courts of law. If Marie's case was to be placed before the King, no man in France but a lawyer could undertake the duty with the slightest chance of serving the interests of the prisoner and the interests of truth.

In this disgraceful emergency a man was found to plead the girl's cause, whose profession secured to him the privilege of examining the evidence against her. This man – a barrister, named Lecauchois – not only undertook to prepare a statement of the case from the records of the court – but further devoted himself to collecting money for Marie, from all the charitably-disposed inhabitants of the town. It is to be said to his credit that he honestly faced the difficulties of his task, and industriously completed the document which he had engaged to furnish. On the other hand, it must be recorded to his shame, that his motives were interested throughout, and that with almost incredible meanness he paid himself for the employment of his time by putting the greater part of the sum which he had collected for his client in his own pocket. With her one friend, no less than with all her enemies, it seems to have been Marie's hard fate to see the worst side of human nature, on every occasion when she was brought into contact with her fellow-creatures.

The statement pleading for the revision of Marie's trial was sent to Paris. An eminent barrister at the Court of Requests framed a petition from it, the prayer of which was granted by the King. Acting under the Royal order, the judges of the Court of Requests furnished themselves with the reports of the evidence as drawn up at Caen; and after examining the whole case, unanimously decided that there was good and sufficient reason for the revision of the trial. The order to that effect was not issued to the parliament of Rouen before the twenty-fourth of May, seventeen hundred and eighty-four – nearly two years after the King's mercy had saved Marie from the executioner. Who can say how slowly that long, long time must have passed to the poor girl who was still languishing in her prison?

The Rouen parliament, feeling that it was held accountable for its pro-ceedings to a high court of judicature, acting under the direct authority of the King himself, recognised at last, readily enough, that the interests of its own reputation and the interests of rigid justice were now intimately bound up together; and applied itself impartially, on this occasion at least, to the consideration of Marie's case.

As a necessary consequence of this change of course, the authorities of Caen began, for the first time, to feel seriously alarmed for themselves. If the parliament of Rouen dealt fairly by the prisoner, a fatal exposure of the whole party would be the certain result. Under these circumstances, Procurator Revel and his friends sent a private requisition to the authorities at Rouen, conjuring them to remember that the respectability of their professional brethren was at stake, and suggesting that the legal establishment of Marie's innocence was the error of all others which it was now most urgently necessary to avoid. The parliament of Rouen was, however, far too cautious, if not too honest, to commit itself to such an atrocious proceeding as was here plainly indicated. After gaining as much time as possible by prolonging their deliberations to the utmost, the authorities resolved on adopting a middle course, which on the one hand should not actually establish the prisoner's innocence, and, on the other, should not publicly expose the disgraceful conduct of the prosecution at Caen. Their decree, not issued until the twelfth of March, seventeen hundred and eighty-five, annulled the sentence of Procurator Revel on technical grounds; suppressed the further publication of the statement of Marie's case, which had been drawn out by the advocate Lecauchois, as libellous towards Monsieur Revel and Madame Duparc; and announced that the prisoner was ordered to remain in confinement until more ample information could be collected relating to the doubtful question of her innocence or her guilt. No such information was at all likely to present itself (more especially after the only existing narrative of the case had been suppressed); and the practical effect of the decree, therefore, was to keep Marie in prison for an indefinite period, after she had been illegally deprived of her liberty already from August, seventeen hundred and eighty-one, to March, seventeen hundred and eighty-five. Who shall say that the respectable classes did not take good care of their respectability on the eve of the French Revolution!

Marie's only hope of recovering her freedom, and exposing her unscrupulous enemies to the obloquy and the punishment which they richly deserved, lay in calling the attention of the higher tribunals of the capital to the cruelly cunning decree of the parliament of Rouen. Accordingly, she once more petitioned the throne. The King referred the document to his council; and the council issued an order submitting the Rouen decree to the final investigation of the parliament of Paris.

At last, then, after more than three miserable years of imprisonment, the victim of Madame Duparc and Procurator Revel had burst her way through all intervening obstacles of law and intricacies of office, to the judgment-seat of that highest law-court in the country, which had the final power of ending her long sufferings and of doing her signal justice on her adversaries of all degrees. The parliament of Paris was now to estimate the unutterable wrong that had been inflicted on her; and the eloquent tongue of one of the first advocates of that famous bar was to plead her cause openly before God, the King, and the country.

The pleading of Monsieur Fournel (Marie's counsel) before the parliament of Paris, remains on record. At the outset, he assumes the highest ground for the prisoner. He disclaims all intention of gaining her liberty by taking the obvious technical objections to the illegal and irregular sentences of Caen and Rouen. He insists on the necessity of vindicating her innocence legally and morally before the world, and of obtaining the fullest compensation that the law allows for the merciless injuries which the original prosecution had inflicted on his client. In pursuance of this design, he then proceeds to examine the evidence of the alleged poisoning and the alleged robbery, step by step, pointing out in the fullest detail the monstrous contradictions and improbabilities which have been already briefly indicated in this narrative. The course thus pursued, with signal clearness and ability, leads, as every one who has followed the particulars of the case from the beginning will readily understand, to a very serious result. The arguments for the defence cannot assert Marie's innocence without shifting the whole weight of suspicion, in the matter of Monsieur de Beaulieu's death by poisoning, on to the shoulders of her mistress, Madame Duparc.

It is necessary, in order to prepare the reader for the extraordinary termination of the proceedings, to examine this question of suspicion in some of its most striking details.

The poisoning of Monsieur de Beaulieu may be accepted, in consideration of the medical evidence, as a proved fact, to begin with. The question that remains is, whether that poisoning was accidental or premeditated. In either case, the evidence points directly at Madame Duparc, and leads to the conclusion that she tried to shift the blame of the poisoning (if accidental) and the guilt of it (if premeditated) from herself to her servant.

Suppose the poisoning to have been accidental. Suppose arsenic to have been purchased for some legitimate domestic purpose, and to have been carelessly left in one of the salt-cellars, on the dresser – who salts the hasty-pudding? Madame Duparc. Who – assuming that the dinner next day really contained some small portion of poison, just enough to swear by – prepared that dinner? Madame Duparc and her daughter, while the servant was asleep. Having caused the death of her father, and having produced symptoms of illness in herself and her guests, by a dreadful accident, how does the circumstantial evidence further show that Madame Duparc tried to fix the responsibility of that accident on her servant, before she openly charged the girl with poisoning?

In the first place, Madame Duparc is the only one of the dinner-party who attributes the general uneasiness to poison. She not only does this, but she indicates the kind of poison used, and declares in the kitchen that it is burnt, – so as to lead to the inference that the servant, who has removed the dishes, has thrown some of the poisoned food on the fire. Here is a foregone conclusion on the subject of arsenic in Madame Duparc's mind, and an inference in connection with it, directed at the servant by Madame Duparc's lips. In the second place, if any trust at all is to be put in the evidence touching the finding of arsenic on or about Marie's person, that trust must be reposed in the testimony of Surgeon Hébert, who first searched the girl. Where does he find the arsenic and the bread crumbs? In Marie's pockets. Who takes the most inexplicably officious notice of such a trifle as Marie's dress, at the most shockingly inappropriate time, when the father of Madame Duparc lies dead in the house? Madame Duparc herself. Who tells Marie to take off her Sunday pockets, and sends her into her own room (which she herself has not entered during the night, and which has been open to the intrusion of any one else in the house) to tie on the very pockets in which the arsenic is found? Madame Duparc. Who put the arsenic into the pockets? Is it jumping to a conclusion to answer once more – Madame Duparc?

Thus far we have assumed that the mistress attempted to shift the blame of a fatal accident on to the shoulders of the servant. Do the facts bear out that theory, or do they lead to the suspicion that the woman was a parricide, and that she tried to fix on the friendless country girl the guilt of her dreadful crime?

If the poisoning of the hasty-pudding (to begin with) was accidental, the salting of it, through which the poisoning was, to all appearance, effected, must have been a part of the habitual cookery of the dish. So far, however, from this being the case, Madame Duparc had expressly warned her servant not to use salt; and only used the salt (or the arsenic) herself, after asking a question which implied a direct contradiction of her own directions, and the inconsistency of which she made no attempt whatever to explain. Again, when her father was taken ill, if Madame Duparc had been only the victim of an accident, would she have remained content with no better help than that of an apothecary's boy? Would she not have sent, as her father grew worse, for the best medical assistance which the town afforded? The facts show that she summoned just help enough, barely to save appearances, and no more. The facts show that she betrayed a singular anxiety to have the body laid out as soon as possible after life was extinct. The facts show that she maintained an unnatural composure on the day of the death. These are significant circumstances. They speak for themselves independently of the evidence given afterwards, in which she and her child contradicted each other as to the time that elapsed when the old man had eaten his fatal meal, before he was taken ill. Add to these serious facts the mysterious disappearance from the house of the eldest son, which was never accounted for; and the rumour of purchased poison, which was never investigated. Consider, besides, whether the attempt to sacrifice the servant's life be not more consistent with the ruthless determination of a criminal, than with the terror of an innocent woman who shrinks from accepting the responsibility of a frightful accident – and determine, at the same time, whether the infinitesimal amount of injury done by the poisoned dinner can be most probably attributed to lucky accident, or to premeditated doctoring of the dishes with just arsenic enough to preserve appearances, and to implicate the servant without too seriously injuring the company on whom she waited. Give all these serious considerations their due weight; then look back to the day of Monsieur de Beaulieu's death: and say if Madame Duparc was the victim of a dreadful accident, or the perpetrator of an atrocious crime!

That she was one or the other, and that, in either case, she was the originator of the vile conspiracy against her servant which these pages disclose, was the conclusion to which Monsieur Fournel's pleading on his client's behalf inevitably led. That pleading satisfactorily demonstrated Marie's innocence of poisoning and theft, and her fair claim to the fullest legal compensation for the wrong inflicted on her. On the twenty-third of May, seventeen hundred and eighty-six, the parliament of Paris issued its decree, discharging her from the remotest suspicion of guilt, releasing her from her long imprisonment, and authorizing her to bring an action for damages against the person or persons who had falsely accused her of murder and theft. The truth had triumphed, and the poor servant-girl had found laws to protect her at last.

Under these altered circumstances, what happened to Madame Duparc? What happened to Procurator Revel and his fellow-conspirators? What happened to the authorities of the parliament of Rouen?

Nothing.

The premonitory rumblings of that great earthquake of nations which History calls the French Revolution, were, at this time, already beginning to make themselves heard; and any public scandal which affected the wealthier and higher classes involved a serious social risk, the importance of which no man in France could then venture to estimate. If Marie claimed the privilege which a sense of justice, or rather a sense of decency, had forced the parliament of Paris to concede to her, – and, through her counsel, she did claim it, – the consequences of the legal inquiry into her case which her demand for damages necessarily involved, would probably be the trying of Madame Duparc, either for parricide, or for homicide by misadventure; the dismissal of Procurator Revel from the functions which he had disgracefully abused; and the suspension from office of the authorities at Caen and Rouen, who had in various ways forfeited public confidence by aiding and abetting him.

Here, then, was no less a prospect in view than the disgrace of a respectable family, and the dishonouring of the highest legal functionaries of two important provincial towns! And for what end was the dangerous exposure to be made? Merely to do justice to the daughter of a common day-labourer, who had been illegally sentenced to torture and burning, and illegally confined in prison for nearly five years. To make a wholesale sacrifice of her superiors, no matter how wicked they might be, for the sake of giving a mere servant-girl compensation for the undeserved obloquy and misery of many years, was too preposterous and too suicidal an act of justice to be thought of for a moment. Accordingly, when Marie was prepared to bring her action for damages, the lawyers laid their heads together, in the interests of society. It was found possible to put her out of court at once and for ever, by taking a technical objection to the proceedings in which she was plaintiff, at the very outset. This disgraceful means of escape once discovered, the girl's guilty persecutors instantly took advantage of it. She was formally put out of court, without the possibility of any further appeal. Procurator Revel and the other authorities retained their distinguished legal positions; and the question of the guilt or innocence of Madame Duparc, in the matter of her father's death, remains a mystery which no man can solve to this day.

After recording this scandalous termination of the legal proceedings, it is gratifying to be able to conclude the story of Marie's unmerited sufferings with a picture of her after-life which leaves an agreeable impression on the mind.

If popular sympathy, after the servant-girl's release from prison, could console her for the hard measure of injustice under which she had suffered so long and so unavailingly, that sympathy was now offered to her heartily and without limit. She became quite a public character in Paris. The people followed her in crowds wherever she went. A subscription was set on foot, which, for the time at least, secured her a comfortable independence. Friends rose up in all directions to show her such attention as might be in their power; and the simple country girl, when she was taken to see the sights of Paris, actually beheld her own name placarded in the showmen's bills, and her presence advertised as the greatest attraction that could be offered to the public. When, in due course of time, all this excitement had evaporated, Marie married prosperously, and the government granted her its licence to open a shop for the sale of stamped papers. The last we hear of her is, that she was a happy wife and mother, and that she performed every duty of life in such a manner as to justify the deep interest which had been universally felt for her by the people of France.

Her story is related here, not only because it seemed to contain some elements of interest in itself, but also because the facts of which it is composed may claim to be of some little historical importance, as helping to expose the unendurable corruptions of society in France before the Revolution. It may not be amiss for those persons whose historical point of view obstinately contracts its range to the Reign of Terror, to look a little farther back – to remember that the hard case of oppression here related had been, for something like one hundred years, the case (with minor changes of circumstance) of the forlorn many against the powerful few, all over France – and then to consider whether there was not a reason and a necessity, a dreadful last necessity, for the French Revolution. That Revolution has expiated, and is still expiating, its excesses, by political failures, which all the world can see. But the social good which it indisputably effected remains to this day. Take, as an example, the administration of justice in France at the present time. Whatever its shortcomings may still be, no innocent French woman could be treated, now, as an innocent French woman was once treated at a period so little remote from our own time as the end of the last century.

Fauntleroy

Originally appeared in *Household Words*, 13 November 1858, as 'A Paradoxical Experience'. The story was included in *The Queen of Hearts* as 'Brother Morgan's Story of Fauntleroy'. Henry Fauntleroy (1785–1824) entered his father's banking-house in 1800. He began as a clerk, but progressed to become a partner, and finally manager. In September 1824 the bank suspended payment, and scandal broke: Fauntleroy had sold the bank's stock by forging trustees' signatures, meanwhile maintaining the books in perfect order, and giving credit in order to pay interest. It was rumoured that he had spent a quarter of a million pounds on mistresses in different establishments, and on gambling. Amid mounting public excitement Fauntleroy was arrested, found guilty and sentenced to death. Despite numerous pleas that the sentence be commuted, Fauntleroy was executed before an estimated 100,000 people on 30 November 1824. The death penalty for forging wills and the power of attorney for transfer of stock was not finally abolished in England until 1837. When the aged Collins read Frances Hodgson Burnett's *Little Lord Fauntleroy* (1887) he wondered if 'Mrs Burnett knows that she has given to her charming little boy the name of the last man hanged for forgery in England.' In *Basil* (1852) the villain Mannion's father is also hanged for forgery.

I

It was certainly a dull little dinner-party. Of the four guests, two of us were men between fifty and sixty, and two of us were youths, between eighteen and twenty; and we had no subjects in common. We were all intimate with our host; but we were only slightly acquainted with each other. Perhaps we should have got on better if there had been some ladies among us; but the master of the house was a bachelor, and, except the parlour-maid, who assisted in waiting on us at dinner, no daughter of Eve was present to brighten the dreary scene.

We tried all sorts of subjects; but they dropped one after the other. The elder gentlemen seemed to be afraid of committing themselves by talking too freely within hearing of us juniors; and we, on our side, restrained our youthful flow of spirits and youthful freedom of conversation, out of deference to our host, who seemed once or twice to be feeling a little nervous about the continued propriety of our behaviour in the presence of his respectable guests. To make matters worse, we had dined at a sensible hour. When the bottles made their first round, at dessert, the clock on the mantelpiece only struck eight. I counted the strokes; and felt certain, from the expression of his face, that the other junior guest, who sat on one side of me at the round table, was counting them also. When we came to the final eight, we exchanged looks of despair. 'Two hours more of this! What on earth is to become of us?' In the language of the eyes, that was exactly what we said to each other.

The wine was excellent; and I think we all came separately and secretly to the same conclusion – that our chance of getting through the evening was intimately connected with our resolution in getting through the bottles.

As a matter of course, we talked wine. No company of Englishmen can assemble together for an evening without doing that. Every man in this country who is rich enough to pay income-tax, has, at one time or other in his life, effected a very remarkable transaction in wine. Sometimes he has made such a bargain as he never expects to make again. Sometimes he is the only man in England, not a peer of the realm, who has got a single drop of a certain famous vintage which has perished from the face of the earth. Sometimes he has purchased, with a friend, a few last left dozens from the cellar of a deceased potentate, at a price so exorbitant that he can only wag his head and decline mentioning it – and if you ask his friend, that friend will wag his head, and decline mentioning it also. Sometimes he has been at an out-of-the-way country inn; has found the sherry not drinkable; has asked if there is no other wine in the house; has been informed that there is some 'sourish foreign stuff that nobody ever drinks;' has called for a bottle of it; has found it Burgundy, such as all France cannot now produce; has cunningly kept his own counsel with the widowed landlady, and has bought the whole stock for 'an old song.' Sometimes he knows the proprietor of a famous tavern in London; and he recommends his one or two particular friends, the next time they are passing that way, to go in and dine, and give his compliments to the landlord, and ask for a bottle of the brown sherry, with the light blue – as distinguished from the dark blue – seal. Thousands of people dine there every year, and think they have got the famous sherry when they get the dark blue seal; but the real wine, the famous wine, is the light blue seal; and nobody in England knows it but the landlord and his friends. In all these wine conversations, whatever variety there may be in the various experiences related, one of two great first principles is invariably assumed by each speaker in succession. Either he knows more about it than anyone else – or he has got better wine of his own even than the excellent wine he is now drinking. Men can get together, sometimes, without talking of women, without talking of horses, without talking of politics; but they cannot assemble to eat a meal together without talking of wine; and they cannot talk of wine without assuming to each one of themselves an absolute infallibility in connection with that single subject, which they would shrink from asserting in relation to any other topic under the sun.

How long the inevitable wine-talk lasted, on the particular social occasion of which I am now writing, is more than I can undertake to say. I had heard so many other conversations of the same sort, at so many other tables, that my attention wandered away wearily; and I began to forget all about the dull little dinner party, and the badly-assorted company of guests of whom I formed one. How long I remained in this not over-courteous condition of mental oblivion, is more than I can tell. But when my attention was recalled, in due course of time, to the little world around me, I found that the good wine had begun to do its good office.

The stream of talk, on either side of the host's chair, was now beginning to flow cheerfully and continuously; the wine conversation had worn itself out; and one of the elder guests – Mr Wendell – was occupied in telling the other guest – Mr Trowbridge – of a small fraud which had lately been committed on him by a clerk in his employment. The first part of the story I missed altogether. The last part, which alone caught my attention, followed the career of the clerk to the dock of the Old Bailey.

'So, as I was telling you,' continued Mr Wendell, 'I made up my mind to prosecute, and I did prosecute. Thoughtless people blamed me for sending the young man to prison, and said I might just as well have forgiven him, seeing that the trifling sum of money I had lost by his breach of trust was barely as much as ten pounds. Of course, personally speaking, I would much rather not have gone into court; but I considered that my duty to society in general, and to my brother merchants in particular, absolutely compelled me to prosecute for the sake of example. I acted on that principle, and I don't regret that I did so. The circumstances under which the man robbed me were particularly disgraceful. He was a hardened reprobate, sir, if ever there was one yet; and I believe, in my conscience, that he wanted nothing but the opportunity, to be as great a villain as Fauntleroy himself.'

At the moment when Mr Wendell personified his idea of consummate villainy by quoting the example of Fauntleroy, I saw the other middle-aged gentleman – Mr Trowbridge – colour up on a sudden, and begin to fidget in his chair.

'The next time you want to produce an instance of a villain, sir,' said Mr Trowbridge, 'I wish you could contrive to quote some other example than Fauntleroy.'

Mr Wendell, naturally enough, looked excessively astonished when he heard these words; which were very firmly, and, at the same time, very politely, addressed to him.

'May I inquire why you object to my example?' he asked.

'I object to it, sir,' said Mr Trowbridge, 'Because it makes me very uncomfortable to hear Fauntleroy called a villain.'

'Good heavens above!' exclaimed Mr Wendell, utterly bewildered. 'Uncomfortable! – you, a mercantile man like myself – you, whose character stands so high everywhere – you uncomfortable when you hear a man who was hanged for forgery called a villain! In the name of wonder – why?'

'Because,' answered Mr Trowbridge, with perfect composure, 'Fauntleroy was a friend of mine.'

'Excuse me, my dear sir,' retorted Mr Wendell, in as polished a tone of sarcasm as he could command – 'but of all the friends whom you have made in the course of your useful and honourable career, I should have thought the friend you have just mentioned would have been the very last to whom you were likely to refer in respectable society – at least, by name.'

'Fauntleroy committed an unpardonable crime, and died a disgraceful death,' said Mr Trowbridge. 'But, for all that, Fauntleroy was a friend of mine; and in that character I shall always acknowledge him boldly to my dying day. I have a tenderness for his memory, though he violated a sacred trust, and died for it on the gallows. Don't look shocked, Mr Wendell. I will tell you, and our other friends here, if they will let me, why I feel that tenderness, which looks so strange and so discreditable in your eyes. It is rather a curious anecdote, sir; and has an interest, I think, for all observers of human nature, quite apart from its connection with the unhappy man of whom we have been talking. You young gentlemen,' continued Mr Trowbridge, addressing himself to us juniors, 'have heard of Fauntleroy, though he sinned and suffered, and shocked all England, long before your time?'

We answered that we had certainly heard of him, as one of the famous criminals of his day. We knew that he had been a partner in a great London banking-house; that he had not led a very virtuous life; that he had possessed himself, by forgery, of trust-moneys which he was doubly bound to respect; and that he had been hanged for his offence, in the year eighteen hundred and twenty-four, when the gallows was still set up for other crimes than murder, and when Jack Ketch was in fashion as one of the hard-working reformers of the age.

'Very good,' said Mr Trowbridge. 'You both of you know quite enough of Fauntleroy to be interested in what I am going to tell you. When the bottles have been round the table, I will start with my story.'

The bottles went round – claret for the degenerate youngsters; port for the sterling, steady-headed, middle-aged gentlemen. Mr Trowbridge sipped his wine – meditated a little – sipped again – and started with the promised anecdote, in these terms:

II

What I am going to tell you, gentlemen, happened when I was a very young man, and when I was just setting up in business on my own account.

My father had been well acquainted for many years with Mr Fauntleroy, of the famous London banking-firm of Marsh, Stracey, Fauntleroy, and Graham. Thinking it might be of some future service to me to make my position known to a great man in the commercial world, my father mentioned to his highly-respected friend that I was about to start in business for myself, in a very small way, and with very little money. Mr Fauntleroy received the intimation with a kind appearance of interest; and said that he would have his eye on me. I expected from this that he would wait to see if I could keep on my legs at starting; and that, if he found I succeeded pretty well, he would then help me forward if it lay in his power. As events turned out, he proved to be a far better friend than that; and he soon showed me that I had very much underrated the hearty and generous interest which he had felt in my welfare from the first.

While I was still fighting with the difficulties of setting up my office, and recommending myself to my connection, and so forth, I got a message from Mr Fauntleroy, telling me to call on him, at the banking-house, the first time I was passing that way. As you may easily imagine, I contrived to be passing that way on a particularly early occasion; and, on presenting myself at the bank, I was shown at once into Mr Fauntleroy's private room.

He was as pleasant a man to speak to as ever I met with – bright and gay and companionable in his manner – with a sort of easy, hearty, jovial bluntness about him that attracted everybody. The clerks all liked him – and that is something to say of a partner in a banking-house, I can tell you!

'Well, young Trowbridge,' says he, giving his papers on the table a brisk push away from him, 'so you are going to set up in business for yourself, are you? I have a great regard for your father, and a great wish to see you succeed. Have you started yet? – No? Just on the point of beginning – eh? Very good. You will have your difficulties, my friend – and I mean to smooth one of them away for you at the outset. A word of advice for your private ear – Bank with us.'

'You are very kind, sir,' I answered, 'and I should ask nothing better than to profit by your suggestion – if I could. But my expenses are heavy at starting, and when they are all paid, I am afraid I shall have very little left to put by for the first year. I doubt if I shall be able to muster much more than three hundred pounds of surplus cash in the world, after paying what I must pay, before I set up my office. And I should be ashamed to trouble your house, sir, to open an account for such a trifle as that.'

'Stuff and nonsense!' says Mr Fauntleroy. 'Are *you* a banker? What business have you to offer an opinion on the matter? Do as I tell you – leave it to me – bank with us – and draw for what you like. Stop! I haven't done yet. When you open the account, speak to the head cashier. Perhaps you may find he has got something to tell you. There! there! go away – don't interrupt me – good-bye – God bless you!'

That was his way – ah, poor fellow! that was his way.

I went to the head cashier the next morning, when I opened my little modicum of an account. He had received orders to pay my drafts without reference to my balance. My cheques, when I had overdrawn, were to be privately shown to Mr Fauntleroy. Do many young men who start in business find their prosperous superiors ready to help them in that way?

Well, I got on – got on very fairly and steadily; being careful not to venture out of my depth, and not to forget that small beginnings may lead in time to great ends. A prospect of one of those great ends – great, I mean, to such a small trader as I was at that period – showed itself to me, when I had been some little time in business. In plain terms, I had a chance of joining in a first-rate transaction, which would give me profit and position and everything I wanted, provided I could qualify myself for engaging in it by getting good security beforehand for a very large amount.

In this emergency, I thought of my kind friend, Mr Fauntleroy, and went to the bank, and saw him once more in his private room.

There he was at the same table, with the same heaps of papers about him, and the same hearty, easy way of speaking his mind to you at once, in the fewest possible words. I explained the business I came upon, with some little hesitation and nervousness; for I was afraid he might think I was taking an unfair advantage of his former kindness to me. When I had done, he just nodded his head, snatched up a blank sheet of paper, scribbled a few lines on it, in his rapid way, handed the writing to me, and pushed me out of the room by the two shoulders before I could say a single word. I looked at the paper in the outer office. It was my security from that great banking-house for the whole amount, and for more, if more was wanted.

I could not express my gratitude then; and I don't know that I can describe it now. I can only say that it has outlived the crime, the disgrace, and the awful death on the scaffold. I am grieved to speak of that death at all. But I have no other alternative. The course of my story must now lead me straight on to the later time, and to the terrible discovery which exposed my benefactor and my friend to all England as the forger Fauntleroy.

I must ask you to suppose a lapse of some time after the occurrence of the events that I have just been relating. During this interval, thanks to the kind assistance I had received at the outset, my position as a man of business had greatly improved. Imagine me now, if you please, on the high road to prosperity, with good large offices and a respectable staff of clerks; and picture me to yourselves sitting alone in my private room, between four and five o'clock, on a certain Saturday afternoon.

All my letters had been written, all the people who had appointments with me had been received – I was looking carelessly over the newspaper, and thinking about going home, when one of my clerks came in, and said that a stranger wished to see me immediately on very important business.

'Did he mention his name?' I inquired.

'No, sir.'

'Did you not ask him for it?'

'Yes, sir. And he said you would be none the wiser if he told me what it was.'

'Does he look like a begging-letter writer?'

'He looks a little shabby, sir; but he doesn't talk at all like a begging-letter writer. He spoke sharp and decided, sir, and said it was in your interests that he came, and that you would deeply regret it afterwards if you refused to see him.'

'He said that, did he? Show him in at once, then.'

He was shown in immediately. A middling sized man, with a sharp, unwholesome-looking face, and with a flippant, reckless manner; dressed in a style of shabby smartness; eyeing me with a bold look; and not so overburdened with politeness as to trouble himself about taking off his hat when he came in. I had never seen him before in my life; and I could not form the slightest conjecture from his appearance to guide me towards guessing his position in the world. He was not a gentleman, evidently; but as to fixing his whereabouts in the infinite downward gradations of vagabond existence in London, that was a mystery which I was totally incompetent to solve.

'Is your name Trowbridge?' he began.

'Yes,' I answered, drily enough.

'Do you bank with Marsh, Stracey, Fauntleroy, and Graham?'

'Why do you ask?'

'Answer my question, and you will know.'

'Very well, I *do* bank with Marsh, Stracey, Fauntleroy, and Graham – and what then?'

'Draw out every farthing of balance you have got, before the bank closes at five to-day.'

I stared at him in speechless amazement. The words, for an instant, absolutely petrified me.

'Stare as much as you like,' he proceeded coolly, 'I mean what I say. Look at your clock there. In twenty minutes it will strike five, and the bank will be shut. Draw out every farthing, I tell you again; and look sharp about it.'

'Draw out my money!' I exclaimed, partially recovering myself. 'Are you in your right senses? Do you know that the firm I bank with represents one of the first houses in the world? What do you mean – you, who are a total stranger to me – by taking this extraordinary interest in my affairs? If you want me to act on your advice, why don't you explain yourself.'

'I have explained myself. Act on my advice, or not, just as you like. It don't matter to me. I have done what I promised, and there's an end of it.'

He turned to the door. The minute hand of the clock was getting on from the twenty minutes to the quarter.

'Done what you promised?' I repeated, getting up to stop him.

'Yes,' he said, with his hand on the lock. 'I have given my message. Whatever happens, remember that. Good afternoon.'

He was gone before I could speak again.

I tried to call after him, but my speech suddenly failed me. It was very foolish, it was very unaccountable, but there was something in the man's last words which had more than half frightened me.

I looked at the clock. The minute hand was on the quarter.

My office was just far enough from the bank to make it necessary for me to decide on the instant. If I had had time to think, I am perfectly certain that I should not have profited by the extraordinary warning that had just been addressed to me. The suspicious appearance and manners of the stranger; the outrageous improbability of the inference against the credit of the bank towards which his words pointed; the chance that some underhand attempt was being made, by some enemy of mine, to frighten me into embroiling myself with one of my best friends, through showing an ignorant distrust of the firm with which he was associated as partner – all these considerations would unquestionably have occurred to me if I could have found time for reflection; and, as a necessary consequence, not one farthing of my balance would have been taken from the keeping of the bank on that memorable day.

As it was, I had just time enough to act, and not a spare moment for thinking. Some heavy payments made at the beginning of the week had so far decreased my balance, that the sum to my credit in the banking-book barely reached fifteen hundred pounds. I snatched up my cheque-book, wrote a draft for the whole amount, and ordered one of my clerks to run to the bank and get it cashed before the doors closed. What impulse urged me on, except the blind impulse of hurry and bewilderment, I can't say. I acted mechanically, under the influence of the vague inexplicable fear which the man's extraordinary parting words had aroused in me, without stopping to analyse my own sensations, – almost without knowing what I was about. In three minutes from the time when the stranger had closed my door, the clerk had started for the bank; and I was alone again in my room, with my hands as cold as ice and my head all in a whirl.

I did not recover my control over myself, until the clerk came back with the notes in his hand. He had just got to the bank in the nick of time. As the cash for my draft was handed to him over the counter, the clock struck five, and he heard the order given to close the doors.

When I had counted the bank-notes and had locked them up in the safe, my better sense seemed to come back to me on a sudden. Never have I reproached myself before or since as I reproached myself at that moment. What sort of return had I made for Mr Fauntleroy's fatherly kindness to me? I had insulted him by the meanest, the grossest distrust of the honour and the credit of his house – and that on the word of an absolute stranger, of a vagabond, if ever there was one yet! It was madness, downright madness, in any man to have acted as I had done. I could not account for my own inconceivably thoughtless proceeding. I could hardly believe in it myself. I opened the safe and looked at the bank notes again. I locked it once more, and flung the key down on the table in a fury of vexation against myself. There the money was, upbraiding me with my own inconceivable folly; telling me in the plainest terms that I had risked depriving myself of my best and kindest friend henceforth and for ever.

It was necessary to do something at once towards making all the atonement that lay in my power. I felt that, as soon as I began to cool down a little. There was but one plain, straightforward way left now out of the scrape in which I had been mad enough to involve myself. I took my hat, and, without stopping an instant to hesitate, hurried off to the bank to make a clean breast of it to Mr Fauntleroy.

When I knocked at the private door, and asked for him, I was told that he had not been at the bank for the last two days. One of the other partners was there, however, and was working at that moment in his own room.

I sent in my name, at once, and asked to see him. He and I were little better than strangers to each other; and the interview was likely to be, on that account, unspeakably embarrassing and humiliating on my side. Still I could not go home. I could not endure the inaction of the next day, the Sunday, without having done my best on the spot, to repair the error into which my own folly had led me. Uncomfortable as I felt at the prospect of the approaching interview, I should have been far more uneasy in my mind if the partner had declined to see me.

To my relief, the bank porter returned with a message requesting me to walk in.

What particular form my explanations and apologies took when I tried to offer them, is more than I can tell now. I was so confused and distressed that I hardly knew what I was talking about at the time. The one circumstance which I remember clearly is, that I was ashamed to refer to my interview with the strange man; and that I tried to account for my sudden withdrawal of my balance by referring it to some inexplicable panic, caused by mischievous reports which I was unable to trace to their source, and which, for anything I knew to the contrary, might, after all, have been only started in jest. Greatly to my surprise, the partner did not seem to notice the lamentable lameness of my excuses, and did not additionally confuse me by asking any questions. A weary, absent look, which I had observed on his face when I came in, remained on it while I was speaking. It seemed to be an effort to him even to keep up the appearance of listening to me. And when, at last, I fairly broke down in the middle of a sentence, and gave up the hope of getting any further, all the answer he gave me was comprised in these few civil, common-place words:

'Never mind, Mr Trowbridge; pray don't think of apologizing. We are all liable to make mistakes. Say nothing more about it, and bring the money back on Monday if you still honour us with your confidence.'

He looked down at his papers, as if he was anxious to be alone again; and I had no alternative, of course, but to take my leave immediately. I went home, feeling a little easier in my mind, now that I had paved the way for making the best practical atonement in my power, by bringing my balance back the first thing on Monday morning. Still, I passed a weary day on Sunday, reflecting, sadly enough, that I had not yet made my peace with Mr Fauntleroy. My anxiety to set myself right with my generous friend was so intense, that I risked intruding myself on his privacy, by calling at his town residence on the Sunday. He was not there; and his servant could tell me nothing of his whereabouts. There was no help for it now but to wait till his week-day duties brought him back to the bank.

I went to business on Monday morning, half-an-hour earlier than usual, so great was my impatience to restore the amount of that unlucky draft to my account as soon as possible after the bank opened.

On entering my office, I stopped with a startled feeling just inside the door. Something serious had happened. The clerks, instead of being at their desks as usual, were all huddled together in a group, talking to each other with blank faces. When they saw me, they fell back behind my managing man, who stepped forward with a circular in his hand.

'Have you heard the news, sir?' he said.

'No. What is it?'

He handed me the circular. My heart gave one violent throb the instant I looked at it. I felt myself turn pale; I felt my knees trembling under me.

Marsh, Stracey, Fauntleroy, and Graham had stopped payment.

'The circular has not been issued more than half an hour,' continued my managing clerk. 'I have just come from the bank, sir. The doors are shut – there is no doubt about it. Marsh and Company have stopped this morning.'

I hardly heard him; I hardly knew who was talking to me. My strange visitor of the Saturday had taken instant possession of all my thoughts; and his words of warning seemed to be sounding once more in my ears. This man had known the true condition of the bank, when not another soul outside the doors was aware of it! The last draft paid across the counter of that ruined house, when the doors closed on Saturday, was the draft that I had so bitterly reproached myself for drawing; the one balance saved from the wreck was my balance. Where had the stranger got the information that had saved me? And why had he brought it to *my* ears?

I was still groping, like a man in the dark, for an answer to those two questions – I was still bewildered by the unfathomable mystery of doubt into which they had plunged me – when the discovery of the stopping of the bank was followed almost immediately by a second shock, far more dreadful, far heavier to bear, so far as I was concerned, than the first.

While I and my clerks were still discussing the failure of the firm, two mercantile men, who were friends of mine, ran into the office, and overwhelmed us with the news that one of the partners had been arrested for forgery. Never shall I forget the terrible Monday morning when those tidings reached me, and when I knew that the partner was Mr Fauntleroy.

I was true to him – I can honestly say I was true to my belief in my generous friend – when that fearful news reached me. My fellow-merchants had got all the particulars of the arrest. They told me that two of Mr Fauntleroy's fellow-trustees had come up to London to make arrangements about selling out some stock. On inquiring for Mr Fauntleroy at the banking-house, they had been informed that he was not there; and, after leaving a message for him, they had gone into the city to make an appointment with their stockbroker for a future day, when their fellow-trustee might be able to attend. The stockbroker volunteered to make certain business inquiries on the spot, with a view to saving as much time as possible; and left them at his office to await his return. He came back, looking very much amazed, with the information that the stock had been sold out, down to the last five hundred pounds. The affair was instantly investigated; the document authorising the selling out was produced; and the two trustees saw on it, side by side with Mr Fauntleroy's signature, the forged signatures of their own names. This happened on the Friday; and the trustees, without losing a moment, sent the officers of justice in pursuit of Mr Fauntleroy. He was arrested, brought up before the magistrate, and remanded, on the Saturday. On the Monday I heard from my friends the particulars which I have just narrated.

But the events of that one morning were not destined to end even yet. I had discovered the failure of the bank, and the arrest of Mr Fauntleroy. I was next to be enlightened, in the strangest and the saddest manner, on the difficult question of his innocence or his guilt.

Before my friends had left my office, before I had exhausted the arguments which my gratitude rather than my reason suggested to me, in favour of the unhappy prisoner, a note, marked immediate, was placed in my hands, which silenced me the instant I looked at it. It was written from the prison by Mr Fauntleroy, and it contained two lines only, entreating me to apply for the necessary order, and to go and see him immediately.

I shall not attempt to describe the flutter of expectation, the strange mixture of dread and hope that agitated me, when I recognised his handwriting, and discovered what it was that he desired me to do. I obtained the order, and went to the prison. The authorities, knowing the dreadful situation in which he stood, were afraid of his attempting to destroy himself, and had set two men to watch him. One came out as they opened his cell door. The other, who was bound not to leave him, very delicately and considerately affected to be looking out of the window the moment I was shown in.

He was sitting on the side of his bed, with his head drooping and his hands hanging listlessly over his knees, when I first caught sight of him. At the sound of my approach he started to his feet, and, without speaking a word, flung both his arms round my neck.

My heart swelled up.

'Tell me it's not true, sir! For God's sake, tell me it's not true!' was all I could say to him.

He never answered – oh, me! he never answered, and he turned away his face.

There was one dreadful moment of silence. He still held his arms round my neck; and on a sudden he put his lips close to my ear.

'Did you get your money out?' he whispered. 'Were you in time on Saturday afternoon?'

I broke free from him, in the astonishment of hearing those words.

'What!' I cried out loud, forgetting the third person at the window. 'That man who brought the message— ?'

'Hush,' he said, putting his hand on my lips. 'There was no better man to be found, after the officers had taken me – I know no more about him than you do – I paid him well, as a chance messenger, and risked his cheating me of his errand.'

'*You* sent him then!'

'I sent him.'

My story is over, gentlemen. There is no need for me to tell you that Mr Fauntleroy was found guilty, and that he died by the hangman's hand. It was in my power to soothe his last moments in this world, by taking on myself the arrangement of some of his private affairs, which, while they remained unsettled, weighed heavily on his mind. They had no connection with the crimes he had committed, so I could do him the last little service he was ever to accept at my hands with a clear conscience.

I say nothing in defence of his character, nothing in palliation of the offence for which he suffered. But I cannot forget that in the time of his most fearful extremity, when the strong arm of the law had already seized him, he thought of the young man whose humble fortunes he had helped to build; whose heartfelt gratitude he had fairly won; whose simple faith he was resolved never to betray. I leave it to greater intellects than mine to reconcile the anomaly of his reckless falsehood towards others, and his steadfast truth towards me. It is as certain as that we sit here, that one of Fauntleroy's last efforts in this world, was the effort he made to preserve me from being a loser by the trust that I had placed in him. There is the secret of my strange tenderness for the memory of a felon. That is why the word villain does somehow still grate on my heart, when I hear it associated with the name – the disgraced name, I grant you – of the forger Fauntleroy. Pass the bottles, young gentlemen, and pardon a man of the old school for having so long interrupted your conversation with a story of the old time.

The Parson's Scruple

Originally appeared in *Household Words*, 1 January 1859 as 'A New Mind'. The story was included in *The Queen of Hearts* as 'Brother Owen's Story of the Parson's Scruple.' Robert Ashley suggests that the discussion of divorce in the story constitutes 'Collins's first protest against the injustice of English marriage laws' (*Wilkie Collins*, p. 56). Catherine Peters claims that the story was 'clearly based' on the experiences of Frances Dickinson, who had played the part of Esther in the 1857 Gallery of Illustration performances of Collins's play *The Frozen Deep*: 'She had been caught up in a ten-year-long matrimonial wrangle, finally decided in her favour on appeal to the House of Lords, of the kind that particularly intrigued and outraged her friend Wilkie. The legal question was over the conflict of Scotch and English law. Frances had left her husband, John Edward Geils, because of his adultery and cruelty, in 1845. He sued for restitution of conjugal rights, but she was granted a divorce a *mensa et toro* (a judicial separation) in the ecclesiastical Court of Arches in 1848, which prevented either party from remarrying during the life of the other. She then tried to get a more complete Scotch divorce a *vinculo matrimonii*. This was at first refused, and it was not until 1855 that she was an entirely free woman' (*The King of Inventors*, p. 173).

I

If you had been in the far West of England about thirteen years since, and if you had happened to take up one of the Cornish newspapers on a certain day of the month, which need not be specially mentioned, you would have seen this notice of a marriage at the top of a column:

> On the third instant, at the parish church, the Reverend Alfred Carling, Rector of Penliddy, to Emily Harriet, relict of the late Fergus Duncan, Esq., of Glendarn, N.B.

The rector's marriage did not produce a very favourable impression in the town, solely in consequence of the unaccountably private and unpretending manner in which the ceremony had been performed. The middle-aged bride and bridegroom had walked quietly to church one morning; had been married by the curate, before anyone was aware of it; and had embarked immediately afterwards in the steamer for Tenby, where they proposed to pass their honeymoon. The bride being a stranger at Penliddy, all inquiries about her previous history were fruitless; and the townspeople had no alternative but to trust to their own investigations for enlightenment when the rector and his wife came home to settle among their friends.

After six weeks' absence, Mr and Mrs Carling returned; and the simple story of the rector's courtship and marriage was gathered together in fragments, by inquisitive friends, from his own lips, and from the lips of his wife.

Mr Carling and Mrs Duncan had met at Torquay. The rector, who had exchanged houses and duties for the season with a brother clergyman settled at Torquay, had called on Mrs Duncan in his clerical capacity, and had come away from the interview deeply impressed and interested by the widow's manners and conversation. The visits were repeated; the acquaintance grew into friendship, and the friendship into love – ardent, devoted love on both sides.

Middle-aged man though he was, this was Mr Carling's first attachment; and it was met by the same freshness of feeling on the lady's part. Her life with her first husband had not been a happy one. She had made the fatal mistake of marrying to please her parents rather than herself, and had repented it ever afterwards. On her husband's death, his family had not behaved well to her; and she had passed her widowhood, with her only child, a daughter, in the retirement of a small Scotch town, many miles away from the home of her married life. After a time, the little girl's health had begun to fail, and, by the doctor's advice, she had migrated southward to the mild climate of Torquay. The change had proved to be of no avail; and, rather more than a year since, the child had died. The place where her darling was buried was a sacred place to her, and she had remained a resident at Torquay. Her position in the world was now a lonely one. She was herself an only child; her father and mother were both dead; and, excepting cousins, her one near relation left alive was a maternal uncle living in London.

These particulars were all related, simply and unaffectedly, before Mr Carling ventured on the confession of his attachment. When he made his proposal of marriage, Mrs Duncan received it with an excess of agitation which astonished and almost alarmed the inexperienced clergyman. As soon as she could speak, she begged, with extraordinary earnestness and anxiety, for a week to consider her answer; and requested Mr Carling not to visit her again, on any account, until the week had expired.

The next morning she and her maid departed for London. They did not return until the week for consideration had expired. On the eighth day Mr Carling called again, and was accepted.

The proposal to make the marriage as private as possible came from the lady. She had been to London to consult her uncle (whose health, she regretted to say, would not allow him to travel to Cornwall to give his niece away at the altar); and he agreed with Mrs Duncan that the wedding could not be too private and unpretending. If it was made public, the family of her first husband would expect cards to be sent to them, and a renewal of intercourse, which would be painful on both sides, might be the consequence. Other friends in Scotland, again, would resent her marrying a second time, at her age; and would distress her and annoy her future husband in many ways. She was anxious to break altogether with her past existence, and to begin a new and happier life, untrammelled by any connection with former times and troubles. She urged these points, as she had received the offer of marriage, with an agitation which was almost painful to see. This peculiarity in her conduct, however, which might have irritated some men, and rendered others distrustful, had no unfavourable effect on Mr Carling. He set it down to an excess of sensitiveness and delicacy which charmed him. He was himself – though he never would confess it – a shy, nervous man by nature. Ostentation of any sort was something which he shrank from instinctively, even in the simplest affairs of daily life; and his future wife's proposal to avoid all the usual ceremony and publicity of a wedding, was therefore more than agreeable to him – it was a positive relief.

The courtship was kept secret at Torquay, and the marriage was celebrated privately at Penliddy. It found its way into the local newspapers as a matter of course; but it was not, as usual in such cases, also advertised in *The Times*. Both husband and wife were equally happy in the enjoyment of their new life, and equally unsocial in taking no measures whatever to publish it to others.

Such was the story of the rector's marriage. Socially, Mr Carling's position was but little affected, either way, by the change in his life. As a bachelor, his circle of friends had been a small one; and, when he married, he made no attempt to enlarge it. He had never been popular with the inhabitants of his parish generally. Essentially a weak man, he was, like other weak men, only capable of asserting himself positively, in serious matters, by running into extremes. As a consequence of this moral defect, he presented some singular anomalies in character. In the ordinary affairs of life, he was the gentlest and most yielding of men; but in all that related to strictness of religious principle, he was the sternest and the most aggressive of fanatics. In the pulpit, he was a preacher of merciless sermons; an interpreter of the Bible, by the letter rather than by the spirit, as pitiless and gloomy as one of the Puritans of old – while, on the other hand, by his own fireside, he was considerate, forbearing, and humble almost to a fault. As a necessary result of this singular inconsistency of character, he was feared, and sometimes even disliked, by the members of his congregation, who only knew him as their pastor; and he was prized and loved by the small circle of friends who also knew him as a man.

Those friends gathered round him more closely and more affectionately than ever after his marriage – not on his own account only, but influenced also by the attractions that they found in the society of his wife. Her refinement and gentleness of manner; her extraordinary accomplishments as a musician; her unvarying sweetness of temper, and her quick, winning, womanly intelligence in conversation charmed every one who approached her. She was quoted as a model wife and woman by all her husband's friends; and she amply deserved the character that they gave her. Although no children came to cheer it, a happier and a more admirable married life has seldom been witnessed in this world than the life which was once to be seen in the rectory-house at Penliddy.

With these necessary explanations, that preliminary part of my narrative of which the events may be massed together generally, for brevity's sake, comes to a close. What I have next to tell is of a deeper and a more serious interest, and must be carefully related in detail.

The rector and his wife had lived together, without, as I honestly believe, a harsh word or an unkind look once passing between them, for upwards of two years, when Mr Carling took his first step towards the fatal future that was awaiting him, by devoting his leisure hours to the apparently simple and harmless occupation of writing a pamphlet.

He had been connected for many years with one of our great Missionary Societies, and had taken as active a part as a country clergyman could in the management of its affairs. At the period of which I speak, certain influential members of the Society had proposed a plan for greatly extending the sphere of its operations, trusting to a proportionate increase in the annual subscriptions to defray the additional expenses of the new movement. The question was not now brought forward for the first time. It had been agitated eight years previously, and the settlement of it had been at that time deferred to a future opportunity. The revival of the project, as usual in such cases, split the working members of the Society into two parties; one party cautiously objecting to run any risks; the other hopefully declaring that the venture was a safe one, and that success was sure to attend it. Mr Carling sided enthusiastically with the members who espoused this latter side of the question; and the object of his pamphlet was to address the subscribers to the Society on the subject, and so to interest them in it as to win their charitable support, on a larger scale than usual, to the new project.

He had worked hard at his pamphlet, and had got more than half way through it, when he found himself brought to a standstill for want of certain facts which had been produced on the discussion of the question eight years since, and which were necessary to the full and fair statement of his case.

At first he thought of writing to the secretary of the Society for information; but, remembering that he had not held his office more than two years, he had thought it little likely that this gentleman would be able to help him, and looked back to his own Diary of the period, to see if he had made any notes in it relating to the original discussion of the affair. He found a note referring, in general terms only, to the matter in hand; but alluding, at the end, to a report in *The Times* of the proceedings of a deputation from the Society, which had waited on a member of the Government of that day, and to certain letters to the Editor which had followed the publication of the report. The note described these letters as 'very important;' and Mr Carling felt, as he put his Diary away again, that the successful conclusion of his pamphlet now depended on his being able to get access to the back numbers of *The Times* of eight years since.

It was winter time when he was thus stopped in his work; and the prospect of a journey to London (the only place he knew of at which files of the paper were to be found) did not present many attractions. And yet he could see no other and easier means of effecting his object. After considering for a little while, and arriving at no positive conclusion, he left the study, and went into the drawing-room to consult his wife.

He found her working industriously by the blazing fire. She looked so happy and comfortable – so gentle and charming in her pretty little lace cap, and her warm brown morning dress, with its bright cherry-coloured ribbons, and its delicate swansdown trimming circling round her neck and nestling over her bosom, that he stooped and kissed her with the tenderness of his bridegroom days before he spoke. When he told her of the cause that had suspended his literary occupation, she listened, with the sensation of the kiss still lingering in her downcast eyes and her smiling lips, until he came to the subject of his Diary, and its reference to the newspaper.

As he mentioned the name of *The Times*, she altered and looked him straight in the face gravely.

'Can you suggest any plan, love,' he went on, 'which may save me the necessity of a journey to London at this bleak time of the year? I must positively have this information; and, so far as I can see, London is the only place at which I can hope to meet with a file of *The Times*.'

'A file of *The Times?*' she repeated.

'Yes; of eight years since,' he said.

The instant the words passed his lips, he saw her face overspread by a ghastly paleness; her eyes fixed on him with a strange mixture of rigidity and vacancy in their look; her hands, with her work held tight in them, dropped slowly on her lap; and a shiver ran through her from head to foot.

He sprang to his feet, and snatched the smelling-salts from her work-table, thinking she was going to faint. She put the bottle from her, when he offered it, with a hand that thrilled him with the deadly coldness of its touch, and said, in a whisper—

'A sudden chill, dear – let me go upstairs and lie down.'

He took her to her room. As he laid her down on the bed, she caught his hand, and said, entreatingly:

'You won't go to London, darling, and leave me here ill?'

He promised that nothing should separate him from her until she was well again; and then ran downstairs to send for the doctor. The doctor came, and pronounced that Mrs Carling was only suffering from a nervous attack; that there was not the least reason to be alarmed; and that, with proper care, she would be well again in a few days.

Both husband and wife had a dinner engagement in the town for that evening. Mr Carling proposed to write an apology, and to remain with his wife. But she would not hear of his abandoning the party on her account. The doctor also recommended that his patient should be left to her maid's care, to fall asleep under the influence of the quieting medicine which he meant to give her. Yielding to this advice, Mr Carling did his best to suppress his own anxieties, and went to the dinner-party.

II

Among the guests whom the rector met, was a gentleman named Rambert – a single man, of large fortune, well-known in the neighbourhood of Penliddy as the owner of a noble country-seat and the possessor of a magnificent library.

Mr Rambert (with whom Mr Carling was well acquainted) greeted him at the dinner-party with friendly expressions of regret at the time that had elapsed since they had last seen each other; and mentioned that he had recently been adding to his collection of books some rare old volumes of theology, which he thought the rector might find it useful to look over. Mr Carling, with the necessity of finishing his pamphlet uppermost in his mind, replied, jestingly, that the species of literature which he was just then most interested in examining happened to be precisely of the sort which (excepting novels, perhaps) had least affinity to theological writing. The necessary explanation followed this avowal, as a matter of course; and to Mr Carling's great delight, his friend turned on him gaily with the most surprising and satisfactory of answers:

'You don't know half the resources of my miles of bookshelves,' he said, 'or you would never have thought of going to London for what you can get from me. A whole side of one of my rooms upstairs is devoted to periodical literature. I have reviews, magazines, and three weekly newspapers, bound, in each case, from the first number; and what is just now more to your purpose, I have *The Times*, for the last fifteen years, in huge half-yearly volumes. Give me the date to-night, and you shall have the volume you want by two o'clock to-morrow afternoon.'

The necessary information was given at once; and, with a great sense of relief, so far as his literary anxieties were concerned, Mr Carling went home early to see what the quieting medicine had done for his wife.

She had dozed a little; but had not slept. However, she was evidently better; for she was able to take an interest in the sayings and doings at the dinner party; and questioned her husband about the guests and the conversation, with all a woman's curiosity about the minutest matters. She lay with her face turned towards him, and her eyes meeting his, until the course of her inquiries drew an answer from him, which informed her of his fortunate discovery in relation to Mr Rambert's library, and of the prospect it afforded of his resuming his labours the next day.

When he mentioned this circumstance, she suddenly turned her head on the pillow, so that her face was hidden from him; and he could see through the counterpane that the shivering, which he had observed when her illness had seized her in the morning, had returned again.

'I am only cold,' she said, in a hurried way, with her face under the clothes.

He rang for the maid, and had a fresh covering placed on the bed. Observing that she seemed unwilling to be disturbed, he did not remove the clothes from her face when he wished her good night; but pressed his lips on her head, and patted it gently with his hand. She shrank at the touch as if it hurt her, light as it was; and he went downstairs, resolved to send for the doctor again if she did not get to rest on being left quiet. In less than half-an-hour afterwards, the maid came down, and relieved his anxiety by reporting that her mistress was asleep.

The next morning, he found her in better spirits. Her eyes, she said, felt too weak to bear the light; so she kept the bedroom darkened. But in other respects, she had little to complain of.

After answering her husband's first inquiries, she questioned him about his plans for the day. He had letters to write which would occupy him until twelve o'clock. At two o'clock he expected the volume of *The Times* to arrive; and he should then devote the rest of the afternoon to his work. After hearing what his plans were, Mrs Carling suggested that he should ride out after he had done his letters, so as to get some exercise at the fine part of the day; and she then reminded him that a longer time than usual had elapsed since he had been to see a certain old pensioner of his, who had nursed him as a child, and who was now bed-ridden, in a village at some distance, called Tringweighton. Although the rector saw no immediate necessity for making this charitable visit, the more especially as the ride to the village and back, and the intermediate time devoted to gossip, would occupy at least two hours and a half, he assented to his wife's proposal, perceiving that she urged it with unusual earnestness, and being unwilling to thwart her, even in a trifle, at a time when she was ill.

Accordingly his horse was at the door at twelve precisely. Impatient to get back to the precious volume of *The Times*, he rode so much faster than usual, and so shortened his visit to the old woman, that he was home again by a quarter past two. Ascertaining from the servant who opened the door, that the volume had been left by Mr Rambert's messenger punctually at two, he ran up to his wife's room to tell her about his visit, before he secluded himself for the rest of the afternoon over his work.

On entering the bedroom, he found it still darkened; and he was struck by a smell of burnt paper in it.

His wife (who was now dressed in her wrapper and lying on the sofa) accounted for the smell by telling him that she had fancied the room felt close, and that she had burnt some paper – being afraid of the cold air if she opened the window – to fumigate it. Her eyes were evidently still weak, for she kept her hand over them while she spoke. After remaining with her long enough to relate the few trivial events of his ride, Mr Carling descended to his study to occupy himself at last with the volume of *The Times*.

It lay on his table, in the shape of a large flat brown paper package. On proceeding to undo the covering, he observed that it had been very carelessly tied up. The strings were crooked and loosely knotted; and the direction bearing his name and address, instead of being in the middle of the paper, was awkwardly folded over at the edge of the volume. However his business was with the inside of the parcel; so he tossed away the covering and the string, and began at once to hunt through the volume for the particular number of the paper which he wished first to consult.

He soon found it, with the report of the speeches delivered by the members of the deputation, and the answer returned by the minister. After reading through the report, and putting a mark in the place where it occurred, he turned to the next day's number of the paper, to see what further hints on the subject the letters addressed to the Editor might happen to contain.

To his inexpressible vexation and amazement, that one number of the paper was missing.

He bent the two sides of the volume back; looked closely between the leaves, and saw immediately that the missing number had been cut out.

A vague sense of something like alarm began to mingle with his first feeling of disappointment. He wrote at once to Mr Rambert, mentioning the discovery he had just made, and sent the note off by his groom, with orders to the man to wait for an answer.

The reply with which the servant returned was almost insolent in the shortness and coolness of its tone. Mr Rambert had no books in his library which were not in perfect condition. The volume of *The Times* had left his house perfect; and whatever blame might attach to the mutilation of it rested therefore on other shoulders than those of the owner.

Like many other weak men, Mr Carling was secretly touchy on the subject of his dignity. After reading the note, and questioning his servants, who were certain that the volume had not been touched till he had opened it, he resolved that the missing number of *The Times* should be procured at any expense and inserted in its place; that the volume should be sent back instantly without a word of comment; and that no more books from Mr Rambert's library should enter his house.

He walked up and down the study, considering what first step he should take to effect the purpose in view. Under the quickening influence of his irritation, an idea occurred to him, which, if it had only entered his mind the day before, might probably have proved the means of saving him from placing himself under an obligation to Mr Rambert. He resolved to write immediately to his bookseller and publisher in London (who knew him well as an old and excellent customer), mentioning the date of the back number of *The Times* that was required, and authorising the publisher to offer any reward he judged necessary to any person who might have the means of procuring it, at the office of the paper, or elsewhere. This letter he wrote and despatched in good time for the London post; and then went upstairs to see his wife and to tell her what had happened.

Her room was still darkened, and she was still on the sofa. On the subject of the missing number she said nothing; but of Mr Rambert and his note, she spoke with the most sovereign contempt. Of course the pompous old fool was mistaken; and the proper thing to do was to send back the volume instantly, and take no more notice of him.

'It shall be sent back,' said Mr Carling, 'but not till the missing number is replaced.' And he then told her what he had done.

The effect of that simple piece of information on Mrs Carling was so extraordinary and so unaccountable, that her husband fairly stood aghast. For the first time since their marriage, he saw her temper suddenly in a flame. She started up from the sofa, and walked about the room, as if she had lost her senses; upbraiding him for making the weakest of concessions to Mr Rambert's insolent assumption that the rector was to blame. If she could only have laid hands on that letter, she would have consulted her husband's dignity and independence by putting it in the fire! She hoped and prayed the number of the paper might not be found! In fact, it was certain that the number, after all these years, could not possibly be hunted up. The idea of his acknowledging himself to be in the wrong, in that way, when he knew himself to be in the right! It was almost ridiculous – no, it was *quite* ridiculous! And she threw herself back on the sofa, and suddenly burst out laughing.

At the first word of remonstrance which fell from her husband's lips, her mood changed again, in an instant. She sprang up once more, kissed him passionately, with the tears streaming from her eyes, and implored him to leave her alone to recover herself. He quitted the room so seriously alarmed about her, that he resolved to go to the doctor privately, and question him on the spot. There was an unspeakable dread in his mind, that the nervous attack from which she had been pronounced to be suffering might be a mere phrase intended to prepare him for the future disclosure of something infinitely and indescribably worse.

The doctor, on hearing Mr Carling's report, exhibited no surprise, and held to his opinion. Her nervous system was out of order, and her husband had been needlessly frightened by an hysterical paroxysm. If she did not get better in a week, change of scene might then be tried. In the meantime, there was not the least cause for alarm.

On the next day she was quieter, but she hardly spoke at all. At night she slept well; and Mr Carling's faith in the medical man revived again.

The morning after was the morning which would bring the answer from the publisher in London. The rector's study was on the ground floor; and when he heard the postman's knock, being especially anxious that morning about his correspondence, he went out into the hall to receive his letters the moment they were put on the table.

It was not the footman who had answered the door, as usual, but Mrs Carling's maid. She had taken the letters from the postman, and she was going away with them upstairs.

He stopped her, and asked her why she did not put the letters on the hall table as usual. The maid, looking very much confused, said that her mistress had desired that whatever the postman had brought that morning should be carried up to her room. He took the letters abruptly from the girl, without asking any more questions, and went back into his study.

Up to this time, no shadow of a suspicion had fallen on his mind. Hitherto, there had been a simple obvious explanation for every unusual event that had occurred during the last three or four days. But this last circumstance in connection with the letters was not to be accounted for. Nevertheless, even now, it was not distrust of his wife that was busy in his mind – he was too fond of her and too proud of her to feel it – the sensation was more like uneasy surprise. He longed to go and question her, and get a satisfactory answer and have done with it. But there was a voice speaking within him that had never made itself heard before; a voice with a persistent warning in it, that said – Wait: and look at your letters first!

He spread them out on the table, with hands that trembled he knew not why. Among them was the back number of *The Times* for which he had written to London, with a letter from the publisher explaining the means by which the copy had been procured.

He opened the newspaper, with a vague feeling of alarm at finding that those letters to the Editor which he had been so eager to read, and that perfecting of the mutilated volume which he had been so anxious to accomplish, had become objects of secondary importance in his mind. An inexplicable curiosity about the general contents of the paper was now the one moving influence which asserted itself within him. He spread open the broad sheet on the table.

The first page on which his eye fell, was the page on the right-hand side. It contained those very letters – three in number – which he had once been so anxious to see. He tried to read them; but no effort could fix his wandering attention. He looked aside, to the opposite page, on the left hand. It was the page that contained the leading articles.

They were three in number. The first was on foreign politics; the second was a sarcastic commentary on a recent division in the House of Lords; the third was one of those articles on social subjects which have greatly and honourably helped to raise the reputation of *The Times* above all contest and all rivalry.

The lines of this third article which first caught his eye, comprised the opening sentence of the second paragraph, and contained these words:

> It appears, from the narrative which will be found in another part of our columns, that this unfortunate woman married, in the spring of the year 18—, one Mr Fergus Duncan, of Glendarn, in the Highlands of Scotland . . .

The letters swam and mingled together under his eyes, before he could go on to the next sentence. His wife exhibited as an object for public compassion in *The Times* newspaper! On the brink of the dreadful discovery that was advancing on him, his mind reeled back; and a deadly faintness came over him. There was water on a side table – he drank a deep draught of it – roused himself – seized on the newspaper with both hands, as if it had been a living thing that could feel the desperate resolution of his grasp – and read the article through, sentence by sentence, word by word.

The subject was the Law of Divorce; and the example quoted was the example of his wife.

At that time, England stood disgracefully alone as the one civilized country in the world having a divorce law for the husband which was not also a divorce law for the wife. The writer in *The Times* boldly and eloquently exposed this discreditable anomaly in the administration of justice; hinted delicately at the unutterable wrongs suffered by Mrs Duncan; and plainly showed that she was indebted to the accident of having been married in Scotland, and to her consequent right of appeal to the Scotch tribunals, for a full and final release from the tie that bound her to the vilest of husbands, which the English law of that day would have mercilessly refused.

He read that. Other men might have gone on to the narrative extracted from the Scotch newspaper. But at the last word of the article *he* stopped.

The newspaper, and the unread details which it contained, lost all hold on his attention in an instant, and, in their stead, living and burning on his mind, like the Letters of Doom on the walls of Belshazzar, there rose up in judgment against him, the last words of a verse in the Gospel of Saint Luke:

'*Whosoever marrieth her that is put away from her husband, committeth adultery.*'

He had preached from these words. He had warned his hearers, with the whole strength of the fanatical sincerity that was in him, to beware of prevaricating with the prohibition which that verse contained, and to accept it as literally, unreservedly, finally forbidding the marriage of a divorced woman.

He had insisted on that plain interpretation of plain words, in terms which had made his congregation tremble. And now, he stood alone in the secrecy of his own chamber, self-convicted of the deadly sin which he had denounced – he stood, as he had told the wicked among his hearers that they would stand, at the Last Day, before the Judgment Seat.

He was unconscious of the lapse of time; he never knew whether it was many minutes or few, before the door of his room was suddenly and softly opened. It did open – and his wife came in.

In her white dress, with a white shawl thrown over her shoulders; her dark hair, so neat and glossy at other times, hanging tangled about her colourless cheeks, and heightening the glassy brightness of terror in her eyes – so he saw her; the woman put away from her husband, the woman whose love had made his life happy and had stained his soul with a deadly sin.

She came on to within a few paces of him, without a word or a tear, or a shadow of change passing over the dreadful rigidity of her face. She looked at him with a strange look; she pointed to the newspaper crumpled in his hand, with a strange gesture; she spoke to him in a strange voice.

'You know it!' she said.

His eyes met hers – she shrank from them – turned – and laid her arms and her head heavily against the wall.

'Oh, Alfred,' she said, 'I was so lonely in the world, and I was so fond of you!'

The woman's delicacy, the woman's trembling tenderness welled up from her heart, and touched her voice with a tone of its old sweetness, as she murmured those simple words.

She said no more. Her confession of her fault, her appeal to their past love for pardon, were both poured forth in that one sentence. She left it to his own heart to tell him the rest. How anxiously her vigilant love had followed his every word, and treasured up his every opinion, in the days when they first met; how weakly and falsely, and yet with how true an affection for him, she had shrunk from the disclosure which she knew but too well would have separated them even at the church door; how desperately she had fought against the coming discovery which threatened to tear her from the bosom she clung to, and to cast her out into the world with the shadow of her own shame to darken her life to the end – all this she left him to feel; for the moment which might part them for ever, was the moment when she knew best how truly, how passionately he had loved her.

His lips trembled as he stood looking at her in silence; and the slow, burning tears dropped heavily, one by one, down his cheeks. The natural human remembrance of the golden days of their companionship, of the nights and nights when that dear head – turned away from him, now, in unutterable misery and shame – had nestled itself so fondly and so happily on his breast, fought hard to silence his conscience, to root out his dreadful sense of guilt, to tear the words of Judgment from their ruthless hold on his mind, to claim him in the sweet names of Pity and of Love. If she had turned and looked at him at that moment, their next words would have been spoken in each other's arms. But the oppression of her despair, under his silence, was too heavy for her, and she never moved.

He forced himself to look away from her; he struggled hard to break the silence between them.

'God forgive you, Emily!' he said.

As her name passed his lips, his voice failed him, and the torture at his heart burst its way out in sobs. He hurried to the door, to spare her the terrible reproof of the grief that had now mastered him. When he passed her, she turned towards him with a faint cry.

He caught her as she sank forward, and saved her from dropping on the floor. For the last time, his arms closed round her. For the last time, his lips touched hers – cold and insensible to him now. He laid her on the sofa and went out.

One of the female servants was crossing the hall. The girl started as she met him, and turned pale at the sight of his face. He could not speak to her, but he pointed to the study-door. He saw her go into the room; and then left the house.

He never entered it more; and he and his wife never met again.

Later on that last day, a sister of Mr Carling's – a married woman living in the town – came to the rectory. She brought an open note with her, addressed to the unhappy mistress of the house. It contained these few lines, blotted and stained with tears:

> May God grant us both the time for repentance! If I had loved you less, I might have trusted myself to see you again. Forgive me, and pity me, and remember me in your prayers, as I shall forgive, and pity, and remember you.

He had tried to write more; but the pen had dropped from his hand. His sister's entreaties had not moved him. After giving her the note to deliver, he had solemnly charged her to be gentle in communicating the tidings that she bore, and had departed alone for London. He heard all remonstrances with patience. He did not deny that the deception of which his wife had been guilty, was the most pardonable of all concealments of the truth, because it sprang from her love for him. But he had the same hopeless answer for everyone who tried to plead with him – the verse from the Gospel of Saint Luke.

His purpose in travelling to London was to make the necessary arrangements for his wife's future existence, and then to get employment which would separate him from his home and from all its associations. A missionary expedition to one of the Pacific Islands accepted him as a volunteer. Broken in body and spirit, his last look of England, from the deck of the ship, was his last look at land. A fortnight afterwards, his brethren read the burial service over him, on a calm cloudless evening at sea. Before he was committed to the deep, his little pocket Bible, which had been a present from his wife, was, in accordance with his dying wishes, placed open on his breast, so that the inscription, 'To my dear Husband,' might rest over his heart.

His unhappy wife still lives. When the farewell lines of her husband's writing reached her, she was incapable of comprehending them. The mental prostration which had followed the parting scene was soon complicated by physical suffering – by fever on the brain. To the surprise of all who attended her, she lived through the shock, recovering with the complete loss of one faculty, which, in her situation, poor thing, was a mercy and a gain to her – the faculty of memory. From that time to this, she has never had the slightest gleam of recollection of anything that happened before her illness. In her happy oblivion, the veriest trifles are as new and as interesting to her, as if she was beginning her existence again. Under the tender care of the friends who now protect her, she lives contentedly the life of a child. When her last hour comes, may she die with nothing on her memory but the recollection of their kindness!

Blow Up With the Brig!

[A Sailor's Story]

Originally appeared in *The Haunted House*, the Christmas number of *All the Year Round* for 1859 as 'The Ghost in the Cupboard Room.' The story was reprinted in *Miss or Mrs? and Other Stories in Outline* (1873). Dickens told Collins it was one of his favourites.

I HAVE GOT an alarming confession to make. I am haunted by a Ghost.
    If you were to guess for a hundred years, you would never guess what
my ghost is. I shall make you laugh to begin with – and afterwards I shall
make your flesh creep. My Ghost is the ghost of a Bedroom Candlestick.

Yes, a bedroom candlestick and candle or a flat candlestick and candle –
put it which way you like – that is what haunts me. I wish it was something
pleasanter and more out of the common way; a beautiful lady, or a mine of
gold and silver, or a cellar of wine and a coach and horses, and such-like. But,
being what it is, I must take it for what it is, and make the best of it – and I
shall thank you kindly if you will help me out by doing the same.

I am not a scholar myself; but I make bold to believe that the haunting of
any man with anything under the sun, begins with the frightening of him. At
any rate, the haunting of me with a bedroom candlestick and candle began
with the frightening of me with a bedroom candlestick and candle – the
frightening of me half out of my life; and, for the time being, the frightening
of me altogether out of my wits. That is not a very pleasant thing to confess,
before stating the particulars; but perhaps you will be the readier to believe
that I am not a downright coward because you find me bold enough to make
a clean breast of it already, to my own great disadvantage, so far.

Here are the particulars, as well as I can put them:

I was apprenticed to the sea when I was about as tall as my own
walking-stick; and I made good enough use of my time to be fit for a mate's
berth at the age of twenty-five years.

It was in the year eighteen hundred and eighteen, or nineteen, I am not
quite certain which, that I reached the before-mentioned age of twenty-five.
You will please to excuse my memory not being very good for dates, names,
numbers, places, and such-like. No fear, though, about the particulars I have
undertaken to tell you of; I have got them all ship-shape in my recollection; I
can see them, at this moment, as clear as noonday in my own mind. But there
is a mist over what went before, and, for the matter of that, a mist likewise over
much that came after – and it's not very likely to lift at my time of life, is it?

Well, in eighteen hundred and eighteen, or nineteen, when there was
peace in our part of the world – and not before it was wanted, you will
say – there was fighting, of a certain scampering, scrambling kind, going
on in that old battle-field, which we seafaring men know by the name of
the Spanish Main.

The possessions that belonged to the Spaniards in South America had
broken into open mutiny and declared for themselves years before. There
was plenty of bloodshed between the new government and the old; but the
new had got the best of it, for the most part, under one General Bolivar –
a famous man in his time, though he seems to have dropped out of people's
memories now. Englishmen and Irishmen with a turn for fighting, and nothing
particular to do at home, joined the general as volunteers; and some of our
merchants here found it a good venture to send supplies across the ocean to
the popular side. There was risk enough, of course, in doing this; but where
one speculation of the kind succeeded, it made up for two, at the least, that
failed. And that's the true principle of trade, wherever I have met with it, all
the world over.

Among the Englishmen who were concerned in this Spanish-American
business, I, your humble servant, happened in a small way to be one.

I was then mate of a brig belonging to a certain firm in the City, which drove a sort of general trade, mostly in queer out-of-the-way places, as far from home as possible; and which freighted the brig, in the year I am speaking of, with a cargo of gunpowder for General Bolivar and his volunteers. Nobody knew anything about our instructions, when we sailed, except the captain; and he didn't half seem to like them. I can't rightly say how many barrels of powder we had on board, or how much each barrel held – I only know we had no other cargo. The name of the brig was the Good Intent – a queer name enough, you will tell me, for a vessel laden with gunpowder, and sent to help a revolution. And as far as this particular voyage was concerned, so it was. I mean that for a joke, and I hope you will encourage me by laughing at it.

The Good Intent was the craziest old tub of a vessel I ever went to sea in, and the worst found in all respects. She was two hundred and thirty, or two hundred and eighty tons burden, I forget which; and she had a crew of eight, all told – nothing like as many as we ought by rights to have had to work the brig. However, we were well and honestly paid our wages; and we had to set that against the chance of foundering at sea, and, on this occasion, likewise, the chance of being blown up into the bargain.

In consideration of the nature of our cargo, we were harassed with new regulations which we didn't at all like, relative to smoking our pipes and lighting our lanterns; and, as usual in such cases, the captain who made the regulations, preached what he didn't practise. Not a man of us was allowed to have a bit of lighted candle in his hand when he went below – except the skipper; and he used his light, when he turned in, or when he looked over his charts on the cabin table, just as usual.

This light was a common kitchen candle or 'dip,' and it stood in an old battered flat candlestick, with all the japan worn and melted off, and all the tin showing through. It would have been more seamanlike and suitable in every respect if he had had a lamp or a lantern; but he stuck to his old candlestick; and that same old candlestick has ever afterwards stuck to *me*. That's another joke, if you please, and a better one than the first, in my opinion.

Well (I said 'well' before, but it's a word that helps a man on like), we sailed in the brig, and shaped our course, first, for the Virgin Islands, in the West Indies; and, after sighting them, we made for the Leeward Islands next; and then stood on due south, till the look-out at the mast-head hailed the deck, and said he saw land. That land was the coast of South America. We had had a wonderful voyage so far. We had lost none of our spars or sails, and not a man of us had been harassed to death at the pumps. It wasn't often the Good Intent made such a voyage as that, I can tell you.

I was sent aloft to make sure about the land, and I did make sure of it.

When I reported the same to the skipper, he went below, and had a look at his letter of instructions and the chart. When he came on deck again, he altered our course a trifle to the eastward – I forget the point on the compass, but that don't matter. What I do remember is, that it was dark before we closed in with the land. We kept the lead going, and hove the brig to in from four to five fathoms water, or it might be six – I can't say for certain. I kept a sharp eye to the drift of the vessel, none of us knowing how the currents ran on that coast. We all wondered why the skipper didn't anchor; but he said, No, he must first show a light at the foretop mast-head, and wait for an answering light on shore. We did wait, and nothing of the sort appeared. It was starlight and calm. What little wind there was came in puffs off the land. I suppose we waited, drifting a little to the westward, as I made it out, best part of an hour before anything happened – and then, instead of seeing the light on shore, we saw a boat coming towards us, rowed by two men only.

We hailed them, and they answered 'Friends!' and hailed us by our name. They came on board. One of them was an Irishman, and the other was a coffee-coloured native pilot, who jabbered a little English.

The Irishman handed a note to our skipper, who showed it to me. It informed us that the part of the coast we were off was not over safe for discharging our cargo, seeing that spies of the enemy (that is to say, of the old government) had been taken and shot in the neighbourhood the day before. We might trust the brig to the native pilot; and he had his instructions to take us to another part of the coast. The note was signed by the proper parties; so we let the Irishman go back alone in the boat, and allowed the pilot to exercise his lawful authority over the brig. He kept us stretching off from the land till noon the next day – his instructions, seemingly, ordering him to keep us well out of sight of the shore. We only altered our course, in the afternoon, so as to close in with the land again a little before midnight.

This same pilot was about as ill-looking a vagabond as ever I saw; a skinny, cowardly, quarrelsome mongrel, who swore at the men, in the vilest broken English, till they were every one of them ready to pitch him overboard. The skipper kept them quiet, and I kept them quiet, for the pilot being given us by our instructions, we were bound to make the best of him. Near nightfall, however, with the best will in the world to avoid it, I was unlucky enough to quarrel with him.

He wanted to go below with his pipe, and I stopped him, of course, because it was contrary to orders. Upon that, he tried to hustle by me, and I put him away with my hand. I never meant to push him down; but, somehow, I did. He picked himself up as quick as lightning, and pulled out his knife. I snatched it out of his hand, slapped his murderous face for him, and threw his weapon overboard. He gave me one ugly look, and walked aft. I didn't think much of the look then; but I remembered it a little too well afterwards.

We were close in with the land again, just as the wind failed us, between eleven and twelve that night; and dropped our anchor by the pilot's directions.

It was pitch dark, and a dead airless calm. The skipper was on deck with two of our best men for watch. The rest were below, except the pilot, who coiled himself up, more like a snake than a man, on the forecastle. It was not my watch till four in the morning. But I didn't like the look of the night, or the pilot, or the state of things generally, and I shook myself down on deck to get my nap there, and be ready for anything at a moment's notice. The last I remember was the skipper whispering to me that he didn't like the look of things either, and that he would go below and consult his instructions again. That is the last I remember, before the slow, heavy, regular roll of the old brig on the ground swell rocked me off to sleep.

I was awoke by a scuffle on the forecastle, and a gag in my mouth. There was a man on my breast, and a man on my legs; and I was bound hand and foot in half a minute.

The brig was in the hands of the Spaniards. They were swarming all over her. I heard six heavy splashes in the water, one after another. I saw the captain stabbed to the heart as he came running up the companion – and I heard a seventh splash in the water. Except myself, every soul of us on board had been murdered and thrown into the sea. Why I was left, I couldn't think, till I saw the pilot stoop over me with a lantern, and look, to make sure of who I was. There was a devilish grin on his face, and he nodded his head at me, as much as to say, *You* were the man who hustled me down and slapped my face, and I mean to play the game of cat and mouse with you in return for it!

I could neither move nor speak; but I could see the Spaniards take off the main hatch and rig the purchases for getting up the cargo. A quarter of an hour afterwards, I heard the sweeps of a schooner, or other small vessel, in the water. The strange craft was laid alongside of us; and the Spaniards set to work to discharge our cargo into her. They all worked hard except the pilot; and he came, from time to time, with his lantern, to have another look at me, and to grin and nod always in the same devilish way. I am old enough now not to be ashamed of confessing the truth; and I don't mind acknowledging that the pilot frightened me.

The fright, and the bonds, and the gag, and the not being able to stir hand or foot, had pretty nigh worn me out, by the time the Spaniards gave over work. This was just as the dawn broke. They had shifted a good part of our cargo on board their vessel, but nothing like all of it; and they were sharp enough to be off with what they had got, before daylight.

I need hardly say that I had made up my mind, by this time, to the worst I could think of. The pilot, it was clear enough, was one of the spies of the enemy, who had wormed himself into the confidence of our consignees without being suspected. He, or more likely his employers, had got knowledge enough of us to suspect what our cargo was; we had been anchored for the night in the safest berth for them to surprise us in; and we had paid the penalty of having a small crew, and consequently an insufficient watch. All this was clear enough – but what did the pilot mean to do with *me?*

On the word of a man, it makes my flesh creep, now, only to tell you what he did with me.

After all the rest of them were out of the brig, except the pilot and two Spanish seamen, these last took me up, bound and gagged as I was, lowered me into the hold of the vessel, and laid me along on the floor; lashing me to it with ropes' ends, so that I could just turn from one side to the other, but could not roll myself fairly over, so as to change my place. They then left me. Both of them were the worse for liquor: but the devil of a pilot was sober – mind that! – as sober as I am at the present moment.

I lay in the dark for a little while, with my heart thumping as if it was going to jump out of me. I lay about five minutes or so, when the pilot came down into the hold, alone.

He had the captain's cursed flat candlestick and a carpenter's awl in one hand, and a long thin twist of cotton yarn, well oiled, in the other. He put the candlestick, with a new 'dip' candle lighted in it, down on the floor, about two feet from my face, and close against the side of the vessel. The light was feeble enough; but it was sufficient to show a dozen barrels of gunpowder or more, left all round me in the hold of the brig. I began to suspect what he was after, the moment I noticed the barrels. The horrors laid hold of me from head to foot; and the sweat poured off my face like water.

I saw him go, next, to one of the barrels of powder standing against the side of the vessel, in a line with the candle, and about three feet, or rather better, away from it. He bored a hole in the side of the barrel with his awl; and the horrid powder came trickling out, as black as hell, and dripped into the hollow of his hand, which he held to catch it. When he had got a good handful, he stopped up the hole by jamming one end of his oiled twist of cotton-yarn fast into it; and he then rubbed the powder into the whole length of the yarn, till he had blackened every hairsbreadth of it.

The next thing he did – as true as I sit here, as true as the heaven above us all – the next thing he did was to carry the free end of his long, lean, black, frightful slow-match to the lighted candle alongside my face. He tied it (the bloody-minded villain!) in several folds, round the tallow dip, about a third of the distance down, measuring from the flame of the wick to the lip of the candlestick. He did that; he looked to see that my lashings were all safe; and then he put his face down close to mine, and whispered in my ear, 'Blow up with the brig!'

He was on deck again the moment after; and he and the two others shoved the hatch on over me. At the farthest end from where I lay, they had not fitted it down quite true, and I saw a blink of daylight glimmering in when I looked in that direction. I heard the sweeps of the schooner fall into the water – splash! splash! fainter and fainter, as they swept the vessel out in the dead calm, to be ready for the wind in the offing. Fainter and fainter, splash! splash! for a quarter of an hour or more.

While those sounds were in my ears, my eyes were fixed on the candle.

It had been freshly lit – if left to itself it would burn for between six and seven hours. The slow-match was twisted round it about a third of the way down; and therefore the flame would be about two hours reaching it. There I lay, gagged, bound, lashed to the floor; seeing my own life burning down with the candle by my side – there I lay, alone on the sea, doomed to be blown to atoms, and to see that doom drawing on, nearer and nearer with every fresh second of time, through nigh on two hours to come; powerless to help myself and speechless to call for help to others. The wonder to me is that I didn't cheat the flame, the slow-match, and the powder, and die of the horror of my situation before my first half-hour was out in the hold of the brig.

I can't exactly say how long I kept the command of my senses after I had ceased to hear the splash of the schooner's sweeps in the water. I can trace back everything I did and everything I thought, up to a certain point; but, once past that, I get all abroad, and lose myself in my memory now, much as I lost myself in my own feelings at the time.

The moment the hatch was covered over me, I began, as every other man would have begun in my place, with a frantic effort to free my hands. In the mad panic I was in, I cut my flesh with the lashings as if they had been knife-blades; but I never stirred them. There was less chance still of freeing my legs, or of tearing myself from the fastenings that held me to the floor. I gave in, when I was all but suffocated for want of breath. The gag, you will please to remember, was a terrible enemy to me; I could only breathe freely through my nose – and that is but a poor vent when a man is straining his strength as far as ever it will go.

I gave in, and lay quiet, and got my breath again; my eyes glaring and straining at the candle all the time.

While I was staring at it, the notion struck me of trying to blow out the flame by pumping a long breath at it suddenly through my nostrils. It was too high above me, and too far away from me, to be reached in that fashion. I tried, and tried, and tried – and then I gave in again and lay quiet again; always with my eyes glaring at the candle, and the candle glaring at *me*. The splash of the schooner's sweeps was very faint by this time. I could only just hear them in the morning stillness. Splash! splash! – fainter and fainter – splash! splash!

Without exactly feeling my mind going, I began to feel it getting queer, as early as this. The snuff of the candle was growing taller and taller, and the length of tallow between the flame and the slow-match, which was the length of my life, was getting shorter and shorter. I calculated that I had rather less than an hour and a half to live.

An hour and a half! Was there a chance, in that time, of a boat pulling off to the brig from shore? Whether the land near which the vessel was anchored was in possession of our side, or in possession of the enemy's side, I made out that they must, sooner or later, send to hail the brig, merely because she was a stranger in those parts. The question for *me* was, how soon? The sun had not risen yet, as I could tell by looking through the chink in the hatch. There was no coast village near us, as we all knew, before the brig was seized, by seeing no lights on shore. There was no wind, as I could tell by listening, to bring any strange vessel near. If I had had six hours to live, there might have been a chance for me, reckoning from sunrise to noon. But with an hour and a half, which had dwindled to an hour and a quarter by this time – or, in other words, with the earliness of the morning, the uninhabited coast, and the dead calm all against me – there was not the ghost of a chance. As I felt that, I had another struggle – the last – with my bonds; and only cut myself the deeper for my pains.

I gave in once more, and lay quiet, and listened for the splash of the sweeps.

Gone! Not a sound could I hear but the blowing of a fish, now and then, on the surface of the sea, and the creak of the brig's crazy old spars, as she rolled gently from side to side with the little swell there was on the quiet water.

An hour and a quarter. The wick grew terribly, as the quarter slipped away; and the charred top of it began to thicken and spread out mushroom-shape. It would fall off soon. Would it fall off red-hot, and would the swing of the brig cant it over the side of the candle, and let it down on the slow-match? If it would, I had about ten minutes to live instead of an hour.

This discovery set my mind for a minute on a new tack altogether. I began to ponder with myself what sort of a death blowing-up might be. Painful? Well, it would be, surely, too sudden for that. Perhaps just one crash, inside me, or outside me, or both, and nothing more? Perhaps not even a crash; that and death and the scattering of this living body of mine into millions of fiery sparks, might all happen in the same instant? I couldn't make it out; I couldn't settle how it would be. The minute of calmness in my mind left it, before I had half done thinking; and I got all abroad again.

When I came back to my thoughts, or when they came back to me (I can't say which), the wick was awfully tall, the flame was burning with a smoke above it, the charred top was broad and red, and heavily spreading out to its fall.

My despair and horror at seeing it, took me in a new way, which was good and right, at any rate, for my poor soul. I tried to pray; in my own heart, you will understand, for the gag put all lip-praying out of my power. I tried, but the candle seemed to burn it up in me. I struggled hard to force my eyes from the slow, murdering flame, and to look up through the chink in the hatch at the blessed daylight. I tried once, tried twice; and gave it up. I tried next only to shut my eyes, and keep them shut – once – twice – and the second time I did it. 'God bless old mother, and sister Lizzie; God keep them both, and forgive *me*.' That was all I had time to say, in my own heart, before my eyes opened again, in spite of me, and the flame of the candle flew into them, flew all over me, and burnt up the rest of my thoughts in an instant.

I couldn't hear the fish blowing now; I couldn't hear the creak of the spars; I couldn't think; I couldn't feel the sweat of my own death agony on my face – I could only look at the heavy, charred top of the wick. It swelled, tottered, bent over to one side, dropped – red hot at the moment of its fall – black and harmless, even before the swing of the brig had canted it over into the bottom of the candlestick.

I caught myself laughing.

Yes! laughing at the safe fall of the bit of wick. But for the gag I should have screamed with laughing. As it was, I shook with it inside me – shook till the blood was in my head, and I was all but suffocated for want of breath. I had just sense enough left to feel that my own horrid laughter, at that awful moment, was a sign of my brain going at last. I had just sense enough left to make another struggle before my mind broke loose like a frightened horse, and ran away with me.

One comforting look at the blink of daylight through the hatch was what I tried for once more. The fight to force my eyes from the candle and to get that one look at the daylight, was the hardest I had had yet; and I lost the fight. The flame had hold of my eyes as fast as the lashings had hold of my hands. I couldn't look away from it. I couldn't even shut my eyes, when I tried that next, for the second time. There was the wick, growing tall once more. There was the space of unburnt candle between the light and the slow match shortened to an inch or less.

How much life did that inch leave me? Three-quarters of an hour? Half an hour? Fifty minutes? Twenty minutes? Steady! an inch of tallow candle would burn longer than twenty minutes. An inch of tallow! the notion of a man's body and soul being kept together by an inch of tallow! Wonderful! Why, the greatest king that sits on a throne can't keep a man's body and soul together; and here's an inch of tallow that can do what the king can't! There's something to tell mother, when I get home, which will surprise her more than all the rest of my voyages put together. I laughed inwardly, again, at the thought of that; and shook and swelled and suffocated myself, till the light of the candle leaped in through my eyes, and licked up the laughter, and burnt it out of me, and made me all empty, and cold, and quiet once more.

Mother and Lizzie. I don't know when they came back; but they did come back – not, as it seemed to me, into my mind this time; but right down bodily before me, in the hold of the brig.

Yes: sure enough, there was Lizzie, just as light-hearted as usual, laughing at me. Laughing! Well, why not? Who is to blame Lizzie for thinking I'm lying on my back, drunk in the cellar, with the beer barrels all round me? Steady! she's crying now – spinning round and round in a fiery mist, wringing her hands, screeching out for help – fainter and fainter, like the splash of the schooner's sweeps. Gone! – burnt up in the fiery mist. Mist? fire? no: neither one nor the other. It's mother makes the light – mother knitting, with ten flaming points at the ends of her fingers and thumbs, and slow-matches hanging in bunches all round her face instead of her own grey hair. Mother in her old arm-chair, and the pilot's long skinny hands hanging over the back of the chair, dripping with gunpowder. No! no gunpowder, no chair, no mother – nothing but the pilot's face, shining red hot, like a sun, in the fiery mist; turning upside down in the fiery mist; running backwards and forwards along the slow-match, in the fiery mist; spinning millions of miles in a minute, in the fiery mist – spinning itself smaller and smaller into one tiny point, and that point darting on a sudden straight into my head – and then, all fire and all mist – no hearing, no seeing, no thinking, no feeling – the brig, the sea, my own self, the whole world, all gone together!

After what I've just told you, I know nothing and remember nothing, till I woke up (as it seemed to me) in a comfortable bed, with two rough and ready men like myself sitting on each side of my pillow, and a gentleman standing watching me at the foot of the bed. It was about seven in the morning. My sleep (or what seemed like my sleep to me) had lasted better than eight months – I was among my own countrymen in the island of Trinidad – the men at each side of my pillow were my keepers, turn and turn about – and the gentleman standing at the foot of the bed was the doctor. What I said and did in those eight months, I never have known and never shall. I woke out of it, as if it had been one long sleep – that's all I know.

It was another two months or more before the doctor thought it safe to answer the questions I asked him.

The brig had been anchored, just as I had supposed, off a part of the coast which was lonely enough to make the Spaniards pretty sure of no interruption, so long as they managed their murderous work quietly under cover of night.

My life had not been saved from the shore, but from the sea. An American vessel, becalmed in the offing, had made out the brig as the sun rose; and the captain having his time on his hands in consequence of the calm, and seeing a vessel anchored where no vessel had any reason to be, had manned one of his boats and sent his mate with it, to look a little closer into the matter, and bring back a report of what he saw.

What he saw, when he and his men found the brig deserted and boarded her, was a gleam of candlelight through the chink in the hatchway. The flame was within about a thread's breath of the slow-match, when he lowered himself into the hold; and if he had not had the sense and coolness to cut the match in two with his knife, before he touched the candle, he and his men might have been blown up along with the brig, as well as me. The match caught and turned into sputtering red fire, in the very act of putting the candle out; and if the communication with the powder barrel had not been cut off, the Lord only knows what might have happened.

What became of the Spanish schooner and the pilot I have never heard from that day to this.

As for the brig, the Yankees took her, as they took me, to Trinidad, and claimed their salvage, and got it, I hope, for their own sakes. I was landed just in the same state as when they rescued me from the brig, that is to say, clean out of my senses. But, please to remember it was a long time ago; and, take my word for it, I was discharged cured, as I have told you. Bless your hearts, I'm all right now, as you may see. I'm a little shaken by telling the story, as is only natural – a little shaken, my good friends, that's all.

Memoirs of an Adopted Son

Originally appeared in *All the Year Round*, 20 April 1861. Included in
My Miscellanies (1863) as a 'Case Worth Looking At'. Collins supplies
the following note to the story: 'The curious legend connected with
the birth of this "Adopted Son," and the facts relating to his
extraordinary career in after life, are derived from the "Records"
of the French police of the period. In this instance, and the instances
of those other papers in the present collection which deal with
foreign incidents and characters [i.e. "The Poisoned Meal" and
"The Cauldron of Oil"], while the facts of each narrative exist in
print, the form in which the narrative is cast is of my own devising.
If these facts had been readily accessible to readers in general, the
papers in question would not have been reprinted. But the scarce and
curious books from which my materials are derived, have long since
been out of print, and are, in all human probability, never likely to
be published again.'

I CIRCUMSTANCES WHICH PRECEDED HIS BIRTH

Towards the beginning of the eighteenth century there stood on a rock in the sea, near a fishing village on the coast of Brittany, a ruined Tower with a very bad reputation. No mortal was known to have inhabited it within the memory of living man. The one tenant whom Tradition associated with the occupation of the place, at a remote period, had moved into it from the infernal regions, nobody knew why – had lived in it, nobody knew how long – and had quitted possession, nobody knew when. Under such circumstances, nothing was more natural than that this unearthly Individual should give a name to his residence; for which reason, the building was thereafter known to all the neighbourhood round as Satanstower.

Early in the year seventeen hundred, the inhabitants of the village were startled, one night, by seeing the red gleam of a fire in the Tower, and by smelling, in the same direction, a preternaturally strong odour of fried fish. The next morning, the fishermen who passed by the building in their boats were amazed to find that a stranger had taken up his abode in it. Judging of him at a distance, he seemed to be a fine tall stout fellow: he was dressed in fisherman's costume, and he had a new boat of his own, moored comfortably in a cleft of the rock. If he had inhabited a place of decent reputation, his neighbours would have immediately made his acquaintance; but, as things were, all they could venture to do was to watch him in silence.

The first day passed, and, though it was fine weather, he made no use of his boat. The second day followed, with a continuance of the fine weather, and still he was as idle as before. On the third day, when a violent storm kept all the boats of the village on the beach – on the third day, in the midst of the tempest, away went the man of the Tower to make his first fishing experiment in strange waters! He and his boat came back safe and sound, in a lull of the storm; and the villagers watching on the cliff above saw him carrying the fish up, by great basketsful, to his Tower. No such haul had ever fallen to the lot of any one of them – and the stranger had taken it in a whole gale of wind!

Upon this, the inhabitants of the village called a council. The lead in the debate was assumed by a smart young fellow, a fisherman named Poulailler, who stoutly declared that the stranger at the Tower was of infernal origin. 'The rest of you may call him what you like,' said Poulailler; 'I call him The Fiend-Fisherman!'

The opinion thus expressed proved to be the opinion of the entire audience – with the one exception of the village priest. The priest said, 'Gently, my sons. Don't make sure about the man of the Tower, before Sunday. Wait and see if he comes to church.'

'And if he doesn't come to church?' asked all the fishermen, in a breath.

'In that case,' replied the priest, 'I will excommunicate him – and then, my children, you may call him what you like.'

Sunday came; and no sign of the stranger darkened the church-doors. He was excommunicated, accordingly. The whole village forthwith adopted Poulailler's idea; and called the man of the Tower by the name which Poulailler had given him – 'The Fiend-Fisherman.'

These strong proceedings produced not the slightest apparent effect on the diabolical personage who had occasioned them. He persisted in remaining idle when the weather was fine; in going out to fish when no other boat in the place dare put to sea; and in coming back again to his solitary dwelling-place, with his nets full, his boat uninjured, and himself alive and hearty. He made no attempts to buy and sell with anybody; he kept steadily away from the village; he lived on fish of his own preternaturally strong frying; and he never spoke to a living soul – with the solitary exception of Poulailler himself. One fine evening, when the young man was rowing home past the Tower, the Fiend-Fisherman darted out on to the rock – said, 'Thank you, Poulailler, for giving me a name' – bowed politely – and darted in again. The young fisherman felt the words run cold down the marrow of his back; and whenever he was at sea again, he gave the Tower a wide berth from that day forth.

Time went on – and an important event occurred in Poulailler's life. He was engaged to be married. On the day when his betrothal was publicly made known, his friends clustered noisily about him on the fishing-jetty of the village to offer their congratulations. While they were all in full cry, a strange voice suddenly made itself heard through the confusion, which silenced everybody in an instant. The crowd fell back, and disclosed the Fiend-Fisherman sauntering up the jetty. It was the first time he had ever set foot – cloven foot – within the precincts of the village.

'Gentlemen,' said the Fiend-Fisherman, 'where is my friend, Poulailler?' He put the question with perfect politeness; he looked remarkably well in his fisherman's costume; he exhaled a relishing odour of fried fish; he had a cordial nod for the men, and a sweet smile for the women – but, with all these personal advantages, everybody fell back from him, and nobody answered his question. The coldness of the popular reception, however, did not in any way abash him. He looked about for Poulailler with searching eyes, discovered the place in which he was standing, and addressed him in the friendliest manner.

'So you are going to be married?' remarked the Fiend-Fisherman.

'What's that to you?' said Poulailler. He was inwardly terrified, but outwardly gruff – not an uncommon combination of circumstances with men of his class, in his mental situation.

'My friend,' pursued the Fiend-Fisherman, 'I have not forgotten your polite attention in giving me a name; and I come here to requite it. You will have a family, Poulailler; and your first child will be a boy. I propose to make that boy my Adopted Son.'

The marrow of Poulailler's back became awfully cold – but he grew gruffer than ever, in spite of his back.

'You won't do anything of the sort,' he replied. 'If I have the largest family in France, no child of mine shall ever go near you.'

'I shall adopt your first-born for all that,' persisted the Fiend-Fisherman. 'Poulailler! I wish you good morning. Ladies and gentlemen! the same to all of you.'

With those words, he withdrew from the jetty; and the marrow of Poulailler's back recovered its temperature.

The next morning was stormy; and all the village expected to see the boat from the Tower put out, as usual, to sea. Not a sign of it appeared. Later in the day, the rock on which the building stood was examined from a distance. Neither boat nor nets were in their customary places. At night, the red gleam of the fire was missed for the first time. The Fiend-Fisherman had gone! He had announced his intentions on the jetty, and had disappeared. What did this mean? Nobody knew.

On Poulailler's wedding-day, a portentous circumstance recalled the memory of the diabolical stranger, and, as a matter of course, seriously discomposed the bridegroom's back. At the moment when the marriage ceremony was complete, a relishing odour of fried fish stole into the nostrils of the company, and a voice from invisible lips said: 'Keep up your spirits, Poulailler; I have not forgotten my promise!'

A year later, Madame Poulailler was in the hands of the midwife of the district, and a repetition of the portentous circumstance took place. Poulailler was waiting in the kitchen to hear how matters ended up-stairs. The nurse came in with a baby. 'Which is it?' asked the happy father; 'girl or boy?' Before the nurse could answer, an odour of supernaturally fried fish filled the kitchen; and a voice from invisible lips replied: 'A boy, Poulailler – *and I've got him!*'

Such were the circumstances under which the subject of this Memoir was introduced to the joys and sorrows of mortal existence.

II HIS BOYHOOD AND EARLY LIFE

When a boy is born under auspices which lead his parents to suppose that, while the bodily part of him is safe at home, the spiritual part is subjected to a course of infernal tuition elsewhere – what are his father and mother to do with him? They must do the best they can – which was exactly what Poulailler and his wife did with the hero of these pages.

In the first place, they had him christened instantly. It was observed with horror that his infant face was distorted with grimaces, and that his infant voice roared with a preternatural lustiness of tone the moment the priest touched him. The first thing he asked for, when he learnt to speak, was 'fried fish;' and the first place he wanted to go to, when he learnt to walk, was the diabolical Tower on the rock. 'He won't learn anything,' said the master, when he was old enough to go to school. 'Thrash him,' said Poulailler – and the master thrashed him. 'He won't come to his first communion,' said the priest. 'Thrash him,' said Poulailler – and the priest thrashed him. The farmers' orchards were robbed; the neighbouring rabbit-warrens were depopulated; linen was stolen from the gardens, and nets were torn on the beach. 'The deuce take Poulailler's boy,' was the general cry. 'The deuce has got him,' was Poulailler's answer. 'And yet he is a nice-looking boy,' said Madame Poulailler. And he was – as tall, as strong, as handsome a young fellow, as could be seen in all France. 'Let us pray for him,' said Madame Poulailler. 'Let us thrash him,' said her husband. 'Our son has been thrashed till all the sticks in the neighbourhood are broken,' pleaded his mother. 'We will try him with the rope's-end next,' retorted his father; 'he shall go to sea and live in an atmosphere of thrashing. Our son shall be a cabin-boy.' It was all one to Poulailler Junior – he knew who had adopted him, as well as his father – he had been instinctively conscious from infancy of the Fiend-Fisherman's interest in his welfare – he cared for no earthly discipline – and a cabin-boy he became at ten years old.

After two years of the rope's-end (applied quite ineffectually), the subject of this Memoir robbed his captain, and ran away in an English port. London became the next scene of his adventures. At twelve years old, he persuaded society in the Metropolis that he was the forsaken natural son of a French duke. British benevolence, after blindly providing for him for four years, opened its eyes and found him out at the age of sixteen; upon which he returned to France, and entered the army in the capacity of drummer. At eighteen, he deserted, and had a turn with the gipsies. He told fortunes, he conjured, he danced on the tight-rope, he acted, he sold quack medicines, he altered his mind again, and returned to the army. Here he fell in love with the vivandière of his new regiment. The sergeant-major of the company, touched by the same amiable weakness, naturally resented his attentions to the lady. Poulailler (perhaps unjustifiably) asserted himself by boxing his officer's ears. Out flashed the swords on both sides, and in went Poulailler's blade through and through the tender heart of the sergeant-major. The frontier was close at hand. Poulailler wiped his sword, and crossed it.

Sentence of death was recorded against him in his absence. When society has condemned us to die, if we are men of any spirit how are we to return the compliment? By condemning society to keep us alive – or, in other words, by robbing right and left for a living. Poulailler's destiny was now accomplished. He was picked out to be the Greatest Thief of his age; and when Fate summoned him to his place in the world, he stepped forward and took it. His life hitherto had been merely the life of a young scamp – he was now to do justice to the diabolical father who had adopted him, and to expand to the proportions of a full-grown Robber.

His first exploits were performed in Germany. They showed such novelty of combination, such daring, such dexterity, and, even in his most homicidal moments, such irresistible gaiety and good humour, that a band of congenial spirits gathered about him in no time. As commander-in-chief of the Thieves' army, his popularity never wavered. His weaknesses – and what illustrious man is without them? – were three in number. First weakness – he was extravagantly susceptible to the charms of the fair sex. Second weakness – he was perilously fond of practical jokes. Third weakness (inherited from his adopted parent) – his appetite was insatiable in the matter of fried fish. As for the merits to set against these defects, some have been noticed already, and others will appear immediately. Let it merely be premised, in this place, that he was one of the handsomest men of his time, that he dressed superbly, and that he was capable of the most exalted acts of generosity wherever a handsome woman was concerned – let this be understood, to begin with; and let us now enter on the narrative of his last exploit in Germany before he returned to France. This adventure is something more than a mere specimen of his method of workmanship – it proved, in the future, to be the fatal event of his life.

On a Monday in the week, he had stopped on the highway, and robbed of all his valuables and all his papers, an Italian nobleman – the Marquis Petrucci of Sienna. On Tuesday, he was ready for another stroke of business. Posted on the top of a steep hill, he watched the road which wound up to the summit on one side, while his followers were ensconced on the road which led down from it on the other. The prize expected, in this case, was the travelling carriage (with a large sum of money inside) of the Baron de Kirbergen.

Before long, Poulailler discerned the carriage afar off, at the bottom of the hill, and in advance of it, ascending the eminence, two ladies on foot. They were the Baron's daughters – Wilhelmina, a fair beauty; Frederica, a brunette – both lovely, both accomplished, both susceptible, both young. Poulailler sauntered down the hill to meet the fascinating travellers. He looked – bowed – introduced himself – and fell in love with Wilhelmina on the spot. Both the charming girls acknowledged in the most artless manner that confinement to the carriage had given them the fidgets, and that they were walking up the hill to try the remedy of gentle exercise. Poulailler's heart was touched, and Poulailler's generosity to the sex was roused in the nick of time. With a polite apology to the young ladies, he ran back, by a short cut, to the ambush on the other side of the hill in which his men were posted.

'Gentlemen!' cried the generous Thief, 'in the charming name of Wilhelmina de Kirbergen, I charge you all, let the Baron's carriage pass free.' The band was not susceptible – the band demurred. Poulailler knew them. He had appealed to their hearts in vain – he now appealed to their pockets. 'Gentlemen!' he resumed, 'excuse my momentary misconception of your sentiments. Here is my one half share of the Marquis Petrucci's property. If I divide it among you, will you let the carriage pass free?' The band knew the value of money – and accepted the terms. Poulailler rushed back up the hill, and arrived at the top just in time to hand the young ladies into the carriage. 'Charming man!' said the white Wilhelmina to the brown Frederica, as they drove off. Innocent soul! what would she have said if she had known that her personal attractions had saved her father's property? Was she ever to see the charming man again? Yes: she was to see him the next day – and, more than that, Fate was hereafter to link her fast to the robber's life and the robber's doom.

Confiding the direction of the band to his first lieutenant, Poulailler followed the carriage on horseback, and ascertained the place of the Baron's residence that night.

The next morning a superbly-dressed stranger knocked at the door. 'What name, sir?' said the servant. 'The Marquis Petrucci of Sienna,' replied Poulailler. 'How are the young ladies after their journey?' The Marquis was shown in, and introduced to the Baron. The Baron was naturally delighted to receive a brother nobleman – Miss Wilhelmina was modestly happy to see the charming man again – Miss Frederica was affectionately pleased on her sister's account. Not being of a disposition to lose time where his affections were concerned, Poulailler expressed his sentiments to the beloved object that evening. The next morning he had an interview with the Baron, at which he produced the papers which proved him to be the Marquis. Nothing could be more satisfactory to the mind of the most anxious parent – the two noblemen embraced. They were still in each other's arms, when a second stranger knocked at the door. 'What name, sir?' said the servant. 'The Marquis Petrucci of Sienna,' replied the stranger. 'Impossible!' said the servant; 'his lordship is now in the house.' 'Show me in, scoundrel,' cried the visitor. The servant submitted, and the two Marquises stood face to face. Poulailler's composure was not shaken in the least; he had come first to the house, and he had got the papers. 'You are the villain who robbed me!' cried the true Petrucci. 'You are drunk, mad, or an impostor,' retorted the false Petrucci. 'Send to Florence, where I am known,' exclaimed one of the Marquises, apostrophising the Baron. 'Send to Florence by all means,' echoed the other, addressing himself to the Baron also. 'Gentlemen,' replied the noble Kirbergen, 'I will do myself the honour of taking your advice' – and he sent to Florence accordingly.

Before the messenger had advanced ten miles on his journey, Poulailler had said two words in private to the susceptible Wilhelmina – and the pair eloped from the baronial residence that night. Once more the subject of this Memoir crossed the frontier, and re-entered France. Indifferent to the attractions of rural life, he forthwith established himself with the beloved object in Paris. In that superb city he met with his strangest adventures, performed his boldest achievements, committed his most prodigious robberies, and, in a word, did himself and his infernal patron the fullest justice, in the character of the Fiend-Fisherman's Adopted Son.

III HIS CAREER IN PARIS

Once established in the French metropolis, Poulailler planned and executed that vast system of perpetual robbery and occasional homicide which made him the terror and astonishment of all Paris. In-doors, as well as out, his good fortune befriended him. No domestic anxieties harassed his mind, and diverted him from the pursuit of his distinguished public career. The attachment of the charming creature with whom he had eloped from Germany, survived the discovery that the Marquis Petrucci was Poulailler the robber. True to the man of her choice, the devoted Wilhelmina shared his fortunes, and kept his house. And why not, if she loved him? – in the all-conquering name of Cupid, why not?

Joined by picked men from his German followers, and by new recruits gathered together in Paris, Poulailler now set society and its safeguards at flat defiance. Cartouche himself was his inferior in audacity and cunning. In course of time, the whole city was panic-stricken by the new robber and his band – the very Boulevards were deserted after nightfall. Monsieur Hérault, lieutenant of police of the period, in despair of laying hands on Poulailler by any other means, at last offered a reward of a hundred pistoles and a place in his office worth two thousand livres a year to any one who would apprehend the robber alive. The bills were posted all over Paris – and, the next morning, they produced the very last result in the world which the lieutenant of police could possibly have anticipated.

Whilst Monsieur Hérault was at breakfast in his study, the Count de Villeneuve was announced as wishing to speak to him. Knowing the Count by name only, as belonging to an ancient family in Provence, or in Languedoc, Monsieur Hérault ordered him to be shown in. A perfect gentleman appeared, dressed with an admirable mixture of magnificence and good taste. 'I have something for your private ear, sir,' said the Count. 'Will you give orders that no one must be allowed to disturb us?'

Monsieur Hérault gave the orders.

'May I enquire, Count, what your business is?' he asked, when the door was closed.

'To earn the reward you offer for taking Poulailler,' answered the Count. 'I am Poulailler.'

Before Monsieur Hérault could open his lips, the robber produced a pretty little dagger and some rose-coloured silk cord. 'The point of this dagger is poisoned,' he observed; 'and one scratch of it, my dear sir, would be the death of you.' With these words Poulailler gagged the lieutenant of police, bound him to his chair with the rose-coloured cord, and lightened his writing-desk of one thousand pistoles. 'I'll take money instead of taking the place in the office which you kindly offer,' said Poulailler. 'Don't trouble yourself to see me to the door. Good morning.'

A few weeks later, while Monsieur Hérault was still the popular subject of ridicule throughout Paris, business took Poulailler on the road to Lille and Cambrai. The only inside passenger in the coach besides himself, was the venerable Dean Potter of Brussels. They fell into talk on the one interesting subject of the time – not the weather, but Poulailler.

'It's a disgrace, sir, to the police,' said the Dean, 'that such a miscreant is still at large. I shall be returning to Paris, by this road, in ten days' time, and I shall call on Monsieur Hérault, to suggest a plan of my own for catching the scoundrel.'

'May I ask what it is?' said Poulailler.

'Excuse me,' replied the Dean; 'you are a stranger, sir, – and, moreover, I wish to keep the merit of suggesting the plan to myself.'

'Do you think the lieutenant of police will see you?' asked Poulailler; 'he is not accessible to strangers, since the miscreant you speak of played him that trick at his own breakfast-table.'

'He will see Dean Potter of Brussels,' was the reply, delivered with the slightest possible tinge of offended dignity.

'Oh, unquestionably!' said Poulailler, – 'pray pardon me.'

'Willingly, sir,' said the Dean – and the conversation flowed into other channels.

Nine days later the wounded pride of Monsieur Hérault was soothed by a very remarkable letter. It was signed by one of Poulailler's band, who offered himself as King's evidence, in the hope of obtaining a pardon. The letter stated that the venerable Dean Potter had been waylaid and murdered by Poulailler, and that the robber, with his customary audacity, was about to re-enter Paris by the Lisle coach, the next day, disguised in the Dean's own clothes, and furnished with the Dean's own papers. Monsieur Hérault took his precautions without losing a moment. Picked men were stationed, with their orders, at the barrier through which the coach must pass to enter Paris; while the lieutenant of police waited at his office, in the company of two French gentlemen who could speak to the Dean's identity, in the event of Poulailler's impudently persisting in the assumption of his victim's name.

At the appointed hour the coach appeared, and out of it got a man in the Dean's costume. He was arrested in spite of his protestations; the papers of the murdered Potter were found on him, and he was dragged off to the police office in triumph. The door opened, and the posse comitatus entered with the prisoner. Instantly the two witnesses burst out with a cry of recognition, and turned indignantly on the lieutenant of police. 'Gracious Heaven, sir, what have you done!' they exclaimed in horror; 'this is not Poulailler – here is our venerable friend; here is the Dean himself!' At the same moment, a servant entered with a letter. 'Dean Potter. To the care of Monsieur Hérault, Lieutenant of Police.' The letter was expressed in these words: 'Venerable sir, – Profit by the lesson I have given you. Be a Christian for the future, and never again try to injure a man unless he tries to injure you. Entirely yours, Poulailler.'

These feats of cool audacity were matched by others, in which his generosity to the sex asserted itself as magnanimously as ever.

Hearing, one day, that large sums of money were kept in the house of a great lady, one Madame de Brienne, whose door was guarded, in anticipation of a visit from the famous thief, by a porter of approved trustworthiness and courage, Poulailler undertook to rob her in spite of her precautions, and succeeded. With a stout pair of leather straps and buckles in his pocket, and with two of his band, disguised as a coachman and footman, he followed Madame de Brienne one night to the theatre. Just before the close of the performance, the lady's coachman and footman were tempted away for five minutes by Poulailler's disguised subordinates to have a glass of wine. No attempt was made to detain them, or to drug their liquor. But, in their absence, Poulailler had slipped under the carriage, had hung his leather straps round the pole – one to hold by, and one to support his feet – and, with these simple preparations, was now ready to wait for events. Madame de Brienne entered the carriage – the footman got up behind – Poulailler hung himself horizontally under the pole, and was driven home with them, under those singular circumstances. He was strong enough to keep his position after the carriage had been taken into the coach-house; and he only left it when the doors were locked for the night. Provided with food beforehand, he waited patiently, hidden in the coach-house, for two days and nights, watching his opportunity of getting into Madame de Brienne's boudoir.

On the third night the lady went to a grand ball – the servants relaxed in their vigilance while her back was turned – and Poulailler slipped into the room. He found two thousand louis d'ors, which was nothing like the sum he expected, and a pocket-book, which he took away with him to open at home. It contained some stock-warrants for a comparatively trifling amount. Poulailler was far too well off to care about taking them, and far too polite, where a lady was concerned, not to send them back again, under those circumstances. Accordingly, Madame de Brienne received her warrants, with a note of apology from the polite thief.

'Pray excuse my visit to your charming boudoir,' wrote Poulailler, 'in consideration of the false reports of your wealth, which alone induced me to enter it. If I had known what your pecuniary circumstances really were, on the honour of a gentleman, Madam, I should have been incapable of robbing you. I cannot return your two thousand louis d'ors by post, as I return your warrants. But if you are at all pressed for money in future, I shall be proud to assist so distinguished a lady by lending her, from my own ample resources, double the sum of which I regret to have deprived her on the present occasion.' This letter was shown to royalty at Versailles. It excited the highest admiration of the Court – especially of the ladies. Whenever the robber's name was mentioned, they indulgently referred to him as the Chevalier de Poulailler. Ah! that was the age of politeness, when good-breeding was recognised, even in a thief. Under similar circumstances, who would recognise it now? O tempora! O mores!

On another occasion, Poulailler was out, one night, taking the air and watching his opportunities on the roofs of the houses; a member of the band being posted in the street below to assist him in case of necessity. While in this position, sobs and groans proceeding from an open back-garret window caught his ear. A parapet rose before the window, which enabled him to climb down and look in. Starving children surrounding a helpless mother, and clamouring for food, was the picture that met his eye. The mother was young and beautiful; and Poulailler's hand impulsively clutched his purse, as a necessary consequence. Before the charitable thief could enter by the window, a man rushed in by the door, with a face of horror; and cast a handful of gold into the lovely mother's lap. 'My honour is gone,' he cried; 'but our children are saved! Listen to the circumstances. I met a man in the street below; he was tall and thin; he had a green patch over one eye; he was looking up suspiciously at this house, apparently waiting for somebody. I thought of you – I thought of the children – I seized the suspicious stranger by the collar. Terror overwhelmed him on the spot. "Take my watch, my money, and my two valuable gold snuff-boxes," he said – "but spare my life." I took them.' 'Noble-hearted man!' cried Poulailler, appearing at the window. The husband started; the wife screamed; the children hid themselves. 'Let me entreat you to be composed,' continued Poulailler. 'Sir! I enter on the scene for the purpose of soothing your uneasy conscience. From your vivid description, I recognise the man whose property is now in your wife's lap. Resume your mental tranquillity. You have robbed a robber – in other words, you have vindicated society. Accept my congratulations on your restored innocence. The miserable coward whose collar you seized, is one of Poulailler's band. He has lost his stolen property, as the fit punishment for his disgraceful want of spirit.'

'Who are you?' exclaimed the husband.

'I am Poulailler,' replied the illustrious man, with the simplicity of an ancient hero. 'Take this purse; and set up in business with the contents. There is a prejudice, Sir, in favour of honesty. Give that prejudice a chance. There was a time when I felt it myself; I regret to feel it no longer. Under all varieties of misfortune, an honest man has his consolation still left. Where is it left? Here!' He struck his heart – and the family fell on their knees before him.

'Benefactor of your species!' cried the husband – 'how can I show my gratitude?'

'You can permit me to kiss the hand of madame,' answered Poulailler.

Madame started to her feet, and embraced the generous stranger. 'What more can I do?' exclaimed this lovely woman eagerly – 'Oh, Heavens! what more?'

'You can beg your husband to light me down stairs,' replied Poulailler. He spoke, pressed their hands, dropped a generous tear, and departed. At that touching moment, his own adopted father would not have known him.

This last anecdote closes the record of Poulailler's career in Paris. The lighter and more agreeable aspects of that career have hitherto been designedly presented, in discreet remembrance of the contrast which the tragic side of the picture must now present. Comedy and Sentiment, twin sisters of French extraction, farewell! Horror enters next on the stage – and enters welcome, in the name of the Fiend-Fisherman's Adopted Son.

IV HIS EXIT FROM THE SCENE

The nature of Poulailler's more serious achievements in the art of robbery may be realised by reference to one terrible fact. In the police records of the period, more than one hundred and fifty men and women are reckoned up as having met their deaths at the hands of Poulailler and his band. It was not the practice of this formidable robber to take life as well as property, unless life happened to stand directly in his way – in which case he immediately swept off the obstacle without hesitation and without remorse. His deadly determination to rob, which was thus felt by the population in general, was matched by his deadly determination to be obeyed, which was felt by his followers in particular. One of their number, for example, having withdrawn from his allegiance, and having afterwards attempted to betray his leader, was tracked to his hiding-place in a cellar, and was there walled up alive in Poulailler's presence; the robber composing the unfortunate wretch's epitaph, and scratching it on the wet plaster with his own hand. Years afterwards, the inscription was noticed, when the house fell into the possession of a new tenant, and was supposed to be nothing more than one of the many jests which the famous robber had practised in his time. When the plaster was removed, the skeleton fell out, and testified that Poulailler was in earnest.

To attempt the arrest of such a man as this by tampering with his followers, was practically impossible. No sum of money that could be offered would induce any one of the members of his band to risk the fatal chance of his vengeance. Other means of getting possession of him had been tried, and tried in vain. Five times over, the police had succeeded in tracking him to different hiding-places; and on all five occasions, the women – who adored him for his gallantry, his generosity, and his good looks – had helped him to escape. If he had not unconsciously paved the way to his own capture, first by eloping with Mademoiselle Wilhelmina de Kirbergen, and secondly by maltreating her, it is more than doubtful whether the long arm of the law would ever have reached far enough to fasten its grasp on him. As it was, the extremes of love and hatred met at last in the bosom of the devoted Wilhelmina; and the vengeance of a neglected woman accomplished what the whole police force of Paris had been powerless to achieve.

Poulailler, never famous for the constancy of his attachments, had wearied, at an early period, of the companion of his flight from Germany – but Wilhelmina was one of those women whose affections, once aroused, will not take No for an answer. She persisted in attaching herself to a man who had ceased to love her. Poulailler's patience became exhausted; he tried twice to rid himself of his unhappy mistress – once by the knife and once by poison – and failed on both occasions. For the third and last time, by way of attempting an experiment of another kind, he established a rival to drive the German woman out of the house. From that moment his fate was sealed. Maddened by jealous rage, Wilhelmina cast the last fragments of her fondness to the winds. She secretly communicated with the police – and Poulailler met his doom.

A night was appointed with the authorities; and the robber was invited by his discarded mistress to a farewell interview. His contemptuous confidence in her fidelity rendered him careless of his customary precautions. He accepted the appointment; and the two supped together, on the understanding that they were henceforth to be friends, and nothing more. Towards the close of the meal, Poulailler was startled by a ghastly change in the face of his companion.

'What is wrong with you?' he asked.

'A mere trifle,' she answered, looking at her glass of wine. 'I can't help loving you still, badly as you have treated me. You are a dead man, Poulailler – and I shall not survive you.'

The robber started to his feet, and seized a knife on the table.

'You have poisoned me?' he exclaimed.

'No,' she replied. 'Poison is my vengeance on myself; not my vengeance on *you*. You will rise from this table as you sat down to it. But your evening will be finished in prison; and your life will be ended on the Wheel.'

As she spoke the words, the door was burst open by the police, and Poulailler was secured. The same night the poison did its fatal work; and his mistress made atonement with her life for the first, last, act of treachery which had revenged her on the man she loved.

Once safely lodged in the hands of justice, the robber tried to gain time to escape in, by promising to make important disclosures. The manoeuvre availed him nothing. In those days, the Laws of the Land had not yet made acquaintance with the Laws of Humanity. Poulailler was put to the torture – was suffered to recover – was publicly broken on the Wheel – and was taken off it alive, to be cast into a blazing fire. By those murderous means, Society rid itself of a murderous man – and the idlers on the Boulevards took their evening stroll again in recovered security.

Paris had seen the execution of Poulailler – but, if legends are to be trusted, our old friends, the people of the fishing village in Brittany saw the end of him afterwards. On the day and hour when he perished, the heavens darkened, and a terrible storm arose. Once more, and for a moment only, the gleam of the unearthly fire reddened the windows of the old Tower. Thunder pealed and struck the building into fragments. Lightning flashed incessantly over the ruins; and, in the scorching glare of it, the boat which, in former years, had put off to sea whenever the storm rose highest, was seen to shoot out into the raging ocean from the cleft in the rock – and was discovered, on this final occasion, to be doubly manned. The Fiend-Fisherman sat at the helm; his Adopted Son tugged at the oars; and a clamour of diabolical voices, roaring awfully through the roaring storm, wished the pair of them a prosperous voyage.

The Cauldron of Oil

Originally appeared in *All the Year Round*, 11 May 1861. Included in *My Miscellanies* (1863) as a 'Case Worth Looking At'.

A BOUT ONE FRENCH league distant from the city of Toulouse, there is a village called Croix-Daurade. In the military history of England, this place is associated with a famous charge of the eighteenth hussars, which united two separated columns of the British army, on the day before the Duke of Wellington fought the battle of Toulouse. In the criminal history of France, the village is memorable as the scene of a daring crime, which was discovered and punished under circumstances sufficiently remarkable to merit preservation in the form of a plain narrative.

I THE PERSONS OF THE DRAMA

In the year seventeen hundred, the resident priest of the village of Croix-Daurade was Monsieur Pierre-Célestin Chaubard. He was a man of no extraordinary energy or capacity, simple in his habits, and sociable in his disposition. His character was irreproachable; he was strictly conscientious in the performance of his duties; and he was universally respected and beloved by all his parishioners.

Among the members of his flock, there was a family named Siadoux. The head of the household, Saturnin Siadoux, had been long established in business at Croix-Daurade as an oil-manufacturer. At the period of the events now to be narrated, he had attained the age of sixty, and was a widower. His family consisted of five children – three young men, who helped him in the business, and two daughters. His nearest living relative was his sister, the widow Mirailhe.

The widow resided principally at Toulouse. Her time in that city was mainly occupied in winding up the business affairs of her deceased husband, which had remained unsettled for a considerable period after his death, through delays in realising certain sums of money owing to his representative. The widow had been left very well provided for – she was still a comely attractive woman – and more than one substantial citizen of Toulouse had shown himself anxious to persuade her into marrying for the second time. But the widow Mirailhe lived on terms of great intimacy and affection with her brother Siadoux and his family; she was sincerely attached to them, and sincerely unwilling, at her age, to deprive her nephews and nieces, by a second marriage, of the inheritance, or even of a portion of the inheritance, which would otherwise fall to them on her death. Animated by these motives, she closed her doors resolutely on all suitors who attempted to pay their court to her, with the one exception of a master-butcher of Toulouse, whose name was Cantegrel.

This man was a neighbour of the widow's, and had made himself useful by assisting her in the business complications which still hung about the realisation of her late husband's estate. The preference which she showed for the master-butcher was, thus far, of the purely negative kind. She gave him no absolute encouragement; she would not for a moment admit that there was the slightest prospect of her ever marrying him – but, at the same time, she continued to receive his visits, and she showed no disposition to restrict the neighbourly intercourse between them, for the future, within purely formal bounds. Under these circumstances, Saturnin Siadoux began to be alarmed, and to think it time to bestir himself. He had no personal acquaintance with Cantegrel, who never visited the village; and Monsieur Chaubard (to whom he might otherwise have applied for advice) was not in a position to give an opinion: the priest and the master-butcher did not even know each other by sight. In this difficulty, Siadoux bethought himself of inquiring privately at Toulouse, in the hope of discovering some scandalous passages in Cantegrel's early life, which might fatally degrade him in the estimation of the widow Mirailhe. The investigation, as usual in such cases, produced rumours and reports in plenty, the greater part of which dated back to a period of the butcher's life when he had resided in the ancient town of Narbonne. One of these rumours, especially, was of so serious a nature, that Siadoux determined to test the truth or falsehood of it, personally, by travelling to Narbonne. He kept his intention a secret not only from his sister and his daughters, but also from his sons; they were young men, not over-patient in their tempers – and he doubted their discretion. Thus, nobody knew his real purpose but himself, when he left home.

His safe arrival at Narbonne was notified in a letter to his family. The letter entered into no particulars relating to his secret errand: it merely informed his children of the day when they might expect him back, and of certain social arrangements which he wished to be made to welcome him on his return. He proposed, on his way home, to stay two days at Castelnaudry, for the purpose of paying a visit to an old friend who was settled there. According to this plan, his return to Croix-Daurade would be deferred until Tuesday, the twenty-sixth of April, when his family might expect to see him about sunset, in good time for supper. He further desired that a little party of friends might be invited to the meal, to celebrate the twenty-sixth of April (which was a feast-day in the village), as well as to celebrate his return. The guests whom he wished to be invited were, first, his sister; secondly, Monsieur Chaubard, whose pleasant disposition made him a welcome guest at all the village festivals; thirdly and fourthly, two neighbours, business-men like himself, with whom he lived on terms of the friendliest intimacy. That was the party; and the family of Siadoux took especial pains, as the time approached, to provide a supper worthy of the guests, who had all shown the heartiest readiness in accepting their invitations.

This was the domestic position, these were the family prospects, on the morning of the twenty-sixth of April – a memorable day, for years afterwards, in the village of Croix-Daurade.

II THE EVENTS OF THE DAY

Besides the curacy of the village church, good Monsieur Chaubard held some small ecclesiastical preferment in the cathedral church of St Stephen at Toulouse. Early in the forenoon of the twenty-sixth, certain matters connected with this preferment took him from his village curacy to the city – a distance which has been already described as not greater than one French league, or between two and three English miles.

After transacting his business, Monsieur Chaubard parted with his clerical brethren, who left him by himself in the sacristy (or vestry) of the church. Before he had quitted the room, in his turn, the beadle entered it, and inquired for the Abbé de Mariotte, one of the officiating priests attached to the cathedral.

'The Abbé has just gone out,' replied Monsieur Chaubard. 'Who wants him?'

'A respectable-looking man,' said the beadle. 'I thought he seemed to be in some distress of mind, when he spoke to me.'

'Did he mention his business with the Abbé?'

'Yes, sir; he expressed himself as anxious to make his confession immediately.'

'In that case,' said Monsieur Chaubard, 'I may be of use to him in the Abbé's absence – for I have authority to act here as confessor. Let us go into the church, and see if this person feels disposed to accept my services.'

When they went into the church, they found the man walking backwards and forwards in a restless, disordered manner. His looks were so strikingly suggestive of some serious mental perturbation, that Monsieur Chaubard found it no easy matter to preserve his composure, when he first addressed himself to the stranger.

'I am sorry,' he began, 'that the Abbé de Mariotte is not here to offer you his services—'

'I want to make my confession,' said the man, looking about him vacantly, as if the priest's words had not attracted his attention.

'You can do so at once, if you please,' said Monsieur Chaubard. 'I am attached to this church, and I possess the necessary authority to receive confessions in it. Perhaps, however, you are personally acquainted with the Abbé de Mariotte? Perhaps you would prefer waiting—'

'No!' said the man, roughly. 'I would as soon, or sooner, confess to a stranger.'

'In that case,' replied Monsieur Chaubard, 'be so good as to follow me.'

He led the way to the confessional. The beadle, whose curiosity was excited, waited a little, and looked after them. In a few minutes, he saw the curtains, which were sometimes used to conceal the face of the officiating priest, suddenly drawn. The penitent knelt with his back turned to the church. There was literally nothing to see – but the beadle waited nevertheless, in expectation of the end.

After a long lapse of time, the curtain was withdrawn, and priest and penitent left the confessional.

The change which the interval had worked in Monsieur Chaubard was so extraordinary, that the beadle's attention was altogether withdrawn, in the interest of observing it, from the man who had made the confession. He did not remark by which door the stranger left the church – his eyes were fixed on Monsieur Chaubard. The priest's naturally ruddy face was as white as if he had just risen from a long sickness – he looked straight before him, with a stare of terror – and he left the church as hurriedly as if he had been a man escaping from prison; left it without a parting word, or a farewell look, although he was noted for his courtesy to his inferiors on all ordinary occasions.

'Good Monsieur Chaubard has heard more than he bargained for,' said the beadle, wandering back to the empty confessional, with an interest which he had never felt in it till that moment.

The day wore on as quietly as usual in the village of Croix-Daurade. At the appointed time, the supper-table was laid for the guests in the house of Saturnin Siadoux. The widow Mirailhe, and the two neighbours, arrived a little before sunset. Monsieur Chaubard, who was usually punctual, did not make his appearance with them; and when the daughters of Saturnin Siadoux looked out from the upper windows, they saw no signs on the high road of their father's return.

Sunset came – and still neither Siadoux nor the priest appeared. The little party sat waiting round the table, and waited in vain. Before long, a message was sent up from the kitchen, representing that the supper must be eaten forthwith, or be spoilt; and the company began to debate the two alternatives, of waiting, or not waiting, any longer.

'It is my belief,' said the widow Mirailhe, 'that my brother is not coming home to-night. When Monsieur Chaubard joins us, we had better sit down to supper.'

'Can any accident have happened to my father?' asked one of the two daughters, anxiously.

'God forbid!' said the widow.

'God forbid!' repeated the two neighbours, looking expectantly at the empty supper-table.

'It has been a wretched day for travelling,' said Louis, the eldest son.

'It rained in torrents, all yesterday,' added Thomas, the second son.

'And your father's rheumatism makes him averse to travelling in wet weather,' suggested the widow, thoughtfully.

'Very true!' said the first of the two neighbours, shaking his head piteously at his passive knife and fork.

Another message came up from the kitchen, and peremptorily forbade the company to wait any longer.

'But where is Monsieur Chaubard?' said the widow. 'Has he been taking a journey too? Why is *he* absent? Has anybody seen him to-day?'

'I have seen him to-day,' said the youngest son, who had not spoken yet. This young man's name was Jean; he was little given to talking, but he had proved himself, on various domestic occasions, to be the quickest and most observant member of the family.

'Where did you see him?' asked the widow.

'I met him, this morning, on his way into Toulouse.'

'He has not fallen ill, I hope? Did he look out of sorts when you met him?'

'He was in excellent health and spirits,' said Jean. 'I never saw him look better—'

'And *I* never saw him look worse,' said the second of the neighbours, striking into the conversation with the aggressive fretfulness of a hungry man.

'What! this morning?' cried Jean, in astonishment.

'No; this afternoon,' said the neighbour. 'I saw him going into our church here. He was as white as our plates will be – when they come up. And what is almost as extraordinary, he passed without taking the slightest notice of me.'

Jean relapsed into his customary silence. It was getting dark; the clouds had gathered while the company had been talking; and, at the first pause in the conversation, the rain, falling again in torrents, made itself drearily audible.

'Dear, dear me!' said the widow. 'If it was not raining so hard, we might send somebody to inquire after good Monsieur Chaubard.'

'I'll go and inquire,' said Thomas Siadoux. 'It's not five minutes' walk. Have up the supper; I'll take a cloak with me; and if our excellent Monsieur Chaubard is out of his bed, I'll bring him back, to answer for himself.'

With those words he left the room. The supper was put on the table forthwith. The hungry neighbour disputed with nobody from that moment, and the melancholy neighbour recovered his spirits.

On reaching the priest's house, Thomas Siadoux found him sitting alone in his study. He started to his feet, with every appearance of the most violent alarm, when the young man entered the room.

'I beg your pardon, sir,' said Thomas; 'I am afraid I have startled you.'

'What do you want?' asked Monsieur Chaubard, in a singularly abrupt, bewildered manner.

'Have you forgotten, sir, that this is the night of our supper?' remonstrated Thomas. 'My father has not come back; and we can only suppose—'

At those words the priest dropped into his chair again, and trembled from head to foot. Amazed to the last degree by this extraordinary reception of his remonstrance, Thomas Siadoux remembered, at the same time, that he had engaged to bring Monsieur Chaubard back with him; and he determined to finish his civil speech, as if nothing had happened.

'We are all of opinion,' he resumed, 'that the weather has kept my father on the road. But that is no reason, sir, why the supper should be wasted, or why you should not make one of us, as you promised. Here is a good warm cloak—'

'I can't come,' said the priest. 'I'm ill; I'm in bad spirits; I'm not fit to go out.' He sighed bitterly, and hid his face in his hands.

'Don't say that, sir,' persisted Thomas. 'If you are out of spirits, let us try to cheer you. And you, in your turn, will enliven us. They are all waiting for you at home. Don't refuse, sir,' pleaded the young man, 'or we shall think we have offended you, in some way. You have always been a good friend to our family—'

Monsieur Chaubard again rose from his chair, with a second change of manner, as extraordinary and as perplexing as the first. His eyes moistened as if the tears were rising in them; he took the hand of Thomas Siadoux, and pressed it long and warmly in his own. There was a curious mixed expression of pity and fear in the look which he now fixed on the young man.

'Of all the days in the year,' he said, very earnestly, 'don't doubt my friendship to-day. Ill as I am, I will make one of the supper-party, for your sake—'

'And for my father's sake?' added Thomas, persuasively.

'Let us go to the supper,' said the priest.

Thomas Siadoux wrapped the cloak round him, and they left the house.

Every one at the table noticed the change in Monsieur Chaubard. He accounted for it by declaring, confusedly, that he was suffering from nervous illness; and then added that he would do his best, notwithstanding, to promote the social enjoyment of the evening. His talk was fragmentary, and his cheerfulness was sadly forced; but he contrived, with these drawbacks, to take his part in the conversation – except in the case when it happened to turn on the absent master of the house. Whenever the name of Saturnin Siadoux was mentioned – either by the neighbours, who politely regretted that he was not present; or by the family, who naturally talked about the resting-place which he might have chosen for the night – Monsieur Chaubard either relapsed into blank silence, or abruptly changed the topic. Under these circumstances, the company, by whom he was respected and beloved, made the necessary allowances for his state of health; the only person among them, who showed no desire to cheer the priest's spirits, and to humour him in his temporary fretfulness, being the silent younger son of Saturnin Siadoux.

Both Louis and Thomas noticed that, from the moment when Monsieur Chaubard's manner first betrayed his singular unwillingness to touch on the subject of their father's absence, Jean fixed his eyes on the priest, with an expression of suspicious attention; and never looked away from him for the rest of the evening. The young man's absolute silence at table did not surprise his brothers, for they were accustomed to his taciturn habits. But the sullen distrust betrayed in his close observation of the honoured guest and friend of the family, surprised and angered them. The priest himself seemed once or twice to be aware of the scrutiny to which he was subjected, and to feel uneasy and offended, as he naturally might. He abstained, however, from openly noticing Jean's strange behaviour; and Louis and Thomas were bound, therefore, in common politeness, to abstain from noticing it also.

The inhabitants of Croix-Daurade kept early hours. Towards eleven o'clock, the company rose and separated for the night. Except the two neighbours, nobody had enjoyed the supper, and even the two neighbours, having eaten their fill, were as glad to get home as the rest. In the little confusion of parting, Monsieur Chaubard completed the astonishment of the guests at the extraordinary change in him, by slipping away alone, without waiting to bid anybody good night.

The widow Mirailhe and her nieces withdrew to their bed-rooms, and left the three brothers by themselves in the parlour.

'Jean,' said Thomas Siadoux, 'I have a word to say to you. You stared at our good Monsieur Chaubard in a very offensive manner all through the evening. What did you mean by it?'

'Wait till to-morrow,' said Jean; 'and perhaps I may tell you.'

He lit his candle, and left them. Both the brothers observed that his hand trembled, and that his manner – never very winning – was, on that night, more serious and more unsociable than usual.

III THE YOUNGER BROTHER

When post-time came on the morning of the twenty-seventh, no letter arrived from Saturnin Siadoux. On consideration, the family interpreted this circumstance in a favourable light. If the master of the house had not written to them, it followed, surely, that he meant to make writing unnecessary by returning on that day.

As the hours passed, the widow and her nieces looked out, from time to time, for the absent man. Towards noon, they observed a little assembly of people approaching the village. Ere long, on a nearer view, they recognised at the head of the assembly, the chief magistrate of Toulouse, in his official dress. He was accompanied by his Assessor (also in official dress), by an escort of archers, and by certain subordinates attached to the town-hall. These last appeared to be carrying some burden, which was hidden from view by the escort of archers. The procession stopped at the house of Saturnin Siadoux; and the two daughters, hastening to the door, to discover what had happened, met the burden which the men were carrying, and saw, stretched on a litter, the dead body of their father.

The corpse had been found that morning on the banks of the river Lers. It was stabbed in eleven places with knife or dagger wounds. None of the valuables about the dead man's person had been touched; his watch and his money were still in his pockets. Whoever had murdered him, had murdered him for vengeance, not for gain.

Some time elapsed before even the male members of the family were sufficiently composed to hear what the officers of justice had to say to them. When this result had been at length achieved, and when the necessary inquiries had been made, no information of any kind was obtained which pointed to the murderer, in the eye of the law. After expressing his sympathy, and promising that every available means should be tried to effect the discovery of the criminal, the chief magistrate gave his orders to his escort, and withdrew.

When night came, the sister and the daughters of the murdered man retired to the upper part of the house, exhausted by the violence of their grief. The three brothers were left once more alone in the parlour, to speak together of the awful calamity which had befallen them. They were of hot Southern blood, and they looked on one another with a Southern thirst for vengeance in their tearless eyes.

The silent younger son was now the first to open his lips.

'You charged me yesterday,' he said to his brother Thomas, 'with looking strangely at Monsieur Chaubard all the evening; and I answered that I might tell you *why* I looked at him when to-morrow came. To-morrow has come, and I am ready to tell you.'

He waited a little, and lowered his voice to a whisper when he spoke again.

'When Monsieur Chaubard was at our supper-table last night,' he said, 'I had it in my mind that something had happened to our father, and that the priest knew it.'

The two elder brothers looked at him in speechless astonishment.

'Our father has been brought back to us a murdered man!' Jean went on, still in a whisper. 'I tell you, Louis – and you, Thomas – that the priest knows who murdered him.'

Louis and Thomas shrank from their younger brother, as if he had spoken blasphemy.

'Listen,' said Jean. 'No clue has been found to the secret of the murder. The magistrate has promised us to do his best – but I saw in his face that he had little hope. We must make the discovery ourselves – or our father's blood will have cried to us for vengeance, and cried in vain. Remember that – and mark my next words. You heard me say yesterday evening, that I had met Monsieur Chaubard on his way to Toulouse in excellent health and spirits. You heard our old friend and neighbour contradict me at the supper-table, and declare that he had seen the priest, some hours later, go into our church here with the face of a panic-stricken man. You saw, Thomas, how he behaved when you went to fetch him to our house. You saw, Louis, what his looks were like when he came in. The change was noticed by everybody – what was the cause of it? *I* saw the cause in the priest's own face, when our father's name turned up in the talk round the supper-table. Did Monsieur Chaubard join in that talk? He was the only person present who never joined in it once. Did he change it, on a sudden, whenever it came his way? It came his way four times; and four times he changed it – trembling, stammering, turning whiter and whiter, but still, as true as the Heaven above us, shifting the talk off himself, every time! Are you men? Have you brains in your heads? Don't you see, as I see, what this leads to? On my salvation I swear it – the priest knows the hand that killed our father!'

The faces of the two elder brothers darkened vindictively, as the conviction of the truth fastened itself on their minds.

'*How* could he know it?' they inquired, eagerly.

'He must tell us himself,' said Jean.

'And if he hesitates – if he refuses to open his lips?'

'We must open them by main force.'

They drew their chairs together after that last answer, and consulted, for some time, in whispers.

When the consultation was over, the brothers rose and went into the room where the dead body of their father was laid out. The three kissed him, in turn, on the forehead – then took hands together, and looked, meaningly, in each other's faces – then separated. Louis and Thomas put on their hats, and went at once to the priest's residence; while Jean withdrew by himself to the great room at the back of the house, which was used for the purposes of the oil-factory.

Only one of the workmen was left in the place. He was watching an immense cauldron of boiling linseed-oil.

'You can go home,' said Jean, patting the man kindly on the shoulder. 'There is no hope of a night's rest for me, after the affliction that has befallen us – I will take your place at the cauldron. Go home, my good fellow – go home.'

The man thanked him, and withdrew. Jean followed, and satisfied himself that the workman had really left the house. He then returned, and sat down by the boiling cauldron.

Meanwhile, Louis and Thomas presented themselves at the priest's house. He had not yet retired to bed, and he received them kindly – but with the same extraordinary agitation in his face and manner which had surprised all who saw him on the previous day. The brothers were prepared beforehand with an answer, when he inquired what they wanted of him. They replied immediately that the shock of their father's horrible death had so seriously affected their aunt and their eldest sister, that it was feared the minds of both might give way, unless spiritual consolation and assistance were afforded to them that night. The unhappy priest – always faithful and self-sacrificing where the duties of his ministry were in question – at once rose to accompany the young men back to the house. He even put on his surplice, and took the crucifix with him, to impress his words of comfort all the more solemnly on the afflicted women whom he was called on to succour.

Thus innocent of all suspicion of the conspiracy to which he had fallen a victim, he was taken into the room where Jean sat waiting by the cauldron of oil; and the door was locked behind him.

Before he could speak, Thomas Siadoux openly avowed the truth.

'It is we three who want you,' he said – 'not our aunt, and not our sister. If you answer our questions truly, you have nothing to fear. If you refuse –' He stopped, and looked toward Jean and the boiling cauldron.

Never, at the best of times, a resolute man; deprived, since the day before, of such resources of energy as he possessed, by the mental suffering which he had undergone in secret – the unfortunate priest trembled from head to foot, as the three brothers closed round him. Louis took the crucifix from him, and held it; Thomas forced him to place his right hand on it; Jean stood in front of him and put the questions.

'Our father has been brought home a murdered man,' he said. 'Do you know who killed him?'

The priest hesitated; and the two elder brothers moved him nearer to the cauldron.

'Answer us, on peril of your life,' said Jean. 'Say, with your hand on the blessed crucifix, do you know the man who killed our father?'

'I do know him.'

'When did you make the discovery?'

'Yesterday.'

'Where?'

'At Toulouse.'

'Name the murderer.'

At those words, the priest closed his hand fast on the crucifix, and rallied his sinking courage.

'Never!' he said firmly. 'The knowledge I possess was obtained in the confessional. The secrets of the confessional are sacred. If I betray them, I commit sacrilege. I will die first!'

'Think!' said Jean. 'If you keep silence, you screen the murderer. If you keep silence, you are the murderer's accomplice. We have sworn over our father's dead body to avenge him – if you refuse to speak, we will avenge him on *you*. I charge you again, name the man who killed him.'

'I will die first,' the priest reiterated, as firmly as before.

'Die then!' said Jean. 'Die in that cauldron of boiling oil.'

'Give him time,' cried Louis and Thomas, earnestly pleading together.

'We will give him time,' said the younger brother. 'There is the clock yonder, against the wall. We will count five minutes by it. In those five minutes, let him make his peace with God – or make up his mind to speak.'

They waited, watching the clock. In that dreadful interval, the priest dropped on his knees and hid his face. The time passed in dead silence.

'Speak! for your own sake, for our sakes, speak!' said Thomas Siadoux, as the minute hand reached the point at which the five minutes expired.

The priest looked up – his voice died away on his lips – the mortal agony broke out on his face in great drops of sweat – his head sank forward on his breast.

'Lift him!' cried Jean, seizing the priest on one side. 'Lift him, and throw him in!'

The two elder brothers advanced a step – and hesitated.

'Lift him, on your oath over our father's body!'

The two brothers seized him on the other side. As they lifted him to a level with the cauldron, the horror of the death that threatened him, burst from the lips of the miserable man in a scream of terror. The brothers held him firm at the cauldron's edge. 'Name the man!' they said for the last time.

The priest's teeth chattered – he was speechless. But he made a sign with his head – a sign in the affirmative. They placed him in a chair, and waited patiently until he was able to speak.

His first words were words of entreaty. He begged Thomas Siadoux to give him back the crucifix. When it was placed in his possession, he kissed it, and said faintly, 'I ask pardon of God for the sin that I am about to commit.' He paused; and then looked up at the younger brother, who still stood in front of him. 'I am ready,' he said. 'Question me, and I will answer.'

Jean repeated the questions which he had put, when the priest was first brought into the room.

'You know the murderer of our father?'

'I know him.'

'Since when?'

'Since he made his confession to me yesterday, in the cathedral of Toulouse.'

'Name him.'

'His name is Cantegrel.'

'The man who wanted to marry our aunt?'

'The same.'

'What brought him to the confessional?'

'His own remorse.'

'What were the motives for his crime?'

'There were reports against his character; and he discovered that your father had gone privately to Narbonne to make sure that they were true.'

'Did our father make sure of their truth?'

'He did.'

'Would those discoveries have separated our aunt from Cantegrel if our father had lived to tell her of them?'

'They would. If your father had lived, he would have told your aunt that Cantegrel was married already; that he had deserted his wife at Narbonne; that she was living there with another man, under another name; and that she had herself confessed it in your father's presence.'

'Where was the murder committed?'

'Between Villefranche and this village. Cantegrel had followed your father to Narbonne; and had followed him back again to Villefranche. As far as that place, he travelled in company with others, both going and returning. Beyond Villefranche, he was left alone at the ford over the river. There Cantegrel drew the knife to kill him, before he reached home and told his news to your aunt.'

'How was the murder committed?'

'It was committed while your father was watering his pony by the bank of the stream. Cantegrel stole on him from behind, and struck him as he was stooping over the saddle-bow.'

'This is the truth, on your oath?'

'On my oath, it is the truth.'

'You may leave us.'

The priest rose from his chair without assistance. From the time when the terror of death had forced him to reveal the murderer's name, a great change had passed over him. He had given his answers with the immoveable calmness of a man on whose mind all human interests had lost their hold. He now left the room, strangely absorbed in himself; moving with the mechanical regularity of a sleepwalker; lost to all perception of things and persons about him. At the door he stopped – woke, as it seemed, from the trance that possessed him –

and looked at the three brothers with a steady changeless sorrow, which they had never seen in him before, which they never afterwards forgot.

'I forgive you,' he said, quietly and solemnly. 'Pray for me, when my time comes.'

With those last words, he left them.

IV THE END

The night was far advanced; but the three brothers determined to set forth instantly for Toulouse, and to place their information in the magistrate's hands, before the morning dawned.

Thus far, no suspicion had occurred to them of the terrible consequences which were to follow their night-interview with the priest. They were absolutely ignorant of the punishment to which a man in holy orders exposed himself, if he revealed the secrets of the confessional. No infliction of that punishment had been known in their neighbourhood – for, at that time, as at this, the rarest of all priestly offences was a violation of the sacred trust confided to the confessor by the Roman Church. Conscious that they had forced the priest into the commission of a clerical offence, the brothers sincerely believed that the loss of his curacy would be the heaviest penalty which the law could exact from him. They entered Toulouse that night, discussing the atonement which they might offer to Monsieur Chaubard, and the means which they might best employ to make his future life easy to him.

The first disclosure of the consequences which would certainly follow the outrage they had committed, was revealed to them when they made their deposition before the officer of justice. The magistrate listened to their narrative with horror vividly expressed in his face and manner.

'Better you had never been born,' he said, 'than have avenged your father's death, as you three have avenged it. Your own act has doomed the guilty and the innocent to suffer alike.'

Those words proved prophetic of the truth. The end came quickly, as the priest had foreseen it, when he spoke his parting words.

The arrest of Cantegrel was accomplished without difficulty, the next morning. In the absence of any other evidence on which to justify this proceeding, the private disclosure to the authorities of the secret which the priest had violated, became inevitable. The Parliament of Languedoc was, under these circumstances, the tribunal appealed to; and the decision of that assembly immediately ordered the priest and the three brothers to be placed in confinement, as well as the murderer Cantegrel. Evidence was then immediately sought for, which might convict this last criminal, without any reference to the revelation that had been forced from the priest – and evidence enough was found to satisfy judges whose minds already possessed the foregone certainty of the prisoner's guilt. He was put on his trial, was convicted of the murder, and was condemned to be broken on the wheel. The sentence was rigidly executed, with as little delay as the law would permit.

The cases of Monsieur Chaubard, and of the three sons of Siadoux, next occupied the judges. The three brothers were found guilty of having forced the secret of a confession from a man in holy orders, and were sentenced to death by hanging. A far more terrible expiation of his offence awaited the unfortunate priest. He was condemned to have his limbs broken on the wheel, and to be afterwards, while still living, bound to the stake, and destroyed by fire.

Barbarous as the punishments of that period were, accustomed as the population was to hear of their infliction, and even to witness it, the sentences pronounced in these two cases dismayed the public mind; and the authorities were surprised by receiving petitions for mercy from Toulouse, and from all the surrounding neighbourhood. But the priest's doom had been sealed. All that could be obtained, by the intercession of persons of the highest distinction, was, that the executioner should grant him the mercy of death, before his body was committed to the flames. With this one modification, the sentence was executed, as the sentence had been pronounced, on the curate of Croix-Daurade.

The punishment of the three sons of Siadoux remained to be inflicted. But the people, roused by the death of the ill-fated priest, rose against this third execution, with a resolution before which the local government gave way. The cause of the young men was taken up by the hot-blooded populace, as the cause of all fathers and all sons; their filial piety was exalted to the skies; their youth was pleaded in their behalf; their ignorance of the terrible responsibility which they had confronted in forcing the secret from the priest, was loudly alleged in their favour. More than this, the authorities were actually warned that the appearance of the prisoners on the scaffold would be the signal for an organised revolt and rescue. Under this serious pressure, the execution was deferred, and the prisoners were kept in confinement until the popular ferment had subsided.

The delay not only saved their lives, it gave them back their liberty as well. The infection of the popular sympathy had penetrated through the prison doors. All three brothers were handsome, well-grown young men. The gentlest of the three in disposition – Thomas Siadoux – aroused the interest and won the affection of the head-gaoler's daughter. Her father was prevailed on at her intercession to relax a little in his customary vigilance; and the rest was accomplished by the girl herself. One morning, the population of Toulouse heard, with every testimony of the most extravagant rejoicing, that the three brothers had escaped, accompanied by the gaoler's daughter. As a necessary legal formality, they were pursued, but no extraordinary efforts were used to overtake them: and they succeeded, accordingly, in crossing the nearest frontier.

Twenty days later, orders were received from the capital, to execute their sentence in effigy. They were then permitted to return to France, on condition that they never again appeared in their native place, or in any other part of the province of Languedoc. With this reservation they were left free to live where they pleased, and to repent the fatal act which had avenged them on the murderer of their father at the cost of the priest's life.

Beyond this point the official documents do not enable us to follow their career. All that is now known has been now told of the village-tragedy at Croix-Daurade.

The Fatal Cradle

[Otherwise, the Heartrending Story
of Mr Heavysides]

Originally appeared in *Tom Tiddler's Ground*, the extra Christmas number of *All the Year Round* for 1861, where it occupied Chapter 4 and was entitled 'Picking Up Waifs at Sea'. It was included in *Miss or Mrs?: and Other Stories in Outline* (1873). Collins broke off in the early stages of writing *No Name* in order to supply the story, and (perhaps because of the success of *The Woman in White* and of the sequence of three long novels which followed it) this turned out to be the last short fiction Collins wrote for a period of ten years. Dickens told Collins the story was one of his favourites. Collins said afterwards the story made him laugh as he was writing it, 'which is what my own fun seldom does.'

T HERE HAS NEVER yet been discovered a man with a grievance, who objected to mention it. I am no exception to this general human rule. I have got a grievance; and I don't object to mention it. Compose your spirits to hear a pathetic story, and kindly picture me in your own mind as a baby five minutes old.

Do I understand you to say that I am too big and too heavy to be pictured in anybody's mind as a baby? Perhaps I may be – but don't mention my weight again, if you please. My weight has been the grand misfortune of my life. It spoilt all my prospects (as you will presently hear) before I was two days old.

My story begins thirty-one years ago, at eleven o'clock in the forenoon; and starts with the great mistake of my first appearance in this world, at sea, on board the merchant ship Adventure, Captain Gillop, five hundred tons burden, coppered and carrying an experienced surgeon.

In presenting myself to you (which I am now about to do) at that eventful period of my life, when I was from five to ten minutes old; and in withdrawing myself again from your notice (so as not to trouble you with more than a short story), before the time when I cut my first tooth, I need not hesitate to admit that I speak on hearsay knowledge only. It is knowledge, however, that may be relied on, for all that. My information comes from Captain Gillop, commander of the Adventure (who sent it to me in the form of a letter); from Mr Jolly, experienced surgeon of the Adventure (who wrote it for me – most unfeelingly, as I think – in the shape of a humorous narrative); and from Mrs Drabble, stewardess of the Adventure (who told it me by word of mouth). Those three persons were, in various degrees, spectators – I may say, astonished spectators – of the events which I have now to relate.

The Adventure, at the time I speak of, was bound out from London to Australia. I suppose you know, without my telling you, that thirty years ago was long before the time of the gold-finding and the famous clipper ships. Building in the new colony, and sheep-farming far up inland, were the two main employments of those days; and the passengers on board our vessel were consequently builders or sheep-farmers, almost to a man.

A ship of five hundred tons, well loaded with cargo, doesn't offer first-rate accommodation to a large number of passengers. Not that the gentlefolks in the cabin had any great reason to complain. There, the passage-money, which was a good round sum, kept them what you call select. One or two berths, in this part of the ship, were even empty and going a begging, in consequence of there being only four cabin passengers. These are their names and descriptions:

Mr Sims, a middle-aged man, going out on a building speculation. Mr Purling, a weakly young gentleman, sent on a long sea-voyage for the benefit of his health. And Mr and Mrs Smallchild, a young married couple with a little independence, which Mr Smallchild proposed to make a large one by sheep-farming.

This gentleman was reported to the captain, as being very good company when on shore. But the sea altered him to a certain extent. When Mr Smallchild was not sick, he was eating and drinking; and when he was not eating and drinking, he was fast asleep. He was perfectly patient and good-humoured, and wonderfully nimble at running into his cabin when the qualms took him on a sudden – but, as for his being good company, nobody heard him say ten words together all through the voyage. And no wonder. A man can't talk, in the qualms; a man can't talk, while he is eating and drinking; and a man can't talk, when he is asleep. And that was Mr Smallchild's life. As for Mrs Smallchild, she kept her cabin from first to last. But you will hear more of her presently.

These four cabin passengers, as I have already remarked, were well enough off for their accommodation. But the miserable people in the steerage – a poor place, at the best of times, on board the Adventure – were all huddled together, men and women and children, higgledy-piggledy, like sheep in a pen; except that they hadn't got the same quantity of fine fresh air to blow over them. They were artisans and farm-labourers, who couldn't make it out in the old country. I have no information either of their exact numbers or of their names. It doesn't matter: there was only one family among them which need be mentioned particularly – namely, the family of the Heavysides. To wit, Simon Heavysides, intelligent and well-educated, a carpenter by trade; Susan Heavysides, his wife; and seven little Heavysides, their unfortunate offspring. My father and mother and brothers and sisters, did I understand you to say? Don't be in a hurry! I recommend you to wait a little before you make quite sure of that circumstance.

Though I myself had not, perhaps – strictly speaking – come on board when the vessel left London, my ill-luck, as I firmly believe, had shipped in the Adventure to wait for me – and decided the nature of the voyage accordingly.

Never was such a miserable time known. Stormy weather came down on us from all points of the compass, with intervals of light baffling winds, or dead calms. By the time the Adventure had been three months out, Captain Gillop's naturally sweet temper began to get soured. I leave you to say whether it was likely to be much improved by a piece of news which reached him from the region of the cabin, on the morning of the ninety-first day. It had fallen to a dead calm again; and the ship was rolling about helpless with her head all round the compass, when Mr Jolly (from whose facetious narrative I repeat all conversations, exactly as they passed) came on deck to the captain, and addressed him in these words:

'I have got some news that will rather surprise you,' said Mr Jolly, smiling and rubbing his hands. (Although the experienced surgeon has not shown much sympathy for my troubles, I won't deny that his disposition was as good as his name. To this day, no amount of bad weather or hard work can upset Mr Jolly's temper.)

'If it's news of a fair wind coming,' grumbled the captain, 'that would surprise me, on board this ship, I can promise you!'

'It's not exactly a wind coming,' said Mr Jolly. 'It's another cabin passenger.'

The captain looked round at the empty sea, with the land thousands of miles away, and with not a ship in sight – turned sharply on the experienced surgeon – eyed him hard – changed colour suddenly – and asked what he meant.

'I mean there's a fifth cabin passenger coming on board,' persisted Mr Jolly, grinning from ear to ear – 'introduced by Mrs Smallchild – likely to join us, I should say, towards evening – size, nothing to speak of – sex, not known at present – manners and customs, probably squally.'

'Do you really mean it?' asked the captain, backing away, and turning paler and paler.

'Yes; I do,' answered Mr Jolly, nodding hard at him.

'Then I'll tell you what,' cried Captain Gillop, suddenly flying into a violent passion, 'I won't have it! the infernal weather has worried me out of my life and soul already – and I won't have it! Put it off, Jolly – tell her there isn't room enough for that sort of thing on board my vessel. What does she mean by taking us all in, in this way? Shameful! shameful!'

'No! no!' remonstrated Mr Jolly. 'Don't look at it in that light. It's her first child, poor thing. How should *she* know? Give her a little more experience, and I dare say—'

'Where's her husband?' broke in the captain, with a threatening look. 'I'll speak my mind to her husband, at any rate.'

Mr Jolly consulted his watch before he answered.

'Half-past eleven,' he said. 'Let me consider a little. It's Mr Smallchild's regular time just now for squaring accounts with the sea. He'll have done in a quarter of an hour. In five minutes more, he'll be fast asleep. At one o'clock he'll eat a hearty lunch, and go to sleep again. At half-past two, he'll square accounts as before – and so on, till night. You'll make nothing of Mr Smallchild, captain. Extraordinary man – wastes tissue, and repairs it again perpetually, in the most astonishing manner. If we are another month at sea, I believe we shall bring him into port totally comatose – Hullo! What do *you* want?'

The steward's mate had approached the quarter deck while the doctor was speaking. Was it a curious coincidence? This man also was grinning from ear to ear, exactly like Mr Jolly.

'You're wanted in the steerage, sir,' said the steward's mate to the doctor. 'A woman taken bad, name of Heavysides.'

'Nonsense!' cried Mr Jolly. 'Ha! ha! ha! You don't mean – Eh?'

'That's it, sir, sure enough,' said the steward's mate, in the most positive manner.

Captain Gillop looked all round him, in silent desperation; lost his sea-legs for the first time these twenty years; staggered back till he was brought up all standing by the side of his own vessel; dashed his fist on the bulwark, and found language to express himself in, at the same moment.

'This ship is bewitched,' said the captain, wildly. 'Stop!' he called out, recovering himself a little, as the doctor bustled away to the steerage. 'Stop! If it's true, Jolly, send her husband here aft to me. Damme, I'll have it out with one of the husbands!' said the captain, shaking his fist viciously at the empty air.

Ten minutes passed; and then there came staggering towards the captain, tottering this way and that with the rolling of the becalmed vessel, a long, lean, melancholy, light-haired man, with a Roman nose, a watery blue eye, and a complexion profusely spotted with large brown freckles. This was Simon Heavysides, the intelligent carpenter, with the wife and the family of seven small children on board.

'Oh! you're the man, are you?' said the captain.

The ship lurched heavily; and Simon Heavysides staggered away with a run to the opposite side of the deck, as if he preferred going straight overboard into the sea, to answering the captain's question.

'You're the man – are you?' repeated the captain, following him, seizing him by the collar, and pinning him up fiercely against the bulwark. 'It's your wife – is it? You infernal rascal! what do you mean by turning my ship into a Lying-In

Hospital? You have committed an act of mutiny; or, if it isn't mutiny, it's next door to it. I've put a man in irons for less! I've more than half a mind to put *you* in irons! Hold up, you slippery lubber! What do you mean by bringing passengers I don't bargain for on board my vessel? What have you got to say for yourself, before I clap the irons on you?'

'Nothing, sir,' answered Simon Heavysides, accepting the captain's strong language without a word of protest. 'As for the punishment you mentioned just now, sir,' continued Simon, 'I wish to say – having seven children more than I know how to provide for, and an eighth coming to make things worse – I respectfully wish to say, sir, that my mind is in irons already: and I don't know as it will make much difference if you put my body in irons along with it.'

The captain mechanically let go of the carpenter's collar: the mild despair of the man melted him in spite of himself.

'Why did you come to sea? Why didn't you wait ashore till it was all over?' asked the captain, as sternly as he could.

'It's no use waiting, sir,' remarked Simon. 'In our line of life as soon as it's over, it begins again. There's no end to it that I can see,' said the miserable carpenter, after a moment's meek consideration – 'except the grave.'

'Who's talking about the grave?' cried Mr Jolly, coming up at that moment. 'It's births we've got to do with on board this vessel – not burials. Captain Gillop, this woman, Mrs Heavysides, can't be left in your crowded steerage, in her present condition. She must be moved off into one of the empty berths – and the sooner the better, I can tell you!'

The captain began to look savage again. A steerage passenger in one of his 'staterooms' was a nautical anomaly subversive of all discipline. He eyed the carpenter once more, as if he was mentally measuring him for a set of irons.

'I'm very sorry, sir,' Simon remarked, politely – 'very sorry that any inadvertence of mine or Mrs Heavysides—'

'Take your long carcase and your long tongue forward!' thundered the captain. 'When talking will mend matters, I'll send for you again. Give your own orders, Jolly,' he went on, resignedly, as Simon staggered off. 'Turn the ship into a nursery as soon as you like!'

Five minutes later – so expeditious was Mr Jolly – Mrs Heavysides appeared horizontally on deck, shrouded in blankets, and supported by three men. When this interesting procession passed the captain, he shrank aside from it with as vivid an appearance of horror as if a wild bull was being carried by him instead of a British matron.

The sleeping berths below opened on either side out of the main cabin. On the left-hand side (looking towards the ship's bowsprit) was Mrs Smallchild. On the right-hand side, opposite to her, the doctor established Mrs Heavysides. A partition of canvas was next run up, entirely across the main cabin. The smaller of the two temporary rooms thus made, lay nearest the stairs leading on deck, and was left free to the public. The larger was kept sacred to the doctor and his mysteries. When an old clothes-basket, emptied, cleaned, and comfortably lined with blankets (to serve for a makeshift cradle), had been, in due course of time, carried into the inner cabin, and had been placed midway between the two sleeping-berths, so as to be easily producible when wanted, the outward and visible preparations of Mr Jolly were complete; the male passengers had all taken refuge on deck; and the doctor and the stewardess were left in undisturbed possession of the lower regions.

While it was still early in the afternoon, the weather changed for the better. For once in a way, the wind came from a fair quarter; and the Adventure bowled along pleasantly before it almost on an even keel. Captain Gillop mixed with the little group of male passengers on the quarter-deck, restored to his sweetest temper; and set them his customary example, after dinner, of smoking a cigar.

'If this fine weather lasts, gentlemen,' he said, 'we shall make out very well with our meals up here; and we shall have our two small extra cabin passengers christened on dry land in a week's time, if their mothers approve of it. How do you feel in your mind, sir, about your good lady?'

Mr Smallchild (to whom the inquiry was addressed) had his points of external personal resemblance to Simon Heavysides. He was neither so tall nor so lean certainly – but he, too, had a Roman nose, and light hair, and watery blue eyes. With careful reference to his peculiar habits at sea, he had been placed conveniently close to the bulwark, and had been raised on a heap of old sails and cushions, so that he could easily get his head over the ship's side when occasion required. The food and drink which assisted in 'restoring his tissue,' when he was not asleep and not 'squaring accounts with the sea,' lay close to his hand. It was then a little after three o'clock; and the snore with which Mr Smallchild answered the captain's inquiry showed that he had got round again, with the regularity of clockwork, to the period of the day when he recruited himself with sleep.

'What an insensible blockhead that man is!' said Mr Sims, the middle-aged passenger; looking across the deck contemptuously at Mr Smallchild.

'If the sea had the same effect on you that it has on him,' retorted the invalid passenger, Mr Purling, 'you would be just as insensible yourself.'

Mr Purling (who was a man of sentiment) disagreed with Mr Sims (who was a man of business) on every conceivable subject, all through the voyage. Before, however, they could continue the dispute about Mr Smallchild, the doctor surprised them by appearing from the cabin.

'Any news from below, Jolly?' asked the captain, anxiously.

'None whatever,' answered the doctor. 'I've come to idle the afternoon away up here, along with the rest of you.'

As events turned out, Mr Jolly idled away an hour and a half exactly. At the end of that time, Mrs Drabble, the stewardess, appeared with a face of mystery, and whispered nervously to the doctor:

'Please to step below directly, sir.'

'Which of them is it?' asked Mr Jolly.

'*Both* of them,' answered Mrs Drabble, emphatically.

The doctor looked grave; the stewardess looked frightened. The two immediately disappeared together.

'I suppose, gentlemen,' said Captain Gillop, addressing Mr Purling, Mr Sims, and the first mate, who had just joined the party, 'I suppose it's only fit and proper, in the turn things have taken, to shake up Mr Smallchild? And I don't doubt but what we ought to have the other husband handy, as a sort of polite attention under the circumstances. Pass the word forward there, for Simon Heavysides. Mr Smallchild, sir! rouse up! Here's your good lady – Hang me, gentlemen, if I know exactly how to put it to him.'

'Yes. Thank you,' said Mr Smallchild, opening his eyes drowsily. 'Biscuit and cold bacon, as usual – when I'm ready. I'm not ready yet. Thank you.

Good afternoon.' Mr Smallchild closed his eyes again, and became, in the doctor's phrase, 'totally comatose.'

Before Captain Gillop could hit on any new plan for rousing this imperturbable passenger, Simon Heavysides once more approached the quarter-deck.

'I spoke a little sharp to you, just now, my man,' said the captain, 'being worried in my mind by what's going on on board this vessel. But I'll make it up to you, never fear. Here's your wife in, what they call, an interesting situation. It's only right you should be within easy hail of her. I look upon you, Heavysides, as a steerage-passenger in difficulties; and I freely give you leave to stop here along with us till it's all over.'

'You are very good, sir,' said Simon; 'and I am indeed thankful to you and to these gentlemen. But, please to remember, I have seven children already in the steerage – and there's nobody left to mind 'em but me. My wife has got over it uncommonly well, sir, on seven previous occasions – and I don't doubt but what she'll conduct herself in a similar manner on the eighth. It will be a satisfaction to her mind, Captain Gillop and gentlemen, if she knows I'm out of the way, and minding the children. For which reason, I respectfully take my leave.' With those words, Simon made his bow, and returned to his family.

'Well, gentlemen, these two husbands take it easy enough, at any rate!' said the captain. 'One of them is used to it, to be sure; and the other is—'

Here a banging of cabin doors below, and a hurrying of footsteps, startled the speaker and his audience into momentary silence and attention.

'Ease her with the helm, Williamson!' said Captain Gillop, addressing the man who was steering the vessel. 'In my opinion, gentlemen, the less the ship pitches the better, in the turn things are taking now.'

The afternoon wore on into evening, and evening into night.

Mr Smallchild performed the daily ceremonies of his nautical existence as punctually as usual. He was aroused to a sense of Mrs Smallchild's situation when he took his biscuit and bacon; lost the sense again when the time came round for 'squaring his accounts;' recovered it in the interval which ensued before he went to sleep: lost it again, as a matter of course, when his eyes closed once more – and so on through the evening and early night. Simon Heavysides received messages occasionally (through the captain's care), telling him to keep his mind easy; returned messages mentioning that his mind was easy, and that the children were pretty quiet, but never approached the deck in his own person. Mr Jolly now and then showed himself; said 'All right, – no news;' took a little light refreshment, and disappeared again, as cheerful as ever. The fair breeze still held; the captain's temper remained unruffled; the man at the helm eased the vessel, from time to time, with the most anxious consideration. Ten o'clock came: the moon rose and shone superbly; the nightly grog made its appearance on the quarter-deck; the captain gave the passengers the benefit of his company; and still nothing happened. Twenty minutes more of suspense slowly succeeded each other – and then, at last, Mr Jolly was seen suddenly to ascend the cabin stairs.

To the amazement of the little group on the quarter-deck, the doctor held Mrs Drabble, the stewardess, fast by the arm, and, without taking the slightest notice of the captain or the passengers, placed her on the nearest seat he could find. As he did this, his face became visible in the moonlight, and displayed to the startled spectators an expression of blank consternation.

'Compose yourself, Mrs Drabble,' said the doctor, in tones of unmistakable alarm. 'Keep quiet, and let the air blow over you. Collect yourself, ma'am – for Heaven's sake, collect yourself!'

Mrs Drabble made no answer. She beat her hands vacantly on her knees, and stared straight before her, like a woman panic-stricken.

'What's wrong?' asked the captain, setting down his glass of grog in dismay. 'Anything amiss with those two unfortunate women?'

'Nothing,' said the doctor. 'Both doing admirably well.'

'Anything queer with their babies?' continued the captain. 'Are there more than you bargained for, Jolly? Twins, for instance?'

'No! no!' replied Mr Jolly, impatiently. 'A baby apiece – both boys – both in first-rate condition. Judge for yourselves,' added the doctor, as the two new cabin-passengers tried their lungs, below, for the first time, and found that they answered their purpose in the most satisfactory manner.

'What the devil's amiss, then, with you and Mrs Drabble?' persisted the captain, beginning to lose his temper again.

'Mrs Drabble and I are two innocent people, and we have got into the most dreadful scrape that ever you heard of!' was Mr Jolly's startling answer.

The captain, followed by Mr Purling and Mr Sims, approached the doctor with looks of horror. Even the man at the wheel stretched himself over it as far as he could to hear what was coming next. The only uninterested person present was Mr Smallchild. His time had come round for going to sleep again, and he was snoring peacefully, with his biscuit and bacon close beside him.

'Let's hear the worst of it at once, Jolly,' said the captain, a little impatiently.

The doctor paid no heed to his request. His whole attention was absorbed by Mrs Drabble. 'Are you better now, ma'am?' he asked, anxiously.

'No better in my mind,' answered Mrs Drabble, beginning to beat her knees again. 'Worse, if anything.'

'Listen to me,' said Mr Jolly, coaxingly. 'I'll put the whole case over again to you, in a few plain questions. You'll find it all come back to your memory, if you only follow me attentively, and if you take time to think and collect yourself before you attempt to answer.'

Mrs Drabble bowed her head in speechless submission – and listened. Everybody else on the quarter-deck listened, except the impenetrable Mr Smallchild.

'Now, ma'am!' said the doctor. 'Our troubles began in Mrs Heavysides' cabin, which is situated on the starboard side of the ship?'

'They did, sir,' replied Mrs Drabble.

'Good! We went backwards and forwards, an infinite number of times, between Mrs Heavysides (starboard) and Mrs Smallchild (larboard) – but we found that Mrs Heavysides, having got the start, kept it – and when I called out, "Mrs Drabble! here's a chopping boy for you: come and take him!" – I called out starboard, didn't I?'

'Starboard, sir – I'll take my oath of it,' said Mrs Drabble.

'Good, again! "Here's a chopping boy," I said. "Take him, ma'am, and make him comfortable in the cradle." And you took him, and made him comfortable in the cradle, accordingly? Now, where was the cradle?'

'In the main cabin, sir,' replied Mrs Drabble.

'Just so! In the main cabin, because we hadn't got room for it in either of the sleeping cabins. You put the starboard baby (otherwise Heavysides) in the clothes-basket cradle in the main cabin. Good, once more. How was the cradle placed?'

'Crosswise to the ship, sir,' said Mrs Drabble.

'Crosswise to the ship? That is to say, with one side longwise towards the stern of the vessel, and one side longwise towards the bows. Bear that in mind – and now follow me a little farther. No! no! don't say you can't, and your head's in a whirl. My next question will steady it. Carry your mind on half an hour, Mrs Drabble. At the end of half an hour, you heard my voice again; and my voice called out – "Mrs Drabble! here's another chopping boy for you: come and take him!" – and you came and took him larboard, didn't you?'

'Larboard, sir, I don't deny it,' answered Mrs Drabble.

'Better and better! "Here is another chopping boy," I said. "Take him, ma'am, and make him comfortable in the cradle, along with number one." And you took the larboard baby (otherwise Smallchild), and made him comfortable in the cradle along with the starboard baby (otherwise Heavysides), accordingly? Now, what happened after that?'

'Don't ask me, sir!' exclaimed Mrs Drabble, losing her self-control, and wringing her hands desperately.

'Steady, ma'am! I'll put it to you as plain as print. Steady! and listen to me. Just as you had made the larboard baby comfortable, I had occasion to send you into the starboard (or Heavysides) cabin, to fetch something which I wanted in the larboard (or Smallchild) cabin; I kept you there a little while along with me; I left you, and went into the Heavysides cabin, and called to you to bring me something I wanted out of the Smallchild cabin, but before you got half-way across the main cabin, I said "No; stop where you are, and I'll come to you"; immediately after which, Mrs Smallchild alarmed you, and you came across to me of your own accord; and, thereupon, I stopped you in the main cabin, and said, "Mrs Drabble, your mind's getting confused, sit down and collect your scattered intellects"; and you sat down, and tried to collect them— ?'

('And couldn't, sir,' interposed Mrs Drabble, parenthetically. 'Oh, my head! my head!')

– 'And tried to collect your scattered intellects, and couldn't?' continued the doctor. 'And the consequence was, when I came out from the Smallchild cabin to see how you were getting on, I found you with the clothes-basket cradle hoisted up on the cabin table, staring down at the babies inside with your mouth dropped open, and both your hands twisted in your hair? And when I said, "Anything wrong with either of those two fine boys, Mrs Drabble?" you caught me by the coat-collar, and whispered in my right ear these words: "Lord save us and help us, Mr Jolly, I've confused the two babies in my mind, and I don't know which is which!"'

'And I don't know now!' cried Mrs Drabble, hysterically. 'Oh, my head! my head! I don't know now!'

'Captain Gillop and gentlemen,' said Mr Jolly, wheeling round and addressing his audience with the composure of sheer despair, 'that is the Scrape – and, if you ever heard of a worse one, I'll trouble you to compose this miserable woman by mentioning it immediately.'

Captain Gillop looked at Mr Purling and Mr Sims. Mr Purling and Mr Sims looked at Captain Gillop. They were all three thunderstruck – and no wonder.

'Can't *you* throw any light on it, Jolly?' inquired the captain, who was the first to recover himself.

'If you knew what I have had to do below, you wouldn't ask me such a question as that,' replied the doctor. 'Remember that I have had the lives of two women and two children to answer for – remember that I have been cramped up in two small sleeping-cabins, with hardly room to turn round in, and just light enough from two miserable little lamps to see my hand before me – remember the professional difficulties of the situation, the ship rolling about under me all the while, and the stewardess to compose into the bargain; – bear all that in mind, will you, and then tell me how much spare time I had on my hands for comparing two boys together inch by inch – two boys born at night, within half an hour of each other, on board a ship at sea. Ha! ha! I only wonder the mothers and the boys and the doctor are all five of them alive to tell the story!'

'No marks on one or other of them, that happened to catch your eye?' asked Mr Sims.

'They must have been strongish marks to catch my eye in the light I had to work by, and in the professional difficulties I had to grapple with,' said the doctor. 'I saw they were both straight, well-formed children – and that's all I saw!'

'Are their infant features sufficiently developed to indicate a family likeness?' inquired Mr Purling. 'Should you say they took after their fathers or their mothers?'

'Both of them have light eyes, and light hair – such as it is,' replied Mr Jolly, doggedly. 'Judge for yourself.'

'Mr Smallchild has light eyes and light hair,' remarked Mr Sims.

'And Simon Heavysides has light eyes and light hair,' rejoined Mr Purling.

'I should recommend waking Mr Smallchild, and sending for Heavysides, and letting the two fathers toss up for it,' suggested Mr Sims.

'The parental feeling is not to be trifled with in that heartless manner,' retorted Mr Purling. 'I should recommend trying the Voice of Nature.'

'What may that be, sir?' inquired Captain Gillop, with great curiosity.

'The maternal instinct,' replied Mr Purling. 'The mother's intuitive knowledge of her own child.'

'Ay, ay!' said the captain. 'Well thought of. What do you say, Jolly, to the Voice of Nature?'

The doctor held up his hand impatiently. He was engaged in resuming the effort to rouse Mrs Drabble's memory by a system of amateur cross-examination, with the unsatisfactory result of confusing her more hopelessly than ever.

Could she put the cradle back, in her own mind, into its original position? No. Could she remember whether she laid the starboard baby (otherwise Heavysides) on the side of the cradle nearest the stern of the ship, or nearest the bows? No. Could she remember any better about the larboard baby (other wise Smallchild)? No. Why did she move the cradle on to the cabin table, and so bewilder herself additionally, when she was puzzled already? Because it came over her, on a sudden, that she had forgotten, in the dreadful confusion of the time, which was which; and of course she wanted to look closer at them, and see; and she couldn't see; and to her dying day she should never forgive herself; and let them throw her overboard, for a miserable wretch, if they liked, – and so on, till the persevering doctor was wearied out at last, and gave up Mrs Drabble, and gave up, with her, the whole case.

'I see nothing for it but the Voice of Nature,' said the captain, holding fast to Mr Purling's idea. 'Try it, Jolly – you can but try it.'

'Something must be done,' said the doctor. 'I can't leave the women alone any longer; and the moment I get below they will both ask for their babies. Wait here, till you're fit to be seen, Mrs Drabble, and then follow me. Voice of Nature!' added Mr Jolly, contemptuously, as he descended the cabin stairs. 'Oh yes, I'll try it – much good the Voice of Nature will do us, gentlemen. You shall judge for yourselves.'

Favoured by the night, Mr Jolly cunningly turned down the dim lamps in the sleeping cabins to a mere glimmer, on the pretext that the light was bad for his patients' eyes. He then took up the first of the two unlucky babies that came to hand, marked the clothes in which it was wrapped with a blot of ink, and carried it in to Mrs Smallchild, choosing her cabin merely because he happened to be nearest to it. The second baby (distinguished by having no mark) was taken by Mrs Drabble to Mrs Heavysides. For a certain time, the two mothers and the two babies were left together. They were then separated again by medical order; and were afterwards reunited, with the difference that the marked baby went on this occasion to Mrs Heavysides, and the unmarked baby to Mrs Smallchild – the result, in the obscurity of the sleeping cabins, proving to be that one baby did just as well as the other, and that the Voice of Nature was (as Mr Jolly had predicted) totally incompetent to settle the existing difficulty.

'While night serves us, Captain Gillop, we shall do very well,' said the doctor, after he had duly reported the failure of Mr Purling's suggested experiment. 'But when morning comes, and daylight shows the difference between the children, we must be prepared with a course of some kind. If the two mothers, below, get the slightest suspicion of the case as it really stands, the nervous shock of the discovery may do dreadful mischief. They must be kept deceived, in the interests of their own health. We must choose a baby for each of them when to-morrow comes, and then hold to the choice, till the mothers are well and up again. The question is, who's to take the responsibility? I don't usually stick at trifles – but I candidly admit that *I'm* afraid of it.'

'I decline meddling in the matter, on the ground that I am a perfect stranger,' said Mr Sims.

'And I object to interfere, from precisely similar motives,' added Mr Purling; agreeing for the first time with a proposition that emanated from his natural enemy all through the voyage.

'Wait a minute, gentlemen,' said Captain Gillop. 'I've got this difficult matter, as I think, in its right bearings. We must make a clean breast of it to the husbands, and let *them* take the responsibility.'

'I believe they won't accept it,' observed Mr Sims.

'And I believe they will,' asserted Mr Purling, relapsing into his old habits.

'If they won't,' said the captain, firmly, 'I'm master on board this ship – and, as sure as my name is Thomas Gillop, I'll take the responsibility!'

This courageous declaration settled all difficulties for the time being; and a council was held to decide on future proceedings. It was resolved to remain passive until the next morning, on the last faint chance that a few hours' sleep might compose Mrs Drabble's bewildered memory. The babies were to be moved into the main cabin before the daylight grew bright – or, in other words, before Mrs Smallchild or Mrs Heavysides could identify the infant who had passed the night with her. The doctor and the captain were to be assisted by Mr Purling, Mr Sims, and the first mate, in the capacity of witnesses: and the assembly so constituted was to meet, in consideration of the emergency of the case, at six o'clock in the morning, punctually.

At six o'clock, accordingly, with the weather fine, and the wind still fair, the proceedings began. For the last time Mr Jolly cross-examined Mrs Drabble, assisted by the captain, and supervised by the witnesses. Nothing whatever was elicited from the unfortunate stewardess. The doctor pronounced her confusion to be chronic, and the captain and the witnesses unanimously agreed with him.

The next experiment tried was the revelation of the true state of the case to the husbands.

Mr Smallchild happened, on this occasion, to be 'squaring his accounts' for the morning; and the first articulate words which escaped him in reply to the disclosure, were: 'Devilled biscuit and anchovy paste.' Further perseverance merely elicited an impatient request that they would 'pitch him overboard at once, and the two babies along with him.' Serious remonstrance was tried next, with no better effect. 'Settle it how you like,' said Mr Smallchild, faintly. 'Do you leave it to me, sir, as commander of this vessel?' asked Captain Gillop. (No answer.) 'Nod your head, sir, if you can't speak.' Mr Smallchild nodded his head roundwise on his pillow – and fell asleep. 'Does that count for leave to me to act?' asked Captain Gillop of the witnesses. And the witnesses answered, decidedly, Yes.

The ceremony was then repeated with Simon Heavysides, who responded, as became so intelligent a man, with a proposal of his own for solving the difficulty.

'Captain Gillop and gentlemen,' said the carpenter, with fluent and melancholy politeness, 'I should wish to consider Mr Smallchild before myself in this matter. I am quite willing to part with my baby (whichever he is); and I respectfully propose that Mr Smallchild should take *both* the children, and so make quite sure that he has really got possession of his own son.'

The only immediate objection to this ingenious proposition was started by the doctor; who sarcastically inquired of Simon 'what he thought Mrs Heavysides would say to it?' The carpenter confessed that this consideration had escaped him; and that Mrs Heavysides was only too likely to be an irremovable obstacle in the way of the proposed arrangement. The witnesses all thought so too; and Heavysides and his idea were dismissed together, after Simon had first gratefully expressed his entire readiness to leave it all to the captain.

'Very well, gentlemen,' said Captain Gillop. 'As commander on board, I reckon next after the husbands in the matter of responsibility – I have considered this difficulty in all its bearings – and I'm prepared to deal with it. The Voice of Nature (which you proposed, Mr Purling) has been found to fail. The tossing up for it (which you proposed, Mr Sims) doesn't square altogether with my notions of what's right in a very serious business. No, sir! I've got my own plan; and I'm now about to try it. Follow me below, gentlemen, to the steward's pantry.'

The witnesses looked round on one another in the profoundest astonishment – and followed.

'Pickerel,' said the captain, addressing the steward, 'bring out the scales.'

The scales were of the ordinary kitchen sort, with a tin tray, on one side, to hold the commodity to be weighed, and a stout iron slab on the other, to support the weights. Pickerel placed these scales upon a neat little pantry table, fitted on the ball-and-socket principle, so as to save the breaking of crockery by swinging with the motion of the ship.

'Put a clean duster in the tray,' said the captain. 'Doctor,' he continued, when this had been done, 'shut the doors of the sleeping-berths (for fear of the women hearing anything); and oblige me by bringing those two babies in here.'

'Oh, sir!' exclaimed Mrs Drabble, who had been peeping guiltily into the pantry – 'oh, don't hurt the little dears! If anybody suffers, let it be me!'

'Hold your tongue, if you please, ma'am,' said the captain. 'And keep the secret of these proceedings, if you wish to keep your place. If the ladies ask for their children, say they will have them in ten minutes' time.'

The doctor came in, and set down the clothes-basket cradle on the pantry floor. Captain Gillop immediately put on his spectacles, and closely examined the two unconscious innocents who lay beneath him.

'Six of one, and half-a-dozen of the other,' said the captain. 'I don't see any difference between them. Wait a bit, though! Yes, I do. One's a bald baby. Very good. We'll begin with that one. Doctor, strip the bald baby, and put him in the scales.'

The bald baby protested – in his own language – but in vain. In two minutes he was flat on his back in the tin tray, with the clean duster under him to take the chill off.

'Weigh him accurately, Pickerel,' continued the captain. 'Weigh him, if necessary, to an eighth of an ounce. Gentlemen! watch this proceeding closely: it's a very important one.'

While the steward was weighing and the witnesses were watching, Captain Gillop asked his first mate for the log-book of the ship, and for pen and ink.

'How much, Pickerel?' asked the captain, opening the book.

'Seven pounds, one ounce, and a quarter,' answered the steward.

'Right, gentlemen?' pursued the captain.

'Quite right,' said the witnesses.

'Bald child – distinguished as Number One – weight, seven pounds, one ounce, and a quarter (avoirdupois),' repeated the captain, writing down the entry in the log-book. 'Very good. We'll put the bald baby back now, doctor; and try the hairy one next.'

The hairy one protested – also in his own language – and also in vain.

'How much, Pickerel?' asked the captain.

'Six pounds, fourteen ounces, and three-quarters,' replied the steward.

'Right, gentlemen?' inquired the captain.

'Quite right,' answered the witnesses.

'Hairy child – distinguished as Number Two – weight, six pounds, fourteen ounces, and three-quarters (avoirdupois),' repeated, and wrote, the captain. 'Much obliged to you, Jolly – that will do. When you have got the other baby back in the cradle, tell Mrs Drabble neither of them must be taken out of it, till further orders; and then be so good as to join me and these gentlemen on deck. If anything of a discussion rises up among us, we won't run the risk of being heard in the sleeping-berths.' With these words Captain Gillop led the way on deck, and the first mate followed with the log-book and the pen and ink.

'Now, gentlemen,' began the captain, when the doctor had joined the assembly, 'my first mate will open these proceedings by reading from the log a statement which I have written myself, respecting this business, from beginning to end. If you find it all equally correct with the statement of what the two children weigh, I'll trouble you to sign it, in your quality of witnesses, on the spot.'

The first mate read the narrative, and the witnesses signed it, as perfectly correct. Captain Gillop then cleared his throat, and addressed his expectant audience in these words:

'You'll all agree with me, gentlemen, that justice is justice; and that like must to like. Here's my ship of five hundred tons, fitted with her spars accordingly. Say, she's a schooner of a hundred and fifty tons, the veriest landsman among you, in that case, wouldn't put such masts as these into her. Say, on the other hand, she's an Indiaman of a thousand tons, would our spars (excellent good sticks as they are, gentlemen) be suitable for a vessel of that capacity? Certainly not. A schooner's spars to a schooner, and a ship's spars to a ship, in fit and fair proportion.'

Here the captain paused, to let the opening of his speech sink well into the minds of the audience. The audience encouraged him with the parliamentary cry of 'Hear! hear!' The captain went on:

'In the serious difficulty which now besets us, gentlemen, I take my stand on the principle which I have just stated to you. And my decision is as follows: Let us give the heaviest of the two babies to the heaviest of the two women; and let the lightest then fall, as a matter of course, to the other. In a week's time, if this weather holds, we shall all (please God) be in port; and if there's a better way out of this mess than *my* way, the parsons and lawyers ashore may find it, and welcome.'

With those words the captain closed his oration; and the assembled council immediately sanctioned the proposal submitted to them, with all the unanimity of men who had no idea of their own to set up in opposition.

Mr Jolly was next requested (as the only available authority) to settle the question of weight between Mrs Smallchild and Mrs Heavysides, and decided it, without a moment's hesitation, in favour of the carpenter's wife, on the indisputable ground that she was the tallest and stoutest woman of the two. Thereupon, the bald baby, 'distinguished as Number One,' was taken into Mrs Heavysides' cabin; and the hairy baby, 'distinguished as Number Two,' was accorded to Mrs Smallchild; the Voice of Nature, neither in the one case nor in the other, raising the slightest objection to the captain's principle of distribution. Before seven o'clock, Mr Jolly reported that the mothers and sons, larboard and starboard, were as happy and comfortable as any four people on board ship could possibly wish to be; and the captain thereupon dismissed the council with these parting remarks:

'We'll get the studding-sails on the ship now, gentlemen, and make the best of our way to port. Breakfast, Pickerel, in half an hour, and plenty of it! I doubt if that unfortunate Mrs Drabble has heard the last of this business yet. We must all lend a hand, gentlemen, and pull her through if we can. In other respects, the job's over, so far as we are concerned; and the parsons and lawyers must settle it ashore.'

The parsons and the lawyers did nothing of the sort, for the plain reason that nothing was to be done. In ten days the ship was in port, and the news was broken to the two mothers. Each one of the two adored her baby, after ten days' experience of it – and each one of the two was in Mrs Drabble's condition of not knowing which was which.

Every test was tried. First, the test by the doctor, who only repeated what he had told the captain. Secondly, the test by personal resemblance; which failed in consequence of the light hair, blue eyes, and Roman noses, shared in common by the fathers, and the light hair, blue eyes, and no noses worth mentioning, shared in common by the children. Thirdly, the test of Mrs Drabble, which began and ended in fierce talking on one side, and floods of tears on the other. Fourthly, the test by legal decision, which broke down through the total absence of any instructions for the law to act on. Fifthly, and lastly, the test by appeal to the husbands, which fell to the ground in consequence of the husbands knowing nothing about the matter in hand. The captain's barbarous test by weight, remained the test still – and here am I, a man of the lower order, without a penny to bless myself with, in consequence.

Yes! I was the bald baby of that memorable period. My excess in weight settled my destiny in life. The fathers and mothers on either side kept the babies according to the captain's principle of distribution, in despair of knowing what else to do. Mr Smallchild – who was sharp enough, when not sea-sick – made his fortune. Simon Heavysides persisted in increasing his family, and died in the workhouse.

Judge for yourself (as Mr Jolly might say) how the two boys born at sea have fared in after-life. I, the bald baby, have seen nothing of the hairy baby for years past. He may be short, like Mr Smallchild – but I happen to know that he is wonderfully like Heavysides, deceased, in the face. I may be tall like the carpenter – but I have the Smallchild eyes, hair, and expression, notwithstanding. Make what you can of that! You will find it come in the end to the same thing. Smallchild, junior, prospers in the world, because he weighed six pounds, fourteen ounces, and three-quarters. Heavysides, junior, fails in the world, because he weighed seven pounds, one ounce, and a quarter. Such is destiny, and such is life. I'll never forgive *my* destiny as long as I live. There is my grievance. I wish you good morning.

John Jago's Ghost

Originally appeared in *The New York Fireside Companion*, 29 December
1873 to 19 January 1874 as 'The Dead Alive'. It ran almost
simultaneously in *The Home Journal* (London) as 'John Jago's Ghost'
(27 December 1873 to February 1874), and carried that title when
it was included in *The Frozen Deep and Other Tales* (1874). The story
was written during Collins's stay in New York in November 1873.
In a 'Note in Conclusion' Collins explains the story's origins: 'The
first idea of this little story was suggested to the author by a printed
account of a trial which actually took place, early in the present
century, in the United States. The recently-published narrative
of the case is entitled "The Trial, Confession, and Conviction
of Jesse and Stephen Boorn for the Murder of Russell Colvin,
and the Return of the Man supposed to have been murdered. By
Hon. Leonard Sargeant, Ex-Lieutenant-Governor of Vermont [one
of the defence-lawyers]. (Manchester, Vermont, Journal Book and
Job Office, 1873)." It may not be amiss to add, for the benefit of
incredulous readers, that all the "improbable events" in the story
are matters of fact, taken from the printed narrative. Anything which
"looks like truth" is, in nine cases out of ten, the invention of the
author.' The plot has a (probably accidental) similarity to that of
Dickens's *The Mystery of Edwin Drood*. See Earle Davis, *The Flint and
the Flame* (Columbia: University of Missouri Press, 1963, p. 289).
This is the first of Collins's works with an American setting.

I THE SICK MAN

'Heart all right,' said the doctor. 'Lungs all right. No organic disease that I can discover. Philip Lefrank, don't alarm yourself. You are not going to die yet. The disease you are suffering from is – overwork. The remedy in your case is – rest.'

So the doctor spoke, in my chambers in the Temple (London); having been sent for to see me about half an hour after I had alarmed my clerk by fainting at my desk. I have no wish to intrude myself needlessly on the reader's attention; but it may be necessary to add, in the way of explanation, that I am a 'junior' barrister in good practice. I come from the Channel Island of Jersey. The French spelling of my name (Lefranc) was Anglicised generations since, in the days when the letter 'k' was still used in England at the end of words which now terminate in 'c'. We hold our heads high, nevertheless, as a Jersey family. It is to this day a trial to my father to hear his son described as a member of the English bar.

'Rest!' I repeated, when my medical adviser had done. 'My good friend, are you aware that it is term time? The courts are sitting. Look at the briefs waiting for me on that table! Rest means ruin in my case.'

'And work,' added the doctor, quietly, 'means death.'

I started. He was not trying to frighten me: he was plainly in earnest.

'It is merely a question of time,' he went on. 'You have a fine constitution; you are a young man; but you cannot deliberately overwork your brain, and derange your nervous system, much longer. Go away at once. If you are a good sailor, take a sea-voyage. The ocean-air is the best of all air to build you up again. No: I don't want to write a prescription. I decline to physic you. I have no more to say.'

With those words my medical friend left the room. I was obstinate: I went into court the same day.

The senior counsel in the case on which I was engaged applied to me for some information which it was my duty to give him. To my horror and amazement, I was perfectly unable to collect my ideas: facts and dates all mingled together confusedly in my mind. I was led out of court thoroughly terrified about myself. The next day my briefs went back to the attorneys; and I followed my doctor's advice by taking my passage for America in the first steamer that sailed for New York.

I had chosen the voyage to America in preference to any other trip by sea, with a special object in view. A relative of my mother's had emigrated to the United States many years since, and had thriven there as a farmer. He had given me a general invitation to visit him if I ever crossed the Atlantic. The long period of inaction, under the name of *rest*, to which the doctor's decision had condemned me, could hardly be more pleasantly occupied, as I thought, than by paying a visit to my relation, and seeing what I could of America in that way. After a brief sojourn at New York, I started by railway for the residence of my host – Mr Isaac Meadowcroft, of Morwick Farm.

There are some of the grandest natural prospects on the face of creation in America. There is also to be found in certain States of the Union, by way of wholesome contrast, scenery as flat, as monotonous, and as uninteresting to the traveller, as any that the earth can show. The part of the country in which Mr Meadowcroft's farm was situated fell within this latter category. I looked round me when I stepped out of the railway-carriage on the platform at Morwick Station; and I said to myself, 'If to be cured means, in my case, to be dull, I have accurately picked out the very place for the purpose.'

I look back at those words by the light of later events; and I pronounce them, as you will soon pronounce them, to be the words of an essentially rash man, whose hasty judgment never stopped to consider what surprises time and chance together might have in store for him.

Mr Meadowcroft's eldest son, Ambrose, was waiting at the station to drive me to the farm.

There was no forewarning, in the appearance of Ambrose Meadowcroft, of the strange and terrible events that were to follow my arrival at Morwick. A healthy, handsome young fellow, one of thousands of other healthy, handsome young fellows, said, 'How d'ye do, Mr Lefrank? Glad to see you, sir. Jump into the buggy: the man will look after your portmanteau.' With equally conventional politeness I answered, 'Thank you. How are you all at home?' So we started on the way to the farm.

Our conversation on the drive began with the subjects of agriculture and breeding. I displayed my total ignorance of crops and cattle before we had travelled ten yards on our journey. Ambrose Meadowcroft cast about for another topic, and failed to find it. Upon this I cast about on my side, and asked, at a venture, if I had chosen a convenient time for my visit. The young farmer's stolid brown face instantly brightened. I had evidently hit, haphazard, on an interesting subject.

'You couldn't have chosen a better time,' he said. 'Our house has never been so cheerful as it is now.'

'Have you any visitors staying with you?'

'It's not exactly a visitor. It's a new member of the family who has come to live with us.'

'A new member of the family? May I ask who it is?'

Ambrose Meadowcroft considered before he replied; touched his horse with the whip; looked at me with a certain sheepish hesitation; and suddenly burst out with the truth, in the plainest possible words:

'It's just the nicest girl, sir, you ever saw in your life.'

'Ay, ay! A friend of your sister's, I suppose?'

'A friend? Bless your heart! it's our little American cousin – Naomi Colebrook.'

I vaguely remembered that a younger sister of Mr Meadowcroft's had married an American merchant in the remote past, and had died many years since, leaving an only child. I was now further informed that the father also was dead. In his last moments he had committed his helpless daughter to the compassionate care of his wife's relations at Morwick.

'He was always a speculating man,' Ambrose went on. 'Tried one thing after another, and failed in all. Died, sir, leaving barely enough to bury him. My father was a little doubtful, before she came here, how his American niece would turn out. We are English, you know; and, though we do live in the United States, we stick fast to our English ways and habits. We don't much like American women in general, I can tell you; but, when Naomi made her appearance, she conquered us all. Such a girl! Took her place as one of the family directly. Learnt to make herself useful in the dairy in a week's time. I tell you this – she hasn't been with us quite two months yet; and we wonder already how we ever got on without her!'

Once started on the subject of Naomi Colebrook, Ambrose held to that one topic, and talked on it without intermission. It required no great gift of penetration to discover the impression which the American cousin had produced in this case. The young fellow's enthusiasm communicated itself, in a certain tepid degree, to me. I really felt a mild flutter of anticipation at the prospect of seeing Naomi, when we drew up, towards the close of evening, at the gates of Morwick Farm.

II THE NEW FACES

Immediately on my arrival, I was presented to Mr Meadowcroft, the father.

The old man had become a confirmed invalid, confined by chronic rheumatism to his chair. He received me kindly, and a little wearily as well. His only unmarried daughter (he had long since been left a widower) was in the room, in attendance on her father. She was a melancholy, middle-aged woman, without visible attractions of any sort – one of those persons who appear to accept the obligation of living, under protest, as a burden which they would never have consented to bear if they had only been consulted first. We three had a dreary little interview in a parlour of bare walls; and then I was permitted to go upstairs, and unpack my portmanteau in my own room.

'Supper will be at nine o'clock, sir,' said Miss Meadowcroft.

She pronounced those words as if 'supper' was a form of domestic offence, habitually committed by the men, and endured by the women. I followed the groom up to my room, not over well pleased with my first experience of the farm.

No Naomi, and no romance, thus far!

My room was clean – oppressively clean. I quite longed to see a little dust somewhere. My library was limited to the Bible and the Prayer-book. My view from the window showed me a dead flat in a partial state of cultivation, fading sadly from view in the waning light. Above the head of my spruce white bed hung a scroll, bearing a damnatory quotation from Scripture in emblazoned letters of red and black. The dismal presence of Miss Meadowcroft had passed over my bedroom, and had blighted it. My spirits sank as I looked round me. Supper-time was still an event in the future. I lit the candles, and took from my portmanteau what I firmly believe to have been the first French novel ever produced at Morwick Farm. It was one of the masterly and charming stories of Dumas the elder. In five minutes I was in a new world, and my melancholy room was full of the liveliest French company. The sound of an imperative and uncompromising bell recalled me in due time to the regions of reality. I looked at my watch. Nine o'clock.

Ambrose met me at the bottom of the stairs, and showed me the way to the supper-room.

Mr Meadowcroft's invalid-chair had been wheeled to the head of the table. On his right-hand side sat his sad and silent daughter. She signed to me, with a ghostly solemnity, to take the vacant place on the left of her father. Silas Meadowcroft came in at the same moment, and was presented to me by his brother. There was a strong family likeness between them, Ambrose being the taller and the handsomer man of the two. But there was no marked character in either face. I set them down as men with undeveloped qualities, waiting (the good and evil qualities alike) for time and circumstances to bring them to their full growth.

The door opened again while I was still studying the two brothers, without, I honestly confess, being very favourably impressed by either of them. A new member of the family-circle, who instantly attracted my attention, entered the room.

He was short, spare, and wiry; singularly pale for a person whose life was passed in the country. The face was in other respects, besides this, a striking face to see. As to the lower part, it was covered with a thick black beard and moustache, at a time when shaving was the rule, and beards the rare exception, in America. As to the upper part of the face, it was irradiated by a pair of wild, glittering brown eyes, the expression of which suggested to me that there was something not quite right with the man's mental balance. A perfectly sane person in all his sayings and doings, so far as I could see, there was still something in those wild brown eyes which suggested to me, that, under exceptionally trying circumstances, he might surprise his oldest friends by acting in some exceptionally violent or foolish way. 'A little cracked' – that, in the popular phrase, was my impression of the stranger who now made his appearance in the supper-room.

Mr Meadowcroft the elder, having not spoken one word thus far, himself introduced the new-comer to me, with a side-glance at his sons, which had something like defiance in it – a glance which, as I was sorry to notice, was returned with a similar appearance of defiance by the two young men.

'Philip Lefrank, this is my overlooker, Mr Jago,' said the old man, formally presenting us. 'John Jago, this is my young relative by marriage, Mr Lefrank. He is not well: he has come over the ocean for rest, and change of scene. Mr Jago is an American, Philip. I hope you have no prejudice against Americans. Make acquaintance with Mr Jago. Sit together.' He cast another dark look at his sons; and the sons again returned it. They pointedly drew back from John Jago as he approached the empty chair next to me, and moved round to the opposite side of the table. It was plain that the man with the beard stood high in the father's favour, and that he was cordially disliked for that or for some other reason by the sons.

The door opened once more. A young lady quietly joined the party at the supper-table.

Was the young lady Naomi Colebrook? I looked at Ambrose, and saw the answer in his face. Naomi at last!

A pretty girl, and, so far as I could judge by appearances, a good girl too. Describing her generally, I may say that she had a small head, well carried, and well set on her shoulders; bright, grey eyes, that looked at you honestly, and meant what they looked; a trim, slight little figure – too slight for our English notions of beauty; a strong American accent; and (a rare thing in America) a pleasantly-toned voice, which made the accent agreeable to English ears. Our first impressions of people are, in nine cases out of ten, the right impressions. I liked Naomi Colebrook at first sight; liked her pleasant smile; liked her hearty shake of the hand when we were presented to each other. 'If I get on well with nobody else in this house,' I thought to myself, 'I shall certainly get on well with *you*.'

For once in a way, I proved a true prophet. In the atmosphere of smouldering enmities at Morwick Farm, the pretty American girl and I remained firm and true friends from first to last.

Ambrose made room for Naomi to sit between his brother and himself. She changed colour for a moment, and looked at him, with a pretty, reluctant tenderness, as she took her chair. I strongly suspected the young farmer of squeezing her hand privately, under cover of the tablecloth.

The supper was not a merry one. The only cheerful conversation was the conversation across the table between Naomi and me.

For some incomprehensible reason, John Jago seemed to be ill at ease in the presence of his young countrywoman. He looked up at Naomi doubtingly from his plate, and looked down again slowly with a frown. When I addressed him, he answered constrainedly. Even when he spoke to Mr Meadowcroft, he was still on his guard – on his guard against the two young men, as I fancied by the direction which his eyes took on these occasions. When we began our meal, I had noticed for the first time that Silas Meadowcroft's left hand was strapped up with surgical plaster; and I now further observed that John Jago's wandering brown eyes, furtively looking at everybody round the table in turn, looked with a curious cynical scrutiny at the young man's injured hand.

By way of making my first evening at the farm all the more embarrassing to me as a stranger, I discovered before long that the father and sons were talking indirectly *at* each other, through Mr Jago and through me. When old Mr Meadowcroft spoke disparagingly to his overlooker of some past mistake made in the cultivation of the arable land of the farm, old Mr Meadowcroft's eyes pointed the application of his hostile criticism straight in the direction of his two sons. When the two sons seized a stray remark of mine about animals in general, and applied it satirically to the mismanagement of sheep and oxen in particular, they looked at John Jago, while they talked to me. On occasions of this sort – and they happened frequently – Naomi struck in resolutely at the right moment, and turned the talk to some harmless topic. Every time she took a prominent part in this way in keeping the peace, melancholy Miss Meadowcroft looked slowly round at her in stern and silent disparagement of her interference. A more dreary and more disunited family-party I never sat at the table with. Envy, hatred, malice, and uncharitableness are never so essentially detestable to my mind as when they are animated by a sense of propriety, and work under the surface. But for my interest in Naomi, and my other interest in the little love-looks which I now and then surprised passing between her and Ambrose, I should never have sat through that supper. I should certainly have taken refuge in my French novel and my own room.

At last the unendurably long meal, served with ostentatious profusion, was at an end. Miss Meadowcroft rose with her ghostly solemnity, and granted me my dismissal in these words:

'We are early people at the farm, Mr Lefrank. I wish you good-night.'

She laid her bony hands on the back of Mr Meadowcroft's invalid-chair, cut him short in his farewell salutation to me, and wheeled him out to his bed as if she were wheeling him out to his grave.

'Do you go to your room immediately, sir? If not, may I offer you a cigar? – provided the young gentlemen will permit it.'

So, picking his words with painful deliberation, and pointing his reference to 'the young gentlemen' with one sardonic sidelook at them, Mr John Jago performed the duties of hospitality on his side. I excused myself from accepting the cigar. With studied politeness, the man of the glittering brown eyes wished me a good night's rest, and left the room.

Ambrose and Silas both approached me hospitably, with their open cigar-cases in their hands.

'You were quite right to say "No,"' Ambrose began. 'Never smoke with John Jago. His cigars will poison you.'

'And never believe a word John Jago says to you,' added Silas. 'He is the greatest liar in America, let the other be whom he may.'

Naomi shook her forefinger reproachfully at them, as if the two sturdy young farmers had been two children.

'What will Mr Lefrank think?' she said, 'if you talk in that way of a person whom your father respects and trusts? Go and smoke. I am ashamed of both of you.'

Silas slunk away without a word of protest. Ambrose stood his ground, evidently bent on making his peace with Naomi before he left her.

Seeing that I was in the way, I walked aside towards a glass door at the lower end of the room. The door opened on the trim little farm-garden, bathed at that moment in lovely moonlight. I stepped out to enjoy the scene, and found my way to a seat under an elm-tree. The grand repose of Nature had never looked so unutterably solemn and beautiful as it now appeared, after what I had seen and heard inside the house. I understood, or thought I understood, the sad despair of humanity which led men into monasteries in the old time. The misanthropical side of my nature (where is the sick man who is not conscious of that side of him?) was fast getting the upper hand of me – when I felt a light touch laid on my shoulder, and found myself reconciled to my species once more by Naomi Colebrook.

III THE MOONLIGHT-MEETING

'I want to speak to you,' Naomi began. 'You don't think ill of me for following you out here? We are not accustomed to stand much on ceremony in America.'

'You are quite right in America. Pray sit down.'

She seated herself by my side, looking at me frankly and fearlessly by the light of the moon.

'You are related to the family here,' she resumed, 'and I am related too. I guess I may say to *you* what I couldn't say to a stranger. I am right glad you have come here, Mr Lefrank; and for a reason, sir, which you don't suspect.'

'Thank you for the compliment you pay me, Miss Colebrook, whatever the reason may be.'

She took no notice of my reply: she steadily pursued her own train of thought.

'I guess you may do some good, sir, in this wretched house,' the girl went on, with her eyes still earnestly fixed on my face. 'There is no love, no trust, no peace at Morwick Farm. They want somebody here – except Ambrose: don't think ill of Ambrose; he is only thoughtless – I say, the rest of them want somebody here to make them ashamed of their hard hearts, and their horrid, false, envious ways. You are a gentleman; you know more than they know: they can't help themselves, they must look up to *you*. Try, Mr Lefrank, when you have the opportunity – pray try, sir, to make peace among them. You heard what went on at supper-time; and you were disgusted with it. Oh, yes, you were! I saw you frown to yourself; and I know what *that* means in you Englishmen.'

There was no choice but to speak one's mind plainly to Naomi. I acknowledged the impression which had been produced on me at supper-time just as plainly as I have acknowledged it in these pages. Naomi nodded her head in undisguised approval of my candour.

'That will do; that's speaking out,' she said. 'But – oh, my! you put it a deal too mildly, sir, when you say the men don't seem to be on friendly terms together here. They hate each other. That's the word, Mr Lefrank – hate; bitter, bitter, bitter hate!' She clenched her little fists; she shook them vehemently, by way of adding emphasis to her last words; and then she suddenly remembered Ambrose. 'Except Ambrose,' she added, opening her hand again, and laying it very earnestly on my arm. 'Don't go and misjudge Ambrose, sir. There is no harm in poor Ambrose.'

The girl's innocent frankness was really irresistible.

'Should I be altogether wrong,' I asked, 'If I guessed that you were a little partial to Ambrose?'

An Englishwoman would have felt, or would at least have assumed, some little hesitation at replying to my question. Naomi did not hesitate for an instant.

'You are quite right, sir,' she said, with the most perfect composure. 'If things go well, I mean to marry Ambrose.'

'If things go well,' I repeated. 'What does that mean? Money?'

She shook her head.

'It means a fear that I have in my own mind,' she answered – 'a fear, Mr Lefrank, of matters taking a bad turn among the men here – the wicked, hard-hearted, unfeeling men. I don't mean Ambrose, sir: I mean his brother Silas, and John Jago. Did you notice Silas's hand? John Jago did that, sir, with a knife.'

'By accident?' I asked.

'On purpose,' she answered. 'In return for a blow.'

This plain revelation of the state of things at Morwick Farm rather staggered me. Blows and knives under the rich and respectable roof-tree of old Mr Meadowcroft! – blows and knives, not among the labourers, but among the masters! My first impression was like *your* first impression, no doubt. I could hardly believe it.

'Are you sure of what you say?' I enquired.

'I have it from Ambrose. Ambrose would never deceive me. Ambrose knows all about it.'

My curiosity was powerfully excited. To what sort of household had I rashly voyaged across the ocean in search of rest and quiet?

'May I know all about it too?' I said.

'Well, I will try and tell you what Ambrose told me. But you must promise me one thing first, sir. Promise you won't go away and leave us when you know the whole truth. Shake hands on it, Mr Lefrank; come, shake hands on it.'

There was no resisting her fearless frankness. I shook hands on it. Naomi entered on her narrative the moment I had given her my pledge, without wasting a word by way of preface.

'When you are shown over the farm here,' she began, 'you will see that it is really two farms in one. On this side of it, as we look from under this tree, they raise crops: on the other side – on much the larger half of the land, mind – they raise cattle. When Mr Meadowcroft got too old and too sick to look after his farm himself, the boys (I mean Ambrose and Silas) divided the work between them. Ambrose looked after the crops, and Silas after the cattle. Things didn't go well, somehow, under their management. I can't tell you why. I am only sure Ambrose was not in fault. The old man got more and more dissatisfied, especially about his beasts. His pride is in his beasts. Without saying a word to the boys, he looked about privately (*I* think he was wrong in that, sir; don't you?) – he looked about privately for help; and, in an evil hour, he heard of John Jago. Do you like John Jago, Mr Lefrank?'

'So far, no. I don't like him.'

'Just my sentiments, sir. But I don't know: it's likely we may be wrong. There's nothing against John Jago, except that he is so odd in his ways. They do say he wears all that nasty hair on his face (I hate hair on a man's face) on account of a vow he made when he lost his wife. Don't you think, Mr Lefrank, a man must be a little mad who shows his grief at losing his wife by vowing that he will never shave himself again? Well, that's what they do say John Jago vowed. Perhaps it's a lie. People are such liars here! Anyway, it's truth (the boys themselves confess *that*), when John came to the farm, he came with a first-rate character. The old father here isn't easy to please; and he pleased the old father. Yes, that's so. Mr Meadowcroft don't like my countrymen in general. He's like his sons – English, bitter English, to the marrow of his bones. Somehow, in spite of that, John Jago got round him; maybe because John does certainly know his business. Oh, yes! Cattle and crops, John knows his business. Since he's been overlooker, things have prospered as they didn't prosper in the time of the boys. Ambrose owned as much to me himself. Still, sir, it's hard to be set aside for a stranger; isn't it? John gives the orders now. The boys do the work; but they have no voice in it when John and the old man put their heads together over the business of the farm. I have been long in telling you of it, sir; but now you know how the envy and the hatred grew among the men, before my time. Since I have been here, things seem to get worse and worse. There's hardly a day goes by that hard words don't pass between the boys and John, or the boys and their father. The old man has an aggravating way, Mr Lefrank – a nasty way, as we do call it – of taking John Jago's part. Do speak to him about it when you get the chance. The main blame of the quarrel between Silas and John the other day lies at his door, I think. I don't want to excuse Silas, either. It was brutal of him – though he *is* Ambrose's brother – to strike John, who is the smaller and weaker man of the two. But it was worse than brutal in John, to out with his knife, and try to stab Silas. Oh, he did it! If Silas had not caught the knife in his hand (his hand's awfully cut, I can tell you; I dressed it myself), it might have ended, for anything I know, in murder—'

She stopped as the word passed her lips, looked back over her shoulder, and started violently.

I looked where my companion was looking. The dark figure of a man was standing, watching us, in the shadow of the elm-tree. I rose directly to approach him. Naomi recovered her self-possession, and checked me before I could interfere.

'Who are you?' she asked, turning sharply towards the stranger. 'What do you want there?'

The man stepped out from the shadow into the moonlight, and stood revealed to us as John Jago.

'I hope I am not intruding?' he said, looking hard at me.

'What do you want?' Naomi repeated.

'I don't wish to disturb you, or to disturb this gentleman,' he proceeded. 'When you are quite at leisure, Miss Naomi, you would be doing me a favour if you would permit me to say a few words to you in private.'

He spoke with the most scrupulous politeness; trying, and trying vainly, to conceal some strong agitation which was in possession of him. His wild brown eyes – wilder than ever in the moonlight – rested entreatingly, with a strange underlying expression of despair, on Naomi's face. His hands, clasped tightly in front of him, trembled incessantly. Little as I liked the man, he did really impress me as a pitiable object at that moment.

'Do you mean that you want to speak to me to-night?' Naomi asked, in undisguised surprise.

'Yes, miss, if you please, at you leisure and at Mr Lefrank's.'

Naomi hesitated.

'Won't it keep till to-morrow?' she said.

'I shall be away on farm-business to-morrow, miss, for the whole day. Please to give me a few minutes this evening.' He advanced a step towards her: his voice faltered, and dropped timidly to a whisper. 'I really have something to say to you, Miss Naomi. It would be a kindness on your part – a very, very great kindness – if you will let me say it before I rest to-night.'

I rose again to resign my place to him. Once more Naomi checked me.

'No,' she said. 'Don't stir.' She addressed John Jago very reluctantly: 'If you are so much in earnest about it, Mr John, I suppose it must be. I can't guess what *you* can possibly have to say to me which cannot be said before a third person. However, it wouldn't be civil, I suppose, to say "No" in my place. You know it's my business to wind up the hall-clock at ten every night. If you choose to come and help me, the chances are that we shall have the hall to ourselves. Will that do?'

'Not in the hall, miss, if you will excuse me.'

'Not in the hall!'

'And not in the house either, if I may make so bold.'

'What do you mean?' She turned impatiently, and appealed to me. 'Do *you* understand him?'

John Jago signed to me imploringly to let him answer for himself.

'Bear with me, Miss Naomi,' he said. 'I think I can make you understand me. There are eyes on the watch, and ears on the watch, in the house; and there are some footsteps – I won't say whose – so soft, that no person can hear them.'

The last allusion evidently made itself understood. Naomi stopped him before he could say more.

'Well, where is it to be?' she asked, resignedly. 'Will the garden do, Mr John?'

'Thank you kindly, miss: the garden will do.' He pointed to a gravel-walk beyond us, bathed in the full flood of the moonlight. 'There,' he said, 'where we can see all round us, and be sure that nobody is listening. At ten o'clock.' He paused, and addressed himself to me. 'I beg to apologise, sir, for intruding myself on your conversation. Please to excuse me.'

His eyes rested with a last, anxious, pleading look on Naomi's face. He bowed to us, and melted away into the shadow of the tree. The distant sound of a door, closed softly, came to us through the stillness of the night. John Jago had re-entered the house.

Now that he was out of hearing, Naomi spoke to me very earnestly:

'Don't suppose, sir, I have any secrets with *him*,' she said. 'I know no more than you do what he wants with me. I have half a mind not to keep the appointment. It's close on ten now. What would you do in my place?'

'Having made the appointment,' I answered, 'it seems to be due to yourself to keep it. If you feel the slightest alarm, I will wait in another part of the garden, so that I can hear if you call me.'

She received my proposal with a saucy toss of the head, and a smile of pity for my ignorance.

'You are a stranger, Mr Lefrank, or you would never talk to me in that way. In America, we don't do the men the honour of letting them alarm us. In America, the women take care of themselves. He has got my promise to meet him, as you say; and I must keep my promise. Only think,' she added, speaking more to herself than to me, 'of John Jago finding out Miss Meadowcroft's nasty, sly, underhand ways in the house! Most men would never have noticed her!'

I was completely taken by surprise. Sad and severe Miss Meadowcroft a listener and a spy! What next at Morwick Farm?

'Was that hint at the watchful eyes and ears, and the soft footsteps, really an allusion to Mr Meadowcroft's daughter?' I asked.

'Of course it was. Ah! she has imposed on you as she imposes on everybody else. The false wretch! She is secretly at the bottom of half the bad feeling among the men. I am certain of it – she keeps Mr Meadowcroft's mind bitter towards the boys. Old as she is, Mr Lefrank, and ugly as she is, she wouldn't object (if she could only make him ask her) to be John Jago's second wife. No, sir; and she wouldn't break her heart if the boys were not left a stick or a stone on the farm when the father dies. I have watched her, and I know it. Ah! I could tell you such things. But there's no time now – there's ten o'clock striking! we must say goodnight. I am right glad I have spoken to you, sir. I say again, at parting, what I have said already: Use your influence, pray use your influence, to soften them, and to make them ashamed of themselves, in this wicked house. We will have more talk about what you can do, to-morrow, when you are shown over the farm. Say goodbye now; I must keep my appointment. Look! here is John Jago stealing out again in the shadow of the tree! Good-night, friend Lefrank; and pleasant dreams.'

With one hand she took mine, and pressed it cordially: with the other she pushed me away without ceremony in the direction of the house. A charming girl! – an irresistible girl! I was nearly as bad as the boys. I declare, *I* almost hated John Jago, too, as we crossed each other in the shadow of the tree.

Arrived at the glass door, I stopped, and looked back at the gravel-walk.

They had met. I saw the two shadowy figures slowly pacing backwards and forwards in the moonlight, the woman a little in advance of the man. What was he saying to her? Why was he so anxious that not a word of it should be heard?

Our presentiments are sometimes, in certain rare cases, the faithful prophecy of the future. A vague distrust of that moonlight-meeting stealthily took a hold on my mind. 'Will mischief come of it?' I asked myself, as I closed the door and entered the house.

Mischief *did* come of it. You shall hear how.

IV THE BEECHEN STICK

Persons of sensitive nervous temperament, sleeping for the first time in a strange house, and in a bed that is new to them, must make up their minds to pass a wakeful night. My first night at Morwick Farm was no exception to this rule. The little sleep I had was broken and disturbed by dreams. Towards six o'clock in the morning my bed became unendurable to me. The sun was shining in brightly at the window. I determined to try the reviving influence of a stroll in the fresh morning air.

Just as I got out of bed, I heard footsteps and voices under my window.

The footsteps stopped, and the voices became recognisable. I had passed the night with my window open: I was able, without exciting notice from below, to look out.

The persons beneath me were Silas Meadowcroft, John Jago, and three strangers, whose dress and appearance indicated plainly enough that they were labourers on the farm. Silas was swinging a stout beechen stick in his hand, and was speaking to Jago, coarsely and insolently enough, of his moonlight-meeting with Naomi on the previous night.

'Next time you go courting a young lady in secret,' said Silas, 'make sure that the moon goes down first, or wait for a cloudy sky. You were seen in the garden, Master Jago; and you may as well tell us the truth for once in a way. Did you find her open to persuasion, sir? Did she say "Yes?"'

John Jago kept his temper.

'If you must have your joke, Mr Silas,' he said, quietly and firmly, 'be pleased to joke on some other subject. You are quite wrong, sir, in what you suppose to have passed between the young lady and me.'

Silas turned about, and addressed himself ironically to the three labourers.

'You hear him, boys? He can't tell the truth, try him as you may. He wasn't making love to Naomi in the garden last night – oh, dear, no! He has had one wife already; and he knows better than to take the yoke on his shoulders for the second time!'

Greatly to my surprise, John Jago met this clumsy jesting with a formal and serious reply.

'You are quite right, sir,' he said. 'I have no intention of marrying for the second time. What I was saying to Miss Naomi doesn't matter to you. It was not at all what you choose to suppose; it was something of quite another kind, with which you have no concern. Be pleased to understand once for all, Mr Silas, that not so much as the thought of making love to the young lady has ever entered my head. I respect her; I admire her good qualities: but if she was the only woman left in the world, and if I was a much younger man than I am, I should never think of asking her to be my wife.' He burst out suddenly into a harsh, uneasy laugh. 'No, no! not my style, Mr Silas – not my style!'

Something in those words, or in his manner of speaking them, appeared to exasperate Silas. He dropped his clumsy irony, and addressed himself directly to John Jago in a tone of savage contempt.

'Not your style?' he repeated. 'Upon my soul, that's a cool way of putting it, for a man in your place! What do you mean by calling her "not your style"? You impudent beggar! Naomi Colebrook is meat for your master!'

John Jago's temper began to give way at last. He approached defiantly a step or two nearer to Silas Meadowcroft.

'Who is my master?' he asked.

'Ambrose will show you, if you go to him,' answered the other. 'Naomi is *his* sweetheart, not mine. Keep out of his way, if you want to keep a whole skin on your bones.'

John Jago cast one of his sardonic side-looks at the farmer's wounded left hand. 'Don't forget your own skin, Mr Silas, when you threaten mine! I have set my mark on you once, sir. Let me by on my business, or I may mark you for a second time.'

Silas lifted his beechen stick. The labourers, roused to some rude sense of the serious turn which the quarrel was taking, got between the two men, and parted them. I had been hurriedly dressing myself while the altercation was proceeding; and I now ran downstairs to try what my influence could do towards keeping the peace at Morwick Farm.

The war of angry words was still going on when I joined the men outside.

'Be off with you on your business, you cowardly hound!' I heard Silas say. 'Be off with you to the town! and take care you don't meet Ambrose on the way!'

'Take *you* care you don't feel my knife again before I go!' cried the other man.

Silas made a desperate effort to break away from the labourers who were holding him.

'Last time you only felt my fist!' he shouted. 'Next time you shall feel *this*!'

He lifted the stick as he spoke. I stepped up, and snatched it out of his hand.

'Mr Silas,' I said, 'I am an invalid, and I am going out for a walk. Your stick will be useful to me. I beg leave to borrow it.'

The labourers burst out laughing. Silas fixed his eyes on me with a stare of angry surprise. John Jago, immediately recovering his self-possession, took off his hat, and made me a deferential bow.

'I had no idea, Mr Lefrank, that we were disturbing you,' he said. 'I am very much ashamed of myself, sir. I beg to apologise.'

'I accept your apology, Mr Jago,' I answered, 'on the understanding that you, as the older man, will set the example of forbearance, if your temper is tried on any future occasion as it has been tried to-day. And I have further to request,' I added, addressing myself to Silas, 'that you will do me a favour, as your father's guest. The next time your good spirits lead you into making jokes at Mr Jago's expense, don't carry them quite so far. I am sure you meant no harm, Mr Silas. Will you gratify me by saying so yourself? I want to see you and Mr Jago shake hands.'

John Jago instantly held out his hand, with an assumption of good feeling which was a little over-acted, to my thinking. Silas Meadowcroft made no advance of the same friendly sort on his side.

'Let him go about his business,' said Silas. 'I won't waste any more words on him, Mr Lefrank, to please *you*. But (saving your presence) I'm damned if I take his hand!'

Further persuasion was plainly useless, addressed to such a man as this. Silas gave me no further opportunity of remonstrating with him, even if I had been inclined to do so. He turned about in sulky silence, and, retracing his steps along the path, disappeared round the corner of the house. The labourers withdrew next, in different directions, to begin the day's work. John Jago and I were alone.

I left it to the man of the wild brown eyes to speak first.

'In half an hour's time, sir,' he said, 'I shall be going on business to Narrabee, our market-town here. Can I take any letters to the post for you? or is there anything else that I can do in the town?'

I thanked him, and declined both proposals. He made me another deferential bow, and withdrew into the house. I mechanically followed the path, in the direction which Silas had taken before me.

Turning the corner of the house, and walking on for a little way, I found myself at the entrance to the stables, and face to face with Silas Meadowcroft once more. He had his elbows on the gate of the yard, swinging it slowly backwards and forwards, and turning and twisting a straw between his teeth. When he saw me approaching him, he advanced a step from the gate, and made an effort to excuse himself, with a very ill grace.

'No offence, mister. Ask me what you will besides, and I'll do it for you. But don't ask me to shake hands with John Jago; I hate him too badly for that. If I touched him with one hand, sir, I tell you this, I should throttle him with the other!'

'That's your feeling towards the man, Mr Silas, is it?'

'That's my feeling, Mr Lefrank; and I'm not ashamed of it, either.'

'Is there any such place as a church in your neighbourhood, Mr Silas?'

'Of course there is.'

'And do you ever go to it?'

'Of course I do.'

'At long intervals, Mr Silas?'

'Every Sunday, sir, without fail.'

Some third person behind me burst out laughing; some third person had been listening to our talk. I turned round, and discovered Ambrose Meadowcroft.

'I understand the drift of your catechism, though my brother doesn't,' he said. 'Don't be hard on Silas, sir. He isn't the only Christian who leaves his Christianity in the pew when he goes out of church. You will never make us friends with John Jago, try as you may. Why, what have you got there, Mr Lefrank? May I die if it isn't my stick! I have been looking for it everywhere!'

The thick beechen stick had been feeling uncomfortably heavy in my invalid hand for some time past. There was no sort of need for my keeping it any longer. John Jago was going away to Narrabee, and Silas Meadowcroft's savage temper was subdued to a sulky repose. I handed the stick back to Ambrose. He laughed as he took it from me.

'You can't think how strange it feels, Mr Lefrank, to be out without one's stick,' he said. 'A man gets used to his stick, sir; doesn't he? Are you ready for your breakfast?'

'Not just yet. I thought of taking a little walk first.'

'All right, sir. I wish I could go with you; but I have got my work to do this morning, and Silas has his work too. If you go back by the way you came, you will find yourself in the garden. If you want to go further, the wicket-gate at the end will lead you into the lane.'

Through sheer thoughtlessness, I did a very foolish thing. I turned back as I was told, and left the brothers together at the gate of the stable-yard.

V THE NEWS FROM NARRABEE

Arrived at the garden, a thought struck me. The cheerful speech and easy manner of Ambrose plainly indicated that he was ignorant thus far of the quarrel which had taken place under my window. Silas might confess to having taken his brother's stick, and might mention whose head he had threatened with it. It was not only useless, but undesirable, that Ambrose should know of the quarrel. I retraced my steps to the stable-yard. Nobody was at the gate. I called alternately to Silas and to Ambrose. Nobody answered. The brothers had gone away to their work.

Returning to the garden, I heard a pleasant voice wishing me 'Good morning.' I looked round. Naomi Colebrook was standing at one of the lower windows of the farm. She had her working-apron on, and she was industriously brightening the knives for the breakfast-table, on an old-fashioned board. A sleek black cat balanced himself on her shoulder, watching the flashing motion of the knife as she passed it rapidly to and fro on the leather-covered surface of the board.

'Come here,' she said: 'I want to speak to you.'

I noticed, as I approached, that her pretty face was clouded and anxious. She pushed the cat irritably off her shoulder: she welcomed me with only the faint reflection of her bright, customary smile.

'I have seen John Jago,' she said. 'He has been hinting at something which he says happened under your bedroom-window this morning. When I begged him to explain himself he only answered, 'Ask Mr Lefrank: I must be off to Narrabee.' What does it mean? Tell me right away, sir! I'm out of temper, and I can't wait!'

Except that I made the best instead of the worst of it, I told her what had happened under my window as plainly as I have told it here. She put down the knife that she was cleaning, and folded her hands before her, thinking.

'I wish I had never given John Jago that meeting,' she said. 'When a man asks anything of a woman, the woman, I find, mostly repents it if she says "Yes."'

She made that quaint reflection with a very troubled brow. The moonlight-meeting had left some unwelcome remembrances in her mind. I saw that as plainly as I saw Naomi herself.

What had John Jago said to her? I put the question with all needful delicacy, making my apologies beforehand.

'I should like to tell *you*,' she began, with a strong emphasis on the last word.

There she stopped. She turned pale; then suddenly flushed again to the deepest red. She took up the knife once more, and went on cleaning it as industriously as ever.

'I mustn't tell you,' she resumed, with her head down over the knife. 'I have promised not to tell anybody. That's the truth. Forget all about it, sir, as soon as you can. Hush! here's the spy who saw us last night on the walk, and who told Silas!'

Dreary Miss Meadowcroft opened the kitchen-door. She carried an ostentatiously large Prayer Book; and she looked at Naomi as only a jealous woman of middle age *can* look at a younger and prettier woman than herself.

'Prayers, Miss Colebrook,' she said, in her sourest manner. She paused, and noticed me standing under the window. 'Prayers, Mr Lefrank,' she added, with a look of devout pity, directed exclusively to my address.

'We will follow you directly, Miss Meadowcroft,' said Naomi.

'I have no desire to intrude on your secrets, Miss Colebrook.'

With that acrid answer, our priestess took herself and her Prayer Book out of the kitchen. I joined Naomi, entering the room by the garden-door. She met me eagerly.

'I am not quite easy about something,' she said. 'Did you tell me that you left Ambrose and Silas together?'

'Yes.'

'Suppose Silas tells Ambrose of what happened this morning?'

The same idea, as I have already mentioned, had occurred to my mind. I did my best to reassure Naomi.

'Mr Jago is out of the way,' I replied. 'You and I can easily put things right in his absence.'

She took my arm.

'Come in to prayers,' she said. 'Ambrose will be there, and I shall find an opportunity of speaking to him.'

Neither Ambrose nor Silas was in the breakfast-room when we entered it. After waiting vainly for ten minutes, Mr Meadowcroft told his daughter to read the prayers. Miss Meadowcroft read, thereupon, in the tone of an injured woman taking the throne of mercy by storm, and insisting on her rights. Breakfast followed; and still the brothers were absent. Miss Meadowcroft looked at her father, and said, 'From bad to worse, sir. What did I tell you?' Naomi instantly applied the antidote: 'The boys are no doubt detained over their work, uncle.' She turned to me. 'You want to see the farm, Mr Lefrank. Come and help me to find the boys.'

For more than an hour we visited one part of the farm after another, without discovering the missing men. We found them at last near the outskirts of a small wood, sitting, talking together, on the trunk of a felled tree.

Silas rose as we approached, and walked away, without a word of greeting or apology, into the wood. As he got on his feet I noticed that his brother whispered something in his ear; and I heard him answer, 'All right!'

'Ambrose, does that mean you have something to keep a secret from us?' asked Naomi, approaching her lover with a smile. 'Is Silas ordered to hold his tongue?'

Ambrose kicked sulkily at the loose stones lying about him. I noticed, with a certain surprise, that his favourite stick was not in his hand, and was not lying near him.

'Business,' he said, in answer to Naomi, not very graciously – 'business between Silas and me. That's what it means, if you must know.'

Naomi went on, woman-like, with her questions, heedless of the reception which they might meet with from an irritated man.

'Why were you both away at prayers and breakfast-time?' she asked next.

'We had too much to do,' Ambrose gruffly replied, 'and we were too far from the house.'

'Very odd,' said Naomi. 'This has never happened before, since I have been at the farm.'

'Well, live and learn. It has happened now.'

The tone in which he spoke would have warned any man to let him alone. But warnings which speak by implication only are thrown away on women. The woman, having still something in her mind to say, said it.

'Have you seen anything of John Jago this morning?'

The smouldering ill temper of Ambrose burst suddenly – why, it was impossible to guess – into a flame.

'How many more questions am I to answer?' he broke out, violently. 'Are you the parson, putting me through my catechism? I have seen nothing of John Jago and I have got my work to go on with. Will that do for you?'

He turned with an oath, and followed his brother into the wood. Naomi's bright eyes looked up at me, flashing with indignation.

'What does he mean, Mr Lefrank, by speaking to me in that way? Rude brute! How dare he do it?' She paused: her voice, look, and manner suddenly changed. 'This has never happened before, sir. Has anything gone wrong? I declare, I shouldn't know Ambrose again, he is so changed. Say, how does it strike you?'

I still made the best of a bad case.

'Something has upset his temper,' I said. 'The merest trifle, Miss Colebrook, upsets a man's temper sometimes. I speak as a man, and I know it. Give him time, and he will make his excuses, and all will be well again.'

My presentation of the case entirely failed to reassure my pretty companion. We went back to the house. Dinner-time came, and the brothers appeared. Their father spoke to them of their absence from morning prayers – with needless severity, as I thought. They resented the reproof with needless indignation on their side, and left the room. A sour smile of satisfaction showed itself on Miss Meadowcroft's thin lips. She looked at her father; then raised her eyes sadly to the ceiling, and said, 'We can only pray for them, sir.'

Naomi disappeared after dinner. When I saw her again, she had some news for me.

'I have been with Ambrose,' she said, 'and he has begged my pardon. We have made it up, Mr Lefrank. Still – still—'

'Still – *what*, Miss Naomi?'

'He is not like himself, sir. He denies it; but I can't help thinking he is hiding something from me.'

The day wore on: the evening came. I returned to my French novel. But not even Dumas himself could keep my attention to the story. What else I was thinking of I cannot say. Why I was out of spirits I am unable to explain. I wished myself back in England: I took a blind, unreasoning hatred to Morwick Farm.

Nine o'clock struck; and we all assembled again at supper, with the exception of John Jago. He was expected back to supper; and we waited for him a quarter of an hour, by Mr Meadowcroft's own directions. John Jago never appeared.

The night wore on, and still the absent man failed to return. Miss Meadowcroft volunteered to sit up for him. Naomi eyed her, a little maliciously I must own, as the two women parted for the night. I withdrew to my room; and again I was unable to sleep. When sunrise came, I went out, as before, to breathe the morning air.

On the staircase I met Miss Meadowcroft ascending to her own room. Not a curl of her stiff grey hair was disarranged: nothing about the impenetrable woman betrayed that she had been watching through the night.

'Has Mr Jago not returned?' I asked.

Miss Meadowcroft slowly shook her head, and frowned at me.

'We are in the hands of Providence, Mr Lefrank. Mr Jago must have been detained for the night at Narrabee.'

The daily routine of the meals resumed its unalterable course. Breakfast-time came and dinner-time came, and no John Jago darkened the doors of Morwick Farm. Mr Meadowcroft and his daughter consulted together, and determined to send in search of the missing man. One of the more intelligent of the labourers was despatched to Narrabee to make enquiries.

The man returned late in the evening, bringing startling news to the farm. He had visited all the inns and all the places of business resort in Narrabee; he had made endless enquiries in every direction, with this result – no one had set eyes on John Jago. Everybody declared that John Jago had not entered the town.

We all looked at each other, excepting the two brothers, who were seated together in a dark corner of the room. The conclusion appeared to be inevitable. John Jago was a lost man.

VI THE LIME-KILN

Mr Meadowcroft was the first to speak.

'Somebody must find John,' he said.

'Without losing a moment,' added his daughter.

Ambrose suddenly stepped out of the dark corner of the room.

'*I* will enquire,' he said.

Silas followed him.

'I will go with you,' he added.

Mr Meadowcroft interposed his authority.

'One of you will be enough; for the present, at least. Go you, Ambrose. Your brother may be wanted later. If any accident has happened (which God forbid), we may have to enquire in more than one direction. Silas, you will stay at the farm.'

The brothers withdrew together – Ambrose to prepare for his journey, Silas to saddle one of the horses for him. Naomi slipped out after them. Left in company with Mr Meadowcroft and his daughter (both devoured by anxiety about the missing man, and both trying to conceal it under an assumption of devout resignation to circumstances), I need hardly add that I, too, retired, as soon as it was politely possible for me to leave the room. Ascending the stairs on my way to my own quarters, I discovered Naomi half hidden in a recess formed by an old-fashioned window-seat on the first landing. My bright little friend was in sore trouble. Her apron was over her face, and she was crying bitterly. Ambrose had not taken his leave as tenderly as usual. She was more firmly persuaded than ever that 'Ambrose was hiding something from her.' We all waited anxiously for the next day. The next day made the mystery deeper than ever.

The horse which had taken Ambrose to Narrabee was ridden back to the farm by a groom from the hotel. He delivered a written message from Ambrose which startled us. Further enquiries had positively proved that the missing man had never been near Narrabee. The only attainable tidings of his whereabouts were tidings derived from vague report. It was said that a man like John Jago had been seen the previous day in a railway car, travelling on the line to New York. Acting on this imperfect information, Ambrose had decided on verifying the truth of the report by extending his enquiries to New York.

This extraordinary proceeding forced the suspicion on me that something had really gone wrong. I kept my doubts to myself; but I was prepared, from that moment, to see the disappearance of John Jago followed by very grave results.

The same day the results declared themselves.

Time enough had now elapsed for report to spread through the district the news of what had happened at the farm. Already aware of the bad feeling existing between the men, the neighbours had been now informed (no doubt by the labourers present) of the deplorable scene that had taken place under my bedroom-window. Public opinion declares itself in America without the slightest reserve, or the slightest care for consequences. Public opinion declared on this occasion that the lost man was the victim of foul play, and held one or both of the brothers Meadowcroft responsible for his disappearance. Later in the day, the reasonableness of this serious view of the case was confirmed in the popular mind by a startling discovery. It was announced that a Methodist preacher lately settled at Morwick, and greatly respected throughout the district, had dreamed of John Jago in the character of a murdered man, whose bones were hidden at Morwick Farm. Before night the cry was general for a verification of the preacher's dream. Not only in the immediate district, but in the town of Narrabee itself, the public voice insisted on the necessity of a search for the mortal remains of John Jago at Morwick Farm.

In the terrible turn which matters had now taken, Mr Meadowcroft the elder displayed a spirit and an energy for which I was not prepared.

'My sons have their faults,' he said – 'serious faults, and nobody knows it better than I do. My sons have behaved badly and ungratefully towards John Jago; I don't deny that either. But Ambrose and Silas are not murderers. Make your search. I ask for it; no, I insist on it, after what has been said, in justice to my family and my name!'

The neighbours took him at his word. The Morwick section of the American nation organised itself on the spot. The sovereign people met in committee, made speeches, elected competent persons to represent the public interests, and began the search the next day. The whole proceeding, ridiculously informal from a legal point of view, was carried on by these extraordinary people with as stern and strict a sense of duty as if it had been sanctioned by the highest tribunal in the land.

Naomi met the calamity that had fallen on the household as resolutely as her uncle himself. The girl's courage rose with the call which was made on it. Her one anxiety was for Ambrose.

'He ought to be here,' she said to me. 'The wretches in this neighbourhood are wicked enough to say that his absence is a confession of his guilt.'

She was right. In the present temper of the popular mind the absence of Ambrose was a suspicious circumstance in itself.

'We might telegraph to New York,' I suggested, 'if you only knew where a message would be likely to find him.'

'I know the hotel which the Meadowcrofts use at New York,' she replied. 'I was sent there, after my father's death, to wait till Miss Meadowcroft could take me to Morwick.'

We decided on telegraphing to the hotel. I was writing the message, and Naomi was looking over my shoulder, when we were startled by a strange voice speaking close behind us.

'Oh! that's his address, is it?' said the voice. 'We wanted his address rather badly.'

The speaker was a stranger to me. Naomi recognised him as one of the neighbours.

'What do you want his address for?' she asked, sharply.

'I guess we've found the mortal remains of John Jago, miss,' the man replied. 'We have got Silas already, and we want Ambrose, too, on suspicion of murder.'

'It's a lie!' cried Naomi, furiously – 'a wicked lie!'

The man turned to me.

'Take her into the next room, mister,' he said, 'and let her see for herself.'

We went together into the next room.

In one corner, sitting by her father, and holding his hand, we saw stern and stony Miss Meadowcroft, weeping silently. Opposite to them, crouched on the window-seat, – his eyes wandering, his hands hanging helpless, – we next discovered Silas Meadowcroft, plainly self-betrayed as a panic-stricken man. A few of the persons who had been engaged in the search were seated near, watching him. The mass of the strangers present stood congregated round a table in the middle of the room. They drew aside as I approached with Naomi, and allowed us to have a clear view of certain objects placed on the table.

The centre object of the collection was a little heap of charred bones. Round this were ranged a knife, two metal buttons, and a stick partially burnt. The knife was recognised by the labourers as the weapon John Jago habitually carried about with him – the weapon with which he had wounded Silas Meadowcroft's hand. The buttons Naomi herself declared to have a peculiar pattern on them, which had formerly attracted her attention to John Jago's coat. As for the stick, burnt as it was, I had no difficulty in identifying the quaintly-carved knob at the top. It was the heavy beechen stick which I had snatched out of Silas's hand, and which I had restored to Ambrose on his claiming it as his own. In reply to my enquiries, I was informed that the bones, the knife, the buttons, and the stick had all been found together in a lime-kiln then in use on the farm.

'Is it serious?' Naomi whispered to me, as we drew back from the table.

It would have been sheer cruelty to deceive her now.

'Yes,' I whispered back; 'it *is* serious.'

The search committee conducted its proceedings with the strictest regularity. The proper applications were made forthwith to a justice of the peace, and the justice issued his warrant. That night Silas was committed to prison; and an officer was despatched to arrest Ambrose in New York.

For my part, I did the little I could to make myself useful. With the silent sanction of Mr Meadowcroft and his daughter, I went to Narrabee, and secured the best legal assistance for the defence which the town could place at my disposal. This done, there was no choice but to wait for news of Ambrose, and for the examination before the magistrate which was to follow. I shall pass over the misery in the house during the interval of expectation: no useful purpose could be served by describing it now. Let me only say that Naomi's conduct strengthened me in the conviction that she possessed a noble nature. I was unconscious of the state of my own feelings at the time; but I am now disposed to think that this was the epoch at which I began to envy Ambrose the wife whom he had won.

The telegraph brought us our first news of Ambrose. He had been arrested at the hotel, and he was on his way to Morwick. The next day he arrived, and followed his brother to prison. The two were confined in separate cells, and were forbidden all communication with each other.

Two days later, the preliminary examination took place. Ambrose and Silas Meadowcroft were charged before the magistrate with the wilful murder of John Jago. I was cited to appear as one of the witnesses; and, at Naomi's own request, I took the poor girl into court, and sat by her during the proceedings. My host also was present in his invalid-chair, with his daughter by his side.

Such was the result of my voyage across the ocean in search of rest and quiet; and thus did time and chance fulfil my first hasty forebodings of the dull life I was to lead at Morwick Farm!

VII THE MATERIALS FOR THE DEFENCE

On our way to the chairs allotted to us in the magistrate's court, we passed the platform on which the prisoners were standing together.

Silas took no notice of us. Ambrose made a friendly sign of recognition, and then rested his hand on the 'bar' in front of him. As she passed beneath him, Naomi was just tall enough to reach his hand on tiptoe. She took it. 'I know you are innocent,' she whispered, and gave him one look of loving encouragement as she followed me to her place. Ambrose never lost his self-control. I may have been wrong; but I thought this a bad sign.

The case, as stated for the prosecution, told strongly against the suspected men.

Ambrose and Silas Meadowcroft were charged with the murder of John Jago (by means of the stick or by use of some other weapon), and with the deliberate destruction of the body by throwing it into the quick-lime. In proof of this latter assertion, the knife which the deceased habitually carried about him, and the metal buttons which were known to belong to his coat, were produced. It was argued that these indestructible substances, and some fragments of the larger bones, had alone escaped the action of the burning lime. Having produced medical witnesses to support this theory by declaring the bones to be human, and having thus circumstantially asserted the discovery of the remains in the kiln, the prosecution next proceeded to prove that the missing man had been murdered by the two brothers, and had been by them thrown into the quick-lime as a means of concealing their guilt.

Witness after witness deposed to the inveterate enmity against the deceased displayed by Ambrose and Silas. The threatening language they habitually used towards him; their violent quarrels with him, which had become a public scandal throughout the neighbourhood, and which had ended (on one occasion at least) in a blow; the disgraceful scene which had taken place under my window; and the restoration to Ambrose, on the morning of the fatal quarrel, of the very stick which had been found among the remains of the dead man – these facts and events, and a host of minor circumstances besides, sworn to by witnesses whose credit was unimpeachable, pointed with terrible directness to the conclusion at which the prosecution had arrived.

I looked at the brothers as the weight of the evidence pressed more and more heavily against them. To outward view at least, Ambrose still maintained his self-possession. It was far otherwise with Silas. Abject terror showed itself in his ghastly face; in his great knotty hands, clinging convulsively to the bar at which he stood; in his staring eyes, fixed in vacant horror on each witness who appeared. Public feeling judged him on the spot. There he stood, self-betrayed already, in the popular opinion, as a guilty man!

The one point gained in cross-examination by the defence related to the charred bones.

Pressed on this point, a majority of the medical witnesses admitted that their examination had been a hurried one, and that it was just possible that the bones might yet prove to be the remains of an animal, and not of a man. The presiding magistrate decided, upon this, that a second examination should be made, and that the number of the medical experts should be increased.

Here the preliminary proceedings ended. The prisoners were remanded for three days.

The prostration of Silas at the close of the enquiry was so complete, that it was found necessary to have two men to support him on his leaving the court. Ambrose leaned over the bar to speak to Naomi before he followed the gaoler out. 'Wait,' he whispered confidently, 'till they hear what I have to say!' Naomi kissed her hand to him affectionately, and turned to me with the bright tears in her eyes.

'Why don't they hear what he has to say at once?' she asked. 'Anybody can see that Ambrose is innocent. It's a crying shame, sir, to send him back to prison. Don't you think so yourself?'

If I had confessed what I really thought, I should have said that Ambrose had proved nothing to my mind, except that he possessed rare powers of self-control. It was impossible to acknowledge this to my little friend. I diverted her mind from the question of her lover's innocence, by proposing that we should get the necessary order and visit him in his prison on the next day. Naomi dried her tears, and gave me a little grateful squeeze of the hand.

'Oh, my! what a good fellow you are!' cried the outspoken American girl. 'When your time comes to be married, sir, I guess the woman won't repent saying "Yes" to *you!*'

Mr Meadowcroft preserved unbroken silence as we walked back to the farm on either side of his invalid-chair. His last reserves of resolution seemed to have given way under the overwhelming strain laid on them by the proceedings in court. His daughter, in stern indulgence to Naomi, mercifully permitted her opinion to glimmer on us only, through the medium of quotation from Scripture-texts. If the texts meant anything, they meant that she had foreseen all that had happened, and that the one sad aspect of the case, to her mind, was the death of John Jago, unprepared to meet his end.

I obtained the order of admission to the prison the next morning.

We found Ambrose still confident of the favourable result, for his brother and for himself, of the enquiry before the magistrate. He seemed to be almost as eager to tell, as Naomi was to hear, the true story of what had happened at the lime-kiln. The authorities of the prison – present, of course, at the interview – warned him to remember that what he said might be taken down in writing and produced against him in court.

'Take it down, gentlemen, and welcome,' Ambrose replied. 'I have nothing to fear; I am only telling the truth.'

With that he turned to Naomi, and began his narrative, as nearly as I can remember, in these words:

'I may as well make a clean breast of it at starting, my girl. After Mr Lefrank left us that morning, I asked Silas how he came by my stick. In telling me how, Silas also told me of the words that had passed between him and John Jago under Mr Lefrank's window. I was angry and jealous; and I own it freely, Naomi, I thought the worst that could be thought about you and John.'

Here Naomi stopped him without ceremony.

'Was that what made you speak to me as you spoke when we found you at the wood?' she asked.

'Yes.'

'And was that what made you leave me, when you went away to Narrabee, without giving me a kiss at parting?'

'It was.'

'Beg my pardon for it before you say a word more.'

'I beg your pardon.'

'Say you are ashamed of yourself.'

'I am ashamed of myself,' Ambrose answered, penitently.

'Now you may go on,' said Naomi. 'Now I'm satisfied.'

Ambrose went on.

'We were on our way to the clearing at the other side of the wood while Silas was talking to me; and, as ill luck would have it, we took the path that led by the lime-kiln. Turning the corner, we met John Jago on his way to Narrabee. I was too angry, I tell you, to let him pass quietly. I gave him a bit of my mind. His blood was up too, I suppose; and he spoke out, on his side, as freely as I did. I own I threatened him with the stick; but I'll swear to it I meant him no harm. You know – after dressing Silas's hand – that John Jago is ready with his knife. He comes from out West, where they are always ready with one weapon or another handy in their pockets. It's likely enough *he* didn't mean to harm me, either; but how could I be sure of that? When he stepped up to me, and showed his weapon, I dropped the stick, and closed with him. With one hand I wrenched the knife away from him; and with the other I caught him by the collar of his rotten old coat, and gave him a shaking that made his bones rattle in his skin. A big piece of the cloth came away in my hand. I shied it into the quick-lime close by us, and I pitched the knife after the cloth; and, if Silas hadn't stopped me, I think it's likely I might have shied John Jago himself into the lime next. As it was, Silas kept hold of me. Silas shouted out to him, "Be off with you! and don't come back again, if you don't want to be burnt in the kiln!" He stood looking at us for a minute, fetching his breath, and holding his torn coat round him. Then he spoke with a deadly-quiet voice and a deadly-quiet look: "Many a true word, Mr Silas," he says, "is spoken in jest. *I shall not come back again.*" He turned about, and left us. We stood staring at each other like a couple of fools. "You don't think he means it?" I says. "Bosh!" says Silas. "He's too sweet on Naomi not to come back." What's the matter now, Naomi?'

I had noticed it too. She started and turned pale, when Ambrose repeated to her what Silas had said to him.

'Nothing is the matter,' Naomi answered. 'Your brother has no right to take liberties with my name. Go on. Did Silas say any more while he was about it?'

'Yes: he looked into the kiln; and he says, "What made you throw away the knife, Ambrose?" – "How does a man know why he does anything," I says, "when he does it in a passion?" – "It's a ripping-good knife," says Silas: "in your place, I should have kept it." I picked up the stick off the ground. "Who says I've lost it yet?" I answered him; and with that I got up on the side of the kiln, and began sounding for the knife, to bring it, you know, by means of the stick, within easy reach of a shovel, or some such thing. "Give us your hand," I says to Silas. "Let me stretch out a bit, and I'll have it in no time." Instead of finding the knife, I came nigh to falling myself into the burning lime. The vapour overpowered me, I suppose. All I know is, I turned giddy, and dropped the stick in the kiln. I should have followed the stick, to a dead certainty, but for Silas pulling me back by the hand. "Let it be," says Silas. "If I hadn't had hold of you, John Jago's knife might have been the death of you, after all!" He led me away by the arm, and we went on together on the road to the wood. We stopped where you found us, and sat down on the felled tree. We had a little more talk about John Jago. It ended in our agreeing to wait and see what happened, and to keep our own counsel in the mean time. You and Mr Lefrank came upon us, Naomi, while we were still talking; and you guessed right when you guessed that we had a secret from you. You know the secret now.'

There he stopped. I put a question to him – the first that I had asked yet.

'Had you or your brother any fear at that time of the charge which has since been brought against you?' I said.

'No such thought entered our heads, sir,' Ambrose answered. 'How could *we* foresee that the neighbours would search the kiln, and say what they have said of us? All we feared was, that the old man might hear of the quarrel, and be bitterer against us than ever. I was the more anxious of the two to keep things secret, because I had Naomi to consider as well as the old man. Put yourself in my place, and you will own, sir, that the prospect at home was not a pleasant one for *me*, if John Jago really kept away from the farm, and if it came out that it was all my doing.'

(This was certainly an explanation of his conduct; but it was not quite satisfactory to my mind.)

'As *you* believe, then,' I went on, 'John Jago has carried out his threat of not returning to the farm? According to you, he is now alive and in hiding somewhere?'

'Certainly!' said Ambrose.

'Certainly!' repeated Naomi.

'Do you believe the report that he was seen travelling on the railway to New York?'

'I believe it firmly, sir; and, what is more, I believe I was on his track. I was only too anxious to find him; and I say I could have found him, if they would have let me stay in New York.'

I looked at Naomi.

'I believe it too,' she said. 'John Jago is keeping away.'

'Do you suppose he is afraid of Ambrose and Silas?'

She hesitated.

'He *may* be afraid of them,' she replied, with a strong emphasis on the word 'may.'

'But you don't think it likely?'

She hesitated again. I pressed her again.

'Do you think there is any other motive for his absence?'

Her eyes dropped to the floor. She answered obstinately, almost doggedly, –

'I can't say.'

I addressed myself to Ambrose.

'Have you anything more to tell us?' I asked.

'No,' he said. 'I have told you all I know about it.'

I rose to speak to the lawyer whose services I had retained. He had helped us to get the order of admission, and he had accompanied us to the prison. Seated apart, he had kept silence throughout, attentively watching the effect of Ambrose Meadowcroft's narrative on the officers of the prison and on me.

'Is this the defence?' I enquired, in a whisper.

'This is the defence, Mr Lefrank. What do you think, between ourselves?'

'Between ourselves, I think the magistrate will commit them for trial.'

'On the charge of murder?'

'Yes; on the charge of murder.'

VIII THE CONFESSION

My replies to the lawyer accurately expressed the conviction in my mind. The narrative related by Ambrose had all the appearance, in my eyes, of a fabricated story, got up, and clumsily got up, to pervert the plain meaning of the circumstantial evidence produced by the prosecution. I reached this conclusion reluctantly and regretfully, for Naomi's sake. I said all I could say to shake the absolute confidence which she felt in the discharge of the prisoners at the next examination.

The day of the adjourned enquiry arrived.

Naomi and I again attended the court together. Mr Meadowcroft was unable, on this occasion, to leave the house. His daughter was present, walking to the court by herself, and occupying a seat by herself.

On his second appearance at the 'bar,' Silas was more composed, and more like his brother. No new witnesses were called by the prosecution. We began the battle over the medical evidence relating to the charred bones; and, to some extent, we won the victory. In other words, we forced the doctors to acknowledge that they differed widely in their opinions. They confessed that they were not certain. Two went still further, and declared that the bones were the bones of an animal, not of a man. We made the most of this; and then we entered upon the defence, founded on Ambrose Meadowcroft's story.

Necessarily, no witnesses could be called on our side. Whether this circumstance discouraged him, or whether he privately shared my opinion of his client's statement, I cannot say – it is only certain that the lawyer spoke mechanically, doing his best, no doubt, but doing it without genuine conviction or earnestness on his own part. Naomi cast an anxious glance at me as he sat down. The girl's hand, when I took it, turned cold in mine. She saw plain signs of the failure of the defence in the look and manner of the counsel for the prosecution; but she waited resolutely until the presiding magistrate announced his decision. I had only too clearly foreseen what he would feel it to be his duty to do. Naomi's head dropped on my shoulder as he said the terrible words which committed Ambrose and Silas Meadowcroft to take their trial on the charge of murder.

I led her out of the court into the air. As I passed the 'bar,' I saw Ambrose, deadly pale, looking after us as we left him; the magistrate's decision had evidently daunted him. His brother Silas had dropped in abject terror on the gaoler's chair; the miserable wretch shook and shuddered dumbly like a cowed dog.

Miss Meadowcroft returned with us to the farm, preserving unbroken silence on the way back. I could detect nothing in her bearing which suggested any compassionate feeling for the prisoners in her stern and secret nature. On Naomi's withdrawal to her own room, we were left together for a few minutes; and then, to my astonishment, the outwardly merciless woman showed me that she, too, was one of Eve's daughters, and could feel and suffer, in her own hard way, like the rest of us. She suddenly stepped close up to me, and laid her hand on my arm.

'You are a lawyer, ain't you?' she asked.

'Yes.'

'Have you had any experience in your profession?'

'Ten years' experience.'

'Do *you* think –' She stopped abruptly; her hard face softened; her eyes dropped to the ground. 'Never mind,' she said, confusedly. 'I'm upset by all this misery, though I may not look like it. Don't notice me.'

She turned away. I waited, in the firm persuasion that the unspoken question in her mind would sooner or later force its way to utterance by her lips. I was right. She came back to me unwillingly, like a woman acting under some influence which the utmost exertion of her will was powerless to resist.

'Do *you* believe John Jago is still a living man?'

She put the question vehemently, desperately, as if the words rushed out of her mouth in spite of her.

'I do *not* believe it,' I answered.

'Remember what John Jago has suffered at the hands of my brothers,' she persisted. 'Is it not in your experience that he should take a sudden resolution to leave the farm?'

I replied, as plainly as before—

'It is *not* in my experience.'

She stood looking at me for a moment with a face of blank despair; then bowed her grey head in silence, and left me. As she crossed the room to the door, I saw her look upward; and I heard her say to herself softly, between her teeth, 'Vengeance is mine, I will repay, saith the Lord.'

It was the requiem of John Jago, pronounced by the woman who loved him.

When I next saw her, her mask was on once more. Miss Meadowcroft was herself again. Miss Meadowcroft could sit by, impenetrably calm, while the lawyers discussed the terrible position of her brothers, with the scaffold in view as one of the possibilities of the 'case'.

Left by myself, I began to feel uneasy about Naomi. I went upstairs, and, knocking softly at her door, made my enquiries from outside. The clear young voice answered me sadly, 'I am trying to bear it: I won't distress you when we meet again.' I descended the stairs, feeling my first suspicion of the true nature of my interest in the American girl. Why had her answer brought the tears into my eyes? I went out walking, alone, to think undisturbedly. Why did the tones of her voice dwell on my ear all the way? Why did my hand still feel the last cold, faint pressure of her fingers when I led her out of court?

I took a sudden resolution to go back to England.

When I returned to the farm, it was evening. The lamp was not yet lit in the hall. Pausing to accustom my eyes to the obscurity in-doors, I heard the voice of the lawyer whom we had employed for the defence, speaking to some one very earnestly.

'I'm not to blame,' said the voice. 'She snatched the paper out of my hand before I was aware of her.'

'Do you want it back?' asked the voice of Miss Meadowcroft.

'No: it's only a copy. If keeping it will help to quiet her, let her keep it by all means. Good evening.'

Saying those last words, the lawyer approached me on his way out of the house. I stopped him without ceremony: I felt an ungovernable curiosity to know more.

'Who snatched the paper out of your hand?' I asked, bluntly.

The lawyer started. I had taken him by surprise. The instinct of professional reticence made him pause before he answered me.

In the brief interval of silence, Miss Meadowcroft replied to my question from the other end of the hall.

'Naomi Colebrook snatched the paper out of his hand.'

'What paper?'

A door opened softly behind me. Naomi herself appeared on the threshold; Naomi herself answered my question.

'I will tell you,' she whispered. 'Come in here.'

One candle only was burning in the room. I looked at her by the dim light. My resolution to return to England instantly became one of the lost ideas of my life.

'Good God!' I exclaimed, 'what has happened now?'

She gave me the paper which she had taken from the lawyer's hand.

The 'copy' to which he had referred, was a copy of the written confession of Silas Meadowcroft on his return to prison. He accused his brother Ambrose of the murder of John Jago. He declared on his oath that he had seen his brother Ambrose commit the crime.

In the popular phrase, I could 'hardly believe my own eyes.' I read the last sentences of the confession for the second time:

> . . . I heard their voices at the lime-kiln. They were having words about Cousin Naomi. I ran to the place to part them. I was not in time. I saw Ambrose strike the deceased a terrible blow on the head with his (Ambrose's) heavy stick. The deceased dropped without a cry. I put my hand on his heart. He was dead. I was horribly frightened. Ambrose threatened to kill *me* next if I said a word to any living soul. He took up the body and cast it into the quick-lime, and threw the stick in after it. We went on together to the wood. We sat down on a felled tree outside the wood. Ambrose made up the story that we were to tell if what he had done was found out. He made me repeat it after him like a lesson. We were still at it when Cousin Naomi and Mr Lefrank came up to us. They know the rest. This, on my oath, is a true confession. I make it of my own free will, repenting me sincerely that I did not make it before.
>
> (Signed) SILAS MEADOWCROFT

I laid down the paper, and looked at Naomi once more. She spoke to me with a strange composure. Immovable determination was in her eye; immovable determination was in her voice.

'Silas has lied away his brother's life to save himself,' she said. 'I see cowardly falsehood and cowardly cruelty in every line on that paper. Ambrose is innocent, and the time has come to prove it.'

'You forget,' I said, 'that we have just failed to prove it.'

She took no notice of my objection.

'John Jago is alive, in hiding from us,' she went on. 'Help me, friend Lefrank, to advertise for him in the newspapers.'

I drew back from her in speechless distress. I own I believed that the new misery which had fallen on her had affected her brain.

'You don't believe it?' she said. 'Shut the door.'

I obeyed her. She seated herself, and pointed to a chair near her.

'Sit down,' she proceeded. 'I am going to do a wrong thing, but there is no help for it. I am going to break a sacred promise. You remember that moonlight night when I met him on the garden-walk?'

'John Jago?'

'Yes. Now listen. I am going to tell you what passed between John Jago and me.'

IX THE ADVERTISEMENT

I waited in silence for the disclosure that was now to come. Naomi began by asking me a question.

'You remember when we went to see Ambrose in prison?' she said.

'Perfectly.'

'Ambrose told us of something which his villain of a brother said of John Jago and me. Do you remember what it was?'

I remembered perfectly. Silas had said, 'John Jago is too sweet on Naomi not to come back.'

'That's so,' Naomi remarked, when I had repeated the words. 'I couldn't help starting when I heard what Silas had said; and I thought you noticed me.'

'I did notice you.'

'Did you wonder what it meant?'

'Yes.'

'I'll tell you. It meant this: What Silas Meadowcroft said to his brother of John Jago, was what I myself was thinking of John Jago at that very moment. It startled me to find my own thought in a man's mind, spoken for me by a man. I am the person, sir, who has driven John Jago away from Morwick Farm; and I am the person who can and will bring him back again.'

There was something in her manner, more than in her words, which let the light in suddenly on my mind.

'You have told me the secret,' I said. 'John Jago is in love with you.'

'Mad about me!' she rejoined, dropping her voice to a whisper. 'Stark, staring mad! – that's the only word for him. After we had taken a few turns on the gravel-walk, he suddenly broke out like a man beside himself. He fell down on his knees; he kissed my gown, he kissed my feet; he sobbed and cried for love of me. I'm not badly off for courage, sir, considering I'm a woman. No man, that I can call to mind, ever really scared me before. But, I own, John Jago frightened me: oh, my! he did frighten me! My heart was in my mouth, and my knees shook under me. I begged and prayed of him to get up and go away. No; there he knelt, and held by the skirt of my gown. The words poured out from him like – well, like nothing I can think of but water from a pump. His happiness and his life, and his hopes in earth and heaven, and Lord only knows what besides, all depended, he said, on a word from me. I plucked up spirit enough at that to remind him that I was promised to Ambrose. "I think you ought to be ashamed of yourself," I said, "to own that you are wicked enough to love me when you know I am promised to another man!" When I spoke to him, he took a new turn: he began abusing Ambrose. *That* straightened me up. I snatched my gown out of his hand, and I gave him my whole mind. "I hate you!" I said. "Even if I wasn't promised to Ambrose, I wouldn't marry you; no! not if there wasn't another man left in the world to ask me. I hate you, Mr Jago! I hate you!" He saw I was in earnest at last. He got up from my feet, and he settled down quiet again, all on a sudden. "You have said enough" (that was how he answered me). "You have broken my life. I have no hopes and no prospects now. I had a pride in the farm, miss, and a pride in my work; I bore with your brutish cousins' hatred of me; I was faithful to Mr Meadowcroft's interests; all for your sake, Naomi Colebrook – all for your sake! I have done with it now; I have done with my life at the farm. You will never be troubled with me again. I am going away, as the dumb creatures go when they are sick, to hide myself in a corner, and die. Do me one last favour. Don't make me the laughing-stock of the whole neighbourhood. I can't bear that: it maddens me, only to think of it. Give me your promise never to tell any living soul what I have said to you to-night – your sacred promise to the man whose life you have broken!" I did as he bade me: I gave him my sacred promise with the tears in my eyes. Yes; that is so. After telling him I hated him (and I did hate him), I cried over his misery; I did. Mercy, what fools

women are! What is the horrid perversity, sir, which makes us always ready
to pity the men? He held out his hand to me; and he said, "Good bye for ever!'
and I pitied him. I said, "I'll shake hands with you if you will give me your
promise in exchange for mine. I beg of you not to leave the farm. What will
my uncle do if you go away? Stay here, and be friends with me; and forget
and forgive, Mr John." He gave me his promise (he can refuse me nothing);
and he gave it again when I saw him again the next morning. Yes, I'll do him
justice, though I do hate him! I believe he honestly meant to keep his word as
long as my eye was on him. It was only when he was left to himself that the
Devil tempted him to break his promise, and leave the farm. I was brought
up to believe in the Devil, Mr Lefrank; and I find it explains many things. It
explains John Jago. Only let me find out where he has gone, and I'll engage
he shall come back and clear Ambrose of the suspicion which his vile brother
has cast on him. Here is the pen all ready for you. Advertise for him, friend
Lefrank; and do it right away, for my sake!'

I let her run on, without attempting to dispute her conclusions, until she
could say no more. When she put the pen into my hand, I began the
composition of the advertisement, as obediently as if I, too, believed that
John Jago was a living man.

In the case of anyone else, I should have openly acknowledged that my
own convictions remained unshaken. If no quarrel had taken place at the
lime-kiln, I should have been quite ready, as I viewed the case, to believe
that John Jago's disappearance was referable to the terrible disappointment
which Naomi had inflicted on him. The same morbid dread of ridicule which
had led him to assert that he cared nothing for Naomi, when he and Silas
had quarrelled under my bedroom-window, might also have impelled him to
withdraw himself secretly and suddenly from the scene of his discomfiture.
But to ask me to believe, after what had happened at the lime-kiln, that he
was still living, was to ask me to take Ambrose Meadowcroft's statement for
granted as a true statement of facts.

I had refused to do this from the first; and I still persisted in taking that
course. If I had been called upon to decide the balance of probability between
the narrative related by Ambrose in his defence and the narrative related by
Silas in his confession. I must have owned, no matter how unwillingly, that
the confession was, to my mind, the least incredible story of the two.

Could I say this to Naomi? I would have written fifty advertisements
enquiring for John Jago rather than say it; and you would have done the
same, if you had been as fond of her as I was.

I drew out the advertisement, for insertion in 'The Morwick Mercury,' in
these terms:

MURDER. – Printers of newspapers throughout the United States are
desired to publish that Ambrose Meadowcroft and Silas Meadowcroft,
of Morwick Farm, Morwick County, are committed for trial on the
charge of murdering John Jago, now missing from the farm and from the
neighbourhood. Any person who can give information of the existence
of said Jago may save the lives of two wrongly accused men by making
immediate communication. Jago is about five feet four inches high. He
is spare and wiry; his complexion is extremely pale; his eyes are dark,
and very bright and restless. The lower part of his face is concealed by

a thick black beard and mustache. The whole appearance of the man
is wild and flighty.

I added the date and address. That evening a servant was sent on horseback
to Narrabee to procure the insertion of the advertisement in the next issue of
the newspaper.

When we parted that night, Naomi looked almost like her brighter and
happier self. Now that the advertisement was on its way to the printing-office,
she was more than sanguine: she was certain of the result.

'You don't know how you have comforted me,' she said, in her frank,
warm-hearted way, when we parted for the night. 'All the newspapers will
copy it, and we shall hear of John Jago before the week is out.' She turned
to go, and came back again to me. 'I will never forgive Silas for writing that
confession!' she whispered in my ear. 'If he ever lives under the same roof
with Ambrose again, I – well, I believe I wouldn't marry Ambrose if he did!
There!'

She left me. Through the wakeful hours of the night my mind dwelt on
her last words. That she should contemplate, under any circumstances, even
the bare possibility of not marrying Ambrose, was, I am ashamed to say, a
direct encouragement to certain hopes which I had already begun to form in
secret. The next day's mail brought me a letter on business. My clerk wrote to
enquire if there was any chance of my returning to England in time to appear
in court at the opening of next law term. I answered, without hesitation, 'It
is still impossible for me to fix the date of my return.' Naomi was in the room
while I was writing. How would she have answered, I wonder, if I had told
her the truth, and said, 'You are responsible for this letter?'

X THE SHERIFF AND THE GOVERNOR

The question of time was now a serious question at Morwick Farm. In
six weeks, the court for the trial of criminal cases was to be opened at
Narrabee.

During this interval, no new event of any importance occurred.

Many idle letters reached us relating to the advertisement for John Jago;
but no positive information was received. Not the slightest trace of the lost
man turned up; not the shadow of a doubt was cast on the assertion of the
prosecution, that his body had been destroyed in the kiln. Silas Meadowcroft
held firmly to the horrible confession that he had made. His brother Ambrose,
with equal resolution, asserted his innocence, and reiterated the statement
which he had already advanced. At regular periods I accompanied Naomi
to visit him in the prison. As the day appointed for the opening of the court
approached, he seemed to falter a little in his resolution; his manner became
restless; and he grew irritably suspicious about the merest trifles. This change
did not necessarily imply the consciousness of guilt: it might merely have
indicated natural nervous agitation as the time for the trial drew near. Naomi
noticed the alteration in her lover. It greatly increased her anxiety, though
it never shook her confidence in Ambrose. Except at meal-times, I was left,
during the period of which I am now writing, almost constantly alone with

the charming American girl. Miss Meadowcroft searched the newspapers for tidings of the living John Jago in the privacy of her own room. Mr Meadowcroft would see nobody but his daughter and his doctor, and occasionally one or two old friends. I have since had reason to believe that Naomi, in these days of our intimate association, discovered the true nature of the feeling with which she had inspired me. But she kept her secret. Her manner towards me steadily remained the manner of a sister: she never over-stepped by a hair's breadth the safe limits of the character she had assumed.

The sittings of the court began. After hearing the evidence, and examining the confession of Silas Meadowcroft, the grand jury found a true bill against both the prisoners. The day appointed for the trial was the first day in the new week.

I had carefully prepared Naomi's mind for the decision of the grand jury. She bore the new blow bravely.

'If you are not tired of it,' she said, 'come with me to the prison to-morrow. Ambrose will need a little comfort by that time.' She paused, and looked at the day's letters lying on the table. 'Still not a word about John Jago,' she said. 'And all the papers have copied the advertisement. I felt so sure we should hear of him long before this!'

'Do you still feel sure that he is living?' I ventured to ask.

'I am as certain of it as ever,' she replied firmly. 'He is somewhere in hiding: perhaps he is in disguise. Suppose we know no more of him than we know now, when the trial begins? Suppose the jury –' She stopped, shuddering. Death – shameful death on the scaffold – might be the terrible result of the consultation of the jury. 'We have waited for news to come to us long enough,' Naomi resumed. 'We must find the tracks of John Jago for ourselves. There is a week yet before the trial begins. Who will help me to make enquiries? Will you be the man, friend Lefrank?'

It is needless to add (though I knew nothing would come of it) that I consented to be the man.

We arranged to apply that day for the order of admission to the prison, and, having seen Ambrose, to devote ourselves immediately to the contemplated search. How that search was to be conducted was more than I could tell, and more than Naomi could tell. We were to begin by applying to the police to help us to find John Jago, and we were then to be guided by circumstances. Was there ever a more hopeless programme than this?

'Circumstances' declared themselves against us at starting. I applied, as usual, for the order of admission to the prison, and the order was for the first time refused; no reason being assigned by the persons in authority for taking this course. Enquire as I might, the only answer given was, 'Not to-day.'

At Naomi's suggestion, we went to the prison to seek the explanation which was refused to us at the office. The gaoler on duty at the outer gate was one of Naomi's many admirers. He solved the mystery cautiously in a whisper. The sheriff and the governor of the prison were then speaking privately with Ambrose Meadowcroft in his cell: they had expressly directed that no persons should be admitted to see the prisoner that day but themselves.

What did it mean? We returned, wondering, to the farm. There Naomi, speaking by chance to one of the female servants, made certain discoveries.

Early that morning the sheriff had been brought to Morwick by an old friend of the Meadowcrofts. A long interview had been held between Mr Meadowcroft and his daughter and the official personage introduced by the friend. Leaving the farm, the sheriff had gone straight to the prison, and had proceeded with the governor to visit Ambrose in his cell. Was some potent influence being brought privately to bear on Ambrose? Appearances certainly suggested that enquiry. Supposing the influence to have been really exerted, the next question followed, What was the object in view? We could only wait and see.

Our patience was not severely tried. The event of the next day enlightened us in a very unexpected manner. Before noon, the neighbours brought startling news from the prison to the farm.

Ambrose Meadowcroft had confessed himself to be the murderer of John Jago! He had signed the confession in the presence of the sheriff and the governor on that very day!

I saw the document. It is needless to reproduce it here. In substance, Ambrose confessed what Silas had confessed; claiming, however, to have only struck Jago under intolerable provocation, so as to reduce the nature of his offence against the law from murder to manslaughter. Was the confession really the true statement of what had taken place? or had the sheriff and the governor, acting in the interests of the family name, persuaded Ambrose to try this desperate means of escaping the ignominy of death on the scaffold? The sheriff and the governor preserved impenetrable silence until the pressure put on them judicially at the trial obliged them to speak.

Who was to tell Naomi of this last and saddest of all the calamities which had fallen on her? Knowing how I loved her in secret, I felt an invincible reluctance to be the person who revealed Ambrose Meadowcroft's degradation to his betrothed wife. Had any other member of the family told her what had happened? The lawyer was able to answer me: Miss Meadowcroft had told her.

I was shocked when I heard it. Miss Meadowcroft was the last person in the house to spare the poor girl: Miss Meadowcroft would make the hard tidings doubly terrible to bear in the telling. I tried to find Naomi, without success. She had been always accessible at other times. Was she hiding herself from me now? The idea occurred to me as I was descending the stairs after vainly knocking at the door of her room. I was determined to see her. I waited a few minutes, and then ascended the stairs again suddenly. On the landing I met her, just leaving her room.

She tried to run back. I caught her by the arm, and detained her. With her free hand she held her handkerchief over her face so as to hide it from me.

'You once told me I had comforted you,' I said to her, gently. 'Won't you let me comfort you now?'

She still struggled to get away, and still kept her head turned from me.

'Don't you see that I am ashamed to look you in the face?' she said, in low, broken tones. 'Let me go.'

I still persisted in trying to sooth her. I drew her to the window-seat. I said I would wait until she was able to speak to me.

She dropped on the seat, and wrung her hands on her lap. Her downcast eyes still obstinately avoided meeting mine.

'Oh!' she said to herself, 'what madness possessed me? Is it possible that I ever disgraced myself by loving Ambrose Meadowcroft?' She shuddered as the idea found its way to expression on her lips. The tears rolled slowly over her cheeks. 'Don't despise me, Mr Lefrank!' she said, faintly.

I tried, honestly tried, to put the confession before her in its least unfavourable light.

'His resolution has given way,' I said. 'He has done this, despairing of proving his innocence, in terror of the scaffold.'

She rose, with an angry stamp of her foot. She turned her face on me with the deep red flush of shame in it, and the big tears glistening in her eyes.

'No more of him!' she said, sternly. 'If he is not a murderer, what else is he? A liar and a coward! In which of his characters does he disgrace me most? I have done with him for ever! I will never speak to him again!' She pushed me furiously away from her; advanced a few steps towards her own door; stopped, and came back to me. The generous nature of the girl spoke in her next words. 'I am not ungrateful to *you*, friend Lefrank. A woman in my place is only a woman; and, when she is shamed as I am, she feels it very bitterly. Give me your hand! God bless you!'

She put my hand to her lips before I was aware of her, and kissed it, and ran back into her room.

I sat down on the place which she had occupied. She had looked at me for one moment when she kissed my hand. I forgot Ambrose and his confession; I forgot the coming trial; I forgot my professional duties and my English friends. There I sat, in a fool's elysium of my own making, with absolutely nothing in my mind but the picture of Naomi's face at the moment when she had last looked at me!

I have already mentioned that I was in love with her. I merely add this to satisfy you that I tell the truth.

XI THE PEBBLE AND THE WINDOW

Miss Meadowcroft and I were the only representatives of the family at the farm who attended the trial. We went separately to Narrabee. Excepting the ordinary greetings at morning and night, Miss Meadowcroft had not said one word to me since the time when I told her that I did *not* believe John Jago to be a living man.

I have purposely abstained from encumbering my narrative with legal details. I now propose to state the nature of the defence in the briefest outline only.

We insisted on making both the prisoners plead 'Not guilty.' This done, we took an objection to the legality of the proceedings at starting. We appealed to the old English law, that there should be no conviction for murder until the body of the murdered person was found, or proof of its destruction obtained beyond a doubt. We denied that sufficient proof had been obtained in the case now before the court.

The judges consulted, and decided that the trial should go on.

We took our next objection when the Confessions were produced in evidence. We declared that they had been extorted by terror, or by undue influence; and we pointed out certain minor particulars in which the two confessions failed to corroborate each other. For the rest, our defence on this occasion was, as to essentials, what our defence had been at the enquiry before the magistrate. Once more the judges consulted, and once more they overruled our objection. The Confessions were admitted in evidence.

On their side, the prosecution produced one new witness in support of their case. It is needless to waste time in recapitulating his evidence. He contradicted himself gravely on cross-examination. We showed plainly, and after investigation proved, that he was not to be believed on his oath.

The Chief Justice summed up.

He charged, in relation to the Confessions, that no weight should be attached to a confession incited by hope or fear; and he left it to the jury to determine whether the Confessions in this case had been so. influenced. In the course of the trial, it had been shown for the defence that the sheriff and the governor of the prison had told Ambrose, with his father's knowledge and sanction, that the case was clearly against him; that the only chance of sparing his family the disgrace of his death by public execution lay in making a confession; and that they would do their best, if he did confess, to have his sentence commuted to transportation for life. As for Silas, he was proved to have been beside himself with terror when he made his abominable charge against his brother. We had vainly trusted to the evidence on these two points to induce the court to reject the Confessions; and we were destined to be once more disappointed in anticipating that the same evidence would influence the verdict of the jury on the side of mercy. After an absence of an hour, they returned into court with a verdict of 'Guilty' against both the prisoners.

Being asked in due form if they had anything to say in mitigation of their sentence, Ambrose and Silas solemnly declared their innocence, and publicly acknowledged that their respective confessions had been wrung from them with the hope of escaping the hangman's hands. This statement was not noticed by the bench. The prisoners were both sentenced to death.

On my return to the farm, I did not see Naomi. Miss Meadowcroft informed her of the result of the trial. Half an hour later, one of the women-servants handed to me an envelope bearing my name on it in Naomi's handwriting.

The envelope enclosed a letter, and with it a slip of paper on which Naomi had hurriedly written these words: 'For God's sake, read the letter I send to you, and do something about it immediately!'

I looked at the letter. It assumed to be written by a gentleman in New York. Only the day before, he had, by the merest accident, seen the advertisement for John Jago, cut out of a newspaper and pasted into a book of 'curiosities' kept by a friend. Upon this he wrote to Morwick Farm to say that he had seen a man exactly answering to the description of John Jago, but bearing another name, working as a clerk in a merchant's office in Jersey City. Having time to spare before the mail went out, he had returned to the office to take another look at the man before he posted his letter. To his surprise, he was informed that the clerk had not appeared at his desk that day. His employer had sent to his lodgings, and had been informed that he had suddenly packed up his hand-bag after reading the newspaper at breakfast; had paid his rent honestly, and had gone away, nobody knew where!

It was late in the evening when I read these lines. I had time for reflection before it would be necessary for me to act.

Assuming the letter to be genuine, and adopting Naomi's explanation of the motive which had led John Jago to absent himself secretly from the farm, I reached the conclusion that the search for him might be usefully limited to Narrabee and to the surrounding neighbourhood.

The newspaper at his breakfast had no doubt given him his first information of the 'finding' of the grand jury, and of the trial to follow. It was in my experience of human nature that he should venture back to Narrabee under these circumstances, and under the influence of his infatuation for Naomi. More than this, it was again in my experience, I am sorry to say, that he should attempt to make the critical position of Ambrose a means of extorting Naomi's consent to listen favourably to his suit. Cruel indifference to the injury and the suffering which his sudden absence might inflict on others, was plainly implied in his secret withdrawal from the farm. The same cruel indifference, pushed to a further extreme, might well lead him to press his proposals privately on Naomi, and to fix her acceptance of them as the price to be paid for saving her cousin's life.

To these conclusions I arrived after much thinking. I had determined, on Naomi's account, to clear the matter up; but it is only candid to add, that my doubts of John Jago's existence remained unshaken by the letter. I believed it to be nothing more nor less than a heartless and stupid 'hoax.'

The striking of the hall-clock roused me from my meditations. I counted the strokes – midnight!

I rose to go up to my room. Everybody else in the farm had retired to bed, as usual, more than an hour since. The stillness in the house was breathless. I walked softly, by instinct, as I crossed the room to look out at the night. A lovely moonlight met my view: it was like the moonlight on the fatal evening when Naomi had met John Jago on the garden-walk.

My bedroom-candle was on the side-table: I had just lit it. I was just leaving the room, when the door suddenly opened, and Naomi herself stood before me!

Recovering the first shock of her sudden appearance, I saw instantly, in her eager eyes, in her deadly pale cheeks, that something serious had happened. A large cloak was thrown over her; a white handkerchief was tied over her head. Her hair was in disorder: she had evidently just risen in fear and in haste from her bed.

'What is it?' I asked, advancing to meet her.

She clung trembling with agitation to my arm.

'John Jago!' she whispered.

You will think my obstinacy invincible. I could hardly believe it, even then!

'Do you mean John Jago's ghost?' I asked.

'I have seen John Jago himself,' she answered.

'Where?'

'In the back yard, under my bedroom-window!'

The emergency was far too serious to allow of any consideration for the small proprieties of every-day life.

'Let *me* see him!' I said.

'I am here to fetch you,' she replied, in her frank and fearless way. 'Come upstairs with me.'

Her room was on the first floor of the house, and was the only bedroom which looked out on the back yard. On our way up the stairs she told me what had happened.

'I was in bed,' she said, 'but not asleep, when I heard a pebble strike against the window-pane. I waited, wondering what it meant. Another pebble was thrown against the glass. So far, I was surprised, but not frightened. I got up, and ran to the window to look out. There was John Jago, looking up at me in the moonlight!'

'Did he see you?'

'Yes. He said, "Come down and speak to me! I have something serious to say to you!"'

'Did you answer him?'

'As soon as I could fetch my breath, I said, "Wait a little," and ran downstairs to you. What shall I do?'

'Let *me* see him, and I will tell you.'

We entered her room. Keeping cautiously behind the window-curtain, I looked out.

There he was! His beard and moustache were shaved off: his hair was cut close. But there was no disguising his wild brown eyes, or the peculiar movement of his spare wiry figure, as he walked slowly to and fro in the moonlight, waiting for Naomi. For the moment, my own agitation almost overpowered me: I had so firmly disbelieved that John Jago was a living man!

'What shall I do?' Naomi repeated.

'Is the door of the dairy open?' I asked.

'No; but the door of the tool-house, round the corner, is not locked.'

'Very good. Show yourself at the window, and say to him, "I am coming directly."'

The brave girl obeyed me without a moment's hesitation.

There had been no doubt about his eyes and his gait: there was no doubt now about his voice, as he answered softly from below—

'All right!'

'Keep him talking to you where he is now,' I said to Naomi, 'until I have time to get round by the other way to the tool-house. Then pretend to be fearful of discovery at the dairy; and bring him round the corner, so that I can hear him behind the door.'

We left the house together, and separated silently. Naomi followed my instructions with a woman's quick intelligence where stratagems are concerned. I had hardly been a minute in the tool-house before I heard him speaking to Naomi on the other side of the door.

The first words which I caught distinctly related to his motive for secretly leaving the farm. Mortified pride – doubly mortified by Naomi's contemptuous refusal, and by the personal indignity offered to him by Ambrose – was at the bottom of his conduct in absenting himself from Morwick. He owned that he had seen the advertisement, and that it had actually encouraged him to keep in hiding!

'After being laughed at and insulted and denied, I was glad,' said the miserable wretch, 'to see that some of you had serious reason to wish me back again. It rests with you, Miss Naomi, to keep me here, and to persuade me to save Ambrose by showing myself, and owning to my name.'

'What do you mean?' I heard Naomi ask, sternly.

He lowered his voice; but I could still hear him.

'Promise you will marry me,' he said, 'and I will go before the magistrate tomorrow, and show him that I am a living man.'

'Suppose I refuse?'

'In that case you will lose me again, and none of you will find me till Ambrose is hanged.'

'Are you villain enough, John Jago, to mean what you say?' asked the girl, raising her voice.

'If you attempt to give the alarm,' he answered, 'as true as God's above us, you will feel my hand on your throat! It's my turn now, miss; and I am not to be trifled with. Will you have me for your husband, – yes or no?'

'No!' she answered, loudly and firmly.

I threw open the door, and seized him as he lifted his hand on her. He had not suffered from the nervous derangement which had weakened me, and he was the stronger man of the two. Naomi saved my life. She struck up his pistol as he pulled it out of his pocket with his free hand, and presented it at my head. The bullet was fired into the air. I tripped up his heels at the same moment. The report of the pistol had alarmed the house. We two together kept him on the ground until help arrived.

XII THE END OF IT

John Jago was brought before the magistrate, and John Jago was identified the next day.

The lives of Ambrose and Silas were, of course, no longer in peril, so far as human justice was concerned. But there were legal delays to be encountered, and legal formalities to be observed, before the brothers could be released from prison in the characters of innocent men.

During the interval which thus elapsed, certain events happened which may be briefly mentioned here before I close my narrative.

Mr Meadowcroft the elder, broken by the suffering which he had gone through, died suddenly of a rheumatic affection of the heart. A codicil attached to his will abundantly justified what Naomi had told me of Miss Meadowcroft's influence over her father, and of the end she had in view in exercising it. A life-income only was left to Mr Meadowcroft's sons. The freehold of the farm was bequeathed to his daughter, with the testator's recommendation added, that she should marry his 'best and dearest friend, Mr John Jago.'

Armed with the power of the will, the heiress of Morwick sent an insolent message to Naomi, requesting her no longer to consider herself one of the inmates at the farm. Miss Meadowcroft, it should be here added, positively refused to believe that John Jago had ever asked Naomi to be his wife, or had ever threatened her, as I had heard him threaten her, if she refused. She accused me, as she accused Naomi, of trying meanly to injure John Jago in her estimation, out of hatred towards 'that much-injured man;' and she sent to me, as she had sent to Naomi, a formal notice to leave the house.

We two banished ones met the same day in the hall, with our travelling bags in our hands.

'We are turned out together, friend Lefrank,' said Naomi, with her quaintly comical smile. 'You will go back to England, I guess; and I must make my own living in my own country. Women can get employment in the States if they have a friend to speak for them. Where shall I find somebody who can give me a place?'

I saw my way to saying the right word at the right moment.

'I have got a place to offer you,' I replied, 'if you see no objection to accepting it.'

She suspected nothing, so far.

'That's lucky, sir,' was all she said. 'Is it in a telegraph-office or in a dry-goods store?'

I astonished my little American friend by taking her then and there in my arms, and giving her my first kiss.

'The office is by my fireside,' I said. 'The salary is anything in reason you like to ask me for. And the place, Naomi, if you have no objection to it, is the place of my wife.'

I have no more to say, except that years have passed since I spoke those words, and that I am as fond of Naomi as ever.

Some months after our marriage, Mrs Lefrank wrote to a friend at Narrabee for news of what was going on at the farm. The answer informed us that Ambrose and Silas had emigrated to New Zealand, and that Miss Meadowcroft was alone at Morwick Farm. John Jago had refused to marry her. John Jago had disappeared again, nobody knew where.

The Frozen Deep

Originally appeared in *Temple Bar*, August to October 1874. This is a 'novelisation' of Collins's celebrated 'drama in three acts' of the same title, which was first performed at Tavistock House, Dickens's London home, on 6 January 1857, and later on at the Gallery of Illustration in Regent Street, and at the Free Trade Hall, Manchester. Dickens played the part of Richard Wardour, finding a personal resonance in the theme of self-sacrifice which was later to feature in the character of Sidney Carton in *A Tale of Two Cities* (1859). The play was revised and printed in 1866, when it enjoyed another run at the Olympic Theatre. Collins made use of a fictionalised version as a public reading on his North American Lecture Tour in 1873–4, which lasted nearly two hours, and proved very successful. When this appeared in book-form in 1874 Collins expanded it considerably, and explained in some 'Introductory Lines' that it departs 'widely from the treatment of the story in the First Act of the dramatic version, but (with the one exception of the Third Scene) follows the play as closely as possible in the succeeding acts.' Catherine Peters suggests that some of the alterations may reflect the reverse influence of *A Tale of Two Cities (The King of Inventors*, p. 365). The story is discussed in T.S. Eliot's essay on 'Wilkie Collins and Dickens' (1927). Eliot views 'The Frozen Deep' as 'a piece of pure melodrama . . . We are asked to accept an improbability, simply for the sake of seeing the thrilling situation which arises in consequence' (T.S. Eliot, *Selected Essays*, 1951, p. 467).

FIRST SCENE

The Ball-room

I

The date is between twenty and thirty years ago. The place is an English seaport. The time is night. And the business of the moment is – dancing.

The Mayor and Corporation of the town are giving a grand ball, in celebration of the departure of an Arctic expedition from their port. The ships of the expedition are two in number – the *Wanderer* and the *Sea-Mew*. They are to sail (in search of the North-West Passage) on the next day, with the morning tide.

Honour to the Mayor and Corporation! It is a brilliant ball. The band is complete. The room is spacious. The large conservatory opening out of it is pleasantly lit with Chinese lanterns, and beautifully decorated with shrubs and flowers. All officers of the army and navy who are present wear their uniforms in honour of the occasion. Among the ladies the display of dresses (a subject which the men don't understand) is bewildering, and the average of beauty (a subject which the men do understand) is the highest average attainable in all parts of the room.

For the moment the dance which is in progress is a quadrille. General admiration selects two of the ladies who are dancing as its favourite objects. One is a dark beauty in the prime of womanhood – the wife of First Lieutenant Crayford, of the *Wanderer*. The other is a young girl, pale and delicate, dressed simply in white, with no ornament on her head but her own lovely brown hair. This is Miss Clara Burnham – an orphan. She is Mrs Crayford's dearest friend, and she is to stay with Mrs Crayford during the Lieutenant's absence in the Arctic regions. She is now dancing, with the Lieutenant himself for partner, and with Mrs Crayford and Captain Helding (Commanding Officer of the *Wanderer*) for *vis-à-vis* – in plain English, for opposite couple.

The conversation between Captain Helding and Mrs Crayford, in one of the intervals of the dance, turns on Miss Burnham. The Captain is greatly interested in Clara. He admires her beauty, but he thinks her manner, for a young girl, strangely serious and subdued. Is she in delicate health?

Mrs Crayford shakes her head, sighs mysteriously, and answers—

'In *very* delicate health, Captain Helding.'

'Consumptive?'

'Not in the least.'

'I am glad to hear that. She is a charming creature, Mrs Crayford. She interests me indescribably. If I was only twenty years younger – perhaps (as I am *not* twenty years younger) I had better not finish the sentence? Is it indiscreet, my dear lady, to inquire what *is* the matter with her?'

'It might be indiscreet on the part of a stranger,' said Mrs Crayford. 'An old friend like you may make any inquiries. I wish I could tell you what is the matter with Clara. It is a mystery to the doctors themselves. Some of the mischief is due, in my humble opinion, to the manner in which she has been brought up.'

'Aye! aye! A bad school, I suppose?'

'Very bad, Captain Helding. But not the sort of school which you have in your mind at this moment. Clara's early years were spent in a lonely old house in the Highlands of Scotland. The ignorant people about her were the people who did the mischief which I have just been speaking of. They filled her mind with the superstitions which are still respected as truths in the wild north – especially the superstition called the Second Sight.'

'God bless me!' cried the captain, 'you don't mean to say she believes in such stuff as that? In these enlightened times, too!'

Mrs Crayford looked at her partner with a satirical smile.

'In these enlightened times, Captain Helding, we only believe in dancing tables, and in messages sent from the other world by spirits who can't spell! By comparison with such superstitions as these, even the Second Sight has something – in the shape of poetry – to recommend it, surely? Estimate for yourself,' she continued seriously, 'the effect of such surroundings as I have described on a delicate sensitive young creature – a girl with a naturally imaginative temperament, leading a lonely neglected life. Is it so very surprising that she should catch the infection of the superstition about her? And is it quite incomprehensible that her nervous system should suffer accordingly at a very critical period of her life?'

'Not at all, Mrs Crayford – not at all, ma'am, as you put it. Still it *is* a little startling, to a commonplace man like me, to meet a young lady at a ball who believes in the Second Sight. Does she really profess to see into the future? Am I to understand that she positively falls into a trance, and sees people in distant countries, and foretells events to come? That is the Second Sight, is it not?'

'That is the Second Sight, Captain. And that is, really and positively, what she does.'

'The young lady who is dancing opposite to us?'

'The young lady who is dancing opposite to us.'

The Captain waited a little – letting the new flood of information which had poured in on him settle itself steadily in his mind. This process accomplished, the Arctic explorer proceeded resolutely on his way to further discoveries.

'May I ask, ma'am, if you have ever seen her in a state of trance with your own eyes?' he inquired.

'My sister and I both saw her in the trance, little more than a month since,' Mrs Crayford replied. 'She had been nervous and irritable all the morning, and we took her out into the garden to breathe the fresh air. Suddenly, without any reason for it, the colour left her face. She stood between us, insensible to touch, insensible to sound, motionless as stone, and cold as death, in a moment. The first change we noticed came after a lapse of some minutes. Her hands began to move slowly, as if she was groping in the dark. Words dropped one by one from her lips, in a lost, vacant tone, as if she was talking in her sleep. Whether what she said referred to past or future I cannot tell you. She spoke of persons in a foreign country – perfect strangers to my sister and to me. After a little interval, she suddenly became silent. A momentary colour appeared in her face, and left it again. Her eyes closed, her feet failed her, and she sank insensible into our arms.'

'Sank insensible into your arms,' repeated the Captain, absorbing his new information. 'Most extraordinary! And – in this state of health – she goes out to parties, and dances. More extraordinary still!'

'You are entirely mistaken,' said Mrs Crayford. 'She is only here to-night to please me. And she is only dancing to please my husband. As a rule, she shuns all society. The doctor recommends change and amusement for her. She won't listen to him. Except on rare occasions like this, she persists in remaining at home.'

Captain Helding brightened at the allusion to the doctor. Something practical might be got out of the doctor. Scientific man. Sure to see this very obscure subject under a new light. 'How does it strike the doctor now?' said the Captain. 'Viewed simply as a case, ma'am, how does it strike the doctor?'

'He will give no positive opinion,' Mrs Crayford answered. 'He told me that such cases as Clara's were by no means unfamiliar to medical practice. "We know," he told me, "that certain disordered conditions of the brain and the nervous system produce results quite as extraordinary as any that you have described – and there our knowledge ends. Neither my science, nor any man's science, can clear up the mystery in this case. It is an especially difficult case to deal with, because Miss Burnham's early associations dispose her to attach a superstitious importance to the malady – the hysterical malady, as some doctors would call it – from which she suffers. I can give you instructions for preserving her general health; and I can recommend you to try some change in her life – provided you first relieve her mind of any secret anxieties that may possibly be preying on it."'

The Captain smiled self-approvingly. The doctor had justified his anticipations. The doctor had suggested a practical solution of the difficulty.

'Aye! aye! At last we have hit the nail on the head! Secret anxieties. Yes! yes! Plain enough now. A disappointment in love – eh, Mrs Crayford?'

'I don't know, Captain Helding; I am quite in the dark. Clara's confidence in me – in other matters unbounded – is, in this matter of her (supposed) anxieties, a confidence still withheld. In all else we are like sisters. I sometimes fear there may indeed be some trouble preying secretly on her mind. I sometimes feel a little hurt at her incomprehensible silence.'

Captain Helding was ready with his own practical remedy for this difficulty.

'Encouragement is all she wants, ma'am. Take my word for it, this matter rests entirely with you. It's all in a nutshell. Encourage her to confide in you – and she *will* confide.'

'I am waiting to encourage her, Captain, until she is left alone with me – after you have all sailed for the Arctic Seas. In the meantime, will you consider what I have said to you as intended for your ear only? And will you forgive me if I own that the turn the subject has taken does not tempt me to pursue it any farther?'

The Captain took the hint. He instantly changed the subject; choosing, on this occasion, safe professional topics. He spoke of ships that were ordered on foreign service; and, finding that these as subjects failed to interest Mrs Crayford, he spoke next of ships that were ordered home again. This last experiment produced its effect – an effect which the Captain had not bargained for.

'Do you know,' he began, 'that the *Atalanta* is expected back from the West Coast of Africa every day? Have you any acquaintances among the officers of that ship?'

As it so happened, he put those questions to Mrs Crayford while they were engaged in one of the figures of the dance which brought them within hearing of the opposite couple. At the same moment – to the astonishment of her friends and admirers – Miss Clara Burnham threw the quadrille into confusion by making a mistake! Everybody waited to see her set the mistake right. She made no attempt to set it right – she turned deadly pale, and caught her partner by the arm.

'The heat!' she said faintly. 'Take me away – take me into the air!'

Lieutenant Crayford instantly led her out of the dance, and took her into the cool and empty conservatory at the end of the room. As a matter of course, Captain Helding and Mrs Crayford left the quadrille at the same time. The Captain saw his way to a joke.

'Is this the trance coming on?' he whispered. 'If it is, as commander of the Arctic Expedition, I have a particular request to make. Will the Second Sight oblige me by seeing the shortest way to the North-West Passage before we leave England?'

Mrs Crayford declined to humour the joke. 'If you will excuse my leaving you,' she said quietly, 'I will try and find out what is the matter with Miss Burnham.'

At the entrance to the conservatory Mrs Crayford encountered her husband. The Lieutenant was of middle age, tall and comely; a man with a winning simplicity and gentleness in his manner, and an irresistible kindness in his brave blue eyes. In one word, a man whom everybody loved – including his wife.

'Don't be alarmed,' said the Lieutenant. 'The heat has overcome her – that's all.'

Mrs Crayford shook her head, and looked at her husband, half satirically, half fondly.

'You dear old Innocent!' she exclaimed, 'that excuse may do for *you*. For my part, I don't believe a word of it. Go and get another partner, and leave Clara to me.'

She entered the conservatory and seated herself by Clara's side.

II

'Now, my dear!' (Mrs Crayford began) 'what does this mean?'

'Nothing.'

'That won't do, Clara. Try again.'

'The heat of the room—'

'That won't do either. Say that you choose to keep your own secrets, and I shall understand what you mean.'

Clara's sad, clear grey eyes looked up for the first time in Mrs Crayford's face, and suddenly became dimmed with tears.

'If I only dared tell you!' she murmured. 'I hold so to your good opinion of me, Lucy – and I am so afraid of losing it.'

Mrs Crayford's manner changed. Her eyes rested gravely and anxiously on Clara's face.

'You know as well as I do that nothing can shake my affection for you,' she said. 'Do justice, my child, to your old friend. There is nobody here to listen to what we say. Open your heart, Clara. I see you are in trouble, and I want to comfort you.'

Clara began to yield. In other words, she began to make conditions.

'Will you promise to keep what I tell you a secret from every living creature?' she began.

Mrs Crayford met that question by putting a question on her side.

'Does "every living creature" include my husband?'

'Your husband more than anybody! I love him, I revere him. He is so noble; he is so good! If I told him what I am going to tell you, he would despise me. Own it plainly, Lucy, if I am asking too much in asking you to keep a secret from your husband.'

'Nonsense, child! When you are married you will know that the easiest of all secrets to keep is a secret from your husband. I give you my promise. Now begin!'

Clara hesitated painfully.

'I don't know how to begin!' she exclaimed with a burst of despair. 'The words won't come to me.'

'Then I must help you. Do you feel ill to-night? Do you feel as you felt that day when you were with my sister and me in the garden?'

'Oh, no.'

'You are not ill, you are not really affected by the heat – and yet you turn as pale as ashes, and you are obliged to leave the quadrille! There must be some reason for this.'

'There *is* a reason. Captain Helding—'

'Captain Helding! What in the name of wonder has the Captain to do with it?'

'He told you something about the *Atalanta*. He said the *Atalanta* was expected back from Africa immediately.'

'Well, and what of that? Is there anybody in whom you are interested coming home in the ship?'

'Somebody whom I am afraid of is coming home in the ship.'

Mrs Crayford's magnificent black eyes opened wide in amazement.

'My dear Clara! do you really mean what you say?'

'Wait a little, Lucy, and you shall judge for yourself. We must go back – if I am to make you understand me – to the year before we knew each other; to the last year of my father's life. Did I ever tell you that my father moved southward, for the sake of his health, to a house in Kent that was lent to him by a friend?'

'No, my dear. I don't remember ever hearing of the house in Kent. Tell me about it.'

'There is nothing to tell – except this. The new house was near a fine country seat standing in its own park. The owner of the place was a gentleman named Wardour. He, too, was one of my father's Kentish friends. He had an only son.'

She paused, and played nervously with her fan. Mrs Crayford looked at her attentively. Clara's eyes remained fixed on her fan – Clara said no more.

'What was the son's name?' asked Mrs Crayford, quietly.

'Richard.'

'Am I right, Clara, in suspecting that Mr Richard Wardour admired you?'

The question produced its intended effect. The question helped Clara to go on.

'I hardly knew at first,' she said, 'whether he admired me or not. He was very strange in his ways – headstrong, terribly headstrong and passionate; but generous and affectionate in spite of his faults of temper. Can you understand such a character?'

'Such characters exist by thousands. I have my faults of temper. I begin to like Richard already. Go on.'

'The days went by, Lucy, and the weeks went by. We were thrown very much together. I began, little by little, to have some suspicion of the truth.'

'And Richard helped to confirm your suspicions, of course?'

'No. He was not – unhappily for me – he was not that sort of man. He never spoke of the feeling with which he regarded me. It was I who saw it. I couldn't help seeing it. I did all I could to show that I was willing to be a sister to him, and that I could never be anything else. He did not understand me, or he would not – I can't say which.'

'"Would not" is the most likely, my dear. Go on.'

'It might have been as you say. There was a strange rough bashfulness about him. He confused and puzzled me. He never spoke out. He seemed to treat me as if our future lives had been provided for while we were children. What could I do, Lucy?'

'Do? You could have asked your father to end the difficulty for you.'

'Impossible! You forget what I have just told you. My father was suffering at that time under the illness which afterwards caused his death. He was quite unfit to interfere.'

'Was there no one else who could help you?'

'No one.'

'No lady in whom you could confide?'

'I had acquaintances among the ladies in the neighbourhood. I had no friends.'

'What did you do, then?'

'Nothing. I hesitated; I put off coming to an explanation with him – unfortunately until it was too late.'

'What do you mean by too late?'

'You shall hear. I ought to have told you that Richard Wardour is in the navy—'

'Indeed? I am more interested in him than ever. Well?'

'One spring day, Richard came to our house to take leave of us before he joined his ship. I thought he was gone, and I went into the next room. It was my own sitting-room, and it opened on to the garden.'

'Yes?'

'Richard must have been watching me. He suddenly appeared in the garden. Without waiting for me to invite him, he walked into the room. I was a little startled as well as surprised, but I managed to hide it. I said, "What is it, Mr Wardour?" He stepped close up to me; he said, in his quick, rough way: "Clara! I am going to the African coast. If I live, I shall come back promoted; and we both know what will happen then." He kissed me. I was half frightened, half angry. Before I could compose myself to say a word, he was out in the garden again – he was gone! I ought to have spoken, I know. It was not honourable, not kind towards *him*. You can't reproach me for my want of courage and frankness more bitterly than I reproach myself!'

'My dear child, I don't reproach you. I only think you might have written to him.'

'I did write.'

'Plainly?'

'Yes. I told him in so many words that he was deceiving himself, and that I could never marry him.'

'Plain enough, in all conscience! Having said that, surely you are not to blame? What are you fretting about now?'

'Suppose my letter has never reached him?'

'Why should you suppose anything of the sort?'

'What I wrote required an answer, Lucy – *asked* for an answer. The answer has never come. What is the plain conclusion? My letter has never reached him. And the *Atalanta* is expected back! Richard Wardour is returning to England – Richard Wardour will claim me as his wife! You wondered just now if I really meant what I said. Do you doubt it still?'

Mrs Crayford leaned back absently in her chair. For the first time since the conversation had begun she let a question pass without making a reply. The truth is, Mrs Crayford was thinking.

She saw Clara's position plainly; she understood the disturbing effect of it on the mind of a young girl. Still, making all allowances, she felt quite at a loss, so far, to account for Clara's excessive agitation. Her quick observing faculty had just detected that Clara's face showed no signs of relief, now that she had unburdened herself of her secret. There was something clearly under the surface here – something of importance, that still remained to be discovered. A shrewd doubt crossed Mrs Crayford's mind, and inspired the next words which she addressed to her young friend.

'My dear,' she said abruptly, 'have you told me all?'

Clara started as if the question terrified her. Feeling sure that she had the clue in her hand, Mrs Crayford deliberately repeated her question in another form of words. Instead of answering, Clara suddenly looked up. At the same moment a faint flush of colour appeared in her face for the first time.

Looking up instinctively on her side, Mrs Crayford became aware of the presence in the conservatory of a young gentleman who was claiming Clara as his partner in the coming waltz. Mrs Crayford fell into thinking once more. Had this young gentleman (she asked herself) anything to do with the untold end of the story? Was *this* the true secret of Clara Burnham's terror at the impending return of Richard Wardour? Mrs Crayford decided on putting her doubts to the test.

'A friend of yours, my dear?' she asked innocently. 'Suppose you introduce us to each other?'

Clara confusedly introduced the young gentleman.

'Mr Francis Aldersley, Lucy. Mr Aldersley belongs to the Arctic Expedition.'

'Attached to the expedition,' Mrs Crayford repeated. 'I am attached to the expedition too – in my way. I had better introduce myself, Mr Aldersley, as Clara seems to have forgotten to do it for me. I am Mrs Crayford. My husband is Lieutenant Crayford of the *Wanderer*. Do you belong to that ship?'

'I have not the honour, Mrs Crayford. I belong to the *Sea-Mew*.'

Mrs Crayford's superb eyes looked shrewdly backwards and forwards between Clara and Francis Aldersley, and saw the untold sequel to Clara's story. The young officer was a bright, handsome, gentleman-like lad – just the person to seriously complicate the difficulty with Richard Wardour! There was no time for making any further inquiries. The band had begun the prelude to the waltz, and Francis Aldersley was waiting for his partner. With a word of apology to the young man, Mrs Crayford drew Clara aside for a moment and spoke to her in a whisper.

'One word, my dear, before you return to the ball-room. It may sound conceited – after the little you have told me – but I think I understand your position *now* better than you do yourself. Do you want to hear my opinion?'

'I am longing to hear it, Lucy! I want your opinion; I want your advice.'

'You shall have both, in the plainest and the fewest words. First, my opinion: You have no choice but to come to an explanation with Mr Wardour as soon as he returns. Second, my advice: If you wish to make the explanation easy to both sides, take care that you make it in the character of a free woman.'

She laid a strong emphasis on the last three words, and looked pointedly at Francis Aldersley as she pronounced them. 'I won't keep you from your partner any longer, Clara,' she resumed, and led the way back to the ballroom.

III

THE burden on Clara's mind weighs on it more heavily than ever after what Mrs Crayford has said to her. She is too unhappy to feel the inspiriting influence of the dance. After a turn round the room, she complains of fatigue. Mr Francis Aldersley looks at the conservatory (still as invitingly cool and empty as ever), leads her back to it, and places her on a seat among the shrubs. She tries – very feebly – to dismiss him.

'Don't let me keep you from dancing, Mr Aldersley.'

He seats himself by her side, and feasts his eyes on the lovely downcast face that dares not turn towards him. He whispers to her:

'Call me Frank.'

She longs to call him Frank – she loves him with all her heart. But Mrs Crayford's warning words are still in her mind. She never opens her lips. Her lover moves a little closer, and asks another favour. Men are all alike on these occasions. Silence invariably encourages them to try again.

'Clara! have you forgotten what I said at the concert yesterday? May I say it again?'

'No!'

'We shall sail to-morrow for the Arctic Seas. I may not return for years. Don't send me away without hope! Think of the long lonely time in the dark North! Make it a happy time for *me*.'

Though he speaks with the fervour of a man, he is little more than a lad; he is only twenty years old – and he is going to risk his young life on the frozen deep! Clara pities him as she never pitied any human creature before. He gently takes her hand. She tries to release it.

'What! Not even that little favour on the last night?'

Her faithful heart takes his part, in spite of her. Her hand remains in his, and feels its soft persuasive pressure. She is a lost woman. It is only a question of time now!

'Clara! do you love me?'

There is a pause. She shrinks from looking at him – she trembles with strange contradictory sensations of pleasure and pain. His arm steals round her; he repeats his question in a whisper; his lips almost touch her little rosy ear as he says it again:

'Do you love me?'

She closes her eyes faintly – she hears nothing but those words – feels nothing but his arm round her – forgets Mrs Crayford's warning – forgets Richard Wardour himself – turns suddenly, with a loving woman's desperate disregard of everything but her love, nestles her head on his bosom, and answers him in that way at last!

He lifts the beautiful drooping head – their lips meet in their first kiss – they are both in heaven – it is Clara who brings them back to earth again with a start – it is Clara who says, 'Oh! what have I done?' – as usual, when it is too late.

Frank answers the question.

'You have made me happy, my angel. Now, when I come back, I come back to make you my wife.'

She shudders. She remembers Richard Wardour again at those words.

'Mind!' she says, 'nobody is to know we are engaged till I permit you to mention it. Remember that!'

He promises to remember it. His arm tries to wind round her once more. No! She is mistress of herself; she can positively dismiss him now – after she has let him kiss her!

'Go!' she says. 'I want to see Mrs Crayford. Find her! Say I am here, waiting to speak to her. Go at once, Frank – for my sake!'

There is no alternative but to obey her. His eyes drink a last draught of her beauty. He hurries away on his errand – the happiest man in the room. Five minutes since, she was only his partner in the dance. He has spoken – and she has pledged herself to be his partner for life!

IV

It was not easy to find Mrs Crayford in the crowd. Searching here and searching there, Frank became conscious of a stranger, who appeared to be looking for somebody on his side. He was a dark, heavy-browed, strongly-built man; dressed in a shabby old naval officer's uniform. His manner – strikingly resolute and self-contained – was unmistakably the manner of a gentleman. He wound his way slowly through the crowd; stopping to look at every lady whom he passed, and then looking away again with a frown. Little by little he approached the conservatory – entered it, after a moment's reflection – detected the glimmer of a white dress in the distance, through the shrubs and flowers – advanced to get a nearer view of the lady – and burst into Clara's presence with a cry of delight.

She sprang to her feet. She stood before him speechless, motionless, struck to stone. All her life was in her eyes – the eyes which told her she was looking at Richard Wardour.

He was the first to speak.

'I am sorry I startled you, my darling. I forgot everything but the happiness of seeing you again. We only reached our moorings two hours since. I was some time inquiring after you, and some time getting my ticket, when they told me you were at the ball. Wish me joy, Clara! I am promoted. I have come back to make you my wife.'

A momentary change passed over the blank terror of her face. Her colour rose faintly, her lips moved. She abruptly put a question to him.

'Did you get my letter?'

He started. 'A letter from you? I never received it.'

The momentary animation died out of her face again. She drew back from him, and dropped into a chair. He advanced towards her, astonished and alarmed. She shrank in the chair – shrank, as if she was frightened of him.

'Clara! you have not even shaken hands with me! What does it mean?'

He paused, waiting, and watching her. She made no reply. A flash of the quick temper in him leapt up in his eyes. He repeated his last words in louder and sterner tones:

'What does it mean?'

She replied this time. His tone had hurt her – his tone had roused her sinking courage.

'It means, Mr Wardour, that you have been mistaken from the first.'

'How have I been mistaken?'

'You have been under a wrong impression, and you have given me no opportunity of setting you right.'

'In what way have I been wrong?'

'You have been too hasty and too confident about yourself and about me. You have entirely misunderstood me. I am grieved to distress you, but for your sake I must speak plainly. I am your friend always, Mr Wardour. I can never be your wife.'

He mechanically repeated the last words. He seemed to doubt whether he had heard her right.

'You can never be my wife?'

'Never!'

'Why?'

There was no answer. She was incapable of telling him a falsehood. She was ashamed to tell him the truth.

He stooped over her, and suddenly possessed himself of her hand. Holding her hand firmly, he stooped a little lower, searching for the signs which might answer him in her face. His own face darkened slowly while he looked. He was beginning to suspect her, and he acknowledged it in his next words.

'Something has changed you towards me, Clara. Somebody has influenced you against me. Is it – you force me to ask the question – is it some other man?'

'You have no right to ask me that.'

He went on without noticing what she had said to him.

'Has that other man come between you and me? I speak plainly on my side. Speak plainly on yours.'

'I *have* spoken. I have nothing more to say.'

There was a pause. She saw the warning light which told of the fire within him, growing brighter and brighter in his eyes. She felt his grasp strengthening on her hand. She heard him appeal to her for the last time.

'Reflect,' he said, 'reflect before it is too late. Your silence will not serve you. If you persist in not answering me, I shall take your silence as a confession. Do you hear me?'

'I hear you.'

'Clara Burnham! I am not to be trifled with. Clara Burnham! I insist on the truth. Are you false to me?'

She resented that searching question with a woman's keen sense of the insult that is implied in doubting her to her face.

'Mr Wardour! you forget yourself when you call me to account in that way. I never encouraged you. I never gave you promise or pledge—'

He passionately interrupted her before she could say more.

'You have engaged yourself in my absence. Your words own it; your looks own it! You have engaged yourself to another man!'

'If I *have* engaged myself, what right have you to complain of it?' she answered firmly. 'What right have you to control my actions— ?'

The next words died away on her lips. He suddenly dropped her hand. A marked change appeared in the expression of his eyes – a change which told her of the terrible passions that she had let loose in him. She read, dimly read, something in his face which made her tremble – not for herself, but for Frank.

Little by little the dark colour faded out of his face. His deep voice dropped suddenly to a low and quiet tone as he spoke the parting words.

'Say no more, Miss Burnham – you have said enough. I am answered; I am dismissed.' He paused, and stepping close up to her laid his hand on her arm.

'The time may come,' he said, 'when I shall forgive *you*. But the man who has robbed me of you shall rue the day when you and he first met.'

He turned, and left her.

A few minutes later, Mrs Crayford, entering the conservatory, was met by one of the attendants at the ball. The man stopped as if he wished to speak to her.

'What do you want?' she asked.

'I beg your pardon, ma'am. Do you happen to have a smelling-bottle about you? There is a young lady in the conservatory who is taken faint.'

BETWEEN THE SCENES

THE LANDING STAGE

V

The morning of the next day – the morning on which the ships were to sail – came bright and breezy. Mrs Crayford, having arranged to follow her husband to the water-side and see the last of him before he embarked, entered Clara's room on her way out of the house, anxious to hear how her young friend had passed the night. To her astonishment, she found Clara had risen and was dressed, like herself, to go out.

'What does this mean, my dear? After what you suffered last night – after the shock of seeing that man – why don't you take my advice and rest in your bed?'

'I can't rest. I have not slept all night. Have you been out yet?'

'No.'

'Have you seen or heard anything of Richard Wardour?'

'What an extraordinary question!'

'Answer my question! Don't trifle with me!'

'Compose yourself, Clara. I have neither seen nor heard anything of Richard Wardour. Take my word for it, he is far enough away by this time.'

'No! He is here! He is near us! All night long the presentiment has pursued me – Frank and Richard Wardour will meet.'

'My dear child, what are you thinking of? They are total strangers to each other.'

'Something will happen to bring them together. I feel it! I know it! They will meet; there will be a mortal quarrel between them, and I shall be to blame. Oh, Lucy! why didn't I take your advice? Why was I mad enough to let Frank know that I loved him? Are you going to the landing-stage? I am all ready; I must go with you.'

'You must not think of it, Clara. There will be crowding and confusion at the water-side. You are not strong enough to bear it. Wait – I won't be long away – wait till I come back.'

'I must, and will, go with you! Crowd! *He* will be among the crowd! Confusion! In that confusion *he* will find his way to Frank! Don't ask me to wait. I shall go mad if I wait. I shall not know a moment's ease until I have seen Frank with my own eyes safe in the boat which takes him to his ship. You have got your bonnet on; what are we stopping here for? Come! or I shall go without you. Look at the clock! We have not a moment to lose!'

It was useless to contend with her. Mrs Crayford yielded. The two women left the house together.

The landing-stage, as Mrs Crayford had predicted, was thronged with spectators. Not only the relatives and friends of the Arctic voyagers, but strangers as well, had assembled in large numbers to see the ships sail. Clara's eyes wandered affrightedly hither and thither among the strange faces in the crowd, searching for the one face that she dreaded to see, and not finding it. So completely were her nerves unstrung, that she started with a cry of alarm on suddenly hearing Frank's voice behind her.

'The *Sea-Mew*'s boats are waiting,' he said. 'I must go, darling. How pale you are looking, Clara! Are you ill?'

She never answered. She questioned him with wild eyes and trembling lips.

'Has anything happened to you, Frank? anything out of the common?'

Frank laughed at the strange question.

'Anything out of the common?' he repeated. 'Nothing that I know of, except sailing for the Arctic Seas. That's out of the common, I suppose; isn't it?'

'Has anybody spoken to you since last night? Has any stranger followed you in the street?'

Frank turned in blank amazement to Mrs Crayford.

'What on earth does she mean?'

Mrs Crayford's lively invention supplied her with an answer on the spur of the moment.

'Do you believe in dreams, Frank? Of course you don't! Clara has been dreaming about you, and Clara is foolish enough to believe in dreams. That's all; it's not worth talking about. Hark! they are calling you. Say good-bye, or you will be too late for the boat.'

Frank took Clara's hand. Long afterwards – in the dark Arctic days, in the dreary Arctic nights – he remembered how coldly and how passively that hand lay in his.

'Courage, Clara!' he said gaily. 'A sailor's sweetheart must accustom herself to partings. The time will soon pass. Good-bye, my darling! Good-bye, my wife!'

He kissed the cold hand; he looked his last – for many a long year perhaps! – at the pale and beautiful face. How she loves me! he thought. How the parting distresses her! He still held her hand; he would have lingered longer, if Mrs Crayford had not wisely waived all ceremony and pushed him away.

The two ladies followed him at a safe distance through the crowd, and saw him step into the boat. The oars struck the water; Frank waved his cap to Clara. In a moment more a vessel at anchor hid the boat from view. They had seen the last of him on his way to the Frozen Deep!

'No Richard Wardour in the boat,' said Mrs Crayford. 'No Richard Wardour on the shore. Let this be a lesson to you, my dear. Never be foolish enough to believe in presentiments again.'

Clara's eyes still wandered suspiciously to and fro among the crowd.

'Are you not satisfied yet?' asked Mrs Crayford.

'No,' Clara answered. 'I am not satisfied yet.'

'What! still looking for him? This is really too absurd. Here is my husband coming. I shall tell him to call a cab and send you home.'

Clara drew back a few steps.

'I won't be in the way, Lucy, while you are taking leave of your good husband,' she said. 'I will wait here.'

'Wait here! What for?'

'For something which I may yet see. Or for something which I may still hear.'

'Richard Wardour?'

'Richard Wardour.'

Mrs Crayford turned to her husband without another word. Clara's infatuation was beyond the reach of remonstrance.

The boats of the *Wanderer* took the place at the landing-stage vacated by the boats of the *Sea-Mew*. A burst of cheering among the outer ranks of the crowd announced the arrival of the commander of the expedition on the scene. Captain Helding appeared, looking right and left for his first lieutenant. Finding Crayford with his wife, the captain made his apologies for interfering with his best grace.

'Give him up to his professional duties for one minute, Mrs Crayford, and you shall have him back again for half an hour. The Arctic Expedition is to blame, my dear lady – not the captain – for parting man and wife. In Crayford's place I should have left it to the bachelors to find the North-West Passage, and have stopped at home with you.'

Excusing himself in those bluntly complimentary terms, Captain Helding drew the lieutenant aside a few steps, accidentally taking a direction that led the two officers close to the place at which Clara was standing. Both the captain and the lieutenant were too completely absorbed in their professional duties to notice her. Neither the one nor the other had the faintest suspicion that she could, and did, hear every word of the talk that passed between them.

'You received my note this morning?' the captain began.

'Certainly, Captain Helding, or I should have been on board the ship before this.'

'I am going on board myself at once,' the captain proceeded. 'But I must ask you to keep your boat waiting for half an hour more. You will be all the longer with your wife, you know. I thought of that, Crayford.'

'I am much obliged to you, Captain Helding. I suppose there is some other reason for inverting the customary order of things, and keeping the lieutenant on shore after the captain is on board?'

'Quite true; there *is* another reason. I want you to wait for a volunteer who has just joined us.'

'A volunteer!'

'Yes; he has his outfit to get in a hurry, and he may be half an hour late.'

'It's rather a sudden appointment, isn't it?'

'No doubt. Very sudden.'

'And, pardon me, it's rather a long time (as we are situated) to keep the ships waiting for one man?'

'Quite true, again. But a man who is worth having is worth waiting for. This man is worth having; this man is worth his weight in gold to such an expedition as ours. Seasoned to all climates and all fatigues, a strong fellow, a brave fellow, a clever fellow – in short, an excellent officer. I know him well, or I should never have taken him. The country gets plenty of work out of my new volunteer, Crayford. He only returned yesterday from foreign service.'

'He only returned yesterday from foreign service, and he volunteers this morning to join the Arctic expedition! You astonish me.'

'I dare say I do; you can't be more astonished than I was when he presented himself at my hotel and told me what he wanted. "Why, my good fellow, you have just got home," I said; "are you weary of your freedom after only a few hours' experience of it?" His answer rather startled me. He said, "I am weary of my life, sir; I have come home and found a trouble to welcome me which goes near to break my heart. If I don't take refuge in absence and hard work, I am a lost man. Will you give me refuge?" That's what he said, Crayford, word for word.'

'Did you ask him to explain himself further?'

'Not I; I knew his value, and I took the poor devil on the spot without pestering him with any more questions. No need to ask him to explain himself; the facts speak for themselves in these cases. The old story, my good friend. There's a woman at the bottom of it, of course.'

Mrs Crayford, waiting for the return of her husband as patiently as she could, was startled by feeling a hand suddenly laid on her shoulder. She looked round and confronted Clara. Her first feeling of surprise changed instantly to alarm. Clara was trembling from head to foot.

'What is the matter? What has frightened you, my dear?'

'Lucy! I *have* heard of him!'

'Richard Wardour again?'

'Remember what I told you. I have heard every word of the conversation between Captain Helding and your husband. A man came to the Captain this morning and volunteered to join the *Wanderer*. The Captain has taken him. The man is Richard Wardour.'

'You don't mean it! Are you sure? Did you hear Captain Helding mention his name?'

'No.'

'Then how do you know it's Richard Wardour?'

'Don't ask me! I am as certain of it as that I am standing here! They are going away together, Lucy – away to the eternal ice and snow. My foreboding has come true! The two will meet – the man who is to marry me, and the man whose heart I have broken!'

'Your foreboding has *not* come true, Clara! The men have not met here – the men are not likely to meet elsewhere. They are appointed to separate ships. Frank belongs to the *Sea-Mew*, and Wardour to the *Wanderer*. See! Captain Helding has done. My husband is coming this way. Let me make sure. Let me speak to him.'

Lieutenant Crayford returned to his wife. She spoke to him instantly.

'William, you have got a new volunteer who joins the *Wanderer*?'

'What! you have been listening to the Captain and me?'

'I want to know his name.'

'How in the world did you manage to hear what we said to each other?'

'His name? has the Captain given you his name?'

'Don't excite yourself, my dear. Look! you are positively alarming Miss Burnham. The new volunteer is a perfect stranger to us. There is his name – last on the ship's list.'

Mrs Crawford snatched the list out of her husband's hand, and read the name:

'RICHARD WARDOUR.'

SECOND SCENE

THE HUT OF THE SEA-MEW

VI

Good-bye to England! Good-bye to inhabited and civilised regions of the earth!

Two years have passed since the voyagers sailed from their native shores. The enterprise has failed – the Arctic Expedition is lost and ice-locked in the Polar wastes. The good ships *Wanderer* and *Sea-Mew*, entombed in ice, will never ride the buoyant waters more. Stripped of their lighter timbers, both vessels have been used for the construction of huts, erected on the nearest land.

The largest of the two buildings which now shelter the lost men is occupied by the surviving officers and crew of the *Sea-Mew*. On one side of the principal room are the sleeping-berths and the fireplace. The other side discloses a broad doorway (closed by a canvas screen), which serves as a means of communication with an inner apartment, devoted to the superior officers. A hammock is slung to the rough raftered roof of the main room as an extra bed. A man, completely hidden by his bedclothes, is sleeping in the hammock. By the fireside there is a second man – supposed to be on the watch – fast asleep, poor wretch! at the present moment. Behind the sleeper stands an old cask, which serves for a table. The objects at present on the table are a pestle and mortar, and a saucepan full of the dry bones of animals. In plain words, the dinner for the day. By way of ornament to the dull brown walls, icicles appear in the crevices of the timber, gleaming at intervals in the red firelight. No wind whistles outside the lonely dwelling – no cry of bird or beast is heard. Indoors and out of doors the awful silence of the Polar desert reigns, for the moment, undisturbed.

VII

The first sound that broke the silence came from the inner apartment. An officer lifted the canvas screen in the hut of the *Sea-Mew* and entered the main room. Cold and privation had sadly thinned the ranks. The commander of the ship – Captain Ebsworth – was dangerously ill. The first lieutenant was dead. An officer of the *Wanderer* filled their places for the time, with Captain Helding's permission. The officer so employed was – Lieutenant Crayford.

He approached the man at the fireside and awakened him.

'Jump up, Bateson! It's your turn to be relieved.'

The relief appeared, rising from a heap of old sails at the back of the hut. Bateson vanished, yawning, to his bed. Lieutenant Crayford walked backwards and forwards briskly, trying what exercise would do towards warming his blood.

The pestle and mortar on the cask attracted his attention. He stopped and looked up at the man in the hammock.

'I must rouse the cook,' he said to himself, with a smile. 'That fellow little thinks how useful he is in keeping up my spirits. The most inveterate croaker and grumbler in the world – and yet, according to his own account, the only cheerful man in the whole ship's company. John Want! John Want! Rouse up, there!'

A head rose slowly out of the bedclothes, covered with a red night-cap. A melancholy nose rested itself on the edge of the hammock. A voice, worthy of the nose, expressed its opinion of the Arctic climate in these words:

'Lord! Lord! here's all my breath on my blanket. Icicles, if you please, sir, all round my mouth and all over my blanket. Every time I have snored I've frozen something. When a man gets the cold into him to that extent that he ices his own bed, it can't last much longer. Never mind! *I* don't grumble.'

Crayford tapped the saucepan of bones impatiently. John Want lowered himself to the floor – grumbling all the way – by a rope attached to the rafters at his bed head. Instead of approaching his superior officer and his saucepan he hobbled, shivering, to the fireplace, and held his chin as close as he possibly could over the fire. Crayford looked after him.

'Hullo! what are you doing there?'

'Thawing my beard, sir.'

'Come here directly, and set to work on these bones.'

John Want remained immovably attached to the fireplace, holding something else over the fire. Crayford began to lose his temper.

'What the devil are you about now?'

'Thawing my watch, sir. It's been under my pillow all night, and the cold has stopped it. Cheerful, wholesome, bracing sort of climate to live in, isn't it, sir? Never mind! *I* don't grumble.'

'No; we all know that. Look here! Are these bones pounded small enough?'

John Want suddenly approached the lieutenant, and looked at him with an appearance of the deepest interest.

'You'll excuse me, sir,' he said; 'how very hollow your voice sounds this morning.'

'Never mind my voice. The bones! the bones!'

'Yes, sir – the bones. They'll take a trifle more pounding. I'll do my best with them, sir, for your sake.'

'What do you mean?'

John Want shook his head, and looked at Crayford with a dreary smile.

'I don't think I shall have the honour of making much more bone soup for you, sir. Do you think yourself you'll last long, sir? I don't, saving your presence. I think about another week or ten days will do for us all. Never mind. *I* don't grumble.'

He poured the bones into the mortar and began to pound them – under protest. At the same moment a sailor appeared, entering from the inner hut.

'A message from Captain Ebsworth, sir.'

'Well?'

'The Captain is worse than ever with his freezing pains, sir. He wants to see you immediately.'

'I will go at once. Rouse the doctor.'

Answering in those terms, Crayford returned to the inner hut, followed by the sailor. John Want shook his head again, and smiled more drearily than ever.

'Rouse the doctor,' he repeated. 'Suppose the doctor should be frozen? He hadn't a ha'porth of warmth in him last night, and his voice sounded like a whisper in a speaking trumpet. Will the bones do now? Yes, the bones will do now. Into the saucepan with you,' cried John Want, suiting the action to the word, 'and flavour the hot water if you can! When I remember that I was once an apprentice at a pastrycook's – when I think of the gallons of turtle-soup that this hand has stirred up in a jolly hot kitchen – and when I find myself mixing bones and hot water for soup, and turning into ice as fast as I can, if I wasn't of a cheerful disposition I should feel inclined to grumble. John Want! John Want! whatever had you done with your natural senses, when you made up your mind to go to sea?'

A new voice hailed the cook, speaking from one of the bedplaces in the side of the hut. It was the voice of Francis Aldersley.

'Who's that croaking over the fire?'

'Croaking?' repeated John Want, with the air of a man who considered himself the object of a gratuitous insult. 'Croaking? You don't find your own voice at all altered for the worse – do you, Mr Frank? I don't give *him*,' John proceeded, speaking confidentially to himself, 'more than six hours to last. He's one of your grumblers.'

'What are you doing there?' asked Frank.

'I'm making bone soup, sir, and wondering why I ever went to sea.'

'Well, and why did you go to sea?'

'I'm not certain, Mr Frank. Sometimes I think it was natural perversity; sometimes I think it was false pride at getting over sea-sickness; sometimes I think it was reading *Robinson Crusoe* and books warning of me *not* to go to sea.'

Frank laughed. 'You're an odd fellow. What do you mean by false pride at getting over sea-sickness? Did you get over sea-sickness in some new way?'

John Want's dismal face brightened in spite of himself. Frank had recalled to the cook's memory one of the noteworthy passages in the cook's life.

'That's it, sir!' he said. 'If ever a man cured sea-sickness in a new way yet, I am that man – I got over it, Mr Frank, by dint of hard eating. I was a passenger on board a packet-boat, sir, when first I saw blue water. A nasty lopp of a sea came on at dinner-time, and I began to feel queer the moment the soup was put on the table. "Sick?" says the captain. "Rather, sir," says I. "Will you try my cure?" says the captain. "Certainly, sir," says I. "Is your heart in your mouth yet?" says the captain. "Not quite, sir," says I. "Mock-turtle soup," says the captain, and helps me. I swallow a couple of spoonfuls, and turn as white as a sheet. The captain cocks his eye at me. "Go on deck, sir," says he, "get rid of the soup, and then come back to the cabin." I got rid of the soup, and then came back to the cabin. "Cod's head-and-shoulders," says the captain, and helps me. "I can't stand it, sir," says I. "You must," says the captain, "because it's the cure." I crammed down a mouthful and turned paler than ever. "Go on deck," says the captain. "Get rid of the cod's head, and come back to the cabin." Off I go, and back I come. "Boiled leg of mutton and trimmings," says the captain, and helps me. "No fat, sir," says I. "Fat's the cure," says the captain, and makes me eat it. "Lean's the cure," says the captain, and makes me eat it. "Steady?" says the captain. "Sick," says I. "Go on deck," says the captain, "get rid of the boiled leg of mutton and trimmings, and come back to the cabin." Off I go, staggering – back I come, more dead than alive. "Devilled kidneys," says the captain. I shut my eyes, and got 'em down. "Cure's beginning," says the captain. "Mutton chop and pickles." I shut my eyes and got *them* down. "Broiled ham and cayenne pepper," says the captain. "Glass of stout and cranberry tart. Want to go on deck again?" "No, sir," says I. "Cure's done," says the captain. "Never you give in to your stomach, and your stomach will end in giving in to *you*."'

Having stated the moral purpose of his story in those unanswerable words, John Want took himself and his saucepan into the kitchen. A moment later Crayford returned to the hut, and astonished Frank Aldersley by an unexpected question.

'Have you anything in your berth, Frank, that you set a value on?'

Frank looked puzzled.

'Nothing that I set the smallest value on – when I am out of it,' he replied. 'What does your question mean?'

'We are almost as short of fuel as we are of provisions,' Crayford proceeded. 'Your berth will make good firing. I have directed Bateson to be here in ten minutes with his axe.'

'Very attentive and considerate on your part,' said Frank. 'What is to become of me, if you please, when Bateson has chopped my bed into firewood?'

'Can't you guess?'

'I suppose the cold has stupefied me. The riddle is beyond my reading. Suppose you give me a hint?'

'Certainly. There will be beds to spare soon – there is to be a change at last in our wretched lives here. Do you see it now?'

Frank's eyes sparkled. He sprang out of his berth and waved his fur cap in triumph.

'See it?' he exclaimed; 'of course I do! The exploring party is to start at last. Do I go with the expedition?'

'It is not very long since you were in the doctor's hands, Frank,' said Crayford, kindly. 'I doubt if you are strong enough yet to make one of the exploring party.'

'Strong enough or not,' returned Frank, 'any risk is better than pining and perishing here. Put me down, Crayford, among those who volunteer to go.'

'Volunteers will not be accepted in this case,' said Crayford. 'Captain Helding and Captain Ebsworth see serious objections, as we are situated, to that method of proceeding.'

'Do they mean to keep the appointments in their own hands?' asked Frank. 'I, for one, object to that.'

'Wait a little,' said Crayford. 'You were playing backgammon the other day with one of the officers. Does the board belong to him or to you?'

'It belongs to me. I have got it in my locker here. What do you want with it?'

'I want the dice and the box, for casting lots. The captains have arranged – most wisely, as I think – that Chance shall decide among us who goes with the expedition, and who stays behind in the huts. The officers and crew of the *Wanderer* will be here in a few minutes to cast the lots. Neither you nor any one can object to that way of settling the question. Officers and men alike take their chance together. Nobody can grumble.'

'*I* am quite satisfied,' said Frank. 'But I know of one man among the officers who is sure to make objections.'

'Who is the man?'

'You know him well enough too. The "Bear of the Expedition," Richard Wardour.'

'Frank! Frank! you have a bad habit of letting your tongue run away with you. Don't repeat that stupid nickname when you talk of my good friend, Richard Wardour.'

'Your good friend? Crayford! your liking for that man amazes me.'

Crayford laid his hand kindly on Frank's shoulder. Of all the officers of the *Sea-Mew*, Crayford's favourite was Frank.

'Why should it amaze you?' he asked. 'What opportunities have *you* had of judging? You and Wardour have always belonged to different ships. I have never seen you in Wardour's society for five minutes together. How can *you* form a fair estimate of his character?'

'I take the general estimate of his character,' Frank answered. 'He has got his nickname because he is the most unpopular man in his ship. Nobody likes him – there must be some reason for that.'

'There is only one reason for it,' Crayford rejoined. 'Nobody understands Richard Wardour. I am not talking at random. Remember I sailed from England with him in the *Wanderer*, and I was only transferred to the *Sea-Mew* long after we were locked up in the ice. I was Richard Wardour's companion on board ship for months, and I learnt there to do him justice. Under all his outward defects, I tell you there beats a great and generous heart. Suspend your opinion, my lad, until you know my friend as well as I do. No more of this now. Give me the dice and the box.'

Frank opened his locker. At the same time the silence of the snowy waste outside was broken by a shouting of voices hailing the hut – '*Sea-Mew*, a-hoy!'

VIII

The sailor on watch opened the outer door. There, plodding over the ghastly white snow, were the officers of the *Wanderer* approaching the hut. There, scattered under the merciless black sky, were the crew, with the dogs and the sledges, waiting the word which was to start them on their perilous and doubtful journey.

Captain Helding of the *Wanderer*, accompanied by his officers, entered the hut – in high spirits at the prospect of a change. Behind them, lounging in slowly by himself, was a dark, sullen, heavy-browed man. He neither spoke nor offered his hand to anybody; he was the one person present who seemed to be perfectly indifferent to the fate in store for him. This was the man whom his brother officers had nicknamed the Bear of the Expedition. In other words – Richard Wardour.

Crayford advanced to welcome Captain Helding. Frank – remembering the friendly reproof which he had just received – passed over the other officers of the *Wanderer*, and made a special effort to be civil to Crayford's friend.

'Good morning, Mr Wardour,' he said. 'We may congratulate each other on the chance of leaving this horrible place.'

'*You* may think it horrible,' Wardour retorted. 'I like it.'

'Like it? Good heavens! why?'

'Because there are no women here.'

Frank turned to his brother officers, without making any further advances in the direction of Richard Wardour. The Bear of the Expedition was more unapproachable than ever.

In the meantime, the hut had become thronged by the able-bodied officers and men of the two ships. Captain Helding, standing in the midst of them, with Crayford by his side, proceeded to explain the purpose of the contemplated expedition to the audience which surrounded him.

He began in these words:

'Brother officers and men of the *Wanderer* and *Sea-Mew*, it is my duty to tell you, very briefly, the reasons which have decided Captain Ebsworth and myself on despatching an exploring party in search of help. Without recalling all the hardships we have suffered for the last two years – the destruction, first of one of our ships, then of the other; the death of some of our bravest and best companions; the vain battles we have been fighting with the ice and snow, and boundless desolation of these inhospitable regions – without dwelling on these things, it is my duty to remind you that this, the last place in which we have taken refuge, is far beyond the track of any previous expedition, and that consequently our chance of being discovered by any rescuing parties that may be sent to look after us is, to say the least of it, a chance of the most uncertain kind. You all agree with me, gentlemen, so far?'

The officers (with the exception of Wardour, who stood apart in sullen silence) all agreed, so far.

The Captain went on.

'It is therefore urgently necessary that we should make another, and probably a last, effort to extricate ourselves. The winter is not far off, game is getting scarcer and scarcer, our stock of provisions is running low, and the sick – especially, I am sorry to say, the sick in the *Wanderer*'s hut – are increasing in number day by day. We must look to our own lives, and to the lives of those who are dependent on us, and we have no time to lose.'

The officers echoed the words cheerfully.

'Right! right! No time to lose.'

Captain Helding resumed:

'The plan proposed is, that a detachment of the able-bodied officers and men among us should set forth this very day, and make another effort to reach the nearest inhabited settlements, from which help and provisions may be despatched to those who remain here. The new direction to be taken, and the various precautions to be adopted, are all drawn out ready. The only question now before us is – Who is to stop here, and who is to undertake the journey?'

The officers answered the question with one accord – 'Volunteers!'

The men echoed their officers. 'Aye, aye, volunteers.'

Wardour still preserved his sullen silence. Crayford noticed him, standing apart from the rest, and appealed to him personally.

'Do you say nothing?' he asked.

'Nothing,' Wardour answered. 'Go or stay, it's all one to me.'

'I hope you don't really mean that?' said Crayford.

'I do.'

'I am sorry to hear it, Wardour.'

Captain Helding answered the general suggestion in favour of volunteering by a question which instantly checked the rising enthusiasm of the meeting.

'Well,' he said, 'suppose we say volunteers. Who volunteers to stop in the huts?'

There was a dead silence. The officers and men looked at each other confusedly. The Captain continued.

'You see we can't settle it by volunteering. You all want to go. Every man among us who has the use of his limbs naturally wants to go. But what is to become of those who have *not* got the use of their limbs? Some of us must stay here and take care of the sick.'

Everybody admitted that this was true.

'So we get back again,' said the Captain, 'to the old question – Who among the able-bodied is to go, and who is to stay? Captain Ebsworth says, and I say, let chance decide it. Here are dice. The numbers run as high as twelve – double sixes. All who throw under six, stay; all who throw over six, go. Officers of the *Wanderer* and the *Sea-Mew*, do you agree to that way of meeting the difficulty?'

All the officers agreed – with the one exception of Wardour, who still kept silence.

'Men of the *Wanderer* and *Sea-Mew*, your officers agree to cast lots. Do you agree too?'

The men agreed without a dissentient voice. Crayford handed the box and the dice to Captain Helding.

'You throw first, sir. Under six, "Stay." Over six, "Go."'

Captain Helding cast the dice; the top of the cask serving for a table. He threw seven.

'Go,' said Crayford. 'I congratulate you, sir. Now for my own chance.' He cast the dice in his turn. Three. 'Stay! Ah, well! well! if I can do my duty and be of use to others, what does it matter whether I go or stay? Wardour, you are next, in the absence of your first lieutenant.'

Wardour prepared to cast without shaking the dice.

'Shake the box, man!' cried Crayford. 'Give yourself a chance of luck!'

Wardour persisted in letting the dice fall out carelessly, just as they lay in the box.

'Not I!' he muttered to himself. 'I've done with luck.' Saying those words, he threw down the empty box, and seated himself on the nearest chest, without looking to see how the dice had fallen.

Crayford examined them. 'Six!' he exclaimed. 'There! you have a second chance, in spite of yourself. You are neither under nor over – you throw again.'

'Bah!' growled the Bear. 'It's not worth the trouble of getting up for. Somebody else throw for me.' He suddenly looked at Frank. 'You! you have got what the women call a lucky face.'

Frank appealed to Crayford. 'Shall I?'

'Yes, if he wishes it,' said Crayford.

Frank cast the dice. 'Five! He stays! Wardour, I am sorry I have thrown against you.'

'Go or stay,' reiterated Wardour, 'it's all one to me. You will be luckier, young one, when you cast for yourself.'

Frank cast for himself.

'Eight. Hurrah! I go!'

'What did I tell you?' said Wardour. 'The chance was yours. You have thriven on my ill luck.'

He rose, as he spoke, to leave the hut. Crayford stopped him.

'Have you anything particular to do, Richard?'

'What has anybody to do here?'

'Wait a little, then. I want to speak to you when this business is over.'

'Are you going to give me any more good advice?'

'Don't look at me in that sour way, Richard. I am going to ask you a question about something which concerns yourself.'

Wardour yielded without a word more. He returned to his chest, and cynically composed himself to slumber. The casting of the lots went on rapidly among the officers and men. In another half hour chance had decided the question of 'Go' or 'Stay' for all alike. The men left the hut. The officers .tered the inner apartment for a last conference with the bedridden captain o. the *Sea-Mew*. Wardour and Crayford were left together, alone.

IX

Crayford touched his friend on the shoulder to rouse him. Wardour looked up, impatiently, with a frown.

'I was just asleep,' he said. 'Why do you wake me?'

'Look round you, Richard. We are alone.'

'Well – and what of that?'

'I wish to speak to you privately, and this is my opportunity. You have disappointed and surprised me today. Why did you say it was all one to you whether you went or stayed? Why are you the only man among us who seems to be perfectly indifferent whether we are rescued or not?'

'Can a man always give a reason for what is strange in his manner or his words?' Wardour retorted.

'He can try,' said Crayford quietly, 'when his friend asks him.'

Wardour's manner softened.

'That's true,' he said. 'I *will* try. Do you remember the first night at sea, when we sailed from England in the *Wanderer*?'

'As well as if it was yesterday.'

'A calm, still night,' the other went on, thoughtfully. 'No clouds, no stars. Nothing in the sky but the broad moon, and hardly a ripple to break the path of light she made in the quiet water. Mine was the middle watch that night. You came on deck, and found me alone—'

He stopped. Crayford took his hand, and finished the sentence for him.

'Alone – and in tears.'

'The last I shall ever shed,' Wardour added bitterly.

'Don't say that. There are times when a man is to be pitied, indeed, if he can shed no tears. Go on, Richard.'

Wardour proceeded – still following the old recollections, still preserving his gentler tones.

'I should have quarrelled with any other man who had surprised me at that moment,' he said. 'There was something, I suppose, in your voice, when you asked my pardon for disturbing me, that softened my heart. I told you I had met with a disappointment which had broken me for life. There was no need to explain further. The only hopeless wretchedness in this world is the wretchedness that women cause.'

'And the only unalloyed happiness,' said Crayford, 'the happiness that women bring.'

'That may be your experience of them,' Wardour answered. 'Mine is different. All the devotion, the patience, the humility, the worship that there is in man I laid at the feet of a woman. She accepted the offering as women do – accepted it easily, gracefully, unfeelingly – accepted it as a matter of course. I left England to win a high place in my profession before I dared to win *her*. I braved danger and faced death. I staked my life in the fever-swamps of Africa to gain the promotion that I only desired for her sake – and gained it. I came back to give her all, and to ask nothing in return but to rest my weary heart in the sunshine of her smile. And her own lips – the lips I had kissed at parting – told me that another man had robbed me of her. I spoke but few words when I heard that confession, and left her for ever. "The time may come," I told her, "when I shall forgive *you*. But the man who has robbed me of you shall rue the day when you and he first met." Don't ask me who he was! I have yet to discover him. The treachery had been kept secret; nobody could tell me where to find him; nobody could tell me who he was. What did it matter? When I had lived out the first agony, I could rely on myself – I could be patient and bide my time.'

'Your time? What time?'

'The time when I and that man shall meet, face to face. I knew it then; I know it now – it was written on my heart then, it is written on my heart now – we two shall meet and know each other! With that conviction strong within me, I volunteered for this service, as I would have volunteered for anything that set work and hardship and danger, like ramparts, between my misery and me. With that conviction strong within me still, I tell you it is no matter whether I stay here with the sick or go hence with the strong. I shall live till I have met that man! There is a day of reckoning appointed between us. Here in the freezing cold, or away in the deadly heat – in battle or in shipwreck – in the face of starvation, under the shadow of pestilence – I, though hundreds are falling round me, I shall live! live for the coming of one day! live for the meeting with one man!'

He stopped, trembling, body and soul, under the hold that his own terrible superstition had fastened on him. Crayford drew back in silent horror. Wardour noticed the action – he resented it – he appealed in defence of his one cherished conviction to Crayford's own experience of him.

'Look at me!' he cried. 'Look how I have lived and thriven, with the heartache gnawing at me at home, and the winds of the icy north whistling round me here! I am the strongest man among you. Why? I have fought through hardships that have laid the best-seasoned men of all our party on their backs. Why? What have *I* done, that my life should throb as bravely through every vein in my body at this minute, and in this deadly place, as ever it did in the wholesome breezes of home? What am I preserved for? I tell you again, for the coming of óne day – for the meeting with one man.'

He paused once more. This time Crayford spoke.

'Richard!' he said, 'since we first met I have believed in your better nature, against all outward appearance. I have believed in you firmly, truly, as your brother might. You are putting that belief to a hard test. If your enemy had told me that you had ever talked as you talk now, that you had ever looked as you look now, I would have turned my back on him as the utterer of a vile calumny against a just, a brave, an upright man. Oh! my friend, my friend, if ever I have deserved well of you, put away those thoughts from your heart! Face me again with the stainless look of a man who has trampled under his feet the bloody superstitions of revenge, and knows them no more! Never, never let the time come when I cannot offer you my hand as I offer it now – to the man I can still admire, to the brother I can still love!'

The heart that no other voice could touch felt that appeal. The fierce eyes, the hard voice, softened under Crayford's influence. Richard Wardour's head sank on his breast.

'You are kinder to me than I deserve,' he said. 'Be kinder still, and forget what I have been talking about. No! no more about me; I am not worth it. We'll change the subject, and never go back to it again. Let's do something. Work, Crayford – that's the true elixir of *our* life! Work, that stretches the muscles and sets the blood a-glowing. Work, that tires the body and rests the mind. Is there nothing in hand that I can do? Nothing to cut? nothing to carry?'

The door opened as he put the question. Bateson – appointed to chop Frank's bedplace into firing – appeared punctually with his axe. Wardour, without a word of warning, snatched the axe out of the man's hand.

'What was this wanted for?' he asked.

'To cut up Mr Aldersley's berth there into firing, sir.'

'I'll do it for you! I'll have it down in no time!' He turned to Crayford. 'You needn't be afraid about me, old friend. I am going to do the right thing. I am going to tire my body and rest my mind.'

The evil spirit in him was plainly subdued – for the time at least. Crayford took his hand in silence, and then (followed by Bateson) left him to his work.

X

Axe in hand, Wardour approached Frank's bedplace.

'If I could only cut the thoughts out of me,' he said to himself, 'as I am going to cut the billets out of this wood!' He attacked the bedplace with the axe like a man who well knew the use of his instrument. 'Oh, me,' he thought, sadly, 'if I had only been born a carpenter instead of a gentleman! A good axe, Master Bateson – I wonder where you got it? Something like a grip, my man, on this handle. Poor Crayford! his words stick in my throat. A fine fellow! a noble fellow! No use thinking, no use regretting; what is said *is* said. Work! work! work!'

Plank after plank fell out on the floor. He laughed over the easy task of destruction. 'Aha! young Aldersley! It doesn't take much to demolish your bedplace. I'll have it down! I would have the whole hut down, if they would only give me the chance of chopping at it!'

A long strip of wood fell to his axe – long enough to require cutting in two. He turned it, and stooped over it. Something caught his eye – letters carved in the wood. He looked closer. The letters were very faintly and badly cut. He could only make out the first three of them; and, even of those, he was not quite certain. They looked like CLA – if they looked like anything. He threw down the strip of wood irritably.

'Damn the fellow (whoever he is) who cut this! Why should he carve *that* name, of all the names in the world?'

He paused, considering – then determined to go on again with his self-imposed labour. He was ashamed of his own outburst. He looked eagerly for the axe. 'Work, work! Nothing for it but work.' He found the axe, and went on again.

He cut out another plank.

He stopped, and looked at it suspiciously.

There was carving again on this plank. The letters F. and A. appeared on it.

He put down the axe. There were vague misgivings in him which he was not able to realise. The state of his own mind was fast becoming a puzzle to him.

'More carving,' he said to himself. 'That's the way these young idlers employ their long hours. F.A.? Those must be *his* initials – Frank Aldersley. Who carved the letters on the other plank? Frank Aldersley, too?'

He turned the piece of wood in his hand nearer to the light, and looked lower down it. More carving again, lower down! Under the initials F. A. were two more letters – C. B.

'C. B.?' he repeated to himself. 'His sweetheart's initials, I suppose? Of course – at his age – his sweetheart's initials.'

He paused once more. A spasm of inner pain showed the shadow of its mysterious passage outwardly on his face.

'*Her* cypher is C. B.,' he said, in low broken tones. 'C. B. – Clara Burnham.'

He waited, with the plank in his hand; repeating the name over and over again, as if it was a question he was putting to himself.

'Clara Burnham? Clara Burnham?'

He dropped the plank and turned deadly pale in a moment. His eyes wandered furtively backwards and forwards between the strip of wood on the floor and the half-demolished berth. 'O God! what has come to me now?' he said to himself, in a whisper. He snatched up the axe with a strange cry – something between rage and terror. He tried – fiercely, desperately tried – to go on with his work. No! strong as he was, he could not use the axe. His hands were helpless; they trembled incessantly. He went to the fire; he held his hands over it. They still trembled incessantly; they infected the rest of him. He shuddered all over. He knew fear. His own thoughts terrified him.

'Crayford!' he cried out. 'Crayford! come here, and let's go hunting.'

No friendly voice answered him. No friendly face showed itself at the door.

An interval passed, and there came over him another change. He recovered his self-possession almost as suddenly as he had lost it. A smile – a horrid, deforming, unnatural smile – spread slowly, stealthily, devilishly over his face. He left the fire; he put the axe away softly in a corner; he sat down in his old place, deliberately self-abandoned to a frenzy of vindictive joy. He had found the man! There, at the end of the world – there, at the last fight of the Arctic voyagers against starvation and death – he had found the man!

The minutes passed.

He became conscious, on a sudden, of a freezing stream of air pouring into the room.

He turned, and saw Crayford opening the door of the hut. A man was behind him. Wardour rose eagerly and looked over Crayford's shoulder.

Was it – could it be – the man who had carved the letters on the plank? Yes! Frank Aldersley!

XI

'Still at work!' Crayford exclaimed, looking at the half-demolished bedplace. 'Give yourself a little rest, Richard. The exploring party is ready to start. If you wish to take leave of your brother officers before they go, you have no time to lose.'

He checked himself there, looking Wardour full in the face.

'Good heavens!' he cried, 'how pale you are. Has anything happened?'

Frank – searching in his locker for articles of clothing which he might require on the journey – looked round. He was startled, as Crayford had been startled, by the sudden change in Wardour since they had last seen him.

'Are you ill?' he asked. 'I hear you have been doing Bateson's work for him. Have you hurt yourself?'

Wardour suddenly moved his head, so as to hide his face from both Crayford and Frank. He took out his handkerchief, and wound it clumsily round his left hand.

'Yes,' he said, 'I hurt myself with the axe. It's nothing. Never mind. Pain always has a curious effect on me. I tell you it's nothing! don't notice it!'

He turned his face towards them again as suddenly as he had turned it away. He advanced a few steps, and addressed himself with an uneasy familiarity to Frank.

'I didn't answer you civilly when you spoke to me some little time since. I mean, when I first came in here, along with the rest of them. I apologize. Shake hands! How are you? Ready for the march?'

Frank met the oddly abrupt advance which had been made to him with perfect good humour.

'I am glad to be friends with you, Mr Wardour. I wish I was as well seasoned to fatigue as you are.'

Wardour burst into a hard, joyless, unnatural laugh.

'Not strong, eh? You don't look it. The dice had better have sent me away and kept you here. I never felt in better condition in my life.' He paused and added, with his eye on Frank, and with a strong emphasis on the words: 'We men of Kent are made of tough material.'

Frank advanced a step on his side, with a new interest in Richard Wardour.

'You come from Kent?' he said.

'Yes. From East Kent.' He waited a little once more, and looked hard at Frank. 'Do you know that part of the country?' he asked.

'I ought to know something about East Kent,' Frank answered. 'Some dear friends of mine once lived there.'

'Friends of yours?' Wardour repeated. 'One of the county families, I suppose?'

As he put the question he abruptly looked over his shoulder. He was standing between Crayford and Frank. Crayford, taking no part in the conversation, had been watching him and listening to him more and more attentively as that conversation went on. Within the last moment or two Wardour had become instinctively conscious of this. He resented Crayford's conduct with needless irritability.

'Why are you staring at me?' he asked.

'Why are you looking unlike yourself?' Crayford answered, quietly.

Wardour made no reply. He renewed the conversation with Frank.

'One of the county families?' he resumed. 'The Witherbys of Yew Grange, I daresay?'

'No,' said Frank; 'but friends of the Witherbys, very likely – the Burnhams.'

Desperately as he struggled to maintain it, Wardour's self-control failed him. He started violently. The clumsily-wound handkerchief fell off his hand. Still looking at him attentively, Crayford picked it up.

'There is your handkerchief, Richard,' he said. 'Strange!'

'What is strange?'

'You told us you had hurt yourself with the axe—'

'Well?'

'There is no blood on your handkerchief.'

Wardour snatched the handkerchief out of Crayford's hand, and, turning away, approached the outer door of the hut. 'No blood on the handkerchief,' he said to himself. 'There may be a stain or two when Crayford sees it again.' He stopped within a few paces of the door, and spoke to Crayford. 'You recommended me to take leave of my brother officers before it was too late,' he said. 'I am going to follow your advice.'

The door was opened from the outer side as he laid his hand on the lock. One of the quartermasters of the *Wanderer* entered the hut.

'Is Captain Helding here, sir?' he asked, addressing himself to Wardour.

Wardour pointed to Crayford.

'The lieutenant will tell you,' he said.

Crayford advanced and questioned the quartermaster.

'What do you want with Captain Helding?' he asked.

'I have a report to make, sir. There has been an accident on the ice.'

'To one of your men?'

'No, sir. To one of our officers.'

Wardour – on the point of going out – paused when the quartermaster made that reply. For a moment he considered with himself. Then he walked slowly back to the part of the room in which Frank was standing. Crayford, directing the quartermaster, pointed to the arched doorway in the side of the hut.

'I am sorry to hear of the accident,' he said. 'You will find Captain Helding in that room.'

For the second time, with singular persistency, Wardour renewed the conversation with Frank.

'So you knew the Burnhams?' he said. 'What became of Clara when her father died?'

Frank's face flushed angrily on the instant.

'Clara?' he repeated. 'What authorises you to speak of Miss Burnham in that familiar manner?'

Wardour seized the opportunity of quarrelling with him.

'What right have you to ask?' he retorted coarsely.

Frank's blood was up. He forgot his promise to Clara to keep their engagement secret – he forgot everything but the unbridled insolence of Wardour's language and manner.

'A right which I insist on your respecting,' he answered. 'The right of being engaged to marry her.'

Crayford's steady eyes were still on the watch, and Wardour felt them on him. A little more, and Crayford might openly interfere. Even Wardour recognised, for once, the necessity of controlling his temper, cost him what it might. He made his apologies with overstrained politeness to Frank.

'Impossible to dispute such a right as yours,' he said. 'Perhaps you will excuse me when you know that I am one of Miss Burnham's old friends. My father and her father were neighbours. We have always met like brother and sister—'

Frank generously stopped the apology there.

'Say no more,' he interposed. 'I was in the wrong – I lost my temper. Pray forgive me.'

Wardour looked at him with a strange reluctant interest while he was speaking. Wardour asked an extraordinary question when he had done.

'Is she very fond of you?'

Frank burst out laughing.

'My dear fellow!' he said, 'come to our wedding, and judge for yourself.'

'Come to your wedding?' As he repeated the words Wardour stole one glance at Frank, which Frank (employed in buckling his knapsack) failed to see. Crayford noticed it – and Crayford's blood ran cold. Comparing the words which Wardour had spoken to him while they were alone together with the words that had just passed in his presence, he could draw but one conclusion. The woman whom Wardour had loved and lost was – Clara Burnham. The man who had robbed him of her was Frank Aldersley. And Wardour had discovered it in the interval since they had last met. 'Thank God!' thought Crayford, 'the dice have parted them! Frank goes with the expedition, and Wardour stays behind with me.'

The reflection had barely occurred to him – Frank's thoughtless invitation to Wardour had just passed his lips – when the canvas screen over the doorway was drawn aside. Captain Helding and the officers who were to leave with the exploring party returned to the main room on their way out. Seeing Crayford, Captain Helding stopped to speak to him.

'I have a casualty to report,' said the captain, 'which diminishes our numbers by one. My second lieutenant, who was to have joined the exploring party, has had a fall on the ice. Judging by what the quartermaster tells me, I am afraid the poor fellow has broken his leg.'

'I will supply his place,' cried a voice at the other end of the hut.

Everybody looked round. The man who had spoken was Richard Wardour.

Crayford instantly interfered – so vehemently as to astonish all who knew him.

'No!' he said. 'Not you, Richard! not you!'

'Why not?' Wardour asked sternly.

'Why not, indeed?' added Captain Helding. 'Wardour is the very man to be useful on a long march. He is in perfect health, and he is the best shot among us. I was on the point of proposing him myself.'

Crayford failed to show his customary respect for his superior officer. He openly disputed the Captain's conclusion.

'Wardour has no right to volunteer,' he rejoined. 'It has been settled, Captain Helding, that chance shall decide who is to go and who is to stay.'

'And chance *has* decided it,' cried Wardour. 'Do you think we are going to cast the dice again, and give an officer of the *Sea-Mew* a chance of replacing an officer of the *Wanderer*? There is a vacancy in our party, not in yours; and we claim the right of filling it as we please. I volunteer, and my captain backs me. Whose authority is to keep me here after that?'

'Gently, Wardour,' said Captain Helding. 'A man who is in the right can afford to speak with moderation.' He turned to Crayford. 'You must admit yourself,' he continued, 'that Wardour is right this time. The missing man belongs to my command, and in common justice one of my officers ought to supply his place.'

It was impossible to dispute the matter further. The dullest man present could see that the Captain's reply was unanswerable. In sheer despair, Crayford took Frank's arm and led him aside a few steps. The last chance left of parting the two men was the chance of appealing to Frank.

'My dear boy,' he began, 'I want to say one friendly word to you on the subject of your health. I have already, if you remember, expressed my doubts whether you are strong enough to make one of an exploring party. I feel those doubts more strongly than ever at this moment. Will you take the advice of a friend who wishes you well?'

Wardour had followed Crayford. Wardour roughly interposed before Frank could reply.

'Let him alone!'

Crayford paid no heed to the interruption. He was too earnestly bent on withdrawing Frank from the expedition to notice anything that was said or done by the persons about him.

'Don't, pray don't, risk hardships which you are unfit to bear!' he went on entreatingly. 'Your place can be easily filled. Change your mind, Frank. Stay here with me.'

Again Wardour interfered. Again he called out, 'Leave him alone!' more roughly than ever. Still deaf and blind to every consideration but one, Crayford pressed his entreaties on Frank.

'You owned yourself just now that you were not well seasoned to fatigue,' he persisted. 'You feel (you *must* feel) how weak that last illness has left you? You know (I am sure you know) how unfit you are to brave exposure to cold and long marches over the snow.'

Irritated beyond endurance by Crayford's obstinacy, seeing, or thinking he saw, signs of yielding in Frank's face, Wardour so far forgot himself as to seize Crayford by the arm, and attempt to drag him away from Frank. Crayford turned and looked at him.

'Richard,' he said, very quietly, 'you are not yourself. I pity you. Drop your hand.'

Wardour relaxed his hold with something of the sullen submission of a wild animal to his keeper. The momentary silence which followed gave Frank an opportunity of speaking at last.

'I am gratefully sensible, Crayford,' he began, 'of the interest which you take in me—'

'And you will follow my advice?' Crayford interposed eagerly.

'My mind is made up, old friend,' Frank answered, firmly and sadly. 'Forgive me for disappointing you. I am appointed to the expedition. With the expedition I go.' He moved nearer to Wardour. In his innocence of all suspicion, he clapped Wardour heartily on the shoulder. 'When I feel the fatigue,' said poor simple Frank, 'you will help me, comrade – won't you? Come along!'

Wardour snatched his gun out of the hands of the sailor who was carrying it for him. His dark face became suddenly irradiated with a terrible joy.

'Come!' he said. 'Over the snow and over the ice! Come! where no human footsteps have ever trodden and where no human trace is ever left.'

Blindly, instinctively, Crayford made an effort to part them. His brother officers, standing near, pulled him back. They looked at each other anxiously. The merciless cold, striking its victims in various ways, had struck in some instances at their reason first. Everybody loved Crayford. Was he, too, going on the dark way that others had taken before him? They forced him to seat himself on one of the lockers. 'Steady, old fellow!' they said kindly – 'steady!' Crayford yielded, writhing inwardly under the sense of his own helplessness. What in God's name could he do? Could he denounce Wardour to Captain Helding on bare suspicion – without so much as the shadow of a proof to justify what he said? The Captain would decline to insult one of his officers by even mentioning the monstrous accusation to him. The Captain would conclude, as others had already concluded, that Crayford's mind was giving way under stress of cold and privation. No hope – literally, no hope now but in the numbers of the expedition. Officers and men, they all liked Frank. As long as they could stir hand or foot they would help him on the way – they would see that no harm came to him.

The word of command was given; the door was thrown open; the hut emptied rapidly. Over the merciless white snow – under the merciless black sky – the exploring party began to move. The sick and helpless men, whose last hope of rescue centred in their departing messmates, cheered faintly. Some few whose days were numbered sobbed and cried like women. Frank's voice faltered as he turned back at the door to say his last words to the friend who had been a father to him.

'God bless you, Crayford!'

Crayford broke away from the officers near him, and, hurrying forward, seized Frank by both hands. Crayford held him as if he would never let him go.

'God preserve you, Frank! I would give all I have in the world to be with you. Good-bye! Good-bye!'

Frank waved his hand – dashed away the tears that were gathering in his eyes – and hurried out. Crayford called after him, the last, the only, warning that he could give:

'While you can stand, keep with the main body, Frank!'

Wardour, waiting till the last – Wardour, following Frank through the snow-drift – stopped, stepped back, and answered Crayford at the door:

'While he can stand, he keeps with Me.'

THIRD SCENE

The Iceberg

XII

Alone! alone on the Frozen Deep!

The Arctic sun is rising dimly in the dreary sky. The beams of the cold northern moon, mingling strangely with the dawning light, clothe the snowy plains in hues of livid grey. An ice-field on the far horizon is moving slowly southward in the spectral light. Nearer, a stream of open water rolls its slow black waves past the edges of the ice. Nearer still, following the drift, an iceberg rears its crags and pinnacles to the sky; here, glittering in the moonbeams; there, looming dim and ghostlike in the ashy light.

Midway on the long sweep of the lower slope of the iceberg, what objects rise and break the desolate monotony of the scene? In this awful solitude can signs appear which tell of human life? Yes! The black outline of a boat just shows itself, hauled up on the berg. In an ice-cavern behind the boat the last red embers of a dying fire flicker from time to time over the figures of two men. One is seated, resting his back against the side of the cavern. The other lies prostrate with his head on his comrade's knee. The first of these men is awake, and thinking. The second reclines, with his still white face turned up to the sky – sleeping or dead. Days and days since, these two have fallen behind on the march of the expedition of relief. Days and days since, these two have been given up by their weary and failing companions as doomed and lost. He who sits thinking is Richard Wardour. He who lies sleeping or dead is Frank Aldersley.

The iceberg drifts slowly, over the black water, through the ashy light. Minute by minute the dying fire sinks. Minute by minute the deathly cold creeps nearer and nearer to the lost men.

Richard Wardour rouses himself from his thoughts, looks at the still white face beneath him, and places his hand on Frank's heart. It still beats feebly. Give him his share of the food and fuel still stored in the boat, and Frank may live through it. Leave him neglected where he lies, and his death is a question of hours, perhaps minutes – who knows?

Richard Wardour lifts the sleeper's head and rests it against the cavern side. He goes to the boat and returns with a billet of wood. He stoops to place the wood on the fire, and stops. Frank is dreaming, and murmuring in his dream. A woman's name passes his lips. Frank is in England again – at the ball – whispering to Clara the confession of his love.

Over Richard Wardour's face there passes the shadow of a deadly thought. He rises from the fire; he takes the wood back to the boat. His iron strength is shaken, but it still holds out. They are drifting nearer and nearer to the open sea. He can launch the boat without help; he can take the food and the fuel with him. The sleeper on the iceberg is the man who has robbed him of Clara

– who has wrecked the hope and the happiness of his life. Leave the man in his sleep, and let him die!

So the tempter whispers. Richard Wardour tries his strength on the boat. It moves; he has got it under control. He stops and looks round. Beyond him is the open sea. Beneath him is the man who has robbed him of Clara. The shadow of the deadly thought grows and darkens over his face. He waits with his hands on the boat – waits and thinks.

The iceberg drifts slowly, over the black water, through the ashy light. Minute by minute the dying fire sinks. Minute by minute the deathly cold creeps nearer to the sleeping man. And still Richard Wardour waits – waits and thinks.

FOURTH SCENE

The Garden

XIII

The spring has come. The air of the April night just lifts the leaves of the sleeping flowers. The moon is queen in the cloudless and starless sky. The stillness of the midnight hour is abroad, over land and over sea.

In a villa on the westward shore of the Isle of Wight, the glass doors which lead from the drawing-room to the garden are yet open. The shaded lamp yet burns on the table. A lady sits by the lamp, reading. From time to time she looks out into the garden, and sees the white-robed figure of a young girl pacing slowly to and fro in the soft brightness of the moonlight on the lawn. Sorrow and suspense have set their mark on the lady. Not rivals only, but friends who formerly admired her, agree now that she looks worn and aged. The more merciful judgment of others remarks, with equal truth, that her eyes, her hair, her simple grace and grandeur of movement have lost but little of their olden charms. The truth lies, as usual, between the two extremes. In spite of sorrow and suffering, Mrs Crayford is the beautiful Mrs Crayford still.

The delicious silence of the hour is softly disturbed by the voice of the younger lady in the garden.

'Go to the piano, Lucy. It is a night for music. Play something that is worthy of the night.'

Mrs Crayford looks round at the clock on the mantlepiece.

'My dear Clara, it is past twelve! Remember what the doctor told you. You ought to have been in bed an hour ago.'

'Half an hour, Lucy – give me half an hour more! Look at the moonlight on the sea. Is it possible to go to bed on such a night as this? Play something, Lucy – something spiritual and divine.'

Earnestly pleading with her friend, Clara advances towards the window. She too has suffered under the wasting influences of suspense. Her face has lost its youthful freshness; no delicate flush of colour rises on it when she speaks. The soft grey eyes which won Frank's heart in the bygone time are sadly altered now. In repose they have a dimmed and wearied look. In action they are wild and restless, like eyes suddenly wakened from startling dreams. Robed in white, her soft brown hair hanging loosely over her shoulders, there is something weird and ghostlike in the girl, as she moves nearer and nearer to the window in the full light of the moon – pleading for music that shall be worthy of the mystery and the beauty of the night.

'Will you come in here if I play to you?' Mrs Crayford asks. 'It is a risk, my love, to be out in the night air.'

'No! no! I like it. Play – while I am out here, looking at the sea. It quiets me; it comforts me; it does me good.'

She glides back, ghostlike over the lawn. Mrs Crayford rises and puts down the volume that she has been reading. It is a record of explorations in the Arctic seas. The time has gone by when the two lonely women could take an interest in subjects not connected with their own anxieties. Now, when hope is fast failing them – now, when their last news of the *Wanderer* and the *Sea-Mew* is news that is more than two years old – they can read of nothing, they can think of nothing, but dangers and discoveries, losses and rescues in the terrible Polar seas.

Unwillingly, Mrs Crayford puts her book aside and goes to the piano – Mozart's 'Air in A, with Variations,' lies open on the instrument. One after another she plays the lovely melodies, so simply, so purely beautiful, of that unpretending and unrivalled work. At the close of the ninth variation (Clara's favourite) she pauses, and turns towards the garden.

'Shall I stop there?' she asks.

There is no answer. Has Clara wandered away out of hearing of the music that she loves – the music that harmonises so subtly with the tender beauty of the night? Mrs Crayford rises and advances to the window.

No! there is the white figure standing alone on the slope of the lawn – the head turned away from the house; the face looking out over the calm sea, whose gently rippling waters end in the dim line on the horizon, which is the line of the Hampshire coast.

Mrs Crayford advances as far as the path before the window and calls to her.

'Clara!'

Again there is no answer. The white figure still stands immovably in its place.

With signs of distress in her face, but with no appearance of alarm, Mrs Crayford returns to the room. Her own sad experience tells her what has happened. She summons the servants, and directs them to wait in the drawing-room until she calls to them. This done, she returns to the garden, and approaches the mysterious figure on the lawn.

Dead to the outer world, as if she lay already in her grave – insensible to touch, insensible to sound, motionless as stone, cold as stone – Clara stands on the moonlit lawn, facing the seaward view. Mrs Crayford waits at her side, patiently watching for the change which she knows is to come. 'Catalepsy,' as some call it – hysteria, as others say – this alone is certain, the same interval always passes; the same change always appears.

It comes now. Not a change in her eyes; they still remain wide open, fixed, and glassy. The first movement is a movement of her hands. They rise slowly from her side, and waver in the air like the hands of a person groping in the dark. Another interval – and the movement spreads to her lips; they part and tremble. A few minutes more, and words begin to drop, one by one, from those parted lips – words spoken in a lost vacant tone, as if she is talking in her sleep.

Mrs Crayford looks back at the house. Sad experience makes her suspicious of the servants' curiosity. Sad experience has long since warned her that the servants are not to be trusted within hearing of the wild words which Clara speaks in the trance. Has any one of them ventured into the garden? No. They are out of hearing at the window, waiting for the signal which tells them that their help is needed.

Turning towards Clara once more, Mrs Crayford hears the vacantly-uttered words falling faster and faster from her lips.

'Frank! Frank! Frank! Don't drop behind – don't trust Richard Wardour. While you can stand, keep with the other men, Frank!'

(The farewell warning of Crayford in the solitudes of the Frozen Deep, repeated by Clara in the garden of her English home!)

A moment of silence follows, and in that moment the vision has changed. She sees him on the iceberg now, at the mercy of the bitterest enemy he has on earth. She sees him drifting, over the black water, through the ashy light.

'Wake, Frank! wake and defend yourself! Richard Wardour knows that I love you. Richard Wardour's vengeance will take your life! Wake, Frank – wake! You are drifting to your death!' A low groan of horror bursts from her, sinister and terrible to hear. 'Drifting! drifting!' she whispers to herself; 'drifting to his death!'

Her glassy eyes suddenly soften, then close. A long shudder runs through her. A faint flush shows itself on the deadly pallor of her face, and fades again. Her limbs fail her. She sinks into Mrs Crayford's arms.

The servants, answering the call for help, carry her into the house. They lay her insensible on her bed. After an hour or more, her eyes open again – this time with the light of life in them – open, and rest languidly on her friend sitting by the bedside.

'I have had a dreadful dream,' she murmurs faintly. 'Am I ill, Lucy? I feel so weak.'

Even as she says the words sleep, gentle, natural sleep, takes her suddenly, as it takes young children weary with their play. Though it is all over now, though no further watching is required, Mrs Crayford still keeps her place by the bedside, too anxious and too wakeful to retire to her own room.

On other occasions she is accustomed to dismiss from her mind the words which drop from Clara in the trance. This time the effort to dismiss them is beyond her power. The words haunt her. Vainly she recalls to memory all that the doctors have said to her in speaking of Clara in the state of trance. 'What she vaguely dreads for the lost man whom she loves, is mingled in her mind with what she is constantly reading of trials, dangers, and escapes in the Arctic Seas. The most startling things that she may say or do are all attributable to this cause, and may be explained in this way.' So the doctors have spoken; and, thus far, Mrs Crayford has shared their view. It is only to-night that the girl's words ring in her ear with a strange prophetic sound in them. It is only to-night that she asks herself: 'Is Clara present, in the spirit, with our loved and lost ones in the lonely North? Can mortal vision see the dead and living in the solitudes of the Frozen Deep?'

XIV

The night had passed.

Far and near, the garden-view looked its gayest and brightest in the light of the noonday sun. The cheering sounds which tell of life and action were audible all round the villa. From the garden of the nearest house rose the voices of children at play. Along the road at the back sounded the roll of wheels, as carts and carriages passed at intervals. Out on the blue sea the distant splash of the paddles, the distant thump of the engines, told from time to time of the passage of steamers, entering or leaving the strait between the island and the mainland. In the trees the birds sang gaily among the rustling leaves. In the house the women-servants were laughing over some jest or story that cheered them at their work. It was a lively and pleasant time – a bright enjoyable day.

The two ladies were out together, resting on a garden seat, after a walk round the grounds.

They exchanged a few trivial words relating to the beauty of the day, and then said no more. Possessing the same consciousness of what she had seen in the trance which persons in general possess of what they have seen in a dream – believing in the vision as a supernatural revelation – Clara's worst forebodings were now, to her mind, realised as truths. Her last faint hope of ever seeing Frank again was now at an end. Intimate experience of her told Mrs Crayford what was passing in Clara's mind, and warned her that the attempt to reason and remonstrate would be little better than a voluntary waste of words and time. The disposition which she had herself felt, on the previous night, to attach a superstitious importance to the words that Clara had spoken in the trance had vanished with the return of the morning. Rest and reflection had quieted her mind, and had restored the composing influence of her sober sense. Sympathising with Clara in all besides, she had no sympathy, as they sat together in the pleasant sunshine, with Clara's gloomy despair of the future. She, who could still hope, had nothing to say to the sad companion who had done with hope. So the quiet minutes succeeded each other, and the two friends sat side by side in silence.

An hour passed – and the gate-bell of the villa rang.

They both started – they both knew the ring. It was the hour when the postman brought their newspapers from London. In past days, what hundreds on hundreds of times they had torn off the cover which enclosed the newspaper, and looked at the same column with the same weary mingling of hope and despair! There to-day – as it was yesterday; as it would be, if they lived, to-morrow – there was the servant with Lucy's newspaper and Clara's newspaper in his hand! Would both of them do again to-day what both of them had done so often in the days that were gone?

No! Mrs Crayford removed the cover from her newspaper as usual. Clara laid *her* newspaper aside, unopened, on the garden seat.

In silence Mrs Crayford looked where she always looked, at the column devoted to the Latest Intelligence from foreign parts. The instant her eye fell on the page she started with a loud cry of joy. The newspaper fell from her trembling hand. She caught Clara in her arms. 'Oh, my darling! my darling! news of them at last.'

Without answering, without the slightest change in look or manner, Clara took the newspaper from the ground, and read the top line in the column, printed in capital letters.

THE ARCTIC EXPEDITION.

She waited, and looked at Mrs Crayford.

'Can you bear to hear it, Lucy,' she asked, 'if I read it aloud?'

Mrs Crayford was too agitated to answer in words. She signed impatiently to Clara to go on.

Clara read the news which followed the heading in capital letters. Thus it ran:

'The following intelligence from St John's, Newfoundland, has reached us for publication. The whaling vessel 'Blythewood' is reported to have met with the surviving officers and men of the expedition in Davis Strait. Many are stated to be dead, and some are supposed to be missing. The list of the saved, as collected by the people of the whaler, is not vouched for as being absolutely correct, the circumstances having been adverse to investigation. The vessel was pressed for time; and the members of the expedition, all more or less suffering from exhaustion, were not in a position to give the necessary assistance to inquiry. Further particulars may be looked for by the next mail.'

The list of the survivors followed, beginning with the officers in the order of their rank. They both read the list together. The first name was Captain Helding. The second was Lieutenant Crayford.

There, the wife's joy overpowered her. After a pause, she put her arm round Clara's waist, and spoke to her.

'Oh, my love!' she murmured, 'are you as happy as I am? Is Frank's name there too? The tears are in my eyes. Read for me – I can't read for myself.'

The answer came, in still sad tones:

'I have read as far as your husband's name. I have no need to read farther.'

Mrs Crayford dashed the tears from her eyes, steadied herself, and looked at the newspaper.

On the list of the survivors the search was vain. Frank's name was not among them. On a second list, headed 'Dead or Missing,' the two first names that appeared were:

FRANCIS ALDERSLEY.

RICHARD WARDOUR.

In speechless distress and dismay Mrs Crayford looked at Clara. Had she force enough, in her feeble health, to sustain the shock that had fallen on her? Yes! She bore it with a strange unnatural resignation; she looked, she spoke, with the sad self-possession of despair.

'I was prepared for it,' she said. 'I saw them in the spirit last night. Richard Wardour has discovered the truth, and Frank has paid the penalty with his life – and I, I alone, am to blame.' She shuddered, and put her hand on her heart. 'We shall not be long parted, Lucy; I shall go to him. He will not return to me.'

Those words were spoken with a calm certainty of conviction that was terrible to see. 'I have no more to say,' she added, after a moment, and rose to return to the house. Mrs Crayford caught her by the hand, and forced her to take her seat again.

'Don't look at me, don't speak to me, in that horrible manner!' she exclaimed. 'Clara, it is unworthy of a reasonable being, it is doubting the mercy of God, to say what you have just said. Look at the newspaper again. See! They tell you plainly that their information is not to be depended upon – they warn you to wait for further particulars. The very words at the top of the list show how little they know of the truth. "Dead, *or* missing!" On their own showing it is quite as likely that Frank is missing as that Frank is dead. For all you know, the next mail may bring a letter from him. Are you listening to me?'

'Yes.'

'Can you deny what I say?'

'No.'

'"Yes!" "No!" Is that the way to answer me when I am so distressed and so anxious about you?'

'I am sorry I spoke as I did, Lucy. We look at some subjects in very different ways. I don't dispute, dear, that yours is the reasonable view.'

'You don't dispute?' retorted Mrs Crayford warmly. 'No! you do what is worse – you believe in your own opinion – you persist in your own conclusion – with the newspaper before you! Do you, or do you not, believe the newspaper?'

'I believe in what I saw last night.'

'In what you saw last night! You, an educated woman, a clever woman, believing in a vision of your own fancy – a mere dream! I wonder you are not ashamed to acknowledge it!'

'Call it a dream if you like, Lucy. I have had other dreams, at other times, and I have known them to be fulfilled.'

'Yes!' said Mrs Crayford. 'For once in a way they may have been fulfilled, by chance – and you notice it, and remember it, and pin your faith on it. Come, Clara, be honest! What about the occasions when the chance has been against you, and your dreams have *not* been fulfilled? You superstitious people are all alike. You conveniently forget when your dreams and your presentiments prove false. For my sake, dear, if not for your own,' she continued, in gentler and tenderer tones, 'try to be more reasonable and more hopeful. Don't lose your trust in the future and your trust in God. God, who has saved my husband, can save Frank. While there is doubt there is hope. Don't embitter my happiness, Clara! Try to think as I think – if it is only to show that you love me.'

She put her arm round the girl's neck and kissed her. Clara returned the kiss; Clara answered sadly and submissively:

'I do love you, Lucy. I *will* try.'

Having answered in those terms, she sighed to herself, and said no more. It would have been plain, only too plain, to far less observant eyes than Mrs Crayford's that no salutary impression had been produced on her. She had ceased to defend her own way of thinking, she spoke of it no more; but there was the terrible conviction of Frank's death at Wardour's hands rooted as firmly as ever in her mind! Discouraged and distressed, Mrs Crayford left her, and walked back towards the house.

XV

At the drawing-room window of the villa there appeared a polite little man, with bright intelligent eyes and cheerful sociable manners. Neatly dressed in professional black, he stood, self-proclaimed, a prosperous country doctor – successful and popular in a wide circle of patients and friends. As Mrs Crayford approached him, he stepped out briskly to meet her on the lawn, with both hands extended in courteous and cordial greeting.

'My dear madam, accept my heartfelt congratulations!' cried the doctor. 'I have seen the good news in the paper; and I could hardly feel more rejoiced than I do now if I had the honour of knowing Lieutenant Crayford personally. We mean to celebrate the occasion at home. I said to my wife before I came out, "A bottle of the old Madeira at dinner to-day, mind! – to drink the Lieutenant's health; God bless him!" And how is our interesting patient? The news is not altogether what we could wish, so far as she is concerned. I felt a little anxious, to tell you the truth, about the effect of it; and I have paid my visit to-day before my usual time. Not that I take a gloomy view of the news myself. No! There is clearly a doubt about the correctness of the information, so far as Mr Aldersley is concerned – and that is a point, a great point, in Mr Aldersley's favour. I give him the benefit of the doubt, as the lawyers say. Does Miss Burnham give him the benefit of the doubt too? I hardly dare hope it, I confess.'

'Miss Burnham has grieved and alarmed me,' Mrs Crayford answered. 'I was just thinking of sending for you, when we met here.'

With those introductory words, she told the doctor exactly what had happened; repeating, not only the conversation of that morning between Clara and herself, but also the words which had fallen from Clara in the trance of the past night.

The doctor listened attentively. Little by little, its easy smiling composure vanished from his face as Mrs Crayford went on, and left him completely transformed into a grave and thoughtful man.

'Let us go and look at her,' he said.

He seated himself by Clara's side, and carefully studied her face, with his hand on her pulse. There was no sympathy here between the dreamy mystical temperament of the patient and the downright practical character of the doctor. Clara secretly disliked her medical attendant. She submitted impatiently to the close investigation of which he made her the object. He questioned her, and she answered irritably. Advancing a step further (the doctor was not easily discouraged) he adverted to the news of the Expedition, and took up the tone of remonstrance which had been already adopted by Mrs Crayford. Clara declined to discuss the question. She rose with formal politeness, and requested permission to return to the house. The doctor attempted no further resistance. 'By all means, Miss Burnham,' he answered, resignedly – having first cast a look at Mrs Crayford which said plainly, 'Stay here with me.' Clara bowed her acknowledgements in cold silence, and left them together. The doctor's bright eyes followed the girl's wasted, yet still graceful, figure, as it slowly receded from view, with an expression of grave anxiety, which Mrs Crayford noticed with grave misgiving on her side. He said nothing until Clara had disappeared under the verandah which ran round the garden-side of the house.

'I think you told me,' he began, 'that Miss Burnham has neither father nor mother living?'

'Yes. Miss Burnham is an orphan.'

'Has she any near relatives?'

'No. You may speak to me as her guardian and her friend. Are you alarmed about her?'

'I am seriously alarmed. It is only two days since I called here last – and I see a marked change in her for the worse. Physically and morally a change for the worse. Don't needlessly alarm yourself! The case is not, I trust, entirely beyond the reach of remedy. The great hope for us is the hope that Mr Aldersley may still be living. In that event, I should feel no misgivings about the future. Her marriage would make a healthy and a happy woman of her. But, as things are, I own I dread that settled conviction in her mind that Mr Aldersley is dead, and that her own death is soon to follow. In her present state of health, that idea (haunting her, as it certainly will, night and day) will have its influence on her body as well as on her mind. Unless we can check the mischief, her last reserves of strength will give way. If you wish for other advice by all means send for it. You have my opinion.'

'I am quite satisfied with your opinion,' Mrs Crayford replied. 'It is your advice I want. For God's sake tell me what can we do?'

'We can try a complete change,' said the doctor. 'We can remove her at once from this place.'

'She will refuse to leave it,' Mrs Crayford rejoined. 'I have more than once proposed a change to her – and she always says No.'

The doctor paused for a moment, like a man collecting his thoughts.

'I heard something on my way here,' he proceeded, 'which suggests to my mind a method of meeting the difficulty that you have just mentioned. Unless I am entirely mistaken, Miss Burnham will not say No to the change that I have in view for her.'

'What is it?' asked Mrs Crayford, eagerly.

'Pardon me if I ask you a question, on my part, before I reply,' said the doctor. 'Are you fortunate enough to possess any interest at the Admiralty?'

'Certainly. My father is in the Secretary's office – and two of the Lords of the Admiralty are friends of his.'

'Excellent! Now I can speak out plainly with little fear of disappointing you. After what I have said, you will agree with me that the only change in Miss Burnham's life which will be of any use to her, is a change that will alter the present tone of her mind on the subject of Mr Aldersley. Place her in a position to discover – not by reference to her own distempered fancies and visions, but by reference to actual evidence and actual fact – whether Mr Aldersley is, or is not, a living man; and there will be an end of the hysterical delusions which now threaten to fatally undermine her health. Even taking matters at their worst – even assuming that Mr Aldersley has died in the Arctic seas – it will be less injurious to her to discover this positively, than to leave her mind to feed on its own morbid superstitions and speculations, for weeks and weeks together, while the next news from the Expedition is on its way to England. In one word, I want you to be in a position, before the week is out, to put Miss Burnham's present convictions to a practical test. Suppose you could say to her: "We differ, my dear, about Mr Francis Aldersley. You declare, without the shadow of a reason for it, that he is certainly dead, and, worse still, that he has died by the act of one of his brother officers. I assert, on the authority of the newspaper, that nothing of the sort has happened, and that the chances are all in favour of his being still a living man. What do you say to crossing the Atlantic, and deciding which of us is right – you or I?" Do you think Miss Burnham will say No to that, Mrs Crayford? If I know anything of human nature, she will seize the opportunity as a means of converting you to a belief in the Second Sight.'

'Good heavens, doctor! do you mean to tell me that we are to go out and meet the Arctic Expedition on its way home?'

'Admirably guessed, Mrs Crayford! That is exactly what I mean.'

'But how is it to be done?'

'I will tell you immediately. I mentioned – didn't I? – that I had heard something on my road to this house.'

'Yes?'

'Well, I met an old friend at my own gate, who walked with me a part of the way here. Last night my friend dined with the Admiral at Portsmouth. Among the guests there was a member of the Ministry, who had brought the news about the Expedition with him from London. This gentleman told the company there was very little doubt that the Admiralty would immediately send out a steam-vessel, to meet the rescued men on the shores of America, and bring them home. Wait a little, Mrs Crayford! Nobody knows, as yet, under what rules and regulations the vessel will sail. Under somewhat similar circumstances, privileged people *have* been received as passengers, or rather as guests, in Her Majesty's ships – and what has been conceded on former occasions may, by bare possibility, be conceded now. I can say no more. If you are not afraid of the voyage for yourself, I am not afraid of it (nay, I am all in favour of it on medical grounds) for my patient. What do you say? Will you write to your father, and ask him to try what his interest will do with his friends at the Admiralty?'

Mrs Crayford rose excitedly to her feet.

'Write!' she exclaimed. 'I will do better than write. The journey to London is no great matter – and my housekeeper here is to be trusted to take care of Clara in my absence. I will see my father tonight! He shall make good use of his interest at the Admiralty – you may rely on that. Oh, my dear doctor, what a prospect it is! My husband! Clara! What a discovery you have made – what a treasure you are! How can I thank you?'

'Compose yourself, my dear madam. Don't make too sure of success. We may consider Miss Burnham's objections as disposed of beforehand. But suppose the Lords of the Admiralty say No?'

'In that case I shall be in London, doctor; and I shall go to them myself. Lords are only men – and men are not in the habit of saying No to *me*.'

So they parted.

In a week from that day Her Majesty's ship *Amazon* sailed for North America. Certain privileged persons, specially interested in the Arctic voyagers, were permitted to occupy the empty state-rooms on board. On the list of these favoured guests of the ship were the names of two ladies – Mrs Crayford and Miss Burnham.

FIFTH SCENE

THE BOAT-HOUSE

XVI

ONCE more the open sea – the sea whose waters break on the shores of Newfoundland! An English steamship lies at anchor in the offing. The vessel is plainly visible through the open doorway of a large boat-house on the shore; one of the buildings attached to a fishing-station on the coast of the island.

The only person in the boat-house at this moment, is a man in the dress of a sailor. He is seated on a chest, with a piece of cord in his hand, looking out idly at the sea. On the rough carpenter's table near him lies a strange object to be left in such a place – a woman's veil.

What is the vessel lying at anchor in the offing?

The vessel is the *Amazon* – despatched from England to receive the surviving officers and men of the Arctic Expedition. The meeting has been successfully effected, on the shores of North America, three days since. But the homeward voyage has been delayed by a storm which has driven the ship out of her course. Taking advantage, on the third day, of the first returning calm, the commander of the *Amazon* has anchored off the coast of Newfoundland, and has sent ashore to increase his supplies of water before he sails for England. The weary passengers have landed for a few hours, to refresh themselves after the discomforts of the tempest. Among them are the two ladies. The veil left on the table in the boat-house is Clara's veil.

And who is the man sitting on the chest, with the cord in his hand, looking out idly at the sea? The man is the only cheerful person in the ship's company. In other words – John Want.

Still reposing on the chest, our friend who never grumbles, is surprised by the sudden appearance of a sailor at the boat-house door.

'Look sharp with your work, there, John Want!' says the sailor; 'Lieutenant Crayford is just coming to look after you.'

With this warning the messenger disappears again. John Want rises with a groan – turns the chest up on one end – and begins to fasten the cord round it. The ship's cook is not a man to look back on his rescue with the feeling of unmitigated satisfaction which animates his companions in trouble. On the contrary, he is ungratefully disposed to regret the North Pole.

'If I had only known' – thus runs the train of thought in the mind of John Want – 'if I had only known, before I was rescued, that I was to be brought to this place, I believe I should have preferred staying at the North Pole. I was very happy keeping up everybody's spirits at the North Pole. Taking one thing with another, I think I must have been very comfortable at the North Pole – if I had only known it. Another man in my place might be inclined to say that this Newfoundland boat-house was rather a sloppy, slimy, draughty, fishy sort of a habitation to take shelter in. Another man might object to perpetual Newfoundland fogs, perpetual Newfoundland codfish, and perpetual

Newfoundland dogs. We had some very nice bears at the North Pole. Never mind! it's all one to me – *I* don't grumble.'

'Have you done cording that box?'

This time the voice is a voice of authority – the man at the doorway is Lieutenant Crayford himself. John Want answers his officer in his own cheerful way.

'I've done it as well as I can, sir – but the damp of this place is beginning to tell upon our very ropes. I say nothing about our lungs – I only say our ropes.'

Crayford answers sharply. He seems to have lost his former relish for the humour of John Want.

'Pooh! To look at your wry face, one would think that our rescue from the Arctic regions was a downright misfortune. You deserve to be sent back again.'

'I could be just as cheerful as ever, sir, if I *was* sent back again. I hope I'm thankful; but I don't like to hear the North Pole run down in such a fishy place as this. It was very clean and snowy at the North Pole – and it's very damp and sandy here. Do you never miss your bone soup, sir? *I* do. It mightn't have been strong; but it was very hot; and the cold seemed to give it a kind of a meaty flavour as it went down. Was it you that was a-coughing so long, last night, sir? I don't presume to say anything against the air of these latitudes – but I should be glad to know it wasn't you that was a-coughing so hollow. Would you be so obliging as just to feel the state of these ropes with the ends of your fingers, sir? You can dry them afterwards on the back of my jacket.'

'You ought to have a stick laid on the back of your jacket. Take that box down to the boat directly. You croaking vagabond! You would have grumbled in the Garden of Eden.'

The philosopher of the Expedition was not a man to be silenced by referring him to the Garden of Eden. Paradise itself was not perfect to John Want.

'I hope I could be cheerful anywhere, sir,' said the ship's cook. 'But you mark my words – there must have been a deal of troublesome work with the flower-beds in the Garden of Eden.'

Having entered that unanswerable protest, John Want shouldered the box, and drifted drearily out of the boat-house.

Left by himself, Crayford looked at his watch, and called to a sailor outside.

'Where are the ladies?' he asked.

'Mrs Crayford is coming this way, sir. She was just behind you when you came in.'

'Is Miss Burnham with her?'

'No, sir; Miss Burnham is down on the beach with the passengers. I heard the young lady asking after you, sir.'

'Asking after me?' Crayford considered with himself, as he repeated the words. He added, in lower and graver tones, 'You had better tell Miss Burnham you have seen me here.'

The man made his salute and went out. Crayford took a turn in the boat-house.

Rescued from death in the Arctic wastes, and reunited to a beautiful wife, the Lieutenant looked, nevertheless, unaccountably anxious and depressed. What could he be thinking of? He was thinking of Clara.

On the first day when the rescued men were received on board the *Amazon*, Clara had embarrassed and distressed, not Crayford only, but the other officers of the Expedition as well, by the manner in which she questioned them on the subject of Francis Aldersley and Richard Wardour. She had shown no signs of dismay or despair when she heard that no news had been received of the two missing men. She had even smiled sadly to herself, when Crayford (out of compassionate regard for her) declared that he and his comrades had not given up the hope of seeing Frank and Wardour yet. It was only when the Lieutenant had expressed himself in those terms – and when he had apparently succeeded in dismissing the painful subject – that Clara had startled every one present by announcing that she had something to say in relation to Richard and Frank, which had not been said yet. Though she spoke guardedly, her next words revealed suspicions of foul play lurking in her mind – exactly reflecting similar suspicions lurking in Crayford's mind – which so distressed the Lieutenant, and so surprised his comrades, as to render them quite incapable of answering her. The warnings of the storm which shortly afterwards broke over the vessel were then visible in sea and sky. Crayford made them his excuse for abruptly leaving the cabin in which the conversation had taken place. His brother officers, profiting by his example, pleaded their duties on deck, and followed him out.

On the next day, and the next, the tempest still raged, and the passengers were not able to leave their state-rooms. But now, when the weather had moderated and the ship had anchored – now, when officers and passengers alike were on shore, with leisure time at their disposal – Clara had opportunities of returning to the subject of the lost men, and of asking questions in relation to them, which would make it impossible for Crayford to plead an excuse for not answering her. How was he to meet those questions? How could he still keep her in ignorance of the truth?

These were the reflections which now troubled Crayford, and which presented him, after his rescue, in the strangely inappropriate character of a depressed and anxious man. His brother officers, as he well knew, looked to him to take the chief responsibility. If he declined to accept it, he would instantly confirm the horrible suspicion in Clara's mind. The emergency must be met; but how to meet it – at once honourably and mercifully – was more than Crayford could tell. He was still lost in his own gloomy thoughts, when his wife entered the boat-house. Turning to look at her, he saw his own perturbations and anxieties plainly reflected in Mrs Crayford's face.

'Have you seen anything of Clara?' he asked. 'Is she still on the beach?'

'She is following me to this place,' Mrs Crayford replied. 'I have been speaking to her this morning. She is just as resolute as ever to insist on your telling her of the circumstances under which Frank is missing. As things are, you have no alternative but to answer her.'

'Help me to answer her, Lucy. Tell me, before she comes in, how this horrible suspicion first took possession of her. All she could possibly have known, when we left England, was that the two men were appointed to separate ships. What could have led her to suspect that they had come together?'

'She was firmly persuaded, William, that they *would* come together, when the Expedition left England. And she had read in books of Arctic travel, of men left behind by their comrades on the march, and of men adrift on icebergs. With her mind full of these images and forebodings, she saw Frank and Wardour (or dreamed of them) in one of her attacks of trance. I was by her side – I heard what she said at the time. She warned Frank that Wardour had discovered the truth. She called out to him, "While you can stand, keep with the other men, Frank!—"'

'Good God!' cried Crayford; 'I warned him myself, almost in those very words, the last time I saw him.'

'Don't acknowledge it, William! Keep her in ignorance of what you have just told me; she will not take it for what it is – a startling coincidence, and nothing more. She will accept it as positive confirmation of the faith, the miserable superstitious faith, that is in her. So long as you don't actually know that Frank is dead, and that he has died by Wardour's hand, deny what she says – mislead her for her own sake – dispute all her conclusions as I dispute them. Help me to raise her to the better and nobler belief in the mercy of God!' She stopped and looked round nervously at the doorway. 'Hush!' she whispered; 'do as I have told you. Clara is here.'

XVII

Clara stopped at the doorway, looking backwards and forwards distrustfully between the husband and wife. Entering the boat-house, and approaching Crayford, she took his arm and led him away a few steps from the place in which Mrs Crayford was standing.

'There is no storm now, and there are no duties to be done on board the ship,' she said, with a faint sad smile which it wrung Crayford's heart to see. 'You are Lucy's husband, and you have an interest in me for Lucy's sake. Don't shrink on that account from giving me pain: I can bear pain. Friend and brother, will you believe that I have courage enough to hear the worst? Will you promise not to deceive me about Frank?'

The gentle resignation in her voice, the sad pleading in her look, shook Crayford's self-possession at the outset. He answered her in the worst possible manner – he answered evasively.

'My dear Clara,' he said, 'what have I done that you should suspect me of deceiving you?'

She looked him searchingly in the face – then glanced with renewed distrust at Mrs Crayford. There was a moment of silence. Before any of the three could speak again, they were interrupted by the appearance of one of Crayford's brother officers, followed by two sailors carrying a hamper between them. Crayford instantly dropped Clara's arm, and seized the welcome opportunity of speaking of other things.

'Any instructions from the ship, Steventon?' he asked, approaching the officer.

'Verbal instructions only,' Steventon replied. 'The ship will sail with the flood tide. We shall fire a gun to collect the people, and send another boat ashore. In the meantime here are some refreshments for the passengers. The vessel is in a state of confusion; the ladies will eat their lunch more comfortably here.'

Hearing this, Mrs Crayford took *her* opportunity of silencing Clara next.

'Come, my dear,' she said, 'let us lay the cloth and put the lunch on the table before the gentlemen come in.'

Clara was too seriously bent on attaining the object which she had in view, to be silenced in that way. 'I will help you directly,' she answered – then crossed the room and addressed herself to the officer whose name was Steventon.

'Can you spare me a few minutes?' she asked; 'I have something to say to you.'

'I am entirely at your service, Miss Burnham.'

Answering in those words, Steventon dismissed the two sailors. Mrs Crayford looked anxiously at her husband. Crayford whispered to her, 'Don't be alarmed about Steventon. I have cautioned him; I believe he is to be depended on.'

Clara beckoned to Crayford to return to her.

'I will not keep you long,' she said; 'I will promise not to distress Mr Steventon. Young as I am, you shall both find that I am capable of self-control. I won't ask you to go back to the story of your past sufferings; I only want to be sure that I am right about one thing – I mean about what happened at the time when the exploring party was despatched in search of help. As I understand it, you cast lots among yourselves who was to go with the party, and who was to remain behind. Frank cast the lot to go.' She paused, shuddering. 'And Richard Wardour,' she went on, 'cast the lot to remain behind. On your honour, as officers and gentlemen, is this the truth?'

'On my honour,' Crayford answered, 'it is the truth.'

'On my honour,' Steventon repeated, 'it is the truth.'

She looked at them, carefully considering her next words before she spoke again.

'You both drew the lot to stay in the huts,' she said, addressing Crayford and Steventon, 'and you are both here. Richard Wardour drew the lot to stay, and Richard Wardour is not here. How does his name come to be with Frank's on the list of the missing?'

The question was a dangerous one to answer. Steventon left it to Crayford to reply. Once again he answered evasively.

'It doesn't follow, my dear,' he said, 'that the two men were missing together, because their names happen to come together on the list.'

Clara instantly drew the inevitable conclusion from that ill-considered reply.

'Frank is missing from the party of relief,' she said. 'Am I to understand that Wardour is missing from the huts?'

Both Crayford and Steventon hesitated. Mrs Crayford cast one indignant look at them, and told the necessary lie without a moment's hesitation!

'Yes!' she said. 'Wardour is missing from the huts.'

Quickly as she had spoken, she had still spoken too late. Clara had noticed the momentary hesitation on the part of the two officers. She turned to Steventon.

'I trust to your honour,' she said, quietly. 'Am I right, or wrong, in believing that Mrs Crayford is mistaken?'

She had addressed herself to the right man of the two. Steventon had no wife present to exercise authority over him. Steventon, put on his honour and fairly forced to say something, owned the truth. Wardour had replaced an officer whom accident had disabled from accompanying the party of relief, and Wardour and Frank were missing together.

Clara looked at Mrs Crayford.

'You hear?' she said. 'It is you who are mistaken; not I. What you call "accident" – what I call "fate" – brought Richard Wardour and Frank together as members of the same Expedition after all.' Without waiting for a reply, she again turned to Steventon and surprised him by changing the painful subject of the conversation of her own accord.

'Have you been in the Highlands of Scotland?' she asked.

'I have never been in the Highlands,' Steventon replied.

'Have you ever read, in books about the Highlands, of such a thing as "The Second Sight?"'

'Yes.'

'Do you believe in the Second Sight?'

Steventon politely declined to commit himself to a direct reply.

'I don't know what I might have done if I had ever been in the Highlands,' he said. 'As it is, I have had no opportunities of giving the subject any serious consideration.'

'I won't put your credulity to the test,' Clara proceeded. 'I won't ask you to believe anything more extraordinary than that I had a strange dream in England not very long since. My dream showed me what you have just acknowledged – and more than that. How did the two missing men come to be parted from their companions? Were they lost by pure accident? or were they deliberately left behind on the march?'

Crayford made a last vain effort to check her enquiries at the point which they had now reached.

'Neither Steventon nor I were members of the party of relief,' he said. 'How are we to answer you?'

'Your brother officers who *were* members of the party must have told you what happened,' Clara rejoined. 'I only ask you and Mr Steventon to tell me what they told you.'

Mrs Crayford interposed again – with a practical suggestion this time.

'The luncheon is not unpacked yet,' she said. 'Come, Clara! this is our business, and the time is passing.'

'The luncheon can wait a few minutes longer,' Clara answered. 'Bear with my obstinacy,' she went on, laying her hand caressingly on Crayford's shoulder. 'Tell me how those two came to be separated from the rest. You have always been the kindest of friends; don't begin to be cruel to me now!'

The tone in which she made her entreaty to Crayford went straight to the sailor's heart. He gave up the hopeless struggle; he let her see a glimpse of the truth.

'On the third day out,' he said, 'Frank's strength failed him. He fell behind the rest from fatigue.'

'Surely they waited for him?'

'It was a serious risk to wait for him, my child. Their lives, and the lives of the men they had left in the huts, depended, in that dreadful climate, on their pushing on. But Frank was a favourite. They waited half a day to give Frank the chance of recovering his strength.'

There he stopped. There the imprudence into which his fondness for Clara had led him showed itself plainly, and closed his lips.

It was too late to take refuge in silence. Clara was determined on hearing more.

She questioned Steventon next.

'Did Frank go on again after the half-day's rest?' she asked.

'He tried to go on—'

'And failed?'

'Yes.'

'What did the men do when he failed? Did they turn cowards? Did they desert Frank?'

She had purposely used language which might irritate Steventon into answering her plainly. He was a young man; he fell into the snare that she had set for him.

'Not one among them was a coward, Miss Burnham!' he replied, warmly. 'You are speaking cruelly and unjustly of as brave a set of fellows as ever lived. The strongest man among them set the example: he volunteered to stay by Frank and to bring him on in the track of the exploring party.'

There Steventon stopped, conscious, on his side, that he had said too much. Would she ask him who this volunteer was? No. She went straight on to the most embarrassing question that she had put yet – referring to the volunteer, as if Steventon had already mentioned his name.

'What made Richard Wardour so ready to risk his life for Frank's sake?' she said to Crayford. 'Did he do it out of friendship for Frank? Surely you can tell me that? Carry your memory back to the days when you were all living in the huts. Were Frank and Wardour friends at that time? Did you never hear any angry words pass between them?'

There Mrs Crayford saw her opportunity of giving her husband a timely hint.

'My dear child!' she said. 'How can you expect him to remember that? There must have been plenty of quarrels among the men, all shut up together, and all weary of each other's company, no doubt.'

'Plenty of quarrels!' Crayford repeated – 'and every one of them made up again.'

'And every one of them made up again,' Mrs Crayford reiterated, in her turn. 'There! a plainer answer than that you can't wish to have. *Now* are you satisfied? Mr Steventon, come and lend a hand (as you say at sea) with the hamper – Clara won't help me. William! Don't stand there doing nothing. This hamper holds a great deal; we must have a division of labour. Your division shall be laying the tablecloth. Don't handle it in that clumsy way! You unfold a tablecloth as if you were unfurling a sail. Put the knives on the right, and the forks on the left, and the napkin and bread between them. Clara! if you are not hungry in this fine air, you ought to be. Come and do your duty – come and have some lunch!'

She looked up as she spoke. Clara appeared to have yielded at last to the conspiracy to keep her in the dark. She had returned slowly to the boat-house doorway; and she was standing alone on the threshold, looking out. Approaching her to lead her to the luncheon-table, Mrs Crayford could hear that she was speaking softly to herself. She was repeating the farewell words which Richard Wardour had spoken to her at the ball.

'"A time may come when I shall forgive *you*. But the man who has robbed me of you shall rue the day when you and he first met." Oh, Frank! Frank! does Richard still live – with your blood on his conscience, and my image in his heart?'

Her lips suddenly closed. She started, and drew back from the doorway, trembling violently. Mrs Crayford looked out at the quiet seaward view.

'Anything there that frightens you, my dear?' she asked. 'I can see nothing – except the boats drawn up on the beach.'

'*I* can see nothing either, Lucy.'

'And yet, you are trembling as if there was something dreadful in the view from this door.'

'There *is* something dreadful! I feel it – though I see nothing. I feel it – nearer and nearer in the empty air, darker and darker in the sunny light. I don't know what it is. Take me away! No. Not out on the beach. I can't pass the door. Somewhere else! somewhere else!'

Mrs Crayford looked round her, and noticed a second door at the inner end of the boat-house. She spoke to her husband.

'See where that door leads to, William.'

Crayford opened the door. It led into a desolate enclosure – half garden, half yard. Some nets, stretched on poles, were hanging up to dry. No other objects were visible – not a living creature appeared in the place. 'It doesn't look very inviting, my dear,' said Mrs Crayford. 'I am at your service, however. What do you say?'

She offered her arm to Clara as she spoke. Clara refused it. She took Crayford's arm, and clung to him.

'I'm frightened, dreadfully frightened!' she said to him, faintly. '*You* keep with me – a woman is no protection; I want to be with *you*.' She looked round again at the boat-house doorway. 'Oh!' she whispered, 'I'm cold all over – I'm frozen with fear of this place. Come into the yard! Come into the yard!'

'Leave her to me,' said Crayford to his wife. 'I will call you, if she doesn't get better in the open air.'

He took her out at once, and closed the yard door behind them.

'Mr Steventon! do you understand this?' asked Mrs Crayford. 'What can she possibly be frightened of?'

She put the question, still looking mechanically at the door by which her husband and Clara had gone out. Receiving no reply, she glanced round at Steventon. He was standing on the opposite side of the luncheon-table, with his eyes fixed attentively on the view from the main doorway of the boat-house. Mrs Crayford looked where Steventon was looking. This time, there was something visible. She saw the shadow of a human figure projected on the stretch of smooth yellow sand in front of the boat-house.

In a moment more, the figure appeared. A man came slowly into view, and stopped on the threshold of the door.

XVIII

The man was a sinister and terrible object to look at. His eyes glared like the eyes of a wild animal; his head was bare; his long grey hair was torn and tangled; his miserable garments hung about him in rags. He stood in the doorway, a speechless figure of misery and want, staring at the well-spread table like a hungry dog.

Steventon spoke to him.

'Who are you?'

He answered in a hollow voice:

'A starving man.'

He advanced a few steps – slowly and painfully, as if he was sinking under fatigue.

'Throw me some bones from the table,' he said. 'Give me my share along with the dogs.'

There was madness as well as hunger in his eyes while he spoke those words. Steventon placed Mrs Crayford behind him, so that he might be easily able to protect her in case of need, and beckoned to two sailors who were passing the door of the boat-house at the time.

'Give the man some bread and meat,' he said, 'and wait near him.'

The outcast seized on the bread and meat with lean, long-nailed hands that looked like claws. After the first mouthful of food, he stopped, considered vacantly with himself, and broke the bread and meat into two portions. One portion he put into an old canvas wallet that hung over his shoulder. The other he devoured voraciously. Steventon questioned him.

'Where do you come from?'

'From the sea.'

'Wrecked?'

'Yes.'

Steventon turned to Mrs Crayford.

'There may be some truth in the poor wretch's story,' he said. 'I heard something of a strange boat having been cast on the beach, thirty or forty miles higher up the coast. When were you wrecked, my man?'

The starving creature looked up from his food, and made an effort to collect his thoughts – to exert his memory. It was not to be done. He gave up the attempt in despair. His language, when he spoke, was as wild as his looks.

'I can't tell you,' he said. 'I can't get the wash of the sea out of my ears. I can't get the shining stars all night, and the burning sun all day, out of my brain. When was I wrecked? When was I first adrift in the boat? When did I get the tiller in my hand and fight against hunger and sleep? When did the gnawing in my breast, and the burning in my head, first begin? I have lost all reckoning of it. I can't think; I can't sleep; I can't get the wash of the sea out of my ears. What are you baiting me with questions for? Let me eat!'

Even the sailors pitied him. The sailors asked leave of their officer to add a little drink to his meal.

'We've got a drop of grog with us, sir, in a bottle. May we give it to him?'

'Certainly!'

He took the bottle fiercely, as he had taken the food – drank a little – stopped – and considered with himself again. He held up the bottle to the light, and, marking how much liquor it contained, carefully drank half of it only. This done, he put the bottle in his wallet along with the food.

'Are you saving it up for another time?' said Steventon.

'I'm saving it up,' the man answered. 'Never mind what for. That's my secret.'

He looked round the boat-house as he made that reply, and noticed Mrs Crayford for the first time.

'A woman among you!' he said. 'Is she English? Is she young? Let me look closer at her.'

He advanced a few steps towards the table.

'Don't be afraid, Mrs Crayford,' said Steventon.

'I'm not afraid,' Mrs Crayford replied. He frightened me at first – he interests me now. Let him speak to me if he wishes it.'

He never spoke. He stood, in dead silence, looking long and anxiously at the beautiful Englishwoman.

'Well?' said Steventon.

He shook his head sadly, and drew back again with a heavy sigh.

'No!' he said to himself, 'that's not *her* face. No! not found yet.'

Mrs Crayford's interest was strongly excited. She ventured to speak to him.

'Who is it you want to find?' she asked. 'Your wife?'

He shook his head again.

'Who then? What is she like?'

He answered that question in words. His hoarse, hollow voice softened little by little into sorrowful and gentle tones.

'Young,' he said; 'with a fair, sad face – with kind, tender eyes – with a soft, clear voice. Young, and loving, and merciful. I keep her face in my mind, though I can keep nothing else. I must wander, wander, wander – restless, sleepless, homeless – till I find *her!* Over the ice and over the snow; tossing on the sea, tramping over the land; awake all night, awake all day; wander, wander, wander, till I find *her!*'

He waved his hand with a gesture of farewell, and turned wearily to go out.

At the same moment Crayford opened the yard door.

'I think you had better come to Clara,' he began – and checked himself, noticing the stranger. 'Who is that?'

The shipwrecked man, hearing another voice in the room, looked round slowly over his shoulder. Struck by his appearance, Crayford advanced a little nearer to him. Mrs Crayford spoke to her husband as he passed her.

'It's only a poor mad creature, William,' she whispered, 'shipwrecked and starving.'

'Mad?' Crayford repeated, approaching nearer and nearer to the man. 'Am *I* in my right senses?' He suddenly sprang on the outcast, and seized him by the throat. 'Richard Wardour!' he cried, in a voice of fury. 'Alive! Alive, to answer for Frank!'

The man struggled. Crayford held him.

'Where is Frank?' he said. 'You villain, where is Frank?'

The man resisted no longer. He repeated vacantly—

'Villain? and where is Frank?'

As the name escaped his lips, Clara appeared at the open yard door, and hurried into the room.

'I heard Richard's name!' she said. 'I heard Frank's name! What does it mean?'

At the sound of her voice the outcast renewed the struggle to free himself, with a sudden frenzy of strength which Crayford was not able to resist. He broke away before the sailors could come to their officer's assistance. Half way down the length of the room he and Clara met one another face to face. A new light sparkled in the poor wretch's eyes; a cry of recognition burst from his lips. He flung one hand up wildly in the air. 'Found!' he shouted, and rushed out to the beach before any of the men present could stop him.

Mrs Crayford put her arms round Clara and held her up. She had not made a movement; she had not spoken a word. The sight of Wardour's face had petrified her.

The minutes passed, and there rose a sudden burst of cheering from the sailors on the beach, near the spot where the fishermen's boats were drawn up. Every man left his work. Every man waved his cap in the air. The passengers, near at hand, caught the infection of enthusiasm, and joined the crew. A moment more, and Richard Wardour appeared again in the doorway, carrying a man in his arms. He staggered, breathless with the effort that he was making, to the place where Clara stood, held up in Mrs Crayford's arms.

'Saved, Clara!' he cried. 'Saved for *you!*'

He released the man, and placed him in Clara's arms.

Frank! Footsore and weary, but living! Saved – saved for *her*! 'Now, Clara,' cried Mrs Crayford, 'which of us is right? I who believed in the mercy of God, or you who believed in a dream?'

She never answered; she clung to Frank in speechless ecstasy. She never even looked at the man who had preserved him – in the first absorbing joy of seeing her lover alive. Step by step, slower and slower, Richard Wardour drew back and left them by themselves.

'I may rest now,' he said, faintly. 'I may sleep at last. The task is done. The struggle is over.'

His last reserves of strength had been given to Frank. He stopped, he staggered, his hands wavered feebly in search of support. But for one faithful friend, he would have fallen. Crayford caught him. Crayford laid his old comrade gently on some sails strewn in a corner, and pillowed Wardour's weary head on his own breast. The tears streamed over his face. 'Richard! Dear Richard!' he said. 'Remember – and forgive me.'

Richard neither heeded nor heard him. His dim eyes still looked across the room at Clara and Frank.

'I have made *her* happy!' he murmured. 'I may lay down my weary head now on the mother earth that hushes all her children to rest at last. Sink, heart! sink, sink to rest! Oh, look at them!' he said to Crayford, with a burst of grief. 'They have forgotten *me* already.'

It was true! The interest was all with the two lovers. Frank was young, and handsome, and popular. Officers, passengers, and sailors, they all crowded round Frank. They all forgot the martyred man who had saved him – the man who was dying in Crayford's arms.

Crayford tried once more to attract his attention – to win his recognition while there was yet time.

'Richard, speak to me! Speak to your old friend!'

He looked round; he vacantly repeated Crayford's last word.

'Friend?' he said. 'My eyes are dim, friend; my mind is dull. I have lost all memories but the memory of *her*. Dead thoughts – all dead thoughts but that one! And yet, you look at me kindly! Why has your face gone down with the wreck of all the rest?'

He paused. His face changed; his thoughts drifted back from present to past. He looked at Crayford vacantly, lost in the terrible remembrances that were rising in him, as the shadows rise with the coming night.

'Hark ye, friend!' he whispered. 'Never let Frank know it. There was a time when the fiend within me hungered for his life. I had my hands on the boat.

I heard the voice of the Tempter speaking to me: "Launch it, and leave him to die!" I waited, with my hands on the boat and my eyes on the place where he slept. "Leave him! leave him!" the Voice whispered. "Love him!" the lad's voice answered, moaning and murmuring in his sleep. "Love him, Clara, for helping *me*!" I heard the morning wind come up in the silence over the great deep. Far and near, I heard the groaning of the floating ice, floating, floating, to the clear water and the balmy air. And the wicked Voice floated away with it – away, away, away for ever! "Love him! love him, Clara, for helping *me*." No wind could float that away. "Love him, Clara"—'

His voice sank into silence; his head dropped on Crayford's breast. Frank saw it. Frank struggled up on his bleeding feet, and parted the friendly throng round him. Frank had not forgotten the man who had saved him.

'Let me go to him!' he cried. 'I must, and will, go to him! Clara, come with me.'

Clara and Steventon supported him between them. He fell on his knees at Wardour's side; he put his hand on Wardour's bosom.

'Richard!'

The weary eyes opened again. The sinking voice was heard feebly once more.

'Ah! poor Frank. I didn't forget you, Frank, when I came here to beg. I remembered you, lying down outside in the shadow of the boats. I saved you your share of the food and drink. Too weak to get at it now! A little rest, Frank! I shall soon be strong enough to carry you down to the ship.'

The end was near. They all saw it now. The men reverently uncovered their heads in the presence of Death. In an agony of despair, Frank appealed to the friends round him.

'Get something to strengthen him, for God's sake! Oh, men! men! I should never have been here but for him! He has given all his strength to my weakness; and now, see how strong I am, and how weak *he* is! Clara! I held by his arm all over the ice and snow. *He* kept watch when I was senseless in the open boat. *His* hand dragged me out of the waves, when we were wrecked. Speak to him, Clara! speak to him!' His voice failed him, and his head dropped on Wardour's breast.

She spoke, as well as her tears would let her.

'Richard! have you forgotten me?'

He rallied at the sound of that beloved voice. He looked up at her, as she knelt at his head.

'Forgotten you?' Still looking at her, he lifted his hand with an effort, and laid it on Frank. 'Should I have been strong enough to save *him*, if I could have forgotten *you*?' He waited a moment, and turned his face feebly towards Crayford. 'Stay!' he said. 'Some one was here and spoke to me.' A faint light of recognition glimmered in his eyes. 'Ah, Crayford! I recollect now. Dear Crayford! Come nearer! My mind clears; but my eyes grow dim. You will remember me kindly for Frank's sake? Poor Frank! why does he hide his face? Is he crying? Nearer, Clara – I want to look my last at *you*. My sister Clara! Kiss me, sister, kiss me before I die!'

She stooped and kissed his forehead. A faint smile trembled on his lips. It passed away; and stillness possessed the face – the stillness of Death.

Crayford's voice was heard in the silence.

'The loss is ours,' he said. 'The gain is his. He has won the greatest of all conquests – the conquest of himself. And he has died in the moment of victory. Not one of us here but may live to envy *his* glorious death.'

The distant report of a gun came from the ship in the offing, and signalled the return to England and to home.

A Mad Marriage

Originally appeared in *All the Year Round*, 17–24 October 1874 as 'A Fatal Fortune'. The story's subsequent publishing history illustrates how fond Collins was of altering the titles of his stories, and of the problems this poses for collector, editor and reader alike. The story appeared as 'A Sane Madman' in *Alicia Warlock (A Mystery) and Other Stories* (Boston: Gill & Co., 1875) and under the same title in *Lotus Leaves* (1875). But the same year Collins also reprinted the story in the second edition of *Miss or Mrs?* (it does not appear in the first), this time calling it 'A Mad Marriage'. He explains in his preface that "A Fatal Fortune", appearing as it does in the present volume, immediately after "The Fatal Cradle", it has been thought desirable, for variety's sake, to alter the title.' Why he did not use the story's American title is not known. In an endnote to the story Collins informs his readers 'that this story is founded, in all essential particulars, on a case which actually occurred in England, eight years since.' In the 1870s, Collins constructed a number of plots which depend on unusual situations within marriages, usually, as here, with obvious polemical purpose. In the novel *Man and Wife* (1870) he examines the vagaries of Irish and Scottish marriage law and condemns the powerlessness in law of a married woman. In *Miss or Mrs?* (1871) a clandestine marriage is arranged so that the heroine may avoid marrying the villain. In *The Law and the Lady* (1874) a woman's marriage stands – despite the fact that her husband gave a false name at the ceremony.

I

One fine morning, more than three months since, you were riding with your brother, Miss Anstell, in Hyde Park. It was a hot day, and you had allowed your horses to fall into a walking pace. As you passed the railing on the right-hand side, near the eastern extremity of the lake in the park, neither you nor your brother noticed a solitary woman loitering on the footpath to look at the riders as they went by.

The solitary woman was my old nurse, Nancy Connell. And these were the words she heard exchanged between you and your brother as you slowly passed her:

Your brother said, 'Is it true that Mary Brading and her husband have gone to America?'

You laughed, as if the question amused you, and answered, 'Quite true.'

'How long will they be away?' your brother asked next.

'As long as they live,' you answered, with another laugh.

By this time you had passed beyond Nancy Connell's hearing. She owns to having followed your horses a few steps, to hear what was said next. She looked particularly at your brother. He took your reply seriously; he seemed to be quite astonished by it.

'Leave England and settle in America!' he exclaimed. 'Why should they do that?'

'Who can tell why?' you answered. 'Mary Brading's husband is mad, and Mary Brading herself is not much better.'

You touched your horse with the whip, and in a moment more you and your brother were out of my old nurse's hearing. She wrote and told me what I here tell you, by a recent mail. I have been thinking of those last words of yours, in my leisure hours, more seriously than you would suppose. The end of it is that I take up my pen, on behalf of my husband and myself, to tell you the story of our marriage, and the reason for our emigration to the United States of America.

It matters little or nothing to him or to me whether our friends in general think us both mad or not. Their opinions, hostile or favourable, are of no sort of importance to us. But you are an exception to the rule. In bygone days at school we were fast and firm friends; and – what weighs with me even more than this – you were heartily loved and admired by my dear mother. She spoke of you tenderly on her death-bed. Events have separated us of late years. But I cannot forget the old times; and I cannot feel indifferent to your opinion of me and of my husband, though an ocean does separate us, and though we are never likely to look on one another again. It is very foolish of me, I daresay, to take seriously to heart what you said in one of your thoughtless moments. I can only plead in excuse that I have gone through a great deal of suffering, and that I was always (as you may remember) a person of sensitive temperament, easily excited and easily depressed.

Enough of this. Do me the last favour I shall ever ask of you. Read what follows, and judge for yourself whether my husband and I are quite so mad as you were disposed to think us when Nancy Connell heard you talking to your brother in Hyde Park.

II

It is now more than a year since I went to Eastbourne, on the coast of Sussex, with my father and my brother James.

My brother had then, as we hoped, recovered from the effects of a fall in the hunting-field. He complained, however, at times, of pain in his head; and the doctors advised us to try the sea air. We removed to Eastbourne, without a suspicion of the serious nature of the injury that he had received. For a few days all went well. We liked the place; the air agreed with us; and we determined to prolong our residence for some weeks to come.

On our sixth day at the seaside – a memorable day to me, for reasons which you have still to hear – my brother complained again of the old pain in his head. He and I went out together to try what exercise would do towards relieving him. We walked through the town to the fort at one end of it, and then followed a footpath running by the side of the sea, over a dreary waste of shingle, bounded at its inland extremity by the road to Hastings and by the marshy country beyond.

We had left the fort at some little distance behind us. I was walking in front, and James was following me. He was talking as quietly as usual – when he suddenly stopped in the middle of a sentence. I turned round in surprise, and discovered my brother prostrate on the path, in convulsions terrible to see.

It was the first epileptic fit I had ever witnessed. My presence of mind entirely deserted me. I could only wring my hands in horror, and scream for help. No one appeared either from the direction of the fort, or of the high road. I was too far off, I suppose, to make myself heard. Looking ahead of me along the path, I discovered, to my infinite relief, the figure of a man running towards me. As he came nearer, I saw that he was unmistakably a gentleman – young, and eager to be of service to me.

'Pray compose yourself,' he said, after a look at my brother. 'It is very dreadful to see, but it is not dangerous. We must wait until the convulsions are over, and then I can help you.'

He seemed to know so much about it that I thought he might be a medical man. I put the question to him plainly.

He coloured, and looked a little confused.

'I am not a doctor,' he said. 'I happen to have seen persons afflicted with epilepsy; and I have heard medical men say it is useless to interfere until the fit is over. See!' he added. 'Your brother is quieter already. He will soon feel a sense of relief which will more than compensate him for what he has suffered. I will help him to get to the fort, and, once there, we can send for a carriage to take him home.'

In five minutes more we were on our way to the fort; the stranger supporting my brother as attentively and tenderly as if he had been an old friend. When the carriage had been obtained, he insisted on accompanying us to our own door, on the chance that his services might still be of some use. He left us, asking permission to call and inquire after James's health the next day. A more modest, gentle, and unassuming person I never met with. He not only excited my warmest gratitude; he interested me at my first meeting with him.

I lay some stress on the impression which this young man produced on me – why, you will soon find out.

The next day the stranger paid his promised visit of inquiry. His card, which he sent upstairs, informed us that his name was Roland Cameron. My father – who is not easily pleased – took a liking to him at once. His visit was prolonged, at our request. He said just enough about himself to satisfy us that we were receiving a person who was at least of equal rank with ourselves. Born in England, of a Scotch family, he had lost both his parents. Not long since, he had inherited a fortune from one of his uncles. It struck us as a little strange that he spoke of this fortune with a marked change to melancholy in his voice and his manner. The subject was, for some inconceivable reason, evidently distasteful to him. Rich as he was, he acknowledged that he led a simple and solitary life. He had little taste for society, and no sympathies in common with the average young men of his age. But he had his own harmless pleasures and occupations; and past sorrow and suffering had taught him not to expect too much from life. All this was said modestly, with a winning charm of look and voice which indescribably attracted me. His personal appearance aided the favourable impression which his manner and his conversation produced. He was of the middle height, lightly and firmly built; his complexion pale; his hands and feet small and finely shaped; his brown hair curling naturally; his eyes large and dark, with an occasional indecision in their expression which was far from being an objection to them, to my taste. It seemed to harmonize with an occasional indecision in his talk; proceeding, as I was inclined to think, from some passing confusion in his thoughts which it always cost him a little effort to discipline and overcome. Does it surprise you to find how closely I observed a man who was only a chance acquaintance, at my first interview with him? or do your suspicions enlighten you, and do you say to yourself, She has fallen in love with Mr Roland Cameron at first sight? I may plead in my own defence, that I was not quite romantic enough to go that length. But I own I waited for his next visit with an impatience which was new to me in my experience of my sober self. And, worse still, when the day came, I changed my dress three times, before my newly-developed vanity was satisfied with the picture which the looking-glass presented to me of myself.

In a fortnight more, my father and my brother began to look on the daily companionship of our new friend as one of the settled institutions of their lives. In a fortnight more, Mr Roland Cameron and I – though we neither of us ventured to acknowledge it – were as devotedly in love with each other as two young people could well be. Ah, what a delightful time it was! and how cruelly soon our happiness came to an end!

During the brief interval which I have just described, I observed certain peculiarities in Roland Cameron's conduct, which perplexed and troubled me when my mind was busy with him in my lonely moments.

For instance, he was subject to the strangest lapses into silence, when he and I were talking together. At these times, his eyes assumed a weary absent look, and his mind seemed to wander away – far from the conversation, and far from me. He was perfectly unaware of his own infirmity; he fell into it unconsciously, and came out of it unconsciously. If I noticed that he had not been attending to me, or if I asked why he had been silent, he was completely at a loss to comprehend what I meant: I puzzled and distressed him. What he was thinking of in these pauses of silence, it was impossible to guess. His face, at other times singularly mobile and expressive, became almost a perfect blank. Had he suffered some terrible shock, at some past period of his life?

and had his mind never quite recovered it? I longed to ask him the question, and yet I shrank from doing it, I was so sadly afraid of distressing him: or to put it in plainer words, I was so truly and so tenderly fond of him.

Then, again, though he was ordinarily, I sincerely believe, the most gentle and most loveable of men; there were occasions when he would surprise me by violent outbreaks of temper, excited by the merest trifles. A dog barking suddenly at his heels, or a boy throwing stones in the road, or an importunate shopkeeper trying to make him purchase something that he did not want, would throw him into a frenzy of rage which was, without exaggeration, really frightful to see. He always apologized for these outbreaks, in terms which showed that he was sincerely ashamed of his own violence. But he could never succeed in controlling himself. The lapses into passion, like the lapses into silence, took him into their own possession, and did with him, for the time being, just what they pleased.

One more example of his peculiarities, and I have done. The strangeness of his conduct in this case was noticed by my father and my brother, as well as by me.

When Roland was with us in the evening, whether he came to dinner or to tea, he invariably left us exactly at nine o'clock. Try as we might to persuade him to stay longer, he always politely but positively refused. Even I had no influence over him in this matter. When I pressed him to remain, though it cost him an effort, he still retired exactly as the clock struck nine. He gave no reason for this strange proceeding; he only said that it was a habit of his, and begged us to indulge him in it without asking for an explanation. My father and my brother (being men) succeeded in controlling their curiosity. For my part (being a woman) every day that passed only made me more and more eager to penetrate the mystery. I privately resolved to choose my time, when Roland was in a particularly accessible humour, and then to appeal to him for the explanation which he had hitherto refused – as a special favour to myself.

In two days more I found my opportunity.

Some friends of ours, who had joined us at Eastbourne, proposed a pic-nic party to the famous neighbouring cliff called Beachey Head. We accepted the invitation. The day was lovely, and the gipsy dinner was, as usual, infinitely preferable (for once in a way) to a formal dinner indoors. Towards evening, our little assembly separated into parties of twos and threes to explore the neighbourhood. Roland and I found ourselves together, as a matter of course. We were happy, and we were alone. Was it the right or the wrong time to ask the fatal question? I am not able to decide? I only know that I asked it.

III

'Mr Cameron,' I said, 'will you make allowances for a weak woman? And will you tell me something that I am dying to know?'

He walked straight into the trap, with that entire absence of ready wit, or small suspicion (I leave you to choose the right phrase), which is so much like men, and so little like women.

'Of course I will,' he answered.

'Then tell me,' I asked, 'why you always insist on leaving us at nine o'clock?'

He started, and looked at me so sadly, so reproachfully, that I would have given everything I possessed to recall the rash words which had just passed my lips.

'If I consent to tell you,' he replied, after a momentary struggle with himself, 'will you let me put a question to you first, and will you promise to answer it?'

I gave him my promise, and waited eagerly for what was coming next.

'Miss Brading,' he said, 'tell me honestly – do you think I am mad?'

It was impossible to laugh at him: he spoke those strange words seriously – sternly, I might almost say.

'No such thought ever entered my head,' I answered.

He looked at me very earnestly.

'You say that, on your word of honour?'

'On my word of honour.'

I answered with perfect sincerity, and I evidently satisfied him that I had spoken the truth. He took my hand, and lifted it gratefully to his lips.

'Thank you,' he said simply. 'You encourage me to tell you a very sad story.'

'Your own story?' I asked.

'My own story. Let me begin by telling you why I persist in leaving your house always at the same early hour. Whenever I go out, I am bound by a promise to the person with whom I am living at Eastbourne, to return at a quarter past nine o'clock.'

'The person with whom you are living,' I repeated. 'You are living at a boarding-house, are you not?'

'I am living, Miss Brading, under the care of a doctor who keeps an asylum for the insane. He has taken a house for some of his wealthier patients at the sea-side; and he allows me my liberty in the daytime, on condition that I faithfully perform my promise at night. It is a quarter of an hour's walk from your house to the doctor's, and it is a rule that the patients retire at half-past nine o'clock.'

Here was the mystery which had so sorely perplexed me, revealed at last! The disclosure literally struck me speechless. Unconsciously and instinctively I drew back from him a few steps. He fixed his sad eyes on me with a touching look of entreaty.

'Don't shrink away from me,' he said. '*You* don't think I am mad?'

I was too confused and distressed to know what to say, and, at the same time, I was too fond of him not to answer that appeal. I took his hand and pressed it in silence. He turned his head aside for a moment. I thought I saw a tear on his cheek. I felt his hand close tremblingly on mine. He mastered himself with surprising resolution: he spoke with perfect composure when he looked at me again.

'Do you care to know my story,' he asked, 'after what I have just told you?'

'I am eager to hear it,' I answered. 'You don't know how I feel for you. I am too distressed to be able to express myself in words.'

'You are the kindest and dearest of women!' he said – with the utmost fervour, and at the same time with the utmost respect.

We sat down together in a grassy hollow of the cliff, with our faces towards the grand grey sea. The daylight was beginning to fade, as I heard the story which made me Roland Cameron's wife.

IV

'My mother died when I was an infant in arms,' he began. 'My father, from my earliest to my latest recollections, was always hard towards me. I have been told that I was an odd child, with strange ways of my own. My father detested anything that was strongly marked, anything out of the ordinary way, in the characters and habits of the persons about him. He himself lived (as the phrase is) by line and rule; and he determined to make his son follow his example. I was subjected to severe discipline at school, and I was carefully watched afterwards at college. Looking back on my early life, I can see no traces of happiness, I can find no tokens of sympathy. Sad submission to a hard destiny, weary wayfaring over unfriendly roads – such is the story of my life, from ten years old to twenty.

'I passed one autumn vacation at the Cumberland lakes – and there I met by accident with a young French lady. The result of that meeting decided my whole after-life.

'She filled the position of nursery governess in the house of a wealthy Englishman. I had frequent opportunities of seeing her. We took an innocent pleasure in each other's society. Her little experience of life was strangely like mine. There was a perfect sympathy of thought and feeling between us. We loved, or thought we loved. I was not twenty-one, and she was not eighteen, when I asked her to be my wife.

'I can understand my folly now, and I can laugh at it, or lament over it, as the humour moves me. And yet, I can't help pitying myself, when I look back at myself at that time – I was so young, so hungry for a little sympathy, so weary of my empty friendless life. Well! everything is comparative in this world. I was soon to regret, bitterly to regret, that friendless life – wretched as it was.

'The poor girl's employer discovered our attachment, through his wife. He at once communicated with my father.

'My father had but one word to say – he insisted on my going abroad, and leaving it to him to release me from my absurd engagement, in my absence. I answered him that I should be of age in a few months, and that I was determined to marry the girl. He gave me three days to reconsider that resolution. I held to my resolution. In a week afterwards I was declared insane by two medical men; and I was placed by my father in a lunatic asylum.

'Was it an act of insanity for the son of a gentleman, with great expectations before him, to propose marriage to a nursery governess? I declare, as Heaven is my witness, I know of no other act of mine which could justify my father, and justify the doctors, in placing me under restraint.

'I was three years in that asylum. It was officially reported that the air did not agree with me. I was removed, for two years more, to another asylum in a remote part of England. For the five best years of my life I have been herded with madmen – and my reason has survived it. The impression I produce on you, on your father, on your brother, on all our friends at this pic-nic, is that I am as reasonable as the rest of my fellow-creatures. Am I rushing to a hasty conclusion, when I assert myself to be now, and always to have been, a sane man?

'At the end of my five years of arbitrary imprisonment in a free country, happily for me – I am ashamed to say it, but I must speak the truth – happily for me, my merciless father died. His trustees, to whom I was now consigned, felt some pity for me. They could not take the responsibility of granting me my freedom. But they placed me under the care of a surgeon, who received me into his private residence, and who allowed me free exercise in the open air.

'A year's trial of this new mode of life satisfied the surgeon, and satisfied everyone else who took the smallest interest in me, that I was perfectly fit to enjoy my liberty. I was freed from all restraint, and was permitted to reside with a near relative of mine, in that very Lake country which had been the scene of my fatal meeting with the French girl, six years before.'

V

'I lived happily in the house of my relative, satisfied with the ordinary pursuits of a country gentleman. Time had long since cured me of my boyish infatuation for the nursery governess. I could revisit with perfect composure the paths along which we had walked, the lake on which we had sailed together. Hearing by chance that she was married in her own country, I could wish her all possible happiness, with the sober kindness of a disinterested friend. What a strange thread of irony runs through the texture of the simplest human life! The early love for which I had sacrificed and suffered so much, was now revealed to me in its true colours, as a boy's passing fancy – nothing more!

'Three years of peaceful freedom passed; freedom which, on the uncontradicted testimony of respectable witnesses, I never abused. Well, that long and happy interval, like all intervals, came to its end – and then the great misfortune of my life fell upon me. One of my uncles died, and left me inheritor of his whole fortune. I, alone, to the exclusion of the other heirs, now received, not only the large income derived from the estates, but seventy thousand pounds in ready money as well.

'The vile calumny which had asserted me to be mad, was now revived by the wretches who were interested in stepping between me and my inheritance. A year ago, I was sent back to the asylum in which I had been last imprisoned. The pretence for confining me was found in an 'act of violence' (as it was called), which I had committed in a momentary outbreak of anger, and which it was acknowledged had led to no serious results. Having got me into the asylum, the conspirators proceeded to complete their work. A Commission in Lunacy was issued against me. It was held by one Commissioner, without a jury, and without the presence of a lawyer to assert my interests. By one man's decision I was declared to be of unsound mind. The custody of my person, as well as the management of my estates, was confided to men chosen from among the conspirators who had declared me to be mad. I am here through the favour of the proprietor of the asylum, who has given me my holiday at the seaside, and who humanely trusts me with my liberty, as you see. At barely thirty years old, I am refused the free use of my money and the free

management of my affairs. At barely thirty years old, I am officially declared
to be a lunatic for life!'

VI

He paused; his head sank on his breast; his story was told.

I have repeated his words as nearly as I can remember them; but I can give
no idea of the modest and touching resignation with which he spoke. To say
that I pitied him with my whole heart, is to say nothing. I loved him with
my whole heart – and I may acknowledge it, now!

'Oh, Mr Cameron,' I said, as soon as I could trust myself to speak, 'can
nothing be done to help you? Is there no hope?'

'There is always hope,' he answered, without raising his head. 'I have to
thank *you*, Miss Brading, for teaching me that.'

'To thank me?' I repeated. 'How have I taught you to hope?'

'You have brightened my dreary life. When I am with you, all my bitter
remembrances leave me. I am a happy man again; and a happy man can
always hope. I dream now of finding what I have never yet had – a dear
and devoted friend, who will rouse the energy that has sunk in me under the
martyrdom that I have endured. Why do I submit to the loss of my rights and
my liberty, without an effort to recover them? I was alone in the world, until
I met with you. I had no kind hand to raise me, no kind voice to encourage
me. Shall I ever find the hand? Shall I ever hear the voice? When I am with
you, the hope that you have taught me answers, Yes. When I am by myself,
the old despair comes back, and says, No.'

He lifted his head for the first time. If I had not understood what his words
meant, his look would have enlightened me. The tears came into my eyes;
my heart heaved and fluttered wildly; my hands mechanically tore up and
scattered the grass round me. The silence became unendurable. I spoke, hardly
knowing what I was saying; tearing faster and faster at the poor harmless grass,
as if my whole business in life was to pull up the greatest quantity in the shortest
possible space of time!

'We have only known each other a little while,' I said; 'and a woman is but
a weak ally in such a terrible position as yours. But useless as I may be, count
on me, now and always, as your friend—'

He moved close to me before I could say more, and took my hand. He
murmured in my ear,

'May I count on you, one day, as the nearest and dearest friend of all? Will
you forgive me, Mary, if I own that I love you? You have taught me to love, as
you have taught me to hope. It is in your power to lighten my hard lot. *You*
can recompense me for all that I have suffered; *you* can rouse me to struggle
for my freedom and my rights. Be the good angel of my life! Forgive me, love
me, rescue me – be my wife!'

I don't know how it happened. I found myself in his arms – and I answered
him in a kiss. Taking all the circumstances into consideration, I dare say I
was guilty, in accepting him, of the rashest act that ever a woman committed.
Very good. I didn't care then – I don't care now. I was then, and I am now,
the happiest woman living.

VII

It was necessary that either he or I should tell my father of what had passed between us. On reflection, I thought it best that I should make the disclosure. The day after the pic-nic, I repeated to my father Roland's melancholy narrative, as a necessary preface to the announcement that I had promised to be Roland's wife.

My father saw the obvious objection to the marriage. He warned me of the imprudence which I contemplated committing, in the strongest terms. Our prospect of happiness, if we married, would depend entirely on our capacity to legally supersede the proceedings of the Lunacy Commission. Success in this arduous undertaking was, to say the least of it, uncertain. The commonest prudence pointed to the propriety of delaying our union until the doubtful experiment had been put to the proof.

This reasoning was unanswerable. It was, nevertheless, completely thrown away upon me.

When did a woman in love ever listen to reason? I believe there is no instance of it on record. My father's wise words of caution had no chance against Roland's fervent entreaties. The days of his residence at Eastbourne were drawing to a close. If I let him return to the asylum an unmarried man, months, years perhaps, might pass before our union could take place. Could I expect him, could I expect any man, to endure that cruel separation, that unrelieved suspense? His mind had been sorely tried already; his mind might give way under it. These were the arguments that carried weight with them, in my judgment! I was of age, and free to act as I pleased. You are welcome, if you like, to consider me the most foolish and the most obstinate of women. In sixteen days from the date of the pic-nic, Roland and I were privately married at Eastbourne.

My father – more grieved than angry, poor man – declined to be present at the ceremony; in justice to himself. My brother gave me away at the altar.

Roland and I spent the afternoon of the wedding-day, and the earlier part of the evening, together. At nine o'clock he returned to the doctor's house, exactly as usual; having previously explained to me that he was in the power of the Court of Chancery, and that until we succeeded in setting aside the proceedings of the Lunacy Commission, there was a serious necessity for keeping the marriage strictly secret. My husband and I kissed, and said good-bye till to-morrow, as the clock struck the hour. I little thought, while I looked after him from the street door, that months on months were to pass before I saw Roland again.

A hurried note from my husband reached me the next morning. Our marriage had been discovered (we never could tell by whom), and we had been betrayed to the doctor. Roland was then on his way back to the asylum. He had been warned that force would be used if he resisted. Knowing that resistance would be interpreted, in his case, as a new outbreak of madness, he had wisely submitted. 'I have made the sacrifice,' the letter concluded, 'it is now for you to help me. Attack the Commission in Lunacy, and be quick about it!'

We lost no time in preparing for the attack. On the day when I received the news of our misfortune, we left Eastbourne for London, and at once took measures to obtain the best legal advice.

My dear father – though I was far from deserving his kindness – entered into the matter heart and soul. In due course of time, we presented a petition to the Lord Chancellor, praying that the decision of the Lunacy Commission might be set aside.

We supported our petition by quoting the evidence of Roland's friends and neighbours, during his three years' residence in the Lake country, as a free man. These worthy people (being summoned before the Lunacy Commission) had one and all agreed that he was, as to their judgment and experience, perfectly quiet, harmless, and sane. Many of them had gone out shooting with him. Others had often accompanied him in sailing excursions on the lake. Do people trust a madman with a gun, and with the management of a boat? As to the 'act of violence,' which the heirs-at-law and the next-of-kin had made the means of imprisoning Roland in the mad-house, it amounted to this. He had lost his temper, and had knocked a man down who had offended him. Very wrong, no doubt – but if that is a proof of madness, what thousands of lunatics are still at large! Another instance produced to prove his insanity was still more absurd. It was solemnly declared that he put an image of the Virgin Mary in his boat, when he went out on his sailing excursions! I have seen the image – it was a very beautiful work of art. Was Roland mad to admire it, and take it with him? His religious convictions leaned towards Catholicism. If he betrayed insanity in adorning his boat with an image of the Virgin Mary, what is the mental condition of most of the ladies in Christendom who wear the Cross as an ornament round their necks? We advanced these arguments in our petition, after quoting the evidence of the witnesses. And more than this, we even went the length of admitting, as an act of respect towards the Court, that my poor husband might be eccentric in some of his opinions and habits. But we put it to the authorities, whether better results might not be expected from placing him under the care of a wife who loved him, and whom he loved, than from shutting him up in an asylum, among incurable madmen, as his companions for life.

Such was our petition, so far as I am able to describe it.

The decision rested with the Lords Justices. They decided against us.

Turning a deaf ear to our witnesses and our arguments, these merciless lawyers declared that the doctor's individual assertion of my husband's insanity was enough for them. They considered Roland's comfort to be sufficiently provided for in the asylum with an allowance of seven hundred pounds a year – and to the asylum they consigned him for the rest of his days.

So far as I was concerned, the result of this infamous judgment was to deprive me of the position of Roland's wife; no lunatic being capable of contracting marriage by law. So far as my husband was concerned, the result may be best stated in the language of a popular newspaper, which published an article on the case. 'It is possible' (said the article – I wish I could personally thank the man who wrote it!) 'for the Court of Chancery to take a man who has a large fortune, and is in the prime of life, but is a little touched in the head, and make a monk of him, and then report to itself that the comfort and happiness of the lunatic have been effectually provided for at the expenditure of seven hundred pounds a year.'

Roland was determined, however, that they should *not* make a monk of him – and, you may rely upon it, so was I!

But one alternative was left to us. The authority of the Court of Chancery (within its jurisdiction) is the most despotic authority on the face of the earth. Our one hope was in taking to flight. The price of our liberty, as citizens of England, was exile from our native country, and the entire abandonment of Roland's fortune. We accepted those hard conditions. Hospitable America offered us a refuge, beyond the reach of mad-doctors and Lords Justices. To hospitable America our hearts turned, as to our second country. The serious question was – how were we to get there?

We had attempted to correspond, and had failed. Our letters had been discovered and seized by the proprietor of the asylum. Fortunately we had taken the precaution of writing in a 'cypher' of Roland's invention, which he had taught me before our marriage. Though our letters were illegible, our purpose was suspected, as a matter of course; and a watch was kept on my husband night and day.

Foiled in our first effort at making arrangements secretly for our flight, we continued our correspondence (still in cypher) by means of advertisement in the newspapers. This second attempt was discovered in its turn. Roland was refused permission to subscribe to the newspapers, and was forbidden to enter the reading-room at the asylum. These tyrannical prohibitions came too late. Our plans had already been communicated; we understood each other, and we had now only to bide our time. We had arranged that my brother and a friend of his, on whose discretion we could thoroughly rely, should take it in turns to watch every evening, for a given time, at an appointed meeting-place, three miles distant from the asylum. The spot had been carefully chosen. It was on the bank of a lonely stream, and close to the outskirts of a thick wood. A waterproof knapsack, containing a change of clothes, a false beard and wig, and some biscuits and preserved meat, was hidden in a hollow tree. My brother and his friend always took their fishing-rods with them, and presented themselves as engaged in the innocent occupation of angling to any chance strangers who might pass within sight of them. On one occasion the proprietor of the asylum himself rode by my brother, on the opposite bank of the stream, and asked politely if he had had good sport!

For a fortnight these staunch allies of ours relieved each other regularly on their watch – and no signs of the fugitive appeared. On the fifteenth evening just as the twilight was changing into night, and just as my brother (whose turn it was) had decided on leaving the place, Roland suddenly joined him on the bank of the stream.

Without wasting a moment in words, the two at once entered the wood, and took the knapsack from its place of shelter in the hollow tree. In ten minutes more my husband was dressed in a suit of workmen's clothes, and was further disguised in the wig and beard. The two then set forth down the course of the stream, keeping in the shadow of the wood until the night had fallen and the darkness hid them. The night was cloudy; there was no moon. After walking two miles or a little more, they altered their course, and made for the high-road to Manchester; entering on it at a point some thirty miles distant from the city.

On their way from the wood, Roland described the manner in which he had effected his escape.

The story was simple enough. He had assumed to be suffering from nervous illness, and had requested to have his meals in his own room. For the first fortnight, the two men appointed to wait upon him in succession, week by week, were both more than his match in strength. The third man employed, at the beginning of the third week, was physically a less formidable person than his predecessors. Seeing this, Roland decided, when evening came, on committing another 'act of violence.' In plain words, he sprang upon the keeper waiting on him in his room, and gagged and bound the man.

This done, he laid the unlucky keeper, face to the wall, on his own bed, covered with his own cloak, so that any one entering the room might suppose he was lying down to rest. He had previously taken the precaution to remove the sheets from the bed, and he had now only to tie them together to escape by the window of his room, situated on the upper floor of the house. The sun was setting, and the inmates of the asylum were then at tea. After narrowly missing discovery by one of the labourers employed in the grounds, he had climbed the garden enclosure, and had dropped on the other side – a free man!

Arrived on the high-road to Manchester, my husband and my brother parted.

Roland, who was an excellent walker, set forth on his way to Manchester on foot. He had food in his knapsack, and he proposed to walk some twelve or fifteen miles on the road to the city, before he stopped at any town or village to rest. My brother, who was physically unable to accompany him, returned to the place in which I was then residing, to tell me the good news.

By the first train the next morning I travelled to Manchester, and took a lodging in a suburb of the city known to my husband as well as to me. A prim, smoky little square was situated in the immediate neighbourhood; and we had arranged that whichever of us first arrived in Manchester should go round that square, between twelve and one in the afternoon, and between six and seven in the evening. In the evening I kept my appointment. A dusty, foot-sore man, in shabby clothes, with a hideous beard, and a knapsack on his back, met me at my first walk round. He smiled as I looked at him. Ah! I knew that smile through all disguises. In spite of the Court of Chancery and the Lords Justices, I was in my husband's arms once more.

We lived quietly in our retreat for a month. During that time (as I heard by letters from my brother) nothing that money and cunning could do towards discovering Roland was left untried by the proprietor of the asylum, and by the persons acting with him. But where is the cunning which can trace a man who, escaping at night in disguise, has not trusted himself to a railway or a carriage, and who takes refuge in a great city in which he has no friends? At the end of our month in Manchester we travelled northward, crossed the Channel to Ireland, and passed a pleasant fortnight in Dublin. Leaving this again, we made our way to Cork and Queenstown, and embarked from that latter place (among a crowd of steerage passengers) in a steam-ship for America.

My story is told. I am writing these lines from a farm in the west of the United States. Our neighbours may be homely enough; but the roughest of them is kinder to us than a mad-doctor or a Lord Justice. Roland is happy in those agricultural pursuits which have always been favourite with him; and I am happy with Roland. Our sole resources consist of my humble little fortune, inherited from my dear mother. After deducting our travelling expenses, the sum total amounts to between seven and eight hundred pounds; and this, as we find, is amply sufficient to start us well in the new life that we have chosen. We expect my father and my brother to pay us a visit next summer; and I think it is just possible that they may find our family circle increased by the presence of a new member in long clothes. Are there no compensations here for exile from England and the loss of a fortune? We think there are! But then, my dear Miss Anstell, 'Mary Brading's husband is mad, and Mary Brading herself is not much better.'

If you feel inclined to alter this opinion, and if you remember our old days at school as tenderly as I remember them, write and tell me so. Your letter will be forwarded, if you send it to the enclosed address at New York.

In the meantime, the moral of our story seems to be worth serious consideration. A certain Englishman legally inherits a large fortune. At the time of his inheritance, he has been living as a free man for three years – without once abusing his freedom, and with the express sanction of the medical superintendent who has had experience and charge of him. His next-of-kin and his heirs-at-law (who are left out of the fortune) look with covetous eyes at the money, and determine to get the management and the ultimate possession of it. Assisted by a doctor, whose honesty and capacity must be taken on trust, these interested persons, in this nineteenth century of progress, can lawfully imprison their relative for life, in a country which calls itself free, and which declares that its justice is equally administered to all alike.

Miss Jéromette and the Clergyman

Originally appeared in *The Canadian Monthly*, August to September 1875. Reprinted in *Little Novels* (1887). The great English writer whose opinion on the subject of ghosts is quoted is Samuel Johnson. The Cremorne Gardens had become notorious by the mid-1870s as a haunt of prostitutes.

I

My brother, the clergyman, looked over my shoulder before I was aware of him, and discovered that the volume which completely absorbed my attention was a collection of famous Trials, published in a new edition and in a popular form.

He laid his finger on the Trial which I happened to be reading at the moment. I looked up at him; his face startled me. He had turned pale. His eyes were fixed on the open page of the book with an expression which puzzled and alarmed me.

'My dear fellow,' I said, 'what in the world is the matter with you?'

He answered in an odd absent manner, still keeping his finger on the open page.

'I had almost forgotten,' he said. 'And this reminds me.'

'Reminds you of what?' I asked. 'You don't mean to say you know anything about the Trial?'

'I know this,' he said. 'The prisoner was guilty.'

'Guilty?' I repeated. 'Why, the man was acquitted by the jury, with the full approval of the judge! What can you possibly mean?'

'There are circumstances connected with that Trial,' my brother answered, 'which were never communicated to the judge or the jury – which were never so much as hinted or whispered in court. *I* know them – of my own knowledge, by my own personal experience. They are very sad, very strange, very terrible. I have mentioned them to no mortal creature. I have done my best to forget them. You – quite innocently – have brought them back to my mind. They oppress, they distress me. I wish I had found you reading any book in your library, except *that* book!'

My curiosity was now strongly excited. I spoke out plainly.

'Surely,' I suggested, 'you might tell your brother what you are unwilling to mention to persons less nearly related to you. We have followed different professions, and have lived in different countries, since we were boys at school. But you know you can trust me.'

He considered a little with himself.

'Yes,' he said. 'I know I can trust you.' He waited a moment; and then he surprised me by a strange question.

'Do you believe,' he asked, 'that the spirits of the dead can return to earth, and show themselves to the living?'

I answered cautiously – adopting as my own the words of a great English writer, touching the subject of ghosts.

'You ask me a question,' I said, 'which, after five thousand years, is yet undecided. On that account alone, it is a question not to be trifled with.'

My reply seemed to satisfy him.

'Promise me,' he resumed, 'that you will keep what I tell you a secret as long as I live. After my death I care little what happens. Let the story of my strange experience be added to the published experience of those other men who have seen what I have seen, and who believe what I believe. The world will not be the worse, and may be the better, for knowing one day what I am now about to trust to your ear alone.'

My brother never again alluded to the narrative which he had confided to me, until the later time when I was sitting by his death-bed. He asked if I still remembered the story of Jéromette. 'Tell it to others,' he said, 'as I have told it to you.'

I repeat it, after his death – as nearly as I can in his own words.

II

On a fine summer evening, many years since, I left my chambers in the Temple, to meet a fellow-student, who had proposed to me a night's amusement in the public gardens at Cremorne.

You were then on your way to India; and I had taken my degree at Oxford. I had sadly disappointed my father by choosing the Law as my profession, in preference to the Church. At that time, to own the truth, I had no serious intention of following any special vocation. I simply wanted an excuse for enjoying the pleasures of a London life. The study of the Law supplied me with that excuse. And I chose the Law as my profession accordingly.

On reaching the place at which we had arranged to meet, I found that my friend had not kept his appointment. After waiting vainly for ten minutes, my patience gave way, and I went into the Gardens by myself.

I took two or three turns round the platform devoted to the dancers, without discovering my fellow-student, and without seeing any other person with whom I happened to be acquainted at that time.

For some reason which I cannot now remember, I was not in my usual good spirits that evening. The noisy music jarred on my nerves, the sight of the gaping crowd round the platform irritated me, the blandishments of the painted ladies of the profession of pleasure saddened and disgusted me. I opened my cigar-case, and turned aside into one of the quiet by-walks of the Gardens.

A man who is habitually careful in choosing his cigar has this advantage over a man who is habitually careless. He can always count on smoking the best cigar in his case, down to the last. I was still absorbed in choosing *my* cigar, when I heard these words behind me – spoken in a foreign accent and in a woman's voice:

'Leave me directly, sir! I wish to have nothing to say to you.'

I turned round and discovered a little lady very simply and tastefully dressed, who looked both angry and alarmed as she rapidly passed me on her way to the more frequented part of the Gardens. A man (evidently the worse for the wine he had drunk in the course of the evening) was following her, and was pressing his tipsy attentions on her with the coarsest insolence of speech and manner. She was young and pretty, and she cast one entreating look at me as she went by, which it was not in manhood – perhaps I ought to say, in young-manhood – to resist.

I instantly stepped forward to protect her, careless whether I involved myself in a discreditable quarrel with a blackguard or not. As a matter of course, the fellow resented my interference, and my temper gave way. Fortunately for me, just as I lifted my hand to knock him down, a policeman appeared who had noticed that he was drunk, and who settled the dispute officially by turning him out of the Gardens.

I led her away from the crowd that had collected. She was evidently frightened – I felt her hand trembling on my arm – but she had one great merit: she made no fuss about it.

'If I can sit down for a few minutes,' she said in her pretty foreign accent, 'I shall soon be myself again, and I shall not trespass any farther on your kindness. I thank you very much, sir, for taking care of me.'

We sat down on a bench in a retired part of the Gardens, near a little fountain. A row of lighted lamps ran round the outer rim of the basin. I could see her plainly.

I have said that she was 'a little lady.' I could not have described her more correctly in three words.

Her figure was slight and small: she was a well-made miniature of a woman from head to foot. Her hair and her eyes were both dark. The hair curled naturally; the expression of the eyes was quiet, and rather sad; the complexion, as I then saw it, very pale; the little mouth perfectly charming. I was especially attracted, I remember, by the carriage of her head; it was strikingly graceful and spirited; it distinguished her, little as she was and quiet as she was, among the thousands of other women in the Gardens, as a creature apart. Even the one marked defect in her – a slight 'cast' in the left eye – seemed to add, in some strange way, to the quaint attractiveness of her face. I have already spoken of the tasteful simplicity of her dress. I ought now to add that it was not made of any costly material, and that she wore no jewels or ornaments of any sort. My little lady was not rich: even a man's eye could see that.

She was perfectly unembarrassed and unaffected. We fell as easily into talk as if we had been friends instead of strangers.

I asked how it was that she had no companion to take care of her. 'You are too young and too pretty,' I said in my blunt English way, 'to trust yourself alone in such a place as this.'

She took no notice of the compliment. She calmly put it away from her as if it had not reached her ears.

'I have no friend to take care of me,' she said simply. 'I was sad and sorry this evening, all by myself, and I thought I would go to the Gardens and hear the music, just to amuse me. It is not much to pay at the gate; only a shilling.'

'No friend to take care of you?' I repeated. 'Surely there must be one happy man who might have been here with you to-night?'

'What man do you mean?' she asked.

'The man,' I answered thoughtlessly, 'whom we call, in England, a Sweetheart.'

I would have given worlds to have recalled those foolish words the moment they passed my lips. I felt that I had taken a vulgar liberty with her. Her face saddened; her eyes dropped to the ground. I begged her pardon.

'There is no need to beg my pardon,' she said. 'If you wish to know, sir – yes, I had once a sweetheart, as you call it in England. He has gone away and left me. No more of him, if you please. I am rested now. I will thank you again, and go home.'

She rose to leave me.

I was determined not to part with her in that way. I begged to be allowed to see her safely back to her own door. She hesitated. I took a man's unfair advantage of her, by appealing to her fears. I said, 'Suppose the blackguard who annoyed you should be waiting outside the gates?' That decided her. She took my arm. We went away together by the bank of the Thames, in the balmy summer night.

A walk of half an hour brought us to the house in which she lodged – a shabby little house in a by-street, inhabited evidently by very poor people.

She held out her hand at the door, and wished me good-night. I was too much interested in her to consent to leave my little foreign lady without the hope of seeing her again. I asked permission to call on her the next day. We were standing under the light of the street-lamp. She studied my face with a grave and steady attention before she made any reply.

'Yes,' she said at last. 'I think I do know a gentleman when I see him. You may come, sir, if you please, and call upon me to-morrow.'

So we parted. So I entered – doubting nothing, foreboding nothing – on a scene in my life, which I now look back on with unfeigned repentance and regret.

III

I am speaking at this later time in the position of a clergyman, and in the character of a man of mature age. Remember that; and you will understand why I pass as rapidly as possible over the events of the next year of my life – why I say as little as I can of the errors and the delusions of my youth.

I called on her the next day. I repeated my visits during the days and weeks that followed, until the shabby little house in the by-street had become a second and (I say it with shame and self-reproach) a dearer home to me.

All of herself and her story which she thought fit to confide to me under these circumstances may be repeated to you in few words.

The name by which letters were addressed to her was 'Mademoiselle Jéromette.' Among the ignorant people of the house and the small tradesmen of the neighbourhood – who found her name not easy of pronunciation by the average English tongue – she was known by the friendly nickname of 'The French Miss.' When I knew her, she was resigned to her lonely life among strangers. Some years had elapsed since she had lost her parents, and had left France. Possessing a small, very small, income of her own, she added to it by colouring miniatures for the photographers. She had relatives still living in France; but she had long since ceased to correspond with them. 'Ask me nothing more about my family,' she used to say. 'I am as good as dead in my own country and among my own people.'

This was all – literally all – that she told me of herself. I have never discovered more of her sad story from that day to this.

She never mentioned her family name – never even told me what part of France she came from, or how long she had lived in England. That she was, by birth and breeding, a lady, I could entertain no doubt; her manners, her accomplishments, her ways of thinking and speaking, all proved it. Looking below the surface, her character showed itself in aspects not common among young women in these days. In her quiet way, she was an incurable fatalist, and a firm believer in the ghostly reality of apparitions from the dead. Then again, in the matter of money, she had strange views of her own. Whenever my purse was in my hand, she held me resolutely at a distance from first to last. She refused to move into better apartments; the shabby little house was clean inside, and the poor people who lived in it were kind to her – and that was enough. The most expensive present that she ever permitted me to offer her was a little enamelled ring, the plainest and cheapest thing of the kind in the jeweller's shop. In all her relations with me she was sincerity itself. On all occasions, and under all circumstances, she spoke her mind (as the phrase is) with the same uncompromising plainness.

'I like you,' she said to me; 'I respect you; I shall always be faithful to you while you are faithful to me. But my love has gone from me. There is another man who has taken it away with him, I know not where.'

Who was the other man?

She refused to tell me. She kept his rank and his name strict secrets from me. I never discovered how he had met with her, or why he had left her, or whether the guilt was his of making her an exile from her country and her friends. She despised herself for still loving him; but the passion was too strong for her – she owned it and lamented it with the frankness which was so pre-eminently a part of her character. More than this, she plainly told me, in the early days of our acquaintance, that she believed he would return to her. It might be to-morrow, or it might be years hence. Even if he failed to repent of his own cruel conduct, the man would still miss her, as something lost out of his life; and, sooner or later, he would come back.

'And will you receive him if he does come back?' I asked.

'I shall receive him,' she replied, 'against my own better judgment – in spite of my own firm persuasion that the day of his return to me will bring with it the darkest days of my life.'

I tried to remonstrate with her.

'You have a will of your own,' I said. 'Exert it, if he attempts to return to you.'

'I have no will of my own,' she answered quietly, 'where *he* is concerned. It is my misfortune to love him.' Her eyes rested for a moment on mine, with the utter self-abandonment of despair. 'We have said enough about this,' she added abruptly. 'Let us say no more.'

From that time we never spoke again of the unknown man. During the year that followed our first meeting, she heard nothing of him directly or indirectly. He might be living, or he might be dead. There came no word of him, or from him. I was fond enough of her to be satisfied with this – he never disturbed us.

IV

The year passed – and the end came. Not the end as you may have anticipated it, or as I might have foreboded it.

You remember the time when your letters from home informed you of the fatal termination of our mother's illness? It is the time of which I am now speaking. A few hours only before she breathed her last, she called me to her bedside, and desired that we might be left together alone. Reminding me that her death was near, she spoke of my prospects in life; she noticed my want of interest in the studies which were then supposed to be engaging my attention, and she ended by entreating me to reconsider my refusal to enter the Church.

'Your father's heart is set upon it,' she said. 'Do what I ask of you, my dear, and you will help to comfort him when I am gone.'

Her strength failed her: she could say no more. Could I refuse the last request she would ever make to me? I knelt at the bedside, and took her wasted hand in mine, and solemnly promised her the respect which a son owes to his mother's last wishes.

Having bound myself by this sacred engagement, I had no choice but to accept the sacrifice which it imperatively exacted from me. The time had come when I must tear myself free from all unworthy associations. No matter what the effort cost me, I must separate myself at once and for ever from the unhappy woman who was not, who never could be, my wife.

At the close of a dull foggy day I set forth with a heavy heart to say the words which were to part us for ever.

Her lodging was not far from the banks of the Thames. As I drew near the place the darkness was gathering, and the broad surface of the river was hidden from me in a chill white mist. I stood for a while, with my eyes fixed on the vaporous shroud that brooded over the flowing water – I stood, and asked myself in despair the one dreary question: 'What am I to say to her?'

The mist chilled me to the bones. I turned from the river-bank, and made my way to her lodgings hard by. 'It must be done!' I said to myself, as I took out my key and opened the house door.

She was not at her work, as usual, when I entered her little sitting-room. She was standing by the fire, with her head down, and with an open letter in her hand.

The instant she turned to meet me, I saw in her face that something was wrong. Her ordinary manner was the manner of an unusually placid and self-restrained person. Her temperament had little of the liveliness which we associate in England with the French nature. She was not ready with her laugh; and, in all my previous experience, I had never yet known her to cry. Now, for the first time, I saw the quiet face disturbed; I saw tears in the pretty brown eyes. She ran to meet me, and laid her head on my breast, and burst into a passionate fit of weeping that shook her from head to foot.

Could she by any human possibility have heard of the coming change in my life? Was she aware, before I had opened my lips, of the hard necessity which had brought me to the house?

It was simply impossible; the thing could not be.

I waited until her first burst of emotion had worn itself out. Then I asked – with an uneasy conscience, with a sinking heart – what had happened to distress her.

She drew herself away from me, sighing heavily, and gave me the open letter which I had seen in her hand.

'Read that,' she said. 'And remember I told you what might happen when we first met.'

I read the letter.

It was signed in initials only; but the writer plainly revealed himself as the man who had deserted her. He had repented; he had returned to her. In proof of his penitence he was willing to do her the justice which he had hitherto refused – he was willing to marry her; on the condition that she would engage to keep the marriage a secret, so long as his parents lived. Submitting this proposal, he waited to know whether she would consent, on her side, to forgive and forget.

I gave her back the letter in silence. This unknown rival had done me the service of paving the way for our separation. In offering her the atonement of marriage, he had made it, on my part, a matter of duty to *her*, as well as to myself, to say the parting words. I felt this instantly. And yet, I hated him for helping me!

She took my hand, and led me to the sofa. We sat down, side by side. Her face was composed to a sad tranquillity. She was quiet; she was herself again.

'I have refused to see him,' she said, 'until I had first spoken to you. You have read his letter. What do you say?'

I could make but one answer. It was my duty to tell her what my own position was in the plainest terms. I did my duty – leaving her free to decide on the future for herself. Those sad words said, it was useless to prolong the wretchedness of our separation. I rose, and took her hand for the last time.

I see her again now, at that final moment, as plainly as if it had happened yesterday. She had been suffering from an affection of the throat; and she had a white silk handkerchief tied loosely round her neck. She wore a simple dress of purple merino, with a black-silk apron over it. Her face was deadly pale; her fingers felt icily cold as they closed round my hand.

'Promise me one thing,' I said, 'before I go. While I live, I am your friend – if I am nothing more. If you are ever in trouble, promise that you will let me know it.'

She started, and drew back from me as if I had struck her with a sudden terror.

'Strange!' she said, speaking to herself. 'He feels as I feel. *He* is afraid of what may happen to me, in my life to come.'

I attempted to reassure her. I tried to tell her what was indeed the truth – that I had only been thinking of the ordinary chances and changes of life, when I spoke.

She paid no heed to me; she came back and put her hands on my shoulders, and thoughtfully and sadly looked up in my face.

'My mind is not your mind in this matter,' she said. 'I once owned to you that I had my forebodings, when we first spoke of this man's return. I may tell you now, more than I told you then. I believe I shall die young, and die miserably. If I am right, have you interest enough still left in me to wish to hear of it?'

She paused, shuddering – and added these startling words:

'You *shall* hear of it.'

The tone of steady conviction in which she spoke alarmed and distressed me. My face showed her how deeply and how painfully I was affected.

'There, there!' she said, returning to her natural manner; 'don't take what I say too seriously. A poor girl who has led a lonely life like mine thinks strangely and talks strangely – sometimes. Yes; I give you my promise. If I am ever in trouble, I will let you know it. God bless you – you have been very kind to me – good-bye!'

A tear dropped on my face as she kissed me. The door closed between us. The dark street received me.

It was raining heavily. I looked up at her window, through the drifting shower. The curtains were parted: she was standing in the gap, dimly lit by the lamp on the table behind her, waiting for our last look at each other. Slowly lifting her hand, she waved her farewell at the window, with the unsought native grace which had charmed me on the night when we first met. The curtains fell again – she disappeared – nothing was before me, nothing was round me, but the darkness and the night.

V

In two years from that time, I had redeemed the promise given to my mother on her deathbed. I had entered the Church.

My father's interest made my first step in my new profession an easy one. After serving my preliminary apprenticeship as a curate, I was appointed, before I was thirty years of age, to a living in the West of England.

My new benefice offered me every advantage that I could possibly desire – with the one exception of a sufficient income. Although my wants were few, and although I was still an unmarried man, I found it desirable, on many accounts, to add to my resources. Following the example of other young clergymen in my position, I determined to receive pupils who might stand in need of preparation for a career at the Universities. My relatives exerted themselves; and my good fortune still befriended me. I obtained two pupils to start with. A third would complete the number which I was at present prepared to receive. In course of time, this third pupil made his appearance, under circumstances sufficiently remarkable to merit being mentioned in detail.

It was the summer vacation; and my two pupils had gone home. Thanks to a neighbouring clergyman, who kindly undertook to perform my duties for me, I too obtained a fortnight's holiday, which I spent at my father's house in London.

During my sojourn in the metropolis, I was offered an opportunity of preaching in a church, made famous by the eloquence of one of the popular pulpit-orators of our time. In accepting the proposal, I felt naturally anxious to do my best, before the unusually large and unusually intelligent congregation which would be assembled to hear me.

At the period of which I am now speaking, all England had been startled by the discovery of a terrible crime, perpetrated under circumstances of extreme provocation. I chose this crime as the main subject of my sermon. Admitting that the best among us were frail mortal creatures, subject to evil promptings and provocations like the worst among us, my object was to show how a Christian man may find his certain refuge from temptation in the safeguards of his religion. I dwelt minutely on the hardship of the Christian's first struggle to resist the evil influence – on the help which his Christianity inexhaustibly held out to him in the worst relapses of the weaker and viler part of his nature – on the steady and certain gain which was the ultimate reward of his faith and his firmness – and on the blessed sense of peace and happiness which accompanied the final triumph. Preaching to this effect, with the fervent conviction which I really felt, I may say for myself, at least, that I did no discredit to the choice which had placed me in the pulpit. I held the attention of my congregation, from the first word to the last.

While I was resting in the vestry on the conclusion of the service, a note was brought to me written in pencil. A member of my congregation – a gentleman – wished to see me, on a matter of considerable importance to himself. He would call on me at any place, and at any hour, which I might choose to appoint. If

I wished to be satisfied of his respectability, he would beg leave to refer me to his father, with whose name I might possibly be acquainted.

The name given in the reference was undoubtedly familiar to me, as the name of a man of some celebrity and influence in the world of London. I sent back my card, appointing an hour for the visit of my correspondent on the afternoon of the next day.

VI

The stranger made his appearance punctually. I guessed him to be some two or three years younger than myself. He was undeniably handsome; his manners were the manners of a gentleman – and yet, without knowing why, I felt a strong dislike to him the moment he entered the room.

After the first preliminary words of politeness had been exchanged between us, my visitor informed me as follows of the object which he had in view.

'I believe you live in the country, sir?' he began.

'I live in the West of England,' I answered.

'Do you make a long stay in London?'

'No. I go back to my rectory tomorrow.'

'May I ask if you take pupils?'

'Yes.'

'Have you any vacancy?'

'I have one vacancy.'

'Would you object to let me go back with you tomorrow, as your pupil?'

The abruptness of the proposal took me by surprise. I hesitated.

In the first place (as I have already said), I disliked him. In the second place, he was too old to be a fit companion for my other two pupils – both lads in their teens. In the third place, he had asked me to receive him at least three weeks before the vacation came to an end. I had my own pursuits and amusements in prospect during that interval, and saw no reason why I should inconvenience myself by setting them aside.

He noticed my hesitation, and did not conceal from me that I had disappointed him.

'I have it very much at heart,' he said, 'to repair without delay the time that I have lost. My age is against me, I know. The truth is – I have wasted my opportunities since I left school, and I am anxious, honestly anxious, to mend my ways, before it is too late. I wish to prepare myself for one of the Universities – I wish to show, if I can, that I am not quite unworthy to inherit my father's famous name. You are the man to help me, if I can only persuade you to do it. I was struck by your sermon yesterday; and, if I may venture to make the confession in your presence, I took a strong liking to you. Will you see my father, before you decide to say No? He will be able to explain whatever may seem strange in my present application; and he will be happy to see you this afternoon, if you can spare the time. As to the question of terms, I am quite sure it can be settled to your entire satisfaction.'

He was evidently in earnest – gravely, vehemently in earnest. I unwillingly consented to see his father.

Our interview was a long one. All my questions were answered fully and frankly.

The young man had led an idle and desultory life. He was weary of it, and ashamed of it. His disposition was a peculiar one. He stood sorely in need of a guide, a teacher, and a friend, in whom he was disposed to confide. If I disappointed the hopes which he had centred in me, he would be discouraged, and he would relapse into the aimless and indolent existence of which he was now ashamed. Any terms for which I might stipulate were at my disposal if I would consent to receive him, for three months to begin with, on trial.

Still hesitating, I consulted my father and my friends.

They were all of opinion (and justly of opinion so far) that the new connection would be an excellent one for me. They all reproached me for taking a purely capricious dislike to a well-born and well-bred young man, and for permitting it to influence me, at the outset of my career, against my own interests. Pressed by these considerations, I allowed myself to be persuaded to give the new pupil a fair trial. He accompanied me, the next day, on my way back to the rectory.

VII

Let me be careful to do justice to a man whom I personally disliked. My senior pupil began well: he produced a decidedly favourable impression on the persons attached to my little household.

The women, especially, admired his beautiful light hair, his crisply-curling beard, his delicate complexion, his clear blue eyes, and his finely-shaped hands and feet. Even the inveterate reserve in his manner, and the downcast, almost sullen, look which had prejudiced *me* against him, aroused a common feeling of romantic enthusiasm in my servants' hall. It was decided, on the high authority of the housekeeper herself, that 'the new gentleman' was in love – and, more interesting still, that he was the victim of an unhappy attachment which had driven him away from his friends and his home.

For myself, I tried hard, and tried vainly, to get over my first dislike to the senior pupil.

I could find no fault with him. All his habits were quiet and regular; and he devoted himself conscientiously to his reading. But, little by little, I became satisfied that his heart was not in his studies. More than this, I had my reasons for suspecting that he was concealing something from me, and that he felt painfully the reserve on his own part which he could not, or dared not, break through. There were moments when I almost doubted whether he had not chosen my remote country rectory, as a safe place of refuge from some person or persons of whom he stood in dread.

For example, his ordinary course of proceeding, in the matter of his correspondence, was, to say the least of it, strange.

He received no letters at my house. They waited for him at the village post-office. He invariably called for them himself, and invariably forbore to trust any of my servants with his own letters for the post. Again, when we were out walking together, I more than once caught him looking furtively over his shoulder, as if he suspected some person of following him, for some evil purpose. Being constitutionally a hater of mysteries, I determined, at an early stage of our intercourse, on making an effort to clear matters up. There might be just a chance of my winning the senior pupil's confidence, if I spoke to him while the last days of the summer vacation still left us alone together in the house.

'Excuse me for noticing it,' I said to him one morning, while we were engaged over our books – 'I cannot help observing that you appear to have some trouble on your mind. Is it indiscreet, on my part, to ask if I can be of any use to you?'

He changed colour – looked up at me quickly – looked down again at his book – struggled hard with some secret fear or secret reluctance that was in him – and suddenly burst out with this extraordinary question:

'I suppose you were in earnest when you preached that sermon in London?'

'I am astonished that you should doubt it,' I replied.

He paused again; struggled with himself again; and startled me by a second outbreak, even stranger than the first.

'I am one of the people you preached at in your sermon,' he said. 'That's the true reason why I asked you to take me for your pupil. Don't turn me out! When you talked to your congregation of tortured and tempted people, you talked of Me.'

I was so astonished by the confession, that I lost my presence of mind. For the moment, I was unable to answer him.

'Don't turn me out!' he repeated. 'Help me against myself. I am telling you the truth. As God is my witness, I am telling you the truth!'

'Tell me the *whole* truth,' I said; 'and rely on my consoling and helping you – rely on my being your friend.'

In the fervour of the moment, I took his hand. It lay cold and still in mine: it mutely warned me that I had a sullen and a secret nature to deal with.

'There must be no concealment between us,' I resumed. 'You have entered my house, by your own confession, under false pretences. It is your duty to me, and your duty to yourself, to speak out.'

The man's inveterate reserve – cast off for the moment only – renewed its hold on him. He considered, carefully considered, his next words before he permitted them to pass his lips.

'A person is in the way of my prospects in life,' he began slowly, with his eyes cast down on his book. 'A person provokes me horribly. I feel dreadful temptations (like the man you spoke of in your sermon) when I am in the person's company. Teach me to resist temptation! I am afraid of myself, if I see the person again. You are the only man who can help me. Do it while you can.'

He stopped, and passed his handkerchief over his forehead.

'Will that do?' he asked – still with his eyes on his book.

'It will *not* do,' I answered. 'You are so far from really opening your heart to me, that you won't even let me know whether it is a man or a woman who stands in the way of your prospects in life. You use the word "person," over and over again – rather than say "he" or "she" when you speak of the provocation which is trying you. How can I help a man who has so little confidence in me as that?'

My reply evidently found him at the end of his resources. He tried, tried desperately, to say more than he had said yet. No! The words seemed to stick in his throat. Not one of them would pass his lips.

'Give me time,' he pleaded piteously. 'I can't bring myself to it, all at once.

I mean well. Upon my soul, I mean well. But I am slow at this sort of thing. Wait till tomorrow.'

Tomorrow came – and again he put it off.

'One more day!' he said. 'You don't know how hard it is to speak plainly. I am half afraid; I am half ashamed. Give me one more day.'

I had hitherto only disliked him. Try as I might (and did) to make merciful allowance for his reserve, I began to despise him now.

VIII

The day of the deferred confession came, and brought an event with it, for which both he and I were alike unprepared. Would he really have confided in me but for that event? He must either have done it, or have abandoned the purpose which had led him into my house.

We met as usual at the breakfast-table. My housekeeper brought in my letters of the morning. To my surprise, instead of leaving the room again as usual, she walked round to the other side of the table, and laid a letter before my senior pupil – the first letter, since his residence with me, which had been delivered to him under my roof.

He started, and took up the letter. He looked at the address. A spasm of suppressed fury passed across his face; his breath came quickly; his hand trembled as it held the letter. So far, I said nothing. I waited to see whether he would open the envelope in my presence or not.

He was afraid to open it, in my presence. He got on his feet; he said, in tones so low that I could barely hear him: 'Please excuse me for a minute' – and left the room.

I waited for half an hour – for a quarter of an hour, after that – and then I sent to ask if he had forgotten his breakfast.

In a minute more, I heard his footstep in the hall. He opened the breakfast-room door, and stood on the threshold, with a small travelling-bag in his hand.

'I beg your pardon,' he said, still standing at the door. 'I must ask for leave of absence for a day or two. Business in London.'

'Can I be of any use?' I asked. 'I am afraid your letter has brought you bad news?'

'Yes,' he said shortly. 'Bad news. I have no time for breakfast.'

'Wait a few minutes,' I urged. 'Wait long enough to treat me like your friend – to tell me what your trouble is before you go.'

He made no reply. He stepped into the hall, and closed the door – then opened it again a little way, without showing himself.

'Business in London,' he repeated – as if he thought it highly important to inform me of the nature of his errand. The door closed for the second time. He was gone.

I went into my study, and carefully considered what had happened.

The result of my reflections is easily described. I determined on discontinuing my relations with my senior pupil. In writing to his father (which I did, with all due courtesy and respect, by that day's post), I mentioned as my reason for arriving at this decision: First, that I had found it impossible to win the confidence of his son. Secondly, that his son had that morning suddenly and mysteriously left my house for London, and that I must decline accepting any further responsibility towards him, as the necessary consequence.

I had put my letter in the post-bag, and was beginning to feel a little easier after having written it, when my housekeeper appeared in the study, with a very grave face, and with something hidden apparently in her closed hand.

'Would you please look, sir, at what we have found in the gentleman's bedroom, since he went away this morning?'

I knew the housekeeper to possess a woman's full share of that amiable weakness of the sex which goes by the name of 'Curiosity.' I had also, in various indirect ways, become aware that my senior pupil's strange departure had largely increased the disposition among the women of my household to regard him as the victim of an unhappy attachment. The time was ripe, as it seemed to me, for checking any further gossip about him, and any renewed attempts at prying into his affairs in his absence.

'Your only business in my pupil's bedroom,' I said to the housekeeper, 'is to see that it is kept clean, and that it is properly aired. There must be no interference, if you please, with his letters, or his papers, or with anything else that he has left behind him. Put back directly whatever you may have found in his room.'

The housekeeper had her full share of a woman's temper as well as of a woman's curiosity. She listened to me with a rising colour, and a just perceptible toss of the head.

'Must I put it back, sir, on the floor, between the bed and the wall?' she inquired, with an ironical assumption of the humblest deference to my wishes. '*That's* where the girl found it when she was sweeping the room. Anybody can see for themselves,' pursued the housekeeper indignantly, 'that the poor gentleman has gone away broken-hearted. And there, in my opinion, is the hussy who is the cause of it!'

With those words, she made me a low curtsey, and laid a small photographic portrait on the desk at which I was sitting.

I looked at the photograph.

In an instant, my heart was beating wildly – my head turned giddy – the housekeeper, the furniture, the walls of the room, all swayed and whirled round me.

The portrait that had been found in my senior pupil's bedroom was the portrait of Jéromette!

IX

I had sent the housekeeper out of my study. I was alone, with the photograph of the Frenchwoman on my desk.

There could surely be little doubt about the discovery that had burst upon me. The man who had stolen his way into my house, driven by the terror of a temptation that he dared not reveal, and the man who had been my unknown rival in the by-gone time, were one and the same!

Recovering self-possession enough to realize this plain truth, the inferences that followed forced their way into my mind as a matter of course. The unnamed person who was the obstacle to my pupil's prospects in life, the unnamed person in whose company he was assailed by temptations which made him tremble for himself, stood revealed to me now as being, in all human probability, no other than Jéromette. Had she bound him in the fetters of the marriage which he had himself proposed? Had she discovered his place of refuge in my house? And was the letter that had been delivered to him of her writing? Assuming these questions to be answered in the affirmative, what, in that case, was his 'business in London?' I remembered how he had spoken to me of his temptations, I recalled the expression that had crossed his face when he recognised the handwriting on the letter – and the conclusion that followed literally shook me to the soul. Ordering my horse to be saddled, I rode instantly to the railway-station.

The train by which he had travelled to London had reached the terminus nearly an hour since. The one useful course that I could take, by way of quieting the dreadful misgivings crowding one after another on my mind, was to telegraph to Jéromette at the address at which I had last seen her. I sent the subjoined message – prepaying the reply:

'If you are in any trouble, telegraph to me. I will be with you by the first train. Answer, in any case.'

There was nothing in the way of the immediate despatch of my message. And yet the hours passed, and no answer was received. By the advice of the clerk, I sent a second telegram to the London office, requesting an explanation. The reply came back in these terms:

'Improvements in street. Houses pulled down. No trace of person named in telegram.'

I mounted my horse, and rode back slowly to the rectory.

'The day of his return to me will bring with it the darkest days of my life.' ... 'I shall die young, and die miserably. Have you interest enough still left in me to wish to hear of it?' ... 'You *shall* hear of it.' Those words were in my memory while I rode home in the cloudless moonlight night. They were so vividly present to me that I could hear again her pretty foreign accent, her quiet clear tones, as she spoke them. For the rest, the emotions of that memorable day had worn me out. The answer from the telegraph-office had struck me with a strange and stony despair. My mind was a blank. I had no thoughts. I had no tears.

I was about half-way on my road home, and I had just heard the clock of a village church strike ten, when I became conscious, little by little, of a chilly sensation slowly creeping through and through me to the bones. The warm balmy air of a summer night was abroad. It was the month of July. In the month of July, was it possible that any living creature (in good health) could feel cold? It was *not* possible – and yet, the chilly sensation still crept through and through me to the bones.

I looked up. I looked all round me.

My horse was walking along an open highroad. Neither trees nor waters were near me. On either side, the flat fields stretched away bright and broad in the moonlight.

I stopped my horse, and looked round me again.

Yes: I saw it. With my own eyes I saw it. A pillar of white mist – between five and six feet high, as well as I could judge – was moving beside me at the edge of the road, on my left hand. When I stopped, the white mist stopped. When I went on, the white mist went on. I pushed my horse to a trot – the pillar of mist was with me. I urged him to a gallop –

the pillar of mist was with me. I stopped him again – the pillar of mist stood still.

The white colour of it was the white colour of the fog which I had seen over the river – on the night when I had gone to bid her farewell. And the chill which had then crept through me to the bones was the chill that was creeping through me now.

I went on again slowly. The white mist went on again slowly – with the clear bright night all round it.

I was awed rather than frightened. There was one moment, and one only, when the fear came to me that my reason might be shaken. I caught myself keeping time to the slow tramp of the horse's feet with the slow utterance of these words, repeated over and over again: 'Jéromette is dead. Jéromette is dead.' But my will was still my own: I was able to control myself, to impose silence on my own muttering lips. And I rode on quietly. And the pillar of mist went quietly with me.

My groom was waiting for my return at the rectory gate. I pointed to the mist, passing through the gate with me.

'Do you see anything there?' I said.

The man looked at me in astonishment.

I entered the rectory. The housekeeper met me in the hall. I pointed to the mist, entering with me.

'Do you see anything at my side?' I asked.

The housekeeper looked at me as the groom had looked at me.

'I am afraid you are not well, sir,' she said. 'Your colour is all gone – you are shivering. Let me get you a glass of wine.'

I went into my study, on the ground-floor, and took the chair at my desk. The photograph still lay where I had left it The pillar of mist floated round the table, and stopped opposite to me, behind the photograph.

The housekeeper brought in the wine. I put the glass to my lips, and set it down again. The chill of the mist was in the wine. There was no taste, no reviving spirit in it. The presence of the housekeeper oppressed me. My dog had followed her into the room. The presence of the animal oppressed me. I said to the woman, 'Leave me by myself, and take the dog with you.'

They went out, and left me alone in the room.

I sat looking at the pillar of mist, hovering opposite to me.

It lengthened slowly, until it reached to the ceiling. As it lengthened, it grew bright and luminous. A time passed, and a shadowy appearance showed itself in the centre of the light. Little by little, the shadowy appearance took the outline of a human form. Soft brown eyes, tender and melancholy, looked at me through the unearthly light in the mist. The head and the rest of the face broke next slowly on my view. Then the figure gradually revealed itself, moment by moment, downward and downward to the feet. She stood before me as I had last seen her, in her purple-merino dress, with the black-silk apron, with the white handkerchief tied loosely round her neck. She stood before me, in the gentle beauty that I remembered so well; and looked at me as she had looked when she gave me her last kiss – when her tears had dropped on my cheek.

I fell on my knees at the table. I stretched out my hands to her imploringly. I said, 'Speak to me – O, once again speak to me, Jéromette.'

Her eyes rested on me with a divine compassion in them. She lifted her hand, and pointed to the photograph on my desk, with a gesture which bade me turn the card. I turned it. The name of the man who had left my house that morning was inscribed on it, in her own handwriting.

I looked up at her again, when I had read it. She lifted her hand once more, and pointed to the handkerchief round her neck. As I looked at it, the fair white silk changed horribly in colour – the fair white silk became darkened and drenched in blood.

A moment more – and the vision of her began to grow dim. By slow degrees, the figure, then the face, faded back into the shadowy appearance that I had first seen. The luminous inner light died out in the white mist. The mist itself dropped slowly downwards – floated a moment in airy circles on the floor – vanished. Nothing was before me but the familiar wall of the room, and the photograph lying face downwards on my desk.

X

The next day, the newspapers reported the discovery of a murder in London. A Frenchwoman was the victim. She had been killed by a wound in the throat. The crime had been discovered between ten and eleven o'clock on the previous night.

I leave you to draw your conclusion from what I have related. My own faith in the reality of the apparition is immovable. I say, and believe, that Jéromette kept her word with me. She died young, and died miserably. And I heard of it from herself.

Take up the Trial again, and look at the circumstances that were revealed during the investigation in court. His motive for murdering her is there.

You will see that she did indeed marry him privately; that they lived together contentedly, until the fatal day when she discovered that his fancy had been caught by another woman; that violent quarrels took place between them, from that time to the time when my sermon showed him his own deadly hatred towards her, reflected in the case of another man; that she discovered his place of retreat in my house, and threatened him by letter with the public assertion of her conjugal rights; lastly, that a man, variously described by different witnesses, was seen leaving the door of her lodgings on the night of the murder. The Law – advancing no farther than this – may have discovered circumstances of suspicion, but no certainty. The Law, in default of direct evidence to convict the prisoner, may have rightly decided in letting him go free.

But *I* persist in believing that the man was guilty. *I* declare that he, and he alone, was the murderer of Jéromette. And now, you know why.

Mr Captain and the Nymph

Originally appeared in *The Spirit of the Times and New York Sportsman*, 23 December 1876. Formerly Wilkes's *Spirit of the Times*, this was an American sporting newspaper concentrating on the turf. Collins contributed to it frequently in the last years of his life. The story appeared almost simultaneously in the British magazine *Belgravia* (January 1877). Reprinted in *Little Novels* (1887). The story was written when Collins's health was deteriorating and he may have been pressing long discarded manuscripts into service. It has been suggested that the story is a distillation of Collins's first, unpublished novel (written 1844), which was set in Tahiti, and declined by 'every publisher of fiction in London.' For an account of the manuscript of *Iolani; or Tahiti as it Was; A Romance*, see Catherine Peters, *The King of Inventors*, Appendix C, pp.441–43.

I

'The Captain is still in the prime of life,' the widow remarked. 'He has given up his ship; he possesses a sufficient income, and he has nobody to live with him. I should like to know why he doesn't marry.'

'The Captain was excessively rude to Me,' the widow's younger sister added, on her side. 'When we took leave of him in London, I asked if there was any chance of his joining us at Brighton this season. He turned his back on me as if I had mortally offended him; and he made me this extraordinary answer: "Miss! I hate the sight of the sea." The man has been a sailor all his life. What does he mean by saying that he hates the sight of the sea?'

These questions were addressed to a third person present – and the person was a man. He was entirely at the mercy of the widow and the widow's sister. The other ladies of the family – who might have taken him under their protection – had gone to an evening concert. He was known to be the Captain's friend, and to be well acquainted with events in the Captain's later life. As it happened, he had reasons for hesitating to revive associations connected with those events. But what polite alternative was left to him? He must either inflict disappointment, and, worse still, aggravate curiosity – or he must resign himself to circumstances, and tell the ladies why the Captain would never marry, and why (sailor as he was) he hated the sight of the sea. They were both young women and handsome women – and the person to whom they had appealed (being a man) followed the example of submission to the sex, first set in the garden of Eden. He enlightened the ladies, in the terms that follow:

II

The British merchantman, *Fortuna*, sailed from the port of Liverpool (at a date which it is not necessary to specify) with the morning tide. She was bound for certain islands in the Pacific Ocean, in search of a cargo of sandal-wood – a commodity which, in those days, found a ready and profitable market in the Chinese Empire.

A large discretion was reposed in the Captain by the owners, who knew him to be not only trustworthy, but a man of rare ability, carefully cultivated during the leisure hours of a seafaring life. Devoted heart and soul to his professional duties, he was a hard reader and an excellent linguist as well. Having had considerable experience among the inhabitants of the Pacific Islands, he had attentively studied their characters, and had mastered their language in more than one of its many dialects. Thanks to the valuable information thus obtained, the Captain was never at a loss to conciliate the islanders. He had more than once succeeded in finding a cargo, under circumstances in which other captains had failed.

Possessing these merits, he had also his fair share of human defects. For instance, he was a little too conscious of his own good looks – of his bright chestnut hair and whiskers, of his beautiful blue eyes, of his fair white skin, which many a woman had looked at with the admiration that is akin to envy. His shapely hands were protected by gloves; a broad-brimmed hat sheltered his complexion in fine weather from the sun. He was nice in the choice of his perfumes; he never drank spirits, and the smell of tobacco was abhorrent to him. New men among his officers and his crew, seeing him in his cabin, perfectly dressed, washed, and brushed until he was an object speckless to look upon – a merchant-captain soft of voice, careful in his choice of words, devoted to study in his leisure hours – were apt to conclude that they had trusted themselves at sea under a commander who was an anomalous mixture of a schoolmaster and a dandy. But if the slightest infraction of discipline took place, or if the storm rose and the vessel proved to be in peril, it was soon discovered that the gloved hands held a rod of iron; that the soft voice could make itself heard through wind and sea from one end of the deck to the other; and that it issued orders which the greatest fool on board discovered to be orders that had saved the ship. Throughout his professional life, the general impression that this variously gifted man produced on the little world about him was always the same. Some few liked him; everybody respected him; nobody understood him. The Captain accepted these results. He persisted in reading his books and protecting his complexion, with this result: his owners shook hands with him, and put up with his gloves.

The *Fortuna* touched at Rio for water, and for supplies of food which might prove useful in case of scurvy. In due time the ship rounded Cape Horn, favoured by the finest weather ever known in those latitudes by the oldest hand on board. The mate – one Mr Duncalf – a boozing, wheezing, self-confident old sea-dog, with a flaming face and a vast vocabulary of oaths, swore that he didn't like it. 'The foul weather's coming, my lads,' said Mr Duncalf. 'Mark my words, there'll be wind enough to take the curl out of the Captain's whiskers before we are many days older!'

For one uneventful week, the ship cruised in search of the islands to which the owners had directed her. At the end of that time the wind took the predicted liberties with the Captain's whiskers; and Mr Duncalf stood revealed to an admiring crew in the character of a true prophet.

For three days and three nights the *Fortuna* ran before the storm, at the mercy of wind and sea. On the fourth morning the gale blew itself out, the sun appeared again towards noon, and the Captain was able to take an observation. The result informed him that he was in a part of the Pacific Ocean with which he was entirely unacquainted. Thereupon, the officers were called to a council in the cabin.

Mr Duncalf, as became his rank, was consulted first. His opinion possessed the merit of brevity. 'My lads, this ship's bewitched. Take my word for it, we shall wish ourselves back in our own latitudes before we are many days older.' Which, being interpreted, meant that Mr Duncalf was lost, like his superior officer, in a part of the ocean of which he knew nothing.

The remaining members of the council, having no suggestions to offer, left the Captain to take his own way. He decided (the weather being fine again) to stand on under an easy press of sail for four-and-twenty hours more, and to see if anything came of it.

Soon after night-fall, something did come of it. The look-out forward hailed the quarter-deck with the dreadful cry, 'Breakers ahead!' In less than a minute more, everybody heard the crash of the broken water. The *Fortuna* was put about, and came round slowly in the light wind. Thanks to the timely alarm and the fine weather, the safety of the vessel was easily provided for. They kept her under short sail; and they waited for the morning.

The dawn showed them in the distance a glorious green island, not marked in the ship's charts – an island girt about by a coral-reef, and having in its midst a high-peaked mountain which looked, through the telescope, like a mountain of volcanic origin. Mr Duncalf, taking his morning draught of rum and water, shook his groggy old head, and said (and swore): 'My lads, I don't like the look of that island.' The Captain was of a different opinion. He had one of the ship's boats put into the water; he armed himself and four of his crew who accompanied him; and away he went in the morning sunlight to visit the island.

Skirting round the coral-reef, they found a natural breach, which proved to be broad enough and deep enough not only for the passage of the boat, but of the ship herself if needful. Crossing the broad inner belt of smooth water, they approached the golden sands of the island, strewed with magnificent shells, and crowded by the dusky islanders – men, women, and children, all waiting in breathless astonishment to see the strangers land.

The Captain kept the boat off, and examined the islanders carefully. The innocent simple people danced, and sang, and ran into the water, imploring their wonderful white visitors by gestures to come on shore. Not a creature among them carried arms of any sort; a hospitable curiosity animated the entire population. The men cried out, in their smooth musical language, 'Come and eat!' and the plump black-eyed women, all laughing together, added their own invitation, 'Come and be kissed!' Was it in mortals to resist such temptations as these? The Captain led the way on shore, and the women surrounded him in an instant, and screamed for joy at the glorious spectacle of his whiskers, his complexion, and his gloves. So, the mariners from the far north were welcomed to the newly-discovered island.

III

The morning wore on. Mr Duncalf, in charge of the ship, cursing the island over his rum and water, as a 'beastly green strip of a place, not laid down in any Christian chart,' was kept waiting four mortal hours before the Captain returned to his command, and reported himself to his officers as follows:

He had found his knowledge of the Polynesian dialects sufficient to make himself in some degree understood by the natives of the new island. Under the guidance of the chief he had made a first journey of exploration, and had seen for himself that the place was a marvel of natural beauty and fertility. The one barren spot in it was the peak of the volcanic mountain, composed of crumbling rock; originally no doubt lava and ashes, which had cooled and consolidated with the lapse of time. So far as he could see, the crater at the top was now an extinct crater. But, if he had understood rightly, the chief had spoken of earthquakes and eruptions at certain bygone periods, some of which lay within his own earliest recollections of the place.

Adverting next to considerations of practical utility, the Captain announced that he had seen sandal-wood enough on the island to load a dozen ships, and that the natives were willing to part with it for a few toys and trinkets generally distributed amongst them. To the mate's disgust, the *Fortuna* was taken inside the reef that day, and was anchored before sunset in a natural harbour. Twelve hours of recreation, beginning with the next morning, were granted to the men, under the wise restrictions in such cases established by the Captain. That interval over, the work of cutting the precious wood and loading the ship was to be unremittingly pursued.

Mr Duncalf had the first watch after the *Fortuna* had been made snug. He took the boatswain aside (an ancient sea-dog like himself), and he said in a gruff whisper: 'My lad, this here ain't the island laid down in our sailing orders. See if mischief don't come of disobeying orders before we are many days older.'

Nothing in the shape of mischief happened that night. But at sunrise the next morning a suspicious circumstance occurred; and Mr Duncalf whispered to the boatswain: 'What did I tell you?' The Captain and the chief of the islanders held a private conference in the cabin; and the Captain, after first forbidding any communication with the shore until his return, suddenly left the ship, alone with the chief, in the chief's own canoe.

What did this strange disappearance mean? The Captain himself, when he took his seat in the canoe, would have been puzzled to answer that question. He asked, in the nearest approach that his knowledge could make to the language used in the island, whether he would be a long time or a short time absent from his ship.

The chief answered mysteriously (as the Captain understood him) in these words: 'Long time or short time, your life depends on it, and the lives of your men.'

Paddling his light little boat in silence over the smooth water inside the reef, the chief took his visitor ashore at a part of the island which was quite new to the Captain. The two crossed a ravine, and ascended an eminence beyond. There the chief stopped, and silently pointed out to sea.

The Captain looked in the direction indicated to him, and discovered a second and a smaller island, lying away to the south-west. Taking out his telescope from the case by which it was slung at his back, he narrowly examined the place. Two of the native canoes were lying off the shore of the new island; and the men in them appeared to be all kneeling or crouching in curiously chosen attitudes. Shifting the range of his glass, he next beheld a white-robed figure, tall and solitary – the one inhabitant of the island whom he could discover. The man was standing on the highest point of a rocky cape. A fire was burning at his feet. Now he lifted his arms solemnly to the sky; now he dropped some invisible fuel into the fire, which made a blue smoke; and now he cast other invisible objects into the canoes floating beneath him, which the islanders reverently received with bodies that crouched in abject submission. Lowering his telescope, the Captain looked round at the chief for an explanation. The chief gave the explanation readily. His language was interpreted by the English stranger in these terms:

'Wonderful white man! the island you see yonder is a Holy Island. As such it is *Taboo* – an island sanctified and set apart. The honourable person whom you notice on the rock is an all-powerful favourite of the gods. He is by vocation a Sorcerer, and by rank a Priest. You now see him casting charms and blessings into the canoes of our fishermen, who kneel to him for fine weather and great plenty of fish. If any profane person, native or stranger, presumes to set foot on that island, my otherwise peaceful subjects will (in the performance of a religious duty) put that person to death. Mention this to your men. They will be fed by my male people, and fondled by my female people, so long as they keep clear of the Holy Isle. As they value their lives, let them respect this prohibition. Is it understood between us? Wonderful white man! my canoe is waiting for you. Let us go back.'

Understanding enough of the chief's language (illustrated by his gestures) to receive in the right spirit the communication thus addressed to him, the Captain repeated the warning to the ship's company in the plainest possible English. The officers and men then took their holiday on shore, with the exception of Mr Duncalf, who positively refused to leave the ship. For twelve delightful hours they were fed by the male people, and fondled by the female people, and then they were mercilessly torn from the flesh-pots and the arms of their new friends, and set to work on the sandal-wood in good earnest. Mr Duncalf superintended the loading, and waited for the mischief that was to come of disobeying the owners' orders with a confidence worthy of a better cause.

IV

Strangely enough, chance once more declared itself in favour of the mate's point of view. The mischief did actually come; and the chosen instrument of it was a handsome young islander, who was one of the sons of the chief.

The Captain had taken a fancy to the sweet-tempered intelligent lad. Pursuing his studies in the dialect of the island, at leisure hours, he had made the chief's son his tutor, and had instructed the youth in English by way of return. More than a month had passed in this intercourse, and the ship's lading was being rapidly completed – when, in an evil hour, the talk between the two turned on the subject of the Holy Island.

'Does nobody live on the island but the Priest?' the Captain asked.

The chief's son looked round him suspiciously. 'Promise me you won't tell anybody!' he began very earnestly.

The Captain gave his promise.

'There is one other person on the island,' the lad whispered; 'a person to feast your eyes upon, if you could only see her! She is the Priest's daughter. Removed to the island in her infancy, she has never left it since. In that sacred solitude she has only looked on two human beings – her father and her mother. I once saw her from my canoe, taking care not to attract her notice, or to approach too near the holy soil. Oh, so young, dear master, and, oh, so beautiful!' The chief's son completed the description by kissing his own hands as an expression of rapture.

The Captain's fine blue eyes sparkled. He asked no more questions; but, later on that day, he took his telescope with him, and paid a secret visit to the eminence which overlooked the Holy Island. The next day, and the next, he privately returned to the same place. On the fourth day, fatal Destiny favoured him. He discovered the nymph of the island.

Standing alone upon the cape on which he had already seen her father, she was feeding some tame birds which looked like turtle-doves. The glass showed the Captain her white robe, fluttering in the sea-breeze; her long black hair falling to her feet; her slim and supple young figure; her simple grace of attitude, as she turned this way and that, attending to the wants of her birds. Before her was the blue ocean; behind her rose the lustrous green of the island forest. He looked and looked until his eyes and arms ached. When she disappeared among the trees, followed by her favourite birds, the Captain shut up his telescope with a sigh, and said to himself: 'I have seen an angel!'

From that hour he became an altered man; he was languid, silent, interested in nothing. General opinion, on board his ship, decided that he was going to be taken ill.

A week more elapsed, and the officers and crew began to talk of the voyage to their market in China. The Captain refused to fix a day for sailing. He even took offence at being asked to decide. Instead of sleeping in his cabin, he went ashore for the night.

Not many hours afterwards (just before daybreak), Mr Duncalf, snoring in his cabin on deck, was aroused by a hand laid on his shoulder. The swinging lamp, still alight, showed him the dusky face of the chief's son, convulsed with terror. By wild signs, by disconnected words in the little English which he had learnt, the lad tried to make the mate understand him. Dense Mr Duncalf, understanding nothing, hailed the second officer, on the opposite side of the deck. The second officer was young and intelligent; he rightly interpreted the terrible news that had come to the ship.

The Captain had broken his own rules. Watching his opportunity, under cover of the night, he had taken a canoe, and had secretly crossed the channel to the Holy Island. No one had been near him at the time, but the chief's son. The lad had vainly tried to induce him to abandon his desperate enterprise, and had vainly waited on the shore in the hope of hearing the sound of the paddle announcing his return. Beyond all reasonable doubt, the infatuated man had set foot on the shores of the tabooed island.

The one chance for his life was to conceal what he had done, until the ship could be got out of the harbour, and then (if no harm had come to him in the interval) to rescue him after nightfall. It was decided to spread the report that he had really been taken ill, and that he was confined to his cabin. The chief's son, whose heart the Captain's kindness had won, could be trusted to do this, and to keep the secret faithfully for his good friend's sake.

Towards noon, the next day, they attempted to take the ship to sea, and failed for want of wind. Hour by hour, the heat grew more oppressive. As the day declined, there were ominous appearances in the western heaven. The natives, who had given some trouble during the day by their anxiety to see the Captain, and by their curiosity to know the cause of the sudden preparations for the ship's departure, all went ashore together, looking suspiciously at the sky, and re-appeared no more. Just at midnight, the ship (still in her snug berth inside the reef) suddenly trembled from her keel to her uppermost masts. Mr Duncalf, surrounded by the startled crew, shook his knotty fist at the island as if he could see it in the dark. 'My lads, what did I tell you? That was a shock of earthquake.'

With the morning the threatening aspect of the weather unexpectedly disappeared. A faint hot breeze from the land, just enough to give the ship steerage-way, offered Mr Duncalf a chance of getting to sea. Slowly the *Fortuna*, with the mate himself at the wheel, half sailed, half drifted into the open ocean. At a distance of barely two miles from the island the breeze was felt no more, and the vessel lay becalmed for the rest of the day.

At night the men waited their orders, expecting to be sent after their Captain in one of the boats. The intense darkness, the airless heat, and a second shock of earthquake (faintly felt in the ship at her present distance from the land) warned the mate to be cautious. 'I smell mischief in the air,' said Mr Duncalf. 'The Captain must wait till I am surer of the weather.'

Still no change came with the new day. The dead calm continued, and the airless heat. As the day declined, another ominous appearance became visible. A thin line of smoke was discovered through the telescope, ascending from the topmost peak of the mountain on the main island. Was the volcano threatening an eruption? The mate, for one, entertained no doubt of it. 'By the Lord, the place is going to burst up!' said Mr Duncalf. 'Come what may of it, we must find the Captain to-night!'

V

What was the lost Captain doing? and what chance had the crew of finding him that night?

He had committed himself to his desperate adventure, without forming any plan for the preservation of his own safety; without giving even a momentary consideration to the consequences which might follow the risk that he had run. The charming figure that he had seen haunted him night and day. The image of the innocent creature, secluded from humanity in her island-solitude, was the one image that filled his mind. A man, passing a woman in the street, acts on the impulse to turn and follow her, and in that one thoughtless moment shapes the destiny of his future life. The Captain had acted on a similar impulse, when he took the first canoe he found on the beach, and shaped his reckless course for the tabooed island.

Reaching the shore while it was still dark, he did one sensible thing – he hid the canoe so that it might not betray him when the daylight came. That done, he waited for the morning on the outskirts of the forest.

The trembling light of dawn revealed the mysterious solitude around him. Following the outer limits of the trees, first in one direction, then in another, and finding no trace of any living creature, he decided on penetrating to the interior of the island. He entered the forest.

An hour of walking brought him to rising ground. Continuing the ascent, he got clear of the trees, and stood on the grassy top of a broad cliff which overlooked the sea. An open hut was on the cliff. He cautiously looked in, and discovered that it was empty. The few household utensils left about, and the simple bed of leaves in a corner, were covered with fine sandy dust. Night-birds flew blundering out of inner cavities in the roof, and took refuge in the shadows of the forest below. It was plain that the hut had not been inhabited for some time past.

Standing at the open doorway and considering what he should do next, the Captain saw a bird flying towards him out of the forest. It was a turtle-dove, so tame that it fluttered close up to him. At the same moment the sound of sweet laughter became audible among the trees. His heart beat fast; he advanced a few steps and stopped. In a moment more the nymph of the island appeared, in her white robe, ascending the cliff in pursuit of her truant bird. She saw the strange man, and suddenly stood still; struck motionless by the amazing discovery that had burst upon her. The Captain approached, smiling and holding out his hand. She never moved; she stood before him in helpless wonderment – her lovely black eyes fixed spell-bound on his face; her dusky bosom palpitating above the fallen folds of her robe; her rich red lips parted in mute astonishment. Feasting his eyes on her beauty in silence, the Captain after a while ventured to speak to her in the language of the main island. The sound of his voice, addressing her in the words that she understood, roused the lovely creature to action. She started, stepped close up to him, and dropped on her knees at his feet.

'My father worships invisible deities,' she said softly. 'Are you a visible deity? Has my mother sent you?' She pointed as she spoke to the deserted hut behind them. 'You appear,' she went on, 'in the place where my mother died. Is it for her sake that you show yourself to her child? Beautiful deity, come to the Temple – come to my father!'

The Captain gently raised her from the ground. If her father saw him, he was a doomed man.

Infatuated as he was, he had sense enough left to announce himself plainly in his own character, as a mortal creature arriving from a distant land. The girl instantly drew back from him with a look of terror.

'He is not like my father,' she said to herself; 'he is not like me. Is he the lying demon of the prophecy? Is he the predestined destroyer of our island?'

The Captain's experience of the sex showed him the only sure way out of the awkward position in which he was now placed. He appealed to his personal appearance.

'Do I look like a demon?' he asked.

Her eyes met his eyes; a faint smile trembled on her lips. He ventured on asking what she meant by the predestined destruction of the island. She held up her hand solemnly, and repeated the prophecy.

The Holy Island was threatened with destruction by an evil being, who would one day appear on its shores. To avert the fatality the place had been sanctified and set apart, under the protection of the gods and their priest. Here was the reason for the taboo, and for the extraordinary rigour with which it was enforced. Listening to her with the deepest interest, the Captain took her hand and pressed it gently.

'Do I feel like a demon?' he whispered.

Her slim brown fingers closed frankly on his hand. 'You feel soft and friendly,' she said with the fearless candour of a child. 'Squeeze me again. I like it!'

The next moment she snatched her hand away from him; the sense of his danger had suddenly forced itself on her mind. 'If my father sees you,' she said, 'he will light the signal fire at the Temple, and the people from the other island will come here and put you to death. Where is your canoe? No! It is daylight. My father may see you on the water.' She considered a little, and, approaching him, laid her hands on his shoulders. 'Stay here till nightfall,' she resumed. 'My father never comes this way. The sight of the place where my mother died is horrible to him. You are safe here. Promise to stay where you are till night-time.'

The Captain gave his promise.

Freed from anxiety so far, the girl's mobile temperament recovered its native cheerfulness, its sweet gaiety and spirit. She admired the beautiful stranger as she might have admired a new bird that had flown to her to be fondled with the rest. She patted his fair white skin, and wished she had a skin like it. She lifted the great glossy folds of her long black hair, and compared it with the Captain's bright curly locks, and longed to change colours with him from the bottom of her heart. His dress was a wonder to her; his watch was a new revelation. She rested her head on his shoulder to listen delightedly to the ticking, as he held the watch to her ear. Her fragrant breath played on his face, her warm supple figure rested against him softly. The Captain's arm stole round her waist, and the Captain's lips gently touched her cheek. She lifted her head with a look of pleased surprise. 'Thank you,' said the child of nature simply. 'Kiss me again; I like it. May I kiss you?' The tame turtle-dove perched on her shoulder as she gave the Captain her first kiss, and diverted her thoughts to the pets that she had left, in pursuit of the truant dove. 'Come,' she said, 'and see my birds. I keep them on this side of the forest. There is no danger, so long as you don't show yourself on the other side. My name is Aimata. Aimata will take care of you. Oh, what a beautiful white neck you have!' She put her arm admiringly round his neck. The Captain's arm held her tenderly to him. Slowly the two descended the cliff, and were lost in the leafy solitudes of the forest. And the tame dove fluttered before them, a winged messenger of love, cooing to his mate.

VI

The night had come, and the Captain had not left the island.

Aimata's resolution to send him away in the darkness was a forgotten resolution already. She had let him persuade her that he was in no danger, so long as he remained in the hut on the cliff; and she had promised, at parting, to return to him while the Priest was still sleeping, at the dawn of day.

He was alone in the hut. The thought of the innocent creature whom he loved was sorrowfully as well as tenderly present to his mind. He almost regretted his rash visit to the island. 'I will take her with me to England,' he said to himself. 'What does a sailor care for the opinion of the world? Aimata shall be my wife.'

The intense heat oppressed him. He stepped out on the cliff, towards midnight, in search of a breath of air.

At that moment, the first shock of earthquake (felt in the ship while she was inside the reef) shook the ground he stood on. He instantly thought of the volcano on the main island. Had he been mistaken in supposing the crater to be extinct? Was the shock that he had just felt a warning from the volcano, communicated through a submarine connection between the two islands? He waited and watched through the hours of darkness, with a vague sense of apprehension, which was not to be reasoned away. With the first light of daybreak he descended into the forest, and saw the lovely being whose safety was already precious to him as his own, hurrying to meet him through the trees.

She waved her hand distractedly, as she approached him. 'Go!' she cried; 'go away in your canoe before our island is destroyed!'

He did his best to quiet her alarm. Was it the shock of earthquake that had frightened her? No: it was more than the shock of earthquake – it was something terrible which had followed the shock. There was a lake near the Temple, the waters of which were supposed to be heated by subterranean fires.

The lake had risen with the earthquake, had bubbled furiously, and had then melted away into the earth and been lost. Her father, viewing the portent with horror, had gone to the cape to watch the volcano on the main island, and to implore by prayers and sacrifices the protection of the gods. Hearing this, the Captain entreated Aimata to let him see the emptied lake, in the absence of the Priest. She hesitated; but his influence was all-powerful. He prevailed on her to turn back with him through the forest.

Reaching the farthest limit of the trees, they came out upon open rocky ground which sloped gently downward towards the centre of the island. Having crossed this space, they arrived at a natural amphitheatre of rock. On one side of it, the Temple appeared, partly excavated, partly formed by a natural cavern. In one of the lateral branches of the cavern was the dwelling of the Priest and his daughter. The mouth of it looked out on the rocky basin of the lake. Stooping over the edge, the Captain discovered, far down in the empty depths, a light cloud of steam. Not a drop of water was visible, look where he might.

Aimata pointed to the abyss, and hid her face on his bosom. 'My father says,' she whispered, 'that it is your doing.'

The Captain started. 'Does your father know that I am on the island?'

She looked up at him with a quick glance of reproach. 'Do you think I would tell him, and put your life in peril?' she asked. 'My father felt the destroyer of the island in the earthquake; my father saw the coming destruction in the disappearance of the lake.' Her eyes rested on him with a loving languor. 'Are you indeed the demon of the prophecy?' she said, winding his hair round her finger. 'I am not afraid of you, if you are. I am a creature bewitched; I love the demon.' She kissed him passionately. 'I don't care if I die,' she whispered between the kisses, 'if I only die with you!'

The Captain made no attempt to reason with her. He took the wiser way – he appealed to her feelings.

'You will come and live with me happily in my own country,' he said. 'My ship is waiting for us. I will take you home with me, and you shall be my wife.'

She clapped her hands for joy. Then she thought of her father, and drew back from him in tears.

The Captain understood her. 'Let us leave this dreary place,' he suggested. 'We will talk about it in the cool glades of the forest, where you first said you loved me.'

She gave him her hand. 'Where I first said I loved you!' she repeated, smiling tenderly as she looked at him. They left the lake together.

VII

The darkness had fallen again; and the ship was still becalmed at sea.

Mr Duncalf came on deck after his supper. The thin line of smoke, seen rising from the peak of the mountain that evening, was now succeeded by ominous flashes of fire from the same quarter, intermittently visible. The faint hot breeze from the land was felt once more. 'There's just an air of wind,' Mr Duncalf remarked. 'I'll try for the Captain while I have the chance.'

One of the boats was lowered into the water – under command of the second mate, who had already taken the bearings of the tabooed island by daylight. Four of the men were to go with him, and they were all to be well-armed. Mr Duncalf addressed his final instructions to the officer in the boat.

'You will keep a look-out, sir, with a lantern in the bows. If the natives annoy you, you know what to do. Always shoot natives. When you get anigh the island, you will fire a gun and sing out for the Captain.'

'Quite needless,' interposed a voice from the sea. 'The Captain is here!'

Without taking the slightest notice of the astonishment that he had caused, the commander of the *Fortuna* paddled his canoe to the side of the ship. Instead of ascending to the deck, he stepped into the boat, waiting alongside. 'Lend me your pistols,' he said quietly to the second officer, 'and oblige me by taking your men back to their duties on board.' He looked up at Mr Duncalf and gave some further directions. 'If there is any change in the weather, keep the ship standing off and on, at a safe distance from the land, and throw up a rocket from time to time to show your position. Expect me on board again by sunrise.'

'What!' cried the mate. 'Do you mean to say you are going back to the island – in that boat – all by yourself?'

'I am going back to the island,' answered the Captain, as quietly as ever; 'in this boat – all by myself.' He pushed off from the ship, and hoisted the sail as he spoke.

'You're deserting your duty!' the old sea-dog shouted, with one of his loudest oaths.

'Attend to my directions,' the Captain shouted back, as he drifted away into the darkness.

Mr Duncalf – violently agitated for the first time in his life – took leave of his superior officer, with a singular mixture of solemnity and politeness, in these words:

'The Lord have mercy on your soul! I wish you good-evening.'

VIII

Alone in the boat, the Captain looked with a misgiving mind at the flashing of the volcano on the main island.

If events had favoured him, he would have removed Aimata to the shelter of the ship on the day when he saw the emptied basin of the lake. But the smoke of the Priest's sacrifice had been discovered by the chief; and he had despatched two canoes with instructions to make inquiries. One of the canoes had returned; the other was kept in waiting off the cape, to place a means of communicating with the main island at the disposal of the Priest. The second shock of earthquake had naturally increased the alarm of the chief. He had sent messages to the Priest, entreating him to leave the island, and other messages to Aimata suggesting that she should exert her influence over her father, if he hesitated. The Priest refused to leave the Temple. He trusted in his gods and his sacrifices – he believed they might avert the fatality that threatened his sanctuary.

Yielding to the holy man, the chief sent reinforcements of canoes to take their turn at keeping watch off the headland. Assisted by torches, the islanders were on the alert (in superstitious terror of the demon of the prophecy) by night as well as by day. The Captain had no alternative but to keep in hiding, and to watch his opportunity of approaching the place in which he had concealed his canoe. It was only after Aimata had left him as usual, to return to her father at the close of evening, that the chances declared themselves in his favour. The fire-flashes from the mountain, visible when the night came, had struck terror into the hearts of the men on the watch. They thought of their wives, their children, and their possessions on the main island, and they one and all deserted their Priest. The Captain seized the opportunity of communicating with the ship, and of exchanging a frail canoe which he was ill able to manage, for a swift-sailing boat capable of keeping the sea in the event of stormy weather.

As he now neared the land, certain small sparks of red, moving on the distant water, informed him that the canoes of the sentinels had been ordered back to their duty.

Carefully avoiding the lights, he reached his own side of the island without accident, and guided by the boat's lantern, anchored under the cliff. He climbed the rocks, advanced to the door of the hut, and was met, to his delight and astonishment, by Aimata on the threshold.

'I dreamed that some dreadful misfortune had parted us for ever,' she said; 'and I came here to see if my dream was true. You have taught me what it is to be miserable; I never felt my heart ache till I looked into the hut and found that you had gone. Now I have seen you, I am satisfied. No! you must not go back with me. My father may be out looking for me. It is you that are in danger, not I. I know the forest as well by dark as by daylight.'

The Captain detained her when she tried to leave him.

'Now you *are* here,' he said, 'why should I not place you at once in safety? I have been to the ship; I have brought back one of the boats. The darkness will befriend us – let us embark while we can.'

She shrank away as he took her hand. 'You forget my father!' she said.

'Your father is in no danger, my love. The canoes are waiting for him at the cape. I saw the lights as I passed.'

With that reply he drew her out of the hut and led her towards the sea. Not a breath of the breeze was now to be felt. The dead calm had returned – and the boat was too large to be easily managed by one man alone at the oars.

'The breeze may come again,' he said. 'Wait here, my angel, for the chance.'

As he spoke, the deep silence of the forest below them was broken by a sound. A harsh wailing voice was heard, calling:

'Aimata! Aimata!'

'My father!' she whispered; 'he has missed me. If he comes here you are lost.'

She kissed him with passionate fervour; she held him to her for a moment with all her strength.

'Expect me at daybreak,' she said, and disappeared down the landward slope of the cliff.

He listened, anxious for her safety. The voices of the father and daughter just reached him from among the trees. The priest spoke in no angry tones; she had apparently found an acceptable excuse for her absence. Little by little, the failing sound of their voices told him that they were on their way back together to the Temple. The silence fell again. Not a ripple broke on the beach. Not a leaf rustled in the forest. Nothing moved but the reflected flashes of the volcano on the mainland over the black sky. It was an airless and an awful calm.

He went into the hut, and laid down on his bed of leaves – not to sleep, but to rest. All his energies might be required to meet the coming events of the morning. After the voyage to and from the ship, and the long watching that had preceded it, strong as he was he stood in need of repose.

For some little time he kept awake, thinking. Insensibly the oppression of the intense heat, aided in its influence by his own fatigue, treacherously closed his eyes. In spite of himself, the weary man fell into a deep sleep.

He was awakened by a roar like the explosion of a park of artillery. The volcano on the main island had burst into a state of eruption. Smoky flame-light overspread the sky, and flashed through the open doorway of the hut. He sprang from his bed – and found himself up to his knees in water.

Had the sea overflowed the land?

He waded out of the hut, and the water rose to his middle. He looked round him by the lurid light of the eruption. The one visible object within the range of view was the sea, stained by reflections from the blood-red sky, swirling and rippling strangely in the dead calm. In a moment more, he became conscious that the earth on which he stood was sinking under his feet. The water rose to his neck; the last vestige of the roof of the hut disappeared.

He looked round again, and the truth burst on him. The island was sinking – slowly, slowly sinking into volcanic depths, below even the depth of the sea! The highest object was the hut, and that had dropped inch by inch under water before his own eyes. Thrown up to the surface by occult volcanic influences, the island had sunk back, under the same influences, to the obscurity from which it had emerged!

A black shadowy object, turning in a wide circle, came slowly near him as the all-destroying ocean washed its bitter waters into his mouth. The buoyant boat, rising as the sea rose, had dragged its anchor, and was floating round in the vortex made by the slowly-sinking island. With a last desperate hope that Aimata might have been saved as *he* had been saved, he swam to the boat, seized the heavy oars with the strength of a giant, and made for the place (so far as he could guess at it now) where the lake and the Temple had once been.

He looked round and round him; he strained his eyes in the vain attempt to penetrate below the surface of the seething dimpling sea. Had the panic-stricken watchers in the canoes saved themselves, without an effort to preserve the father and daughter? Or had they both been suffocated before they could make an attempt to escape? He called to her in his misery, as if she could hear him out of the fathomless depths, 'Aimata! Aimata!' The roar of the distant eruption answered him. The mounting fires lit the solitary sea far and near over the sinking island. The boat turned slowly and more slowly in the lessening vortex. Never again would those gentle eyes look at him with unutterable love! Never again would those fresh lips touch his lips with their fervent kiss! Alone, amid the savage forces of Nature in conflict, the miserable mortal lifted his hands in frantic supplication – and the burning sky glared down on him in its pitiless grandeur, and struck him to his knees in the boat. His reason sank with his sinking limbs. In the merciful frenzy that succeeded the shock, he saw her afar off, in her white robe, an angel poised on the waters; beckoning him to follow her to the brighter and the better world. He loosened the sail, he seized the oars; and the faster he pursued it, the faster the mocking vision fled from him over the empty and endless sea.

IX

The boat was discovered, on the next morning, from the ship.

All that the devotion of the officers of the *Fortuna* could do for their unhappy commander was done on the homeward voyage. Restored to his own country, and to skilled medical help, the Captain's mind by slow degrees recovered its balance. He has taken his place in society again – he lives and moves and manages his affairs like the rest of us. But his heart is dead to all new emotions; nothing remains in it but the sacred remembrance of his lost love. He neither courts nor avoids the society of women. Their sympathy finds him grateful, but their attractions seem to be lost on him; they pass from his mind as they pass from his eyes – they stir nothing in him but the memory of Aimata.

'Now you know, ladies, why the Captain will never marry, and why (sailor as he is) he hates the sight of the sea.'

Mr Percy and the Prophet

Originally appeared as the Extra Summer Number of *All the Year Round*, 2 July 1877, as 'Percy and the Prophet'. Reprinted in *Little Novels* (1887). This story was written at the instigation of *All the Year Round's* editor, Charles Dickens Junior. The quasi-supernatural framing device is a throw-back to early sensational stories such as 'Nine O'Clock!'; the duel motif recalls *Mad Monkton*.

Part One

I THE QUACK

The disasters that follow the hateful offence against Christianity, which men call war, were severely felt in England during the peace that ensued on the overthrow of Napoleon at Waterloo. With rare exceptions, distress prevailed among all classes of the community. The starving nation was ripe and ready for a revolutionary rising against its rulers, who had shed the people's blood and wasted the people's substance in a war which had yielded to the popular interests absolutely nothing in return.

Among the unfortunate persons who were driven, during the disastrous early years of this century, to strange shifts and devices to obtain the means of living, was a certain obscure medical man, of French extraction, named Lagarde. The Doctor (duly qualified to bear the title) was an inhabitant of London; living in one of the narrow streets which connect the great thoroughfare of the Strand with the bank of the Thames.

The method of obtaining employment chosen by poor Lagarde, as the one alternative left in the face of starvation, was, and is still considered by the medical profession to be, the method of a quack. He advertised in the public journals.

Addressing himself especially to two classes of the community, the Doctor proceeded in these words:

'I have the honour of inviting to my house, in the first place: Persons afflicted with maladies which ordinary medical practice has failed to cure – and, in the second place: Persons interested in investigations, the object of which is to penetrate the secrets of the future. Of the means by which I endeavour to alleviate suffering and to enlighten doubt, it is impossible to speak intelligibly within the limits of an advertisement. I can only offer to submit my system to public inquiry, without exacting any preliminary fee from ladies and gentlemen who may honour me with a visit. Those who see sufficient reason to trust me, after personal experience, will find a money-box fixed on the waiting-room table, into which they can drop their offerings according to their means. Those whom I am not fortunate enough to satisfy will be pleased to accept the expression of my regret, and will not be expected to give anything. I shall be found at home every evening between the hours of six and ten.'

Towards the close of the year 1816, this strange advertisement became a general topic of conversation among educated people in London. For some weeks, the Doctor's invitations were generally accepted – and, all things considered, were not badly remunerated. A faithful few believed in him, and told wonderful stories of what he had pronounced and prophesied in the sanctuary of his consulting-room. The majority of his visitors simply viewed him in the light of a public amusement, and wondered why such a gentlemanlike man should have chosen to gain his living by exhibiting himself as a quack.

II THE NUMBERS

On a raw and snowy evening towards the latter part of January, 1817, a gentleman, walking along the Strand, turned into the street in which Doctor Lagarde lived, and knocked at the physician's door.

He was admitted by an elderly male servant to a waiting-room on the first floor. The light of one little lamp, placed on a bracket fixed to the wall, was so obscured by a dark green shade as to make it difficult, if not impossible, for visitors meeting by accident to recognise each other. The metal money-box fixed to the table was just visible. In the flickering light of a small fire, the stranger perceived the figures of three men seated, apart and silent, who were the only occupants of the room beside himself.

So far as objects were to be seen, there was nothing to attract attention in the waiting-room. The furniture was plain and neat, and nothing more. The elderly servant handed a card, with a number inscribed on it, to the new visitor, said in a whisper, 'Your number will be called, sir, in your turn,' and disappeared. For some minutes nothing disturbed the deep silence but the faint ticking of a clock. After a while a bell rang from an inner room, a door opened, and a gentleman appeared, whose interview with Doctor Lagarde had terminated. His opinion of the sitting was openly expressed in one emphatic word – 'Humbug!' No contribution dropped from his hand as he passed the money-box on his way out.

The next number (being Number Fifteen) was called by the elderly servant, and the first incident occurred in the strange series of events destined to happen in the Doctor's house that night.

One after another the three men who had been waiting rose, examined their cards under the light of the lamp, and sat down again surprised and disappointed.

The servant advanced to investigate the matter. The numbers possessed by the three visitors, instead of being Fifteen, Sixteen, and Seventeen, proved to be Sixteen, Seventeen, and Eighteen. Turning to the stranger who had arrived the last, the servant said:

'Have I made a mistake, sir? Have I given you Number Fifteen instead of Number Eighteen?'

The gentleman produced his numbered card.

A mistake had certainly been made, but not the mistake that the servant supposed. The card held by the latest visitor turned out to be the card previously held by the dissatisfied stranger who had just left the room – Number Fourteen! As to the card numbered Fifteen, it was only discovered the next morning lying in a corner, dropped on the floor!

Acting on his first impulse, the servant hurried out, calling to the original holder of Fourteen to come back and bear his testimony to that fact. The street-door had been opened for him by the landlady of the house. She was a pretty woman – and the gentleman had fortunately lingered to talk to her. He was induced, at the intercession of the landlady, to ascend the stairs again.

On returning to the waiting-room, he addressed a characteristic question to the assembled visitors. '*More* humbug?' asked the gentleman who liked to talk to a pretty woman.

The servant – completely puzzled by his own stupidity – attempted to make his apologies.

'Pray forgive me, gentlemen,' he said. 'I am afraid I have confused the cards I distribute with the cards returned to me. I think I had better consult my master.'

Left by themselves, the visitors began to speak jestingly of the strange situation in which they were placed. The original holder of Number Fourteen described his experience of the Doctor in his own pithy way. 'I applied to the fellow to tell my fortune. He first went to sleep over it, and then he said he could tell me nothing. I asked why. "I don't know," says he. "*I* do," says I – "humbug!" I'll bet you the long odds, gentlemen, that *you* find it humbug, too.'

Before the wager could be accepted or declined, the door of the inner room was opened again. The tall, spare, black figure of a new personage appeared on the threshold, relieved darkly against the light in the room behind him. He addressed the visitors in these words:

'Gentlemen, I must beg your indulgence. The accident – as we now suppose it to be – which has given to the last comer the number already held by a gentleman who has unsuccessfully consulted me, may have a meaning which we can none of us at present see. If the three visitors who have been so good as to wait, will allow the present holder of Number Fourteen to consult me out of his turn – and if the earlier visitor who left me dissatisfied with his consultation will consent to stay here a little longer – something may happen which will justify a trifling sacrifice of your own convenience. Is ten minutes' patience too much to ask of you?'

The three visitors who had waited longest consulted among themselves, and (having nothing better to do with their time) decided on accepting the doctor's proposal. The visitor who believed it all to be 'humbug' coolly took a gold coin out of his pocket, tossed it into the air, caught it in his closed hand, and walked up to the shaded lamp on the bracket.

'Heads, stay,' he said, 'Tails, go.' He opened his hand, and looked at the coin. 'Heads! Very good. Go on with your hocus-pocus, Doctor – I'll wait.'

'You believe in chance,' said the Doctor, quietly observing him. 'That is not my experience of life.'

He paused to let the stranger who now held Number Fourteen pass him into the inner room – then followed, closing the door behind him.

III THE CONSULTATION

The consulting-room was better lit than the waiting-room, and that was the only difference between the two. In the one as in the other, no attempt was made to impress the imagination. Everywhere, the commonplace furniture of a London lodging-house was left without the slightest effort to alter or improve it by changes of any kind.

Seen under the clearer light, Doctor Lagarde appeared to be the last person living who would consent to degrade himself by an attempt at imposture of any kind. His eyes were the dreamy eyes of a visionary; his look was the prematurely-aged look of a student, accustomed to give the hours to his book which ought to have been given to his bed. To state it briefly, he was a man who might easily be deceived by others, but who was incapable of consciously practising deception himself.

Signing to his visitor to be seated, he took a chair on the opposite side of the small table that stood between them – waited a moment with his face hidden in his hands, as if to collect himself – and then spoke.

'Do you come to consult me on a case of illness?' he inquired, 'or do you ask me to look into the darkness which hides your future life?'

The answer to those questions was frankly and briefly expressed: 'I have no need to consult you about my health. I come to hear what you can tell me of my future life.'

'I can try,' pursued the Doctor; 'but I cannot promise to succeed.'

'I accept your conditions,' the stranger rejoined. 'I neither believe nor disbelieve. If you will excuse my speaking frankly, I mean to observe you closely, and to decide for myself.'

Doctor Lagarde smiled sadly.

'You have heard of me as a charlatan who contrives to amuse a few idle people.' he said. 'I don't complain of that; my present position leads necessarily to misinterpretation of myself and my motives. Still, I may at least say that I am the victim of a sincere avowal of my belief in a great science. Yes! I repeat it, a great science! New, I dare say, to the generation we live in, though it was known and practised in the days when the pyramids were built. The age is advancing; and the truths which it is my misfortune to advocate, before the time is ripe for them, are steadily forcing their way to recognition. I am resigned to wait. My sincerity in this matter has cost me the income that I derived from my medical practice. Patients distrust me; doctors refuse to consult with me. I could starve if I had no one to think of but myself. But I have another person to consider, who is very dear to me; and I am driven, literally driven, either to turn beggar in the streets, or to do what I am doing now.'

He paused, and looked round towards the corner of the room behind him. 'Mother,' he said gently, 'are you ready?'

An elderly lady, dressed in deep mourning, rose from her seat in the corner. She had been, thus far, hidden from notice by the high back of the easy-chair in which her son sat. Excepting some folds of fine black lace, laid over her white hair so as to form a head-dress at once simple and picturesque, there was nothing remarkable in her attire. The visitor rose and bowed. She gravely returned his salute, and moved so as to place herself opposite to her son.

'May I ask what this lady is going to do?' said the stranger.

'To be of any use to you,' answered Doctor Lagarde, 'I must be thrown into the magnetic trance. The person who has the strongest influence over me is the person who will do it to-night.'

He turned to his mother. 'When you like,' he said.

Bending over him, she took both the Doctor's hands, and looked steadily into his eyes. No words passed between them; nothing more took place. In a minute or two, his head was resting against the back of the chair, and his eyelids had closed.

'Are you sleeping?' asked Madame Lagarde.

'I am sleeping,' he answered.

She laid his hands gently on the arms of the chair, and turned to address the visitor.

'Let the sleep gain on him for a minute or two more,' she said. 'Then take one of his hands, and put to him what questions you please.'

'Does he hear us now, madam?'

'You might fire off a pistol, sir, close to his ear, and he would not hear it. The vibration might disturb him; that is all. Until you or I touch him, and so establish the nervous sympathy, he is as lost to all sense of our presence here, as if he were dead.'

'Are you speaking of the thing called Animal Magnetism, madam?'

'Yes, sir.'

'And you believe in it, of course?'

'My son's belief, sir, is my belief in this thing as in other things. I have heard what he has been saying to you. It is for me that he sacrifices himself by holding these exhibitions; it is in my poor interests that his hardly-earned money is made. I am in infirm health; and remonstrate as I may, my son persists in providing for me, not the bare comforts only, but even the luxuries of life. Whatever I may suffer, I have my compensation; I can still thank God for giving me the greatest happiness that a woman can enjoy, the possession of a good son.'

She smiled fondly as she looked at the sleeping man. 'Draw your chair nearer to him,' she resumed, 'and take his hand. You may speak freely in making your inquiries. Nothing that happens in this room goes out of it.'

With those words she returned to her place, in the corner behind her son's chair.

The visitor took Doctor Lagarde's hand. As they touched each other, he was conscious of a faintly-titillating sensation in his own hand – a sensation which oddly reminded him of bygone experiments with an electrical machine, in the days when he was a boy at school!

'I wish to question you about my future life,' he began. 'How ought I to begin?'

The Doctor spoke his first words in the monotonous tones of a man talking in his sleep.

'Own your true motive before you begin,' he said. 'Your interest in your future life is centred in a woman. You wish to know if her heart will be yours in the time that is to come – and there your interest in your future life ends.'

This startling proof of the sleeper's capacity to look, by sympathy, into his mind, and to see there his most secret thoughts, instead of convincing the stranger, excited his suspicions. 'You have means of getting information,' he said, 'that I don't understand.'

The Doctor smiled, as if the idea amused him. Madame Lagarde rose from her place, and interposed.

'Hundreds of strangers come here to consult my son,' she said quietly. 'If you believe that we know who those strangers are, and that we have the means of inquiring into their private lives before they enter this room, you believe in something much more incredible than the magnetic sleep!'

This was too manifestly true to be disputed. The visitor made his apologies.

'I should like to have *some* explanation,' he added. 'The thing is so very extraordinary. How can I prevail upon Doctor Lagarde to enlighten me?'

'He can only tell you what he sees,' Madame Lagarde answered; 'ask him that, and you will get a direct reply. Say to him: "Do you see the lady?"'

The stranger repeated the question. The reply followed at once, in these words:

'I see two figures standing side by side. One of them is your figure. The other is the figure of a lady. She only appears dimly. I can discover nothing but that she is taller than women generally are, and that she is dressed in pale blue.'

The man to whom he was speaking started at those last words. 'Her favourite colour!' he thought to himself – forgetting that, while he held the Doctor's hand, the Doctor could think with *his* mind.

'Yes,' added the sleeper quietly, 'her favourite colour, as you know. She fades and fades as I look at her,' he went on. 'She is gone. I only see *you*, under a new aspect. You have a pistol in your hand. Opposite to you, there stands the figure of another man. He, too, has a pistol in his hand. Are you enemies? Are you meeting to fight a duel? Is the lady the cause? I try, but I fail to see her.'

'Can you describe the man?'

'Not yet. So far, he is only a shadow in the form of a man.'

There was another interval. An appearance of disturbance showed itself on the sleeper's face. Suddenly, he waved his free hand in the direction of the waiting-room.

'Send for the visitors who are there,' he said. 'They are all to come in. Each one of them is to take one of my hands in turn – while you remain where you are, holding the other hand. Don't let go of me, even for a moment. My mother will ring.'

Madame Lagarde touched a bell on the table. The servant received his orders from her and retired. After a short absence, he appeared again in the consulting-room, with one visitor only waiting on the threshold behind him.

IV THE MAN

'The other three gentlemen have gone away, madam,' the servant explained, addressing Madame Lagarde. 'They were tired of waiting. I found *this* gentleman fast asleep; and I am afraid he is angry with me for taking the liberty of waking him.'

'Sleep of the common sort is evidently not allowed in this house.' With that remark the gentleman entered the room, and stood revealed as the original owner of the card numbered Fourteen.

Viewed by the clear lamplight, he was a tall, finely-made man, in the prime of life, with a florid complexion, golden-brown hair, and sparkling blue eyes. Noticing Madame Lagarde, he instantly checked the flow of his satire, with the instinctive good-breeding of a gentleman. 'I beg your pardon,' he said; 'I have a great many faults, and a habit of making bad jokes is one of them. Is the servant right, madam, in telling me that I have the honour of presenting myself here at your request?'

Madame Lagarde briefly explained what had passed.

The florid gentleman (still privately believing it to be all 'humbug') was delighted to make himself of any use. 'I congratulate you, sir,' he said, with his easy humour, as he passed the visitor who had become possessed of his card. 'Number Fourteen seems to be a luckier number in your keeping than it was in mine.'

As he spoke, he took Doctor Lagarde's disengaged hand. The instant they touched each other, the sleeper started. His voice rose; his face flushed. 'You are the man!' he exclaimed. 'I see you plainly, now!'

'What am I doing?'

'You are standing opposite to the gentleman here who is holding my other hand; and (as I have said already) you have met to fight a duel.'

The unbeliever cast a shrewd look at his companion in the consultation.

'Considering that you and I are total strangers, sir,' he said, 'don't you think the Doctor had better introduce us, before he goes any farther? We have got to fighting a duel already, and we may as well know who we are, before the pistols go off.' He turned to Doctor Lagarde. 'Dramatic situations don't amuse me out of the theatre,' he resumed. 'Let me put you to a very commonplace test. I want to be introduced to this gentleman. Has he told you his name?'

'No.'

'Of course, you know it, without being told?'

'Certainly. I have only to look into your own knowledge of yourselves, while I am in this trance, and while you have got my hands, to know both your names as well as you do.'

'Introduce us, then!' retorted the jesting gentleman. 'And take my name first.'

'Mr Percy Linwood,' replied the Doctor; 'I have the honour of presenting you to Captain Bervie, of the Artillery.'

With one accord, the gentlemen both dropped Doctor Lagarde's hands, and looked at each other in blank amazement.

'Of course he has discovered our names somehow!' said Mr Percy Linwood, explaining the mystery to his own perfect satisfaction in that way.

Captain Bervie had not forgotten what Madame Lagarde had said to him, when he too had suspected a trick. He now repeated it (quite ineffectually) for Mr Linwood's benefit. 'If you don't feel the force of that argument as I feel it,' he added, 'perhaps, as a favour to me, sir, you will not object to our each taking the Doctor's hand again, and hearing what more he can tell us while he remains in the state of trance?'

'With the greatest pleasure!' answered good-humoured Mr Linwood. 'Our friend is beginning to amuse me; I am as anxious as you are to know what he is going to see next.'

Captain Bervie put the next question.

'You have seen us ready to fight a duel – can you tell us the result?'

'I can tell you nothing more than I have told you already. The figures of the duellists have faded away, like the other figures I saw before them. What I see now looks like the winding gravel-path of a garden. A man and a woman are walking towards me. The man stops, and places a ring on the woman's finger, and kisses her.'

Captain Bervie opened his lips to continue his enquiries – turned pale – and checked himself. Mr Linwood put the next question.

'Who is the happy man?' he asked.

'*You* are the happy man,' was the instantaneous reply.

'Who is the woman?' cried Captain Bervie, before Mr Linwood could speak again.

'The same woman whom I saw before; dressed in the same colour, in pale blue.'

Captain Bervie positively insisted on receiving clearer information than this.

'Surely you can see *something* of her personal appearance?' he said.

'I can see that she has long dark-brown hair, falling below her waist. I can see that she has lovely dark-brown eyes. She has the look of a sensitive nervous person. She is quite young. I can see no more.'

'Look again at the man who is putting the ring on her finger,' said the Captain. 'Are you sure that the face you see is the face of Mr Percy Linwood?'

'I am absolutely sure.'

Captain Bervie rose from his chair.

'Thank you, madam,' he said to the Doctor's mother. 'I have heard enough.'

He walked to the door. Mr Percy Linwood dropped Doctor Lagarde's hand, and appealed to the retiring Captain with a broad stare of astonishment.

'You don't really believe this?' he said.

'I only say I have heard enough,' Captain Bervie answered.

Mr Linwood could hardly fail to see that any further attempt to treat the matter lightly might lead to undesirable results.

'It is difficult to speak seriously of this kind of exhibition,' he resumed quietly. 'But I suppose I may mention a mere matter of fact, without meaning or giving offence. The description of the lady, I can positively declare, does not apply in any single particular to anyone whom I know.'

Captain Bervie turned round at the door. His patience was in some danger of failing him. Mr Linwood's unruffled composure, assisted in its influence by the presence of Madame Lagarde, reminded him of the claims of politeness. He restrained the rash words as they rose to his lips. 'You may make new acquaintances, sir,' was all that he said. '*You* have the future before you.'

Upon that, he went out. Percy Linwood waited a little, reflecting on the Captain's conduct.

Had Doctor Lagarde's description of the lady accidentally answered the description of a living lady whom Captain Bervie knew? Was he by any chance in love with her? and had the Doctor innocently reminded him that his love was not returned? Assuming this to be likely, was it really possible that he believed in prophetic revelations offered to him under the fantastic influence of a trance? Could any man in the possession of his senses go to those lengths? The Captain's conduct was simply incomprehensible.

Pondering these questions, Percy decided on returning to his place by the Doctor's chair. 'Of one thing I am certain, at any rate,' he thought to himself. 'I'll see the whole imposture out before I leave the house!'

He took Doctor Lagarde's hand. 'Now, then! what is the next discovery?' he asked.

The sleeper seemed to find some difficulty in answering the question.

'I indistinctly see the man and the woman again,' he said.

'Am I the man still?' Percy enquired.

'No. The man, this time, is the Captain. The woman is agitated by something that he is saying to her. He seems to be trying to persuade her to go away with him. She hesitates. He whispers something in her ear. She yields. He leads her away. The darkness gathers behind them. I look and look, and I can see no more.'

'Shall we wait awhile?' Percy suggested, 'and then try again?'

Doctor Lagarde sighed, and reclined in his chair. 'My head is heavy,' he said; 'my spirits are dull. The darkness baffles me. I have toiled long enough for you. Drop my hand and leave me to rest.'

Hearing those words, Madame Lagarde approached her son's chair.

'It will be useless, sir, to ask him any more questions tonight,' she said. 'He has been weak and nervous all day, and he is worn out by the effort he has made. Pardon me, if I ask you to step aside for a moment, while I give him the repose that he needs.'

She laid her right hand gently on the Doctor's head, and kept it there for a minute or so. 'Are you at rest now?' she asked.

'I am at rest,' he answered, in faint drowsy tones.

Madame Lagarde returned to Percy. 'If you are not yet satisfied,' she said, 'my son will be at your service tomorrow evening, sir.'

'Thank you, madam, I have only one more question to ask, and you can no doubt answer it. When your son wakes, will he remember what he has said to Captain Bervie and to myself?'

'My son will be as absolutely ignorant of everything that he has seen, and of everything that he has said in the trance, as if he had been at the other end of the world.'

Percy Linwood swallowed this last outrageous assertion with an effort which he was quite unable to conceal. 'Many thanks, madam,' he said; 'I wish you good-night.'

Returning to the waiting-room, he noticed the money-box fixed to the table. 'These people look poor,' he thought to himself, 'and I feel really indebted to them for an amusing evening. Besides, I can afford to be liberal, for I shall certainly never go back.' He dropped a five-pound note into the money-box, and left the house.

Walking towards his club, Percy's natural serenity of mind was a little troubled by the remembrance of Captain Bervie's language and conduct. The Captain had interested the young man in spite of himself. His first idea was to write to Bervie, and mention what had happened at the renewed consultation with Doctor Lagarde. On second thoughts, he saw reason to doubt how the Captain might receive such an advance as this, on the part of a stranger. 'After all,' Percy decided, 'the whole thing is too absurd to be worth thinking about seriously. Neither he nor I are likely to meet again, or to see the Doctor again – and there's an end of it.'

He never was more mistaken in his life. The end of it was not to come for many a long day yet.

Part Two: The Fulfilment

V THE BALL-ROOM

While the consultation at Doctor Lagarde's was still fresh in the memory of the persons present at it, Chance or Destiny, occupied in sowing the seeds for the harvest of the future, discovered as one of its fit instruments a retired military officer named Major Mulvany.

The Major was a smart little man, who persisted in setting up the appearance of youth as a means of hiding the reality of fifty. Being still a bachelor, and being always ready to make himself agreeable, he was generally popular in the society of women. In the ballroom he was a really welcome addition to the company. The German waltz had then been imported into England little more than three years since. The outcry raised against the dance, by persons skilled in the discovery of latent impropriety, had not yet lost its influence in certain quarters. Men who could waltz were scarce. The Major had successfully grappled with the difficulties of learning the dance in mature life; and the young ladies rewarded him nobly for the effort. That is to say, they took the assumption of youth for granted in the palpable presence of fifty.

Knowing everybody and being welcome everywhere, playing a good hand at whist, and having an inexhaustible fancy in the invention of a dinner, Major Mulvany naturally belonged to all the best clubs of his time. Percy Linwood and he constantly met in the billiard-room or at the dinner-table. The Major approved of the easy, handsome, pleasant-tempered young man. 'I have lost the first freshness of youth,' he used to say with pathetic resignation, 'and I see myself revived, as it were, in Percy. Naturally I like Percy.'

About three weeks after the memorable evening at Doctor Lagarde's, the two friends encountered each other on the steps of a club.

'Have you got anything to do to-night?' asked the Major.

'Nothing that I know of,' said Percy, 'unless I go to the theatre.'

'Let the theatre wait, my boy. My old regiment gives a ball at Woolwich tonight. I have got a ticket to spare; and I know several sweet girls who are going. Some of them waltz, Percy! Gather your rosebuds while you may. Come with me.'

The invitation was accepted as readily as it was given. The Major found the carriage, and Percy paid for the post-horses. They entered the ballroom among the earlier guests; and the first person whom they met, waiting near the door, was – Captain Bervie.

Percy bowed, a little uneasily. 'I feel some doubt,' he said, laughing, 'whether we have been properly introduced to one another or not.'

'Not properly introduced!' cried Major Mulvany. 'I'll soon set that right. My dear friend, Percy Linwood; my dear friend, Arthur Bervie – be known to each other! esteem each other!'

Captain Bervie acknowledged the introduction by a cold salute. Percy, yielding to the good-natured impulse of the moment, alluded to what had happened in Doctor Lagarde's consulting-room.

'You missed something worth hearing when you left the Doctor the other night,' he said. 'We continued the sitting; and *you* turned up again among the persons of the drama, in a new character—'

'Excuse me for interrupting you,' said Captain Bervie. 'I am a member of the committee, charged with the arrangements of the ball, and I must really attend to my duties.'

He withdrew without waiting for a reply. Percy looked round wonderingly at Major Mulvany. 'Strange!' he said, 'I feel rather attracted towards Captain

Bervie; and he seems to have taken such a dislike to me, that he can hardly behave with common civility. What does it mean?'

'I'll tell you,' answered the Major confidentially. 'Arthur Bervie is madly in love – madly is really the word – with a Miss Bowmore. And (this is between ourselves) the young lady doesn't feel it quite in the same way. A sweet girl; I've often had her on my knee when she was a child. Her father and mother are old friends of mine. She is coming to the ball tonight. That's the true reason why Arthur left you just now. Look at him – waiting to be the first to speak to her. If he could have his way, he wouldn't let another man come near the poor girl all through the evening; he really persecutes her. I'll introduce you to Miss Bowmore; and you will see how he looks at us for presuming to approach her. It's a great pity; she will never marry him. Arthur Bervie is a man in a thousand; but he's fast becoming a perfect bear under the strain on his temper. What's the matter? You don't seem to be listening to me.'

This last remark was perfectly justified. In telling the Captain's love-story, Major Mulvany had revived his young friend's memory of the lady in the blue dress, who had haunted the visions of Doctor Lagarde.

'Tell me,' said Percy, 'what is Miss Bowmore like? Is there anything remarkable in her personal appearance? I have a reason for asking.'

As he spoke, there arose among the guests in the rapidly-filling ballroom a low murmur of surprise and admiration. The Major laid one hand on Percy's shoulder, and, lifting the other, pointed to the door.

'What is Miss Bowmore like?' he repeated. 'There she is! Let her answer for herself.'

Percy turned towards the lower end of the room.

A young lady was entering, dressed in plain silk, and the colour of it was a pale blue! Excepting a white rose at her breast, she wore no ornament of any sort. Doubly distinguished by the perfect simplicity of her apparel, and by her tall, supple, commanding figure, she took rank at once as the most remarkable woman in the room Moving nearer to her through the crowd, under the guidance of the complaisant Major, young Linwood gained a clearer view of her hair, her complexion, and the colour of her eyes. In every one of these particulars, she was the living image of the woman described by Doctor Lagarde!

While Percy was absorbed over this strange discovery, Major Mulvany had got within speaking distance of the young lady and of her mother, as they stood together in conversation with Captain Bervie. 'My dear Mrs Bowmore, how well you are looking! My dear Miss Charlotte, what a sensation you have made already! The glorious simplicity (if I may so express myself) of your dress is – is – what was I going to say? – the ideas come thronging on me; I merely want words.'

Miss Bowmore's magnificent brown eyes, wandering from the Major to Percy, rested on the young man with a modest and momentary interest, which Captain Bervie's jealous attention instantly detected.

'They are forming a dance,' he said, pressing forward impatiently to claim his partner. 'If we don't take our places, we shall be too late.'

'Stop! stop!' cried the Major. 'There is a time for everything, and this is the time for presenting my dear friend here, Mr Percy Linwood. He is like me, Miss Charlotte – *he* has been struck by your glorious simplicity, and *he* wants words.' At this part of the presentation, he happened to look toward the irate Captain, and instantly gave him a hint on the subject of his temper. 'I say, Arthur Bervie! we are all good-humoured people here. What have you got on your eyebrows? It looks like a frown; and it doesn't become you. Send for a skilled waiter, and have it brushed off and taken away directly!'

'May I ask, Miss Bowmore, if you are disengaged for the next dance?' said Percy, the moment the Major gave him an opportunity of speaking.

'Miss Bowmore is engaged to *me* for the next dance,' said the angry Captain, before the young lady could answer.

'The third dance, then?' Percy persisted, with his brightest smile.

'With pleasure, Mr Linwood,' said Miss Bowmore. She would have been no true woman if she had not resented the open exhibition of Arthur's jealousy; it was like asserting a right over her to which he had not the shadow of a claim. She threw a look at Percy as her partner led her away, which was the severest punishment she could inflict on the man who ardently loved her.

The third dance stood in the programme as a waltz.

In jealous distrust of Percy, the Captain took the conductor of the band aside, and used his authority as committeeman to substitute another dance. He had no sooner turned his back on the orchestra than the wife of the Colonel of the regiment, who had heard him, spoke to the conductor in her turn, and insisted on the original programme being retained. 'Quote the Colonel's authority,' said the lady, 'if Captain Bervie ventures to object.' In the meantime, the Captain, on his way to rejoin Charlotte, was met by one of his brother officers, who summoned him officially to an impending debate of the committee charged with the administrative arrangements of the supper-table.

Bervie had no choice but to follow his brother officer to the committee-room.

Barely a minute later the conductor appeared at his desk, and the first notes of the music rose low and plaintive, introducing the third dance.

'Percy, my boy!' cried the Major, recognising the melody, 'you're in luck's way – it's going to be a waltz!'

Almost as he spoke, the notes of the symphony glided by subtle modulations into the inspiriting air of the waltz. Percy claimed his partner's hand. Miss Charlotte hesitated, and looked at her mother.

'Surely you waltz?' said Percy.

'I have learnt to waltz,' she answered modestly; 'but this is such a large room, and there are so many people!'

'Once round,' Percy pleaded; 'only once round!'

Miss Bowmore looked again at her mother. Her foot was keeping time with the music, under her dress; her heart was beating with a delicious excitement; kind-hearted Mrs Bowmore smiled and said, 'Once round, my dear, as Mr Linwood suggests.'

In another moment, Percy's arm took possession of her waist, and they were away on the wings of the waltz!

Could words describe, could thought realize, the exquisite enjoyment of the dance? Enjoyment? It was more – it was an epoch in Charlotte's life – it was the first time she had waltzed with a man. What a difference between the fervent clasp of Percy's arm and the cold formal contact of the mistress who had taught her! How brightly his eyes looked down into hers; admiring her with such a tender restraint, that there could surely be no harm in looking up at him now and then in return. Round and round they glided, absorbed in the music and in themselves. Occasionally her bosom just touched him, at those critical moments when she was most in need of support. At other intervals, she almost let her head sink on his shoulder in trying to hide from him the smile which acknowledged his admiration too boldly. 'Once round,' Percy had suggested; 'once round,' her mother had said. They had been ten, twenty, thirty times round; they had never stopped to rest like other dancers; they had centred the eyes of the whole room on them – including the eyes of Captain Bervie – without knowing it; her delicately pale complexion had changed to rosy-red; the neat arrangement of her hair had become disturbed; her bosom was rising and falling faster and faster in the effort to breathe – before fatigue and heat overpowered her at last, and forced her to say to him faintly, 'I'm very sorry – I can't dance any more!'

Percy led her into the cooler atmosphere of the refreshment-room, and revived her with a glass of lemonade. Her arm still rested on his – she was just about to thank him for the care he had taken of her – when Captain Bervie entered the room.

'Mrs Bowmore wishes me to take you back to her,' he said to Charlotte. Then, turning to Percy, he added: 'Will you kindly wait here while I take Miss Bowmore to the ballroom? I have a word to say to you – I will return directly.'

The Captain spoke with perfect politeness – but his face betrayed him. It was pale with the sinister whiteness of suppressed rage.

Percy sat down to cool and rest himself. With his experience of the ways of men, he felt no surprise at the marked contrast between Captain Bervie's face and Captain Bervie's manner. 'He has seen us waltzing, and he is coming back to pick a quarrel with me.' Such was the interpretation which Mr Linwood's knowledge of the world placed on Captain Bervie's politeness. In a minute or two more the Captain returned to the refreshment-room, and satisfied Percy that his anticipations had not deceived him.

VI LOVE

Four days had passed since the night of the ball.

Although it was no later in the year than the month of February, the sun was shining brightly, and the air was as soft as the air of a day in spring. Percy and Charlotte were walking together in the little garden at the back of Mr Bowmore's cottage, near the town of Dartford in Kent.

'Mr Linwood,' said the young lady, 'you were to have paid us your first visit the day after the ball. Why have you kept us waiting? Have you been too busy to remember your new friends?'

'I have counted the hours since we parted, Miss Charlotte. If I had not been detained by business—'

'I understand! For three days business has controlled you. On the fourth day, you have controlled business – and here you are? I don't believe one word of it, Mr Linwood!'

There was no answering such a declaration as this. Guiltily conscious that Charlotte was right in refusing to accept his well-worn excuse, Percy made an awkward attempt to change the topic of conversation.

They happened, at the moment, to be standing near a small conservatory at the end of the garden. The glass door was closed, and the few plants and shrubs inside had a lonely, neglected look. 'Does nobody ever visit this secluded place?' Percy asked jocosely, 'or does it hide discoveries in the rearing of plants, which are forbidden mysteries to a stranger?'

'Satisfy your curiosity, Mr Linwood, by all means,' Charlotte answered in the same tone. 'Open the door, and I will follow you.'

Percy obeyed. In passing through the doorway, he encountered the bare hanging branches of some creeping plant, long since dead, and detached from its fastenings on the woodwork of the roof. He pushed aside the branches so that Charlotte could easily follow him in, without being aware that his own forced passage through them had a little deranged the folds of spotless white cambric which a well-dressed gentleman wore round his neck in those days. Charlotte seated herself, and directed Percy's attention to the desolate conservatory with a saucy smile.

'The mystery which your lively imagination has associated with this place,' she said, 'means, being interpreted, that we are too poor to keep a gardener. Make the best of your disappointment, Mr Linwood, and sit here by me. We are out of hearing and out of sight of mamma's other visitors. You have no excuse now for not telling me what has really kept you away from us.'

She fixed her eyes on him as she said those words. Before Percy could think of another excuse, her quick observation detected the disordered condition of his cravat, and discovered the upper edge of a black plaster attached to one side of his neck.

'You have been hurt in the neck!' she said. 'That is why you have kept away from us for the last three days!'

'A mere trifle,' he answered, in great confusion; 'please don't notice it.'

Her eyes, still resting on his face, assumed an expression of suspicious enquiry, which Percy was entirely at a loss to understand. Suddenly, she started to her feet, as if a new idea had occurred to her. 'Wait here,' she said, flushing with excitement, 'till I come back: I insist on it!'

Before Percy could ask for an explanation, she had left the conservatory.

In a minute or two, Miss Bowmore returned, with a newspaper in her hand. 'Read that,' she said, pointing to a paragraph distinguished by a line drawn round it in ink.

The passage that she indicated contained an account of a duel which had recently taken place in the neighbourhood of London. The names of the duellists were not mentioned. One was described as an officer, and the other as a civilian. They had quarrelled at cards, and had fought with pistols. The civilian had had a narrow escape of his life. His antagonist's bullet had passed near enough to the side of his neck to tear the flesh, and had missed the vital parts, literally, by a hair's-breadth.

Charlotte's eyes, riveted on Percy, detected a sudden change of colour in his face the moment he looked at the newspaper. That was enough for her. 'You *are* the man!' she cried. 'Oh, for shame, for shame! To risk your life for a paltry dispute about cards.'

'I would risk it again,' said Percy, 'to hear you speak as if you set some value on it.'

She looked away from him without a word of reply. Her mind seemed to be busy again with its own thoughts. Did she meditate returning to the subject of the duel? Was she not satisfied with the discovery which she had just made?

No such doubts as these troubled the mind of Percy Linwood. Intoxicated by the charm of her presence, emboldened by her innocent betrayal of the interest that she felt in him, he opened his whole heart to her as unreservedly as if they had known each other from the days of their childhood. There was but one excuse for him. Charlotte was his first love.

'You don't know how completely you have become a part of my life, since we met at the ball,' he went on. 'That one delightful dance seemed, by some magic which I can't explain, to draw us together in a few minutes as if we had known each other for years. Oh, dear! I could make such a confession of what I felt – only I am afraid of offending you by speaking too soon. Women are so dreadfully difficult to understand. How is a man to know at what time it is considerate towards them to conceal his true feelings; and at what time it is equally considerate to express his true feelings? One doesn't know whether it is a matter of days or weeks or months – there ought to be a law to settle it. Dear Miss Charlotte, when a poor fellow loves you at first sight, as he has never loved any other woman, and when he is tormented by the fear that some other man may be preferred to him, can't you forgive him if he lets out the truth a little too soon?' He ventured, as he put that very downright question, to take her hand. 'It really isn't my fault,' he said simply. 'My heart is so full of you, I can talk of nothing else.'

To Percy's delight, the first experimental pressure of his hand, far from being resented, was softly returned. Charlotte looked at him again, with a new resolution in her face.

'I'll forgive you for talking nonsense, Mr Linwood,' she said; 'and I will even permit you to come and see me again, on one condition – that you tell the whole truth about the duel. If you conceal the smallest circumstance, our acquaintance is at an end.'

'Haven't I owned everything already?' Percy inquired, in great perplexity. 'Did I say No, when you told me I was the man?'

'Could you say No, with that plaster on your neck?' was the ready rejoinder. 'I am determined to know more than the newspaper tells me. Will you declare, on your word of honour, that Captain Bervie had nothing to do with the duel? Can you look me in the face, and say that the real cause of the quarrel was a disagreement at cards? When you were talking with me just before I left the ball, how did you answer a gentleman who asked you to make one at the whist-table? You said, "I don't play at cards." Ah! You thought I had forgotten that? Don't kiss my hand! Trust me with the whole truth, or say good-bye for ever.'

'Only tell me what you wish to know, Miss Charlotte,' said Percy humbly. 'If you will put the question, I will give the answers – as well as I can.'

On this understanding, Percy's evidence was extracted from him as follows:

'Was it Captain Bervie who quarrelled with you?'

'Yes.'

'Was it about me?'

'Yes.'

'What did he say?'

'He said I had committed an impropriety in waltzing with you.'

'Why?'

'Because your parents disapproved of your waltzing in a public ballroom.'

'That's not true! What did he say next?'

'He said I had added tenfold to my offence, by waltzing with you in such a manner as to make you the subject of remark to the whole room.'

'Oh! did you let him say that?'

'No; I contradicted him instantly. And I said, besides, "It's an insult to Miss Bowmore, to suppose that she would permit any impropriety."'

'Quite right! And what did he say?'

'Well, he lost his temper; I would rather not repeat what he said when he was mad with jealousy. There was nothing to be done with him but to give him his way.'

'Give him his way? Does that mean fight a duel with him?'

'Don't be angry – it does.'

'And you kept my name out of it, by pretending to quarrel at the card-table?'

'Yes. We managed it when the card-room was emptying at supper-time, and nobody was present but Major Mulvany and another friend as witnesses.'

'And when did you fight the duel?'

'The next morning.'

'You never thought of *me*, I suppose?'

'Indeed, I did; I was very glad that you had no suspicion of what we were at.'

'Was that all?'

'No; I had your flower with me, the flower you gave me out of your nosegay, at the ball.'

'Well?'

'Oh, never mind, it doesn't matter.'

'It does matter. What did you do with my flower?'

'I gave it a sly kiss while they were measuring the ground; and (don't tell anybody!) I put it next to my heart to bring me luck.'

'Was that just before he shot at you?'

'Yes.'

'How did he shoot?'

'He walked (as the seconds had arranged it) ten paces forward; and then he stopped, and lifted his pistol—'

'Don't tell me any more! Oh, to think of my being the miserable cause of such horrors! I'll never dance again as long as I live. Did you think he had killed you, when the bullet wounded your poor neck?'

'No; I hardly felt it at first.'

'Hardly felt it? How he talks! And when the wretch had done his best to kill you, and when it came to your turn, what did you do?'

'Nothing.'

'What! You didn't walk your ten paces forward?'

'No.'

'And you never shot at him in return?'

'No; I had no quarrel with him, poor fellow; I just stood where I was, and fired in the air—'

Before he could stop her, Charlotte seized his hand, and kissed it with an hysterical fervour of admiration, which completely deprived him of his presence of mind.

'Why shouldn't I kiss the hand of a hero?' she cried, with tears of enthusiasm sparkling in her eyes. 'Nobody but a hero would have given that man his life; nobody but a hero would have pardoned him, while the blood was streaming from the wound that he had inflicted. I respect you, I admire you. Oh, don't think me bold! I can't control myself when I hear of anything noble and good. You will understand me better when we get to be old friends – won't you?'

She spoke in low sweet tones of entreaty. Percy's arm stole softly round her.

'Are we never to be nearer and dearer to each other than old friends?' he asked in a whisper. 'I am not a hero – your goodness overrates me, dear Miss Charlotte. My one ambition is to be the happy man who is worthy enough to win *you*. At your own time! I wouldn't distress you, I wouldn't confuse you, I wouldn't for the whole world take advantage of the compliment which your sympathy has paid to me. If it offends you, I won't even ask if I may hope.'

She sighed as he said the last words; trembled a little, and silently looked at him.

Percy read his answer in her eyes. Without meaning it on either side, their heads drew nearer together; their cheeks, then their lips, touched. She started back from him, and rose to leave the conservatory. At the same moment, the sound of slowly-approaching footsteps became audible on the gravel walk of the garden. Charlotte hurried to the door.

'My father!' she exclaimed, turning to Percy. 'Come, and be introduced to him.'

Percy followed her into the garden.

VII POLITICS

Judging by appearances, Mr Bowmore looked like a man prematurely wasted and worn by the cares of a troubled life. His eyes presented the one feature in which his daughter resembled him. In shape and colour they were exactly reproduced in Charlotte; the difference was in the expression. The father's look was habitually restless, eager, and suspicious. Not a trace was to be seen in it of the truthfulness and gentleness which made the charm of the daughter's expression. A man whose bitter experience of the world had soured his temper and shaken his faith in his fellow-creatures – such was Mr Bowmore as he presented himself on the surface. He received Percy politely – but with a preoccupied air. Every now and then, his restless eyes wandered from the visitor to an open letter in his hand. Charlotte, observing him, pointed to the letter.

'Have you any bad news there, papa?' she asked.

'Dreadful news!' Mr Bowmore answered. 'Dreadful news, my child, to every Englishman who respects the liberties which his ancestors won. My correspondent is a man who is in the confidence of the Ministers,' he continued, addressing Percy. 'What do you think is the remedy that the

Government proposes for the universal distress among the population, caused by an infamous and needless war? Despotism, Mr Linwood; despotism in this free country is the remedy! In one week more, sir, Ministers will bring in a Bill for suspending the Habeas Corpus Act!'

Before Percy could do justice in words to the impression produced on him, Charlotte innocently asked a question which shocked her father.

'What is the Habeas Corpus Act, papa?'

'Good God!' cried Mr Bowmore, 'is it possible that a child of mine has grown up to womanhood, in ignorance of the palladium of English liberty? Oh, Charlotte! Charlotte!'

'I am very sorry, papa. If you will only tell me, I will never forget it.'

Mr Bowmore reverently uncovered his head, saluting an invisible Habeas Corpus Act. He took his daughter by the hand, with a certain parental sternness: his voice trembled with emotion as he spoke his next words:

'The Habeas Corpus Act, my child, forbids the imprisonment of an English subject, unless that imprisonment can be first justified by law. Not even the will of the reigning monarch can prevent us from appearing before the judges of the land, and summoning them to declare whether our committal to prison is legally just.'

He put on his hat again. 'Never forget what I have told you, Charlotte!' he said solemnly. 'I would not remove my hat, sir,' he continued, turning to Percy, 'in the presence of the proudest autocrat that ever sat on a throne. I uncover, in homage to the grand law which asserts the sacredness of human liberty. When Parliament has sanctioned the infamous Bill now before it, English patriots may be imprisoned, may even be hanged, on warrants privately obtained by the paid spies and informers of the men who rule us. Perhaps I weary you, sir. You are a young man; the conduct of the Ministry may not interest you.'

'On the contrary,' said Percy, 'I have the strongest personal interest in the conduct of the Ministry.'

'How? in what way?' cried Mr Bowmore eagerly.

'My late father had a claim on Government,' Percy answered, 'for money expended in foreign service. As his heir, I inherit the claim, which has been formally recognised by the present Ministers. My petition for a settlement will be presented by friends of mine who can advocate my interests in the House of Commons.'

Mr Bowmore took Percy's hand, and shook it warmly.

'In such a matter as this you cannot have too many friends to help you,' he said. 'I myself have some influence, as representing opinion outside the House; and I am entirely at your service. Come tomorrow, and let us talk over the details of your claim at my humble dinner-table. Today I must attend a meeting of the Branch-Hampden-Club, of which I am vice-president, and to which I am now about to communicate the alarming news which my letter contains. Excuse me for leaving you – and count on a hearty welcome when we see you to-morrow.'

The amiable patriot saluted his daughter with a smile, and disappeared.

'I hope you like my father?' said Charlotte. 'All our friends say he ought to be in Parliament. He has tried twice. The expenses were dreadful; and each time the other man defeated him. The agent says he would be certainly elected if he tried again; but there is no money, and we mustn't think of it.'

A man of a suspicious turn of mind might have discovered, in those artless words, the secret of Mr Bowmore's interest in the success of his young friend's claim on the Government. One British subject, with a sum of ready money at his command, may be an inestimably useful person to another British subject (without ready money) who cannot sit comfortably unless he sits in Parliament. But honest Percy Linwood was not a man of a suspicious turn of mind. He had just opened his lips to echo Charlotte's filial glorification of her father, when a shabbily-dressed man-servant met them with a message, for which they were both alike unprepared:

'Captain Bervie has called, Miss, to say good-bye, and my mistress requests your company in the parlour.'

VIII THE WARNING

Having delivered his little formula of words, the shabby servant cast a look of furtive curiosity at Percy and withdrew. Charlotte turned to her lover, with indignation sparkling in her eyes and flushing on her cheeks at the bare idea of seeing Captain Bervie again. 'Does he think I will breathe the same air,' she exclaimed, 'with the man who attempted to take your life!'

Percy gently remonstrated with her.

'You are sadly mistaken,' he said. 'Captain Bervie stood to receive my fire as fairly as I stood to receive his. When I discharged my pistol in the air, he was the first man who ran up to me, and asked if I was seriously hurt. They told him my wound was a trifle; and he fell on his knees and thanked God for preserving my life from his guilty hand. "I am no longer the rival who hates you," he said. "Give me time to try if change of scene will quiet my mind; and I will be *your* brother, and *her* brother." Whatever his faults may be, Charlotte, Arthur Bervie has a great heart. Go in, I entreat you, and be friends with him as I am.'

Charlotte listened with downcast eyes and changing colour. 'You believe him?' she asked, in low trembling tones.

'I believe him as I believe You,' Percy answered.

She secretly resented the comparison, and detested the Captain more heartily than ever. 'I will go in and see him, if you wish it,' she said. 'But not by myself. I want you to come with me.'

'Why?' Percy asked.

'I want to see what his face says, when you and he meet.'

'Do you still doubt him, Charlotte?'

She made no reply. Percy had done his best to convince her, and had evidently failed.

They went together into the cottage. Fixing her eyes steadily on the Captain's face, Charlotte saw it turn pale when Percy followed her into the parlour. The two men greeted one another cordially. Charlotte sat down by her mother, preserving her composure so far as appearances went. 'I hear you have called to bid us goodbye,' she said to Bervie. 'Is it to be a long absence?'

'I have got two months' leave,' the Captain answered, without looking at her while he spoke.

'Are you going abroad?'

'Yes. I think so.'

She turned away to her mother. Bervie seized the opportunity of speaking to Percy. 'I have a word of advice for your private ear.' At the same moment, Charlotte whispered to her mother: 'Don't encourage him to prolong his visit.'

The Captain showed no intention to prolong his visit. To Charlotte's surprise, when he took leave of the ladies, Percy also rose to go. 'His carriage,' he said, 'was waiting at the door; and he had offered to take Captain Bervie back to London.'

Charlotte instantly suspected an arrangement between the two men for a confidential interview. Her obstinate distrust of Bervie strengthened tenfold. She reluctantly gave him her hand, as he parted from her at the parlour-door. The effort of concealing her true feeling towards him, gave a colour and a vivacity to her face which made her irresistibly beautiful. Bervie looked at the woman whom he had lost with an immeasurable sadness in his eyes. 'When we meet again,' he said, 'you will see me in a new character.' He hurried out to the gate, as if he feared to trust himself for a moment longer in her presence.

Charlotte followed Percy into the passage. 'I shall be here to-morrow, dearest!' he said, and tried to raise her hand to his lips. She abruptly drew it away. 'Not that hand!' she answered. 'Captain Bervie has just touched it. Kiss the other!'

'Do you still doubt the Captain?' said Percy, amused by her petulance.

She put her arm over his shoulder, and touched the plaster on his neck gently with her finger. 'There's one thing I don't doubt,' she said: 'the Captain did *that!*'

Percy left her, laughing. At the front gate of the cottage, he found Arthur Bervie in conversation with the same shabbily-dressed man-servant who had announced the Captain's visit to Charlotte.

'What has become of the other servant?' Bervie asked. 'I mean the old man who has been with Mr Bowmore for so many years.'

'He has left his situation, sir.'

'Why?'

'As I understand, sir, he spoke disrespectfully to the master.'

'Oh? And how came the master to hear of *you?*'

'I advertised; and Mr Bowmore answered my advertisement.'

Bervie looked hard at the man for a moment, and then joined Percy at the carriage door. The two gentlemen started for London.

'What do you think of Mr Bowmore's new servant?' asked the Captain, as they drove away from the cottage. 'I don't like the look of the fellow.'

'I didn't particularly notice him,' Percy answered.

There was a pause. When the conversation was resumed, it turned on common-place subjects. The Captain looked uneasily out of the carriage window. Percy looked uneasily at the Captain.

They had left Dartford about two miles behind them, when Percy noticed an old gabled house, sheltered by magnificent trees, and standing on an eminence well removed from the high-road. Carriages and saddle-horses were visible on the drive in front, and a flag was hoisted on a staff placed in the middle of the lawn.

'Something seems to be going on there,' Percy remarked. 'A fine old house! Who does it belong to?'

Bervie smiled. 'It belongs to my father,' he said. 'He is chairman of the bench of local magistrates, and he receives his brother justices today, to celebrate the opening of the sessions.'

He stopped, and looked at Percy with some embarrassment. 'I am afraid I have surprised and disappointed you,' he resumed, abruptly changing the subject. 'I told you when we met just now at Mr Bowmore's cottage that I had something to say to you; and I have not yet said it. The truth is, I don't feel sure whether I have been long enough your friend to take the liberty of advising you.'

'Whatever your advice is,' Percy answered, 'trust me to take it kindly on my side.'

Thus encouraged, the Captain spoke out.

'You will probably pass much of your time at the cottage,' he began, 'and you will be thrown a great deal into Mr Bowmore's society. I have known him for many years. Speaking from that knowledge, I most seriously warn you against him as a thoroughly unprincipled and thoroughly dangerous man.'

This was strong language – and, naturally enough, Percy said so. The Captain justified his language.

'Without alluding to Mr Bowmore's politics,' he went on, 'I can tell you that the motive of everything he says and does is vanity. To the gratification of that one passion he would sacrifice you or me, his wife or his daughter, without hesitation and without remorse. His one desire is to get into Parliament. You are wealthy and you can help him. He will leave no effort untried to reach that end; and, if he gets you into political difficulties, he will desert you without scruple.'

Percy made a last effort to take Mr Bowmore's part – for the one irresistible reason that he was Charlotte's father.

'Pray don't think I am unworthy of your kind interest in my welfare,' he pleaded. 'Can you tell me of any *facts* which justify what you have just said?'

'I can tell you of three facts,' Bervie answered. 'Mr Bowmore belongs to one of the most revolutionary clubs in England; he has spoken rank sedition at public meetings; and his name is already in the black book at the Home Office. So much for the past. As to the future, if the rumour be true that Ministers mean to stop the insurrectionary risings among the population by suspending the Habeas Corpus Act, Mr Bowmore will certainly be in danger; and it may be my father's duty to grant the warrant that apprehends him. Write to my father to verify what I have said, and I will forward your letter, by way of satisfying him that he can trust you. In the meantime, refuse to accept Mr Bowmore's assistance in the matter of your claim on Parliament; and, above all things, stop him at the outset, when he tries to steal his way into your intimacy. I need not caution you to say nothing against him to his wife and daughter. His wily tongue has long since deluded them. Don't let it delude *you!* Have you thought any more of our evening at Doctor Lagarde's?' he asked, abruptly changing the subject.

'I hardly know,' said Percy, still under the impression of the formidable warning which he had just received.

'Let me jog your memory,' the other continued. 'You went on with the consultation by yourself, after I had left the Doctor's house. It will be really doing me a favour, if you can call to mind what Lagarde saw in the trance – in my absence?'

Thus entreated Percy roused himself. His memory of events was still fresh enough to answer the call that his friend had made on it. In describing what had happened, he accurately repeated all that the Doctor had said.

Bervie dwelt on the words with alarm in his face as well as surprise.

'A man like me, trying to persuade a woman like –,' he checked himself, as if he was afraid to let Charlotte's name pass his lips. 'Trying to induce a woman to go away with me,' he resumed, 'and persuading her at last? Pray go on! What did the Doctor see next?'

'He was too much exhausted, he said, to see any more.'

'Surely you returned to consult him again?'

'No; I had had enough of it.'

'When we get to London,' said the Captain, 'we shall pass along the Strand, on the way to your chambers. Will you kindly drop me at the turning that leads to the Doctor's lodgings?'

Percy looked at him in amazement. 'You still take it seriously?' he said.

'Is it *not* serious?' Bervie asked. 'Have you and I, so far, not done exactly what this man saw us doing? Did we not meet, in the days when we were rivals (as he saw us meet), with the pistols in our hands? Did you not recognise his description of the lady when you met her at the ball, as I recognised it before you?'

'Mere coincidences!' Percy answered, quoting Charlotte's opinion when they had spoken together of Doctor Lagarde, but taking care not to cite his authority. 'How many thousand men have been crossed in love? How many thousand men have fought duels for love? How many thousand women choose blue for their favourite colour, and answer to the vague description of the lady whom the Doctor pretended to see?'

'Say that it is so,' Bervie rejoined. 'The thing is remarkable, even from your point of view. And if more coincidences follow, the result will be more remarkable still.'

Arrived at the Strand, Percy set the Captain down at the turning which led to the Doctor's lodgings. 'You will call on me or write me word, if anything remarkable happens,' he said.

'You shall hear from me without fail,' Bervie replied.

That night, the Captain's pen performed the Captain's promise, in few and startling words.

Melancholy news! Madame Lagarde is dead. Nothing is known of her son but that he has left England. I have found out that he is a political exile. If he has ventured back to France, it is barely possible that I may hear something of him. I have friends at the English embassy in Paris who will help me to make enquiries; and I start for the Continent in a day or two. Write to me while I am away, to the care of my father, at 'The Manor House, near Dartford.' He will always know my address abroad, and will forward your letters. For your own sake, remember the warning I gave you this afternoon! Your faithful friend, A. B.

IX OFFICIAL SECRETS

There was a more serious reason than Bervie was aware of, at the time, for the warning which he had thought it his duty to address to Percy Linwood. The new footman who had entered Mr Bowmore's service was a Spy.

Well practised in the infamous vocation that he followed, the wretch had been chosen, by the Department of Secret Service at the Home Office, to watch the proceedings of Mr Bowmore and his friends, and to report the result to his superiors. It may not be amiss to add that the employment of paid spies and informers, by the English Government of that time, was openly acknowledged in the House of Lords, and was defended as a necessary measure in the speeches of Lord Redesdale and Lord Liverpool.

The reports furnished by the Home Office Spy, under these circumstances, begin with the month of March, and take the form of a series of notes introduced as follows:

Mr Secretary:
Since I entered Mr Bowmore's service, I have the honour to inform you that my eyes and ears have been kept in a state of active observation; and I can further certify that my means of making myself useful in the future to my honourable employers are in no respect diminished. Not the slightest suspicion of my true character is felt by any person in the house.

FIRST NOTE
The young gentleman now on a visit to Mr Bowmore is, as you have been correctly informed, Mr Percy Linwood. Although he is engaged to be married to Miss Bowmore, he is not discreet enough to conceal a certain want of friendly feeling, on his part, towards her father. The young lady has noticed this, and has resented it. She accuses her lover of having allowed himself to be prejudiced against Mr Bowmore by some slanderous person unknown.

Mr Percy's clumsy defence of himself led (in my hearing) to a quarrel! Nothing but his prompt submission prevented the marriage engagement from being broken off.

'If you showed a want of confidence in Me' (I heard Miss Charlotte say), 'I might forgive it. But when you show a want of confidence in a man so noble as my father, I have no mercy on you.' After such an expression of filial sentiment as this, Mr Percy wisely took the readiest way of appealing to the lady's indulgence. The young man has a demand on Parliament for moneys due to his father's estate; and he pleased and flattered Miss Charlotte by asking Mr Bowmore to advise him as to the best means of asserting his claim. By way of advancing his political interests, Mr Bowmore introduced him to the local Hampden Club; and Miss Charlotte rewarded him with a generosity which must not be passed over in silence. Her lover was permitted to put an engagement ring on her finger, and to kiss her afterwards to his heart's content.

SECOND NOTE

Mr Percy has paid more visits to the Republican Club; and Justice Bervie (father of the Captain) has heard of it, and has written to his son. The result that might have been expected has followed. Captain Bervie announces his return to England, to exert his influence for political good against the influence of Mr Bowmore for political evil.

In the meanwhile, Mr Percy's claim has been brought before the House of Commons, and has been adjourned for further consideration in six months' time. Both the gentlemen are indignant – especially Mr Bowmore. He has called a meeting of the Club to consider his young friend's wrongs, and has proposed the election of Mr Percy as a member of that revolutionary society.

THIRD NOTE

Mr Percy has been elected. Captain Bervie has tried to awaken his mind to a sense of the danger that threatens him, if he persists in associating with his republican friends – and has utterly failed. Mr Bowmore and Mr Percy have made speeches at the Club, intended to force the latter gentleman's claim on the immediate attention of Government. Mr Bowmore's flow of frothy eloquence has its influence (as you know from our shorthand writers' previous reports) on thousands of ignorant people. As it seems to me, the reasons for at once putting this man in prison are beyond dispute. Whether it is desirable to include Mr Percy in the order of arrest, I must not venture to decide. Let me only hint that his seditious speech rivals the more elaborate efforts of Mr Bowmore himself.

So much for the present. I may now respectfully direct your attention to the future.

On the second of April next, the Club assembles a public meeting, 'in aid of British liberty,' in a field near Dartford. Mr Bowmore is to preside, and is to be escorted afterwards to Westminster Hall on his way to plead Mr Percy's cause, in his own person, before the House of Commons. He is quite serious in declaring that 'the minions of Government dare not touch a hair of his head.' Miss Charlotte agrees with her father. And Mr Percy agrees with Miss Charlotte. Such is the state of affairs at the house in which I am acting the part of domestic servant.

I enclose shorthand reports of the speeches recently delivered at the Hampden Club, and have the honour of waiting for further orders.

FOURTH NOTE

Your commands have reached me by this morning's post.

I immediately waited on Justice Bervie (in plain clothes, of course), and gave him your official letter, instructing me to arrest Mr Bowmore and Mr Percy Linwood.

The venerable magistrate hesitated.

He quite understood the necessity for keeping the arrest a strict secret, in the interests of Government. The only reluctance he felt in granting the warrant related to his son's intimate friend. But for the peremptory tone of your letter, I really believe he would have asked you to give Mr Percy time for consideration. Not being rash enough to proceed to such an extreme as this, he slily consulted the young man's interests by declining, on formal grounds, to date the warrant earlier than the second of April. Please note that my visit to him was paid at noon, on the thirty-first of March.

If the object of this delay (to which I was obliged to submit) is to offer a chance of escape to Mr Percy, the same chance necessarily includes Mr Bowmore, whose name is also in the warrant. Trust me to keep a watchful eye on both these gentlemen; especially on Mr Bowmore. He is the most dangerous man of the two, and the most likely, if he feels any suspicions, to slip through the fingers of the law.

I have also to report that I discovered three persons in the hall of Justice Bervie's house, as I went out.

One of them was his son, the Captain; one was his daughter, Miss Bervie; and the third was that smooth-tongued old soldier, Major Mulvany. If the escape of Mr Bowmore and Mr Linwood is in contemplation, mark my words: the persons whom I have just mentioned will be concerned in it – and perhaps Miss Charlotte herself as well. At present, she is entirely unsuspicious of any misfortune hanging over her head; her attention being absorbed in the preparation of her bridal finery. As an admirer myself of the fair sex, I must own that it seems hard on the girl to have her lover clapped into prison, before the wedding-day.

I will bring you word of the arrest myself. There will be plenty of time to catch the afternoon coach to London.

Here – unless something happens which it is impossible to foresee – my report may come to an end.

X THE ELOPEMENT

On the evening of the first of April, Mrs Bowmore was left alone with the servants. Mr Bowmore and Percy had gone out together to attend a special meeting of the Club. Shortly afterwards Miss Charlotte had left the cottage, under very extraordinary circumstances.

A few minutes only after the departure of her father and Percy, she received a letter, which appeared to cause her the most violent agitation. She said to Mrs Bowmore:

'Mamma, I must see Captain Bervie for a few minutes in private, on a matter of serious importance to all of us. He is waiting at the front gate, and he will come in if I show myself at the hall door.'

Upon this, Mrs Bowmore had asked for an explanation.

'There is no time for explanation,' was the only answer she received; 'I ask you to leave me for five minutes alone with the Captain.'

Mrs Bowmore still hesitated. Charlotte snatched up her garden hat, and declared wildly that she would go out to Captain Bervie, if she was not permitted to receive him at home. In the face of this declaration, Mrs Bowmore yielded, and left the room.

In a minute more the Captain made his appearance.

Although she had given way, Mrs Bowmore was not disposed to trust her daughter, without supervision, in the society of a man whom Charlotte herself had reviled as a slanderer and a false friend. She took up her position in the veranda outside the parlour, at a safe distance from one of the two windows of the room, which had been left partially open to admit the fresh air. Here she waited and listened.

The conversation was for some time carried on in whispers.

As they became more and more excited, both Charlotte and Bervie ended in unconsciously raising their voices.

'I swear it to you on my faith as a Christian!' Mrs Bowmore heard the Captain say. 'I declare before God who hears me that I am speaking the truth!'

And Charlotte had answered, with a burst of tears:

'I can't believe you! I daren't believe you! Oh, how can you ask me to do such a thing? Let me go! let me go!'

Alarmed at those words, Mrs Bowmore advanced to the window, and looked in.

Bervie had put her daughter's arm on his arm, and was trying to induce her to leave the parlour with him. She resisted, and implored him to release her. He dropped her arm, and whispered in her ear. She looked at him – and instantly made up her mind.

'Let me tell my mother where I am going,' she said; 'and I will consent.'

'Be it so!' he answered. 'And remember one thing; every minute is precious; the fewest words are the best.'

Mrs Bowmore re-entered the cottage by the adjoining room, and met them in the passage. In few words, Charlotte spoke.

'I must go at once to Justice Bervie's house. Don't be afraid, mamma! I know what I am about, and I know I am right.'

'Going to Justice Bervie's!' cried Mrs Bowmore, in the utmost extremity of astonishment. 'What will your father say, what will Percy think, when they come back from the Club?'

'My sister's carriage is waiting for me close by,' Bervie answered. 'It is entirely at Miss Bowmore's disposal. She can easily get back, if she wishes to keep her visit a secret, before Mr Bowmore and Mr Linwood return.'

He led her to the door as he spoke. She ran back, and kissed her mother tenderly. Mrs Bowmore called to them to wait.

'I daren't let you go,' she said to her daughter, 'without your father's leave!'

Charlotte seemed not to hear, the Captain seemed not to hear. They ran across the front garden, and through the gate – and were out of sight in less than a minute.

More than two hours passed; the sun sank below the horizon, and still there were no signs of Charlotte's return.

Feeling seriously uneasy, Mrs Bowmore crossed the room to ring the bell, and send the man-servant to Justice Bervie's house to hasten her daughter's return.

As she approached the fireplace, she was startled by a sound of stealthy footsteps in the hall, followed by a loud noise as of some heavy object that had dropped on the floor. She rang the bell violently, and opened the door of the parlour. At the same moment, the spy-footman passed her, running out, apparently in pursuit of somebody, at the top of his speed. She followed him, as rapidly as she could, across the little front garden, to the gate. Arrived in the road, she was in time to see him vault upon the luggage-board at the back of a post-chaise before the cottage, just as the postilion started the horses on their way to London. The spy saw Mrs Bowmore looking at him, and pointed, with an insolent nod of his head, first to the inside of the vehicle, and then over it to the high-road; signing to her that he designed to accompany the person in the post-chaise to the end of the journey.

Turning to go back, Mrs Bowmore saw her own bewilderment reflected in the faces of the two female servants, who had followed her out.

'Who can the footman be after, ma'am?' asked the cook. 'Do you think it's a thief?'

The housemaid pointed to the post-chaise, barely visible in the distance.

'Simpleton!' she said. 'Do thieves travel in that way? I wish my master had come back,' she proceeded, speaking to herself; 'I'm afraid there's something wrong.'

Mrs Bowmore, returning through the garden-gate, instantly stopped and looked at the woman.

'What makes you mention your master's name, Amelia, when you fear that something is wrong?' she asked.

Amelia changed colour, and looked confused.

'I am loath to alarm you, ma'am,' she said; 'and I can't rightly see what it is my duty to do.'

Mrs Bowmore's heart sank within her under the cruellest of all terrors, the terror of something unknown. 'Don't keep me in suspense,' she said faintly. 'Whatever it is, let me know it.'

She led the way back to the parlour. The housemaid followed her. The cook (declining to be left alone) followed the housemaid.

'It was something I heard early this afternoon, ma'am,' Amelia began. 'Cook happened to be busy—'

The cook interposed: she had not forgiven the housemaid for calling her a simpleton. 'No, Amelia, if you *must* bring me into it – not busy. Uneasy in my mind on the subject of the soup.'

'I don't know that your mind makes much difference,' Amelia resumed. 'What it comes to is this – it was I, and not you, who went into the kitchen-garden for the vegetables.'

'Not by *my* wish, Heaven knows!' persisted the cook.

'Leave the room!' said Mrs Bowmore. Even her patience had given way at last.

The cook looked as if she declined to believe her own ears. Mrs Bowmore pointed to the door. The cook said 'Oh?' – accenting it as a question. Mrs Bowmore's finger still pointed. The cook, in solemn silence, yielded to circumstances, and banged the door.

'I was getting the vegetables, ma'am,' Amelia proceeded, 'when I heard voices on the other side of the paling. The wood is so old that one can see through the cracks easy enough. I saw my master, and Mr Linwood, and Captain Bervie. The Captain seemed to have stopped the other two on the pathway that leads to the field; he stood, as it might be, between them and the back way to the house – and he spoke severely, that he did!'

'What did Captain Bervie say?'

'He said these words, ma'am: "For the last time, Mr Bowmore," says he, "will you understand that you are in danger, and that Mr Linwood is in danger, unless you both leave this neighbourhood to-night?" My master made light of it. "For the last time," says he, "will you refer us to a proof of what you say, and allow us to judge for ourselves?" "I have told you already," says the Captain, "I am bound by my duty towards another person to keep what I know a secret." "Very well," says my master, "*I* am bound by my duty to my country. And I tell you this," says he, in his high and mighty way, "neither Government, nor the spies of Government, dare touch a hair of my head: they know it, sir, for the head of the people's friend!'"

'That's quite true,' said Mrs Bowmore, still believing in her husband as firmly as ever.

Amelia went on:

'Captain Bervie didn't seem to think so,' she said. 'He lost his temper. "What stuff!" says he; "there's a Government spy in your house at this moment, disguised as your footman." My master looked at Mr Linwood, and burst out laughing. "You won't beat that, Captain," says he, "if you talk till doomsday." He turned about without a word more, and went home. The Captain caught Mr Linwood by the arm, as soon as they were alone. "For God's sake," says he, "don't follow that madman's example!"'

Mrs Bowmore was shocked. 'Did he really call my husband a madman?' she asked.

'He did indeed, ma'am – and he was in earnest about it too. "If you value your liberty," he says to Mr Linwood; "if you hope to become Charlotte's husband, consult your own safety. I can give you a passport. Escape to France and wait till this trouble is over." Mr Linwood was not in the best of tempers – Mr Linwood shook him off. "Charlotte's father will soon be my father," says he; "do you think I will desert him? My friends at the Club have taken up my claim; do you think I will forsake them at the meeting to-morrow? You ask me to be unworthy of Charlotte, and unworthy of my friends – you insult me, if you say more." He whipped round on his heel, and followed my master.'

'And what did the Captain do?'

'Lifted up his hands, ma'am, to the heavens, and looked – I declare it turned my blood to see him. If there's truth in mortal man, it's my firm belief—'

What the housemaid's belief was, remained unexpressed. Before she could get to her next word, a shriek of horror from the hall announced that the cook's powers of interruption were not exhausted yet.

Mistress and servant both hurried out, in terror of they knew not what. There stood the cook, alone in the hall, confronting the stand on which the overcoats and hats of the men of the family were placed.

'Where's the master's travelling-coat?' cried the cook, staring wildly at an unoccupied peg. 'And where's his cap to match? Oh Lord, he's off in the post-chaise! and the footman's after him!'

Simpleton as she was, the woman had blundered on a very serious discovery.

Coat and cap – both made after a foreign pattern, and both strikingly remarkable in form and colour to English eyes – had unquestionably disappeared. It was equally certain that they were well known to the footman, whom the Captain had declared to be a spy, as the coat and cap which his master used in travelling. Had Mr Bowmore discovered (since the afternoon) that he was really in danger? Had the necessities of instant flight only allowed him time enough to snatch his coat and cap out of the hall? And had the treacherous man-servant seen him as he was making his escape to the post-chaise? The cook's conclusion answered all these questions in the affirmative – and, if Captain Bervie's words of warning had been correctly reported, the cook's conclusion for once was not to be despised.

Under this last trial of her fortitude, Mrs Bowmore's feeble reserves of endurance completely gave way. The poor lady turned faint and giddy. Amelia placed her on a chair in the hall, and told the cook to open the front door, and let in the fresh air.

The cook obeyed; and instantly broke out with a second terrific scream; announcing nothing less, this time, than the appearance of Mr Bowmore himself, alive and hearty, returning with Percy from the meeting at the Club!

The inevitable enquiries and explanations followed.

Fully assured, as he had declared himself to be, of the sanctity of his person (politically speaking), Mr Bowmore turned pale, nevertheless, when he looked at the unoccupied peg on his clothes stand. Had some man unknown personated him? And had a post-chaise been hired to lead an impending pursuit of him in the wrong direction? What did it mean? Who was the friend to whose services he was indebted? As for the proceedings of the man-servant, but one interpretation could now be placed on them. They distinctly justified what Captain Bervie had said of him. Mr Bowmore thought of the Captain's other assertion, relating to the urgent necessity for making his escape; and looked at Percy in silent dismay; and turned paler than ever.

Percy's thoughts, diverted for the moment only from the lady of his love, returned to her with renewed fidelity. 'Let us hear what Charlotte thinks of it,' he said. 'Where is she?'

It was impossible to answer this question plainly and in few words.

Terrified at the effect which her attempt at explanation produced on Percy, helplessly ignorant when she was called upon to account for her daughter's absence, Mrs Bowmore could only shed tears and express a devout trust in Providence. Her husband looked at the new misfortune from a political point of view. He sat down, and slapped his forehead theatrically with the palm of his hand. 'Thus far,' said the patriot, 'my political assailants have only struck at me through the newspapers. *Now* they strike at me through my child!'

Percy made no speeches. There was a look in his eyes which boded ill for Captain Bervie if the two met. 'I am going to fetch her,' was all he said, 'as fast as a horse can carry me.'

He hired his horse at an inn in the town, and set forth for Justice Bervie's house at a gallop.

During Percy's absence, Mr Bowmore secured the front and back entrances to the cottage with his own hands.

These first precautions taken, he ascended to his room, and packed his travelling-bag. 'Necessaries for my use in prison,' he remarked. 'The bloodhounds of Government are after me.' 'Are they after Percy, too?' his wife ventured to ask. Mr Bowmore looked up impatiently, and cried 'Pooh!' – as if Percy was of no consequence. Mrs Bowmore thought otherwise: the good woman privately packed a bag for Percy, in the sanctuary of her own room.

For an hour, and more than an hour, no event of any sort occurred.

Mr Bowmore stalked up and down the parlour, meditating. At intervals, ideas of flight presented themselves attractively to his mind. At intervals, ideas of the speech that he had prepared for the public meeting on the next day took their place. 'If I fly to-night,' he wisely observed, 'what will become of my speech? I will *not* fly to-night! The people shall hear me.'

He sat down, and crossed his arms fiercely. As he looked at his wife to see what effect he had produced on her, the sound of heavy carriage-wheels and the trampling of horses penetrated to the parlour from the garden-gate.

Mr Bowmore started to his feet, with every appearance of having suddenly altered his mind on the question of flight. Just as he reached the hall, Percy's voice was heard at the front-door. 'Let me in. Instantly! Instantly!'

Mrs Bowmore drew back the bolts, before the servants could help her. 'Where is Charlotte?' she cried; seeing Percy alone on the doorstep.

'Gone!' Percy answered furiously. 'Eloped to Paris, with Captain Bervie! Read her own confession. They were just sending the messenger with it, when I reached the house.'

He handed a note to Mrs Bowmore, and turned aside to speak to her husband while she read it. Charlotte wrote to her mother very briefly; promising to explain everything on her return. In the meantime, she had left home under careful protection – she had a lady for her companion on the journey – and she would write again from Paris. So the letter, evidently written in great haste, began and ended.

Percy took Mr Bowmore to the window, and pointed to a carriage and four horses waiting at the garden-gate.

'Do you come with me, and back me with your authority as her father?' he asked sternly. 'Or do you leave me to go alone?'

Mr Bowmore was famous among his admirers for his 'happy replies.' He made one now.

'I am not Brutus,' he said. 'I am only Bowmore. My daughter before everything. Fetch my travelling-bag.'

While the travellers' bags were being placed in the chaise, Mr Bowmore was struck by an idea.

He produced from his coat-pocket a roll of many papers thickly covered with writing. On the blank leaf in which they were tied up, he wrote in the largest letters: 'Frightful domestic calamity! Vice-President Bowmore obliged to leave England! Welfare of a beloved daughter! His speech will be read at the meeting by Secretary Joskin, of the Club. (Private to Joskin. Have these lines printed and posted everywhere. And, when you read my speech, for God's sake don't drop your voice at the ends of the sentences.)'

He threw down the pen, and embraced Mrs Bowmore in the most summary manner. The poor woman was ordered to send the roll of paper to the Club, without a word to comfort and sustain her from her husband's lips. Percy spoke to her hopefully and kindly, as he kissed her cheek at parting.

On the next morning, a letter, addressed to Mrs Bowmore, was delivered at the cottage by private messenger.

Opening the letter, she recognised the handwriting of her husband's old friend, and her old friend – Major Mulvany. In breathless amazement, she read these lines:

Dear Mrs Bowmore:
In matters of importance, the golden rule is never to waste words.

I have performed one of the great actions of my life – I have saved your husband.

How I discovered that my friend was in danger, I must not tell you at present. Let it be enough if I say that I have been a guest under Justice Bervie's hospitable roof, and that I know of a Home Office spy who has taken you unawares under pretence of being your footman. If I had not circumvented him, the scoundrel would have imprisoned your husband, and another dear friend of mine. This is how I did it.

I must begin by appealing to your memory.

Do you happen to remember that your husband and I are as near as may be of about the same height? Very good, so far. Did you, in the next place, miss Bowmore's travelling coat and cap from their customary peg? I am the thief, dearest lady; I put them on my own humble self. Did you hear a sudden noise in the hall? Oh, forgive me – I made the noise! And it did just what I wanted of it. It brought the spy up from the kitchen, suspecting that something might be wrong.

What did the wretch see when he got into the hall? His master, in travelling costume, running out. What did he find when he reached the garden? His master escaping, in a post-chaise, on the road to London. What did he do, the born blackguard that he was? Jumped up behind the chaise, to make sure of his prisoner. It was dark when we got to London. In a hop, skip, and jump, I was out of the carriage, and in at my own door, before he could look me in the face.

The date of the warrant, you must know, obliged him to wait till the morning. All that night, he and the Bow Street runners kept watch. They came in with the sunrise – and who did they find? Major Mulvany snug in his bed, and as innocent as the babe unborn. Oh, they did their duty! Searched the place from the kitchen to the garrets – and gave it up. There's but one thing I regret – I let the spy off without a good thrashing. No matter. I'll do it yet, one of these days.

Let me know the first good news of our darling fugitives, and I shall be more than rewarded for what little I have done.

Your always devoted,

TERENCE MULVANY

XI PURSUIT AND DISCOVERY

Feeling himself hurried away on the road to Dover, as fast as four horses could carry him, Mr Bowmore had leisure to criticise Percy's conduct, from his own purely selfish point of view.

'If you had listened to my advice,' he said, 'you would have treated that man Bervie like the hypocrite and villain that he is. But no! you trusted to your own crude impressions. Having given him your hand after the duel (I would have given him the contents of my pistol!) you hesitated to withdraw it again, when that slanderer appealed to your friendship not to cast him off. Now you see the consequence!'

'Wait till we get to Paris!' All the ingenuity of Percy's travelling companion failed to extract from him any other answer than that.

Foiled so far, Mr Bowmore began to start difficulties next. Had they money enough for the journey? Percy touched his pocket, and answered shortly, 'Plenty.' Had they passports? Percy sullenly showed a letter. 'There is the necessary voucher from a magistrate,' he said. 'The consul at Dover will give us our passports. Mind this!' he added, in warning tones, 'I have pledged my word of honour to Justice Bervie, that we have no political object in view in travelling to France. Keep your politics to yourself, on the other side of the Channel.'

Mr Bowmore listened in blank amazement.

Charlotte's lover was appearing in a new character – the character of a man who had lost his respect for Charlotte's father!

It was useless to talk to him. He deliberately checked any further attempts at conversation, by leaning back in the carriage, and closing his eyes. The truth is, Mr Bowmore's own language and conduct were insensibly producing the salutary impression on Percy's mind, which Bervie had vainly tried to convey, under the disadvantage of having Charlotte's influence against him. Throughout the journey, Percy did exactly what Bervie had once entreated him to do – he kept Mr Bowmore at a distance.

At every stage, they inquired after the fugitives. At every stage, they were answered by a more or less intelligible description of Bervie and Charlotte, and of the lady who accompanied them. No disguise had been attempted; no person had in any case been bribed to conceal the truth.

When the first tumult of his emotions had in some degree subsided, this strange circumstance associated itself in Percy's mind with the equally unaccountable conduct of Justice Bervie, on his arrival at the manor house.

The old gentleman met his visitor in the hall, without expressing, and apparently without feeling, any indignation at his son's conduct. It was even useless to appeal to him for information. He only said, 'I am not in Arthur's confidence; he is of age, and my daughter (who has volunteered to accompany him) is of age. I have no claim to control them. I believe they have taken Miss Bowmore to Paris; and that is all I know about it.'

He had shown the same dense insensibility in giving his official voucher for the passports. Percy had only to satisfy him on the question of politics; and the document was drawn out as a matter of course. Such had been the father's behaviour; and the conduct of the son now exhibited the same shameless composure. To what conclusion did this discovery point? Percy abandoned the attempt to answer that question in despair.

They reached Dover towards two o'clock in the morning.

At the pier-head they found a coast-guardsman on duty, and received more information.

In 1817 the communication with France was still by sailing-vessels. Arriving long after the departure of the regular packet, Bervie had hired a lugger, and had sailed with the two ladies for Calais, having a fresh breeze in his favour. Percy's first angry impulse was to follow him instantly. The next moment he remembered the insurmountable obstacle of the passports. The Consul would certainly not grant those essentially necessary documents at two in the morning!

The only alternative was to wait for the regular packet, which sailed some hours later – between eight and nine o'clock in the forenoon. In this case, they might apply for their passports before the regular office hours, if they explained the circumstances, backed by the authority of the magistrate's letter.

Mr Bowmore followed Percy to the nearest inn that was open, sublimely indifferent to the delays and difficulties of the journey. He ordered refreshments with the air of a man who was performing a melancholy duty to himself, in the name of humanity.

'When I think of my speech,' he said, at supper, 'my heart bleeds for the people. In a few hours more, they will assemble in their thousands, eager to hear me. And what will they see? Joskin in my place! Joskin with a manuscript in his hand! Joskin, who drops his voice at the ends of his sentences! I will never forgive Charlotte. Waiter, another glass of brandy and water.'

After an unusually quick passage across the Channel, the travellers landed on the French coast, before the defeated spy had returned from London to Dartford by stage-coach. Continuing their journey by post as far as Amiens, they reached that city in time to take their places by the diligence to Paris.

Arrived in Paris, they encountered another incomprehensible proceeding on the part of Captain Bervie.

Among the persons assembled in the yard to see the arrival of the diligence was a man with a morsel of paper in his hand, evidently on the look-out for some person whom he expected to discover among the travellers. After consulting his bit of paper, he looked with steady attention at Percy and Mr Bowmore, and suddenly approached them. 'If you wish to see the Captain,' he said, in broken English, 'you will find him at that hotel.' He handed a printed card to Percy, and disappeared among the crowd before it was possible to question him.

Even Mr Bowmore gave way to human weakness, and condescended to feel astonished in the face of such an event as this. 'What next!' he exclaimed.

'Wait till we get to the hotel,' said Percy.

In half an hour more the landlord had received them, and the waiter had led them to the right door. Percy pushed the man aside, and burst into the room.

Captain Bervie was alone, reading a newspaper. Before the first furious words had escaped Percy's lips, Bervie silenced him by pointing to a closed door on the right of the fireplace.

'She is in that room,' he said; 'speak quietly, or you may frighten her. I know what you are going to say,' he added, as Percy stepped nearer to him. 'Will you hear me in my own defence, and then decide whether I am the greatest scoundrel living, or the best friend you ever had?'

He put the question kindly, with something that was at once grave and tender in his look and manner. The extraordinary composure with which he acted and spoke had its tranquillising influence over Percy. He felt himself surprised into giving Bervie a hearing.

'I will tell you first what I have done,' the Captain proceeded, 'and next why I did it. I have taken it on myself, Mr Linwood, to make an alteration in your wedding arrangements. Instead of being married at Dartford church, you will be married (if you see no objection) at the chapel of the embassy in Paris, by my old college friend the chaplain.'

This was too much for Percy's self-control. 'Your audacity is beyond belief,' he broke out.

'And beyond endurance,' Mr Bowmore added. 'Understand this, sir! Whatever your defence may be, I object, under any circumstances, to be made the victim of a trick.'

'You are the victim of your own obstinate refusal to profit by a plain warning,' Bervie rejoined. 'At the eleventh hour, I entreated you, and I entreated Mr Linwood, to provide for your own safety; and I spoke in vain.'

Percy's patience gave way once more.

'To use your own language,' he said, 'I have still to decide whether you have behaved towards me like a scoundrel or a friend. You have said nothing to justify yourself yet.'

'Very well put!' Mr Bowmore chimed in. 'Come to the point, sir! My daughter's reputation is in question.'

'Miss Bowmore's reputation is not in question for a single instant,' Bervie answered. 'My sister has been the companion of her journey from first to last.'

'Journey?' Mr Bowmore repeated indignantly. 'I want to know, sir, what the journey means. As an outraged father, I ask one plain question. Why did you run away with my daughter?'

Bervie took a slip of paper from his pocket, and handed it to Percy with a smile.

It was a copy of the warrant which Justice Bervie's duty had compelled him to issue for the 'arrest of Orlando Bowmore and Percy Linwood.' There was no danger in divulging the secret now. British warrants were waste-paper in France, in those days.

'I ran away with the bride,' Bervie said coolly, 'in the certain knowledge that you and Mr Bowmore would run after me. If I had not forced you both to follow me out of England on the first of April, you would have been made State prisoners on the second. What do you say to my conduct now?'

'Wait, Percy, before you answer him,' Mr Bowmore interposed. 'He is ready enough at excusing himself. But, observe – he hasn't a word to say in justification of my daughter's readiness to run away with him.'

'Have you quite done?' Bervie asked as quietly as ever.

Mr Bowmore reserved the right of all others which he most prized, the right of using his tongue. 'For the present,' he answered in his loftiest manner, 'I have done.'

Bervie proceeded: 'Your daughter consented to run away with me, because I took her to my father's house, and prevailed upon him to trust her with the secret of the coming arrests. She had no choice left but to let her obstinate father and her misguided lover go to prison – or to take her place with my sister and me in the travelling-carriage.' He appealed once more to Percy. 'My friend, you remember the day when you spared my life. Have I remembered it, too?'

For once, there was an Englishman who was not contented to express the noblest emotions that humanity can feel by the commonplace ceremony of shaking hands. Percy's heart overflowed. In an outburst of unutterable gratitude he threw himself on Bervie's breast. As brothers the two men embraced. As brothers they loved and trusted one another, from that day forth.

The door on the right was softly opened from within. A charming face – the dark eyes bright with happy tears, the rosy lips just opening into a smile – peeped into the room. A low sweet voice, with an under-note of trembling in it, made this modest protest, in the form of an inquiry:

'When you have quite done, Percy, with our good friend, perhaps you will have something to say to ME?'

LAST WORDS

The persons immediately interested in the marriage of Percy and Charlotte were the only persons present at the ceremony.

At the little breakfast afterwards, in the French hotel, Mr Bowmore insisted on making a speech to a select audience of six – namely the bride and bridegroom, the bridesmaid, the Chaplain, the Captain, and Mrs Bowmore. But what does a small audience matter? The English frenzy for making speeches is not to be cooled by such a trifle as that. At the end of the world, the expiring forces of Nature will hear a dreadful voice – the voice of the last Englishman delivering the last speech.

Percy wisely made his honeymoon a long one; he determined to be quite sure of his superior influence over his wife, before he trusted her within reach of her father again.

Mr and Mrs Bowmore accompanied Captain Bervie and Miss Bervie on their way back to England, as far as Boulogne. In that pleasant town, the banished patriot set up his tent. It was a cheaper place to live in than Paris, and it was conveniently close to England, when he had quite made up his mind whether to be an exile on the Continent, or to go back to his own country and be a martyr in prison. In the end, the course of events settled that question for him. Mr Bowmore returned to England, with the return of the Habeas Corpus Act.

The years passed. Percy and Charlotte (judged from the romantic point of view) became two uninteresting married people. Bervie (always remaining a bachelor) rose steadily in his profession, through the higher grades of military rank. Mr Bowmore, wisely overlooked by a new Government, sank back again into the obscurity from which shrewd Ministers would never have assisted him to emerge. The one subject of interest left, among the persons of this little drama, was now represented by Doctor Lagarde. Thus far, not a trace had been discovered of the French physician, who had so strangely associated the visions of his magnetic sleep with the destinies of the two men who had consulted him.

Steadfastly maintaining his own opinion of the prediction and the fulfilment, Bervie persisted in believing that he and Lagarde (or Percy and Lagarde) were yet destined to meet, and resume the unfinished consultation at the point where it had been broken off. Persons, happy in the possession of 'sound common sense,' who declared the prediction to be skilled guess-work, and the fulfilment manifest coincidence, ridiculed the idea of finding Doctor Lagarde as closely akin to that other celebrated idea of finding the needle in the bottle of hay. But Bervie's obstinacy was proverbial. Nothing shook his confidence in his own convictions.

More than thirteen years had elapsed since the consultation at the Doctor's lodgings, when Bervie went to Paris to spend a summer holiday with his friend, the chaplain to the English embassy. His last words to Percy and Charlotte when he took his leave were: 'Suppose I meet with Doctor Lagarde?'

It was then the year 1830. Bervie arrived at his friend's rooms on the 24th of July. On the 27th of the month, the famous revolution broke out which dethroned Charles the Tenth in three days.

On the second day, Bervie and his host ventured into the streets, watching the revolution (like other reckless Englishmen) at the risk of their lives. In the confusion around them, they were separated. Bervie, searching for his companion, found his progress stopped by a barricade, which had been desperately attacked, and desperately defended. Men in blouses and men in uniform lay dead and dying together: the tricoloured flag waved over them, in token of the victory of the people.

Bervie had just revived a poor wretch with a drink from an overthrown bowl of water, which still had a few drops left in it, when he felt a hand laid on his shoulder from behind. He turned and discovered a National Guard, who had been watching his charitable action. 'Give a helping hand to that poor fellow,' said the citizen-soldier, pointing to a workman standing near, grimed with blood and gunpowder. The tears were rolling down the man's cheeks. 'I can't see my way, sir, for crying,' he said. 'Help me to carry that sad burden into the next street.' He pointed to a rude wooden litter, on which lay a dead or wounded man, his face and breast covered with an old cloak. 'There is the best friend the people ever had,' the workman said. 'He cured us, comforted us, respected us, loved us. And there he lies, shot dead while he was binding up the wounds of friends and enemies alike!'

'Whoever he is, he has died nobly,' Bervie answered. 'May I look at him?'

The workman signed that he might look.

Bervie lifted the cloak – and met with Doctor Lagarde once more.

Miss Bertha and the Yankee

[Preliminary Statements of Witnesses for the Defence, Collected at the Office of the Solicitor]

Originally appeared in *The Spirit of the Times*, 22 December 1877 as 'The Duel in Herne Wood'. Reprinted in *Little Novels* (1887). This is the third story the ailing Wilkie Collins had produced in 1877, and depends on a condensation of the duel plot from 'Mr Percy and the Prophet'. Catherine Peters has remarked that 'it almost seems a self-plagiarism' (*The King of Inventors*, p.382). Once again there are echoes of 'Mad Monkton', but the mixture of duelling and insanity also perhaps owes something to Tennyson's *Maud*. Collins was again to use duelling as a mechanism in his novel *The Black Robe* (1881), where the neurotic husband is beset by feelings of remorse for the man he has killed.

I

No. 1 – Miss Bertha Laroche, of Nettlegrove Hall, testifies and says:

Towards the middle of June, in the year 1817, I went to take the waters at Maplesworth, in Derbyshire, accompanied by my nearest living relative – my aunt.

I am an only child; and I was twenty-one years old at my last birthday. On coming of age I inherited a house and lands in Derbyshire, together with a fortune in money of one hundred thousand pounds. The only education which I have received has been obtained within the last two or three years of my life; and I have thus far seen nothing of Society, in England or in any other civilized part of the world. I can be a competent witness, it seems, in spite of these disadvantages. Anyhow, I mean to tell the truth.

My father was a French colonist in the island of Saint Domingo. He died while I was very young; leaving to my mother and to me just enough to live on, in the remote part of the island in which our little property was situated. My mother was an Englishwoman. Her delicate health made it necessary for her to leave me, for many hours of the day, under the care of our household slaves. I can never forget their kindness to me; but, unfortunately, their ignorance equalled their kindness. If we had been rich enough to send to France or England for a competent governess we might have done very well. But we were not rich enough. I am ashamed to say that I was nearly thirteen years old before I had learnt to read and write correctly.

Four more years passed – and then there came a wonderful event in our lives, which was nothing less than the change from Saint Domingo to England.

My mother was distantly related to an ancient and wealthy English family. She seriously offended these proud people by marrying an obscure foreigner, who had nothing to live on but his morsel of land in the West Indies. Having no expectations from her relatives, my mother preferred happiness with the man she loved to every other consideration; and I, for one, think she was right. From that moment she was cast off by the head of the family. For eighteen years of her life, as wife, mother, and widow, no letters came to her from her English home. We had just celebrated my seventeenth birthday when the first letter came. It informed my mother that no less than three lives, which stood between her and the inheritance of certain portions of the family property, had been swept away by death. The estate and the fortune which I have already mentioned had fallen to her in due course of law, and her surviving relatives were magnanimously ready to forgive her at last!

We wound up our affairs at Saint Domingo, and we went to England to take possession of our new wealth.

At first, the return to her native air seemed to have a beneficial effect on my mother's health. But it was a temporary improvement only. Her constitution had been fatally injured by the West Indian climate, and just as we had engaged a competent person to look after my neglected education, my constant attendance was needed at my mother's bedside. We loved each other dearly, and we wanted no strange nurses to come between us. My aunt (my mother's sister) relieved me of my cares in the intervals when I wanted rest.

For seven sad months our dear sufferer lingered. I have only one remembrance to comfort me; my mother's last kiss was mine – she died peacefully with her head on my bosom.

I was nearly nineteen years old before I had sufficiently rallied my courage to be able to think seriously of myself and my prospects.

At that age one does not willingly submit one's self for the first time to the authority of a governess. Having my aunt for a companion and protectress, I proposed to engage my own masters and to superintend my own education.

My plans failed to meet with the approval of the head of the family. He declared (most unjustly, as the event proved) that my aunt was not a fit person to take care of me. She had passed all the later years of her life in retirement. A good creature, he admitted, in her own way, but she had no knowledge of the world and no firmness of character. The right person to act as my chaperon, and to superintend my education, was the high-minded and accomplished woman who had taught his own daughters.

I declined, with all needful gratitude and respect, to take his advice. The bare idea of living with a stranger so soon after my mother's death revolted me. Besides, I liked my aunt and my aunt liked me. Being made acquainted with my decision, the head of the family cast me off, exactly as he had cast off my mother before me.

So I lived in retirement with my good aunt, and studied industriously to improve my mind until my twenty-first birthday came. I was now an heiress, privileged to think and act for myself. My aunt kissed me tenderly. We talked of my poor mother, and we cried in each other's arms on the memorable day which made a wealthy woman of me. In a little time more, other troubles than vain regrets for the dead were to try me, and other tears were to fill my eyes than the tears which I had given to the memory of my mother.

II

I may now return to my visit, in June, 1817, to the healing springs at Maplesworth.

This famous inland watering-place was only between nine and ten miles from my new home called Nettlegrove Hall. I had been feeling weak and out of spirits for some months, and our medical adviser recommended change of scene and a trial of the waters at Maplesworth. My aunt and I established ourselves in comfortable apartments, with a letter of introduction to the chief doctor in the place. This otherwise harmless and worthy man proved, strangely enough, to be the innocent cause of the trials and troubles which beset me at the outset of my new life.

The day after we had presented our letter of introduction, we met the doctor on the public walk. He was accompanied by two strangers, both young men, and both (so far as my ignorant opinion went) persons of some distinction, judging by their dress and manners. The doctor said a few kind words to us, and rejoined his two companions. Both the gentlemen looked at me, and both took off their hats as my aunt and I proceeded on our walk.

I own I thought occasionally of the well-bred strangers during the rest of the day, especially of the shortest of the two, who was also the handsomest of the two to my thinking. If this confession seems rather a bold one, remember, if you please, that I had never been taught to conceal my feelings at Saint Domingo, and that the events which followed our arrival in England had kept me completely secluded from the society of other young ladies of my age.

The next day, while I was drinking my glass of healing water (extremely nasty water, by the way), the doctor joined us.

While he was asking me about my health, the two strangers made their appearance again, and took off their hats again. They both looked expectantly at the doctor, and the doctor (in performance of a promise which he had already made, as I privately suspected) formally introduced them to my aunt and to me. First (I put the handsomest man first) Captain Arthur Stanwick, of the army, home from India on leave, and staying at Maplesworth to take the waters; secondly, Mr Lionel Varleigh, of Boston, in America, visiting England, after travelling all over Europe, and stopping at Maplesworth to keep company with his friend the Captain.

On their introduction, the two gentlemen, observing, no doubt, that I was a little shy, forbore delicately from pressing their society on us.

Captain Stanwick, with a beautiful smile, and with teeth worthy of the smile, stroked his whiskers, and asked me if I had found any benefit from taking the waters. He afterwards spoke in great praise of the charming scenery in the neighbourhood of Maplesworth, and then turning away, addressed his next words to my aunt. Mr Varleigh took his place. Speaking with perfect gravity, and with no whiskers to stroke, he said:

'I have once tried the waters here out of curiosity. I can sympathize, Miss, with the expression which I observed on your face when you emptied your glass just now. Permit me to offer you something nice to take the taste of the waters out of your mouth.' He produced from his pocket a beautiful little box filled with sugar-plums. 'I bought it in Paris,' he explained. 'Having lived a good deal in France, I have got into a habit of making little presents of this sort to ladies and children. I wouldn't let the doctor see it, Miss, if I were you. He has the usual medical prejudice against sugar-plums.' With that quaint warning he, too, made his bow and discreetly withdrew.

Thinking it over afterwards, I acknowledged to myself that the English Captain – although he was the handsomest man of the two, and possessed the smoothest manners – had failed, nevertheless, to overcome my shyness. The American traveller's unaffected sincerity and good-humour, on the other hand, set me quite at my ease. I could look at him and thank him, and feel amused at his sympathy with the grimace I had made, after swallowing the illflavoured waters. And yet, while I lay awake at night, wondering whether we should meet our new acquaintances on the next day, it was the English Captain that I most wanted to see again, and not the American traveller! At the time, I set this down to nothing more important than my own perversity. Ah, dear! dear! I know better than that now.

The next morning brought the doctor to our hotel on a special visit to my aunt. He invented a pretext for sending me into the next room, which was so plainly a clumsy excuse, that my curiosity was aroused. I gratified my curiosity. Must I make my confession plainer still? Must I acknowledge that I was mean enough to listen on the other side of the door?

I heard my dear innocent old aunt say, 'Doctor! I hope you don't see anything alarming in the state of Bertha's health?'

The doctor burst out laughing. 'My dear Madam! there is nothing in the state of the young lady's health which need cause the smallest anxiety to you or to me. The object of my visit is to justify myself for presenting those two gentlemen to you yesterday. They are both greatly struck by Miss Bertha's beauty, and they both urgently entreated me to introduce them. Such introductions, I need hardly say, are marked exceptions to my general rule. In ninety-nine cases out of a hundred I should have said No. In the cases of Captain Stanwick and Mr Varleigh, however, I saw no reason to hesitate. Permit me to assure you that I am not intruding on your notice two fortune-hunting adventurers. They are both men of position and men of property. The family of the Stanwicks has been well known to me for years; and Mr Varleigh brought me a letter from my oldest living friend, answering for him as a gentleman in the highest sense of the word. He is the wealthiest man of the two; and it speaks volumes for him, in my opinion, that he has preserved his simplicity of character after a long residence in such places as Paris and Vienna. Captain Stanwick has more polish and ease of manner, but, looking under the surface, I rather fancy there may be something a little impetuous and domineering in his temper. However, we all have our faults. I can only say, for both these young friends of mine, that you need feel no scruple about admitting them to your intimacy, if they happen to please you – and your niece. Having now, I hope, removed any doubts which may have troubled you, pray recall Miss Bertha. I am afraid I have interrupted you in discussing your plans for the day.'

The smoothly eloquent doctor paused for the moment; and I darted away from the door.

Our plans for the day included a drive through the famous scenery near the town. My two admirers met us on horseback. Here, again, the Captain had the advantage over his friend. His seat in the saddle and his riding-dress were both perfect things in their way. The Englishman rode on one side of the carriage and the American on the other. They both talked well, but Mr Varleigh had seen more of the world in general than Captain Stanwick, and he made himself certainly the most interesting and most amusing companion of the two.

On our way back my admiration was excited by a thick wood, beautifully situated on rising ground at a little distance from the high-road. 'Oh, dear,' I said, 'how I should like to take a walk in that wood!' Idle thoughtless words; but, oh, what remembrances crowd on me as I think of them now!

Captain Stanwick and Mr Varleigh at once dismounted and offered themselves as my escort. The coachman warned them to be careful; people had often lost themselves, he said, in that wood. I asked the name of it. The name was Herne Wood. My aunt was not very willing to leave her comfortable seat in the carriage, but it ended in her going with us.

Before we entered the wood, Mr Varleigh noted the position of the high-road by his pocket-compass. Captain Stanwick laughed at him, and offered me his arm. Ignorant as I was of the ways of the world and the rules of coquetry, my instinct (I suppose) warned me not to distinguish one of the gentlemen too readily at the expense of the other. I took my aunt's arm and settled it in that way.

A winding path led us into the wood.

On a nearer view, the place disappointed me; the farther we advanced, the more horribly gloomy it grew. The thickly-growing trees shut out the light;

the damp stole over me little by little until I shivered; the undergrowth of bushes and thickets rustled at intervals mysteriously, as some invisible creeping creature passed through it. At a turn in the path we reached a sort of clearing, and saw the sky and the sunshine once more. But, even here, a disagreeable incident occurred. A snake wound his undulating way across the open space, passing close by me, and I was fool enough to scream. The Captain killed the creature with his riding-cane, taking a pleasure in doing it which I did not like to see.

We left the clearing and tried another path, and then another. And still the horrid wood preyed on my spirits. I agreed with my aunt that we should do well to return to the carriage. On our way back we missed the right path, and lost ourselves for the moment. Mr Varleigh consulted his compass, and pointed in one direction. Captain Stanwick, consulting nothing but his own jealous humour, pointed in the other. We followed Mr Varleigh's guidance, and got back to the clearing. He turned to the Captain, and said good-humouredly, 'You see the compass was right.' Captain Stanwick answered sharply, 'There are more ways than one out of an English wood; you talk as if we were in one of your American forests.'

Mr Varleigh seemed to be at a loss to understand his rudeness: there was a pause. The two men looked at each other, standing face to face on the brown earth of the clearing – the Englishman's ruddy countenance, light auburn hair and whiskers, and well-opened bold blue eyes, contrasting with the pale complexion, the keenly-observant look, the dark closely-cut hair, and the delicately-lined face of the American. It was only for a moment: I had barely time to feel uneasy before they controlled themselves and led us back to the carriage, talking as pleasantly as if nothing had happened. For days afterwards, nevertheless, that scene in the clearing – the faces and figures of the two men, the dark line of trees hemming them in on all sides, the brown circular patch of ground on which they stood – haunted my memory, and got in the way of my brighter and happier thoughts. When my aunt inquired if I had enjoyed the day, I surprised her by saying, No. And when she asked why, I could only answer, 'It was all spoilt by Herne Wood.'

III

Three weeks passed.

The terror of those dreadful days creeps over me again when I think of them. I mean to tell the truth without shrinking; but I may at least consult my own feelings by dwelling on certain particulars as briefly as I can. I shall describe my conduct towards the two men who courted me, in the plainest terms, if I say that I distinguished neither of them. Innocently and stupidly I encouraged them both.

In books, women are generally represented as knowing their own minds in matters which relate to love and marriage. This is not my experience of myself. Day followed day; and, ridiculous as it may appear, I could not decide which of my two admirers I liked best!

Captain Stanwick was, at first, the man of my choice. While he kept his temper under control, he charmed me. But when he let it escape him, he sometimes disappointed, sometimes irritated me. In that frame of mind I turned for relief to Lionel Varleigh, feeling that he was the more gentle and the more worthy man of the two, and honestly believing, at such times, that I preferred him to his rival. For the first few days after our visit to Herne Wood I had excellent opportunities of comparing them. They paid their visits to us together, and they divided their attentions carefully between me and my aunt. At the end of the week, however, they began to present themselves separately. If I had possessed any experience of the natures of men, I might have known what this meant, and might have seen the future possibility of some more serious estrangement between the two friends, of which I might be the unfortunate cause. As it was, I never once troubled my head about what might be passing out of my presence. Whether they came together, or whether they came separately, their visits were always agreeable to me, and I thought of nothing and cared for nothing more.

But the time that was to enlighten me was not far off.

One day Captain Stanwick called much earlier than usual. My aunt had not yet returned from her morning walk. The Captain made some excuse for presenting himself under these circumstances which I have now forgotten.

Without actually committing himself to a proposal of marriage, he spoke with such tender feeling, he managed his hold on my inexperience so delicately, that he entrapped me into saying some words, on my side, which I remembered with a certain dismay as soon as I was left alone again. In half an hour more, Mr Lionel Varleigh was announced as my next visitor. I at once noticed a certain disturbance in his look and manner which was quite new in my experience of him. I offered him a chair. To my surprise he declined to take it.

'I must trust to your indulgence to permit me to put an embarrassing question to you,' he began. 'It rests with you, Miss Laroche, to decide whether I shall remain here, or whether I shall relieve you of my presence by leaving the room.'

'What can you possibly mean?' I asked.

'Is it your wish,' he went on, 'that I should pay you no more visits except in Captain Stanwick's company, or by Captain Stanwick's express permission?'

My astonishment deprived me for the moment of the power of answering him. 'Do you really mean that Captain Stanwick has forbidden you to call on me?' I asked as soon as I could speak.

'I have exactly repeated what Captain Stanwick said to me half an hour since,' Lionel Varleigh answered.

In my indignation at hearing this, I entirely forgot the rash words of encouragement which the Captain had entrapped me into speaking to him. When I think of it now, I am ashamed to repeat the language in which I resented this man's presumptuous assertion of authority over me. Having committed one act of indiscretion already, my anxiety to assert my freedom of action hurried me into committing another. I bade Mr Varleigh welcome whenever he chose to visit me, in terms which made his face flush under the emotions of pleasure and surprise which I had aroused in him. My wounded vanity acknowledged no restraints. I signed to him to take a seat on the sofa at my side; I engaged to go to his lodgings the next day, with my aunt, and see the collection of curiosities which he had amassed in the course of his travels. I almost believe, if he had tried to kiss me, that I was angry enough with the Captain to have let him do it!

Remember what my life had been – remember how ignorantly I had passed the precious days of my youth, how insidiously a sudden accession of wealth and importance had encouraged my folly and my pride – and try, like good Christians, to make some allowance for me!

My aunt came in from her walk before Mr Varleigh's visit had ended. She received him rather coldly, and he perceived it. After reminding me of our appointment for the next day, he took his leave.

'What appointment does Mr Varleigh mean?' my aunt asked, as soon as we were alone. 'Is it wise, under the circumstances, to make appointments with Mr Varleigh?' she said, when I had answered her question. I naturally inquired what she meant. My aunt replied, 'I have met Captain Stanwick while I was out walking. He has told me something which I am quite at a loss to understand. Is it possible, Bertha, that you have received a proposal of marriage from him favourably, without saying one word about your intentions to me?'

I instantly denied it. However rashly I might have spoken, I had certainly said nothing to justify Captain Stanwick in claiming me as his promised wife. In his mean fear of a fair rivalry with Mr Varleigh, he had deliberately misinterpreted me. 'If I marry either of the two,' I said, 'it will be Mr Varleigh!'

My aunt shook her head. 'These two gentlemen seem to be both in love with you, Bertha. It is a trying position for you between them, and I am afraid you have acted with some indiscretion. Captain Stanwick tells me that he and his friend have come to a separation already. I fear you are the cause of it. Mr Varleigh has left the hotel at which he was staying with the Captain, in consequence of a disagreement between them this morning. You were not aware of that when you accepted his invitation. Shall I write an excuse for you? We must, at least, put off the visit, my dear, until you have set yourself right with Captain Stanwick.'

I began to feel a little alarmed, but I was too obstinate to yield without a struggle. 'Give me time to think over it,' I said. 'To write an excuse seems like acknowledging the Captain's authority. Let us wait till to-morrow morning.'

IV

The morning brought with it another visit from Captain Stanwick. This time my aunt was present. He looked at her without speaking, and turned to me, with his fiery temper showing itself already in his eyes.

'I have a word to say to you in private,' he began.

'I have no secrets from my aunt,' I answered. 'Whatever you have to say, Captain Stanwick, may be said here.'

He opened his lips to reply, and suddenly checked himself. He was controlling his anger by so violent an effort that it turned his ruddy face pale. For the moment he conquered his temper – he addressed himself to me with the outward appearance of respect at least.

'Has that man Varleigh lied?' he asked; 'or have you given *him* hopes too – after what you said to me yesterday?'

'I said nothing to you yesterday which gives you any right to put that question to me,' I rejoined. 'You have entirely misunderstood me if you think so.'

My aunt attempted to say a few temperate words, in the hope of sooth-ing him. He waved his hand, refusing to listen to her, and advanced closer to me.

'*You* have misunderstood *me*,' he said, 'if you think I am a man to be made a plaything of in the hands of a coquette!'

My aunt interposed once more, with a resolution which I had not expected from her.

'Captain Stanwick,' she said, 'you are forgetting yourself.'

He paid no heed to her; he persisted in speaking to me. 'It is my misfortune to love you,' he burst out. 'My whole heart is set on you. I mean to be your husband, and no other man living shall stand in my way. After what you said to me yesterday, I have a right to consider that you have favoured my addresses. This is not a mere flirtation. Don't think it! I say it's the passion of a life! Do you hear? It's the passion of a man's whole life! I am not to be trifled with. I have had a night of sleepless misery about you – I have suffered enough for you – and you're not worth it. Don't laugh! This is no laughing matter. Take care, Bertha! Take care!'

My aunt rose from her chair. She astonished me. On all ordinary occasions the most retiring, the most feminine of women, she now walked up to Captain Stanwick and looked him full in the face, without flinching for an instant.

'You appear to have forgotten that you are speaking in the presence of two ladies,' she said. 'Alter your tone, sir, or I shall be obliged to take my niece out of the room.'

Half angry, half frightened, I tried to speak in my turn. My aunt signed to me to be silent. The Captain drew back a step as if he felt her reproof. But his eyes, still fixed on me, were as fiercely bright as ever. *There* the gentleman's superficial good-breeding failed to hide the natural man beneath.

'I will leave you in undisturbed possession of the room,' he said to my aunt with bitter politeness. 'Before I go, permit me to give your niece an opportunity of reconsidering her conduct before it is too late.' My aunt drew back, leaving him free to speak to me. After considering for a moment, he laid his hand firmly, but not roughly, on my arm. 'You have accepted Lionel Varleigh's invitation to visit him,' he said, 'under pretence of seeing his curiosities. Think again before you decide on keeping that engagement. If you go to Varleigh tomorrow, you will repent it to the last day of your life.' Saying those words, in a tone which made me tremble in spite of myself, he walked to the door. As he laid his hand on the lock, he turned towards me for the last time. 'I forbid you go to Varleigh's lodgings,' he said, very distinctly and quietly. 'Understand what I tell you. I forbid it.'

With those words he left us.

My aunt sat down by me and took my hand kindly. 'There is only one thing to be done,' she said; 'we must return at once to Nettlegrove. If Captain Stanwick attempts to annoy you in your own house, we have neighbours who will protect us, and we have Mr Loring, our Rector, to appeal to for advice. As for Mr Varleigh, I will write our excuses myself before we go away.'

She put out her hand to ring the bell and order the carriage. I stopped her. My childish pride urged me to assert myself in some way, after the passive position that I had been forced to occupy during the interview with Captain Stanwick.

'No,' I said, 'it is not acting fairly towards Mr Varleigh to break our engagement with him. Let us return to Nettlegrove by all means, but let us first call on Mr Varleigh and take our leave. Are we to behave rudely to a gentleman who has always treated us with the utmost consideration, because Captain Stanwick has tried to frighten us by cowardly threats? The commonest feeling of self-respect forbids it.'

My aunt protested against this outbreak of folly with perfect temper and good sense. But my obstinacy (my firmness as I thought it!) was immovable. I left her to choose between going with me to Mr Varleigh, or letting me go to him by myself. Finding it useless to resist, she decided, it is needless to say, on going with me.

We found Mr Varleigh very courteous, but more than usually grave and quiet. Our visit only lasted for a few minutes; my aunt using the influence of her age and her position to shorten it. She mentioned family affairs as the motive which recalled us to Nettlegrove. I took it on myself to invite Mr Varleigh to visit me at my own house. He bowed, and thanked me, without engaging himself to accept the invitation. When I offered him my hand at parting, he raised it to his lips, and kissed it with a fervour that agitated me. His eyes looked into mine with a sorrowful admiration, with a lingering regret, as if they were taking their leave of me for a long while. 'Don't forget me!' he whispered, as he stood at the door, while I followed my aunt out. 'Come to Nettlegrove,' I whispered back. His eyes dropped to the ground; he let me go without a word more.

This, I declare solemnly, was all that passed at our visit. By some unexpressed consent among us, no allusion whatever was made to Captain Stanwick; not even his name was mentioned. I never knew that the two men had met, just before we called on Mr Varleigh. Nothing was said which could suggest to me the slightest suspicion of any arrangement for another meeting between them later in the day. Beyond the vague threats which had escaped Captain Stanwick's lips – threats which I own I was rash enough to despise – I had no warning whatever of the dreadful events which happened at Maplesworth on the day after our return to Nettlegrove Hall.

I can only add that I am ready to submit to any questions that may be put to me. Pray don't think me a heartless woman. My worst fault was ignorance. In those days, I knew nothing of the false pretences under which men hide what is selfish and savage in their natures from the women whom it is their interest to deceive.

No. 2 – Julius Bender, fencing-master, testifies and says:

I am of German nationality; established in England as teacher of the use of the sword and the pistol since the beginning of the present year.

Finding business slack in London, it unfortunately occurred to me to try what I could do in the country. I had heard of Maplesworth as a place largely frequented by visitors on account of the scenery, as well as by invalids in need of taking the waters; and I opened a gallery there at the beginning of the season of 1817, for fencing and pistol practice. About the visitors I had not been deceived; there were plenty of idle young gentlemen among them who might have been expected to patronise my establishment. They showed the most barbarous indifference to the noble art of attack and defence – came by twos and threes, looked at my gallery, and never returned. My small means began to fail me. After paying my expenses, I was really at my wits' end to find a few pounds to go on with, in the hope of better days.

One gentleman I remember, who came to see me, and who behaved most liberally.

He described himself as an American, and said he had travelled a great deal. As my ill luck would have it, he stood in no need of my instructions. On the two or three occasions when he amused himself with my foils and my pistols, he proved to be one of the most expert swordsmen and one of the finest shots that I ever met with. It was not wonderful: he had by nature cool nerves and a quick eye; and he had been taught by the masters of the art in Vienna and Paris.

Early in July – the 9th or 10th of the month, I think – I was sitting alone in my gallery, looking ruefully enough at the last two sovereigns in my purse, when a gentleman was announced who wanted a lesson. 'A *private* lesson,' he said with emphasis, looking at the man who cleaned and took care of my weapons.

I sent the man out of the room. The stranger (an Englishman, and, as I fancied, judging by outward appearances, a military man as well) took from his pocket-book a fifty-pound bank-note, and held it up before me. 'I have a heavy wager depending on a fencing match,' he said, 'and I have no time to improve myself. Teach me a trick which will make me a match for a man skilled in the use of the foil, and keep the secret – and there are fifty pounds for you.'

I hesitated. I did indeed hesitate, poor as I was. But this devil of a man held his bank-note before me whichever way I looked, and I had only two pounds left in the world!

'Are you going to fight a duel?' I asked.

'I have already told you what I am going to do,' he answered.

I waited a little. The infernal bank-note still tempted me. In spite of myself, I tried him again.

'If I teach you the trick,' I persisted, 'will you undertake to make no bad use of your lesson?'

'Yes,' he said, impatiently enough.

I was not quite satisfied yet.

'Will you promise it, on your word of honour?' I asked.

'Of course I will,' he answered. 'Take the money, and don't keep me waiting any longer!'

I took the money, and I taught him the trick – and I regretted it almost as soon as it was done. Not that I knew, mind, of any serious consequences that followed; for I returned to London the next morning. My sentiments were those of a man of honour, who felt that he had degraded his art, and who could not be quite sure that he might not have armed the hand of an assassin as well. I have no more to say.

No. 3 – Thomas Outwater, servant to Captain Stanwick, testifies and says:

If I did not firmly believe my master to be out of his senses, no punishment that I could receive would prevail upon me to tell of him what I am going to tell now.

But I say he is mad, and therefore not accountable for what he has done – mad for love of a young woman. If I could have my way, I should like to twist her neck, though she *is* a lady, and a great heiress into the bargain. Before she came between them, my master and Mr Varleigh were more like brothers than anything else. She set them at variance, and whether she meant to do it or not is all the same to me. I own I took a dislike to her when I first saw her. She was one of the light-haired, blue-eyed sort, with an innocent look and a snaky waist – not at all to be depended on, as I have found them.

I hear I am not expected to give an account of the disagreement between the two gentlemen, of which this lady was the cause. I am to state what I did in Maplesworth, and what I saw afterwards in Herne Wood. Poor as I am, I would give a five-pound note to anybody who could do it for me. Unfortunately, I must do it for myself.

On the 10th of July, in the evening, my master went, for the second time that day, to Mr Varleigh's lodgings.

I am certain of the date, because it was the day of publication of the town newspaper, and there was a law report in it which set everybody talking. There had been a duel with pistols, a day or two before, between a resident in the town and a visitor, caused by some dispute about horses. Nothing very serious came of the meeting. One of the men only was hurt, and the wound proved to be of no great importance. The awkward part of the matter was that the constables appeared on the ground, before the wounded man had been removed. He and his two seconds were caught, and the prisoners were committed for trial. Duelling (the magistrates said) was an inhuman and unchristian practice, and they were determined to put the law in force and stop it. This sentence made a great stir in the town, and fixed the date, as I have just said, in my mind.

Having been accidentally within hearing of some of the disputes concerning Miss Laroche between my master and Mr Varleigh, I had my misgivings about the Captain's second visit to the friend with whom he had quarrelled already. A gentleman called on him, soon after he had gone out, on important business. This gave me an excuse for following him to Mr Varleigh's rooms with the visitor's card, and I took the opportunity.

I heard them at high words on my way upstairs, and waited a little on the landing. The Captain was in one of his furious rages; Mr Varleigh was firm and cool as usual. After listening for a minute or so, I heard enough (in my opinion) to justify me in entering the room. I caught my master in the act of lifting his cane – threatening to strike Mr Varleigh. He instantly dropped his hand, and turned on me in a fury at my intrusion. Taking no notice of this outbreak of temper, I gave him his friend's card, and went out. A talk followed in voices too low for me to hear outside the room, and then the Captain approached the door. I got out of his way, feeling very uneasy about what was to come next. I could not presume to question Mr Varleigh. The only thing I could think of was to tell the young lady's aunt what I had seen and heard, and to plead with Miss Laroche herself to make peace between them. When I inquired for the ladies at their lodgings, I was told that they had left Maplesworth.

I saw no more of the Captain that night.

The next morning he seemed to be quite himself again. He said to me, 'Thomas, I am going sketching in Herne Wood. Take the paint-box and the rest of it, and put this into the carriage.'

He handed me a packet as thick as my arm, and about three feet long, done up in many folds of canvas. I made bold to ask what it was. He answered that it was an artist's sketching umbrella, packed for travelling.

In an hour's time, the carriage stopped on the road below Herne Wood. My master said he would carry his sketching things himself, and I was to wait with the carriage. In giving him the so-called umbrella, I took the occasion of his eye being off me for the moment to pass my hand over it carefully; and I felt, through the canvas, the hilt of a sword. As an old soldier, I could not be mistaken – the hilt of a sword.

What I thought, on making this discovery, does not much matter. What I did was to watch the Captain into the wood, and then to follow him.

I tracked him along the path to where there was a clearing in the midst of the trees. There he stopped, and I got behind a tree. He undid the canvas, and produced *two* swords concealed in the packet. If I had felt any doubts before, I was certain of what was coming now. A duel without seconds or witnesses, by way of keeping the town magistrates in the dark – a duel between my master and Mr Varleigh! As his name came into my mind the man himself appeared, making his way into the clearing from the other side of the wood.

What could I do to stop it? No human creature was in sight. The nearest village was a mile away, reckoning from the farther side of the wood. The coachman was a stupid old man, quite useless in a difficulty, even if I had had time enough to go back to the road and summon him to help me. While I was thinking about it, the Captain and Mr Varleigh had stripped to their shirts and trousers. When they crossed their swords, I could stand it no longer – I burst in on them. 'For God Almighty's sake, gentlemen,' I cried out, 'don't fight without seconds!' My master turned on me, like the madman he was, and threatened me with the point of his sword. Mr Varleigh pulled me back out of harm's way. 'Don't be afraid,' he whispered, as he led me back to the verge of the clearing; 'I have chosen the sword instead of the pistol expressly to spare his life.'

Those noble words (spoken by as brave and true a man as ever breathed) quieted me. I knew Mr Varleigh had earned the repute of being one of the finest swordsmen in Europe.

The duel began. I was placed behind my master, and was consequently opposite to his antagonist. The Captain stood on his defence, waiting for the other to attack. Mr Varleigh made a pass. I was opposite the point of his sword; I saw it touch the Captain's left shoulder. In the same instant of time my master struck up his opponent's sword with his own weapon, seized Mr Varleigh's right wrist in his left hand, and passed his sword clean through Mr Varleigh's breast. He fell, the victim of a murderous trick – fell without a word or a cry.

The Captain turned slowly, and faced me with his bloody sword in his hand. I can't tell you how he looked; I can only say that the sight of him turned me faint with terror. I was at Waterloo – I am no coward. But I tell you the cold sweat poured down my face like water. I should have dropped if I had not held by the branch of a tree.

My master waited until I had in a measure recovered myself. 'Feel if his heart beats,' he said, pointing to the man on the ground.

I obeyed. He was dead – the heart was still; the beat of the pulse was gone. I said 'You have killed him!'

The Captain made no answer. He packed up the two swords again in the canvas, and put them under his arm. Then he told me to follow him with the sketching materials. I drew back from him without speaking; there was a horrid hollow sound in his voice that I did not like. 'Do as I tell you,' he said: 'you have yourself to thank for it if I refuse to lose sight of you now,' I managed to say that he might trust me to say nothing. He refused to trust me; he put out his hand to take hold of me. I could not stand that. 'I'll go with you,' I said; 'don't touch me!' We reached the carriage and returned to Maplesworth. The same day we travelled by post to London.

In London I contrived to give the Captain the slip. By the first coach the next morning I went back to Maplesworth, eager to hear what had happened, and if the body had been found. Not a word of news reached me; nothing seemed to be known of the duel in Herne Wood.

I went to the wood – on foot, fearing that I might be traced if I hired a carriage. The country round was as solitary as usual. Not a creature was near when I entered the wood; not a creature was near when I looked into the clearing.

There was nothing on the ground. The body was gone.

No. 4 – The Reverend Alfred Loring, Rector of Nettlegrove, testifies and says:

Early in the month of October, 1817, I was informed that Miss Bertha Laroche had called at my house, and wished to see me in private.

I had first been presented to Miss Laroche on her arrival, with her aunt, to take possession of her property at Nettlegrove Hall. My opportunities of improving my acquaintance with her had not been so numerous as I could have desired, and I sincerely regretted it. She had produced a very favourable impression on me. Singularly inexperienced and impulsive – with an odd mixture of shyness and vivacity in her manner, and subject now and then to outbursts of vanity and petulance which she was divertingly incapable of concealing – I could detect, nevertheless, under the surface the signs which told of a true and generous nature, of a simple and pure heart. Her personal appearance, I should add, was attractive in a remarkable degree. There was something in it so peculiar, and at the same time so fascinating, that I am conscious it may have prejudiced me in her favour. For fear of this acknowledgment being misunderstood, I think it right to add that I am old enough to be her grandfather, and that I am also a married man.

I told the servant to show Miss Laroche into my study.

The moment she entered the room, her appearance alarmed me: she looked literally panic-stricken. I offered to send for my wife; she refused the proposal. I entreated her to take time at least to compose herself. It was not in her impulsive nature to do this. She said, 'Give me your hand to encourage me, and let me speak while I can.' I gave her my hand, poor soul. I said, 'Speak to me, my dear, as if I were your father.'

So far as I could understand the incoherent statement which she addressed to me, she had been the object of admiration (while visiting Maplesworth) to two gentlemen, who both desired to marry her. Hesitating between them, and perfectly inexperienced in such matters, she had been the unfortunate cause of enmity between the rivals, and had returned to Nettlegrove, at her aunt's suggestion, as the best means of extricating herself from a very embarrassing position. The removal failing to alleviate her distressing recollections of what had happened, she and her aunt had tried a further change by making a tour of two months on the Continent. She had returned in a more quiet frame of mind. To her great surprise, she had heard nothing of either of her two suitors, from the day when she left Maplesworth to the day when she presented herself at my rectory.

Early that morning she was walking, after breakfast, in the park at Nettlegrove, when she heard footsteps behind her. She turned, and found herself face to face with one of her suitors at Maplesworth. I am informed that there is no necessity now for my suppressing the name. The gentleman was Captain Stanwick.

He was so fearfully changed for the worse that she hardly knew him again.

After his first glance at her, he held his hand over his bloodshot eyes as if the sunlight hurt them. Without a word to prepare her for the disclosure, he confessed that he had killed Mr Varleigh in a duel. His remorse (he declared) had unsettled his reason: only a few days had passed since he had been released from confinement in an asylum.

'You are the cause of it,' he said wildly. 'It is for love of you. I have but one hope left to live for – my hope in you. If you cast me off, my mind is made up. I will give my life for the life that I have taken; I will die by my own hand. Look at me, and you will see that I am in earnest. My future as a living man depends on your decision. Think of it today, and meet me here tomorrow. Not at this time; the horrid daylight feels like fire in my eyes, and goes like fire to my brain. Wait till sunset – you will find me here.'

He left her as suddenly as he had appeared. When she had sufficiently recovered herself to be able to think, she decided on saying nothing of what had happened to her aunt. She took her way to the rectory, to seek my advice.

It is needless to encumber my narrative by any statement of the questions which I felt it my duty to put to her, under these circumstances.

My inquiries informed me that Captain Stanwick had, in the first instance, produced a favourable impression on her. The less showy qualities of Mr Varleigh had afterwards grown on her liking; aided greatly by the repelling effect on her mind of the Captain's violent language and conduct when he had reason to suspect that his rival was being preferred to him. When she knew the horrible news of Mr Varleigh's death, she 'knew her own heart' (to repeat her exact words to me) by the shock that she felt. Towards Captain Stanwick the only feeling of which she was now conscious was, naturally, a feeling of the strongest aversion.

My own course in this difficult and painful matter appeared to me to be clear.

'It is your duty as a Christian to see this miserable man again,' I said. 'And it is my duty, as your friend and pastor, to sustain you under the trial. I will go with you tomorrow to the place of meeting.'

The next evening we found Captain Stanwick waiting for us in the park.

He drew back on seeing me. I explained to him, temperately and firmly, what my position was. With sullen looks he resigned himself to endure my presence. By degrees I won his confidence. My first impression of him remains unshaken – the man's reason was unsettled. I suspected that the assertion of his release was a falsehood, and that he had really escaped from the asylum. It was impossible to lure him into telling me where the place was. He was too cunning to do this – too cunning to say anything about his relations, when I tried to turn the talk that way next. On the other hand, he spoke with a revolting readiness of the crime that he had committed, and of his settled resolution to destroy himself if Miss Laroche refused to be his wife. 'I have nothing else to live for; I am alone in the world,' he said. 'Even my servant has deserted me. He knows how I killed Lionel Varleigh.' He paused, and spoke his next words in a whisper to me. 'I killed him by a trick – he was the best swordsman of the two.'

This confession was so horrible that I could only attribute it to an insane delusion. On pressing my inquiries, I found that the same idea must have occurred to the poor wretch's relations, and to the doctors who signed the certificates for placing him under medical care. This conclusion (as I afterwards heard) was greatly strengthened by the fact that Mr Varleigh's body had not been found on the reported scene of the duel. As to the servant, he had deserted his master in London, and had never reappeared. So far as my poor judgment went, the question before me was not of delivering a self-accused murderer to justice (with no corpse to testify against him), but of restoring an insane man to the care of the persons who had been appointed to restrain him.

I tried to test the strength of his delusion in an interval when he was not urging his shocking entreaties on Miss Laroche.

'How do you know that you killed Mr Varleigh?' I said.

He looked at me with a wild terror in his eyes. Suddenly he lifted his right hand, and shook it in the air, with a moaning cry, which was unmistakably a cry of pain. 'Should I see his ghost,' he asked, 'if I had not killed him? I know it, by the pain that wrings me in the hand that stabbed him. Always in my right hand! always the same pain at the moment when I see him!' He stopped, and ground his teeth in the agony and reality of his delusion. 'Look!' he cried. 'Look between the two trees behind you. There he is – with his dark hair, and his shaven face, and his steady look! There he is, standing before me as he stood in the wood, with his eyes on my eyes, and his sword feeling mine!' He turned to Miss Laroche. 'Do *you* see him too?' he asked eagerly. 'Tell me the truth. My whole life depends on your telling me the truth.'

She controlled herself with a wonderful courage. 'I don't see him,' she answered.

He took out his handkerchief, and passed it over his face with a gasp of relief. 'There is my last chance!' he said. 'If she will be true to me – if she will be always near me, morning, noon, and night, I shall be released from the sight of him. See! he is fading away already. Gone!' he cried, with a scream of exultation. He fell on his knees, and looked at Miss Laroche like a savage adoring his idol. 'Will you cast me off now?' he asked humbly. 'Lionel was fond of you in his lifetime. His spirit is a merciful spirit. He shrinks from frightening you; he has left me for your sake; he will release me for your sake. Pity me, take me to live with you – and I shall never see him again!'

It was dreadful to hear him. I saw that the poor girl could endure no more. 'Leave us,' I whispered to her; 'I will join you at the house.'

He heard me, and instantly placed himself between us. 'Let her promise, or she shan't go.'

She felt, as I felt, the imperative necessity of saying anything that might soothe him. At a sign from me she gave him her promise to return.

He was satisfied – he insisted on kissing her hand, and then he let her go. I had by this time succeeded in inducing him to trust me. He proposed, of his own accord, that I should accompany him to the inn in the village at which he had been staying. The landlord (naturally enough distrusting his wretched guest) had warned him that morning to find some other place of shelter. I engaged to use my influence with the man to make him change his purpose, and I succeeded in effecting the necessary arrangements for having the poor wretch properly looked after. On my return to my own house, I wrote to a brother magistrate living near me, and to the superintendent of our county asylum, requesting them to consult with me on the best means of lawfully restraining Captain Stanwick until we could communicate with his relations. Could I have done more than this? The event of the next morning answered that question – answered it at once and for ever.

Presenting myself at Nettlegrove Hall towards sunset, to take charge of Miss Laroche, I was met by an obstacle in the shape of a protest from her aunt.

This good lady had been informed of the appearance of Captain Stanwick in the park, and she strongly disapproved of encouraging any further communication with him on the part of her niece. She also considered that I had failed in my duty in still leaving the Captain at liberty. I told her that I was only waiting to act on the advice of competent persons, who would arrive the next day to consult with me; and I did my best to persuade her of the wisdom of the course that I had taken in the meantime. Miss Laroche, on her side, was resolved to be true to the promise that she had given. Between us, we induced her aunt to yield on certain conditions.

'I know the part of the park in which the meeting is to take place,' the old lady said; 'it is my niece's favourite walk. If she is not brought back to me in half an hour's time, I shall send the men-servants to protect her.'

The twilight was falling when we reached the appointed place. We found Captain Stanwick angry and suspicious; it was not easy to pacify him on the subject of our delay. His insanity seemed to me to be now more marked than ever. He had seen, or dreamed of seeing, the ghost during the past night. For the first time (he said) the apparition of the dead man had spoken to him. In solemn words it had condemned him to expiate his crime by giving his life for the life that he had taken. It had warned him not to insist on marriage with Bertha Laroche: 'She shall share your punishment if she shares your life. And you shall know it by this sign – *She shall see me as you see me.*'

I tried to compose him. He shook his head in immovable despair. 'No,' he answered; 'if she sees him when I see him, there ends the one hope of release that holds me to life. It will be good-bye between us, and good-bye for ever!'

We had walked on, while we were speaking, to a part of the park through which there flowed a rivulet of clear water. On the farther bank the open ground led down into a wooded valley. On our side of the stream rose a thick plantation of fir-trees, intersected by a winding path. Captain Stanwick stopped as we reached the place. His eyes rested, in the darkening twilight, on the narrow space pierced by the path among the trees. On a sudden he lifted his right hand, with the same cry of pain which we had heard before:

with his left hand he took Miss Laroche by the arm. 'There!' he said. 'Look where I look! Do you see him there?'

As the words passed his lips, a dimly-visible figure appeared, advancing towards us along the path.

Was it the figure of a living man? or was it the creation of my own excited fancy? Before I could ask myself the question, the man advanced a step nearer to us. A last gleam of the dying light fell on his face through an opening in the trees. At the same instant Miss Laroche started back from Captain Stanwick with a scream of terror. She would have fallen if I had not been near enough to support her. The Captain was instantly at her side again. 'Speak!' he cried. 'Do *you* see it too?'

She was just able to say 'Yes,' before she fainted in my arms.

He stooped over her, and touched her cold cheek with his lips. 'Good-bye!' he said, in tones suddenly and strangely changed to the most exquisite tenderness. 'Goodbye, for ever!'

He leapt the rivulet; he crossed the open ground; he was lost to sight in the valley beyond.

As he disappeared, the visionary man among the fir-trees advanced; passed in silence; crossed the rivulet at a bound; and vanished as the figure of the Captain had vanished before him.

I was left alone with the swooning woman. Not a sound, far or near, broke the stillness of the coming night.

No. 5 – Mr Frederic Darnel, Member of the College of Surgeons, testifies and says:

In the intervals of my professional duty I am accustomed to occupy myself in studying Botany, assisted by a friend and neighbour, whose tastes in this respect resemble my own. When I can spare an hour or two from my patients, we go out together searching for specimens. Our favourite place is Herne Wood. It is rich in material for the botanist, and it is only a mile distant from the village in which I live.

Early in July, my friend and I made a discovery in the wood of a very alarming and unexpected kind. We found a man in the clearing, prostrated by a dangerous wound, and to all appearance dead.

We carried him to the gamekeeper's cottage, on the outskirts of the wood, and on the side of it nearest to our village. He and his boy were out, but the light cart in which he makes his rounds, in the remoter part of his master's property, was in the outhouse. While my friend was putting the horse to, I examined the stranger's wound. It had been quite recently inflicted, and I doubted whether it had (as yet, at any rate) really killed him. I did what I could with the linen and cold water which the gamekeeper's wife offered to me, and then my friend and I removed him carefully to my house in the cart.

I applied the necessary restoratives, and I had the pleasure of satisfying myself that the vital powers had revived. He was perfectly unconscious, of course, but the action of the heart became distinctly perceptible, and I had hopes.

In a few days more I felt fairly sure of him. Then the usual fever set in. I was obliged, in justice to his friends, to search his clothes in presence of a witness.

We found his handkerchief, his purse, and his cigar-case, and nothing more. No letters or visiting cards; nothing marked on his clothes but initials. There was no help for it but to wait to identify him until he could speak.

When that time came, he acknowledged to me that he had divested himself purposely of any clue to his identity, in the fear (if some mischance happened to him) of the news of it reaching his father and mother abruptly, by means of the newspapers. He had sent a letter to his bankers in London, to be forwarded to his parents, if the bankers neither saw him nor heard from him in a month's time. His first act was to withdraw this letter. The other particulars which he communicated to me are, I am told, already known. I need only add that I willingly kept his secret, simply speaking of him in the neighbourhood as a traveller from foreign parts who had met with an accident.

His convalescence was a long one. It was the beginning of October before he was completely restored to health. When he left us he went to London. He behaved most liberally to me; and we parted with sincere good wishes on either side.

No. 6 – Mr Lionel Varleigh, of Boston, U.S.A., testifies and says:

My first proceeding, on my recovery, was to go to the relations of Captain Stanwick in London, for the purpose of making inquiries about him.

I do not wish to justify myself at the expense of that miserable man. It is true that I loved Miss Laroche too dearly to yield her to any rival except at her own wish. It is also true that Captain Stanwick more than once insulted me, and that I endured it. He had suffered from sunstroke in India, and in his angry moments he was hardly a responsible being. It was only when he threatened me with personal chastisement that my patience gave way. We met sword in hand. In my mind was the resolution to spare his life. In his mind was the resolution to kill me. I have forgiven him. I will say no more.

His relations informed me of the symptoms of insane delusion which he had shown after the duel; of his escape from the asylum in which he had been confined; and of the failure to find him again.

The moment I heard this news the dread crossed my mind that Stanwick had found his way to Miss Laroche. In an hour more I was travelling to Nettlegrove Hall.

I arrived late in the evening, and found Miss Laroche's aunt in great alarm about her niece's safety. The young lady was at that very moment speaking to Stanwick in the park, with only an old man (the Rector) to protect her. I volunteered to go at once, and assist in taking care of her. A servant accompanied me to show me the place of meeting. We heard voices indistinctly, but saw no one. The servant pointed to a path through the fir-trees. I went on quickly by myself, leaving the man within call. In a few minutes I came upon them suddenly, at a little distance from me, on the bank of a stream.

The fear of seriously alarming Miss Laroche, if I showed myself too suddenly, deprived me for a moment of my presence of mind. Pausing to consider what it might be best to do, I was less completely protected from discovery by the trees than I had supposed. She had seen me; I heard her cry of alarm. The instant afterwards I saw Stanwick leap over the rivulet and take to flight. That action roused me. Without stopping for a word of explanation, I pursued him.

Unhappily, I missed my footing in the obscure light, and fell on the open ground beyond the stream. When I had gained my feet once more, Stanwick had disappeared among the trees which marked the boundary of the park beyond me. I could see nothing of him, and I could hear nothing of him, when I came out on the high-road. There I met with a labouring man who showed me the way to the village.

From the inn I sent a letter to Miss Laroche's aunt, explaining what had happened, and asking leave to call at the Hall on the next day.

Early in the morning the Rector came to me at the inn. He brought sad news. Miss Laroche was suffering from a nervous attack, and my visit to the Hall must be deferred. Speaking next of the missing man, I heard all that Mr Loring could tell me. My intimate knowledge of Stanwick enabled me to draw my own conclusion from the facts. The thought instantly crossed my mind that the poor wretch might have committed his expiatory suicide at the very spot on which he had attempted to kill me. Leaving the Rector to institute the necessary inquiries, I took post-horses to Maplesworth on my way to Herne Wood.

Advancing from the high-road to the wood, I saw two persons at a little distance from me – a man in the dress of a gamekeeper and a lad. I was too much agitated to take any special notice of them; I hurried along the path which led to the clearing. My presentiment had not misled me. There he lay, dead on the scene of the duel, with a blood-stained razor by his side! I fell on my knees by the corpse; I took his cold hand in mine; and I thanked God that I had forgiven him in the first days of my recovery.

I was still kneeling, when I felt myself seized from behind. I struggled to my feet, and confronted the gamekeeper. He had noticed my hurry in entering the wood; his suspicions had been aroused, and he and the lad had followed me. There was blood on my clothes, there was horror in my face. Appearances were plainly against me; I had no choice but to accompany the gamekeeper to the nearest magistrate.

My instructions to my solicitor forbade him to vindicate my innocence by taking any technical legal objections to the action of the magistrate or of the coroner. I insisted on my witnesses being summoned to the lawyer's office, and allowed to state, in their own way, what they could truly declare on my behalf; and I left my defence to be founded upon the materials thus obtained. In the meanwhile I was detained in custody, as a matter of course.

With this event the tragedy of the duel reached its culminating point. I was accused of murdering the man who had attempted to take my life!

This last incident having been related, all that is worth noticing in my contribution to the present narrative comes to an end. I was tried in due course of law. The evidence taken at my solicitor's office was necessarily altered in form, though not in substance, by the examination to which the witnesses were subjected in a court of justice. So thoroughly did our defence satisfy the jury, that they became restless towards the close of the proceedings, and returned their verdict of Not Guilty without quitting the box.

When I was a free man again, it is surely needless to dwell on the first use that I made of my honourable acquittal. Whether I deserved the enviable place that I occupied in Bertha's estimation, it is not for me to say. Let me leave the decision to the lady who has ceased to be Miss Laroche – I mean the lady who has been good enough to become my wife.

Miss Mina and the Groom

Originally appeared in *Barnes' International Review*, 2 November 1878 as 'A Shocking Story', and also in the *Belgravia Annual* for 1878. Reprinted in *Little Novels* (1887). The story's preoccupation with love across class-barriers may owe something to Collins's own liaisons with lower-class women, and foreshadows the themes of a number of Hardy short stories. This was the story that landed Collins in difficulties for trying to sell the same copy twice over, at a time when he was particularly pressed for money. Catherine Peters writes: 'The *International Review* also circulated in England, and Chatto & Windus, the proprietors of *Belgravia*, protested. Wilkie claimed he had no reason to suppose there would be a clash of interest, and reminded Chatto that, at £31 10s, they had got the story cheap' (*The King of Inventors*, p. 384).

I

I hear that the 'shocking story of my conduct' was widely circulated at the ball, and that public opinion (among the ladies), in every part of the room, declared I had disgraced myself.

But there was one dissentient voice in this chorus of general condemnation. You spoke, Madam, with all the authority of your wide celebrity and your high rank. You said: 'I am personally a stranger to the young lady who is the subject of remark. If I venture to interfere, it is only to remind you that there are two sides to every question. May I ask if you have waited to pass sentence, until you have heard what the person accused has to say in her own defence?'

These just and generous words produced, if I am correctly informed, a dead silence. Not one of the women who had condemned me had heard me in my own defence. Not one of them ventured to answer you.

How I may stand in the opinions of such persons as these, is a matter of perfect indifference to me. My one anxiety is to show that I am not quite unworthy of your considerate interference in my favour. Will you honour me by reading what I have to say for myself in these pages?

I will pass as rapidly as I can over the subject of my family; and I will abstain (in deference to motives of gratitude and honour) from mentioning surnames in my narrative.

My father was the second son of an English nobleman. A German lady was his first wife, and my mother. Left a widower, he married for the second time; the new wife being of American birth. She took a stepmother's dislike to me – which, in some degree at least, I must own that I deserved.

When the newly-married pair went to the United States they left me in England, by my own desire, to live under the protection of my uncle – a General in the army. This good man's marriage had been childless; and his wife (Lady Claudia) was, perhaps on that account, as kindly ready as her husband to receive me in the character of an adopted daughter. I may add here, that I bear my German mother's Christian name, Wilhelmina. All my friends, in the days when I had friends, used to shorten this to Mina. Be my friend so far, and call me Mina, too.

After these few words of introduction, will your patience bear with me, if I try to make you better acquainted with my uncle and aunt, and if I allude to circumstances connected with my new life which had, as I fear, some influence in altering my character for the worse?

II

When I think of the good General's fatherly kindness to me, I really despair of writing about him in terms that do justice to his nature. To own the truth, the tears get into my eyes, and the lines mingle in such confusion that I cannot read them myself. As for my relations with my aunt, I only tell the truth when I say that she performed her duties towards me without the slightest pretension, and in the most charming manner.

At nearly fifty years old, Lady Claudia was still admired, though she had lost the one attraction which distinguished her before my time – the attraction of a perfectly beautiful figure. With fine hair and expressive eyes, she was otherwise a plain woman. Her unassuming cleverness and her fascinating manners were the qualities no doubt which made her popular everywhere. We never quarrelled. Not because I was always amiable, but because my aunt would not allow it. She managed me, as she managed her husband, with perfect tact. With certain occasional checks, she absolutely governed the General. There were eccentricities in his character which made him a man easily ruled by a clever woman. Deferring to his opinion, so far as appearances went, Lady Claudia generally contrived to get her own way in the end. Except when he was at his club, happy in his gossip, his good dinners, and his whist, my excellent uncle lived under a despotism, in the happy delusion that he was master in his own house.

Prosperous and pleasant as it appeared on the surface, my life had its sad side for a young woman.

In the commonplace routine of our existence, as wealthy people in the upper rank, there was nothing to ripen the growth of any better capacities which may have been in my nature. Heartily as I loved and admired my uncle, he was neither of an age nor of a character to be the chosen depositary of my most secret thoughts, the friend of my inmost heart who could show me how to make the best and the most of my life. With friends and admirers in plenty, I had found no one who could hold this position towards me. In the midst of society I was, unconsciously, a lonely woman.

As I remember them, my hours of happiness were the hours when I took refuge in my music and my books. Out of the house, my one diversion, always welcome and always fresh, was riding. Without any false modesty, I may mention that I had lovers as well as admirers; but not one of them produced an impression on my heart. In all that related to the tender passion, as it is called, I was an undeveloped being. The influence that men have on women, *because* they are men, was really and truly a mystery to me. I was ashamed of my own coldness – I tried, honestly tried, to copy other girls; to feel my heart beating in the presence of the one chosen man. It was not to be done. When a man pressed my hand, I felt it in my rings, instead of my heart.

These confessions made, I have done with the past, and may now relate the events which my enemies, among the ladies, have described as presenting a shocking story.

III

We were in London for the season. One morning, I went out riding with my uncle, as usual, in Hyde Park.

The General's service in the army had been in a cavalry regiment – service distinguished by merits which justified his rapid rise to the high places in his profession. In the hunting-field, he was noted as one of the most daring and most accomplished riders in our county. He had always delighted in riding young and high-spirited horses; and the habit remained with him after he had quitted the active duties of his profession in later life. From first to last he had met with no accidents worth remembering, until the unlucky morning when he went out with me.

His horse, a fiery chestnut, ran away with him, in that part of the Park-ride called Rotten Row. With the purpose of keeping clear of other riders, he spurred his runaway horse at the rail which divides the Row from the grassy enclosure at its side. The terrified animal swerved in taking the leap, and dashed him against a tree. He was dreadfully shaken and injured; but his strong constitution carried him through to recovery – with the serious drawback of an incurable lameness in one leg.

The doctors, on taking leave of their patient, united in warning him (at his age, and bearing in mind his weakened leg) to ride no more restive horses. 'A quiet cob, General,' they all suggested. My uncle was sorely mortified and offended. 'If I am fit for nothing but a quiet cob,' he said bitterly, 'I will ride no more.' He kept his word. No one ever saw the General on horseback again.

Under these sad circumstances (and my aunt being no horsewoman), I had apparently no other choice than to give up riding also. But my kind-hearted uncle was not the man to let me be sacrificed to his own disappointment. His riding-groom had been one of his soldier-servants in the cavalry regiment – a quaint sour-tempered old man, not at all the sort of person to attend on a young lady taking her riding-exercise alone. 'We must find a smart fellow who can be trusted,' said the General. 'I shall inquire at the club.'

For a week afterwards, a succession of grooms, recommended by friends, applied for the vacant place.

The General found insurmountable objections to all of them. 'I'll tell you what I have done,' he announced one day, with the air of a man who had hit on a grand discovery; 'I have advertised in the papers.'

Lady Claudia looked up from her embroidery with the placid smile that was peculiar to her. 'I don't quite like advertising for a servant,' she said. 'You are at the mercy of a stranger; you don't know that you are not engaging a drunkard or a thief.'

'Or you may be deceived by a false character,' I added, on my side. I seldom ventured, at domestic consultations, on giving my opinion unasked – but the new groom represented a subject in which I felt a strong personal interest. In a certain sense, he was to be *my* groom.

'I'm much obliged to you both for warning me that I am so easy to deceive,' the General remarked satirically. 'Unfortunately, the mischief is done. Three men have answered my advertisement already. I expect them here to-morrow to be examined for the place.'

Lady Claudia looked up from her embroidery again. 'Are you going to see them yourself?' she asked softly. 'I thought the steward—'

'I have hitherto considered myself a better judge of a groom than my steward,' the General interposed. 'However, don't be alarmed; I won't act on my own sole responsibility, after the hint you have given me. You and Mina shall lend me your valuable assistance, and discover whether they are thieves, drunkards, and what not, before I feel the smallest suspicion of it, myself.'

IV

We naturally supposed that the General was joking. No. This was one of those rare occasions on which Lady Claudia's tact – infallible in matters of importance – proved to be at fault in a trifle. My uncle's self-esteem had been touched in a tender place; and he had resolved to make us feel it. The next morning a polite message came, requesting our presence in the library, to see the grooms. My aunt (always ready with her smile, but rarely tempted into laughing outright) did for once laugh heartily. 'It is really too ridiculous!' she said. However, she pursued her policy of always yielding, in the first instance. We went together to the library.

The three grooms were received in the order in which they presented themselves for approval. Two of them bore the ineffaceable mark of the public-house so plainly written on their villainous faces, that even I could see it. My uncle ironically asked us to favour him with our opinions. Lady Claudia answered with her sweetest smile: 'Pardon me, General – we are here to learn.' The words were nothing; but the manner in which they were spoken was perfect. Few men could have resisted that gentle influence – and the General was not one of the few. He stroked his moustache, and returned to his petticoat government. The two grooms were dismissed.

The entry of the third and last man took me completely by surprise.

If the stranger's short coat and tight trousers had not proclaimed his vocation in life, I should have taken it for granted that there had been some mistake, and that we were favoured with a visit from a gentleman unknown. He was between dark and light in complexion, with frank clear blue eyes; quiet and intelligent, if appearances were to be trusted; easy in his movements; respectful in his manner, but perfectly free from servility. 'I say!' the General blurted out, addressing my aunt confidentially, '*he* looks as if he would do, doesn't he?'

The appearance of the new man seemed to have had the same effect on Lady Claudia which it had produced on me. But she got over her first feeling of surprise sooner than I did. 'You know best,' she answered, with the air of a woman who declined to trouble herself by giving an opinion.

'Step forward, my man,' said the General. The groom advanced from the door, bowed, and stopped at the foot of the table – my uncle sitting at the head, with my aunt and myself on either side of him. The inevitable questions began.

'What is your name?'

'Michael Bloomfield.'

'Your age?'

'Twenty-six.'

My aunt's want of interest in the proceedings expressed itself by a little weary sigh. She leaned back resignedly in her chair.

The General went on with his questions: 'What experience have you had as a groom?'

'I began learning my work, sir, before I was twelve years old.'

'Yes! yes! I mean, what private families have you served in?'

'Two, sir.'

'How long have you been in your two situations?'

'Four years in the first; and three in the second.'

The General looked agreeably surprised. 'Seven years in only two situations is a good character in itself,' he remarked. 'Who are your references?'

The groom laid two papers on the table.

'I don't take written references,' said the General.

'Be pleased to read my papers, sir,' answered the groom.

My uncle looked sharply across the table. The groom sustained the look with respectful but unshaken composure. The General took up the papers, and seemed to be once more favourably impressed as he read them. 'Personal references in each case if required, in support of strong written recommendations from both his employers,' he informed my aunt. 'Copy the addresses, Mina. Very satisfactory, I must say. Don't you think so yourself?' he resumed, turning again to my aunt.

Lady Claudia replied by a courteous bend of her head. The General went on with his questions. They related to the management of horses; and they were answered to his complete satisfaction.

'Michael Bloomfield, you know your business,' he said, 'and you have a good character. Leave your address. When I have consulted your references, you shall hear from me.'

The groom took out a blank card, and wrote his name and address on it. I looked over my uncle's shoulder when he received the card. Another surprise! The handwriting was simply irreproachable – the lines running perfectly straight, and every letter completely formed. As this perplexing person made his modest bow, and withdrew, the General, struck by an after-thought, called him back from the door.

'One thing more,' said my uncle. 'About friends and followers? I consider it my duty to my servants to allow them to see their relations; but I expect them to submit to certain conditions in return—'

'I beg your pardon, sir,' the groom interposed. 'I shall not give you any trouble on that score. I have no relations.'

'No brothers or sisters?' asked the General.

'None, sir.'

'Father and mother both dead?'

'I don't know, sir.'

'You don't know! What does that mean?' ·

'I am telling you the plain truth, sir. I never heard who my father and mother were – and I don't expect to hear now.'

He said those words with a bitter composure which impressed me painfully. Lady Claudia was far from feeling it as I did. Her languid interest in the engagement of the groom seemed to be completely exhausted – and that was all. She rose, in her easy graceful way, and looked out of the window at the courtyard and fountain, the house-dog in his kennel, and the box of flowers in the coachman's window.

In the meanwhile, the groom remained near the table, respectfully waiting for his dismissal. The General spoke to him sharply, for the first time. I could see that my good uncle had noticed the cruel tone of that passing reference to the parents, and thought of it as I did.

'One word more, before you go,' he said. 'If I don't find you more mercifully inclined towards my horses than you seem to be towards your father and mother, you won't remain long in my service. You might have told me you had never heard who your parents were, without speaking as if you didn't care to hear.'

'May I say a bold word, sir, in my own defence?'

He put the question very quietly, but, at the same time, so firmly that he even surprised my aunt. She looked round from the window – then turned back again, and stretched out her hand towards the curtain, intending, as I supposed, to alter the arrangement of it. The groom went on.

'May I ask, sir, why I should care about a father and mother who deserted me? Mind what you are about, my lady!' he cried – suddenly addressing my aunt. 'There's a cat in the folds of that curtain; she might frighten you.'

He had barely said the words, before the housekeeper's large tabby cat, taking its noonday siesta in the looped-up fold of the curtain, leaped out and made for the door.

Lady Claudia was, naturally enough, a little perplexed by the man's discovery of an animal completely hidden in the curtain. She appeared to think that a person who was only a groom had taken a liberty in presuming to puzzle her. Like her husband, she spoke to Michael sharply.

'Did you see the cat?' she asked.

'No, my lady.'

'Then how did you know the creature was in the curtain?'

For the first time since he had entered the room, the groom looked a little confused.

'It's a sort of presumption for a man in my position to be subject to a nervous infirmity,' he answered. 'I am one of those persons (the weakness is not uncommon, as your ladyship is aware) who know by their own unpleasant sensations when a cat is in the room. It goes a little farther than that with me. The "antipathy," as the gentlefolks call it, tells me in what part of the room the cat is.'

My aunt turned to her husband, without attempting to conceal that she took no sort of interest in the groom's antipathies.

'Haven't you done with the man yet?' she asked.

The General gave the groom his dismissal.

'You shall hear from me in three days' time. Good-morning.'

Michael Bloomfield seemed to have noticed my aunt's ungracious manner. He looked at her for a moment with steady attention, before he left the room.

V

'You don't mean to engage that man?' said Lady Claudia as the door closed.

'Why not?' asked my uncle.

'I have taken a dislike to him.'

This short answer was so entirely out of the character of my aunt, that the General took her kindly by the hand, and said:

'I am afraid you are not well.'

She irritably withdrew her hand.

'I don't feel well. It doesn't matter.'

'It does matter, Claudia. What can I do for you?'

'Write to the man –' She paused and smiled contemptuously. 'Imagine a groom with an antipathy to cats!' she said, turning to me. 'I don't know what you think, Mina. I have a strong objection, myself, to servants who hold themselves above their position in life. Write,' she resumed, addressing her husband, 'and tell him to look for another place.'

'What objection can I make to him?' the General asked helplessly.

'Good heavens! can't you make an excuse? Say he is too young.'

My uncle looked at me in expressive silence – walked slowly to the writing-table – and glanced at his wife, in the faint hope that she might change her mind. Their eyes met – and she seemed to recover the command of her temper. She put her hand caressingly on the General's shoulder.

'I remember the time,' she said softly, 'when any caprice of mine was a command to you. Ah, I was younger then!'

The General's reception of this little advance was thoroughly characteristic of him. He first kissed Lady Claudia's hand, and then he wrote the letter. My aunt rewarded him by a look, and left the library.

'What the deuce is the matter with her?' my uncle said to me, when we were alone. 'Do you dislike the man too?'

'Certainly not. So far as I can judge, he appears to be just the sort of person we want.'

'And knows thoroughly well how to manage horses, my dear. What *can* be your aunt's objection to him?'

As the words passed his lips, Lady Claudia opened the library door.

'I am so ashamed of myself,' she said sweetly. 'At my age, I have been behaving like a spoilt child. How good you are to me, General! Let me try to make amends for my misconduct. Will you permit me?'

She took up the General's letter, without waiting for permission; tore it to pieces, smiling pleasantly all the while; and threw the fragments into the waste-paper basket. 'As if you didn't know better than I do!' she said, kissing him on the forehead. 'Engage the man by all means.'

She left the room for the second time. For the second time my uncle looked at me in blank perplexity – and I looked back at him in the same condition of mind. The sound of the luncheon bell was equally a relief to both of us. Not a word more was spoken on the subject of the new groom. His references were verified; and he entered the General's service in three days' time.

VI

Always careful in anything that concerned my welfare, no matter how trifling it might be, my uncle did not trust me alone with the new groom when he first entered our service. Two old friends of the General accompanied me at his special request, and reported the man to be perfectly competent and trustworthy. After that, Michael rode out with me alone; my friends among young ladies seldom caring to accompany me, when I abandoned the Park for the quiet country roads, on the north and west of London. Was it wrong in me to talk to him on these expeditions? It would surely have been treating a man like a brute never to take the smallest notice of him – especially as his conduct was uniformly respectful towards me. Not once, by word or look, did he presume on the position which my favour permitted him to occupy.

Ought I to blush, when I confess (though he was only a groom) that he interested me?

In the first place, there was something romantic in the very blankness of the story of his life.

He had been left, in his infancy, in the stables of a gentleman living in Kent, near the high-road between Gravesend and Rochester. The same day, the stable-boy had met a woman running out of the yard, pursued by the dog. She was a stranger and was not well dressed. While the boy was protecting her by chaining the dog to his kennel, she was quick enough to place herself beyond the reach of pursuit.

The infant's clothing proved, on examination, to be of the finest linen. He was warmly wrapt in a beautiful shawl of some foreign manufacture, entirely unknown to all the persons present, including the master and mistress of the house. Among the folds of the shawl there was discovered an open letter, without date, signature, or address, which it was presumed the woman must have forgotten.

Like the shawl, the paper was of foreign manufacture. The handwriting presented a strongly marked character; and the composition plainly revealed the mistakes of a person imperfectly acquainted with the English language. The contents of the letter, after alluding to the means supplied for the support of the child, announced that the writer had committed the folly of enclosing a sum of a hundred pounds in a bank-note, 'to pay expenses.' In a postscript, an appointment was made for a meeting, in six months' time, on the eastward side of London Bridge. The stable-boy's description of the woman who had passed him showed that she belonged to the lower class. To such a person a hundred pounds would be a fortune. She had, no doubt, abandoned the child, and made off with the money.

No trace of her was ever discovered. On the day of the appointment the police watched the eastward side of London Bridge without obtaining any result. Through the kindness of the gentleman in whose stable he had been found, the first ten years of the boy's life were passed under the protection of a charitable asylum. They gave him the name of one of the little inmates who had died; and they sent him out to service before he was eleven years old. He was harshly treated, and ran away; wandered to some training-stables near Newmarket; attracted the favourable notice of the head-groom, was employed among the other boys, and liked the occupation. Growing up to manhood, he had taken service in private families as a groom. This was the story of twenty-six years of Michael's life!

But there was something in the man himself which attracted attention, and made one think of him in his absence.

I mean by this, that there was a spirit of resistance to his destiny in him, which is very rarely found in serving-men of his order. I remember accompanying the General 'on one of his periodical visits of inspection to the stable.' He was so well satisfied, that he proposed extending his investigations to the groom's own room.

'If you don't object, Michael?' he added, with his customary consideration for the self-respect of all persons in his employment. Michael's colour rose a little; he looked at me. 'I am afraid the young lady will not find my room quite so tidy as it ought to be,' he said as he opened the door for us.

The only disorder in the groom's room was produced, to our surprise, by the groom's books and papers.

Cheap editions of the English poets, translations of Latin and Greek classics, handbooks for teaching French and German 'without a master,' carefully written 'exercises' in both languages, manuals of shorthand, with more 'exercises' in that art, were scattered over the table, round the central object of a reading-lamp, which spoke plainly of studies by night. 'Why, what is all this?' cried the General. 'Are you going to leave me, Michael, and set up a school?' Michael answered in sad submissive tones. 'I try to improve myself, sir – though I sometimes lose heart and hope.' 'Hope of what?' asked my uncle. 'Are you not content to be a servant? Must you rise in the world, as the saying is?' The groom shrank a little at that abrupt question. 'If I had relations to care for me and help me along the hard ways of life,' he said, 'I might be satisfied, sir, to remain as I am. As it is, I have no one to think about but myself – and I am foolish enough sometimes to look beyond myself.'

So far, I had kept silence; but I could no longer resist giving him a word of encouragement – his confession was so sadly and so patiently made. 'You speak too harshly of yourself,' I said; 'the best and greatest men have begun like you by looking beyond themselves.' For a moment our eyes met. I admired the poor lonely fellow trying so modestly and so bravely to teach himself – and I did not care to conceal it. He was the first to look away; some suppressed emotion turned him deadly pale. Was I the cause of it? I felt myself tremble as that bold question came into my mind. The General, with one sharp glance at me, diverted the talk (not very delicately, as I thought) to the misfortune of Michael's birth.

'I have heard of your being deserted in your infancy by some woman unknown,' he said. 'What has become of the things you were wrapped in, and the letter that was found on you? They might lead to a discovery, one of these days.' The groom smiled. 'The last master I served thought of it as you do, sir. He was so good as to write to the gentleman who was first burdened with the care of me – and the things were sent to me in return.'

He took up an unlocked leather bag, which opened by touching a brass knob, and showed us the shawl, the linen (sadly faded by time), and the letter. We were puzzled by the shawl. My uncle, who had served in the East, thought it looked like a very rare kind of Persian work. We examined with interest the letter, and the fine linen. When Michael quietly remarked, as we handed them back to him, 'They keep the secret, you see,' we could only look at each other, and own there was nothing more to be said.

VII

That night, lying awake thinking, I made my first discovery of a great change that had come over me. I felt like a new woman.

Never yet had my life been so enjoyable to me as it was now. I was conscious of a delicious lightness of heart. The simplest things pleased me; I was ready to be kind to everybody, and to admire everything. Even the familiar scenery of my rides in the Park developed beauties which I had never noticed before. The enchantments of music affected me to tears. I was absolutely in love with my dogs and my birds – and, as for my maid, I bewildered the girl with presents, and gave her holidays almost before she could ask for them. In a bodily sense, I felt an extraordinary accession of strength and activity. I romped with the dear old General, and actually kissed Lady Claudia, one morning, instead of letting her kiss me as usual. My friends noticed my new outburst of gaiety and spirit – and wondered what had produced it. I can honestly say that I wondered too! Only on that wakeful night which followed our visit to Michael's room, did I arrive at something like a clear understanding of myself. The next morning completed the process of enlightenment. I went out riding as usual. The instant when Michael put his hand under my foot as I sprang into the saddle, his touch flew all over me like a flame. I knew who had made a new woman of me from that moment.

As to describing the first sense of confusion that overwhelmed me, even if I were a practised writer I should be incapable of doing it. I pulled down my veil, and rode on in a sort of trance. Fortunately for me, our house looked on the Park, and I had only to cross the road. Otherwise, I should have met with some accident if I had ridden through the streets. To this day, I don't know where I rode. The horse went his own way quietly – and the groom followed me.

The groom! Is there any human creature so free from the hateful and anti-Christian pride of rank as a woman who loves with all her heart and soul, for the first time in her life? I only tell the truth (in however unfavourable a light it may place me) when I declare that my confusion was entirely due to the discovery that I was in love. I was not ashamed of myself for being in love with the groom. I had given my heart to the *man*. What did the accident of his position matter? Put money into his pocket and a title before his name – by another accident: in speech, manners, and attainments, he would be a gentleman worthy of his wealth and worthy of his rank.

Even the natural dread of what my relations and friends might say, if they discovered my secret, seemed to be a sensation so unworthy of me and of him, that I looked round, and called to him to speak to me, and asked him questions about himself which kept him riding nearly side by side with me. Ah, how I enjoyed the gentle deference and respect of his manner as he answered me! He was hardly bold enough to raise his eyes to mine, when I looked at him. Absorbed in the Paradise of my own making, I rode on slowly, and was only aware that friends had passed and had recognised me, by seeing him touch his hat. I looked round and discovered the women smiling ironically as they rode by. That one circumstance roused me rudely from my dream. I let Michael fall back again to his proper place, and quickened my horse's pace; angry with myself, angry with the world in general – then suddenly changing, and being fool enough and child enough to feel ready to cry. How long these varying moods lasted, I don't know. On returning, I slipped off my horse without waiting for Michael to help me, and ran into the house without even wishing him 'Good-day.'

VIII

After taking off my riding-habit, and cooling my hot face with eau-de-cologne and water, I went down to the room which we called the morning-room. The piano there was my favourite instrument – and I had the idea of trying what music would do towards helping me to compose myself.

As I sat down before the piano, I heard the opening of the door of the breakfast room (separated from me by a curtained archway), and the voice of Lady Claudia asking if Michael had returned to the stable. On the servant's reply in the affirmative, she desired that he might be sent to her immediately.

No doubt, I ought either to have left the morning-room, or to have let my aunt know of my presence there. I did neither the one nor the other. Her first dislike of Michael had, to all appearance, subsided. She had once or twice actually taken opportunities of speaking to him kindly. I believed this was due to the caprice of the moment. The tone of her voice too suggested, on this occasion, that she had some spiteful object in view, in sending for him. I knew it was unworthy of me – and yet, I deliberately waited to hear what passed between them.

Lady Claudia began.

'You were out riding to-day with Miss Mina?'

'Yes, my lady.'

'Turn to the light. I wish to see people when I speak to them. You were observed by some friends of mine; your conduct excited remark. Do you know your business as a lady's groom?'

'I have had seven years' experience, my lady.'

'Your business is to ride at a certain distance behind your mistress. Has your experience taught you that?'

'Yes, my lady.'

'You were not riding behind Miss Mina – your horse was almost side by side with hers. Do you deny it?'

'No, my lady.'

'You behaved with the greatest impropriety – you were seen talking to Miss Mina. Do you deny that?'

'No, my lady.'

'Leave the room. No! come back. Have you any excuse to make?'

'None, my lady.'

'Your insolence is intolerable! I shall speak to the General.'

The sound of the closing door followed.

I knew now what the smiles meant on the false faces of those women-friends of mine who had met me in the Park. An ordinary man, in Michael's place, would have mentioned my own encouragement of him as a sufficient excuse. *He*, with the inbred delicacy and reticence of a gentleman, had taken all the blame on himself. Indignant and ashamed, I advanced to the breakfast-room, bent on instantly justifying him. Drawing aside the curtain, I was startled by a sound as of a person sobbing. I cautiously looked in. Lady Claudia was prostrate on the sofa, hiding her face in her hands, in a passion of tears.

I withdrew, completely bewildered. The extraordinary contradictions in my aunt's conduct were not at an end yet. Later in the day, I went to my uncle, resolved to set Michael right in *his* estimation, and to leave him to speak to Lady Claudia. The General was in the lowest spirits; he shook his head ominously the moment I mentioned the groom's name. 'I dare say the man meant no harm – but the thing has been observed. I can't have you made the subject of scandal, Mina. My wife makes a point of it – Michael must go.'

'You don't mean to say that she has insisted on your sending Michael away?'

Before he could answer me, a footman appeared with a message. 'My lady wishes to see you, sir.'

The General rose directly. My curiosity had got, by this time, beyond all restraint. I was actually indelicate enough to ask if I might go with him! He stared at me, as well he might. I persisted; I said I particularly wished to see Lady Claudia. My uncle's punctilious good breeding still resisted me. 'Your aunt may wish to speak to me in private,' he said. 'Wait a moment, and I will send for you.'

I was incapable of waiting; my obstinacy was something superhuman. The bare idea that Michael might lose his place, through my fault, made me desperate, I suppose. 'I won't trouble you to send for me,' I persisted; 'I will go with you at once as far as the door, and wait to hear if I may come in.' The footman was still present, holding the door open; the General gave way. I kept so close behind him, that my aunt saw me as her husband entered the room. 'Come in, Mina,' she said, speaking and looking like the charming Lady Claudia of everyday life. Was this the woman whom I had seen crying her heart out on the sofa hardly an hour ago?

'On second thoughts,' she continued, turning to the General, 'I fear I may have been a little hasty. Pardon me for troubling you about it again – have you spoken to Michael yet? No? Then let us err on the side of kindness; let us look over his misconduct this time.'

My uncle was evidently relieved. I seized the opportunity of making my confession, and taking the whole blame on myself. Lady Claudia stopped me with the perfect grace of which she was mistress.

'My good child, don't distress yourself! don't make mountains out of molehills!' She patted me on the cheek with two plump white fingers which felt deadly cold. 'I was not always prudent, Mina, when I was your age. Besides, your curiosity is naturally excited about a servant who is – what shall I call him? – a foundling.'

She paused and fixed her eyes on me attentively. 'What did he tell you?' she asked. 'Is it a very romantic story?'

The General began to fidget in his chair. If I had kept my attention on him, I should have seen in his face a warning to me to be silent. But my interest at the moment was absorbed in my aunt. Encouraged by her amiable reception, I was not merely unsuspicious of the trap that she had set for me – I was actually foolish enough to think that I could improve Michael's position in her estimation (remember that I was in love with him!) by telling his story exactly as I have already told it in these pages. I spoke with fervour. Will you believe it? – her humour positively changed again! She flew into a passion with me for the first time in her life.

'Lies!' she cried. 'Impudent lies on the face of them – invented to appeal to your interest. How dare you repeat them? General! If Mina had not brought it on herself, this man's audacity would justify you in instantly dismissing him. Don't you agree with me?'

The General's sense of fair play roused him for once into openly opposing his wife. 'You are completely mistaken,' he said. 'Mina and I have both had the shawl and the letter in our hands – and (what was there besides?) – ah, yes, the very linen the child was wrapped in.'

What there was in those words to check Lady Claudia's anger in its full flow, I was quite unable to understand. If her husband had put a pistol to her head, he could hardly have silenced her more effectually. She did not appear to be frightened, or ashamed of her outbreak of rage – she sat vacant and speechless, with her eyes on the General and her hands crossed on her lap. After waiting a moment (wondering as I did what it meant) my uncle rose with his customary resignation and left her. I followed him. He was unusually silent and thoughtful; not a word passed between us. I afterwards discovered that he was beginning to fear, poor man, that his wife's mind must be affected in some way, and was meditating a consultation with the physician who helped us in cases of need.

As for myself, I was either too stupid or too innocent to feel any positive forewarning of the truth, so far. After luncheon, while I was alone in the conservatory, my maid came to me from Michael, asking if I had any commands for him in the afternoon. I thought this rather odd; but it occurred to me that he might want some hours to himself. I made the inquiry.

To my astonishment, the maid announced that Lady Claudia had employed Michael to go on an errand for her. The nature of the errand was to take a letter to her bookseller, and to bring back the books which she had ordered. With three idle footmen in the house, whose business it was to perform such service as this, why had she taken the groom away from his work? The question obtained such complete possession of my mind, that I actually summoned courage enough to go to my aunt. I said I had thought of driving out in my pony-carriage that afternoon, and I asked if she objected to sending one of the three indoor servants for her books in Michael's place.

She received me with a strange hard stare, and answered with obstinate self-possession, 'I wish Michael to go.' No explanation followed. With reason or without it, agreeable to me or not agreeable to me, she wished Michael to go.

I begged her pardon for interfering, and replied that I would give up the idea of driving on that day. She made no further remark. I left the room, determining to watch her. There is no defence for my conduct; it was mean and unbecoming, no doubt. I was drawn on, by some force in me which I could not even attempt to resist. Indeed, indeed I am not a mean person by nature!

At first, I thought of speaking to Michael; not with any special motive, but simply because I felt drawn towards him as the guide and helper in whom my heart trusted at this crisis in my life. A little consideration, however, suggested to me that I might be seen speaking to him, and might so do him an injury. While I was still hesitating, the thought came to me that my aunt's motive for sending him to her bookseller might be to get him out of her way.

Out of her way in the house? No: his place was not in the house. Out of her way in the stable? The next instant, the idea flashed across my mind of watching the stable door.

The best bedrooms, my room included, were all in front of the house. I went up to my maid's room, which looked on the court-yard; ready with my excuse, if she happened to be there. She was not there. I placed myself at the window, in full view of the stable opposite.

An interval elapsed – long or short, I cannot say which; I was too much excited to look at my watch. All I know is that I discovered her! She crossed the yard, after waiting to make sure that no one was there to see her; and she entered the stable by the door which led to that part of the building occupied by Michael. This time I looked at my watch.

Forty minutes passed before I saw her again. And then, instead of appearing at the door, she showed herself at the window of Michael's room; throwing it wide open. I concealed myself behind the window curtain, just in time to escape discovery, as she looked up at the house. She next appeared in the yard, hurrying back. I waited a while, trying to compose myself in case I met anyone on the stairs. There was little danger of a meeting at that hour. The General was at his club; the servants were at their tea. I reached my own room without being seen by anyone, and locked myself in.

What had my aunt been doing for forty minutes in Michael's room? And why had she opened the window?

I spare you my reflections on these perplexing questions. A convenient head-ache saved me from the ordeal of meeting Lady Claudia at the dinner-table. I passed a restless and miserable night; conscious that I had found my way blindly, as it were, to some terrible secret which might have its influence on my whole future life, and not knowing what to think, or what to do next. Even then, I shrank instinctively from speaking to my uncle. This was not wonderful. But I felt afraid to speak to Michael – and that perplexed and alarmed me. Consideration for Lady Claudia was certainly not the motive that kept me silent, after what I had seen.

The next morning, my pale face abundantly justified the assertion that I was still ill.

My aunt, always doing her maternal duty towards me, came herself to inquire after my health before I was out of my room. So certain was she of not having been observed on the previous day – or so prodigious was her power of controlling herself – that she actually advised me to go out riding before lunch, and try what the fresh air and the exercise would do to relieve me! Feeling that I must end in speaking to Michael, it struck me that this would be the one safe way of consulting him in private. I accepted her advice, and had another approving pat on the cheek from her plump white fingers. They no longer struck cold on my skin; the customary vital warmth had returned to them. Her ladyship's mind had recovered its tranquillity.

IX

I left the house for my morning ride.

Michael was not in his customary spirits. With some difficulty, I induced him to tell me the reason. He had decided on giving notice to leave his situation in the General's employment. As soon as I could command myself, I asked what had happened to justify this incomprehensible proceeding on his part. He silently offered me a letter. It was written by the master whom he had served before he came to us; and it announced that an employment as secretary was offered to him, in the house of a gentleman who was 'interested in his creditable efforts to improve his position in the world.'

What it cost me to preserve the outward appearance of composure as I handed back the letter, I am ashamed to tell. I spoke to him with some bitterness. 'Your wishes are gratified,' I said; 'I don't wonder that you are eager to leave your place.' He reined back his horse, and repeated my words. 'Eager to leave my place? I am heart-broken at leaving it.' I was reckless enough to ask why. His head sank. 'I daren't tell you,' he said. I went on from one imprudence to another. 'What are you afraid of?' I asked. He suddenly looked up at me. His eyes answered: '*You.*'

Is it possible to fathom the folly of a woman in love? Can any sensible person imagine the enormous importance which the veriest trifles assume in her poor little mind? I was perfectly satisfied – even perfectly happy, after that one look. I rode on briskly for a minute or two – then the forgotten scene at the stable recurred to my memory. I resumed a foot-pace and beckoned to him to speak to me.

'Lady Claudia's bookseller lives in the City, doesn't he?' I began.

'Yes, Miss.'

'Did you walk both ways?'

'Yes.'

'You must have felt tired when you got back?'

'I hardly remember what I felt when I got back – I was met by a surprise.'

'May I ask what it was?'

'Certainly, Miss. Do you remember a black bag of mine?'

'Perfectly.'

'When I returned from the City, I found the bag open; and the things I kept in it – the shawl, the linen, and the letter—'

'Gone?'

'Gone.'

My heart gave one great leap in me, and broke into vehement throbbings, which made it impossible for me to say a word more. I reined up my horse, and fixed my eyes on Michael. He was startled; he asked if I felt faint. I could only sign to him that I was waiting to hear more.

'My own belief,' he proceeded, 'is that some person burnt the things in my absence, and opened the window to prevent any suspicion being excited by the smell. I am certain I shut the window before I left my room. When I closed it on my return, the fresh air had not entirely removed the smell of burning; and, what is more, I found a heap of ashes in the grate. As to the person who has done me this injury, and why it has been done, those are mysteries beyond my fathoming – I beg your pardon, Miss, I am sure you are not well. Might I advise you to return to the house?'

I accepted his advice, and turned back.

In the tumult of horror and amazement that filled my mind, I could still feel a faint triumph stirring in me through it all, when I saw how alarmed and how anxious he was about me. Nothing more passed between us on the way back. Confronted by the dreadful discovery that I had now made, I was silent and helpless. Of the guilty persons concerned in the concealment of the birth, and in the desertion of the infant, my nobly-born, highly-bred, irreproachable aunt now stood revealed before me as one! An older woman than I was might have been hard put to it to preserve her presence of mind, in such a position as mine. Instinct, not reason, served me in my sore need. Instinct, not reason, kept me passively and stupidly silent when I got back to the house. 'We will talk about it to-morrow,' was all I could say to Michael, when he gently lifted me from my horse.

I excused myself from appearing at the luncheon-table; and I drew down the blinds in my sitting-room, so that my face might not betray me when Lady Claudia's maternal duty brought her upstairs to make inquiries. The same excuse served in both cases – my ride had failed to relieve me of my headache. My aunt's brief visit led to one result which is worth mentioning. The indescribable horror of her that I felt, forced the conviction on my mind that we two could live no longer under the same roof. While I was still trying to face this alternative with the needful composure, my uncle presented himself, in some anxiety about my continued illness. I should certainly have burst out crying, when the kind and dear old man condoled with me, if he had not brought news with him which turned back all my thoughts on myself and my aunt. Michael had shown the General his letter, and had given notice to leave. Lady Claudia was present at the time. To her husband's amazement, she abruptly interfered with a personal request to Michael to think better of it, and to remain in his place!

'I should not have troubled you, my dear, on this unpleasant subject,' said my uncle, 'if Michael had not told me that you were aware of the circumstances under which he feels it his duty to leave us. After your aunt's interference (quite incomprehensible to *me*), the man hardly knows what to do. Being your groom, he begs me to ask if there is any impropriety in his leaving the difficulty to your decision. I tell you of his request, Mina; but I strongly advise you to decline taking any responsibility on yourself.'

I answered mechanically, accepting my uncle's suggestion, while my thoughts were wholly absorbed in this last of the many extraordinary proceedings on Lady Claudia's part since Michael had entered the house. There are limits – out of books and plays – to the innocence of a young unmarried woman. After what I had just heard, the doubts which had thus far perplexed me were suddenly and completely cleared up. I said to my secret self: 'She has some human feeling left. If her son goes away, she knows that they may never meet again!'

From the moment when my mind emerged from the darkness, I recovered the use of such intelligence and courage as I naturally possessed. From this point, you will find that, right or wrong, I saw my way before me, and took it.

To say that I felt for the General with my whole heart, is merely to own that I could be commonly grateful. I sat on his knee, and laid my cheek against his cheek, and thanked him for his long, long years of kindness to me. He stopped me in his simple generous way. 'Why, Mina, you talk as if you were going to leave us!' I started up, and went to the window, opening it and complaining of the heat, and so concealing from him that he had unconsciously anticipated the event that was indeed to come. When I returned to my chair, he helped me to recover myself by alluding once more to his wife. He feared that her health was in some way impaired. In the time when they had first met, she was subject to nervous maladies, having their origin in a 'calamity' which was never mentioned by either of them in later days. She might possibly be suffering again, from some other form of nervous derangement, and he seriously thought of persuading her to send for medical advice.

Under ordinary circumstances, this vague reference to a 'calamity' would not have excited any special interest in me. But my mind was now in a state of morbid suspicion. I had not heard how long my uncle and aunt had been married; but I remembered that Michael had described himself as being twenty-six years old. Bearing these circumstances in mind, it struck me that I might be acting wisely (in Michael's interest) if I persuaded the General to speak further of what had happened, at the time when he met the woman whom an evil destiny had bestowed on him for a wife. Nothing but the consideration of serving the man I loved, would have reconciled me to making my own secret use of the recollections which my uncle might innocently confide to me. As it was, I thought the means would, in this case, be for once justified by the end. Before we part, I have little doubt that you will think so too.

I found it an easier task than I had anticipated to turn the talk back again to the days when the General had seen Lady Claudia for the first time. He was proud of the circumstances under which he had won his wife. Ah, how my heart ached for him as I saw his eyes sparkle, and the colour mount in his fine rugged face!

This is the substance of what I heard from him. I tell it briefly, because it is still painful to me to tell it at all.

My uncle had met Lady Claudia at her father's country house. She had then reappeared in society, after a period of seclusion, passed partly in England, partly on the Continent. Before the date of her retirement, she had been engaged to marry a French nobleman, equally illustrious by his birth, and by his diplomatic services in the East. Within a few weeks of the wedding-day, he was drowned by the wreck of his yacht. This was the calamity to which my uncle had referred.

Lady Claudia's mind was so seriously affected by the dreadful event, that the doctors refused to answer for the consequences, unless she was at once placed in the strictest retirement. Her mother, and a French maid devotedly attached to her, were the only persons whom it was considered safe for the young lady to see, until time and care had in some degree composed her. Her return to her friends and admirers, after the necessary interval of seclusion, was naturally a subject of sincere rejoicing among the guests assembled in her father's house. My uncle's interest in Lady Claudia soon developed into love. They were equals in rank, and well suited to each other in age. The parents raised no obstacles; but they did not conceal from their guest that the disaster which had befallen their daughter was but too likely to disincline her to receive his addresses, or any man's addresses, favourably. To their surprise, they proved to be wrong. The young lady was touched by the simplicity and the delicacy with which her lover urged his suit. She had lived among worldly people. This was a man whose devotion she could believe to be sincere. They were married.

Had no unusual circumstances occurred? Had nothing happened which the General had forgotten? Nothing.

X

It is surely needless that I should stop here, to draw the plain inferences from the events just related.

Any person who remembers that the shawl in which the infant was wrapped came from those Eastern regions which were associated with the French nobleman's diplomatic services – also, that the faults of composition in the letter found on the child were exactly the faults likely to have been committed by the French maid – any person who follows these traces can find his way to the truth as I found mine.

Returning for a moment to the hopes which I had formed of being of some service to Michael, I have only to say that they were at once destroyed, when I heard of the death by drowning of the man to whom the evidence pointed as his father. The prospect looked equally barren when I thought of the miserable mother. That she should openly acknowledge her son in her position, was perhaps not to be expected of any woman. Had she courage enough, or, in plainer words, heart enough to acknowledge him privately?

I called to mind again some of the apparent caprices and contradictions in Lady Claudia's conduct, on the memorable day when Michael had presented himself to fill the vacant place. Look back with me to the record of what she said and did on that occasion, by the light of your present knowledge, and you will see that his likeness to his father must have struck her when he entered the room, and that his statement of his age must have correctly described the age of her son. Recall the actions that followed, after she had been exhausted by her first successful efforts at self-control – the withdrawal to the window to conceal her face; the clutch at the curtain when she felt herself sinking; the harshness of manner under which she concealed her emotions when she ventured to speak to him; the reiterated inconsistencies and vacillations of conduct that followed, all alike due to the protest of Nature, desperately resisted to the last – and say if I did her injustice when I believed her to be incapable of running the smallest risk of discovery at the prompting of maternal love.

There remained, then, only Michael to think of. I remembered how he had spoken of the unknown parents whom he neither expected nor cared to discover. Still, I could not reconcile it to my conscience to accept a chance outbreak of temper, as my sufficient justification for keeping him in ignorance of a discovery which so nearly concerned him. It seemed at least to be my duty to make myself acquainted with the true state of his feelings, before I decided to bear the burden of silence with me to my grave.

What I felt it my duty to do in this serious matter, I determined to do at once. Besides, let me honestly own that I felt lonely and desolate, oppressed by the critical situation in which I was placed, and eager for the relief that it would be to me only to hear the sound of Michael's voice. I sent my maid to say that I wished to speak to him immediately. The crisis was already hanging over my head. That one act brought it down.

XI

He came in, and stood modestly waiting at the door.

After making him take a chair, I began by saying that I had received his message, and that, acting on my uncle's advice, I must abstain from interfering in the question of his leaving, or not leaving, his place. Having in this way established a reason for sending for him, I alluded next to the loss that he had sustained, and asked if he had any prospect of finding out the person who had entered his room in his absence. On his reply in the negative, I spoke of the serious results to him of the act of destruction that had been committed. 'Your last chance of discovering your parents,' I said, 'has been cruelly destroyed.'

He smiled sadly. 'You know already, Miss, that I never expected to discover them.'

I ventured a little nearer to the object I had in view.

'Do you never think of your mother?' I asked. 'At your age, she might be still living. Can you give up all hope of finding her, without feeling your heart ache?'

'If I have done her wrong, in believing that she deserted me,' he answered, 'the heart-ache is but a poor way of expressing the remorse that I should feel.'

I ventured nearer still. 'Even if you were right,' I began – 'even if she did desert you—'

He interrupted me sternly. 'I would not cross the street to see her,' he said. 'A woman who deserts her child is a monster. Forgive me for speaking so, Miss! When I see good mothers and their children, it maddens me when I think of what *my* childhood was.'

Hearing those words, and watching him attentively while he spoke, I could see that my silence would be a mercy, not a crime. I hastened to speak of other things. 'If you decide to leave us,' I said, 'when shall you go?'

His eyes softened instantly. Little by little the colour faded out of his face as he answered me.

'The General kindly said, when I spoke of leaving my place –' His voice faltered, and he paused to steady it. 'My master,' he resumed, 'said that I need not keep my new employer waiting by staying for the customary month, provided – provided you were willing to dispense with my services.'

So far, I had succeeded in controlling myself. At that reply I felt my resolution failing me. I saw how he suffered; I saw how manfully he struggled to conceal it.

'I am not willing,' I said. 'I am sorry – very, very sorry to lose you. But I will do anything that is for your good. I can say no more.'

He rose suddenly, as if to leave the room; mastered himself; stood for a moment silently looking at me – then looked away again, and said his parting words.

'If I succeed, Miss Mina, in my new employment – if I get on perhaps to higher things – is it – is it presuming too much, to ask if I might, some day – perhaps when you are out riding alone – if I might speak to you – only to ask if you are well and happy—'

He could say no more. I saw the tears in his eyes; saw him shaken by the convulsive breathings which break from men in the rare moments when they cry. He forced it back even then. He bowed to me – oh, God, he bowed to me, as if he were only my servant! as if he were too far below me to take my hand, even at that moment! I could have endured anything else; I believe I could still have restrained myself under any other circumstances. It matters little now; my confession must be made, whatever you may think of me. I flew to him like a frenzied creature – I threw my arms round his neck – I said to him, 'Oh, Michael, don't you know that I love you?' And then I laid my head on his breast, and held him to me, and said no more.

In that moment of silence, the door of the room was opened. I started, and looked up. Lady Claudia was standing on the threshold.

I saw in her face that she had been listening – she must have followed him when he was on his way to my room. That conviction steadied me. I took his hand in mine, and stood side by side with him, waiting for her to speak first. She looked at Michael, not at me. She advanced a step or two, and addressed him in these words: 'It is just possible that *you* have some sense of decency left. Leave the room.'

That deliberate insult was all I wanted to make me completely mistress of myself. I told Michael to wait a moment, and opened my writing-desk. I wrote on an envelope the address in London of a faithful old servant, who had attended my mother in her last moments. I gave it to Michael. 'Call there to-morrow morning,' I said. 'You will find me waiting for you.'

He looked at Lady Claudia, evidently unwilling to leave me alone with her. 'Fear nothing,' I said; 'I am old enough to take care of myself. I have only a word to say to this lady before I leave the house.' With that, I took his arm, and walked with him to the door, and said good-bye almost as composedly as if we had been husband and wife already.

Lady Claudia's eyes followed me as I shut the door again, and crossed the room to a second door which led into my bed-chamber. She suddenly stepped up to me, just as I was entering the room, and laid her hand on my arm.

'What do I see in your face?' she asked, as much of herself as of me – with her eyes fixed in keen inquiry on mine.

'You shall know directly,' I answered. 'Let me get my bonnet and cloak first.'

'Do you mean to leave the house?'

'I do.'

She rang the bell. I quietly dressed myself, to go out. The servant answered the bell, as I returned to the sitting-room.

'Tell your master I wish to see him instantly,' said Lady Claudia.

'My master has gone out, my lady.'

'To his club?'

'I believe so, my lady.'

'I will send you with a letter to him. Come back when I ring again.' She turned to me as the man withdrew. 'Do you refuse to stay here until the General returns?'

'I shall be happy to see the General, if you will enclose my address in your letter to him.'

Replying in those terms, I wrote the address for the second time. Lady Claudia knew perfectly well, when I gave it to her, that I was going to a respectable house kept by a woman who had nursed me when I was a child.

'One last question,' she said. 'Am I to tell the General that it is your intention to marry your groom?'

Her tone stung me into making an answer which I regretted the moment it had passed my lips.

'You can put it more plainly, if you like,' I said. 'You can tell the General that it is my intention to marry *your son.*'

She was near the door, on the point of leaving me. As I spoke, she turned with a ghastly stare of horror – felt about her with her hands as if she was groping in darkness – and dropped on the floor.

I instantly summoned help. The women-servants carried her to my bed. While they were restoring her to herself, I wrote a few lines telling the miserable woman how I had discovered her secret.

'Your husband's tranquillity,' I added, 'is as precious to me as my own. As for your son, you know what he thinks of the mother who deserted him. Your secret is safe in my keeping – safe from your husband, safe from your son, to the end of my life.'

I sealed up those words, and gave them to her when she had come to herself again. I never heard from her in reply. I have never seen her from that time to this. She knows she can trust me.

And what did my good uncle say, when we next met? I would rather report what he did, when he had got the better of his first feelings of anger and surprise on hearing of my contemplated marriage. He consented to receive us on our wedding-day; and he gave my husband the appointment which places us both in an independent position for life.

But he had his misgivings. He checked me when I tried to thank him.

'Come back in a year's time,' he said. 'I will wait to be thanked till the experience of your married life tells me that I have deserved it.'

The year passed; and the General received the honest expression of my gratitude. He smiled and kissed me; but there was something in his face which suggested that he was not quite satisfied yet.

'Do you believe that I have spoken sincerely?' I asked.

'I firmly believe it,' he answered – and there he stopped.

A wiser woman would have taken the hint and dropped the subject. My folly persisted in putting another question:

'Tell me, uncle. Haven't I proved that I was right when I married my groom?'

'No, my dear. You have only proved that you are a lucky woman!'

Mr Marmaduke and the Minister

Originally appeared in *The Spirit of the Times*, 28 December 1878, as 'The Mystery of Marmaduke'. Reprinted in *Little Novels* (1887). The Minister of Cauldkirk is one of Collins's many satirical portraits of Puritanism. Compare Joanna Grice in *Hide and Seek* (1854) and Drusilla Clack and Godfrey Ablewhite in *The Moonstone* (1868). Exeter Hall was a rallying-point for evangelicals, staging many missions, lecture-courses and revival-meetings.

I

September 13*th* – Winter seems to be upon us, on the Highland Border, already.

I looked out of window, as the evening closed in, before I barred the shutters and drew the curtains for the night. The clouds hid the hilltops on either side of our valley. Fantastic mists parted and met again on the lower slopes, as the varying breeze blew them. The blackening waters of the lake before our window seemed to anticipate the coming darkness. On the more distant hills the torrents were just visible, in the breaks of the mist, stealing their way over the brown ground like threads of silver. It was a dreary scene. The stillness of all things was only interrupted by the splashing of our little waterfall at the back of the house. I was not sorry to close the shutters, and confine the view to the four walls of our sitting-room.

The day happened to be my birthday. I sat by the peat-fire, waiting for the lamp and the tea-tray, and contemplating my past life from the vantage-ground, so to speak, of my fifty-fifth year.

There was wonderfully little to look back on. Nearly thirty years since, it pleased an all-wise Providence to cast my lot in this remote Scottish hamlet, and to make me Minister of Cauldkirk, on a stipend of seventy-four pounds sterling per annum. I and my surroundings have grown quietly older and older together. I have outlived my wife; I have buried one generation among my parishioners, and married another; I have borne the wear and tear of years better than the kirk in which I minister and the manse (or parsonage-house) in which I live – both sadly out of repair, and both still trusting for the means of reparation to the pious benefactions of persons richer than myself. Not that I complain, be it understood, of the humble position which I occupy. I possess many blessings; and I thank the Lord for them. I have my little bit of land and my cow. I have also my good daughter, Felicia; named after her deceased mother, but inheriting her comely looks, it is thought, rather from myself.

Neither let me forget my elder sister, Judith; a friendless single person, sheltered under my roof, whose temperament I could wish somewhat less prone to look at persons and things on the gloomy side, but whose compensating virtues Heaven forbid that I should deny. No; I am grateful for what has been given me (from on high), and resigned to what has been taken away. With what fair prospects did I start in life! Springing from a good old Scottish stock, blest with every advantage of education that the institutions of Scotland and England in turn could offer; with a career at the Bar and in Parliament before me – and all cast to the winds, as it were, by the measureless prodigality of my unhappy father, God forgive him! I doubt if I had five pounds left in my purse, when the compassion of my relatives on the mother's side opened a refuge to me at Cauldkirk, and hid me from the notice of the world for the rest of my life.

September 14*th* – Thus far I had posted up my Diary on the evening of the 13th, when an event occurred so completely unexpected by my household and myself, that the pen, I may say, dropped incontinently from my hand.

It was the time when we had finished our tea, or supper – I hardly know which to call it. In the silence, we could hear the rain pouring against the window, and the wind that had risen with the darkness howling round the house. My sister Judith, taking the gloomy view according to custom – copious draughts of good Bohea and two helpings of such a mutton ham as only Scotland can produce had no effect in raising her spirits – my sister, I say, remarked that there would be ships lost at sea and men drowned this night. My daughter Felicia, the brightest-tempered creature of the female sex that I have ever met with, tried to give a cheerful turn to her aunt's depressing prognostication. 'If the ships must be lost,' she said, 'we may surely hope that the men will be saved.' 'God willing,' I put in – thereby giving to my daughter's humane expression of feeling the fit religious tone that was all it wanted – and then went on with my written record of the events and reflections of the day. No more was said. Felicia took up a book. Judith took up her knitting.

On a sudden, the silence was broken by a blow on the house-door.

My two companions, as is the way of women, set up a scream. I was startled myself, wondering who could be out in the rain and the darkness, and striking at the door of the house. A stranger it must be. Light or dark, any person in or near Cauldkirk, wanting admission, would know where to find the bell-handle at the side of the door. I waited awhile to hear what might happen next. The stroke was repeated, but more softly. It became me as a man and a minister to set an example. I went out into the passage, and I called through the door, 'Who's there?'

A man's voice answered – so faintly that I could barely hear him – 'A lost traveller.'

Immediately upon this my cheerful sister expressed her view of the matter through the open parlour door. 'Brother Noah, it's a robber. Don't let him in!'

What would the Good Samaritan have done in my place? Assuredly he would have run the risk and opened the door. I imitated the Good Samaritan.

A man, dripping wet, with a knapsack on his back and a thick stick in his hand, staggered in, and would I think have fallen in the passage if I had not caught him by the arm. Judith peeped out at the parlour door, and said, 'He's drunk.' Felicia was behind her, holding up a lighted candle the better to see what was going on. 'Look at his face, aunt,' says she. 'Worn out with fatigue, poor man. Bring him in, father – bring him in.'

Good Felicia! I was proud of my girl. 'He'll spoil the carpet,' says sister Judith. I said, 'Silence, for shame!' and brought him in, and dropped him dripping into my own armchair. Would the Good Samaritan have thought of his carpet or his chair? I did think of them, but I overcame it. Ah, we are a decadent generation in these latter days!

'Be quick, father!' says Felicia; 'he'll faint if you don't give him something!'

I took out one of our little drinking cups (called among us a 'Quaigh'), while Felicia, instructed by me, ran to the kitchen for the cream-jug. Filling the cup with whisky and cream in equal proportions, I offered it to him. He drank it off as if it had been so much water. 'Stimulant and nourishment, you'll observe, sir, in equal portions,' I remarked to him. 'How do you feel now?'

'Ready for another,' says he.

Felicia burst out laughing. I gave him another. As I turned to hand it to him, sister Judith came behind me, and snatched away the cream-jug. Never a generous person, sister Judith, at the best of times – more especially in the matter of cream.

He handed me back the empty cup. 'I believe, sir, you have saved my life,' he said. 'Under Providence,' I put in – adding, 'But I would remark, looking to the state of your clothes, that I have yet another service to offer you, before you tell us how you came into this pitiable state.' With that reply, I led him upstairs, and set before him the poor resources of my wardrobe, and left him to do the best he could with them. He was rather a small man, and I am in stature nigh on six feet. When he came down to us in my clothes, we had the merriest evening that I can remember for years past. I thought Felicia would have had an hysteric fit; and even sister Judith laughed – he did look such a comical figure in the minister's garments.

As for the misfortune that had befallen him, it offered one more example of the preternatural rashness of the English traveller in countries unknown to him. He was on a walking tour through Scotland; and he had set forth to go twenty miles a-foot, from a town on one side of the Highland Border to a town on the other, without a guide. The only wonder is that he found his way to Cauldkirk, instead of perishing of exposure among the lonesome hills.

'Will you offer thanks for your preservation to the Throne of Grace, in your prayers to-night?' I asked him. And he answered, 'Indeed I will!'

We have a spare room at the manse; but it had not been inhabited for more than a year past. Therefore we made his bed, for that night, on the sofa in the parlour; and so left him, with the fire on one side of his couch, and the whisky and the mutton ham on the other in case of need. He mentioned his name when we bade him good-night. Marmaduke Falmer of London, son of a minister of the English Church Establishment, now deceased. It was plain, I may add, before he spoke, that we had offered the hospitality of the manse to a man of gentle breeding.

September 15*th* – I have to record a singularly pleasant day; due partly to a return of the fine weather, partly to the good social gifts of our guest.

Attired again in his own clothing, he was, albeit wanting in height, a finely proportioned man, with remarkably small hands and feet; having also a bright mobile face, and large dark eyes of an extraordinary diversity of expression. Also, he was of a sweet and cheerful humour; easily pleased with little things, and amiably ready to make his gifts agreeable to all of us. At the same time, a person of my experience and penetration could not fail to perceive that he was most content when in company with Felicia. I have already mentioned my daughter's comely looks and good womanly qualities. It was in the order of nature that a young man (to use his own phrase) getting near to his thirty-first birthday should feel drawn by sympathy towards a well-favoured young woman in her four-and-twentieth year. In matters of this sort I have always cultivated a liberal turn of mind, not forgetting my own youth.

As the evening closed in, I was sorry to notice a certain change in our guest for the worse. He showed signs of fatigue – falling asleep at intervals in his chair, and waking up and shivering. The spare room was now well aired, having had a roaring fire in it all day.

I begged him not to stand on ceremony, and to betake himself at once to his bed. Felicia (having learned the accomplishment from her excellent mother) made him a warm sleeping-draught of eggs, sugar, nutmeg, and spirits, delicious alike to the senses of smell and taste. Sister Judith waited until he had closed the door behind him, and then favoured me with one of her dismal predictions. 'You'll rue the day, brother, when you let him into the house. He is going to fall ill on our hands.'

II

November 28th – God be praised for all His mercies! This day, our guest, Marmaduke Falmer, joined us downstairs in the sitting-room for the first time since his illness.

He is sadly deteriorated, in a bodily sense, by the wasting rheumatic fever that brought him nigh to death; but he is still young, and the doctor (humanly speaking) has no doubt of his speedy and complete recovery. My sister takes the opposite view. She remarked, in his hearing, that nobody ever thoroughly got over a rheumatic fever. Oh, Judith! Judith! it's well for humanity that you're a single person! If, haply, there had been any man desperate enough to tackle such a woman in the bonds of marriage, what a pessimist progeny must have proceeded from you!

Looking back over my Diary for the last two months and more, I see one monotonous record of the poor fellow's sufferings; cheered and varied, I am pleased to add, by the devoted services of my daughter at the sick man's bedside. With some help from her aunt (most readily given when he was nearest to the point of death), and with needful services performed in turn by two of our aged women in Cauldkirk, Felicia could not have nursed him more assiduously if he had been her own brother. Half the credit of bringing him through it belonged (as the doctor himself confessed) to the discreet young nurse, always ready through the worst of the illness, and always cheerful through the long convalescence that followed. I must also record to the credit of Marmaduke that he was indeed duly grateful. When I led him into the parlour, and he saw Felicia waiting by the armchair, smiling and patting the pillows for him, he took her by the hand, and burst out crying. Weakness, in part, no doubt – but sincere gratitude at the bottom of it, I am equally sure.

November 29th – However, there are limits even to sincere gratitude. Of this truth Mr Marmaduke seems to be insufficiently aware. Entering the sitting-room soon after noon to-day, I found our convalescent guest and his nurse alone. His head was resting on her shoulder; his arm was round her waist – and (the truth before everything) Felicia was kissing him.

A man may be of a liberal turn of mind, and may yet consistently object to freedom when it takes the form of unlicensed embracing and kissing; the person being his own daughter, and the place his own house. I signed to my girl to leave us; and I advanced to Mr Marmaduke, with my opinion of his conduct just rising in words to my lips – when he staggered me with amazement by asking for Felicia's hand in marriage.

'You need feel no doubt of my being able to offer to your daughter a position of comfort and respectability,' he said. 'I have a settled income of eight-hundred pounds a year.'

His raptures over Felicia; his protestations that she was the first woman he had ever really loved; his profane declaration that he preferred to die, if I refused to let him be her husband – all these flourishes, as I may call them, passed in at one of my ears and out at the other. But eight hundred pounds sterling per annum, descending as it were in a golden avalanche on the mind of a Scottish minister (accustomed to thirty years' annual contemplation of seventy-four pounds) – eight hundred a year, in one young man's pocket, I say, completely overpowered me. I just managed to answer, 'Wait till tomorrow' – and hurried out of doors to recover my self-respect, if the thing was to be anywise done. I took my way through the valley. The sun was shining, for a wonder. When I saw my shadow on the hillside, I saw the Golden Calf as an integral part of me, bearing this inscription in letters of flame – 'Here's another of them!'

November 30*th* – I have made amends for yesterday's backsliding; I have acted as becomes my parental dignity and my sacred calling.

The temptation to do otherwise has not been wanting. Here is sister Judith's advice: 'Make sure that he has got the money first; and, for Heaven's sake, nail him!' Here is Mr Marmaduke's proposal: 'Make any conditions you please, so long as you give me your daughter.' And, lastly, here is Felicia's confession: 'Father, my heart is set on him. Oh, don't be unkind to me for the first time in your life!'

But I have stood firm. I have refused to hear any more words on the subject from any one of them, for the next six months to come.

'So serious a venture as the venture of marriage,' I said, 'is not to be undertaken on impulse. As soon as Mr Marmaduke can travel, I request him to leave us, and not to return again for six months. If, after that interval, he is still of the same mind, and my daughter is still of the same mind, let him return to Cauldkirk, and (premising that I am in all other respects satisfied) let him ask me for his wife.'

There were tears, there were protestations; I remained immovable. A week later, Mr Marmaduke left us, on his way by easy stages to the south. I am not a hard man. I rewarded the lovers for their obedience by keeping sister Judith out of the way, and letting them say their farewell words (accompaniments included) in private.

III

May 28*th* – A letter from Mr Marmaduke, informing me that I may expect him at Cauldkirk, exactly at the expiration of the six months' interval – viz., on June the seventh.

Writing to this effect, he added a timely word on the subject of his family. Both his parents were dead; his only brother held a civil appointment in India, the place being named. His uncle (his father's brother) was a merchant resident in London; and to this near relative he referred me, if I wished to make inquiries about him. The names of his bankers, authorised to give me every information in respect to his pecuniary affairs, followed. Nothing could be more plain and straight-forward. I wrote to his uncle, and I wrote to his bankers. In both cases the replies were perfectly satisfactory – nothing in the slightest degree doubtful, no prevarications, no mysteries. In a word, Mr Marmaduke himself was thoroughly well vouched for, and Mr Marmaduke's income was invested in securities beyond fear and beyond reproach. Even sister Judith, bent on picking a hole in the record somewhere, tried hard, and could make nothing of it.

The last sentence in Mr Marmaduke's letter was the only part of it which I failed to read with pleasure.

He left it to me to fix the day for the marriage, and he entreated that I would make it as early a day as possible. I had a touch of the heartache when I thought of parting with Felicia, and being left at home with nobody but Judith. However, I got over it for that time; and, after consulting my daughter, we decided on naming a fortnight after Mr Marmaduke's arrival – that is to say, the twenty-first of June. This gave Felicia time for her preparations, besides offering to me the opportunity of becoming better acquainted with my son-in-law's disposition. The happiest marriage does indubitably make its demands on human forbearance; and I was anxious, among other things, to assure myself of Mr Marmaduke's good temper.

IV

June 22nd – The happy change in my daughter's life (let me say nothing of the change in *my* life) has come: they were married yesterday. The manse is a desert; and sister Judith was never so uncongenial a companion to me as I feel her to be now. Her last words to the married pair, when they drove away, were: 'Lord help you both; you have all your troubles before you!'

I had no heart to write yesterday's record, yesterday evening, as usual. The absence of Felicia at the supper-table completely overcame me. I, who have so often comforted others in their afflictions, could find no comfort for myself. Even now that the day has passed, the tears come into my eyes, only with writing about it. Sad, sad weakness! Let me close my Diary, and open the Bible – and be myself again.

June 23rd – More resigned since yesterday; a more becoming and more pious frame of mind – obedient to God's holy will, and content in the belief that my dear daughter's married life will be a happy one.

They have gone abroad for their holiday – to Switzerland, by way of France. I was anything rather than pleased when I heard that my son-in-law proposed to take Felicia to that sink of iniquity, Paris. He knows already what I think of balls and playhouses, and similar devils' diversions, and how I have brought up my daughter to think of them – the subject having occurred in conversation among us more than a week since. That he could meditate taking a child of mine to the headquarters of indecent jiggings and abominable stage-plays, of spouting rogues and painted Jezebels, was indeed a heavy blow.

However, Felicia reconciled me to it in the end. She declared that her only desire in going to Paris was to see the picture-galleries, the public buildings, and the fair outward aspect of the city generally. 'Your opinions, father, are my opinions,' she said; 'and Marmaduke, I am sure, will so shape our arrangements as to prevent our passing a Sabbath in Paris.' Marmaduke not only consented to this (with the perfect good temper of which I have observed more than one gratifying example in him), but likewise assured me that, speaking for himself personally, it would be a relief to him when they got to the mountains and the lakes. So that matter was happily settled. Go where they may, God bless and prosper them!

Speaking of relief, I must record that Judith has gone away to Aberdeen on a visit to some friends. 'You'll be wretched enough here,' she said at parting, 'all by yourself.' Pure vanity and self-complacence! It may be resignation to her absence, or it may be natural force of mind, I began to be more easy and composed the moment I was alone, and this blessed state of feeling has continued uninterruptedly ever since.

V

September 5th – A sudden change in my life, which it absolutely startles me to record. I am going to London!

My purpose in taking this most serious step is of a twofold nature. I have a greater and a lesser object in view.

The greater object is to see my daughter, and to judge for myself whether certain doubts on the vital question of her happiness, which now torment me night and day, are unhappily founded on truth. She and her husband returned in August from their wedding-tour, and took up their abode in Marmaduke's new residence in London. Up to this time, Felicia's letters to me were, in very truth, the delight of my life – she was so entirely happy, so amazed and delighted with all the wonderful things she saw, so full of love and admiration for the best husband that ever lived. Since her return to London, I perceive a complete change.

She makes no positive complaint, but she writes in a tone of weariness and discontent; she says next to nothing of Marmaduke, and she dwells perpetually on the one idea of my going to London to see her. I hope with my whole heart that I am wrong; but the rare allusions to her husband, and the constantly repeated desire to see her father (while she has not been yet three months married), seem to me to be bad signs. In brief, my anxiety is too great to be endured. I have so arranged matters with one of my brethren as to be free to travel to London cheaply by steamer; and I begin the journey tomorrow.

My lesser object may be dismissed in two words. Having already decided on going to London, I propose to call on the wealthy nobleman who owns all the land hereabouts, and represent to him the discreditable, and indeed dangerous, condition of the parish kirk for want of means to institute the necessary repairs. If I find myself well received, I shall put in a word for the manse, which is almost in as deplorable a condition as the church. My lord is a wealthy man – may his heart and his purse be opened unto me!

Sister Judith is packing my portmanteau. According to custom, she forebodes the worst. 'Never forget,' she says, 'that I warned you against Marmaduke, on the first night when he entered the house.'

VI

September 10th – After more delays than one, on land and sea, I was at last set ashore near the Tower, on the afternoon of yesterday. God help us, my worst anticipations have been realized! My beloved Felicia has urgent and serious need of me.

It is not to be denied that I made my entry into my son-in-law's house in a disturbed and irritated frame of mind. First, my temper was tried by the almost interminable journey, in the noisy and comfortless vehicle which they call a cab, from the river-wharf to the west-end of London, where Marmaduke lives. In the second place, I was scandalised and alarmed by an incident which took place – still on the endless journey from east to west – in a street hard by the market of Covent Garden.

We had just approached a large building, most profusely illuminated with gas, and exhibiting prodigious coloured placards having inscribed on them nothing but the name of Barrymore. The cab came suddenly to a standstill; and looking out to see what the obstacle might be, I discovered a huge concourse of men and women, drawn across the pavement and road alike, so that it seemed impossible to pass by them. I inquired of my driver what this assembling of the people meant. 'Oh,' says he, 'Barrymore has made another hit.' This answer being perfectly unintelligible to me, I requested some further explanation, and discovered that 'Barrymore' was the name of a stage-player favoured by the populace; that the building was a theatre; and that all these creatures with immortal souls were waiting, before the doors opened, to get places at the show!

The emotions of sorrow and indignation caused by this discovery so absorbed me, that I failed to notice an attempt the driver made to pass through, where the crowd seemed to be thinner, until the offended people resented the proceeding. Some of them seized the horse's head; others were on the point of pulling the driver off his box, when providentially the police interfered. Under their protection, we drew back, and reached our destination in safety, by another way. I record this otherwise unimportant affair, because it grieved and revolted me (when I thought of the people's souls), and so indisposed my mind to take cheerful views of anything. Under these circumstances, I would fain hope that I have exaggerated the true state of the case, in respect to my daughter's married life.

My good girl almost smothered me with kisses. When I at last got a fair opportunity of observing her, I thought her looking pale and worn and anxious. Query: Should I have arrived at this conclusion if I had met with no example of the wicked dissipations of London, and if I had ridden at my ease in a comfortable vehicle?

They had a succulent meal ready for me, and, what I call, fair enough whisky out of Scotland. Here again I remarked that Felicia ate very little, and Marmaduke nothing at all. He drank wine too – and, good heavens, champagne wine! – a needless waste of money surely when there was whisky on the table. My appetite being satisfied, my son-in-law went out of the room, and returned with his hat in his hand. 'You and Felicia have many things to talk about on your first evening together. I'll leave you for a while – I shall only be in the way.' So he spoke. It was in vain that his wife and I assured him he was not in the way at all. He kissed his hand, and smiled pleasantly, and left us.

'There, father!' says Felicia. 'For the last ten days, he has gone out like that, and left me alone for the whole evening. When we first returned from Switzerland, he left me in the same mysterious way, only it was after breakfast then. Now he stays at home in the daytime, and goes out at night.'

I inquired if she had not summoned him to give her some explanation.

'I don't know what to make of his explanation,' says Felicia. 'When he went away in the daytime, he told me he had business in the City. Since he took to going out at night, he says he goes to his club.'

'Have you asked where his club is, my dear?'

'He says it's in Pall Mall. There are dozens of clubs in that street – and he has never told me the name of *his* club. I am completely shut out of his confidence. Would you believe it, father? he has not introduced one of his friends to me since we came home. I doubt if they know where he lives, since he took this house.'

What could I say?

I said nothing, and looked round the room. It was fitted up with perfectly palatial magnificence. I am an ignorant man in matters of this sort, and partly to satisfy my curiosity, partly to change the subject, I asked to see the house. Mercy preserve us, the same grandeur everywhere! I wondered if even such an income as eight hundred a year could suffice for it all. In a moment when I was considering this, a truly frightful suspicion crossed my mind. Did these mysterious absences, taken in connection with the unbridled luxury that surrounded us, mean that my son-in-law was a gamester? a shameless shuffler of cards, or a debauched bettor on horses? While I was still completely overcome by my own previsions of evil, my daughter put her arm in mine to take me to the top of the house.

For the first time I observed a bracelet of dazzling gems on her wrist. 'Not diamonds?' I said. She answered, with as much composure as if she had been the wife of a nobleman, 'Yes, diamonds – a present from Marmaduke.' This was too much for me; my previsions, so to speak, forced their way into words. 'Oh, my poor child!' I burst out, 'I'm in mortal fear that your husband's a gamester!'

She showed none of the horror I had anticipated; she only shook her head and began to cry.

'Worse than that, I'm afraid,' she said.

I was petrified; my tongue refused its office, when I would fain have asked her what she meant. Her besetting sin, poor soul, is a proud spirit. She dried her eyes on a sudden, and spoke out freely, in these words: 'I am not going to cry about it. The other day, father, we were out walking in the park. A horrid, bold, yellow-haired woman passed us in an open carriage. She kissed her hand to Marmaduke, and called out to him, 'How are you, Marmy?' I was so indignant that I pushed him away from me, and told him to go and take a drive with his lady. He burst out laughing. "Nonsense!" he said; "she has known me for years – you don't understand our easy London manners." We have made it up since then; but I have my own opinion of the creature in the open carriage.'

Morally speaking, this was worse than all. But, logically viewed, it completely failed as a means of accounting for the diamond bracelet and the splendour of the furniture.

We went on to the uppermost story. It was cut off from the rest of the house by a stout partition of wood, and a door covered with green baize.

When I tried the door it was locked. 'Ha!' says Felicia, 'I wanted you to see it for yourself!' More suspicious proceedings on the part of my son-in-law! He kept the door constantly locked, and the key in his pocket. When his wife asked him what it meant, he answered: 'My study is up there – and I like to keep it entirely to myself.' After such a reply as that, the preservation of my daughter's dignity permitted but one answer: 'Oh, keep it to yourself, by all means!'

My previsions, upon this, assumed another form.

I now asked myself – still in connection with my son-in-law's extravagant expenditure – whether the clue to the mystery might not haply be the forging of banknotes on the other side of the baize door. My mind was prepared for anything by this time. We descended again to the dining-room. Felicia saw how my spirits were dashed, and came and perched upon my knee. 'Enough of my troubles for to-night, father,' she said. 'I am going to be your little girl again, and we will talk of nothing but Cauldkirk, until Marmaduke comes back.' I am one of the firmest men living, but I could not keep the hot tears out of my eyes when she put her arm round my neck and said those words. By good fortune I was sitting with my back to the lamp; she didn't notice me.

A little after eleven o'clock, Marmaduke returned. He looked pale and weary. But more champagne, and this time something to eat with it, seemed to set him to rights again – no doubt by relieving him from the reproaches of a guilty conscience.

I had been warned by Felicia to keep what had passed between us a secret from her husband for the present; so we had (superficially speaking) a merry end to the evening. My son-in-law was nearly as good company as ever, and wonderfully fertile in suggestions and expedients when he saw they were wanted. Hearing from his wife, to whom I had mentioned it, that I purposed representing the decayed condition of the kirk and manse to the owner of Cauldkirk and the country round about, he strongly urged me to draw up a list of repairs that were most needful, before I waited on my lord. This advice, vicious and degraded as the man who offered it may be, is sound advice nevertheless. I shall assuredly take it.

So far I had written in my Diary, in the forenoon. Returning to my daily record, after a lapse of some hours, I have a new mystery of iniquity to chronicle. My abominable son-in-law now appears (I blush to write it) to be nothing less than an associate of thieves!

After the meal they call luncheon, I thought it well, before recreating myself with the sights of London, to attend first to the crying necessities of the kirk and the manse. Furnished with my written list, I presented myself at his lordship's residence. I was immediately informed that he was otherwise engaged, and could not possibly receive me. If I wished to see my lord's secretary, Mr Helmsley, I could do so. Consenting to this, rather than fail entirely in my errand, I was shown into the secretary's room.

Mr Helmsley heard what I had to say civilly enough; expressing, however, grave doubts whether his lordship would do anything for me, the demands on his purse being insupportably numerous already. However, he undertook to place my list before his employer, and to let me know the result. 'Where are you staying in London?' he asked. I answered, 'With my son-in-law, Mr Marmaduke Falmer.' Before I could add the address, the secretary started to his feet, and tossed my list back to me across the table in the most uncivil manner.

'Upon my word,' says he, 'your assurance exceeds anything I ever heard of. Your son-in-law is concerned in the robbery of her ladyship's diamond bracelet – the discovery was made not an hour ago. Leave the house, sir, and consider yourself lucky that I have no instructions to give you in charge to the police.' I protested against this unprovoked outrage, with a violence of language which I would rather not recall. As a minister I ought, under every provocation, to have preserved my self-control.

The one thing to do next was to drive back to my unhappy daughter. Her guilty husband was with her. I was too angry to wait for a fit opportunity of speaking. The Christian humility which I have all my life cultivated as the first of virtues sank, as it were, from under me. In terms of burning indignation I told them what had happened. The result was too distressing to be described. It ended in Felicia giving her husband back the bracelet. The hardened reprobate laughed at us. 'Wait till I have seen his lordship and Mr Helmsley,' he said, and left the house.

Does he mean to escape to foreign parts? Felicia, womanlike, believes in him still; she is quite convinced that there must be some mistake. I am myself in hourly expectation of the arrival of the police.

With gratitude to Providence, I note before going to bed the harmless termination of the affair of the bracelet – so far as Marmaduke is concerned. The agent who sold him the jewel has been forced to come forward and state the truth. His lordship's wife is the guilty person; the bracelet was hers – a present from her husband. Harassed by debts that she dare not acknowledge, she sold it; my lord discovered that it was gone; and in terror of his anger the wretched woman took refuge in a lie.

She declared that the bracelet had been stolen from her. Asked for the name of the thief, the reckless woman (having no other name in her mind at the moment) mentioned the man who had innocently bought the jewel of her agent, otherwise my unfortunate son-in-law. Oh, the profligacy of the modern Babylon! It was well I went to the secretary when I did, or we should really have had the police in the house. Marmaduke found them in consultation over the supposed robbery, asking for his address. There was a dreadful exhibition of violence and recrimination at his lordship's residence: in the end he repurchased the bracelet. My son-in-law's money has been returned to him; and Mr Helmsley has sent me a written apology.

In a worldly sense, this would, I suppose, be called a satisfactory ending.

It is not so, to my mind. I freely admit that I too hastily distrusted Marmaduke; but am I, on that account, to give him back immediately the place which he once occupied in my esteem? Again this evening he mysteriously quitted the house, leaving me alone with Felicia, and giving no better excuse for his conduct than that he had an engagement. And this when I have a double claim on his consideration, as his father-in-law and his guest!

September 11*th* – The day began well enough. At breakfast, Marmaduke spoke feelingly of the unhappy result of my visit to his lordship, and asked me to let him look at the list of repairs. 'It's just useless to expect anything from my lord, after what has happened,' I said. 'Besides, Mr Helmsley gave me no hope when I stated my case to him.' Marmaduke still held out his hand for the list. 'Let me try if I can get some subscribers,' he replied. This was kindly meant, at any rate. I gave him the list; and I began to recover some of my old friendly feeling for him. Alas! the little gleam of tranquillity proved to be of short duration.

We made out our plans for the day pleasantly enough. The check came when Felicia spoke next of our plans for the evening. 'My father has only four days more to pass with us,' she said to her husband. 'Surely you won't go out again to-night, and leave him?' Marmaduke's face clouded over directly; he looked embarrassed and annoyed. I sat perfectly silent, leaving them to settle it by themselves.

'You will stay with us this evening, won't you?' says Felicia. No: he was not free for that evening. 'What! another engagement? Surely you can put it off?' No; impossible to put it off. 'Is it a ball, or a party of some kind?' No answer; he changed the subject – he offered Felicia the money repaid to him for the bracelet. 'Buy one for yourself, my dear, this time.' Felicia handed him back the money, rather too haughtily perhaps. 'I don't want a bracelet,' she said; 'I want your company in the evening.'

He jumped up, good-tempered as he was, in something very like a rage – then looked at me, and checked himself on the point (as I believe) of using profane language. 'This is downright persecution!' he burst out, with an angry turn of his head towards his wife. Felicia got up, in her turn. 'Your language is an insult to my father and to me!' He looked thoroughly staggered at this: it was evidently their first serious quarrel.

Felicia took no notice of him. 'I will get ready directly, father; and we will go out together.' He stopped her as she was leaving the room – recovering his good temper with a readiness which it pleased me to see. 'Come, come, Felicia! We have not quarrelled yet, and we won't quarrel now. Let me off this one time more, and I will devote the next three evenings of your father's visit to him and to you. Give me a kiss, and make it up.' My daughter doesn't do things by halves. She gave him a dozen kisses, I should think – and there was a happy end to it.

'But what shall we do to-morrow evening?' says Marmaduke, sitting down by his wife, and patting her hand as it lay in his.

'Take us somewhere,' says she. Marmaduke laughed. 'Your father objects to public amusements. Where does he want to go to?' Felicia took up the newspaper. 'There is an oratorio at Exeter Hall,' she said; 'my father likes music.' He turned to me. 'You don't object to oratorios, sir?' 'I don't object to music,' I answered, 'so long as I am not required to enter a theatre.' Felicia handed the newspaper to me. 'Speaking of theatres, father, have you read what they say about the new play? What a pity it can't be given out of a theatre!' I looked at her in speechless amazement. She tried to explain herself. 'The paper says that the new play is a service rendered to the cause of virtue; and that the great actor, Barrymore, has set an example in producing it which deserves the encouragement of all truly religious people. Do read it, father!' I held up my hands in dismay. My own daughter perverted! pinning her faith on a newspaper! speaking, with a perverse expression of interest, of a stage-play and an actor! Even Marmaduke witnessed this lamentable exhibition of backsliding with some appearance of alarm. 'It's not her fault, sir,' he said, interceding with me. 'It's the fault of the newspaper. Don't blame her!' I held my peace; determining inwardly to pray for her. Shortly afterwards my daughter and I went out. Marmaduke accompanied us part of the way, and left us at a telegraph-office. 'Who are you going to telegraph to?' Felicia asked. Another mystery! He answered, 'Business of my own, my dear' – and went into the office.

September 12*th* – Is my miserable son-in-law's house under a curse? The yellow-haired woman in the open carriage drove up to the door at half-past ten this morning, in a state of distraction. Felicia and I saw her from the drawing-room balcony – a tall woman in gorgeous garments. She knocked with her own hand at the door – she cried out distractedly, 'Where is he? I must see him!' At the sound of her voice, Marmaduke (playing with his little dog in the drawing-room) rushed downstairs, and out into the street. 'Hold your tongue!' we heard him say to her. 'What are you here for?'

What she answered we failed to hear; she was certainly crying. Marmaduke stamped on the pavement like a man beside himself – took her roughly by the arm, and led her into the house.

Before I could utter a word, Felicia left me, and flew headlong down the stairs.

She was in time to hear the dining-room door locked. Following her, I prevented the poor jealous creature from making a disturbance at the door. God forgive me – not knowing how else to quiet her – I degraded myself by advising her to listen to what they said. She instantly opened the door of the back dining-room, and beckoned to me to follow. I naturally hesitated. 'I shall go mad,' she whispered, 'if you leave me by myself!' What could I do? I degraded myself for the second time. For my own child – in pity for my own child!

We heard them, through the flimsy modern folding-doors, at those times when he was most angry, and she most distracted. That is to say, we heard them when they spoke in their loudest tones.

'How did you find out where I live?' says he. 'Oh, you're ashamed of me?' says she. 'Mr Helmsley was with us yesterday evening. That's how I found out!' 'What do you mean?' 'I mean that Mr Helmsley had your card and address in his pocket. Ah, you were obliged to give your address when you had to clear up that matter of the bracelet! You cruel, cruel man, what have I done to deserve such a note as you sent me this morning?' 'Do what the note tells you!' 'Do what the note tells me? Did anybody ever hear a man talk so, out of a lunatic asylum? Why, you haven't even the grace to carry out your own wicked deception – you haven't even gone to bed!' There the voices grew less angry, and we missed what followed. Soon the lady burst out again, piteously entreating him this time. 'Oh, Marmy, don't ruin me! Has anybody offended you? Is there anything you wish to have altered? Do you want more money? It is too cruel to treat me in this way – it is indeed!' He made some answer, which we were not able to hear; we could only suppose that he had upset her temper again. She went on louder than ever. 'I've begged and prayed of you – and you're as hard as iron. I've told you about the Prince – and *that* has had no effect on you. I have done now. We'll see what the doctor says.' He got angry, in his turn; we heard him again. 'I won't see the doctor!' 'Oh, you refuse to see the doctor? I shall make your refusal known – and if there's law in England, you shall feel it!' Their voices dropped again; some new turn seemed to be taken by the conversation. We heard the lady once more, shrill and joyful this time. 'There's a dear! You see it, don't you, in the right light? And you haven't forgotten the old times, have you? You're the same dear, honourable, kind-hearted fellow that you always were!'

I caught hold of Felicia, and put my hand over her mouth.

There was a sound in the next room which might have been – I cannot be certain – the sound of a kiss. The next moment, we heard the door of the room unlocked. Then the door of the house was opened, and the noise of retreating carriage-wheels followed. We met him in the hall, as he entered the house again.

My daughter walked up to him, pale and determined.

'I insist on knowing who that woman is, and what she wants here.' Those were her first words. He looked at her like a man in utter confusion. 'Wait till this evening; I am in no state to speak to you now!' With that, he snatched his hat off the hall table, and rushed out of the house.

It is little more than three weeks since they returned to London from their happy wedding-tour – and it has come to this!

The clock has just struck seven; a letter has been left by a messenger, addressed to my daughter. I had persuaded her, poor soul, to lie down in her own room. God grant that the letter may bring her some tidings of her husband! I please myself in the hope of hearing good news.

My mind has not been kept long in suspense. Felicia's waiting-woman has brought me a morsel of writing-paper, with these lines pencilled on it in my daughter's handwriting: 'Dearest father, make your mind easy. Everything is explained. I cannot trust myself to speak to you about it to-night – and *he* doesn't wish me to do so. Only wait till tomorrow, and you shall know all. He will be back about eleven o'clock. Please don't wait up for him – he will come straight to me.'

September 13*th* – The scales have fallen from my eyes; the light is let in on me at last. My bewilderment is not to be uttered in words – I am like a man in a dream.

Before I was out of my room in the morning, my mind was upset by the arrival of a telegram addressed to myself. It was the first thing of the kind I ever received; I trembled under the prevision of some new misfortune as I opened the envelope.

Of all the people in the world, the person sending the telegram was sister Judith! Never before did this distracting relative confound me as she confounded me now. Here is her message: 'You can't come back. An architect from Edinburgh asserts his resolution to repair the kirk and the manse. The man only waits for his lawful authority to begin. The money is ready – but who has found it? Mr Architect is forbidden to tell. We live in awful times. How is Felicia?'

Naturally concluding that Judith's mind must be deranged, I went downstairs to meet my son-in-law (for the first time since the events of yesterday) at the late breakfast which is customary in this house. He was waiting for me – but Felicia was not present. 'She breakfasts in her room this morning,' says Marmaduke; 'and I am to give you the explanation which has already satisfied your daughter. Will you take it at great length, sir? or will you have it in one word?' There was something in his manner that I did not at all like – he seemed to be setting me at defiance. I said, stiffly, 'Brevity is best; I will have it in one word.'

'Here it is then,' he answered. 'I am Barrymore.'

POSTSCRIPT ADDED BY FELICIA

If the last line extracted from my dear father's Diary does not contain explanation enough in itself, I add some sentences from Marmaduke's letter to me, sent from the theatre last night. (N.B. – I leave out the expressions of endearment: they are my own private property.)

* * * 'Just remember how your father talked about theatres and actors, when I was at Cauldkirk, and how you listened in dutiful agreement with him. Would he have consented to your marriage if he had known that I was one of the "spouting rogues," associated with the "painted Jezebels" of the play-house? He would never have consented – and you yourself, my darling, would have trembled at the bare idea of marrying an actor.

'Have I been guilty of any serious deception? and have my friends been guilty in helping to keep my secret? My birth, my name, my surviving relatives, my fortune inherited from my father – all these important particulars have been truly stated. The name of Barrymore is nothing but the name that I assumed when I went on the stage.

'As to what has happened, since our return from Switzerland, I own that I ought to have made my confession to you. Forgive me if I weakly hesitated. I was so fond of you; and I so distrusted the Puritanical convictions which your education had rooted in your mind, that I put it off from day to day. Oh, my angel * * *!

'Yes, I kept the address of my new house a secret from all my friends, knowing they would betray me if they paid us visits. As for my mysteriously-closed study, it was the place in which I privately rehearsed my new part. When I left you in the mornings, it was to go to the theatre rehearsals. My evening absences began of course with the first performance.

'Your father's arrival seriously embarrassed me. When you (most properly) insisted on my giving up some of my evenings to him, you necessarily made it impossible for me to appear on the stage. The one excuse I could make to the theatre was, that I was too ill to act. It did certainly occur to me to cut the Gordian knot by owning the truth. But your father's horror, when you spoke of the newspaper review of the play, and the shame and fear you showed at your own boldness, daunted me once more.

'The arrival at the theatre of my written excuse brought the manageress down upon me, in a state of distraction. Nobody could supply my place; all the seats were taken; and the Prince was expected. There was, what we call, a scene between the poor lady and myself. I felt I was in the wrong; I saw that the position in which I had impulsively placed myself was unworthy of me – and it ended in my doing my duty to the theatre and the public. But for the affair of the bracelet, which obliged me as an honourable man to give my name and address, the manageress would not have discovered me. She, like everyone else, only knew of my address at my bachelor chambers. How could you be jealous of the old theatrical comrade of my first days on the stage? Don't you know yet that you are the one woman in the world * * *?

'A last word relating to your father, and I have done.

'Do you remember my leaving you at the telegraph-office? It was to send a message to a friend of mine, an architect in Edinburgh, instructing him to go immediately to Cauldkirk, and provide for the repairs at my expense. The theatre, my dear, more than trebles my paternal income, and I can well afford it. Will your father refuse to accept a tribute of respect to a Scottish minister, because it is paid out of an actor's pocket? You shall ask him the question.

'And, I say, Felicia – will you come and see me act? I don't expect your father to enter a theatre; but, by way of further reconciling him to his son-in-law, suppose you ask him to hear me read the play?'

Mrs Zant and the Ghost

Originally appeared in the Tauchnitz edition of the novella *My Lady's
Money* (1879) as 'The Ghost's Touch'. Also published (in USA) in
Harper's Weekly, 23 October 1885. Reprinted in *Little Novels* (1887).
Collins claimed he had written the story, and especially the character
of the little girl, Lucy, for his twelve-year-old protegée Nannie Wynne,
with whom he was on especially close terms at this time (though
it looks as though the story preceded the friendship). 'Wilkie was
undoubtedly extremely fond of Nannie,' writes Catherine Peters.
'He wrote to her as "his dearest little wife", "darling", "Mia sposa
adorata". We, in our more anxious sexual climate, may wonder about
[the 61-year-old Wilkie's] underlying feelings. But Nannie was no
Rose la Touche' (*The King of Inventors*, p. 412). Lucy might be a
first sketch for the very lively little girl Zo (short for Zoe) in *Heart
and Science* (1883). Like so many of Collins's fictions, 'Mrs Zant and
the Ghost' makes play with the ramifications of marriage-law – in
this case the prohibition on a man's marrying his deceased wife's
sister, which was confirmed by Lord Lyndhurst's Act of 1835. For
an entertaining discussion of the mid-Victorian controversy over this
issue, see Matthew Arnold's *Culture and Anarchy* (1869), chapter 6,
and *Friendship's Garland* (1871), letter 8. Collins was paid £150 for
this story.

I

The course of this narrative describes the return of a disembodied spirit to earth and leads the reader on new and strange ground.

Not in the obscurity of midnight, but the searching light of day, did the supernatural influence assert itself. Neither revealed by a vision, nor announced by a voice, it reached mortal knowledge through the sense which is least easily self-deceived: the sense that feels.

The record of this event will of necessity produce conflicting impressions. It will raise, in some minds, the doubt which reason asserts; it will invigorate, in other minds, the hope which faith justifies; and it will leave the terrible question of the destinies of man, where centuries of vain investigation have left it – in the dark.

Having only undertaken in the present narrative to lead the way along a succession of events, the writer declines to follow modern examples by thrusting himself and his opinions on the public view. He returns to the shadow from which he has emerged, and leaves the opposing forces of incredulity and belief to fight the old battle over again, on the old ground.

II

The events happened soon after the first thirty years of the present century had come to an end.

On a fine morning, early in the month of April, a gentleman of middle age (named Rayburn) took his little daughter Lucy out for a walk, in the woodland pleasure-ground of Western London, called Kensington Gardens.

The few friends whom he possessed reported of Mr Rayburn (not unkindly) that he was a reserved and solitary man. He might have been more accurately described as a widower devoted to his only surviving child. Although he was not more than forty years of age, the one pleasure which made life enjoyable to Lucy's father was offered by Lucy herself.

Playing with her ball, the child ran on to the southern limit of the Gardens, at that part of it which still remains nearest to the old Palace of Kensington. Observing close at hand one of those spacious covered seats, called in England 'alcoves,' Mr Rayburn was reminded that he had the morning's newspaper in his pocket, and that he might do well to rest and read. At that early hour, the place was a solitude.

'Go on playing, my dear,' he said; 'but take care to keep where I can see you.'

Lucy tossed up her ball; and Lucy's father opened his newspaper. He had not been reading for more than ten minutes, when he felt a familiar little hand laid on his knee.

'Tired of playing?' he inquired – with his eyes still on the newspaper.

'I'm frightened, papa.'

He looked up directly. The child's pale face startled him. He took her on his knee, kissed her.

'You oughtn't to be frightened, Lucy, when I am with you,' he said gently.

'What is it?' He looked out of the alcove as he spoke, and saw a little dog among the trees. 'Is it the dog?' he asked.

Lucy answered:

'It's not the dog – it's the lady.'

The lady was not visible from the alcove.

'Has she said anything to you?' Mr Rayburn inquired.

'No.'

'What has she done to frighten you?'

The child put her arms round her father's neck.

'Whisper, papa,' she said; 'I'm afraid of her hearing us. I think she's mad.'

'Why do you think so, Lucy?'

'She came near to me. I thought she was going to say something. She seemed to be ill.'

'Well? And what then?'

'She looked at me.'

There, Lucy found herself at a loss how to express what she had to say next – and took refuge in silence.

'Nothing very wonderful, so far,' her father suggested.

'Yes, papa – but she didn't seem to see me when she looked.'

'Well, and what happened then?'

'The lady was frightened – and that frightened me. I think,' the child repeated positively, 'she's mad.'

It occurred to Mr Rayburn that the lady might be blind. He rose at once to set the doubt at rest.

'Wait here,' he said, 'and I'll come back to you.'

But Lucy clung to him with both hands; Lucy declared that she was afraid to be by herself. They left the alcove together.

The new point of view at once revealed the stranger, leaning against the trunk of a tree. She was dressed in the deep mourning of a widow. The pallor of her face, the glassy stare in her eyes, more than accounted for the child's terror – it excused the alarming conclusion at which she had arrived.

'Go nearer to her,' Lucy whispered.

They advanced a few steps. It was now easy to see that the lady was young, and wasted by illness – but (arriving at a doubtful conclusion perhaps under present circumstances) apparently possessed of rare personal attractions in happier days. As the father and daughter advanced a little, she discovered them. After some hesitation, she left the tree; approached with an evident intention of speaking; and suddenly paused. A change to astonishment and fear animated her vacant eyes. If it had not been plain before, it was now beyond all doubt that she was not a poor blind creature, deserted and helpless. At the same time, the expression of her face was not easy to understand. She could hardly have looked more amazed and bewildered, if the two strangers who were observing her had suddenly vanished from the place in which they stood.

Mr Rayburn spoke to her with the utmost kindness of voice and manner.

'I am afraid you are not well,' he said. 'Is there anything that I can do—'

The next words were suspended on his lips. It was impossible to realize such a state of things; but the strange impression that she had already produced on him was now confirmed. If he could believe his senses, her face did certainly tell him that he was invisible and inaudible to the woman whom he had just addressed! She moved slowly away with a heavy sigh, like a person disappointed and distressed. Following her with his eyes, he saw the dog once more – a little smooth-coated terrier of the ordinary English breed. The dog showed none of the restless activity of his race. With his head down and his tail depressed, he crouched like a creature paralyzed by fear. His mistress roused him by a call. He followed her listlessly as she turned away.

After walking a few paces only, she suddenly stood still.

Mr Rayburn heard her talking to herself.

'Did I feel it again?' she said, as if perplexed by some doubt that awed or grieved her. After a while, her arms rose slowly, and opened with a gentle caressing action – an embrace strangely offered to the empty air! 'No,' she said to herself sadly, after waiting a moment. 'More perhaps when to-morrow comes – no more to-day.' She looked up at the clear blue sky. 'The beautiful sunlight! the merciful sunlight!' she murmured. 'I should have died if it had happened in the dark.'

Once more she called to the dog; and once more she walked slowly away.

'Is she going home, papa?' the child asked.

'We will try and find out,' the father answered.

He was by this time convinced that the poor creature was in no condition to be permitted to go out without someone to take care of her. From motives of humanity, he was resolved on making the attempt to communicate with her friends.

III

The lady left the Gardens by the nearest gate; stopping to lower her veil before she turned into the busy thoroughfare which leads to Kensington. Advancing a little way along the High Street, she entered a house of respectable appearance, with a card in one of the windows which announced that apartments were to let.

Mr Rayburn waited a minute – then knocked at the door, and asked if he could see the mistress of the house. The servant showed him into a room on the ground floor, neatly but scantily furnished. One little white object varied the grim brown monotony of the empty table. It was a visiting-card.

With a child's unceremonious curiosity Lucy pounced on the card, and spelt the name, letter by letter:

'Z, A, N, T,' she repeated. 'What does that mean?'

Her father looked at the card, as he took it away from her, and put it back on the table. The name was printed, and the address was added in pencil: 'Mr John Zant, Purley's Hotel.'

The mistress made her appearance. Mr Rayburn heartily wished himself out of the house again, the moment he saw her. The ways in which it is possible to cultivate the social virtues are more numerous and more varied than is generally supposed. This lady's way had apparently accustomed her to meet her fellow-creatures on the hard ground of justice without mercy. Something in her eyes, when she looked at Lucy, said:

'I wonder whether that child gets punished when she deserves it?'

'Do you wish to see the rooms which I have to let?' she began.

Mr Rayburn at once stated the object of his visit – as clearly, as civilly, and as concisely as a man could do it. He was conscious (he added) that he had been guilty perhaps of an act of intrusion.

The manner of the mistress of the house showed that she entirely agreed with him. He suggested, however, that his motive might excuse him. The mistress's manner changed, and asserted a difference of opinion.

'I only know the lady whom you mention,' she said, 'as a person of the highest respectability, in delicate health. She has taken my first-floor apartments, with excellent references; and she gives remarkably little trouble. I have no claim to interfere with her proceedings, and no reason to doubt that she is capable of taking care of herself.'

Mr Rayburn unwisely attempted to say a word in his own defence.

'Allow me to remind you –' he began.

'Of what, sir?'

'Of what I observed, when I happened to see the lady in Kensington Gardens.'

'I am not responsible for what you observed in Kensington Gardens. If your time is of any value, pray don't let me detain you.'

Dismissed in those terms, Mr Rayburn took Lucy's hand and withdrew. He had just reached the door, when it was opened from the outer side. The Lady of Kensington Gardens stood before him. In the position which he and his daughter now occupied, their backs were towards the window. Would she remember having seen them for a moment in the Gardens?

'Excuse me for intruding on you,' she said to the landlady. 'Your servant tells me my brother-in-law called while I was out. He sometimes leaves a message on his card.'

She looked for the message, and appeared to be disappointed: there was no writing on the card.

Mr Rayburn lingered a little in the doorway, on the chance of hearing something more. The landlady's vigilant eyes discovered him.

'Do you know this gentleman?' she said maliciously to her lodger.

'Not that I remember.'

Replying in those words, the lady looked at Mr Rayburn for the first time; and suddenly drew back from him.

'Yes,' she said, correcting herself; 'I think we met—'

Her embarrassment overpowered her; she could say no more.

Mr Rayburn compassionately finished the sentence for her.

'We met accidentally in Kensington Gardens,' he said.

She seemed to be incapable of appreciating the kindness of his motive. After hesitating a little she addressed a proposal to him, which seemed to show distrust of the landlady.

'Will you let me speak to you upstairs in my own rooms?' she asked.

Without waiting for a reply, she led the way to the stairs. Mr Rayburn and Lucy followed. They were just beginning the ascent to the first floor, when the spiteful landlady left the lower room, and called to her lodger over their heads:

'Take care what you say to this man, Mrs Zant! He thinks you're mad.'

Mrs Zant turned round on the landing, and looked at him. Not a word fell from her lips. She suffered, she feared, in silence. Something in the sad submission of her face touched the springs of innocent pity in Lucy's heart. The child burst out crying.

That artless expression of sympathy drew Mrs Zant down the few stairs which separated her from Lucy.

'May I kiss your dear little girl?' she said to Mr Rayburn. The landlady, standing on the mat below, expressed her opinion of the value of caresses, as compared with a sounder method of treating young persons in tears: 'If that child was mine,' she remarked, 'I would give her something to cry for.'

In the meantime, Mrs Zant led the way to her rooms.

The first words she spoke showed that the landlady had succeeded but too well in prejudicing her against Mr Rayburn.

'Will you let me ask your child,' she said to him, 'why you think me mad?'

He met this strange request with a firm answer.

'You don't know yet what I really do think. Will you give me a minute's attention?'

'No,' she said positively. 'The child pities me, I want to speak to the child. What did you see me do in the Gardens, my dear, that surprised you?' Lucy turned uneasily to her father; Mrs Zant persisted. 'I first saw you by yourself, and then I saw you with your father,' she went on. 'When I came nearer to you, did I look very oddly – as if I didn't see you at all?'

Lucy hesitated again; and Mr Rayburn interfered.

'You are confusing my little girl,' he said. 'Allow me to answer your questions – or excuse me if I leave you.'

There was something in his look, or in his tone, that mastered her. She put her hand to her head.

'I don't think I'm fit for it,' she answered vacantly. 'My courage has been sorely tried already. If I can get a little rest and sleep, you may find me a different person. I am left a great deal by myself; and I have reasons for trying to compose my mind. Can I see you tomorrow? Or write to you? Where do you live?'

Mr Rayburn laid his card on the table in silence. She had strongly excited his interest. He honestly desired to be of some service to this forlorn creature – abandoned so cruelly, as it seemed, to her own guidance. But he had no authority to exercise, no sort of claim to direct her actions, even if she consented to accept his advice. As a last resource he ventured on an allusion to the relative of whom she had spoken downstairs.

'When do you expect to see your brother-in-law again?' he said.

'I don't know,' she answered. 'I should like to see him – he is so kind to me.'

She turned aside to take leave of Lucy.

'Good-bye, my little friend. If you live to grow up, I hope you will never be such a miserable woman as I am.' She suddenly looked round at Mr Rayburn. 'Have you got a wife at home?' she asked.

'My wife is dead.'

'And *you* have a child to comfort you! Please leave me; you harden my heart. Oh, sir, don't you understand? You make me envy you!'

Mr Rayburn was silent when he and his daughter were out in the street again. Lucy, as became a dutiful child, was silent, too. But there are limits to human endurance – and Lucy's capacity for self-control gave way at last.

'Are you thinking of the lady, papa?' she said.

He only answered by nodding his head. His daughter had interrupted him at that critical moment in a man's reflections, when he is on the point of making up his mind. Before they were at home again Mr Rayburn had arrived at a decision.

Mrs Zant's brother-in-law was evidently ignorant of any serious necessity for his interference – or he would have made arrangements for immediately repeating his visit. In this state of things, if any evil happened to Mrs Zant, silence on Mr Rayburn's part might be indirectly to blame for a serious misfortune. Arriving at that conclusion, he decided upon running the risk of being rudely received, for the second time, by another stranger.

Leaving Lucy under the care of her governess, he went at once to the address that had been written on the visiting-card left at the lodging-house, and sent in his name. A courteous message was returned. Mr John Zant was at home, and would be happy to see him.

IV

Mr Rayburn was shown into one of the private sitting-rooms of the hotel.

He observed that the customary position of the furniture in a room had been, in some respects, altered. An armchair, a side-table, and a footstool had all been removed to one of the windows, and had been placed as close as possible to the light. On the table lay a large open roll of morocco leather, containing rows of elegant little instruments in steel and ivory. Waiting by the table, stood Mr John Zant. He said 'Good-morning' in a bass voice, so profound and so melodious that those two commonplace words assumed a new importance, coming from his lips. His personal appearance was in harmony with his magnificent voice – he was a tall finely-made man of dark complexion; with big brilliant black eyes, and a noble curling beard, which hid the whole lower part of his face. Having bowed with a happy mingling of dignity and politeness, the conventional side of this gentleman's character suddenly vanished; and a crazy side, to all appearance, took its place. He dropped on his knees in front of the footstool. Had he forgotten to say his prayers that morning, and was he in such a hurry to remedy the fault that he had no time to spare for consulting appearances? The doubt had hardly suggested itself, before it was set at rest in a most unexpected manner. Mr Zant looked at his visitor with a bland smile, and said:

'Please let me see your feet.'

For the moment, Mr Rayburn lost his presence of mind. He looked at the instruments on the side-table.

'Are you a corn-cutter?' was all he could say.

'Excuse me, sir,' returned the polite operator, 'the term you use is quite obsolete in our profession.' He rose from his knees, and added modestly: 'I am a Chiropodist.'

'I beg your pardon.'

'Don't mention it! You are not, I imagine, in want of my professional services. To what motive may I attribute the honour of your visit?'

By this time Mr Rayburn had recovered himself.

'I have come here,' he answered, 'under circumstances which require apology as well as explanation.'

Mr Zant's highly polished manner betrayed signs of alarm; his suspicions pointed to a formidable conclusion – a conclusion that shook him to the innermost recesses of the pocket in which he kept his money.

'The numerous demands on me –' he began.

Mr Rayburn smiled.

'Make your mind easy,' he replied. 'I don't want money. My object is to speak with you on the subject of a lady who is a relation of yours.'

'My sister-in-law!' Mr Zant exclaimed. 'Pray, take a seat.'

Doubting if he had chosen a convenient time for his visit, Mr Rayburn hesitated.

'Am I likely to be in the way of persons who wish to consult you?' he asked.

'Certainly not. My morning hours of attendance on my clients are from eleven to one.' The clock on the mantelpiece struck the quarter-past one as he spoke. 'I hope you don't bring me bad news?' he said, very earnestly. 'When I called on Mrs Zant this morning, I heard that she had gone out for a walk. Is it indiscreet to ask how you became acquainted with her?'

Mr Rayburn at once mentioned what he had seen and heard in Kensington Gardens; not forgetting to add a few words, which described his interview afterwards with Mrs Zant.

The lady's brother-in-law listened with an interest and sympathy, which offered the strongest possible contrast to the unprovoked rudeness of the mistress of the lodging-house. He declared that he could only do justice to his sense of obligation by following Mr Rayburn's example, and expressing himself as frankly as if he had been speaking to an old friend.

'The sad story of my sister-in-law's life,' he said, 'will, I think, explain certain things which must have naturally perplexed you. My brother was introduced to her at the house of an Australian gentleman, on a visit to England. She was then employed as governess to his daughters. So sincere was the regard felt for her by the family that the parents had, at the entreaty of their children, asked her to accompany them when they returned to the Colony. The governess thankfully accepted the proposal.'

'Had she not relations in England?' Mr Rayburn asked.

'She was literally alone in the world, sir. When I tell you that she had been brought up in the Foundling Hospital, you will understand what I mean. Oh, there is no romance in my sister-in-law's story! She never has known, or will know, who her parents were or why they deserted her. The happiest moment in her life was the moment when she and my brother first met. It was an instance, on both sides, of love at first sight. Though not a rich man, my brother had earned a sufficient income in mercantile pursuits. His character spoke for itself. In a word, he altered all the poor girl's prospects, as we then hoped and believed, for the better. Her employers deferred their return to Australia, so that she might be married from their house. After a happy life of a few weeks only—'

His voice failed him; he paused, and turned his face from the light.

'Pardon me,' he said; 'I am not able, even yet, to speak composedly of my brother's death. Let me only say that the poor young wife was a widow, before the happy days of the honeymoon were over. That dreadful calamity struck her down. Before my brother had been committed to the grave, her life was in danger from brain-fever.'

Those words placed in a new light Mr Rayburn's first fear that her intellect might be deranged. Looking at him attentively, Mr Zant seemed to understand what was passing in the mind of his guest.

'No!' he said. 'If the opinions of the medical men are to be trusted, the result of the illness is injury to her physical strength – not injury to her mind. I have observed in her, no doubt, a certain waywardness of temper since her illness;

but that is a trifle. As an example of what I mean, I may tell you that I invited her, on her recovery, to pay me a visit. My house is not in London – the air doesn't agree with me – my place of residence is at St Sallins-on-Sea. I am not myself a married man; but my excellent housekeeper would have received Mrs Zant with the utmost kindness. She was resolved – obstinately resolved, poor thing – to remain in London. It is needless to say that, in her melancholy position, I am attentive to her slightest wishes. I took a lodging for her; and, at her special request, I chose a house which was near Kensington Gardens.'

'Is there any association with the Gardens which led Mrs Zant to make that request?'

'Some association, I believe, with the memory of her husband. By the way, I wish to be sure of finding her at home, when I call to-morrow. Did you say (in the course of your interesting statement) that she intended – as you supposed – to return to Kensington Gardens to-morrow? Or has my memory deceived me?'

'Your memory is perfectly accurate.'

'Thank you. I confess I am not only distressed by what you have told me of Mrs Zant – I am at a loss to know how to act for the best. My only idea, at present, is to try change of air and scene. What do you think yourself?'

'I think you are right.'

Mr Zant still hesitated.

'It would not be easy for me, just now,' he said, 'to leave my patients and take her abroad.'

The obvious reply to this occurred to Mr Rayburn. A man of larger worldly experience might have felt certain suspicions, and might have remained silent. Mr Rayburn spoke.

'Why not renew your invitation and take her to your house at the seaside?' he said.

In the perplexed state of Mr Zant's mind, this plain course of action had apparently failed to present itself. His gloomy face brightened directly.

'The very thing!' he said. 'I will certainly take your advice. If the air of St Sallins does nothing else, it will improve her health, and help her to recover her good looks. Did she strike you as having been (in happier days) a pretty woman?'

This was a strangely familiar question to ask – almost an indelicate question, under the circumstances. A certain furtive expression in Mr Zant's fine dark eyes seemed to imply that it had been put with a purpose. Was it possible that he suspected Mr Rayburn's interest in his sister-in-law to be inspired by any motive which was not perfectly unselfish and perfectly pure? To arrive at such a conclusion as this, might be to judge hastily and cruelly of a man who was perhaps only guilty of a want of delicacy of feeling. Mr Rayburn honestly did his best to assume the charitable point of view. At the same time, it is not to be denied that his words, when he answered, were carefully guarded, and that he rose to take his leave.

Mr John Zant hospitably protested.

'Why are you in such a hurry? Must you really go? I shall have the honour of returning your visit to-morrow, when I have made arrangements to profit by that excellent suggestion of yours. Good-bye. God bless you.'

He held out his hand: a hand with a smooth surface and a tawny colour, that fervently squeezed the fingers of a departing friend.

'Is that man a scoundrel?' was Mr Rayburn's first thought, after he had left the hotel. His moral sense set all hesitation at rest – and answered: 'You're a fool if you doubt it.'

V

Disturbed by presentiments, Mr Rayburn returned to his house on foot, by way of trying what exercise would do towards composing his mind.

The experiment failed. He went upstairs and played with Lucy; he drank an extra glass of wine at dinner; he took the child and her governess to a circus in the evening; he ate a little supper, fortified by another glass of wine, before he went to bed – and still those vague forebodings of evil persisted in torturing him. Looking back through his past life, he asked himself if any woman (his late wife of course excepted!) had ever taken the predominant place in his thoughts which Mrs Zant had assumed – without any discernible reason to account for it? If he had ventured to answer his own question, the reply would have been: Never!

All the next day he waited at home, in expectation of Mr John Zant's promised visit, and waited in vain.

Towards evening the parlour-maid appeared at the family tea-table, and presented to her master an unusually large envelope sealed with black wax, and addressed in a strange handwriting. The absence of stamp and postmark showed that it had been left at the house by a messenger.

'Who brought this?' Mr Rayburn asked.

'A lady, sir – in deep mourning.'

'Did she leave any message?'

'No, sir.'

Having drawn the inevitable conclusion, Mr Rayburn shut himself up in his library. He was afraid of Lucy's curiosity and Lucy's questions, if he read Mrs Zant's letter in his daughter's presence.

Looking at the open envelope after he had taken out the leaves of writing which it contained, he noticed these lines traced inside the cover:

My one excuse for troubling you, when I might have consulted my brother-in-law, will be found in the pages which I enclose. To speak plainly, you have been led to fear that I am not in my right senses. For this very reason, I now appeal to you. Your dreadful doubt of me, sir, is my doubt too. Read what I have written about myself – and then tell me, I entreat you, which I am: A person who has been the object of a supernatural revelation? or an unfortunate creature who is only fit for imprisonment in a mad-house?

Mr Rayburn opened the manuscript. With steady attention, which soon quickened to breathless interest, he read what follows:

VI THE LADY'S MANUSCRIPT

Yesterday morning, the sun shone in a clear blue sky – after a succession of cloudy days, counting from the first of the month.

The radiant light had its animating effect on my poor spirits. I had passed the night more peacefully than usual; undisturbed by the dream, so cruelly familiar to me, that my lost husband is still living – the dream from which I always wake in tears. Never, since the dark days of my sorrow, have I been so little troubled by the self-tormenting fancies and fears which beset miserable women, as when I left the house, and turned my steps towards Kensington Gardens – for the first time since my husband's death.

Attended by my only companion, the little dog who had been his favourite as well as mine, I went to the quiet corner of the Gardens which is nearest to Kensington.

On that soft grass, under the shade of those grand trees, we had loitered together in the days of our betrothal. It was his favourite walk; and he had taken me to see it in the early days of our acquaintance. There, he had first asked me to be his wife. There, we had felt the rapture of our first kiss. It was surely natural that I should wish to see once more a place sacred to such memories as these? I am only twenty-three years old; I have no child to comfort me, no companion of my own age, nothing to love but the dumb creature who is so faithfully fond of me.

I went to the tree under which we stood, when my dear one's eyes told his love before he could utter it in words. The sun of that vanished day shone on me again; it was the same noontide hour; the same solitude was round me. I had feared the first effect of the dreadful contrast between past and present. No! I was quiet and resigned. My thoughts, rising higher than earth, dwelt on the better life beyond the grave. Some tears came into my eyes. But I was not unhappy. My memory of all that happened may be trusted, even in trifles which relate only to myself – I was not unhappy.

The first object that I saw, when my eyes were clear again, was the dog. He crouched a few paces away from me, trembling pitiably, but uttering no cry. What had caused the fear that overpowered him?

I was soon to know.

I called to the dog; he remained immovable – conscious of some mysterious coming thing that held him spellbound. I tried to go to the poor creature, and fondle and comfort him.

At the first step forward that I took, something stopped me.

It was not to be seen, and not to be heard. It stopped me.

The still figure of the dog disappeared from my view: the lonely scene round me disappeared – excepting the light from heaven, the tree that sheltered me, and the grass in front of me. A sense of unutterable expectation kept my eyes riveted on the grass. Suddenly, I saw its myriad blades rise erect and shivering. The fear came to me of something passing over them with the invisible swiftness of the wind. The shivering advanced. It was all round me. It crept into the leaves of the tree over my head; they shuddered, without a sound to tell of their agitation: their pleasant natural rustling was struck dumb. The songs of the birds had ceased. The cries of the water-fowl on the pond were heard no more. There was a dreadful silence.

But the lovely sunshine poured down on me, as brightly as ever.

In that dazzling light, in that fearful silence, I felt an Invisible Presence near me.

It touched me gently.

At the touch, my heart throbbed with an overwhelming joy. Exquisite pleasure thrilled through every nerve in my body. I knew him! From the unseen world – himself unseen – he had returned to me. Oh, I knew him!

And yet, my helpless mortality longed for a sign that might give me assurance of the truth. The yearning in me shaped itself into words. I tried to utter the words. I would have said, if I could have spoken: 'Oh, my angel, give me a token that it is You!' But I was like a person struck dumb – I could only think it.

The Invisible Presence read my thought. I felt my lips touched, as my husband's lips used to touch them when he kissed me. And that was my answer. A thought came to me again. I would have said, if I could have spoken: 'Are you here to take me to the better world?'

I waited. Nothing that I could feel touched me.

I was conscious of thinking once more. I would have said, if I could have spoken: 'Are you here to protect me?'

I felt myself held in a gentle embrace, as my husband's arms used to hold me when he pressed me to his breast. And that was my answer.

The touch that was like the touch of his lips, lingered and was lost; the clasp that was like the clasp of his arms, pressed me and fell away. The garden-scene resumed its natural aspect. I saw a human creature near, a lovely little girl looking at me.

At that moment, when I was my own lonely self again, the sight of the child soothed and attracted me. I advanced, intending to speak to her. To my horror I suddenly ceased to see her. She disappeared as if I had been stricken blind.

And yet I could see the landscape round me; I could see the heaven above me. A time passed – only a few minutes, as I thought – and the child became visible to me again; walking hand-in-hand with her father. I approached them; I was close enough to see that they were looking at me with pity and surprise. My impulse was to ask if they saw anything strange in my face or my manner. Before I could speak, the horrible wonder happened again. They vanished from my view.

Was the Invisible Presence still near? Was it passing between me and my fellow-mortals; forbidding communication, in that place and at that time?

It must have been so. When I turned away in my ignorance, with a heavy heart, the dreadful blankness which had twice shut out from me the beings of my own race, was not between me and my dog. The poor little creature filled me with pity; I called him to me. He moved at the sound of my voice, and followed me languidly; not quite awakened yet from the trance of terror that had possessed him.

Before I had retired by more than a few steps, I thought I was conscious of the Presence again. I held out my longing arms to it. I waited in the hope of a touch to tell me that I might return. Perhaps I was answered by indirect means? I only know that a resolution to return to the same place, at the same hour, came to me, and quieted my mind.

The morning of the next day was dull and cloudy; but the rain held off. I set forth again to the Gardens.

My dog ran on before me into the street – and stopped: waiting to see in which direction I might lead the way. When I turned towards the Gardens, he dropped behind me. In a little while I looked back. He was following me no longer; he stood irresolute. I called to him. He advanced a few steps – hesitated – and ran back to the house.

I went on by myself. Shall I confess my superstition? I thought the dog's desertion of me a bad omen.

Arrived at the tree, I placed myself under it. The minutes followed each other uneventfully. The cloudy sky darkened. The dull surface of the grass showed no shuddering consciousness of an unearthly creature passing over it.

I still waited, with an obstinacy which was fast becoming the obstinacy of despair. How long an interval elapsed, while I kept watch on the ground before me, I am not able to say. I only know that a change came.

Under the dull gray light I saw the grass move – but not as it had moved, on the day before. It shrivelled as if a flame had scorched it. No flame appeared. The brown underlying earth showed itself winding onward in a thin strip – which might have been a footpath traced in fire. It frightened me. I longed for the protection of the Invisible Presence; I prayed for a warning of it, if danger was near.

A touch answered me. It was as if a hand unseen had taken my hand – had raised it, little by little – had left it, pointing to the thin brown path that wound towards me under the shrivelled blades of grass.

I looked to the far end of the path.

The unseen hand closed on my hand with a warning pressure: the revelation of the coming danger was near me – I waited for it; I saw it.

The figure of a man appeared, advancing towards me along the thin brown path. I looked in his face as he came nearer. It showed me dimly the face of my husband's brother – John Zant.

The consciousness of myself as a living creature left me. I knew nothing; I felt nothing; I was dead.

When the torture of revival made me open my eyes, I found myself on the grass. Gentle hands raised my head, at the moment when I recovered my senses. Who had brought me to life again? Who was taking care of me?

I looked upward, and saw – bending over me – John Zant.

VII

There, the manuscript ended.

Some lines had been added on the last page; but they had been so carefully erased as to be illegible. These words of explanation appeared below the cancelled sentences:

'I had begun to write the little that remains to be told, when it struck me that I might, unintentionally, be exercising an unfair influence on your opinion. Let me only remind you that I believe absolutely in the supernatural revelation which I have endeavoured to describe. Remember this – and decide for me what I dare not decide for myself.'

There was no serious obstacle in the way of compliance with this request.

Judged from the point of view of the materialist, Mrs Zant might no doubt be the victim of illusions (produced by a diseased state of the nervous system), which have been known to exist – as in the celebrated case of the bookseller, Nicolai, of Berlin – without being accompanied by derangement of the intellectual powers. But Mr Rayburn was not asked to solve any such intricate problem as this. He had been merely instructed to read the manuscript, and to say what impression it had left on him of the mental condition of the writer; whose doubt of herself had been, in all probability, first suggested by remembrance of the illness from which she had suffered – brain-fever.

Under these circumstances, there could be little difficulty in forming an opinion. The memory which had recalled, and the judgment which had arranged, the succession of events related in the narrative revealed a mind in full possession of its resources.

Having satisfied himself so far, Mr Rayburn abstained from considering the more serious question suggested by what he had read.

At any time, his habits of life and his ways of thinking would have rendered him unfit to weigh the arguments, which assert or deny supernatural revelation among the creatures of earth. But his mind was now so disturbed by the startling record of experience which he had just read, that he was only conscious of feeling certain impressions – without possessing the capacity to reflect on them. That his anxiety on Mrs Zant's account had been increased, and that his doubts of Mr John Zant had been encouraged, were the only practical results of the confidence placed in him of which he was thus far aware. In the ordinary exigencies of life a man of hesitating disposition, his interest in Mrs Zant's welfare, and his desire to discover what had passed between her brother-in-law and herself, after their meeting in the Gardens, urged him into instant action. In half an hour more, he had arrived at her lodgings. He was at once admitted.

VIII

Mrs Zant was alone, in an imperfectly lit room. 'I hope you will excuse the bad light,' she said; 'my head has been burning as if the fever had come back again. Oh, don't go away! After what I have suffered, you don't know how dreadful it is to be alone.'

The tone of her voice told him that she had been crying. He at once tried the best means of setting the poor lady at ease, by telling her of the conclusion at which he had arrived, after reading her manuscript. The happy result showed itself instantly: her face brightened, her manner changed; she was eager to hear more.

'Have I produced any other impression on you?' she asked.

He understood the allusion. Expressing sincere respect for her own convictions, he told her honestly that he was not prepared to enter on the obscure and terrible question of supernatural interposition. Grateful for the tone in which he had answered her, she wisely and delicately changed the subject.

'I must speak to you of my brother-in-law,' she said. 'He has told me of your visit; and I am anxious to know what you think of him. Do you like Mr John Zant?'

Mr Rayburn hesitated.

The care-worn look appeared again in her face. 'If you had felt as kindly towards him as he feels towards you,' she said, 'I might have gone to St Sallins with a lighter heart.'

Mr Rayburn thought of the supernatural appearances, described at the close of her narrative. 'You believe in that terrible warning,' he remonstrated; 'and yet, you go to your brother-in-law's house!'

'I believe,' she answered, 'in the spirit of the man who loved me in the days of his earthly bondage. I am under *his* protection. What have I to do but to cast away my fears, and to wait in faith and hope? It might have helped my resolution if a friend had been near to encourage me.' She paused and smiled sadly. 'I must remember,' she resumed, 'that your way of understanding my position is not my way. I ought to have told you that Mr John Zant feels needless anxiety about my health. He declares that he will not lose sight of me until his mind is at ease. It is useless to attempt to alter his opinion. He says my nerves are shattered – and who that sees me can doubt it? He tells me that my only chance of getting better is to try change of air and perfect repose – how can I contradict him? He reminds me that I have no relation but himself, and no house open to me but his own – and God knows he is right!'

She said those last words in accents of melancholy resignation, which grieved the good man whose one merciful purpose was to serve and console her. He spoke impulsively with the freedom of an old friend.

'I want to know more of you and Mr John Zant, than I know now,' he said. 'My motive is a better one than mere curiosity. Do you believe that I feel a sincere interest in you?'

'With my whole heart.'

That reply encouraged him to proceed with what he had to say. 'When you recovered from your fainting-fit,' he began, 'Mr John Zant asked questions, of course?'

'He asked what could possibly have happened, in such a quiet place as Kensington Gardens, to make me faint.'

'And how did you answer?'

'Answer? I couldn't even look at him!'

'You said nothing?'

'Nothing. I don't know what he thought of me; he might have been surprised, or he might have been offended.'

'Is he easily offended?' Mr Rayburn asked.

'Not in my experience of him.'

'Do you mean your experience of him before your illness?'

'Yes. Since my recovery, his engagements with country patients have kept him away from London. I have not seen him since he took these lodgings for me. But he is always considerate. He has written more than once to beg that I will not think him neglectful, and to tell me (what I knew already through my poor husband) that he has no money of his own, and must live by his profession.'

'In your husband's lifetime, were the two brothers on good terms?'

'Always. The one complaint I ever heard my husband make of John Zant was that he didn't come to see us often enough, after our marriage. Is there some wickedness in him which we have never suspected? It may be – but *how* can it be? I have every reason to be grateful to the man against whom I have been supernaturally warned! His conduct to me has been always perfect. I can't tell you what I owe to his influence in quieting my mind, when a dreadful doubt arose about my husband's death.'

'Do you mean doubt if he died a natural death?'

'Oh, no! no! He was dying of rapid consumption – but his sudden death took the doctors by surprise. One of them thought that he might have taken an overdose of his sleeping drops, by mistake. The other disputed this conclusion, or there might have been an inquest in the house. Oh, don't speak of it any more! Let us talk of something else. Tell me when I shall see you again.'

'I hardly know. When do you and your brother-in-law leave London?'

'Tomorrow.' She looked at Mr Rayburn with a piteous entreaty in her eyes; she said timidly: 'Do you ever go to the seaside, and take your dear little girl with you?'

The request, at which she had only dared to hint, touched on the idea which was at that moment in Mr Rayburn's mind.

Interpreted by his strong prejudice against John Zant, what she had said of her brother-in-law filled him with forebodings of peril to herself; all the more powerful in their influence, for this reason – that he shrank from distinctly realizing them. If another person had been present at the interview, and had said to him afterwards: 'That man's reluctance to visit his sister-in-law, while her husband was living, is associated with a secret sense of guilt which her innocence cannot even imagine: he, and he alone, knows the cause of her husband's sudden death: his feigned anxiety about her health is adopted as the safest means of enticing her into his house' – if those formidable conclusions had been urged on Mr Rayburn, he would have felt it his duty to reject them, as unjustifiable aspersions on an absent man. And yet, when he took leave that evening of Mrs Zant, he had pledged himself to give Lucy a holiday at the seaside; and he had said, without blushing, that the child really deserved it, as a reward for general good conduct and attention to her lessons!

IX

Three days later, the father and daughter arrived towards evening at St Sallins-on-Sea. They found Mrs Zant at the station.

The poor woman's joy, on seeing them, expressed itself like the joy of a child. 'Oh, I am so glad! so glad!' was all she could say when they met. Lucy was half-smothered with kisses, and was made supremely happy by a present of the finest doll she had ever possessed. Mrs Zant accompanied her friends to the rooms which had been secured at the hotel. She was able to speak confidentially to Mr Rayburn, while Lucy was in the balcony hugging her doll, and looking at the sea.

The one event that had happened during Mrs Zant's short residence at St Sallins, was the departure of her brother-in-law that morning, for London. He had been called away to operate on the feet of a wealthy patient who knew the value of his time: his housekeeper expected that he would return to dinner.

As to his conduct towards Mrs Zant, he was not only as attentive as ever – he was almost oppressively affectionate in his language and manner. There was no service that a man could render which he had not eagerly offered to her. He declared that he already perceived an improvement in her health; he congratulated her on having decided to stay in his house; and (as a proof, perhaps, of his sincerity) he had repeatedly pressed her hand. 'Have you any idea what all this means?' she said simply.

Mr Rayburn kept his idea to himself. He professed ignorance; and asked next what sort of person the housekeeper was.

Mrs Zant shook her head ominously.

'Such a strange creature,' she said, 'and in the habit of taking such liberties, that I begin to be afraid she is a little crazy.'

'Is she an old woman?'

'No – only middle-aged. This morning, after her master had left the house, she actually asked me what I thought of my brother-in-law! I told her, as coldly as possible, that I thought he was very kind. She was quite insensible to the tone in which I had spoken; she went on from bad to worse. "Do you call him the sort of man who would take the fancy of a young woman?" was her next question. She actually looked at me (I might have been wrong; and I hope I was) as if the "young woman" she had in her mind was myself! I said, "I don't think of such things, and I don't talk about them." Still, she was not in the least discouraged; she made a personal remark next: "Excuse me – but you do look wretchedly pale." I thought she seemed to enjoy the defect in my complexion; I really believe it raised me in her estimation. "We shall get on better in time," she said; "I'm beginning to like you." She walked out humming a tune. Don't you agree with me? Don't you think she's crazy?'

'I can hardly give an opinion until I have seen her. Does she look as if she might have been a pretty woman at one time of her life?'

'Not the sort of pretty woman whom I admire!'

Mr Rayburn smiled. 'I was thinking,' he resumed, 'that this person's odd conduct may perhaps be accounted for. She is probably jealous of any young lady who is invited to her master's house – and (till she noticed your complexion) she began by being jealous of you.'

Innocently at a loss to understand how *she* could become an object of the housekeeper's jealousy, Mrs Zant looked at Mr Rayburn in astonishment. Before she could give expression to her feeling of surprise, there was an interruption – a welcome interruption. A waiter entered the room, and announced a visitor; described as 'a gentleman.'

Mrs Zant at once rose to retire.

'Who is the gentleman?' Mr Rayburn asked – detaining Mrs Zant as he spoke.

A voice which they both recognised answered gaily, from the outer side of the door:

'A friend from London.'

X

'Welcome to St Sallins!' cried Mr John Zant. 'I knew that you were expected, my dear sir, and I took my chance of finding you at the hotel.' He turned to his sister-in-law, and kissed her hand with an elaborate gallantry worthy of Sir Charles Grandison himself. 'When I reached home, my dear, and heard that you had gone out, I guessed that your object was to receive our excellent friend. You have not felt lonely while I have been away? That's right! that's right!' He looked towards the balcony, and discovered Lucy at the open window, staring at the magnificent stranger. 'Your little daughter, Mr Rayburn? Dear child! Come, and kiss me.'

Lucy answered in one positive word: 'No.'

Mr John Zant was not easily discouraged. 'Show me your doll, darling,' he said. 'Sit on my knee.'

Lucy answered in two positive words – 'I won't.'

Her father approached the window to administer the necessary reproof. Mr John Zant interfered in the cause of mercy with his best grace. He held up his hands in cordial entreaty. 'Dear Mr Rayburn! The fairies are sometimes shy; and *this* little fairy doesn't take to strangers at first sight. Dear child! All in good time. And what stay do you make at St Sallins? May we hope that our poor attractions will tempt you to prolong your visit?'

He put his flattering little question with an ease of manner which was rather too plainly assumed; and he looked at Mr Rayburn with a watchfulness which appeared to attach undue importance to the reply. When he said: 'What stay do you make at St Sallins?' did he really mean: 'How soon do you leave us?' Inclining to adopt this conclusion, Mr Rayburn answered cautiously, that his stay at the seaside would depend on circumstances. Mr John Zant looked at his sister-in-law, sitting silent in a corner with Lucy on her lap. 'Exert your attractions,' he said; 'make the circumstances agreeable to our good friend. Will you dine with us today, my dear sir, and bring your little fairy with you?'

Lucy was far from receiving this complimentary allusion in the spirit in which it had been offered. 'I'm not a fairy,' she declared. 'I'm a child.'

'And a naughty child,' her father added, with all the severity that he could assume.

'I can't help it, papa; the man with the big beard puts me out.'

The man with the big beard was amused – amiably, paternally amused – by Lucy's plain speaking. He repeated his invitation to dinner; and he did his best to look disappointed when Mr Rayburn made the necessary excuses.

'Another day,' he said (without, however, fixing the day). 'I think you will find my house comfortable. My housekeeper may perhaps be eccentric – but in all essentials a woman in a thousand. Do you feel the change from London already? Our air at St Sallins is really worthy of its reputation. Invalids who come here are cured as if by magic. What do you think of Mrs Zant? How does she look?'

Mr Rayburn was evidently expected to say that she looked better. He said it. Mr John Zant seemed to have anticipated a stronger expression of opinion.

'Surprisingly better!' he pronounced. 'Infinitely better! We ought both to be grateful. Pray believe that we *are* grateful.'

'If you mean grateful to me,' Mr Rayburn remarked, 'I don't quite understand—'

'You don't quite understand? Is it possible that you have forgotten our conversation when I first had the honour of receiving you? Look at Mrs Zant again.'

Mr Rayburn looked; and Mrs Zant's brother-in-law explained himself.

'You notice the return of her colour, the healthy brightness of her eyes. (No, my dear, I am not paying you idle compliments; I am stating plain facts.) For that happy result, Mr Rayburn, we are indebted to you.'

'Surely not?'

'Surely yes! It was at your valuable suggestion that I thought of inviting my sister-in-law to visit me at St Sallins. Ah, you remember it now. Forgive me if I look at my watch; the dinner hour is on my mind. Not, as your dear little daughter there seems to think, because I am greedy, but because I am always punctual, in justice to the cook. Shall we see you to-morrow? Call early, and you will find us at home.'

He gave Mrs Zant his arm, and bowed and smiled, and kissed his hand to Lucy, and left the room. Recalling their interview at the hotel in London, Mr Rayburn now understood John Zant's object (on that occasion) in assuming the character of a helpless man in need of a sensible suggestion. If Mrs Zant's residence under his roof became associated with evil consequences, he could declare that she would never have entered the house but for Mr Rayburn's advice.

With the next day came the hateful necessity of returning this man's visit.

Mr Rayburn was placed between two alternatives. In Mrs Zant's interests he must remain, no matter at what sacrifice of his own inclinations, on good terms with her brother-in-law – or he must return to London, and leave the poor woman to her fate. His choice, it is needless to say, was never a matter of doubt. He called at the house, and did his innocent best – without in the least deceiving Mr John Zant – to make himself agreeable during the short duration of his visit. Descending the stairs on his way out, accompanied by Mrs Zant, he was surprised to see a middle-aged woman in the hall, who looked as if she was waiting there expressly to attract notice.

'The housekeeper,' Mrs Zant whispered. 'She is impudent enough to try to make acquaintance with you.'

This was exactly what the housekeeper was waiting in the hall to do.

'I hope you like our watering-place, sir,' she began. 'If I can be of service to you, pray command me. Any friend of this lady's has a claim on me – and you are an old friend, no doubt. I am only the housekeeper; but I presume to take a sincere interest in Mrs Zant; and I am indeed glad to see you here. We none of us know – do we? – how soon we may want a friend. No offence, I hope? Thank you, sir. Good morning.'

There was nothing in the woman's eyes which indicated an unsettled mind; nothing in the appearance of her lips which suggested habits of intoxication. That her strange outburst of familiarity proceeded from some strong motive seemed to be more than probable. Putting together what Mrs Zant had already told him, and what he had himself observed, Mr Rayburn suspected that the motive might be found in the housekeeper's jealousy of her master.

XI

Reflecting in the solitude of his own room, Mr Rayburn felt that the one prudent course to take would be to persuade Mrs Zant to leave St Sallins. He tried to prepare her for this strong proceeding, when she came the next day to take Lucy out for a walk.

'If you still regret having forced yourself to accept your brother-in-law's invitation,' was all he ventured to say, 'don't forget that you are perfect mistress of your own actions. You have only to come to me at the hotel, and I will take you back to London by the next train.'

She positively refused to entertain the idea.

'I should be a thankless creature indeed,' she said, 'if I accepted your proposal. Do you think I am ungrateful enough to involve you in a personal quarrel with John Zant? No! If I find myself forced to leave the house, I will go away alone.'

There was no moving her from this resolution. When she and Lucy had gone out together, Mr Rayburn remained at the hotel, with a mind ill at ease. A man of readier mental resources might have felt at a loss how to act for the best, in the emergency that now confronted him. While he was still as far as ever from arriving at a decision, some person knocked at the door.

Had Mrs Zant returned? He looked up as the door was opened, and saw to his astonishment – Mr John Zant's housekeeper.

'Don't let me alarm you, sir,' the woman said. 'Mrs Zant has been taken a little faint, at the door of our house. My master is attending to her.'

'Where is the child?' Mr Rayburn asked.

'I was bringing her back to you, sir, when we met a lady and her little girl at the door of the hotel. They were on their way to the beach – and Miss Lucy begged hard to be allowed to go with them. The lady said the two children were playfellows, and she was sure you would not object.'

'The lady is quite right. Mrs Zant's illness is not serious, I hope?'

'I think not, sir. But I should like to say something in her interests. May I? Thank you.' She advanced a step nearer to him, and spoke her next words in a whisper. 'Take Mrs Zant away from this place, and lose no time in doing it.'

Mr Rayburn was on his guard. He merely asked:

'Why?'

The housekeeper answered in a curiously indirect manner – partly in jest, as it seemed, and partly in earnest.

'When a man has lost his wife,' she said, 'there's some difference of opinion in Parliament, as I hear, whether he does right or wrong, if he marries his wife's sister. Wait a bit! I'm coming to the point. My master is one who has a long head on his shoulders; he sees consequences which escape the notice of people like me. In his way of thinking, if one man may marry his wife's sister, and no harm done, where's the objection if another man pays a compliment to the family, and marries his brother's widow? My master, if you please, is that other man. Take the widow away before she marries him.'

This was beyond endurance.

'You insult Mrs Zant,' Mr Rayburn answered, 'if you suppose that such a thing is possible!'

'Oh! I insult her, do I? Listen to me. One of three things will happen. She will be entrapped into consenting to it – or frightened into consenting to it – or drugged into consenting to it—'

Mr Rayburn was too indignant to let her go on.

'You are talking nonsense,' he said. 'There can be no marriage; the law forbids it.'

'Are you one of the people who see no farther than their noses?' she asked insolently. 'Won't the law take his money? Is he obliged to mention that he is related to her by marriage, when he buys the license?' She paused; her humour changed; she stamped furiously on the floor. The true motive that animated her showed itself in her next words, and warned Mr Rayburn to grant a more favourable hearing than he had accorded to her yet. 'If you won't stop it,' she burst out, 'I will! If he marries anybody, he is bound to marry ME. Will you take her away? I ask you, for the last time – *will* you take her away?'

The tone in which she made that final appeal to him had its effect.

'I will go back with you to John Zant's house,' he said, 'and judge for myself.'

She laid her hand on his arm:

'I must go first – or you may not be let in. Follow me in five minutes; and don't knock at the street door.'

On the point of leaving him, she abruptly returned.

'We have forgotten something,' she said. 'Suppose my master refuses to see you. His temper might get the better of him; he might make it so unpleasant for you that you would be obliged to go.'

'*My* temper might get the better of *me*,' Mr Rayburn replied; 'and – if I thought it was in Mrs Zant's interests – I might refuse to leave the house unless she accompanied me.'

'That will never do, sir.'

'Why not?'

'Because I should be the person to suffer.'

'In what way?'

'In this way. If you picked a quarrel with my master, I should be blamed for it because I showed you upstairs. Besides, think of the lady. You might frighten her out of her senses, if it came to a struggle between you two men.'

The language was exaggerated; but there was a force in this last objection which Mr Rayburn was obliged to acknowledge.

'And, after all,' the housekeeper continued, 'he has more right over her than you have. He is related to her, and you are only her friend.'

Mr Rayburn declined to let himself be influenced by this consideration.

'Mr John Zant is only related to her by marriage,' he said. 'If she prefers trusting in me – come what may of it, I will be worthy of her confidence.'

The housekeeper shook her head.

'That only means another quarrel,' she answered. 'The wise way, with a man like my master, is the peaceable way. We must manage to deceive him.'

'I don't like deceit.'

'In that case, sir, I'll wish you good-bye. We will leave Mrs Zant to do the best she can for herself.'

Mr Rayburn was unreasonable. He positively refused to adopt this alternative.

'Will you hear what I have got to say?' the housekeeper asked.

'There can be no harm in that,' he admitted. 'Go on.'

She took him at his word.

'When you called at our house,' she began, 'did you notice the doors in the passage, on the first floor? Very well. One of them is the door of the drawing-room, and the other is the door of the library. Do you remember the drawing-room, sir?'

'I thought it a large well-lit room,' Mr Rayburn answered. 'And I noticed a doorway in the wall, with a handsome curtain hanging over it.'

'That's enough for our purpose,' the housekeeper resumed. 'On the other side of the curtain, if you had looked in, you would have found the library. Suppose my master is as polite as usual, and begs to be excused for not receiving you, because it is an inconvenient time. And suppose you are polite on your side, and take yourself off by the drawing-room door. You will find me waiting downstairs, on the first landing. Do you see it now?'

'I can't say I do.'

'You surprise me, sir. What is to prevent us from getting back softly into the library, by the door in the passage? And why shouldn't we use that second way into the library as a means of discovering what may be going on in the drawing-room? Safe behind the curtain, you will see him if he behaves uncivilly to Mrs Zant, or you will hear her if she calls for help. In either case, you may be as rough and ready with my master as you find needful; it will be he who has frightened her, and not you. And who can blame the poor housekeeper because Mr Rayburn did his duty, and protected a helpless woman? There is my plan, sir. Is it worth trying?'

He answered, sharply enough: 'I don't like it.'

The housekeeper opened the door again, and wished him good-bye.

If Mr Rayburn had felt no more than an ordinary interest in Mrs Zant, he would have let the woman go. As it was, he stopped her; and, after some further protest (which proved to be useless), he ended in giving way.

'You promise to follow my directions?' she stipulated.

He gave the promise. She smiled, nodded, and left him. True to his instructions, Mr Rayburn reckoned five minutes by his watch, before he followed her.

XII

The housekeeper was waiting for him, with the street-door ajar.

'They are both in the drawing-room,' she whispered, leading the way upstairs. 'Step softly, and take him by surprise.'

A table of oblong shape stood midway between the drawing-room walls. At the end of it which was nearest to the window, Mrs Zant was pacing to and fro across the breadth of the room. At the opposite end of the table, John Zant was seated. Taken completely by surprise, he showed himself in his true character. He started to his feet, and protested with an oath against the intrusion which had been committed on him.

Heedless of his action and his language, Mr Rayburn could look at nothing, could think of nothing, but Mrs Zant. She was still walking slowly to and fro, unconscious of the words of sympathy which he addressed to her, insensible even as it seemed to the presence of other persons in the room.

John Zant's voice broke the silence. His temper was under control again: he had his reasons for still remaining on friendly terms with Mr Rayburn.

'I am sorry I forgot myself just now,' he said.

Mr Rayburn's interest was concentrated on Mrs Zant; he took no notice of the apology.

'When did this happen?' he asked.

'About a quarter of an hour ago. I was fortunately at home. Without speaking to me, without noticing me, she walked upstairs like a person in a dream.'

Mr Rayburn suddenly pointed to Mrs Zant.

'Look at her!' he said. 'There's a change!'

All restlessness in her movements had come to an end. She was standing at the farther end of the table which was nearest to the window, in the full flow of sunlight pouring at that moment over her face. Her eyes looked out straight before her – void of all expression. Her lips were a little parted; her head drooped slightly towards her shoulder, in an attitude which suggested listening for something or waiting for something. In the warm brilliant light, she stood before the two men, a living creature self-isolated in a stillness like the stillness of death.

John Zant was ready with the expression of his opinion.

'A nervous seizure,' he said. 'Something resembling catalepsy, as you see.'

'Have you sent for a doctor?'

'A doctor is not wanted.'

'I beg your pardon. It seems to me that medical help is absolutely necessary.'

'Be so good as to remember,' Mr John Zant answered, 'that the decision rests with me, as the lady's relative. I am sensible of the honour which your visit confers on me. But the time has been unhappily chosen. Forgive me if I suggest that you will do well to retire.'

Mr Rayburn had not forgotten the housekeeper's advice, or the promise which she had exacted from him. But the expression in John Zant's face was a serious trial to his self-control. He hesitated, and looked back at Mrs Zant.

If he provoked a quarrel by remaining in the room, the one alternative would be the removal of her by force. Fear of the consequences to herself, if she was suddenly and roughly roused from her trance, was the one consideration which reconciled him to submission. He withdrew.

The housekeeper was waiting for him below, on the first landing. When the door of the drawing-room had been closed again, she signed to him to follow her, and returned up the stairs. After another struggle with himself, he obeyed. They entered the library from the corridor – and placed themselves behind the closed curtain which hung over the doorway. It was easy so to arrange the edge of the drapery as to observe, without exciting suspicion, whatever was going on in the next room.

Mrs Zant's brother-in-law was approaching her, at the time when Mr Rayburn saw him again.

In the instant afterwards, she moved – before he had completely passed over the space between them. Her still figure began to tremble. She lifted her drooping head. For a moment, there was a shrinking in her – as if she had been touched by something. She seemed to recognise the touch: she was still again.

John Zant watched the change. It suggested to him that she was beginning to recover her senses. He tried the experiment of speaking to her.

'My love, my sweet angel, come to the heart that adores you!'

He advanced again; he passed into the flood of sunlight pouring over her.

'Rouse yourself!' he said.

She still remained in the same position; apparently at his mercy, neither hearing him nor seeing him.

'Rouse yourself!' he repeated. 'My darling, come to me!'

At the instant when he attempted to embrace her – at the instant when Mr Rayburn rushed into the room – John Zant's arms, suddenly turning rigid, remained outstretched. With a shriek of horror, he struggled to draw them back – struggled, in the empty brightness of the sunshine, as if some invisible grip had seized him.

'What has got me?' the wretch screamed. 'Who is holding my hands? Oh, the cold of it! the cold of it!'

His features became convulsed; his eyes turned upwards until only the white eyeballs were visible. He fell prostrate with a crash that shook the room.

The housekeeper ran in. She knelt by her master's body. With one hand she loosened his cravat. With the other she pointed to the end of the table.

Mrs Zant still kept her place; but there was another change. Little by little, her eyes recovered their natural living expression – then slowly closed. She tottered backwards from the table, and lifted her hands wildly, as if to grasp at something which might support her. Mr Rayburn hurried to her before she fell – lifted her in his arms – and carried her out of the room.

One of the servants met them in the hall. He sent her for a carriage. In a quarter of an hour more, Mrs Zant was safe under his care at the hotel.

XIII

That night a note, written by the housekeeper, was delivered to Mrs Zant.

'The doctors give little hope. The paralytic stroke is spreading upwards to his face. If death spares him, he will live a helpless man. I shall take care of him to the last. As for you – forget him.'

Mrs Zant gave the note to Mr Rayburn.

'Read it, and destroy it,' she said. 'It is written in ignorance of the terrible truth.'

He obeyed – and looked at her in silence, waiting to hear more. She hid her face. The few words that she addressed to him, after a struggle with herself, fell slowly and reluctantly from her lips.

She said, 'No mortal hand held the hands of John Zant. The guardian spirit was with me. The promised protection was with me. I know it. I wish to know no more.'

Having spoken, she rose to retire. He opened the door for her, seeing that she needed rest in her own room.

Left by himself, he began to consider the prospect that was before him in the future. How was he to regard the woman who had just left him? As a poor creature weakened by disease, the victim of her own nervous delusion? or as the chosen object of a supernatural revelation – unparalleled by any similar revelation that he had heard of, or had found recorded in books? His first discovery of the place that she really held in his estimation dawned on his mind, when he felt himself recoiling from the conclusion which presented her to his pity, and yielding to the nobler conviction which felt with her faith, and raised her to a place apart among other women.

XIV

They left St Sallins the next day.

Arrived at the end of the journey, Lucy held fast by Mrs Zant's hand. Tears were rising in the child's eyes. 'Are we to bid her good-bye?' she said sadly to her father.

He seemed to be unwilling to trust himself to speak; he only said, 'My dear, ask her yourself.'

But the result justified him. Lucy was happy again.

The Devil's Spectacles

Originally appeared in *The Spirit of the Times* on 20 December 1879.
It was reprinted in *The Seaside Library* as 'The Magic Spectacles',
25 June 1880. According to R.V. Andrew, 'In *The Bolton Weekly
Journal* and syndicated papers it appeared on various dates in 1886
as "The Devil's Spectacles".' There is in the Berg Collection, New
York Public Library, a note signed by Collins and dated January
1887, stating that he does not want 'The Devil's Spectacles', 'Love's
Random Shot' or 'Fie! Fie! or, the Fair Physician' to be republished
after his death. The story was never collected in book-form. The prologue to the story revamps the Polar Expedition material employed in
'The Frozen Deep', with the cannibalism deriving (ultimately) from
accounts of Franklin's ill-fated search for the North-West Passage in
1846; the occult element recalls the prophetic mirror of polished coal
in Collins's nonfictional sketch 'My Black Mirror' (*Household Words*,
1856). Collins's own eyesight had deteriorated greatly by the time
he wrote 'The Devil's Spectacles'. He was paid £35 for the story.

I MEMOIRS OF AN ARCTIC VOYAGER

'He says, sir, he thinks he's nigh to his latter end, and he would like, if convenient, to see you before he goes.'

'Do you mean before he dies?'

'That's about it, sir.'

I was in no humor (for reasons to be hereafter mentioned) for seeing anybody, under disastrous circumstances of any sort; but the person who had sent me word that he was 'nigh to his latter end' had special claims on my consideration.

He was an old sailor, who had first seen blue water under the protection of my father, then a post-captain in the navy. Born on our estate, and the only male survivor of our head gamekeeper's family of seven children, he had received a good education through my father's kindness, and he ought to have got on well in the world; but he was one of those born vagabonds who set education at defiance. His term of service having expired, he disappeared for many years. During part of the time he was supposed to have been employed in the merchant navy. At the end of that long interval he turned up one day at our country house, an invalided man, without a penny in his pocket. My good father, then nearing the end of his life, was invalided too. Whether he had a fellow-feeling for the helpless creature whom he had once befriended, or whether he only took counsel of his own generous nature, it is now needless to inquire. He appointed Septimus Notman to be lodge-keeper at the second of our two park gates, and he recommended Septimus to my personal care on his deathbed. 'I'm afraid he's an old scoundrel,' my father confessed; 'but somebody must look after him as long as he lasts, and if you don't take his part, Alfred, nobody else will.' After this Septimus kept his place at the gate while we were in the country. When we returned to our London house the second gate was closed. The old sailor was lodged (by a strong exertion of my influence) in a room over a disused stable, which our coachman had proposed to turn into a hayloft. Everybody disliked Septimus Notman. He was said to be mad; to be a liar, a hypocrite, a vicious wretch, and a disagreeable brute. There were people who even reported that he had been a pirate during the time when we lost sight of him and who declared, when they were asked for their proof, that his crimes were written in his face. He was not in the least affected by the opinions of his neighbors; he chewed his tobacco and drank his grog, and, in the words of the old song, 'He cared for nobody, no, not he!' Well had my poor father said, that if I didn't take his part nobody else would. And shall I tell you a secret? Though I strictly carried out my father's wishes, and though Septimus was disposed in his own rough way to be grateful to me, I didn't like him either.

So I went to the room over the stables (we were in London at the time) with dry eyes and I sat down by his bed and cut up a cake of tobacco for him, and said, 'Well, what's the matter?' as coolly as if he had sent me word that he thought he had caught a cold in the head.

'I'm called away.' Septimus answered, 'and before I go I've got a confession to make, and something useful to offer you. It's reported among the servants, Mr Alfred, that you're in trouble just now between two ladies. You may see your way clear in that matter, sir, if death spares me long enough to say a few last words.'

'Never mind me, Septimus. Has a doctor seen you?'

'The doctor knows no more about me than I know myself. The doctor be— !'

'Have you any last wishes that I can attend to?'

'None, sir.'

'Shall I send for a clergyman?'

Septimus Notman looked at me as directly as he could – he was afflicted with a terrible squint. Otherwise he was a fine, stoutly-built man, with a ruddy face profusely encircled by white hair and whiskers, a hoarse, heavy voice, and the biggest hands I ever saw. He put one of these enormous hands under his pillow before he answered me.

'If you think,' he said, 'that a clergyman will come to a man who has got the Devil's Spectacles here, under his pillow, and who has only to put those Spectacles on to see through that clergyman's clothes, flesh, and what not, and read everything that's written in his secret mind as plain as print, fetch him, Master Alfred – fetch him!'

I thought the clergyman might not like this, and withdrew my suggestion accordingly. The least I could do, as a matter of common politeness, after giving up the clergyman, was to ask if I might look at the Devil's Spectacles.

'Hear how I came by them first!' said Septimus.

'Will it take long?' I inquired.

'It will take long, and it will make your flesh creep.'

I remembered my promise to my father, and placed myself and my flesh at the mercy of Septimus Notman. But he was not ready to begin yet.

'Do you see that white jug?' he said, pointing to the wash-hand stand.

'Yes. Do you want water?'

'I want grog. There's grog in the white jug. And there's a pewter mug on the chimney-piece. I must be strung up, Master Alfred – I must be strung up.'

The white jug contained at least half a gallon of rum and water, roughly calculated. I strung him up. In the case of any other dying person I might have hesitated. But a man who possessed the Devil's Spectacles was surely an exception to ordinary rules, and might finish his career and finish his grog at one and the same time.

'Now, I'm ready,' he said, 'What do you think I was up to in the time when you all lost sight of me? The latter part of that time, I mean?'

'They say you were a pirate,' I replied.

'Worse than that. Guess again.'

I tried to persuade myself that there might be such a human anomaly as a merciful pirate, and guessed once more.

'A murderer,' I suggested.

'Worse than that. Guess again.'

I declined to guess again. 'Tell me yourself what you have been,' I said.

He answered without the least appearance of discomposure, 'I've been a Cannibal.'

Perhaps it was weak of me – but I did certainly start to my feet and make for the door.

'Hear the circumstances,' said Septimus. 'You know the proverb, sir? Circumstances alter cases.'

There was no disputing the proverb. I sat down again. I was a young and tender man, which, in my present position, was certainly against me. But I had very little flesh on my bones and that was in my favor.

'It happened when I went out with the Arctic expedition,' Septimus proceeded. 'I've forgotten all my learning, and lost my memory for dates. The year escapes me, and the latitude and longitude escape me. But I can tell you the rest of it. We were an exploring party, you must know, with sledges. It was getting close to the end of the summer months in those parts, and we were higher than any of them have ever got since to the North Pole. We should have found our way there – don't you doubt it – but for three of our best men who fell sick of the scurvy. The second lieutenant, who was in command, called a halt, as the soldiers say. "With this loss of strength," says he, "it's my duty to take you back to the ships. We must let the North Pole be, and pray God that we may have no more invalided men to carry. I give you half an hour's rest before we turn back." The carpenter was one of our sound men. He spoke next. He reported one of the two sledges not fit for service. "How long will you be making it fit?" says the lieutenant. "In a decent climate," says the carpenter, "I should say two or three hours, sir. Here, double that time, at least." You may say why not do without the sledge? I'll tell you why. On account of the sick men to be carried. "Be as quick about it as you can," says the lieutenant: "time means life in our predicament." Most of the men were glad enough to rest. Only two of us murmured at not going on. One was a boatswain's mate; t'other was me. "Do you think the North Pole's the other side of that rising ground there?" says the lieutenant. The boatswain's mate was young and self-conceited. "I should like to try, sir," he says, "if any other man has pluck enough to go along with me." He looked at me when he said that. I wasn't going to have my courage called in question publicly by a slip of a lad; and, moreover, I had a fancy to try for the North Pole, too. I volunteered to go along with him. Our notion, you will understand, was to take a compass and some grub with us; to try what we could find in a couple of hours' march forward; and to get back in good time for our duty on the return journey. The lieutenant wouldn't hear of it. "I'm responsible for every man in my charge," says he. "You're a couple of fools. Stay where you are." We *were* a couple of fools. We watched our opportunity, while they were all unloading the broken-down sledge; and slipped off to try our luck, and get the reward for discovering the North Pole.'

There he stopped, and pointed to the grog. 'Dry-work, talking,' he said. 'Give us a drop more.'

I filled the pewter mug again. And again Septimus Notman emptied it.

'We set our course northwest by north,' he went on; 'and after a while (seeing the ground favored us) we altered it again to due north. I can't tell you how long we walked (we neither of us had watches) – but this I'll swear to. Just as the last of the daylight was dying out, we got to the top of a hillock; and there we saw the glimmer of the open Polar Sea! No! not the Sound that enters Kennedy's Channel, which has been mistaken for it, I know – but the real thing, the still and lonesome Polar Sea! What would you have done in our place? I'll tell you what we did. We sat down on some nice dry snow, and took out our biscuits and grog. Freezing work, do you say? You'll find it in the books, if you don't believe me – the further north you get in those parts, the less cold there is, and the more open water you find. Ask Captain M'Clure what sort of a bed he slept upon, on the night of October thirtieth, 'fifty-one. Well, and what do you think we did when we had eaten and drunk? Lit our pipes. And what next? Fell fast asleep, after our long walk, on our nice dry snow. And what sort of prospect met us when we woke? Darkness and drizzle and mist. I had the compass, and I tried to set our course on the way back. I could no more see the compass than if I had been blind. We had no means of striking a light, except my match-box. I had left it on the snow by my side when I fell asleep. Not a match would light. As for help of any sort, it was not to be thought of. We couldn't have been less than five miles distant from the place where we had left our messmates. So there we were, the boatswain's mate and me, alone in the desert, lost at the North Pole.'

I began to feel interested. 'You tried to get back, I suppose, dark as it was?' I said.

'We walked till we dropped,' Septimus answered; 'and then we yelled and shouted till we had no voices left; and then we hollowed out a hole in the snow, and waited for daylight.'

'What did you expect when daylight came?'

'*I* expected nothing, Master Alfred. The boatswain's mate (beginning to get a little light-headed, you know) expected the lieutenant to send in search of us, or to wait till we returned. A likely thing for an officer in charge to do, with the lives of the sledging party depending on his getting them back to the ships, and only two men missing, who had broken orders and deserted their duty. A good riddance of bad rubbish – that's what he said of us when we were reported missing, I'll be bound. When the light came we tried to get back; and we did set our course cleverly enough. But, bless you, we had nothing left to eat or drink! When the light failed us again we were done up. We dropped on the snow, under the lee of a rock, and gave out. The boatswain's mate said his prayers, and I said Amen. Not the least use! On the contrary, as the night advanced it got colder and colder. We were both close together, to keep each other warm. I don't know how long it was, I only know it was still pitch dark, when I heard the boatswain's mate give a little flutter of a sigh, and no more. I opened his clothes, and put my hand on his heart. Dead, of cold and exhaustion, and no mistake. I shouldn't have been long after him but for my own presence of mind.'

'Your presence of mind? What did you do?'

'Stripped every rag of clothes off him, and put them all on myself. What are you shivering about? *He* couldn't feel it, could he? I tell you, he'd have been frozen stiff before the next day's light came – but for my presence of mind again. As well as my failing strength would let me, I buried him under the snow. Virtue, they say, Master Alfred, is its own reward. That good action proved to be the saving of my life.'

'What do you mean?'

'Didn't I tell you I buried him?'

'Well!'

'Well, in that freezing air, the burying of him kept him eatable. Don't you see?'

'You wretch!'

'Put yourself in my place, and don't call names. I held out till I was mad with hunger. And then I did open my knife with my teeth. And I did burrow down in the snow till I felt him—.'

I could hear no more of it. 'Get on to the end!' I said. 'Why didn't you die at the North Pole?'

'Because somebody helped me to get away.'

'Who helped you?'

'The Devil.'

He showed his yellow old teeth in a horrible grin. I could draw but one conclusion – his mind was failing him before death. Anything that spared me his hideous confession of cannibalism was welcome. I asked how the supernatural rescue happened.

'More grog first,' he said. 'The horrors come on me when I think of it.' He was evidently sinking. Without the grog I doubt if he could have said much more.

'I can't tell you how many days passed,' he went on; 'I only know that the time was nigh when it was all dark and no light. The darker it got, the deeper I scooped the sort of cavern I'd made for myself under the snow. Whether it was night, or whether it was day I know no more than you do. On a sudden, in the awful silence and solitude, I heard a voice, high up, as it were, on the rock behind me. It was a cheering and a pleasant voice, and it said, "Well, Septimus Notman, is there much left of the boatswain's mate by this time? Did he eat short while he lasted?" I cried out in a fright, "Who the devil— ?" The voice stopped me before I could say the rest. "You've hit it," says the voice, "I am that person; and it's about time the Devil helped you out of this." "No," says I, "I'd rather perish by cold than fire any day." "Make your mind easy," says he, taking the point, "I don't want you at my place yet. I expect you to do a deal more in the way of degrading your humanity before you come to me, and I offer you a safe passage back to the nearest settlement. Friend Septimus, you're a man after my own heart." "As how, sir?" says I. "Because you're such a complete beast," says he. "A human being who elevates himself, and rises higher and higher to his immortal destiny, is a creature I hate. He gets above me, even in his earthly lifetime. But you have dropped – you dear good fellow – to the level of a famished wolf. You have gobbled up your dead companion; and if you ever had such a thing as a soul – ha, Septimus! – it parted company with you at the first morsel you tasted of the Boatswain's mate. Do you think I'll leave such a prime specimen of the Animal Man as you are, deserted at the North Pole? No, no; I grant you a free pass by my railway; darkness and distance are no obstacles to Me. Are you ready?" You may not believe me; but I felt myself being lifted up, as it were, against my own will. "Give us a light," I says, "I can't travel in the dark." "Take my spectacles," says he, "they'll help you to see more than you bargain for. Look through them at your fellow mortals, and you'll see the inmost thoughts of their hearts as plain as I do, and, considering your nature, Septimus, that will drop you even below the level of a wolf." "Suppose I don't want to look," says I, "may I throw the spectacles away?" "They'll come back to you," says he. "May I smash them up?" "They'll put themselves together again." "What am I to do with them?" "Give them to another man. Now, then! One, two, three – and away!" You may not believe me again; I lost my senses, Master Alfred. Hold me up; I'm losing them now. More grog – that's right – more grog. I came to myself at Upernavik, with the Devil's Spectacles in my pocket. Take them, sir. And read those two ladies' hearts. And act accordingly. Hush! I hear him speaking to me again. Behind my pillow. Just as he spoke on the rock. Most polite and cheering. Calling to me, as it were, "Come, Cannibal – come!" Like a song, isn't it? "Come, Cannibal – come!"'

He sang the last words faintly, and died with a smile on his face. Delirium or lies? With the Spectacles actually in my hands, I was inclined to think lies. They were of the old-fashioned sort, with big, circular glasses, and stout tortoise-shell frames; they smelt musty, but not sulphurous. I possess a sense of humour, I am happy to say. When they were thoroughly cleaned, I determined to try the Devil's Spectacles on the two ladies, and submit to the consequences, whatever they might be.

II MEMOIRS OF MYSELF

Who were the two ladies?

They were both young and unmarried. As a matter of delicacy, I ask permission to mention them by their Christian names only. Zilla, aged seventeen. Cecilia, aged two and twenty.

And what was my position between them?

I was of the same age as Cecilia. She was my mother's companion and reader; handsome, well-born and poor. I had made her a proposal, and had been accepted. There were no money difficulties in the way of our marriage, in spite of my sweetheart's empty purse. I was an only child, and I had inherited, excepting my mother's jointure, the whole of the large property that my father left at his death. In social rank Cecilia was more than my equal; we were therefore not ill-matched from the worldly point of view. Nevertheless, there was an obstacle to our union, and a person interested in making the most of it. The obstacle was Zilla. The person interested was my mother. Zilla was her niece – her elder brother's daughter. The girl's parents had died in India, and she had been sent to school in England, under the care of her uncle and guardian. I had never seen her, and had hardly even heard of her, until there was a question of her spending the Christmas holidays (in the year when Septimus Notman died) at our house.

'Her uncle has no objection,' my mother said; 'and I shall be more than glad to see her. A most interesting creature, as I hear. So lovely, and so good, that they call her The Angel, at school. I say nothing about her nice little fortune or the high military rank that her poor father possessed. You don't care for these things. But, oh, Alfred, it would make me so happy if you fell in love with Zilla and married her!'

Three days before, I had made my proposal to Cecilia, and had been accepted – subject to my mother's approval. I thought this a good opportunity of stating my case plainly; and I spoke out. Never before had I seen my mother so outraged and disappointed – enraged with Cecilia; disappointed in me. 'A woman without a farthing of dowry; a woman who was as old as I was; a woman who had taken advantage of her position in the house to mislead and delude me!' and so on, and so on. Cecilia would certainly have been sent away if I had not declared that I should feel it my duty, in that event, to marry her immediately. My mother knew my temper, and refrained from giving Cecilia any cause of offence. Cecilia, on her side, showed what is called a proper pride; she declined to become my wife until my mother approved of her. She considered herself to be a martyr; and I considered myself to be an abominably ill-treated man. Between us, I am afraid we made my good mother's life unendurable – she was obliged to be the first who gave way. It was understood that we were to be married in the spring. It was also understood that Zilla was bitterly disappointed at having her holiday visit to us put off. 'She was so anxious to see you, poor child.' my mother said to me; 'but I really daren't ask her here under present circumstances. She is so fresh, so innocent, so infinitely superior in personal attractions to Cecilia, that I don't know what might happen if you saw her now. You are the soul of honor, Alfred; but you and Zilla had better remain strangers to each other – you *might* repent your rash engagement.' After this, it is needless to say that I was dying to see Zilla; while, at the same time, I never for an instant swerved from my fidelity to Cecilia.

Such was my position, on the memorable day when Septimus Notman died, leaving me possessor of the Devil's Spectacles.

III THE TEST OF THE SPECTACLES

The first person whom I encountered on returning to the house was the butler. He met me in the hall, with a receipted account in his hand which I had sent him to pay. The amount was close on a hundred pounds, and I had paid it immediately. 'Is there no discount?' I asked, looking at the receipt.

'The parties expect cash, sir, and charge accordingly.'

He looked so respectable when he made this answer, he had served us for so many years, that I felt an irresistible temptation to try the Devil's Spectacles on the butler, before I ventured to look through them at the ladies of my family. Our honest old servant would be such an excellent test.

'I am afraid my sight is failing me,' I said.

With this exceedingly simple explanation I put on the spectacles and looked at the butler.

The hall whirled round with me; on my word of honor I tremble and turn cold while I write of it now. Septimus Notman had spoken the truth!

In an instant the butler's heart became hideously visible – a fat organ seen through the medium of the infernal glasses. The thought in him was plainly legible to me in these words: 'Does my master think I'm going to give *him* the five per cent off the bill? Beastly meanness, interfering with the butler's perquisites.'

I took off my spectacles and put them in my pocket.

'You are a thief,' I said to the butler. 'You have got the discount money on this bill – five pounds all but a shilling or two – in your pocket. Send in your accounts; you leave my service.'

'To-morrow, sir, if you like!' answered the butler, indignantly. 'After serving your family for five-and-twenty years, to be called a thief for only taking my perquisites is an insult, Mr Alfred, that I have not deserved.' He put his handkerchief to his eyes and left me.

It was true that he had served us for a quarter of a century; it was also true that he had taken his perquisite and told a fib about it. But he had his compensating virtues. When I was a child he had given me many a ride on his knee and many a stolen drink of wine and water. His cellar-book had always been honestly kept; and his wife herself admitted that he was a model husband.

At other times I should have remembered this, I should have felt that I had been hasty, and have asked his pardon. At this time I failed to feel the slightest compassion for him, and never faltered for a moment in my resolution to send him away. What change had passed over me?

The library door opened, and an old schoolfellow and college friend of mine looked out. 'I thought I heard your voice in the hall,' he said; 'I have been waiting an hour for you.'

'Anything very important,' I asked, leading the way back to the library.

'Nothing of the least importance to *you*,' he replied, modestly.

I wanted no further explanation. More than once already I had lent him money, and, sooner or later, he had always repaid me. 'Another little loan?' I inquired, smiling pleasantly.

'I am really ashamed to ask you again, Alfred. But if you could lend me fifty pounds – just look at that letter.'

What mean impulse led me to repeat the excuse about my failing sight, and to read his heart on pretence of reading his letter?

He made some joke, suggested by the quaint appearance of the Spectacles. I was too closely occupied to appreciate his sense of humor. What had he just said to me? He had said. 'I am ashamed to ask you again.' And what had he thought while he was speaking? He had thought. 'When one has a milch cow at one's disposal, who but a fool would fail to take advantage of it?'

I handed him back the letter (from a lawyer, threatening 'proceedings') and I said, in my hardest tones, 'It's not convenient to oblige you this time.'

He stared at me like a man thunderstruck. 'Is this a joke, Alfred?' he asked.

'Do I look as if I was joking?'

He took up his hat. 'There is but one excuse for you,' he said. 'Your social position is too much for your weak brain – your money has got into your head. Good morning.'

I had been indebted to him for all sorts of kind services at school and college. He was an honorable man, and a faithful friend. If the galling sense of his own narrow means made him unjustly contemptuous towards rich people, it was a fault (in my case, an exasperating fault), no doubt. But who is perfect? And what are fifty pounds to me? This is what I should once have felt, before he could have found time enough to get to the door. As things were, I let him go, and thought myself well rid of a mean hanger-on who only valued me for my money.

Being now free to visit the ladies, I rang the bell and asked if my mother was at home. She was in her boudoir. And where was Miss Cecilia? In the boudoir, too.

On entering the room I found visitors in the way, and put off the trial of the Spectacles until they had taken their leave. Just as they were going a thundering knock at the door announced more visitors. This time, fortunately, we escaped with no worse consequences than the delivery of cards. We actually had two minutes to ourselves. I seized the opportunity of reminding my mother that I was constitutionally inaccessible to the claims of Society, and that I thought we might as well have our house to ourselves for half an hour or so. 'Send word down stairs,' I said, 'that you are not at home.'

My mother – magnificent in her old lace, her admirably-dressed gray hair, and her finely falling robe of purple silk – looked across the fireplace at Cecilia

– tall, and lazy, and beautiful, with lovely brown eyes, luxuriant black hair, a warmly-pale complexion, and an amber-colored dress – and said to me, 'You forget Cecilia. She likes Society.'

Cecilia looked at my mother with an air of languid surprise. 'What an extraordinary mistake!' she answered. 'I hate Society.'

My mother smiled – rang the bell – and gave the order – Not at home. I produced my Spectacles. There was an outcry at the hideous ugliness of them. I laid the blame on 'my oculist,' and waited for what was to follow between the two ladies. My mother spoke. Consequently I looked it my mother.

[I present her words first, and her thoughts next, in parenthesis.]

'So you hate society, my dear? Surely you have changed your opinion lately?' ('She doesn't mind how she lies as long as she can curry favor with Alfred. False creature.')

[I report Cecilia's answer on the same plan.]

'Pardon me; I haven't in the least changed my opinion – I was only afraid to express it. I hope I have not given offence by expressing it now.' ('She can't exist without gossip, and then she tries to lay it on me. Worldly old wretch!')

What I began to think of my mother, I am ashamed to record. What I thought of Cecilia may be stated in two words. I was more eager than ever to see 'The Angel of the school,' the good and lovely Zilla.

My mother stopped the further progress of my investigations. 'Take off those hideous Spectacles, Alfred, or leave us to our visitors. I don't say your sight may not be failing; I only say change your oculist.'

I took off the Spectacles, all the more willingly that I began to be really afraid of them. The talk between the ladies went on.

'Yours is a strange confession, my dear,' my mother said to Cecilia. 'May I ask what motive so young a lady can have for hating Society?'

'Only the motive of wanting to improve myself,' Cecilia answered. 'If I knew a little more of modern languages, and if I could be something better than a feeble amateur when I paint in water colours, you might think me worthier to be Alfred's wife. But Society is always in the way when I open my book or take up my brushes. In London I have no time to myself, and, I really can't disguise it, the frivolous life I lead is not to my taste.'

I thought this – (my Spectacles being in my pocket, remember) – very well and very prettily said. My mother looked at me. 'I quite agree with Cecilia,' I said, answering the look. 'We cannot count on having five minutes to ourselves in London from morning to night.' Another knock at the street door contributed its noisy support to my views as I spoke. 'We daren't even look out of the window,' I remarked, 'for fear Society may look up at the same moment, and see that we are at home.'

My mother smiled. 'You are certainly two remarkable young people,' she said, with an air of satirical indulgence – and paused for a moment, as if an idea had occurred to her which was more than usually worthy of consideration. If her eye had not been on me at the moment, I believe I should have taken my Spectacles out of my pocket. 'You are both so thoroughly agreed in disliking Society and despising London,' she resumed, 'that I feel it my duty, as a good mother, to make your lives a little more in harmony with your tastes, if I can. You complain, Alfred, that you can never count on having five minutes to yourself with Cecilia, Cecilia complains that she is perpetually interrupted in the laudable effort to improve her mind. I offer you both the whole day to yourselves, week after week, for the next three months. We will spend the winter at Long Fallas.'

Long Fallas was our country seat. There was no hunting; the shooting was let; the place was seven miles from Timbercombe town and station; and our nearest neighbor was a young Ritualistic clergyman, popularly reported in the village to be starving himself to death. I declined my mother's extraordinary proposal without a moment's hesitation. Cecilia, with the readiest and sweetest submission, accepted it.

This was our first open difference of opinion. Even without the Spectacles I could see that my mother hailed it as a good sign. She had consented to our marriage in the spring, without in the least altering her opinion that the angelic Zilla was the right wife for me. 'Settle it between yourselves, my dears,' she said, and left her chair to look for her work. Cecilia rose immediately to save her the trouble.

The instant their backs were turned on me I put on the terrible glasses. Is there such a thing in anatomy as a back view of the heart? There is such a thing assuredly when you look through the Devil's Spectacles. My mother's private sentiments presented themselves to me, as follows: 'If they don't get thoroughly sick of each other in a winter at Long Fallas I give up all knowledge of human nature. He shall marry Zilla yet.' Cecilia's motives asserted themselves with transparent simplicity in these words, 'His mother fully expects me to say "No." Horrible as the prospect is, I'll disappoint her by saying "Yes."'

'Horrible as the prospect is' was to my mind a very revolting expression, considering that I was personally included in the prospect. My mother's mischievous test of our affection for each other now presented itself to me in the light of a sensible proceeding. In the solitude of Long Fallas, I should surely discover whether Cecilia was about to marry me for my money or for myself. I concealed my Spectacles, and said nothing at the time. But later, when my mother entered the drawing-room dressed to go out for dinner, I waylaid her, and, after announcing that I had reconsidered the matter, declared that I was quite willing to go to Long Fallas. Cecilia came in dressed for dinner also. She had never looked so irresistibly lovely as when she was informed of my change of opinion. 'What a happy time we shall have,' she said, and smiled as if she really meant it?

They went away to their party. I was in the library when they returned. Hearing the carriage stop at the door I went out into the hall, and was suddenly checked on my way to the ladies by the sound of a man's voice: 'Many thanks; I am close at home now.' My mother's voice followed: 'I will let you know if we go to the country, Sir John. You will ride over and see us?' 'With the greatest pleasure. Good-night, Miss Cecilia.' There was no mistaking the tone in which those last four words were spoken. Sir John's accent expressed indescribable tenderness. I retired again to the library.

My mother came in, followed by her charming companion.

'Here is a new complication,' she said. 'Cecilia doesn't want to go to Long Fallas.' I asked why. Cecilia answered, without looking at me, 'Oh, I have changed my mind.' She turned aside to relieve my mother of her fur cloak. I instantly consulted my Spectacles, and obtained my information in these mysterious terms: 'Sir John goes to Timbercombe.'

Very short, and yet suggestive of more than one interpretation. A little inquiry made the facts more clear. Sir John had been one of the guests at the dinner, and he and Cecilia had shaken hands like old friends. At my mother's request, he had been presented to her. He had produced such an excellent impression that she had taken him in her carriage part of his way home. She had also discovered that he was about to visit a relative living at Timbercombe (already mentioned, I think, as our nearest town). Another momentary opportunity with the Spectacles completed my discoveries. Sir John had proposed marriage (unsuccessfully) to Cecilia, and being still persistently in love with her, only wanted a favorable opportunity to propose again. The excellent impression which he had produced on my mother was perfectly intelligible now.

In feeling reluctant to give her rejected lover that other opportunity, was Cecilia afraid of Sir John, or afraid of herself? My Spectacles informed me that she deliberately declined to face that question, even in her thoughts.

Under these circumstances, the test of a dreary winter residence at Long Fallas became, to my mind, more valuable than ever. Single-handed, Cecilia might successfully keep up appearances and deceive other people, though she might not deceive me. But, in combination with Sir John, there was a chance that she might openly betray the true state of her feelings. If I was really the favored man, she would, of course, be dearer to me than ever. If not (with more producable proof than the Devil's Spectacles to justify me), I need not hesitate to break off the engagement.

'Second thoughts are not always best, dear Cecilia,' I said. 'Do me a favour. Let us try Long Fallas, and if we find the place quite unendurable, let us return to London.'

Cecilia looked at me and hesitated – looked at my mother, and submitted to Long Fallas in the sweetest manner. The more they were secretly at variance, the better the two ladies appeared to understand each other.

We did not start for the country until three days afterward. The packing up was a serious matter to begin with, and my mother prolonged the delay by paying a visit to her niece at the school in the country. She kept the visit a secret from Cecilia, of course. But even when we were alone, and when I asked about Zilla, I was only favoured with a very brief reply. She merely lifted her eyes to Heaven, and said, 'Perfectly charming!'

IV THE TEST OF LONG FALLAS

We had had a week of it. If we had told each other the truth we should have said, 'Let us go back to London.'

Thus far there had been no signs of Sir John. The Spectacles informed me that he had arrived at Timbercombe, and that Cecilia had written to him. But, strangely enough, they failed to disclose what she had said. Had she forgotten it already, or was there some defect, hitherto unsuspected, in my supernatural glasses?

Christmas Day was near at hand. The weather was, so far, almost invariably misty and wet. Cecilia began to yawn over her favorite intellectual resources. My mother waited with superhuman patience for events. As for myself, having literally nothing else to amuse me, I took to gratifying an improper curiosity in the outlying regions of the family circle. In plain English, I discovered a nice little needle-woman, who was employed at Long Fallas. Her name was Miss Peskey. When nobody was looking, I amused myself with Miss Peskey.

Let no person of strict principles be alarmed. It was an innocent flirtation, on my side; and the nice little needle-woman rigidly refused to give me the smallest encouragement. Quite a young girl, Miss Peskey had the self-possession of a mature woman. She allowed me time enough to see that she had a trim little figure, soft blue eyes, and glossy golden hair; and then, in the sweetest of voices, respectfully requested me to leave her to her work. If I tried to persuade her to let me stay a little longer, she rose meekly, and said 'I shall, most unwillingly, be compelled to place myself under the protection of the housekeeper.' Once I attempted to take her hand. She put her handkerchief to her eyes, and said, 'Is it manly, sir, to insult a defenceless girl?' In one word, Miss Peskey foiled me at every point. For the first week I never even got the chance of looking at her through the Devil's Spectacles.

On the first day of the new week the weather cleared up wonderfully; spring seemed to have come to us in the middle of winter.

Cecilia and I went out riding. On our return, having nothing better to do, I accompanied the horses back to the stables, and naturally offended the groom, who thought I was 'watching him.' Returning toward the house, I passed the window of the ground-floor room, at the back of the building, devoted to the needlewoman. A railed yard kept me at a respectful distance, but at the same time gave me a view of the interior of the room. Miss Peskey was not alone; my mother was with her. They were evidently talking, but not a word reached my ears. It mattered nothing. While I could see them through my Spectacles, their thoughts were visible to me before they found their way into words.

My mother was speaking – 'Well, my dear, have you formed your opinion of him yet?'

Miss Peskey replied, 'Not quite yet.'

'You are wonderfully cautious in arriving at a conclusion. How much longer is this clever contrivance of yours to last?'

'Give me two days more, dear madam; I can't decide until Sir John helps me.'

'Is Sir John really coming here?'

'I think so.'

'And have *you* managed it?'

'If you will kindly excuse me, I would rather not answer just yet.'

The housekeeper entered the room, and called my mother away on some domestic business. As she walked to the door, I had time to read her thought before she went out – 'Very extraordinary to find such resources of clever invention in such a young girl!'

Miss Peskey, left in maiden meditation with her work on her lap, smiled to herself. I turned the glasses on her, and made a discovery that petrified me. To put it plainly, the charming needlewoman was deceiving us all (with the one exception of my mother) under an assumed name and vocation in life. Miss Peskey was no other than my cousin Zilla, 'the Angel of the school!'

Let me do my poor mother justice. She was guilty of the consenting to the deception, and of no more. The invention of the trick, and the entire responsibility of carrying it out, rested wholly and exclusively with Miss Zilla, aged seventeen.

I followed the train of thought which my mother's questions had set going in the mind of this young person. To justify my own conduct, I must report the result as briefly as I can. Have you heard of 'fasting' girls? have you heard of 'mesmeric' girls? have you heard of girls (in the newspapers) who have invented the most infamous charges against innocent men? Then don't accuse my Spectacles of seeing impossible sights!

My report of Miss Zilla's thoughts, as they succeeded each other, begins as follows:

First Thought: 'My small fortune is all very well; but I want to be mistress of a great establishment, and to get away from school. Alfred, dear fellow, is reported to have fifteen thousand a year. Is his mother's companion to be allowed to catch this rich fish, without the least opposition? Not if I know it!'

Second Thought: 'How very simple old people are! His mother visits me, invites me to Long Fallas, and expects me to cut out Cecilia. Men are such fools (the writing master has fallen in love with me) that she would only have to burst out crying, and keep him to herself. I have proposed a better way than fair fighting for Alfred, suggested by a play I read the other day. The old mother consents, with conditions. "I am sure you will do nothing, my dear, unbecoming to a young lady. Win him, as Miss Hardcastle won Mr Marlow in She Stoops to Conquer, if you like; but do nothing to forfeit your self-respect." What astonishing simplicity! Where *did* she go to school when she was young?'

Third Thought: 'How amazingly lucky that Cecilia's maid is lazy, and that the needlewoman dines in the servants' hall! The maid had the prospect of getting up before six in the morning, to be ready to go in the chaise-car with the servant who does the household errands at Timbercombe – and for what? To take a note from her mistress to Sir John, and wait for an answer. The good little neddlewoman hears this, smiles, and says, "I don't mind how early I get up; I'll take it for you, and bring back the answer."'

Fourth Thought: 'What a blessing it is to have blue eyes and golden hair! Sir John was quite struck with me. I thought at the time he would do instead of Alfred. Fortunately I have since asked the simple old mother about him. He is a poor baronet. Not to be thought of for an instant. "My Lady" – without a corresponding establishment! Too dreadful! But I didn't throw away my fascinations. I saw him wince when he read the letter. "No bad news, I hope, sir," I ventured to say. He shook his head solemnly. "Your mistress" (he took me, of course, for Cecilia's maid) forbids me to call at Long Fallas." I thought to myself what a hypocrite Cecilia must be, and I said modestly to Sir John, "Do you think it wise, sir, always to take a young lady at her word?" What a wonderful effect a well-put question sometimes has, especially when it is followed by sound advice. I took back a conventional answer from Sir John, to keep up appearances. Our private arrangement is that he is to ride over to Long Fallas to-morrow, and wait in the shrubbery at half-past two. If it rains or snows he is to try the next fine day. In either case the poor needlewoman will ask for a half holiday, and will induce Miss Cecilia to take a little walk in the right direction. Sir John gave me two sovereigns and a kiss at parting. I accepted both tributes with the most becoming humility. He shall have his money's worth, though he is a poor baronet; he shall meet his young lady in the shrubbery. And I may catch the rich fish, after all!'

Fifth Thought: 'Bother this horrid work! It is all very well to be clever with one's needle, but how it disfigures one's forefinger! No matter, I must play my part while it lasts, or I shall be reported lazy by the most detestable woman I ever met with – the housekeeper at Long Fallas.'

She threaded her needle, and I put my Spectacles in my pocket.

I don't think I suspected it at the time; but I am now well aware that Septimus Notman's diabolical gift was exerting its influence over me. I was wickedly cool, under circumstances which would have roused my righteous indignation in the days before my Spectacles. Sir John and the Angel; my mother and her family interests; Cecilia and her unacknowledged lover – what a network of conspiracy and deception was wound about me! and what a perfectly fiendish pleasure I felt in planning to match them on their own ground! The method of obtaining this object presented itself to me in the simplest form. I had only to take my mother for a walk in the near neighbourhood of the shrubbery – and the exposure would be complete! That night I studied the barometer with unutterable anxiety. The prospect of the weather was all that I could wish.

V THE TRUTH IN THE SHRUBBERY

On the next day, the friendly sun shone, the balmy air invited everybody to go out. I made no further use of the Spectacles that morning: my purpose was to keep them in my pocket until the interview in the shrubbery was over. Shall I own the motive? It was simply fear – fear of making further discoveries, and of losing the masterly self-control on which the whole success of my project depended.

We lunched at one o'clock. Had Cecilia and Zilla come to a private understanding on the subject of the interview in the shrubbery? By way of ascertaining this, I asked Cecilia if she would like to go out riding in the afternoon. She declined the proposal – she wanted to finish a sketch. I was sufficiently answered.

'Cecilia complains that your manner has grown cold toward her lately,' my mother said, when we were left together.

My mind was dwelling on Cecilia's letter to Sir John. Would any man have so easily adopted Zilla's suggestion not to take Cecilia at her word, unless there had been something to encourage him? I could only trust myself to answer my mother very briefly. 'Cecilia is changed toward me' – was all my reply.

My mother was evidently gratified by this prospect of a misunderstanding between us. 'Ah!' she said, 'if Cecilia only had Zilla's sweet temper.'

This was a little too much to endure – but I did endure it. 'Will you come out with me, mamma, for a walk in the grounds?' I asked.

My mother accepted the invitation so gladly, that I really think I should have felt ashamed of myself – if I had not had the contaminating Spectacles in my pocket. We had just settled to start soon after two o'clock, when there was a timid knock at the door. The angelic needlewoman appeared to ask for her half holiday. My mother actually blushed! Old habits will cling to the members of the past generation. 'What is it?' she said, in low uncertain tones. 'Might I go to the village, ma'am, to buy some little things?' 'Certainly.' The door closed again. 'Now for the shrubbery!' I thought. 'Make haste, mamma,' I said, 'the best of the day is going. And mind one thing – put on your thickest boots!'

On one side of the shrubbery were the gardens. The other side was bounded by a wooden fence. A footpath, running part of the way beside the fence, crossed the grass beyond, and made a short cut between the nearest park gate and the servants' offices. This was the safe place that I had chosen. We could hear perfectly – though the closely-planted evergreens might prevent the exercise of sight. I had recommended 'thick boots' because there was no help but to muffle the sound of our footsteps by walking on the wet grass. At its further end, the shrubbery joined the carriage road up to the house.

My mother's surprise at the place that I had chosen for our walk would have been expressed in words, as well as by looks, if I had not stopped her by a whispered warning. 'Keep perfectly quiet,' I said, 'and listen. I have a motive for bringing you here.'

The words had hardly passed my lips, before we heard the voices of Cecilia and the needlewoman in the shrubbery.

'Wait a minute,' said Cecilia; 'you must be a little more explicit, before I consent to go any farther. How came you to take my letter to Sir John, instead of my maid?'

'Only to oblige her, Miss. She was not very well, and she didn't fancy going all the way to Timbercombe. I can buy no good needles in the village, and I was glad of the opportunity of getting to the town.'

There was a pause. Cecilia was reflecting, as I supposed. My mother began to turn pale.

Cecilia resumed. 'There is nothing in Sir John's answer to my letter,' she said, 'that leads me to suppose he can be guilty of an act of rudeness. I have always believed him to be a gentleman. No gentleman would force his way into my presence, when I wrote expressly to ask him to spare me. Pray how did you know he was determined only to take his dismissal from my lips?'

'Gentlemen's feelings sometimes get the better of them, Miss. Sir John was very much distressed—'

Cecilia interrupted her. 'There was nothing in my letter to distress him,' she said.

'He *was* distressed, Miss; and he *did* say, "I cannot take my answer this way – I must and will see her." And then he asked me to get you to walk out to-day, and to say nothing so that he might take you by surprise. He is so madly in love with you, Miss, that he is all but beside himself. I am really afraid of what might happen, if you don't soften his disappointment to him in some way. How any lady can treat such a handsome gentleman so cruelly, passes my poor judgment!'

Cecilia instantly resented the familiarity implied in those last words. 'You are not called upon to exercise your judgment,' she said. 'You can go back to the house.'

'Hadn't I better see Sir John first, Miss?'

'Certainly not! You and Sir John have seen quite enough of each other already.'

There was another pause. My mother stood holding by my arm, pale and trembling. We could neither of us speak. My own mind was strangely agitated. Either Cecilia was a monster of deceit, or she had thus far spoken and acted as became a true and highly-bred woman. The distant sound of horses' hoofs on the park road, told us both that the critical moment was at hand. In another minute, the sound ceased. Sir John had probably dismounted, and tied up his horse at the entrance of the shrubbery. After an interval, we heard Cecilia's voice again, farther away from us. We followed the voice. The interview which was to decide my future destiny in life had begun.

'No, Sir John; I must have my question answered first. Is there anything in my letter – was there anything in my conduct, when we met in London – which justifies this?'

'Love justifies everything, Cecilia!'

'You are not to call me Cecilia, if you please. Have you no plainer answer to give me?'

'Have *you* no mercy on a man, who cannot live without you? Is there really nothing in myself and my title to set against the perfectly obscure person, to whom you have so rashly engaged yourself? It would be an insult to suppose that his wealth has tempted you. What can be his merit in your eyes? His own friends can say no more in his favour than that he is a good-natured fool. I don't blame you; women often drift into engagements that they repent of afterwards. Do yourself justice! Be true to your own nobility of character – and be the angel who makes our two lives happy, before it is too late!'

'Have you done, Sir John?'

There was a moment of silence. It was impossible to mistake her tone – Sir John's flow of eloquence came to a full stop.

'Before I answer you,' Cecilia proceeded, 'I have something to say first. The girl who took my letter to you, was not my maid, as you may have supposed. She is a stranger to me; and I suspect her of being a false creature with some purpose of her own to serve. I find a difficulty in attributing to a person in your rank of life the mean deceit which answers my letter in terms that lead me to trust you, and then takes me by surprise in this way. My messenger (as I believe) is quite insolent enough to have suggested this course to you. Am I right? I expect a reply, Sir John, that is worthy in its entire truthfulness of you and your title. Am I right?'

'You are right, Miss Cecilia. Pray don't despise me. The temptation to plead with you once more—'

'I will speak to you, Sir John, as candidly as you have spoken to me. You are entirely wrong in supposing it possible for me to repent of my marriage engagement. The man, whose false friends have depreciated him in your estimation, is the only man I love, and the only man I will marry. And I beg you to understand, if he lost the whole of his fortune to-morrow, I would marry him the next day, if he asked me. Must I say more? or will you treat me with the delicacy of a gentleman, and take your leave?'

I don't remember whether he said anything or not, before he left her. I only know that they parted. Don't ask me to confess what I felt. Don't ask me to describe what my mother felt. Let the scene be changed, and the narrative be resumed at a later hour of the day.

VI THE END OF THE SPECTACLES

I asked myself a question, which I beg to repeat here. What did I owe to the Devil's Spectacles?

In the first place, I was indebted to my glasses for seeing all the faults, and none of the merits, in the persons about me. In the second place, I arrived at the great discovery that, if we are to live usefully and happily with our fellow-creatures, we must take them at their best, and not at their worst. Having reached these conclusions, I trusted to my own unassisted insight, and set myself to ascertain what the Devil had *not* helped me to discover in the two persons who were dearest to me – my mother and Cecilia.

I began with Cecilia, leaving my mother time to recover after the shock that had fallen on her.

It was impossible to acknowledge what I had seen through the Spectacles, or what I had heard at the shrubbery fence. In speaking to Cecilia, I could only attribute my coldness of manner to jealousy of the mere name of 'Sir John,' and ask to be pardoned for even a momentary distrust of the most constant and charming of women. There was something, I suppose, in my contrite consciousness of having wronged her, that expressed itself in my looks and my tones. We were sitting together on the sofa. For the first time since our engagement, she put her arm round my neck, and kissed me, without waiting to be kissed first.

'I am not very demonstrative,' she said, softly; 'and I don't think, Alfred, you have ever known how fond I am of you. My dear, when Sir John and I met again at that dinner party, I was too faithful to you even to allow myself to *think* of him. Your poor mother irritated me by seeming to doubt whether I could trust myself within reach of Timbercombe, or I should never have consented to go to Long Fallas. You remember that she invited Sir John to ride over and see us. I wrote to him, informing him of my engagement to you, and telling him, in the plainest words, that if he did call at this house, nothing would induce me to see him. I had every reason to suppose that he would understand and respect my motives—'

She paused. The rich color rose in her lovely face. I refused to let her distress herself by saying a word of what had happened in the shrubbery. Look back, if you have forgotten it, and see how completely the Spectacles failed to show me the higher and nobler motives that had animated her. The little superficial irritabilities and distrusts, they exhibited to perfection; but the true regard for each other, hidden below the surface in my mother and in my promised wife, was completely beyond them.

'Shall we go back to London, to-morrow?' I asked.

'Are you tired of being here with me, Alfred?'

'I am tired of waiting till the spring, my angel. I will live with you wherever you like, if you will only consent to hasten the transformation which makes you my wife. Will you consent?'

'If your mother asks me. Don't hurry her, Alfred.'

But I did hurry her. After what we had heard in the shrubbery I could look into my mother's heart (without assistance), and feel sure that the nobler part of her nature would justify my confidence in it. She was not only ready to 'ask Cecilia,' then and there – she was eager, poor soul, to confess how completely she had been misled by her natural interest in her brother's child. Being firmly resolved to keep the secret of my discovery of her niece, I refused to hear her, as I had refused to hear Cecilia. Did I not know, without being told, what child's play it would be to Zilla to dazzle and delude my innocent mother? I merely asked if 'the needlewoman was still in the house.' The answer was thoroughly explicit: 'She is at the railway station by this time, and she will never enter any house of mine again.'

We returned to London the next morning.

I had a moment's private talk with the station-master at Timbercombe. Sir John had left his friends at the town, on the previous day. He and Zilla had met on the platform, waiting for the London train. She had followed him into the smoking-carriage. Just as the station-master was going to start the train, Sir John opened the door, with a strong expression of disgust, and took refuge in another carriage. She had tried the baronet as a last resource, and *he* had slipped through her fingers too. What did it matter to Zilla? She had plenty of time before her, and she belonged to the order of persons who never fail to make the most of her advantages. The other day I saw the announcement of her marriage to a great ironmaster, a man worth millions of money, with establishments to correspond. Brava, Zilla! No need to look for *your* nobler motives with the naked eye.

A few days before I became a married man I was a guest at the dinner table of a bachelor friend, and I met Sir John. It would have been ridiculous to leave the room; I merely charged my host to keep my name concealed. I sat next to the baronet, and he doesn't know, to this day, who his 'very agreeable neighbour' was.

Instead of spending our honeymoon abroad, Cecilia and I went back to Long Fallas. We found the place delightful, even in the winter time.

Did I take the Devil's Spectacles back with me?

No.

Did I throw them away or smash them into small morsels?

Neither. I remembered what Septimus Notman had told me. The one way of getting rid of them was to give them to some other man.

And to what other man did I give them?

I had not forgotten what my rival had said of me in the shrubbery. I gave the Devil's Spectacles to Sir John.

VII BETWEEN THE READER AND THE EDITOR

Are we to have no satisfactory explanation of the supernatural element in the story? How did it come into the Editor's hands? Was there neither name nor address on the manuscript?

There was an address, if you must know. But I decline to mention it.

Suppose I guess that the address was at a lunatic asylum? What would you say to that?

I should say I suspected you of being a critic, and I should have the honour of wishing you good morning.

Mr Policeman and the Cook

Originally appeared in *The Seaside Library*, 26 January 1881, as
'Who Killed Zebedee?' Reprinted in *Little Novels* (1887). In this
late whodunnit, Norman Page points out that 'there is a strong
sense of the profession of detective and the techniques of detection
having made considerable strides since Collins's own stories of the
1850s.' The police are now able to send photographs of the murder
weapon 'to every police station in the kingdom.' See Introduction to
Mad Monkton and Other Stories, p. xxvi. After the anti-Jesuit excesses
of *The Black Robe* (1881), Collins seems to have returned to a more
sympathetic handling of Roman Catholicism in this story. It earned
him £35.

A FIRST WORD FOR MYSELF

Before the Doctor left me one evening, I asked him how much longer I was likely to live. He answered: 'It's not easy to say; you may die before I can get back to you in the morning, or you may live to the end of the month.'

I was alive enough on the next morning to think of the needs of my soul, and (being a member of the Roman Catholic Church) to send for the priest.

The history of my sins, related in confession, included blameworthy neglect of a duty which I owed to the laws of my country. In the priest's opinion – and I agreed with him – I was bound to make public acknowledgement of my fault, as an act of penance becoming to a Catholic Englishman. We concluded, thereupon, to try a division of labour. I related the circumstances, while his reverence took the pen, and put the matter into shape.

Here follows what came of it:

I

When I was a young man of five-and-twenty, I became a member of the London police force. After nearly two years' ordinary experience of the responsible and ill-paid duties of that vocation, I found myself employed on my first serious and terrible case of official inquiry – relating to nothing less than the crime of Murder.

The circumstances were these:

I was then attached to a station in the northern district of London – which I beg permission not to mention more particularly. On a certain Monday in the week, I took my turn of night duty. Up to four in the morning, nothing occurred at the station-house out of the ordinary way. It was then spring time, and, between the gas and the fire, the room became rather hot. I went to the door to get a breath of fresh air – much to the surprise of our Inspector on duty, who was constitutionally a chilly man. There was a fine rain falling; and a nasty damp in the air sent me back to the fireside. I don't suppose I had sat down for more than a minute when the swinging-door was violently pushed open. A frantic woman ran in with a scream, and said: 'Is this the station-house?'

Our Inspector (otherwise an excellent officer) had, by some perversity of nature, a hot temper in his chilly constitution. 'Why, bless the woman, can't you *see* it is?' he says. 'What's the matter now?'

'Murder's the matter!' she burst out. 'For God's sake come back with me. It's at Mrs Crosscapel's lodging-house, number 14, Lehigh Street. A young woman has murdered her husband in the night! With a knife, sir. She says she thinks she did it in her sleep.'

I confess I was startled by this; and the third man on duty (a sergeant) seemed to feel it too. She was a nice-looking young woman, even in her terrified condition, just out of bed, with her clothes huddled on anyhow. I was partial in those days to a tall figure – and she was, as they say, my style. I put a chair for her; and the sergeant poked the fire. As for the Inspector, nothing ever upset *him*. He questioned her as coolly as if it had been a case of petty larceny.

'Have you seen the murdered man?' he asked.

'No, sir.'

'Or the wife?'

'No, sir. I didn't dare go into the room; I only heard about it!'

'Oh? And who are You? One of the lodgers?'

'No, sir. I'm the cook.'

'Isn't there a master in the house?'

'Yes, sir. He's frightened out of his wits. And the housemaid's gone for the Doctor. It all falls on the poor servants, of course. Oh, why did I ever set foot in that horrible house?'

The poor soul burst out crying, and shivered from head to foot. The Inspector made a note of her statement, and then asked her to read it, and sign it with her name. The object of this proceeding was to get her to come near enough to give him the opportunity of smelling her breath. 'When people make extraordinary statements,' he afterwards said to me, 'it sometimes saves trouble to satisfy yourself that they are not drunk. I've known them to be mad – but not often. You will generally find *that* in their eyes.'

She roused herself, and signed her name – 'Priscilla Thurlby.' The Inspector's own test proved her to be sober; and her eyes – of a nice light blue colour, mild and pleasant, no doubt, when they were not staring with fear, and red with crying – satisfied him (as I supposed) that she was not mad. He turned the case over to me, in the first instance. I saw that he didn't believe in it, even yet.

'Go back with her to the house,' he says. 'This may be a stupid hoax, or a quarrel exaggerated. See to it yourself, and hear what the Doctor says. If it *is* serious, send word back here directly, and let nobody enter the place or leave it till we come. Stop! You know the form if any statement is volunteered?'

'Yes, sir. I am to caution the persons that whatever they say will be taken down, and may be used against them.'

'Quite right. You'll be an Inspector yourself one of these days. Now, Miss!' With that he dismissed her, under my care.

Lehigh Street was not very far off – about twenty minutes' walk from the station. I confess I thought the Inspector had been rather hard on Priscilla. She was herself naturally angry with him. 'What does he mean,' she says, 'by talking of a hoax? I wish he was as frightened as I am. This is the first time I have been out at service, sir – and I did think I had found a respectable place.'

I said very little to her – feeling, if the truth must be told, rather anxious about the duty committed to me. On reaching the house the door was opened from within, before I could knock. A gentleman stepped out, who proved to be the Doctor. He stopped the moment he saw me.

'You must be careful, policeman,' he says. 'I found the man lying on his back, in bed, dead – with the knife that had killed him left sticking in the wound.'

Hearing this, I felt the necessity of sending at once to the station. Where could I find a trustworthy messenger? I took the liberty of asking the Doctor if he would repeat to the police what he had already said to me. The station was not much out of his way home. He kindly granted my request.

The landlady (Mrs Crosscapel) joined us while we were talking. She was still a young woman; not easily frightened, as far as I could see, even by a murder in the house. Her husband was in the passage behind her. He looked old enough to be her father; and he so trembled with terror that some people might have taken him for the guilty person. I removed the key from the street door, after locking it; and I said to the landlady: 'Nobody must leave the house, or enter the house, till the Inspector comes. I must examine the premises to see if anyone has broken in.'

'There is the key of the area gate,' she said, in answer to me. 'It's always kept locked. Come downstairs, and see for yourself.' Priscilla went with us. Her mistress set her to work to light the kitchen fire. 'Some of us,' says Mrs Crosscapel, 'may be the better for a cup of tea.' I remarked that she took things easy, under the circumstances. She answered that the landlady of a London lodging-house could not afford to lose her wits, no matter what might happen.

I found the gate locked, and the shutters of the kitchen window fastened. The back kitchen and back door were secured in the same way. No person was concealed anywhere. Returning upstairs, I examined the front parlour window. There again, the barred shutters answered for the security of that room. A cracked voice spoke through the door of the back parlour. 'The policeman can come in,' it said, 'if he will promise not to look at me.' I turned to the landlady for information. 'It's my parlour lodger, Miss Mybus,' she said, 'a most respectable lady.' Going into the room, I saw something rolled up perpendicularly in the bed curtains. Miss Mybus had made herself modestly invisible in that way. Having now satisfied my mind about the security of the lower part of the house, and having the keys safe in my pocket, I was ready to go upstairs.

On our way to the upper regions I asked if there had been any visitors on the previous day. There had been only two visitors, friends of the lodgers – and Mrs Crosscapel herself had let them both out. My next inquiry related to the lodgers themselves. On the ground floor there was Miss Mybus. On the first floor (occupying both rooms) Mr Barfield, an old bachelor, employed in a merchant's office. On the second floor, in the front room, Mr John Zebedee, the murdered man, and his wife. In the back room, Mr Deluc; described as a cigar agent, and supposed to be a Creole gentleman from Martinique. In the front garret, Mr and Mrs Crosscapel. In the back garret, the cook and the housemaid. These were the inhabitants, regularly accounted for. I asked about the servants. 'Both excellent characters,' says the landlady, 'or they would not be in my service.'

We reached the second floor, and found the housemaid on the watch outside the door of the front room. Not as nice a woman, personally, as the cook, and sadly frightened of course. Her mistress had posted her, to give the alarm in the case of an outbreak on the part of Mrs Zebedee, kept locked up in the room. My arrival relieved the housemaid of further responsibility. She ran downstairs to her fellow-servant in the kitchen.

I asked Mrs Crosscapel how and when the alarm of the murder had been given.

'Soon after three this morning,' says she, 'I was woke by the screams of Mrs Zebedee. I found her out here on the landing, and Mr Deluc, in great alarm, trying to quiet her. Sleeping in the next room, he had only to open his door, when her screams woke him. "My dear John's murdered! I am the miserable wretch – I did it in my sleep!" She repeated those frantic words over and over again, until she dropped in a swoon. Mr Deluc and I carried her back into the bedroom. We both thought the poor creature had been driven distracted by some dreadful dream. But when we got to the bedside – don't ask me what we saw; the Doctor has told you about it already. I was once a nurse in a hospital, and accustomed, as such, to horrid sights. It turned me cold and giddy, notwithstanding. As for Mr Deluc, I thought *he* would have had a fainting fit next.'

Hearing this, I inquired if Mrs Zebedee had said or done any strange things since she had been Mrs Crosscapel's lodger.

'You think she's mad?' says the landlady. 'And anybody would be of your mind, when a woman accuses herself of murdering her husband in her sleep. All I can say is that, up to this morning, a more quiet, sensible, well-behaved little person than Mrs Zebedee I never met with. Only just married, mind, and as fond of her unfortunate husband as a woman could be. I should have called them a pattern couple, in their own line of life.'

There was no more to be said on the landing. We unlocked the door and went into the room.

II

He lay in bed on his back as the Doctor had described him. On the left side of his nightgown, just over his heart, the blood on the linen told its terrible tale. As well as one could judge, looking unwillingly at a dead face, he must have been a handsome young man in his life-time. It was a sight to sadden anybody – but I think the most painful sensation was when my eyes fell next on his miserable wife.

She was down on the floor, crouched up in a corner – a dark little woman, smartly dressed in gay colours. Her black hair and her big brown eyes made the horrid paleness of her face look even more deadly white than perhaps it really was. She stared straight at us without appearing to see us. We spoke to her, and she never answered a word. She might have been dead – like her husband – except that she perpetually picked at her fingers, and shuddered every now and then as if she was cold. I went to her and tried to lift her up. She shrank back with a cry that well-nigh frightened me – not because it was loud, but because it was more like the cry of some animal than of a human being. However quietly she might have behaved in the landlady's previous experience of her, she was beside herself now. I might have been moved by a natural pity for her, or I might have been completely upset in my mind – I only know this, I could not persuade myself that she was guilty. I even said to Mrs Crosscapel, 'I don't believe she did it.'

While I spoke, there was a knock at the door. I went downstairs at once, and admitted (to my great relief) the Inspector, accompanied by one of our men.

He waited downstairs to hear my report, and he approved of what I had done. 'It looks as if the murder had been committed by somebody in the house.' Saying this, he left the man below, and went up with me to the second floor.

Before he had been a minute in the room, he discovered an object which had escaped my observation.

It was the knife that had done the deed.

The Doctor had found it left in the body – had withdrawn it to probe the wound – and had laid it on the bedside table. It was one of those useful knives which contain a saw, a corkscrew, and other like implements. The big blade fastened back, when open, with a spring. Except where the blood was on it, it was as bright as when it had been purchased. A small metal plate was fastened to the horn handle, containing an inscription, only partly engraved, which ran thus: '*To John Zebedee, from—*' There it stopped, strangely enough.

Who or what had interrupted the engraver's work? It was impossible even to guess. Nevertheless, the Inspector was encouraged.

'This ought to help us,' he said – and then he gave an attentive ear (looking all the while at the poor creature in the corner) to what Mrs Crosscapel had to tell him.

The landlady having done, he said he must now see the lodger who slept in the next bedchamber.

Mr Deluc made his appearance, standing at the door of the room, and turning away his head with horror from the sight inside.

He was wrapped in a splendid blue dressing-gown, with a golden girdle and trimmings. His scanty brownish hair curled (whether artificially or not, I am unable to say) in little ringlets. His complexion was yellow; his greenish-brown eyes were of the sort called 'goggle' – they looked as if they might drop out of his face, if you held a spoon under them. His moustache and goat's beard were beautifully oiled; and, to complete his equipment, he had a long black cigar in his mouth.

'It isn't insensibility to this terrible tragedy,' he explained. 'My nerves have been shattered, Mr Policeman, and I can only repair the mischief in this way. Be pleased to excuse and feel for me.'

The Inspector questioned this witness sharply and closely. He was not a man to be misled by appearances; but I could see that he was far from liking, or even trusting, Mr Deluc. Nothing came of the examination, except what Mrs Crosscapel had in substance already mentioned to me. Mr Deluc returned to his room.

'How long has he been lodging with you?' the Inspector asked, as soon as his back was turned.

'Nearly a year,' the landlady answered.

'Did he give you a reference?'

'As good a reference as I could wish for.' Thereupon, she mentioned the names of a well-known firm of cigar merchants in the City. The Inspector noted the information in his pocket-book.

I would rather not relate in detail what happened next: it is too distressing to be dwelt on. Let me only say that the poor demented woman was taken away in a cab to the station-house. The Inspector possessed himself of the knife, and of a book found on the floor, called 'The World of Sleep.' The portmanteau containing the luggage was locked – and then the door of the room was secured, the keys in both cases being left in my charge. My instructions were to remain in the house, and allow nobody to leave it, until I heard again shortly from the Inspector.

III

The coroner's inquest was adjourned; and the examination before the magistrate ended in a remand – Mrs Zebedee being in no condition to understand the proceedings in either case. The surgeon reported her to be completely prostrated by a terrible nervous shock. When he was asked if he considered her to have been a sane woman before the murder took place, he refused to answer positively at that time.

A week passed. The murdered man was buried; his old father attending the funeral. I occasionally saw Mrs Crosscapel, and the two servants, for the purpose of getting such further information as was thought desirable. Both the cook and the housemaid had given their month's notice to quit; declining, in the interest of their characters, to remain in a house which had been the scene of a murder. Mr Deluc's nerves led also to his removal; his rest was now disturbed by frightful dreams. He paid the necessary forfeit-money, and left without notice. The first-floor lodger, Mr Barfield, kept his rooms, but obtained leave of absence from his employers, and took refuge with some friends in the country. Miss Mybus alone remained in the parlours. 'When I am comfortable,' the old lady said, 'nothing moves me, at my age. A murder up two pairs of stairs is nearly the same thing as a murder in the next house. Distance, you see, makes all the difference.'

It mattered little to the police what the lodgers did. We had men in plain clothes watching the house night and day. Everybody who went away was privately followed; and the police in the district to which they retired were warned to keep an eye on them, after that. As long as we failed to put Mrs Zebedee's extraordinary statement to any sort of test – to say nothing of having proved unsuccessful, thus far, in tracing the knife to its purchaser – we were bound to let no person living under Mrs Crosscapel's roof, on the night of the murder, slip through our fingers.

IV

In a fortnight more, Mrs Zebedee had sufficiently recovered to make the necessary statement – after the preliminary caution addressed to persons in such cases. The surgeon had no hesitation, now, in reporting her to be a sane woman.

Her station in life had been domestic service. She had lived for four years in her last place as lady's-maid, with a family residing in Dorsetshire. The one objection to her had been the occasional infirmity of sleep-walking, which made it necessary that one of the other female servants should sleep in the same room, with the door locked and the key under her pillow. In all other respects the lady's-maid was described by her mistress as 'a perfect treasure.'

In the last six months of her service, a young man named John Zebedee entered the house (with a written character) as footman. He soon fell in love with the nice little lady's-maid, and she heartily returned the feeling. They might have waited for years before they were in a pecuniary position to marry, but for the death of Zebedee's uncle, who left him a little fortune of two thousand pounds. They were now, for persons in their station, rich enough to please themselves; and they were married from the house in which they had served together, the little daughters of the family showing their affection for Mrs Zebedee by acting as her bridesmaids.

The young husband was a careful man. He decided to employ his small capital to the best advantage, by sheep-farming in Australia. His wife made no objection; she was ready to go wherever John went.

Accordingly they spent their short honeymoon in London, so as to see for themselves the vessel in which their passage was to be taken. They went to Mrs Crosscapel's lodging-house because Zebedee's uncle had always stayed there when he was in London. Ten days were to pass before the day of embarkation arrived. This gave the young couple a welcome holiday, and a prospect of amusing themselves to their hearts' content among the sights and shows of the great city.

On their first evening in London they went to the theatre. They were both accustomed to the fresh air of the country, and they felt half stifled by the heat and the gas. However, they were so pleased with an amusement which was new to them that they went to another theatre on the next evening. On this second occasion, John Zebedee found the heat unendurable. They left the theatre, and got back to their lodgings towards ten o'clock.

Let the rest be told in the words used by Mrs Zebedee herself. She said:

'We sat talking for a little while in our room, and John's headache got worse and worse. I persuaded him to go to bed, and I put out the candle (the fire giving sufficient light to undress by), so that he might the sooner fall asleep. But he was too restless to sleep. He asked me to read him something. Books always made him drowsy at the best of times.

'I had not myself begun to undress. So I lit the candle again, and I opened the only book I had. John had noticed it at the railway bookstall by the name of "The World of Sleep." He used to joke with me about my being a sleep-walker; and he said, "Here's something that's sure to interest you" – and he made me a present of the book.

'Before I had read to him for more than half an hour he was fast asleep. Not feeling that way inclined, I went on reading to myself.

'The book did indeed interest me. There was one terrible story which took a hold on my mind – the story of a man who stabbed his own wife in a sleep-walking dream. I thought of putting down my book after that, and then changed my mind again and went on. The next chapters were not so interesting; they were full of learned accounts of why we fall asleep, and what our brains do in that state, and such like. It ended in my falling asleep, too, in my armchair by the fireside.

'I don't know what o'clock it was when I went to sleep. I don't know how long I slept, or whether I dreamed or not. The candle and the fire had both burned out, and it was pitch dark when I woke. I can't even say why I woke – unless it was the coldness of the room.

'There was a spare candle on the chimney-piece. I found the match-box, and got a light. Then, for the first time, I turned round towards the bed; and I saw—'

She had seen the dead body of her husband, murdered while she was unconsciously at his side – and she fainted, poor creature, at the bare remembrance of it.

The proceedings were adjourned. She received every possible care and attention; the chaplain looking after her welfare as well as the surgeon.

I have said nothing of the evidence of the landlady and the servants. It was taken as a mere formality. What little they knew proved nothing against Mrs Zebedee. The police made no discoveries that supported her first frantic accusation of herself. Her master and mistress, where she had been last in service, spoke of her in the highest terms. We were at a complete deadlock.

It had been thought best not to surprise Mr Deluc, as yet, by citing him as a witness. The action of the law was, however, hurried in this case by a private communication received from the chaplain.

After twice seeing, and speaking with, Mrs Zebedee, the reverend gentleman was persuaded that she had no more to do than himself with the murder of her husband. He did not consider that he was justified in repeating a confidential communication – he would only recommend that Mr Deluc should be summoned to appear at the next examination. This advice was followed.

The police had no evidence against Mrs Zebedee when the inquiry was resumed. To assist the ends of justice she was now put into the witness-box. The discovery of her murdered husband, when she woke in the small hours of the morning, was passed over as rapidly as possible. Only three questions of importance were put to her.

First, the knife was produced. Had she ever seen it in her husband's possession? Never. Did she know anything about it? Nothing whatever.

Secondly: Did she, or did her husband, lock the bedroom door when they returned from the theatre? No. Did she afterwards lock the door herself? No.

Thirdly: Had she any sort of reason to give for supposing that she had murdered her husband in a sleep-walking dream? No reason, except that she was beside herself at the time, and the book put the thought into her head.

After this the other witnesses were sent out of court. The motive for the chaplain's communication now appeared. Mrs Zebedee was asked if anything unpleasant had occurred between Mr Deluc and herself.

Yes. He had caught her alone on the stairs at the lodging-house; had presumed to make love to her; and had carried the insult still further by attempting to kiss her. She had slapped his face, and had declared that her husband should know of it, if his misconduct was repeated. He was in a furious rage at having his face slapped; and he said to her: 'Madam, you may live to regret this.'

After consultation, and at the request of our Inspector, it was decided to keep Mr Deluc in ignorance of Mrs Zebedee's statement for the present. When the witnesses were recalled, he gave the same evidence which he had already given to the Inspector – and he was then asked if he knew anything of the knife. He looked at it without any guilty signs in his face, and swore that he had never seen it until that moment. The resumed inquiry ended, and still nothing had been discovered.

But we kept an eye on Mr Deluc. Our next effort was to try if we could associate him with the purchase of the knife.

Here again (there really did seem to be a sort of fatality in this case) we reached no useful result. It was easy enough to find out the wholesale cutlers, who had manufactured the knife at Sheffield, by the mark on the blade. But they made tens of thousands of such knives, and disposed of them to retail dealers all over Great Britain – to say nothing of foreign parts. As to finding out the person who had engraved the imperfect inscription (without knowing where, or by whom, the knife had been purchased) we might as well have looked for the proverbial needle in the bundle of hay. Our last resource was to have the knife photographed, with the inscribed side uppermost, and to send copies to every police-station in the kingdom.

At the same time we reckoned up Mr Deluc – I mean that we made investigations into his past life – on the chance that he and the murdered man might have known each other, and might have had a quarrel, or a rivalry about a woman, on some former occasion. No such discovery rewarded us.

We found Deluc to have led a dissipated life, and to have mixed with very bad company. But he had kept out of reach of the law. A man may be a profligate vagabond; may insult a lady; may say threatening things to her, in the first stinging sensation of having his face slapped – but it doesn't follow from these blots on his character that he has murdered her husband in the dead of the night.

Once more, then, when we were called upon to report ourselves, we had no evidence to produce. The photographs failed to discover the owner of the knife, and to explain its interrupted inscription. Poor Mrs Zebedee was allowed to go back to her friends, on entering into her own recognisance to appear again if called upon. Articles in the newspapers began to inquire how many more murderers would succeed in baffling the police. The authorities at the Treasury offered a reward of a hundred pounds for the necessary information. And the weeks passed, and nobody claimed the reward.

Our Inspector was not a man to be easily beaten. More inquiries and examinations followed. It is needless to say anything about them. We were defeated – and there, so far as the police and the public were concerned, was an end of it.

The assassination of the poor young husband soon passed out of notice, like other undiscovered murders. One obscure person only was foolish enough, in his leisure hours, to persist in trying to solve the problem of Who Killed Zebedee? He felt that he might rise to the highest position in the police force if he succeeded where his elders and betters had failed – and he held to his own little ambition, though everybody laughed at him. In plain English, I was the man.

V

Without meaning it, I have told my story ungratefully.

There were two persons who saw nothing ridiculous in my resolution to continue the investigation, single-handed. One of them was Miss Mybus; and the other was the cook, Priscilla Thurlby.

Mentioning the lady first, Miss Mybus was indignant at the resigned manner in which the police accepted their defeat. She was a little bright-eyed wiry woman; and she spoke her mind freely.

'This comes home to me,' she said. 'Just look back for a year or two. I can call to mind two cases of persons found murdered in London – and the assassins have never been traced. I am a person too; and I ask myself if my turn is not coming next. You're a nice-looking fellow – and I like your pluck and perseverance. Come here as often as you think right; and say you are my visitor, if they make any difficulty about letting you in. One thing more! I have nothing particular to do, and I am no fool. Here, in the parlours, I see everybody who comes into the house or goes out of the house. Leave me your address – I may get some information for you yet.'

With the best intentions, Miss Mybus found no opportunity of helping me. Of the two, Priscilla Thurlby seemed more likely to be of use.

In the first place, she was sharp and active, and (not having succeeded in getting another situation as yet) was mistress of her own movements.

In the second place, she was a woman I could trust. Before she left home to try domestic service in London, the parson of her native parish gave her a written testimonial, of which I append a copy. Thus it ran:

> I gladly recommend Priscilla Thurlby for any respectable employment which she may be competent to undertake. Her father and mother are infirm old people, who have lately suffered a diminution of their income; and they have a younger daughter to maintain. Rather than be a burden on her parents, Priscilla goes to London to find domestic employment, and to devote her earnings to the assistance of her father and mother. This circumstance speaks for itself. I have known the family many years; and I only regret that I have no vacant place in my own household which I can offer to this good girl.
>
> (Signed)
> HENRY DERRINGTON, Rector of Roth

After reading those words, I could safely ask Priscilla to help me in reopening the mysterious murder case to some good purpose.

My notion was that the proceedings of the persons in Mrs Crosscapel's house, had not been closely enough inquired into yet. By way of continuing the investigation, I asked Priscilla if she could tell me anything which associated the housemaid with Mr Deluc. She was unwilling to answer. 'I may be casting suspicion on an innocent person,' she said. 'Besides, I was for so short a time the housemaid's fellow servant—'

'You slept in the same room with her,' I remarked; 'and you had opportunities of observing her conduct towards the lodgers. If they had asked you, at the examination, what I now ask, you would have answered as an honest woman.'

To this argument she yielded. I heard from her certain particulars which threw a new light on Mr Deluc, and on the case generally. On that information I acted. It was slow work, owing to the claims on me of my regular duties; but with Priscilla's help, I steadily advanced towards the end I had in view.

Besides this, I owed another obligation to Mrs Crosscapel's nice-looking cook. The confession must be made sooner or later – and I may as well make it now. I first knew what love was, thanks to Priscilla. I had delicious kisses, thanks to Priscilla. And, when I asked if she would marry me, she didn't say No. She looked, I must own, a little sadly, and she said: 'How can two such poor people as we are ever hope to marry?' To this I answered: 'It won't be long before I lay my hand on the clue which my Inspector has failed to find. I shall be in a position to marry you, my dear, when that time comes.'

At our next meeting we spoke of her parents. I was now her promised husband. Judging by what I had heard of the proceedings of other people in my position, it seemed to be only right that I should be made known to her father and mother. She entirely agreed with me; and she wrote home that day, to tell them to expect us at the end of the week.

I took my turn of night-duty, and so gained my liberty for the greater part of the next day. I dressed myself in plain clothes, and we took our tickets on the railway for Yateland, being the nearest station to the village in which Priscilla's parents lived.

VI

The train stopped, as usual, at the big town of Waterbank. Supporting herself by her needle, while she was still unprovided with a situation, Priscilla had been at work late in the night – she was tired and thirsty. I left the carriage to get her some soda-water. The stupid girl in the refreshment room failed to pull the cork out of the bottle, and refused to let me help her. She took a corkscrew, and used it crookedly. I lost all patience, and snatched the bottle out of her hand. Just as I drew the cork, the bell rang on the platform. I only waited to pour the soda-water into a glass – but the train was moving as I left the refreshment-room. The porters stopped me when I tried to jump on to the step of the carriage. I was left behind.

As soon as I had recovered my temper, I looked at the time-table. We had reached Waterbank at five minutes past one. By good-luck, the next train was due at forty-four minutes past one, and arrived at Yateland (the next station) ten minutes afterwards. I could only hope that Priscilla would look at the time-table too, and wait for me. If I had attempted to walk the distance between the two places, I should have lost time instead of saving it. The interval before me was not very long; I occupied it in looking over the town.

Speaking with all due respect to the inhabitants, Waterbank (to other people) is a dull place. I went up one street and down another – and stopped to look at a shop which struck me; not from anything in itself, but because it was the only shop in the street with the shutters closed.

A bill was posted on the shutters, announcing that the place was to let. The out-going tradesman's name and business, announced in the customary painted letters, ran thus: *James Wycomb, Cutler, etc.*

For the first time, it occurred to me that we had forgotten an obstacle in our way, when we distributed our photographs of the knife. We had none of us remembered that a certain proportion of cutlers might be placed, by circumstances, out of our reach – either by retiring from business or by becoming bankrupt. I always carried a copy of the photograph about me; and I thought to myself, 'Here is the ghost of a chance of tracing the knife to Mr Deluc!'

The shop door was opened, after I had twice rung the bell, by an old man, very dirty and very deaf. He said: 'You had better go upstairs, and speak to Mr Scorrier – top of the house.'

I put my lips to the old fellow's ear-trumpet, and asked who Mr Scorrier was.

'Brother-in-law to Mr Wycomb. Mr Wycomb's dead. If you want to buy the business apply to Mr Scorrier.'

Receiving that reply, I went upstairs, and found Mr Scorrier engaged in engraving a brass door-plate. He was a middle-aged man, with a cadaverous face and dim eyes. After the necessary apologies, I produced my photograph.

'May I ask, sir, if you know anything of the inscription on that knife?' I said.

He took his magnifying glass to look at it.

'This is curious,' he remarked quietly. 'I remember the queer name – Zebedee. Yes, sir; I did the engraving, as far as it goes. I wonder what prevented me from finishing it?'

The name of Zebedee, and the unfinished inscription on the knife, had appeared in every English newspaper. He took the matter so coolly, that I was doubtful how to interpret his answer. Was it possible that he had not seen the account of the murder? Or was he an accomplice with prodigious powers of self-control?

'Excuse me,' I said, 'do you read the newspapers?'

'Never! My eyesight is failing me. I abstain from reading, in the interests of my occupation.'

'Have you not heard the name of Zebedee mentioned – particularly by people who do read the newspapers?'

'Very likely; but I didn't attend to it. When the day's work is done, I take my walk. Then I have my supper, my drop of grog, and my pipe. Then I go to bed. A dull existence you think, I dare say! I had a miserable life, sir, when I was young. A bare subsistence, and a little rest, before the last perfect rest in the grave – that is all I want. The world has gone by me long ago. So much the better.'

The poor man spoke honestly. I was ashamed of having doubted him. I returned to the subject of the knife.

'Do you know where it was purchased, and by whom?' I asked.

'My memory is not so good as it was,' he said; 'but I have got something by me that helps it.'

He took from a cupboard a dirty old scrap-book. Strips of paper, with writing on them, were pasted on the pages, as well as I could see. He turned to an index, or table of contents, and opened a page. Something like a flash of life showed itself on his dismal face.

'Ha! now I remember,' he said. 'The knife was bought of my late brother-in-law, in the shop downstairs. It all comes back to me, sir. A person in a state of frenzy burst into this very room, and snatched the knife away from me, when I was only half way through the inscription!'

I felt that I was now close on discovery. 'May I see what it is that has assisted your memory?' I asked.

'Oh yes. You must know, sir, I live by engraving inscriptions and addresses, and I paste in this book the manuscript instructions which I receive, with marks of my own on the margin. For one thing, they serve as a reference to new customers. And for another thing, they do certainly help my memory.'

He turned the book towards me, and pointed to a slip of paper which occupied the lower half of a page.

I read the complete inscription, intended for the knife that killed Zebedee, and written as follows:

'To John Zebedee. From Priscilla Thurlby.'

VII

I declare that it is impossible for me to describe what I felt, when Priscilla's name confronted me like a written confession of guilt. How long it was before I recovered myself in some degree, I cannot say. The only thing I can clearly call to mind is, that I frightened the poor engraver.

My first desire was to get possession of the manuscript inscription. I told him I was a policeman, and summoned him to assist me in the discovery of a crime. I even offered him money. He drew back from my hand. 'You shall have it for nothing,' he said, 'if you will only go away and never come here again.' He tried to cut it out of the page – but his trembling hands were helpless. I cut it out myself, and attempted to thank him. He wouldn't hear me. 'Go away!' he said, 'I don't like the look of you.'

It may be here objected that I ought not to have felt so sure as I did of the woman's guilt, until I had got more evidence against her. The knife might have been stolen from her, supposing she was the person who had snatched it out of the engraver's hands, and might have been afterwards used by the thief to commit the murder. All very true. But I never had a moment's doubt in my own mind, from the time when I read the damnable line in the engraver's book.

I went back to the railway without any plan in my head. The train by which I had proposed to follow her had left Waterbank. The next train that arrived was for London. I took my place in it – still without any plan in my head.

At Charing Cross a friend met me. He said, 'You're looking miserably ill. Come and have a drink.'

I went with him. The liquor was what I really wanted; it strung me up, and cleared my head. He went his way, and I went mine. In a little while more, I determined what I would do.

In the first place, I decided to resign my situation in the police, from a motive which will presently appear. In the second place, I took a bed at a public-house. She would no doubt return to London, and she would go to my lodgings to find out why I had broken my appointment. To bring to justice the one woman whom I had dearly loved was too cruel a duty for a poor creature like me. I preferred leaving the police force. On the other hand, if she and I met before time had helped me to control myself, I had a horrid fear that I might turn murderer next, and kill her then and there. The wretch had not only all but misled me into marrying her, but also into charging the innocent housemaid with being concerned in the murder.

The same night I hit on a way of clearing up such doubts as still harassed my mind. I wrote to the rector of Roth, informing him that I was engaged to marry her, and asking if he would tell me (in consideration of my position) what her former relations might have been with the person named John Zebedee.

By return of post I got this reply:

Sir, – Under the circumstances, I think I am bound to tell you confidentially what the friends and well-wishers of Priscilla have kept secret, for her sake.

'Zebedee was in service in this neighbourhood. I am sorry to say it, of a man who has come to such a miserable end – but his behaviour to Priscilla proves him to have been a vicious and heartless wretch. They were engaged – and, I add with indignation, he tried to seduce her under a promise of marriage. Her virtue resisted him, and he pretended to be ashamed of himself. The banns were published in my church. On the next day Zebedee disappeared, and cruelly deserted her. He was a capable servant; and I believe he got another place. I leave you to imagine what the poor girl suffered under the outrage inflicted on her. Going to London, with my recommendation, she answered the first advertisement that she saw, and was unfortunate enough to begin her career in domestic service in the very lodging house, to which (as I gather from the newspaper report of the murder) the man Zebedee took the person whom he married, after deserting Priscilla. Be assured that you are about to unite yourself to an excellent girl, and accept my best wishes for your happiness.

It was plain from this that neither the rector nor the parents and friends knew anything of the purchase of the knife. The one miserable man who knew the truth, was the man who had asked her to be his wife.

I owed it to myself – at least so it seemed to me – not to let it be supposed that I, too, had meanly deserted her. Dreadful as the prospect was, I felt that I must see her once more, and for the last time.

She was at work when I went into her room. As I opened the door she started to her feet. Her cheeks reddened, and her eyes flashed with anger. I stepped forward – and she saw my face. My face silenced her.

I spoke in the fewest words I could find.

'I have been to the cutler's shop at Waterbank,' I said. 'There is the unfinished inscription on the knife, completed in your handwriting. I could hang you by a word. God forgive me – I can't say the word.'

Her bright complexion turned to a dreadful clay-colour. Her eyes were fixed and staring, like the eyes of a person in a fit. She stood before me, still and silent. Without saying more, I dropped the inscription into the fire. Without saying more, I left her.

I never saw her again.

VIII

But I heard from her a few days later.

The letter has been long since burnt. I wish I could have forgotten it as well. It sticks to my memory. If I die with my senses about me, Priscilla's letter will be my last recollection on earth.

In substance it repeated what the rector had already told me. Further, it informed me that she had bought the knife as a keepsake for Zebedee, in place of a similar knife which he had lost. On the Saturday, she made the purchase, and left it to be engraved. On the Sunday, the banns were put up. On the Monday, she was deserted; and she snatched the knife from the table while the engraver was at work.

She only knew that Zebedee had added a new sting to the insult inflicted on her, when he arrived at the lodgings with his wife. Her duties as cook kept her in the kitchen – and Zebedee never discovered that she was in the house. I still remember the last lines of her confession:

'The devil entered into me when I tried their door, on my way up to bed, and found it unlocked, and listened awhile, and peeped in. I saw them by the dying light of the candle – one asleep on the bed, the other asleep by the fireside. I had the knife in my hand, and the thought came to me to do it, so that they might hang *her* for the murder. I couldn't take the knife out again, when I had done it. Mind this! I did really like you – I didn't say Yes, because you could hardly hang your own wife, if you found out who killed Zebedee.'

Since that past time I have never heard again of Priscilla Thurlby; I don't know whether she is living or dead. Many people may think I deserve to be hanged myself for not having given her up to the gallows. They may, perhaps, be disappointed when they see this confession, and hear that I have died decently in my bed. I don't blame them. I am a penitent sinner. I wish all merciful Christians good-bye for ever.

Mr Cosway and the Landlady

Originally appeared in *The People's Library*, 17 December 1881, as 'Your Money or Your Life.' Reprinted in *Little Novels* (1887). The anecdote in which, as Collins explains at the end of the story, the 'improbable events' of its First Epoch are based, is to be found in *The Life of Sir Walter Scott*, by J.G. Lockhart, Vol. V, pp. 388–9, dated 2 January 1825: 'My cousin Watty Scott . . . was a midshipman some 40 years ago in a ship at Portsmouth; he and 2 other companions had gone on shore, and had overstaid their leave, spent all their money, and run up an immense bill at a tavern on the Point – the ship made the signal for sailing, but their landlady said, "No, gentlemen – you shall not escape without paying your reckoning;" – and she accompanied her words by appropriate actions, and placed them under the tender keeping of a sufficient party of bailiffs. They felt they were in a scrape, and petitioned very hard to be released; "No, no," said Mrs Quickly, "I must be satisfied one way or t'other: you must be well aware, gentlemen, that you will be totally ruined if you don't get on board in time." They made long faces, and confessed that it was but too true. "Well," said she, "I'll give you one more chance – I am so circumstanced here that I cannot carry on my business as a single woman, and I must continue to have a husband, or at all events I must be able to produce a marriage certificate; and therefore the only terms on which you shall all three have leave to go on board to-morrow morning is, that one of you consent to marry me. I don't care a d— which it is, but, by all that's holy, one of you I will have, or else you all 3 go to jail, and your ship sails without you!" The virago was not to be pacified, and the poor youths, left to themselves, agreed after a time to draw lots, and it happened to fall on my cousin. No time was lost, and off they marched to church, and my poor relative was forthwith spliced. The bride, on returning, gave them a good substantial dinner and several bottles of wine a piece, and having tumbled them into a wherry sent them off. The ship sailed, and the young men religiously adhered to the oath of secrecy they had taken previous to drawing lots. The bride, I should have said, merely wanted to be married, and was the first to propose an eternal separation. Some months later, at Jamaica, a file of papers reached the midshipman's berth, and Watty, who was observed to be looking them over carelessly, suddenly jumped up, in his ecstacy forgot his obligation of secrecy, and cried out "Thanks be to God, my wife is hanged."' Collins thought Scott 'the greatest novelist that has ever written,' and Lockhart's *Life* was his favourite biography after Boswell's *Johnson*. When the Landlady declares to the cornered Stone and Cosway 'So long as the bride and bridegroom agree to it, they may be married in any name they like, and it stands good' she is referring to a legal technicality which Collins had used in his novel *The Law and the Lady* (1875).

I

The guests would have enjoyed their visit to Sir Peter's country house – but for Mr Cosway.

And to make matters worse, it was not Mr Cosway but the guests who were to blame. They repeated the old story of Adam and Eve, on a larger scale. The women were the first sinners; and the men were demoralised by the women.

Mr Cosway's bitterest enemy could not have denied that he was a handsome, well-bred, unassuming man. No mystery of any sort attached to him. He had adopted the Navy as a profession – had grown weary of it after a few years' service – and now lived on the moderate income left to him, after the death of his parents. Out of this unpromising material the lively imaginations of the women built up a romance. The men only noticed that Mr Cosway was rather silent and thoughtful; that he was not ready with his laugh; and that he had a fancy for taking long walks by himself. Harmless peculiarities, surely? And yet, they excited the curiosity of the women as signs of a mystery in Mr Cosway's past life, in which some beloved object unknown must have played a chief part.

As a matter of course, the influence of the sex was tried, under every indirect and delicate form of approach, to induce Mr Cosway to open his heart, and tell the tale of his sorrows. With perfect courtesy, he baffled curiosity, and kept his supposed secret to himself. The most beautiful girl in the house was ready to offer herself and her fortune as consolations, if this impenetrable bachelor would only have taken her into his confidence. He smiled sadly, and changed the subject.

Defeated so far, the women accepted the next alternative.

One of the guests staying in the house was Mr Cosway's intimate friend – formerly his brother-officer on board ship. This gentleman was now subjected to the delicately directed system of investigation which had failed with his friend. With unruffled composure he referred the ladies, one after another, to Mr Cosway. His name was Stone. The ladies decided that his nature was worthy of his name.

The last resource left to our fair friends was to rouse the dormant interest of the men, and to trust to the confidential intercourse of the smoking-room for the enlightenment which they had failed to obtain by other means.

In the accomplishment of this purpose, the degree of success which rewarded their efforts was due to a favouring state of affairs in the house. The shooting was not good for much; the billiard-table was under repair; and there were but two really skilled whist-players among the guests. In the atmosphere of dulness thus engendered, the men not only caught the infection of the women's curiosity, but were even ready to listen to the gossip of the servants' hall, repeated to their mistresses by the ladies'-maids. The result of such an essentially debased state of feeling as this was not slow in declaring itself. But for a lucky accident, Mr Cosway would have discovered to what extremities of illbred curiosity idleness and folly can lead persons holding the position of ladies and gentlemen, when he joined the company at breakfast on the next morning.

The newspapers came in before the guests had risen from table. Sir Peter handed one of them to the lady who sat on his right hand.

She first looked, it is needless to say, at the list of births, deaths, and marriages; and then she turned to the general news – the fires, accidents, fashionable departures, and so on. In a few minutes, she indignantly dropped the newspaper in her lap.

'Here is another unfortunate man,' she exclaimed, 'sacrificed to the stupidity of women! If I had been in his place, I would have used my knowledge of swimming to save myself, and would have left the women to go to the bottom of the river as they deserved!'

'A boat accident, I suppose?' said Sir Peter.

'Oh yes – the old story. A gentleman takes two ladies out in a boat. After a while they get fidgety, and feel an idiotic impulse to change places. The boat upsets as usual; the poor dear man tries to save them – and is drowned along with them for his pains. Shameful! shameful!'

'Are the names mentioned?'

'Yes. They are all strangers to me; I speak on principle.' Asserting herself in those words, the indignant lady handed the newspaper to Mr Cosway, who happened to sit next to her. 'When you were in the navy,' she continued, 'I dare say *your* life was put in jeopardy by taking women in boats. Read it yourself, and let it be a warning to you for the future.'

Mr Cosway looked at the narrative of the accident – and revealed the romantic mystery of his life by a burst of devout exclamation, expressed in these words:

'Thank God, my wife's drowned!'

II

To declare that Sir Peter and his guests were all struck speechless, by discovering in this way that Mr Cosway was a married man, is to say very little. The general impression appeared to be that he was mad. His neighbours at the table all drew back from him, with the one exception of his friend. Mr Stone looked at the newspaper: pressed Mr Cosway's hand in silent sympathy – and addressed himself to his host.

'Permit me to make my friend's apologies,' he said, 'until he is composed enough to act for himself. The circumstances are so extraordinary that I venture to think they excuse him. Will you allow us to speak to you privately?'

Sir Peter, with more apologies addressed to his visitors, opened the door which communicated with his study. Mr Stone took Mr Cosway's arm, and led him out of the room. He noticed no one, spoke to no one – he moved mechanically, like a man walking in his sleep.

After an unendurable interval of nearly an hour's duration, Sir Peter returned alone to the breakfast-room. Mr Cosway and Mr Stone had already taken their departure for London, with their host's entire approval.

'It is left to my discretion,' Sir Peter proceeded, 'to repeat to you what I have heard in the study. I will do so, on one condition – that you all consider yourselves bound in honour not to mention the true names and the real places, when you tell the story to others.'

Subject to this wise reservation, the narrative is here repeated by one of the company. Considering how he may perform his task to the best advantage, he finds that the events which preceded and followed Mr Cosway's disastrous marriage resolve themselves into certain well-marked divisions. Adopting this arrangement, he proceeds to relate:

THE FIRST EPOCH IN MR COSWAY'S LIFE

The sailing of her Majesty's ship *Albicore* was deferred by the severe illness of the captain. A gentleman not possessed of political influence might, after the doctor's unpromising report of him, have been superseded by another commanding officer. In the present case, the Lords of the Admiralty showed themselves to be models of patience and sympathy. They kept the vessel in port, waiting the captain's recovery.

Among the unimportant junior officers, not wanted on board under these circumstances, and favoured accordingly by obtaining leave to wait for orders on shore, were two young men, aged respectively twenty-two and twenty-three years, and known by the names of Cosway and Stone. The scene which now introduces them opens at a famous seaport on the south coast of England, and discloses the two young gentlemen at dinner in a private room at their inn.

'I think that last bottle of champagne was corked,' Cosway remarked. 'Let's try another. You're nearest the bell, Stone. Ring.'

Stone rang, under protest. He was the elder of the two by a year, and he set an example of discretion.

'I am afraid we are running up a terrible bill,' he said. 'We have been here more than three weeks—'

'And we have denied ourselves nothing,' Cosway added. 'We have lived like princes. Another bottle of champagne, waiter. We have our riding-horses, and our carriage, and the best box at the theatre, and such cigars as London itself could not produce. I call that making the most of life. Try the new bottle. Glorious drink, isn't it? Why doesn't my father have champagne at the family dinner-table?'

'Is your father a rich man, Cosway?'

'I should say not. He didn't give me anything like the money I expected, when I said good-bye – and I rather think he warned me solemnly, at parting, to take the greatest care of it. "There's not a farthing more for you," he said, "till your ship returns from her South American station." *Your* father is a clergyman, Stone.'

'Well, and what of that?'

'And some clergymen are rich.'

'My father is not one of them, Cosway.'

'Then let us say no more about him. Help yourself, and pass the bottle.'

Instead of adopting this suggestion, Stone rose with a very grave face, and once more rang the bell. 'Ask the landlady to step up,' he said, when the waiter appeared.

'What do you want with the landlady?' Cosway inquired.

'I want the bill.'

The landlady – otherwise, Mrs Pounce – entered the room. She was short, and old, and fat, and painted, and a widow. Students of character, as revealed in the face, would have discovered malice and cunning in her bright little black eyes, and a bitter vindictive temper in the lines about her thin red lips. Incapable of such subtleties of analysis as these, the two young officers differed widely, nevertheless, in their opinions of Mrs Pounce. Cosway's reckless sense of humour delighted in pretending to be in love with her. Stone took a dislike to her from the first. When his friend asked for the reason, he made a strangely obscure answer. 'Do you remember that morning in the wood when you killed the snake?' he said. 'I took a dislike to the snake.' Cosway made no further inquiries.

'Well, my young heroes,' cried Mrs Pounce (always loud, always cheerful, and always familiar with her guests), 'what do you want with me now?'

'Take a glass of champagne, my darling,' said Cosway; 'and let me try if I can get my arm round your waist. That's all *I* want with you.'

The landlady passed this over without notice. Though she had spoken to both of them, her cunning little eyes rested on Stone from the moment when she appeared in the room. She knew by instinct the man who disliked her – and she waited deliberately for Stone to reply.

'We have been here some time,' he said, 'and we shall be obliged, ma'am, if you will let us have our bill.'

Mrs Pounce lifted her eyebrows with an expression of innocent surprise.

'Has the captain got well, and must you go on board tonight?' she asked.

'Nothing of the sort!' Cosway interposed. 'We have no news of the captain, and we are going to the theatre to-night.'

'But,' persisted Stone, 'we want, if you please, to have the bill.'

'Certainly, sir,' said Mrs Pounce, with a sudden assumption of respect. 'But we are very busy downstairs, and we hope you will not press us for it tonight?'

'Of course not!' cried Cosway.

Mrs Pounce instantly left the room, without waiting for any further remark from Cosway's friend.

'I wish we had gone to some other house,' said Stone. 'You mark my words – that woman means to cheat us.'

Cosway expressed his dissent from this opinion in the most amiable manner. He filled his friend's glass, and begged him not to say ill-natured things of Mrs Pounce.

But Stone's usually smooth temper seemed to be ruffled: he insisted on his own view. 'She's impudent and inquisitive, if she is not downright dishonest,' he said. 'What right had she to ask you where we lived when we were at home; and what our Christian names were; and which of us was oldest, you or I? Oh, yes – it's all very well to say she only showed a flattering interest in us! I suppose she showed a flattering interest in my affairs, when I woke a little earlier than usual, and caught her in my bedroom with my pocket-book in her hand. Do you believe she was going to lock it up for safety's sake? She knows how much money we have got as well as we know it ourselves. Every halfpenny we have will be in her pocket to-morrow. And a good thing too – we shall be obliged to leave the house.'

Even this cogent reasoning failed in provoking Cosway to reply. He took Stone's hat, and handed it with the utmost politeness to his foreboding friend. 'There's only one remedy for such a state of mind as yours,' he said. 'Come to the theatre.'

At ten o'clock the next morning, Cosway found himself alone at the breakfast table. He was informed that Mr Stone had gone out for a little walk, and would be back directly. Seating himself at the table, he perceived an envelope on his plate, which evidently enclosed the bill. He took up the envelope, considered a little, and put it back again unopened. At the same moment Stone burst into the room in a high state of excitement.

'News that will astonish you!' he cried. 'The captain arrived yesterday evening. His doctors say that the sea-voyage will complete his recovery. The ship sails today – and we are ordered to report ourselves on board in an hour's time. Where's the bill?'

Cosway pointed to it. Stone took it out of the envelope.

It covered two sides of a prodigiously long sheet of paper. The sum-total was brightly decorated with lines in red ink. Stone looked at the total, and passed it in silence to Cosway. For once, even Cosway was prostrated. In dreadful stillness, the two young men produced their pocket-books; added up their joint stores of money, and compared the result with the bill. Their united resources amounted to a little more than one-third of their debt to the landlady of the inn.

The only alternative that presented itself was to send for Mrs Pounce; to state the circumstances plainly; and to propose a compromise on the grand commercial basis of credit.

Mrs Pounce presented herself superbly dressed in walking costume. Was she going out? or had she just returned to the inn? Not a word escaped her; she waited gravely to hear what the gentlemen wanted. Cosway, presuming on his position as favourite, produced the contents of the two pocket-books, and revealed the melancholy truth.

'There is all the money we have,' he concluded. 'We hope you will not object to receive the balance in a bill at three months.'

Mrs Pounce answered with a stern composure of voice and manner entirely new in the experience of Cosway and Stone.

'I have paid ready money, gentlemen, for the hire of your horses and carriages,' she said; 'here are the receipts from the livery stables to vouch for me; I never accept bills unless I am quite sure beforehand that they will be honoured. I defy you to find an overcharge in the account now rendered; and I expect you to pay it before you leave my house.'

Stone looked at his watch. 'In three-quarters of an hour,' he said, 'we must be on board.'

Mrs Pounce entirely agreed with him. 'And if you are not on board,' she remarked, 'you will be tried by court-martial, and dismissed the service with your characters ruined for life.'

'My dear creature, we haven't time to send home, and we know nobody in the town,' pleaded Cosway. 'For God's sake take our watches and jewellery, and our luggage – and let us go.'

'I am not a pawnbroker,' said the inflexible lady. 'You must either pay your lawful debt to me in honest money, or—'

She paused and looked at Cosway. Her fat face brightened – she smiled graciously for the first time.

Cosway stared at her in unconcealed perplexity. He helplessly repeated her last words. 'We must either pay the bill,' he said, 'or – what?'

'Or,' answered Mrs Pounce, 'one of you must marry ME.'

Was she joking? Was she intoxicated? Was she out of her senses? Neither of the three; she was in perfect possession of herself; her explanation was a model of lucid and convincing arrangement of facts.

'My position here has its drawbacks,' she began. 'I am a lone widow; I am known to have an excellent business, and to have saved money. The result is that I am pestered to death by a set of needy vagabonds who want to marry me. In this position, I am exposed to slanders and insults. Even if I didn't know that the men were after my money, there is not one of them whom I would venture to marry. He might turn out a tyrant, and beat me; or a drunkard, and disgrace me; or a betting man, and ruin me. What I want, you see, for my own peace and protection, is to be able to declare myself married, and to produce the proof in the shape of a certificate. A born gentleman, with a character to lose, and so much younger in years than myself that he wouldn't think of living with me – there is the sort of husband who suits my book! I'm a reasonable woman, gentlemen. I would undertake to part with my husband at the church door – never to attempt to see him or write to him afterwards – and only to show my certificate when necessary, without giving any explanations. Your secret would be quite safe in my keeping. I don't care a straw for either of you, so long as you answer my purpose. What do you say to paying my bill (one or the other of you) in this way? I am ready dressed for the altar; and the clergyman has notice at the church. My preference is for Mr Cosway,' proceeded this terrible woman with the cruellest irony, 'because he has been so particular in his attentions towards me. The licence (which I provided on the chance a fortnight since) is made out in his name. Such is my weakness for Mr Cosway. But that don't matter if Mr Stone would like to take his place. He can hail by his friend's name. Oh yes, he can! I have consulted my lawyer. So long as the bride and bridegroom agree to it, they may be married in any name they like, and it stands good. Look at your watch again, Mr Stone. The church is in the next street. By my calculation, you have just got five minutes to decide. I'm a punctual woman, my little dears; and I will be back to the moment.'

She opened the door, paused, and returned to the room.

'I ought to have mentioned,' she resumed, 'that I shall make you a present of the bill, receipted, on the conclusion of the ceremony. You will be taken to the ship in my own boat, with all your money in your pockets, and a hamper of good things for the mess. After that, I wash my hands of you. You may go to the devil your own way.'

With this parting benediction, she left them.

Caught in the landlady's trap, the two victims looked at each other in expressive silence. Without time enough to take legal advice; without friends on shore; without any claim on officers of their own standing in the ship, the prospect before them was literally limited to Marriage or Ruin. Stone made a proposal worthy of a hero.

'One of us must marry her,' he said; 'I'm ready to toss up for it.'

Cosway matched him in generosity. 'No,' he answered. 'It was I who brought you here; and I who led you into these infernal expenses. I ought to pay the penalty – and I will.'

Before Stone could remonstrate, the five minutes expired. Punctual Mrs Pounce appeared again in the doorway.

'Well?' she inquired, 'which is it to be – Cosway, or Stone?'

Cosway advanced as reckless as ever, and offered his arm.

'Now then, Fatsides,' he said, 'come and be married!'

In five-and-twenty minutes more, Mrs Pounce had become Mrs Cosway; and the two officers were on their way to the ship.

THE SECOND EPOCH IN MR COSWAY'S LIFE

Four years elapsed before the *Albicore* returned to the port from which she had sailed.

In that interval, the death of Cosway's parents had taken place. The lawyer who managed his affairs, during his absence from England, wrote to inform him that his inheritance from his late father's 'estate' was eight hundred a year. His mother only possessed a life interest in her fortune; she had left her jewels to her son, and that was all.

Cosway's experience of the life of a naval officer on foreign stations (without political influence to hasten his promotion) had thoroughly disappointed him. He decided on retiring from the service when the ship was 'paid off.' In the meantime, to the astonishment of his comrades, he seemed to be in no hurry to make use of the leave granted him to go on shore. The faithful Stone was the only man on board who knew that he was afraid of meeting his 'wife.' This good friend volunteered to go to the inn, and make the necessary investigation with all needful prudence. 'Four years is a long time, at *her* age,' he said. 'Many things may happen in four years.'

An hour later, Stone returned to the ship, and sent a written message on board, addressed to his brother-officer, in these words: 'Pack up your things at once, and join me on shore.'

'What news?' asked the anxious husband.

Stone looked significantly at the idlers on the landing-place. 'Wait,' he said, 'till we are by ourselves.'

'Where are we going?'

'To the railway station.'

They got into an empty carriage; and Stone at once relieved his friend of all further suspense.

'Nobody is acquainted with the secret of your marriage but our two selves,' he began quietly. 'I don't think, Cosway, you need go into mourning.'

'You don't mean to say she's dead!'

'I have seen a letter (written by her own lawyer) which announces her death,' Stone replied. 'It was so short that I believe I can repeat it, word for word: "Dear Sir, – I have received information of the death of my client. Please address your next and last payment, on account of the lease and goodwill of the inn, to the executors of the late Mrs Cosway." There, that is the letter. "Dear Sir," means the present proprietor of the inn. He told me your wife's previous history in two words. After carrying on the business with her customary intelligence for more than three years, her health failed, and she went to London to consult a physician. There she remained under the doctor's care. The next event was the appearance of an agent, instructed to sell the business in consequence of the landlady's declining health. Add the death at a later time – and there is the beginning and the end of the story. Fortune owed you a good turn, Cosway – and Fortune has paid the debt. Accept my best congratulations.'

Arrived in London, Stone went on at once to his relations in the North. Cosway proceeded to the office of the family lawyer (Mr Atherton), who had taken care of his interests in his absence. His father and Mr Atherton had been schoolfellows and old friends. He was affectionately received, and was invited to pay a visit the next day to the lawyer's villa at Richmond.

'You will be near enough to London to attend to your business at the Admiralty,' said Mr Atherton, 'and you will meet a visitor at my house, who is one of the most charming girls in England – the only daughter of the great Mr Restall. Good heavens! have you never heard of him? My dear sir, he's one of the partners in the famous firm of Benshaw, Restall, and Benshaw.'

Cosway was wise enough to accept this last piece of information as quite conclusive. The next day, Mrs Atherton presented him to the charming Miss Restall; and Mrs Atherton's young married daughter (who had been his playfellow when they were children) whispered to him, half in jest, half in earnest: 'Make the best use of your time; she isn't engaged yet.'

Cosway shuddered inwardly at the bare idea of a second marriage.

Was Miss Restall the sort of woman to restore his confidence?

She was small and slim and dark – a graceful, well-bred, brightly intelligent person, with a voice exquisitely sweet and winning in tone. Her ears, hands, and feet were objects to worship; and she had an attraction, irresistibly rare among the women of the present time – the attraction of a perfectly natural smile. Before Cosway had been an hour in the house, she discovered that his long term of service on foreign stations had furnished him with subjects of conversation which favourably contrasted with the commonplace gossip addressed to her by other men. Cosway at once became a favourite, as Othello became a favourite in his day.

The ladies of the household all rejoiced in the young officer's success, with the exception of Miss Restall's companion (supposed to hold the place of her lost mother, at a large salary), one Mrs Margery.

Too cautious to commit herself in words, this lady expressed doubt and disapprobation by her looks. She had white hair, iron-gray eyebrows, and protuberant eyes; her looks were unusually expressive. One evening, she caught poor Mr Atherton alone, and consulted him confidentially on the subject of Mr Cosway's income. This was the first warning which opened the eyes of the good lawyer to the nature of the 'friendship' already established between his two guests. He knew Miss Restall's illustrious father well, and he feared that it might soon be his disagreeable duty to bring Cosway's visit to an end.

On a certain Saturday afternoon, while Mr Atherton was still considering how he could most kindly and delicately suggest to Cosway that it was time to say good-bye, an empty carriage arrived at the villa. A note from Mr Restall was delivered to Mrs Atherton, thanking her with perfect politeness for her kindness to his daughter. 'Circumstances,' he added, 'rendered it necessary that Miss Restall should return home that afternoon.'

The 'circumstances' were supposed to refer to a garden-party to be given by Mr Restall in the ensuing week. But why was his daughter wanted at home before the day of the party?

The ladies of the family, still devoted to Cosway's interests, entertained no doubt that Mrs Margery had privately communicated with Mr Restall, and that the appearance of the carriage was the natural result. Mrs Atherton's married daughter did all that could be done: she got rid of Mrs Margery for one minute, and so arranged it that Cosway and Miss Restall took leave of each other in her own sitting-room.

When the young lady appeared in the hall she had drawn her veil down. Cosway escaped to the road and saw the last of the carriage as it drove away. In little more than a fortnight, his horror of a second marriage had become one of the dead and buried emotions of his nature. He stayed at the villa until Monday morning, as an act of gratitude to his good friends and then accompanied Mr Atherton to London. Business at the Admiralty was the excuse. It imposed on nobody. He was evidently on his way to Miss Restall.

'Leave your business in my hands,' said the lawyer, on the journey to town, 'and go and amuse yourself on the Continent. I can't blame you for falling in love with Miss Restall; I ought to have foreseen the danger, and waited till she had left us before I invited you to my house. But I may at least warn you to carry the matter no further. If you had eight thousand instead of eight hundred a year, Mr Restall would think it an act of presumption on your part to aspire to his daughter's hand, unless you had a title to throw into the bargain. Look at it in the true light, my dear boy; and one of these days you will thank me for speaking plainly.'

Cosway promised to 'look at it in the true light.'

The result, from his point of view, led him into a change of residence. He left his hotel and took a lodging in the nearest by-street to Mr Restall's palace at Kensington.

On the same evening, he applied (with the confidence due to a previous arrangement) for a letter at the neighbouring post office, addressed to E. C. – the initials of Edwin Cosway. 'Pray be careful,' Miss Restall wrote; 'I have tried to get you a card for our garden-party. But that hateful creature, Margery, has evidently spoken to my father; I am not trusted with any invitation cards. Bear it patiently, dear, as I do, and let me hear if you have succeeded in finding a lodging near us.'

Not submitting to this first disappointment very patiently, Cosway sent his reply to the post-office, addressed to A. R. – the initials of Adela Restall. The next day, the impatient lover applied for another letter. It was waiting for him, but it was not directed in Adela's handwriting. Had their correspondence been discovered? He opened the letter in the street; and read, with amazement, these lines:

Dear Mr Cosway, my heart sympathizes with two faithful lovers, in spite of my age and my duty. I enclose an invitation to the party to-morrow. Pray don't betray me, and don't pay too marked attention to Adela. Discretion is easy. There will be twelve hundred guests. Your friend, in spite of appearances, Louisa Margery.

How infamously they had all misjudged this excellent woman! Cosway went to the party a grateful, as well as a happy, man. The first persons known to him, whom he discovered among the crowd of strangers, were the Athertons. They looked, as well they might, astonished to see him. Fidelity to Mrs Margery forbade him to enter into any explanations. Where was that best and truest friend? With some difficulty he succeeded in finding her. Was there any impropriety in seizing her hand, and cordially pressing it? The result of this expression of gratitude was, to say the least of it, perplexing.

Mrs Margery behaved like the Athertons! She looked astonished to see him, and she put precisely the same question, 'How did you get here?' Cosway could only conclude that she was joking. 'Who should know that, dear lady, better than yourself?' he rejoined. 'I don't understand you,' Mrs Margery answered sharply. After a moment's reflection, Cosway hit on another solution of the mystery. Visitors were near them; and Mrs Margery had made her own private use of one of Mr Restall's invitation cards. She might have serious reasons for pushing caution to its last extreme. Cosway looked at her significantly. 'The least I can do is not to be indiscreet,' he whispered – and left her.

He turned into a side walk; and there he met Adela at last!

It seemed like a fatality. *She* looked astonished; and *she* said, 'How did you get here?' No intrusive visitors were within hearing, this time. 'My dear!' Cosway remonstrated, 'Mrs Margery must have told you, when she sent me my invitation.' Adela turned pale. 'Mrs Margery?' she repeated. 'Mrs Margery has said nothing to me; Mrs Margery detests you. We must have this cleared up. No; not now – I must attend to our guests. Expect a letter; and, for heaven's sake, Edwin, keep out of my father's way. One of our visitors whom he particularly wished to see has sent an excuse – and he is dreadfully angry about it.'

She left him before Cosway could explain that he and Mr Restall had thus far never seen each other.

He wandered away towards the extremity of the grounds, troubled by vague suspicions; hurt at Adela's cold reception of him. Entering a shrubbery, which seemed intended to screen the grounds, at this point, from a lane outside, he suddenly discovered a pretty little summer-house among the trees. A stout gentleman, of mature years, was seated alone in this retreat. He looked up with a frown. Cosway apologized for disturbing him, and entered into conversation as an act of politeness.

'A brilliant assembly today, sir.'

The stout gentleman replied by an inarticulate sound – something between a grunt and a cough.

'And a splendid house and grounds,' Cosway continued.

The stout gentleman repeated the inarticulate sound.

Cosway began to feel amused. Was this curious old man deaf and dumb?

'Excuse my entering into conversation,' he persisted. 'I feel like a stranger here. There are so many people whom I don't know.'

The stout gentleman suddenly burst into speech. Cosway had touched a sympathetic fibre at last.

'There are a good many people here whom *I* don't know,' he said gruffly. 'You are one of them. What's your name?'

'My name is Cosway, sir. What's yours?'

The stout gentleman rose with fury in his looks. He burst out with an oath; and added the intolerable question, already three times repeated by others, 'How did you get here?' The tone was even more offensive than the oath. 'Your age protects you, sir,' said Cosway, with the loftiest composure. 'I'm sorry I gave my name to so rude a person.'

'Rude?' shouted the old gentleman. 'You want my name in return, I suppose? You young puppy, you shall have it! My name is Restall.'

He turned his back, and walked off. Cosway took the only course now open to him. He returned to his lodgings.

The next day, no letter reached him from Adela. He went to the post office. No letter was there. The day wore on to evening – and, with the evening, there appeared a woman who was a stranger to him. She looked like a servant; and she was the bearer of a mysterious message.

'Please be at the garden-door that opens on the lane, at ten o'clock to-morrow morning. Knock three times at the door – and then say "Adela." Some one who wishes you well will be alone in the shrubbery, and will let you in. No, sir! I am not to take anything; and I am not to say a word more.' She spoke – and vanished.

Cosway was punctual to his appointment. He knocked three times; he pronounced Miss Restall's Christian name. Nothing happened. He waited a while, and tried again. This time, Adela's voice answered strangely from the shrubbery in tones of surprise: 'Edwin! is it really you?'

'Did you expect anyone else?' Cosway asked. 'My darling, your message said ten o'clock – and here I am.'

The door was suddenly unlocked.

'I sent no message,' said Adela, as they confronted each other on the threshold.

In the silence of utter bewilderment they went together into the summer-house. At Adela's request, Cosway repeated the message that he had received, and described the woman who had delivered it. The description applied to no person known to Miss Restall. 'Mrs Margery never sent you the invitation; and I repeat, I never sent you the message. This meeting has been arranged by some one who knows that I always walk in the shrubbery after breakfast. There is some underhand work going on—'

Still mentally in search of the enemy who had betrayed them, she checked herself, and considered a little. 'Is it possible –?' she began, and paused again. Her eyes filled with tears. 'My mind is so completely upset,' she said, 'that I can't think clearly of anything. Oh, Edwin, we have had a happy dream, and it has come to an end. My father knows more than we think for. Some friends of ours are going abroad tomorrow – and I am to go with them. Nothing I can say has the least effect upon my father. He means to part us for ever – and this is his cruel way of doing it!'

She put her arm round Cosway's neck, and lovingly laid her head on his shoulder. With tenderest kisses they reiterated their vows of eternal fidelity until their voices faltered and failed them. Cosway filled up the pause by the only useful suggestion which it was now in his power to make – he proposed an elopement.

Adela received this bold solution of the difficulty in which they were placed, exactly as thousands of other young ladies have received similar proposals before her time, and after.

She first said positively No. Cosway persisted. She began to cry, and asked if he had no respect for her. Cosway declared that his respect was equal to any sacrifice, except the sacrifice of parting with her for ever. He could, and would, if she preferred it, die for her, but while he was alive he must refuse to give her up. Upon this, she shifted her ground. Did he expect her to go away with him alone? Certainly not. Her maid could go with her, or, if her maid was not to be trusted, he would apply to his landlady, and engage 'a respectable elderly person' to attend on her until the day of their marriage. Would she have some mercy on him, and just consider it? No: she was afraid to consider it. Did she prefer misery for the rest of her life? Never mind *his* happiness: it was *her* happiness only that he had in his mind. Travelling with unsympathetic people; absent from England, no one could say for how long; married, when she did return, to some rich man whom she hated – would she, could she, contemplate that prospect? She contemplated it through tears; she contemplated it to an accompaniment of sighs, kisses, and protestations – she trembled, hesitated, gave way. At an appointed hour of the coming night, when her father would be in the smoking-room, and Mrs Margery would be in bed, Cosway was to knock at the door in the lane once more; leaving time to make all the necessary arrangements in the interval.

The one pressing necessity, under these circumstances, was to guard against the possibility of betrayal and surprise. Cosway discreetly alluded to the unsolved mysteries of the invitation and the message.

'Have you taken anybody into our confidence?' he asked.

Adela answered with some embarrassment. 'Only one person,' she said – 'dear Miss Benshaw.'

'Who is Miss Benshaw?'

'Don't you really know, Edwin? She is richer even than papa – she has inherited from her late brother one half-share in the great business in the City. Miss Benshaw is the lady who disappointed papa by not coming to the garden-party. You remember, dear, how happy we were, when we were together at Mr Atherton's? I was very miserable when they took me away. Miss Benshaw happened to call the next day, and she noticed it. "My dear," she said (Miss Benshaw is quite an elderly lady now), "I am an old maid, who has missed the happiness of her life, through not having had a friend to guide and advise her when she was young. Are you suffering as I once suffered?" She spoke so nicely – and I was so wretched – that I really couldn't help it. I opened my heart to her.'

Cosway looked grave. 'Are you sure she is to be trusted?' he asked.

'Perfectly sure.'

'Perhaps, my love, she has spoken about us (not meaning any harm) to some friend of hers? Old ladies are so fond of gossip. It's just possible – don't you think so?'

Adela hung her head.

'I have thought it just possible myself,' she admitted. 'There is plenty of time to call on her to-day. I will set our doubts at rest, before Miss Benshaw goes out for her afternoon drive.'

On that understanding they parted.

Towards evening, Cosway's arrangements for the elopement were completed. He was eating his solitary dinner when a note was brought to him. It had been left at the door by a messenger. The man had gone away without waiting for an answer. The note ran thus:

Miss Benshaw presents her compliments to Mr Cosway, and will be obliged if he can call on her at nine o'clock this evening, on business which concerns himself.

This invitation was evidently the result of Adela's visit earlier in the day. Cosway presented himself at the house, troubled by natural emotions of anxiety and suspense. His reception was not of a nature to compose him. He was shown into a darkened room. The one lamp on the table was turned down low, and the little light thus given was still further obscured by a shade. The corners of the room were in almost absolute darkness.

A voice out of one of the corners addressed him in a whisper:

'I must beg you to excuse the darkened room. I am suffering from a severe cold. My eyes are inflamed, and my throat is so bad that I can only speak in a whisper. Sit down, sir. I have got news for you.'

'Not bad news, I hope, ma'am?' Cosway ventured to inquire.

'The worst possible news,' said the whispering voice. 'You have an enemy striking at you in the dark.'

Cosway asked who it was, and received no answer. He varied the form of inquiry, and asked why the unnamed person struck at him in the dark. The experiment succeeded; he obtained a reply.

'It is reported to me,' said Miss Benshaw, 'that the person thinks it necessary to give you a lesson, and takes a spiteful pleasure in doing it as mischievously as possible. The person, as I happen to know, sent you your invitation to the party, and made the appointment which took you to the door in the lane. Wait a little, sir; I have not done yet. The person has put it into Mr Restall's head to send his daughter abroad to-morrow.'

Cosway attempted to make her speak more plainly.

'Is this wretch a man or a woman?' he said.

Miss Benshaw proceeded without noticing the interruption.

'You needn't be afraid, Mr Cosway; Miss Restall will not leave England. Your enemy is all-powerful. Your enemy's object could only be to provoke you into planning an elopement – and, your arrangements once completed, to inform Mr Restall, and to part you and Miss Adela quite as effectually as if you were at opposite ends of the world. Oh, you will undoubtedly be parted! Spiteful, isn't it? And, what is worse, the mischief is as good as done already.'

Cosway rose from his chair.

'Do you wish for any further explanation?' asked Miss Benshaw.

'One thing more,' he replied. 'Does Adela know of this?'

'No,' said Miss Benshaw; 'it is left to you to tell her.'

There was a moment of silence. Cosway looked at the lamp. Once roused, as usual with men of his character, his temper was not to be trifled with.

'Miss Benshaw,' he said, 'I dare say you think me a fool; but I can draw my own conclusion, for all that. *You* are my enemy.'

The only reply was a chuckling laugh. All voices can be more or less effectually disguised by a whisper – but a laugh carries the revelation of its own identity with it. Cosway suddenly threw off the shade over the lamp, and turned up the wick.

The light flooded the room, and showed him – His Wife.

THE THIRD EPOCH IN MR COSWAY'S LIFE

Three days had passed. Cosway sat alone in his lodging – pale and worn: the shadow already of his former self.

He had not seen Adela since the discovery. There was but one way in which he could venture to make the inevitable disclosure – he wrote to her; and Mr Atherton's daughter took care that the letter should be received. Inquiries made afterwards, by help of the same good friend, informed him that Miss Restall was suffering from illness.

The mistress of the house came in

'Cheer up, sir,' said the good woman. 'There is better news of Miss Restall today.'

He raised his head.

'Don't trifle with me!' he answered fretfully; 'tell me exactly what the servant said.'

The mistress repeated the words. Miss Restall had passed a quieter night, and had been able for a few hours to leave her room. He asked next if any reply to his letter had arrived. No reply had been received.

If Adela definitely abstained from writing to him, the conclusion would be too plain to be mistaken. She had given him up – and who could blame her?

There was a knock at the street-door. The mistress looked out.

'Here's Mr Stone come back, sir!' she exclaimed joyfully – and hurried away to let him in.

Cosway never looked up when his friend appeared.

'I knew I should succeed,' said Stone. 'I have seen your wife.'

'Don't speak of her,' cried Cosway. 'I should have murdered her when I first saw her face, if I had not instantly left the house. I may be the death of the wretch yet, if you persist in speaking of her!'

Stone put his hand kindly on his friend's shoulder.

'Must I remind you that you owe something to your old comrade?' he asked. 'I left my father and mother, the morning I got your letter – and my one thought has been to serve you. Reward me. Be a man, and hear what it is your right and duty to know. After that, if you like, we will never refer to the woman again.'

Cosway took his hand, in silent acknowledgment that he was right. They sat down together. Stone began.

'She is so entirely shameless,' he said, 'that I had no difficulty in getting her to speak. And she so cordially hates you that she glories in her own falsehood and treachery.'

'Of course, she lies,' Cosway said bitterly, 'when she calls herself Miss Benshaw?'

'No; she is really the daughter of the man who founded the great house in the City. With every advantage that wealth and position could give her, the perverse creature married one of her father's clerks, who had been deservedly dismissed from his situation. From that moment her family discarded her. With the money procured by the sale of her jewels, her husband took the inn which we have such bitter cause to remember – and she managed the house after his death. So much for the past. Carry your mind on now to the time when our ship brought us back to England. At that date, the last surviving member of your wife's family – her elder brother – lay at the point of death. He had taken his father's place in the business, besides inheriting his father's fortune. After a happy married life, he was left a widower, without children; and it became necessary that he should alter his will. He deferred performing this duty. It was only at the time of his last illness that he had dictated instructions for a new will, leaving his wealth (excepting certain legacies to old friends) to the hospitals of Great Britain and Ireland. His lawyer lost no time in carrying out the instructions. The new will was ready for signature (the old will having been destroyed by his own hand), when the doctors sent a message to say that their patient was insensible, and might die in that condition.'

'Did the doctors prove to be right?'

'Perfectly right. Our wretched landlady, as next of kin, succeeded, not only to the fortune, but (under the deed of partnership) to her late brother's place in the firm: on the one easy condition of resuming the family name. She calls herself "Miss Benshaw." But as a matter of legal necessity she is set down in the deed as "Mrs Cosway Benshaw." Her partners only now know that her husband is living, and that you are the Cosway whom she privately married. Will you take a little breathing-time? or shall I go on, and get done with it?'

Cosway signed to him to go on.

'She doesn't in the least care,' Stone proceeded, 'for the exposure. "I am the head partner," she says, "and the rich one of the firm; they daren't turn their backs on Me." You remember the information I received – in perfect good faith on his part – from the man who now keeps the inn? The visit to the London doctor, and the assertion of failing health, were adopted as the best means of plausibly severing the lady's connection (the great lady now!) with a calling so unworthy of her as the keeping of an inn. Her neighbours at the seaport were all deceived by the stratagem, with two exceptions. They were both men – vagabonds who had pertinaciously tried to delude her into marrying them in the days when she was a widow. They refused to believe in the doctor and the declining health; they had their own suspicion of the motives which had led to the sale of the inn, under very unfavourable circumstances; and they decided on going to London, inspired by the same base hope of making discoveries which might be turned into a means of extorting money.'

'She escaped them, of course,' said Cosway. 'How?'

'By the help of her lawyer, who was not above accepting a handsome private fee. He wrote to the new landlord of the inn, falsely announcing his client's death, in the letter which I repeated to you in the railway carriage on our journey to London. Other precautions were taken to keep up the deception, on which it is needless to dwell. Your natural conclusion that you were free to pay your addresses to Miss Restall, and the poor young lady's innocent confidence in "Miss Benshaw's" sympathy, gave this unscrupulous woman the means of playing the heartless trick on you which is now exposed. Malice and jealousy – I have it, mind, from herself! – were not her only motives. "But for that Cosway," she said (I spare you the epithet which she put before your name), "with my money and position, I might have married a needy lord, and sunned myself in my old age in the full blaze of the peerage." Do you understand how she hated you, now? Enough of the subject! The moral of it, my dear Cosway, is to leave this place, and try what change of scene will do for you. I have time to spare; and I will go abroad with you. When shall it be?'

'Let me wait a day or two more,' Cosway pleaded.

Stone shook his head. 'Still hoping, my poor friend, for a line from Miss Restall? You distress me.'

'I am sorry to distress you, Stone. If I can get one pitying word from *her*, I can submit to the miserable life that lies before me.'

'Are you not expecting too much?'

'You wouldn't say so, if you were as fond of her as I am.'

They were silent. The evening slowly darkened; and the mistress came in as usual with the candles. She brought with her a letter for Cosway.

He tore it open; read it in an instant; and devoured it with kisses. His highly wrought feelings found their vent in a little allowable exaggeration. 'She has saved my life!' he said, as he handed the letter to Stone.

It only contained these lines:

'My love is yours, my promise is yours. Through all trouble, through all profanation, through the hopeless separation that may be before us in this world, I live yours – and die yours. My Edwin, God bless and comfort you.'

THE FOURTH EPOCH IN MR COSWAY'S LIFE

The separation had lasted for nearly two years, when Cosway and Stone paid that visit to the country house which is recorded at the outset of the present narrative. In the interval, nothing had been heard of Miss Restall, except through Mr Atherton. He reported that Adela was leading a very quiet life. The one remarkable event had been an interview between 'Miss Benshaw' and herself. No other person had been present; but the little that was reported placed Miss Restall's character above all praise. She had forgiven the woman who had so cruelly injured her!

The two friends, it may be remembered, had travelled to London, immediately after completing the fullest explanation of Cosway's startling behaviour at the breakfast-table. Stone was not by nature a sanguine man. 'I don't believe in our luck,' he said. 'Let us be quite sure that we are not the victims of another deception.'

The accident had happened on the Thames; and the newspaper narrative proved to be accurate in every respect. Stone personally attended the inquest. From a natural feeling of delicacy towards Adela, Cosway hesitated to write to her on the subject. The ever-helpful Stone wrote in his place.

After some delay, the answer was received. It enclosed a brief statement (communicated officially by legal authority) of a last act of malice on the part of the late head-partner in the house of Benshaw and Company. She had not died intestate, like her brother. The first clause of her will contained the testator's grateful recognition of Adela Restall's Christian act of forgiveness. The second clause (after stating that there were neither relatives nor children to be benefited by the will) left Adela Restall mistress of Mrs Cosway Benshaw's fortune – on the one merciless condition that she did *not* marry Edwin Cosway. The third clause – if Adela Restall violated the condition – handed over the whole of the money to the firm in the

City, 'for the extension of the business, and the benefit of the surviving partners.'

Some months later, Adela came of age. To the indignation of Mr Restall, and the astonishment of the 'Company,' the money actually went to the firm. The fourth epoch in Mr Cosway's life witnessed his marriage to a woman who cheerfully paid half a million of money for the happiness of passing her life, on eight hundred a year, with the man whom she loved.

But Cosway felt bound in gratitude to make a rich woman of his wife, if work and resolution could do it. When Stone last heard of him, he was reading for the Bar; and Mr Atherton was ready to give him his first brief.

Note – That 'most improbable' part of the present narrative, which is contained in the division called The First Epoch, is founded on an adventure which actually occurred to no less a person than a cousin of Sir Walter Scott. In Lockhart's delightful 'Life,' the anecdote will be found as told by Sir Walter to Captain Basil Hall. The remainder of the present story is entirely imaginary. The writer wondered what such a woman as the landlady would do, under certain given circumstances, after her marriage to the young midshipman – and here is the result.

Miss Morris and the Stranger

Originally appeared in *The Spirit of the Times*, 24 December 1881, as 'How I Married Him'. Reprinted in *Little Novels* (1887). Collins liked to champion women struggling to earn their own living, and this is by no means his only sortie into governess fiction. Compare the presentation of Harriet Garth in *No Name* (1862). Collins's mother, Harriet Geddes, had wanted to go on the stage, but was persuaded to become a governess instead. Perhaps this is why Katherine West, in *Chapter of Governesses: A Study of the Governess in English Fiction 1800–1949* (London: Cohen and West, 1949) was able to declare that 'all Wilkie Collins's material on governesses rings true.'

I

When I first saw him, he was lost in one of the Dead Cities of England – situated on the south coast, and called Sandwich.

Shall I describe Sandwich? I think not. Let us own the truth; descriptions of places, however nicely they may be written, are always more or less dull. Being a woman, I naturally hate dulness. Perhaps some description of Sandwich may drop out, as it were, from my report of our conversation when we first met as strangers in the street.

He began irritably. 'I've lost myself,' he said.

'People who don't know the town often do that,' I remarked.

He went on: 'Which is my way to the Fleur de Lys Inn?'

His way was, in the first place, to retrace his steps. Then to turn to the left. Then to go on until he found two streets meeting. Then to take the street on the right. Then to look out for the second turning on the left. Then to follow the turning until he smelt stables – and there was the inn. I put it in the clearest manner, and never stumbled over a word.

'How the devil am I to remember all that?' he said.

This was rude. We are, naturally and properly, indignant with any man who is rude to us. But whether we turn our backs on him in contempt, or whether we are merciful and give him a lesson in politeness, depends entirely on the man. He may be a bear, but he may also have his redeeming qualities. This man had redeeming qualities. I cannot positively say that he was either handsome or ugly, young or old, well or ill dressed. But I can speak with certainty to the personal attractions which recommended him to notice. For instance, the tone of his voice was persuasive. (Did you ever read a story, written by one of *us*, in which we failed to dwell on our hero's voice?) Then, again, his hair was reasonably long. (Are you acquainted with any woman who can endure a man with a cropped head?) Moreover, he was of a good height. (It must be a very tall woman who can feel favourably inclined towards a short man.) Lastly, although his eyes were not more than fairly presentable in form and colour, the wretch had in some unaccountable manner become possessed of beautiful eyelashes. They were even better eyelashes than mine. I write quite seriously. There is one woman who is above the common weakness of vanity – and she holds the present pen.

So I gave my lost stranger a lesson in politeness. The lesson took the form of a trap. I asked if he would like me to show him the way to the inn. He was still annoyed at losing himself. As I had anticipated, he bluntly answered: 'Yes.'

'When you were a boy, and you wanted something,' I said, 'did your mother teach you to say "Please"?'

He positively blushed. 'She did,' he admitted; 'and she taught me to say "Beg your pardon" when I was rude. I'll say it now: "Beg your pardon."'

This curious apology increased my belief in his redeeming qualities. I led the way to the inn. He followed me in silence. No woman who respects herself can endure silence when she is in the company of a man. I made him talk.

'Do you come to us from Ramsgate?' I began. He only nodded his head. 'We don't think much of Ramsgate here,' I went on. 'There is not an old building in the place. And their first Mayor was only elected the other day!'

This point of view seemed to be new to him. He made no attempt to dispute

it; he only looked round him, and said, 'Sandwich is a melancholy place, Miss.'
He was so rapidly improving in politeness, that I encouraged him by a smile.
As a citizen of Sandwich, I may say that we take it as a compliment when we are
told that our town is a melancholy place. And why not? Melancholy is connected
with dignity. And dignity is associated with age. And *we* are old. I teach my
pupils logic, among other things – there is a specimen. Whatever may be said
to the contrary, women can reason. They can also wander; and I must admit
that *I* am wandering. Did I mention, at starting, that I was a governess? If not,
that allusion to 'pupils' must have come in rather abruptly. Let me make my
excuses, and return to my lost stranger.

'Is there any such thing as a straight street in all Sandwich?' he asked.

'Not one straight street in the whole town.'

'Any trade, Miss?'

'As little as possible – and *that* is expiring.'

'A decayed place, in short?'

'Thoroughly decayed.'

My tone seemed to astonish him. 'You speak as if you were proud of its being
a decayed place,' he said.

I quite respected him: this was such an intelligent remark to make. We do
enjoy our decay: it is our chief distinction. Progress and prosperity everywhere
else; decay and dissolution here. As a necessary consequence, we produce our
own impression, and we like to be original. The sea deserted us long ago: it once
washed our walls, it is now two miles away from us – we don't regret the sea.
We had sometimes ninety-five ships in our harbour, Heaven only knows how
many centuries ago; we now have one or two small coasting vessels, half their
time aground in a muddy little river – we don't regret our harbour. But one
house in the town is daring enough to anticipate the arrival of resident visitors,
and announces furnished apartments to let. What a becoming contrast to our
modern neighbour, Ramsgate! Our noble market-place exhibits the laws made
by the corporation; and every week there are fewer and fewer people to obey
the laws. How convenient! Look at our one warehouse by the river side – with
the crane generally idle, and the windows mostly boarded up; and perhaps one
man at the door, looking out for the job which his better sense tells him cannot
possibly come. What a wholesome protest against the devastating hurry and
over-work elsewhere, which has shattered the nerves of the nation! 'Far from
me and from my friends' (to borrow the eloquent language of Doctor Johnson)
'be such frigid enthusiasm as shall conduct us indifferent and unmoved' over
the bridge by which you enter Sandwich, and pay a toll if you do it in a
carriage. 'That man is little to be envied' (Doctor Johnson again) who can
lose himself in our labyrinthine streets, and not feel that he has reached the
welcome limits of progress, and found a haven of rest in an age of hurry.

I am wandering again. Bear with the unpremeditated enthusiasm of a citizen
who only attained years of discretion at her last birthday. We shall soon have
done with Sandwich; we are close to the door of the inn.

'You can't mistake it now, sir,' I said. 'Good-morning.'

He looked down at me from under his beautiful eyelashes (have I mentioned
that *I* am a little woman?), and he asked in his persuasive tones, 'Must we say
good-bye?'

I made him a bow.

'Would you allow me to see you safe home?' he suggested.

Any other man would have offended me. This man blushed like a boy, and looked at the pavement instead of looking at me. By this time I had made up my mind about him. He was not only a gentleman beyond all doubt, but a shy gentleman as well. His bluntness and his odd remarks were, as I thought, partly efforts to disguise his shyness, and partly refuges in which he tried to forget his own sense of it. I answered his audacious proposal amiably and pleasantly. 'You would only lose your way again,' I said, 'and I should have to take you back to the inn for the second time.'

Wasted words! My obstinate stranger only made another proposal.

'I have ordered lunch here,' he said, 'and I am quite alone.' He stopped in confusion, and looked as if he rather expected me to box his ears. 'I shall be forty next birthday,' he went on; 'I am old enough to be your father.' I all but burst out laughing, and stepped across the street, on my way home. He followed me. 'We might invite the landlady to join us,' he said, looking the picture of a headlong man, dismayed by the consciousness of his own imprudence. 'Couldn't you honour me by lunching with me if we had the landlady?' he asked.

This was a little too much. 'Quite out of the question, sir – and you ought to know it,' I said with severity. He half put out his hand. 'Won't you even shake hands with me?' he inquired piteously. When we have most properly administered a reproof to a man, what *is* the perversity which makes us weakly pity him the minute afterwards? I was fool enough to shake hands with this perfect stranger. And, having done it, I completed the total loss of my dignity by running away. Our dear crooked little streets hid me from him directly.

As I rang at the door-bell of my employer's house, a thought occurred to me which might have been alarming to a better regulated mind than mine.

'Suppose he should come back to Sandwich?'

II

Before many more days passed I had troubles of my own to contend with, which put the eccentric stranger out of my head for the time.

Unfortunately, my troubles are part of my story; and my early life mixes itself up with them. In consideration of what is to follow, may I say two words relating to the period before I was a governess?

I am the orphan daughter of a shop-keeper of Sandwich. My father died, leaving to his widow and child an honest name and a little income of £80 a year. We kept on the shop – neither gaining nor losing by it. The truth is, nobody would buy our poor little business. I was thirteen years old at the time; and I was able to help my mother, whose health was then beginning to fail. Never shall I forget a certain bright summer's day, when I saw a new customer enter our shop. He was an elderly gentleman; and he seemed surprised to find so young a girl as myself in charge of the business, and, what is more, competent to support the charge. I answered his questions in a manner which seemed to please him. He soon discovered that my education (excepting my knowledge of the business) had been sadly neglected; and he inquired if he could see my mother. She was resting on the sofa in the back parlour – and she received him there. When he came out, he patted me on the cheek. 'I have taken a fancy to you,' he said, 'and perhaps I shall come back again.' He did come back again. My mother had referred him to the rector for our characters in the town, and he had heard what our clergyman could say for us. Our only relations had emigrated to Australia, and were not doing well there. My mother's death would leave me, so far as relatives were concerned, literally alone in the world. 'Give this girl a first-rate education,' said our elderly customer, sitting at our tea-table in the back parlour, 'and she will do. If you will send her to school, ma'am, I'll pay for her education.' My poor mother began to cry at the prospect of parting with me. The old gentleman said, 'Think of it,' and got up to go. He gave me his card as I opened the shop-door for him. 'If you find yourself in trouble,' he whispered, so that my mother could not hear him, 'be a wise child, and write and tell me of it.' I looked at the card. Our kind-hearted customer was no less a person than Sir Gervase Damian, of Garrum Park, Sussex – with landed property in our county as well! He had made himself (through the rector, no doubt) far better acquainted than I was with the true state of my mother's health. In four months from the memorable day when the great man had taken tea with us, my time had come to be alone in the world. I have no courage to dwell on it; my spirits sink, even at this distance of time, when I think of myself in those days. The good rector helped me with his advice – I wrote to Sir Gervase Damian.

A change had come over his life as well as mine in the interval since we had met.

Sir Gervase had married for the second time – and, what was more foolish still, perhaps, at his age, had married a young woman. She was said to be consumptive, and of a jealous temper as well. Her husband's only child by his first wife, a son and heir, was so angry at his father's second marriage, that he left the house. The landed property being entailed, Sir Gervase could only express his sense of his son's conduct by making a new will, which left all his property in money to his young wife.

These particulars I gathered from the steward, who was expressly sent to visit me at Sandwich.

'Sir Gervase never makes a promise without keeping it,' this gentleman informed me. 'I am directed to take you to a first-rate ladies' school in the neighbourhood of London, and to make all the necessary arrangements for your remaining there until you are eighteen years of age. Any written communications in the future are to pass, if you please, through the hands of the rector of Sandwich. The delicate health of the new Lady Damian makes it only too likely that the lives of her husband and herself will be passed, for the most part, in a milder climate than the climate of England. I am instructed to say this, and to convey to you Sir Gervase's best wishes.'

By the rector's advice, I accepted the position offered to me in this unpleas-antly formal manner – concluding (quite correctly, as I afterwards discovered) that I was indebted to Lady Damian for the arrangement which personally separated me from my benefactor. Her husband's kindness and my gratitude, meeting on the neutral ground of Garrum Park, were objects of conjugal distrust to this lady. Shocking! shocking! I left a sincerely grateful letter to be forwarded to Sir Gervase; and, escorted by the steward, I went to school – being then just fourteen years old.

I know I am a fool. Never mind. There is some pride in me, though I am only a small shopkeeper's daughter. My new life had its trials – my pride held me up.

For the four years during which I remained at the school, my poor welfare might be a subject of inquiry to the rector, and sometimes even to the steward

– never to Sir Gervase himself. His winters were no doubt passed abroad; but in the summer time he and Lady Damian were at home again. Not even for a day or two in the holiday time was there pity enough felt for my lonely position to ask me to be the guest of the housekeeper (I expected nothing more) at Garrum Park. But for my pride, I might have felt it bitterly. My pride said to me, 'Do justice to yourself.' I worked so hard, I behaved so well, that the mistress of the school wrote to Sir Gervase to tell him how thoroughly I had deserved the kindness that he had shown to me. No answer was received. (Oh, Lady Damian!) No change varied the monotony of my life – except when one of my schoolgirl friends sometimes took me home with her for a few days at vacation time. Never mind. My pride held me up.

As the last half-year of my time at school approached, I began to consider the serious question of my future life.

Of course, I could have lived on my eighty pounds a year; but what a lonely, barren existence it promised to be! – unless somebody married me; and where, if you please, was I to find him? My education had thoroughly fitted me to be a governess. Why not try my fortune, and see a little of the world in that way? Even if I fell among ill-conditioned people, I could be independent of them, and retire on my income.

The rector, visiting London, came to see me. He not only approved of my idea – he offered me a means of carrying it out. A worthy family, recently settled at Sandwich, were in want of a governess. The head of the household was partner in a business (the exact nature of which it is needless to mention) having 'branches' out of London. He had become superintendent of a new 'branch' – tried as a commercial experiment, under special circumstances, at Sandwich. The idea of returning to my native place pleased me – dull as the place was to others. I accepted the situation.

When the steward's usual half-yearly letter arrived soon afterwards, inquiring what plans I had formed on leaving school, and what he could do to help them, acting on behalf of Sir Gervase, a delicious tingling filled me from head to foot when I thought of my own independence. It was not ingratitude towards my benefactor; it was only my little private triumph over Lady Damian. Oh, my sisters of the sex, can you not understand and forgive me?

So to Sandwich I returned; and there, for three years, I remained with the kindest people who ever breathed the breath of life. Under their roof I was still living when I met with my lost gentleman in the street.

Ah me! the end of that quiet, pleasant life was near. When I lightly spoke to the odd stranger of the expiring trade of the town, I never suspected that my employer's trade was expiring too. The speculation had turned out to be a losing one; and all his savings had been embarked in it. He could no longer remain at Sandwich, or afford to keep a governess. His wife broke the sad news to me. I was so fond of the children, I proposed to her to give up my salary. Her husband refused even to consider the proposal. It was the old story of poor humanity over again. We cried, we kissed, we parted.

What was I to do next? – write to Sir Gervase?

I had already written, soon after my return to Sandwich; breaking through the regulations by directly addressing Sir Gervase. I expressed my grateful sense of his generosity to a poor girl who had no family claim on him; and I promised to make the one return in my power by trying to be worthy of the interest he had taken in me. The letter was written without any alloy of mental reserve. My new life as a governess was such a happy one, that I had forgotten my paltry bitterness of feeling against Lady Damian.

It was a relief to think of this change for the better, when the secretary at Garrum Park informed me that he had forwarded my letter to Sir Gervase, then at Madeira with his sick wife. She was slowly and steadily wasting away in a decline. Before another year had passed, Sir Gervase was left a widower for the second time, with no child to console him under his loss. No answer came to my grateful letter. I should have been unreasonable indeed if I had expected the bereaved husband to remember me in his grief and loneliness. Could I write to him again, in my own trumpery little interests, under these circumstances? I thought (and still think) that the commonest feeling of delicacy forbade it. The only other alternative was to appeal to the ever-ready friends of the obscure and helpless public. I advertised in the newspapers.

The tone of one of the answers which I received impressed me so favourably, that I forwarded my references. The next post brought my written engagement, and the offer of a salary which doubled my income.

The story of the past is told; and now we may travel on again, with no more stoppages by the way.

III

The residence of my present employer was in the north of England. Having to pass through London, I arranged to stay in town for a few days to make some necessary additions to my wardrobe. An old servant of the rector, who kept a lodging-house in the suburbs, received me kindly, and guided my choice in the serious matter of a dressmaker. On the second morning after my arrival, an event happened. The post brought me a letter forwarded from the rectory. Imagine my astonishment when my correspondent proved to be Sir Gervase Damian himself!

The letter was dated from his house in London. It briefly invited me to call and see him, for a reason which I should hear from his own lips. He naturally supposed that I was still at Sandwich, and requested me, in a postscript, to consider my journey as made at his expense.

I went to the house the same day. While I was giving my name, a gentleman came out into the hall. He spoke to me without ceremony.

'Sir Gervase,' he said, 'believes he is going to die. Don't encourage him in that idea. He may live for another year or more, if his friends will only persuade him to be hopeful about himself.'

With that, the gentleman left me; the servant said it was the doctor.

The change in my benefactor, since I had seen him last, startled and distressed me. He lay back in a large arm-chair, wearing a grim black dressing-gown, and looking pitiably thin and pinched and worn. I do not think I should have known him again, if we had met by accident. He signed to me to be seated on a little chair by his side.

'I wanted to see you,' he said quietly, 'before I die. You must have thought me neglectful and unkind, with good reason. My child, you have not been forgotten. If years have passed without a meeting between us, it has not been altogether my fault—'

He stopped. A pained expression passed over his poor worn face; he was evidently thinking of the young wife whom he had lost. I repeated – fervently and sincerely repeated – what I had already said to him in writing. 'I owe everything, sir, to your fatherly kindness.' Saying this, I ventured a little further. I took his wan white hand, hanging over the arm of the chair, and respectfully put it to my lips.

He gently drew his hand away from me, and sighed as he did it. Perhaps *she* had sometimes kissed his hand.

'Now tell me about yourself,' he said.

I told him of my new situation, and how I had got it. He listened with evident interest.

'I was not self-deceived,' he said, 'when I first took a fancy to you in the shop. I admire your independent feeling; it's the right kind of courage in a girl like you. But you must let me do something more for you – some little service, to remember me by when the end has come. What shall it be?'

'Try to get better, sir; and let me write to you now and then,' I answered. 'Indeed, indeed, I want nothing more.'

'You will accept a little present, at least?' With those words he took from the breast-pocket of his dressing-gown an enamelled cross attached to a gold chain. 'Think of me sometimes,' he said, as he put the chain round my neck. He drew me to him gently, and kissed my forehead. It was too much for me. 'Don't cry, my dear,' he said; 'don't remind me of another sad young face—'

Once more he stopped; once more he was thinking of the lost wife. I pulled down my veil, and ran out of the room.

IV

The next day I was on my way to the north. My narrative brightens again – but let us not forget Sir Gervase Damian.

I ask permission to introduce some persons of distinction: Mrs Fosdyke, of Carsham Hall, widow of General Fosdyke; also Master Frederick, Miss Ellen, and Miss Eva, the pupils of the new governess; also two ladies and three gentlemen, guests staying in the house.

Discreet and dignified; handsome and well-bred – such was my impression of Mrs Fosdyke, while she harangued me on the subject of her children, and communicated her views on education. Having heard the views before from others, I assumed a listening position, and privately formed my opinion of the schoolroom. It was large, lofty, perfectly furnished for the purpose; it had a big window and a balcony looking out over the garden terrace and the park beyond – a wonderful schoolroom, in my limited experience. One of the two doors which it possessed was left open, and showed me a sweet little bedroom, with amber draperies and maplewood furniture, devoted to myself. Here were wealth and liberality, in that harmonious combination so seldom discovered by the spectator of small means. I controlled my first feeling of bewilderment just in time to answer Mrs Fosdyke on the subject of reading and recitation – viewed as minor accomplishments which a good governess might be expected to teach.

'While the organs are young and pliable,' the lady remarked, 'I regard it as of great importance to practise children in the art of reading aloud, with an agreeable variety of tone and correctness of emphasis. Trained in this way, they will produce a favourable impression on others, even in ordinary conversation, when they grow up. Poetry, committed to memory and recited, is a valuable means towards this end. May I hope that your studies have enabled you to carry out my views?'

Formal enough in language, but courteous and kind in manner. I relieved Mrs Fosdyke from anxiety by informing her that we had a professor of elocution at school. And then I was left to improve my acquaintance with my three pupils.

They were fairly intelligent children; the boy, as usual, being slower than the girls. I did my best – with many a sad remembrance of the far dearer pupils whom I had left – to make them like me and trust me; and I succeeded in winning their confidence. In a week from the time of my arrival at Carsham Hall, we began to understand each other.

The first day in the week was one of our days for reciting poetry, in obedience to the instructions with which I had been favoured by Mrs Fosdyke. I had done with the girls, and had just opened (perhaps I ought to say profaned) Shakespeare's *Julius Cæsar*, in the elocutionary interests of Master Freddy. Half of Mark Antony's first glorious speech over Cæsar's dead body he had learnt by heart; and it was now my duty to teach him, to the best of my small ability, how to speak it. The morning was warm. We had our big window open; the delicious perfume of flowers in the garden beneath filled the room.

I recited the first eight lines, and stopped there, feeling that I must not exact too much from the boy at first. 'Now, Freddy,' I said, 'try if you can speak the poetry as I have spoken it.'

'Don't do anything of the kind, Freddy,' said a voice from the garden; 'it's all spoken wrong.'

Who was this insolent person? A man unquestionably – and, strange to say, there was something not entirely unfamiliar to me in his voice. The girls began to giggle. Their brother was more explicit. 'Oh,' says Freddy, 'it's only Mr Sax.'

The one becoming course to pursue was to take no notice of the interruption. 'Go on,' I said. Freddy recited the lines, like a dear good boy, with as near an imitation of my style of elocution as could be expected from him.

'Poor devil!' cried the voice from the garden, insolently pitying my attentive pupil.

I imposed silence on the girls by a look – and then, without stirring from my chair, expressed my sense of the insolence of Mr Sax in clear and commanding tones. 'I shall be obliged to close the window if this is repeated.' Having spoken to that effect, I waited in expectation of an apology. Silence was the only apology. It was enough for me that I had produced the right impression. I went on with my recitation.

> 'Here, under leave of Brutus, and the rest
> (For Brutus is an honourable man;
> So are they all, all honourable men),
> Come I to speak in Cæsar's funeral.
> He was my friend, faithful and just to me—'

'Oh, good heavens, I can't stand *that!* Why don't you speak the last line properly? Listen to me.'

Dignity is a valuable quality, especially in a governess. But there are limits to the most highly trained endurance. I bounced out into the balcony – and there, on the terrace, smoking a cigar, was my lost stranger in the streets of Sandwich!

He recognised me, on his side, the instant I appeared. 'Oh, Lord!' he cried in tones of horror, and ran round the corner of the terrace as if my eyes had been mad bulls in close pursuit of him. By this time it is, I fear, useless for me to set myself up as a discreet person in emergencies. Another woman might have controlled herself. *I* burst into fits of laughter. Freddy and the girls joined me. For the time, it was plainly useless to pursue the business of education. I shut up Shakespeare, and allowed – no, let me tell the truth, encouraged – the children to talk about Mr Sax.

They only seemed to know what Mr Sax himself had told them. His father and mother and brothers and sisters had all died in course of time. He was the sixth and last of the children, and he had been christened 'Sextus' in consequence, which is Latin (here Freddy interposed) for sixth. Also christened 'Cyril' (here the girls recovered the lead) by his mother's request; 'Sextus' being such a hideous name. And which of his christian names does he use? You wouldn't ask if you knew him! 'Sextus' of course, because it is the ugliest. Sextus Sax? Not the romantic sort of name that one likes, when one is a woman. But I have no right to be particular. My own name (is it possible that I have not mentioned it in these pages yet?) is only Nancy Morris. Do not despise me – and let us return to Mr Sax.

Is he married? The eldest girl thought not. She had heard mamma say to a lady, 'An old German family, my dear, and, in spite of his oddities, an excellent man; but so poor – barely enough to live on – and blurts out the truth, if people ask his opinion, as if he had twenty thousand a year!' Your mamma knows him well, of course? I should think so, and so do we. He often comes here. They say he's not good company among grown-up people. *We* think him jolly. He understands dolls, and he's the best back at leap-frog in the whole of England.

Thus far we had advanced in the praise of Sextus Sax, when one of the maids came in with a note for me. She smiled mysteriously, and said, 'I'm to wait for an answer, Miss.'

I opened the note, and read these lines:

I am so ashamed of myself, I daren't attempt to make my apologies personally. Will you accept my written excuses? Upon my honour, nobody told me when I got here yesterday that you were in the house. I heard the recitation, and – can you excuse my stupidity? – I thought it was a stage-struck housemaid amusing herself with the children. May I accompany you when you go out with the young ones for your daily walk? One word will do. Yes or no. Penitently yours, – S. S.

In my position, there was but one possible answer to this. Governesses must not make appointments with strange gentlemen – even when the children are present in the capacity of witnesses. I said, No. Am I claiming too much for my readiness to forgive injuries, when I add that I should have preferred saying Yes?

We had our early dinner, and then got ready to go out walking as usual. These pages contain a true confession. Let me own that I hoped Mr Sax would understand my refusal, and ask Mrs Fosdyke's leave to accompany us. Lingering a little as we went downstairs, I heard him in the hall – actually speaking to Mrs Fosdyke! What was he saying? That darling boy, Freddy, got into a difficulty with one of his boot-laces exactly at the right moment. I could help him, and listen – and be sadly disappointed by the result. Mr Sax was offended with me.

'You needn't introduce me to the new governess,' I heard him say. 'We have met on a former occasion, and I produced a disagreeable impression on her. I beg you will not speak of me to Miss Morris.'

Before Mrs Fosdyke could say a word in reply, Master Freddy changed suddenly from a darling boy to a detestable imp. 'I say, Mr Sax!' he called out, 'Miss Morris doesn't mind you a bit – she only laughs at you.'

The answer to this was the sudden closing of a door. Mr Sax had taken refuge from me in one of the ground-floor rooms. I was so mortified, I could almost have cried.

Getting down into the hall, we found Mrs Fosdyke with her garden hat on, and one of the two ladies who were staying in the house (the unmarried one) whispering to her at the door of the morning-room. The lady – Miss Melbury – looked at me with a certain appearance of curiosity which I was quite at a loss to understand, and suddenly turned away towards the farther end of the hall.

'I will walk with you and the children,' Mrs Fosdyke said to me. 'Freddy, you can ride your tricycle if you like.' She turned to the girls. 'My dears, it's cool under the trees. You may take your skipping-ropes.'

She had evidently something special to say to me; and she had adopted the necessary measures for keeping the children in front of us, well out of hearing. Freddy led the way on his horse on three wheels; the girls followed, skipping merrily. Mrs Fosdyke opened her business by the most embarrassing remark that she could possibly have made under the circumstances.

'I find that you are acquainted with Mr Sax,' she began; 'and I am surprised to hear that you dislike him.'

She smiled pleasantly, as if my supposed dislike of Mr Sax rather amused her. What 'the ruling passion' may be among men, I cannot presume to consider. My own sex, however, I may claim to understand. The ruling passion among women is Conceit. My ridiculous notion of my own consequence was wounded in some way. I assumed a position of the loftiest indifference.

'Really, ma'am,' I said, 'I can't undertake to answer for any impression that Mr Sax may have formed. We met by the merest accident. I know nothing about him.'

Mrs Fosdyke eyed me slily, and appeared to be more amused than ever.

'He is a very odd man,' she admitted, 'but I can tell you there is a fine nature under that strange surface of his. However,' she went on, 'I am forgetting that he forbids me to talk about him in your presence. When the opportunity offers, I shall take my own way of teaching you two to understand each other: you will both be grateful to me when I have succeeded. In the meantime, there is a third person who will be sadly disappointed to hear that you know nothing about Mr Sax.'

'May I ask, ma'am, who the person is?'

'Can you keep a secret, Miss Morris? Of course you can! The person is Miss Melbury.'

(Miss Melbury was a dark woman. It cannot be because I am a fair woman myself – I hope I am above such narrow prejudice as that – but it is certainly true that I don't admire dark women.)

'She heard Mr Sax telling me that you particularly disliked him,' Mrs Fosdyke proceeded. 'And just as you appeared in the hall, she was asking me to find out what your reason was. My own opinion of Mr Sax, I ought to tell you, doesn't satisfy her; I am his old friend, and I present him of course from my own favourable point of view. Miss Melbury is anxious to be made acquainted with his faults – and she expected you to be a valuable witness against him.'

Thus far we had been walking on. We now stopped, as if by common consent, and looked at one another.

In my previous experience of Mrs Fosdyke, I had only seen the more constrained and formal side of her character. Without being aware of my own success, I had won the mother's heart in winning the goodwill of her children. Constraint now seized its first opportunity of melting away; the latent sense of humour in the great lady showed itself, while I was inwardly wondering what the nature of Miss Melbury's extraordinary interest in Mr Sax might be. Easily penetrating my thoughts, she satisfied my curiosity without committing herself to a reply in words. Her large gray eyes sparkled as they rested on my face, and she hummed the tune of the old French song, '*C'est l'amour, l'amour, l'amour!*' There is no disguising it – something in this disclosure made me excessively angry. Was I angry with Miss Melbury? or with Mr Sax? or with myself? I think it must have been with myself.

Finding that I had nothing to say on my side, Mrs Fosdyke looked at her watch, and remembered her domestic duties. To my relief, our interview came to an end.

'I have a dinner-party to-day,' she said, 'and I have not seen the housekeeper yet. Make yourself beautiful, Miss Morris, and join us in the drawing-room after dinner.'

V

I wore my best dress; and, in all my life before, I never took such pains with my hair. Nobody will be foolish enough, I hope, to suppose that I did this on Mr Sax's account. How could I possibly care about a man who was little better than a stranger to me? No! the person I dressed at was Miss Melbury.

She gave me a look, as I modestly placed myself in a corner, which amply rewarded me for the time spent on my toilette. The gentlemen came in. I looked at Mr Sax (mere curiosity) under shelter of my fan. His appearance was greatly improved by evening dress. He discovered me in my corner, and seemed doubtful whether to approach me or not. I was reminded of our first odd meeting; and I could not help smiling as I called it to mind. Did he presume to think that I was encouraging him? Before I could decide that question, he took the vacant place on the sofa. In any other man – after what had passed in the morning – this would have been an audacious proceeding. *He* looked so painfully embarrassed, that it became a species of Christian duty to pity him.

'Won't you shake hands?' he said, just as he had said it at Sandwich.

I peeped round the corner of my fan at Miss Melbury. She was looking at us. I shook hands with Mr Sax.

'What sort of sensation is it,' he asked, 'when you shake hands with a man whom you hate?'

'I really can't tell you,' I answered innocently; 'I have never done such a thing.'

'You would not lunch with me at Sandwich,' he protested; 'and, after the humblest apology on my part, you won't forgive me for what I did this morning. Do you expect me to believe that I am not the special object of your antipathy? I wish I had never met with you! At my age, a man gets angry when he is treated cruelly and doesn't deserve it. You don't understand that, I dare say.'

'Oh yes, I do. I heard what you said about me to Mrs Fosdyke, and I heard you bang the door when you got out of my way.'

He received this reply with every appearance of satisfaction. 'So you listened, did you? I'm glad to hear that.'

'Why?'

'It shows you take some interest in me, after all.'

Throughout this frivolous talk (I only venture to report it because it shows that I bore no malice on my side) Miss Melbury was looking at us like the basilisk of the ancients. She owned to being on the wrong side of thirty; and she had a little money – but these were surely no reasons why she should glare at a poor governess. Had some secret understanding of the tender sort been already established between Mr Sax and herself? She provoked me into trying to find out – especially as the last words he had said offered me the opportunity.

'I can prove that I feel a sincere interest in you,' I resumed. 'I can resign you to a lady who has a far better claim to your attention than mine. You are neglecting her shamefully.'

He stared at me with an appearance of bewilderment, which seemed to imply that the attachment was on the lady's side, so far. It was of course impossible to mention names; I merely turned my eyes in the right direction. He looked where I looked – and his shyness revealed itself, in spite of his resolution to conceal it. His face flushed; he looked mortified and surprised. Miss Melbury could endure it no longer. She rose, took a song from the music-stand, and approached us.

'I am going to sing,' she said, handing the music to him. 'Please turn over for me, Mr Sax.'

I think he hesitated – but I cannot feel sure that I observed him correctly. It matters little. With or without hesitation, he followed her to the piano.

Miss Melbury sang – with perfect self-possession, and an immense compass of voice. A gentleman near me said she ought to be on the stage. I thought so too. Big as it was, our drawing-room was not large enough for her. The gentleman sang next. No voice at all – but so sweet, such true feeling! I turned over the leaves for him. A dear old lady, sitting near the piano, entered into conversation with me. She spoke of the great singers at the beginning of the present century. Mr Sax hovered about, with Miss Melbury's eye on him. I was so entranced by the anecdotes of my venerable friend, that I could take no notice of Mr Sax. Later, when the dinner-party was over, and we were retiring for the night, he still hovered about, and ended in offering me a bedroom candle. I immediately handed it to Miss Melbury. Really a most enjoyable evening!

VI

The next morning we were startled by an extraordinary proceeding on the part of one of the guests. Mr Sax had left Carsham Hall, by the first train – nobody knew why.

Nature has laid – so at least philosophers say – some heavy burdens upon women. Do those learned persons include in their list the burden of hysterics? If so, I cordially agree with them. It is hardly worth speaking of in my case – a constitutional outbreak in the solitude of my own room, treated with eau-de-cologne and water, and quite forgotten afterwards in the absorbing employment of education. My favourite pupil, Freddy, had been up earlier than the rest of us – breathing the morning air in the fruit-garden. He had seen Mr Sax and had asked when he was coming back again. And Mr Sax had said, 'I shall be back again next month.' (Dear little Freddy!)

In the meanwhile we, in the schoolroom, had the prospect before us of a dull time in an empty house. The remaining guests were to go away at the end of the week, their hostess being engaged to pay a visit to some old friends in Scotland.

During the next three or four days, though I was often alone with Mrs Fosdyke, she never said one word on the subject of Mr Sax. Once or twice I caught her looking at me with that unendurably significant smile of hers. Miss Melbury was equally unpleasant in another way. When we accidentally met on the stairs, her black eyes shot at me passing glances of hatred and scorn. Did these two ladies presume to think— ?

No; I abstained from completing that inquiry at the time, and I abstain from completing it here.

The end of the week came, and I and the children were left alone at Carsham Hall.

I took advantage of the leisure hours at my disposal to write to Sir Gervase; respectfully inquiring after his health, and informing him that I had been again most fortunate in my engagement as a governess. By return of post an answer arrived. I eagerly opened it. The first lines informed me of Sir Gervase Damian's death.

The letter dropped from my hand. I looked at my little enamelled cross. It is not for me to say what I felt. Think of all that I owed to him; and remember how lonely my lot was in the world. I gave the children a holiday; it was only the truth to tell them that I was not well.

How long an interval passed before I could call to mind that I had only read the first lines of the letter, I am not able to say. When I did take it up I was surprised to see that the writing covered two pages. Beginning again where I had left off, my head, in a moment more, began to swim. A horrid fear overpowered me that I might not be in my right mind, after I had read the first three sentences. Here they are, to answer for me that I exaggerate nothing:

'The will of our deceased client is not yet proved. But, with the sanction of the executors, I inform you confidentially that you are the person chiefly interested in it. Sir Gervase Damian bequeaths to you, absolutely, the whole of his personal property, amounting to the sum of seventy thousand pounds.'

If the letter had ended there, I really cannot imagine what extravagances I might not have committed. But the writer (head partner in the firm of Sir

Gervase's lawyers) had something more to say on his own behalf. The manner in which he said it strung up my nerves in an instant. I cannot, and will not, copy the words here. It is quite revolting enough to give the substance of them.

The man's object was evidently to let me perceive that he disapproved of the will. So far I do not complain of him – he had, no doubt, good reason for the view he took. But, in expressing his surprise 'at this extraordinary proof of the testator's interest in a perfect stranger to the family,' he hinted his suspicion of an influence, on my part, exercised over Sir Gervase, so utterly shameful, that I cannot dwell on the subject. The language, I should add, was cunningly guarded. Even I could see that it would bear more than one interpretation, and would thus put me in the wrong if I openly resented it. But the meaning was plain; and part at least of the motive came out in the following sentences:

'The present Sir Gervase, as you are doubtless aware, is not seriously affected by his father's will. He is already more liberally provided for, as heir under the entail to the whole of the landed property. But, to say nothing of old friends who are forgotten, there is a surviving relative of the late Sir Gervase passed over, who is nearly akin to him by blood. In the event of this person disputing the will, you will of course hear from us again, and refer us to your legal adviser.'

The letter ended with an apology for delay in writing to me, caused by difficulty in discovering my address.

And what did I do? – Write to the rector, or to Mrs Fosdyke, for advice? Not I!

At first I was too indignant to be able to think of what I ought to do. Our post-time was late, and my head ached as if it would burst into pieces. I had plenty of leisure to rest and compose myself. When I got cool again, I felt able to take my own part, without asking any one to help me.

Even if I had been treated kindly, I should certainly not have taken the money when there was a relative living with a claim to it. What did *I* want with a large fortune? To buy a husband with it, perhaps? No, no! from all that I have heard, the great Lord Chancellor was quite right when he said that a woman with money at her own disposal was 'either kissed out of it or kicked out of it, six weeks after her marriage.' The one difficulty before me was not to give up my legacy, but to express my reply with sufficient severity, and at the same time with due regard to my own self-respect. Here is what I wrote:

> Sir, – I will not trouble you by attempting to express my sorrow on hearing of Sir Gervase Damian's death. You would probably form your own opinion on that subject also; and I have no wish to be judged by your unenviable experience of humanity for the second time.
>
> With regard to the legacy, feeling the sincerest gratitude to my generous benefactor, I nevertheless refuse to receive the money.
>
> Be pleased to send me the necessary document to sign, for transferring my fortune to that relative of Sir Gervase mentioned in your letter. The one condition on which I insist is, that no expression of thanks shall be addressed to me by the person in whose favour I resign the money. I do not desire (even supposing that justice is done to my motives on this occasion) to be made the object of expressions of gratitude for only doing my duty.

So it ended. I may be wrong, but I call that strong writing.

In due course of post a formal acknowledgment arrived. I was requested to wait for the document until the will had been proved, and was informed that my name should be kept strictly secret in the interval. On this occasion, the executors were almost as insolent as the lawyer. They felt it their duty to give me time to reconsider a decision which had been evidently formed on impulse. Ah, how hard men are – at least, some of them! I locked up the acknowledgment in disgust, resolved to think no more of it until the time came for getting rid of my legacy. I kissed poor Sir Gervase's little keepsake. While I was still looking at it, the good children came in, of their own accord, to ask how I was. I was obliged to draw down the blind in my room, or they would have seen the tears in my eyes. For the first time since my mother's death, I felt the heartache. Perhaps the children made me think of the happier time when I was a child myself.

VII

The will had been proved, and I was informed that the document was in course of preparation, when Mrs Fosdyke returned from her visit to Scotland.

She thought me looking pale and worn.

'The time seems to me to have come,' she said, 'when I had better make you and Mr Sax understand each other. Have you been thinking penitently of your own bad behaviour?'

I felt myself blushing. I *had* been thinking of my conduct to Mr Sax – and I was heartily ashamed of it, too.

Mrs Fosdyke went on, half in jest, half in earnest.

'Consult your own sense of propriety!' she said. 'Was the poor man to blame for not being rude enough to say No, when a lady asked him to turn over her music? Could *he* help it, if the same lady persisted in flirting with him? He ran away from her the next morning. Did you deserve to be told why he left us? Certainly not – after the vixenish manner in which you handed the bedroom candle to Miss Melbury. You foolish girl! Do you think I couldn't see that you were in love with him? Thank Heaven, he's too poor to marry you, and take you away from my children, for some time to come. There will be a long marriage engagement, even if he is magnanimous enough to forgive you. Shall I ask Miss Melbury to come back with him?'

She took pity on me at last, and sat down to write to Mr Sax. His reply, dated from a country house some twenty miles distant, announced that he would be at Carsham Hall in three days' time.

On that third day the legal paper that I was to sign arrived by post. It was Sunday morning; I was alone in the schoolroom.

In writing to me, the lawyer had only alluded to 'a surviving relative of Sir Gervase, nearly akin to him by blood.' The document was more explicit. It described the relative as being a nephew of Sir Gervase, the son of his sister. The name followed.

It was Sextus Cyril Sax.

I have tried on three different sheets of paper to describe the effect which this discovery produced on me – and I have torn them up one after another. When I only think of it, my mind seems to fall back into the helpless surprise and confusion of that time. After all that had passed between us – the man himself being then on his way to the house! – what would he think of me when he saw my name at the bottom of the document? what, in Heaven's name, was I to do?

How long I sat petrified, with the document on my lap, I never knew. Somebody knocked at the schoolroom door, and looked in and said something, and went out again. Then there was an interval. Then the door was opened again. A hand was laid kindly on my shoulder. I looked up – and there was Mrs Fosdyke, asking, in the greatest alarm, what was the matter with me.

The tone of her voice roused me into speaking. I could think of nothing but Mr Sax; I could only say, 'Has he come?'

'Yes – and waiting to see you.'

Answering in those terms, she glanced at the paper in my lap. In the extremity of my helplessness, I acted like a sensible creature at last. I told Mrs Fosdyke all that I have told here.

She neither moved nor spoke until I had done. Her first proceeding, after that, was to take me in her arms and give me a kiss. Having so far encouraged me, she next spoke of poor Sir Gervase.

'We all acted like fools,' she announced, 'in needlessly offending him by protesting against his second marriage. I don't mean you – I mean his son, his nephew, and myself. If his second marriage made him happy, what business had we with the disparity of years between husband and wife? I can tell you this, Sextus was the first of us to regret what he had done. But for his stupid fear of being suspected of an interested motive, Sir Gervase might have known there was that much good in his sister's son.'

She snatched up a copy of the will, which I had not even noticed thus far.

'See what the kind old man says of you,' she went on, pointing to the words. I could not see them; she was obliged to read them for me. 'I leave my money to the one person living who has been more than worthy of the little I have done for her, and whose simple unselfish nature I know that I can trust.'

I pressed Mrs Fosdyke's hand; I was not able to speak. She took up the legal paper next.

'Do justice to yourself, and be above contemptible scruples,' she said. 'Sextus is fond enough of you to be almost worthy of the sacrifice that you are making. Sign – and I will sign next as the witness.'

I hesitated.

'What will he think of me?' I said.

'Sign!' she repeated, 'and we will see to that.'

I obeyed. She asked for the lawyer's letter. I gave it to her, with the lines which contained the man's vile insinuation folded down, so that only the words above were visible, which proved that I had renounced my legacy, not even knowing whether the person to be benefited was a man or a woman. She took this, with the rough draft of my own letter, and the signed renunciation – and opened the door.

'Pray come back, and tell me about it!' I pleaded.

She smiled, nodded, and went out.

Oh, what a long time passed before I heard the long-expected knock at the door! 'Come in,' I cried impatiently.

Mrs Fosdyke had deceived me. Mr Sax had returned in her place. He closed the door. We two were alone.

He was deadly pale; his eyes, as they rested on me, had a wild startled look. With icy cold fingers he took my hand, and lifted it in silence to his lips. The sight of his agitation encouraged me – I don't to this day know why, unless it appealed in some way to my compassion. I was bold enough to look at him. Still silent, he placed the letters on the table – and then he laid the signed paper beside them. When I saw that, I was bolder still. I spoke first.

'Surely you don't refuse me?' I said.

He answered, 'I thank you with my whole heart; I admire you more than words can say. But I can't take it.'

'Why not?'

'The fortune is yours,' he said gently. 'Remember how poor I am, and feel for me if I say no more.'

His head sank on his breast. He stretched out one hand, silently imploring me to understand him. I could endure it no longer. I forgot every consideration which a woman, in my position, ought to have remembered. Out came the desperate words, before I could stop them.

'You won't take my gift by itself?' I said.

'No.'

'Will you take Me with it?'

That evening, Mrs Fosdyke indulged her sly sense of humour in a new way. She handed me an almanack.

'After all, my dear,' she remarked, 'you needn't be ashamed of having spoken first. You have only used the ancient privilege of the sex. This is Leap Year.'

Fie! Fie! or, the Fair Physician

First published simultaneously in *The Spirit of the Times* and *The Pictorial World Christmas Supplement* on 23 December 1882. The story appeared subsequently in *The Seaside Library* on 5 April 1883. This is one of the stories Collins did not want reprinted after his death. It was never collected in book-form. With its smug medical jokes about the hero's 'overburdened heart' as Dr Sillico plies the stethoscope, the story comes over today as a glibly anti-feminist piece, demonstrating that Collins may have championed the rights of female casualties of tyrannic marriage laws or sexual double standards, but he was not about to campaign for their admission into the ancient male professions. For an equally unsympathetic portrait of a lady doctor (PhD, not MD), see the alarming Miss Olivia Q. Fleabody in Trollope's *Is He Popenjoy?* (1878); for a more sympathetic portrait the drily humorous Dr Mary J. Prance in Henry James's *The Bostonians* (1886). Catherine Peters points out that 'one of Collins's last letters to Andrew Chatto complained of "a German *Female* Doctor" who wanted to translate *Heart and Science*: "I felt inclined to . . . tell her to 'go to hell". But even when a woman is a doctor, she is a woman still' (*The King of Inventors*, p. 425).

I

On Christmas Eve, Mrs Crossmichael made an interesting announcement in her family circle. She said, 'I am positively determined to write an account of it; I shall furnish the raw material, and an editor shall manufacture the narrative.'

Whatever is said of Mrs Crossmichael's family in these pages must be said from Mrs Crossmichael's point of view. The Editor would prefer his own point of view; but he knows his lady, and uses his pen cautiously when he mentions her father, her mother, and her unmarried sister. A profound scholar and a handsome old man; a venerable lady with grand remains of beauty; a sweet girl, who is also an accomplished musician – named respectively Reverend and Mrs Skirton, and Miss Salome Skirton – comprise the audience addressed by Mrs Crossmichael, when she expressed her resolution to produce the present narrative.

'My mind being quite made up,' she said, 'I am now ready to hear what you think of it.' Her husband came in at the moment; but she took no notice of him.

Mrs Skirton smiled over her knitting, and made no remark. In the cases of some rare persons, silent smiles have a meaning of their own: Mrs Skirton's smile meant gentle encouragement. Reverend Mr Skirton expressed himself in words. 'Have it privately printed, my dear, and it cannot fail to be productive of advantage to others.' Miss Salome modestly exhibited her father's view in detail. 'It will be productive,' she said 'of a warning to young ladies.' Nobody consulted Mr Crossmichael, sitting modestly in a corner. Like the present Editor (but with infinitely superior opportunities), he knew his lady, and he kept his opinions to himself. Had he not promised at the altar (as Mrs Crossmichael frequently reminded him) to love, honour, and obey his wife? They were the happiest married couple in all England.

Venerable and learned and charming as they were, the family had failed, nevertheless, to penetrate the object which Mrs Crossmichael had in view. It was not to please her excellent mother; it was not to 'prove of advantage to others;' it was not to 'offer a warning to young ladies,' that she had determined to take up her pen. Her one motive for favouring the Editor with his 'raw material' shall be stated in the lady's own words:—

'I hate her.'

Who was she? And why did Mrs Crossmichael hate her?

Here, again, the expressive brevity of 'the raw material' may be quoted with advantage. The instructions run as follows: 'Say the worst you can of her at starting; and condemn her unheard by means of her own visiting card.'

Here it is:

Sophia Pillico, M.D.

Is M.D. sufficiently intelligible? Let no hasty persons answer, 'Of course!' There are full-grown inhabitants of the civilised universe who have never heard of Julius Cæsar, Oliver Cromwell, or Napoleon the Great. There may be other inhabitants, who are not aware that we have invented fair physicians in these latter days. M.D. (let it be known to these benighted brethren) means that Sophia has passed her examination, and has taken her Doctor's degree. Mrs Crossmichael is further willing to admit that Miss Pillico is sufficiently young, and – we all know there is no accounting for tastes – passably pretty. (NOTE, attached to the instructions: 'We are not on oath, and we may be allowed our own merciful little reserves. Never mind her figure – oh dear no, never mind her figure: Men-doctors get on very well with clumsy legs and no waists. Why should women doctors not do the same? Equal justice to the two sexes, Sophia, was the subject of your last lecture – I was present, and heard you say it!')

The second question still remains unanswered. Why did Mrs Crossmichael hate her?

For three good reasons. Because she delivered lectures on the rights of women in our Assembly Room. Because she set herself up in medical practice, in our south-eastern suburb of London, and within five minutes walk of our house. Because she became acquainted with our next-door neighbours, and took advantage of that circumstance to behave in the most abominable manner to my sister Salome. The Editor can bear witness to this. (He bears witness with pleasure.) The Editor can describe our next-door neighbours. (No: he is not sufficiently well acquainted with them. He knows a lady who can take the story, at the present stage of it, out of his hands – and to that lady he makes his bow, and offers his pen.)

Mrs Crossmichael abhors flattery, and considers descriptions to be the bane of literature. If she is to accept the pen, it must be on one condition. The next-door neighbours shall describe themselves.

II

Our suburb possesses the most convenient detached houses in all England. The gardens are worthy of the houses – and the rents are frightful. A sudden death, and an executor in a hurry, offered the lease of the next house a bargain. Alderman Sir John Dowager took it on speculation, and is waiting to dispose of it on his own outrageous terms. In the meantime, he and his family occupy the premises. Sir John is stingy; his wife is deaf; his daughter is sour, his son is sulky. The one other member of this detestable family is an interesting exception to the rest: he is Lady Dowager's son, by her first husband. Let this gentleman wait a little while, and be introduced presently by himself.

Our new neighbours took possession during an excessively hot summer. On the first day, they were occupied in settling themselves in their house. On the second day, they enjoyed their garden. We were sitting on our lawn; and they were sitting on their lawn. In consideration of Lady Dowager's deafness, they talked loud enough (especially the daughter, Miss Bess, and the son, Young John) to be heard all over our grounds. This said, let them describe their own characters in an extract from their conversation. I am the reporter. And I own I peeped over the wall.

Stingy Sir John. – I gave orders, my dear, about those two pieces of bread that were left yesterday; and I find nobody can give any account of them. Is this the manner in which I am to be treated by my own servants?

Deaf Lady Dowager (addressing her daughter). – What does your papa say, Bess?

Sour Bess. – Pa's abusing the servants; and all about two bits of bread.

Sir John. – I'll thank you, miss, not to misrepresent me to my own face. You do it on purpose.

Sulky Young John. – She does everything on purpose.

Miss Bess. – That's a lie.

Lady Dowager. – What is it? I can't hear. What is it?

Sir John. – My dear, your deafness is certainly growing on you.

Young John. – And a good thing too, in such a family as ours.

Sir John. – That is a most improper observation to make.

Miss Bess. – He looked at me when he made it.

Lady Dowager. – Who's speaking now? Bess! what *is* the matter?

Miss Bess. – Papa and John are quarrelling with me as usual.

Sir John. – How dare you speak in that way of your father? Over and over again, Miss Elizabeth, I have had occasion to remark—

Young John. – It's a perfect misery to live in the same house with her.

Sir John. – What do you mean, sir, by interrupting me?

Lady Dowager. – I think it's rather hard on *me* that nobody speaks loud enough to be heard. I shall go into the house.

Sir John (looking after his wife). – Her temper gets more irritable every day.

Bess (looking at Young John ⎫
Young John (looking at Bess ⎭ No wonder!

There are our next-door neighbours presented by themselves. Why do I introduce such people into these pages? Alas! I am not able to keep them out. They are mixed up, by the inscrutable decrees of Providence, with Sophia Pillico's wickedness, and with my sister Salome's dearest hopes in life. Does my sister's Christian name sound disagreeably? Let me mention the associations; and no reasonable person will object to it. She was called Salome, and I was called Lois, after my father's two maiden sisters. Excellent women! They lived in the West of England – they left us their money – and they went to Heaven. (Instructions to the Editor: Now go on.)

III

The Editor introduces Mr and Mrs Wholebrook; directors of the famous Hydropathic Establishment at Cosgrove.

As man and wife, they were naturally accustomed to talk over the affairs of the day, in bed. The affairs of the day, in their case, meant the incoming and outgoing patients. One night, they held an especially interesting conversation. Both agreed – they had not been very long married – in lamenting the departure of a retiring member of the household; registered in the books by the odd name of, 'Otto Fitzmark.'

'Why should he leave us?' Mr Wholebrook asked. 'He has not gone through the cure; and, when I inquired if he had any complaint to make, he spoke in the most gratifying manner of the comfort of the house, and the excellence of the cooking.'

'My dear, if you knew him as well as I do—'

'What do you mean, Louisa? Has Mr Fitzmark been— ?'

'Don't be a fool, James. Mr Fitzmark is a ladies' man; young and handsome, and in delicate health. He likes to confide in women, poor fellow; especially when they happen to be – there! that will do; I forgive you: don't interrupt me again. And understand this: I, who am in Mr Otto's confidence, expected him to say he was going back to London, at least a week since.'

'Is it business, my dear?'

'Business! Mr Fitzmark has absolutely nothing to do. His valet is a treasure; and he has a comfortable income left him by his father.'

'His father was a foreigner, wasn't he?'

'Good Heavens! what has that got to do with it?'

'I only spoke. If I am to be taken up short because I only speak, we'll say good night.'

'Don't be angry, darling! Won't you forgive me? won't you? won't you?'

'What were we talking about, dear?'

'What, indeed! Wasn't it Mr Fitzmark's father? You were quite right about him: he was a sort of half foreigner. He settled in England, and married an Englishwoman; she led him a horrid life. Mr Otto – you don't mind my calling him by his Christian name? I like manly men, James, like you; I only pity Mr Otto. Always delicate, brought up at home, indulged in everything. His stupid mother married again; and he didn't get on with the new family; and he had a private tutor; and he and the tutor went abroad; and there he had it all his own way, and was flattered by everybody. Are you going to sleep, dear?'

'No! No!'

'You see I want you to understand that Mr Otto has his whim and caprices – and soon gets tired when the novelty of a thing wears off. But, there's another reason for his leaving our place; there's a lady in the case. He hasn't mentioned her name to me: she lives in London or in the neighbourhood, I'm not sure which. Plays divinely on the piano, and is lovely and elegant, and all that. He hasn't openly avowed his admiration – not having made up his mind yet about her family. She has a married sister, who rather frightens him; clever, and a will of her own, and so on. However, to come to the point, his main reason for trying our place – What? his main reason must be his health? Nothing of the sort, you dear simple creature! He never expects to be well again. Not that he disbelieves in the cold water cure; but what he really wanted was to try if absence from the young lady would weaken the impression – or, as he put it, rather funnily, if deluges of cold water could drown his memory of a charming girl. She's not to be disposed of, James, in that way. Wet sheets won't pack her out; and ten tumblers of cold water a day only make her more lively than ever. Well, it's past a joke; he is really going back to her to-morrow. Love – ah, We know it, don't we? – love is a wonderful thing! What? Asleep? He *is* asleep. Snoring, positively snoring. And kicking me. Brute! brute!'

IV

Mr Otto Fitzmark reached London, late in the evening.

He was so fatigued by the journey, that he went straight to the rooms prepared for him in Sir John's house. On those occasions when he visited his mother, his step-father arranged – with the absolute shamelessness peculiar to misers – to receive compensation privately for trouble and expense. When Lady Dowager sometimes complained that her son treated the house as if it were an hotel, she little thought what a defence of his conduct lay hidden in Sir John's guilty pocket.

The next morning, the valet – a grave, ponderous, and respectable English servant – came in with the coffee and the news, as usual.

'I have had a wretched night, Frederick. Sir John must have got this beastly bed a bargain. What's the news? The last time I was here I was driven away by a row in the family. Any more quarrels this time?'

'The worst row I remember, sir (if I may be allowed to say so), in all our experience,' Frederick answered.

'Is my mother in it?'

'It's said to be Lady Dowager's doing, sir.'

'The devil it is! Give me some more sugar. Did you make this coffee yourself?'

'Certainly, sir.'

'Go to the place in Piccadilly, and buy something that really is coffee: this is muck. Well? what's the new row about?'

'About a woman, sir.'

'You don't mean to say Sir John—'

'I beg your pardon, sir, I ought to have expressed myself more correctly. The woman in question is a She-Doctor.'

'No wonder there's a row! The fair physician is a bony old wretch with a wig and spectacles, of course?'

'That's not the account given to me, sir, by the footman. Except Miss Salome, next door, Sir John's man says she's the prettiest young woman he's seen for many a long day past.'

Otto stared at the valet in astonishment. Frederick went steadily on with his story.

'The lady has lately set up in practice, in this neighbourhood. And, what with her good looks and her lectures, she's turned the people's heads hereabouts, already. The resident medical man has got a red nose, and is suspected of drinking. He's losing his lady-patients as fast as he can. They say Miss Pillico—'

'Miss – who?'

'The lady's name, sir, is Miss Sophia Pillico.'

'I pity Sophia with all my heart. The sooner she changes her name the better.'

'That's the joke among the women downstairs, sir. I was about to say that Miss Pillico is not content to doctor her own sex only. She considers it a part of the Rights of Women to doctor the men; and she has begun with Sir John—'

Here Frederick incomprehensibly checked himself, and prepared for shaving his master by sharpening the razor.

'Why don't you go on?' said Otto. 'Sophia means to doctor the men; and she's beginning with Sir John—'

He suddenly checked himself, and started up in the bed. His next question seemed to burst out of him irrepressibly. 'You don't mean to say, Frederick, that my mother is jealous?'

The valet, still sharpening the razor, looked up. 'That's the row, sir,' he answered as gravely as ever.

Otto fell back on the bed, and pulled the clothes over his face. Deaf Lady Dowager owned to having arrived at sixty years of age. Sir John's biography (in the past time when he had been Lord Mayor of London) fixed the date of his birth at a period of seventy-four years since. The bedclothes heaved, and the bed shook; violent emotion of some kind was overwhelming Lady Dowager's son. Not the ghost of a smile – though he was at liberty to indulge his sense of humour as things were now – appeared on the wooden face of Frederick. He laid out his shaving materials, and waited until Mr Fitzmark's beard was ready for him.

Otto rose again above the horizon of the bedclothes. He looked completely exhausted – but that was all. The altar of appearances, waiting for the sacrifice, claimed and received the necessary recognition. Having first got out of bed – by way of separating himself from irreverent associations possibly lurking in the mind of his valet – Otto posed, as the French say, in an attitude of severe propriety.

'Drop the subject,' he said.

Frederick gently lathered his master's chin, and answered, 'Just so, sir.'

V

Otto breakfasted in his own room.

His mother's maid brought word that her ladyship was ill in bed, with a sick headache: she would see Mr Fitzmark towards luncheon time. The valet not being present to draw his own conclusions, Otto privately extracted information from the maid. Miss Doctor Pillico would professionally visit Sir John, at her usual hour – two o'clock. And in what part of the house would Sir John receive her? He looked at himself in the glass when he put that question. The maid began to understand the nature of his interest in the medical young woman. She took the liberty of smiling, and answered, 'In the library, sir.'

Towards two o'clock, Otto called for his hat and cane, and said he would take a turn in the garden.

Before he went downstairs he once more surveyed himself in the glass. Yes: he could not have been more becomingly dressed – and he looked, in his own delicate way, surprisingly well. His auburn hair and whiskers; his fair complexion; his sensitive mouth, and his long white hands were in perfect order. In the garden he met Young John, sulkily smoking.

'How is Bess?' he asked indulgently. Young John answered, 'I don't know; I've not been on speaking terms with my sister since yesterday.' 'And how is your father?' Young John answered, 'I don't care. He told me last week I was a sulky lout, and he has not apologised yet; I don't speak to *him*, either.' Otto left his half-brother, cordially agreeing with his half-brother's father.

The library opened, by means of French windows, on the terrace. He picked a flower for his button-hole, and sauntered that way. The windows being open, he entered the room in a genial impulsive manner. 'Ha, Sir John, how are you? Oh, I beg your pardon!'

Sir John was seated bolt upright in his chair, looking at vacancy, and drawing in and puffing out his breath in a highly elaborate manner. A finely-developed young woman, with brown hair and eyes, and warm rosy cheeks, dressed to perfection in a style of severe simplicity, was sitting close by him. Her arm was round his neck, and her ear was at his breast. So absorbed was this charming creature in listening, that she held up a pretty plump little hand, in mute entreaty for silence. 'Yes,' she said, in clear, positive tones, 'you confirm my diagnosis, Sir John; I persist in saying that your medical attendant has mistaken the case.' Her bright resolute eyes, turning towards Otto, softened as they rested on his beautiful hair and his sensitive lips: a little increase of colour deepened the delicately ruddy tint of her cheeks. 'Pray excuse me,' she resumed, with a captivating smile; 'I am, in a professional point of view, naturally interested in Sir John. His life is public property: if I make any mistake here, I disgrace myself – and my cause! – in the eyes of the nation.' Otto's countenance preserved a gravity worthy of his valet. 'Permit me to introduce myself,' he said, 'before I renew my apologies. I am Sir John's step-son, Otto Fitzmark.' The charming Doctor bowed with a look of modest interest. Sir John did what he had done from the first – he sat in solemn silence, looking foolish. It was not everybody who remembered that he had once been Lord Mayor of London, and who attended to him as a famous personage. It was also the first occasion (for at least forty years past) on which he had felt the arm of a handsome young woman round his neck, and the head of a handsome young woman on his breast. Add that the fair physician had said, on the first day of her attendance, 'It is a rule of mine never to accept fees from public characters' – and the catalogue of Sir John's overwhelming emotions will be complete.

'I can only atone for my intrusion in one way,' Otto proceeded. 'Permit me to hope for an early opportunity of improving our acquaintance – and to return to the garden.'

'Not on *my* account, Mr Fitzmark! In any other case, my visit would be at an end. But I am perhaps morbidly anxious to "make assurance doubly sure" (the words of Shakespeare, I think?) in the case of Sir John. Besides, I have the prejudice of the world against me; always on the look-out for an opportunity of asserting that a woman is not fit to be a doctor.'

This seemed to be the right place for a burst of enthusiasm: Otto did it with perfect tact and dexterity. 'Miss Pillico, I sincerely sympathise with you in the battle you are fighting against ignorance and stupidity. The Woman-Movement, in all its departments, has my heartfelt admiration and good wishes!' His heavenly blue eyes became irresistible as this expression of generous feeling escaped him.

Sophia was too proud and too grateful to be able to reply in words. She rewarded the friend of the Women by a look – and turned with a sigh to business and Sir John.

'May I try once more before I write my prescription?' she asked. 'No, my dear sir, your back this time. Lean well forward – so – and now draw a long breath.' Her pretty hand grasped his shoulder, and her little rosy ear pressed (medically pressed) Sir John's broad back.

At this interesting moment the library door opened. Lady Dowager appeared – and paused indignantly on the threshold. Otto advanced to salute his mother. Her ladyship waved him back with one hand, and pointed to the Doctor and the patient with the other. Sir John visibly trembled. Sophia kept her ear at his back as composedly as if nothing had happened.

'Look at her!' said Lady Dowager, addressing Otto in the muffled monotonous tones peculiar to the deaf. 'Hugging my husband before my face – and he seventy-four years old, last birthday. You unnatural hussy, let go of him. *You* a doctor indeed? I know what you are. Fie! fie!'

'My dear mother!'

'I can't hear you, Otto.'

'My dear mother!'

'Yes, yes; I'll kiss you directly. Look at that old fool, your step-father! *He* a knight; *he* an alderman? Ha! ha! a nasty, mangy, rusty old Tom-cat. I won't live with him any longer. You're a witness, Otto – you see what's going on in that chair – I'll have a divorce. Ha! look at her hair,' said Lady Dowager, as Sir John's physician quietly lifted her head from Sir John's back – 'look at her hair, all rumpled with her horrid passions. I blush for my sex. Fie, Miss Pillico – fie!'

Sophia sat down at the desk, and wrote her prescription. 'Two tablespoon-fuls, Sir John, by measure glass, three times in the twenty-four hours. Your lungs are as sound as mine. Suppressed gout – that's what is the matter with you – suppressed gout.'

She put on her bonnet (laid aside in the interests of auscultation), and held out her hand to Otto, with modest frankness. 'A friend to my cause, Mr

Fitzmark, is *my* friend. Your excellent mother,' she continued, encountering the furious eyes of Lady Dowager with a little pleasant smile, 'is naturally prejudiced against me. Early education – on the narrow stand-point of fifty years since – has much to answer for. I am sorry to have made this excellent lady angry; and I heartily forgive the hard words she has said to me. On the day after to-morrow, Sir John, I will look in, and see what my prescription has done for you. Thank you, Mr Fitzmark, I have no carriage to call; I am not rich enough to keep a carriage. Besides, my next visit is only next door. Ah, you know the Skirtons? The daughter is indeed a sweet girl. And the dear old father,' Miss Pillico added, demurely announcing the medical conquest of another elderly gentleman, 'is my patient. Neuralgia, ignorantly treated as pure rheumatism. Good morning, my lady.'

She bowed respectfully to the formidable enemy of the Rights of Women – posted at the doorway, and following her with glaring eyes as she glided out.

'Ha! she's going to the other old fool now,' said Lady Dowager. 'Susannah and the Elders! Do you hear, Miss Pillico? I call you Susannah and the Elders!' She turned to her guilty husband (rising to retreat), with a look which threw him back into his chair. '*Now*, Sir John!'

Otto was too wise to remain in the room. He slipped into the garden.

After taking a turn or two, reflection convinced him that it was his duty to pay a visit next door. He had an opportunity of comparing two different orders of beauty, as represented by Sophia and Salome, which it would be injudicious on his part to neglect. A man of his tastes would be naturally interested in comparing the two girls together. At the same time, he had not ceased to feel the attraction that had lured him back to London: he was true to his young lady. When he entered Mr Skirton's house, it was with a loyal conviction that Salome's superiority would be proved by comparison.

VI

In ten days' time events had made a great advance. Miss Pillico's patients felt the powerful influence of Miss Pillico's treatment. Sir John's improved health bore witness to the capacity of his new doctor; Mr Skirton was well enough to give a small musical party at his house; Mr Otto Fitzmark, false to Mrs Wholebrook and Hydropathy, was entered triumphantly on Miss Pillico's sick list. Last, but by no means least, Lady Dowager had anticipated her divorce by retiring to the seaside.

The case of Mr Fitzmark was not sufficiently formidable, in the opinion of his new physician, to seclude him from the pleasures of Society. He was allowed to accept an invitation to Mr and Mrs Skirton's musical entertainment – and, by a happy combination of circumstances, he and his medical adviser entered the drawing-room together.

The primitive little party began at eight o'clock. By half-past eleven, the guests had retired, the master and mistress of the house had gone to bed – and Mr and Mrs Crossmichael and Salome were left together in an empty room.

Mrs Crossmichael issued her orders to her husband. 'Go to the club, and return in half-an-hour. You needn't come in again. Wait for me in the cab.'

The one person in the way having been disposed of, the conference between the sisters began.

'Now, Salome, we can have a little talk. You have been wretchedly out of spirits all the evening.'

'You would have been out of spirits, Lois, in my place, if you had seen them come into the room together as if they were man and wife already!'

'Aggravating,' Mrs Crossmichael admitted; 'but you might have controlled yourself when you went to the piano; I never heard you play so badly. Let us get back to Mr Fitzmark. My opinion of him doesn't matter – I may, and do, think him a poor effeminate creature, quite unworthy of such a girl as you are. The question is, what do *you* think? Are you, or are you not, seriously in love with him?'

'I know it's weak of me,' Salome answered piteously; 'and I haven't got any reasons to give. Oh, Lois, I do love him!'

'Stop!' said Mrs Crossmichael. 'If you begin to cry, I leave you to your fate. Stop it! stop it! I won't have your eyes dim; I won't have your nose red. I want your eyes, and I want your nose, for my argument.'

This extraordinary announcement effectually controlled the flow of Salome's tears.

'Now look at me,' the resolute lady resumed. 'Yes, you will do. You see the glass, at the other end of the room. Go, and look at yourself. I mean what I say. Go!'

Salome obeyed, and contemplated the style of beauty, immortalised by Byron in one line: 'A kind of sleepy Venus was Dudu.' The glass drew a pretty picture, presenting soft drowsy languishing grey eyes – plentiful hair, bright with the true golden colour, as distinguished from the hideous counterfeit – a pure pale complexion, a mild smile, and a weak little chin, made to be fondled and kissed. A more complete contrast to the brown and brisk beauty of Sophia Pillico could not have been found, through the whole range of female humanity.

'Well,' said Mrs Crossmichael, 'are you quite satisfied that you have no reason to be afraid of Sophia, on personal grounds? Yes! yes! I know it's *his* opinion that is of importance to us – but I want you to be confident. Sophia is confident; and humility is thrown away upon the molly-coddle who has taken your foolish fancy. Come, and sit down by me. There was a fat guest in my way, when Mr Fitzmark said good night. Did he squeeze your hand; and did he look at you – like this?'

Mrs Crossmichael's eyes assumed an amorous expression.

Salome blushed, and said, 'Yes, he did.'

'Now another question. When you got up from the piano (Chopin would have twisted your neck, and you would have deserved it, for murdering his music) Mr Fitzmark followed you into a corner. I saw that he was tender and confidential – did he come to the point? How stupid you are, Salome! Did he make a proposal?'

'Not exactly, in words, dear. But if you had seen how he looked at me—'

'Nonsense! He must be made to speak out – and I will help you to do it. I want a perfect bonnet for the flower-show next month; and I have ordered my husband to take me to Paris. For your sake, I will put if off for a week; and we will come and stay here, instead – so that I may be ready on the spot for anything that happens. No; you needn't kiss me – you will do infinitely better if you listen to what I have to say. I have been carefully watching Sophia and your young man, and I have arrived at the conclusion that his doctor is certainly in love with him. (Haven't I told you to listen? Then why don't you let me go on?) I am equally certain, Salome, that he is not in love with her. (*Will* you listen?) But she flatters his conceit – and many a woman has caught her man in that way. Besides this danger, she has one terrible advantage over you: she is his doctor. And she has had the devil's own luck – I am too excited to choose my language – with papa and Sir John. Otto is disposed to believe in her; and papa and that wretched Alderman just get well enough to encourage him. Did you notice, at supper, that she ordered him to take this, and forbade him to take that – and treated the poor creature like a child? Oh, I can tell you, we have no time to lose!'

'What are we to do, Lois?'

'*Will* you listen? This is the second of the month. Give my love to the dear old people upstairs, and say that we must have another party, a garden-party, on the fifth. It is the safest way of getting at Pillico. If I call on her, she's quite sharp enough to suspect that I have a reason for it. What's the matter now?'

Salome looked towards the door. 'Don't I hear the cab? Oh, dear, your husband has come back already!'

'Haven't I told him to wait? They say marriage strengthens girls' minds – and I sincerely hope they are right! In all probability Mr Fitzmark will call to-morrow, to make polite inquiries. You must not be at home. What do you mean by saying, "Oh!" If you don't take my advice, I shall go to Paris.'

'I beg your pardon, Lois: I'll do whatever you tell me.'

Mrs Crossmichael rose, and rang for her cloak. 'There's one thing more you must do – provoke his jealousy. The mother of that other young fellow who is dangling after you is just the person you want for the purpose. I heard her ask you to fix a day for visiting them at Windsor. You promised to write. Write to-morrow; and propose the day after, for your visit – returning the next morning, of course, for the garden-party. Leave word where you have gone, when the beautiful Otto calls again. In the language of Miss Pillico, my dear, he wants a stimulant. I know what I am about. Good night.'

VII

Mr Fitzmark called the next day, as Mrs Crossmichael had anticipated, and returned to his quarters at Sir John's a disappointed man. An hour later his doctor arrived, and found him in the garden, consoling himself with a cigarette. She took it out of his mouth with a fascinating familiarity, and threw it away.

'I find I must speak seriously, Mr Fitzmark. There's nobody in the garden. Suppose we sit down in the summer-house?'

They took their chairs, and Miss Pillico produced her stethoscope.

'Open your waistcoat, please. Thank you – that will do.' She used her stethoscope, and then she used her ear; and then she took his hand. Not to press it! Only to put him into the right position to have his pulse felt. 'I have already told you that there is really no danger,' she said. 'The action of your heart is irregular – and I find I have underrated the necessity of taking certain precautions. But I have no doubt of being able to restore you to health, if –' she let go of his hand, and looked at him tenderly – 'if you will believe in your doctor, and do your best to help me.'

Otto only waited for his instructions. 'I am careful about my diet,' he said; 'I never hurry myself in going upstairs; and, now I know you object to it, I won't smoke. Is there anything more?'

'One thing more,' said Sophia softly. 'After what I saw last night, I cannot conceal from myself that Society is bad for you. You were excited – oh, you were! Your doctor thought of your heart, and had her eye on you when you were talking to that lovely girl. Of course you are invited to the garden-party? Do me a favour (in my medical capacity) – help your poor heart; write an excuse.'

Otto consented, not very willingly, to make a sacrifice to the necessities, as distinguished from the inclinations, of his heart. Sophia's pretty brown eyes stole a look at him – a gentle, appealing look. 'I am afraid you hate me for keeping you away from Miss Salome,' she said.

This demand on Otto's gallantry only admitted of one reply. 'Miss Pillico, the man doesn't live who could hate you.'

The Doctor blushed. 'I wonder whether I may put a bold question,' she murmured – 'entirely in the interest of your health?' She hesitated, and toyed confusedly with her stethoscope. 'I hardly know how to put it. Pray remember what I have already told you about your heart! Pleasurable excitement is just as bad for it as painful excitement. Bear that in mind, and let me suppose something quite likely – an event in which all your friends must feel the deepest interest. Let me suppose (professionally) that you are going to be married.'

Otto denied it, without stopping to think first. The effect he produced on Miss Pillico rather alarmed him. She clasped her hands, and exclaimed fervently, 'What a relief!'

She was a strong-minded woman, and she followed a man's profession. Would she take a man's privilege, and make him an offer of marriage? Otto's weak heart began to flutter. Sophia still played with her stethoscope.

'I was thinking of my medical responsibility,' she explained. 'Please let me listen again.'

Otto submitted. There was prolonged examination. 'Yes,' she said, 'under present conditions there can be no doubt of it. You mustn't! Indeed, you mustn't!'

'Mustn't – what?' Otto asked.

'Marry!' Miss Pillico answered sternly.

'Never?' Otto persisted, piteously.

Sophia informed him that it depended on the treatment. 'What I have said to you,' she proceeded, not unmindful of the future in her own interests, 'refers to the present time. If you had been engaged to marry some young lady, for instance, I should have said, Put it off. Or, if you only contemplated such a thing, I should say, Pause. In one word, we have an interval to pass: long or short, is more than I can yet tell.' She rose, and laid her hand persuasively on his arm. 'Pray be regular with your medicine,' she pleaded; 'and let me know directly if you feel any change in your heart.' They passed a flower-bed on their way back to the house. Miss Pillico admired the roses. Otto instantly presented her with a rose. She put it in her bosom – and sighed – and gave him a farewell look. For the first time he left the look unreturned. He had accidentally picked the rose which bore Salome's favourite colour – he was thinking of the grey-eyed girl with the golden hair. Before Sophia could win back his attention to herself, Young John, with his pipe in his mouth, appeared at a turn in the path. The Doctor took her leave in depressed spirits.

Otto hesitated about giving up the garden-party. It was only on the next day that he decided on staying at home. He wrote his excuses to Salome.

In the meanwhile Young John advanced lazily towards the summer-house, and discovered his sister in ambush at the back of the building. Sour Bess was in such a state of excitement that she actually forgot her quarrel with her brother. 'I've heard every word they said to each other!' she burst out. 'That hateful wretch is sweet on Otto, and means to make him marry her. Oh, Johnny! how can I stop it? Who can I speak to first?'

Young John's sympathy with his sister – when she happened to be in an especially malicious mood – expressed itself in a broad grin. United by their mutual interest in making mischief, these amiable young people met, in reconciliation, on common ground. 'It's no use speaking to Otto,' Johnny remarked, 'he's such a fool. And, as for my father, he'd sooner believe Pillico than either of us. The girl next door is fond of Otto. How would it be if you told her?'

Bess refused even to consider the suggestion. 'No,' she said; 'it might be doing a service to Salome, and we are not on speaking terms.'

Young John, under these circumstances, counselled patience. 'Don't throw away a good chance, Bess, by being in a hurry. It won't hurt to wait for the Skirton's garden-party. Miss Pillico will be there; she'll give you another opportunity.'

Bess was struck by this last suggestion. 'I didn't intend to go to the party,' she said. 'You're quite right; I'll accept the invitation.'

VIII

The servant who had delivered Otto's written excuses came back with a message. His letter would be given to Miss Salome on her return from Windsor.

This announcement at once proved Mrs Crossmichael's calculations to be correct. Otto was at no loss to interpret the meaning of Salome's absence at Windsor. She was visiting the mother of his rival, at a time when her son was staying in the house. In other words, she was indirectly encouraging a man who was reported to have already made her an unsuccessful offer of marriage, and to be prepared to try again. Otto sent the servant back to ascertain the exact time at which Miss Salome was expected to return. The reply informed him that she was to travel by an early train, and that she would be at home on the morning of the garden-party by twelve o'clock. A second letter was thereupon despatched, asking for an interview soon after that time. Jealousy had determined Otto to take the gloomiest view of the state of his heart. Instead of asking Salome to make loving allowance for the formidable revelations of the stethoscope, he proposed to retire from the field in favour of the 'fortunate gentleman whom she preferred.' Such was the vindictive feeling with which this otherwise inoffensive young man regarded his sweetheart's visit to Windsor; and so had Mrs Crossmichael's clever calculations defeated themselves.

At two o'clock on the day of the party, Salome's devoted sister performed her promise.

She and her husband arrived, to occupy the room which was always reserved for them in Mr Skirton's house. Asking at once for her sister, she was informed that Salome was behaving very strangely; she had locked herself up in her room, and would open the door to nobody. Mrs Crossmichael applied for admission, with the energy peculiar to herself. 'You know that my husband invariably obeys my orders, and that he is one of the biggest men in England. If you don't let me in, I shall call him up, and say, Burst open that door.' Salome gave way. Her eyes were red, her cheeks were stained with tears. 'You're the worst enemy I have!' she cried passionately, as her sister entered the room; 'I'll never forgive you for sending me to Windsor.'

'A row with Otto?' Mrs Crossmichael asked quietly.

'Otto has given me up! Otto leaves the other man (whom I hate and detest) free to marry me! That's what comes of taking your advice.'

Mrs Crossmichael preserved her temper. 'Had he any other reason to give,' she continued, 'besides jealousy of the other man? If that was his only motive, you will have reason to be grateful to me, Salome, as long as you live.'

'He *had* another reason – a dreadful reason – a mysterious reason. Marriage is forbidden to him. And, when I wanted to know why, he looked the picture of despair, and said, "Ask no more!"'

'Is he coming to the party?'

'Of course not!'

'What's his excuse?'

'Ill-health.'

'Wait here, Salome, till I come back.'

Mrs Crossmichael immediately presented herself at the next house. Mr Fitzmark was not well enough to see her. The message was positive; and the wooden-faced valet was impenetrable. Not daunted yet, the obstinate visitor asked for Miss Pillico. Miss Pillico was not in the house. Mrs Crossmichael returned, defeated, but not discouraged yet.

She appeared to be quite satisfied when Salome told her that the fair physician would be present at the garden-party.

The guests began to arrive; and Sophia was among them.

Her two faithful patients, Sir John and Mr Skirton, noticed that she was serious and silent. Mr Skirton asked if she had visited Otto that day. No; she had not thought it necessary, and he had not sent to say that he wanted her. Mrs Crossmichael, waiting her opportunity, got into conversation with Sophia, in a quiet part of the grounds. Salome waylaid her sister, when the interview was over: 'What have you found out?' Mrs Crossmichael whispered back, 'Pillico was not born yesterday. She has some reason for being discontented with Otto – that's all I can discover so far. Hush! don't turn round too suddenly. Do you see that cat?'

The 'cat' was Sir John's daughter. She had just met Miss Pillico on the lawn, and had only been noticed by a formal bow. Sour Bess looked after the lady-doctor with an expression of devilish malice which was not lost on Mrs Crossmichael. 'An enemy to Sophia!' she whispered to her sister. 'Ah, Miss Dowager, it's a long time since we have seen each other. You're looking remarkably well. Have you, too, been consulting Miss Pillico?' She took Bess's arm in the friendliest manner, and walked away with her to the farther end of the garden.

IX

'Well, Lois!'

'Don't come near me, or you will spoil everything! One word. Did that man make you another offer when you were at Windsor?'

'Yes.'

'And you refused him again?'

'Certainly!'

'And you still think Otto is worth having?'

'I can't live without him!'

'Otto is yours.'

Half an hour afterwards, Mr Fitzmark received a letter, marked Private: 'After such conduct as yours no young lady, in my sister's position, could condescend to explain herself. I think it right, however, to inform you – merely to remove a false impression from your mind – that the gentleman who has excited your jealousy (and no wonder, for he is in every way your superior) has made her a proposal of marriage, and has, to my sincere regret, been refused. It is needless to add that you will not be received, if you venture to call again at my father's house. – L. C.'

The despatch of this letter was followed by a bolder experiment still.

When the garden-party had come to an end, and the guests were at home again, Miss Pillico received Mrs Crossmichael's visiting card – with a line on it in pencil: 'I should be glad to say two words, if quite convenient.' Mrs Crossmichael had produced a favourable impression in the garden – the interview was immediately granted.

'You are naturally surprised to see me again, after I have already had the pleasure of meeting you. Events have happened – no! I had better not trouble you with the events, except on condition. The condition is, that you will kindly reply to a question which I must ask first.' So Salome's sister opened fire on the enemy. The enemy only bowed.

'A lady possessed of your personal advantages, who follows your profession,' Mrs Crossmichael proceeded, 'excites admiration (especially among the men) for other qualities besides her medical ability—'

'I don't desire such admiration,' Miss Pillico interposed; 'and I never notice it.'

'Not even in the case of one of your most ardent admirers – Mr Otto Fitzmark?'

'Certainly not!'

'Allow me to beg your pardon, Miss Pillico, for an intrusion which has, *now*, no excuse. I came here – without Mr Fitzmark's knowledge – to make a very painful communication (so far as our family is concerned), in which, as I foolishly imagined, a duty – a friendly duty – might be involved towards yourself. Pray accept my excuses. Good evening.'

'Stop, Mrs Crossmichael! Did you say duty was involved?'

'I did, Miss Pillico.'

'An act of duty is too serious to be trifled with. Will it help you if we *suppose* that I have noticed the feeling of admiration to which you refer?'

'Thank you – it will help me very much.'

'Pray go on.'

'I trust to your honour, Miss Pillico, to keep what I am about to say, a profound secret. Before Mr Fitzmark had the honour of becoming acquainted with you, his attentions to my sister were a subject of general remark among our friends. He called this morning in a state of indescribable confusion and distress, to inform her that his sentiments had undergone a change; the attractions of some other lady, as I strongly suspect, being answerable for this result. I have merely to add (speaking from my own experience) that he is an exceedingly shy man. He is also – according to his own account of it – subject to some extraordinary delusion, which persuades him that he can never marry. My own idea is, that this is a mere excuse; a stupid falsehood invented to palliate his conduct to my sister. As I think, she is well out of it. I have no opinion of Mr Fitzmark; and I should consider it my duty,' Mrs Crossmichael proceeded, with an expression of undisguised malignity – 'my bounden duty to warn any lady, in whom I was interested, against encouraging the addresses of such a false and fickle man. If you ask how you are interested in hearing all this, I can only own that, like other foolish women, I act on impulse, and often regret it too late. Once more, good evening.'

Salome was waiting at home, eager to know how the interview had ended. Mrs Crossmichael described it in these words:

'I have assumed the character, my dear, of your vindictive sister; eager to lower the man who has jilted you, in Sophia's estimation. The trap is set – thanks to that charming girl, Sir John's daughter. To-morrow will show if Pillico walks into it.'

X

To-morrow did show. Mrs Crossmichael received a reply to her letter, from Mr Fitzmark.

'I entreat you to intercede for me. No words can tell how ashamed I am of my conduct, and how I regret the inexcusable jealousy which led to it. Salome – no! I dare not speak of her in that familiar way – Miss Salome is too good and too noble not to forgive a sincerely penitent man. I know how utterly unworthy of her I am; and I dare not hope to obtain more than my pardon. May she be happy! – is the only wish I can now presume to form.

'One word more, relating to myself, before I close these lines.

'I was foolish enough, when I made that ever-to-be-regretted visit, to hint at an obstacle to my entering the marriage state. It all originated in a mistaken view, taken by Miss Sophia Pillico, of the state of my heart. She called medically this morning, and applied the stethoscope as before: the result seemed to surprise her. She asked how many times I had taken my medicine, – I said, Twice. Digitalis, she thereupon remarked, was a wonderful remedy. She also said that she might, in her anxiety, have taken an exaggerated view of my case, and have alarmed me without reason. Her conduct, after this, was so extraordinary that I cannot pretend to describe it. She waited, after the examination was over, and seemed to expect me to say something more. I waited, on my side, for a word of explanation. She flew into a rage, and told me to provide myself with another doctor. What does it mean?

'Being naturally interested in finding out whether there was anything the matter with me or not, I called on the resident medical man in this neighbourhood. He took great pains with me; and he admitted that I had an overburdened heart.

'God knows this is true enough! But the cause he assigned makes me blush while I write. It seems that I eat too much – and my full stomach presses against my heart. "Live moderately, and take a long walk every day," the doctor said; "and there isn't an Office in London that won't be glad to insure your life."

'Do me one last favour. Pray don't let Miss Salome know about my stomach!'

Private Note by the Editor – When Mrs Crossmichael showed this letter to her sister, she said, 'Now I have bowled Pillico out at last!' Quite a mistake. Sophia publicly alluded to her brief professional connection with Mr Fitzmark, in these terms: 'Other women view the approach of age with horror – I look to it myself with impatience and hope. At my present time of life, stupid male patients persist in falling in love with me. Mr Fitzmark was a particularly offensive instance of this. No words can say what a relief it is to me to hear, that he is going to marry Miss Salome Skirton.'

Mr Lismore and the Widow

Originally appeared in *The Spirit of the Times* 22 December 1883 with the combatively sensational title of 'She Loves and Lies'. Reprinted in *Little Novels* (1887). This memorable little story provides a modernised analogue of Chaucer's *The Wife of Bath's Tale*.

I

Late in the autumn, not many years since, a public meeting was held at the Mansion House, London, under the direction of the Lord Mayor.

The list of gentlemen invited to address the audience had been chosen with two objects in view. Speakers of celebrity, who would rouse public enthusiasm, were supported by speakers connected with commerce, who would be practically useful in explaining the purpose for which the meeting was convened. Money wisely spent in advertising had produced the customary result – every seat was occupied before the proceedings began.

Among the late arrivals, who had no choice but to stand or to leave the hall, were two ladies. One of them at once decided on leaving the hall. 'I shall go back to the carriage,' she said, 'and wait for you at the door.' Her friend answered, 'I shan't keep you long. He is advertised to support the second Resolution; I want to see him – and that is all.'

An elderly gentleman, seated at the end of a bench, rose and offered his place to the lady who remained. She hesitated to take advantage of his kindness, until he reminded her that he had heard what she said to her friend. Before the third Resolution was proposed, his seat would be at his own disposal again. She thanked him, and without further ceremony took his place. He was provided with an opera-glass, which he more than once offered to her, when famous orators appeared on the platform; she made no use of it until a speaker – known in the City as a shipowner – stepped forward to support the second Resolution.

His name (announced in the advertisements) was Ernest Lismore.

The moment he rose, the lady asked for the opera-glass. She kept it to her eyes for such a length of time, and with such evident interest in Mr Lismore, that the curiosity of her neighbours was aroused. Had he anything to say in which a lady (evidently a stranger to him) was personally interested? There was nothing in the address that he delivered which appealed to the enthusiasm of women. He was undoubtedly a handsome man, whose appearance proclaimed him to be in the prime of life – midway perhaps between thirty and forty years of age. But why a lady should persist in keeping an opera-glass fixed on him all through his speech, was a question which found the general ingenuity at a loss for a reply.

Having returned the glass with an apology, the lady ventured on putting a question next. 'Did it strike you, sir, that Mr Lismore seemed to be out of spirits?' she asked.

'I can't say it did, ma'am.'

'Perhaps you noticed that he left the platform the moment he had done?'

This betrayal of interest in the speaker did not escape the notice of a lady, seated on the bench in front. Before the old gentleman could answer, she volunteered an explanation.

'I am afraid Mr Lismore is troubled by anxieties connected with his business,' she said. 'My husband heard it reported in the City yesterday that he was seriously embarrassed by the failure—'

A loud burst of applause made the end of the sentence inaudible. A famous member of Parliament had risen to propose the third Resolution. The polite old man took his seat, and the lady left the hall to join her friend.

*

'Well, Mrs Callender, has Mr Lismore disappointed you?'

'Far from it! But I have heard a report about him which has alarmed me: he is said to be seriously troubled about money matters. How can I find out his address in the City?'

'We can stop at the first stationer's shop we pass, and ask to look at the Directory. Are you going to pay Mr Lismore a visit?'

'I am going to think about it.'

II

The next day a clerk entered Mr Lismore's private room at the office, and presented a visiting-card. Mrs Callender had reflected, and had arrived at a decision. Underneath her name she had written these explanatory words: 'On important business.'

'Does she look as if she wanted money?' Mr Lismore inquired.

'Oh dear, no! She comes in her carriage.'

'Is she young or old?'

'Old, sir.'

To Mr Lismore – conscious of the disastrous influence occasionally exercised over busy men by youth and beauty – this was a recommendation in itself. He said:

'Show her in.'

Observing the lady, as she approached him, with the momentary curiosity of a stranger, he noticed that she still preserved the remains of beauty. She had also escaped the misfortune, common to persons at her time of life, of becoming too fat. Even to a man's eye, her dressmaker appeared to have made the most of that favourable circumstance. Her figure had its defects concealed, and its remaining merits set off to advantage. At the same time she evidently held herself above the common deceptions by which some women seek to conceal their age. She wore her own gray hair; and her complexion bore the test of daylight. On entering the room, she made her apologies with some embarrassment. Being the embarrassment of a stranger (and not of a youthful stranger), it failed to impress Mr Lismore favourably.

'I am afraid I have chosen an inconvenient time for my visit,' she began.

'I am at your service,' he answered a little stiffly; 'especially if you will be so kind as to mention your business with me in few words.'

She was a woman of some spirit, and that reply roused her.

'I will mention it in one word,' she said smartly. 'My business is – gratitude.'

He was completely at a loss to understand what she meant, and he said so plainly. Instead of explaining herself, she put a question.

'Do you remember the night of the eleventh of March, between five and six years since?'

He considered for a moment.

'No,' he said, 'I don't remember it. Excuse me, Mrs Callender, I have affairs of my own to attend to which cause me some anxiety—'

'Let me assist your memory, Mr Lismore; and I will leave you to your affairs. On the date that I have referred to you were on your way to the railway-station at Bexmore, to catch the night express from the North to London.'

As a hint that his time was valuable the shipowner had hitherto remained standing. He now took his customary seat, and began to listen with some interest. Mrs Callender had produced her effect on him already.

'It was absolutely necessary,' she proceeded, 'that you should be on board your ship in the London Docks at nine o'clock the next morning. If you had lost the express, the vessel would have sailed without you.'

The expression of his face began to change to surprise.

'Who told you that?' he asked.

'You shall hear directly. On your way into the town, your carriage was stopped by an obstruction on the highroad. The people of Bexmore were looking at a house on fire.'

He started to his feet.

'Good heavens! Are you the lady?'

She held up her hand in satirical protest.

'Gently, sir! You suspected me just now of wasting your valuable time. Don't rashly conclude that I am the lady, until you find that I am acquainted with the circumstances.'

'Is there no excuse for my failing to recognise you?' Mr Lismore asked. 'We were on the dark side of the burning house; you were fainting, and I—'

'And you,' she interposed, 'after saving me at the risk of your own life, turned a deaf ear to my poor husband's entreaties, when he asked you to wait till I had recovered my senses.'

'Your poor husband? Surely, Mrs Callender, he received no serious injury from the fire?'

'The firemen rescued him under circumstances of peril,' she answered, 'and at his great age he sank under the shock. I have lost the kindest and best of men. Do you remember how you parted from him – burnt and bruised in saving me? He liked to talk of it in his last illness. "At least" (he said to you) "tell me the name of the man who has preserved my wife from a dreadful death." You threw your card to him out of the carriage window, and away you went at a gallop to catch your train! In all the years that have passed I have kept that card, and have vainly inquired for my brave sea-captain. Yesterday I saw your name on the list of speakers at the Mansion House. Need I say that I attended the meeting? Need I tell you now why I come here and interrupt you in business-hours?'

She held out her hand. Mr Lismore took it in silence, and pressed it warmly.

'You have not done with me yet,' she resumed with a smile. 'Do you remember what I said of my errand, when I first came in?'

'You said it was an errand of gratitude.'

'Something more than the gratitude which only says "Thank you,"' she added. 'Before I explain myself, however, I want to know what you have been doing, and how it was that my inquiries failed to trace you after that terrible night.'

The appearance of depression which Mrs Callender had noticed at the public meeting showed itself again in Mr Lismore's face. He sighed as he answered her.

'My story has one merit,' he said; 'it is soon told. I cannot wonder that you failed to discover me. In the first place, I was not captain of my ship at that time; I was only mate. In the second place, I inherited some money, and ceased to lead a sailor's life, in less than a year from the night of the fire. You will now understand what obstacles were in the way of your tracing me. With my little capital I started successfully in business as a shipowner. At the time, I naturally congratulated myself on my own good fortune. We little know, Mrs Callender, what the future has in store for us.'

He stopped. His handsome features hardened – as if he was suffering (and concealing) pain. Before it was possible to speak to him, there was a knock at the door. Another visitor, without an appointment, had called; the clerk appeared again, with a card and a message.

'The gentleman begs you will see him, sir. He has something to tell you which is too important to be delayed.'

Hearing the message, Mrs Callender rose immediately.

'It is enough for today that we understand each other,' she said. 'Have you any engagement tomorrow, after the hours of business?'

'None.'

She pointed to her card on the writing-table. 'Will you come to me tomorrow evening at that address? I am like the gentleman who has just called; I too have my reason for wishing to see you.'

He gladly accepted the invitation. Mrs Callender stopped him as he opened the door for her.

'Shall I offend you,' she said, 'if I ask a strange question before I go? I have a better motive, mind, than mere curiosity. Are you married?'

'No.'

'Forgive me again,' she resumed. 'At my age, you cannot possibly misunderstand me; and yet—'

She hesitated. Mr Lismore tried to give her confidence. 'Pray don't stand on ceremony, Mrs Callender. Nothing that *you* can ask me need be prefaced by an apology.'

Thus encouraged, she ventured to proceed.

'You may be engaged to be married?' she suggested. 'Or you may be in love?'

He found it impossible to conceal his surprise. But he answered without hesitation.

'There is no such bright prospect in *my* life,' he said. 'I am not even in love.'

She left him with a little sigh. It sounded like a sigh of relief.

Ernest Lismore was thoroughly puzzled. What could be the old lady's object in ascertaining that he was still free from a matrimonial engagement? If the idea had occurred to him in time, he might have alluded to her domestic life, and might have asked if she had children? With a little tact he might have discovered more than this. She had described her feeling towards him as passing the ordinary limits of gratitude; and she was evidently rich enough to be above the imputation of a mercenary motive. Did she propose to brighten those dreary prospects to which he had alluded in speaking of his own life? When he presented himself at her house the next evening, would she introduce him to a charming daughter?

He smiled as the idea occurred to him. 'An appropriate time to be thinking of my chances of marriage!' he said to himself. 'In another month I may be a ruined man.'

III

The gentleman who had so urgently requested an interview was a devoted friend – who had obtained a means of helping Ernest at a serious crisis in his affairs.

It had been truly reported that he was in a position of pecuniary embarrassment, owing to the failure of a mercantile house with which he had been intimately connected. Whispers affecting his own solvency had followed on the bankruptcy of the firm. He had already endeavoured to obtain advances of money on the usual conditions, and had been met by excuses for delay. His friend had now arrived with a letter of introduction to a capitalist, well known in commercial circles for his daring speculations, and for his great wealth.

Looking at the letter, Ernest observed that the envelope was sealed. In spite of that ominous innovation on established usage, in cases of personal introduction, he presented the letter. On this occasion, he was not put off with excuses. The capitalist flatly declined to discount Mr Lismore's bills, unless they were backed by responsible names.

Ernest made a last effort.

He applied for help to two mercantile men whom he had assisted in *their* difficulties, and whose names would have satisfied the money-lender. They were most sincerely sorry – but they too refused.

The one security that he could offer was open, it must be owned, to serious objections on the score of risk. He wanted an advance of twenty thousand pounds, secured on a homeward-bound ship and cargo. But the vessel was not insured; and, at that stormy season, she was already more than a month overdue. Could grateful colleagues be blamed if they forgot their obligations when they were asked to offer pecuniary help to a merchant in this situation? Ernest returned to his office, without money and without credit.

A man threatened by ruin is in no state of mind to keep an engagement at a lady's tea-table. Ernest sent a letter of apology to Mrs Callender, alleging extreme pressure of business as the excuse for breaking his engagement.

'Am I to wait for an answer, sir?' the messenger asked.

'No; you are merely to leave the letter.'

IV

In an hour's time – to Ernest's astonishment – the messenger returned with a reply.

'The lady was just going out, sir, when I rang at the door,' he explained, 'and she took the letter from me herself. She didn't appear to know your handwriting, and she asked me who I came from. When I mentioned your name, I was ordered to wait.'

Ernest opened the letter.

Dear Mr Lismore,

One of us must speak out, and your letter of apology forces me to be that one. If you are really so proud and so distrustful as you seem to be, I shall offend you. If not, I shall prove myself to be your friend.

Your excuse is 'pressure of business.' The truth (as I have good reason to believe) is 'want of money.' I heard a stranger, at that public meeting, say that you were seriously embarrassed by some failure in the City.

Let me tell you what my own pecuniary position is in two words. I am the childless widow of a rich man—'

Ernest paused. His anticipated discovery of Mrs Callender's 'charming daughter' was in his mind for the moment. 'That little romance must return to the world of dreams,' he thought – and went on with the letter.

After what I owe to you, I don't regard it as repaying an obligation – I consider myself as merely performing a duty when I offer to assist you by a loan of money.

Wait a little before you throw my letter into the wastepaper-basket.

Circumstances (which it is impossible for me to mention before we meet) put it out of my power to help you – unless I attach to my most sincere offer of service a very unusual and very embarrassing condition. If you are on the brink of ruin, that misfortune will plead my excuse – and your excuse too, if you accept the loan on my terms. In any case, I rely on the sympathy and forbearance of the man to whom I owe my life.

After what I have now written, there is only one thing to add. I beg to decline accepting your excuses; and I shall expect to see you to-morrow evening, as we arranged. I am an obstinate old woman – but I am also your faithful friend and servant,

MARY CALLENDER

Ernest looked up from the letter. 'What can this possibly mean?' he wondered.

But he was too sensible a man to be content with wondering – he decided on keeping his engagement.

V

What Doctor Johnson called 'the insolence of wealth' appears far more frequently in the houses of the rich than in the manners of the rich. The reason is plain enough. Personal ostentation is, in the very nature of it, ridiculous. But the ostentation which exhibits magnificent pictures, priceless china, and splendid furniture, can purchase good taste to guide it, and can assert itself without affording the smallest opening for a word of depreciation, or a look of contempt. If I am worth a million of money, and if I am dying to show it, I don't ask you to look at me – I ask you to look at my house.

Keeping his engagement with Mrs Callender, Ernest discovered that riches might be lavishly and yet modestly used.

In crossing the hall and ascending the stairs, look where he might, his notice was insensibly won by proofs of the taste which is not to be purchased, and the wealth which uses but never exhibits its purse. Conducted by a man-servant to the landing on the first floor, he found a maid at the door of the boudoir waiting to announce him. Mrs Callender advanced to welcome her guest, in a simple evening dress perfectly suited to her age. All that had looked worn and faded in her fine face, by daylight, was now softly obscured by shaded lamps. Objects of beauty surrounded her, which glowed with subdued radiance from their background of sober colour. The influence of appearances is the strongest of all outward influences, while it lasts. For the moment, the scene produced its impression on Ernest, in spite of the terrible anxieties which consumed him. Mrs Callender, in his office, was a woman who had stepped out of her appropriate sphere. Mrs Callender, in her own house, was a woman who had risen to a new place in his estimation.

'I am afraid you don't thank me for forcing you to keep your engagement,' she said, with her friendly tones and her pleasant smile.

'Indeed I do thank you,' he replied. 'Your beautiful house and your gracious welcome have persuaded me into forgetting my troubles – for a while.'

The smile passed away from her face. 'Then it is true?' she said gravely.

'Only too true.'

She led him to a seat beside her, and waited to speak again until her maid had brought in the tea.

'Have you read my letter in the same friendly spirit in which I wrote it?' she asked when they were alone again.

'I have read your letter gratefully, but—'

'But you don't know yet what I have to say. Let us understand each other before we make any objections on either side. Will you tell me what your present position is – at its worst? I can, and will, speak plainly when my turn comes, if you will honour me with your confidence. Not if it distresses you,' she added, observing him attentively.

He was ashamed of his hesitation – and he made amends for it.

'Do you thoroughly understand me?' he asked, when the whole truth had been laid before her without reserve.

She summed up the result in her own words.

'If your overdue ship returns safely, within a month from this time, you can borrow the money you want, without difficulty. If the ship is lost, you have no alternative (when the end of the month comes) but to accept a loan from me or to suspend payment. Is that the hard truth?'

'It is.'

'And the sum you require is – twenty thousand pounds?'

'Yes.'

'I have twenty times as much money as that, Mr Lismore, at my sole disposal – on one condition.'

'The condition alluded to in your letter?'

'Yes.'

'Does the fulfilment of the condition depend in some way on any decision of mine?'

'It depends entirely on you.'

That answer closed his lips.

With a composed manner and a steady hand she poured herself out a cup of tea.

'I conceal it from you,' she said; 'but I want confidence. Here' (she pointed to the cup) 'is the friend of women, rich or poor, when they are in trouble. What I have now to say obliges me to speak in praise of myself. I don't like it – let me get it over as soon as I can. My husband was very fond of me: he had the most absolute confidence in my discretion, and in my sense of duty to him and to myself. His last words, before he died, were words that thanked me for making the happiness of his life. As soon as I had in some degree recovered, after the affliction that had fallen on me, his lawyer and executor produced a copy of his will, and said there were two clauses in it which my husband had expressed a wish that I should read. It is needless to say that I obeyed.'

She still controlled her agitation – but she was now unable to conceal it. Ernest made an attempt to spare her.

'Am I concerned in this?' he asked.

'Yes. Before I tell you why, I want to know what you would do – in a certain case which I am unwilling even to suppose. I have heard of men, unable to pay the demands made on them, who began business again, and succeeded, and in course of time paid their creditors.'

'And you want to know if there is any likelihood of my following their example?' he said. 'Have you also heard of men who have made that second effort – who have failed again – and who have doubled the debts they owed to their brethren in business who trusted them? I knew one of those men myself. He committed suicide.'

She laid her hand for a moment on his.

'I understand you,' she said. 'If ruin comes—'

'If ruin comes,' he interposed, 'a man without money and without credit can make but one last atonement. Don't speak of it now.'

She looked at him with horror.

'I didn't mean *that!*' she said.

'Shall we go back to what you read in the will?' he suggested.

'Yes – if you will give me a minute to compose myself.'

VI

In less than the minute she had asked for, Mrs Callender was calm enough to go on.

'I now possess what is called a life-interest in my husband's fortune,' she said. 'The money is to be divided, at my death, among charitable institutions; excepting a certain event—'

'Which is provided for in the will?' Ernest added, helping her to go on.

'Yes. I am to be absolute mistress of the whole of the four hundred thousand pounds –' her voice dropped, and her eyes looked away from him as she spoke the next words – 'on this one condition, that I marry again.'

He looked at her in amazement.

'Surely I have mistaken you,' he said. 'You mean on this one condition, that you do *not* marry again?'

'No, Mr Lismore; I mean exactly what I have said. You now know that the recovery of your credit and your peace of mind rests entirely with yourself.'

After a moment of reflection he took her hand, and raised it respectfully to his lips. 'You are a noble woman!' he said.

She made no reply. With drooping head and downcast eyes she waited for his decision. He accepted his responsibility.

'I must not, and dare not, think of the hardship of my own position,' he said; 'I owe it to you to speak without reference to the future that may be in store for me. No man can be worthy of the sacrifice which your generous forgetfulness of yourself is willing to make. I respect you; I admire you; I thank you with my whole heart. Leave me to my fate, Mrs Callender – and let me go.'

He rose. She stopped him by a gesture.

'A *young* woman,' she answered, 'would shrink from saying – what I, as an old woman, mean to say now. I refuse to leave you to your fate. I ask you to prove that you respect me, admire me, and thank me with your whole heart. Take one day to think – and let me hear the result. You promise me this?'

He promised.

'Now go,' she said.

VII

The next morning Ernest received a letter from Mrs Callender. She wrote to him as follows:

There are some considerations which I ought to have mentioned yesterday evening, before you left my house.

I ought to have reminded you – if you consent to reconsider your decision – that the circumstances do not require you to pledge yourself to me absolutely.

At my age, I can with perfect propriety assure you that I regard our marriage simply and solely as a formality which we must fulfil, if I am to carry out my intention of standing between you and ruin.

Therefore – if the missing ship appears in time, the only reason for the marriage is at an end. We shall be as good friends as ever; without the encumbrance of a formal tie to bind us.

In the other event, I should ask you to submit to certain restrictions which, remembering my position, you will understand and excuse.

We are to live together, it is unnecessary to say, as mother and son. The marriage ceremony is to be strictly private; and you are so to arrange your affairs that, immediately afterwards, we leave England for any foreign place which you prefer. Some of my friends, and (perhaps) some of your friends, will certainly misinterpret our motives – if we stay in our own country – in a manner which would be unendurable to a woman like me.

As to our future lives, I have the most perfect confidence in you, and I should leave you in the same position of independence which you occupy now. When you wish for my company, you will always be welcome. At other times, you are your own master. I live on my side of the house, and you live on yours – and I am to be allowed my hours of solitude every day, in the pursuit of musical occupations, which have been happily associated with all my past life, and which I trust confidently to your indulgence.

A last word, to remind you of what you may be too kind to think of yourself.

At my age, you cannot, in the course of Nature, be troubled by the society of a grateful old woman for many years. You are young enough to look forward to another marriage, which shall be something more than a mere form. Even if you meet with the happy woman in my lifetime, honestly tell me of it – and I promise to tell her that she has only to wait.

In the meantime, don't think, because I write composedly, that I write heartlessly. You pleased and interested me, when I first saw you, at the public meeting. I don't think I could have proposed, what you call this sacrifice of myself, to a man who had personally repelled me – though I might have felt my debt of gratitude as sincerely as ever. Whether your ship is saved, or whether your ship is lost, old Mary Callender likes you – and owns it without false shame.

Let me have your answer this evening, either personally or by letter – whichever you like best.

VIII

Mrs Callender received a written answer long before the evening. It said much in few words:

A man impenetrable to kindness might be able to resist your letter. I am not that man. Your great heart has conquered me.

The few formalities which precede marriage by special license were observed by Ernest. While the destiny of their future lives was still in suspense, an unacknowledged feeling of embarrassment, on either side, kept Ernest and Mrs Callender apart. Every day brought the lady her report of the state of affairs in the City, written always in the same words: 'No news of the ship.'

IX

On the day before the shipowner's liabilities became due, the terms of the report from the City remained unchanged – and the special license was put to its contemplated use. Mrs Callender's lawyer and Mrs Callender's maid were the only persons trusted with the secret. Leaving the chief clerk in charge of the business, with every pecuniary demand on his employer satisfied in full, the strangely married pair quitted England.

They arranged to wait for a few days in Paris, to receive any letters of importance which might have been addressed to Ernest in the interval. On the evening of their arrival, a telegram from London was waiting at their hotel. It announced that the missing ship had passed up Channel – undiscovered in a fog, until she reached the Downs – on the day before Ernest's liabilities fell due.

'Do you regret it?' Mrs Lismore said to her husband.

'Not for a moment!' he answered.

They decided on pursuing their journey as far as Munich.

Mrs Lismore's taste for music was matched by Ernest's taste for painting. In his leisure hours he cultivated the art, and delighted in it. The picture galleries of Munich were almost the only galleries in Europe which he had not seen. True to the engagements to which she had pledged herself, his wife was willing to go wherever it might please him to take her. The one suggestion she made was, that they should hire furnished apartments. If they lived at an hotel, friends of the husband or the wife (visitors like themselves to the famous city) might see their names in the book, or might meet them at the door.

They were soon established in a house large enough to provide them with every accommodation which they required.

Ernest's days were passed in the galleries; Mrs Lismore remaining at home, devoted to her music, until it was time to go out with her husband for a drive. Living together in perfect amity and concord, they were nevertheless not living happily. Without any visible reason for the change, Mrs Lismore's spirits were depressed. On the one occasion when Ernest noticed it she made an effort to be cheerful, which it distressed him to see. He allowed her to think that she had relieved him of any further anxiety. Whatever doubts he might feel were doubts delicately concealed from that time forth.

But when two people are living together in a state of artificial tranquillity, it seems to be a law of Nature that the elements of disturbance gather unseen, and that the outburst comes inevitably with the lapse of time.

In ten days from the date of their arrival at Munich the crisis came. Ernest returned later than usual from the picture-gallery, and – for the first time in his wife's experience – shut himself up in his own room.

He appeared at the dinner-hour with a futile excuse. Mrs Lismore waited until the servant had withdrawn.

'Now, Ernest,' she said, 'it's time to tell me the truth.'

Her manner, when she said those few words, took him by surprise. She was unquestionably confused; and, instead of looking at him, she trifled with the fruit on her plate. Embarrassed on his side, he could only answer:

'I have nothing to tell.'

'Were there many visitors at the gallery?' she asked.

'About the same as usual.'

'Any that you particularly noticed?' she went on. 'I mean, among the ladies.'

He laughed uneasily.

'You forget how interested I am in the pictures,' he said.

There was a pause. She looked up at him – and suddenly looked away again. But he saw it plainly: there were tears in her eyes.

'Do you mind turning down the gas?' she said. 'My eyes have been weak all day.'

He complied with her request – the more readily, having his own reasons for being glad to escape the glaring scrutiny of the light.

'I think I will rest a little on the sofa,' she resumed. In the position which he occupied, his back would have been now turned on her. She stopped him when he tried to move his chair. 'I would rather not look at you, Ernest,' she said, 'when you have lost confidence in me.'

Not the words, but the tone, touched all that was generous and noble in his nature. He left his place, and knelt beside her – and opened to her his whole heart.

'Am I not unworthy of you?' he asked when it was over.

She pressed his hand in silence.

'I should be the most ungrateful wretch living,' he said, 'if I did not think of you, and you only, now that my confession is made. We will leave Munich tomorrow – and, if resolution can help me, I will only remember the sweetest woman my eyes ever looked on as the creature of a dream.'

She hid her face on his breast, and reminded him of that letter of her writing, which had decided the course of their lives.

'When I thought you might meet the happy woman in my lifetime, I said to you, "Tell me of it – and I promise to tell *her* that she has only to wait." Time must pass, Ernest, before it can be needful to perform my promise. But you might let me see her. If you find her in the gallery tomorrow, you might bring her here.'

Mrs Lismore's request met with no refusal. Ernest was only at a loss to know how to grant it.

'You tell me she is a copyist of pictures,' his wife reminded him. 'She will be interested in hearing of the portfolio of drawings by the great French artists which I bought for you in Paris. Ask her to come and see them, and to tell you if she can make some copies. And say, if you like, that I shall be glad to become acquainted with her.'

He felt her breath beating fast on his bosom. In the fear that she might lose all control over herself, he tried to relieve her by speaking lightly. 'What an invention yours is!' he said. 'If my wife ever tries to deceive me, I shall be a mere child in her hands.'

She rose abruptly from the sofa – kissed him on the forehead – and said wildly, 'I shall be better in bed!' Before he could move or speak, she had left him.

X

The next morning he knocked at the door of his wife's room, and asked how she had passed the night.

'I have slept badly,' she answered, 'and I must beg you to excuse my absence at breakfast-time.' She called him back as he was about to withdraw. 'Remember,' she said, 'when you return from the gallery today, I expect that you will not return alone.'

Three hours later he was at home again. The young lady's services as a copyist were at his disposal; she had returned with him to look at the drawings.

The sitting-room was empty when they entered it. He rang for his wife's maid – and was informed that Mrs Lismore had gone out. Refusing to believe the woman, he went to his wife's apartments. She was not to be found.

When he returned to the sitting-room, the young lady was not unnaturally offended. He could make allowances for her being a little out of temper at the slight that had been put on her; but he was inexpressibly disconcerted by the manner – almost the coarse manner – in which she expressed herself.

'I have been talking to your wife's maid, while you have been away,' she said. 'I find you have married an old lady for her money. She is jealous of me, of course?'

'Let me beg you to alter your opinion,' he answered. 'You are wronging my wife; she is incapable of any such feeling as you attribute to her.'

The young lady laughed. 'At any rate you are a good husband,' she said satirically. 'Suppose you own the truth? Wouldn't you like her better if she was young and pretty like me?'

He was not merely surprised – he was disgusted. Her beauty had so completely fascinated him, when he first saw her, that the idea of associating any want of refinement and good breeding with such a charming creature never entered his mind. The disenchantment of him was already so complete that he was even disagreeably affected by the tone of her voice: it was almost as repellent to him as the exhibition of unrestrained bad temper which she seemed perfectly careless to conceal.

'I confess you surprise me,' he said coldly.

The reply produced no effect on her. On the contrary, she became more insolent than ever.

'I have a fertile fancy,' she went on, 'and your absurd way of taking a joke only encourages me! Suppose you could transform this sour old wife of yours, who has insulted me, into the sweetest young creature that ever lived, by only holding up your finger – wouldn't you do it?'

This passed the limits of his endurance. 'I have no wish,' he said, 'to forget the consideration which is due to a woman. You leave me but one alternative.' He rose to go out of the room.

She ran to the door as he spoke, and placed herself in the way of his going out.

He signed to her to let him pass.

She suddenly threw her arms round his neck, kissed him passionately, and whispered, with her lips at his ear, 'Oh, Ernest, forgive me! Could I have asked you to marry me for my money if I had not taken refuge in a disguise?'

XI

When he had sufficiently recovered to think, he put her back from him. 'Is there an end of the deception now?' he asked sternly. 'Am I to trust you in your new character?'

'You are not to be harder on me than I deserve,' she answered gently. 'Did you ever hear of an actress named Miss Max?'

He began to understand her. 'Forgive me if I spoke harshly,' he said. 'You have put me to a severe trial.'

She burst into tears. 'Love,' she murmured, 'is my only excuse.'

From that moment she had won her pardon. He took her hand, and made her sit by him.

'Yes,' he said, 'I have heard of Miss Max, and of her wonderful powers of personation – and I have always regretted not having seen her while she was on the stage.'

'Did you hear anything more of her, Ernest?'.

'I heard that she was a pattern of modesty and good conduct, and that she gave up her profession, at the height of her success, to marry an old man.'

'Will you come with me to my room?' she asked. 'I have something there which I wish to show you.'

It was the copy of her husband's will.

'Read the lines, Ernest, which begin at the top of the page. Let my dead husband speak for me.'

The lines ran thus:

My motive in marrying Miss Max must be stated in this place, in justice to her – and, I will venture to add, in justice to myself. I felt the sincerest sympathy for her position. She was without father, mother, or friends; one of the poor forsaken children, whom the mercy of the Foundling

Hospital provides with a home. Her after-life on the stage was the life of a virtuous woman: persecuted by profligates; insulted by some of the baser creatures associated with her, to whom she was an object of envy. I offered her a home, and the protection of a father – on the only terms which the world would recognise as worthy of us. My experience of her since our marriage has been the experience of unvarying goodness, sweetness, and sound sense. She has behaved so nobly, in a trying position, that I wish her (even in this life) to have her reward. I entreat her to make a second choice in marriage, which shall not be a mere form. I firmly believe that she will choose well and wisely – that she will make the happiness of a man who is worthy of her – and that, as wife and mother, she will set an example of inestimable value in the social sphere that she occupies. In proof of the heartfelt sincerity with which I pay my tribute to her virtues, I add to this my will the clause that follows.

With the clause that followed, Ernest was already acquainted.

'Will you now believe that I never loved till I saw your face for the first time?' said his wife. 'I had no experience to place me on my guard against the fascination – the madness some people might call it – which possesses a woman when all her heart is given to a man. Don't despise me, my dear! Remember that I had to save you from disgrace and ruin. Besides, my old stage remembrances tempted me. I had acted in a play in which the heroine did – what I have done! It didn't end with me, as it did with her in the story. *She* was represented as rejoicing in the success of her disguise. *I* have known some miserable hours of doubt and shame since our marriage. When I went to meet you in my own person at the picture-gallery – oh, what relief, what joy I felt, when I saw how you admired me – it was not because I could no longer carry on the disguise. I was able to get hours of rest from the effort; not only at night but in the daytime, when I was shut up in my retirement in the music-room; and when my maid kept watch against discovery. No, my love! I hurried on the disclosure, because I could no longer endure the hateful triumph of my own deception. Ah, look at that witness against me! I can't bear even to see it!'

She abruptly left him. The drawer that she had opened to take out the copy of the will also contained the false gray hair which she had discarded. It had only that moment attracted her notice. She snatched it up, and turned to the fireplace.

Ernest took it from her, before she could destroy it. 'Give it to me,' he said.

'Why?'

He drew her gently to his bosom, and answered, 'I must not forget my old wife.'

Love's Random Shot

According to R.V. Andrew the story appeared in *The Seaside Library*, Vol. LXXXVII, No. 1770. The story also appeared in *Love's Random Shot and Other Stories* by Wilkie Collins (New York: George Munro's Sons, possibly 1894). This reprint provides the text for the present edition, which was kindly supplied by Andrew Gasson. 'Love's Random Shot' is one of the stories Collins did not want reprinted after his death. Its theme of mature infatuation is one Kipling might have handled exceptionally well, but in Collins's hands it remains gratuitously sensational.

I

The scene is a famous city in Scotland.

The chief personage is the best police-officer we had in the time when I served the office of Sheriff.

He was an old man, about to retire on a well-earned pension at the period of his life to which my narrative refers. A theft of a priceless picture, which had escaped discovery by the other members of our police force, roused old Benjamin Parley to exert himself for the last time. The money motive was not the motive that mainly influenced him, although the large reward originally offered for the recovery of the picture had been doubled. 'If the rest of you can't find the thief,' he said, 'I must take the case in hand, for the honor of Scotland.'

Having arrived at his decision, Parley presented himself at my house. I gave him a letter of introduction to the proprietor of the picture – then on the point of applying for help to London.

You have heard of Lord Dalton's famous gallery. A Madonna, by Raphael, was the gem of the collection. Early one morning the servants discovered the empty frame, without finding a trace of the means by which the audacious robbery had been committed. Having allowed our veteran officer to make his own preliminary investigations, my lord (a man of rare ability and of marked originality of character) was at once impressed by the startling novelty of the conclusion at which Parley arrived, and by the daring nature of the plan that he devised for solving the mystery of the theft.

Lord Dalton pointed to a letter on his library table, addressed to the Chief of the London Detective Police Force.

'I will delay posting this for a week,' he said. 'If, at the end of the time, you send me a sufficiently encouraging first report, the case shall be left unreservedly in your hands.'

At the end of the week the report was sent in. Lord Dalton first destroyed his letter to London, and then spoke to Parley on the subject of the reward.

'As a well-informed police-officer,' he said, 'you are no doubt aware that I am one of the three richest men in Scotland. Have you also heard that I am a stingy man?'

'I have heard exactly the contrary, my lord,' Parley answered, with perfect truth.

'Very good. You will be inclined to believe me, when I tell you that the money value of my picture (large as it may be) is the least part of its value in my estimation. The sheriff tells me that you have a wife and two daughters at home, and that you were about to retire on a pension when you offered me your services. At your age, I must take that circumstance into consideration. Do you mind telling me what income you have to look forward to; adding your other pecuniary resources (if you have any) to your pension?'

Parley answered the question without hesitation, and without reserve. He was not an easy man to astonish; but Lord Dalton's next words literally struck him speechless.

'Put my Raphael back in the frame, within a month from this day,' said his lordship, 'and I will treble your income, and secure it to your widow and children after you.'

In less than three weeks from that date, Benjamin Parley (just arrived from

Brussels) walked into the picture gallery, and put the Raphael back into the frame with his own hands. He refused to say how he had recovered the picture. But he announced, with an appearance of self-reproach which entirely failed to deceive Lord Dalton, the disastrous escape of his prisoner on the journey to Scotland. At a later period, scandal whispered that this same prisoner was a vagabond member of my lord's family, and that Parley's success had been due, in the first instance, to his wise courage in daring to suspect a nobleman's relative. I don't know what your experience may be. For my own part, I have now and then found scandal building on a well-secured foundation.

II

In relating the circumstances which made the generous nobleman and the skilled police-officer acquainted with each other, I have borne in mind certain results, the importance of which you have yet to estimate. The day on which Benjamin Parley received his magnificent reward proved to be the fatal day in his life.

He had originally planned to retire to the village in Perthshire in which he had been born. Being now possessed of an income which enabled him to indulge the ambition of his wife and his daughters, it was decided that he should fix his residence in one of the suburbs of the city. Mrs Parley and her two girls, established in 'a genteel villa,' assumed the position of 'ladies'; and old Benjamin, when time hung heavy on his hands, was within half an hour's walk of his colleagues in the police force. 'But for my lord's generosity,' his wife remarked, 'he would not have had that resource. If we had gone to Perthshire, he would never, in all likelihood, have seen our city again.'

To give you some idea of this poor fellow's excellent character, and of the high estimation in which he was deservedly held, I may mention that his retirement was celebrated by the presentation of a testimonial. It assumed the quaint form of a receipted bill, representing the expenses incurred in furnishing his new house. I took the chair at the meeting. The landed gentry, the lawyers, and the merchants were present in large numbers; all equally desirous of showing their respect for a man who, in a position beset by temptations, had set an example of incorruptible integrity from first to last.

Some family troubles of mine, at that time, obliged me to apply for leave of absence. For two months my duties were performed by deputy.

Examining the letters and cards which covered the study-table on my return, I found a morsel of paper with some lines of writing on it in pencil, signed by Parley's wife. 'When you can spare a little time, sir, pray be so good as to let me say a word to you – at your house.'

The handwriting showed plain signs of agitation; and the last three words were underlined. Was the good woman burdened with a domestic secret? and were her husband and children not admitted to her confidence?

I was so busily occupied, after my absence, that I could only make an appointment to see Mrs Parley at my breakfast time. The hour was so early that she would be sure to find me alone.

The moment she entered the room I saw a change in her, which prepared me for something serious. It may be, perhaps, desirable to add, by way of explaining a certain tendency to excitement and exaggeration in

Mrs Parley's ways of thinking and speaking, that she was a Welsh woman.

'Is there anything wrong at home?' I asked.

She began to cry. 'You know how proud I was, sir, of our grand house, and our splendid income. I wish we had gone where we first thought of going – hundreds of miles away from this place! I wish Parley had never seen his lordship, and never earned that great reward!'

'You don't mean to tell me,' I said, 'that you and your husband have quarrelled?'

'Worse, sir, – worse than that. Parley is so changed that my own husband is like a stranger to me. For God's sake, don't mention it! In our old age, after sleeping together for thirty years and more, I'm cast off. Parley has his bedroom, and I have mine!' She looked at me – and blushed. At nearly sixty years of age, the poor creature blushed like a young girl!

It is needless to say that the famous question of the French philosopher was on the tip of my tongue: 'Who is she?' But I owed it to Parley's unblemished reputation to hesitate before I committed myself to a positive opinion. The question of the beds was clearly beyond the reach of my interference. 'In what other ways does Parley seem to be changed?' I inquired.

'Seem?' she repeated. 'Why even the girls notice it! They say their father doesn't care about them now. And it's true! In our present prosperity, we can afford to pay a governess; and when we first settled in the new house, Parley agreed with me that the poor things ought to be better educated. He has lost all interest in their welfare. If I only mention the matter now, he says, "Oh! bother!" and discourages me in that way. You know, sir, he always dressed respectably, according to his station and time of life. That's all altered now. He has gone to a new tailor; he wears smart cutaway coats, like the young men; I found an elastic belt among his clothes – the sort of thing they advertise to keep down fat, and preserve the figure. You were so kind as to give him a snuff-box, on his last birthday. It's of no more use to him now. Benjamin has given up taking snuff.'

Here I thought it desirable, in the interests of good Mrs Parley herself, to bring the recital of her grievances to a close. The domestic situation (to speak the language of the stage) was more than sufficiently revealed to me. After an exemplary life, the model husband and father had fallen in the way of one of those temptations which are especially associated with the streets of a great city – and had yielded at the end of his career. A disastrous downfall; not altogether without precedent in the history of frail humanity, even at the wintry period of life! I was sorry, truly sorry; but in my position what could I do?

'I am at your service,' I said, 'if you will only tell me how I can advise you.'

'Some hussy has got hold of Benjamin!' cried the poor woman. 'And I don't know where to find her. What am I to do? Benjamin's too deep for me – I believe I shall go mad!'

She fell back on her chair, and began to beat her hands on her lap. If I permitted this hysterical agitation to proceed in its usual course of development, the household would be alarmed by an outburst of screaming. There was but one way of composing Mrs Parley, and I took it.

'Suppose I speak to your husband?' I suggested.

'Oh, Mr Sheriff— !'

In Mrs Parley's excitable Welsh nature even gratitude threatened to express itself hysterically. I checked the new outbreak by putting some necessary questions. The few facts which I succeeded in eliciting did not present my coming interview with the husband in an encouraging light.

After moving into the new house, Parley had found some difficulty (naturally enough) in reconciling himself to the change in his life. From time to time (as his wife had suggested) he looked in at the police office, and offered the benefit of his experience to his colleagues when they were in need of advice. For a while these visits to the city produced the good results which had been anticipated. Then followed the very complete and very suspicious change in him, already related to me. While the husband and wife still occupied the same room at night, Mrs Parley discovered that Benjamin was disturbed by dreams. For the first time in all her experience, she heard him talking in his sleep. Here and there, words escaped him which seemed to allude to a woman – a woman whom he called 'my dear' – a woman who had apparently placed some agitating confidence in him. Sensible enough under other circumstances, Mrs Parley's jealousy had hurried her into an act of folly. She woke her husband and insisted on an explanation. The result had been the institution of separate bedrooms – on the pretence that Parley's sense of conjugal duty would not permit him to be the means of disturbing his wife's rest. Arriving, correctly enough, at the conclusion that he was afraid of betraying himself, Mrs Parley had tried the desperate experiment of following him privately when he next left the house. A police-officer of forty years' experience, with a secret to keep, sees before him and behind him, and on his right hand and his left, at one and the same time. Poor Mrs Parley, discovered as a spy, felt the look that her husband gave her (to use her own expression) 'in the marrow of her bones.' His language had been equally alarming. 'Try it again,' he had said, 'and you will have seen the last of me.' She had naturally been afraid to try it again; and there she was, at my breakfast table, with but one hope left – the hope that the Sheriff would assist her!

III

Such was my interview with the wife. My interview with the husband produced one result, for which I was in some degree prepared. It satisfied me that any interference on my part would be worse than useless.

I had certain claims on Parley's gratitude and respect, which he had hitherto recognized with heartfelt sincerity. When we now stood face to face – before a word had passed between us – I saw one thing clearly: my hold over him was lost.

For Mrs Parley's sake I could not allow myself to be discouraged at the outset. 'Your wife was with me yesterday,' I said, 'in great distress.'

'I am sorry, sir, that my wife should have troubled you.'

His voice told me that he had suffered – and was still suffering – keenly. I also noticed that the lines marked by age in his face had deepened. He evidently felt that he stood before me a man self-degraded in his old age. On the other hand, it was just as plain that he was determined to deceive me if I attempted to penetrate his secret.

My one chance of producing the right impression was to appeal to his sense of self-respect, if any such sense was still left in him.

'Don't suppose that I presume to interfere between you and your wife,' I resumed. 'In what little I have now to say to you, I shall bear in mind the high character that you have always maintained, not only among your own friends, but among persons like myself, who are placed above you by the accidents of birth and position.'

'You are very good, sir. I assure you I feel—'

He paused. I waited to let him go on. His eyes dropped before mine. He seemed to be afraid to follow the good impulse that I had roused in him. I tried again.

'Without repeating what Mrs Parley has said to me,' I proceeded, 'I may tell you at what conclusion I have myself arrived. It is only doing you justice to suppose that your wife has been misled by false appearances. Will you go back to her, and satisfy her that she has been mistaken?'

'She wouldn't believe me, sir.'

'Will you, at least, try the experiment?'

He shook his head doggedly. 'Quite useless,' he answered. 'My wife's temper—'

I stopped him there.

'Make some allowance for your wife's temper,' I said, 'and don't forget that you owe some consideration to your daughters. Spare them the shame and distress of seeing their father and mother at enmity.'

His manner changed: I had said something which appeared to give him confidence.

'Did my wife say anything to you about our girls?' he asked.

'Yes.'

'What did she say?'

'She thought you neglectful of your daughters.'

'Anything else, sir?'

'She said you had, at one time, acknowledged that the girls ought to have a good governess; but she now finds you indifferent to the best interests of your children.'

He lifted one of his hands, with a theatrical exaggeration of gesture, quite new in my experience of him.

'She said that, did she? Now, Mr Sheriff, judge for yourself what my wife's complaints of me are worth! I have this day engaged a governess for my children.'

I looked at him.

Once more his eyes dropped before mine.

'Does Mrs Parley know what you have done?' I inquired.

'She shall know,' he answered loudly, almost insolently, 'when I return home.'

'I am obliged to you for coming here, Mr Parley. Don't let me detain you any longer.'

'Does that mean, sir, that you disapprove of what I have done?'

'I pronounce no opinion.'

'Does it mean that you doubt the governess's character?'

'It means that I regret having troubled you to come here – and that I have no more to say.'

He walked to the door – opened it – hesitated – and came back to me.

'I ask your pardon, sir, if I have been in any way rough in speaking to you. You will understand perhaps that I am a little troubled in my mind.' He considered with himself, and took from his pocket the snuff-box to which his wife had alluded. 'I've given up the habit, sir, of taking snuff. It's slovenly, and – and not good for the health. But I don't feel the less honored by your gift. I shall prize it gratefully, as long as I live.'

He turned his head away – but not quickly enough to hide the tears that filled his eyes. For a moment all that was best and truest in the nature of Benjamin Parley had forced its way to expression. But the devil in possession of him was not to be cast out. He became basely ashamed of the good impulse that did him honor. 'The sun is very bright this morning,' he muttered confusedly; 'my eyes are rather weak, sir. I wish you good morning.'

IV

Left by myself I rang the bell, and gave the servant his instructions. If Mr or Mrs Parley called again at the house they were to be told that I was not able to see them.

Was this a harsh act on my part? Let us look the matter fairly in the face and see.

It is possible that some persons, not having had my experience of the worst aspects of human nature, might have been inclined to attribute Mrs Parley's suspicions to her jealous temper, and might have been not unwilling to believe that her husband had engaged a governess for his children in perfect good faith. No such merciful view of the matter presented itself to my mind. Nothing could be plainer to me than that Parley was an instrument in the hands of a bold and wicked woman; who had induced him, for reasons of her own, to commit an act which was nothing less than an outrage on his wife. To what purpose could I interfere? The one person who could help poor Mrs Parley must be armed with the authority of a relation. And, even in this case, what good result could be anticipated if the woman played her part as governess discreetly, and if Parley held firm? A more hopeless domestic prospect, so far, had never presented itself to my view. It vexed and humiliated me to find myself waiting helplessly for events. What else could I do?

On the next day Mrs Parley called, and the servant followed his instructions.

On the day after (with the pardonable pertinacity of a woman in despair), she wrote to me.

The letter has been long since destroyed; but the substance of it remains in my memory. It informed me that the governess was actually established in the house; and described her, it is needless to say, as the most shameless wretch that had ever breathed the breath of life. Asked if he had obtained a reference to her character, Parley had replied that he was old enough to know how to engage a governess: that he refused to answer impertinent questions; and that he had instructed 'Miss Beaumont' (this was the lady's well-sounding name) to follow his example. She had already contrived to steal her way into the confidence of her two innocent pupils, and to produce a favorable impression on a visitor who had called at the house that morning. In one word, Mrs Parley's position was, on her own showing, beyond the reach of help. As I had anticipated, the false governess played her part with discretion, and the infatuated husband asserted his authority.

Ten days later, I happened to be driving through the suburb of our city, and I discovered Mrs Parley in close conversation with one of the younger members of the detective police force, named Butler. They were walking slowly along a retired path which led out of the high-road; so interested apparently in what they had to say to each other that they failed to notice me, though I passed close by them.

The next morning Butler presented himself at my office, and asked leave to speak to me. Being busy that day, I sent a message back, inquiring if the matter was of any importance. The answer was, 'Of most serious importance.' He was immediately admitted to my private room.

V

The little I had heard of this young police officer represented him to be 'a rising man,' resolute and clever, and not very scrupulous in finding his way to his own ends. 'Thoroughly useful, but wants looking after.' There was the superintendent's brief description of Mr Butler.

I warned him at the outset that I had but little time to spare. 'Say what is necessary, but put it in few words. What is your business with me?'

'My business relates, sir, to something that has happened in the house of Benjamin Parley. He has got himself into a serious scrape.'

I should have made a bad detective policeman. When I hear anything that interests or excites me, my face has got a habit of owning it. Butler had merely to look at me, and to see that he might pass over certain explanations which he had been prepared to offer.

'Mrs Parley told me, sir, that you had permitted her husband to speak to you. May I take it for granted that you have heard of the governess? Parley met the woman in the street. He was struck by her personal appearance; he got into conversation with her; he took her into a restaurant, and gave her a dinner; he heard her interesting story; he fell in love with her, like an infernal old fool – oh, I beg your pardon!'

'Quite needless to apologize, Mr Butler. When he permitted the woman to be governess to his children, he behaved like a scoundrel, as well as a fool. Go on. You have discovered, of course, what object she has in establishing herself in Parley's house?'

'I will ask leave to tell you first, sir, how I made the discovery.'

'Why?'

'Because you won't believe who the woman really is, unless I convince you beforehand that I have committed no mistake.'

'Is she a person of celebrity?'

'She is known wherever there is a newspaper published.'

'And conceals herself, of course,' I said, 'under an assumed name?'

'And, what is more, sir, she would never have been found out – but for the wife's jealousy. Everybody but that old woman was wheedled into liking Miss Beaumont. Mrs Parley believed the charming governess to be an impostor, and, being determined to expose her, applied to me for advice. The one morsel of evidence that induced me to look into the matter, came from the servant girl. Miss Beaumont's bedroom was at the back of the house. One night the servant heard her softly open her window, and saw her empty her wash-hand basin into the garden. The customary means of emptying her basin were, of course, ready and waiting in her room. Have you ever dropped into an actor's dressing-room, sir, when he has done his work on the stage?'

'Sometimes.'

'Have you accidentally looked at the basin when he washes his face before he goes home?'

'Not that I remember.'

'In such cases, sir, the actor often leaves, what you may call, a tinge of his complexion in the water; and the colour might strike an observant person. If I had not begun life on the stage, it would never have occurred to me that Miss Beaumont's reason for privately emptying her basin might be connected with a false complexion – occasionally removed, you know, at night, and put on again the next morning. A mere guess, you will say, and more likely to be wrong than right. I don't dispute it; I only say that my guess encouraged me to make one or two inquiries. It's needless to trouble you, sir, by speaking of the difficulties that I found in my way. Let me only say that I contrived to get the better of them. Last night, after old Parley was safe in bed, his wife and his servant and I invaded the sanctuary of Miss Beaumont's room. We were not at all afraid of waking the lady, having taken the precaution (at supper time) of giving her – let us say, the blessing of a good night's rest. She had seemingly been a little irritable and restless before she went to sleep. At any rate, her wig was thrown on the floor. We passed by that, and went to the bed. She lay on her back; her mouth was open, and her arms were flung out on either side of her. Her own pretty fair hair was not very long; and her false colour (she was disguised, sir, as a dark lady in public) was left that night on her face and neck and hands. So far, we had only discovered that she was, what Mrs Parley believed her to be – an impostor, unknown. It was left for *me* to find out who the woman really was. The fastening of her night-dress round the throat had given way. Her bosom was exposed. Upon my soul I was terrified when the truth burst on me! There it was, sir, and no mistake – there, on the right side, under the right breast—'

I started out of my chair. On my writing-table lay a handbill, which I had read and re-read till I knew it by heart. It had been distributed by the London authorities throughout the United Kingdom; and it contained the description of a woman suspected of a terrible crime, who had baffled the pursuit of the police. I looked at the handbill; I looked at the man who was speaking to me.

'Good God!' I cried, 'did you see the scar?'

'I saw it, Mr Sheriff, as plainly as I see you.'

'And the false eye-tooth on the left side of her mouth?'

'Yes, sir – with the gold fastening to speak for it.'

Years have passed since the conversation took place which I have just related. But some persons must remember a famous criminal trial in London – and would recognize, if I felt myself at liberty to mention it, the name of the most atrocious murderess of modern times.

VI

The warrant was issued for the woman's arrest. Competent witnesses identified her, and the preliminaries of the law took their course.

To me, the serious part of the discovery was the part which cast suspicion on the unfortunate Benjamin Parley. Appearances were indisputably against him. He was not only suspected; he was actually charged with assisting the murderess to escape from justice. For the trouble that had now fallen on him, I could be of some use in assisting Parley, and in comforting his unhappy family.

You will hardly believe the assertion, but I declare it to be true, the man's infatuation kept its hold on him more firmly than ever. His own interests were of no sort of importance to him; he seemed to be but little affected even by the distress of his wife and family; his one over-whelming anxiety was for the prisoner. 'I believe in her innocence,' he actually said to me, 'as I believe in my religion. She is falsely accused, sir, of that horrible crime.' He was incapable of resenting, he was even incapable of appreciating the cruel deception that she had practised on him. In one word, he was more devotedly in love with her than ever.

And, mind, there was no madness in this! I can answer for it, from my own experience; he was in perfect possession of his faculties.

The order came to have the woman removed to London, to be tried at the Central Criminal Court. Parley heard of it. In the most moving terms he entreated me to have him set at liberty, and to trust him with the duty of taking charge of the prisoner!

It was my business to see her placed in the railway carriage, under proper guard. The train started in the morning. She refused to leave her bed. As a matter of course, I was sent for in this emergency.

The murderess was not a beautiful woman; she was not even a pretty woman. But she had a voluptuous smile, a singularly musical voice, a fine figure, and a supreme confidence in herself. The moment I entered the room, the horrible creature tried her powers of fascination on the Sheriff – she assumed the character of an innocent victim, overwhelmed by suffering of body and mind. I looked at my watch, and told her she had no time to lose. Not in the least disconcerted, she shifted to a new character; she took me, gayly and cynically, into her confidence. 'My dear sir, you would never have caught me,' she said, 'if I had not made one mistake. As governess in the family of an ex-police-officer I should have been safe from discovery if I had not taken it for granted that I could twist Parley's old woman round my little finger, like the rest of them. Who would have thought she could have been jealous of an ugly old husband at her time of life? Wouldn't you have said yourself, "All that sort of thing must have been over long ago, when a woman is sixty years old and more?" Can there be jealousy without love? And do we love when we are hideous flabby creatures covered with wrinkles? Oh, fie! fie!'

I took out my watch once more.

'If I don't hear that you are up and dressed in ten minutes,' I said, 'I will have you wrapped in a blanket and taken to the railway station by main force.'

With that warning I left the room. The women in charge of her told me afterward that her language was too terrible to be repeated. But she was quick enough to see that I was in earnest; and she was up and dressed in time for the train.

VII

When I tell you that Parley was one of the witnesses examined at the trial, you will understand that we had relieved him from the serious charge of being (in the legal phrase) 'an accessory after the fact.' He went to London as firmly convinced of her innocence as ever. She was found guilty on irresistible evidence, and sentenced to death.

On the conclusion of the trial, Parley had not returned to his family; he had not even written. His wife followed him to London. He seemed hardly to know her again.

The one idea in possession of him was the hopeless idea of obtaining a reprieve. He was absolutely indifferent to every other earthly consideration. Ignorant people thought him mad. He wrote to the newspapers; he haunted the Government offices; he forced his way into the house of the judge who had presided at the trial. An eminent medical man was consulted. After careful examination he pronounced the patient to be perfectly sane.

Through the influence of friends in London, who were known to the city authorities, the poor wretch gained admittance to the prison, while the criminal was waiting for execution. His wife heard what happened at the interview; but she was never able to repeat it; to me or to any one. The same miserable cry always escaped her if she was pressed on the subject. 'Oh don't ask me! Don't ask me!'

On the evening before the execution, he burst into a fit of hysterical crying. That outbreak of violent emotion was followed by a cataleptic seizure. More than eight and forty hours passed before consciousness returned. They feared the loss of reason when he had regained the capacity to feel and to suffer. No such result attended his recovery.

On the same day he spoke of her to others for the first and last time. He said, very quietly, with a remarkable stillness in his face, 'Is she dead?' They answered, Yes. He said no more.

The next morning his wife asked if he would go back to Scotland with her. He was quite ready to do anything that she wished. Two or three days after their return I saw him. His gray hair had become perfectly white; his manner was subdued; his face, full of vivid expression in past days, seemed to have fallen into a state of changeless repose. That was all.

After an interval, I asked his wife and children if they noticed any change for the worse in him. Except that he was very silent, they noticed no change for the worse. He was once more the good husband and kind father of their past happy experience. Did he ever speak of the woman? Never.

I was not quite satisfied. A month later Mrs Parley asked me if I thought a friend of mine, who was one of our greatest living physicians, could do Benjamin any good. I asked what was the matter with him. 'He seems to be getting weak,' was the only reply.

The same day I took my friend with me to Parley's house. After looking at the patient, and putting some questions, he asked to be allowed to make a complete examination. The two retired. When they returned, Mrs Parley was naturally a little alarmed. 'Is there anything that's wrong, sir?' she asked. And to my astonishment, the doctor answered, 'Nothing that I can find out.'

When we had left the house, I put the question to him, 'What does this mean?'

'It means,' he answered, 'that the old man is dying; and I can't find out why.'

Once in every week the great physician visited Parley, always refusing to take his fee; but now and then asking permission to bring a medical friend with him. One day he called on me, and said, 'If you want to say "good-bye" to the old police-officer, you have no time to lose.' I went to the house the same day. Parley was asleep. I returned some hours later. Parley was dead. I asked what he had died of, and the doctor said, 'We have obtained the widow's permission to make a post mortem examination. Wait a little.'

I waited until the funeral was over, and then I returned to the subject.

'What discoveries did you make at the post-mortem examination?'

'We made no discoveries.'

'But there must have been some cause for his death?'

'I called it "decay of nature" on the certificate,' my friend answered. 'A mere pretence! The man's constitution was sound; and he had not reached seventy years of age. A registrar of deaths has nothing to do with questions of sentiment. A doctor's certificate is bound to deal with facts, otherwise—'

He paused, and drew me out of hearing of the mourners lingering in the churchyard.

'Don't mention it among my colleagues,' he said. 'If there really *is* such a thing – Benjamin Parley has died of a broken heart.'

Mr Lepel and the Housekeeper

Originally appeared in *The Spirit of the Times*, 6 December 1884, as 'The Girl at the Gate'. Reprinted in *Little Novels* (1887). The 'First Epoch' of the story gives Collins opportunity to make use of a lifetime's theatregoing, and the main plot, which depends upon the device of a marriage of convenience running out of hand, is a variation on the theme of 'Mr Cosway and the Landlady.' Once again Collins handles Roman Catholic materials sympathetically.

FIRST EPOCH

The Italians are born actors.

At this conclusion I arrived, sitting in a Roman theatre – now many years since. My friend and travelling companion, Rothsay, cordially agreed with me. Experience had given us some claim to form an opinion. We had visited, at that time, nearly every city in Italy. Wherever a theatre was open, we had attended the performances of the companies which travel from place to place; and we had never seen bad acting from first to last. Men and women, whose names are absolutely unknown in England, played (in modern comedy and drama for the most part) with a general level of dramatic ability which I have never seen equalled in the theatres of other nations. Incapable Italian actors there must be, no doubt. For my own part I have only discovered them, by ones and twos, in England; appearing among the persons engaged to support Salvini and Ristori before the audiences of London.

On the occasion of which I am now writing, the night's performances consisted of two plays. An accident, to be presently related, prevented us from seeing more than the introductory part of the second piece. That one act – in respect of the influence which the remembrance of it afterwards exercised over Rothsay and myself – claims a place of its own in the opening pages of the present narrative.

The scene of the story was laid in one of the principalities of Italy, in the bygone days of the Carbonaro conspiracies. The chief persons were two young noblemen, friends affectionately attached to each other, and a beautiful girl born in the lower ranks of life.

On the rising of the curtain, the scene before us was the courtyard of a prison. We found the beautiful girl (called Celia as well as I can recollect) in great distress; confiding her sorrows to the gaoler's daughter. Her father was pining in the prison, charged with an offence of which he was innocent; and she herself was suffering the tortures of hopeless love. She was on the point of confiding her secret to her friend, when the appearance of the young noblemen closed her lips. The girls at once withdrew; and the two friends – whom I now only remember as The Marquis and The Count – began the dialogue which prepared us for the story of the play.

The Marquis has been tried for conspiracy against the reigning Prince and his government; has been found guilty, and is condemned to be shot that evening. He accepts his sentence with the resignation of a man who is weary of his life. Young as he is, he has tried the round of pleasures without enjoyment; he has no interests, no aspirations, no hopes; he looks on death as a welcome release. His friend the Count, admitted to a farewell interview, has invented a stratagem by which the prisoner may escape and take to flight. The Marquis expresses a grateful sense of obligation, and prefers being shot. 'I don't value my life,' he says; 'I am not a happy man like you.' Upon this the Count mentions circumstances which he has hitherto kept secret. He loves the charming Celia, and loves in vain. Her reputation is unsullied; she possesses every good quality that a man can desire in a wife – but the Count's social position forbids him to marry a woman of low birth. He is heartbroken; and he too finds life without hope a burden that is not to be borne. The Marquis at once sees a way of devoting himself to his friend's interests. He is rich; his money is at his own disposal; he will bequeath a marriage portion to Celia which will make her one of the richest women in Italy. The Count receives this proposal with a sigh. 'No money,' he says, 'will remove the obstacle that still remains. My father's fatal objection to Celia is her rank in life.' The Marquis walks apart – considers a little – consults his watch – and returns with a new idea. 'I have nearly two hours of life still left,' he says. 'Send for Celia: she was here just now, and she is probably in her father's cell.' The Count is at a loss to understand what this proposal means. The Marquis explains himself. 'I ask your permission,' he resumes, 'to offer marriage to Celia – for your sake. The chaplain of the prison will perform the ceremony. Before dark, the girl you love will be my widow. My widow is a lady of title – a fit wife for the greatest nobleman in the land.' The Count protests and refuses in vain. The gaoler is sent to find Celia. She appears. Unable to endure the scene, the Count rushes out in horror. The Marquis takes the girl into his confidence, and makes his excuses. If she becomes a widow of rank, she may not only marry the Count, but will be in a position to procure the liberty of the innocent old man, whose strength is failing him under the rigours of imprisonment. Celia hesitates. After a struggle with herself, filial love prevails, and she consents. The gaoler announces that the chaplain is waiting; the bride and bridegroom withdraw to the prison chapel. Left on the stage, the gaoler hears a distant sound in the city, which he is at a loss to understand. It sinks, increases again, travels nearer to the prison, and now betrays itself as the sound of multitudinous voices in a state of furious uproar. Has the conspiracy broken out again? Yes! The whole population has risen; the soldiers have refused to fire on the people; the terrified Prince has dismissed his ministers, and promises a constitution. The Marquis, returning from the ceremony which has just made Celia his wife, is presented with a free pardon, and with the offer of a high place in the reformed ministry. A new life is opening before him – and he has innocently ruined his friend's prospects! On this striking situation the drop-curtain falls.

While we were still applauding the first act, Rothsay alarmed me: he dropped from his seat at my side, like a man struck dead. The stifling heat in the theatre had proved too much for him. We carried him out at once into the fresh air. When he came to his senses, my friend entreated me to leave him, and see the end of the play. To my mind, he looked as if he might faint again. I insisted on going back with him to our hotel.

On the next day I went to the theatre, to ascertain if the play would be repeated. The box-office was closed. The dramatic company had left Rome.

My interest in discovering how the story ended led me next to the booksellers' shops – in the hope of buying the play. Nobody knew anything about it. Nobody could tell me whether it was the original work of an Italian writer, or whether it had been stolen (and probably disfigured) from the French. As a fragment I had seen it. As a fragment it has remained from that time to this.

SECOND EPOCH

One of my objects in writing these lines is to vindicate the character of an innocent woman (formerly in my service as housekeeper) who has been cruelly slandered. Absorbed in the pursuit of my purpose, it has only now occurred to me that strangers may desire to know something more than they know now of myself and my friend. 'Give us some idea,' they may say, 'of what sort of persons you are, if you wish to interest us at the outset of your story.'

A most reasonable suggestion, I admit. Unfortunately, I am not the right man to comply with it.

In the first place, I cannot pretend to pronounce judgment on my own character. In the second place, I am incapable of writing impartially of my friend. At the imminent risk of his own life, Rothsay rescued me from a dreadful death by accident, when we were at college together. Who can expect me to speak of his faults? I am not even capable of seeing them.

Under these embarrassing circumstances – and not forgetting, at the same time, that a servant's opinion of his master and his master's friends may generally be trusted not to err on the favourable side – I am tempted to call my valet as a witness to character.

I slept badly on our first night at Rome; and I happened to be awake while the man was talking of us confidentially in the courtyard of the hotel – just under my bedroom window. Here, to the best of my recollection, is a faithful report of what he said to some friend among the servants who understood English:

'My master's well connected, you must know – though he's only plain Mr Lepel. His uncle's the great lawyer, Lord Lepel; and his late father was a banker. Rich, did you say? I should think he *was* rich – and be hanged to him! No; not married, and not likely to be. Owns he was forty last birthday; a regular old bachelor. Not a bad sort, taking him altogether. The worst of him is, he is one of the most indiscreet persons I ever met with. Does the queerest things, when the whim takes him, and doesn't care what other people think of it. They say the Lepels have all got a slate loose in the upper story. Oh, no; not a very old family – I mean, nothing compared to the family of his friend, young Rothsay. *They* count back, as I have heard, to the ancient Kings of Scotland. Between ourselves, the ancient Kings haven't left the Rothsays much money. They would be glad, I'll be bound, to get my rich master for one of their daughters. Poor as Job, I tell you. This young fellow, travelling with us, has never had a spare five-pound note since he was born. Plenty of brains in his head, I grant you; and a little too apt sometimes to be suspicious of other people. But liberal – oh, give him his due – liberal in a small way. Tips me with a sovereign now and then. I take it – Lord bless you, I take it. What do you say? Has he got any employment? Not he! Dabbles in chemistry (experiments, and that sort of thing) by way of amusing himself; and tells the most infernal lies about it. The other day he showed me a bottle about as big as a thimble, with what looked like water in it, and said it was enough to poison everybody in the hotel. What rot! Isn't that the clock striking again? Near about bedtime, I should say. Wish you goodnight.'

There are our characters – drawn on the principle of justice without mercy, by an impudent rascal who is the best valet in England. Now you know what sort of persons we are; and now we may go on again.

*

Rothsay and I parted, soon after our night at the theatre. He went to Civita Vecchia to join a friend's yacht, waiting for him in the harbour. I turned homeward, travelling at a leisurely rate through the Tyrol and Germany.

After my arrival in England, certain events in my life occurred, which did not appear to have any connection at the time. They led nevertheless to consequences which seriously altered the relations of happy past years between Rothsay and myself.

The first event took place on my return to my house in London. I found among the letters waiting for me, an invitation from Lord Lepel to spend a few weeks with him at his country seat in Sussex.

I had made so many excuses, in past years, when I received invitations from my uncle, that I was really ashamed to plead engagements in London again. There was no unfriendly feeling between us. My only motive for keeping away from him took its rise in dislike of the ordinary modes of life in an English country-house. A man who feels no interest in politics, who cares nothing for field sports, who is impatient of amateur music and incapable of small talk, is a man out of his element in country society. This was my unlucky case. I went to Lord Lepel's house sorely against my will; longing already for the day when it would be time to say good-bye.

The routine of my uncle's establishment had remained unaltered since my last experience of it.

I found my lord expressing the same pride in his collection of old masters, and telling the same story of the wonderful escape of his picture-gallery from fire – I renewed my acquaintance with the same members of Parliament among the guests, all on the same side in politics – I joined in the same dreary amusements – I saluted the same resident priest (the Lepels are all born and bred Roman Catholics) – I submitted to the same rigidly early breakfast hour; and inwardly cursed the same peremptory bell, ringing as a means of reminding us of our meals. The one change that presented itself was a change out of the house. Death had removed the lodge-keeper at the park-gate. His widow and daughter (Mrs Rymer and little Susan) remained in their pretty cottage. They had been allowed by my lord's kindness to take charge of the gate.

Out walking, on the morning after my arrival, I was caught in a shower on my way back to the park, and took shelter in the lodge.

In the bygone days, I had respected Mrs Rymer's husband as a thoroughly worthy man – but Mrs Rymer herself was no great favourite of mine. She had married beneath her, as the phrase is, and she was a little too conscious of it. A woman with a sharp eye to her own interests; selfishly discontented with her position in life, and not very scrupulous in her choice of means when she had an end in view: that is how I describe Mrs Rymer. Her daughter, whom I only remembered as a weakly child, astonished me when I saw her again after the interval that had elapsed. The backward flower had bloomed into perfect health. Susan was now a lovely little modest girl of seventeen – with a natural delicacy and refinement of manner, which marked her to my mind as one of Nature's gentlewomen. When I entered the lodge she was writing at a table in a corner, having some books on it, and rose to withdraw. I begged that she would proceed with her employment, and asked if I might know what it was. She answered me with a blush, and a pretty brightening of her clear blue eyes. 'I am trying, sir, to teach myself French,' she said. The weather showed no signs of improving – I volunteered to help her, and found her such an attentive and intelligent pupil that I looked in at the lodge from time to time afterwards, and continued my instructions. The younger men among my uncle's guests set their own stupid construction on my attentions to 'the girl at the gate,' as they called her – rather too familiarly, according to my notions of propriety. I contrived to remind them that I was old enough to be Susan's father, in a manner which put an end to their jokes; and I was pleased to hear, when I next went to the lodge, that Mrs Rymer had been wise enough to keep these facetious gentlemen at their proper distance.

The day of my departure arrived. Lord Lepel took leave of me kindly, and asked for news of Rothsay. 'Let me know when your friend returns,' my uncle said; 'he belongs to a good old stock. Put me in mind of him when I next invite you to come to my house.'

On my way to the train I stopped of course at the lodge to say good-bye. Mrs Rymer came out alone. I asked for Susan.

'My daughter is not very well to-day.'

'Is she confined to her room?'

'She is in the parlour.'

I might have been mistaken, but I thought Mrs Rymer answered me in no very friendly way. Resolved to judge for myself, I entered the lodge, and found my poor little pupil sitting in a corner, crying. When I asked her what was the matter, the excuse of a 'bad headache' was the only reply that I received. The natures of young girls are a hopeless puzzle to me. Susan seemed, for some reason which it was impossible to understand, to be afraid to look at me.

'Have you and your mother been quarrelling?' I asked.

'Oh, no!'

She denied it with such evident sincerity that I could not for a moment suspect her of deceiving me. Whatever the cause of her distress might be, it was plain that she had her own reasons for keeping it a secret.

Her French books were on the table. I tried a little allusion to her lessons.

'I hope you will go on regularly with your studies,' I said.

'I will do my best, sir – without you to help me.'

She said it so sadly that I proposed – purely from the wish to encourage her – a continuation of our lessons through the post.

'Send your exercises to me once a week,' I suggested; 'and I will return them corrected.'

She thanked me in low tones, with a shyness of manner which I had never noticed in her before. I had done my best to cheer her – and I was conscious, as we shook hands at parting, that I had failed. A feeling of disappointment overcomes me when I see young people out of spirits. I was sorry for Susan.

THIRD EPOCH

One of my faults (which has not been included in the list set forth by my valet) is a disinclination to occupy myself with my own domestic affairs. The proceedings of my footman, while I had been away from home, left me no alternative but to dismiss him on my return. With this exertion of authority my interference as chief of the household came to an end. I left it to my excellent housekeeper, Mrs Mozeen, to find a sober successor to the drunken vagabond who had been sent away. She discovered a respectable young man – tall, plump, and rosy – whose name was Joseph, and whose character was beyond reproach. I have but one excuse for noticing such a trifling event as this. It took its place, at a later period, in the chain which was slowly winding itself round me.

My uncle had asked me to prolong my visit; and I should probably have consented, but for anxiety on the subject of a near and dear relative – my sister. Her health had been failing since the death of her husband, to whom she was tenderly attached. I heard news of her while I was in Sussex, which hurried me back to town. In a month more, her death deprived me of my last living relation. She left no children; and my two brothers had both died unmarried while they were still young men.

This affliction placed me in a position of serious embarrassment, in regard to the disposal of my property after my death.

I had hitherto made no will; being well aware that my fortune (which was entirely in money) would go in due course of law to the person of all others who would employ it to the best purpose – that is to say, to my sister as my nearest of kin. As I was now situated, my property would revert to my uncle if I died intestate. He was a richer man than I was. Of his two children, both sons, the eldest would inherit his estates: the youngest had already succeeded to his mother's ample fortune. Having literally no family claims on me, I felt bound to recognise the wider demands of poverty and misfortune, and to devote my superfluous wealth to increasing the revenues of charitable institutions. As to minor legacies, I owed it to my good housekeeper, Mrs Mozeen, not to forget the faithful services of past years. Need I add – if I had been free to act as I pleased – that I should have gladly made Rothsay the object of a handsome bequest? But this was not to be. My friend was a man morbidly sensitive on the subject of money. In the early days of our intercourse, we had been for the first and only time on the verge of a quarrel, when I had asked (as a favour to myself) to be allowed to provide for him in my will.

'It is because I am poor,' he explained, 'that I refuse to profit by your kindness – though I feel it gratefully.'

I failed to understand him – and said so plainly.

'You will understand this,' he resumed; 'I should never recover my sense of degradation, if a mercenary motive on my side was associated with our friendship. Don't say it's impossible! You know as well as I do that appearances would be against me, in the eyes of the world. Besides, I don't want money; my own small income is enough for me. Make me your executor if you like, and leave me the customary present of five hundred pounds. If you exceed that sum I declare on my word of honour that I will not touch one farthing of it.' He took my hand, and pressed it fervently. 'Do me a favour,' he said. 'Never let us speak of this again!'

I understood that I must yield – or lose my friend.

In now making my will, I accordingly appointed Rothsay one of my executors, on the terms that he had prescribed. The minor legacies having been next duly reduced to writing, I left the bulk of my fortune to public charities.

My lawyer laid the fair copy of the will on my table.

'A dreary disposition of property for a man of your age,' he said. 'I hope to receive a new set of instructions before you are a year older.'

'What instructions?' I asked.

'To provide for your wife and children,' he answered.

My wife and children! The idea seemed to be so absurd that I burst out laughing. It never occurred to me that there could be any absurdity in my own point of view.

I was sitting alone, after my legal adviser had taken his leave, looking absently at the newly-engrossed will, when I heard a sharp knock at the house-door which I thought I recognised. In another minute Rothsay's bright face enlivened my dull room. He had returned from the Mediterranean that morning.

'Am I interrupting you?' he asked, pointing to the leaves of manuscript before me. 'Are you writing a book?'

'I am making my will.'

His manner changed; he looked at me seriously.

'Do you remember what I said, when we once talked of your will?' he asked. I set his doubts at rest immediately – but he was not quite satisfied yet. 'Can't you put your will away?' he suggested. 'I hate the sight of anything that reminds me of death.'

'Give me a minute to sign it,' I said – and rang to summon the witnesses.

Mrs Mozeen answered the bell. Rothsay looked at her, as if he wished to have my housekeeper put away as well as my will. From the first moment when he had seen her, he conceived a great dislike to that good creature. There was nothing, I am sure, personally repellent about her. She was a little slim quiet woman, with a pale complexion and bright brown eyes. Her movements were gentle; her voice was low; her decent gray dress was adapted to her age. Why Rothsay should dislike her was more than he could explain himself. He turned his unreasonable prejudice into a joke – and said he hated a woman who wore slate-coloured cap-ribbons!

I explained to Mrs Mozeen that I wanted witnesses to the signature of my will. Naturally enough – being in the room at the time – she asked if she could be one of them.

I was obliged to say No; and not to mortify her, I gave the reason.

'My will recognises what I owe to your good services,' I said. 'If you are one of the witnesses, you will lose your legacy. Send up the men-servants.'

With her customary tact, Mrs Mozeen expressed her gratitude silently, by a look, – and left the room.

'Why couldn't you tell that woman to send the servants, without mentioning her legacy?' Rothsay asked. 'My friend Lepel, you have done a very foolish thing.'

'In what way?'

'You have given Mrs Mozeen an interest in your death.'

It was impossible to make a serious reply to this ridiculous exhibition of Rothsay's prejudice against poor Mrs Mozeen.

'When am I to be murdered?' I asked. 'And how is it to be done? Poison?'

'I'm not joking,' Rothsay answered. 'You are infatuated about your housekeeper. When you spoke of her legacy, did you notice her eyes?'

'Yes.'

'Did nothing strike you?'

'It struck me that they were unusually well preserved eyes for a woman of her age.'

The appearance of the valet and the footman put an end to this idle talk. The will was executed, and locked up. Our conversation turned on Rothsay's travels by sea. The cruise had been in every way successful. The matchless shores of the Mediterranean defied description; the sailing of the famous yacht had proved to be worthy of her reputation; and, to crown all, Rothsay had come back to England, in a fair way, for the first time is his life, of making money.

'I have discovered a treasure,' he announced.

'What is it?'

'It *was* a dirty little modern picture, picked up in a by-street at Palermo. It *is* a Virgin and Child, by Guido.'

On further explanation it appeared that the picture exposed for sale was painted on copper. Noticing the contrast between the rare material and the wretchedly bad painting that covered it, Rothsay had called to mind some of the well-known stories of valuable works of art that had been painted over for purposes of disguise. The price asked for the picture amounted to little more than the value of the metal. Rothsay bought it. His knowledge of chemistry enabled him to put his suspicion successfully to the test; and one of the guests on board the yacht – a famous French artist – had declared his conviction that the picture now revealed to view was a genuine work by Guido. Such an opinion as this convinced me that it would be worth while to submit my friend's discovery to the judgment of other experts. Consulted independently, these critics confirmed the view taken by the celebrated personage who had first seen the work. This result having been obtained, Rothsay asked my advice next on the question of selling his picture. I at once thought of my uncle. An undoubted work by Guido would surely be an acquisition to his gallery. I had only (in accordance with his own request) to let him know that my friend had returned to England. We might take the picture with us, when we received our invitation to Lord Lepel's house.

FOURTH EPOCH

My uncle's answer arrived by return of post. Other engagements obliged him to defer receiving us for a month. At the end of that time, we were cordially invited to visit him, and to stay as long as we liked.

In the interval that now passed, other events occurred – still of the trifling kind.

One afternoon, just as I was thinking of taking my customary ride in the Park, the servant appeared charged with a basket of flowers, and with a message from Mrs Rymer, requesting me to honour her by accepting a little offering from her daughter. Hearing that she was then waiting in the hall, I told the man to show her in. Susan (as I ought to have already mentioned) had sent her exercises to me regularly every week. In returning them corrected, I had once or twice added a word of well-deserved approval. The offering of flowers was evidently intended to express my pupil's grateful sense of the interest taken in her by her teacher.

I had no reason, this time, to suppose that Mrs Rymer entertained an unfriendly feeling towards me. At the first words of greeting that passed between us I perceived a change in her manner, which ran into the opposite extreme. She overwhelmed me with the most elaborate demonstrations of politeness and respect; dwelling on her gratitude for my kindness in receiving her, and on her pride at seeing her daughter's flowers on my table, until I made a resolute effort to stop her by asking (as if it was actually a matter of importance to me!) whether she was in London on business or on pleasure.

'Oh, on business, sir! My poor husband invested his little savings in bank stock, and I have just been drawing my dividend. I do hope you don't think my girl over-bold in venturing to send you a few flowers. She wouldn't allow me to interfere. I do assure you she would gather and arrange them with her own hands. In themselves I know they are hardly worth accepting; but if you will allow the motive to plead—'

I made another effort to stop Mrs Rymer; I said her daughter could not have sent me a prettier present.

The inexhaustible woman only went on more fluently than ever.

'She is so grateful, sir, and so proud of your goodness in looking at her exercises. The difficulties of the French language seem as nothing to her, now her motive is to please you. She is so devoted to her studies that I find it difficult to induce her to take the exercise necessary to her health; and, as you may perhaps remember, Susan was always rather weakly as a child. She inherits her father's constitution, Mr Lepel – not mine.'

Here, to my infinite relief, the servant appeared, announcing that my horse was at the door.

Mrs Rymer opened her mouth. I saw a coming flood of apologies on the point of pouring out – and seized my hat on the spot. I declared I had an appointment; I sent kind remembrances to Susan (pitying her for having such a mother with my whole heart); I said I hoped to return to my uncle's house soon, and to continue the French lessons. The one thing more that I remember was finding myself safe in the saddle, and out of the reach of Mrs Rymer's tongue.

Reflecting on what had passed, it was plain to me that this woman had some private end in view and that my abrupt departure had prevented her from finding the way to it. What motive could she possibly have for that obstinate persistence in presenting poor Susan under a favourable aspect, to a man who had already shown that he was honestly interested in her pretty modest daughter? I tried hard to penetrate the mystery – and gave it up in despair.

Three days before the date at which Rothsay and I were to pay our visit to Lord Lepel, I found myself compelled to undergo one of the minor miseries of human life. In other words, I became one of the guests at a large dinner-party. It was a rainy day in October. My position at the table placed me between a window that was open, and a door that was hardly ever shut. I went to bed shivering; and woke the next morning with a headache and a difficulty in breathing. On consulting the doctor, I found that I was suffering from an attack of bronchitis. There was no reason to be alarmed. If I remained indoors, and submitted to the necessary treatment, I might hope to keep my engagement with my uncle in ten days or a fortnight.

There was no alternative but to submit. I accordingly arranged with Rothsay that he should present himself at Lord Lepel's house (taking the picture with him), on the date appointed for our visit, and that I should follow as soon as I was well enough to travel.

On the day when he was to leave London, my friend kindly came to keep me company for awhile. He was followed into my room by Mrs Mozeen, with a bottle of medicine in her hand. This worthy creature, finding that the doctor's directions occasionally escaped my memory, devoted herself to the duty of administering the remedies at the prescribed intervals of time. When she left the room, having performed her duties as usual, I saw Rothsay's eyes follow her to the door with an expression of sardonic curiosity. He put a strange question to me as soon as we were alone.

'Who engaged that new servant of yours?' he asked. 'I mean that fat fellow, with the curly flaxen hair.'

'Hiring servants,' I replied, 'is not much in my way. I left the engagement of the new man to Mrs Mozeen.'

Rothsay walked gravely up to my bedside.

'Lepel,' he said, 'your respectable housekeeper is in love with the fat young footman.'

It is not easy to amuse a man suffering from bronchitis. But this new outbreak of absurdity was more than I could resist, even with a mustard-plaster on my chest.

'I thought I should raise your spirits,' Rothsay proceeded. 'When I came to your house this morning, the valet opened the door to me. I expressed my surprise at his condescending to take that trouble. He informed me that Joseph was otherwise engaged. "With anybody in particular?" I asked, humouring the joke. "Yes, sir, with the housekeeper. She's teaching him how to brush his hair, so as to show off his good looks to the best advantage." Make up your mind, my friend, to lose Mrs Mozeen – especially if she happens to have any money.'

'Nonsense, Rothsay! The poor woman is old enough to be Joseph's mother.'

'My good fellow, that won't make any difference to Joseph. In the days when we were rich enough to keep a manservant, our footman – as handsome a fellow as ever you saw, and no older than I am – married a witch with a lame leg. When I asked him why he had made such a fool of himself he looked quite indignant, and said, "Sir! she has got six hundred pounds." He and the witch keep a public-house. What will you bet me that we don't see your housekeeper drawing beer at the bar, and Joseph getting drunk in the parlour, before we are a year older?'

I was not well enough to prolong my enjoyment of Rothsay's boyish humour. Besides, exaggeration to be really amusing must have some relation, no matter how slender it may be, to the truth. My housekeeper belonged to a respectable family, and was essentially a person accustomed to respect herself. Her brother occupied a position of responsibility in the establishment of a firm of chemists whom I had employed for years past. Her late husband had farmed his own land, and had owed his ruin to calamities for which he was in no way responsible. Kind-hearted Mrs Mozeen was just the woman to take a motherly interest in a well-disposed lad like Joseph; and it was equally characteristic of my valet – especially when Rothsay was thoughtless enough to encourage him – to pervert an innocent action for the sake of indulging in a stupid jest. I took advantage of my privilege as an invalid, and changed the subject.

A week passed. I had expected to hear from Rothsay. To my surprise and disappointment no letter arrived.

Susan was more considerate. She wrote, very modestly and prettily, to say that she and her mother had heard of my illness from Mr Rothsay, and to express the hope that I should soon be restored to health. A few days later, Mrs Rymer's politeness carried her to the length of taking the journey to London, to make inquiries at my door. I did not see her, of course. She left word that she would have the honour of calling again.

The second week followed. I had by that time perfectly recovered from my attack of bronchitis – and yet I was too ill to leave the house.

The doctor himself seemed to be at a loss to understand the symptoms that now presented themselves. A vile sensation of nausea tried my endurance, and an incomprehensible prostration of strength depressed my spirits. I felt such a strange reluctance to exert myself, that I actually left it to Mrs Mozeen to write to my uncle in my name, and say that I was not yet well enough to visit him. My medical adviser tried various methods of treatment; my housekeeper administered the prescribed medicines with unremitting care; but nothing came of it. A physician of great authority was called into consultation. Being completely puzzled, he retreated to the last refuge of bewildered doctors. I asked him what was the matter with me. And he answered:

'Suppressed gout.'

FIFTH EPOCH

Midway in the third week, my uncle wrote to me as follows:

I have been obliged to request your friend Rothsay to bring his visit to a conclusion. Although he refuses to confess it, I have reason to believe that he has committed the folly of falling seriously in love with the young girl at my lodge gate. I have tried remonstrance in vain; and I write to his father at the same time that I write to you. There is much more that I might say. I reserve it for the time when I hope to have the pleasure of seeing you, restored to health.

Two days after the receipt of this alarming letter, Rothsay returned to me.

Ill as I was, I forgot my sufferings the moment I looked at him. Wild and haggard, he stared at me with bloodshot eyes like a man demented.

'Do you think I am mad? I dare say I am. I can't live without her.' Those were the first words he said when we shook hands.

But I had more influence over him than any other person; and, weak as I was, I exerted it. Little by little, he became more reasonable; he began to speak like his old self again.

To have expressed any surprise, on my part, at what had happened, would have been not only imprudent, but unworthy of him and of me. My first inquiry was suggested by the fear that he might have been hurried into openly confessing his passion to Susan – although his position forbade him to offer marriage. I had done him an injustice. His honourable nature had shrunk from the cruelty of raising hopes, which, for all he knew to the contrary, might never be realized. At the same time, he had his reasons for believing that he was at least personally acceptable to her.

'She was always glad to see me,' said poor Rothsay. 'We constantly talked of you. She spoke of your kindness so prettily and so gratefully. Oh, Lepel, it is not her beauty only that has won my heart! Her nature is the nature of an angel.'

His voice failed him. For the first time in my remembrance of our long companionship, he burst into tears.

I was so shocked and distressed that I had the greatest difficulty in preserving my own self-control. In the effort to comfort him, I asked if he had ventured to confide in his father.

'You are the favourite son,' I reminded him. 'Is there no gleam of hope in the future?'

He had written to his father. In silence he gave me the letter in reply.

It was expressed with a moderation which I had hardly dared to expect. Mr Rothsay the elder admitted that he had himself married for love, and that his wife's rank in the social scale (although higher than Susan's) had not been equal to his own.

'In such a family as ours,' he wrote – perhaps with pardonable pride – 'we raise our wives to our own degree. But this young person labours under a double disadvantage. She is obscure, and she is poor. What have you to offer her? Nothing. And what have I to give you? Nothing.'

This meant, as I interpreted it, that the main obstacle in the way was Susan's poverty. And I was rich! In the excitement that possessed me, I followed the impulse of the moment headlong, like a child.

'While you were away from me,' I said to Rothsay, 'did you never once think of your old friend? Must I remind you that I can make Susan your wife with one stroke of my pen?' He looked at me in silent surprise. I took my cheque-book from the drawer of the table, and placed the inkstand within reach. 'Susan's marriage portion,' I said, 'is a matter of a line of writing, with my name at the end of it.'

He burst out, with an exclamation that stopped me, just as my pen touched the paper.

'Good heavens!' he cried, 'you are thinking of that play we saw at Rome! Are we on the stage? Are you performing the part of the Marquis – and am I the Count?'

I was so startled by this wild allusion to the past – I recognised with such astonishment the reproduction of one of the dramatic situations in the play, at a crisis in his life and mine – that the use of the pen remained suspended in my hand. For the first time in my life, I was conscious of a sensation which resembled superstitious dread.

Rothsay recovered himself first. He misinterpreted what was passing in my mind.

'Don't think me ungrateful,' he said. 'You dear, kind, good fellow, consider for a moment, and you will see that it can't be. What would be said of her and of me, if you made Susan rich with your money, and if I married her? The poor innocent would be called your cast-off mistress. People would say, "He has behaved liberally to her, and his needy friend has taken advantage of it."'

The point of view which I had failed to see was put with terrible directness of expression: the conviction that I was wrong was literally forced on me. What reply could I make? Rothsay evidently felt for me.

'You are ill,' he said gently; 'let me leave you to rest.'

He held out his hand to say good-bye. I insisted on his taking up his abode with me, for the present at least. Ordinary persuasion failed to induce him to yield. I put it on selfish grounds next.

'You have noticed that I am ill,' I said; 'I want you to keep me company.'

He gave way directly.

Through the wakeful night, I tried to consider what moral remedies might be within our reach. The one useful conclusion at which I could arrive was to induce Rothsay to try what absence and change might do to compose his mind. To advise him to travel alone was out of the question. I wrote to his one other old friend besides myself – the friend who had taken him on a cruise in the Mediterranean.

The owner of the yacht had that very day given directions to have his vessel laid up for the winter season. He at once countermanded the order by telegraph. 'I am an idle man,' he said, 'and I am as fond of Rothsay as you are. I will take him wherever he likes to go.' It was not easy to persuade the object of these kind intentions to profit by them. Nothing that I could say roused him. I spoke to him of his picture. He had left it at my uncle's house, and neither knew nor cared to know whether it had been sold or not. The one consideration which ultimately influenced Rothsay was presented by the doctor; speaking as follows (to quote his own explanation) in the interests of my health:

'I warned your friend,' he said, 'that his conduct was causing anxiety which you were not strong enough to bear. On hearing this he at once promised to follow the advice which you had given to him, and to join the yacht. As you know, he has kept his word. May I ask if he has ever followed the medical profession?'

Replying in the negative, I begged the doctor to tell me why he had put his question.

He answered, 'Mr Rothsay requested me to tell him all that I knew about your illness. I complied, of course; mentioning that I had lately adopted a new method of treatment, and that I had every reason to feel confident of the results. He was so interested in the symptoms of your illness, and in the remedies being tried, that he took notes in his pocket-book of what I had said. When he paid me that compliment, I thought it possible that I might be speaking to a colleague.'

I was pleased to hear of my friend's anxiety for my recovery. If I had been in better health, I might have asked myself what reason he could have had for making those entries in his pocket-book.

Three days later, another proof reached me of Rothsay's anxiety for my welfare.

The owner of the yacht wrote to beg that I would send him a report of my health, addressed to a port on the south coast of England, to which they were then bound. 'If we don't hear good news,' he added, 'I have reason to fear that Rothsay will overthrow our plans for the recovery of his peace of mind by leaving the vessel, and making his own inquiries at your bedside.'

With no small difficulty I roused myself sufficiently to write a few words with my own hand. They were words that lied – for my poor friend's sake. In a postscript, I begged my correspondent to let me hear if the effect produced on Rothsay had answered to our hopes and expectations.

SIXTH EPOCH

The weary days followed each other – and time failed to justify the doctor's confidence in his new remedies. I grew weaker and weaker.

My uncle came to see me. He was so alarmed that he insisted on a consultation being held with his own physician. Another great authority was called in, at the same time, by the urgent request of my own medical man. These distinguished persons held more than one privy council, before they would consent to give a positive opinion. It was an evasive opinion (encumbered with hard words of Greek and Roman origin) when it was at last pronounced. I waited until they had taken their leave, and then appealed to my own doctor. 'What do those men really think?' I asked. 'Shall I live, or die?'

The doctor answered for himself as well as for his illustrious colleagues. 'We have great faith in the new prescriptions,' he said.

I understood what that meant. They were afraid to tell me the truth. I insisted on the truth.

'How long shall I live?' I said. 'Till the end of the year?'

The reply followed in one terrible word:

'Perhaps.'

It was then the first week in December. I understood that I might reckon – at the utmost – on three weeks of life. What I felt, on arriving at this conclusion, I shall not say. It is the one secret I keep from the readers of these lines.

The next day, Mrs Rymer called once more to make inquiries. Not satisfied with the servant's report, she entreated that I would consent to see her. My housekeeper, with her customary kindness, undertook to convey the message. If she had been a wicked woman, would she have acted in this way? 'Mrs Rymer seems to be sadly distressed,' she pleaded. 'As I understand, sir, she is suffering under some domestic anxiety which can only be mentioned to yourself.'

Did this anxiety relate to Susan? The bare doubt of it decided me. I consented to see Mrs Rymer. Feeling it necessary to control her in the use of her tongue, I spoke the moment the door was opened.

'I am suffering from illness; and I must ask you to spare me as much as possible. What do you wish to say to me?'

The tone in which I addressed Mrs Rymer would have offended a more sensitive woman. The truth is, she had chosen an unfortunate time for her visit. There were fluctuations in the progress of my malady: there were days when I felt better, and days when I felt worse – and this was a bad day. Moreover, my uncle had tried my temper that morning. He had called to see me, on his way to winter in the south of France by his physician's advice; and he recommended a trial of change of air in my case also. His country house (only thirty miles from London) was entirely at my disposal; and the railway supplied beds for invalids. It was useless to answer that I was not equal to the effort. He reminded me that I had exerted myself to leave my bedchamber for my arm-chair in the next room, and that a little additional resolution would enable me to follow his advice. We parted in a state of irritation on either side which, so far as I was concerned, had not subsided yet.

'I wish to speak to you, sir, about my daughter,' Mrs Rymer answered.

The mere allusion to Susan had its composing effect on me. I said kindly that I hoped she was well.

'Well in body,' Mrs Rymer announced. 'Far from it, sir, in mind.'

Before I could ask what this meant, we were interrupted by the appearance of the servant, bringing the letters which had arrived for me by the afternoon post. I told the man, impatiently, to put them on the table at my side.

'What is distressing Susan?' I inquired, without stopping to look at the letters.

'She is fretting, sir, about your illness. Oh, Mr Lepel, if you would only try the sweet country air! If you only had my good little Susan to nurse you!'

She too taking my uncle's view! And talking of Susan as my nurse!

'What are you thinking of?' I asked her. 'A young girl like your daughter nursing Me! You ought to have more regard for Susan's good name!'

'I know what *you* ought to do!' She made that strange reply with a furtive look at me; half in anger, half in alarm.

'Go on,' I said.

'Will you turn me out of your house for my impudence?' she asked.

'I will hear what you have to say to me. What ought I to do?'

'Marry Susan.'

I heard the woman plainly – and yet, I declare I doubted the evidence of my senses.

'She's breaking her heart for you,' Mrs Rymer burst out. 'She's been in love with you, since you first darkened our doors – and it will end in the neighbours finding it out. I did my duty to her; I tried to stop it; I tried to prevent you from seeing her, when you went away. Too late; the mischief was done. When I see my girl fading day by day – crying about you in secret, talking about you in her dreams – I can't stand it; I must speak out. Oh, yes, I know how far beneath you she is – the daughter of your uncle's servant. But she's your equal, sir, in the sight of Heaven. My lord's priest converted her only last year – and my Susan is as good a Papist as yourself.'

How could I let this go on? I felt that I ought to have stopped it before.

'It's possible,' I said, 'that you may not be deliberately deceiving me. If you are yourself deceived, I am bound to tell you the truth. Mr Rothsay loves your daughter, and, what is more, Mr Rothsay has reason to know that Susan—'

'That Susan loves him?' she interposed, with a mocking laugh. 'Oh, Mr Lepel, is it possible that a clever man like you can't see clearer than that? My girl in love with Mr Rothsay! She wouldn't have looked at him a second time if he hadn't talked to her about *you*. When I complained privately to my lord of Mr Rothsay hanging about the lodge, do you think she turned as pale as ashes, and cried when *he* passed through the gate, and said good-bye?'

She had complained of Rothsay to Lord Lepel – I understood her at last! She knew that my friend and all his family were poor. She had put her own construction on the innocent interest that I had taken in her daughter. Careless of the difference in rank, blind to the malady that was killing me, she was now bent on separating Rothsay and Susan, by throwing the girl into the arms of a rich husband like myself!

'You are wasting your breath,' I told her; 'I don't believe one word you say to me.'

'Believe Susan, then!' cried the reckless woman. 'Let me bring her here. If she's too shamefaced to own the truth, look at her – that's all I ask – look at her, and judge for yourself!'

This was intolerable. In justice to Susan, in justice to Rothsay, I insisted on silence. 'No more of it!' I said. 'Take care how you provoke me. Don't you see that I am ill? don't you see that you are irritating me to no purpose?'

She altered her tone. 'I'll wait,' she said quietly, 'while you compose yourself.'

With those words, she walked to the window, and stood there with her back towards me. Was the wretch taking advantage of my helpless condition? I stretched out my hand to ring the bell, and have her sent away – and hesitated to degrade Susan's mother, for Susan's sake. In my state of prostration, how could I arrive at a decision? My mind was dreadfully disturbed; I felt the imperative necessity of turning my thoughts to some other subject. Looking about me, the letters on the table attracted my attention. Mechanically, I took them up; mechanically, I put them down again. Two of them slipped from my trembling fingers; my eyes fell on the uppermost of the two. The address was in the handwriting of the good friend with whom Rothsay was sailing.

Just as I had been speaking of Rothsay, here was the news of him for which I had been waiting.

I opened the letter and read these words:

There is, I fear, but little hope for our friend – unless this girl on whom he has set his heart can (by some lucky change of circumstances) become his wife. He has tried to master his weakness; but his own infatuation is too much for him. He is really and truly in a state of despair. Two evenings since – to give you a melancholy example of what I mean – I was in my cabin, when I heard the alarm of a man overboard. The man was Rothsay. My sailing-master, seeing that he was unable to swim, jumped into the sea and rescued him, as I got on deck. Rothsay declares it to have been an accident; and everybody believes him but myself. I know the state of his mind. Don't be alarmed; I will have him well looked after; and I won't give him up just yet. We are still bound southward, with a fair wind. If the new scenes which I hope to show him prove to be of no avail, I must reluctantly take him back to England. In that case, which I don't like to contemplate, you may see him again – perhaps in a month's time.

He might return in a month's time – return to hear of the death of the one friend, on whose power and will to help him he might have relied. If I failed to employ in his interests the short interval of life still left to me, could I doubt (after what I had just read) what the end would be? How could I help him? Oh, God! how could I help him?

Mrs Rymer left the window, and returned to the chair which she had occupied when I first received her.

'Are you quieter in your mind now?' she asked.

I neither answered her nor looked at her.

Still determined to reach her end, she tried again to force her unhappy daughter on me. 'Will you consent,' she persisted, 'to see Susan?'

If she had been a little nearer to me, I am afraid I should have struck her. 'You wretch!' I said, 'do you know that I am a dying man?'

'While there's life there's hope,' Mrs Rymer remarked.

I ought to have controlled myself; but it was not to be done.

'Hope of your daughter being my rich widow?' I asked.

Her bitter answer followed instantly.

'Even then,' she said, 'Susan wouldn't marry Rothsay.'

A lie! If circumstances favoured her, I knew, on Rothsay's authority, what Susan would do.

The thought burst on my mind, like light bursting on the eyes of a man restored to sight. If Susan agreed to go through the form of marriage with a dying bridegroom, my rich widow could (and would) become Rothsay's wife. Once more, the remembrance of the play at Rome returned, and set the last embers of resolution which sickness and suffering had left to me, in a flame. The devoted friend of that imaginary story had counted on death to complete his generous purpose in vain: *he* had been condemned by the tribunal of man, and had been reprieved. I – in his place, and with his self-sacrifice in my mind – might found a firmer trust in the future; for I had been condemned by the tribunal of God.

Encouraged by my silence, the obstinate woman persisted. 'Won't you even send a message to Susan?' she asked.

Rashly, madly, without an instant's hesitation, I answered:

'Go back to Susan, and say I leave it to *her.*'

Mrs Rymer started to her feet. 'You leave it to Susan to be your wife, if she likes?'

'I do.'

'And if she consents?'

'*I* consent.'

In two weeks and a day from that time, the deed was done. When Rothsay returned to England, he would ask for Susan – and he would find my virgin-widow rich and free.

SEVENTH EPOCH

Whatever may be thought of my conduct, let me say this in justice to myself – I was resolved that Susan should not be deceived.

Half an hour after Mrs Rymer had left my house, I wrote to her daughter, plainly revealing the motive which led me to offer marriage, solely in the future interest of Rothsay and herself. 'If you refuse,' I said, in conclusion, 'you may depend on my understanding you and feeling for you. But, if you consent – then I have a favour to ask. Never let us speak to one another of the profanation that we have agreed to commit, for your faithful lover's sake.'

I had formed a high opinion of Susan – too high an opinion as it seemed. Her reply surprised and disappointed me. In other words, she gave her consent.

I stipulated that the marriage should be kept strictly secret, for a certain period. In my own mind I decided that the interval should be held to expire, either on the day of my death, or on the day when Rothsay returned.

My next proceeding was to write in confidence to the priest whom I have already mentioned, in an earlier part of these pages. He has reasons of his own for not permitting me to disclose the motive which induced him to celebrate my marriage privately in the chapel at Lord Lepel's house. My uncle's desire that I should try change of air, as offering a last chance of recovery, was known to my medical attendant, and served as a sufficient reason (although he protested against the risk) for my removal to the country. I was carried to the station, and placed on a bed – slung by ropes to the ceiling of a saloon carriage, so as to prevent me from feeling the vibration when the train was in motion. Faithful Mrs Mozeen entreated to be allowed to accompany me. I was reluctantly compelled to refuse compliance with this request, in justice to the claims of my lord's housekeeper; who had been accustomed to exercise undivided authority in the household, and who had made every preparation for my comfort. With her own hands, Mrs Mozeen packed everything that I required, including the medicines prescribed for the occasion. She was deeply affected, poor soul, when we parted.

I bore the journey – happily for me, it was a short one – better than had been anticipated. For the first few days that followed, the purer air of the country seemed, in some degree, to revive me. But the deadly sense of weakness, the slow sinking of the vital power in me, returned as the time drew near for the marriage. The ceremony was performed at night. Only Susan and her mother were present. No persons in the house but ourselves had the faintest suspicion of what had happened.

I signed my new will (the priest and Mrs Rymer being the witnesses) in my bed that night. It left everything that I possessed, excepting a legacy to Mrs Mozeen, to my wife.

Obliged, it is needless to say, to preserve appearances, Susan remained at the lodge as usual. But it was impossible to resist her entreaty to be allowed to attend on me, for a few hours daily, as assistant to the regular nurse. When she was alone with me, and had no inquisitive eyes to dread, the poor girl showed a depth of feeling, which I was unable to reconcile with the motives that could alone have induced her (as I then supposed) to consent to the mockery of our marriage. On occasions when I was so far able to resist the languor that oppressed me as to observe what was passing at my bedside – I saw Susan look at me, as if there were thoughts in her pressing for utterance which she hesitated to express. Once, she herself acknowledged this. 'I have so much to say to you,' she owned, 'when you are stronger and fitter to hear me.' At other times, her nerves seemed to be shaken by the spectacle of my sufferings. Her kind hands trembled and made mistakes, when they had any nursing duties to perform near me. The servants, noticing her, used to say, 'That pretty girl seems to be the most awkward person in the house.' On the day that followed the ceremony in the chapel, this want of self-control brought about an accident which led to serious results.

In removing the small chest which held my medicines from the shelf on which it was placed, Susan let it drop on the floor. The two full bottles still left were so completely shattered that not even a teaspoonful of the contents was saved.

Shocked at what she had done, the poor girl volunteered to go herself to my chemist in London, by the first train. I refused to allow it. What did it matter to me now, if my death from exhaustion was hastened by a day or two? Why need my life be prolonged artificially by drugs, when I had nothing left to live for? An excuse for me which would satisfy others was easily found. I said that I had been long weary of physic, and that the accident had decided me on refusing to take more.

That night I did not wake quite so often as usual. When she came to me the next day, Susan noticed that I looked better. The day after, the other nurse made the same observation. At the end of the week, I was able to leave my bed, and sit by the fireside, while Susan read to me. Some mysterious change in my health had completely falsified the prediction of the medical men. I sent to London for my doctor – and told him that the improvement in me had begun on the day when I left off taking my remedies. 'Can you explain it?' I asked.

He answered that no such 'resurrection from the dead' (as he called it) had

ever happened in his long experience. On leaving me, he asked for the latest
prescriptions that had been written. I inquired what he was going to do with
them. 'I mean to go to the chemist,' he replied, 'and to satisfy myself that your
medicines have been properly made up.'

I owed it to Mrs Mozeen's true interest in me, to tell her what had happened.
The same day I wrote to her. I also mentioned what the doctor had said, and
asked her to call on him, and ascertain if the prescriptions had been shown
to the chemist, and if any mistake had been made.

A more innocently intended letter than this never was written. And yet,
there are people who have declared that it was inspired by suspicion of Mrs
Mozeen!

EIGHTH EPOCH

Whether I was so weakened by illness as to be incapable of giving my mind
to more than one subject for reflection at a time (that subject being now the
extraordinary recovery of my health) – or whether I was preoccupied by the
effort, which I was in honour bound to make, to resist the growing attraction
to me of Susan's society – I cannot presume to say. This only I know: when
the discovery of the terrible position towards Rothsay in which I now stood
suddenly overwhelmed me, an interval of some days had passed. I cannot
account for it. I can only say – so it was.

Susan was in the room. I was wholly unable to hide from her the sudden
change of colour which betrayed the horror that had overpowered me. She
said anxiously: 'What has frightened you?'

I don't think I heard her. The play was in my memory again – the fatal
play, which had wound itself into the texture of Rothsay's life and mine. In
vivid remembrance, I saw once more the dramatic situation of the first act,
and shrank from the reflection of it in the disaster which had fallen on my
friend and myself.

'What has frightened you?' Susan repeated.

I answered in one word – I whispered his name: 'Rothsay!'

She looked at me in innocent surprise. 'Has he met with some misfortune?'
she asked quietly.

'Misfortune' – did she call it? Had I not said enough to disturb her
tranquillity in mentioning Rothsay's name? 'I am living!' I said. 'Living –
and likely to live!'

Her answer expressed fervent gratitude. 'Thank God for it!'

I looked at her, astonished as she had been astonished when she looked at
me.

'Susan, Susan,' I cried – 'must I own it? I love you!'

She came nearer to me with timid pleasure in her eyes – with the first faint
light of a smile playing round her lips.

'You say it very strangely,' she murmured. 'Surely, my dear one, you ought
to love me? Since the first day when you gave me my French lesson – haven't
I loved You?'

'*You* love *me?*' I repeated. 'Have you read –?' My voice failed me; I could
say no more.

She turned pale. 'Read – what?' she asked.

'My letter.'

'What letter?'

'The letter I wrote to you before we were married.'

Am I a coward? The bare recollection of what followed that reply makes me tremble. Time has passed. I am a new man now; my health is restored; my happiness is assured: I ought to be able to write on. No: it is not to be done. How can I think coolly? how force myself to record the suffering that I innocently, most innocently, inflicted on the sweetest and truest of women? Nothing saved us from a parting as absolute as the parting that follows death, but the confession that had been wrung from me at a time when my motive spoke for itself. The artless avowal of her affection had been justified, had been honoured, by the words which laid my heart at her feet when I said 'I love you.'

She had risen to leave me. In a last look, we had silently resigned ourselves to wait, apart from each other, for the day of reckoning that must follow Rothsay's return, when we heard the sound of carriage-wheels on the drive that led to the house. In a minute more, the man himself entered the room.

He looked first at Susan – then at me. In both of us he saw the traces that told of agitation endured, but not yet composed. Worn and weary he waited, hesitating, near the door.

'Am I intruding?' he asked.

'We were thinking of you, and speaking of you,' I replied, 'just before you came in.'

'*We?*' he repeated, turning towards Susan once more. After a pause, he offered me his hand – and drew it back.

'You don't shake hands with me,' he said.

'I am waiting, Rothsay, until I know that we are the same firm friends as ever.'

For the third time he looked at Susan.

'Will *you* shake hands?' he asked.

She gave him her hand cordially. 'May I stay here?' she said, addressing herself to me.

In my situation at that moment, I understood the generous purpose that animated her. But she had suffered enough already – I led her gently to the door. 'It will be better,' I whispered, 'if you will wait down stairs in the library.' She hesitated. 'What will they say in the house?' she objected, thinking of the servants, and of the humble position which she was still supposed to occupy. 'It matters nothing what they say, now,' I told her. She left us.

'There seems to be some private understanding between you,' Rothsay said, when we were alone.

'You shall hear what it is,' I answered. 'But I must beg you to excuse me if I speak first of myself.'

'Are you alluding to your health?'

'Yes.'

'Quite needless, Lepel. I met your doctor this morning. I know that a council of physicians decided you would die before the year was out.'

He paused there.

'And they proved to be wrong,' I added.

'They might have proved to be right,' Rothsay rejoined, 'but for the accident which spilt your medicine, and the despair of yourself which decided you on taking no more.'

I could hardly believe that I understood him. 'Do you assert,' I said, 'that my medicine would have killed me, if I had taken the rest of it?'

'I have no doubt that it would.'

'Will you explain what you mean?'

'Let me have your explanation first. I was not prepared to find Susan in your room. I was surprised to see traces of tears in her face. Something has happened in my absence. Am I concerned in it?'

'You are.'

I said it quietly – in full possession of myself. The trial of fortitude through which I had already passed seemed to have blunted my customary sense of feeling. I approached the disclosure which I was now bound to make with steady resolution, resigned to the worst that could happen when the truth was known.

'Do you remember the time,' I resumed, 'when I was so eager to serve you that I proposed to make Susan your wife by making her rich?'

'Yes.'

'Do you remember asking me if I was thinking of the play we saw together at Rome? Is the story as present to your mind now, as it was then?'

'Quite as present.'

'You asked if I was performing the part of the Marquis – and if you were the Count. Rothsay! the devotion of that ideal character to his friend has been *my* devotion; his conviction that his death would justify what he had done for his friend's sake, has been *my* conviction; and as it ended with him, so it has ended with me – his terrible position is *my* terrible position towards you, at this moment.'

'Are you mad?' Rothsay asked sternly.

I passed over that first outbreak of his anger in silence.

'Do you mean to tell me you have married Susan?' he went on.

'Bear this in mind,' I said. 'When I married her, I was doomed to death. Nay more. In your interests – as God is my witness – I welcomed death.'

He stepped up to me, in silence, and raised his hand with a threatening gesture.

That action at once deprived me of my self-possession. I spoke with the ungovernable rashness of a boy.

'Carry out your intention,' I said. 'Insult me.'

His hand dropped.

'Insult me,' I repeated; 'it is one way out of the unendurable situation in which we are placed. You may trust me to challenge you. Duels are still fought on the Continent; I will follow you abroad; I will choose pistols; I will take care that we fight on the fatal foreign system; and I will purposely miss you. Make her what I intended her to be – my rich widow.'

He looked at me attentively.

'Is *that* your refuge?' he asked scornfully. 'No! I won't help you to commit suicide.'

God forgive me! I was possessed by a spirit of reckless despair; I did my best to provoke him.

'Reconsider your decision,' I said; 'and remember – you tried to commit suicide yourself.'

He turned quickly to the door, as if he distrusted his own powers of self-control.

'I wish to speak to Susan,' he said, keeping his back turned on me.

'You will find her in the library.'

He left me.

I went to the window. I opened it, and let the cold wintry air blow over my burning head. I don't know how long I sat at the window. There came a time when I saw Rothsay on the house steps. He walked rapidly towards the park gate. His head was down; he never once looked back at the room in which he had left me.

As he passed out of my sight, I felt a hand laid gently on my shoulder. Susan had returned to me.

'He will not come back,' she said. 'Try still to remember him as your old friend. He asks you to forgive and forget.'

She had made the peace between us. I was deeply touched; my eyes filled with tears as I looked at her. She kissed me on the forehead and went out. I afterwards asked what had passed between them when Rothsay spoke with her in the library. She never has told me what they said to each other; and she never will. She is right.

Later in the day, I was told that Mrs Rymer had called, and wished to 'pay her respects.'

I refused to see her. Whatever claim she might have otherwise had on my consideration had been forfeited by the infamy of her conduct, when she intercepted my letter to Susan. Her sense of injury, on receiving my message, was expressed in writing, and was sent to me the same evening. The last sentence in her letter was characteristic of the woman.

'However your pride may despise me,' she wrote, 'I am indebted to you for the rise in life that I have always desired. You may refuse to see me – but you can't prevent my being the mother-in-law of a gentleman.'

Soon afterwards, I received a visit which I had hardly ventured to expect. Busy as he was in London, my doctor came to see me. He was not in his usual good spirits.

'I hope you don't bring me any bad news,' I said.

'You shall judge for yourself,' he replied. 'I come from Mr Rothsay, to say for him what he is not able to say for himself.'

'Where is he?'

'He has left England.'

'For any purpose that you know of?'

'Yes. He has sailed to join the expedition of rescue – I ought rather to call it the forlorn hope – which is to search for the lost explorers in Central Australia.'

In other words, he had gone to seek death in the fatal footsteps of Burke and Wills. I could not trust myself to speak.

The doctor saw that there was a reason for my silence, and that he would do well not to notice it. He changed the subject.

'May I ask,' he said, 'if you have heard from the servants left in charge at your house in London?'

'Has anything happened?'

'Something has happened which they are evidently afraid to tell you; knowing the high opinion which you have of Mrs Mozeen. She has suddenly quitted your service, and has gone, nobody knows where. I have taken charge of a letter which she left for you.'

He handed me the letter. As soon as I had recovered myself, I looked at it.

There was this inscription on the address: 'For my good master, to wait until he returns home.'

The few lines in the letter itself ran thus:

> Distressing circumstances oblige me to leave you, sir, and do not permit me to enter into particulars. In asking your pardon, I offer my sincere thanks for your kindness, and my fervent prayers for your welfare.

That was all. The date had a special interest for me. Mrs Mozeen had written on the day when she must have received my letter – the letter which has already appeared in these pages.

'Is there really nothing known of the poor woman's motives?' I asked.

'There are two explanations suggested,' the doctor informed me. 'One of them, which is offered by your female servants, seems to me absurd. They declare that Mrs Mozeen, at her mature age, was in love with the young man who is your footman! It is even asserted that she tried to recommend herself to him, by speaking of the money which she expected to bring to the man who would make her his wife. The footman's reply, informing her that he was already engaged to be married, is alleged to be the cause which has driven her from your house.'

I begged that the doctor would not trouble himself to repeat more of what my women servants had said. 'If the other explanation,' I added, 'is equally unworthy of notice—'

'The other explanation,' the doctor interposed, 'comes from Mr Rothsay, and is of a very serious kind.'

Rothsay's opinion demanded my respect. 'What view does he take?' I inquired.

'A view that startles me,' the doctor said. 'You remember my telling you of the interest he took in your symptoms, and in the remedies I had employed? Well! Mr Rothsay accounts for the incomprehensible recovery of your health by asserting that poison – probably administered in small quantities, and intermitted at intervals in fear of discovery – has been mixed with your medicine; and he asserts that the guilty person is Mrs Mozeen.'

It was impossible that I could openly express the indignation that I felt on hearing this. My position towards Rothsay forced me to restrain myself.

'May I ask,' the doctor continued, 'if Mrs Mozeen was aware that she had a legacy to expect at your death?'

'Certainly.'

'Has she a brother who is one of the dispensers employed by your chemists?'

'Yes.'

'Did she know that I doubted if my prescriptions had been properly prepared, and that I intended to make inquiries?'

'I wrote to her myself on the subject.'

'Do you think her brother told her that I was referred to *him*, when I went to the chemists?'

'I have no means of knowing what her brother did.'

'Can you at least tell me when she received your letter?'

'She must have received it on the day when she left my house.'

The doctor rose with a grave face. 'These are rather extraordinary coincidences,' he remarked.

I merely replied, 'Mrs Mozeen is as incapable of poisoning as I am.'

The doctor wished me good morning.

I repeat here my conviction of my housekeeper's innocence. I protest against the cruelty which accuses her. And, whatever may have been her motive in suddenly leaving my service, I declare that she still possesses my sympathy and esteem, and I invite her to return to me if she ever sees these lines.

I have only to add, by way of postscript, that we have heard of the safe return of the expedition of rescue. Time, as my wife and I both hope, may yet convince Rothsay that he will not be wrong in counting on Susan's love – the love of a sister.

In the meanwhile, we possess a memorial of our absent friend. We have bought his picture.

Mr Medhurst and the Princess

Originally appeared in the Christmas Number of *Longman's Magazine* 1884 as 'Royal Love'. Reprinted in *Little Novels* (1887).

I

The day before I left London, to occupy the post of second secretary of legation at a small German Court, I took leave of my excellent French singing-master, Monsieur Bonnefoy, and of his young and pretty daughter named Jeanne.

Our farewell interview was saddened by Monsieur Bonnefoy's family anxieties. His elder brother, known in the household as Uncle David, had been secretly summoned to Paris by order of a republican society. Anxious relations in London (whether reasonably or not, I am unable to say) were in some fear of the political consequences that might follow.

At parting, I made Mademoiselle Jeanne a present, in the shape of a plain gold brooch. For some time past, I had taken my lessons at Monsieur Bonnefoy's house; his daughter and I often sang together under his direction. Seeing much of Jeanne, under these circumstances, the little gift that I had offered to her was only the natural expression of a true interest in her welfare. Idle rumour asserted – quite falsely – that I was in love with her. I was sincerely the young lady's friend: no more, no less.

Having alluded to my lessons in singing, it may not be out of place to mention the circumstances under which I became Monsieur Bonnefoy's pupil, and to allude to the change in my life that followed in due course of time.

Our family property – excepting the sum of five thousand pounds left to me by my mother – is landed property, strictly entailed. The estates were inherited by my only brother, Lord Medhurst: the kindest, the best, and, I grieve to say it, the unhappiest of men. He lived separated from a bad wife; he had no children to console him; and he only enjoyed at rare intervals the blessing of good health. Having myself nothing to live on but the interest of my mother's little fortune, I had to make my own way in the world. Poor younger sons, not possessed of the commanding ability which achieves distinction, find the roads that lead to prosperity closed to them, with one exception. They can always apply themselves to the social arts which make a man agreeable in society. I had naturally a good voice, and I cultivated it. I was ready to sing, without being subject to the wretched vanity which makes objections and excuses – I pleased the ladies – the ladies spoke favourably of me to their husbands – and some of their husbands were persons of rank and influence. After no very long lapse of time, the result of this combination of circumstances declared itself. Monsieur Bonnefoy's lessons became the indirect means of starting me on a diplomatic career – and the diplomatic career made poor Ernest Medhurst, to his own unutterable astonishment, the hero of a love story!

The story being true, I must beg to be excused, if I abstain from mentioning names, places, and dates, when I enter on German ground. Let it be enough to say that I am writing of a bygone year in the present century, when no such thing as a German Empire existed, and when the revolutionary spirit of France was still an object of well-founded suspicion to tyrants by right divine on the continent of Europe.

II

On joining the legation, I was not particularly attracted by my chief, the Minister. His manners were oppressively polite; and his sense of his own importance was not sufficiently influenced by diplomatic reserve. I venture to describe him (mentally speaking) as an empty man, carefully trained to look full on public occasions.

My colleague, the first secretary, was a far more interesting person. Bright, unaffected, and agreeable, he at once interested me when we were introduced to each other. I pay myself a compliment, as I consider, when I add that he became my firm and true friend.

We took a walk together in the palace gardens on the evening of my arrival. Reaching a remote part of the grounds, we were passed by a lean sallow sour-looking old man, drawn by a servant in a chair on wheels. My companion stopped, whispered to me, 'Here is the Prince,' and bowed bareheaded. I followed his example as a matter of course. The Prince feebly returned our salutation. 'Is he ill?' I asked, when we had put our hats on again.

'Shakespeare,' the secretary replied, 'tells us that "one man in his time plays many parts." Under what various aspects the Prince's character may have presented itself, in his younger days, I am not able to tell you. Since I have been here, he has played the part of a martyr to illness, misunderstood by his doctors.'

'And his daughter, the Princess – what do you say of her?'

'Ah, she is not so easily described! I can only appeal to your memory of other women like her, whom you must often have seen – women who are tall and fair, and fragile and elegant; who have delicate aquiline noses and melting blue eyes – women who have often charmed you by their tender smiles and their supple graces of movement. As for the character of this popular young lady, I must not influence you either way; study it for yourself.'

'Without a hint to guide me?'

'With a suggestion,' he replied, 'which may be worth considering. If you wish to please the Princess, begin by endeavouring to win the good graces of the Baroness.'

'Who is the Baroness?'

'One of the ladies in waiting – bosom friend of her Highness, and chosen repository of all her secrets. Personally, not likely to attract you; short and fat, and ill-tempered and ugly. Just at this time, I happen myself to get on with her better than usual. We have discovered that we possess one sympathy in common – we are the only people at Court who don't believe in the Prince's new doctor.'

'Is the new doctor a quack?'

The secretary looked round, before he answered, to see that nobody was near us.

'It strikes me,' he said, 'that the Doctor is a spy. Mind! I have no right to speak of him in that way; it is only my impression – and I ought to add that appearances are all in his favour. He is in the service of our nearest royal neighbour, the Grand Duke; and he has been sent here expressly to relieve the sufferings of the Duke's good friend and brother, our invalid Prince. This is an honourable mission no doubt. And the man himself is handsome, well-bred, and (I don't quite know whether this is an additional recommendation) a countryman of ours. Nevertheless I doubt him, and the Baroness doubts him. You are an independent witness; I shall be anxious to hear if your opinion agrees with ours.'

I was presented at Court, towards the end of the week; and, in the course of the next two or three days, I more than once saw the Doctor. The impression that he produced on me surprised my colleague. It was my opinion that he and the Baroness had mistaken the character of a worthy and capable man.

The secretary obstinately adhered to his own view.

'Wait a little,' he answered, 'and we shall see.'

He was quite right. We did see.

III

But the Princess – the gentle, gracious, beautiful Princess – what can I say of her Highness? I can only say that she enchanted me.

I had been a little discouraged by the reception that I met with from her father. Strictly confining himself within the limits of politeness, he bade me welcome to his Court in the fewest possible words, and then passed me by without further notice. He afterwards informed the English Minister that I had been so unfortunate as to try his temper: 'Your new secretary irritates me, sir – he is a person in an offensively perfect state of health.' The Prince's charming daughter was not of her father's way of thinking; it is impossible to say how graciously, how sweetly I was received. She honoured me by speaking to me in my own language, of which she showed herself to be a perfect mistress. I was not only permitted, but encouraged, to talk of my family, and to dwell on my own tastes, amusements, and pursuits. Even when her Highness's attention was claimed by other persons waiting to be presented, I was not forgotten. The Baroness was instructed to invite me for the next evening to the Princess's tea-table; and it was hinted that I should be especially welcome if I brought my music with me, and sang.

My friend the secretary, standing near us at the time, looked at me with a mysterious smile. He had suggested that I should make advances to the Baroness – and here was the Baroness (under royal instructions) making advances to Me!

'We know what *that* means,' he whispered.

In justice to myself, I must declare that I entirely failed to understand him.

On the occasion of my second reception by the Princess, at her little evening party, I detected the Baroness, more than once, in the act of watching her Highness and myself, with an appearance of disapproval in her manner, which puzzled me. When I had taken my leave, she followed me out of the room.

'I have a word of advice to give you,' she said. 'The best thing you can do, sir, is to make an excuse to your Minister, and go back to England.'

I declare again, that I entirely failed to understand the Baroness.

IV

Before the season came to an end, the Court removed to the Prince's
country-seat, in the interests of his Highness's health. Entertainments were
given (at the Doctor's suggestion), with a view of raising the patient's depressed
spirits. The members of the English legation were among the guests invited.
To me it was a delightful visit. I had again every reason to feel gratefully
sensible of the Princess's condescending kindness. Meeting the secretary one
day in the library, I said that I thought her a perfect creature. Was this an
absurd remark to make? I could see nothing absurd in it – and yet my friend
burst out laughing.

'My good fellow, nobody is a perfect creature,' he said. 'The Princess has
her faults and failings, like the rest of us.'

I denied it positively.

'Use your eyes,' he went on; 'and you will see, for example, that she is
shallow and frivolous. Yesterday was a day of rain. We were all obliged
to employ ourselves somehow, indoors. Didn't you notice that she had no
resources in herself? She can't even read.'

'There you are wrong at any rate,' I declared. 'I saw her reading the
newspaper.'

'You saw her with the newspaper in her hand. If you had not been deaf and
blind to her defects, you would have noticed that she couldn't fix her attention
on it. She was always ready to join in the chatter of the ladies about her. When
even their stores of gossip were exhausted, she let the newspaper drop on her
lap, and sat in vacant idleness smiling at nothing.'

I reminded him that she might have met with a dull number of the
newspaper. He took no notice of this unanswerable reply.

'You were talking the other day of her warmth of feeling,' he proceeded. 'She
has plenty of sentiment (German sentiment), I grant you, but no true feeling.
What happened only this morning, when the Prince was in the breakfast-room,
and when the Princess and her ladies were dressed to go out riding? Even
she noticed the wretchedly depressed state of her father's spirits. A man
of that hypochondriacal temperament suffers acutely, though he may only
fancy himself to be ill. The Princess overflowed with sympathy, but she never
proposed to stay at home, and try to cheer the old man. Her filial duty was
performed to her own entire satisfaction, when she had kissed her hand to the
Prince. The moment after, she was out of the room – eager to enjoy her ride.
We all heard her laughing gaily among the ladies in the hall.'

I could have answered this also, if our discussion had not been interrupted at
the moment. The Doctor came into the library in search of a book. When he had
left us, my colleague's strong prejudice against him instantly declared itself.

'Be on your guard with that man,' he said.

'Why?' I asked.

'Haven't you noticed,' he replied, 'that when the Princess is talking to you,
the Doctor always happens to be in that part of the room?'

'What does it matter where the Doctor is?'

My friend looked at me with an oddly mingled expression of doubt and
surprise. 'Do you really not understand me?' he said.

'I don't indeed.'

'My dear Ernest, you are a rare and admirable example to the rest of us – you are a truly modest man.'

What did he mean?

V

Events followed, on the next day, which (as will presently be seen) I have a personal interest in relating.

The Baroness left us suddenly, on leave of absence. The Prince wearied of his residence in the country; and the Court returned to the capital. The charming Princess was reported to be 'indisposed,' and retired to the seclusion of her own apartments.

A week later, I received a note from the Baroness, marked 'private and confidential.' It informed me that she had resumed her duties as lady-in-waiting, and that she wished to see me at my earliest convenience. I obeyed at once; and naturally asked if there were better accounts of her Highness's health.

The Baroness's reply a little surprised me. She said, 'The Princess is perfectly well.'

'Recovered already!' I exclaimed.

'She has never been ill,' the Baroness answered. 'Her indisposition was a sham; forced on her by me, in her own interests. Her reputation is in peril; and you – you hateful Englishman – are the cause of it.'

Not feeling disposed to put up with such language as this, even when it was used by a lady, I requested that she would explain herself. She complied without hesitation. In another minute my eyes were opened to the truth. I knew – no; that is too positive – let me say I had reason to believe that the Princess loved me!

It is simply impossible to convey to the minds of others any idea of the emotions that overwhelmed me at that critical moment of my life. I was in a state of confusion at the time; and, when my memory tries to realize it, I am in a state of confusion now. The one thing I can do is to repeat what the Baroness said to me when I had in some degree recovered my composure.

'I suppose you are aware,' she began, 'of the disgrace to which the Princess's infatuation exposes her, if it is discovered? On my own responsibility I repeat what I said to you a short time since. Do you refuse to leave this place immediately?'

Does the man live, honoured as I was, who would have hesitated to refuse? Find him if you can!

'Very well,' she resumed. 'As the friend of the Princess, I have no choice now but to take things as they are, and to make the best of them. Let us realize your position to begin with. If you were (like your elder brother) a nobleman possessed of vast estates, my royal mistress might be excused. As it is, whatever you may be in the future, you are nothing now but an obscure young man, without fortune or title. Do you see your duty to the Princess? or must I explain it to you?'

I saw my duty as plainly as she did. 'Her Highness's secret is a sacred secret,' I said. 'I am bound to shrink from no sacrifice which may preserve it.'

The Baroness smiled maliciously. 'I may have occasion,' she answered, 'to remind you of what you have just said. In the meanwhile, the Princess's secret is in danger of discovery.'

'By her father?'

'No. By the Doctor.'

At first, I doubted whether she was in jest or in earnest. The next instant, I remembered that the secretary had expressly cautioned me against that man.

'It is evidently one of your virtues,' the Baroness proceeded, 'to be slow to suspect. Prepare yourself for a disagreeable surprise. The Doctor has been watching the Princess, on every occasion when she speaks to you, with some object of his own in view. During my absence, young sir, I have been engaged in discovering what that object is. My excellent mother lives at the Court of the Grand Duke, and enjoys the confidence of his Ministers. He is still a bachelor; and, in the interests of the succession to the throne, the time has arrived when he must marry. With my mother's assistance, I have found out that the Doctor's medical errand here is a pretence. Influenced by the Princess's beauty, the Grand Duke has thought of her first as his future Duchess. Whether he has heard slanderous stories, or whether he is only a cautious man, I can't tell you. But this I know: he has instructed his physician – if he had employed a professed diplomatist, his motive might have been suspected – to observe her Highness privately, and to communicate the result. The object of the report is to satisfy the Duke that the Princess's reputation is above the reach of scandal; that she is free from entanglements of a certain kind; and that she is in every respect a person to whom he can with propriety offer his hand in marriage. The Doctor, Mr Ernest, is not disposed to allow you to prevent him from sending in a favourable report. He has drawn his conclusions from the Princess's extraordinary kindness to the second secretary of the English legation; and he is only waiting for a little plainer evidence to communicate his suspicions to the Prince. It rests with you to save the Princess.'

'Only tell me how I am to do it!' I said.

'There is but one way of doing it,' she answered; 'and that way has (comically enough) been suggested to me by the Doctor himself.'

Her tone and manner tried my patience.

'Come to the point!' I said.

She seemed to enjoy provoking me.

'No hurry, Mr Ernest – no hurry! You shall be fully enlightened, if you will only wait a little. The Prince, I must tell you, believes in his daughter's indisposition. When he visited her this morning he was attended by his medical adviser. I was present at the interview. To do him justice, the Doctor is worthy of the trust reposed in him – he boldly attempted to verify his suspicions of the daughter, in the father's presence.'

'How?'

'Oh, in the well-known way that has been tried over and over again, under similar circumstances! He merely invented a report that you were engaged in a love-affair with some charming person in the town. Don't be angry; there's no harm done.'

'But there *is* harm done,' I insisted. 'What must the Princess think of me?'

'Do you suppose she is weak enough to believe the Doctor? Her Highness beat him at his own weapons; not the slightest sign of agitation on her part rewarded his ingenuity. All that you have to do is to help her to mislead this medical spy. It's as easy as lying, and easier. The Doctor's slander declares that you have a love-affair in the town. Take the hint – and astonish the Doctor by proving that he has hit on the truth.'

It was a hot day; the Baroness was beginning to get excited. She paused and fanned herself.

'Do I startle you?' she asked.

'You disgust me.'

She laughed.

'What a thick-headed man this is!' she said pleasantly. 'Must I put it more plainly still? Engage in what your English prudery calls a "flirtation," with some woman here – the lower in degree the better, or the Princess might be jealous – and let the affair be seen and known by everybody about the Court. Sly as he is, the Doctor is not prepared for that! At your age, and with your personal advantages, he will take appearances for granted; he will conclude that he has wronged you, and misinterpreted the motives of the Princess. The secret of her Highness's weakness will be preserved – thanks to that sacrifice, Mr Ernest, which you are so willing and so eager to make.'

It was useless to remonstrate with such a woman as this. I simply stated my own objection to her artfully devised scheme.

'I don't wish to appear vain,' I said; 'but the woman to whom I am to pay these attentions may believe that I really admire her – and it is just possible that she may honestly return the feeling which I am only assuming.'

'Well – and what then?'

'It's hard on the woman, surely?'

The Baroness was shocked, unaffectedly shocked.

'Good heavens!' she exclaimed, 'how can anything that you do for the Princess be hard on a woman of the lower orders? There must be an end of this nonsense, sir! You have heard what I propose; and you know what the circumstances are. My mistress is waiting for your answer. What am I to say?'

'Let me see her Highness, and speak for myself,' I said.

'Quite impossible today, without running too great a risk. Your reply must be made through me.'

There was to be a Court concert at the end of the week. On that occasion I should be able to make my own reply. In the meanwhile I only told the Baroness I wanted time to consider.

'What time?' she asked.

'Until to-morrow. Do you object?'

'On the contrary, I cordially agree. Your base hesitation may lead to results which I have not hitherto dared to anticipate.'

'What do you mean?'

'Between this and tomorrow,' the horrid woman replied, 'the Princess may end in seeing you with my eyes. In that hope I wish you good-morning.'

VI

My enemies say that I am a weak man, unduly influenced by persons of rank
– because of their rank. If this were true, I should have found little difficulty in
consenting to adopt the Baroness's suggestion. As it was, the longer I reflected
on the scheme the less I liked it. I tried to think of some alternative that might
be acceptably proposed. The time passed, and nothing occurred to me. In this
embarrassing position my mind became seriously disturbed; I felt the necessity
of obtaining some relief, which might turn my thoughts for a while into a new
channel. The secretary called on me, while I was still in doubt what to do. He
reminded me that a new prima-donna was advertised to appear on that night;
and he suggested that we should go to the opera. Feeling as I did at the time,
I readily agreed.

We found the theatre already filled, before the performance began. Two
French gentlemen were seated in the row of stalls behind us. They were talking
of the new singer.

'She is advertised as "Mademoiselle Fontenay,"' one of them said. 'That
sounds like an assumed name.'

'It *is* an assumed name,' the other replied. 'She is the daughter of a French
singing-master, named Bonnefoy.'

To my friend's astonishment I started to my feet, and left him without a
word of apology. In another minute I was at the stage-door, and had sent
in my card to 'Mademoiselle Fontenay.' While I was waiting, I had time
to think. Was it possible that Jeanne had gone on the stage? Or were
there two singing-masters in existence named Bonnefoy? My doubts were
soon decided. The French woman-servant whom I remembered when I
was Monsieur Bonnefoy's pupil, made her appearance, and conducted me
to her young mistress's dressing-room. Dear good Jeanne, how glad she was
to see me!

I found her standing before the glass, having just completed her preparations
for appearing on the stage. Dressed in her picturesque costume, she was so
charming that I expressed my admiration heartily, as became her old friend.
'Do you really like me?' she said, with the innocent familiarity which I
recollected so well. 'See how I look in the glass – that is the great test.' It
was not easy to apply the test. Instead of looking at her image in the glass,
it was far more agreeable to look at herself. We were interrupted – too soon
interrupted – by the call-boy. He knocked at the door, and announced that
the overture had begun.

'I have a thousand things to ask you,' I told her. 'What has made this
wonderful change in your life? How is it that I don't see your father—'

Her face instantly saddened; her hand trembled as she laid it on my arm
to silence me.

'Don't speak of him now,' she said, 'or you will unnerve me! Come to
me tomorrow when the stage will not be waiting; Annette will give you my
address.' She opened the door to go out, and returned. 'Will you think me
very unreasonable if I ask you not to make one of my audience to-night? You
have reminded me of the dear old days that can never come again. If I feel
that I am singing to *you* –' She left me to understand the rest, and turned away
again to the door. As I followed her out, to say good-bye, she drew from her

bosom the little brooch which had been my parting gift, and held it out to me. 'On the stage, or off,' she said, 'I always wear it. Goodnight, Ernest.'

I was prepared to hear sad news, when we met the next morning.

My good old friend and master had died suddenly. To add to the bitterness of that affliction, he had died in debt to a dear and intimate friend. For his daughter's sake he had endeavoured to add to his little savings by speculating with borrowed money on the Stock Exchange. He had failed, and the loan advanced had not been repaid, when a fit of apoplexy struck him down. Offered the opportunity of trying her fortune on the operatic stage, Jeanne made the attempt, and was now nobly employed in earning the money to pay her father's debt.

'It was the only way in which I could do justice to his memory,' she said simply. 'I hope you don't object to my going on the stage?'

I took her hand, poor child – and let that simple action answer for me. I was too deeply affected to be able to speak.

'It is not in me to be a great actress,' she resumed; 'but you know what an admirable musician my father was. He has taught me to sing, so that I can satisfy the critics, as well as please the public. There was what they call a great success last night. It has earned me an engagement for another year to come, and an increase of salary. I have already sent some money to our good old friend at home, and I shall soon send more. It is my one consolation – I feel almost happy again when I am paying my poor father's debt. No more now of my sad story! I want to hear all that you can tell me of yourself.' She moved to the window, and looked out. 'Oh, the beautiful blue sky! We used sometimes to take a walk, when we were in London, on fine days like this. Is there a park here?'

I took her to the palace gardens, famous for their beauty in that part of Germany.

Arm in arm we loitered along the pleasant walks. The lovely flowers, the bright sun, the fresh fragrant breeze, all helped her to recover her spirits. She began to be like the happy Jeanne of my past experience, as easily pleased as a child. When we sat down to rest, the lap of her dress was full of daisies. 'Do you remember,' she said, 'when you first taught me to make a daisy-chain? Are you too great a man to help me again, now?'

We were still engaged with our chain, seated close together, when the smell of tobacco-smoke was wafted to us on the air.

I looked up and saw the Doctor passing us, enjoying his cigar. He bowed; eyed my pretty companion with a malicious smile; and passed on.

'Who is that man?' she asked.

'The Prince's physician,' I replied.

'I don't like him,' she said; 'why did he smile when he looked at me?'

'Perhaps,' I suggested, 'he thought we were lovers.'

She blushed. 'Don't let him think that! tell him we are only old friends.'

We were not destined to finish our flower chain on that day.

Another person interrupted us, whom I recognised as the elder brother of Monsieur Bonnefoy – already mentioned in these pages, under the name of Uncle David. Having left France for political reasons, the old republican had taken care of his niece after her father's death, and had accepted the position of Jeanne's business manager in her relations with the stage. Uncle David's object, when he joined us in the garden, was to remind her that she was wanted at rehearsal, and must at once return with him to the theatre. We parted, having arranged that I was to see the performance on that night.

Later in the day, the Baroness sent for me again.

'Let me apologize for having misunderstood you yesterday,' she said; 'and let me offer you my best congratulations. You have done wonders already in the way of misleading the Doctor. There is only one objection to that girl at the theatre – I hear she is so pretty that she may possibly displease the Princess. In other respects, she is just in the public position which will make your attentions to her look like the beginning of a serious intrigue. Bravo, Mr Ernest – bravo!'

I was too indignant to place any restraint on the language in which I answered her.

'Understand, if you please,' I said, 'that I am renewing an old friendship with Mademoiselle Jeanne – begun under the sanction of her father. Respect that young lady, madam, as I respect her.'

The detestable Baroness clapped her hands, as if she had been at the theatre.

'If you only say that to the Princess,' she remarked, 'as well as you have said it to me, there will be no danger of arousing her Highness's jealousy. I have a message for you. At the concert, on Saturday, you are to retire to the conservatory, and you may hope for an interview when the singers begin the second part of the programme. Don't let me detain you any longer. Go back to your young lady, Mr Ernest – pray go back!'

VII

On the second night of the opera the applications for places were too numerous to be received. Among the crowded audience, I recognised many of my friends. They persisted in believing an absurd report (first circulated, as I imagine, by the Doctor), which asserted that my interest in the new singer was something more than the interest of an old friend. When I went behind the scenes to congratulate Jeanne on her success, I was annoyed in another way – and by the Doctor again. He followed me to Jeanne's room, to offer *his* congratulations; and he begged that I would introduce him to the charming prima-donna. Having expressed his admiration, he looked at me with his insolently suggestive smile, and said he could not think of prolonging his intrusion. On leaving the room, he noticed Uncle David, waiting as usual to take care of Jeanne on her return from the theatre – looked at him attentively – bowed, and went out.

The next morning, I received a note from the Baroness, expressed in these terms:

'More news! My rooms look out on the wing of the palace in which the Doctor is lodged. Half an hour since, I discovered him at his window, giving a letter to a person who is a stranger to me. The man left the palace immediately afterwards. My maid followed him, by my directions. Instead of putting the letter in the post, he took a ticket at the railway-station – for what place the servant was unable to discover. Here, you will observe, is a letter important enough to be despatched by special messenger, and written at a time when we have succeeded in freeing ourselves from the Doctor's suspicions. It is at least possible that he has decided on sending a favourable report of the Princess to the Grand Duke. If this is the case, please consider whether you will not act wisely (in her Highness's interests) by keeping away from the concert.'

Viewing this suggestion as another act of impertinence on the part of the Baroness, I persisted in my intention of going to the concert. It was for the Princess to decide what course of conduct I was bound to follow. What did I care for the Doctor's report to the Duke! Shall I own my folly? I do really believe I was jealous of the Duke.

VIII

Entering the Concert Room, I found the Princess alone on the daïs, receiving the company. 'Nervous prostration' had made it impossible for the Prince to be present. He was confined to his bed-chamber; and the Doctor was in attendance on him.

I bowed to the Baroness, but she was too seriously offended with me for declining to take her advice to notice my salutation. Passing into the conservatory, it occurred to me that I might be seen, and possibly suspected, in the interval between the first and second parts of the programme, when the music no longer absorbed the attention of the audience. I went on, and waited outside on the steps that led to the garden; keeping the glass door open, so as to hear when the music of the second part of the concert began.

After an interval which seemed to be endless, I saw the Princess approaching me.

She had made the heat in the Concert Room an excuse for retiring for a while; and she had the Baroness in attendance on her to save appearances. Instead of leaving us to ourselves, the malicious creature persisted in paying the most respectful attentions to her mistress. It was impossible to make her understand that she was not wanted any longer until the Princess said sharply, 'Go back to the music!' Even then, the detestable woman made a low curtsey, and answered: 'I will return, Madam, in five minutes.'

I ventured to present myself in the conservatory.

The Princess was dressed with exquisite simplicity, entirely in white. Her only ornaments were white roses in her hair and in her bosom. To say that she looked lovely is to say nothing. She seemed to be the ethereal creature of some higher sphere; too exquisitely delicate and pure to be approached by a mere mortal man like myself. I was awed; I was silent. Her Highness's sweet smile encouraged me to venture a little nearer. She pointed to a footstool which the Baroness had placed for her. 'Are you afraid of me, Ernest?' she asked softly.

Her divinely beautiful eyes rested on me with a look of encouragement. I dropped on my knees at her feet. She had asked if I was afraid of her. This, if I may use such an expression, roused my manhood. My own boldness astonished me. I answered: 'Madam, I adore you.'

She laid her fair hand on my head, and looked at me thoughtfully. 'Forget my rank,' she whispered – 'have I not set you the example? Suppose that I am nothing but an English Miss. What would you say to Miss?'

'I should say, I love you.'

'Say it to Me.'

My lips said it on her hand. She bent forward. My heart beats fast at the bare remembrance of it. Oh, Heavens, her Highness kissed me!

'There is your reward,' she murmured, 'for all that you have sacrificed for my sake. What an effort it must have been to offer the pretence of love to an obscure stranger! The Baroness tells me this actress – this singer – what is she? – is pretty. Is it true?'

The Baroness was quite mischievous enough to have also mentioned the false impression, prevalent about the Court, that I was in love with Jeanne. I attempted to explain. The gracious Princess refused to hear me.

'Do you think I doubt you?' she said. 'Distinguished by me, could you waste a look on a person in *that* rank of life?' She laughed softly, as if the mere idea of such a thing amused her. It was only for a moment: her thoughts took a new direction – they contemplated the uncertain future. 'How is this to end?' she asked. 'Dear Ernest, we are not in Paradise; we are in a hard cruel world which insists on distinctions in rank. To what unhappy destiny does the fascination which you exercise over me condemn us both?'

She paused – took one of the white roses out of her bosom – touched it with her lips – and gave it to me.

'I wonder whether you feel the burden of life as I feel it?' she resumed. 'It is immaterial to me, whether we are united in this world or in the next. Accept my rose, Ernest, as an assurance that I speak with perfect sincerity. I see but two alternatives before us. One of them (beset with dangers) is elopement. And the other,' she added, with truly majestic composure, 'is suicide.'

Would Englishmen in general have rightly understood such fearless confidence in them as this language implied? I am afraid they might have attributed it to, what my friend the secretary called, 'German sentiment.' Perhaps they might even have suspected the Princess of quoting from some old-fashioned German play. Under the irresistible influence of that glorious creature, I contemplated with such equal serenity the perils of elopement and the martyrdom of love, that I was for the moment at a loss how to reply. In that moment, the evil genius of my life appeared in the conservatory. With haste in her steps, with alarm in her face, the Baroness rushed up to her royal mistress, and said, 'For God's sake, Madam, come away! The Prince desires to speak with you instantly.'

Her Highness rose, calmly superior to the vulgar excitement of her lady in waiting. 'Think of it to-night,' she said to me, 'and let me hear from you to-morrow.'

She pressed my hand; she gave me a farewell look. I sank into the chair that she had just left. Did I think of elopement? Did I think of suicide? The elevating influence of the Princess no longer sustained me; my nature became degraded. Horrid doubts rose in my mind. Did her father suspect us?

IX

Need I say that I passed a sleepless night?

The morning found me with my pen in my hand, confronting the serious responsibility of writing to the Princess, and not knowing what to say. I had already torn up two letters, when Uncle David presented himself with a message from his niece. Jeanne was in trouble, and wanted to ask my advice.

My state of mind, on hearing this, became simply inexplicable. Here was an interruption which ought to have annoyed me. It did nothing of the kind – it inspired me with a feeling of relief!

I naturally expected that the old Frenchman would return with me to his niece, and tell me what had happened. To my surprise, he begged that I would excuse him, and left me without a word of explanation. I found Jeanne walking up and down her little sitting-room, flushed and angry. Fragments of torn paper and heaps of flowers littered the floor; and three unopened jewel-cases appeared to have been thrown into the empty fireplace. She caught me excitedly by the hand the moment I entered the room.

'You are my true friend,' she said; 'you were present the other night when I sang. Was there anything in my behaviour on the stage which could justify men who call themselves gentlemen in insulting me?'

'My dear, how can you ask the question?'

'I must ask it. Some of them send flowers, and some of them send jewels; and every one of them writes letters – infamous abominable letters – saying they are in love with me, and asking for appointments as if I was—'

She could say no more. Poor dear Jeanne – her head dropped on my shoulder; she burst out crying. Who could see her so cruelly humiliated – the faithful loving daughter, whose one motive for appearing on the stage had been to preserve her father's good name – and not feel for her as I did? I forgot all considerations of prudence; I thought of nothing but consoling her; I took her in my arms; I dried her tears; I kissed her; I said, 'Tell me the name of any one of the wretches who has written to you, and I will make him an example to the rest!' She shook her head, and pointed to the morsels of paper on the floor. 'Oh, Ernest, do you think I asked you to come here for any such purpose as that? Those jewels, those hateful jewels, tell me how I can send them back! spare me the sight of them!'

So far, it was easy to console her. I sent the jewels at once to the manager of the theatre – with a written notice to be posted at the stage door, stating that they were waiting to be returned to the persons who could describe them.

'Try, my dear, to forget what has happened,' I said. 'Try to find consolation and encouragement in your art.'

'I have lost all interest in my success on the stage,' she answered, 'now I know the penalty I must pay for it. When my father's memory is clear of reproach, I shall leave the theatre never to return to it again.'

'Take time to consider, Jeanne.'

'I will do anything you ask of me.'

For a while we were silent. Without any influence to lead to it that I could trace, I found myself recalling the language that the Princess had used in alluding to Jeanne. When I thought of them now, the words and the tone in which they had been spoken jarred on me. There is surely something mean in an assertion of superiority which depends on nothing better than the accident of birth. I don't know why I took Jeanne's hand; I don't know why I said, 'What a good girl you are! how glad I am to have been of some little use to you!' Is my friend the secretary right, when he reproaches me with acting on impulse, like a woman? I don't like to think so; and yet, this I must own – it was well for me that I was obliged to leave her, before I had perhaps said other words which might have been alike unworthy of Jeanne, of the Princess, and of myself. I was called away to speak to my servant. He brought with him the secretary's card, having a line written on it: 'I am waiting at your rooms, on business which permits of no delay.'

As we shook hands, Jeanne asked me if I knew where her uncle was. I could only tell her that he had left me at my own door. She made no remark; but she seemed to be uneasy on receiving that reply.

X

When I arrived at my rooms, my colleague hurried to meet me the moment I opened the door.

'I am going to surprise you,' he said; 'and there is no time to prepare you for it. Our chief, the Minister, has seen the Prince this morning, and has been officially informed of an event of importance in the life of the Princess. She is engaged to be married to the Grand Duke.'

Engaged to the Duke – and not a word from her to warn me of it! Engaged – after what she had said to me no longer ago than the past night! Had I been made a plaything to amuse a great lady? Oh, what degradation! I was furious; I snatched up my hat to go to the palace – to force my way to her – to overwhelm her with reproaches. My friend stopped me. He put an official document into my hand.

'There is your leave of absence from the legation,' he said; 'beginning from today. I have informed the Minister, in strict confidence, of the critical position in which you are placed. He agrees with me that the Princess's inexcusable folly is alone to blame. Leave us, Ernest, by the next train. There is some intrigue going on, and I fear you may be involved in it. You know that the rulers of these little German States can exercise despotic authority when they choose?'

'Yes! yes!'

'Whether the Prince has acted of his own free will – or whether he has been influenced by some person about him – I am not able to tell you. He has issued an order to arrest an old Frenchman, known to be a republican, and suspected of associating with one of the secret societies in this part of Germany. The conspirator has taken to flight; having friends, as we suppose, who warned him in time. But this, Ernest, is not the worst of it. That charming singer, that modest pretty girl—'

'You don't mean Jeanne?'

'I am sorry to say I do. Advantage has been taken of her relationship to the old man, to include that innocent creature in political suspicions which it is simply absurd to suppose that she has deserved. She is ordered to leave the Prince's dominions immediately. – Are you going to her?'

'Instantly!' I replied.

Could I feel a moment's hesitation, after the infamous manner in which the Princess had sacrificed me to the Grand Duke? Could I think of the poor girl, friendless, helpless – with nobody near her but a stupid woman-servant, unable to speak the language of the country – and fail to devote myself to the protection of Jeanne? Thank God, I reached her lodgings in time to tell her what had happened, and to take it on myself to receive the police.

XI

In three days more, Jeanne was safe in London; having travelled under my escort. I was fortunate enough to find a home for her, in the house of a lady who had been my mother's oldest and dearest friend.

We were separated, a few days afterwards, by the distressing news which reached me of the state of my brother's health. I went at once to his house in the country. His medical attendants had lost all hope of saving him: they told me plainly that his release from a life of suffering was near at hand.

While I was still in attendance at his bedside, I heard from the secretary. He enclosed a letter, directed to me in a strange handwriting. I opened the envelope and looked for the signature. My friend had been entrapped into sending me an anonymous letter.

Besides addressing me in French (a language seldom used in my experience at the legation), the writer disguised the identity of the persons mentioned by the use of classical names. In spite of these precautions, I felt no difficulty in arriving at a conclusion. My correspondent's special knowledge of Court secrets, and her malicious way of communicating them, betrayed the Baroness.

I translate the letter; restoring to the persons who figure in it the names under which they are already known. The writer began in these satirically familiar terms:

'When you left the Prince's dominions, my dear sir, you no doubt believed yourself to be a free agent. Quite a mistake! You were a mere puppet; and the strings that moved you were pulled by the Doctor.

'Let me tell you how.

'On a certain night, which you well remember, the Princess was unexpectedly summoned to the presence of her father. His physician's skill had succeeded in relieving the illustrious Prince, prostrate under nervous miseries. He was able to attend to a state affair of importance, revealed to him by the Doctor – who then for the first time acknowledged that he had presented himself at Court in a diplomatic, as well as in a medical capacity.

'This state affair related to a proposal for the hand of the Princess, received from the Grand Duke through the authorised medium of the Doctor. Her Highness, being consulted, refused to consider the proposal. The Prince asked for her reason. She answered, "I have no wish to be married." Naturally irritated by such a ridiculous excuse, her father declared positively that the marriage should take place.

'The impression produced on the Grand Duke's favourite and emissary was of a different kind.

'Certain suspicions of the Princess and yourself, which you had successfully contrived to dissipate, revived in the Doctor's mind when he heard the lady's reason for refusing to marry his royal master. It was now too late to regret that he had suffered himself to be misled by cleverly managed appearances. He could not recall the favourable report which he had addressed to the Duke – or withdraw the proposal of marriage which he had been commanded to make.

'In this emergency, the one safe course open to him was to get rid of You – and, at the same time, so to handle circumstances as to excite against you the pride and anger of the Princess. In the pursuit of this latter object he was assisted by one of the ladies in waiting, sincerely interested in the welfare of her gracious mistress, and therefore ardently desirous of seeing her Highness married to the Duke.

'A wretched old French conspirator was made the convenient pivot on which the intrigue turned.

'An order for the arrest of this foreign republican having been first obtained, the Prince was prevailed on to extend his distrust of the Frenchman to the Frenchman's niece. You know this already; but you don't know why it was done. Having believed from the first that you were really in love with the young lady, the Doctor reckoned confidently on your devoting yourself to the protection of a friendless girl, cruelly exiled at an hour's notice.

'The one chance against us was that tender considerations, associated with her Highness, might induce you to hesitate. The lady in waiting easily moved this obstacle out of the way. She abstained from delivering a letter addressed to you, entrusted to her by the Princess. When the great lady asked why she had not received your reply, she was informed (quite truly) that you and the charming opera singer had taken your departure together. You may imagine what her Highness thought of you, and said of you, when I mention in conclusion that she consented, the same day, to marry the Duke.

'So, Mr Ernest, these clever people tricked you into serving their interests, blindfold. In relating how it was done, I hope I may have assisted you in forming a correct estimate of the state of your own intelligence. You have made a serious mistake in adopting your present profession. Give up diplomacy – and get a farmer to employ you in keeping his sheep.'

Do I sometimes think regretfully of the Princess?

Permit me to mention a circumstance, and to leave my answer to be inferred. Jeanne is Lady Medhurst.

The Poetry Did It

[An Event in the Life of Major Evergreen]

———————

Originally appeared in *The Spirit of the Times* on 26 December 1885, and almost simultaneously in *The English Illustrated Magazine* for January 1866. The poem which has influenced Major Evergreen's 'They say she's dark' is Byron's 'She walks in beauty' from *Hebrew Melodies* (1815).

I

An employment which he enjoyed represented the bright side, and an enemy whom he abhorred personified the dark side, of Major Evergreen's life. He had plenty of money, excellent health, and a hare-brained little niece who might have caused some anxiety to other men in his position. The major's constitutional tranquillity accepted responsibilities of all sorts with a good-humoured indifference which set them at defiance. If Miss Mabel had eloped with the footman, he would have said: 'Well, I hope they may be happy.' If she had come down one morning to breakfast, and had announced that she felt a vocation to be a nun, he would have answered: 'You know best, my dear; I only beg you won't trouble me to find the convent.'

Persons who wished to see Major Evergreen in earnest – terribly in earnest – had only to look at him when he had pen, ink, and paper before him, and was writing poetry.

This was the employment that he enjoyed; this was the occupation of every day in his life. He must have written hundreds of thousands of lines, without a single thought in them which was not unconsciously borrowed from somebody else. Every form that poetry can take was equally easy and delightful to him. Blank verse and rhyming verse; epic poems and sonnets; tragedies, satires, epigrams; passionate poetry in the manner of Byron; narrative poetry in the manner of Scott; philosophical poetry in the manner of Wordsworth; poetry of the modern type which gets into the pulpit, and reminds us of our moral duties – this wonderful man was equal to every imaginable effort in verse; and, more deplorable still, being rich, he published his works. They appeared in volumes (first edition), and disappeared as waste paper – and appeared again (second edition), and disappeared as before. The printing was perfection; the paper was expressly manufactured to make it worthy of the printing; and the happy major, closing his eyes on facts, firmly believed in his own popularity.

One day, towards the end of summer, the poet had laid down his pen, and was considering whether he should write a few hundred lines more, when his niece looked over his shoulder, and asked if she might speak to him.

Miss Mabel was little and dark, and slim and active; her brightly restless eyes were never in repose, except when she was asleep; her voice was cheerful, her manner was brisk, and her figure was plump. She was further entitled to claim general admiration by a system of dress which was the perfection of elegance, and by possessing a fortune of eighty thousand pounds. And last, not least on the list of her virtues, she read Major Evergreen's poetry.

'Well, Mabel, what is it?'

'It's about my marriage, uncle.'

'Marry anybody you like, my dear.'

'Even your ugly old publisher?'

'Yes, if you prefer him.'

'Or anybody else!'

'Certainly, if you like him better.'

'The fact is, uncle, you don't care what becomes of me.'

'I am of your way of thinking, my dear.'

'What do you mean?'

'Do *you* care what becomes of you?'

'Of course I do!'

'Then I care too.'

There was an interval of silence. Mabel was considering what she should say next. She decided on speaking plainly, come what might of it.

'This is serious,' she resumed.

The major was glad to hear it.

'I'm only afraid of one thing – I'm afraid I shall offend you.'

The major declared that it was impossible to offend him.

'Remember what you have said, uncle! I have just had an offer of marriage.'

'From my ugly publisher?'

'No; from Sir John Bosworth.'

Major Evergreen – usually the laziest of men – jumped out of his chair, and walked up and down the room, transformed from a pleasant uncle who wrote poetry to a disagreeable old bachelor who was angry with his niece.

And for what reason? For this excellent reason: she had mentioned the name of the enemy whom he abhorred.

Sir John Bosworth was a gentleman who indulged in the hazardous speculations of modern life. He owned racehorses, and he built theatres; he was also proprietor of a weekly journal. In that newspaper had appeared the only review of Major Evergreen's poems which had ever noticed them at any length. Of the tone adopted by the critic, it is merely necessary to say that it hurried away the easy-tempered major to his lawyer's office, to bring an action for libel against Sir John Bosworth. The wise lawyer pronounced the article to be simply inhuman, but not libellous. Sir John (already under the influence of Mabel) expressed his regret in the handsomest manner; and declared that the article had been published by his editor without his knowledge. Major Evergreen submitted to circumstances – recovered his customary good spirits – and went on writing poetry more industriously than ever. But what author has succeeded in forgetting an inhuman review? To mention the name of the proprietor of the paper was to wound the poet in his tenderest place. When Sir John Bosworth paid visits to the charming niece, the unforgiving uncle was never in his way. Major Evergreen was 'engaged in his study.'

'I couldn't help mentioning the name, uncle,' Mabel pleaded. 'I was obliged to tell you who it was that had asked me to marry him.'

The major received this apology with a word of serious advice. 'You might have spared me the name, my dear – you might have said, That Man. I should have known whom you meant.'

Mabel accepted the suggestion. 'I wished to tell you that I didn't engage to marry That Man,' she proceeded; 'I only said I wanted time to consider. I don't think I like him. I rather believe I want to get away from him, before he calls again.'

The major returned quietly to his chair.

'Very right indeed,' he said – and looked at his pen and ink. He was longing to get rid of his niece and go back to his poetry.

'This is about the time of year,' Mabel persisted, 'when we go to the country.'

The major was quite willing. 'Just as you please; they're ready for us at Stillbrook.'

'Stillbrook won't do, uncle. If we go to your country house That Man will follow us. Suppose we take refuge at Oakapple Hall?'

'With all my heart.'

'Then I may write to Mrs Corydon?'

'Certainly.'

Mabel went away to write a letter; and Mabel's uncle remained, to write poetry.

II

A widow of mild and retiring character, married late in life; and possessed of one son who exactly resembled her in disposition: there is the briefly sufficient description of Mrs Corydon.

Arriving at Oakapple Hall, Major Evergreen and his niece encountered a surprise held in reserve for them by their amiable hostess. They were received at the housedoor by Mrs Corydon's son. On the last two occasions when they had enjoyed the widow's hospitality, Mr Cyril Corydon had been absent, pursuing his studies at Oxford. Mabel had not seen him since he had left school.

Cyril had greatly improved in the interval. Still modest and a little reserved, he was no longer awkward; he kept his hands out of his pockets, and his nails exhibited no black rims; his fair complexion was without pimples; his vacant smile of former days had meaning in it now; and, to complete the transformation, Mabel saw a slim young man who fed delicately, in place of a devouring fat boy who approached his dinner as a pig approaches a trough. She also noticed his pretty little flaxen moustache, and a shy tenderness in the expression of his gentle blue eyes. Upon the whole, he reminded her of a description of a Troubadour, in one of her uncle's poems.

Oakapple Hall, in one respect, resembled the famous abbey described by Rabelais – the inhabitants did as they pleased. When luncheon was over Major Evergreen retired to his room and his pen and ink. Mrs Corydon resumed work on an immense embroidered counterpane, which had already occupied her patient fingers for the greater part of her life. The two young people took a walk in the park: Cyril offered his arm, and Mabel started the conversation.

'Have you really left Oxford for good?' she began. 'And are you sorry for it?'

'I was sorry for it, until to-day.'

Cyril laid a strong emphasis on the last three words, and ventured on a look which sent his artful compliment straight to its right address. Mabel acknowledged the look by an innocent little question: 'Do you think I am improved, since you saw me last?'

Cyril burst into an exclamation. Expressed in letters, it was only, 'Oh!' The manner and the tone made it eloquent, and ought to be described. But description requires appropriate words. Where, in this case, are the words? Mabel's innocence, requiring no description, pursued its artless way: 'Mr Corydon, you mustn't flatter me.' Mr Corydon immediately proceeded to flatter her.

'Don't call me "Mr"! You used to call me "Cyril," in the days when I was insensible to that honour and happiness. My one ambition is to hear you call me "Cyril" now.'

'You were a boy then, Mr Corydon: you are a young man now. I am afraid it wouldn't be quite right.'

Cyril hit on a poetical allusion which might have fallen from the lips of the major himself. 'Juliet didn't hesitate,' he remarked, 'to call Romeo by his Christian name.'

This – for a shy man – was, as Mabel thought, getting on at rather too rapid a rate. She turned the talk back into the prosaic channels of modern life. 'I thought your mother and you were serious people,' she said. 'Have you really been to the play?'

'Only to Shakespeare,' Cyril reminded her. 'I was taken to the theatre, in the last vacation, by a man of high position, and large experience, whom I am proud to call my friend. His younger brother read with me under the same tutor – and I first came to know him in that way.'

'Who is this remarkable gentleman?'

'Sir John Bosworth.'

Mabel stood stock-still, and looked at the unsuspecting heir of Oakapple Hall. That good fellow was honestly pleased. 'Sir John's fame has reached you,' he said. 'And perhaps you may have met him in society?'

Mabel acknowledged that she had met him, and said no more. Cyril sang his praises.

'What a man! He builds places of public amusement, he wins money on racecourses, he sits on the throne of the Press and dictates the policy of Europe – and, only think, he is My Friend!'

But Mabel's thoughts were otherwise employed.

A young person, hitherto free from any weak leanings towards superstition, she now dimly perceived the hand of Fate, mysteriously pointing to Sir John, at the very time when she had determined to dismiss him from her mind and from her list of visitors. What would be the next event? Would he discover Oakapple Hall? Preceded by his celebrity, would he obtain an introduction to Mrs Corydon, and renew his offer of marriage? With the ready inconsistency of her sex and age, Mabel began to feel a certain reluctant interest in Sir John. He assumed romantic proportions in his absence. She had left him a shadowy figure disappearing, as it were, in the background. And here he was in the front of the picture again; presenting himself through the innocent medium of this nice boy – so proud of him, so grateful to him! Her curiosity was excited by the very man whom she had despised not three days since. She encouraged poor Cecil to talk of Sir John. One of Eve's daughters – there is nothing else to be said for her: one of Eve's daughters.

The course of their walk had brought them back, by this time, to the house. Cyril suddenly made an apology.

'Excuse me for one moment; I have something to show you.' He ran into the house, and ran out again with the local newspaper in his hand.

'Nothing that I can say of our gifted friend will be as interesting to you as this,' he announced, and pointed to the column of the newspaper filled by the London correspondent with news from the fashionable world. There was Sir John again! 'A brilliant circle had assembled' at the country seat of a great nobleman, situated within an hour's drive of Oakapple Hall – and in two days more Sir John Bosworth was expected as a welcome addition to the number of his lordship's guests.

Mabel made the first excuse that occurred to her, and escaped from Cyril to the solitude of her own room. It was high time to consider what she had better do next.

III

Decision of character is, generally speaking, a plant of slow growth in the human constitution. When the age is seventeen, the sex female, and the question: What am I to do next? – perplexing circumstances wait for an answer, and seldom get it. Mabel could not venture to consult her uncle – and if Mrs Corydon had an amiable weakness, it took the form of habitual reliance on other people's advice. In this emergency, Mabel's temper escaped from control; and Cyril's position in the estimation of his charming friend receded, without any reason for that deplorable event which it was possible to discover. Ignorant of the ways of women – in love, with the ready inflammability of a young man who has led an innocent life – Cyril was foolish enough to ask if he had offended Mabel. He made the mistake with the utmost humility of manner and language – and was received with a toss of the head, and a reply which expressed surprise that a member of an English University should prove to be an ill-bred man.

Three days passed. Sir John Bosworth (if the newspaper could be trusted) was already established as a guest at the country seat of his noble friend. In sheer despair of recovering the ground that he had lost by any effort of his own, Cyril decided on asking the advice of the one competent and trustworthy person within his reach.

Sir John was in the house; Sir John hurried into the room in which Cyril was waiting for him, and shook hands with a cordial squeeze. This inestimable friend of Cyril's was a tall finely-made man, rather dark than light in complexion, and a little bald; otherwise remarkable for bushy eyebrows, a strong Roman nose, and magnificent whiskers; eyes bright and striking in themselves, but a little shifty in expression at times: in one word, a most agreeable person – with a false nature, concealed from the mass of mankind under a surface of easy humour and hearty good spirits.

'My dear boy, how glad I am to see you! You are one of *us*, of course? and you have come to luncheon? No? You are not invited by my lord? Come along and see him. Between ourselves, he's a bit of a bore – and a bright young fellow like you will be a perfect godsend to the rest of us. You won't? Now I look at you again, I see signs of something wrong. Am I rushing at rash conclusions if I suspect that my young friend is in a scrape? No explanations! At your age there is only one scrape – a woman.'

'The loveliest girl in the world, Sir John. I am in sore need of your advice. Can we speak here without interruption?'

'Of course we can!'

He rang the bell as he replied, and gave his orders to the servant as coolly as if he had been in his own house. He was obsequiously obeyed. The servant knew him to be the proprietor of a newspaper; and, like his betters (including some of the highest personages in the land) the footman was afraid of the Press.

Sir John administered his first dose of advice. 'Sit down, my good fellow – take a cigar – and out with it!'

Cyril told his melancholy story. 'She treats me cruelly,' he said, by way of conclusion. 'And I assure you, on my word of honour, I haven't deserved it.'

Sir John administered the second dose. 'Exactly my case,' he remarked coolly. 'I am devoted to the loveliest girl in the world, and she treats me cruelly. Would you believe it? – she has left London to avoid me, and I don't know where to find her. Do as I do: take it easy.'

'I'm too fond of her, Sir John, to take it easy.'

'Oh, if you come to that, *I'm* broken-hearted. At the same time, I don't disguise from myself that we are both rowing in the same boat. You're the favourite plaything of one coquette; and I'm the favourite plaything of another. There it is in a nutshell.'

This off-hand way of speaking of the beloved object shocked Cyril. 'You may be right about your lady,' he answered. 'Excuse me for saying that you are wrong about mine.'

Sir John laughed. 'I was as innocent once as you are,' he said. 'Let's get at the facts first. Mine is quite a young one. Is yours quite a young one too?'

'In the first lovely bloom of youth!'

'You curious boy! Your imagination is misleading you – and you don't know it. All girls are alike.'

Cyril indignantly struck his fist on the table. 'There isn't another girl in the world like my Mabel!'

Sir John suddenly became serious.

'Mabel?' he repeated. 'There's something in that name which sounds familiar to me. Not the niece of Major Evergreen, surely?'

'Yes!' cried simple Cyril, 'the same. How stupid of me not to have thought of it before! She has met you in society; and she is naturally interested in a celebrated man like yourself. *You* would have some influence over her. Oh, Sir John, if you would only see Mabel, and say a word to her in my interests, how truly obliged to you I should be!'

The impenetrable face of the man of the world expressed nothing but perfect readiness to make himself useful. Far more experienced eyes than Cyril's would have discovered nothing in Sir John Bosworth's manner even remotely suggesting that the two lovers had been, all this time, talking of the same lady.

'With pleasure!' cried Sir John. 'But where shall we find her?'

Cyril seized his hand. 'You good friend!' he exclaimed, with tears in his eyes. 'She's staying with my mother at our house – only a short ride from this place. When will you let me introduce you to my mother?'

'Whenever you like.'

'At once?'

And that excellent man smiled, and cheerfully echoed the words: 'At once!'

IV

The two gentlemen discovered Miss Mabel walking up and down the garden terrace in front of Oakapple Hall, reading a book. Good girl! It was a volume of her uncle's poetry.

'I felt sure you would be glad to meet Sir John Bosworth again,' Cyril began.

His manner was a great deal too humble. Before he could get any farther, Sir John spoke for himself.

'The happiness is all mine,' he said in his easy way. 'If I happen, however, to be intruding, pray don't scruple to say so.'

Mabel raised her eyes from her book. She had only to look at Cyril, and to see what had happened. Angry, perplexed, flattered, amused – in this conflict of small emotions she was completely at a loss how to assert herself to the best advantage; and she took refuge in a cold composure which, for the time being at least, committed her to nothing. 'I was certainly engaged in reading,' she replied – and put a mark in her book with a sigh of resignation.

Impenetrable Sir John received the blow without flinching. 'You led me to hope for the honour of being introduced to Mrs Corydon,' he said to Cyril. 'Shall we find her at home?'

He took Cyril's arm and led him to the house. 'That's the way to manage her,' he whispered. 'I'll bet you five to one she's vexed at our leaving her – and ten to one that she receives us more civilly when she sees us again. Don't look back! You're a lost man if she discovers that you're thinking of her. Which is the way to the drawing-room?'

Sir John Bosworth effected the conquest of Mrs Corydon at the first interview. She treated him as she was accustomed to treat her best friends. In other words, she offered to show him over the house. Oakapple Hall was a place of great age and celebrity. In the upper regions two Kings of England had slept, and the ground floor still showed traces of the passage of Oliver Cromwell and his men. Sir John made his excuses for that day. Having heard that Mabel's uncle was in the house, he was courteously unwilling to disturb the major in the agonies of poetical composition. When he had taken his leave he whispered to Cyril, on his way to the house door: 'I'll lay you another wager, if you like – we shall see Miss Mabel still on the terrace.' And they did see her.

She was seated, with her closed book on her lap, deep in thought.

Hesitating between her two lovers, she had decided at first in favour of Cyril: he had youth on his side, he was handsome, he was modest and amiable. If he had happened to appear on the terrace, at that moment, he would have been the man preferred. But he was indoors, in attendance on his friend; and he left Mabel time to remember that there was a weak side to his character. In Cyril's place would Sir John have consulted another man, and have brought him to visit her, without once suspecting that he might be a rival in disguise? Mabel was already leaning to the side of Sir John, when she heard footsteps on the walk – and, looking up, saw the man himself approaching her, alone.

In the present state of her inclinations, she was disposed, as an accomplished flirt, to begin by trifling with him. He saw her intention in the bright malice of her eyes, and put an obstacle in her way. Taking the book off her lap, he assumed to be interested in her reading.

'Tired of poetry, Miss Mabel?'

'Never tired of it, Sir John.'

'You read a great deal of poetry.'

'I believe I have read all the English poets.'

'Including the major. Do you find him equal to the others?'

'My uncle reminds me of the others – always pleasantly.'

Sir John opened the book, at that part of it in which a mark had been left, and read the title of the poem: *The Rival Minstrels: a Contest in Verse.*

'Is it very interesting?' he asked.

His tone irritated Mabel. 'It is perfectly charming,' she answered – 'and reminds me of Walter Scott. Two minstrels are in love with the same fair lady; she challenges them to an exhibition of their art; they are each to address her in verse; and she offers her hand to the poet whose lines she most admires. Ah, what a position women occupied in those days!'

'You would like to have been that fair lady, I suppose?'

'I should indeed! Especially,' she added with a saucy smile, 'if you were a minstrel.'

'I never wrote anything in my life – except letters. A proprietor of a newspaper, Miss Mabel, leaves prose and verse to his editor and his contributors. Are you looking for anything?'

'I am looking for Mr Corydon. Where is he?' Mabel asked, with an appearance of the deepest interest.

Sir John determined to stop the coming flirtation in another way.

'Staying in the house,' he answered gravely, 'by my advice.'

'And why does he want your advice?'

'Because he is under my protection. I feel the truest regard for him, and the sincerest sympathy with him in his present trying situation.'

Sir John knew his young lady well. His object was to puzzle her by presenting himself in an angry and jealous character entirely new to her experience – to keep her flighty mind by this means employed in trying to understand him, when he was obliged to leave her – to return the next day, and, by means of humble excuses and ardent entreaties for a reconciliation, to place poor Cyril's mild and modest fidelity in a light of comparison which it would be little likely to endure.

Thus far he had succeeded. Mabel listened, and looked at him, and said, 'I don't understand you.'

'I will make myself understood,' Sir John rejoined. 'Have you forgotten the offer of marriage which I ventured to address to you in London? You didn't say No; you told me you wished for time to consider. I called again, to hear what your decision might be; and I found that you had not only gone away into the country, without a word of apology, but had left strict instructions that the place of your retreat was not to be mentioned to anybody. If this was not a deliberate insult, it was something extremely like it. When I told you just now that Mr Corydon was under my protection, I meant that I would not allow that excellent young man to be treated as you have treated me.'

Mabel's indignation was equal to the one possible reply to this.

'Make your mind easy,' she said; 'Mr Corydon is in no danger of being treated as I have treated you.'

'I sincerely hope for my young friend's sake,' Sir John answered, 'that you really mean what you say.'

Mabel got more and more angry. 'Mr Corydon is charming!' she burst out. 'Mr Corydon is a young man whom I esteem and admire!'

'Allow me to thank you, Miss Mabel, for your candour. You relieve me from the anxiety that I have been feeling on my friend's account. If you will only say to him what you have just said to me I shall retire, happy in the conviction that my intercession in Mr Corydon's favour has been crowned with success. Good morning.'

V

Left by herself, Mabel felt the composing influence of solitude. Little by little, her cheeks recovered their every-day delicacy of colour; her eyebrows took their proper places on her forehead; and her pulse returned to the customary moderation of its beat. She was able to listen to the gentle promptings of her own vanity; and, as a matter of course, she began to look at Sir John's insolence from a new point of view. He, the self-possessed man of the world, had completely forgotten himself, and there could be but one reason for it. 'Mad with jealousy,' she concluded complacently. 'How fond he must be of me!'

Who was this, approaching slowly from the house with steps that hesitated? This was the fatal young man who was under Sir John's protection, and who had repaid the obligation by rousing emotions of jealous rage in Sir John's breast. Mabel was not sure whether she despised him or pitied him. In this difficulty, she took a middle course, and only said, 'What do you want?'

'May I not have the happiness of speaking to you?'

'It depends, Mr Corydon, on what you have to say. I forbid you to speak of Sir John Bosworth; I won't hear you if you speak of yourself; and I shall retire to my room if you speak of me. Have you any harmless remarks to make? Suppose you try the weather?'

Humble Cyril looked up at the sky. 'Beautiful weather,' he said submissively.

'Or politics?' Miss Mabel continued.

'Conservative,' Cyril answered, as if he were saying his catechism.

'Or literature?'

'I haven't got any.'

'What do you mean by that?'

'I mean, I wish I was as well read as you are. Oh, Miss Mabel, don't be so hard on a poor fellow who loves you with all his heart. I didn't mean any harm when I asked Sir John—'

'Be quiet!'

'If there is any sort of atonement that I can make – if you could only tell me what a young lady wants – I mean, what she looks for in a young man—'

'She looks, Mr Corydon, for what she doesn't find in you.'

'May I ask what that is?'

'May I ask if you object to the form of vulgarity which is called – Slang?'

'I object to nothing from You. Pray tell me in what I am deficient.'

'Pluck!'

She looked at him with a moment's saucy attention – bowed, and returned to the house. Even Cyril discovered that she was not positively angry this time.

VI

Sir John Bosworth appeared again on the next day – with an excellent reason for returning so soon. He had not yet been shown over Oakapple Hall.

On this occasion, the servant conducted him to the music-room. Mabel was at the piano; and Cyril was turning the leaves of the music for her. Sir John had only to look at them, and to suspect that his modest young friend had been gaining ground in his absence. He approached the piano with his genial smile, and examined the music. 'Maiden Musings' was the title; and, in one respect at least, the composer had deserved well of the public of the present day – he had given them plenty of notes for their money. 'Go on, please,' said the amiable visitor. Mabel went on. Notes that thundered, notes that shrieked, notes in cataracts of sound represented the maiden's musings. 'What were those remarks,' Sir John asked when it was over, 'that Mozart made on the subject of melody? Cyril, my dear fellow, have you got Kelly's *Reminiscences* in the library? Kelly was Mozart's pupil. Do try to find the book.'

Before he complied with this request, Cyril looked at Mabel, and received a look in return. Then, and only then, he left the room. Sir John saw that he had not a moment to lose. The door had barely closed on his young rival, before he possessed himself of Mabel's hand, and said, 'Oh, forgive me!'

She released her hand, and assumed an icy composure. 'I confess I am a little surprised to see you again,' she remarked.

'You see a man crushed by sorrow and shame,' Sir John proceeded. 'Some devil must have possessed me when I spoke to you yesterday. I have not had one quiet moment since. You are literally the one hope of my life. Try, pray try to imagine what I felt, when I had every reason to fear that I had lost you – and to what a man!'

'A very agreeable man, Sir John.'

'Torture me, if you like; I have deserved it. But don't tell me that you – with your bright intelligence, your tact and delicacy, your superiority to the little weaknesses and vanities of ordinary women – can feel a serious attachment to such a person as Cyril Corydon. No! Despise me as you may, Mabel; destroy all the hopes that I have centred in you; doom me to be a wretched man for the rest of my life – there is one thing you can *not* do: I defy you to lower yourself in my estimation. You have been the one woman in the world to me since I first saw you; and the one woman you will remain to the day of my death!'

He caught her by the hand again: it trembled in his hand; her ready tongue had literally nothing to say. The power of nonsense, in every form which it can take, is one of the great moral forces to which humanity instinctively submits. When Cyril returned (without having discovered the book) Sir John's nonsense, admirably spoken, had answered Sir John's purpose. Placed between her two admirers, Mabel was not able to determine which she really preferred.

'There's no such book in the library,' Cyril announced. 'If he wanted to get rid of me, don't you think, Miss Mabel, he might have said so plainly?'

For the moment Sir John was thunderstruck. Was this the same confiding helpless young gentleman who had brought him to Oakapple Hall? He recovered himself directly.

'My dear boy, is there gout in your family?' he asked. 'I am at a loss to understand this extraordinary outbreak of temper – unless there is a first fit coming on, at an unusually early age.'

Cyril passed this question over without notice. His fair complexion reddened with anger. Never had love wrought such a transformation in a man since the time of Cymon.

'I saw you take Miss Mabel's hand just now, when I came in,' he declared stoutly. 'I consider that to be a liberty.'

Sir John's satirical composure was not disturbed even by this. 'May I inquire, merely as a matter of curiosity, whether you claim a right of property in this young lady's hand?'

'Yes, I do! I have reason to hope that this young lady will do me the honour of marrying me.'

'So have I!'

'I have a prior claim on her, Sir John.'

'Nothing of the sort. I asked Miss Mabel to marry me last week.'

Cyril turned indignantly to Mabel. 'Is that true?'

Sir John cautioned her. 'You're not bound to answer,' he said.

'She *is* bound!'

'No, Cyril – no.'

'Do you hear him, Mabel?'

Sir John pointed to Cyril's flaming cheeks. 'Do you see him, Mabel?'

She burst out laughing. This disconcerted both the men: there was an awful pause. 'Must I decide between you,' she asked, 'without any time to think first?' Neither the one nor the other offered her time to think first. Mabel's eyes suddenly brightened: a new idea had occurred to her. She turned to Sir John.

'I see a way out of the difficulty,' she said. 'Do you remember my uncle's poem – the *Contest of the Minstrels?* Suppose you and Mr Corydon each address me in a little poem of your own composing – and suppose I imitate the fair lady of the ballad, and choose the minstrel whose verses I like best?'

Cyril was reduced to silence. Even Sir John could only say: 'You're joking.'

She *was* joking. But the consternation visible in the faces of the two men roused the spirit of mischief in her. 'I'm quite in earnest,' she answered. 'If you wish me to decide between you, you have heard the only terms on which I consent. The day is before you: do your best.'

As she opened the door to leave them, Mrs Corydon came in. The amiable old lady said she was at Sir John's service when he wished to see the house.

VII

Major Evergreen proved to be useless, on this occasion, as a means for making an excuse; he had gone out for a walk. All the rooms at Oakapple Hall were open to Sir John. He heard how the two Kings had slept in the house, how Oliver Cromwell had battered the house, how one part of it was built in one century, and another part in another. He was not even spared the interesting spectacle of Major Evergreen's study. 'So characteristic of a poet,' Mrs Corydon said; 'look at the manuscripts all scattered about!' Sir John looked at the manuscripts. Mrs Corydon left him, and led the way to the window. 'And now look at the view!' Sir John looked at the view.

Released at last, he had leisure to consider whether he should humour Mabel's absurd caprice, or decline to make himself ridiculous, and leave her to recover her senses. He was a man greedy for money, as well as a man in love. Remembering that she had a handsome fortune, and that a rival younger than himself was also courting her, he made his way to the library.

At one of the writing-tables, Cyril was sitting forlorn, surrounded by morsels of torn paper. 'What have you done?' the elder minstrel asked of the younger. The melancholy answer was, 'Nothing!' Cyril's voice sounded as if he was a child again, and was ready to cry.

Sir John sat down at a second table, in a distant part of the room, and began to write. The quiet in the library was only disturbed, now and then, by the heavy sighs of Cyril, and the sound of paper that was being torn up.

VIII

There was a knock at the door. A fresh young voice asked gaily: 'May I come in?'

'Don't let me disturb you,' said Mabel. 'The fair ladies of past times were remarkable for their patience – especially with minstrels. I can wait.'

She looked at Cyril, who was seated nearest to her. Too cruelly mortified to speak, he took her hand, and put it on his hot forehead; he pointed to the mass of torn paper all round him. The tears rose in his eyes – he opened the door and went out.

Mabel's face lost its expression of malicious enjoyment. She looked ashamed of herself; and she said softly: 'Poor fellow!'

Sir John crossed the room, with a smile of conscious superiority. He was not a man who did anything by halves. Having decided on humouring the young lady, he presented his poetic offering with chivalrous humility, dropping on one knee.

Mabel read his verses. They had one great merit – there were very few of them.

> They say she's dark; yes, like the night
>   Whose beauty shines from starry skies:
> Oh, my sweet saint, how darkly bright
>   The mellow radiance of those eyes!
> I love in you the tender light—
>   The light that gaudy day denies.

'Very pretty,' Mabel said – 'and reminds me of Byron. Did you ever read his Hebrew Melodies?'

'Never!' Sir John declared fervently. 'Allow me, my angel, to kiss your hand, and claim your promise.'

At that critical moment, Major Evergreen returned from his walk, and entered the library in search of a book. He stood petrified at the sight of the enemy whom he abhorred. 'That Man!' he cried – and ran out of the room with a furious look at his niece.

She ran out after him. Sir John followed on tiptoe, and listened at the half-opened door.

'There's more excuse for me, uncle, than you think,' Mabel pleaded. 'Sir John Bosworth has one merit which you really ought to allow. He is a poet like yourself – he has just written this.'

She began to read the verses:

> They say she's dark; yes, like the night
> Whose beauty shines from starry skies—

Her uncle snatched the paper out of her hand. 'My Poetry!' he shouted.

Before his niece could stop him, he was back again in the library. 'Thief!' he called out at the top of his voice.

Mabel made a vain attempt to quiet him. She had forgotten the inhuman review. Not so the major. Even at that trying moment he could have repeated the most atrocious insults inflicted on him in the newspaper without missing a word.

'The scoundrel has been among My Manuscripts!' cried the infuriated poet. 'I've longed to murder him for the last six months. And now I'll do it!'

It was useless to search the room. Sir John Bosworth had made his escape.

At a later period, when Mabel was asked why she had married Cyril instead of Sir John, she used to answer—
'The Poetry did it.'

A Sad Death and Brave Life

Originally appeared in the American *Youth's Companion* on 19 August 1886. This was the first of two stories collectively entitled 'The Victims of Circumstances: Discovered in Records of Old Trials' which dealt with serious miscarriages of justice. It was reprinted in *The Boy's Own Paper* on 23 October 1886.

A T THAT MEMORABLE period in the early history of the United States when American citizens resented the tyranny of George the Third and his Parliament by destroying a cargo of taxed tea, a Bristol trader arrived in the harbour of Boston, having one passenger on board. This person was a young English woman, named Esther Calvert, daughter of a shopkeeper at Cheltenham, and niece of the captain of the ship.

Some years before her departure from England, Esther had suffered an affliction – associated with a deplorable public event – which had shaken her attachment to her native land. Free, at a later period, to choose for herself, she resolved on leaving England, as soon as employment could be found for her in another country. After a weary interval of expectation, the sea-captain had obtained a situation for his niece, as housekeeper in the family of Mrs Anderkin – a widow lady living in Boston.

Esther had been well practised in domestic duties during the long illness of her mother. Intelligent, modest and sweet-tempered, she soon became a favourite with Mrs Anderkin and the members of her young family. The children found but one fault with the new housekeeper; she dressed invariably in dismal black; and it was impossible to prevail upon her to give the cause. It was known that she was an orphan, and she had acknowledged that no relation of hers had recently died – and yet she persisted in wearing mourning. Some great grief had evidently overshadowed the life of the gentle English housekeeper.

In her intervals of leisure, she soon became the chosen friend of Mrs Anderkin's children; always ready to teach them new games, clever at dressing the girls' dolls and at mending the boys' toys, Esther was in one respect only not in sympathy with her young friends – she never laughed. One day, they boldly put the question to her: 'When we are all laughing, why don't you laugh too?'

Esther took the right way to silence children whose earliest lessons had taught them the golden rule: Do unto others as you would they should do unto you. She only replied in these words:

'I shall think it kind of you if you won't ask me that question again.'

The young people deserved her confidence in them: they never mentioned the subject from that time forth.

But there was another member of the family, whose desire to know something of the housekeeper's history was, from motives of delicacy, concealed from Esther herself. This was the governess – Mrs Anderkin's well-loved friend, as well as the teacher of her children.

On the day before he sailed on his homeward voyage, the sea-captain called to take leave of his niece – and then asked if he could also pay his respects to Mrs Anderkin. He was informed that the lady of the house had gone out, but that the governess would be happy to receive him. At the interview which followed they talked of Esther, and agreed so well in their good opinion of her, that the captain paid a long visit. The governess had persuaded him to tell the story of his niece's wasted life.

But he insisted on one condition.

'If we had been in England,' he said, 'I should have kept the matter secret, for the sake of the family. Here, in America, Esther is a stranger – here she will stay – and no slur will be cast on the family name at home. But mind one thing! I trust to your honour to take no one into your confidence – excepting only the mistress of the house.'

More than one hundred years have passed since those words were spoken.

Esther's sad story may be harmlessly told now. In the year 1762, a young man named John Jennings, employed as waiter at a Yorkshire inn, astonished his master by announcing that he was engaged to be married, and that he purposed retiring from service on next quarter-day.

Further inquiry showed that the young woman's name was Esther Calvert, and that Jennings was greatly her inferior in social rank. Her father's consent to the marriage depended on her lover's success in rising in the world. Friends with money were inclined to trust Jennings, and to help him to start a business of his own, if Miss Calvert's father would do something for the young people on his side. He made no objection, and the marriage engagement was sanctioned accordingly.

One evening, when the last days of Jennings's service were drawing to an end, a gentleman on horseback stopped at the inn. In a state of great agitation, he informed the landlady that he was on his way to Hull, but that he had been so frightened as to make it impossible for him to continue his journey. A highwayman had robbed him of a purse containing twenty guineas. The thief's face (as usual in those days) was concealed by a mask; and there was but one chance of bringing him to justice. It was the traveller's custom to place a private mark on every gold piece that he carried with him on a journey: and the stolen guineas might possibly be traced in that way.

The landlord (one Mr Brunell) attended on his guest at supper. His wife had only that moment told him of the robbery; and he had a circumstance to mention which might lead to the discovery of the thief. In the first place, however, he wished to ask at what time the crime had been committed. The traveller answered that he had been robbed late in the evening, just as it was beginning to get dark. On hearing this, Mr Brunell looked very much distressed.

'I have got a waiter here, named Jennings,' he said; 'a man superior to his station in life – good manners and a fair education – in fact, a general favourite. But for some little time past I have observed that he has been rather free with his money and that habits of drinking have grown on him. I am afraid he is not worthy of the good opinion entertained of him by myself and by other persons. This evening I sent him out to get some small silver for me; giving him a guinea to change. He came back intoxicated, telling me that change was not to be had. I ordered him to bed – and then happened to look at the guinea which he had brought back. Unfortunately I had not at that time, heard of the robbery; and I paid the guinea away with some other money, in settlement of a tradesman's account. But this I am sure of – there was a mark on the guinea which Jennings gave back to me. It is, of course, possible that there might have been a mark (which escaped my notice) on the guinea which I took out of my purse when I sent for change.'

'Or,' the traveller suggested, 'it may have been one of my stolen guineas, given back by mistake by this drunken waiter of yours instead of the guinea handed to him by yourself. Do you think he is asleep?'

'Sure to be asleep, sir, in his condition.'

'Do you object, Mr Brunell, after what you have told me, to setting this matter at rest by searching the man's clothes?'

The landlord hesitated.

'It seems hard on Jennings,' he said, 'if we prove to have been suspicious of him without a cause. Can you speak positively, sir, to the mark which you put on your money?'

The traveller declared that he could swear to his mark. Mr Brunell yielded. The two went up together to the waiter's room.

Jennings was fast asleep. At the very outset of the search they found the stolen bag of money in his pocket. The guineas – nineteen in number – had a mark on each one of them, and that mark the traveller identified. After this discovery there was but one course to take. The waiter's protestations of innocence, when they woke him and accused him of the robbery, were words flatly contradicted by facts. He was charged before a magistrate with the theft of the money, and, as a matter of course, was committed for trial.

The circumstances were so strongly against him that his own friends recommended Jennings to plead guilty, and appeal to the mercy of the Court. He refused to follow their advice, and he was bravely encouraged to persist in that decision by the poor girl, who believed in his innocence with her whole heart. At that dreadful crisis in her life she secured the best legal assistance, and took from her little dowry the money that paid the expenses.

At the next assizes the case was tried. The proceedings before the judge were a repetition (at great length and with more solemnity) of the proceedings before the magistrate. No skill in cross-examination could shake the direct statements of the witnesses. The evidence was made absolutely complete by the appearance of the tradesman to whom Mr Brunell had paid the marked guinea. The coin (so marked) was a curiosity: the man had kept it, and he now produced it in court.

The judge summed up, finding literally nothing that he could say, as an honest man, in favour of the prisoner. The jury returned a verdict of guilty, after a consultation which was a mere matter of form. Clearer circumstantial evidence of guilt had never been produced, in the opinion of every person – but one – who was present at the trial. The sentence on Jennings for highway robbery was, by the law of those days, death on the scaffold.

Friends were found to help Esther in the last effort that the faithful creature could now make – the attempt to obtain a commutation of the sentence. She was admitted to an interview with the Home Secretary, and her petition was presented to the king. Here, again, the indisputable evidence forbade the exercise of mercy. Esther's betrothed husband was hanged at Hull. His last words declared his innocence – with the rope round his neck.

Before a year had passed the one poor consolation that she could hope for in this world found Esther in her misery. The proof that Jennings had died a martyr to the fallibility of human justice was made public by the confession of the guilty man.

Another criminal trial took place at the assizes. The landlord of an inn was found guilty of having stolen the property of a person staying in his house. It was stated in evidence that this was not his first offence. He had been habitually a robber on the highway, and his name was Brunell.

The wretch confessed that he was the masked highwayman who had stolen the bag of guineas. Riding, by a nearer way than was known to the traveller, he had reached the inn first. There he found a person in trade waiting by appointment for the settlement of a bill. Not having enough money of his own about him to pay the whole amount, Brunell had made use of one of the stolen guineas, and had only heard the traveller declare that his money was marked after the tradesman had left the house. To ask for the return of the fatal guinea was more than he dared to attempt. But one other alternative presented itself. The merciless villain ensured his own safety by the sacrifice of an innocent man.

After the time when the sea-captain had paid his visit at Mrs Anderkin's house, Esther's position became subject to certain changes. One little domestic privilege followed another, so gradually and so modestly that the housekeeper found herself a loved and honoured member of the family, without being able to trace by what succession of events she had risen to the new place that she occupied. The secret confided to the two ladies had been strictly preserved; Esther never even suspected that they knew the deplorable story of her lover's death. Her life, after what she had suffered, was not prolonged to a great age. She died, peacefully unconscious of the terrors of death. Her last words were spoken with a smile. She looked at the loving friends assembled round her bed, and said to them, 'My dear one is waiting for me. Good-bye.'

Farmer Fairweather

Originally appeared in the American *Youth's Companion* on 19 August 1886. This was the second of two stories collectively entitled 'The Victims of Circumstances: Discovered in Records of Old Trials' which dealt with serious miscarriages of justice. It was reprinted in *The Boy's Own Paper* on 26 February 1887.

I AM THE last surviving witness who appeared at the trial, and unless I reduce to writing what I happen to know, there will be no record of the true particulars left after my death.

In the town of Betminster, and round about it for many a good English mile, I am known as Dame Roundwood. I have never been married, and at my present age, I never shall be. My one living relative, at the past time of which I now write, was my sister – married to a man named Morcom. He was settled in France, as a breeder of horses. Now and then he crossed over to England on his business, and went back again.

I took such a dislike to Morcom that I refused to be present at the wedding. This led, of course, to a quarrel. Nephews and nieces, if there had been any, might perhaps have reconciled me with my sister. As it was, we never wrote to each other after she went to France with her husband. And I never saw her again until she lay on her deathbed. So much about myself, to begin with.

Circumstances, which it is neither needful nor pleasant to dwell on in this place, occasioned the loss of my income, while I was still in the prime of my life. I had no choice but to make the best of a bad bargain, and to earn my bread by going out to service.

Having provided myself with good recommendations, I applied for the vacant place of housekeeper to Farmer Fairweather. I had heard of him as a well-to-do old bachelor, cultivating his land nigh on five miles in a northerly direction beyond Betminster. But I positively declare that I had never been in his house, or exchanged a word with him, on the day when I set forth for the farm.

The door was opened to me by a nice little girl. I noticed that her manners were pretty, and her voice was a remarkably strong one for her age. She had, I may also mention, the finest blue eyes I ever saw in any young creature's face. When she looked at you, there was just a cast, as they call it, in her left eye, barely noticeable, and not a deformity in any sense of the word. The one drawback that I could find in this otherwise pleasing young person was that she had rather a sullen look, and that she seemed to be depressed in her spirits.

But, like most people the girl was ready enough to talk about herself. I found that her name was Dina Coomb, and that she had lost both her parents. Farmer Fairweather was her guardian, as well as her uncle, and held a fortune of ten thousand pounds ready and waiting for her when she came of age.

What would become of the money if she died in her youth, was more than Dina could tell me. Her mother's timepiece had been already given to her, by directions in her mother's will. It looked of great value to my eyes, and it flattered her vanity to see how I admired her grand gold watch.

'I hope you are coming to stay here,' she said to me.

This seemed, as I thought, rather a sudden fancy to take to a stranger. 'Why do you want me to stay with you?' I asked.

And she hung her head, and had nothing to say. The farmer came in from his fields, and I entered on my business with him. At the same time I noticed, with some surprise, than Dina slipped out of the room by one door when her uncle came in by the other.

He was pleased with my recommendations, and he civilly offered me sufficient wages. Moreover, he was still fair to look upon, and not (as some farmers are) slovenly in his dress. So far from being an enemy to this miserable man, as has been falsely asserted, I gladly engaged to take my place at the farm on the next day at twelve o'clock, noon.

A friendly neighbour at Betminster, one Master Gouch, gave me a cast in his gig. We arrived true to the appointed time. While Master Gouch waited to bring my box after me, I opened the garden gate and rang the bell at the door. There was no answer. I had just rung once more, when I heard a scream in the house. These were the words that followed the scream, in a voice which I recognised as the voice of Dina Coomb:

'Oh, uncle, don't kill me!'

I was too frightened to know what to do. Master Gouch, having heard that dreadful cry as I did, jumped out of the gig and tried the door. It was not fastened inside. Just as he was stepping over the threshold, the farmer bounced out of a room that opened into the passage, and asked what he did there.

My good neighbour answered, 'Here, sir, is Dame Roundwood, come to your house by your own appointment.'

Thereupon Farmer Fairweather said he had changed his mind, and meant to do without a housekeeper. He spoke in an angry manner, and he took the door in his hand, as if he meant to shut us out. But before he could do this, we heard a moaning in the room that he had just come out of. Says my neighbour,

'There's somebody hurt, I'm afraid.'

Says I, 'Is it your niece, sir?'

The farmer slammed the door in our faces, and then locked it against us. There was no help for it after this but to go back to Betminster.

Master Gouch, a cautious man in all things, recommended that we should wait awhile before we spoke of what had happened, on the chance of receiving an explanation and apology from the farmer when he recovered his temper. I agreed to this. But there! I am a woman, and I did take a lady (a particular friend of mine) into my confidence. The next day it was all over the town. Inquiries were made; some of the labourers on the farm said strange things; the mayor and aldermen heard of what was going on. When I next saw Farmer Fairweather he was charged with the murder of his niece, and I was called, along with Master Gouch and the labourers, as witness against him.

The ins and outs of the law are altogether beyond me. I can only report that Dina Coomb was certainly missing, and this, taken with what Master Gouch and I had heard and seen, was (as the lawyers said) the case against the farmer. His defence was that Dina was a bad girl. He found it necessary, standing towards her in the place of her father, to correct his niece with a leather strap from time to time; and we upset his temper by trying to get into his house when strangers were not welcome, and might misinterpret his actions. As for the disappearance of Dina, he could only conclude that she had run away, and where she had gone to was more than he had been able to discover.

To this the law answered, 'You have friends to help you, and you are rich enough to pay the expense of a strict search. Find Dina Coomb, and produce her here to prove what you have said. We will give you reasonable time. Make the best use of it.'

Ten days passed, and we, the witnesses, were summoned again. How it came out I don't know. Everybody in Betminster was talking of it; Farmer Fairweather's niece had been found.

The girl told her story, and the people who had discovered her told *their* story. It was all plain and straightforward, and I had just begun to wonder what I was wanted for, when up got the lawyer who had the farmer's interests in charge, and asked that the witnesses might be ordered to leave the court. We were turned out under care of an usher; and we were sent for as the authorities wanted us, to speak to the identity of Dina, one at a time. The parson of Farmer Fairweather's parish church was the first witness called. Then came the turn of the labourers. I was sent for last.

When I had been sworn, and when the girl and I were, for the first time, set close together face to face, a most extraordinary interest seemed to be felt in my evidence. How I first came to be in Dina's company, and how long a time passed while I was talking with her, were questions which I answered as I had answered them once already, ten days since.

When a voice warned me to be careful and to take my time, and another voice said. 'Is that Dina Coomb?' I was too much excited – I may even say, too much frightened – to turn my head and see who was speaking to me. The longer I looked at the girl, the more certain I felt that I was *not* looking at Dina.

What could I do? As an honest woman giving evidence on her oath I was bound, come what might of it, to tell the truth. To the voice which had asked me if that was Dina Coomb, I answered positively, 'No.'

My reasons, when given, were two in number. First, both this girl's eyes were as straight as straight could be – not so much as the vestige of a cast could I see in her left eye. Secondly, she was fatter than Dina in the face, and fatter in the neck and arms, and rounder in the shoulders. I owned, when the lawyer put the question to me, that she was of the same height as Dina, and had the same complexion and the same fine blue colour in her eyes. But I stuck fast to the differences that I had noticed – and they said I turned the scale against the prisoner.

As I afterwards discovered, we witnesses had not been agreed. The labourers declared that the girl was Dina. The parson, who had seen Dina hundreds of times at his school, said exactly what I had said. Other competent witnesses were sought for and found the next day. Their testimony was our testimony repeated again and again. Later still, the abominable father and mother who had sold their child for purposes of deception were discovered, and were afterwards punished, along with the people who had paid the money.

Driven to the wall, the prisoner owned that he had failed to find his runaway niece; and that, in terror of being condemned to die on the scaffold for murder, he had made this desperate attempt to get himself acquitted by deceiving the law. His confession availed him nothing; his solemn assertion of innocence availed him nothing. Farmer Fairweather was hanged.*

With the passing away of time the memory of things passes away too. I was beginning to be an old woman, and the trial was only remembered by elderly people like myself, when I got a letter relating to my sister. It was written for her by the English consul at the French town in which she lived. He informed me that she had been a widow for some years past; and he

---

* This terrible miscarriage of justice happened before the time when trials were reported in the newspapers, and led to one valuable result: Since that time it has been a first and foremost condition of a trial for murder that the body of the slain person shall have been discovered and identified. – W. C.

summoned me instantly to her bedside if I wished to see her again before she died.

I was just in time to find her living. She was past speaking to me but, thank God, she understood what I meant when I kissed her and asked her to forgive me. Towards evening the poor soul passed away quietly, with her head resting on my breast.

The consul had written down what she wanted to say to me. I leave the persons who may read this to judge what my feelings were when I discovered that my sister's husband was the wretch who had assisted the escape of Dina Coomb, and who had thus been the means of condemning an innocent man to death on the scaffold.

On one of those visits on business to England of which I have already spoken he had met a little girl sitting under a hedge at the side of the high road, lost, footsore, and frightened, and had spoken to her. She owned that she had run away from home after a most severe beating. She showed the marks. A worthy man would have put her under the protection of the nearest magistrate.

My rascally brother-in-law noticed her valuable watch, and, suspecting that she might be connected with wealthy people, he encouraged her to talk. When he was well assured of her expectations, and of the use to which he might put them in her friendless situation, he offered to adopt her, and he took her away with him to France.

My sister, having no child of her own took a liking to Dina, and readily believed what her husband chose to tell her. For three years the girl lived with them. She cared little for the good woman who was always kind to her, but she was most unreasonably fond of the villain who had kidnapped her.

After his death this runaway creature – then aged fifteen – was missing again. She left a farewell letter to my sister, saying that she had found another friend: and from that time forth nothing more had been heard of her, for years on years. This had weighed on my sister's mind, and this was what she had wanted to tell me on her deathbed. Knowing nothing of the trial, she was aware that Dina belonged to the neighbourhood of Betminster, and she thought in her ignorance that I might communicate with Dina's friends, if such persons existed.

On my return to England I thought it a duty to show to the Mayor of Betminster what the consul had written from my sister's dictation. He read it and heard what I had to tell him. Then he reckoned up the years that had passed. Says he, 'The girl must be of age by this time: I shall cause inquiries to be made in London.'

In a week more we did hear of Dina Coomb. She had returned to her own country, with a French husband at her heels, had proved her claim, and had got her money.

Miss Dulane and My Lord

Originally appeared in *The Spirit of the Times*, 25 December 1886, as 'An Old Maid's Husband'. Reprinted in *Little Novels* (1887). The situation of the old wife who toys with giving way to a younger woman recalls 'Mr Lismore and the Widow.' The story is noteworthy for a number of gratuitous anti-feminist asides, and the slightly caustic presentation of a Jewish private detective.

Part One: Two Remonstrances

I

One afternoon old Miss Dulane entered her drawing-room; ready to receive visitors, dressed in splendour, and exhibiting every outward appearance of a defiant frame of mind.

Just as a saucy bronze nymph on the mantelpiece struck the quarter to three on an elegant clock under her arm, a visitor was announced – 'Mrs Newsham.'

Miss Dulane wore her own undisguised gray hair, dressed in perfect harmony with her time of life. Without an attempt at concealment, she submitted to be too short and too stout. Her appearance (if it had only been made to speak) would have said, in effect: 'I am an old woman, and I scorn to disguise it.'

Mrs Newsham, tall and elegant, painted and dyed, acted on the opposite principle in dressing, which confesses nothing. On exhibition before the world, this lady's disguise asserted that she had reached her thirtieth year on her last birthday. Her husband was discreetly silent, and Father Time was discreetly silent; they both knew that her last birthday had happened thirty years since.

'Shall we talk of the weather and the news, my dear? Or shall we come to the object of your visit at once?' So Miss Dulane opened the interview.

'Your tone and manner, my good friend, are no doubt provoked by the report in the newspaper of this morning. In justice to you, I refuse to believe the report.' So Mrs Newsham adopted her friend's suggestion.

'Your kindness is thrown away, Elizabeth. The report is true.'

'Matilda, you shock me!'

'Why?'

'At your age!'

'If *he* doesn't object to my age, what does it matter to *you?*'

'Don't speak of that man!'

'Why not?'

'He is young enough to be your son; and he is marrying you – impudently, undisguisedly marrying you – for your money!'

'And I am marrying him – impudently, undisguisedly marrying him – for his rank.'

'You needn't remind me, Matilda, that you are the daughter of a tailor.'

'In a week or two more, Elizabeth, I shall remind you that I am the wife of a nobleman's son.'

'A younger son; don't forget that.'

'A younger son, as you say. He finds the social position, and I find the money – half a million at my own sole disposal. My future husband is a good fellow in his way, and his future wife is another good fellow in her way. To look at your grim face, one would suppose there were no such things in the world as marriages of convenience.'

'Not at your time of life. I tell you plainly, your marriage will be a public scandal.'

'That doesn't frighten us,' Miss Dulane remarked. 'We are resigned to every ill-natured thing that our friends can say of us. In course of time, the next nine days' wonder will claim public attention, and we shall be forgotten. I shall be none the less on that account Lady Howel Beaucourt. And my husband will be happy in the enjoyment of every expensive taste which a poor man can gratify, for the first time in his life. Have you any more objections to make? Don't hesitate to speak plainly.'

'I have a question to ask, my dear.'

'Charmed, I am sure, to answer it – if I can.'

'Am I right in supposing that Lord Howel Beaucourt is about half your age?'

'Yes, dear; my future husband is as nearly as possible half as old as I am.'

Mrs Newsham's uneasy virtue shuddered. 'What a profanation of marriage!' she exclaimed.

'Nothing of the sort,' her friend pronounced positively. 'Marriage, by the law of England (as my lawyer tells me), is nothing but a contract. Who ever heard of profaning a contract?'

'Call it what you please, Matilda. Do you expect to live a happy life, at your age, with a young man for your husband?'

'A happy life,' Miss Dulane repeated, 'because it will be an innocent life.' She laid a certain emphasis on the last word but one.

Mrs Newsham resented the emphasis, and rose to go. Her last words were the bitterest words that she had spoken yet.

'You have secured such a truly remarkable husband, my dear, that I am emboldened to ask a great favour. Will you give me his lordship's photograph?'

'No,' said Miss Dulane, 'I won't give you his lordship's photograph.'

'What is your objection, Matilda?'

'A very serious objection, Elizabeth. You are not pure enough in mind to be worthy of my husband's photograph.'

With that reply the first of the remonstrances assumed hostile proportions, and came to an untimely end.

II

The second remonstrance was reserved for a happier fate. It took its rise in a conversation between two men who were old and true friends. In other words, it led to no quarrelling.

The elder man was one of those admirable human beings who are cordial, gentle, and good-tempered, without any conscious exercise of their own virtues. He was generally known in the world about him by a fond and familiar use of his Christian name. To call him 'Sir Richard' in these pages (except in the character of one of his servants) would be simply ridiculous. When he lent his money, his horses, his house, and (sometimes, after unlucky friends had dropped to the lowest social depths) even his clothes, this general benefactor was known, in the best society and the worst society alike, as 'Dick.' He filled the hundred mouths of Rumour with his nickname, in the days when there was an opera in London, as the proprietor of the 'Beauty-box.' The ladies who occupied the box were all invited under the same circumstances. They enjoyed operatic music; but their husbands and fathers were not rich enough to be able to gratify that expensive taste. Dick's carriage called for them, and took them home again; and the beauties all agreed (if he ever married) that Mrs Dick would be the most enviable woman on the face of the civilised earth. Even the false reports, which declared that he was privately married already, and on bad terms with his wife, slandered him cordially under the popular name. And his intimate companions, when they alluded among each other to a romance in his life which would remain a hidden romance to the end of his days, forgot that the occasion justified a serious and severe use of his surname, and blamed him affectionately as 'poor dear Dick.'

The hour was midnight; and the friends, whom the most hospitable of men delighted to assemble round his dinner-table, had taken their leave – with the exception of one guest specially detained by the host, who led him back to the dining-room.

'You were angry with our friends,' Dick began, 'when they asked you about that report of your marriage. You won't be angry with Me. Are you really going to be the old maid's husband?'

This plain question received a plain reply: 'Yes, I am.'

Dick took the young lord's hand. Simply and seriously, he said: 'Accept my congratulations.'

Howel Beaucourt started as if he had received a blow instead of a compliment.

'There isn't another man or woman in the whole circle of my acquaintance,' he declared, 'who would have congratulated me on marrying Miss Dulane. I believe you would make allowances for me if I had committed murder.'

'I hope I should,' Dick answered gravely. 'When a man is my friend – murder or marriage – I take it for granted that he has a reason for what he does. Wait a minute. You mustn't give me more credit than I deserve. I don't agree with you. If I were a marrying man myself, I shouldn't pick an old maid – I should prefer a young one. That's a matter of taste. You are not like me. *You* always have a definite object in view. I may not know what the object is. Never mind! I wish you joy all the same.'

Beaucourt was not unworthy of the friendship that he had inspired. 'I should be ungrateful indeed,' he said, 'if I didn't tell you what my object is. You know that I am poor?'

'The only poor friend of mine,' Dick remarked, 'who has never borrowed money of me.'

Beaucourt went on without noticing this. 'I have three expensive tastes,' he said. 'I want to get into Parliament; I want to have a yacht; I want to collect pictures. Add, if you like, the selfish luxury of helping poverty and wretchedness, and hearing my conscience tell me what an excellent man I am. I can't do all this on five hundred a year – but I can do it on forty times five hundred a year. Moral: marry Miss Dulane.'

Listening attentively until the other had done, Dick showed a sardonic side to his character never yet discovered in Beaucourt's experience of him.

'I suppose you have made the necessary arrangements,' he said. 'When the old lady releases you, she will leave consolation behind her in her will.'

'That's the first ill-natured thing I ever heard you say, Dick. When the old lady dies, my sense of honour takes fright, and turns its back on her will. It's a condition on my side, that every farthing of her money shall be left to her relations.'

'Don't you call yourself one of them?'

'What a question! Am I her relation because the laws of society force a mock marriage on us? How can I make use of her money unless I am her husband? and how can she make use of my title unless she is my wife? As long as she lives I stand honestly by my side of the bargain. But when she dies the transaction is at an end, and the surviving partner returns to his five hundred a year.'

Dick exhibited another surprising side to his character. The most compliant of men now became as obstinate as the proverbial mule.

'All very well,' he said, 'but it doesn't explain why – if you must sell yourself – you have sold yourself to an old lady. There are plenty of young ones and pretty ones with fortunes to tempt you. It seems odd that you haven't tried your luck with one of them.'

'No, Dick. It would have been odd, and worse than odd, if I had tried my luck with a young woman.'

'I don't see that.'

'You shall see it directly. If I marry an old woman for her money, I have no occasion to be a hypocrite; we both know that our marriage is a mere matter of form. But if I make a young woman my wife because I want her money, and if that young woman happens to be worth a straw, I must deceive her and disgrace myself by shamming love. That, my boy, you may depend upon it, I will never do.'

Dick's face suddenly brightened with a mingled expression of relief and triumph.

'Ha! my mercenary friend,' he burst out, 'there's something mixed up in this business which is worthier of you than anything I have heard yet. Stop! I'm going to be clever for the first time in my life. A man who talks of love as you do, must have felt love himself. Where is the young one and the pretty one? And what has she done, poor dear, to be deserted for an old woman? Good God! how you look at me! I have hurt your feelings – I have been a greater fool than ever – I am more ashamed of myself than words can say!'

Beaucourt stopped him there, gently and firmly.

'You have made a very natural mistake,' he said. 'There *was* a young lady. She has refused me – resolutely refused me. There is no more love in my life. It's a dark life and an empty life for the rest of my days. I must see what money can do for me next. When I have thoroughly hardened my heart I may not feel my misfortune as I feel it now. Pity me or despise me. In either case let us say good-night.'

He went out into the hall and took his hat. Dick went out into the hall and took *his* hat.

'Have your own way,' he answered, 'I mean to have mine – I'll go home with you.'

The man was simply irresistible. Beaucourt sat down resignedly on the nearest of the hall chairs. Dick asked him to return to the dining-room. 'No,' he said; 'it's not worth while. What I can tell you may be told in two minutes.' Dick submitted, and took the next of the hall chairs. In that inappropriate place the young lord's unpremeditated confession was forced out of him, by no more formidable exercise of power than the kindness of his friend.

'When you hear where I met with her,' he began, 'you will most likely not want to hear any more. I saw her, for the first time, on the stage of a music hall.'

He looked at Dick. Perfectly quiet and perfectly impenetrable, Dick only said, 'Go on.' Beaucourt continued in these words:

'She was singing Arne's delicious setting of Ariel's song in the "Tempest," with a taste and feeling completely thrown away on the greater part of the audience. That she was beautiful – in my eyes at least – I needn't say. That she had descended to a sphere unworthy of her and new to her, nobody could doubt. Her modest dress, her refinement of manner, seemed rather to puzzle than to please most of the people present; they applauded her, but not very warmly, when she retired. I obtained an introduction through her music-master, who happened to be acquainted professionally with some relatives of mine. He told me that she was a young widow; and he assured me that the calamity through which her family had lost their place in the world had brought no sort of disgrace on them. If I wanted to know more, he referred me to the lady herself. I found her very reserved. A long time passed before I could win her confidence – and a longer time still before I ventured to confess the feeling with which she had inspired me. You know the rest.'

'You mean, of course, that you offered her marriage?'

'Certainly.'

'And she refused you on account of your position in life.'

'No. I had foreseen that obstacle, and had followed the example of the adventurous nobleman in the old story. Like him, I assumed a name, and presented myself as belonging to her own respectable middle class of life. You are too old a friend to suspect me of vanity if I tell you that she had no objection to me, and no suspicion that I had approached her (personally speaking) under a disguise.'

'What motive could she possibly have had for refusing you?' Dick asked.

'A motive associated with her dead husband,' Beaucourt answered. 'He had married her – mind, innocently married her – while his first wife was living. The woman was an inveterate drunkard; they had been separated for years. Her death had been publicly reported in the newspapers, among the persons killed in a railway accident abroad. When she claimed her unhappy husband he was in delicate health. The shock killed him. His widow – I can't, and won't, speak of her misfortune as if it was her fault – knew of no living friends who were in a position to help her. Not a great artist with a wonderful voice, she could still trust to her musical accomplishments to provide for the necessities of life. Plead as I might with her to forget the past, I always got the same reply: "If I was base enough to let myself be tempted by the happy future that you offer, I should deserve the unmerited disgrace which has fallen on me. Marry a woman whose reputation will bear inquiry, and forget me." I was mad enough to press my suit once too often. When I visited her on the next day she was gone. Every effort to trace her has failed. Lost, my friend – irretrievably lost to me!'

He offered his hand and said good-night. Dick held him back on the doorstep.

'Break off your mad engagement to Miss Dulane,' he said. 'Be a man, Howel; wait and hope! You are throwing away your life when happiness is within your reach, if you will only be patient. That poor young creature is worthy of you. Lost? Nonsense! In this narrow little world, people are never hopelessly lost till they are dead and underground. Help me to recognise her by a description, and tell me her name. I'll find her; I'll persuade her to come back to you – and, mark my words, you will live to bless the day when you followed my advice.'

This well-meant remonstrance was completely thrown away. Beaucourt's despair was deaf to every entreaty that Dick had addressed to him.

'Thank you with all my heart,' he said. 'You don't know her as I do. She is one of the very few women who mean No when they say No. Useless, Dick – useless!'

Those were the last words he said to his friend in the character of a single man.

Part Two: Platonic Marriage

III

'Seven months have passed, my dear Dick, since my "inhuman obstinacy" (those were the words you used) made you one of the witnesses at my marriage to Miss Dulane, sorely against your will. Do you remember your parting prophecy, when you were out of the bride's hearing? "A miserable life is before that woman's husband – and, by Jupiter, he has deserved it!"

'Never, my dear boy, attempt to forecast the future again. Viewed as a prophet you are a complete failure. I have nothing to complain of in my married life.

'But you must not mistake me. I am far from saying that I am a happy man; I only declare myself to be a contented man. My old wife is a marvel of good temper and good sense. She trusts me implicitly, and I have given her no reason to regret it. We have our time for being together, and our time for keeping apart. Within our inevitable limits we understand each other and respect each other, and have a truer feeling of regard on both sides than many people far better matched than we are in point of age. But you shall judge for yourself. Come and dine with us, when I return on Wednesday next from the trial trip of my new yacht. In the meantime I have a service to ask of you.

'My wife's niece has been her companion for years. She has left us to be married to an officer, who has taken her to India; and we are utterly at a loss how to fill her place. The good old lady doesn't want much. A nice-tempered refined girl, who can sing and play to her with some little taste and feeling, and read to her now and then when her eyes are weary – there is what we require; and there, it seems, is more than we can get, after advertising for a week past. Of all the "companions" who have presented themselves, not one has turned out to be the sort of person whom Lady Howel wants.

'Can you help us? In any case, my wife sends you her kind remembrances; and (true to the old times) I add my love.'

On the day which followed the receipt of this letter, Dick paid a visit to Lady Howel Beaucourt.

'You seem to be excited,' she said. 'Has anything remarkable happened?'

'Pardon me if I ask a question first,' Dick replied. 'Do you object to a young widow?'

'That depends on the widow.'

'Then I have found the very person you want. And, oddly enough, your husband has had something to do with it.'

'Do you mean that my husband has recommended her?'

There was an undertone of jealousy in Lady Howel's voice – jealousy excited not altogether without a motive. She had left it to Beaucourt's sense of honour to own the truth, if there had been any love affair in his past life which ought to make him hesitate before he married. He had justified Miss Dulane's confidence in him; acknowledging an attachment to a young widow, and adding that she had positively refused him. 'We have not met since,' he said, 'and we shall never meet again.' Under those circumstances, Miss Dulane had considerately abstained from asking for any further details. She had not thought of the young widow again, until Dick's language had innocently inspired her first doubt. Fortunately for both of them, he was an outspoken man; and he reassured her unreservedly in these words: 'Your husband knows nothing about it.'

'Now,' she said, 'you may tell me how you came to hear of the lady.'

'Through my uncle's library,' Dick replied. 'His will has left me his collection of books – in such a wretchedly neglected condition that I asked Beaucourt (not being a reading man myself) if he knew of any competent person who could advise me how to set things right. He introduced me to Farleigh and Halford, the well-known publishers. The second partner is a book-collector himself, as well as a bookseller. He kindly looks in now and then, to see how his instructions for mending and binding are being carried out. When he called yesterday I thought of you, and I found he could help us to a young lady employed in his office at correcting proof sheets.'

'What is the lady's name?'

'Mrs Evelin.'

'Why does she leave her employment?'

'To save her eyes, poor soul. When the senior partner, Mr Farleigh, met with her, she was reduced by family misfortunes to earn her own living. The publishers would have been only too glad to keep her in their office, but for the oculist's report. He declared that she would run the risk of blindness, if she fatigued her weak eyes much longer. There is the only objection to this otherwise invaluable person – she will not be able to read to you.'

'Can she sing and play?'

'Exquisitely. Mr Farleigh answers for her music.'

'And her character?'

'Mr Halford answers for her character.'

'And her manners?'

'A perfect lady. I have seen her and spoken to her; I answer for her manners, and I guarantee her personal appearance. Charming! charming!'

For a moment Lady Howel hesitated. After a little reflection, she decided that it was her duty to trust her excellent husband. 'I will receive the charming widow,' she said, 'tomorrow at twelve o'clock; and, if she produces the right impression, I promise to overlook the weakness of her eyes.'

IV

Beaucourt had prolonged the period appointed for the trial trip of his yacht by a whole week. His apology when he returned delighted the kind-hearted old lady who had made him a present of the vessel.

'There isn't such another yacht in the whole world,' he declared. 'I really hadn't the heart to leave that beautiful vessel after only three days' experience of her.' He burst out with a torrent of technical praises of the yacht, to which his wife listened as attentively as if she really understood what he was talking about. When his breath and his eloquence were exhausted alike, she said, 'Now, my dear, it's my turn. I can match your perfect vessel with my perfect lady.'

'What! you have found a companion?'

'Yes.'

'Did Dick find her for you?'

'He did indeed. You shall see for yourself how grateful I ought to be to your friend.'

She opened a door which led into the next room. 'Mary, my dear, come and be introduced to my husband.'

Beaucourt started when he heard the name, and instantly recovered himself. He had forgotten how many Marys there are in the world.

Lady Howel returned, leading her favourite by the hand, and gaily introducing her the moment they entered the room.

'Mrs Evelin; Lord—'

She looked at her husband. The utterance of his name was instantly suspended on her lips. Mrs Evelin's hand, turning cold at the same moment in her hand, warned her to look round. The face of the woman more than reflected the inconcealable agitation in the face of the man.

The wife's first words, when she recovered herself, were addressed to them both.

'Which of you can I trust,' she asked, 'to tell me the truth?'

'You can trust both of us,' her husband answered.

The firmness of his tone irritated her. 'I will judge of that for myself,' she said. 'Go back to the next room,' she added, turning to Mrs Evelin; 'I will hear you separately.'

The companion, whose duty it was to obey – whose modesty and gentleness had won her mistress's heart – refused to retire.

'No,' she said; 'I have been deceived too. I have *my* right to hear what Lord Howel has to say for himself.'

Beaucourt attempted to support the claim that she had advanced. His wife sternly signed to him to be silent. 'What do you mean?' she said, addressing the question to Mrs Evelin.

'I mean this. The person whom you speak of as a nobleman was presented to me as "Mr Vincent, an artist." But for that deception I should never have set foot in your ladyship's house.'

'Is this true, my lord?' Lady Howel asked, with a contemptuous emphasis on the title of nobility.

'Quite true,' her husband answered. 'I thought it possible that my rank might prove an obstacle in the way of my hopes. The blame rests on me, and on me alone. I ask Mrs Evelin to pardon me for an act of deception which I deeply regret.'

Lady Howel was a just woman. Under other circumstances she might have shown herself to be a generous woman. That brighter side of her character was incapable of revealing itself in the presence of Mrs Evelin, young and beautiful, and in possession of her husband's heart. She could say, 'I beg your pardon, madam; I have not treated you justly.' But no self-control was strong enough to restrain the next bitter words from passing her lips. 'At my age,' she said, 'Lord Howel will soon be free; you will not have long to wait for him.'

The young widow looked at her sadly – answered her sadly.

'Oh, my lady, your better nature will surely regret having said that!'

For a moment her eyes rested on Beaucourt, dim with rising tears. She left the room – and left the house.

There was silence between the husband and wife. Beaucourt was the first to speak again.

'After what you have just heard, do you persist in your jealousy of that lady, and your jealousy of me?' he asked.

'I have behaved cruelly to her and to you. I am ashamed of myself,' was all she said in reply. That expression of sorrow, so simple and so true, did not appeal in vain to the gentler side of Beaucourt's nature. He kissed his wife's hand; he tried to console her.

'You may forgive me,' she answered. 'I cannot forgive myself. That poor lady's last words have made my heart ache. What I said to her in anger I ought to have said generously. Why should she not wait for you? After your life with me – a life of kindness, a life of self-sacrifice – you deserve your reward. Promise me that you will marry the woman you love – after my death has released you.'

'You distress me, and needlessly distress me,' he said. 'What you are thinking of, my dear, can never happen; no, not even if –' He left the rest unsaid.

'Not even if you were free?' she asked.

'Not even then.'

She looked towards the next room. 'Go in, Howel, and bring Mrs Evelin back; I have something to say to her.'

The discovery that she had left the house caused no fear that she had taken to flight with the purpose of concealing herself. There was a prospect before the poor lonely woman which might be trusted to preserve her from despair, to say the least of it.

During her brief residence in Beaucourt's house she had shown to Lady Howel a letter received from a relation, who had emigrated to New Zealand with her husband and her infant children some years since. They had steadily prospered; they were living in comfort, and they wanted for nothing but a trustworthy governess to teach their children. The mother had accordingly written, asking if her relative in England could recommend a competent person, and offering a liberal salary. In showing the letter to Lady Howel, Mrs Evelin had said: 'If I had not been so happy as to attract your notice, I might have offered to be the governess myself.' Assuming that it had now occurred to her to act on this idea, Lady Howel felt assured that she would apply for advice either to the publishers who had recommended her, or to Lord Howel's old friend.

Beaucourt at once offered to make the inquiries which might satisfy his wife that she had not been mistaken. Readily accepting his proposal, she asked at the same time for a few minutes of delay.

'I want to say to you,' she explained, 'what I had in my mind to say to Mrs Evelin. Do you object to tell me why she refused to marry you? I couldn't have done it in her place.'

'You would have done it, my dear, as I think, if her misfortune had been your misfortune.' With those prefatory words he told the miserable story of Mrs Evelin's marriage.

Lady Howel's sympathies, strongly excited, appeared to have led her to a conclusion which she was not willing to communicate to her husband. She asked him, rather abruptly, if he would leave it to her to find Mrs Evelin. 'I promise,' she added, 'to tell you what I am thinking of, when I come back.'

In two minutes more she was ready to go out, and had hurriedly left the house.

V

After a long absence Lady Howel returned, accompanied by Dick. His face and manner betrayed unusual agitation; Beaucourt noticed it.

'I may well be excited,' Dick declared, 'after what I have heard, and after what we have done. Lady Howel, yours is the brain that thinks to some purpose. Make our report – I wait for you.'

But my lady preferred waiting for Dick. He consented to speak first, for the thoroughly characteristic reason that he could 'get over it in no time.'

'I shall try the old division,' he said, 'into First, Second, and Third. Don't be afraid; I am not going to preach – quite the contrary; I am going to be quick about it. First, then, Mrs Evelin has decided, under sound advice, to go to New Zealand. Second, I have telegraphed to her relations at the other end of the world to tell them that she is coming. Third, and last, Farleigh and Halford have sent to the office, and secured a berth for her in the next ship that sails – date the day after to-morrow. Done in half a minute. Now Lady Howel!'

'I will begin and end in half a minute too,' she said, 'if I can. First,' she continued, turning to her husband, 'I found Mrs Evelin at your friend's house. She kindly let me say all that I could say for the relief of my poor heart. Secondly—'

She hesitated, smiled uneasily, and came to a full stop.

'I can't do it, Howel,' she confessed; 'I must speak to you as usual, or I can never get on. Saying many things in few words – if the ladies who assert our Rights will forgive me for confessing it – is an accomplishment in which we are completely beaten by the men. You must have thought me rude, my dear, for leaving you very abruptly, without a word of explanation. The truth is, I had an idea in my head, and I kept it to myself (old people are proverbially cautious, you know) till I had first found out whether it was worth mentioning. When you were speaking of the wretched creature who had claimed Mrs Evelin's husband as her own, you said she was an inveterate drunkard. A woman in that state of degradation is capable, as I persist in thinking, of any wickedness. I suppose this put it into my head to doubt her – no; I mean, to wonder whether Mrs Evelin – do you know that she keeps her husband's name by his own entreaty addressed to her on his deathbed? – oh, I am losing myself in a crowd of words of my own collecting! Say the rest of it for me, Sir Richard!'

'No, Lady Howel. Not unless you call me "Dick."'

'Then say it for me – Dick.'

'No, not yet, on reflection. Dick is too short, say "Dear Dick."'

'Dear Dick – there!'

'Thank you, my lady. Now we had better remember that your husband is present.' He turned to Beaucourt. 'Lady Howel had the idea,' he proceeded, 'which ought to have presented itself to you and to me. It was a serious misfortune (as she thought) that Mr Evelin's sufferings in his last illness, and his wife's anxiety while she was nursing him, had left them unfit to act in their own defence. They might otherwise not have submitted to the drunken wretch's claim, without first making sure that she had a right to advance it. Taking her character into due consideration, are we quite certain that she was herself free to marry, when Mr Evelin unfortunately made her his wife? To that serious question we now mean to find an answer. With Mrs Evelin's knowledge of the affair to help us, we have discovered the woman's address, to begin with. She keeps a small tobacconist's shop at the town of Grailey in the north of England. The rest is in the hands of my lawyer. If we make the discovery that we all hope for, we have your wife to thank for it.' He paused, and looked at his watch. 'I've got an appointment at the club. The committee will blackball the best fellow that ever lived if I don't go and stop them. Good-bye.'

The last day of Mrs Evelin's sojourn in England was memorable in more ways than one.

On the first occasion in Beaucourt's experience of his married life, his wife wrote to him instead of speaking to him, although they were both in the house at the time. It was a little note, only containing these words: 'I thought you would like to say good-bye to Mrs Evelin. I have told her to expect you in the library, and I will take care that you are not disturbed,'

Waiting at the window of her sitting-room, on the upper floor, Lady Howel perceived that the delicate generosity of her conduct had been gratefully felt. The interview in the library barely lasted for five minutes. She saw Mrs Evelin leave the house with her veil down. Immediately afterwards, Beaucourt ascended to his wife's room to thank her. Carefully as he had endeavoured to hide them, the traces of tears in his eyes told her how cruelly the parting scene had tried him. It was a bitter moment for his admirable wife. 'Do you wish me dead?' she asked with sad self-possession. 'Live,' he said, 'and live happily, if you wish to make me happy too.' He drew her to him and kissed her forehead. Lady Howel had her reward.

Part Three: News from the Colony

VI

Furnished with elaborate instructions to guide him, which included golden materials for bribery, a young Jew holding the place of third clerk in the office of Dick's lawyer was sent to the town of Grailey to make discoveries. In the matter of successfully instituting private inquiries, he was justly considered to be a match for any two Christians who might try to put obstacles in his way. His name was Moses Jackling.

Entering the cigar-shop, the Jew discovered that he had presented himself at a critical moment.

A girl and a man were standing behind the counter. The girl looked like a maid-of-all-work: she was rubbing the tears out of her eyes with a big red fist. The man, smart in manner and shabby in dress, received the stranger with a peremptory eagerness to do business. 'Now, then! what for you?' Jackling bought the worst cigar he had ever smoked, in the course of an enormous experience of bad tobacco, and tried a few questions with this result. The girl had lost her place; the man was in 'possession'; and the stock and furniture had been seized for debt. Jackling thereupon assumed the character of a creditor, and asked to speak with the mistress.

'She's too ill to see you, sir,' the girl said.

'Tell the truth, you fool,' cried the man in possession. He led the way to a door with glass in the upper part of it, which opened into a parlour behind the shop. As soon as his back was turned, Jackling whispered to the maid, 'When I go, slip out after me; I've got something for you.' The man lifted the curtain over the glass. 'Look through,' he said, 'and see what's the matter with her for yourself.'

Jackling discovered the mistress flat on her back on the floor, helplessly drunk. That was enough for the clerk – so far. He took leave of the man in possession, with the one joke which never wears out in the estimation of Englishmen; the joke that foresees the drinker's headache in the morning. In a minute or two more the girl showed herself, carrying an empty jug. She had been sent for the man's beer, and she was expected back directly. Jackling, having first overwhelmed her by a present of five shillings, proposed another appointment in the evening. The maid promised to be at the place of meeting; and in memory of the five shillings she kept her word.

'What wages do you get?' was the first question that astonished her.

'Three pounds a year, sir,' the unfortunate creature replied.

'All paid?'

'Only one pound paid – and I say it's a crying shame.'

'Say what you like, my dear, so long as you listen to me. I want to know everything that your mistress says and does – first when she's drunk, and then when she's sober. Wait a bit; I haven't done yet. If you tell me everything you can remember – mind, *everything* – I'll pay the rest of your wages.'

Madly excited by this golden prospect, the victim of domestic service answered inarticulately with a scream. Jackling's right hand and left hand entered his pockets, and appeared again holding two sovereigns separately between two fingers and thumbs. From that moment, he was at liberty to empty the maid-of-all-work's memory of every saying and doing that it contained.

The sober moments of the mistress yielded little or nothing to investigation. The report of her drunken moments produced something worth hearing. There were two men whom it was her habit to revile bitterly in her cups. One of them was Mr Evelin, whom she abused – sometimes for the small allowance that he made to her; sometimes for dying before she could prosecute him for bigamy. Her drunken remembrances of the other man were associated with two names. She called him 'Septimus'; she called him 'Darts'; and she despised him occasionally for being a 'common sailor.' It was clearly demonstrated that he was one man, and not two. Whether he was 'Septimus,' or whether he was 'Darts,' he had always committed the same atrocities. He had taken her money away from her; he had called her by an atrocious name; and he had knocked her down on more than one occasion. Provided with this information, Jackling rewarded the girl, and paid a visit to her mistress the next day.

The miserable woman was exactly in the state of nervous prostration (after the excess of the previous evening) which offered to the clerk his best chance of gaining his end. He presented himself as the representative of friends, bent on helping her, whose modest benevolence had positively forbidden him to mention their names.

'What sum of money must you pay,' he asked, 'to get rid of the man in possession?'

Too completely bewildered to speak, her trembling hand offered to him a slip of paper on which the amount of the debt and the expenses was set forth: £51 12s 10d.

With some difficulty the Jew preserved his gravity. 'Very well,' he resumed. 'I will make it up to sixty pounds (to set you going again) on two conditions.'

She suddenly recovered her power of speech. 'Give me the money!' she cried, with greedy impatience of delay.

'First condition,' he continued, without noticing the interruption: 'you are not to suffer, either in purse or person, if you give us the information that we want.'

She interrupted him again. 'Tell me what it is, and be quick about it.'

'Second condition,' he went on as impenetrably as ever: 'you take me to the place where I can find the certificate of your marriage to Septimus Darts.'

Her eyes glared at him like the eyes of a wild animal. Furies, hysterics, faintings, denials, threats – Jackling endured them all by turns. It was enough for him that his desperate guess of the evening before, had hit the mark on the morning after. When she had completely exhausted herself he returned to the experiment which he had already tried with the maid. Well aware of the advantage of exhibiting gold instead of notes, when the object is to tempt poverty, he produced the promised bribe in sovereigns, pouring them playfully backwards and forwards from one big hand to the other.

The temptation was more than the woman could resist. In another half-hour the two were travelling together to a town in one of the midland counties.

The certificate was found in the church register, and duly copied. It also appeared that one of the witnesses to the marriage was still living. His name and address were duly noted in the clerk's pocket-book. Subsequent inquiry, at the office of the Customs Comptroller, discovered the name of Septimus Darts on the captain's official list of the crew of an outward bound merchant vessel. With this information, and with a photographic portrait to complete it, the man was discovered, alive and hearty, on the return of the ship to her port.

His wife's explanation of her conduct included the customary excuse that she had every reason to believe her husband to be dead, and was followed by a bold assertion that she had married Mr Evelin for love. In Moses Jackling's opinion she lied when she said this, and lied again when she threatened to prosecute Mr Evelin for bigamy. 'Take my word for it,' said this new representative of the Unbelieving Jew, 'she would have extorted money from him if he had lived.' Delirium tremens left this question unsettled, and closed the cigar shop soon afterwards, under the authority of death.

The good news, telegraphed to New Zealand, was followed by a letter containing details.

At a later date, a telegram arrived from Mrs Evelin. She had reached her destination, and had received the despatch which told her that she had been lawfully married. A letter to Lady Howel was promised by the next mail.

While the necessary term of delay was still unexpired, the newspapers received intelligence of a volcanic eruption in the northern island of the New Zealand group. Later particulars, announcing a terrible destruction of life and property, included the homestead in which Mrs Evelin was living. The farm had been overwhelmed, and every member of the household had perished.

Part Four: The Night Nurse

VII

Endorsed as follows: 'Reply from Sir Richard, addressed to Farleigh and Halford.'

'Your courteous letter has been forwarded to my house in the country.

'I really regret that you should have thought it necessary to apologise for troubling me. Your past kindness to the unhappy Mrs Evelin gives you a friendly claim on me which I gladly recognise – as you shall soon see.

'"The extraordinary story," as you very naturally call it, is nevertheless true. I am the only person, now at your disposal, who can speak as an eye-witness of the events.

'In the first place I must tell you that the dreadful intelligence, received from New Zealand, had an effect on Lord Howel Beaucourt which shocked his friends, and inexpressibly distressed his admirable wife. I can only describe him, at that time, as a man struck down in mind and body alike.

'Lady Howel was unremitting in her efforts to console him. He was thankful and gentle. It was true that no complaint could be made of him. It was equally true that no change for the better rewarded the devotion of his wife.

'The state of feeling which this implied embittered the disappointment that

Lady Howel naturally felt. As some relief to her overburdened mind, she associated herself with the work of mercy, carried on under the superintendence of the Rector of the parish. I thought he was wrong in permitting a woman, at her advanced time of life, to run the risk encountered in visiting the sick and suffering poor at their own dwelling-places. Circumstances, however, failed to justify my dread of the perilous influences of infection and foul air. The one untoward event that happened, seemed to be too trifling to afford any cause for anxiety. Lady Howel caught cold.

'Unhappily, she treated that apparently trivial accident with indifference. Her husband tried in vain to persuade her to remain at home. On one of her charitable visits she was overtaken by a heavy fall of rain; and a shivering fit seized her on returning to the house. At her age the results were serious. A bronchial attack followed. In a week more, the dearest and best of women had left us nothing to love but the memory of the dead.

'Her last words were faintly whispered to me in her husband's presence: "Take care of him," the dying woman said, "when I am gone."

'No effort of mine to be worthy of that sacred trust was left untried. How could I hope to succeed where *she* had failed? My house in London and my house in the country were both open to Beaucourt; I entreated him to live with me, or (if he preferred it) to be my guest for a short time only, or (if he wished to be alone) to choose the place of abode which he liked best for his solitary retreat. With sincere expressions of gratitude, his inflexible despair refused my proposals.

'In one of the ancient "Inns", built centuries since for the legal societies of London, he secluded himself from friends and acquaintances alike. One by one, they were driven from his dreary chambers by a reception which admitted them with patient resignation, and held out little encouragement to return. After an interval of no great length, I was the last of his friends who intruded on his solitude.

'Poor Lady Howel's will (excepting some special legacies) had left her fortune to me in trust, on certain conditions with which it is needless to trouble you. Beaucourt's resolution not to touch a farthing of his dead wife's money laid a heavy responsibility on my shoulders; the burden being ere long increased by forebodings which alarmed me on the subject of his health.

'He devoted himself to the reading of old books, treating (as I was told) of that branch of useless knowledge generally described as "occult science." These unwholesome studies so absorbed him, that he remained shut up in his badly ventilated chambers for weeks together, without once breathing the outer air even for a few minutes. Such defiance of the ordinary laws of nature as this could end but in one way; his health steadily declined, and feverish symptoms showed themselves. The doctor said plainly, "There is no chance for him if he stays in this place."

'Once more he refused to be removed to my London house. The development of the fever, he reminded me, might lead to consequences dangerous to me and to my household. He had heard of one of the great London hospitals, which reserved certain rooms for the occupation of persons capable of paying for the medical care bestowed on them. If he were to be removed at all, to that hospital he would go. Many advantages, and no objections of importance, were presented by this course of proceeding. We conveyed him to the hospital without a moment's loss of time.

'When I think of the dreadful illness that followed, and when I recall the days of unrelieved suspense passed at the bedside, I have not courage enough to dwell on this part of my story. Besides, you know already that Beaucourt recovered – or, as I might more correctly describe it, that he was snatched back to life when the grasp of death was on him. Of this happier period of his illness I have something to say which may surprise and interest you.

'On one of the earlier days of his convalescence my visit to him was paid later than usual. A matter of importance, neglected while he was in danger, had obliged me to leave town for a few days, after there was nothing to be feared. Returning, I had missed the train which would have brought me to London in better time.

'My appearance evidently produced in Beaucourt a keen feeling of relief. He requested the day-nurse, waiting in the room, to leave us by ourselves.

'"I was afraid you might not have come to me today," he said. "My last moments would have been embittered, my friend, by your absence."

'"Are you anticipating your death," I asked, "at the very time when the doctors answer for your life?"

'"The doctors have not seen her," he said; "I saw her last night."

'"Of whom are you speaking?"

'"Of my lost angel, who perished miserably in New Zealand. Twice, her spirit has appeared to me. I shall see her for the third time tonight; I shall follow her to the better world."

'Had the delirium of the worst time of the fever taken possession of him again? In unutterable dread of a relapse, I took his hand. The skin was cool. I laid my fingers on his pulse. It was beating calmly.

'"You think I am wandering in my mind," he broke out. "Stay here tonight – I command you, stay! – and see her as I have seen her."

'I quieted him by promising to do what he had asked of me. He had still one more condition to insist on.

'"I won't be laughed at," he said. "Promise that you will not repeat to any living creature what I have just told you."

'My promise satisfied him. He wearily closed his eyes. In a few minutes more his poor weak body was in peaceful repose.

'The day-nurse returned, and remained with us later than usual. Twilight melted into darkness. The room was obscurely lit by a shaded lamp, placed behind a screen that kept the sun out of the sick man's eyes in the daytime.

'"Are we alone?" Beaucourt asked.

'"Yes."

'"Watch the door."

'"Why?"

'"You will see her on the threshold."

'As he said those words the door slowly opened. In the dim light I could only discern at first the figure of a woman. She slowly advanced towards me. I saw the familiar face in shadow; the eyes were large and faintly luminous – the eyes of Mrs Evelin.

'The wild words spoken to me by Beaucourt, the stillness and the obscurity in the room, had their effect, I suppose, on my imagination. You will think me a poor creature when I confess it. For the moment I did assuredly feel a thrill of superstitious terror.

'My delusion was dispelled by a change in her face. Its natural expression of surprise, when she saw me, set my mind free to feel the delight inspired by the discovery that she was a living woman. I should have spoken to her if she had not stopped me by a gesture.

'Beaucourt's voice broke the silence. "Ministering Spirit!" he said, "free me from the life of earth. Take me with you to the life eternal."

'She made no attempt to enlighten him. "Wait," she answered calmly, "wait and rest."

'Silently obeying her, he turned his head on the pillow; we saw his face no more.

'I have related the circumstances exactly as they happened; the ghost story which report has carried to your ears has no other foundation than this.

'Mrs Evelin led the way to that farther end of the room in which the screen stood. Placing ourselves behind it, we could converse in whispers without being heard. Her first words told me that she had been warned by one of the hospital doctors to respect my friend's delusion for the present. His mind partook in some degree of the weakness of his body, and he was not strong enough yet to bear the shock of discovering the truth.

'She had been saved almost by a miracle.

'Released (in a state of insensibility) from the ruins of the house, she had been laid with her dead relatives awaiting burial. Happily for her, an English traveller visiting the island was among the first men who volunteered to render help. He had been in practice as a medical man, and he saved her from being buried alive. Nearly a month passed before she was strong enough to bear removal to Wellington (the capital city), and to be received into the hospital.

'I asked why she had not telegraphed or written to me.

'"When I was strong enough to write," she said, "I was strong enough to bear the sea-voyage to England. The expenses so nearly exhausted my small savings that I had no money to spare for the telegraph."

'On her arrival in London, only a few days since, she had called on me at the time when I had left home on the business which I have already mentioned. She had not heard of Lady Howel's death, and had written ignorantly to prepare that good friend for seeing her. The messenger sent with the letter had found the house in the occupation of strangers, and had been referred to the agent employed in letting it. She went herself to this person, and so heard that Lord Howel Beaucourt had lost his wife, and was reported to be dying in one of the London hospitals.

'"If he had been in his usual state of health," she said, "it would have been indelicate on my part – I mean it would have seemed like taking a selfish advantage of the poor lady's death – to have let him know that my life had been saved, in any other way than by writing to him. But when I heard he was dying, I forgot all customary considerations. His name was so well-known in London that I easily discovered at what hospital he had been received. There I heard that the report was false, and that he was out of danger. I ought to have been satisfied with that – but oh, how could I be so near him and not long to see him? The old doctor with whom I had been speaking discovered, I suppose, that I was in trouble about something. He was so kind and fatherly, and he seemed to take such interest in me, that I confessed everything to him. After he had made me promise to be careful, he told the night-nurse to let me take her place for a little while, when the dim light in the room would not permit his patient to see me too plainly. He waited at the door when we tried the experiment. Neither he nor I foresaw that poor Lord Howel would put such a strange interpretation on my presence. The nurse doesn't approve of my coming back – even for a little while only – and taking her place again to-night. She is right. I have had my little glimpse of happiness, and with that little I must be content."

'What I said in answer to this, and what I did as time advanced, it is surely needless to tell you. You have read the newspapers which announce their marriage and their departure for Italy. What else is there left for me to say?

'There is, perhaps, a word more still wanting.

'Obstinate Lord Howel persisted in refusing to take the fortune that was waiting for him. In this difficulty, the conditions under which I was acting permitted me to appeal to the bride. When she too said No, I was not to be trifled with. I showed her poor Lady Howel's will. After reading the terms in which my dear old friend alluded to her she burst out crying. I interpreted those grateful tears as an expression of repentance for the ill-considered reply which I had just received. As yet, I have not been told that I was wrong.'

The First Officer's Confession

First appeared in *The Spirit of the Times* on 24 December 1887. Never reprinted. Like the heroine of the story, Collins was devoted to dogs. A dog – based on one of Collins's own pets – does some sterling detective work in *My Lady's Money* (1879).

I

She is at the present time, as I have every reason to believe, the most distinguished woman in England – she has never written a novel.

I first saw her on board of our steamship, bound from New York to Liverpool. She was accompanied by her dog; and there occurred a little difference of opinion between the commander of the vessel and herself.

The captain began it with his customary politeness:

'Excuse me, Miss: I must beg you to submit to a little disappointment. You can't have your dog with you in the saloon. Dogs are not allowed, on board our ships, among the passengers.'

To this the young lady answered: 'And pray, sir, – if these tyrannical regulations are to be carried out – where is my dog to go?'

'Your dog is to go Miss, to the butcher.'

'You brute!'

I declare it on my word of honour, she did actually express her opinion in those terms to the only absolute despot now to be found on the face of the earth – the commander of a ship, afloat on his own vessel. What an ill-natured man might have done under these circumstances I hardly like to guess. Our captain's sweet temper saw the humorous side of the insult offered to him; he burst out laughing. I stepped up, before the lady's answer could express itself in stronger language still, and tried the effect of polite explanation.

'The butcher at sea.' I said, 'is like the butcher on shore. In spite of his calling, Miss, he is not, generally speaking, of a bloodthirsty disposition. Our man here is accustomed to take care of passenger's dogs. He will let you see *your* dog whenever you please; and the one risk your pet will be likely to run is the risk of being too well fed. May I be allowed to lead you to the forward part of the vessel, so that you can judge for yourself?'

We were rolling, at the time, as usual in all well-regulated Atlantic steam ships. I took the greatest care of our charming passenger; and she took the greatest care of her dog. The captain gave me a look as we passed him. I was sacrificing some of the precious time included in my turn of rest below. He attributed this act of folly (as he afterwards told me) to the influence of love at first sight. Having suffered, as will be presently seen, from concealment of the truth by other persons, I am all the readier to speak frankly of myself. The captain's interpretation of my conduct was undeniably correct. While the young lady, the butcher, and the dog were all three in course of arriving at a friendly understanding. I reached a conclusion in my own private mind. 'Whether she is above me, or whether she is below me,' I said to myself, 'is something which remains to be discovered. But this I know already. Either I have found my wife, or I shall live and die an unmarried man.'

Who am I? And who is she?

I am Evan Fencote, first officer of the ship, and third son of a country gentleman; left a widower at my birth. He spent all his money in a great lawsuit, and died leaving barely enough to pay his debts and to bury him. I had to get my own living, and I got it at sea. My stature is five feet ten inches; my age is thirty-two; my temper is considered impetuous – and that is all I have to say for myself on the present occasion.

My young lady is Miss Mira Ringmore, daughter of an Englishman established in business in the United States. Her father had recently married for the second time. The new wife hated Miss Ringmore and Miss Ringmore hated the new wife. Being of age, and having her own little income (inherited from her mother), she had nothing to do but to please herself. Happening to notice our ship in the harbour – dressed in flags in honour of the captain's birthday – she took a fancy to our pretty colours; felt an impulse to go back to the old country with us; and followed the lead of her own feelings at a day's notice. Having friends on the other side – I mean in England – she purposed to visit them, beginning with her maternal aunt, a single lady whose kindness she remembered with gratitude in the time when she was a child.

As for her personal appearance. I call it delicious. Her colour is dark; her stature is (I say it thankfully) not remarkable in the matter of height, and not encumbered by what I particularly dislike in a young woman, excess of flesh. Her manner I may describe as modestly irresistible. And I sum up the list of her perfections when I declare that she is not sick at sea.

II

How other men pay their addresses to women, and pave the way for favourable consideration of a proposal of marriage. I have not contrived to discover. Never yet has a friend come in my way who could tell me how he made himself acceptable, in the days of his courtship, to his wife. The obstacles to success, in the case of my own love-affair, raised perpetually by my professional duties on board, would, I am inclined to believe, have disheartened and defeated me if I had been left to contend against them single-handed. Let me be permitted to thank my stars for having provided me with two powerful friends, whose generous assistance was rendered to me in my hour of need.

One of them was the captain; and the other was the dog.

'He is so kind, he is so attentive, and he offers us the great advantage of being a steady married man.' Hundreds of times I have heard these words spoken of my commanding officer by fathers, husbands and brothers when circumstances compelled them to let their female relatives cross the Atlantic alone. As a guardian of the fair sex, afloat, our captain was, I firmly believe, without an equal in the honorable profession to which he belonged. He made kind inquiries, through their cabin doors, when the ladies were ill below; his gallant arm was ready for them when they got well enough to promenade the deck: and he exercised a fascinating influence over their timid appetites, when they ventured to appear at the dinner table for the first time. His experience of the sex, obtained in this way, (and in other ways not so well known to me) was ready for any emergency that might call on it. I was myself indebted to his instructions for precious private interviews with Miss Ringmore; and, let me add, it was not the captain's fault that consequences followed which the most cautious man in existence must have failed to foresee.

Never neglecting his own duties, our commander never permitted neglect on the part of his subordinates. After waiting a day, and satisfying himself that his chief officer attended to the service of the ship as devotedly as ever, he favoured me, in private, with invaluable advice.

'If I was in love with that young lady,' he said, 'do you know how I should recommend myself to her favourable notice?'

'I can't say I do, sir.'

'In your place, Evan, I should begin by making a friend of the dog.'

From the lips of Solomon himself wiser words than those never dropped. I at once relieved the butcher of the trouble of feeding the dog. He was a clever little smooth haired terrier of the English breed. Miss Mira found her favourite pleased and flattered, when she saw us together, and was naturally pleased and flattered herself. A common ground of sympathy was, in this way, established between us. I stole time from my sleep and stole time from my meals, and made the most of my opportunities. To crown all, the captain favoured me with another offering from his stores of good advice:

'The art of making love, my friend, has one great merit – it succeeds by simple means. Are you acquainted with the means?'

'I am afraid not, sir.'

'Then listen to me. Bear in mind, Evan, that the sex (excepting the blackguard members, of course) hates violence. In making your advances, gain ground by fine degrees; never let a loud word or sudden action escape you. The serpentine way succeeded with the first woman, in the Garden of Eden; and it has succeeded with her posterity from that time to this.'

I followed the serpentine way as cleverly as I could. But the truth is, I was too fond of her to prove myself worthy of my instructions. If I try to put on record the various steps by which I advanced to my end, I may possibly produce a sort of guide book to the art of making love at sea. How useful it may be to passengers crossing the Atlantic!

First Day: The dog is the subject of conversation. Miss Mira tells anecdotes of his affectionate disposition and his rare intelligence. I listen with interest. A message arrives which informs me that the first officer is wanted. The little terrier whines when I get up to go. His mistress caresses him, and looks at me with approving smiles. 'He is almost as fond of you as he is of me,' she says. – First step forward in Miss Mira's affections.

Second Day: The story of my life forms the new subject of conversation. I tell it as shortly as possible. Miss Mira is interested when she hears that I am the son of a ruined father, who was once a country gentleman. She puts an intelligent question: 'Why do I follow an arduous profession, which exposes me to be drowned, when my father's surviving friends must be persons with influence who might do something better for me?' I can only reply that a man, like myself, who is alone in the world, feels no interest in improving his position. We look at each other. Miss Mira's attention devotes itself, with some appearance of confusion, to the dog on her lap. – Second step forward.

Third Day: The story of my young lady's life came, next. She begins, however, by noticing (with a woman's nicety of observation) that there is a change in my dress. I have just been relieved from my watch on deck; and I happen to be wearing a warmer waistcoat than usual, knitted in bright-coloured wool. 'Who made your waistcoat, Mr Fencote?' 'Mrs Jennet made it.' 'And who is Mrs Jennet?' 'A grateful woman, Miss Ringmore.' 'A young woman?' 'No: an old woman.' 'And why was she grateful to you?' There is but one way in which I can answer this last question. I am obliged to mention a common place event in the life of every good swimmer employed on board ship. One of our boys, being in danger of drowning, I happen to save his life. He mentions the circumstance to a grateful old grandmother, and my waistcoat ends the story. With some difficulty, I induce Miss Ringmore to drop the subject and talk of herself. Her social prospects are not very brilliant; she can only hope to be kindly received by her good aunt. Name of the aunt, Miss Urban; station in life, mistress of a ladies' school since the death of her elder sister who founded the establishment; address, Lewk-Bircot, West Riding, Yorkshire; attractions of Lewk-Bircot, beautiful scenery in the neighbourhood. The first officer is eager to visit the scenery; and the fair passenger would be pleased to show it to him, as a means of expressing her sense of his kindness. – Third step.

Fourth Day: A gentle breeze, a fine sun, a bright sea. She comes on deek at the time when we are passing a large merchantman, under all sail. Impressed by that fine sight, she encourages me to tell her the names of the ship's masts and sails. After the first few moments her attention begins to wander: she listens absently. I express the fear that she must be getting tired of the voyage. Answer, 'If I could feel tired of the voyage, I should be ungrateful indeed to You.' – Fourth step.

Fifth Day: A dreadful blank. She has got a nervous headache, and the doctor keeps her in her cabin. But she is good enough to correspond with me. That is to say, she sends me a slip of paper with a line written on it in pencil. 'Pray take care of my dear little dog.' – Fifth step.

Sixth Day: Perfect recovery of the invalid. The dog is still an invaluable friend to me; the care I have taken of him is gratefully acknowledged. Beyond this circumstance my recollections of the sixth day do not carry me. In whatever way I may have gained my next step in advance, it ceases to be of any importance by comparison with the great, I may say the final, event which made a new man of me in four and twenty hours more.

Seventh Day: When we meet on this grand occasion she notices that I am not in good spirits. I own that my mind is ill at ease. Our voyage is coming to an end. On the next evening the ship will probably be passing the Fastnet light, off the Irish coast. 'I hope you won't be offended.' I venture to say: 'my spirits sink, Miss Ringmore, at the prospect of bidding you goodbye.' She makes no reply in words; her eyes rest on me for a moment and then look away again. I find it quite impossible to explain the effect which she produces on me. The captain's excellent advice loses its hold on my mind. I forget the importance of making my advances by fine degrees. I become incapable of taking the serpentine way with this charming creature which once succeeded with Mother Eve in the Garden of Eden. What I intend to say is, that the happiness of my life depends on persuading Miss Mira to let me be her husband. What I actually do say, it is impossible for me to relate. She understands me, although I am incapable of understanding myself. There is one private place of retreat, and one only, on the deck of an ocean steamship in the day time. Between the after end of the vessel, called the taff rail, and the stout little wooden house which shelters the man at the helm, lucky lovers may sometimes find an unoccupied and unobserved interval of space. There I receive my reply: and there we register her favourable decision in our first kiss. My own impression is that the dog, at the other end of the ship, sees (or smells) reason to be jealous of me. He howls furiously. We have no alternative but to hurry to the butcher's quarters and comfort him. Who is the author of the remark, that serious things and comic things tread close on each other's heels? What a first officer that great observer would have made!

III

Mira's interests were my interests now.

Her sudden departure from New York had rendered it impossible to communicate by letter with her aunt. When the vessel reached Liverpool, my first proceeding was to send a telegraphic message, in her name, to Miss Urban: 'Expect me by the afternoon train; explanations when we meet.' I begged hard to be allowed to travel with her. In this case I deserved a refusal, and I got what I deserved.

'It is quite bad enough,' Mira said, 'for me to take Miss Urban by surprise. I must not venture to bring a stranger with me, until I have secured a welcome for him by telling my aunt of our marriage engagement. When she has heard all that I can say in your favour, expect a letter from me with an invitation.'

'May I hope for your letter to-morrow?'

She smiled at my impatience. 'I will do all I can,' she said kindly, 'to hurry my aunt.'

Some people, as I have heard, feel presentiments of evil when unexpected troubles are lying in wait for them. No such forebodings weighed on Mira's mind or on mine. When I put her into the railway carriage, she asked if I had any message for her aunt. I sent my love. She laughed over my audacious familiarity, as gaily as a child.

The next day came, and brought with it no letter. I tried to quiet my impatience by anticipating the arrival of a telegram. The day wore on to evening, and no telegram appeared.

My first impulse was to follow Mira, without waiting for a formal invitation from her aunt. On reflection, however. I felt that such a headlong proceeding as this might perhaps injure me in Miss Urban's estimation. There was nothing for it but to practise self-restraint, and hope to find myself rewarded on the next morning.

I was up and ready at the door of the lodging to take my expected letter from the postman's hand. There were letters for other people in the house – nothing had arrived for me. For two hours more I waited on the chance of getting a telegram, and still waited in vain. My suspense and anxiety were no longer to be trifled with. Come what might of it, I resolved to follow Mira to her aunt's house.

There was no difficulty in discovering Miss Urban. Everybody at Lewk-Bircot knew the schoolmistress's spacious and handsome establishment for young ladies. The fear had come to me, in the railway, that Mira might not have met with the reception which she had anticipated, and might have left her aunt, under a sense of injury only too natural in a high-spirited young woman. In horrid doubt, I asked if Miss Ringmore was at home. When the man servant said 'Yes, sir,' so great was my sense of relief that I protest I could have hugged him.

I was shown into a little drawing-room, while the servant took my card upstairs. The window looked out on a garden. It was the hour of recreation: the young ladies were amusing themselves. They failed to interest me. The one object I cared to look at was the door of the room. At last it was opened; suddenly, violently opened. Mira came in with such an altered expression in her face, such a singular mingling of alarm in her eyes and confusion in her manner, that I stood like a fool, looking at her in silence. She was the first to speak.

'Why have you come here?' That was what she said to me.

A man of my temper, finding himself treated in this way by any woman – and especially when she is a woman whom he adores – feels the serious necessity of preserving his self-control. Instead of complaining of the ungracious welcome that I had received, I told her how I had waited, and what I had suffered: and I said in conclusion: 'Surely, you might make some allowance for the anxieties of a man who loves you, left without news of you.'

'You might have been content with writing to me,' she answered.

'I couldn't have waited for the reply.'

'Why not?'

'Because your silence alarmed me. Come, come, Mira! speak as plainly to me as I have spoken to you. I appear to have arrived here at an unfortunate time. Is your aunt ill?'

'No.'

'Does she object to your marrying me?'

'She is too kind and too just to object to a person whom she has never seen.'

That something had gone wrong nevertheless, and that there were reasons for not letting me know what it was, admitted by this time of no doubt. I took Mira's hand, led her to the sofa, and made her sit down by me. Then I ventured on one more inquiry, the last.

'Have you changed your mind?' I asked her. 'Are you sorry you promised to be my wife?'

All her own pretty self came back in an instant. She put her arm round my neck, and rested her head on my shoulder, and began to cry. How would a landsman have taken such an answer as this? A sailor received it with gratitude; repaid it with kisses; and then remembered what was due to his dear's peace of mind.

'Its plain to me,' I said, 'that I ought not to have come here without first asking leave. Let me set that right. My heart's at ease about you now: I'll go back again at once, and wait for our next meeting till you allow of it.' She looked at me, surprised to find that I was such a biddable man. I said: 'My darling, I will do anything to please you; and whether you choose to tell me your secrets, or whether you prefer keeping them to yourself, will make no difference to me. I shall believe in you all the same.'

She came close to me, and laid her hands on my shoulders. Her hands trembled.

'Suppose,' she said, 'that you see things and hear things which you don't understand, will your confidence in me take my good faith for granted, without asking for an explanation?'

'I won't even wish for an explanation.'

Somewhere or other, I have read of the language of flowers. Mira stood up on tiptoe, and thanked me in the language of kisses. I had my hat in my hand ready to go. She took it away.

'You are to stay here with me,' she said, 'and be introduced to my aunt?'

Was this pleasant change of purpose a reward? It was that and something more; it proved to be the first of many tests to which my sincerity was submitted. No fear of this troubled me at the time! I was too happy to think of consequences.

IV

The door of the room was opened again. A tall, elegant woman came in, looking neither old nor young. She was dressed plainly in dark coloured garments; there were furrows on her handsome face, and tinges of gray in her fine thick hair, which gave me the idea of a person who had seen troubled days in the course of her life. She had a slip of paper in her hand and gave it to Mira with these words:

'Here is a list of invitations to the party, my dear. If you will write on the cards we can send them round to my friends this evening.' As she laid the cards on the writing-table she noticed me. 'Who is the gentleman?'

'I have already spoken of him, aunt. He is the gentleman to whom I am engaged. Evan, let me present you to Miss Urban.'

The grand schoolmistress shook hands with me civilly enough. She was a little majestic in offering her congratulations; but I had heard of the manners of the old school and took it for granted that I saw them now. I made my apologies for having presumed to present myself without a formal invitation.

Miss Urban's lofty courtesy paid me a compliment, in reply: 'Excuses are quite needless, Mr Fencote. You might have been sure of your welcome from Mrs Motherwell and from me.'

I looked round the room. No other lady was to be seen 'Where is Mrs Motherwell?' I asked.

Miss Urban lifted her hand – a large strong hand that looked capable of boxing little girls' ears – and smiling sweetly, waved it towards Mira.

'There is Mrs Motherwell,' she said.

Mira heard her, and never denied it. I looked backwards and forwards from the aunt to the niece and from the niece to the aunt. In the infernal confusion of the moment I presumed to correct the schoolmistress. I said.

'No. Miss Ringmore.'

Miss Urban assumed the duties of correction, on her side

'Mrs Motherwell, formerly Miss Ringmore,' she reminded me. 'Are you doing me the honour, sir, of attending to what I say?'

I was not attending. My eyes and my mind were both fixed on Mira. To my dismay, she kept her back turned on me – afraid, evidently afraid, to let me see her face. A second opportunity had been offered to her of denying that she was a married woman – and again she was silent, when silence meant a confession of guilt. It is all very well to say that a man is bound to restrain himself, no matter how angry he may be, in the presence of a woman. There are occasions on which it is useless to expect a man to restrain himself. I was certainly loud, I dare say I was fierce.

'You have infamously deceived me.' I called out: 'I loved you. I trusted you. You are a heartless woman!'

Instead of looking at me, she looked at her aunt. I saw reproach in her eyes; I saw anger in the flush of her face. I heard her say to herself: 'Cruel! cruel!'

The schoolmistress – Lord! how I hated her – interfered directly. 'I can't allow you, Mr Fencote, to frighten my niece. Control yourself, or I must ask you to leave the room.'

In justice to myself, I took the woman's advice. The most stupid thing I could possibly do would be to give her an excuse for turning me out. Besides, I now had an object in view, in which I was especially interested. I may have been a brute, or I may have been only a fool. The prospect of avenging my wrongs on Mira's husband presented the first ray of comfort which had dawned on me yet.

'Is Mr Motherwell in the house?' I inquired.

To this the schoolmistress replied mysteriously.

'Mr Motherwell is in the last house of all.'

'What do you mean, ma'am?'

'I mean the churchyard.'

'A widow?' I burst out.

'What else should she be, sir?'

I was determined to have it, in words – and from Mira's own lips. 'Are you a widow?' I asked.

She turned round, and faced me. What thoughts had been in her mind, up to that time, it was impossible for me to divine. I could only see that she was mistress of herself again – a little pale perhaps: and (I did really think) a little sorry for me.

'Evan,' she began gently, 'what did we say to each other, before my aunt came in?'

She was my charming girl, before her aunt came in. She was my deceitful widow now. I remembered that, and remembered nothing more. 'I don't understand you.' I said.

My face no doubt showed some perplexity. It seemed to amuse her; she smiled. What are women made of? Oh, if my father had only sent me to be educated in a monastery and brought up to the business (whatever it may be) of a monk! She remembered everything: 'I led you to suppose, Evan, that things might happen here for which you were not at all prepared, and I asked you if your confidence in me would take my good faith for granted, without wanting an explanation. And how did you answer me? You even went beyond what I had expected. You declared that you would not even *wish* for an explanation. Has my memory misled me?'

'No.'

'Did you mean what you said?'

'I did.'

'Will you be as good as your word?'

The aunt and the niece looked at each other. I am not skilled in interpreting looks which pass between women – and it is, I dare say, natural to be suspicious of what we cannot understand. Anyway, I found myself making a cautious reply.

'You have put me to a hard trial,' I said. 'All through our voyage, you have kept back the truth. You even accepted my proposal of marriage, without taking me into your confidence. After the discoveries that I have made in this room, how can I engage to be as good as my word, when I don't know what confessions may be coming next. I can promise to try – and that's all.'

'It's all that I have a right to expect.' Saying that, Mira turned away to the window.

Miss Urban consulted her watch. A deep-toned bell was rung at the same time in the lower part of the house. The schoolmistress begged me to excuse her. 'Our young ladies,' she explained, 'are returning to their studies; my duties are waiting for me.' Passing her niece, on her way out of the room, she whispered something. I could only hear Mira's reply: 'I can't do it! I won't do it!' Her aunt considered a little, and came back to me.

'Mr Fencote,' she said, 'do you like little boys?'

I had got so distrustful of both of them, that I made another cautious reply to this effect:

'Suppose I say Yes, or suppose I say No, what difference does it make?'

'Ask my niece.'

Only three words! Having spoken them, Miss Urban attempted to leave the room. I stopped her; my dull mind was beginning to be enlightened by something like a gleam of truth.

'You began it,' I told her: 'I shall not ask your niece to explain what you mean – I shall ask you. What am I to understand by your talking of little boys?'

'I ought to have mentioned one little boy, Mr Fencote.'

'Who is he?'

She pointed to Mira, still standing at the window.

'Mrs Motherwell's little boy,' she answered; 'the sweetest child I ever met with.'

I had been holding the schoolmistress by the arm, to prevent her from leaving me. My hand dropped. She must have made her way out; I neither saw her, nor heard her.

Having already suffered the shock of discovering that Mira had been a married woman, it would seem likely to most people that I might have been prepared to hear next of the existence of her child. I was not prepared; I felt the revelation of the child – why, God only knows – more keenly than I had felt the revelation of her husband. At that horrid moment, not a word would pass my lips. In the silence that had now fallen on us, Mira confronted me once more. Something in my face – I am afraid, something cruel – appeared to strike her with terror. She burst, poor soul, into wild entreaties:

'Evan! don't look at me like that. Try, dear, to do me justice. If you only knew what my position is! Believe me you are wrong to trust to appearances. I love you, my darling. I love you with all my heart and soul. Oh, he doesn't believe me! There's no enduring this. Come what may of it, I don't care; I'll tell you—'

'Tell me nothing more,' I said, 'I have heard enough.'

It was beyond what I could bear, to see what I saw at that moment; I made for the door. She called me back with a cry of misery:

'You're not going to leave me?'

When I look back now at that miserable time, I thank God that my heart was moved with pity for her, and that I gave her my promise to return. I could do no more. My head was in a whirl; my longing for solitude and quiet was not to be told in words. I ran down the stairs. At one end of the hall, a glass door led into the garden; not a creature was to be seen there. The bright flowers, the fine old trees looked like glimpses of Heaven after what I had gone through. In a minute more, I was breathing the fresh air: I was sheltered under the peaceful shade.

V

As for the state of my mind, I can say no more about it than I have said already.

If I can trust my memory I may, however, mention that my thoughts were now more busy with Miss Urban than with her niece. I had turned a deaf ear to Mira's entreaties at the time; but they had their own irresistible influence when I found myself alone; and they led me to the conviction that the schoolmistress must be answerable for what had befallen me since I entered her house. How was she answerable? To find the right reply to this, was the one obstacle that no effort of mine could overcome. There was a provocation in constantly trying, and constantly failing, to hit on a reasonable interpretation of what Mira had said, which ended in making me too restless to remain in my place of repose. I left the pleasant shade, and wandered away; still battling with my difficulties, and neither knowing nor caring whither I went.

On a sudden, I found myself called back to present things, oddly enough, by a pull at my coat-tail.

Looking around, I discovered a little boy who seemed to be about five or six years of age – a really pretty child, with bright merry eyes and beautiful dark red hair. Here no doubt was the fatal creature who had caused me such suffering when I heard who his mother was. If he had not spoken first, I am afraid I should have gone on without taking any notice of him.

'Do come, sir, and see my garden.'

He took hold of my hand as he preferred that request, and he looked up in my face with a smile, so innocent and so pretty, that Herod himself must have felt the charm of it.

We took the way to his garden. 'My little man,' I said, 'suppose you tell me your name?'

'The boys call me Blazes – because of my red hair.'

'Have you no other name besides that?'

'Yes; I'm Kit.'

'Well, Kit, and who do you belong to?'

'I belong to Aunt Urban.'

'Have you got no father and mother?'

'I don't know that I've got a father. They tell me mother lives far away, somewhere.'

'Have you any playfellows?'

The child shook his head: 'I'm left to play by myself. Here's my garden.'

It was a barren little spot in a corner between two walls. Kit's pride in his few sickly-looking flowers, and his small crookedly directed walks, might have made some people laugh; it made me feel readier to cry.

'I hope you like my garden?' the boy said.

'Indeed I do like it.'

'And you call me a good boy?'

'Yes, certainly.'

'I like to be praised – I don't get much of it,' poor little Kit confessed. He took up his small toy spade. 'I want to make a new walk. You're a goodnatured fellow. Will you help me?'

I marked out the course of a new path, and left him hard at work on it. The sooner we separated the better it would be for me: the poor boy innocently embittered my mind against the mother who had deserted him – who had ignored his existence at the very time when she had promised to be my wife. I was afraid to go back to her until I had mastered my own indignation by the help of time.

Walking straight on, and still failing to compose myself, experience reminded me of the comforting and companionable friend of man through the journey of life. In a moment more, my pipe and pouch were in my hand – but I had lost or mislaid the means of lighting the tobacco. While I was still vainly searching my pockets, I noticed a thin blue column of smoke rising through a clump of trees on my left hand. Advancing in that direction, I reached the limit of the grounds and discovered a gate with the customary Lodge by the side of it.

An old woman was knitting at an open window. I asked her if she would kindly give me a light for my pipe.

'Surely, sir,' was the cheerful reply. 'Please to come round to the door.'

She was waiting for me on the threshold. When I approached her, she lifted her withered brown hands in amazement. Her brightening face made her look ten years younger directly. 'Lord bless us and save us, Mr Fencote, don't you know me?'

I was near enough to her now to make a likely guess. 'Not Mrs Jennet?' I said.

'Come in, sir! come in! Who but Mrs Jennet should it be?' She insisted on placing me in her own arm chair; and she spoke of her grandson, 'thriving and married and happy, when he might have been dead at the bottom of the sea, sir, but for you.' I listened with every appearance of interest that I could command, and flattered myself that I had concealed the state of my mind from the good old soul who was so honestly glad to see me. It soon appeared that I was mistaken.

'You don't look like your own bright and cheery self, sir. Has anything happened to trouble you at the school-house?'

'Yes,' I said, 'something has happened to trouble me.'

Why I suddenly changed my mind, and owned the truth in this offhand way, I hardly know. People sometimes act on impulses which they are not themselves able to explain. That I had no distinct purpose in view, I am quite sure; the result that I produced took me completely by surprise.

My old friend eyed me attentively. 'Any misunderstanding, sir, between my mistress and you?' she asked. 'I make no doubt you're a friend of Miss Urban's, or why should you be here in the grounds?'

'I can't call myself a friend of Miss Urban,' I said; 'I was only introduced to her about an hour ago.'

The temperature of Mrs Jennet's curiosity rose a little higher.

'Will it be considered a liberty,' she went on, 'if I ask who made you and Miss Urban known to one another?'

Now, when it was probably too late, prudence suggested the necessity of speaking with reserve. I refrained from mentioning Mira's name.

'The person who introduced me,' I answered, 'was a young lady.'

Mrs Jennet's eyes fastened on me with an expression of dismay; Mrs Jennet's voice sank to a whisper.

'Miss Urban's niece?' she said.

'Yes.'

'Perhaps some relation of yours?'

'She may be.'

'May be? What does that mean?'

'It means that she may be a very near relation of mine – if I marry her.'

That reply put an end to all further hesitation, on Mrs Jennet's side and on mine. 'I know what has happened now,' she said; 'as well as if I had seen you and heard you. Mr Fencote, I warned my mistress, at the time, that she might expect to meet with some such ill-luck as the misfortune that has fallen on her now. When that telegram surprised us with the news that her niece was coming, I resisted temptation; I didn't say "I told you so" – I only thought it. Ha! I don't doubt you have been hardly dealt with. But there's another person – you know who she is! – whom I pity more than I pity you. No! you mustn't tempt me to enter into particulars. What am I to do,' the poor woman asked, 'between you who saved my grandson's life, and my mistress who trusts me after thirty years spent in her service? Why don't you ask the young lady to tell you that miserable story?'

'I don't want to distress the young lady,' I said. 'My temper is quieter by this time. I find I'm too fond of my darling to desert her. Whether you take me into your confidence, or whether you don't – I'll marry her all the same.'

Mrs Jennet seemed to be strongly impressed by this.

'Upon your soul, sir?' she said solemnly.

'Upon my soul,' I answered.

What I had done to make the good old dame as reckless of consequences as I was, let others find out. 'Light your pipe,' she said; 'and I'll tell you all about it.'

VI

'A great deal of mischief is sometimes done, sir,' Mrs Jennet began, 'among pleasure parties who go to enjoy themselves at the seaside. It was in the Midsummer holidays, six or seven years ago (I don't rightly recollect which), that we went wrong. When I say We I only mean the eldest Miss Urban, who was then alive – the youngest Miss Urban, now mistress of the school – and my old self, in past days lady's maid, and afterwards keeper of the gate. My health was not as good in those days as it is now. So the two Misses Urban, as good creatures as ever lived, took me with them to the seaside. We had been about a fortnight in comfortable lodgings, when Miss Esther, (who was the eldest one) says to me: "I'm afraid my sister is going to do a very foolish thing." You will not be surprised to hear, sir, that a man was at the bottom of it. Also, that he was thought to be a perfect gentleman. Also, that he was handsome and clever and reputed to be well born. Also, that Miss Arabella (that is to say the present Miss Urban) was determined to marry him – and did marry him.'

'And they are now separated,' I ventured to guess. 'And Miss Arabella has returned to her maiden name?'

'Worse than that, Mr Fencote. She never was married at all. A lady – a perfect lady if ever there was one yet – heard where the newly-married couple had gone for their honeymoon. She says to my mistress, breaking it very kindly to her. "I am his victim, and you are his victim; look at my marriage certificate." You will ask if he was caught and punished. Not he! Early in the morning, the wretch said he was going out for a walk. He never came back, and has never been heard of since. It all happened within the six weeks of the Midsummer holidays; a hundred miles, and more, away from this place. We were saved, owing to those circumstances, from a scandal that might have ruined the school; and, like foolish women, we thought ourselves well out of it. Who could have foreseen, sir, that more misfortunes were going to fall on us? The first of them was the death of the eldest Miss Urban. The second – well some people might blame me for calling it a misfortune. What else is it, I should be glad to know, when a single lady, left sole mistress of a thriving school for girls, finds herself in a way to be a mother – cheated out of her lawful marriage by a villain who went to church with her, the husband of another woman?'

I thought of the little lovable boy whom I had left at work in his garden. But I had not courage enough to speak of him; remembering with shame how cruelly my headlong anger had injured Mira in my thoughts.

'There's but little more for me to say,' Mrs Jennet resumed. 'You don't need to be told that a time came when the "health" of the mistress obliged her to leave the management of the school, for a few weeks, to the teachers, and that I was the servant who attended on her. But please notice this: I am not to blame for the story which Miss Urban's cleverness made up (when the child was put out at nurse) to save her reputation. From first to last, I was against that story. Miss Mira was then settled in America with her father and mother, and there was no prospect of the parents or the daughter returning to the old country. What does my mistress do but turn her niece into "Mrs Motherwell, a widow," living abroad, and obliged by circumstances to confide her little boy to the care of her aunt in England. That lie succeeded very well. But I have had a good education, Mr Fencote; and I was taught to observe things, before family troubles forced me to take to domestic service. This I have noticed, that lies turn traitors, in the long run, against the very people whom they have served. Miss Urban found this to be true, when your young lady unexpectedly returned to England. Ah, sir, I see what you are thinking of!'

I was thinking of the first interview between the aunt and the niece – and of how my intrusion must have complicated their deplorable position towards each other.

These were Mrs Jennet's last words:

'Miss Urban sent for me to bear witness, before her niece, to the cruel deception by which she had suffered. It was the only excuse she could offer by way of appeasing Miss Mira's indignation – natural indignation, just indignation, I say! The next thing was to offer atonement, so far as it could be done. My mistress proposed to retire from the school, and to sell the business; and to live out her life (with her boy) among strangers. Until this could be done, she threw herself, as the saying is, on Miss Mira's mercy. "It rests with you," she said, going down on her knees, "to promise to keep up the deception for a few weeks, or to ruin me for life." You know how it ended. In having the chance of getting that noble young woman for your wife, I consider you, sir, to be the luckiest man I ever set eyes on. And remember this, if you had not said that your mind was made up to marry her – or, to put it more plainly still, if you had not shown yourself ready to trust her, when you were quite ignorant of what had really happened – not one word of all that I have said to you would have passed my lips. Now I have spoken my mind – and there is an end of it.'

POSTSCRIPT

There is an end of it also, so far as this narrative is concerned.

It is plainly needless to describe what happened when I got back to the house. Results alone are important enough to deserve notice. Mrs Jennet paid the penalty of taking me into her confidence by the loss of her situation, and entered my service on the spot. She accompanied Mira when we went back to Liverpool to be married. Miss Urban, safe in our silence on the subject of her private affairs, was left in possession of her school, her reputation, and her (adopted) son. At the time when I write my confession – offering it as a valuable lesson to my children, and inventing nothing in it but names of persons and places – my wife and I are old people; little Kit has become a fine man and a thorough sailor; our aunt and our good housekeeper have long since been reconciled in death; and I have been, for a quarter of a century past, the happiest man that ever drew a prize in the lottery of marriage.